W9-CBV-913

SANDRA BROWN

Three Complete Novels

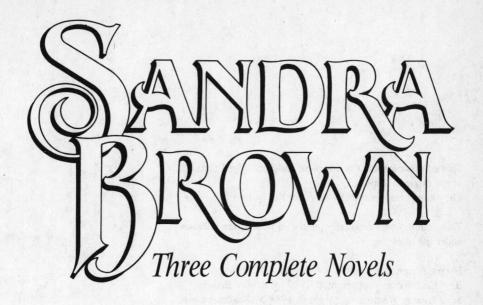

SANDRA BROWN

Three Complete Novels

MIRROR IMAGE

BEST KEPT SECRETS

SLOW HEAT IN HEAVEN

WINGS BOOKS
NEW YORK • AVENEL, NEW JERSEY

This edition contains the complete and unabridged texts
of the original editions.
They have been completely reset for this volume.

This omnibus was originally published in separate volumes
under the titles:

Mirror Image, copyright © 1990 by Sandra Brown.
Best Kept Secrets, copyright © 1989 by Sandra Brown.
Slow Heat in Heaven, copyright © 1988 by Sandra Brown.

This 1992 edition is published by Wings Books,
distributed by Random House Value Publishing, Inc.,
40 Engelhard Avenue, Avenel, New Jersey 07001,
by arrangement with Warner Books.

Random House
New York • Toronto • London • Sydney • Auckland

Book design by Jamila Miller

Printed and Bound in the United States of America

Library of Congress Cataloging-in-Publication Data

Brown, Sandra, 1948–
    [Novels. Selections]
    Three complete novels / Sandra Brown.
        p.   cm.
    Contents: Mirror image—Best kept secrets—Slow heat in
heaven.
    ISBN 0-517-07774-4
    I. Title.
PS3552.R718A6   1992
813′.54—dc20   91-38481
                                                    CIP

15 14 13 12 11 10

CONTENTS

MIRROR IMAGE

⋙ PROLOGUE

The hell of it was that it couldn't have been a better day for flying. The January sky was cloudless and so blue it was almost painful to look at. Visibility was unlimited. There was a cool, harmless breeze out of the north.

Airport traffic was moderate to heavy at that time of day, but efficient ground crews were keeping to schedules. No planes were circling, awaiting permission to land, and there were only a couple of aircraft in line to take off.

It was an ordinary Friday morning at the San Antonio International Airport. The only thing the passengers of AireAmerica's Flight 398 had found troublesome was getting into the airport itself. Road construction on 410 West, the major freeway artery in front of the airport, had caused bumper-to-bumper traffic for nearly a mile.

Yet ninety-seven passengers had boarded on schedule, stowing carryon baggage in overhead compartments, buckling up, settling into their seats with books, magazines, newspapers. The cockpit crew routinely went through the preflight check. Flight attendants joked among themselves as they loaded up drink dollies and brewed coffee that would never be poured. A final head count was taken and anxious standby passengers were allowed to board. The jetway was withdrawn. The plane taxied to the end of the runway.

The captain's friendly drawl came over the speakers and informed his passengers that they were next in line on the runway. After he reported that the current weather conditions in their destination city of Dallas were perfect, he instructed the attendants to prepare for takeoff.

Neither he nor anyone on board guessed that Flight 398 would be airborne less than thirty seconds.

"Irish!"

"Hmm?"

"A plane just went down at the airport."

Irish McCabe's head snapped up. "Crashed?"

"And burning. It's a hell of a fire at the end of the runway."

The news director dropped the latest Nielsen ratings onto his messy desk. Moving with admirable agility for a man of his age and untended physical condition, Irish rounded the corner of his desk and barreled through the door of his private glass cubicle, almost mowing down the reporter who had brought him the bulletin from the newsroom.

"Taking off or landing?" he asked over his shoulder.

"Unconfirmed."

"Survivors?"

"Unconfirmed."

"Airline or private craft?"

3

"Unconfirmed."

"Hell, are you sure there's even been a crash?"

A somber group of reporters, photographers, secretaries, and gofers had already collected at the bank of police radios. Irish elbowed them aside and reached for a volume knob.

". . . runway. No sign of survivors at this time. Airport firefighting equipment is rushing toward the site. Smoke and flames are evident. Choppers are airborne. Ambulances are—"

Irish began barking orders louder than the radios, which were squawking noisily. "You," he said, pointing toward the male reporter who had barged into his office only seconds earlier, "take a live remote unit and get the hell out there on the double." The reporter and a video cameraman peeled away from the group and raced for the exit. "Who called this in?" Irish wanted to know.

"Martinez. He was driving to work and got caught up in traffic on 410."

"Is he standing by?"

"He's still there, talking on his car phone."

"Tell him to get as close to the wreckage as he can, and shoot as much video as possible until the mobile unit arrives. Let's get a chopper in the air, too. Somebody get on the phone and chase down the pilot. Meet him at the heliport."

He scanned the faces, looking for one in particular. "Ike still around?" he asked, referring to the morning news anchorman.

"He's in the john taking a crap."

"Go get him. Tell him to get on the studio set. We'll do a break-in bulletin. I want a statement from somebody in the tower, from the airport officials, the airline, police—*something* to go on the air with before the NTSB boys put a gag on everybody. Get on it, Hal. Somebody else call Avery at home. Tell her—"

"Can't. She's going to Dallas today, remember?"

"Shit. I forgot. No, wait," Irish said, snapping his fingers and looking hopeful. "She might still be at the airport. If she is, she'll be there ahead of everyone else. If she can get into the AireAmerica terminal, she can cover the story from the human interest angle. When she calls in, I want to be notified immediately."

Eager for an update, he turned back to the radios. Adrenaline rushed through his system. This would mean he would have no weekend. It meant overtime and headaches, cold meals and stale coffee, but Irish was in his element. There was nothing like a good plane crash to round out a news week and boost ratings.

Tate Rutledge stopped his car in front of the house. He waved to the ranch foreman who was pulling out of the driveway in his pickup. A mongrel, mostly collie, bounded up and tackled him around the knees.

"Hey, Shep." Tate reached down and petted the dog's shaggy head. The dog looked up at him with unabashed hero worship.

Tens of thousands of people regarded Tate Rutledge with that same kind of reverent devotion. There was a lot about the man to admire. From the crown of his tousled brown hair to the toes of his scuffed boots, he was a man's man and a woman's fantasy.

But for every ardent admirer, he had an equally ardent enemy.

Instructing Shep to stay outdoors, he entered the wide foyer of the house and peeled off his sunglasses. His boot heels echoed on the quarry tile flooring as he headed toward the kitchen, where he could smell coffee brewing. His stomach rumbled, reminding him that he hadn't eaten before making the early trip to San Antonio. He fantasized about a breakfast steak, grilled to perfection; a pile of fluffy scrambled eggs; and a few slices of hot, buttered toast. His stomach growled more aggressively.

His parents were in the kitchen, seated at the round oak table that had been there for as long as Tate could remember. As he walked in, his mother turned toward him, a stricken expression on her face. She was alarmingly pale. Nelson Rutledge, his father, immediately left his place at the table and moved toward him, arms outstretched.

"Tate."

"What's going on?" he asked, puzzled. "To look at the two of you, you'd think somebody just died."

Nelson winced. "Weren't you listening to your car radio?"

"No. Tapes. Why?" The first stirring of panic seized his heart. "What the hell's happened?" His eyes flickered to the portable television on the tile countertop. It had been the focus of his parents' attention when he walked in.

"Tate," Nelson said in an emotionally ragged voice, "Channel Two just broke into 'Wheel of Fortune' with a news bulletin. A plane crashed on takeoff a few minutes ago at the airport." Tate's chest rose and fell on a quick, soundless gasp.

"It's still unconfirmed exactly which flight number it was, but they think—" Nelson stopped and shook his head mournfully. At the table, Zee crammed a damp Kleenex to her compressed lips.

"Carole's plane?" Tate asked hoarsely.

Nelson nodded.

ONE

She clawed her way up through the gray mist.

The clearing beyond it must exist, she reassured herself, even if she couldn't see it yet. For a minute, she thought that reaching it couldn't possibly be worth the struggle, but something behind her was so terrifying it propelled her ever forward.

She was steeped in pain. With increasing frequency she emerged from blessed oblivion into a glaring awareness that was accompanied by pain so intense, so encompassing, she couldn't localize it. It was everywhere—inside her, on the surface. It was a saturating pain. Then, just when she didn't think she could stand it an instant longer, she would be flooded with a warm rush of numbness—a magic elixir that washed through her veins. Soon after, the prayed-for oblivion would embrace her again.

Her conscious moments became extended, however. Muffled sounds reached her despite her muzziness. By concentrating very hard, she began to identify them: the incessant whooshing of a respirator, the constant bleeping of electronic machinery, rubber soles squeaking on tile floors, ringing telephones.

Once when she surfaced from unconsciousness, she overheard a hushed conversation taking place nearby.

". . . incredibly lucky . . . with that much fuel splashed on her . . . burns, but they're mostly superficial."

"How long . . . to respond?"

". . . patience . . . trauma like this injures more . . . the body."

"What will . . . look like when . . . is finished?"

". . . surgeon tomorrow. He'll . . . procedure with you."

"When?"

". . . no longer danger . . . infection."

"Will . . . effects on the fetus?"

"Fetus? Your wife wasn't pregnant."

The words were meaningless. They hurtled toward her like meteors out of a dark void. She wanted to dodge them, because they intruded on the peaceful nothingness. She craved the bliss of knowing and feeling absolutely nothing, so she tuned out the voices and sank once again into the cushiony pillows of forgetfulness.

"Mrs. Rutledge? Can you hear me?"

Reflexively, she responded, and a low moan escaped her sore chest. She tried to lift her eyelids, but she couldn't do it. One was prized open and a beam of light painfully pierced her skull. At last the hateful light was extinguished.

"She's coming out of it. Notify her husband immediately," the disembodied voice said. She tried turning her head in its direction, but found it impossible to move. "Have you got the number of their hotel handy?"

"Yes, Doctor. Mr. Rutledge gave it to all of us in case she came in while he wasn't here."

Lingering tendrils of the gray mist evaporated. Words she couldn't previously decipher now linked up with recognizable definitions in her brain. She understood the words, and yet they made no sense.

"I know you're experiencing a great deal of discomfort, Mrs. Rutledge. We're doing everything possible to alleviate that. You won't be able to speak, so don't try. Just relax. Your family will be here shortly."

Her rapid pulse reverberated through her head. She wanted to breathe, but she couldn't. A machine was breathing for her. Through a tube in her mouth, air was being pumped directly into her lungs.

Experimentally she tried opening her eyes again. One was coaxed into opening partially. Through the slit, she could see fuzzy light. It hurt to focus, but she concentrated on doing so until indistinct forms began to take shape.

Yes, she was in a hospital. That much she had known.

But how? Why? It had something to do with the nightmare she had left behind in the mist. She didn't want to remember it now, so she left it alone and dwelled on the present.

She was immobile. Her arms and legs wouldn't move no matter how hard she concentrated. Nor could she move her head. She felt like she was sealed inside a stiff cocoon. The paralysis terrified her. Was it permanent?

Her heart started beating more furiously. Almost immediately a presence materialized at her side. "Mrs. Rutledge, there's no need to be afraid. You're going to be fine."

"Her heart rate is too high," a second presence remarked from the other side of her bed.

"She's just scared, I think." She recognized the first voice. "She's disoriented—doesn't know what to make of all this."

A form clothed in white bent over her. "Everything's going to be all right. We've called Mr. Rutledge and he's on his way. You'll be glad to see him, won't you? He's so relieved that you've regained consciousness."

"Poor thing. Can you imagine waking up and having this to cope with?"

"I can't imagine living through a plane crash."

An unvoiced scream echoed loudly through her head.

She remembered

Screaming metal. Screaming people. Smoke, dense and black. Then flames, and stark terror.

She had automatically performed the emergency instructions drilled into her by hundreds of flight attendants on as many flights.

Once she had escaped the burning fuselage, she began running blindly through a world bathed in red blood and black smoke. Even though it was agonizing to run, she did so, clutching—

Clutching what? She remembered it was something precious—something she had to carry to safety.

She remembered falling. As she had gone down, she had taken what she had then believed to be her last look at the world. She hadn't even felt the pain of colliding with the hard ground. By then she had been enveloped by oblivion, which until now had protected her from the agony of remembering.

"Doctor!"

"What is it?"

"Her heartbeat has escalated dramatically."

"Okay, let's take her down a bit. Mrs. Rutledge," the doctor said imperiously, "calm down. Everything is all right. There is nothing to worry about."

"Dr. Martin, Mr. Rutledge just arrived."

"Keep him outside until we've stabilized her."

"What's the matter?" The new voice seemed to come from miles away, but carried a ring of authority.

"Mr. Rutledge, please give us a few—"

"Carole?"

She was suddenly aware of him. He was very close, bending over her, speaking to her with soft reassurance. "You're going to be fine. I know you're frightened and worried, but you're going to be all right. So is Mandy, thank God. She has a few broken bones and some superficial burns on her arms. Mom's staying in the hospital room with her. She's going to be fine. Hear me, Carole? You and Mandy survived, and that's what's important now."

There was a bright fluorescent light directly behind his head, so his features were indistinct, but she could piece together enough strong features to form a vague impression of what he looked like. She clung to each comforting word he spoke. And because he spoke them with such conviction, she believed them.

She reached for his hand—or rather, tried to. He must have sensed her slight plea for human contact because he placed his hand lightly upon her shoulder.

Her anxiety began to wane at his touch, or perhaps because the powerful sedative that had been injected into her IV began to take effect. She allowed herself to be lured, feeling safer somehow by having this stranger with the compelling voice beside her, within reach.

"She's drifting off. You can leave now, Mr. Rutledge."

"I'm staying."

She closed her eye, blotting out his blurred image. The drug was seductive. It gently rocked her like a small boat, lulling her into the safe harbor of uncaring.

Who is Mandy? she wondered.

Was she supposed to know this man who referred to her as Carole?

Why did everyone keep calling her Mrs. Rutledge?

Did everybody think she was married to him?

They were wrong, of course.

She didn't even know him.

He was there when she woke up again. Minutes, hours, days could have elapsed for all she knew. Since time had no relevance in an intensive care unit, her disorientation was augmented further.

The moment she opened her eye, he leaned over her and said, "Hi."

It was nerve-racking, not being able to see him clearly. Only one of her eyes would open. She realized now that her head was swathed in bandages and that's why she couldn't move it. As the doctor had warned her, she couldn't speak. The lower portion of her face seemed to have solidified.

"Can you understand me, Carole? Do you know where you are? Blink if you can understand me."

She blinked.

He made a motion with his hand. She thought he raked it through his hair, but she couldn't be certain. "Good," he said with a sigh. "They said you shouldn't be upset by anything, but knowing you, you'll want all the facts. Am I right?"

She blinked.

"Do you remember boarding the airplane? It was the day before yesterday. You and Mandy were going to shop in Dallas for a few days. Do you remember the crash?''

She tried desperately to convey to him that she wasn't Carole and didn't know who Mandy was, but she blinked in response to his question about the crash.

"Only fourteen of you survived."

She didn't realize that her eye was shedding tears until he used a tissue to blot them away. His touch was gentle for a man with such strong-looking hands.

"Somehow—God knows how—you were able to get out of the burning wreckage with Mandy. Do you remember that?''

She didn't blink.

"Well, it doesn't matter. However you managed it, you saved her life. She's upset and frightened, naturally. I'm afraid her injuries are more emotional than physical, and therefore harder to deal with. Her broken arm has been set. No permanent damage was done. She won't even need skin grafts for the burns. You,'' and here he gave her a penetrating stare, "you protected her with your own body.''

She didn't comprehend his stare, but it was almost as though he doubted the facts as he knew them. He was the first to break the stare and continue with the explanation.

"The NTSB's investigating. They found the black recorder box. Everything seemed normal, then one of the engines just blew up. That ignited the fuel. The plane became a fireball. But before the fuselage was completely engulfed in flames, you managed to get out through an emergency exit onto the wing, carrying Mandy with you.

"One of the other survivors said he saw you struggling to unlatch her seat belt. He said the three of you found your way to the door through the smoke. Your face was already covered with blood, he said, so the injuries to it must have happened on impact.''

She remembered none of these details. All she recalled was the terror of thinking she was going to die the suffocating death of smoke inhalation, if she didn't burn to death first. He was giving her credit for operating courageously during a disaster. All she had done was react to every living creature's survival instinct.

Perhaps the memories of the tragedy would unfold gradually. Perhaps they never would. She wasn't certain she wanted to remember. Reliving those terrifying minutes following the crash would be like experiencing hell again.

If only fourteen passengers had survived, then scores had died. That she had survived perplexed her. By a twist of fate, she had been selected to live, and she would never know why.

Her vision grew blurry and she realized that she was crying again. Wordlessly, he applied the tissue to her exposed eye. "They tested your blood for gases and decided to put you on a respirator. You've got a concussion, but there was no serious head injury. You broke your right tibia when you jumped from the wing.

"Your hands are bandaged and in splints because of burns. Thank God, though, that all your injuries, except for the smoke inhalation, were external.

"I know you're concerned about your face," he said uneasily. "I won't bullshit you, Carole. I know you don't want me to.''

She blinked. He paused, gazing down at her with uncertainty. "Your face sustained serious damage. I've retained the best plastic surgeon in the state. He specializes in reconstructive surgery on accident and trauma victims just like you.''

Her eye was blinking furiously now, not with understanding, but with anxiety. Feminine vanity had asserted itself, even though she was lying flat on her back in a hospital ICU, lucky to be alive. She wanted to know just how badly her face had been damaged. Reconstructive surgery sounded ominous.

"Your nose was broken. So was one cheekbone. The other cheekbone was pulverized. That's why your eye is bandaged. There's nothing there to support it."

She made a small sound of pure terror. "No, you didn't lose your eye. That's a blessing. Your upper jawbone was also broken. But this surgeon can repair it—all of it. Your hair will grow back. You'll have dental implants that will look exactly like your front teeth."

She had no teeth and no hair.

"We've brought him pictures of you—recent pictures, taken from every angle. He'll be able to reconstruct your features perfectly. The burns on your face affected only the outer skin, so you won't have to have grafts. When the skin peels, it will be like taking off ten years, the doctor said. You should appreciate that."

The subtle inflections in his speech slipped past her comprehension while she focused on key words. The message that had come through loud and clear was that beneath the bandages, she looked like a monster.

Panic welled up inside her. It must have communicated itself to him because he laid his hand on her shoulder again. "Carole, I didn't tell you the extent of your injuries to upset you. I know that you're worried about it. I thought it best to be frank so you could mentally prepare yourself for the ordeal ahead of you.

"It won't be easy, but everybody in the family is behind you one hundred percent." He paused and lowered his voice. "For the time being, I'm laying personal considerations aside and concentrating on putting you back together again. I'll stick by you until you are completely satisfied with the surgeon's results. I promise you that. I owe it to you for saving Mandy's life."

She tried to shake her head in denial of everything he was saying, but it was no use. She couldn't move. Making an effort to speak around the tube in her throat caused pain to her chemically scorched esophagus.

Her frustration increased until a nurse came in and ordered him to leave. When he lifted his hand off her shoulder, she felt forsaken and alone.

The nurse administered a dose of narcotic. It stole through her veins, but she fought its anesthetizing effects. It was stronger than she, however, and gave her no choice but to submit.

"Carole, can you hear me?"

Roused, she moaned pitiably. The medication made her feel weighted down and lifeless, as though the only living cells in her entire body resided in her brain and the rest of her was dead.

"Carole?" the voice hissed close to her bandaged ear.

It wasn't the man named Rutledge. She would have recognized his voice. She couldn't remember if he had left her. She didn't know who was speaking to her now. She wanted to shrink from this voice. It wasn't soothing, like Mr. Rutledge's.

"You're still in bad shape and might succumb yet. But if you feel you're fixing to die, don't make any deathbed confessions, even if you're able to."

She wondered if she was dreaming. Frightened, she opened her eye. As usual, the room was brightly lit. Her respirator hissed rhythmically. The person speaking to her was standing outside her peripheral vision. She could sense him there, but she couldn't see him.

"We're still in this together, you and I. And you're in too deep to get out now, so don't even consider it."

To no avail, she tried to blink away her grogginess and disorientation. The person remained only a presence, without form or distinction—a disembodied, sinister voice.

"Tate will never live to take office. This plane crash has been an inconvenience, but we can work it to our advantage if you don't panic. Hear me? If you come out of this, we'll pick up where we left off. There'll never be a Senator Tate Rutledge. He'll die first."

She squeezed her eye closed in an attempt to stave off her mounting panic.

"I know you can hear me, Carole. Don't pretend you can't."

After several moments, she reopened her eye and rolled it as far back as she could. She still couldn't see anybody, but she sensed her visitor had left.

Several minutes more ticked by, measured by the maddening cycle of the respirator. She hovered between sleep and wakefulness, valiantly fighting the effects of drugs, panic, and the disorientation, inherent to an ICU.

Shortly afterward, a nurse came, checked her IV bottle, and took her blood pressure. She behaved routinely. Surely if someone were in her room, or had been there recently, the nurse would have acknowledged it. Satisfied with her patient's condition, she left.

By the time she fell asleep again, she had convinced herself that she had only had a bad dream.

 # TWO

Tate Rutledge stood at the window of his hotel room, gazing down at the traffic moving along the freeway. Taillights and headlights were reflected on the wet pavement, leaving watery streaks of red and white.

When he heard the door opening behind him, he turned on the heels of his boots and nodded a greeting to his brother. "I called your room a few minutes ago," he said. "Where have you been?"

"Drinking a beer down in the bar. The Spurs are playing the Lakers."

"I'd forgotten. Who's winning?"

His brother's derisive frown indicated the silliness of that question. "Dad's not back yet?"

Tate shook his head, let the drape fall back into place, and moved away from the window.

"I'm starving," Jack said. "You hungry?"

"I guess so. I hadn't thought about it." Tate dropped into the easy chair and rubbed his eyes.

"You're not going to do Carole or Mandy any good if you don't take care of yourself through this, Tate. You look like shit."

"Thanks."

"I mean it."

"I know you do," Tate said, lowering his hands and giving his older brother a wry smile. "You're all candor and no tact. That's why I'm a politician and you're not."

"Politician is a bad word, remember? Eddy's coached you not to use it."

"Even among friends and family?"

"You might develop a bad habit of it. Best not to use it at all."

"Jeez, don't you ever let up?"

"I'm only trying to help."

Tate lowered his head, ashamed of his ill-tempered outburst. "I'm sorry." He toyed with the TV's remote control, punching through the channels soundlessly. "I told Carole about her face."

"You did?"

Lowering himself to the edge of the bed, Jack Rutledge leaned forward, propping his elbows on his knees. Unlike his brother, he was clad in suit slacks, a white dress shirt, and a necktie. This late in the day, however, he looked rumpled. The starched shirt had wilted, the tie had been loosened, and his sleeves were rolled back. The slacks were wrinkled across his lap because he'd been sitting most of the day.

"How did she react when you told her?"

"How the hell do I know?" Tate muttered. "You can't see anything except her right eye. Tears came out of it, so I know she was crying. Knowing her, how vain she is, I would imagine she's hysterical underneath all those bandages. If she could move at all, she would probably be running up and down the corridors of the hospital screaming. Wouldn't you be?"

Jack hung his head and studied his hands, as though trying to imagine what it would feel like to have them burned and bandaged. "Do you think she remembers the crash?"

"She indicated that she did, although I'm not sure how much she remembers. I left out the grisly details and only told her that she and Mandy and twelve others had survived."

"They said on the news tonight that they're still trying to match up the charred pieces and parts of bodies and identify them."

Tate had read the accounts in the newspaper. According to the report, it was a scene straight out of hell. Hollywood couldn't have created a slasher picture more gruesome than the grim reality that faced the coroner and his army of assistants.

Whenever Tate remembered that Carole and Mandy could have been among those victims, his stomach became queasy. He couldn't sleep nights for thinking about it. Each casualty had a story, a reason for being on that particular flight. Each obituary was poignant.

In his imagination, Tate added Carole's and Mandy's names to the list of casualties: *The wife and three-year-old daughter of senatorial candidate Tate Rutledge were among the victims of Flight 398.*

But fate had dictated otherwise. They hadn't died. Because of Carole's surprising bravery, they had come out of it alive.

"Good Lord, it's coming down in buckets out there." Nelson's voice boomed through the silence as he came in, balancing a large, square pizza box on his shoulder and shaking out a dripping umbrella with his other hand.

"We're famished," Jack said.

"I got back as soon as I could."

"Smells great, Dad. What'll you have to drink?" Tate asked as he moved toward the small, built-in refrigerator that his mother had stocked for him the first night there. "Beer or something soft?"

"With pizza? Beer."

"Jack?"

"Beer."

"How were things at the hospital?"

"He told Carole about her injuries," Jack said before Tate had a chance to answer.

"Oh?" Nelson lifted a wedge of steaming pizza to his mouth and took a bite. Around it, he mumbled, "Are you sure that was wise?"

"No. But if I were where she is, I'd want to know what the hell was going on, wouldn't you?"

"I suppose." Nelson took a sip of the beer Tate had brought him. "How was your mother when you left?"

"Worn out. I begged her to come back here and let me stay with Mandy tonight, but she said they were into their routine now, and for Mandy's sake, she didn't want to break it."

"That's what she told you," Nelson said. "But she probably took one look at you and decided that you needed a good night's sleep more than she does. You're the one who's worn out."

"That's what I told him," Jack said.

"Well, maybe the pizza will help revive me." Tate tried to inject some humor into his voice.

"Don't make light of our advice, Tate," Nelson warned sternly. "You can't let your own health deteriorate."

"I don't intend to." He saluted them with his can of beer, drank from it, then solemnly added, "Now that Carole's regained consciousness and knows what's ahead of her, I'll rest better."

"It's going to be a long haul. For everybody," Jack remarked.

"I'm glad you brought that up, Jack." Tate blotted his mouth with a paper napkin and mentally braced himself. He was about to test their mettle. "Maybe I should wait another six years to run for office."

For the beat of several seconds, there was an air of suspended animation around the table, then Nelson and Jack spoke simultaneously, each trying to make himself heard over the other.

"You can't make a decision like that until you see how her operation goes."

"What about all the work we've put in?"

"Too many folks are counting on you."

"Don't even think of quitting now, little brother. This election is the one."

Tate held up his hands for silence. "You know how badly I want it. Jesus, all I've ever wanted to be was a legislator. But I can't sacrifice the welfare of my family to anything, even my political career."

"Carole doesn't deserve that kind of consideration from you."

Tate's razor-sharp gray eyes found his brother's. "She's my *wife*," he enunciated.

Another taut silence ensued. Clearing his throat, Nelson said, "Of course, you must be at Carole's side as much as possible during the ordeal she's facing. It's admirable of you to think of her first and your political career second. I would expect that kind of unselfishness from you."

To emphasize his next point, Nelson leaned across the ravaged pizza that had been opened over the small, round table. "But remember how much Carole herself encouraged you to throw your hat into the ring. I think she would be terribly upset if you withdrew from the race on her account. Terribly upset," he said, jabbing the space between them with his blunt index finger.

"And looking at it from a very cold and crass viewpoint," he went on, "this unfortunate accident might be turned to our advantage. It'll generate free publicity."

Disgusted by the observation, Tate tossed down his wadded napkin and left his chair. For several moments he prowled aimlessly around the room. "Did you confer with Eddy on this? Because he said virtually the same thing when I called him earlier to discuss it."

"He's your campaign manager." Jack had turned pale and speechless at the thought that his brother might give up before his campaign even got off the ground. "He's paid to give you good advice."

"Harp on me, you mean."

"Eddy wants to see Tate Rutledge become a United States senator, just like all the rest of us, and his desire for that has nothing to do with the salary he draws." Smiling broadly, Nelson got up and slapped Tate on the back. "You'll run in the November election. Carole would be the first in line to encourage you to."

"All right then," Tate said evenly. "I had to know that I could depend on your unqualified support. The demands placed on me in the coming months will be all I can handle, and then some."

"You've got our support, Tate," Nelson said staunchly.

"Will I have your patience and understanding when I can't be two places at once?" Tate divided his inquiring look between them. "I'll do my best not to sacrifice one responsibility to the other, but I'm only one person."

Nelson assured him, "We'll take up the slack for you."

"What else did Eddy say?" Jack asked, greatly relieved that the crisis had passed.

"He has volunteers stuffing questionnaires into envelopes to be mailed later this week."

"What about public appearances? Has he scheduled any more?"

"A tentative speech to a high school in the valley. I told him to decline."

"Why?" Jack asked.

"High school kids don't vote," Tate said reasonably.

"But their parents do. And we need those Mexicans in the valley on our side."

"We've got them on our side."

"Don't take anything for granted."

"I don't," Tate said, "but this is one of those instances where I have to weigh my priorities. Carole and Mandy are going to require a lot of my time. I'll have to be more selective about where I go and when. Each speech will have to count, and I don't think a high school audience would be that beneficial."

"You're probably right," Nelson said, diplomatically intervening.

Tate realized that his father was humoring him, but he didn't care. He was tired, worried, and wanted to go to bed and at least try to sleep. As tactfully as possible, he conveyed that to his brother and father.

As he saw them out, Jack turned and gave him an awkward hug. "Sorry I badgered you tonight. I know you've got a lot on your mind."

"If you didn't, I'd get fat and lazy in no time. I rely on you to badger me." Tate flashed him the engaging smile that was destined to appear on campaign posters.

"If it's okay with y'all, I think I'll go home tomorrow morning," Jack said. "Somebody needs to check on things at the house, and see how everybody is making out."

"How is everything there?" Nelson asked.

"Okay."

"It didn't look okay the last time I was home. Your daughter Francine hadn't been heard from in days, and your wife . . . well, you know the state she was in." He shook his finger at his elder son. "Things have come to a sad pass when a man doesn't exercise any more influence over his family than you do." He glanced at Tate. "Or you, either, for that matter. Both of you have let your wives do as they damn well please."

Addressing Jack again, he said, "You should see to getting help for Dorothy Rae before it's too late."

"Maybe after the election," he mumbled. Looking at his brother, he added. "I'll only be an hour's drive away if you need me."

"Thanks, Jack. I'll call as developments warrant."

"Did the doctor give you any indication when they'd do the surgery?"

"Not until the risk of infection goes down," Tate told them. "The smoke inhalation damaged her lungs, so he might have to wait as long as two weeks. For him it's a real dilemma, because if he waits too long the bones of her face will start to heal the way they are."

"Jesus," Jack said. Then, on a falsely cheerful note, he said, "Well, give her my regards. Dorothy Rae's and Fancy's too."

"I will."

Jack went down the hall toward his own room. Nelson lingered. "I talked to Zee this morning. While Mandy was asleep, she slipped down to the ICU. Zee said Carole was a sight to behold."

Tate's wide shoulders drooped slightly. "She is. I hope to God that surgeon knows what he's talking about."

Nelson laid a hand on Tate's arm in a silent gesture of reassurance. For a moment, Tate covered his father's hand with his own. "Dr. Sawyer, the surgeon, did the video imaging today. He electronically painted Carole's face onto a TV screen, going by the pictures we'd given him. It was remarkable."

"And he thinks he can reproduce this video imaging during surgery?"

"That's what he says. He told me there might be some slight differences, but most of them will be in her favor." Tate laughed dryly. "Which she should like."

"Before this is over, she might believe that every woman in America should be so lucky," Nelson said with his characteristic optimism.

But Tate was thinking about that single eye, bloodshot and swollen, yet still the same dark coffee brown, looking up at him with fear. He wondered if she was afraid of dying. Or of living without the striking face that she had used to every advantage.

Nelson said good night and retired to his own room. Deep in thought, Tate turned off the TV and the lights, stripped, and slid into bed.

Lightning flashes penetrated the drapes, momentarily illuminating the room. Thunder crashed near the building, rattling panes of glass. He stared at the flickering patterns with dry, gritty eyes.

They hadn't even kissed good-bye.

Because of their recent, vicious argument, there had been a lot of tension between them that morning. Carole had been anxious to be off for a few days of shopping in Dallas, but they'd arrived at the airport in time to have a cup of coffee in the restaurant.

Mandy had accidentally dribbled orange juice on her dress. Naturally, Carole had overreacted. As they left the coffee shop, she blotted at the stained, ruffled pinafore and scolded Mandy for being so careless.

"Fore crissake, Carole, you can't even see the spot," he had said.

"*I* can see it."

"Then don't look at it."

She had shot her husband that drop-dead look that no longer fazed him. He carried Mandy through the terminal, chatting with her about all the exciting things she would see and do in Dallas. At the gate, he knelt and gave her a hug. "Have fun, sweetheart. Will you bring me back a present?"

"Can I, Mommy?"

"Sure," Carole replied distractedly.

"Sure," Mandy told him with a big smile.

"I'll look forward to that." He drew her to him for one last good-bye hug.

Straightening up, he asked Carole if she wanted him to wait until their plane left the gate. "There's no reason for you to."

He hadn't argued, but only made certain they had all their carryon luggage. "Well, see you on Tuesday then."

"Don't be late picking us up," Carole called as she pulled Mandy toward the jetway, where an airline attendant was waiting to take their boarding passes. "I hate hanging around airports."

Just before they entered the passageway, Mandy turned and waved at him. Carole hadn't even looked back. Self-confident and assured, she had walked purposefully forward.

Maybe that's why that single eye was filled with such anxiety now. The foundation of Carole's confidence—her looks—had been stolen by fate. She despised ugliness. Perhaps her tears hadn't been for those who had died in the crash, as he had originally thought. Perhaps they had been for herself. She might wish that she had died instead of being disfigured, even temporarily.

Knowing Carole, he wouldn't be surprised.

In the pecking order of assistants to the Bexar County coroner, Grayson was on the lowest rung. That's why he checked and rechecked the information before approaching his immediate supervisor with his puzzling findings.

"Got a minute?"

An exhausted, querulous man wearing a rubber apron and gloves gave him a quelling glance over his shoulder. "What'd you have in mind—a round of golf?"

"No, this."

"What?" The supervisor turned back to his work on the charred heap of matter that had once been a human body.

"The dental records of Avery Daniels," Grayson said. "Casualty number eighty-seven."

"She's already been IDed and autopsied." The supervisor consulted the chart on the wall, just to make certain. A red line had been drawn through her name. "Yep."

"I know, but—"

"She had no living relatives. A close family friend IDed her this afternoon."

"But these records—"

"Look, pal," the supervisor said with asperity, "I got bodies with no heads, hands without arms, feet without legs. And they're on my ass to finish this tonight. So if somebody's been positively IDed, autopsied, and sealed shut, don't bother me with records, okay?"

Grayson stuffed the dental X-rays back into the manila envelope they had arrived in and sailed it toward a trash barrel. "Okay. Fine. And in the meantime, fuck you."

"Sure, sure—any time. As soon as we get these stiffs IDed."

Grayson shrugged. They weren't paying him to be Dick Tracy. If nobody else gave a damn about a mysterious inconsistency, why should he? He went back to matching up dental records with the corpses as yet to be identified.

THREE

The weather seemed to be in mourning, too.

It rained the day of Avery Daniels's funeral. The night before, thunderstorms had rumbled through the Texas hill country. This morning, all that was left of them was a miserable, cold, gray rain.

Bareheaded, impervious to the inclement weather, Irish McCabe stood beside the casket. He had insisted on a spray of yellow roses, knowing they had been her favorite. Vivid and flamboyant, they seemed to be mocking death. He took comfort in that.

Tears rolled down his ruddy cheeks. His fleshy, veined nose was redder than usual, although he hadn't been drinking so much lately. Avery nagged him about it, saying an excessive amount of alcohol wasn't good for his liver, his blood pressure, or his expanding midsection.

She nagged Van Lovejoy about his chemical abuses, too, but he had showed up at her funeral high on cheap Scotch and the joint he had smoked on the drive to the chapel. The outmoded necktie around his ill-fitting collar was a concession to the solemnity of the occasion and attested to the fact that he held Avery in higher regard than he did most members of the human family.

Other people regarded Van Lovejoy no more favorably than he did them. Avery had numbered among the very few who could tolerate him. When the reporter assigned to cover the story of her tragic death for KTEX's news asked Van if he would shoot the video, the photographer had glared at him with contempt, shot him the finger, and slunk out of the newsroom without a word. This rude mode of self-expression was typical of Van, and just one of the reasons for his alienation from mankind.

At the conclusion of the brief interment service, the mourners began making their way down the gravel path toward the row of cars parked in the lane, leaving only Irish and Van at the grave. At a discreet distance, cemetery employees were waiting to finish up so they could retreat indoors, where it was warm and dry.

Van was fortyish and string-bean thin. His belly was concave and there was a pronounced stoop to his bony shoulders. His thin hair hung straight down from a central part, reaching almost to his shoulders and framing a thin, narrow face. He was an aging hippie who had never evolved from the sixties.

By contrast, Irish was short and robust. While Van looked like he could be carried off by a strong gust of wind, Irish looked like he could stand forever if he firmly planted his feet on solid ground. As different as they were physically, today their postures and bleak expressions were reflections of each other. Of the two, however, Irish's suffering was the more severe.

In a rare display of compassion, Van laid a skinny, pale hand on Irish's shoulder. "Let's go get shit-faced."

Irish nodded absently. He stepped forward the plucked one of the yellow rose-buds off the spray, then turned and let Van precede him from beneath the tem-porary tent and down the path. Raindrops splashed against his face and on the shoulders of his overcoat, but he didn't increase his stolid pace.

"I, uh, rode here in the limousine," he said, as though just remembering that when he reached it.

"Wanna go back that way?"

Irish looked toward Van's battered heap of a van. "I'll go with you." He dismissed the funeral home driver with a wave of his hand and climbed inside the van. The interior was worse than the exterior. The ripped upholstery was covered with a ratty beach towel, and the maroon carpet lining the walls reeked of stale marijuana smoke.

Van climbed into the driver's seat and started the motor. While it was reluctantly warming up, he lit a cigarette with long, nicotine-stained fingers and passed it to Irish.

"No thanks." Then, after a seconds' reconsideration, Irish took the cigarette and inhaled deeply. Avery had gotten him to quit smoking. It had been months since he'd had a cigarette. Now, the tobacco smoke stung his mouth and throat. "God, that's good," he sighed as he inhaled again.

"Where to?" Van asked around the cigarette he was lighting for himself.

"Any place where we're not known. I'm likely to make a spectacle of myself."

"I'm known in all of them." Left unsaid was that Van frequently made a spectacle of himself, and, in the places he patronized, it didn't matter. He engaged the protesting gears.

Several minutes later Van ushered Irish through the tufted red vinyl door of a lounge located on the seedy outskirts of downtown. "Are we going to get rolled in here?" Irish asked.

"They check you for weapons as you go in."

"And if you don't have one, they issue you one," Irish said, picking up the tired joke.

The atmosphere was murky. The booth they slid into was secluded and dark. The midmorning customers were as morose as the tinsel that had been strung from the dim, overhead light several Christmases ago. Spiders had made permanent residences of it. A naked señorita smiled beguilingly from the field of black velvet on which she had been painted. In stark contrast to the dismal ambience, lively mariachi music blared from the jukebox.

Van called for a bottle of scotch. "I really should eat something," Irish mumbled without much conviction.

When the bartender unceremoniously set down the bottle and two glasses, Van ordered Irish some food. "You didn't have to," Irish objected.

The video photographer shrugged as he filled both glasses. "His old lady'll cook if you ask her to."

"You eat here often?"

"Sometimes," Van replied with another laconic shrug.

The food arrived, but after taking only a few bites, Irish decided he wasn't hungry after all. He pushed aside the chipped plate and reached for his glass of whiskey. The first swallow played like a flamethrower in his stomach. Tears filled his eyes. He sucked in a wheezing breath.

But with the expertise of a professional drinker, he recovered quickly and took another swig. The tears, however, remained in his eyes. "I'm going to miss her like hell." Idly, he twirled his glass on the greasy tabletop.

"Yeah, me, too. She could be a pain in the ass, but not nearly as much as most."

The brassy song currently playing on the jukebox ended. No one made another selection, which came as a relief to Irish. The music intruded on his bereavement.

"She was like my own kid, you know?" he asked rhetorically. Van continued smoking, lighting another cigarette from the tip of the last. "I remember the day she was born. I was there at the hospital, sweating it out with her father. Waiting. Pacing. Now I'll have to remember the day she died."

He slammed back a shot of whiskey and refilled his glass. "You know, it never occurred to me it was her plane that went down. I was only thinking about the story, the goddamn news story. It was such a piss-ant story that I didn't even send a photographer along. She was going to borrow one from a station in Dallas.''

"Hey, man, don't blame yourself for doing your job. You couldn't have known.''

Irish stared into the amber contents of his glass. "Ever had to identify a body, Van?'' He didn't wait for a reply. "They had them all lined up, like . . .'' He released an unsteady sigh. "Hell, I don't know. I never had to go to war, but it must have been like that.

"She was zipped up in a black plastic bag. She didn't have any hair left,'' he said, his voice cracking. "It was all burned off. And her skin . . . oh, Jesus.'' He covered his eyes with his stubby fingers. Tears leaked through them. "If it weren't for me, she wouldn't have been on that plane.''

"Hey, man.'' Those two words exhausted Van's repertoire of commiserating phrases. He refreshed Irish's drink, lit another cigarette,and silently passed it to the grieving man. For himself, he switched to marijuana.

Irish drew on his cigarette. "Thank God her mother didn't have to see her like that. If she hadn't been clutching her locket in her hand, I wouldn't even have known the corpse was Avery.'' His stomach almost rebelled when he recalled what the crash had done to her.

"I never thought I'd say this, but I'm glad Rosemary Daniels isn't alive. A mother should never have to see her child in that condition.''

Irish nursed his drink for several minutes before lifting his tearful eyes to his companion. "I loved her—Rosemary, I mean. Avery's mother. Hell, I couldn't help it. Cliff, her father, was gone nearly all the time, away in some remote hellhole of the world. Every time he left he asked me to keep an eye on them. He was my best friend, but more than once I wanted to kill him for that.''

He sipped his drink. "Rosemary knew, I'm sure, but there was never a word about it spoken between us. She loved Cliff. I knew that.''

Irish had been a surrogate parent to Avery since her seventeenth year. Cliff Daniels, a renowned photojournalist, had been killed in a battle over an insignificant, unpronounceable village in Central America. With very little fuss, Rosemary had ended her own life only a few weeks after her husband's death, leaving Avery bereft and without anyone to turn to except Irish, a steadfast family friend.

"I'm as much Avery's daddy as Cliff was. Maybe more. When her folks died, it was me she turned to. I was the one she came running to last year after she got herself in that mess up in D.C.''

"She might have fucked up real bad that one time, but she was still a good reporter,'' Van commented through a cloud of sweet, pungent smoke.

"It's just so tragic that she died with that screwup on her conscience.'' He drank from his glass. "See, Avery had this hang-up about failing. That's what she feared most. Cliff wasn't around much when she was a kid, so she was still trying to win his approval, live up to his legacy.

"We never discussed it,'' he continued morosely. "I just know. That's why that snafu in D.C. was so devastating to her. She wanted to make up for it, win back her credibility and self-esteem. Time ran out before she got a chance. Goddammit, she died thinking of herself as a failure.''

The older man's misery struck a rare, responsive chord in Van. He gave the task of consoling Irish his best shot. "About that other—you know, how you felt about her mother? Well, Avery knew.''

Irish's red, weepy eyes focused on him. "How do you know?''

"She told me once,'' Van said. "I asked her just how long you two had known each other. She said you were in her memory as far back as it went. She had guessed that you secretly loved her mother.''

"Did she seem to care?" Irish asked anxiously. "I mean, did it seem to bother her?"

Van shook his long stringy hair.

Irish withdrew the wilting rose from the breast pocket of his dark suit and rubbed his pudgy fingers over the fragile petals. "Good. I'm glad. I loved them both."

His heavy shoulders began to shake. He curled his fingers into a tight fist around the rose. "Oh, hell," he groaned, "I'm going to miss her."

He lowered his head to the table and sobbed brokenly while Van sat across from him, nursing his own grief in his own way.

 # FOUR

Avery woke up knowing who she was.

She had never exactly forgotten. It was just that her medication, along with her concussion, had left her confused.

Yesterday—or at least she guessed it had been yesterday, since everyone who had recently come within her range of vision had greeted her with a "good morning"—she had been disoriented, which was understandable. Waking after having been comatose for several days to find that she couldn't move, couldn't speak, and couldn't see beyond a very limited range would confound anyone. She was rarely ill, certainly not seriously, so being this injured was shocking.

The ICU, with its constant light and activity, was enough to hamper anyone's mental process. But what really had Avery puzzled was that everyone was addressing her incorrectly. How had she come to be mistaken for a woman named Carole Rutledge? Even Mr. Rutledge seemed convinced that he was speaking to his wife.

Somehow, she must communicate this mistake to them. But she didn't know how, and that frightened her.

Her name was Avery Daniels. It was clearly printed on her driver's license, her press pass, and all the other forms of identification in her wallet. They had probably been destroyed in the crash, she thought.

Memories of the crash tended to panic her still, so she determinedly put them aside to be dealt with later, when she was stronger and had this temporary mix-up straightened out.

Where was Irish? Why hadn't he come to her rescue?

The obvious answer startled her unexpectedly. Her whole body reacted as though it had been electrically charged. It was unthinkable, untenable, yet it was glaringly apparent. If she had been mistaken for Mrs. Rutledge, and Mrs. Rutledge was believed alive, then Avery Daniels was believed dead.

She imagined the anguish Irish must be going through. Her "death" would hit him hard. For the present, however, she was helpless to alleviate his suffering. No! As long as she was alive, she wasn't helpless. She must think. She must concentrate.

"Good morning."

She recognized his voice immediately. The swelling in her eye must have gone down some because she could see him more clearly. His previously blurred features were now distinct.

His heavy, well-shaped brows almost met above the bridge of a long, straight nose. He had a strong, stubborn jawline and chin, yet it fell short of being pugnacious, despite the vertical cleft at the edge of it. His lips were firm, wide, and thin, the lower one slightly fuller than the upper.

He was smiling, but not with his eyes, she noted. He didn't really feel the smile. It didn't come from his soul. Avery wondered why not.

"They said you had a restful night. Still no sign of pulmonary infection. That's terrific news."

She knew this face, this voice. Not from yesterday. It was before that, but she couldn't recall when she had met this man.

"Mom left Mandy's room long enough to come say hello to you." He turned his head and signaled someone to move closer. "You have to stand here, Mom, or she can't see you."

An exceptionally pretty, middle-aged face materialized in Avery's patch of vision. The woman's soft, dark hair had a very flattering silver streak that waved up and away from her smooth, unlined forehead.

"Hello, Carole. We're all very relieved that you're doing so well. Tate said the doctors are pleased with your progress."

Tate Rutledge! Of course.

"Tell her about Mandy, Mom."

Dutifully, the stranger reported on another stranger. "Mandy ate most of her breakfast this morning. They sedated her last night so she would sleep better. The cast on her arm bothers her, but that's to be expected, I suppose. She's the sweetheart of the pediatric wing, and has the entire staff wrapped around her little finger." Tears formed in her eyes and she blotted at them with a tissue. "When I think of what . . ."

Tate Rutledge placed his arm across his mother's shoulders. "But it didn't happen. Thank God it didn't."

Avery realized then that it must have been Mandy Rutledge she had carried from the plane. She remembered hearing the child's screams and frantically trying to unfasten her jammed seat belt. When it came free, she had gathered the terrified child against her and, with the assistance of another passenger, had plunged through the dense, acrid smoke toward an emergency exit.

Because she had had the child, they had assumed she was Mrs. Carole Rutledge. But that wasn't all—they had been in each other's seats.

Her mind clumsily pieced together a puzzle of which only she was aware. She recalled that her boarding pass had designated the window seat, but when she had arrived, a woman was already sitting there. She hadn't pointed out the error, but had taken the seat on the aisle instead. The child had been sitting in the seat between them.

The woman had worn her dark hair shoulder length, much like Avery wore hers. She also had dark eyes. They bore a resemblance to each other. In fact, the flight attendant, who had made a fuss over the little girl, had asked who was the mother and who was the aunt, implying that Avery and Carole Rutledge were sisters.

Her face had been smashed beyond recognition. Mrs. Rutledge had probably been burned beyond recognition. They had misidentified her on the basis of the child and a seating rearrangement that no one knew about. My God, she had to tell them!

"You'd better go back now before Mandy becomes anxious, Mom," Tate was saying. "Tell her I'll be there shortly."

"Good-bye for now, Carole," the woman said to her. "I'm sure when Dr. Sawyer's done, you'll be as pretty as ever."

Her eyes don't smile either, Avery thought as the woman moved away.

"Before I forget it," Tate said, stepping close to the bed so that she could see him again, "Eddy, Dad, and Jack send their regards. I think Dad's coming to the meeting with the plastic surgeon this afternoon, so you'll see him then.

"Jack went home this morning," Tate continued talking, not knowing he wasn't speaking to his wife. "I'm sure he's worried about Dorothy Rae. God only knows what Fancy is up to without any supervision, although Eddy has got her working as a volunteer at the headquarters. None of them will be allowed to see you until you're moved to a private room, but I don't think you'll miss them, will you?"

He assumed that she knew who and what he was talking about. How could she convey that she hadn't the foggiest idea? These people were unknown to her. Their comings and goings were no concern of hers. She must contact Irish. She must let this man know that he was a widower.

"Listen, Carole, about the campaign." By the motion his shoulders made, she thought he had probably slid his hands into his hip pockets. He bowed his head for a moment, almost resting his chin on his chest, before looking at her again. "I'm going ahead with it as planned. Dad, Jack, and Eddy agree. They've pledged their support. It was going to be a tough fight before, but nothing I was afraid to tackle. Now, with this, it's going to be even tougher. Still, I'm committed."

Tate Rutledge had been making news recently. That's why his name and face were familiar to her, though she had never met him personally. He was hoping to win the primary election in May and then go up against an incumbent senator in the November election.

"I won't shirk any of my responsibilities to you and Mandy while you're recovering, but going to Congress is what I've been preparing for all my life. I don't want to wait another six years to run or I'll lose the momentum I've built. I need to do it now."

After consulting his wristwatch, he said, "I'd better get back to Mandy. I promised to feed her some ice cream. With her arms bandaged and all, well," he added, glancing toward her bandaged hands, resting in their splints, "you can understand. The psychologist has the first session with her today. Nothing to worry about," he rushed to say. "More precautionary than anything. I don't want her to be permanently traumatized."

He paused, looking down at her meaningfully. "That's why I don't think she should see you just yet. I know that sounds cruel, but these bandages would scare her half to death, Carole. Once the surgeons rebuild your face and you start looking like yourself, I'll bring her in for short visits. Besides, I'm sure you don't feel up to seeing her now, either."

Avery struggled to speak, but her mouth had the breathing tube taped inside it. She had overheard a nurse say that smoke inhalation had rendered her vocal cords temporarily inoperable. She couldn't move her jaw anyway. She batted her eye to convey her distress.

Misconstruing the reason for it, he laid a consoling hand on her shoulder. "I promise that your disfigurement is temporary, Carole. Dr. Sawyer says it looks much worse to us than it actually is. He'll be in later today to explain the procedure to you. He knows what you looked like before and guarantees that you'll look the same when he gets finished."

She tried to shake her head no. Tears of panic and fear overflowed her eye. A nurse came in and edged him aside. "I think you'd better let her rest now, Mr. Rutledge. I've got to change her bandages anyway."

"I'll be with my daughter."

"We'll call if you're needed," the nurse told him kindly. "Oh, and while I'm thinking of it, they called from downstairs to remind you that Mrs. Rutledge's jewelry is in the hospital safe. They took it off her when she arrived in the emergency room.''

''Thanks. I'll get it later.''

Now! Get it now, Avery's mind screamed. It wouldn't be Carole Rutledge's jewelry in the hospital safe—it would be hers. Once they saw it, they would realize that a horrible mistake had been made. Mr. Rutledge would learn that his wife was dead. It would come as a blow to him, but it would be better that he discover the error now rather than later. She would lament the Rutledges' tragic loss, but Irish would be overjoyed. Dear Irish. His bereavement would end.

But what if Mr. Rutledge failed to retrieve his wife's jewelry before the plastic surgeon began to change her face into Carole Rutledge's?

That was her last conscious thought before the pain-relieving medication claimed her once again.

Tate will never live to take office.

She was reliving the nightmare again. She tried desperately to ward it off. Again, she couldn't see him, but she could feel his sinister presence hovering above her, just beyond her field of vision. His breath fanned across her exposed eye. It was like being taunted in the dark with a sheer veil—unseen but felt, ghostly.

There will never be a Senator Tate Rutledge. Tate will never live. Senator Tate Rutledge will die first. There'll never be . . . Never live . . .

Avery woke up screaming. It was a silent scream, of course, but it reverberated through her skull. She opened her eye and recognized the lights overhead, the medicinal smell she associated with hospitals, the hissing sound of her respirator. She had been asleep, so this time it had been a nightmare.

But last night it had been real. Last night she hadn't even known Mr. Rutledge's first name! She couldn't have dreamed it if she hadn't known it, but she distinctly remembered hearing that menacing, faceless voice contemptuously whispering it into her ear.

Was her mind playing games with her, or was Tate Rutledge in real danger? Surely she was becoming panicked prematurely. After all, she had been heavily sedated and disoriented. Maybe she wasn't keeping the chronology straight. Was she getting events out of order? Who could possibly want him dead?

God, these were staggering questions. She had to know the answers to them. But her powers of deductive reasoning seemed to have deserted her, along with her other faculties. She couldn't think logically.

The threat to Tate Rutledge's life had far-reaching and enormous ramifications, but she was helpless to do anything about it. She was too woozy to formulate an explanation or solution. Her mind was operating sluggishly. It wouldn't, couldn't function properly, even though a man's life was at stake.

Avery almost resented this intrusion into her own problem. Didn't she already have enough to cope with without worrying about a senatorial candidate's safety?

She was incapable of motion, yet on the inside she was roiling with frustration. It was exhausting. Eventually, it was no match for the void that continued to remain at the fringes of her consciousness. She combated it, but finally gave up the struggle and was sucked into its peacefulness again.

FIVE

"**I**'m not at all surprised by her reaction. It's to be expected in accident victims." Dr. Sawyer, the esteemed plastic surgeon, smiled placidly. "Imagine how you would feel if your handsome face had been pulverized."

"Thanks for the compliment," Tate said tightly.

At that moment, he would have liked to crush the surgeon's complacent face. Despite his sterling reputation, the man seemed to have ice water flowing through his veins.

He had done fine-tuning on some of the most celebrated faces in the state, including debutantes who possessed as much money as vanity, corporate executives who wanted to stay ahead of the aging process, models, and TV stars. Although his credentials were impressive, Tate didn't like the cocky way he dismissed Carole's apprehensions.

"I've tried to put myself in Carole's place," he explained. "Under the circumstances, I think she's bearing up very well—better than I would ever have guessed she could."

"You're contradicting yourself, Tate," Nelson remarked. He was sitting beside Zee on a sofa in the ICU waiting room. "You just told Dr. Sawyer that Carole seemed terribly upset at the mention of the surgery."

"I know it sounds contradictory. What I mean is that she seemed to take the news about Mandy and the crash itself very well. But when I began telling her about the surgery on her face, she started crying. Jesus," he said, raking a hand through his hair. "You can't imagine how pitiful she looks when she cries out of that one eye. It's like something out of 'The Twilight Zone.' "

"Your wife was a beautiful woman, Mr. Rutledge," the doctor said. "The damage to her face panics her. Naturally, she's afraid of looking like a monster for the rest of her life. Part of my job is to assure her that her face can be reconstructed, even improved upon."

Sawyer paused to make eye contact with each of them. "I sense hesitation and reluctance from you. I can't have that. I must have your cooperation and whole-hearted confidence in my ability."

"If you didn't have my confidence, I wouldn't have retained your services," Tate said bluntly. "I don't think you're lacking in skill, just sympathy."

"I save my bedside manner for my patients. I don't waste time or energy bullshitting their families, Mr. Rutledge. I leave that to politicians. Like you."

Tate and the surgeon stared each other down. Eventually Tate smiled, then laughed dryly. "I don't bullshit either, Dr. Sawyer. You're necessary. That's why you're here. You're also the most pompous son of a bitch I've ever run across, but by all accounts, you're the best. So I'll cooperate with you in order to see Carole returned to normal."

"Okay, then," the surgeon said, unaffected by the insult, "let's go see the patient."

When they entered the ICU, Tate moved ahead, arriving first at her beside. "Carole? Are you awake?"

She responded immediately by opening her eye. As best he could tell, she was lucid. "Hi. Mom and Dad are here." He moved aside. They approached the bed.

"Hello again, Carole," Zee said. "Mandy said to tell you she loves you."

Tate had forgotten to caution his mother against telling Carole about Mandy's initial session with the child psychologist. It hadn't gone well, but thankfully, Zee was sensitive enough not to mention it. She moved aside and let Nelson take her place.

"Hi, Carole. You gave us all a fright. Can't tell you how pleased we are that you're going to be okay."

He relinquished his position to Tate. "The surgeon's here, Carole."

Tate exchanged places with Dr. Sawyer, who smiled down at his patient. "We've already met, Carole. You just don't remember it. At the request of your family, I came in to examine you on your second day here. The staff plastic surgeon had done all the preliminary treatment in the emergency room when you arrived. I'll take over from here."

She registered alarm. Tate was gratified to see that Sawyer had noticed it. He patted her shoulder. "The bone structure of your face was seriously damaged. I'm sure you're aware of that. I know your husband has already told you that it will be fully restored, but I want you to hear it from me. I'll make you look like a better Carole Rutledge than you were before."

Beneath the bandages, her body tensed. She tried to shake her head vigorously, and she began to make desperate guttural sounds.

"What the hell is she trying to say?" Tate asked the doctor.

"That she doesn't believe me," he calmly replied. "She's frightened. That's customary." He leaned over her. "Most of the pain you're experiencing is from the burns, but they're superficial. The burn specialist here at the hospital is treating them with antibiotics. I'm going to delay surgery until the risk of infection both to your skin and your lungs is minimal.

"It will be a week or two before you can move your hands. You'll start physical therapy then. The damage isn't permanent, I assure you."

He bent down closer. "Now, let's talk about your face. X-rays were taken while you were still unconscious. I've studied them. I know what must be done. I have a staff of excellent surgeons who will assist me during the operation."

He touched her face with the tip of his ballpoint pen, as though tracing over the bandages. "We'll rebuild your nose and cheekbones by using bone grafts. Your jaw will be put back into place with pins, screws, and wires. I've got a whole bag of tricks.

"You'll have an invisible scar across the top of your head from temple to temple. We'll also make incisions beneath each eye at the lash line. They're invisible, too. Some of the work on your nose will be done from inside, so there will be no scars at all there.

"After the surgery you'll be swollen and bruised and you'll generally look like hell. Be prepared for that. It will take a few weeks before you're a raving beauty again."

"What about her hair, Dr. Sawyer?" Zee asked.

"I'll have to shave off a patch because I'll be taking a graft from her skull to use as part of her new nose. But if you're asking if the hair that was burned off will grow back, the burn specialist says yes. That's the least of our problems," he said, smiling down into the bandaged face.

"You won't be eating solid foods for a while, I'm afraid. A prosthodontist will take out the roots of your teeth during the surgery and install implants. Two or three weeks later, you'll get your new teeth, which he'll make to look exactly like the ones you lost. Until you get the replacements, you'll be fed through a tube from your mouth to your stomach, then progress to a soft diet."

Tate noticed, even if the surgeon failed to acknowledge it, that Carole's eye was roving as though looking for a friend among them, or possibly a means of escape. He kept telling himself that Sawyer knew what he was doing. The surgeon might be accustomed to anxiety like this among his patients, but it was as disturbing as hell to Tate.

Sawyer extracted a glossy eight-by-ten color photograph from the folder he had carried in with him. "I want you to look at this, Mrs. Rutledge." It was a picture of Carole. She was smiling the beguiling smile that had caused Tate to fall in love with her. Her eyes were shining and mischievous. Glossy dark hair framed her face.

"It'll be an all day, bring-your lunch operation," he told her, "but my staff and I will fix you up. Give us eight to ten weeks from the day of your surgery and this is what you'll look like, only younger and prettier, and with shorter hair. Who could ask for more than that?"

Apparently Carole could. Tate noticed that, rather than assuaging her fears, the surgeon's visit had seemed to heighten them.

Avery tried moving her extremities and coaxing motion out of her fingers and toes, but her limbs still felt too heavy to lift. She couldn't move her head at all. Meanwhile, each passing minute brought her closer to a disaster she seemed incapable of preventing.

For days—it was difficult to calculate exactly how many, but she guessed around ten—she had tried to figure out a means of letting everyone else in on the truth that only she knew. Thus far, she hadn't arrived at a solution. As the days passed and her body healed, her anxiety increased. Everyone thought it was caused by the delay of her reconstructive operation.

Finally, Tate announced one evening that her surgery had been scheduled for the next day. "All the doctors involved consulted this afternoon. They agreed that you're out of the danger zone. Sawyer issued the go-ahead. I came as soon as I was notified."

She had until tomorrow to let him know that a dreadful mistake had been made. It was strange but, even though he was partially responsible for this tragic chain of events, she didn't blame him. Indeed, she had come to anticipate his visits. She felt safer somehow when he was with her.

"I guess it's all right to tell you now that I didn't like Sawyer at first," he said, sitting gingerly on the edge of her bed. "Hell, I still don't like him, but I trust him. You know that he wouldn't be doing the operation if I didn't think he would do the best job."

She believed that, so she blinked.

"Are you afraid?"

She blinked again.

"Can't say that I blame you," he said grimly. "The next few weeks are going to be tough, Carole, but you'll get through them." His smile stiffened slightly. "You always land on your feet."

"Mr. Rutledge?"

When he turned his head toward the feminine voice who had spoken to him from the doorway, he provided Avery a rare view of his profile. Carole Rutledge had been a lucky woman.

"You asked me to remind you about Mrs. Rutledge's jewelry," the nurse said. "It's still in the safe."

Avery's mind quickened. She had envisioned him entering her room and dumping her jewelry onto the bed. "These aren't Carole's things," he would say. "Who are you?" But that scenario hadn't occurred. Maybe there was hope yet.

"I keep forgetting to stop by the office and pick it up," he told the nurse with chagrin. "Could you possibly send somebody down to get it for me?"

"I'll call down and check."

"I'd appreciate that. Thank you."

Avery's heart began to pound. She offered up a silent prayer of thanksgiving. Here, at the eleventh hour, she would be saved from disaster. Reconstructive surgery would have to be done to her face, but she would come out of it looking like Avery Daniels, and not someone else.

"The jewelry won't do you much good in the operating room," Tate was saying, "but I know you'll feel better once your things are in my possession."

In her mind, she was smiling hugely. It was going to be all right. The mistake would be discovered in plenty of time, and she could leave the emotional rollercoaster she had been riding behind.

"Mr. Rutledge, I'm afraid it's against hospital regulations for anyone except the patient himself or next of kin to retrieve possessions from the safe. I can't send anyone down for it. I'm sorry."

"No problem. I'll try to get down there sometime tomorrow."

Avery's spirits plummeted. Tomorrow would be too late. She asked herself why God was doing this to her. Hadn't she been punished enough for her mistake? Would the rest of her life be an endless and futile endeavor to make up for one failure? She had already lost her credibility as a journalist, the esteem of her colleagues, her career status. Must she give up her identity, too?

"There's something else, Mr. Rutledge," the nurse said hesitantly. "There are two reporters down the hall who want to speak with you."

"Reporters?"

"From one of the TV stations."

"Here? Now? Did Eddy Paschal send them?"

"No. That's the first thing I asked them. They're after a scoop. Apparently word has leaked out about Mrs. Rutledge's surgery tomorrow. They want to talk to you about the effect of the crash on your family and senatorial race. What should I tell them?"

"Tell them to go to hell."

"Mr. Rutledge, I can't."

"No, you can't. If you did, Eddy would kill me," he muttered to himself. "Tell them that I'm not making any statements until my wife and daughter are drastically improved. Then, if they don't leave, call hospital security. And tell them for me that if they go anywhere near the pediatric wing and try to see my mother or daughter, I'll sue their asses for all they've got."

"I'm sorry to have bothered you with—"

"It's not your fault. If they give you any trouble, come get me."

When his head came back around, Avery noticed through her tears that his face was lined with worry and exhaustion. "Media vultures. Yesterday the newspaper took a statement I had made about the shrimping business along the coast and printed it out of context. This morning my phone rang incessantly until Eddy could issue a counterstatement and demand a retraction." He shook his head with disgust over the unfairness.

Avery sympathized. She had spent enough time in Washington to know that the only politicians who didn't suffer were the unscrupulous ones. Men with integrity, as Tate Rutledge seemed to be, had a much more difficult time of it.

It was little wonder that he appeared so tired. He was not only burdened with running for public office, but he had to cope with an emotionally traumatized child and a wife facing her own ordeal.

Only she wasn't his wife. She was a stranger. She couldn't tell him that he was confiding in an outsider. She couldn't protect him from media assaults or help him through Mandy's difficulties. She couldn't even warn him that someone might be planning to kill him.

*   *   *

He stayed with her through the night. Each time she awakened, he instantly materialized at her bedside. The character lines in his face became more pronounced by the hour as fatigue settled in. The whites of his eyes grew rosy with sleeplessness. Once, Avery was aware of a nurse urging him to leave and get some rest, but he refused.

"I can't run out on her now," he said. "She's scared."

Inside she was crying, *No, please don't go. Don't leave me. I need someone.*

It must have been dawn when another nurse brought him a cup of fresh coffee. It smelled delicious; Avery craved a sip.

Technicians came in to adjust her respirator. She was gradually being weaned from it as her lungs recovered from their injury. The machine's job had been drastically scaled down from what it had originally done for her, but she would need it a few days more.

Orderlies prepped her for surgery. Nurses monitored her blood pressure. She tried to catch someone's eye and alert them to the mix-up, but no one paid any attention to the mummified patient.

Tate stepped out for a while, and when he returned, Dr. Sawyer was with him. The surgeon was brisk and buoyant. "How are you, Carole? Mr. Rutledge told me you spent some anxious hours last night, but this is your big day."

He methodically perused her chart. Much of what he said was by rote, she realized. As a human being, she didn't like him any better than Tate did.

Satisfied with her vital signs, he shut the metal file and passed it to a nurse. "Physically, you're doing fine. In a few hours, you'll have the framework of a new face and be on your way to a full recovery."

She put all her strength into the guttural sounds she made, trying to convey the wrongness of what they were about to do. They misinterpreted her distress. The surgeon thought she was arguing with him. "It can be done. I promise. In about half an hour we'll be underway."

Again, she protested, using the only means available to her, her single eye. She batted it furiously.

"Give her a pre-op sedative to calm her down," he ordered the nurse before bustling out.

Avery screamed inside her head.

Tate stepped forward and pressed her shoulder. "Carole, it's going to be all right."

The nurse injected a syringe of narcotic into the IV in her arm. Avery felt the slight tug on the needle in the bend of her elbow. Seconds later, the now-familiar warmth began stealing through her, until even the pads of her toes tingled. It was the nirvana that junkies would kill for—a delicious jolt of numbness. Almost instantly she became weightless and transparent. Tate's features began to blur and become distorted.

"You're going to be all right. I swear it, Carole."

I'm not Carole.

She struggled to keep her eye open, but it closed and became too heavy to reopen.

". . . waiting for you, Carole," he said gently.

I'm Avery. I'm Avery. I'm not Carole.

But when she came out of the operating room, she would be.

SIX

"I don't understand what you're so upset about."

Tate spun around and angrily confronted his campaign manager. Eddy Paschal suffered the glare with equanimity. Experience had taught him that Tate's temper was short, but just as short-lived.

As Eddy expected, the fire in Tate's eyes downgraded to a hot glow. He lowered his hands from his hips, making his stance less antagonistic.

"Eddy, for crissake, my wife had just come out of a delicate operation that had lasted for hours."

"I understand."

"But you can't understand why I was upset when hordes of reporters surrounded me, asking questions?" Tate shook his head, incredulous. "Let me spell it out for you. I was in no mood for a press conference."

"Granted, they were out of line."

"Way out of line."

"But you got forty seconds of airtime on the six and ten o'clock newscasts—all three networks. I taped them and played them back later. You appeared testy, but that's to be expected, considering the circumstances. All in all, I think it went in our favor. You look like a victim of the insensitive media. Voters will sympathize. That's definitely a plus."

Tate laughed mirthlessly as he slumped into a chair. "You're as bad as Jack. You never stop campaigning, measuring which way this or that went—in our favor, against us." He dragged his hands down his face. "Christ, I'm tired."

"Have a beer." Eddy handed him a cold can he'd taken from the compact refrigerator. Taking one for himself, he sat down on the edge of Tate's hotel room bed. For a moment they drank in silence. Finally, Eddy asked, "What's her prognosis, Tate?"

Tate sighed. "Sawyer was braying like a jackass when he came out of the operating room. Said he was perfectly satisfied with the results—that it was the finest work his team had ever done."

"Was that P.R. bullshit or the truth?"

"I hope to God it's the truth."

"When will you be able to see for yourself?"

"She doesn't look like much now. But in a few weeks . . ."

He made a vague gesture and slouched down deeper into the chair, stretching his long legs out in front of him. His boots almost came even with Eddy's polished dress shoes. The jeans Tate had on were at the opposite end of the wardrobe scale from Eddy's creased and pressed navy flannel slacks.

For the present, Eddy didn't badger his candidate about his casual attire. The political platform they were building was one that common folk—hardworking middle-class Texans—would adhere to. Tate Rutledge was going to be the champion of the downtrodden. He dressed the part—not as a political maneuver, but because that's the way he had dressed since the early seventies, when Eddy had met him at the University of Texas.

"One of the crash survivors died today," Tate informed him in a quiet voice. "A man my age, with a wife and four kids. He had a lot of internal injuries, but they had patched him up and thought he was going to make it. He died of infection. God," he said, shaking his head, "can you imagine making it that far and then dying from *infection*?"

Eddy could see that his friend was sinking into a pit of melancholia. That was bad for Tate personally and for the campaign. Jack had expressed his concern for

Tate's mental attitude. So had Nelson. An important part of Eddy's job was to boost Tate's morale when it flagged.

"How's Mandy?" he asked, making his voice sound bright. "All the volunteers miss her."

"We hung that get well banner they had all signed on her bedroom wall today. Be sure to thank them for me."

"Everyone wanted to do something special to commemorate her release from the hospital. I'll warn you that tomorrow she's going to receive a teddy bear that's bigger than you are. She's the princess of this election, you know."

Eddy was rewarded with a wan smile. "The doctors tell me that her broken bones will heal. The burns won't leave any scars. She'll be able to play tennis, cheerlead, dance—anything she wants."

Tate got up and went for another two beers. When he was once again relaxing in the chair, he said, "Physically, she'll recover. Emotionally, I'm not so sure."

"Give the kid a chance. Adults have a hard time coping with this kind of trauma. That's why the airline has counselors trained to deal with people who survive crashes and with the families of those who don't."

"I know, but Mandy was shy to begin with. Now she seems completely withdrawn, suppressed. Oh, I can get a smile out of her if I try hard enough, but I think she does it just to please me. She has no animation, no vitality. She just lies there and stares into space. Mom says she cries in her sleep and wakes up screaming from nightmares."

"What does the psychologist say?"

"That dyke," Tate said, cursing impatiently. "She says it'll take time and patience, and that I shouldn't expect too much from Mandy."

"I say ditto."

"I'm not angry with Mandy for not performing on command," he snapped irritably. "That's what the psychologist implied, and it made me mad as hell. But my little girl sits and stares like she's got the weight of the world on her shoulders, and that's just not normal behavior for a three-year-old."

"Neither is living through a plane crash," Eddy pointed out reasonably. "Her emotional wounds aren't going to heal overnight, any more than her physical ones will."

"I know. It's just . . . hell, Eddy, I don't know if I can be what Carole and Mandy and the voting public need, all at the same time."

Eddy's greatest fear was that Tate would second-guess his decision to remain in the race. When Jack had told him that there were rumors in journalistic circles of Tate withdrawing from the race, he'd wanted to hunt down the gossiping reporters and kill them single-handedly. Luckily, Tate hadn't heard the rumors. Eddy had to keep the candidate's fighting spirit high.

Sitting forward, he said, "You remember the time you played in that fraternity tennis tournament and won it for us our sophomore year?"

Tate regarded him blankly. "Vaguely."

"Vaguely," Eddy scoffed. "The reason the recollection is dim is because you had such a hangover. You'd forgotten all about the tournament and had spent the previous night drinking beer and banging a Delta Gamma. I had to rout you out of her bed, get you into a cold shower and onto the court by nine o'clock to keep us from getting a forfeit."

Tate was chuckling with self-derision. "Is this story going somewhere? Does it have a point?"

"The point is," Eddy said, scooting farther forward so that his hips were barely on the edge of the bed, "that you came through, under the worst possible conditions, because you knew you had to. You were the only chance we had of winning that tournament and you knew it. You won it for us, even though minutes before your first match you were massaging your blue balls and puking up two six-packs of beer.''

"This is different from a college tennis tournament.''

"But you,'' Eddy said, aiming an index finger at him, "are exactly the same. Since I've known you, you've never failed to rise to the occasion. Through those two years we spent together at UT, through flight training, through Nam, when you were carrying me out of that goddamn jungle, when have you ever failed to be a fucking hero?''

"I don't want to be a hero. I just want to be an effective congressman for the people of Texas.''

"And you will be.''

Slapping his knees as though an important decision had been reached, Eddy stood up and set his empty beer can on the dresser. Tate stood up, too, and he happened to catch a glimpse of his reflection in the mirror.

"Good God.'' He ran his hand over the heavy stubble on his jaw. "Who'd vote for *that*? Why didn't you tell me I looked so bad?''

"I didn't have the heart.'' Eddy slapped him lightly between the shoulder blades. "All you need is some rest. And I recommend a close shave in the morning.''

"I'll be leaving for the hospital early. They told me that Carole will be taken out of the recovery room about six and moved into a private room. I want to be there.''

Eddy studied the shiny toes of his shoes for a moment before raising his eyes to his slightly taller friend. "The way you're sticking so close to her through this—well, uh, I think it's damned admirable.''

Tate bobbed his head once, tersely. "Thanks.''

Eddy started to say more, thought better of it, and gave Tate's arm a companionable slap. Tate wouldn't welcome marriage counseling from anyone, but especially not from a bachelor.

"I'll leave and let you get to bed. Stay in touch tomorrow. We'll be standing by for word on Carole's condition.''

"How are things at home?''

"Status quo.''

"Jack said you'd put Fancy to work at headquarters.''

Eddy laughed and, knowing that Tate wouldn't take offense at an off-color comment about his niece, added, "By day I've got her stuffing envelopes. By night, God only knows who's stuffing her.''

Francine Angela Rutledge crossed the cattle guard doing seventy-five miles per hour in a year-old car that she'd inflicted with five years' worth of abuse. Because she didn't like safety belts, she was jounced out of her seat a good six inches. When she landed, she was laughing. She loved feeling the wind tear through her long, blond hair, even in wintertime. Driving fast, with flagrant disregard for traffic laws, was just one of Fancy's passions.

Another was Eddy Paschal.

Her desire for him was recent and, so far, unfulfilled and unreciprocated. She had all the confidence in the world that he would eventually come around.

In the meantime, she was occupying herself with a bellhop at the Holiday Inn in Kerrville. She'd met him at a twenty-four-hour truck stop several weeks earlier. She had stopped there after a late movie, since it was one of the few places in town that stayed open after ten o'clock and it was on her way home.

At the truck stop Buck and Fancy made smoldering eye contact over the orange vinyl booths while she nursed a vanilla Coke through a large straw. Buck gobbled down a bacon cheeseburger. The way his mouth savagely gnawed at the greasy sandwich aroused her, just as intended. So on her way past his booth, she had slowed down as though to speak, then went on by. She settled her tab quickly, wasting no time to chat with the cashier as she usually did, and went directly to her convertible parked outside.

Sliding beneath the steering wheel, she smiled smugly. It was only a matter of time now. Watching through the wide windows of the café, she saw the young man stuff the last few bites of the cheeseburger into his mouth and toss enough currency to cover his bill onto the table before charging for the door in hot pursuit.

After exchanging names and innuendos, Buck had suggested that they meet there the following night, same time, for dinner. Fancy had an even better idea—breakfast at the motel.

Buck said that suited him just fine since he had access to all the unoccupied rooms at the Holiday Inn. The illicit and risky arrangement appealed to Fancy enormously. Her lips had formed the practiced smile that she knew was crotch-teasing. It promised a wicked good time.

''I'll be there at seven o'clock sharp,'' she had said in her huskiest drawl. ''I'll bring the doughnuts, you bring the rubbers.'' While she exercised no more morals than an alley cat, she was too smart and too selfish to risk catching a fatal disease for a mere roll in the hay.

Buck hadn't been a disappointment. What he lacked in finesse he made up for with stamina. He'd been so potent and eager to please that she'd pretended not to notice the pimples on his ass. Overall, he had a pretty good body. That's why she'd slept with him six times since that first morning.

They'd spent tonight, his night off, in the tacky apartment he was so proud of, eating bad Mexican TV dinners, drinking cheap wine, smoking expensive grass—Fancy's contribution to the evening's entertainment—and screwing on the carpet because it had looked marginally cleaner to her than the sheets on the bed.

Buck was sweet. He was earnest. He was horny. He told her often that he loved her. He was okay. Nobody was perfect.

Except Eddy.

She sighed now, expanding the cotton sweater across her braless breasts. Much to the disapproval of her grandmother, Zee, Fancy didn't believe in the restraints imposed by brassieres any more than those imposed by seat belts.

Eddy was beautiful. He was always perfectly groomed, and he dressed like a man, not a boy. The local louts, mostly shit-kickers and rednecks, wore cowboy clothes. God! Western wear was okay in its place. Hadn't she worn the gaudiest outfit she could find the year she was rodeo queen? But it belonged exclusively in the rodeo arena, as far as she was concerned.

Eddy wore dark three-piece suits and silk shirts and Italian leather shoes. He always smelled like he'd just stepped out of the shower. Thinking about him in the shower made her cream. She lived for the day she could touch his naked body, kiss it, lick him all over. She just knew he would taste good.

She squirmed with pleasure at the thought, but a frown of consternation soon replaced her expression of bliss. First she had to cure him of his hang-up over the gap in their ages. Then she'd have to help him get over the fact that she was his best friend's niece. Eddy hadn't come right out and said that's why he was resistant, but Fancy couldn't think of any other reason he would avoid the blatant invitation in her eyes every time she looked at him.

Everybody in the family had been tickled to death when she had volunteered to work at campaign headquarters. Grandpa had given her a hug that had nearly wrung the breath out of her. Grandma had smiled that vapid, ladylike smile Fancy detested and said in her soft, tepid voice, "How wonderful, dear." Daddy had stammered his surprised approval. Mama had even sobered up long enough to tell her she was glad she was doing something useful for a change.

Fancy had hoped Eddy's response would be equally as enthusiastic, but he had only appeared amused. All he had said was, "We need all the help down there we can get. By the way, can you type?"

Screw you, she had wanted to say. She didn't because her grandparents would have gone into cardiac arrest and because Eddy probably knew that's exactly what she was dying to say and she wouldn't give him the satisfaction of seeing her rattled.

So she had looked up at him with proper respect and said earnestly, "I do my best at whatever I undertake, Eddy."

The high-performance Mustang convertible sent up a cloud of dust as she wheeled up to the front door of the ranch house and cut the engine. She had hoped to get to the wing she shared with her parents without encountering anyone, but no such luck. As soon as she closed the door, her grandfather called out from the living room. "Who's that?"

"It's me, Grandpa."

He intercepted her in the hallway. "Hi, baby." He bent down to kiss her cheek. Fancy knew that he was sneakily checking her breath for alcohol. In preparation for that, she had consumed three breath mints on the way home to cover the smell of the cheap wine and strong pot.

He pulled away, satisfied. "Where'd you go tonight?"

"To the movies," she lied blithely. "How's Aunt Carole? Did the surgery go okay?"

"The doctor says it went fine. It'll be hard to tell for a week or so."

"God, it's just awful what happened to her face, isn't it?" Fancy pulled her own lovely face into a suitably sad frown. When she wanted to, she could bat her long lashes over her big blue eyes and look positively angelic. "I hope it turns out okay."

"I'm sure it will."

She could tell by his gentle smile that her concern had touched him. "Well, I'm tired. The movie was so boring, I nearly fell asleep in it. 'Night, Grandpa." She went up on tiptoe to kiss his cheek and mentally cringed. He would horsewhip her if he knew how her lips had been occupied barely an hour ago.

She moved along the central hallway and turned left into another. Through wide double doors at the end of it, she entered the wing of the house that she shared with her mother and father. She had her hand on the door to her room and was about to open it when Jack poked his head through his bedroom door.

"Fancy?"

"Hi, Daddy," she said with a sweet smile.

"Hi."

He didn't ask where she'd been because he didn't really want to know. That's why she told him. "I was at a . . . friend's." Her pause was deliberate, strategic, and rewarded by a pinched look that came to her father's mouth and eyes. "Where's Mama?"

He glanced over his shoulder into the room. "Sleeping."

Even from where she stood, Fancy could hear her mother's resonant snores. She wasn't just "sleeping," she was sleeping it off.

"Well, good night," Fancy said, edging into her bedroom.

He detained her. "How's it going down at headquarters?"

"Fine."

"You enjoying the work?"

"It's okay. Something to do."

"You could go back to college."

"Fuck that."

He winced but didn't chide. She had known he wouldn't. "Well, good night, Fancy."

" 'Night," she replied flippantly and soundly closed her bedroom door behind her.

⟫⟫⟫ SEVEN

"**I** might bring Mandy to see you tomorrow." Tate regarded her closely. "Since the swelling's gone down some, she'll be able to recognize you."

Avery gazed back at him. Even though he smiled encouragingly every time he looked at her face, she knew it was still frightful. There were no bandages to hide behind. As Irish would say, she could make a buzzard puke.

However, in the week since her operation, Tate had never avoided looking at her. She appreciated that charitable quality in him. As soon as her hands were capable of holding a pencil, she would write a note and tell him so.

The bandages had been removed from her hands several days ago. She had been dismayed at the sight of the red, raw, hairless skin. Her nails had been clipped short, making her hands look different, ugly. Each day she did physical therapy with a rubber ball, squeezing it in her weak fists, but she hadn't quite graduated to grasping a pencil and controlling it well enough to write. As soon as she could, there would be much she had to tell Tate Rutledge.

She had finally been weaned from the despised respirator. To her mortification, she hadn't been able to make a single sound—a traumatizing occurrence for a broadcast journalist who was already insecure in her career.

However, the doctors had cautioned her against becoming alarmed with the assurance that her voice would be restored gradually. They told her that the first few times she tried to speak she probably wouldn't be able to make herself understood, but that this was normal, considering the damage done to her vocal cords by the smoke she had inhaled.

Beyond that, she was virtually hairless, toothless, and taking liquid nourishment through a straw. Overall, she was still a mess.

"What do you think about that?" Tate asked her. "Do you feel up to having a visit with Mandy?"

He smiled, but Avery could tell his heart wasn't in it. She pitied him. He tried so valiantly to be cheerful and optimistic. Her earliest postoperative recollections were of him speaking soft words of encouragement. He had told her then and continued to tell her daily that the surgery had gone splendidly. Dr. Sawyer and all the nurses on the floor continued to commend her on her rapid progress and good disposition.

In her situation, what other kind of disposition could one have? She could cope with a broken leg if her hands could handle crutches, which they couldn't. She was still a prisoner to the hospital bed. Good disposition be damned. How did they know that she wasn't raging on the inside? She wasn't, but only because it wouldn't do any good. The damage had already been done. Avery Daniels's face had been replaced by someone else's. That recurring thought brought scalding tears to her eyes.

Tate misinterpreted them. "I promise not to keep Mandy here long, but I believe even a short visit with you would do her good. She's home now, you know. Everybody's pampering her, even Fancy. But she's still having a tough go of it at night. Seeing you might reassure her. Maybe she thinks we're lying to her when we say that you're coming back. Maybe she thinks you're really dead. She hasn't said so, but then, she doesn't say much of anything."

Dejectedly, he bent his head down and studied his hands. Avery stared at the crown of his head. His hair grew around a whorl that was slightly off-center. She enjoyed looking at him. More than her gifted surgeon, or the hospital's capable nursing staff, Tate Rutledge had become the center of her small universe.

As promised, sight in her left eye had been restored once the shelf to support her eyeball had been rebuilt. Three days following her surgery, the sutures on her eyelids had been taken out. She'd been promised that the packs inside her nose and the splint covering it would be removed tomorrow.

Tate had had fresh flowers delivered to her private room every day, as though to mark each tiny step toward full restoration. He was always smiling when he came in. He never failed to dispense a small bit of flattery.

Avery felt sorry for him. Though he tried to pretend otherwise, she could tell that these visits to her room were taxing. Yet if he stopped coming to see her, she thought she would die.

There were no mirrors in the room—nothing in fact that would reflect an image. She was sure that was by design. She longed to know what she looked like. Was her ghastly appearance the reason for the aversion that Tate tried so hard to conceal?

Like anyone with a physical disability, her senses had become keener. She had developed an acute perception into what people were thinking and feeling. Tate was being kind and considerate to his "wife." Common decency demanded it. There was, however, a discernible distance between them that Avery didn't understand.

"Should I bring her or not?"

He was sitting on the edge of her bed, being careful of her broken leg, which was elevated. It must be a cold day out, she reasoned, because he was wearing a suede jacket over his casual shirt. But the sun was shining. He'd been wearing sunglasses when he had come in. He had taken them off and slipped them into his breast pocket. His eyes were gray-green, straightforward, disarming. He was an extremely attractive man, she thought, mustering what objectivity she could.

How could she refuse to grant his request? He'd been so kind to her. Even though the little girl wasn't her daughter, if it would make Tate happier, she would pretend to be Mandy's mother just this once.

She nodded yes, something she'd been able to do since her surgery.

"Good." His sudden bright smile was sincere. "I checked with the head nurse and she said you could start wearing your own things if you wanted to. I took the liberty of packing some nightgowns and robes. It might be better for Mandy if you were wearing something familiar."

Again Avery nodded.

Motion at the door drew her eyes toward it. She recognized the man and woman as Tate's parents. Nelson and Zinnia, or Zee, as everybody called her.

"Well, looky here." Nelson crossed the room ahead of his wife and came to stand at the foot of Avery's bed. "You're looking fine, just fine, isn't she, Zee?"

Zee's eyes connected with Avery's. Kindly she replied, "Much better than yesterday even."

"Maybe that doctor is worth his fancy fee after all," Nelson remarked, laughing. "I never put much stock in plastic surgery. Always thought it was something vain, rich women threw away their husbands' money on. But this," he said, lifting his hand and indicating Avery's face, "this is going to be worth every penny."

Avery resented their hearty compliments when she knew she still looked every bit the victim of a plane crash.

Apparently Tate sensed that she was uncomfortable because he changed the subject. "She's agreed to let Mandy come see her tomorrow."

Zee's head snapped toward her son. Her hands met at her waist, where she clasped them tightly. "Are you sure that's wise, Tate? For Carole's sake, as well as Mandy's?"

"No, I'm not sure. I'm flying by the seat of my pants."

"What does Mandy's psychologist say?"

"Who the hell cares what she says?" Nelson asked crossly. "How could a shrink know more what's good for a kid than the kid's own daddy?" He clapped Tate on the shoulder. "I believe you're right. I think it'll do Mandy a world of good to see her mother."

"I hope you're right."

Zee didn't sound convinced, Avery noticed. She shared Zee's concern, but was powerless to express it. She only hoped that the benevolent gesture she was making for Tate's sake wouldn't backfire and do his emotionally fragile daughter more harm than good.

Zee went around the bright room watering the plants and flowers Avery had received, not only from Tate, but from people she didn't even know. Since no mention had ever been made of Carole's family, she deduced that she didn't have one. Her in-laws were her family.

Nelson and Tate were discussing the campaign, a topic that seemed never to be far from their minds. When they referred to Eddy, she mentally matched the name with a smooth-shaven face and impeccable clothing. He had come to see her on two occasions, accompanied by Tate each time. He seemed a pleasant chap, sort of the cheerleader of the group.

Tate's brother was named Jack. He was older and had a much more nervous nature than Tate. Or perhaps it just seemed so since during most of the time he'd been in her room, he had stammered apologies because his wife and daughter hadn't come to see her along with him.

Avery had gathered that Dorothy Rae, Jack's wife, was permanently indisposed by some sort of malady, though no one had referred to a debilitating illness. Fancy was obviously a bone of contention to everyone in the family. Avery had pieced together from their remarks that she was old enough to drive, but not old enough to live alone. They all lived together somewhere within an hour's drive of San Antonio. She vaguely recalled references to a ranch in the news stories about Tate. The family evidently had money and the prestige and power that accompanied it.

They were all friendly and cheerful when speaking to her. They chose their words carefully, so as not to alarm or distress her. What they didn't say interested her more than what they did.

She studied their expressions, which were generally guarded. Their smiles were tentative or strained. Tate's family treated his wife courteously, but there were undercurrents of dislike.

"This is a lovely gown," Zee said, drawing Avery's thoughts back into the

room. She was unpacking the things that Tate had brought from home and hanging
them in the narrow closet. "Maybe you should wear this tomorrow for Mandy's
visit."

Avery gave her a slight nod.

"Are you about finished there, Mom? I think she's getting tired." Tate moved
closer to the bed and looked deeply into her eyes. "You'll have a full day tomorrow. We'd better let you get some rest."

"Don't worry about a thing," Nelson said to her. "You're getting along fine,
just like we knew you would. Come on, Zee, let's give them a minute alone."

"Good-bye, Carole," Zee said.

They slipped out. Tate lowered himself to the edge of her bed again. He looked
weary. She wished she had the courage to reach out and touch him, but she didn't.
He'd never touched her with anything except consolation—certainly not affection.

"We'll come in the middle of the afternoon, after Mandy's nap." He paused
inquiringly; she nodded. "Look for us around three o'clock. I think it would be
best if Mandy and I came alone—without anybody else."

He glanced away, and drew a hesitant breath. "I have no idea how she'll
respond, Carole, but take into account all that she's been through. I know you've
been through a lot, too—a hell of a lot—but you're an adult. You've got more
power to cope than she does."

He met her eyes again. "She's just a little girl. Remember that." Then he
straightened and smiled briefly. "But, hey, I'm sure the visit will go well."

He stood to go. As usual when he was about to leave, Avery experienced a flurry
of panic. He was the only link she had with the world. He was her only reality.
When he left, he took her courage with him, leaving her to feel alone, afraid, and
alienated.

"Have a restful evening and get a good night's sleep. I'll see you tomorrow."

In farewell, he brushed her fingertips with his own, but he didn't kiss her. He
never kissed her. There wasn't too much of her that was accessible to kiss, but
Avery thought that a husband would have found a way to kiss his wife if he had
really wanted to.

She watched his retreating back until it disappeared through the door of her
room. Loneliness crept in from all sides to smother her. The only way she could
combat it was to think. She spent her waking hours planning how she was going
to tell Tate Rutledge the heartbreaking news that she wasn't who he thought she
was. His Carole was no doubt buried in a grave marked Avery Daniels. How
would she tell him that?

How could she tell him that somebody close to him wanted him dead?

At least a thousand times during the past week, she had tried convincing herself
that her ghostly visitor had been a nightmare. Any one of a number of contributing
factors could have made her hallucinate. It was easier to believe that the speaker
of those malevolent words had been a delusion.

But she knew better. He had been real. In her mind, his words were as clear as
a tropical lagoon. She had memorized them. The sinister tone and inflection were
indelibly recorded on her brain. He had meant what he had said. There was no
mistaking that.

He had to have been someone in the Rutledge family because only immediate
family was allowed in the intensive care unit. But who? None seemed to show any
malice toward Tate; quite the contrary, everyone seemed to adore him.

She considered each of them: His father? Unthinkable. It was evident that both
parents doted on him. Jack? He didn't appear to harbor any grudges toward his
younger brother. Though Eddy wasn't a blood relation, he was treated like a

member of the family, and the camaraderie between Tate and his best friend was plain to see. She had yet to hear Dorothy Rae or Fancy speak, but she was fairly certain the voice she had heard had been masculine.

None of the voices she had heard recently belonged to her visitor. But how could a stranger have sneaked into her room? The man had been no stranger to Carole; he had spoken to her as a confidante and coconspirator.

Did Tate realize that his wife was conspiring to have him killed? Did he guess she meant him harm? Was that why he administered comfort and encouragement from behind an invisible barrier? Avery knew he gave her what he was expected to give, but nothing more.

Lord, she wished she could sit down with Irish and lay out all the components of this tangle, as she often did before tackling a complex story. They would try to piece together the missing elements. Irish possessed almost supernatural insight into human behavior, and she valued his opinion above all others.

Thinking about the Rutledges had given Avery a splitting headache, so she welcomed the sedative that was injected into her IV that evening to help her sleep. Unlike the constant brilliance of the ICU, only one small night-light was left burning in her room every night.

Wavering between sleep and consciousness, Avery allowed herself to wonder what would happen if she assumed the role of Carole Rutledge indefinitely. It would postpone Tate's becoming a widower. Mandy would have a mother's support during her emotional recuperation. Avery Daniels could perhaps expose an attempted assassin and be hailed a heroine.

In her mind, she laughed. Irish would think she had gone crazy for sure. He would rant and rave and probably threaten to bend her over his knee and spank her for even thinking up such a preposterous idea.

Still, it was a provocative one. What a story she would have when the charade was over—politics, human relationships, and intrigue.

The fantasy lulled her to sleep.

 # EIGHT

She was more nervous than she had been before her first television audition at that dumpy little TV station in Arkansas eight years earlier. With damp palms and a dry throat, she had stood ankle deep in mud and swill, gripping the microphone with bloodless fingers and bluffing her way through an on-location story about a parasite currently affecting swine farmers. Afterward, the news director had drolly reminded her that the disease was affecting the swine, not the farmers. But he had given her the job of field reporter anyway.

This was an audition, too. Would Mandy detect what no one else had been able to—that the woman behind the battered face was not Carole Rutledge?

During the day, while the caring, talkative nurses had bathed and dressed her, while the physical therapist had gone through her exercises with her, a haunting question persisted: Did she want the truth to be revealed?

She had arrived at no definite answer. For the time being, what difference did it make who they perceived her to be? She couldn't alter fate. She was alive and Carole Rutledge was dead. Some cosmic force had deemed the outcome of that plane crash, not she.

She had tried desperately, with her severely limited capabilities, to alert everyone to their error, but without success. There was nothing she could do about the consequences of it now. Until she could use a tablet and pencil to communicate, she must remain Carole. While playing that role, she could do some undercover research into a bizarre news story and repay Tate Rutledge for his kindness. If he believed that Mandy would benefit from seeing her "mother," then Avery would temporarily go along with that. She thought the child might be better off by knowing the truth of her mother's death right away, but she wasn't in a position to tell her. Hopefully, her appearance wouldn't frighten the child so badly that she regressed.

The nurse adjusted the scarf covering her head, where her hair was still no more than an inch long. "There. Not bad at all," she said, appraising her handiwork. "In a couple more weeks, that handsome husband of yours won't be able to take his eyes off you. You know, of course, that all the single nurses, as well as a few married ones," she amended dryly, "are wildly in love with him."

She was moving around the bed, straightening the sheets and fussing with the flowers, pinching off blooms that had already peaked and were withering.

"You don't mind, do you?" she asked. "Surely you're used to other women lusting after him by now. How long have y'all been married? Four years, I believe he said when one of the nurses asked." She patted Avery's shoulder. "Dr. Sawyer works miracles. Wait and see. Y'all will be the best-looking couple in Washington."

"You're taking a lot for granted, aren't you?"

At the sound of his voice, Avery's heart fluttered. She looked toward the door to find him filling it. As he came farther into the room, he said to the nurse, "I'm convinced that Dr. Sawyer can work miracles. But are you sure that I'll win the election?"

"You've got my vote."

His laugh was deep and rich and as comfortable as an old, worn blanket. "Good. I'll need all the votes I can get."

"Where's your little girl?"

"I left her at the nurses' station. I'll get her in a few minutes."

Taking his subtle cue for what it was, the nurse smiled down at Avery and winked. "Good luck."

As soon as they were alone, Tate moved to Avery's side. "Hi. You look nice." He expelled a deep breath. "Well, she's here. I'm not sure how it'll go. Don't be disappointed if she—"

He broke off as his eyes flickered across her breasts. She didn't adequately fill the bodice of Carole's nightgown, modest as it was. Avery saw the puzzlement register on his face and her heart began to pound.

"Carole?" he said huskily.

He knew!

"My God."

How could she explain?

"You've lost so much weight," he whispered. Gently, he pressed his hand against the side of her breast. He looked over her body. Avery's blood flowed toward the contact of his hand. A small, helpless sound issued out of her throat.

"I don't mean to imply that you look bad—just . . . different. Stands to reason, I guess, that you would lose several pounds." Their eyes met and held for a moment, then he withdrew his hand. "I'll go get Mandy."

Avery took a deep breath to steady her jangled nerves. Until now she hadn't realized how unnerving the discovery of the truth was going to be to both of them.

Nor had she realized how far her feelings for him had extended. His touch had left her insides as weak as her extremities.

But she didn't have the luxury of letting her emotions crumble now. She braced herself for what was to come. She even closed her eyes, dreading the horror she would see on the child's face when she first looked at her disfigured "mother." She heard them enter and approach the bed. "Carole?"

Slowly, Avery opened her eyes. Tate was carrying Mandy against his chest. She was dressed in a white pinafore with a navy blue and white print dress beneath it. Her legs were encased in white stockings and she had on navy leather shoes. There was a cast on her left arm.

Her hair was dark and glossy. It was very thick and heavy, but not as long as Avery remembered it. As though reading her mind, Tate explained, "We had to cut her hair because some of it was singed." It was bobbed to chin length. She wore straight bangs above solemn brown eyes as large and round as quarters and as resigned as a doe's caught in cross hairs.

She was a beautiful child, yet she was unnaturally impassive. Instead of registering repulsion or fear or curiosity, which would have been the expected reactions, she registered nothing.

"Give Mommy the present you brought her," Tate prompted.

With her right fist she was strangling the stems of a bouquet of daises. She timidly extended them toward Avery. When Avery's fingers failed to grasp them, Tate took them from Mandy and gently laid them on Avery's chest.

"I'm going to set you here on the bed while I find some water to put the flowers in." Tate eased Mandy down on the edge of the bed, but when he moved away, she whimpered and fearfully clutched the lapels of his sports jacket.

"Okay," he said, "guess not." He shot Avery a wry smile and gingerly sat down behind Mandy, barely supporting his hip on the edge of the mattress.

"She colored this for you today," he said, addressing Avery over Mandy's head. From the breast pocket of his jacket, he withdrew a folded piece of manila paper and shook it out. "Tell her what it is, Mandy."

The multicolored scribbles didn't look like anything, but Mandy whispered, "Horses."

"Grandpa's horses," Tate said. "He took her riding yesterday, so this morning I suggested that she color you a picture of the horses while I was working."

Avery lifted her hand and signaled for him to hold the picture in front of her. She studied it at length before Tate laid it on her chest, along with the bouquet of daises.

"I think Mommy likes your picture." Tate continued looking at Avery with that odd expression.

The child wasn't much interested in whether or not her artwork was appreciated. She pointed at the splint on Avery's nose. "What that?"

"That's part of the bandages Grandma and I told you about, remember?" To Avery he said, "I thought it was coming off today."

She rolled her hand from a palm down position to palm up.

"Tomorrow?" he asked.

She nodded.

"What's it doing?" Mandy asked, still intrigued by the splint.

"It's sort of like your cast. It's protecting Mommy's face until it gets well, like the cast is protecting your arm while the bone inside grows back together."

Mandy listened to the explanation, then turned her solemn stare back onto Avery. "Mommy's crying."

"I think it's because she's very glad to see you."

Avery nodded, closed her eyes, held them closed for several seconds, then opened them. In that way she hoped to convey an emphatic yes. She was glad to see the child, who could so easily have died a fiery death. The crash had left emotional scars, but Mandy had survived and she would live to overcome her residual fear and timidity. Avery was also assailed by guilt and sorrow that she wasn't who they thought she was.

In one of those sudden, unexpected moves that only a child can execute, Mandy thrust out her hand, ready to touch Avery's bruised cheek. Tate reached around her and caught her hand just before it made contact. Then, thinking better of it, he guided her hand down.

"You can touch it very gently. Don't hurt Mommy."

Tears welled up in the child's eyes. "Mommy's hurt." Her lower lip began to tremble and she inclined toward Avery.

Avery couldn't bear to witness Mandy's anguish. Responding to a spontaneous maternal urge, she reached up and cradled Mandy's head with her scarred hand. Applying only as much pressure as her strength and pain would afford, she guided Mandy's head down to her breasts. Mandy came willingly, curling her small body against Avery's side. Avery smoothed her hand over Mandy's head and crooned to her wordlessly.

That inarticulate reassurance communicated itself to the child. In a few moments she stopped crying, sat up, and meekly announced, "I didn't spill my milk, Mommy."

Avery's heart melted. She wanted to take the child in her arms and hold her tight. She wanted to tell her that spilled milk didn't matter a damn because they had both survived a disaster. Instead, she watched Tate stand and pull Mandy back up into his arms.

"We don't want to wear out our welcome," he said. "Blow Mommy a kiss, Mandy." She didn't. Instead, she shyly wrapped her arms around his neck and turned her face into his collar. "Some other time," he told Avery with an apologetic shrug. "I'll be right back."

He was gone for a few minutes and returned alone. "I left her at the nurses' station. They gave her a Dixie cup of ice cream."

He lowered himself to the edge of the bed and sat with his hands between his knees. Rather than look at her, he stared at his hands. "Since it went so well, I may bring her back later in the week. At least *I* felt it went well. Did you?" He glanced over his shoulder for her answer. She nodded.

He diverted his attention back to his hands. "I'm not sure how Mandy felt about it. It's hard to tell how she feels about anything. We can't seem to get through, Carole." The despair in his voice tore at Avery's heart. "A trip to McDonald's used to make her do cartwheels. Now, nothing." His elbows settled on his knees and he dropped his head into his waiting palms. "I've tried everything I know of to reach her. Nothing works. I don't know what else to do."

Avery lifted her arm and smoothed back the hair that grew away from his temple.

He flinched and whipped his head around, almost knocking her hand away. She snatched it back so quickly and reflexively that it sent a pain shooting up her arm. She moaned.

"I'm sorry," he said, instantly coming to his feet. "Are you all right? Should I call somebody?"

She made a negative motion with her head, then self-consciously repositioned the slipping scarf. More than ever before, she felt exposed and naked. She wished she could conceal her ugliness from him.

When he was convinced she was no longer in pain, he said, "Don't worry about Mandy. Given time, I'm sure she'll be fine. I shouldn't have brought it up. I'm just tired. The campaign is escalating and . . . never mind. Those are my concerns, not yours. I've got to be going. I know our visit has been hard on you. Good-bye, Carole."

This time, he didn't even brush her fingertips in farewell.

 # NINE

"Are we boring you, Tate?"

Guiltily, he glanced up at his campaign manager. "Sorry."

Tate, acknowledging that Eddy had every right to be perturbed with him, cleared his throat and sat up straighter in the leather easy chair. He stopped mindlessly twirling a pencil between his fingers.

They were spending the day at home, holding a powwow to outline campaign strategy for these last few weeks before the primary.

"Exactly where did you drift off?"

"Somewhere in El Paso and Sweetwater," Tate answered. "Look, Eddy, are you sure that sweep through West Texas is essential?"

"Absolutely essential," Jack chimed in. "With the price of Texas crude where it is, those folks out there need all the pep talks you can give them."

"I'll tell it like it is. You know how I feel about false hopes and empty promises."

"We understand your position completely, Tate," Nelson said. "But Senator Dekker is partly responsible for the fix the oil business is in. He favored that trade agreement with the Arabs. Those unemployed roughnecks need to be reminded of that."

Tate tossed the pencil onto the conference table and stood up. Sliding his hands into the hip pockets of his jeans, he went to stand in front of the window.

It was a spectacular day. Spring was still a fledgling chick, but redbud trees and daffodils were blooming. Grass in the pastures was gradually turning green.

"You don't agree with Nelson's observation?" Eddy asked.

"I agree wholeheartedly," Tate replied, keeping his back to them. "I know I need to be out there citing Dekker's bad judgment and doling out optimism, but I also need to be here."

"With Carole."

"Yes. And with Mandy."

"I thought Mandy's shrink said all she needed was time, and that after Carole returned home, Mandy would naturally improve," Jack said.

"She did."

"So, whether you're here or not won't matter a whole hell of a lot to Mandy. There's not a thing you can do for Carole, either."

"I can be with her," Tate said impatiently. Feeling defensive, he turned to face them.

"Doing what? Just standing there and staring at those two big, bruised eyes," Jack said. "Jesus, they give me the creeps." Tate's face grew taut with anger over his brother's insensitive remark.

"Shut up, Jack," Nelson snapped.

Tate said crisply, "Just standing there staring might be all I can do for her, Jack, but it's still my responsibility to do it. Didn't I make that clear to you weeks ago?"

With a long-suffering sigh, Eddy lowered himself into a chair. "I thought we had all agreed that Carole was better off in that private clinic than here at home."

"We did."

"She's treated like royalty there—better than she was in the hospital," Jack observed. "She's looking better every day. I was just kidding about her eyes. Once the redness goes away and her hair grows back, she'll look great. So what's the problem?"

"The problem is that she's still recovering from trauma and serious physical injury," Tate said testily.

"No one is arguing that point," Nelson said. "But you've got to seize every opportunity, Tate. You've got a responsibility to your campaign that can't be neglected any more than you can neglect your wife."

"Don't you think I realize that?" he asked the three of them.

"You realize it," Eddy said. "And so does Carole."

"Maybe. But she doesn't do as well when I'm away. Dr. Sawyer told me she becomes very depressed."

"How the hell does he know whether she's depressed or laughing her head off? She still can't say a goddamned—"

"Jack!" Nelson spoke in the tone he had frequently used during the course of his military career to reduce cocky airmen to groveling penitents. Every inch the retired air force colonel, he glared at his older son.

He had rarely spanked his children when they were growing up, resorting to corporal punishment only when he felt it was absolutely necessary. Usually a single, quelling look and that harsh tone of voice would whip them back into line. "Have a little consideration for your brother's predicament, please."

Parental respect silenced Jack, but he flopped back in his chair with obvious exasperation.

"Carole would be the first to tell you to go on this trip," Nelson said to Tate in a quieter voice. "I wouldn't say that if I didn't believe it."

"I agree with Nelson," Eddy said.

"And I agree with both of you. Before the accident, she would have been packing right along with me." Tate rubbed the back of his neck, trying to work out some of the tension and fatigue.

"Now when I tell her I'm leaving, I see panic in her eyes. It haunts me. She's still so pathetic. I feel guilty. Before I leave for any extended time, I have to take into account how she's going to respond to my being away."

He took a silent inventory of their reactions. On each of their faces was an argument wanting to be spoken. Out of consideration, they were keeping their opposing opinions to themselves.

He expelled a deep breath. "Shit. I'm going out for a while."

He stamped from the room and left the house. In under five minutes, he was mounted on horseback and galloping across one of the ranch's pastures, skirting heads of lazily grazing hybrid beef cattle. No particular destination was on his mind; he just needed the privacy and peace that the open air afforded.

These days, he was rarely by himself, but he had never felt more alone in his entire life. His father, Eddy, and Jack could all advise him on political issues, but personal decisions were just that—personal. Only he could make them.

He kept thinking about the way Carole had touched him. He wondered what it meant.

In the two weeks since it had happened, he had reviewed and analyzed it to death and still couldn't get it off his mind. Because of his stunned reaction to it, it hadn't lasted more than a split second—just long enough for her fingertips to rake gently through the hair at his temples. But he considered it the most important caress he and Carole had ever shared—more important than their first kiss, than the first time they had made love . . . than the last time they had made love.

He reined in and dismounted beside a single-fed stream that trickled down from the limestone hills. Scrub oak, cedar, and mesquite trees dotted the rocky ground. The wind was strong, out of the north. It stung his cheeks and made his eyes water. He'd left without a jacket, but the sun was warm.

That touch had surprised the hell out of him because it was such an uncharacteristic thing for her to do. She knew how to touch a man, all right. Even now, after all that had happened between them, memories of their earlier days together could make him hard with desire. Very skillfully, Carole had used touching to communicate when she wanted him. Whether she chose to be teasing, subtle, or downright dirty, she knew how to convey her desires.

This one had been different. He had felt the difference. It had been a touch of concern and caring and compassion. It had been untutored—spawned by a guileless heart, not a calculating mind. Unselfish, not the reverse.

Very unlike Carole.

The sound of a horse approaching brought his head around. Nelson reined in and dismounted with almost as much agility as Tate had minutes before. "Thought I'd ride out, too. Good day for it." He tilted his head back and gazed at the cloudless, cerulean sky.

"Bullshit. You came to aid and abet."

Nelson chuckled and indicated with a nod that they should sit on one of the bleached white boulders. "Zee spotted you taking off. She suggested it was time to call a break in the meeting. She served sandwiches to the others and sent me after you. Said you looked upset."

"I am."

"Well, get over it," Nelson ordered.

"It's not that easy."

"We knew from the beginning that this campaign was going to be a bitch, Tate. What did you expect?"

"It's not the campaign. I'm ready for that," he said with a determined jut of his cleft chin.

"Then it's this business with Carole. You knew that wasn't going to be a picnic, either."

Tate swiveled his head around and asked bluntly, "Have you noticed the changes in her?"

"The doctor warned you that there would be some slight alterations in her appearance, but they're hardly noticeable."

"Not physical changes. I'm talking about the way she reacts to things."

"Can't say that I have. Like what?"

Tate cited several instances when Carole's eyes had registered uncertainty, insecurity, fear.

Nelson listened to every word, then ruminated for a long time before saying anything. "I'd say her anxiety was natural, wouldn't you? Her face was torn up to a fare-thee-well. That would make any woman uncertain, but a woman who looked like Carole—well, the thought of losing her beauty would be enough to shake her confidence."

"I suppose you're right," Tate muttered, "but I would expect rage from her before fear. I really can't explain it. It's just something I feel." Absently, he recounted Mandy's first visit to Carole. "I've taken her back three times, and during each visit Carole cries and holds Mandy against her."

"She's thinking how easily she could have lost her."

"It's more than that, Dad. One day while she was still at the hospital, when we stepped off the elevator, she was sitting there in the hall in a wheelchair, waiting for our arrival. It was before her teeth were replaced. Her head was wrapped in a scarf. Her leg was propped up in that cast." Perplexed, he shook his head. "She looked like hell, but there she was, bold as brass. Now, is that something Carole would do?"

"She was eager to see you, to show off her ability to get out of bed."

Tate considered that for a moment, but it still didn't gel. When had Carole ever put herself out to please someone else? He could have sworn that despite her inability to smile, she was beaming at the sight of Mandy and him when the elevator doors opened. "So you think it's all an act?"

"No," Nelson said hesitantly. "I just think it's—"

"Temporary."

"Yes," he said flatly. "I face facts, Tate. You know that. I don't mean to butt into your personal life. Zee and I want you and Jack and your families to stay here on the ranch with us. And because we do, we've made it a point never to interfere with your private business. If I did what I felt inclined to, I'd see to it that Dorothy Rae got professional help for her problem and I'd blister Fancy's butt for all the times it should have been blistered and wasn't."

He paused before continuing. "Maybe I should have said something before now, but I was hoping that you would take the initiative to set your marriage straight. I know that you and Carole have sort of grown apart over the last couple of years." He held up both hands. "You don't have to tell me why. I don't need to know. It's just something that I've sensed, you know?

"Hell, every marriage goes through rough spots now and then. Zee and I hope that you and Carole will iron out your differences, have another baby, go to Washington, and live to grow old together. Maybe this tragedy will patch up the problems you had and bring you closer together.

"But," he said, "don't expect Carole to change entirely as a result of what's happened to her. If anything, it'll take more patience to get along with her than it has up till now."

Tate edited his father's speech, picking out the pertinent points and reading between the lines. "You're telling me that I'm looking for something that isn't there, is that it?"

"I'm saying it's a possibility," the older man stressed. "Usually when someone has a close brush with death, he goes through a period of smelling the roses. I've seen it happen with pilots who ditched their planes and lived to tell about it.

"You know, they contemplate all that could have been taken from them in the blink of an eye, feel guilty for not appreciating their loved ones, and promise to make amends, improve their general attitude toward life, become a better person—that kind of thing." He rested his hand on Tate's knee. "I think that's what you're seeing in Carole.

"I don't want you to start hoping that this incident has rid her of all her faults and left her a paragon of what a wife should be. Dr. Sawyer guaranteed to remove some of the imperfections in her face, but he never said a word about her soul," he added with a smile.

"I guess you're right," Tate said tautly. "I *know* you're right. That's exactly what I was doing, looking for improvements that aren't really there."

Nelson used Tate's shoulder as a prop as he stood up. "Don't be so hard on yourself or on her. Time and patience are indispensable investments. Anything worth having is worth waiting for, no matter how long it takes—even a lifetime.''

They mounted and turned the horses toward the house. On the way back, they said very little. As they drew up in front of the stable, Tate leaned on his saddle horn and turned to address his father.

"About that trip to West Texas.''

"Yeah?'' Nelson threw his right leg over and stepped to the ground.

"I'll compromise. One week. I can't be gone any longer than that.''

Nelson slapped Tate's thigh with the reins he was holding, then handed them to Tate. "I figured you'd come around. I'll tell Eddy and Jack." He headed for the house.

"Dad?'' Nelson stopped and turned. "Thanks,'' Tate said.

Nelson waved off the gratitude. "Put those horses up properly.''

Tate walked his horse into the stable, pulling Nelson's along behind. He dismounted and began the rubdown procedure he'd been taught to do as early as he'd been taught to ride.

But after several minutes, his hands fell idle on the horse's rump and he stared into space.

He had needed her compassion and tenderness that night. He had wanted to trust the motives behind her touch. For the sake of their marriage and Mandy, he had hoped these changes in her would be permanent.

Only time would tell, but his father was probably right. It was wishful thinking to believe that Carole had changed, when her previous actions had shown her to be faithless and untrustworthy. He couldn't give her the benefit of the doubt without everybody, chiefly himself, thinking he was a fool for trusting her even that far.

"Damn.''

 TEN

"After that, we intend to send him up to the panhandle for a speech at Texas Tech.'' As Jack detailed Tate's itinerary to his sister-in-law, a fresh thought occurred to him. "You know, Tate, there are a lot of cotton farmers in that region. I wonder if Eddy's considered having you speak to a co-op or something?''

"If he hasn't, he should. I definitely want to.''

"I'll make a mental note to have him schedule something.''

From her bed, Avery observed the two brothers. There was enough resemblance to place them in the same family, but enough difference to make them drastically unlike each other.

Jack appeared more than three years older that Tate. His hair, several shades darker than Tate's, was thinning on top. He wasn't exactly paunchy, but his physique wasn't well honed, as Tate's was.

Of the two, Tate was much better looking. Although there was nothing offensive about Jack's appearance, there wasn't anything distinguishing about it, either. He faded into the woodwork. Tate couldn't if he tried.

"Forgive us for taking him away from you for so long, Carole.'' She noticed that Jack never looked directly at her when speaking to her. He would always address some other area of her body besides her face—her chest, her hand, the cast on her leg. "We wouldn't if we didn't feel it was important to the campaign."

Her fingers closed around the oversized pencil in her hand and she scrawled "okay" on the tablet. Jack tilted his head, read what she'd written, shot her a weak smile, and nodded curtly. There were unpleasant undercurrents between Jack and his sister-in-law. Avery wondered what they were.

"Tate said you managed to say some words today," he said. "That's great news. We'll all be glad to hear what you've got to say once you can talk again."

Avery knew Tate wouldn't be glad to hear what she had to say. He would want to know why she hadn't written down her name, why she had let him go on believing that she was his wife, even after she'd regained enough coordination in her hand to use the pencil on the tablet.

She wanted to know that herself.

Anxiety over it brought tears to her eyes. Jack immediately stood and began backing toward the door. "Well, it's getting late, and I'm facing that long drive home. Good luck, Carole. You coming, Tate?"

"Not quite yet, but I'll walk you to the lobby." After telling her that he would be back in a few minutes, he accompanied his brother from the room.

"I think I upset her by talking about your trip," Jack remarked.

"She's been touchy the last few days."

"You'd think she'd be glad she was getting her voice back, wouldn't you?"

"I guess it's frustrating to try and speak plainly when you can't." Tate moved to the tinted glass doors of the exclusive clinic and pulled one open.

"Uh, Tate, have you noticed something weird when she writes?"

"Weird?"

He moved aside to admit a pair of nurses into the lobby, followed by a man carrying an arrangement of copper chrysanthemums. Jack stepped outside, but used his hand to prevent the door from closing behind him.

"Carole's right-handed, isn't she?"

"Yeah."

"So why is she writing with her left hand?" As soon as Jack posed the puzzling question, he shrugged. "I just thought it was odd." His hand fell to his side and the hydraulic door began to close. "See you at home, Tate."

"Drive carefully."

Tate stood staring after his brother until someone else approached the door and looked at him inquiringly. He pivoted on his heels and thoughtfully retraced his steps toward Carole's room.

While Tate was gone, Avery thought about how he had changed. She had sensed a difference in his attitude more than a week ago. He still paid her regular visits, but they were no longer on a daily basis. At first she had excused this, knowing that his campaign was in full swing.

Whenever he came, he still brought flowers and magazines. Now that she could eat solid foods, he brought her junk food to augment the hospital's excellent, but boring cuisine. He'd even had a VCR installed and had supplied her with a variety of movies to help entertain her. But he was often withdrawn and moody, guarded in what he said to her. He never stayed for very long.

As Carole's face became more distant, Tate became more distant.

He hadn't brought Mandy to see her, either. She had printed Mandy's name, followed by a question mark, on the tablet and held it up to him. He had shrugged. "I thought the visits were probably doing her more harm than good. You'll have plenty of time to spend with her once you're back home."

The insensitive words had wounded her. Mandy's visits had become highlights in her monotonous existence. On the other hand, it was probably better that he had suspended them. She was growing too attached to the child and wanted desperately to help see her through this crisis in her young life. Since she wouldn't have that opportunity, it was wise to sever any emotional bonds now.

The attachment she had developed for Tate was more complex and would be considerably harder to sever when she moved out of his world and back into her own.

At least she would be taking something back with her: the ingredients of a juicy inside story on the man running for the U.S. Senate whom someone wanted murdered.

Avery's journalistic curiosity ran rampant. What had been amiss in the Rutledges' marriage? Why had Carole wanted her husband dead? She wanted to exhaust all the possibilities until she arrived at the truth. Telling that truth might lift her out of the muck she'd made of her professional life. Yet it left a bad taste in her mouth to think about broadcasting that truth.

Tate Rutledge's problems belonged to her now just as much as they did to him. She hadn't asked for them; they'd been imposed on her. But she couldn't just turn her back on them. For some bizarre reason that defied explanation, she felt compelled to make up for Carole's shortcomings.

The one time she had extended a compassionate hand to him, he had emphatically rebuffed her, but the strife between Tate and Carole went beyond the normal marriage in trouble. There was another almost malevolent dimension to it. He treated her as one might a caged wild beast. He saw to all her needs, but from a careful distance. His approach was mistrustful, as though her behavior couldn't be depended on.

As Avery knew, Tate's wariness of his wife was well-founded. Carole, along with another individual, had plotted to kill him. How and why were the questions that haunted her more than any others.

The troubling thoughts were temporarily shelved when he returned from escorting Jack out. However, her welcoming smile wavered as he approached her chair. He was scowling.

"Why are you writing with your left hand?"

Avery froze. So, this was to be the moment of truth. She had hoped to choose the time herself, but it had been chosen for her. How stupid she'd been to make such a blunder! Percentages were strongly against Carole Rutledge being left-handed.

She looked up at him with appeal and managed to speak a guttural version of his name.

God help me, she prayed as she fumbled for the pencil with her left hand. As soon as she revealed her identity, she must warn him of the planned assassination. The only time limit placed on it was that he would never live to take office. It could happen tomorrow, tonight. It might not happen until next November, but he had to be warned immediately.

Who in his family would she accuse? She hadn't revealed herself as soon as she could control a pencil because she didn't have enough facts. She had vainly hoped that each new day would provide her with some.

Once she had outlined the meager facts she knew, would he believe her?

Why should he?

Why should he even listen to a woman who had, for almost two months, passed herself off as his wife? He would think she was an unconscionable opportunist, which could be uncomfortably close to the truth if she weren't genuinely concerned for his and Mandy's welfare.

The pencil moved beneath the painstaking coaxing of her fingers. She drew the letter *h*. Her hand was shaking so badly, she dropped the pencil. It rolled downward, slid across her lap, and finally became lodged between her hip and the seat of the upholstered chair.

Tate went after it. His strong fingers nudged her flesh. He replaced the pencil in her hand and guided it back onto the tablet. "*H* what?"

Beseechingly, she looked up at him, silently asking for his forgiveness. Then she finished the word she had begun. When she had printed it, she turned the tablet toward him.

"Hurts," he read. "It hurts to use your right hand?"

Immersed in guilt, Avery nodded her head. "It hurts," she croaked, and raised her right hand where the skin was still sensitive.

Her lie was justified, she assured herself. She couldn't tell him the truth until she could explain everything in detail. A scrawled message, a few key words without any elaboration, would only pitch him into a frenzy of anger and confusion. In that kind of mental state, he would never believe that someone wanted to kill him.

He gave her a soft, short laugh. "You had Jack spooked. I can't believe I didn't notice it myself. I guess I've had too much on my mind to sweat the details."

He placed his hands in the small of his back and arched it, stretching luxuriantly. "Well, I've got that drive ahead of me, and it's getting late. I understand your cast comes off tomorrow. That's good. You'll be able to move around better."

Avery's eyes clouded with tears. This man, who had been so kind to her, was going to hate her when he discovered the truth. Through the weeks of her recuperation, he had unwittingly become her lifeline. Whether he was aware of it or not, she had depended on him for physical and emotional healing.

Now, she must repay his kindness by telling him three ugly truths: his wife was dead; in her place was a broadcast journalist who was privy to aspects of his personal life; and someone was going to try to assassinate him.

Rather than eliciting his pity, her tears provoked him. He glanced away in irritation, and as he did, he noticed the newspapers stacked on the deep windowsill. She had requested them from the deferential staff. They were back issues, containing accounts of the plane crash. Tate gestured toward them.

"I don't understand your tears, Carole. Your face looks great. You could have died, for crissake. So could Mandy. Can't you consider yourself lucky to be alive?"

After that outburst, he drew himself up and took a deep breath, controlling his temper by an act of will. "Look, I'm sorry. I didn't mean to lash out like that. I know you've suffered a lot. It's just that you could have suffered a hell of a lot more. We all could have."

He reached for the sports jacket he frequently wore with his jeans and pulled it on. "I'll see you later."

With no more than that, he left her.

Avery stared at the empty doorway for a long while. A nurse came in and helped her prepare for sleep. She had graduated from a wheelchair to crutches for her broken leg, but was still awkward on them. Gripping them hurt her hands. By the time she was settled and left alone, she was exhausted.

Her mind was as tired as her body, and yet she couldn't sleep. She tried to envision the expression that would break across Tate's face when he discovered the truth. His life would undergo another upheaval, and at a time when he was most vulnerable.

The instant the word vulnerable formed in her mind, Avery was struck by a new and terrifying thought. As soon as she was exposed, she, too, would be vulnerable to whoever planned to kill Tate!

Why hadn't she thought of that before? When Avery Daniels, a television news reporter, was revealed, the culprit would realize his grave error and be forced to do something about it. She would be as susceptible to attack as Tate. Judging by the deadly calculation she had heard in his voice, the would-be assassin wouldn't hesitate to murder both of them.

She sat up and peered into the shadows of the room, as if expecting her faceless, nameless nemesis to leap out at her. Her rapid heartbeats echoed loudly against her eardrums.

Lord, what could she do? How could she protect herself? How could she protect Tate? If only she really were Carole, she—

Before the idea was even fully developed, her mind began hurling objections, both conscientious and practical. It couldn't be done. Tate would know. The assassin would know.

But if she could keep playing the role long enough to determine who Tate's secret enemy was, she could save his life.

Yet it was inconceivable to step into another woman's life. And what about her own? Officially, Avery Daniels no longer existed. No one would be missing her. She had no husband, no children, no family.

Her career was in a shambles. Because of one mistake—one gross error in judgment—she was deemed a failure by anyone's standards. Not only had she failed to live up to her father's sterling reputation, she'd taken the glint off it. Working at KTEX in San Antonio was like being sentenced to years of hard labor. While the station had a solid reputation for a market its size, and while she would be eternally grateful to Irish for giving her a job when no one else would even grant her an interview, employment there was tantamount to banishment in Siberia. She was alienated from journalistic circles that really counted. KTEX was a long step down from a network job and a Washington, D.C., beat.

But now, a sensational story had been dropped into her lap. If she became Mrs. Tate Rutledge, she could document a senatorial campaign and an attempted murder from an insider's point of view. She wouldn't just be covering the story, she would be living it.

What better vehicle to launch herself back to the top echelon of broadcast news? How many reporters had ever been given an opportunity like this? She knew scores who would give their right arm for it.

She smiled wanly. Her right arm hadn't been required of her, but she had given her face, her name, and her own identity already. Saving a man's life and getting a career boost would be repayment enough for such an indignity. And when the truth finally came out, no one could accuse her of exploitation. She hadn't asked for this chance; it had been forced on her. She wouldn't be exploiting Tate, either. Even above her desire to restore her professional credibility, she wanted to preserve his life, which had become precious to her.

The risks involved were astronomical, but she couldn't name a single ace reporter who hadn't stuck his neck out to get where he was. Her father had taken daily risks in the pursuit of his profession. His courage had paid off with a Pulitzer prize. If he was willing to risk everything for his stories, could less be expected of her?

However, she realized that this had to be a rational business decision. She must approach it pragmatically, not emotionally. She would be assuming the role of Tate's wife and all that the relationship implied and entailed. She would be living with his family, constantly observed by people who knew Carole intimately.

The enormity of the challenge was intimidating, but it was also irresistible. The consequences could be severe, but the rewards would be worth any price.

She would make a million mistakes, like writing with the wrong hand. But she'd always had a knack for thinking on her feet. She would talk her way out of mistakes.

Could it work? Could she do it? *Dare* she try?

She threw off the covers, propped herself on her crutches, and hobbled into the bathroom. Beneath the glaring, merciless fluorescent lighting, she stared at the face in the mirror and compared it to the photograph of Carole that had been taped to the wall for encouragement.

The skin looked new, as pink and smooth as a baby's butt, just as Dr. Sawyer had promised. She peeled her lips back and studied the dental prostheses that were duplicates of Carole Rutledge's front teeth. She ran her hand over the close cap of dark hair. No scars were discernible, unless one looked very closely. In time, all traces would fade into invisibility.

She didn't allow herself the luxury of sadness, though regret and homesickness for her own familiar image tugged at her heart. This was her destiny now. She had a new face. It could be her ticket to a new life.

Tomorrow, she would assume the identity of Carole Rutledge.

Avery Daniels had nothing else to lose.

 # ELEVEN

The nurse gave her a satisfied once-over. "You've got wonderful hair, Mrs. Rutledge."

"Thanks," Avery said ruefully. "What there is of it."

During the seven days that Tate had been away, she had fully regained her voice. He was due to arrive at any moment, and she was nervous.

"No," the nurse was saying, "that's my point. Not everybody can wear such a short style. On you, it's a knockout."

Avery glanced into the hand mirror, plucked at the spiky bangs on her forehead, and said dubiously, "I hope so."

She was seated in a chair with her right leg elevated on a footstool. A cane was propped against the chair. Her hands were folded together in her lap.

The nurses were as aflutter as she over Tate's imminent arrival after being out of town for more than a week. They had primed her like a bride waiting for her groom.

"He's here," one of them announced in a stage whisper, poking her head around the door. The nurse with Avery squeezed her shoulder. "You look terrific. He's going to be bowled over."

He wasn't exactly bowled over, but he was momentarily stunned. She watched his eyes widen marginally when he spotted her sitting in the chair, wearing street clothes—Carole's street clothes—which Zee had brought her several days earlier.

"Hello, Tate."

At the sound of her voice, he registered even more surprise.

Her heart lurched. *He knew!*

Had she made another blunder? Did Carole have a pet name she always addressed him by? She held her breath, waiting for him to point an accusing finger at her and shout, "You lying impostor!"

Instead, he cleared his throat uneasily and returned her greeting. "Hello, Carole."

Through her finely fashioned nose, she exhaled thin little wisps of air, not wanting to give away her relief by expelling the deep breath she'd been holding for so long it had made her chest ache.

He came farther into the room, and absently laid a bunch of flowers and a package on the nightstand. "You look great."

"Thank you."

"You can talk," he said with an awkward laugh.

"Yes. Finally."

"Your voice sounds different."

"We were warned of that, remember?" she said quickly.

"Yeah, but I didn't expect the . . ." He made a motion with his fingers across his throat. "The hoarseness."

"It might eventually fade."

"I like it."

He couldn't take his eyes off her. If things between them had been what they should have been, he would be kneeling in front of her, skimming her new face with his fingertips like a blind man, marveling over its smoothness, and telegraphing his love. To her disappointment, he maintained a careful distance.

As usual, he was wearing jeans. They were pressed and creased, but old and soft enough to glove his lower body. Avery didn't want to be trapped by her own feminine curiosity, so she resolutely kept her eyes above the lapel of his sports jacket.

The view from there was very good, too. Her gaze was almost as penetrating as his.

She nervously raised her hand to her chest. "You're staring."

His head dropped forward, but only for a split second before he raised it again. "I'm sorry. I guess I really didn't expect you to ever look like yourself again. And . . . and you do. Except for the hair."

She gave a little shiver of joy because her ruse had worked.

"Are you cold?"

"What? Cold? No." She recklessly groped for something to divert him. "What's that?"

He followed her nod to the package he had carried in with him. "Oh, it's your jewelry."

"Jewelry?" Her bubble of happiness burst. She swallowed with difficulty.

"What you were wearing the day of the plane crash. The hospital called the law office today to remind me it was still in their safe. I stopped there on my way here to pick it up. I kept forgetting about it." He extended the envelope to her. Avery stared at it as though it were a poisonous snake and was just as loath to touch it. Seeing no way to avoid it, however, she took it from him. "I didn't take the time to inventory the contents," he said, "but maybe you should now."

She laid the envelope in her lap. "I will later."

"I thought you'd want your things back."

"Oh, I do. It's just not very comfortable to wear jewelry right now." She formed a fist, then slowly opened it, extending her fingers. "My hands are almost back to normal, but they still get sore. I think I'd have trouble slipping my rings on and off."

"That would be a first, wouldn't it? For your wedding ring, anyway."

The harsh words took her aback. He wasn't wearing a wedding ring, either, she noted, and was tempted to point that out in Carole's defense, but she curbed the impulse. If Carole had removed her wedding ring for illicit purposes, as he'd insinuated, the subject was best avoided—for now.

Tate sat down on the edge of the bed. The hostile silence stretched out. Avery was the first to break it. "Did the trip go as well as you had hoped?"

"Yeah, it was fine. Tiring as hell."

"I saw you on television nearly every night. The crowds seemed enthusiastic."

"Everybody was pleased with the response I got."

"All the political analysts are predicting that you'll win the primary by a landslide."

"I hope so."

They lapsed into another silence while each tried, without much success, to keep from staring at the other.

"How is Mandy?"

He gave a dismissive shrug. "She's fine."

Avery frowned doubtfully.

"Okay, not so fine." He stood again and began pacing the length of the bed, his boot heels making crescent impressions in the carpeting. "Mom says she's still having nightmares. She wakes up screaming nearly every night, sometimes even during her nap. She moves around the house like a little ghost." He extended his hands as though reaching for something, then closed them around nothingness. "Not quite there, you know? Nobody's getting through—not me, not the psychologist."

"I asked Zee to bring her to see me. She said you had told her not to."

"That's right."

"Why?"

"I didn't think it would be a good idea for her to come when I wasn't here."

She didn't press her luck by asking why. It might spark another argument she wasn't yet equipped to handle. "I miss her. Once I'm at home, she'll do better."

His skepticism was plain. "Maybe."

"Does she ever ask for me?"

"No."

Avery lowered her gaze to her lap. "I see."

"Well, what do you expect, Carole? You only get back what you give."

For a moment their eyes clashed, then her hand came up to her forehead. Tears filled her eyes. She cried for the child who hadn't had enough of her mother's love. Poor little Mandy. Avery knew how it felt to be deprived of a parent's attention. That's why she justified pretending to be Mandy's mother when, initially, she had felt Mandy would profit from being told of Carole's demise immediately.

"Aw, shit," Tate said beneath his breath. He crossed the room and lightly rested his hand on the top of her head. His fingers worked their way through her stubby hair until the pads were gently massaging her scalp. "I'm sorry. I didn't mean to make you cry. Mandy's going to get better—much better." After a moment he said, "Maybe I should go."

"No!" Her head snapped up. Tears still drenched her eyes. "I wish you wouldn't."

"It's time I did."

"Please stay a while longer."

"I'm tired and cranky from the trip—not good company."

"I don't mind."

He shook his head.

Valiantly, she masked her immense disappointment. "I'll see you out then."

She reached for her cane and placed her weight on it as she stood up. But her nervously perspiring hand slipped on the crook and caused her to lose her balance.

"Christ, be careful."

Tate's arms went around her. The manila envelope fell from her lap onto the floor, but neither noticed. His arm supported her back, and his strong fingers aligned with her ribs beneath the soft weight of her breast.

As he inched her toward the bed, Avery clung to him, curling her fingers into the cloth of his jacket. She deeply inhaled his scent—clean but outdoorsy, fragrant but masculine, with a trace of citrus. His strength permeated her and she imbibed it like an elixir.

She acknowledged then what she had avoided acknowledging during the long, torturous days he had been away. She wanted to become Mrs. Rutledge so she could be close to Tate. Based on the misery she'd felt during his absence and the joy she'd experienced when he had entered her room, that was no less valid a reason than the others. At least, it was just as strong.

He eased her onto the side of the bed, and gingerly touched the thigh of her injured leg. "That was a multiple fracture. The bone's still not as strong as you'd like to think."

"I guess not."

"We were right to decide you should stay here until after the primary. All that activity would be too much for you."

"Probably."

Her reply was qualified, because when Zee had told her that had been the decision reached without her consent or consultation, she had felt abandoned, like a family embarrassment that had been hidden away, out of the public eye.

"I can't wait to come home, Tate."

Their heads were close. She could see her new face reflected in the pupils of his eyes. His breath wafted over it. She wanted to be held. She wanted to hold him. *Touch me, Tate. Hold me. Kiss me,* she wanted to say.

For several heartbeats he seemed to be considering it, then he pulled back.

"I'll go now," he said gruffly, "so you can rest."

She reached for his hand and clasped it as tightly as she was able to. "Thank you."

"For what?"

"For . . . the flowers and . . . and for helping me back to bed."

"That's nothing," he said dismissively, pulling his hand free.

She made a wounded sound. "Why do you always refuse my thanks?"

"Don't play dumb, Carole," he whispered testily. "Your thanks don't mean anything to me and you know why." He said a curt good-bye and left.

Avery was crushed. She had hoped for so much more out of their reunion. Her fantasies of it hadn't been anything like the grim reality. But what could she expect from a husband who obviously didn't care a great deal about his wife?

At least he hadn't detected her lie. From a professional standpoint, she was still on firm ground.

She returned to the chair and picked up the envelope, pried open the metal brad, lifted the flap, and shook the contents into her hand. Her wristwatch was no longer ticking—the crystal had been shattered. A gold earring was missing, but it was no great loss. The item that was most important to her wasn't there. Where was her locket?

Then she remembered. She hadn't been wearing her locket when the accident had occurred. Carole Rutledge had had it.

Avery slumped against the chair, lamenting the loss of that treasured piece of jewelry, but she roused herself immediately. She would mourn the loss later. Right now, she had to act.

A few minutes later, a nurse at the central station glanced up from the keyboard of her computer terminal. "Good evening, Mrs. Rutledge. Did you enjoy your visit with your husband?"

"Very much, thank you." She handed the nurse the envelope. "I have a favor to ask. Would you please mail this for me tomorrow?" The nurse read the address Avery printed on it. "Please," Avery pressed, before the nurse could ask any questions.

"I'd be glad to," she said, though obviously found it a strange request. "It'll go out in the morning's mail."

"I would rather you not mention this to anyone. My husband accuses me of being too sentimental as it is."

"All right."

Avery handed her several folded bills, pilfered from the generous allowance Tate had left with her before his trip. "That's enough money to cover the postage, I believe. Thank you."

That represented another severance with Avery Daniels. She returned to the room assigned to Mrs. Carole Rutledge.

 # TWELVE

In stocking feet, Irish McCabe went to his refrigerator for another beer. He pulled off the tab and, as he sipped the malty foam from the top of the can, inspected his freezer for dinner possibilities. Finding nothing there that was a better option than hunger, he decided to do without food and fill up on beer.

On his way back into the living room, he picked up the stack of mail he'd dropped on the table when he had come in earlier. While idly watching a TV game show, he sorted through the correspondence, culling junk mail and setting aside bills.

"Humph." A puzzled frown pulled together salt-and-pepper eyebrows when he came across the manila envelope. There was no return address, but it bore a local postmark. He unfastened the brad and wedged his index finger beneath the flap. He upended the envelope and dumped the contents into his lap.

He sucked in a quick breath and recoiled, as though something foul had landed on him. He stared at the damaged jewelry while his lungs struggled for air and his heart labored in his chest.

It was several moments before he calmed down enough to reach out and touch the shattered wristwatch. He had immediately recognized it as Avery's. Gingerly he picked it up and tentatively investigated the gold earring he'd last seen decorating Avery's ear.

Quickly coming to his feet, he rushed across the room to a desk that he rarely used, except as a catchall. He pulled open the lap drawer and took out the envelope he'd been given at the morgue the day he had identified Avery's body. "Her things," the forensic assistant had told him apologetically.

He remembered dropping her locket into the envelope without even looking inside. Up till now he hadn't had the heart to open it and touch her personal effects. He was superstitious. To paw through Avery's belongings would be as distasteful to him as grave robbing.

He'd had to empty her apartment because her landlady had insisted on it. He hadn't kept a single thing, except a few photographs. Her clothes and all other usable items had been donated to various charities.

The only thing that Irish had deemed worth keeping was the locket that had identified her body. Her daddy had given it to her when she was just a kid, and Irish had never seen Avery without it.

He opened the envelope that had been in his desk all this time and dumped the contents onto the desk's littered surface. Along with Avery's locket, there was a pair of diamond earrings, a gold bracelet watch, two bangle bracelets, and three rings, two of which comprised a wedding set. The third ring was a cluster of sapphires and diamonds. Together it added up to a hell of a lot more money than Avery's jewelry, but it wasn't worth a plug nickel to Irish McCabe.

Obviously, the pieces belonged to one of the other crash victims, possibly to one of the survivors. Was somebody grieving its misplacement? Or had it even been missed?

He would have to check on that and try to get it back to the rightful owner. Now, all he could think about was Avery's jewelry—the watch and earring that had been delivered today to his post office box. Who had sent them? Why now? Where had they been all this time?

He studied the envelope, searching for possible clues as to its sender. There were none. It didn't look like it had come from a municipal office. The printed lettering was rickety and uneven, almost childish.

"Who the hell?" he asked his empty apartment.

The pain of his grief over Avery should have been blunted by now, but it wasn't. He dropped heavily into his easy chair and stared at the locket with misty eyes. He rubbed it between his finger and thumb like a talisman that might make her miraculously materialize.

Later, he would try to solve the mystery of how her jewelry had become switched with that of another crash victim. For the present, however, he only wanted to wallow in the morass of his bereavement.

"I don't see why not."

"I told you why not."

"What would be wrong with me going down to Corpus Christi with you when you go later this week?"

"It's a business trip. I'll be busy setting up rallies for Tate."

Fancy's mouth drew into a petulant pout. "You could let me tag along if you really wanted to."

Eddy Paschal looked at her from the corner of his eye. "Guess that gives you the answer."

He switched out the lights at campaign headquarters. The property was located in a shopping center and had previously been a pet store. The rent was cheap. It was a central location, easily accessible to just about any point in the city. About its only drawback was the remnant odor of caged pets.

"Why are you so mean to me, Eddy?" Fancy whined as he used his key to secure the dead bolt.

"Why are you such a pest?"

Together they walked across the parking lot to his parked car, a serviceable Ford sedan that she privately scorned. He unlocked the passenger door and opened it for her. As she got in, she brushed the front of her body against his.

As he rounded the hood on his way to the driver's side, she noticed that he'd recently gotten a haircut. The barber had clipped his hair too short. Topping her list of Eddy "redos" was his car. Second was his barber.

He slid in behind the wheel and turned on the ignition. The air conditioner came on automatically and began filling the interior with hot, humid air. Eddy made a concession to his fresh-out-of-the-bandbox appearance by loosening his tie and unbuttoning his collar button.

Fancy went considerably further than that in her quest for comfort. She unbuttoned her blouse to her waist, then fanned it open and shut, providing Eddy with an excellent view of her breasts if he chose to take it, which she was peeved to note that he didn't. He was maneuvering the car through the intersection and up the entrance ramp to the freeway.

"Are you gay, or what?" she demanded crossly.

He burst out laughing. "Why do you ask?"

"Because if I gave away to other guys half of what I give away to you, I'd spend all my time on my back."

"To hear you tell it, you do anyhow." He glanced at her. "Or is that just so much talk?"

Fancy's blue eyes fairly smoked, but she was too clever to lose her temper. Instead, she curled up into the car seat with the sinuous laziness of a cat and asked slyly, "Why don't you find out for yourself, Mr. Paschal?"

He shook his head. "You're an incorrigible brat, Fancy, know that?"

"I should," she said breezily, pulling her fingers through her mass of dark-blond curls. "That's what everybody tells me." She leaned toward the air-conditioning vent, which was blowing out frigid air now. She held her hair up off her neck and let the air blow against her skin, which was dewy with perspiration. "Well, are you?"

"Am I what?"

"Gay."

"No, I'm not."

She sat up and angled her body toward him. Her hands were still holding her hair up off her neck—a pose that emphasized her breasts. The cold air had made her nipples hard. They jutted against the cloth of her shirt. "Then, how can you resist me?"

Congested freeway traffic had been left behind and they were now heading northwest toward the ranch. Eddy's gaze roved over her slowly, taking in all the alluring details. It gave her satisfaction to watch his Adam's apple slide up and down as he swallowed with difficulty.

"You're a beautiful child, Fancy." His eyes rested briefly on her breasts, where the dark impressions of their pert centers could be seen beneath her shirt. "A beautiful *woman*."

Gradually she lowered her arms, letting her hair fall loosely around her face and onto her shoulders. "Well, then?"

"You're my best friend's niece."

"So?"

"So to me that means you're off limits."

"How prudish!" she exclaimed. "You're a Victorian, Eddy, that's what you are. A throwback. A stuffy prude. Ridiculous."

"It wouldn't be ridiculous to your Uncle Tate. Or to your grandfather or father. If I laid a hand on you, any one or all three of them would come after me with a shotgun."

She reached across the seat and ran her finger up his thigh, whispering, "Now, wouldn't that be exciting?"

He removed her hand and pushed it back across the car. "Not if you're the target."

She flopped back in her seat, annoyed, and turned her head to gaze at the passing scenery. That morning she had deliberately left her car at the ranch and hitched a ride into San Antonio with her father, planning all along to stay late and finagle a ride home with Eddy. Months of subtle invitation had gotten her nowhere. Since patience had never been one of her virtues, she had decided to step up the pace of her pursuit.

Buck, the bellhop, had lasted less than a month before he had become possessive and jealous. Then the man who had come to spray the house for cockroaches had ended up in her bed. That affair had lasted until she discovered he was married. It wasn't his marital status that bothered her so much as his postcoital guilt, which he morosely discussed with her. Remorse took all the fun out of fucking.

Since the exterminator there had been an assortment of partners, but all had simply been diversions to occupy her until Eddy surrendered. She was getting tired of waiting.

Indeed, she was getting tired of everything. The last three months had put a real strain on her generally good disposition. There had even been times when she had envied her Aunt Carole all the attention she was getting.

While Fancy was spending interminable hours stuffing envelopes and taking telephone polls in that noisy, crowded, stinky, tacky campaign headquarters, with people who could get off on a ten-dollar contribution, Carole was being waited on hand and foot in that posh private clinic.

Mandy was another thorn in her side. As if the little brat hadn't always been spoiled rotten, it was even worse now since the plane crash. Just last week Fancy had been sternly reprimanded by her grandmother when she had yelled at her young cousin for eating all the Oreos.

In Fancy's opinion, the kid was off her beam. Her hollow, vacant eyes were damn spooky. She was turning into a zombie and, in the meantime, everybody kissed her ass.

Her daddy had gone positive ape shit when she had gotten her most recent speeding ticket, and he had threatened to take away her car if she got another. He even warned that she would have to pay the fine out of money she earned herself. Of course her daddy's threats never panned out, but his shouting had really gotten on her nerves.

She couldn't believe the fuss everyone made over that primary election. You would have thought her uncle was running for fuckin' president the way everybody had carried on about it. He had won by a landslide, which had come as no surprise to her. She couldn't understand why they had paid a political analyst big bucks to predict the outcome a week before the election, when she could have given it to them months ago for free. Her uncle's smile made women cream their jeans. It didn't matter what his speeches were about; women would vote for him on the basis of his looks. But had anyone asked her? No. Nobody asked her opinion about anything.

Things were looking up, however. Now that the primary election was out of the way, Eddy wouldn't have so many distractions. His mind would be freer to think about her. She had been optimistic of a successful seduction when she had first launched the project. Now she wasn't so sure. He'd eluded her charms more adroitly than she would have guessed it was possible for a man to do. As far as she could tell, he wasn't even close to the breaking point.

She swiveled her head to glare at him. On the surface, at least, he looked as cool as a cucumber. She could have been as ugly as a warthog's ass for all the attention he was paying her. Maybe it was time she threw caution to the wind, stopped pussyfooting around, and, if nothing else, shocked the shit out of Mr. Clean.

"How 'bout a blow job?"

Moving with studied casualness, Eddy draped his right arm along the seat backs. "Come to think of it, that would feel real good about now."

Heat rushed to her face. She gritted her teeth. "Don't you dare patronize me, you son of a bitch."

"Then stop throwing yourself at me like a cheap streetwalker. Dirty talk doesn't turn me on, any more than a ringside view of your chest. I'm not interested, Fancy, and this juvenile game of yours is getting tiresome."

"You *are* a fag."

He snorted. "Believe that if you want to, if it salves your ego."

"Then you're bound to be getting it from somebody, because it's just not normal for a man to go without." She scooted closer to him and clutched his sleeve. "Who are you sleeping with, Eddy—somebody who works at headquarters?"

"Fancy—"

"That redhead with the skinny butt? I'll bet it's her! She's divorced, I hear, and probably real hot." She clutched his sleeve tighter. "Why would you want to screw somebody old like her when you could have me?"

He brought the car to a stop in the circular drive in front of the house. He caught her by both shoulders and shook her hard. "Because I don't screw children— especially one who opens her thighs to every stiff dick that comes along."

His anger only fanned her desire. Passion of any kind aroused and excited her. Eyes alight, she reached down and pressed his crotch with the palm of her hand. Her lips curved into a smug smile. "Why, Eddy, darlin'!" she exclaimed in a sultry whisper. "Yours is stiff."

Cursing, he pushed her away and got out of the car. "As far as you're concerned, that's how it'll stay."

Fancy took time to rebutton her blouse and compose herself before following him into the house. The contest had resulted in a tie. He hadn't dragged her off to bed, but he had wanted to. That was progress she could live with for a while . . . but not indefinitely.

As she reached the door leading to her wing, her mother emerged. Dorothy Rae was walking straight, but her eyes were glazed with the effects of several drinks.

"Hello, Fancy."

"I'm going to Corpus Christi for a few days," she announced. If Eddy refused to take her, she'd just surprise him in the coastal city. "I'm leaving in the morning. Give me some money."

"You can't leave town right now."

Fancy's fist found a prop on her shapely hip. Her eyes narrowed the way they were wont to do when she didn't immediately get her way. "Why the hell not?"

"Nelson said everybody had to be here," her mother said. "Carole's coming home tomorrow."

"Oh, piss," Fancy muttered. "Just what I need."

 # THIRTEEN

She saw him in the mirror.

Seated at the small dressing table in her room at the clinic, Avery made eye contact with Tate as he came in. They held their stare as she gradually lowered the powder puff to the mirrored surface of the table, then swiveled on the stool and met him face-to-face.

He tossed his coat and several department store shopping bags onto the bed while his eyes remained on her. Tightly clasping her hands in her lap, Avery laughed nervously. "The suspense is killing me."

"You look beautiful."

She moistened her lips, which were already shiny with carefully applied gloss. "The resident cosmetologist came today and gave me a makeup lesson. I've been using cosmetics for years, but I figured I needed a refresher course. Besides, the consultation comes with the room." Again she gave him a nervous little smile.

Actually, she had wanted an excuse to improve Carole's mode of makeup, which, in Avery's opinion, had been applied with too heavy a hand. "I tried a new technique. Do you think it looks all right?"

She offered her face up for his review. In spite of his reluctance to come any closer, he did. Placing his hands on his knees, he bent from the waist and gave her uplifted face a thorough inspection. "Can't even see the scars. Nothing. It's incredible."

"Thank you." She gave him a smile a woman gives her loving husband.

Except Tate wasn't her husband and he wasn't loving. He straightened up and turned his back on her. Avery closed her eyes momentarily, tamping down her discouragement. He didn't have a forgiving nature, she'd learned. Carole had shattered his trust in her. It was going to be difficult to win him back.

"Are you accustomed to my new look yet?"

"It's growing on me."

"There are differences," she remarked in an unsure voice.

"You look younger." He shot her a glance over his shoulder, then added beneath his breath, "Prettier."

Avery left the dressing table and moved toward him. She laid her hand on his arm and drew him around. "Really? Prettier?"

"Yeah."

"Prettier how? In what way?"

Just as she had learned the extent of his inability to forgive, she had also learned the extent of his ability to control his temper. She was waving a red flag at it now. Lightning was flashing in his eyes, but she didn't back down. She felt compelled to know the discernible differences he saw between her and his wife. Research, she assured herself.

He swore impatiently, raking a hand through his hair. "I don't know. You're just different. Maybe it's the makeup, the hair—I don't know. You look good, okay? Can we leave it at that? You look . . ." His eyes lowered to take in more than her face. They swept down her body, moved up again, looked away. "You look good."

He dug into his shirt pocket and produced a handwritten list. "Mom and I got the things you asked for." Nodding toward the shopping bags, he read off the items. "Ysatis spray perfume. They were out of the bath stuff you wanted."

"I'll get it later."

"Panty hose. Is that the color you had in mind? You said light beige."

"It's fine." She rummaged in the bags, locating the items as he named them. She withdrew the boxed bottle of fragrance from the sack. Uncapping it, she mister her wrist with the atomizer. "Hmm. Smell."

She laid her wrist against his cheek, so that he had to turn his head toward it in order to sniff. When he did, his lips brushed her inner arm. Their eyes met instantly.

"Nice," he said and turned his head away before Avery lowered her arm. "A nightgown with sleeves." Again he questioned her. "Since when have you started sleeping in anything, but especially something with sleeves?"

Avery, tired of being put on the defensive, fired back, "Since I lived through a plane crash and got second-degree burns on my arms."

His mouth, open and ready to make a quick comeback, clicked shut. Returning to the last item on the list, he read, "Bra, 34-B."

"I'm sorry about that." Taking the garment from the sack, she removed the tags and refolded it. The bras that had been brought to her from Carole's drawers at home had been way too large.

"About what?"

"Coming down a full size."

"What possible difference could that make to me?"

The scorn in his expression made her look away. "None, I guess."

She emptied the shopping bags, adding the items to the things she had laid out to wear home the following day. The clothes Zee and Tate had brought her from Carole's closet had fit fairly well. They were only a trifle large. Carole's breasts and hips had been fuller, curvier, but Avery had explained that away by the liquid diet she had been on for so long. Even Carole's shoes fit her.

Whenever possible she kept her arms and legs covered, preferring pants to skirts. She was afraid that the shape of her calves and ankles would give her away. So far, no one had made a comparison. To the Rutledges, she was Carole. They were convinced.

Or were they?

Why hadn't Carole's coconspirator spoken to her again?

That worry was as persistent as a gnat that continually buzzed through Avery's head. Dwelling on it made her ill with fear, so she concentrated more on Carole's personality in an effort to avoid making mistakes that would give her away.

As far as she could tell, she'd been lucky. She wasn't aware of having made any major blunders.

Now that departure was imminent, she was nervous. Being under the same roof with the Rutledges, especially with Tate, would increase the opportunities for making errors.

In addition, she would resurface as a congressional candidate's wife and be called upon to cope with the problems associated with that.

"What's going to happen in the morning, Tate?"

"Eddy told me to prepare you. Sit down."

"This sounds serious," she teased once they were facing each other in matching chairs.

"It is."

"Are you afraid I'll commit a faux pas in front of the press?"

"No," he replied, "but I can damn well guarantee that they'll commit some social taboos."

Because he was criticizing her profession, she took umbrage. "Like what?"

"They'll ask you hundreds of personal questions. They'll study your face, looking for scars, that kind of thing. You'll probably have your picture taken more times tomorrow than at any other time during the campaign."

"I'm not camera shy."

He laughed dryly. "I know that. But tomorrow when you leave here, you'll be swarmed. Eddy's going to try to keep it orderly, but these things have a way of getting out of hand."

He fished into his breast pocket again, produced another piece of paper, and passed it to her. "Familiarize yourself with this tonight. It's a brief statement Eddy wrote for you to read. He'll have a microphone set—What's the matter?"

"This," she said, shaking the paper at him. "If I read this, I'll sound like a moron."

He sighed and rubbed his temples. "Eddy was afraid you'd think that."

"Anybody hearing this would think the crash had damaged my brain more than my face. Everyone would assume you had locked me away in this private hospital until I regained my sanity, like something out of *Jane Eyre*. Keep the mentally disturbed wife—"

"*Jane Eyre*? You've certainly gotten literary."

She was taken aback for a moment, but retorted quickly, "I saw the movie. Anyway, I don't want people to think I'm mentally dysfunctional and must have everything I say written out for me beforehand."

"Just don't let your mouth overload your ass, okay?"

"I know how to speak the English language, Tate," she snapped. "I can put more than three words together at any given time, and I know how to conduct myself in public." She ripped the prepared statement in half and tossed it to the floor.

"Apparently, you've forgotten that incident in Austin. We can't afford mistakes like that, Carole."

Since she didn't know what mistake Carole had made in Austin, she could neither defend herself nor apologize. One thing she must remember, however, was that Avery Daniels had experience speaking before television cameras. She was media sophisticated. Carole Rutledge obviously had not been.

In a calmer voice, she said, "I know how important every public appearance is from now until November. I'll try to conduct myself properly and watch what I say." She smiled ruefully and bent to pick up the torn paper. "I'll even memorize this valid little speech. I want to do what's best for you."

"Don't put yourself out trying to please me. If it were up to me, you wouldn't even be making a statement. Eddy feels that you should, to alleviate the public's curiosity. Jack and Dad go along with his opinion. So you've got to please them, not me."

He stood to go. Avery rose quickly. "How's Mandy?"

"The same."

"Did you tell her I was coming home tomorrow?"

"She listened, but it's hard to tell what she was thinking."

Distressed that there had been no measurable improvement in the child's condition, Avery raised her hand to the base of her throat and rubbed it absently.

Tate touched the back of her hand. "That reminds me." He went for his jacket, which was still lying across the foot of her bed, and removed something from his pocket. "Since the hospital screwed up and lost your jewelry after all, Eddy thought I should replace your wedding ring. He said voters would expect you to be wearing one."

She hadn't exactly lied to him. When he had inquired about her jewelry, she had told him that when she had opened the envelope taken from the hospital safe, it had contained someone else's jewelry, not Carole Rutledge's. "I gave it to one of the nurses here to handle."

"Then where is yours?" he had asked at the time.

"God knows. Just one of those mix-ups that can't be explained, I guess. Take it up with the insurance company."

Tate was now removing a simple, wide gold band from the gray velvet lining of the ring box. "It's not as fancy as your other one, but it'll do."

"I like this one," she said as he slid the ring onto her third finger. When he tried to withdraw his hand, she noticed that he was wearing a matching band. She clutched his hand and called his name on a quick intake of breath.

She bowed her head over their clasped hands, holding them between their chests. Bending her head down farther, she softly kissed the ridge of his knuckles.

"Carole," he said, trying to pull his hand free. "Don't."

"Please, Tate. I want to thank you for all you've done. Please let me."

She implored him to accept her gratitude. "There were so many times—even from the very beginning, when I first regained consciousness—that I wanted to die. I probably would have willed myself to if it hadn't been for your unflagging encouragement. You've been . . ." She choked up and made no attempt to stem the tears that ran down her flawless cheeks. "You've been a wonderful source of strength through all this. Thank you."

She spoke from her heart. Each word was the truth. Responding to the prompting of her emotions, she came up on tiptoe and touched his lips with hers.

He yanked his head back. She heard the swift surprised breath he took. She sensed his hesitation as his eyes roved over her face. Then he lowered his head. His lips made contact with hers briefly, airily, barely glancing them.

She inclined her body closer to his, reached higher for his lips with her own, and murmured, "Tate, kiss me, please."

With a low moan, his mouth pressed down on hers. His arm went around her waist and pulled her against him. He unraveled their clasped fingers and curved his hand around her throat, stroking it with his thumb while his tongue played at getting between her lips.

Once it had, he sent it deep.

He instantly broke off the kiss and raised his head. "What the—"

He peered deeply into her eyes while his chest soughed against hers. Though he wrestled against it, his eyes were drawn back to her mouth. He closed his eyes and shook his head in denial of something he couldn't explain before covering her mouth with his own.

Avery returned his kiss, releasing all the yearning she had secretly nurtured for months. Their mouths melded together with hunger and heat. The more he got of hers, the more he wanted and the more she wanted to give.

With his hand on her hips, he tilted her forward against his erection. Arching into it, she raised her hands to the back of his neck and drew his head down, loving the blend of textures encountered by her fingertips—his hair, his clothing, his skin.

And then it stopped.

He shoved her away, putting several feet between them. She watched with anguish as he drew the back of his fist across his mouth, wiping off her kiss. She emitted a small, pained noise.

"It won't work, Carole," he said tightly. "I'm unfamiliar with this new game you're playing, but until I learn the rules, I refuse to participate. I feel sorry for what happened to you. Since you're my legal wife, I did what duty demanded of me. But it has no bearing on my feelings. They haven't changed. Got that? Nothing's changed."

He snatched up his sports coat, slung it over his shoulder, and sauntered from the room without looking back.

Eddy stepped out into the courtyard. The May sunshine had brought out the blooming plants. Oleander bushes bloomed in pottery urns bordering the deck around the swimming pool. Moss rose carpeted the flower beds.

It was dark now, however, and the blossoms had closed for the night. The courtyard was illumined by spotlights placed in the ground among the plants. They cast tall, spindly shadows upon the white stucco walls of the house.

"What are you doing out here?" Eddy asked.

The loner, slouched in a patio lounger, answered curtly. "Thinking."

He was thinking about Carole—about how her face had looked reflected in the mirror when he had entered her room. It had been incandescent. Her dark eyes had glowed as though his arrival signified something special to her. He decided it was quite an act. For an insane moment or two, he'd even fallen for it. What an idiot.

If he had just walked out, never touched her, never tasted her, never wished that things were different, he wouldn't be snarling at his friend now, nursing a bottle of scotch and fighting a losing battle with an erection that wouldn't subside. Aggravated with himself, he reached for the bottle of Chivas Regal again and splashed some over the melting ice in the bottom of his tumbler.

Eddy sat down in a lounge chair close to Tate's and eyed him with concern. Tate, catching his friend's candidly critical gaze, said, "If you don't like what you see, look at something else."

"My, my. Cranky, aren't we?"

He was horny and lusting for an unfaithful wife. The unfaithfulness he *might* forgive, eventually, but not the other. Never the other.

"Did you see Carole?" Eddy asked, guessing the source of Tate's dark mood.

"Yes."

"Did you give her the statement to read?"

"Yes. Know what she did?"

"Told you to shove it?"

"Essentially. She tore it in half."

"I wrote it for her own good."

"Tell that to her yourself."

"The last time I told her something for her own good, she called me an asshole."

"She fell just short of spelling that out tonight."

"Whether she believes it or not, meeting the press for the first time since the crash is going to be a bitch, even on somebody as tough as Carole. Their curiosity alone will have them whipped into a frenzy."

"I told her that, but she resents getting unasked-for advice and having words put in her mouth."

"Well," Eddy said, rubbing his neck tiredly, "don't worry about it until you have to. She'll probably do fine."

"She seems confident that she will." Tate took a sip of his drink, then rolled the tumbler between his palms as he watched a moth making suicidal dives toward one of the spotlights in the shrubbery. "She's . . ."

Eddy leaned forward. "She's what?"

"Hell, I don't know." Tate sighed. "Different."

"How so?"

For starters, she tasted different, but he didn't tell his friend that. "She's more subdued. Congenial."

"Congenial? Sounds to me like she pitched a temper tantrum tonight."

"Yeah, but this is the first one. The crash and everything she's been through since then have sobered her up, I think. She looks younger, but she acts more mature."

"I've noticed that. Understandable, though, isn't it? Carole's suddenly realized that she's mortal.'' Eddy stared at the terrazzo tiles between his widespread feet. "How, uh, how are personal things between the two of you?'' Tate shot him a hot, fierce glance. "If it's none of my business, just say so.''

"It's none of your business.''

"I know what happened in Fort Worth last week.''

"I don't know what the hell you're talking about.''

"The woman, Tate.''

"There were a lot of women around.''

"But only one invited you to her house after the rally. At least, only one that I know of.''

Tate rubbed his forehead. "Jesus, doesn't anything escape your attention?''

"Not where you're concerned. Not until you're elected senator.''

"Well, rest easy. I didn't go.''

"I know that.''

"So what's the point of bringing it up?''

"Maybe you should have.''

Tate barked a short laugh of surprise.

"Did you want to?''

"Maybe.''

"You did,'' Eddy said, answering for him. "You're human. Your wife's been incapacitated for months, and even before then—''

"You're out of line, Eddy.''

"Everybody in the family knows that the two of you weren't getting along. I'm only stating the obvious. Let's be frank.''

"You be frank. I'm going to bed.''

Eddy caught his arm before he could stand up. "For God's sake, don't get mad at me and go off half-cocked. I'm trying to do you a favor here.'' He waited for several moments, giving Tate time to contain his anger.

"All I'm saying is that you've been doing without for a long time,'' Eddy said calmly. "The deprivation has got you uptight and edgy, and that's no good for anybody. If all it takes to get you happy again is a roll in the hay, let me know.''

"And you'll do what?'' Tate asked dangerously. "Pimp?''

Eddy looked disappointed in him. "There are ways to arrange it discreetly.''

"Tell that to Gary Hart.''

"He wasn't smart.''

"And you are?''

"Damn right I am.''

"Do you know what Dad would think if he heard you making me this offer?''

"He's an idealist,'' Eddy said dismissively. "Nelson really believes in motherhood and apple pie. Morality is his middle name. I, on the other hand, am a realist. We clean up pretty, but underneath our affectations, man is still an animal.

"If you need to get laid and your wife isn't accommodating, you get laid by somebody else.'' After his crude summation, Eddy gave an eloquent shrug. "In your situation, Tate, a little marital infidelity would be healthy.''

"What makes you so sure I'm in desperate need of getting laid?''

Eddy smiled as he came to his feet. "I've watched you in action, remember? You've got that tension around your mouth that says you haven't gotten off lately. I recognize the black scowl. You might be running for public office, but you're still Tate Rutledge. Your cock doesn't know that it's expected to be a good little boy until you get elected.''

"I'm investing my future in this election, Eddy. You know that. I'm about to realize my ambition to go to Washington as a senator. Do you think I'd risk that dream on twenty minutes of marital infidelity?''

"No, I guess not," Eddy said with a rueful sigh. "I was only trying to help you out."

Tate stood and offered a crooked smile. "The next thing you're going to say is, what are friends for?"

Eddy chuckled. "Something that trite? Are you kidding?"

They headed toward the door leading into the main part of the house. Tate companionably rested his arm across Eddy's shoulders. "You're a good friend."

"Thanks."

"But Carole was right about one thing."

"What's that?"

"You are an asshole."

Laughing together, they entered the house.

 # FOURTEEN

A very slid on a pair of sunglasses.

"I think it would be better not to wear them," Eddy told her. "We don't want to look like we're hiding something unsightly."

"All right." She removed the sunglasses and pocketed them in the raw silk jacket, which matched her pleated trousers. "Do I look okay?" she nervously asked Tate and Eddy.

Eddy gave her a thumbs-up sign. "Smashing."

"Lousy pun," Tate remarked with a grin.

Avery ran her hand over the short hair at the back of her skull. "Does my hair . . . ?"

"Very chic," Eddy said. Then he clapped his hands together and rubbed them vigorously. "Well, we've kept the baited hounds at bay long enough. Let's go."

Together, the three of them left her room for the last time and walked down the hallway toward the lobby. Good-byes to the staff had already been said, but good-luck wishes were called out to them as they passed the nurses' station.

"A limo?" Avery asked when they reached the tinted glass facade of the building. The horde of reporters couldn't yet see them, but she could see outside. A black Cadillac limousine was parked at the curb with a uniformed chauffeur standing by.

"So both of us would be free to protect you," Eddy explained.

"From what?"

"The crush. The driver's already stowed your things in the trunk. Go to the mike, say your piece, politely decline to field any questions, then head for the car."

He looked at her for a moment, as though wanting to make certain his instructions had sunk in, then turned to Tate. "You can take a couple of questions if you want to. Gauge how friendly they are. As long as it's comfortable, milk it for all it's worth. If it gets sticky, use Carole as your excuse to cut it short. Ready?"

He went ahead to open the door. Avery looked up at Tate. "How do you abide his bossiness?"

"That's what he's being paid for."

She made a mental note not to criticize Eddy. In Tate's estimation, his campaign manager was above reproach.

Eddy was holding the door for them. Tate encircled her elbow and nudged her forward. The reporters and photographers had been a clamoring, squirming mass moments before. Now an expectant hush fell over them as they waited for the sensational candidate's wife to emerge after months of seclusion.

Avery cleared the doorway and moved to the microphone as Eddy had instructed her. She looked like Carole Rutledge. She knew that. It was remarkable to her that the charade hadn't been detected by those closest to Carole, even her husband. Of course, none had reason to doubt that she was who she was supposed to be. They weren't looking for an impostor, and therefore, they didn't see one.

But as she approached the microphone, Avery was afraid that strangers might discern what intimates hadn't. Someone might rise above the crowd, aim an accusatory finger at her, and shout, "Impostor!"

Therefore, the spontaneous burst of applause astonished her. It took her, Tate, and even Eddy, who was always composed, by complete surprise. Her footsteps faltered. She glanced up at Tate with uncertainty. He smiled that dazzling, all-American hero smile at her and it was worth all the pain and anguish she had suffered since the crash. It boosted her confidence tremendously.

She graciously signaled for the applause to cease. As it tapered off, she said a timid thank-you. Then, clearing her throat, giving a slight toss of her head, and moistening her lips with her tongue, she began reciting her brief, prepared speech.

"Thank you, ladies and gentlemen, for being here to welcome me back after my long hospitalization. I wish to publicly extend my sympathy to those who lost loved ones in the dreadful crash of AireAmerica Flight 398. It's still incredible to me that my daughter and I survived such a tragic and costly accident. I probably wouldn't have, had it not been for the constant support and encouragement of my husband."

The last line had been her addition to Eddy's prepared speech. Boldly, she slipped her hand into Tate's. After a moment's hesitation, which only she was aware of, he gave her hand a gentle squeeze.

"Mrs. Rutledge, do you hold AireAmerica responsible for the crash?"

"We can't comment until the investigation is completed and the results have been announced by the NTSB," Tate said.

"Mrs. Rutledge, do you plan to sue for damages?"

"We have no plans to pursue litigation at this time." Again, Tate answered for her.

"Mrs. Rutledge, do you remember saving your daughter from the burning wreckage?"

"I do now," she said before Tate could speak. "But I didn't at first. I responded to survival instinct. I don't remember making a conscious decision."

"Mrs. Rutledge, at any point during the reconstructive procedure on your face, did you doubt it could be done?"

"I had every confidence in the surgeon my husband selected."

Tate leaned into the mike to make himself heard above the din. "As you might guess, Carole is anxious to get home. If you'll excuse us, please."

He ushered her forward, but the crowd surged toward them. "Mr. Rutledge, will Mrs. Rutledge be going with you on the campaign trail?" A particularly pushy reporter blocked their path and shoved a microphone into Tate's face.

"A few trips for Carole have been scheduled. But there will be many times when she'll feel it's best to stay at home with our daughter."

"How is your daughter, Mr. Rutledge?"

"She's well, thank you. Now, if we could—"

"Is she suffering any aftereffects from the crash?"

"What does your daughter think of the slight alterations in your appearance, Mrs. Rutledge?"

"No more questions now, please."

With Eddy clearing a path for them, they made their way through the obstinate crowd. It was friendly, for the most part, but even so, being surrounded by so many people gave Avery a sense of suffocation.

Up till now, she'd always been on the other side, a reporter poking a microphone at someone in the throes of a personal crisis. The reporter's job was to get the story, get the sound bite that no one else got, take whatever measures were deemed necessary. Little consideration was ever given to what it was like on the other side of the microphone. She'd never enjoyed that aspect of the job. Her fatal mistake in broadcasting hadn't arisen from having too little sensitivity, but having too much.

From the corner of her eye she spotted the KTEX logo stenciled on the side of a Betacam. Instinctively, she turned her head in that direction. It was Van!

For a split second she forgot that he was supposed to be a stranger to her. She came close to calling out his name and waving eagerly. His pale, thin face and lanky ponytail looked wonderfully familiar and dear! She longed to throw herself against his bony chest and hug him hard.

Thankfully, her face remained impassive. She turned away, giving no sign of recognition. Tate ushered her into the limo. Once inside the backseat and screened by the tinted glass, she looked out the rear window. Van, like all the others, was shoving his way through the throng, video camera riding atop his shoulder, his eye glued to the viewfinder.

How she missed the newsroom, with its ever-present pall of tobacco smoke, jangling telephones, squawking police radios, and clacking teletypes. The constant ebb and flow of reporters, cameramen and gofers seemed to Avery to be light-years in the past.

As the limo pulled away from the address that had been her refuge for weeks, she experienced an overwhelming homesickness for Avery Daniels's life. What had happened to her apartment, her things? Had they been boxed up and parceled out to strangers? Who was wearing her clothes, sleeping on her sheets, using her towels? She suddenly felt as though she'd been stripped and violated. But she had made an irrevocable decision to leave Avery Daniels indefinitely dead. Not only her career, but her life, and Tate's, were at stake.

Beside her, Tate adjusted himself into the seat. His leg brushed hers. His elbow grazed her breast. His hip settled reassuringly against hers.

For the time being, she was where she wanted to be.

Eddy, sitting on the fold-down seat in front of her, patted her knee. "You did great, even on the ad libs. Nice touch, reaching for Tate's hand that way. What'd you think, Tate?"

Tate was loosening his tie and unbuttoning his collar. "She did fine." He wagged his finger at Eddy. "But I don't like those questions about Mandy. What possible bearing does she have on the campaign issues or the election?"

"None. People are just curious."

"Screw curious. She's my daughter. I want her protected."

"Maybe she's too protected." Avery's husky voice sharply drew Tate's eyes to her.

"Meaning?"

"Now that they've seen me," she said, "they'll stop pestering you with questions about me and concentrate on the important issues."

During her convalescence, she had kept close tabs on his campaign by reading every newspaper available and watching television news. He had blitzed the primary election, but the real battle was still ahead of him. His opponent in November would be the incumbent senior senator, Rory Dekker.

Dekker was an institution in Texas politics. For as long as Avery remembered, he had been a senator. It was going to be a David-and-Goliath contest. The incredible odds in Dekker's favor, coupled with Tate's audacious courage against such an impressive foe, had sparked more interest in this election than any in recent memory.

On nearly every newscast there was at least a fifteen-second mention of the senate race, and, as Avery well knew, even fifteen seconds was an enviable amount of time. But while Dekker wisely used his time to state his platform, Tate's allotment had been squandered on questions regarding Carole's medical progress.

"If we don't keep Mandy under such lock and key," she said carefully, "their curiosity over her will soon abate. Hopefully, they'll get curious about something else, like your relief plan for the farmers who have been foreclosed on."

"She might have a point, Tate." Eddy eyed her suspiciously, but with grudging respect.

Tate's expression bordered between anger and indecision. "I'll think about it," was all he said before turning his head to stare out the window.

They rode in silence until they reached campaign headquarters. Eddy said, "Everybody's anxious to see you, Carole. I've asked them not to gape, but I can't guarantee that they won't," he warned her as she alighted with the chauffeur's assistance. "I think the goodwill would go a long way if you could stick around for a while."

"She will." Giving her no choice, Tate took her arm and steered her toward the door.

His chauvinism raised the hair on the back of her neck, but she was curious to see his campaign headquarters, so she went peaceably. As they approached the door, however, her stomach grew queasy with fear. Each new situation was a testing ground, a mine field that she must navigate gingerly, holding her breath against making a wrong move.

The doors admitted them into a place of absolute chaos. The volunteer workers were taking calls, making calls, sealing envelopes, opening envelopes, stapling, unstapling, standing up, sitting down. Everyone was in motion. After the silence and serenity of the clinic, Avery felt as though she had just been thrust into an ape house.

Tate removed his jacket and rolled up the sleeves of his shirt. Once he was spotted, each volunteer stopped his particular chore in favor of speaking to him. It was apparent to Avery that everyone in the room looked to him as a hero and was dedicated to helping him win the election.

It also became clear to her that Eddy Paschal's word was considered law, because while the volunteers looked at her askance and spoke polite hellos, she wasn't subjected to avidly curious stares. Feeling awkward and uncertain over what was expected of her, she tagged along behind Tate as he moved through the room. In his element, he emanated contagious confidence.

"Hello, Mrs. Rutledge," one young man said to her. "You're looking extremely well."

"Thank you."

"Tate, this morning the governor issued a statement congratulating Mrs. Rutledge on her full recovery. He commended her courage, but he called you, and I paraphrase, a bleeding-heart liberal that Texans should be wary of. He cautioned the voting public not to let sympathy for Mrs. Rutledge influence their votes in November. How do you want to respond?"

"I don't. Not right away. The pompous son of a bitch wants to provoke me and make me look like a fire-breathing dragon. I won't give him the satisfaction. Oh, and that 'pompous son of a bitch' is off the record."

The young man laughed and scurried toward a word processor to compose his press release.

"What does the current poll show?" Tate asked the room at large.

"We aren't paying attention to the polls," Eddy said smoothly, moving toward them. Somewhere along the way, he had picked up Fancy. She was eyeing Carole with her usual recalcitrance.

"The hell you're not," Tate said, countering Eddy's glib response. "How many points am I behind?"

"Fourteen."

"Up one from last week. I've been saying all along there's nothing to sweat." Everyone laughed at his optimistic analysis.

"Hi, Uncle Tate. Hi, Aunt Carole."

"Hello, Fancy."

The girl's face broke into an angelic smile, but there was malice behind it that Avery found unsettling. The one time Fancy had come to see her in the hospital, she had snickered at her scars, which had still been visible. The girl's insensitivity had angered Nelson so much that he'd sent her from the room and banished her from returning. She hadn't seemed to mind.

Just to look at her, one could tell that she was a calculating, selfish little bitch. If Fancy were ten years younger, Avery would think a hard spanking would be in order. Her regard for Carole, however, seemed to go beyond teenage sullenness. She seemed to hold a deep and abiding grudge against her.

"Is that your new wedding ring?" Fancy asked now, nodding down at Avery's left hand.

"Yes. Tate gave it to me last night."

She lifted Avery's hand by the fingertips and scornfully assessed the ring. "He wouldn't spring for more diamonds, huh?"

"I have a job for you," Eddy said tersely. "Back here." Taking Fancy's elbow, he spun her around and gave her a push in the opposite direction.

"Such a sweet child," Avery said from the corner of her mouth.

"She could stand a good paddling."

"I agree."

"Hello, Mrs. Rutledge." A middle-aged woman approached them and shook Avery's hand.

"Hello. It's nice to see you again, Mrs. Baker," she said after surreptitiously consulting the name tag pinned to the woman's breast pocket.

Mrs. Baker's smile faltered. She nervously glanced at Tate. "Eddy said you should read over these press releases, Tate. They're scheduled to be sent out tomorrow."

"Thanks. I'll do it tonight and send them back with Eddy tomorrow."

"That'll be fine. There's no rush."

"I made a mistake, didn't I?" Avery asked him as the woman moved away.

"We'd better go."

He called out a good-bye that encompassed everybody. Eddy waved to him from across the room but continued speaking into the telephone receiver he had cradled between his ear and shoulder. From her perch on the corner of his desk, Fancy gave them a negligent wave.

Tate escorted Avery outside and toward a parked silver sedan. "No limo this time?"

"We're just plain folks now."

Avery drank up the sights and sounds of the city as they slogged their way through noon traffic. It had been so long since her world had consisted of more than only a few sterile walls. The hectic pace at which everything moved, the racket, color, and light, were intimidating after her months of isolation. They were also thrilling. Everything was fondly familiar yet excitingly new, as spring must be to an animal emerging from hibernation.

When they passed the airport and she saw the jets taking off, chill bumps broke out over her arms and her insides tensed to the point of pain.

"Are you okay?"

Quickly, she averted her eyes from the airfield and caught Tate watching her closely. "Sure. I'm fine."

"Will you ever be able to fly again?"

"I don't know. I suppose. The first time is sure to be the toughest."

"I don't know if we'll ever get Mandy on a plane again."

"She might overcome her fear easier than I will. Children are often more resilient than adults."

"Maybe."

"I'm so anxious to see her. It's been weeks."

"She's growing."

"Is she?"

A smile broke across his face. "The other day I pulled her into my lap and noticed that the top of her head almost reaches my chin now."

They shared a smile for several seconds. Then his eyes dimmed, his smile relaxed, and he returned his attention to the traffic. Feeling shut out, Avery asked, "What about Mrs. Baker? What did I do wrong?"

"She only started working for us two weeks ago. You've never met her."

Avery's heart fluttered. This was bound to happen. She would make these little mistakes that she had to rapidly think up excuses for.

She lowered her head and rubbed her temples with her middle finger and thumb. "I'm sorry, Tate. I must have looked and sounded very phony."

"You did."

"Have patience with me. The truth is, I have lapses of memory. Sometimes the sequence of events confuses me. I can't remember people or places clearly."

"I noticed that weeks ago. Things you said didn't make any sense."

"Why didn't you say something when you first noticed?"

"I didn't want to worry you, so I asked the neurologist about it. He said your concussion probably erased part of your memory."

"Forever?"

He shrugged. "He couldn't say. Things might gradually come back to you, or they might be irretrievable."

Secretly, Avery was glad to hear the neurologist's prognosis. If she committed a faux pas, she could use a lapse of memory as her excuse.

Reaching across the car, she covered Tate's hand with her own. "I'm sorry if I embarrassed you."

"I'm sure she'll understand when I explain."

He slid his hand from beneath hers and placed both on the steering wheel to take an exit ramp off the divided highway. Avery paid close attention to the route they were taking. She would have to know how to find her way home, wouldn't she?

She had been born in Denton, a college town in north central Texas, and spent most of her childhood in Dallas, the base from which Cliff Daniels had worked as a freelance photojournalist.

Like most native Texans, regional pride had been bred into her. Though she'd spent hundreds of dollars on speech teachers in an effort to eradicate her accent, at heart she was all Texan. The hill country had always been one of her favorite areas of the state. The gently rolling hills and underground, spring-fed streams were beautiful any season of the year.

The bluebonnets were in full bloom now, covering the ground like a sapphire rash. More brilliantly colored wildflowers were splashed across the natural canvas, and the borders of color blurred to resemble a Monet painting. Giant boulders jutted out of the earth like crooked molars, saving the landscape from being merely pastoral.

Passion teemed in this countryside where Spanish *dons* had established empires, Comanche warriors had chased mustang herds, and colonists had shed blood to win autonomy. The land seemed to pulse with the ghosts of those indomitable peoples who had domesticated but never tamed it. Their fiercely independent spirits lurked there, like the wildcats that lived in the natural caves of the area, unseen but real.

Hawks on the lookout for prey spiraled on motionless wings. Rust-colored Herefords grazed on the sparse grass growing between cedar bushes. Like benevolent overseers, occasional live oaks spread their massive branches over the rocky ground, providing shade for cattle, deer, elk, and smaller game. Cypress trees grew along the rushing riverbeds; the swollen banks of the Guadalupe were densely lined with their ropy trunks, knobby knees, and feathery branches.

It was a land rich in contrasts and folklore. Avery loved it.

So, apparently, did Tate. While driving, he gazed at the scenery with the appreciation of one seeing it for the first time. He turned into a road bracketed by two native stone pillars. Suspended between them was a sign made of wrought iron that spelled out "Rocking R Ranch."

From the articles about the Rutledges that she had secretly read during her convalescence, Avery had learned that the Rocking R covered more than five thousand acres and was home to an impressive herd of prime beef cattle. Two tributaries from the Guadalupe River and one from the Blanco supplied it with coveted water.

Nelson had inherited the land from his father. Since his retirement from the air force, he had devoted his time to building the ranch into a profitable enterprise, traveling to other parts of the country to study breeds of cattle and ways to improve the Rocking R's stock.

An article in *Texas Monthly* had carried an accompanying picture of the house, but Avery couldn't tell much about it from the photograph.

Now, as they topped a rise, she could see it in the distance. It was built of white adobe like a Spanish *hacienda,* with three wings that formed a horseshoe around a central courtyard. From the center, one had a spectacular view of the valley and the river beyond. The expansive house had a red tile roof that was currently reflecting the noon sun.

The driveway arced, forming a half circle in front of the main entrance. A majestic live oak shaded the entire front of the house, with curly gray moss dripping from its branches. Geraniums, scarlet and profuse, were blooming in terracotta pots on either side of the front door, which Tate guided her toward once she had alighted from the car.

It was quintessential Texana, breathtakingly beautiful, and, Avery suddenly realized, home.

FIFTEEN

The entire house was furnished with a taste and style one would expect from Zee. The decor was traditional, very cozy, and comfortable. All the rooms were spacious, with high, beamed ceilings and wide windows. Zee had made a good home for her family.

Lunch was waiting for them in the courtyard. It was served at a round redwood picnic table with a bright yellow umbrella shading it. After Avery had been embraced by Nelson and Zee, she approached Mandy and knelt down.

"Hi, Mandy. It's so good to see you."

Mandy stared at the ground. "I have been good."

"Of course you have. Daddy's been telling me. And you look so pretty." She smoothed her hand over Mandy's glossy page boy. "Your hair's growing out and you've got your cast off."

"Can I have my lunch now? Grandma said I could when you got here."

Her indifference broke Avery's heart. She should have been bursting with exciting things to tell her mother after such a lengthy separation.

As they took their places around the table, a maid carried a tray of food out from the kitchen and welcomed her home.

"Thank you. It's good to be back." A vapid, but safe response, Avery thought.

"Get Carole some iced tea, Mona," Nelson said, providing Avery with the housekeeper's name. "And remember to add real sugar."

The family unwittingly supplied her with clues like that. From them she gleaned Carole's habits, likes and dislikes. She remained constantly alert for the clues she might be unwittingly giving away, as well, although only Tate's parents and Mandy were present.

Just when she was congratulating herself on her excellent performance, a large, shaggy dog loped into the courtyard. He came to within a few feet of Avery before realizing she was a stranger. All four of his legs stiffened, then he crouched down and began to growl deep in his throat.

A dog—the family pet! Why hadn't she thought of that? Rather than waiting for the others to react, she seized the initiative.

"What's wrong with him? Am I that changed? Doesn't he recognize me?"

Tate threw one leg over to straddle the bench of the picnic table and patted his thigh. "Come here, Shep, and stop that growling."

Keeping a wary eye on Avery, the dog crept forward and laid his chin on Tate's thigh. Tate scratched him behind the ears. Tentatively, Avery extended her hand and petted the dog's muzzle. "Hey, Shep. It's me."

He sniffed her hand suspiciously. Finally satisfied that she posed no danger, he gave her palm a warm, wet stroke with his tongue. "That's better." Laughing, she looked up at Tate, who was regarding her strangely.

"Since when have you wanted to become friends with my dog?"

Avery glanced around helplessly. Nelson and Zee also seemed baffled by her behavior. "Since . . . since I came so close to dying. I feel a bond with all living creatures, I guess."

The awkward moment passed and lunch continued without further mishap. Once it was over, however, Avery was ready to retire to their room and use the bathroom—only she didn't know where, within the sprawling house, their room was located.

"Tate," she asked, "have my bags been brought in yet?"

"I don't think so. Why, do you need them?"

"Yes, please."

Leaving Mandy in her grandparents' care, Avery followed him from the court-yard and back to the car still parked out front. She carried the smaller bag; he took the larger.

"I could have gotten both," he told her over his shoulder as he reentered the house.

"It's all right." She lagged behind so she could follow him. Wide double doors opened into a long corridor. One wall of the hallway was made of windows overlooking the courtyard. Several rooms gave off from the other side. Tate entered one of them and set her suitcase down in front of a louvered closet door.

"Mona will help you unpack."

Avery nodded an acknowledgment, but she was distracted by the bedroom. It was spacious and light, with a saffron-colored carpet and blond wood furniture. The bedspread and drapes were made of a floral print chintz. It was a little too flowery for Avery's taste, but obviously expensive and well made.

She took in every detail at a glance, from the digital alarm clock on the night-stand to the silver framed photo of Mandy on the dresser.

Tate said, "I'm going to the office for a while. You probably ought to take it easy this afternoon, get back into the flow slowly. If you—"

Avery's sharp gasp stopped him. He followed the direction of her gaze to the life-size portrait of Carole mounted on the opposite wall. "What's the matter?"

A hand at her throat, Avery swallowed and said, "Nothing. It's . . . it's just that I don't look much like that anymore." It was disconcerting to look into the eyes of the one person who knew unequivocally that she was an impostor. Those dark, knowing eyes mocked her.

Looking away from them, she smiled up at Tate timorously and ran a hand through her short hair. "I guess I'm not completely used to the changes yet. Would you mind if I took the portrait down?"

"Why would I mind? This is your room. Do whatever the hell you want with it." He headed for the door. "I'll see you at dinner." He soundly closed the door behind him when he left.

His disregard was unarguable. She felt like she'd been dumped in Antarctica and was watching the last plane out disappear over the horizon. He had deposited her where she belonged and considered that the extent of his duty.

This is your room.

The bedroom was museum clean, like it hadn't been occupied for a long time. She guessed it had been three months—since Carole had left it the morning of the plane crash.

She slid open the closet doors. There were enough clothes hanging inside to outfit an army, but every single article was feminine, from the fur coat to the fussiest peignoir. Nothing in the closet belonged to Tate, nor did anything on the bureau or in any of the many drawers.

Avery dejectedly lowered herself to the edge of the wide, king-size bed. *Your room,* he had said. Not *our* room.

Well, she thought dismally, she didn't have to entertain any more qualms about the first time he claimed conjugal rights, did she? That worry could be laid aside. She wouldn't be intimately involved with Tate because he no longer shared that kind of relationship with his wife.

Given his attitude over the last several weeks, it came as no surprise, but it was a vast disappointment. Coupled with her disappointment, however, was shame. It hadn't been her intention to sleep with him under false pretenses; she didn't even know if she wanted that. It would be wrong—very wrong. Yet. . . .

She glared up at the portrait. Carole Rutledge seemed to be smiling down at her with malicious amusement. "You bitch," Avery whispered scathingly. "I'm going to undo whatever you did that caused him to stop loving you. See if I dont."

"You getting enough to eat down there?"

When Avery realized that Nelson was addressing her, she smiled at him down the length of the table. "Plenty, thank you. As good as the food was at the clinic, this tastes delicious."

"You've lost a lot of weight," he observed. "We've got to fatten you up. I don't tolerate puniness in my family."

She laughed and reached for her wine. She didn't like wine, but obviously Carole had. A glass had been poured for her without anyone asking if she wanted it or not. By sipping slowly throughout the meal, she had almost emptied the glass of burgundy that had accompanied the steak dinner.

"Your boobs have practically disappeared." Seated across from Avery, Fancy was balancing her forks between two fingers, insolently wagging it up and down as she made the snide observation.

"Fancy, you'll refrain from making rude remarks, please," Zee admonished.

"I wasn't being rude. Just honest."

"Tact is as admirable a trait as honesty, young lady," her grandfather said sternly from his chair at the head of the table.

"Jeez, I just—"

"And it's unbecoming for any woman to take the Lord's name in vain," he added coldly. "I certainly won't have it from you."

Fancy dropped her fork onto her plate with a loud clatter. "I don't get it. Everybody in this family has been talking about how skinny she is. I'm the only one with enough guts to say something out loud, and I get my head bitten off."

Nelson shot Jack a hard look, which he correctly took as his cue to do something about his daughter's misbehavior. "Fancy, please be nice. This is Carole's homecoming dinner."

Avery read her lips as she mouthed, "Big fuckin' deal." Slouching in her chair, she lapsed into sullen silence and toyed with her remaining food, obviously killing time until she could be excused from the table.

"I think she looks damn good."

"Thank you, Eddy." Avery smiled across the table at him.

He saluted her with his wineglass. "Anybody catch her performance on the steps of the clinic this morning? They aired it on all three local stations during the news."

"Couldn't have asked for better coverage," Nelson remarked. "Pour me some coffee, please, Zee?"

"Of course."

She filled his cup before passing the carafe down the table. Dorothy Rae declined coffee and reached instead for the wine bottle. Her eyes locked with Avery's across the table. Avery's sympathetic smile was met with rank hostility. Dorothy Rae defiantly refilled her wineglass.

She was an attractive woman, though excessive drinking had taken its toll on her appearance. Her face was puffy, particularly around her eyes, which otherwise were a fine, deep blue. She'd made an attempt to groom herself for dinner, but she hadn't quite achieved neatness. Her hair had been haphazardly clamped back with two barrettes, and she would have looked better without any makeup than she did in what had been ineptly and sloppily applied. She didn't enter the conversation unless specifically spoken to. All her interactions were with an inanimate object—the wine bottle.

Avery had readily formed the opinion that Dorothy Rae Rutledge was an extremely unhappy woman. Nothing had changed that first impression. The reason for Dorothy Rae's unhappiness was still unknown, but Avery was certain of one thing, she loved her husband. She responded to Jack defensively, as now, when he tried to discreetly place the wine bottle beyond her reach. She swatted his hand aside, lunged for the neck of the bottle, and topped off the portion already in her glass. In unguarded moments, however, Avery noticed her watching Jack with palpable desperation.

"Did you see those mock-ups of the new posters?" Jack was asking his brother.

Avery was flanked by Tate on one side and Mandy on the other. Though she had been conversant with everybody during the meal, she had been particularly aware of the two of them, but for distinctly different reasons.

After Avery had cut Mandy's meat into bite-size chunks, the child had eaten carefully and silently. Avery's experience with children was limited, but whenever she had observed them, they were talkative, inquisitive, fidgety, and sometimes annoyingly active.

Mandy was abnormally subdued. She didn't complain. She didn't entreat. She didn't do anything except mechanically take small bites of food.

Tate ate efficiently, as though he resented the time it took to dine. Once he had finished, he toyed with his wineglass between sips, giving Avery the impression that he was anxious for the others to finish.

"I looked at them this afternoon," he said in response to Jack's question. "My favorite slogan was the one about the foundation."

" 'Tate Rutledge, a solid new foundation,' " Jack quoted.

"That's the one."

"I submitted it," Jack said.

Tate fired a fake pistol at his brother and winked. "That's probably why I liked it best. You're always good at cutting to the heart of the matter. What do you think, Eddy?"

"Sounds good to me. It goes along with our platform of getting Texas out of its current economic slump and back on its feet. You're something the state can build its future on. At the same time, it subtly suggests that Dekker's foundation is crumbling."

"Dad?"

Nelson was thoughtfully tugging on his lower lip. "I liked the one that said something about fair play for all Texans."

"It was okay," Tate said, "but kinda corny."

"Maybe that's what your campaign needs," he said, frowning.

"It has to be something Tate feels comfortable with, Nelson," Zee said to her husband. She lifted the glass cover off a multilayered coconut cake and began slicing it. The first slice went to Nelson, who was about to dig in before he remembered what the dinner was commemorating.

"Tonight, the first slice belongs to Carole. Welcome home." The plate was passed down to her.

"Thank you."

She didn't like coconut any more than she did wine, but apparently Carole had, so she began eating the dessert while Zee served the men and the men resumed their discussion about campaign strategy.

"So, should we go with that slogan and have them start printing up the posters?"

"Let's hold off making a definite decision for a couple of days, Jack." Tate glanced at his father. Though Nelson was appreciatively demolishing his slice of cake, he was still wearing a frown because his favorite slogan hadn't met with their approval. "I only glanced at them today. That was just my first impression."

"Which is usually the best one," Jack argued.

"Probably. But we've got a day or two to think about it, don't we?"

Jack accepted a plate with a slice of cake on it. Dorothy Rae declined the one passed to her. "We should get those posters into production by the end of the week."

"I'll give you my final decision well before then."

"For God's sake. Would somebody please . . ." Fancy was waving her hand toward Mandy. Getting the cake from plate to mouth had proved to be too much of a challenge for the three-year-old. Crumbs had fallen onto her dress and frosting was smeared across her mouth. She had tried to remedy the problem by wiping it away, but had only succeeded in getting her hands coated with sticky icing. "It's just too disgusting to watch the little spook eat. Can I be excused?"

Without waiting for permission, Fancy scraped her chair back and stood, tossing her napkin into her plate. "I'm going into Kerrville and see if there's a new movie on. Anybody want to go?" She included everybody in the invitation, but her eyes fell on Eddy. He was studiously eating his dessert. "Guess not." Spinning around, she flounced from the room.

Avery was glad to see the little snot go. How dare she speak to a defenseless child so cruelly? Avery scooped Mandy into her lap. "Cake is just too good to eat without dropping a few crumbs, isn't it, darling?" She wrapped a corner of her linen napkin around her index finger, dunked it into her water glass, and went to work on the frosting covering Mandy's face.

"Your girl is getting out of hand, Dorothy Rae," Nelson observed. "That skirt she was wearing was so short, it barely covered her privates."

Dorothy Rae pushed her limp bangs off her forehead. "I try, Nelson. It's Jack who lets her get by with murder."

"That's a goddamn lie," he exclaimed in protest. "I've got her going to work every day, don't I? That's more constructive than anything you've been able to get her to do."

"She should be in school," Nelson declared. "Never should have let her up and quit like that without even finishing the semester. What's going to become of her? What kind of life will she have without an education?" He shook his head with dire premonition. "She'll pay dearly for her bad choices. So will you. You reap what you sow, you know."

Avery agreed with him. Fancy was entirely out of control, and it was no doubt her parents' fault. Still, she didn't think Nelson should discuss their parental shortcomings with everybody else present.

"I don't think anything short of a bath is going to do Mandy any good," she said, grateful for the excuse to leave the table. "Will you please excuse us?"

"Do you need any help?" Zee asked.

"No, thank you." Then, realizing that she was usurping the bedtime ritual from Zee, who must have enjoyed it very much, she added, "Since this is my first night home, I'd like to put her to bed myself. It was a lovely dinner, Zee. Thank you."

"I'll be in to tell Mandy good night later," Tate called after them as Avery carried the child from the dining room.

"Well, I see that nothing's changed."

Dorothy Rae weaved her way across the sitting room and collapsed into one of the two chairs parked in front of a large-screen TV set. Jack was occupying the other chair. "Did you hear me?" she asked when several seconds ticked by and he still hadn't said anything."

"I heard you, Dorothy Rae. And if by 'nothing's changed' you mean that you're shit-faced again tonight, then you're right. Nothing's changed."

"What I mean is that you can't keep your eyes off your brother's wife."

Jack was out of his chair like a shot. He slapped his palm against the switch on the TV, shutting up Johnny Carson in midjoke. "You're drunk and disgusting. I'm going to bed." He stamped into the connecting bedroom. Dorothy Rae struggled to get out of her chair and follow him. The hem of her robe trailed behind her.

"Don't try to deny it," she said with a sob. "I was watching you. All through dinner, you were drooling over Carole and her pretty new face."

Jack removed his shirt, balled it up, and flung it into the clothes hamper. He bent over to unlace his shoes. "The only one who drools in this family is you, when you get so drunk you can't control yourself."

Reflexively, she wiped the back of her hand across her mouth. People who had known Dorothy Rae Hancock when she was growing up wouldn't believe what she had become in middle age. She'd been the belle of Lampasas High School; her rein had lasted all four years.

Her daddy had been a prominent attorney in town. She, his only child, was the apple of his eye. The way he doted on her had made her the envy of everybody who knew her. He'd taken her to Dallas twice a year to shop at Neiman-Marcus for her seasonal wardrobes. He'd given her a brand new Corvette convertible on her sixteenth birthday.

Her mother had had a fit and said it was too much car for a young girl to be driving, but Hancock had poured his wife another stiff drink and told her that if he'd wanted her worthless opinion about anything, he would have asked for it.

After graduating from high school, Dorothy Rae had gone off in a blaze of glory to enter the University of Texas in Austin. She met Jack Rutledge during her junior year, fell madly in love, and became determined to have him for her very own. She'd never been denied anything in her life, and she didn't intend to start with missing out on the only man she would every truly love.

Jack, struggling through his second year in law school, was in love with Dorothy Rae, too, but couldn't even think about marriage until after he finished school. His daddy expected him not only to graduate, but to rank high in his class. His daddy also expected him to be chivalrous where women were concerned.

So when Jack finally succumbed to temptation and relieved Dorothy Rae Hancock of her virginity, he was in a quandary as to which had priority—chivalry toward the lady or responsibility toward parental expectations. Dorothy Rae spurred him into making a decision when she weepily told him that she was late getting her period.

Panicked, Jack figured that an untimely marriage was better than an untimely baby and prayed that Nelson would figure it that way, too. He and Dorothy Rae drove to Oklahoma over the weekend, wed in secret, and broke the glad tidings to their parents after the fact.

Nelson and Zee were disappointed, but after getting Jack's guarantee that he had no intention of dropping out of law school, they welcomed Dorothy Rae into the family.

The Hancocks of Lampasas didn't take the news quite so well. Her elopement nearly killed Dorothy Rae's daddy. In fact, he dropped dead of a heart attack one month after the nuptials. Dorothy Rae's unstable mother was committed to an alcohol abuse hospital. On the day of her release several weeks later, she was deemed dried out and cured. Three days later, she ran her car into a bridge abutment while driving drunk. She died on impact.

Francine Angela wasn't born until eighteen months after Dorothy Rae's marriage to Jack. It was either the longest pregnancy in history or she had tricked him into marriage.

He had never accused her of either, but, as though in self-imposed penance, she had had two miscarriages in quick succession when Fancy was still a baby.

The last miscarriage had proved to be life-threatening, so the doctor had tied her tubes to prevent future pregnancies. To blunt the physical, mental, and emotional pain this caused her, Dorothy Rae began treating herself to a cocktail every afternoon. And when that didn't work, she treated herself to two.

"How can you look at yourself in the mirror," she demanded of her husband now, "knowing that you love your brother's wife?"

"I don't love her."

"No, you don't, do you?" Leaning close, she poisoned the air between them with the intoxicating fumes of her breath. "You hate her because she treats you like dirt. She wipes her feet on you. You can't even see that all these changes in her are just—"

"What changes?" Instead of hanging his pants on the hanger in his hand, he dropped them into a chair. "She explained about using her left hand, you know."

Having won his attention, Dorothy Rae pulled herself up straight and assumed the air of superiority that only drunks can assume. "Other changes," she said loftily. "Haven't you noticed them?"

"Maybe. Like what?"

"Like the attention she's showering on Mandy and the way she's sucking up to Tate."

"She's been through a lot. She's mellowed."

"Ha!" she crowed indelicately. "Her? Mellowed? God above, you're blind where she's concerned." Her blue eyes tried to focus on his face. "Since that plane crash, she's like a different person, and you know it. But it's all for show," she stated knowingly.

"Why should she bother?"

"Because she wants something." She swayed toward him and tapped his chest for emphasis. "Probably, she's playing the good little senator's wife so she'll get to move to Washington with Tate. What'll you do then, Jack? Huh? What'll you do with your sinful lust then?"

"Maybe I'll start drinking and keep you company."

She raised a shaky hand and pointed her finger at him. "Don't get off the subject. You want Carole. I know you do," she finished with another sob.

Jack, once more bored with her inebriated rambling, finished hanging up his clothes, then methodically went around the room, switching off lamps and turning down the bed. "Come to bed, Dorothy Rae," he said wearily.

She caught his arm. "You never loved me."

"That's not true."

"You think I tricked you into marrying me."

"I never said that."

"I thought I was pregnant. I did!"

"I know you did."

"Because you don't love me, you thought it was okay to go after other women." Her eyes narrowed on him accusingly. "I know there have been others. You've cheated on me so many times, it's no wonder I drink."

Tears were streaming down her face. Ineffectually, she slapped his bare shoulder. "I drink because my husband doesn't love me. Never did. And now he's in love with his brother's wife."

Jack crawled into bed, turned onto his side, and pulled the covers up over himself. His nonchalance enraged her. On her knees, she walked to the center of the bed and began pounding on his back with her fists. "Tell me the truth. Tell me how much you love her. Tell me how much you despise me."

Her anger and strength were rapidly exhausted, as he had known they would be. She collapsed beside him, losing consciousness instantly. Jack rolled to his side and adjusted the covers over her. Then, heaving an unhappy sigh, he lay back down and tried to sleep.

 # SIXTEEN

"I thought she would be in bed by now."

Tate spoke from the doorway of Mandy's bathroom. Avery was kneeling beside the tub, where Mandy was worming her fingers through a mound of bubbles.

"She probably should be, but we went a little overboard with the bubble bath."

"So I see."

Tate came in and sat down on the lid of the commode. Mandy smiled up at him. "Do your trick for Daddy," Avery told her.

Obediently, the child cupped a handful of suds and blew on them hard, sending clumps of white foam flying in all directions. Several landed on Tate's knee. He made a big deal of it. "Whoa, there, Mandy, girl! You're taking the bath, not me."

She giggled and scooped up another handful. This time a dollop of suds landed on Avery's nose. To Mandy's delight, she sneezed. "I'd better put a stop to this before it gets out of hand." She bent over the tub, slid her hands into Mandy's armpits, and lifted her out.

"Here, give her to me." Tate was waiting to wrap up his daughter in a towel. "Careful. Slippery when wet."

Mandy, bundled in soft pink terry cloth, was carried into her adjoining bedroom and set down beside her bed. Her chubby little feet sank into the thick rug. Its luxuriant nap swallowed all ten toes. Tate sat down on the edge of her bed and began drying her with experienced hands.

"Nightie?" he asked, looking up at Avery expectantly.

"Oh, yes. Coming right up." There was a tall, six-drawer chest and a wide, three-drawer bureau. Where would the nighties be kept? She moved toward the bureau and opened the top drawer. Socks and panties.

"Carole? Second drawer."

Avery responded with aplomb. "She'll need underwear, too, won't she?" He unwound the towel from around Mandy and helped her step into her underwear, then pulled the nightgown over her head while Avery turned down her bed. He lifted Mandy into it.

Avery brought a hairbrush from the bureau, sat down beside Tate on the edge of the bed, and began brushing Mandy's hair. "You smell so clean," she whispered, bending down to kiss her rosy cheek once she'd finished with her hair. "Want some powder on?"

"Like yours?" Mandy asked.

"Hmm, like mine." Avery went back to the bureau for the small music box of dusting powder she'd spotted there earlier. Returning to the bed, she opened the lid. A Tchaikovsky tune began to play. She dipped the plush puff into the powder, then applied it to Mandy's chest, tummy, and arms. Mandy tilted her head back. Avery stroked her exposed throat with the powder puff. Giggling, Mandy hunched her shoulders and dug her fists into her lap.

"That tickles, Mommy."

The form of address startled Avery and brought tears to her eyes. She pulled the child into a tight hug. It was a moment before she could speak. "Now you really smell good, doesn't she, Daddy?"

"She sure does. 'Night, Mandy." He kissed her, eased her back onto the pillows, and tucked the summer-weight covers around her.

"Good night." Avery leaned down to softly peck her cheek, but Mandy flung her arms around Avery's neck and gave her mouth a smacking, moist kiss. She then turned onto her side, pulled a well-loved Pooh Bear against her, and closed her eyes.

Somewhat dazed by Mandy's spontaneous show of affection, Avery replaced the music box, turned out the light, and preceded Tate through the doorway and down the hall toward her own room.

"For our first day—"

She got no further before he grabbed her upper arm and shoved her inside her bedroom and against the nearest wall. Keeping one hand firmly around her biceps, he closed the door so they wouldn't be overheard and flattened his other palm against the wall near her head.

"What's the matter with you?" she demanded.

"Shut up and listen to me." He moved in closer, his face taut with anger. "I don't know what game you're playing with me. What's more, I don't give a shit. But if you start messing with Mandy, I'll kick you out so fast your head will spin, understand?"

"No. I don't understand."

"The hell you don't," he snarled. "This sweetness and light act is a bunch of crap."

"Act?"

"I'm an adult."

"You're a bully. Let go of my arm."

"I recognize your act for what it is. But Mandy is a child. To her it's real, and she'll respond to it." He inclined his body even closer. "Then, when you go back to being your old self, you'll leave her irreparably damaged."

"I—"

"I can't let that happen to her. I won't."

"You give me very little credit, Tate."

"I give you none."

She sucked in a quick, harsh breath.

He looked her over rudely. "Okay, so this morning you dazzled the press on my behalf. Thank you. You took my hand during the press conference. Sweet. We're wearing matching wedding bands. How romantic," he sneered.

"You've even got members of my family, who should know better, speculating that you had some kind of conversion experience in the hospital—found Jesus or something."

He lowered his head to within inches of hers. "I know you too well, Carole. I know that you are at your sweetest and kindest just before you go in for the kill." Increasing the pressure on her arm, he added, "I know that for a fact, remember?"

Distressed, Avery said fervently, "I have changed. I am different."

"Like hell. You've just changed tactics, that's all. But I don't care how well you play the part of the perfect candidate's wife, you're out. What I told you before the crash still stands. After the election, no matter the outcome, you're gone, baby."

His threat of dispossession didn't frighten her. Avery Daniels had been dispossessed of everything already—even her identity. What stunned Avery was that Tate Rutledge, on whose integrity she would have staked her life, was a phony after all.

"You would manipulate the public that way?" she hissed. "You'd go through the campaign with me playing your devoted wife, standing at your side, waving and smiling and delivering silly speeches that are composed for me, only as a means of getting more votes?" Her voice had risen a full octave. "Because a happily married candidate has a better chance of winning than one caught up in a divorce procedure. Isn't that right?"

His eyes turned as hard as flint. "Good try, Carole. Shift the blame to me if it makes you feel better about your own manipulations. You know damn good and well why I didn't kick you out a long time ago. I want this election for myself and for the following I've cultivated. I won't let those voters down. I can't do anything that might prevent me from winning, even if it means pretending to live in wedded bliss with you."

Once again he subjected her to a contemptuous once-over. "Your surgery made the packaging look fresher, but you're still rotten on the inside."

Avery was having a difficult time keeping the aspersions he was casting on Carole separate from herself. She took each insult to heart, as though it were aimed at her and not his late wife. She wanted to defend herself against his criticism, to fight back with a woman's weapons. Because, while his fierce temperament was intimidating, it was also arousing.

His anger only intensified his sexiness. It emanated from him as potently as the scent of his after-shave. His mouth looked hard and cruel. It became Avery's goal to soften it.

She raised her head, defying his resentful glare. "Are you sure I'm the same?"

"Damn sure."

Sliding her arms over his shoulders, she clasped her hands behind his neck. "Are you sure, Tate?" Coming up on tiptoes, she brushed her parted lips across his. "Absolutely sure?"

"Don't do this. It only makes you more of a whore."

"I'm not!"

The insult smarted. In a way, she was prostituting herself with another woman's husband for the sake of a story. But that wasn't motivating her as much as a growing sexual need more powerful than any she had ever experienced. With or without her story, she had a genuine desire to give Tate the tenderness and love that had been missing from his marriage to Carole.

"I'm not the woman I was before. I swear to you I'm not."

She tilted her head to one side and aligned her lips with his. Her hands cupped the back of his head, her fingers curling through his hair and drawing him down. If he really wanted to, he could resist, Avery assured herself.

But he allowed his head to be drawn closer to hers. Encouraged, she daintily used the moist tip of her tongue to probe at his lips. His muscles tensed, but it was a sign of weakness, not endurance.

"Tate?" She gently nipped his lower lip with her teeth.

"Christ."

The hand bracing him against the wall fell away. Avery was propelled backward when she absorbed the weight of his body, becoming sandwiched between him and the wall. One arm curled hard and tight around her waist. His other hand captured her jaw, almost crushing it between his strong fingers. It held her head in place while he kissed her ravenously. He sealed her open mouth to his with gentle suction, then burrowed his tongue into the silky wet cavity.

Leaving her gasping for breath, he angled his head the opposite way and tormented her with quick, deft flicks of his tongue across her lips and barely inside them. Her hands moved to his cheeks. She laid her palms against them and ran her fingertips across his cheekbones as she gave herself totally to his kiss.

He fumbled with her clothing, thrusting his hand beneath her skirt, into her underpants, and filling it with soft woman flesh. She moaned pleasurably when he tilted her middle up against his swollen pelvis and ground it with her cleft.

Avery felt fluid and feverish. Her sex was wet and warm. Her breasts ached. The nipples tingled.

Then she was abruptly deserted.

She blinked her eyes into focus. Her head landed hard against the wall behind her. She flattened her hands against it to keep herself from sliding to the floor.

"I'll grant you that it's a polished act," he said woodenly. His cheeks were flushed and his eyes were dilated. His breathing was rapid and shallow. "You're not as blatant as you used to be, but classier. Different, but just as sexy. Maybe even sexier."

She looked down at the distended fly of his jeans, a look that made words superfluous.

"Okay, I'm hard," he admitted with an angry growl. "But I'll die of it before I'll sleep with you again."

He walked out. He didn't slam the door behind him, but left it standing open, more of an insult than if he had stormed out. Heartsick and wounded, Avery was left alone in Carole's room, with Carole's chintz, Carole's mess.

Everyone in the family had noticed the puzzling inconsistencies in Carole's personality, but her odd behavior was keeping one person in particular awake at night. After hours of prowling the grounds surrounding the house, looking for answers in the darkness, the insomniac posed a question to the moon.

What is the bitch up to?

No radical changes in her could be pinpointed. The differences in her face were subtle, the result of the reconstructive surgery. Shorter hair made her look different, but that was inconsequential. She had lost a few pounds, making her appear slimmer than before, but it was certainly no drastic weight loss. Physically, she was virtually the same as before the crash. It was the nonphysical changes that were noticeable and so damned baffling.

What is the bitch up to?

Judging by her behavior since the crash, one would think her brush with death had given her a conscience. But that couldn't be. She didn't know the meaning of the word. Although for the goodwill she was dispensing, that's apparently what she wanted everybody to believe.

Could Carole Rutledge have had a change of heart? Could she be seeking her husband's approval? Could she ever be a loving, attentive mother?

Don't make me laugh.

She was stupid to switch tactics now. She'd been doing fine at what she'd been hired to do: destroy Tate Rutledge's soul, so that by the time that bullet exploded in his head, it would almost be a blessing to him.

Carole Navarro had been perfect for the job. Oh, she'd had to be scrubbed down, tidied up, dressed correctly, and taught not to spike her speech with four-letter words. But by the time the overhaul had been completed, she had been a stunning package of wit, intellect, sophistication, and sexiness that Tate hadn't been able to resist.

He hadn't known that her wit had been cleansed of all ribaldry, that her intellect was only refined street smarts, her sophistication acquired, and her sexiness tempered with false morality. Just as planned, he'd fallen for the package, because it had promised everything he had been looking for in a wife.

Carole had perpetuated the myth until after Mandy was born—that had also been according to plan. It had been a relief for her to put phase two into action and start having affairs. The shackles of respectability had been chafing her for a long time. Her patience had worn thin. Once let loose, she performed beautifully.

God, it had been marvelous to witness Tate in his misery!

Except for that indiscreet visit in the hospital ICU, there'd been no mention made of their secret alliance since she was introduced to Tate four years ago. Neither by word or deed had they given away the pact that they had made when she had been recruited for the job.

But since the crash, she'd been even more evasive than usual. She bore watching—closely. She was doing some strange and unusual things, even for Carole. The whole family was noticing the unfamiliar personality traits.

Maybe she was acting strange for the hell of it. That would be like her. She enjoyed being perverse for perversity's sake alone. That wasn't serious, but it rankled that she had seized the initiative to change the game plan without prior consultation.

Perhaps she hadn't had an opportunity to consult yet. Perhaps she knew something about Tate that no one else was privy to and which needed to be acted upon immediately.

Or perhaps the bitch—and this was the most likely possibility—had decided that being a senator's wife was worth more to her than the payoff she was due to receive the day Tate was laid in a casket. After all, her metamorphosis had coincided with the primary election.

Whatever her motive, this new behavior pattern was as annoying as hell. She'd better watch herself, or she'd be cut out. At this point, it could all go down with or without her participation. Didn't the stupid bitch realize that?

Or had she finally realized that a second bullet was destined for her?

SEVENTEEN

"**M**rs. Rutledge, what a surprise."

The secretary stood up to greet Avery as she entered the anteroom of the law office Tate shared with his brother. To learn where it was, she had had to look up the address in the telephone directory.

"Hello. How are you?" She didn't address the secretary by name. The nameplate on the desk read "Mary Crawford," but she was taking no chances.

"I'm fine, but you look fabulous."

"Thank you."

"Tate told me that you were prettier than ever, but seeing is believing."

Tate had told her that? They hadn't engaged in a private conversation since the night he had kissed her. She found it hard to believe that he'd said something flattering about her to his secretary.

"Is he in?" He was. His car was parked out front.

"He's with a client."

"I didn't think he was handling any cases."

"He's not." Mary Crawford smoothed her skirt beneath her hips and sat back down. "He's with Barney Bridges. You know what a character he is. Anyway, he pledged a hefty donation to Tate's campaign, so when he hand delivered it, Tate made time to see him."

"Well, I've come all this way. Will they be long? Shall I wait?"

"Please do. Have a seat." The secretary indicated the grouping of waiting room sofas and chairs upholstered in burgundy and navy striped corduroy. "Would you like some coffee?"

"No thanks. Nothing."

She often passed up coffee now, preferring none at all to the liberally sweetened brew Carole had drunk. Sitting down in one of the armchairs, she picked up a current issue of *Field and Stream* and began idly thumbing through it. Mary resumed typing, as she'd been doing before Avery had come in.

This impetuous visit to Tate's law office was chancy, but it was a desperation measure she felt she had to take or go mad. What had Carole Rutledge done all day?

Avery had been living in the ranch house for over two weeks, and she had yet to discover a single constructive activity that Tate's wife had been involved in.

It had taken Avery several days to locate everything in her bedroom and the other rooms of the house to which she had access. She was constantly looking over her shoulder, not wanting to alert anyone to what she was doing. Eventually, she felt comfortable with the house's layout and where everyday items were stored.

Gradually, she began to learn her way around outside, as well. She took Mandy with her on these missions so they would appear to be nothing more than innocent strolls.

Carole had driven an American sports car. To Avery's consternation, it had a standard transmission. She wasn't too adept at driving standard transmissions. The first few times she took the car out, she nearly gave herself whiplash and stripped all the gears.

But once she felt adequate, she invented errands that would get her out of the house. Carole's way of life was dreadfully boring. Her routine lacked diversion and spontaneity. The ennui was making Avery Daniels crazy.

The day she had discovered an engagement calendar in a nightstand drawer, she had clutched it to her chest like a miner would a gold nugget. But a scan of its pages revealed very little except the days that Carole had had her hair and nails done.

Avery never called for an appointment. It would be a luxury to spend several hours a week being pampered in a salon—something Avery Daniels had never had time for—but she couldn't risk letting Carole's hairdresser touch her hair or a manicurist her nails. They might detect giveaways that others couldn't.

The engagement book had shed no light on what Carole did to fill her days. Obviously, she wasn't a member of any clubs. She had few or no friends because no one called. That came both as a surprise and a relief to Avery, who had been afraid that a covey of confidantes would descend, expecting to pick up where they had left off before Carole's accident.

Apparently, no such close friends existed. The flowers and cards she had received during her convalescence must have come from friends of the family.

Carole had held no job, had no hobbies. Avery reasoned that she should be thankful for that. What if Carole had been an expert sculptress, artist, harpist, or calligrapher? It had been difficult enough teaching herself in private to write and eat with her right hand.

She was expected to do no chores, not even make her own bed. Mona took care of the house and did all the cooking. A yard man came twice a week to tend to the plants in the courtyard. A retired cowboy, too old to herd cattle or rodeo, managed the stable of horses. No one encouraged her to resume an activity or interest that had been suspended as a result of her injuries.

Carole Rutledge had been a lazy idiot. Avery Daniels was not.

The door to Tate's private office opened. He emerged in the company of a barrel-chested, middle-aged man. They were laughing together.

Avery's heart accelerated at the sight of Tate, who was wearing a genuinely warm smile. His eyes were crinkled at the corners with the sense of humor he never shared with her. Eddy constantly nagged him to trade in his jeans, boots, and casual shirts for a coat and tie. He refused unless he was making a scheduled public appearance.

"Who am I trying to impress?" he had asked his perturbed campaign manager during a discussion relating to his wardrobe.

"Several million voters," Eddy had replied.

"If I can't impress them by what I'm standing for, they sure as hell aren't going to be impressed by what I'm standing in."

Nelson had drolly remarked, "Unless it's bullshit."

Everybody had laughed and that had been the end of the discussion.

Avery was glad Tate dressed as he did. He looked sensational. His head was bent at the listening angle that she had come to recognize and find endearing. One lock of hair dipped low over his forehead. His mouth was split in a wide grin, showing off strong, white teeth.

He hadn't seen her yet. At unguarded moments like this, she reveled in looking at him before contempt for his wife turned his beautiful smile into something ugly.

"Now, this is a treat!"

The booming bass voice snapped Avery out of her love-struck daze. Tate's visitor came swiftly toward her on short, stocky legs that were reminiscent of Irish. She was scooped up into a smothering bear hug and her back was hammered upon with exuberant affection. "Gawddamn, you look better than you ever have, and I didn't think that was possible."

"Hello, Mr. Bridges."

" 'Mr. Bridges?' Shee-ut. Where'd that come from? I told Mama when we saw you on TV that you're prettier now than you were before. She thought so, too."

"I'm glad I have your approval."

He wagged two stubby fingers, holding a cigar, near the tip of her nose. "Now you listen to ol' Barney, darlin', those polls don't meant a gawddamn thing, you hear? Not a gawddamn thing. I told Mama just the other day that those polls ain't worth shee-ut. You think I'd put my money on the boy here," he said, walloping Tate between the shoulder blades, "if I didn't think he was gonna put the screws to that gawddamn Dekker on election day? Huh?"

"No sir, not you, Barney," she replied, laughing.

"You're gawddamn right I wouldn't." Cramming the cigar into the corner of his mouth, he reached for her and gave her another rib-crunching hug. "I'd purely love to take y'all to lunch, but I got a deacons' meetin' at the church."

"Don't let us keep you," Tate said, trying to keep a straight face. "Thank you again for the contribution."

Barney waved away the thanks. "Mama's mailin' hers in today."

Tate swallowed with difficulty. "I . . . I thought the check was from both of you."

"Hell no, boy. That was only my half. Gotta go. The church is a long way from here, and Mama gets pissed if I drive the Vette over seventy in town, so I promised not to. Too many gawddamn crazies on the road. Y'll take care, you hear?"

He lumbered out. After the door had closed behind him, the secretary looked up at Tate and wheezed, "Did he say half?"

"That's what he said." Tate shook his head in disbelief. "Apparently he really believes that the polls aren't worth shee-ut."

Mary laughed. So did Avery. But Tate's smile had disappeared by the time he had ushered her into his office and closed the door. "What are you doing here? Need some money?"

When he addressed her in that curt, dismissive tone of voice, which he reserved for the times when they were alone, each word was like a shard of glass being gouged into her vitals. It made her ache. It also made her mad as hell.

"No, I don't need money," she said tightly as she sat down in the chair opposite his desk. "As you suggested, I went to the bank and signed a new card. I explained about the change in my handwriting," she said, flexing her right hand. "So I can write a check against the account whenever I get low on cash."

"So why are you here?"

"I need something else."

"What's that?"

"Something to do."

Her unexpected statement served its purpose. It won her his undivided attention. Skeptically holding her stare, he leaned back in his chair and raised his boots to the corner of his desk. "Something to do?"

"That's right."

He laced his fingers together across his belt buckle. "I'm listening."

"I'm bored, Tate." Her frustration boiled over. Restlessly, she left the chair. "I'm stuck out there on the ranch all day with nothing productive to do. I'm sick of being idle. My mind's turning to mush. I'm actually beginning to discuss the soap operas with Mona."

As she aimlessly roamed his office, she made note of several things—primarily that there were framed photographs of Mandy everywhere, but none of Carole.

Framed diplomas and photographs were attractively arranged on the wall behind the credenza. Looking for clues into his past, she paused in front of an eight-by-ten blowup of a snapshot taken in Vietnam.

Tate and Eddy were standing in front of a jet bomber, their arms draped across each other's shoulders in a pose of camaraderie. One's grin was as cocky as the other's. Avery had inadvertently learned that they'd been college roommates until Tate had postponed his education to enlist in the air force. Until now, she hadn't realized that Eddy had accompanied him to war.

"Since when have you been concerned with your mind?" he asked her, bringing her around.

"I need activity."

"Join an aerobics class."

"I did—the same day the doctor examined my tibia and gave me the go-ahead. But the class only lasts one hour three times a week."

"Join another one."

"Tate!"

"What? What the hell is all this about?"

"I'm trying to tell you. You're stubbornly refusing to listen."

He glanced at the closed door, mindful of the secretary seated just beyond it. Lowering his voice, he said, "You enjoy riding, but you haven't saddled up once since you got home."

No, she hadn't. Avery enjoyed riding, too, but she didn't know how good an equestrian Carole had been and hadn't wanted to tip her hand by being either too adept or too inexperienced.

"I've lost interest," she said lamely.

"I thought you would," he said sardonically, "just as soon as you cut the price tags off all that expensive gear."

Avery had seen the riding clothes in Carole's closet and wondered if she had ever actually worn the jodhpurs and short, tailored jacket. "I'll go back to it eventually." Giving herself time to collect her thoughts, she gazed at a picture of Nelson with Lyndon B. Johnson while he was still a congressman. Impressive.

There were several photos of Nelson in uniform, providing her a chronical of his military career. One picture in particular caught her eye because it was reminiscent of the snapshot of Tate and Eddy.

In the photo, Nelson's arm was draped companionably around another Air Force cadet—a young man as strikingly handsome and cavalier as young Nelson. Looming in the background, like a behemoth, was a monstrous bomber plane. Typed neatly across the bottom of the photograph was "Majors Nelson Rutledge and Bryan Tate, South Korea, 1951."

Bryan Tate. A relative of Nelson's? A friend? Presumably, because Nelson had named his son after him.

Avery turned again to face him, trying not to show more interest in the photograph than it should warrant for someone already familiar with it. "Put me to work at campaign headquarters."

"No."

"Why? Fancy's working there."

"Which is reason enough to keep you out. There might be bloodshed."

"I'll ignore her."

He shook his head. "We've got a slew of new volunteers. They're stepping over each other. Eddy's inventing work to accommodate all of them."

"I've got to get involved in something, Tate."

"Why, for God's sake?"

Because Avery Daniels performed best under pressure, she was accustomed to moving at a hectic pace, and couldn't tolerate inactivity. The sedentary life Carole Rutledge had lived was driving her insane.

She could neither protect him from assassination or do a story on the attempt if he continued to keep her at a safe distance. Her future, as well as his, hinged on her becoming as actively involved in his campaign as all the suspects.

"I feel like I should be helping you in some way."

He barked a short laugh. "Who do you think you're kidding?"

"I'm your wife!"

"Only for the time being!"

His sharp put-down silenced her. Tate, seeing her wounded expression, swore beneath his breath. "Okay, if you want to do something for me, continue being a decent mother to Mandy. She's opening up a little, I think."

"She's opening up a lot. And I intend for her to improve further every day."

She braced her hands on his desk and leaned over it, as she had when she had appealed to Irish for permission to pursue a story that met with his disapproval. "Even Mandy and her problems don't consume enough time. I can't be with her constantly. She goes to nursery school three mornings a week."

"You agreed with the psychologist that she should."

"I still do. Interaction with other children is extremely beneficial to her. She needs to develop social skills. But while she's at school, I wander through the house, killing time until it's time to pick her up. Every afternoon she takes a long nap." She leaned farther forward. "Please, Tate. I'm withering on the vine."

He held her stare for a long moment. Eventually, his eyes ventured down into the gaping vee of her silk shirt, but he quickly raised them and looked annoyed with himself for even that merest slip of his control.

He cleared his throat and asked crossly, "Okay, what do you suggest?"

Her tension eased somewhat. At least he was open to discussing it. She straightened up. "Let me work at headquarters."

"Nix."

"Then let me accompany you on that campaign trip next week."

"No," he said with taut finality.

"Please."

"I said no." Angrily he swung his feet to the floor, stood up, and rounded the desk.

"Why not?"

"Because you're not a trouper, Carole, and I won't put up with the disharmony you create."

"Like what?"

"Like what?" he demanded, incredulous that her memory didn't serve her. "When you went before, you complained about the rooms, the banquet food, everything. You ran consistently late when you knew how tightly Eddy wanted to keep to schedule. You made wisecracks to the press, which you considered cute and everybody else thought were tasteless and unbecoming. And that was only a three-day trip to test the waters before I had made my final decision to run."

"It won't be like that this time."

"I won't have any time to entertain you. When I'm not making a speech, I'll be writing one. Hours into the trip, you'd be whining that I was ignoring you and that you had nothing to do."

"I'll find things to do. I can make coffee, order sandwiches, sharpen pencils, take calls, return calls, run errands."

"Menial labor. We've got gofers and hangers-on who do all that."

"I can do *something*." She had been following closely on his heels as he moved around the office. When he stopped abruptly, she collided with him from behind.

He turned. "The novelty would wear off after the first day, and you'd be tired of it, complaining, wanting to come home."

"No, I wont."

"Why do you want to become involved all of a sudden?"

"Because," she said with rising ire, "you're running for a Senate seat, and it's my responsibility as your wife to help you win."

"Bullshit!"

There were three sharp raps on the door. Seconds later it was opened to admit Eddy and Jack. "Excuse us," the former said, "but we heard all the shouting when we came in and thought you might need us to referee."

"What's going on?" Jack closed the door behind them. "What are you doing here?"

"I came to see my husband," Avery retorted. "If that's all right with you, Jack." She pushed her bangs off her forehead, a belligerent gesture that dared him to make something of it.

"Calm down, for crissake. I was just asking." Jack sat down on the short sofa against the wall.

Eddy shoved his hands into his pants pockets and stared at the Oriental rug between his gleaming shoes. Tate returned to his desk and sat down. Avery was too keyed up to sit, so she crossed to the credenza and backed against it, supporting herself on her hips.

"Carole wants to go on the campaign trip with us next week," Tate said.

Jack said, "Jesus, not again."

Avery cried, "Well, why not?"

Eddy said, "Let's discuss it."

Tate took them in turn. "You don't like the idea, Jack?"

Jack glared at her, then shrugged and swore beneath his breath. "She's your wife."

Tate's attention moved to Avery. "You already know my objections."

"Some of them are justified," she said in a conciliatory tone, admiring him for not criticizing his wife in front of other men. "I'll do better this time, now that I know what to expect and what is expected of me."

"Eddy?"

Eddy's contemplation of the rug ended when Tate spoke his name. He raised his head. "There's no doubt that a handsome couple is an easier package to sell than a handsome man alone."

"Why?"

"Image, mainly. A couple represents all the things America stands for—hearth and home, the American dream. Marriage signifies that once you get to Washington you aren't going to squander taxpayers' money on bimbo secretaries who can't type."

"At least in theory," Jack said with a guffaw.

Eddy smiled crookedly and conceded, "At least in theory. Women voters will respect you for being a faithful husband and conscientious father. Men will like that you aren't either gay or on the make.

"For all our modern sophistication, voters might feel uneasy about voting a suspected homosexual into office. A good-looking candidate is inherently resented by male voters. Having a wife by your side makes you one of the guys."

"In other words, misery loves company," Avery said snidely.

Eddy gave a helpless lift of his shoulders and apologetically replied, "I didn't make up the rules, Carole."

She divided her disgusted look among the three of them. "So, what's the verdict?"

"I have a suggestion."

"You have the floor, Eddy." As before, Tate's feet were resting on the corner of his desk, and he was reclining in the tall leather chair. Avery was tempted to sweep his boots off the desk just to unbalance his posture and his insouciance.

Eddy said, "On Carole's behalf, I declined her invitation to attend that dinner coming up this Friday night."

"The southern governors' thing in Austin?"

"Right. I excused her from going by saying that for all the progress she's made, she wasn't quite up to a black tie evening."

He turned toward her. "I could call them back and accept. It's a bipartisan group, so there'll be no active campaigning, just a chance to glad-hand, see, and be seen. We'll see how that evening goes and make a decision about the trip based on that.''

''An audition, in other words,'' Avery said.

''If that's how you want to see it,'' Eddy returned calmly. He looked toward Jack and Tate. ''She did a pretty good job at that press conference when she left the hospital.''

Eddy's opinion mattered a great deal to Tate, but final decisions were always left to him. He glanced at his older brother, who had remained irascibly silent. ''What do you think, Jack?''

''I guess it'd be okay,'' he said, glancing at her resentfully. ''I know Mom and Dad would rather the two of you present a unified front.''

''Thank you both for your advice.''

They took the subtle hint. Jack left the office without saying another word. Eddy nodded an unspoken good-bye to Avery and closed the door behind himself.

Tate held her stare for several moments. ''All right,'' he said grudgingly. ''You've won a chance to convince me that you'd be more of an asset than a liability when we begin campaigning in earnest.''

''You won't be disappointed, Tate. I promise.''

He frowned doubtfully. ''Friday night. We'll leave the house at seven sharp. Be ready.''

 # EIGHTEEN

''I'll get it.''

The front doorbell had rung twice. Avery was the first to reach it. She grabbed the knob and pulled it open. Van Lovejoy stood between the pots of geraniums.

Avery froze. Her expectant, welcoming smile turned to stone, her knees to water. Her stomach tightened.

Van reacted with similar disquiet. His slumped posture was instantly corrected. A cigarette fell from between his fingers. He blinked numerous times.

Avery, hoping that his pupils had been dilated by marijuana and not shock, mustered as much composure as she could. ''Hello.''

''Hi, uh . . .'' He closed his eyes for a moment and shook his head of stringy hair. ''Uh, Mrs. Rutledge?''

''Yes?''

He covered his heart with a bony hand. ''Jesus, for a minute there, you looked just like—''

''Come in, please.'' She didn't want to hear him speak her name. She had barely curbed her impulse to joyously cry out his. It had been nearly impossible to keep from hugging him fiercely and telling him that she was onto the hottest story of her career.

From the beginning, however, she had been in this alone. Telling Van would place him in danger, too. As comforting as it would be to have an ally, she couldn't afford the luxury. Besides, she didn't want to risk blowing the opportunity by confiding in him. Van wasn't all that trustworthy.

She stepped aside and he joined her in the entry. It would have been natural for him to gaze around at the unfamiliar and impressive surroundings, but instead, he stared into her face. Avery pitied him his confusion. "You are . . . ?"

"Oh, sorry." He rubbed his palms self-consciously on the seat of his jeans, then extended his right hand. She shook it quickly. "Van Lovejoy."

"I'm Carole Rutledge."

"I know. I was there the day you left the clinic. I work for KTEX."

"I see."

Even though he was making an attempt at normal conversation, his eyes hadn't left her. It was agony to be this close to a friend and not be able to behave normally. She had a million and one questions to ask him, but settled for the one that Carole would logically ask next.

"If you're here representing the television station, shouldn't you have cleared it first with Mr. Paschal, my husband's campaign manager?"

"He knows I'm coming. The production company sent me over."

"Production company?"

"I'm shooting a TV commercial here next Wednesday. I came today to scout my locations. Didn't anybody tell you I was coming?"

"I—"

"Carole?"

Nelson moved into the hallway, subjecting Van to a glare of stern disapproval. Nelson was always military neat. He never had a wrinkle in his clothing or a single gray hair out of place.

Van was the antithesis. His dingy T-shirt had come from a Cajun restaurant that specialized in oysters on the half shell. The lewdly suggestive slogan on the shirt read, "Shuck me, suck me, eat me raw." His jeans had gone beyond being fashionably ragged to downright threadbare. There were no laces in his scuffed jogging shoes. Avery doubted he owned a pair of socks because he always went without.

He looked unhealthy and underfed to the point of emaciation. Sharp shoulder blades poked against the T-shirt. If he had stood up straight, each rib would have been delineated. As it was, his back bowed over a concave torso.

Avery knew that those nicotine-stained hands with the chipped and dirty fingernails were gifted in handling a video camera. His vacuous eyes were capable of incredible artistic insight. All Nelson could see, however, was an eternal hippie, a wasted life. Van's talent was as well disguised as her real identity.

"Nelson, this is Mr. Lovejoy. Mr. Lovejoy, Colonel Rutledge." Nelson seemed reluctant to shake hands with Van and made short business of it. "He's here to look over the house in preparation for the television commercial they're taping next week."

"You work for MB Productions?" Nelson asked stiffly.

"I freelance for them sometimes. When they want the best."

"Hmm. They said somebody would be out today." Apparently, Van wasn't what Nelson had expected. "I'll show you around. What do you want to see—indoors or out?"

"Both. Any place that Rutledge, his wife, and his kid might spend an average day. Folksy is what they said they wanted. Sentimental crap."

"You can see all of the house you want, but you'll have no access to my family, Mr. Lovejoy. My wife would be affronted by the crude wording on your shirt."

"She's not wearing it, so why the fuck should she care?"

Nelson's blue eyes turned arctic. He was accustomed to being treated with more deference by anyone he considered of inferior rank. Avery wouldn't have been surprised if Nelson had grabbed him by the seat of his pants and the scruff of his

neck and thrown him out. If Van's business hadn't dealt directly with Tate's campaign, he probably would have.

As it was, he said, "Carole, I apologize for what you just heard. You'll excuse us?"

Van turned back to her. "See you around, Mrs. Rutledge. Sorry I stared, but you look so much like—"

"I'm used to people staring at my face now," she interrupted quickly. "Everyone's naturally curious about it."

Nelson impatiently inclined his head. "This way, Lovejoy."

Van gave one last puzzled shake of his head before ambling off down the hallway behind Nelson. Avery retreated to her room, leaning against the door after she had closed it behind her. She breathed deeply and blinked back tears of nervousness and remorse.

She had wanted to grab Van's skinny arm and, after a jubilant reunion, pump him for information. How was Irish? Was he still grieving over her death? Was he taking care of himself? What had become of the new weatherman? Had he been canned or had he left of his own volition? Had the pregnant secretary delivered a boy or a girl? What was the latest gossip from the sales department? Was the general manager still cheating on his wife with the socialite?

She realized, however, that Van might not be as glad to see her as she was to see him. Oh, he'd be thrilled that she was alive, but once he'd recovered from the shock, she could almost hear him saying, "Just what the fuck do you think you're doing?"

Frequently, she had been asking herself that same question. She wanted the story, yes, but her motivation wasn't entirely self-fulfilling.

Saving Tate's life had been her ultimate reason for taking the place of his late wife. But was that still operative? Where was the threat that was supposed to exist?

Since coming home, she had been a curious observer. There was some discord between Jack and Dorothy Rae. Fancy could provoke a saint. Nelson was autocratic. Zee was aloof. Eddy was competent to a fault. But none had exhibited anything but adoration and love toward Tate. She wanted to rout out a potential killer, and get the story that would win back the respect and credibility that had been so stupidly sacrificed to poor judgment. Seeing Van had served as a reminder of that.

He'd brought with him the realization that she wasn't concentrating as much on the incredible story as she was on the people living it. That wasn't surprising. Detachment had always been the most difficult aspect of her career. It was the only essential element of journalism that had escaped her.

She had inherited journalistic interest and skill from her father. But his ability to discount the human factor hadn't been part of his legacy. She tried to develop objectivity but so far she had failed. She feared that she wasn't going to learn it by becoming involved with the Rutledges.

But she could not leave now. The biggest flaw in her carefully laid plan was that she hadn't left herself an escape route. Short of ripping the whole thing wide open, she had no choice but to stay and take things as they came—even surprise visits from old friends.

Friday arrived. Avery whiled away the long hours of the afternoon by playing with Mandy in her room after she woke up from her nap. Seated at a small table, they made clay dinosaurs until Mandy got hungry and was turned over to Mona.

At five o'clock Avery bathed. While she applied her evening makeup, she nibbled from a snack plate that Mona had brought her.

She styled her hair with mousse. It was still short and chic, but not as severe as it had been. The top had grown out long enough for her to creatively style it. She accented the smart, sexy, final results with a lavish pair of diamond earrings.

By quarter of seven, fifteen minutes ahead of schedule, she was ready. She was in her bathroom, dabbing fragrance behind her ears, when Tate suddenly strode in.

His unheralded and unprecedented appearance stunned her. He slept on the convertible sofa in the study/parlor next to her room. There was a connecting door between them, but it was always kept shut and locked from his side.

The study was decorated in subdued, masculine tones resembling a gentleman's club. It had a small adjoining bathroom. The sink was no bigger than a dentist's basin, the shower barely large enough to accommodate an adult. Yet Tate preferred those cramped facilities to sharing his wife's spacious bedroom and bathroom, which had two large dressing areas connected by a wall of mirrors, and a marble Roman tub with a skylight overhead, and yards of plush carpeting.

Avery's first sinking thought when he barged in was that he had changed his mind and had come to tell her that she couldn't go with him. He didn't appear angry, however, only harassed. He was brought up short when he spied her image in the mirror.

Gratified to know that her efforts had paid off, Avery turned to face him and held her arms out to her sides. "Like it?"

"The dress? The dress is great."

"Our Frost Brothers bill will reflect just how great."

She knew it was a terrific dress. Black illusion, irregularly sprinkled with sequins, covered her chest, shoulders, upper back, and arms, down to the wrists. From the first suggestion of cleavage, the knee-length sheath was lined with black silk. The dress was further enhanced by bands of black iridescent sequins at her neck and around her wrists.

It was a sexy dress, but in a respectable way, reminiscent of Audrey Hepburn. She hadn't splurged on it for selfish reasons. She hadn't wanted to wear anything belonging to Carole tonight. She had wanted to be new for Tate, different, unlike Carole had ever been.

Besides, all Carole's formal dresses had been low-cut and flamboyant, not to Avery's liking. She had needed something seasonably lightweight, but with long sleeves. She was very conscientious about revealing too much skin, which might give her false identity away. This dress had offered it all.

"Money well spent," Tate muttered reluctantly.

"Did you want something in particular? Or did you come to see if I was running late?"

"I'm the one who's late, I'm afraid. I can't find my studs. Have you seen them?"

It hadn't escaped her notice that he was only partially dressed. There was a speck of fresh blood on his chin, attesting to a quick, close shave. He was still barefoot, his hair was still damp and uncombed after a haphazard towel drying, and his starched, pleated shirt was unbuttoned. The long shirttail hung over his dark tuxedo trousers.

The sight of his hairy, bare chest made her mouth water. His belly was as tight and flat as a drum. Since he hadn't yet fastened the fly to his trousers, she had an unrestricted view all the way down, past his navel, to the white elastic waistband of his briefs.

Reflexively, she moistened her lips. Her heart was beating so hard she could actually feel the fabric of her dress moving against her skin. "Studs?" she asked faintly.

"I thought I might have left them in here."

"Feel free to look." She gestured toward the dressing area, where she had discovered a cache of masculine toiletries and grooming utensils during one of her explorations.

He rifled through two drawers before finding the black jewelry box with the flip-top lid. A set of onyx studs and a pair of matching cuff links were inside. "Do you need help?"

"No."

"Yes." She moved to block his exit from the room.

"I can do it."

"And wrinkle your shirt while wrestling with them. Let me." Waving away his protests and his hands, she inserted the first stud. Her knuckles brushed against the dense hair on his chest. It was soft, damp. She wanted to bury her face in it.

"What's all that?" She glanced up at him, then followed his indicating chin. "Oh. Mandy's artwork." There were several scribbled pictures attached to her mirror with strips of Scotch tape. "Didn't she give you some?"

"Sure. I just didn't expect yours to be so prominently displayed. You used to say you couldn't stand the clutter. Finished?" He bent his head down to cheek her slow progress. They almost bumped heads.

"One more. Stand still. Is that your stomach growling? Help yourself to a snack."

He paused for a moment, then reached toward the snack plate for an apple slice and a chunk of cheese. His teeth crunched into the apple. The sound of his munching was wildly erotic.

"Cuff links?"

He passed them to her and extended his left arm. She speared the cuff link through the holes, then flipped it open so it would hold. She patted it into place. "Next?" He gave her his right arm. After it was done, she declined to put distance between them. Instead, she angled her head back and looked up at him from close range.

"What about your bow tie?"

He swallowed the food. "In my room."

"Can you handle it?"

"I'll manage. Thanks."

"Any time."

Then, when he could leave, he didn't. He stayed for several moments longer, staring down at her, with the lingering mist of her long bath and the smell of her perfume swirling around them.

Finally, he stepped back and moved toward the door. "I'll be out in five minutes."

Tate felt like he had just made a narrow escape when he reentered the room he slept in. His shower must have been too hot. Why else couldn't he cool down? He blamed his clumsiness on necessary haste and the important evening facing him.

He bungled tying his tie several times before getting it right; he couldn't find matching socks; it took him ten minutes to finish dressing. However, when his wife emerged from her bedroom after his soft tap on her door, she didn't remark on the delay.

Together they went into the living room, where Zee was reading Mandy a story. Nelson was watching his favorite TV detective chase down the bad guys and bring them to justice.

He glanced up when they walked in and gave a long wolf whistle. "You two look like the bride and groom on the wedding cake."

"Thanks, Dad," Tate answered for both of them.

"She hardly looks like a bride in that black dress, Nelson."

Tate was sure his mother hadn't meant for her comment to be insulting, but that's how it sounded. It was followed by an awkward pause that was finally broken when Zee added, "But you do look very nice, Carole."

"Thank you," she replied in a subdued voice.

From the day they were introduced, Zee had been reserved in her relationship with Carole. She would have preferred that their love affair had died before it had come to marriage, though she would never have said so.

She had warmed up to Carole while she was carrying Mandy, but that maternal affection soon cooled. For months prior to the plane crash, Zee had been more openly critical than before. Tate knew why, of course. Neither of his parents was stupid or blind, and they had always disparaged anything that hurt Jack or him.

Tonight, however, he had hoped that everything would go smoothly. It already promised to be a strained evening. While his mother's thoughtless comment hadn't ruined it entirely, it certainly hadn't helped relieve any tension.

Mandy revived the festive mood somewhat when she slid from her grandmother's lap and shyly approached them. He knelt down. "Come give me a big hug." Mandy placed her arms around him and buried her face in his neck.

To his surprise, Carole crouched down beside them. "I'll come kiss you when we get home. Okay?"

Mandy raised her head and nodded solemnly. "Okay, Mommy."

"Be a good girl for Grandma and Grandpa."

Mandy nodded again, then removed her arms from Tate's neck and hugged Carole. "Bye-bye."

"Bye-bye. Give me good night sugars."

"Do I have to go to bed now?"

"No, but I want my sugars ahead of time."

Mandy kissed Carole's mouth noisily, then scampered back to her grandmother. Ordinarily, Carole complained when Mandy ruined her makeup or mussed her clothing. All she did now was lightly dab at her lips with a Kleenex.

He couldn't figure it, except that she was playing the good-mother role to the hilt. God only knew what her motive was. This newfound affection for Mandy was probably phony as hell. No doubt she had picked up pointers from talk shows and magazine articles during her convalescence.

He placed his hand beneath her elbow and guided her toward the front door. "It might be late before we're back."

"Drive carefully," Zee called after them.

Nelson left his detective with gun drawn and followed them to the door. "If this was a beauty contest and ballots were handed out tonight, y'all would win. Can't tell you how proud and pleased I am to see the two of you stepping out with each other all dressed up."

Was his father suggesting that whatever had come between them should be forgiven and forgotten? Tate appreciated his concern; he just didn't think he could oblige him. Forgive? He'd always found that hard to do. Forget? It just wasn't in his nature.

But as he seated Carole in the silver leather interior of his car, he wished he could. If he could erase all the anger, pain, and contempt, and start over with this woman tonight, would he want to?

Tate had always been as scrupulously honest with himself as he was with everyone. Looking and behaving as Carole did tonight, yes, he told himself, he would want to make a new start.

Plainly, he wanted her. He liked her when she was like this, soft-spoken and even-tempered and sexy. He didn't expect her to be a doormat. She had too much vivacity and intelligence to be a silent, submissive partner. He didn't want her to be. He liked sparks—of anger, of humor. Without them, a relationship was as bland as unseasoned food.

She smiled at him as he slid behind the wheel. "Nelson's right. You look very nice tonight, Tate."

"Thanks." And just because he was weary of being scornful all the time, he added, "So do you."

She dazzled him with a smile. In the old days, he would have said, "Screw being late, I'm going to make love to my wife," and taken her right there in the car.

A fantasy of doing that flashed into his mind; nuzzling her flushed breasts; sinking into her deep, wet heat; hearing her gasps of pleasure when she came.

He groaned, quickly covering it with a cough.

He missed the spontaneity, the fun of having hot sex with someone he loved.

To conceal the fierce light in his eyes, which she would instantly recognize as arousal, he slid on his sunglasses, even though the sun had already set.

Driving away from the house, he admitted that he missed what they had had, but he didn't miss *her*. Because while the sex had been hot and good and frequent, there had been little real intimacy. That cerebral exchange and spiritual bonding had been lacking in their marriage from the very beginning, though he hadn't put a name to the missing component until much later.

He couldn't miss what he'd never had, but he still yearned for it. Winning the Senate seat was going to be sweet. It would mark the beginning of what he hoped would be a lifetime career in public service. But the victory would be tainted by his marital unhappiness.

It would be much sweeter, and his political future would look much brighter, if he could share it with a loving, supportive wife.

He might just as well wish for the moon, he thought. Even if Carole had that kind of love to give, which she didn't, he wouldn't take it. She had destroyed any possibility of that long ago.

The physical attraction was still there, inexplicably stronger than ever, but the emotional attachments were dead. And he'd be damned if he would accept one while being cheated of the other.

He figured the resolution just hadn't reached his cock yet.

He glanced at Carole from out of the corner of his eye. She looked fantastic. His mother had called it correctly. She had too much poise and sophistication and sexiness for a bride.

She looked like a well-loved, well-sated wife—very unlike Carole.

 # NINETEEN

Eddy Paschal stepped out of the shower. He quickly patted the towel over his arms and chest and down both legs. Flinging it over his shoulder, he caught the other end and rubbed it back and forth across his back as he moved from bathroom to bedroom. As soon as he cleared the door, he drew up short. "What the—"

"Hi, there. Didn't know you were into dirty pictures."

Fancy was stretched diagonally across the bed. She was propped up on one elbow, thumbing through the *Penthouse* she had found lying on his nightstand. After a dispassionate glance at one particularly provocative pose, she looked up at him and smiled slyly. "You naughty boy, you."

"What the hell are you doing in here?" He hastily secured the towel around his middle.

Fancy stretched with feline laziness. "I was sunbathing out by the pool and came in here to get cool."

Eddy lived in an apartment over the ranch's garage. Shortly after he was hired to be Tate's campaign manager, he had asked if he could rent the efficiency. The Rutledges had vehemently protested.

Zee had been the most vocal. "Servant's quarters? I wouldn't hear of it."

Tate had added his own protests, stating that if Eddy was going to live at the ranch, he would live in the house with the family.

Eddy had explained that he needed the convenience of living close to them while maintaining his privacy. The garage apartment satisfied both requirements. They had relented and he had moved in.

His privacy had now been invaded. "Why cool off in here?" he asked querulously. "Is the air conditioner in the house on the blink?"

"Don't be tacky." Fancy tossed the magazine aside and came to a sitting position. "Aren't you glad to see me?"

"There's certainly plenty to see," he muttered, ruffling his wet hair. It was fine, straight, and pale. "I've seen Band-Aids bigger than that bikini. Does Nelson approve of you running around like that?" Abundant flesh was overflowing the skimpy swimsuit.

"Grandpa doesn't approve of anything erogenous," she snorted. "I swear I don't know how my daddy and Uncle Tate ever got conceived. I bet Grandpa sings 'The Battle Hymn of the Republic' while he's balling Grandma. Or maybe 'Off We Go, into the Wild, Blue Yonder.' " She drew a thoughtful expression. "I just can't imagine her coming, can you?"

"You're hopeless, Fancy." In spite of himself, he chuckled at the images she had conjured. Then he propped his hands on his hips and looked at her reprovingly. "Will you please scram so I can dress? I told Tate I'd meet him and Carole at the Waller Creek, and I'm already running late."

"Can I go with you?"

"No."

"Why?" she wheedled.

"No more tickets."

"You could manage it." He shook his head no. "Why not? I could get ready in a jiff."

"It'll be a stuffy, grown-up affair, Fancy. You'd be bored stiff."

"You'd be stiff if I went along. But I guarantee you wouldn't be bored." She gave him a licentious wink.

"Are you going to leave, or what?"

"What, I think," she replied flippantly. She unclasped her bikini bra and let it fall. Leaning back, she propped herself up on her elbows. "How do you like my . . . tan?"

Her breasts were full and soft, rising from a band of baby pinkness between her suntanned chest and stomach. The areolas were oversized, and her nipples were rosy and raised.

Tilting his face ceilingward, Eddy pinched his eyes shut. "Why are you doing this now? Come on, get up. Put your top back on and get the hell out of here."

He moved toward the bed and extended his hand down to assist her up. Fancy took his hand, but she didn't use it as leverage. Instead, she carried it to her breast and pressed his palm against the distended center. Her eyes were alight with mischief and arousal. As she slowly rotated his palm over her nipple, she used her other hand to pull away his towel and affected a gasp of surprised pleasure.

"Hmm, Eddy, you have a beautiful cock."

She gazed at it avidly as she inched to the edge of the bed. Her fingers encircled his penis, then she squeezed it through her fist, elongating and stretching it. "So big. Who are you saving it for? That ugly redhead down at headquarters? Or my Aunt Carole?"

She flung her head back and looked up the length of his torso. The cold glint in his eyes alarmed her for an instant before she decided that she liked him best when he was being a bastard. He posed more of a challenge that way.

"I can and will do more for you than either of them." Having made that breathy pledge, she bent her head over him to prove it.

At the first deft, damp stroke of her tongue, Eddy's knees buckled. In seconds, Fancy was on her back in the middle of his bed and he was lying above her, his tongue inside her mouth, spearing toward the back of her throat.

"Oh, God. Oh, Jesus. Yes. Yes," Fancy panted when his hands roughly caressed her.

He threw her arms behind her head and attacked her breasts with his mouth, sucking ardently, biting hungrily, licking furiously while the girl writhed beneath him. She became so lost in his rowdy foreplay that it took several seconds for her to realize that he was no longer doing it.

She opened her eyes. Once again he was standing at the foot of the bed, smiling with amusement.

"Wha—"

Only when she tried to sit up did she discover that her arms were tied above her head. She swung them forward. Her bikini bra was wrapped around her wrists, the ends knotted.

"You son of a bitch," she yelled. "Untie my fuckin' hands."

Calmly, Eddy went to the bureau and took a pair of briefs from the top drawer. As he pulled them on, he made a tsking sound. "Such language."

"Untie me, you bastard."

"I'm sure that a resourceful young *lady,*" he stressed with one eyebrow skeptically raised, "will think of a way to free herself."

He took his rented tuxedo out of the plastic bag and began dressing. For as long as that took, Fancy lambasted him with every epithet her fertile mind and unlimited vocabulary could produce.

"Save it," Eddy said tersely when the crude tirade had ceased to be amusing. "I just want to know one thing."

"Screw you."

"What did you mean by that remark about Carole and me?"

"What do you think?"

He reached the bed in three strides, grabbed a handful of Fancy's hair, and wound it around his fist until it pulled against her scalp. "I don't know what to think. That's why I'm asking."

He frightened her. She lost some of her defiance. "You're getting it from somewhere. Why not from Aunt Carole?"

"First and foremost, because she doesn't appeal to me."

"That's bullshit."

"Why bullshit?"

"Because you watch her like a hawk, especially since she came home."

Eddy continued to stare at her coldly. "She's my best friend's wife. They've had their problems. I'm concerned how their marriage might effect the outcome of the campaign."

"Some marriage," Fancy scoffed. "He can't stand her because she's screwed around on him. My true blue Uncle Tate won't put up with that kind of crap from his wife. He's only staying married to her until the election is over."

Then Fancy smiled. She was almost purring. "But, you know what? If you do want in Carole's pants, I think you're out of luck. I think they're patching things up. I think she's giving to him—if he wants it—what she was giving to you before the airplane crash."

Gradually, his hand relaxed and he released her hair. "That's quite a theory, Fancy." His voice was cool and calm. He moved to the dresser, stuffed a handkerchief into his pants pocket, and slid on his wristwatch. "It just happens to be wrong. There never has been or will be anything between Carole and me."

"I might ask her and see what she says."

"If I were you," he said softly, addressing her over his shoulder, "I'd keep my jealous speculations to myself."

Without the benefit of her hands to assist her, Fancy wiggled off the bed and came to her feet. "This is getting old, Eddy. Untie my hands."

He angled his head to one side, as though giving her demand careful consideration. "No, I don't believe so. I think I'd rather put some distance between us before you get loose."

"I can't leave here until I get my hands free."

"That's right."

She padded after him to the door. "Please, Eddy," she wailed. Tears formed in her large blue eyes. "You're being cruel. This isn't a game to me. I know you think I'm a slut for throwing myself at you, but I felt like I had to make the first move or you never would. I love you. Please love me back. Please."

He laid his hand in the curve of her waist and squeezed it gently. "I'm sure you can find some other guy who'll appreciate me warming you up for him."

Her cheeks bloomed scarlet. "You son of a bitch." The wheedling humility vanished. Her low voice now vibrated with rage. "You're goddamn right I'll find a man. I'll fuck his brains out. I'll suck him dry. I'll—"

"Have a good evening, Fancy." Unceremoniously, he pushed her out of his way and jogged down the exterior stairs to his parked car.

Fancy put her foot to the door and slammed it hard behind him.

As Avery came out of the ladies' room, she didn't even notice the man at the pay telephone. She was anxious to get back to the party. The banquet had been interminable, the after-dinner speaker ponderous.

However, once they were free to mingle, Tate had been the center of attention. It seemed that everyone in the room wanted to meet him and shake his hand, whether they shared a party affiliation or not. Even political rivals were friendly. None was hostile—certainly not enough to want him dead.

He was respected even if his ideas weren't unanimously popular. It was a heady feeling just to be standing next to him as his wife. Each time he made an introduction, he did so with a certain degree of pride that thrilled her. She hadn't made any social blunders. She had covertly taken her cues from him when someone Carole would have known approached. Everything was going splendidly.

Tate had touched her arm briefly as she excused herself to go to the powder room, as though he dreaded even that brief a separation.

Now, as she passed the bank of telephones, a hand shot out and manacled her wrist. She emitted a cry of astonishment and spun around to confront the man who had accosted her. He was wearing a tuxedo, signifying that he belonged to the crowd in the banquet hall.

"How's it going, baby?" he drawled.

"Let go of me." Taking him for someone who'd had too much to drink, she made a painful attempt to wrench her arm free.

"Not so fast, Mrs. Rutledge." He slurred the name insultingly. "I want to get a close-up look at the new face I've heard so much about." He pulled her closer. "Except for your hair, you look the same. But tell me what I really want to know. Are you still as hot?"

"Let me go, I said."

"What's the matter? Afraid your husband is going to catch you? He won't. He's too busy campaigning."

"I'll scream bloody murder if you don't release my arm this instant."

He laughed. "Are you pissed because I didn't come see you in the hospital? Now, would it have been seemly for one of your lovers to elbow your husband away from your bedside?"

She glared at him with cold fury. "Things have changed."

"Oh, yeah?" He put his face close to hers. "Doesn't your pussy itch like it used to?"

Incensed and afraid, she renewed her struggle to release her arm, which only seemed to incite him. He bent her arm up behind her and hauled her against the front of his body. His breath was humid and boozy against her face. She tried to turn her head away, but he trapped her jaw with his free hand.

"What's with you, Carole? Do you think you're high and mighty now that Tate's actually in the race? What a joke! Rory Dekker's gonna kick his ass, you know." He closed his fingers, hurting her jaw. She whimpered with pain and outrage.

"Now that you think he might make it to Washington, you're really sucking up to him, aren't you? Tonight you looked straight through me. Just who the hell do you think you are, bitch, to ignore me like that?"

He ground a hard kiss upon her lips, smearing her fresh lipstick and making her sick by poking his tongue between her lips. She doubled her fists and pushed with all her might against his shoulders. She tried to drive a knee into his crotch, but her slim skirt prevented that. He was strong; she couldn't budge him. He consumed all her air. She felt herself weakening, growing faint.

Dimly at first, and then louder, she heard approaching voices. So did he. He shoved her away and gave her a smirking smile. "You'd do well to remember who your friends are," he sneered. He rounded the corner seconds ahead of two women who were on their way to the powder room.

Their conversation died when they saw Avery. She quickly turned her back and fumbled with the telephone receiver as though she were about to place a call. They went past and entered the ladies' room. As soon as the door swished closed behind them, she collapsed against the shelf beneath the public phone.

She broke a nail in her haste to undo the clasp on Carole's beaded evening bag in search of a Kleenex. Finding one, she wiped her mouth, rubbing it hard, ridding it of the smeared lipstick and any taste of the hateful kiss she had endured from Carole's ex-lover. She unwrapped a peppermint and put it in her mouth, then dabbed her tearful eyes with the tissue. During the tussle an earring had come off, she clipped it back on.

The two women came out, speaking in hushed tones as they walked past. Avery murmured needlessly into the receiver, feeling like a fool for enacting such a ridiculous charade.

But then, she had become very good at playing charades, hadn't she? She'd fooled one of Carole's lovers.

When she finally felt composed enough to face the crowd again, she hung up the telephone receiver and turned to go. As she did, a man quickly rounded the corner and ran right into her. Seeing only the front of his tux, she cried out in fear.

"Carole? For God's sake, what's wrong?"

"Tate!"

Avery slumped against him, tightly wrapping her arms around his waist. Resting her cheek on his lapel, she closed her eyes to block out the vision of the other man.

Hesitantly, Tate placed his arms around her. His hands stirred the silk against her body as he stroked her back. "What's the matter? What happened? A lady drew me aside and said you looked upset. Are you sick?"

He had immediately deserted the limelight and rushed to her assistance, even though she was an unfaithful wife. Whatever scruples she had had against sleeping with another woman's husband vanished in that single moment. Carole hadn't deserved him.

"Oh, Tate, I'm sorry." She lifted her face to his. "So sorry."

"For what?" He took her firmly by the shoulders and shook her lightly. "Will you tell me what the hell is going on?"

Because she couldn't tell him the truth, she foundered for a logical explanation. When she arrived at one, she realized that it wasn't entirely untrue. "I guess I'm not ready to be surrounded by so many people. The crowd was overwhelming me. I felt smothered."

"You seemed to be doing fine."

"I was. I was enjoying it. But all of a sudden everybody seemed to close in. It was like being wrapped up in those bandages again. I couldn't breathe, couldn't—"

"Okay. I get the picture. You should have said something. Come on." He took her by the arm.

She dug her heels in. "We don't have to leave."

"The party's breaking up anyway. We'll beat everybody to the valet parking."

"You're sure?" She wanted to leave. To return to the banquet hall and possibly confront that gloating face again would be untenable. However, this was her audition. She didn't want to blow it and be left at the ranch when he went campaigning.

"I'm sure. Let's go."

They didn't say much on the way home. Avery tucked her feet beneath her hips and turned in the seat to face him. She wanted to touch him, to comfort and be comforted, but she satisfied herself with simply facing him.

Everyone was in bed when they arrived home. Silently they went together in Mandy's room, and, as they had promised, kissed her good night. She mumbled sleepily in response but didn't wake up.

As they moved down the hallway toward their respective bedrooms, Tate said offhandedly, "We'll be attending several formal functions. You probably should take that dress on the trip."

Avery spun around to face him. "You mean you want me to go?"

He looked at a spot beyond her head. "Everybody thinks it would be a good idea."

Unwilling to let him off that lightly, she gave his lapel a tug. His eyes connected with hers. "I'm only interested in what you think, Tate."

He deliberated for several tense moments before giving his answer. "Yeah, I think it's a good idea. Eddy'll give you an itinerary in a day or two so you'll know what else to pack. Good night."

Bitterly disappointed in his lukewarm enthusiasm, Avery watched him walk down the hall and enter his room. Dejectedly, she went into hers alone and prepared for bed. She examined her dress, looking for damage done by Carole's ex-lover, whoever he'd been, but thankfully found none.

She was exhausted by the time she turned off the lamps, but when an hour went by and she still hadn't fallen asleep, she got out of bed and left her room.

Fancy decided to enter through the kitchen in case her grandfather had set up an ambush in the living room. She unlocked the door, disengaged the alarm system, and quietly reset it.

"Who's that? Fancy?"

Fancy nearly jumped out of her skin. "Jesus Christ, Aunt Carole! You scared the living shit out of me!" She reached for the light switch.

"Oh, my God." Avery sprang from her chair at the kitchen table and turned Fancy's face up toward the light. "What happened to you?" She grimaced as she examined the girl's swollen eye and bleeding lip.

"Maybe you can lend me your plastic surgeon," Fancy quipped before she discovered that it hurt to smile. Touching the bleeding cut with the tip of her tongue, she disengaged herself from her aunt. "I'll be all right." She moved to the refrigerator, took out a carton of milk, and poured herself a glass.

"Shouldn't you see a doctor? Do you want me to drive you to the emergency room?"

"Hell, no. And would you please keep your voice down? I don't want Grandma and Grandpa to see this. I'd never hear the end of it."

"What happened?"

"Well, it was like this." She scraped the cream filling out of an Oreo with her lower front teeth. "I went to this shit-kicker's dance hall. The place was swinging. Friday night, you know—payday. Everybody was in a party mood. There was this one guy with a really cute ass." She ate the two disks of chocolate cookie and dug into the ceramic jar for another.

"He took me to a motel. We drank some beer and smoked some grass. He got a little too sublime, I guess, because when we got down to business, he couldn't get it up. Naturally, he took it out on me." As she summed up the tale, she dusted her hands of cookie crumbs and reached for the glass of milk.

"He hit you?"

Fancy gaped at her, then gave a semblance of a laugh.

" 'He hit you?' " she mimicked. "What the hell do you think? Of course he hit me."

"You could have been seriously hurt, Fancy."

"I can't believe this," she said, rolling her eyes ceilingward in disbelief. "You always enjoyed hearing about my romantic interludes, said they gave you a vicarious thrill, whatever the hell that means."

"I'd hardly classify getting hit in the face romantic. Did he tie you up, too?"

Fancy followed her aunt's gaze down to the red circles around each of her wrists. "Yeah," she answered bitterly, "the bastard tied my hands together." Carole didn't have to know that the "bastard" she referred to wasn't the drunken, impotent cowboy.

"You're crazy to go to a motel room with a stranger like that, Fancy."

"I'm crazy? You're the one stuffing ice cubes in a Baggie."

"For your eye."

Fancy slapped away the makeshift ice pack. "Don't do me any favors, okay?"

"Your eye is turning black and blue. It's about to swell shut. Do you want your parents to see it like that and have to tell them the story you just told me?"

Irritably, Fancy snatched up the ice pack and held it against her eye. She knew her aunt was right.

"Do you want some peroxide for your lip? An aspirin? Something for the pain?"

"I had enough beer and grass to dull the pain."

Fancy was confused. Why was Carole being so nice to her? Since coming home from that luxury palace of a clinic, she had been freaking weird. She didn't yell at the kid anymore. She looked for things to do instead of sitting on her ass all day. She actually seemed to like Uncle Tate again.

Fancy had always considered Carole stupid for playing Russian roulette with her marriage. Uncle Tate was good-looking. All the girls she knew drooled over him. If her instincts in this field were any good, and she believed them to be excellent, he'd be terrific in bed.

She wished she had somebody who loved her as much as Uncle Tate had loved Carole when they had first gotten married. He'd treated her like a queen. She had been a fool to throw that away. Maybe she had reached that conclusion herself and was trying to win him back.

Fat chance, Fancy thought derisively. Once you crossed Uncle Tate, you were on his shit list for life.

"What are you doing up so late," she asked, "sitting all by yourself in the dark?"

"I couldn't sleep. I thought cocoa might help." There was a half-empty cup of chocolate on the table."

"Cocoa? That's a hoot."

"A proper insomnia remedy for a senator's wife," she replied with a wistful smile.

Fancy, never one to beat around the bush, asked, "You're mending your ways, aren't you?"

"What do you mean?"

"You know damn well what I mean. You're changing your image in the hopes that Uncle Tate will get elected and keep you on when he goes to Washington." She assumed a confidential, just-between-us-girls pose. "Tell me, did you give up humping all your boyfriends, or just Eddy?"

Her aunt's head snapped up. Her face went pale. She pulled her lower lip between her teeth and wheezed, "What did you say?"

"Don't play innocent. I suspected it all along," Fancy said breezily. "I confronted Eddy with it."

"And what did he say?"

"Nothing. Didn't deny it. Didn't admit it. He responded as a gentleman should." Snorting rudely, she headed for the door that led to the other rooms of the house. "Don't worry. There's enough shit flying around here already. I'm not going to tell Uncle Tate. Unless . . ."

She spun around, her attitude combative. "Unless you pick up your affair with Eddy again. It's me he's gonna be screwing from now on, not you. G'night."

Feeling smug and satisfied for having made herself so unequivocally understood, Fancy sashayed from the kitchen. One look in the mirror over her bedroom dresser confirmed that her face was a mess.

It didn't occur to Fancy until days later that Carole was the only one in the family who had even noticed that she was sporting a black eye and a busted lip, and that she hadn't ratted on her.

TWENTY

Van Lovejoy's apartment was *House Beautiful*'s worst nightmare. He slept on a narrow mattress supported by concrete building blocks. Other pieces of furniture were just as ramshackle, salvaged from flea markets and junk stores.

There was a sad, dusty piñata, a sacrilegious effigy of Elvis Presley, dangling from the light fixture. It was a souvenir he'd brought back from a visit to Nuevo Laredo. The goodies inside—several kilos of marijuana—were but a memory. Except for the piñata, the apartment was unadorned.

The otherwise empty rooms were filled with videotapes. That and the equipment he used to duplicate, edit, and play back his tapes were the only things of any value in the apartment, and their worth was inestimable. Van was better equipped than many small video production companies.

Video catalogs were stacked everywhere. He subscribed to all of them and scoured them monthly in search of a video he didn't already have or hadn't seen. Nearly all his income went to keeping his library stocked and updated.

His collection of movies rivaled any video rental store. He studied directing and cinematographic techniques. His taste was ecletic, ranging from Orson Welles to Frank Capra, Sam Peckinpah to Steven Spielberg. Whether filmed in black and white or Technicolor, camera moves fascinated him.

Besides the movies, his collection included serials and documentaries, along with every inch of tape he had shot himself in the span of his career. It was known throughout the state that if stock footage of an event was needed and it couldn't be found elsewhere, Van Lovejoy of KTEX in San Antonio would have it.

He spent all his free time watching tapes. Tonight, his fascination was centered on the raw footage he had shot at the Rocking R Ranch a few days earlier. He'd delivered the tapes to MB Productions, but not before making copies of them for himself. He never knew when something he'd shot years earlier might prove useful or valuable, so he kept copies of everything.

In post-production, MBP would write scripts, edit, record voice-overs, mix music, and end up with slick, fully produced commercials of varying lengths. Van's camera work would look sterilized and staged by the time the commercials went out over the air. He didn't care. He'd been paid. What interested him were the candid shots.

Tate Rutledge was charismatic on or off camera. Handsome and affluent, he was a walking success story—the kind of man Van usually despised on principle. But if Van had been a voter, the guy would get his vote just because he seemed to shoot straight from the hip. He didn't bullshit, even when what he was saying wasn't particularly what people wanted to hear. He might lose the election, but it wouldn't be because he lacked integrity.

He kept thinking that there was something wrong with the kid. She was cute enough, although, in Van's opinion, one kid looked like another. He usually wasn't called upon to videotape children, but when he was, his experience had been that they had to be threatened or cajoled into settling down, behaving, and cooperating, especially when shooting retakes or reverse questions.

That hadn't been the case with the Rutledge kid. She was quiet and didn't do anything ornery. She didn't do anything, period, unless she was told to, and then she moved like a little wind-up doll. The one who got the most response out of her was Carole Rutledge.

It was she who really held Van enthralled.

Time and again he had played the tapes—those he'd shot of her at the ranch, and those he'd shot on the day she left the clinic. The lady knew what to do in front of a camera.

He'd had to direct Rutledge and the kid, but not her. She was a natural, always turning toward the light, knowing instinctively where to look. She seemed to know what he was about to do before he did it. Her face begged for close-ups. Her body language wasn't stilted or robotized, like most amateurs.

She was a pro.

Her resemblance to another pro he had known and worked with was damned spooky.

For hours he had sat in front of his console, replaying the tapes and studying Carole Rutledge. When she did make an awkward move, he believed it was deliberate, as if she realized just how good she was and wanted to cover it up.

He ejected one tape and inserted another, one he had shot so it could be played back in slow motion. He was familiar with the scene. It showed the threesome walking through a pasture of verdant grass, Rutledge carrying his daughter, his wife at his side. Van had planned his shot so that the sun was sinking behind the nearest hill, casting them in silhouette. It was a great effect, he thought now as he watched it for the umpteenth time.

And then he saw it! Mrs. Rutledge turned her head and smiled up at her husband. She touched his arm. His smile turned stiff. He moved his arm—slightly, but enough to shrug off her wifely caress. If the tape hadn't been in slow motion, Van might not have even noticed the candidate's subtle rejection of his wife's touch.

He didn't doubt when the post-production was done, the shot would be edited out. The Rutledges would come out looking like Ozzie and Harriet. But there was something wrong with the marriage, just like there was something wrong with the kid. Something stunk in Camelot.

Van was a cynic by nature. It came as no surprise to him that the marriage was shaky. He figured they all were, and he didn't give a flying fig.

Yet the woman still fascinated him. He could swear that she had recognized him the other day before he had introduced himself. He was constantly aware of expressions and reactions, and he couldn't have mistaken that momentary widening of her eyes or the quick rush of her breath. Even though the features weren't identical, and the hairstyle was wrong, the resemblance between Carole Rutledge and Avery Daniels was uncanny. Carole's moves were right on target and the subconscious mannerisms eerily reminiscent.

He let the tape play out. Closing his eyes, Van pinched the bridge of his nose between two of his fingers until it hurt, as if wanting to force the notion out of his head, because what he was thinking was just too weird—"Twilight Zone" time. But the idea was fucking with his mind something fierce and he couldn't get rid of it, crazy as it was.

Several days ago he'd walked into Irish's office. Dropping into one of the armchairs, he'd asked, "Get a chance to watch that tape I gave you?"

Irish, as usual, was doing six different things at once. He ran his hand over his burred gray hair. "Tape? Oh, the one of Rutledge? Who've we got on that human bone pile they found in Comal County?" he had shouted through his office door to a passing reporter.

"What'd you think about it?" Van asked, once Irish's attention swung back to him.

Irish had taken up smoking again since Avery wasn't there to hound him about it. He seemed to want to make up for lost time. He lit a new cigarette from the smoldering butt of another and spoke through the plume of unfiltered smoke. "About what?"

"The tape," Van said testily.

"Why? You moonlighting as a pollster?"

"Jesus," Van had muttered and made to rise. Irish cantankerously signaled him to sit back down. "What'd you want me to look at? Specifically, I mean."

"The broad."

Irish coughed. "You got the hots for her?"

Van remembered being annoyed that Irish hadn't noticed the similarities between Carole Rutledge and Avery Daniels. That should have been an indication of just how ridiculous his thinking was, because nobody knew Avery better than Irish. He had known her for two decades before Van had ever laid eyes on her. Mulishly, however, Irish's flippancy compelled him to prove himself right.

"I think she looks a lot like Avery."

Irish had been pouring himself a cup of viscous coffee from the hot plate on his littered credenza. He gave Van a sharp glance. "So, what else is new? Somebody remarked on that as soon as Rutledge got into politics and we started seeing him and his wife in the news."

"Guess I wasn't around that day."

"Or you were too stoned to remember."

"Could be."

Irish returned to his desk and sat down heavily. He worked harder than ever, putting in unnecessarily long hours. Everybody in the newsroom talked about it. Work was a panacea for his bereavement. A Catholic, he wouldn't commit suicide outright, but he would eventually kill himself through too much work, too much booze, too much smoking, too much stress—all the things about which Avery had affectionately berated him.

"You ever figure out who sent you her jewelry?" Van asked. Irish had confided that bizarre incident to him, and he had thought it strange at the time, but had forgotten about it until he had stood eyeball to eyeball with Carole Rutledge.

Irish thoughtfully shook his head. "No."

"Ever try?"

"I made a few calls."

Obviously, he didn't want to talk about it. Van was persistent. "And?"

"I got some asshole on the phone who didn't want to be bothered. He said that following the crash, things were so chaotic just about anything was possible."

Like mixing up bodies? Van wondered.

He wanted to ask that question, but didn't. Irish was coping as best he could with Avery's death, and he still wasn't doing very well. He didn't need to hear Van's harebrained hypothesis. Besides, even if it were possible, it made no sense. If Avery were alive, she'd be living her life, not somebody else's.

So he hadn't broached the possibility with Irish. His imagination had run amok, that's all. He'd compiled a bunch of creepy coincidences and shaped them into an outlandish, illogical theory.

Irish would probably have said that his brains were fried from doing too much dope, which was probably the truth. He was nothing but a bum—a washout. A reprobate. What the fuck did he know?

But he loaded another of the Rutledge tapes into the VCR anyway.

The first scream woke her. The second registered. The third prompted her to throw off the covers and scramble out of bed.

Avery grabbed a robe, flung open the door to her bedroom, and charged down the hall toward Mandy's room. Within seconds of leaving her bed, she was bending over the child's. Mandy was thrashing her limbs and screaming.

"Mandy, darling, wake up." Avery dodged a flailing fist.

"Mandy?"

Tate materialized on the other side of the bed. He dropped to his knees on the rug and tried to restrain his daughter. Once he had captured her small hands, her body bucked and twisted while her head thrashed on the pillow and her heels pummeled the mattress. She continued to scream.

Avery placed her hands on Mandy's cheeks and pressed hard. "Mandy, wake up. Wake up, darling. Tate, what should we do?"

"Keep trying to wake her up."

"Is she having another nightmare?" Zee asked as she and Nelson rushed in. Zee moved behind Tate. Nelson stood at the foot of his granddaughter's bed.

"We could hear her screams all the way in our wing," he said. "Poor little thing."

Avery slapped Mandy's cheeks lightly. "It's Mommy. Mommy and Daddy are here. You're safe, darling. You're safe."

Eventually, the screams subsided. As soon as she opened her eyes, she launched herself into Avery's waiting arms. Avery gathered her close and cupped the back of her head, pressing the tear-drenched face into her neck. Mandy's shoulders shook; her whole body heaved with sobs.

"My God, I had no idea it was this bad."

"She had them nearly every night while you were still in the hospital," Tate told her. "Then they started tapering off. She hasn't had one for several weeks. I was hoping that once you got home they would stop altogether." His face was drawn with concern.

"Is there anything you want us to do?"

Tate glanced at Nelson. "No. I think she'll calm down now and go back to sleep, Dad, but thanks."

"You two need to put a stop to this. Immediately." He took Zee's arm and propelled her toward the door. She seemed reluctant to leave and looked at Avery anxiously.

"She'll be all right," Avery said, rubbing Mandy's back. She was still hiccuping sobs, but the worst was over.

"Sometimes they come back," Zee said uneasily.

"I'll stay with her for the rest of the night." When she and Tate were left alone with the child, Avery said, "Why didn't you tell me her nightmares were this severe?"

He sat down in the rocking chair near the bed. "You had your own problems to deal with. The dreams stopped happening with such regularity, just like the psychologist predicted they would. I thought she was getting over them."

"I still should have known."

Avery continued to hold Mandy tight against her, rocking back and forth and murmuring reassurances. She wouldn't let go until Mandy indicated that she was ready. Eventually, she raised her head.

"Better now?" Tate asked her. Mandy nodded.

"I'm sorry you had such a bad dream," Avery whispered, wiping Mandy's damp cheeks with the pads of her thumbs. "Do you want to tell Mommy about it?"

"It's going to get me," she stammered on choppy little breaths.

"What is, darling?"

"The fire."

Avery shuddered with her own terrifying recollections. They seized her sometimes unexpectedly and it often took several minutes to recover from them. As an adult, she found it hard to deal with her memories of the crash. What must it be like for a child?

"I got you out of the fire, remember?" Avery asked softly. "It's not there anymore. But it's still scary to think about, isn't it?" Mandy nodded.

Avery had once done a news story with a renowned child psychologist. During the interview she recalled him saying that denying the authenticity of a child's fears was the worst thing a parent could do. Fears had to be acknowledged before they could be dealt with and, hopefully, overcome.

"Maybe a cool, damp cloth would feel good on her face," Avery suggested to Tate. He left the rocker, and returned shortly with a washcloth. "Thank you."

He sat down beside her as she bathed Mandy's face. In a move that endeared him to Avery, he picked up the Pooh Bear and pressed it into Mandy's arms. She clutched it to her chest.

"Ready to lie back down?" Avery asked her gently.

"No." Apprehensively, her eyes darted around the room.

"Mommy's not going to leave you. I'll lie down with you."

She eased Mandy back, then lay down beside her, facing her as their heads shared the pillow. Tate pulled the covers over both of them, then bridged their pillow with his arms and leaned down to kiss Mandy.

He was wearing nothing but a pair of briefs. His body looked exceptionally strong and beautiful in the soft glow of the night-light. As he started to stand up, his eyes locked with Avery's. Acting on impulse, she laid her hand on his furry chest and raised her head to lightly kiss his lips. "Good night, Tate."

He straightened up slowly. As he did, her hand slid down his chest; over the hard, curved muscles; across the nipple; through the dense, crisp hair; to the smoother plane of his belly; until her fingertips brushed against the elastic waistband of his briefs before falling away.

"I'll be right back," he mumbled.

He was gone only a few minutes, but by the time he returned, Mandy was sleeping peacefully. He had pulled on a lightweight robe, but had left it unbelted. As he lowered himself into the rocking chair, he noticed that Avery's eyes were still open. "That bed's not meant for two. Are you comfortable."

"I'm fine."

"I don't think Mandy would know if you got up now and went to your own room."

"I would know. And I told her I'd stay with her the rest of the night." She stroked Mandy's flushed cheek with the back of her finger. "What are we going to do, Tate?"

Resting his elbows on his knees, he sat forward and dug his thumbs into his eye sockets. A tousled lock of hair fell over his forehead. With stubble surrounding it, the vertical cleft at the edge of his chin seemed more pronounced. He sighed, expanding his bare chest beneath the open robe. "I don't know."

"Do you think the psychologist is doing her any good?"

He raised his head. "Don't you?"

"I shouldn't second-guess the choice you and your parents made while I was indisposed."

She knew she shouldn't get involved at all. This was a personal problem and Avery Daniels had no right to poke her nose into it. But she couldn't just stand by and let a child's emotional stability deteriorate.

"If you have an opinion, be my guest and say so," Tate urged. "This is our child we're talking about. I'm not going to get petty about who had the best idea."

"I know of a doctor in Houston," she began. One of his eyebrows arched inquisitively. "He . . . I saw him on a talk show once and was very impressed with what he had to say and how he conducted himself. He wasn't pompous. He was very straightforward and practical. Since the current doctor isn't making much progress, maybe we should take Mandy to see him."

"We haven't got anything to lose. Make an appointment."

"I'll call tomorrow." Her head sank deeper into the pillow, but she kept her eyes on him. He sat back in the rocking chair and rested his head against the stuffed pink cushion. "You don't have to sit there all night, Tate," she said softly.

Their eyes met and held. "Yes, I do."

She fell asleep watching him watch her.

TWENTY-ONE

Avery woke up first. It was early, and the room was dim, although the night-light still burned. She smiled wistfully when she realized that Mandy's small hand was resting on her cheek. Her muscles were cramped from lying so long in one position; otherwise, she probably would have gone back to sleep. Needing to stretch, she eased Mandy's hand off her face and laid it on the pillow. Taking agonizing care not to awaken the child, she got up.

Tate was asleep in the rocker. His head was lying at such an angle to one side that it was almost resting on his shoulder. It looked like a very uncomfortable position, but his abdomen was rising and falling rhythmically, and she could hear his even breathing in the quiet room.

His robe lay parted, revealing his torso and thighs. His right leg was bent at the knee; the left was stretched out in front of him. His calves and feet were well-shaped. His hands were heavily veined and sprinkled with hair. One was dangling from the arm of the chair, the other lay against his stomach.

Sleep had erased the furrow of concern from between his brows. His lashes formed sooty crescents against his cheeks. Relaxed, his mouth looked sensual, capable of giving a woman enormous pleasure. Avery imagined that he would make love intently, passionately, and well, just as he did everything. Emotion brimmed inside Avery's chest until it ached. She wanted badly to cry.

She loved him.

As much as she wanted to make recompense for her professional failures, she realized now that she had also assumed the role of wife because she had fallen in love with him before she could even speak his name. She had loved him when she had had to look at him through a veil of bandages and rely only on the sound of his voice to inspire her to fight for her life.

She was playing his wife because she wanted to *be* his wife. She wanted to protect him. She wanted to heal the hurts inflicted on him by a selfish, spiteful woman. She wanted to sleep with him.

If he claimed his conjugal rights, she would gladly oblige him. That would be her greatest lie yet—one he wouldn't be able to forgive when her true identity was revealed. He would despise her more than he had Carole because he would think she had tricked him. He would never believe her love was genuine. But it was.

He stirred. When he brought his head upright, he winced. His eyelids fluttered, came open with a start, then focused on her. She was standing within touching distance.

"What time is it?" he asked with sleepy huskiness.

"I don't know. Early. Does your neck hurt?" She ran her hand through his tousled hair, then curved her hand around his neck.

"A little."

She squeezed the cords of his neck, working the kinks out.

"Hmm."

After a moment, he yanked his robe together, folding one side over the other. He drew in his extended leg and sat up straighter. She wondered if her tender massage had given him an early morning erection he didn't want her to see.

"Mandy's still asleep," he commented rhetorically.

"Want some breakfast?"

"Coffee's fine."

"I'll make breakfast."

Dawn was just breaking. Mona wasn't even up yet and the kitchen was dark. Tate began spooning coffee into the disposable paper filter of a coffeemaker. Avery went to the refrigerator.

"Don't bother," he said.

"Aren't you hungry?"

"I can wait for Mona to get up."

"I'd like to cook you something."

Turning his back, he said nonchalantly, "All right. A couple of eggs, I guess."

She was familiar enough with the kitchen by now to assemble the makings for breakfast. Everything went fine until she started whisking eggs in a bowl.

"What are you doing?"

"Making scrambled eggs. F . . . for me," she bluffed when he gave her a puzzled look. She had no idea how he liked his eggs. "Here. You finish this and let me get the toast started."

She busied herself with buttering the slices of toast as they popped from the toaster while covertly watching him fry two eggs for himself. He slid them onto a plate and brought it to the table, along with her serving of scrambled eggs.

"We haven't had breakfast together in a long time." She bit into a slice of toast, scooped a bite of egg into her mouth, and reached for her glass of orange juice before she realized that she was the only one eating. Tate was sitting across from her with his chin propped in his hands, elbows on the table.

"We've never eaten breakfast together, Carole. You hate breakfast."

It was difficult for her to swallow. Her hand clenched the glass of juice. "They made me eat breakfast while I was in the hospital. You know, after I got the dental implants and could eat solid food. I had to gain my weight back."

His gaze hadn't wavered. He wasn't buying it.

"I . . . I got used to eating it and now I miss it when I don't." Defensively, she added, "Why are you making such a big deal of it?"

Tate picked up his fork and began to eat. His movements were too controlled to be automatic. He was angry. "Save yourself the trouble."

She was afraid he meant the trouble of lying to him. "What trouble?"

"Cooking my breakfast is just another of your machinations to worm your way back into my good graces."

Her appetite deserted her. The smell of the food now made her nauseated. "Machinations?"

Apparently he, too, had lost his appetite. He shoved his plate away. "Breakfast. Domesticity. Those displays of affection like touching my hair, rubbing my neck."

"You seemed to enjoy them."

"They don't mean a goddamn thing."

"They do!"

"The hell they do!" He sat back, glowering at her, his jaw working with pent-up rage. "The touches and sweet good-night kisses I can stomach if I have to. If you want to pretend that we're a loving, affectionate couple, go ahead. Make a fool of yourself. Just don't expect me to return the phony affection. Even the Senate seat wouldn't be enough inducement to get me into bed with you again, so that should tell you how much I despise you." He paused for breath. "But the thing that really galls me is your sudden concern for Mandy. You put on quite a show for her last night."

"It wasn't a show."

He ignored her denial. "You'd damn sure better plan to follow through with the maternal act until she's completely cured. She couldn't take another setback."

"You sanctimonious . . ." Avery was getting angry in her own right. "I'm as interested in Mandy's recovery as you are."

"Yeah. Sure."

"You don't believe me?"

"No."

"That's not fair."

"You're a fine one to talk about fair."

"I'm worried to death about Mandy."

"Why?"

"*Why?*" she cried. "Because she's our child."

"So was the one you aborted! That didn't stop you from killing it!"

The words knifed through her. She actually laid an arm across her middle and bent forward as though her vital organs had been impaled. She held her breath for several seconds while she stared at him speechlessly.

As though loath to look at her, he got up and turned his back. At the counter he refilled his coffee cup. "I would have found out eventually, of course." His voice sounded as cold as ice. When he turned back around to confront her, his eyes looked just as piercingly cold.

"But to be informed by a stranger that my wife was no longer pregnant . . ." Seething, he glanced away. Again, it was as though he couldn't bear looking at her. "Can you imagine how I felt, Carole? Jesus! There you were, close to death, and I wanted to kill you myself." He swung his head back around and, as his eyes bore into hers, he clenched his free hand into a fist.

Out of her cottony memory, Avery conjured up voices.

Tate's: *The child . . . effects on the fetus?*

And someone else's: *Child? Your wife wasn't pregnant.*

The fractured conversation had meant nothing. Its significance had escaped her. It had blended into the myriad confusing conversations she had overheard before she had fully regained consciousness. She had forgotten it until now.

"Didn't you think I'd notice that you failed to produce a baby? You were so eager to flaunt it in my face that you were pregnant, why didn't you let me know about your abortion, too?''

Avery shook her head miserably. She had no words to say to him. No excuses. No explanations. But now she knew why Tate hated Carole so.

''When did you do it? It must have been just a few days before your scheduled trip to Dallas. Didn't want to be hampered by a baby, did you? It would have cramped your style.''

He bore down on her and loudly slapped the surface of the table. ''Answer me, damn you. Say something. It's about time we talked about this, don't you think?''

Avery stammered, ''I . . . I didn't think it would matter so much.'' His expression turned so ferocious, she thought he might actually strike her. Rushing to her own defense, she lashed out, ''I know your policy on abortion, Mr. Rutledge. How many times have I heard you preach that it's a woman's right to choose? Does that pertain to every woman in the state of Texas except your wife?''

''Yes, dammit!''

''How hypocritical.''

He grabbed her arm and hauled her to her feet. ''The principle that applies to the public at large doesn't necessarily carry over into my personal life. *This* abortion wasn't an *issue*. It was my baby.''

His eyes narrowed to slits. ''Or was it? Was that another lie to keep me from throwing you out, along with the other trash?''

She tried to imagine how Carole might have responded. ''It takes two to make a baby, Tate.''

As she had hoped, she had struck a chord. He released her arm immediately and backed away from her. ''I sorely regret that night. I made that clear as soon as it happened. I'd sworn never to touch your whoring body again.

''But you've always known which buttons to push, Carole. For days you'd been curling up against me like a cat in heat, mewing your apologies and promises to be a loving wife. If I hadn't had too much to drink that night, I would have recognized it for the trap it was.''

He gave her a scornful once-over. ''Is that what you're doing now, laying another trap? Is that why you've been the model wife since you got out of the hospital?

''Tell me,'' he said, propping his hands on his hips, ''did you slip up that night and get pregnant by accident? Or was getting pregnant and having an abortion part of your plan to torment me? Is that what you're trying to do again—make me want you? Prove that you can get me into your bed again, even if it means sacrificing your own daughter's welfare in order to prove it?''

''No,'' Avery declared hoarsely. She couldn't endure his hatred, even though it wasn't intended for her.

''You no longer have any power over me, Carole. I don't even hate you anymore. You're not worth the energy it requires to hate you. Take all the lovers you want. See if I give a damn.

''The only way you could possibly hurt me now is through Mandy, and I'll see you in hell first.

That afternoon she went horseback riding. She needed the space and open air in which to think. Feeling silly wearing the formal riding clothes, she asked the stable hand to saddle her a mount.

The mare shied away from her. As the aging cowboy gave her a boost up, he said, ''Guess she hasn't forgotten the whipping you gave her last time.'' The mare was skittish because she didn't recognize her rider's smell, but Avery let the man believe what he wanted.

Carole Rutledge had been a monster—abusive to her husband, her child, everything she had come into contact with, it seemed. The scene over breakfast had left Avery's nerves raw, but at least she knew what she was up against. The extent of Tate's contempt for his wife was understandable now. Carole had planned to abort his child—or one she claimed was his—though whether she had done so before the crash would forever remain a mystery.

Avery pieced together the scenario. Carole had been unfaithful and had made no secret of it. Her faithlessness would be intolerable to Tate, but with his political future at risk, he decided to remain married until after the election.

For an unspecified period of time, he hadn't slept with his wife. He'd even moved out of their bedroom. But Carole had seduced him into making love to her one more time.

Whether the child was Tate's or not, Carole's abortion *was* a political issue, and Avery believed she had planned it that way. It made her ill to think about the negative publicity and grave repercussions if anyone ever found out. The public effect on Tate would be as profound as the personal one.

When Avery returned from her ride, Mandy was assisting Mona with baking cookies. The housekeeper was very good with Mandy, so Avery complimented Mandy's cookies and left her in the older woman's care.

The house was quiet. She had seen Fancy roar off in her Mustang earlier. Jack, Eddy, and Tate were always in the city at this time of day, working at either the campaign headquarters or the law office. Dorothy Rae was secluded in her wing of the house, as usual. Mona had told her that Nelson and Zee had gone into Kerrville for the afternoon. Reaching her room, Avery tossed the riding quirt onto the bed and used the bootjack to remove the tall riding boots. She padded into the bathroom and turned on the taps of the shower.

Not for the first time, an eerie feeling came over her. She sensed that someone had been in the rooms during her absence. Goose bumps broke out over her arms as she examined the top of her dressing table.

She couldn't remember if she had left her hairbrush lying there. Had her bottle of hand lotion been moved? She was certain she hadn't left the lid of the jewelry box open with a strand of pearls spilling out. She noticed things in the bedroom, too, that had been disturbed while she was out. She did something she hadn't done since moving into Carole's room—she locked the door.

She showered and pulled on a thick robe. Still uneasy and distressed, she decided to lie down for a while before dressing. As her head sank into the pillow, it crackled.

A sheet of paper had been slipped between the pillow and the pillowcase.

Avery studied it with misgivings. The paper had been folded twice, but nothing was written on the outside. She dreaded opening it. What had the intruder expected to find? What had he been searching for?

One thing was certain—the note was no accident. It had been cleverly and deliberately placed where she, and only she, would find it.

She unfolded it. There was one line typed in the center of the white, unlined sheet.

Whatever you're doing, it's working on him. Keep it up.

"Nelson?"

"Hmm?"

His absent reply drew a frown from Zinnia. She laid her hairbrush aside and swiveled on her dressing table stool. "This is important."

Nelson tipped down the corner of his newspaper. Seeing that she was troubled, he folded the paper and depressed the footrest of his lounge chair, bringing himself to a sitting position. "I'm sorry, darling. What'd you say?"

"Nothing yet."

"Is something wrong?"

They were in their bedroom. The ten o'clock news, which they watched ritualistically, was over. They were preparing for bed.

Zee's dark hair was shining after its recent brushing. The silver streak was accented by the lamplight. Her skin, well tended because of the harsh Texas sun, was smooth. There weren't many worry lines to mar it. There weren't many laugh lines, either.

"Something is going on between Tate and Carole," she said.

"I think they had a tiff today." He left his chair and began removing his clothing. "They were both awfully quiet at supper."

Zee had also noticed the hostility in the air tonight. Where her younger son's moods were concerned, she was particularly sensitive. "Tate wasn't just sullen, he was mad."

"Carole probably did something that didn't sit well with him."

"And when Tate is mad," Zee continued as though he hadn't spoken, "Carole is usually her most ebullient. Whenever he's angry, she antagonizes him further by being frivolous and silly."

Nelson neatly hung his trousers in the closet on the rod where all his other trousers were hung. Messiness was anathema. "She wasn't frivolous tonight. She barely said a word."

Zee gripped the back of her vanity stool. "That's my point, Nelson. She was as edgy and upset as Tate. Their fights never used to be like that."

Dressed only in his boxer shorts now, he neatly folded back the bedspread and climbed into bed. He stacked his hands beneath his head and stared at the ceiling. "I've noticed several things here lately that aren't like Carole at all."

"Thank God," Zee said. "I thought I was losing my mind. I'm relieved to know somebody besides me has noticed." She turned out the lamps and got into bed beside her husband. "She's not as superficial as she used to be, is she?"

"That close call with death sobered her up."

"Maybe."

"You don't think so?"

"If that were all, I might think that was the reason."

"What else?" he asked.

"Mandy, for one. Carole's a different person around her. Have you ever seen Carole as worried about Mandy as she was last night after her nightmare? I remember once when Mandy was running a temperature of a hundred and three. I was frantic and thought she should be taken to the emergency room. Carole was blasé. She said that all kids ran fevers. But last night, Carole was as shaken as Mandy."

Nelson shifted uncomfortably. Zee knew why. Deductive reasoning annoyed him. Issues were either black or white. He believed only in absolutes, with the exception of God, which, to him, was an absolute as sure as heaven and hell. Other than that, he didn't believe in anything intangible. He was skeptical of psycho-analysis and psychiatry. In his opinion, anyone worth his salt could solve his own problems without whining for help from someone else.

"Carole's growing up, that's all," he said. "The ordeal she was put through matured her. She's looking at things in a whole new light. She finally appreciates what she's got—Tate, Mandy, this family. 'Bout time she got her head on straight.''

Zee wished she could believe that. "I only hope it lasts."

Nelson rolled to his side, facing her, and placed his arm in the hollow of her waist. He kissed her hairline where the gray streak started. "What do you hope lasts?"

"Her loving attitude toward Tate and Mandy. On the surface, she seems to care for them."

"That's good, isn't it?"

"If it's sincere. Mandy is so fragile I'm afraid she couldn't handle the rejection if Carole reverted to her short-tempered, impatient self. And Tate." Zee sighed. "I want him to be happy, especially at this turning point in his life, whether he wins the election or not. He deserves to be happy. He deserves to be loved."

"You've always seen to the happiness of your sons, Zee."

"But neither of them has a happy marriage, Nelson," she said wistfully. "I had hoped they would."

His finger touched her lips, trying to trace a smile that wasn't there. "You haven't changed. You're still so romance-minded."

He drew her delicate body against his and kissed her. His large hands removed her nightgown and possessively caressed her naked flesh. They made love in the dark.

TWENTY-TWO

Avery agonized for days over how to contact Irish. Once she had reached the soul-searching conclusion that she needed counsel, she was faced with the problem of how to go about informing him that she hadn't died a fiery death in the crash of Flight 398.

No matter how she went about it, it would be cruel. If she simply appeared on his doorstep, he might not survive the shock. He would think a phone call was a prank because her voice no longer sounded the same. So she settled on sending a note to the post office box where she had mailed her jewelry weeks earlier. Surely he had puzzled over receiving that through the mail without any explanation. Wouldn't he already suspect that there had been mysterious circumstances surrounding her death?

She deliberated for hours over how to word such an unprecedented letter. There were no guidelines that she knew of, no etiquette to follow when you informed a loved one who believed you to be dead that you were, in fact, alive. Straightforwardness, she finally decided, was the only way to go about it.

Dear Irish,
    I did not die in the airplane crash. I will explain the bizarre sequence of events next Wednesday evening at your apartment, six o'clock.
    Love, Avery.

She wrote it with her left hand—a luxury these days—so that he would immediately recognize her handwriting, and mailed it without a return address on the envelope.

Tate had barely been civil to her since their argument over breakfast the previous Saturday. She was almost glad. Even though his antipathy wasn't aimed at her, she bore the brunt of it for her alter ego. Distance made it easier to endure.

She dared not think about how he would react when he discovered the truth. His hatred for Carole would pale against what he would feel for Avery Daniels. The best she could hope for was an opportunity to explain herself. Until then, she could only demonstrate how unselfish her motives were. Early Monday morning, she made an appointment with Dr. Gerald Webster, the famed Houston child psychologist. His calendar was full, but she didn't take no for an answer. She used Tate's current celebrity in order to secure an hour of the doctor's coveted time. For Mandy's sake, she pulled rank with a clear conscience.

When she informed Tate of the appointment, he nodded brusquely. "I'll make a note of it on my calendar." She had made the appointment to coincide with one of the days their campaign would have them in Houston anyway.

Beyond that brief exchange, they'd had little to say to each other. That gave her more time to rehearse what she was going to say when she stood face-to-face with Irish.

However, by Wednesday evening, when she pulled her car to a stop in front of his modest house, she still had no idea what to say to him or even how to begin.

Her heart was in her throat as she went up the walk, especially when she saw movement behind the window blinds. Before she reached the front porch, the door was hauled open. Irish, looking ready to tear her limb from limb with his bare hands, strode out and demanded, "Who the fuck are you and what the fuck is your game?"

Avery didn't let his ferocity intimidate her. She continued moving forward until she reached him. He was only a shade taller than she. Since she wore high heels, they met eye to eye.

"It's me, Irish." She smiled gently. "Let's go inside."

At the touch of her hand on his arm, his militancy evaporated. The furious Irishman wilted like the most fragile of flower petals. It was a pathetic sight to see. In a matter of seconds he was transformed from a belligerent pugilist into a confused old man. The icy disclaimer in his blue eyes was suddenly clouded by tears of doubt, dismay, joy.

"Avery? Is it . . .? How . . .? Avery?"

"I'll tell you everything inside."

She took his arm and turned him around because it seemed he had forgotten how to use his feet and legs. A gentle nudge pushed him over the threshold. She closed the door behind him.

The house, she noted sadly, looked as much a wreck as Irish, whose appearance had shocked her. He'd gained weight around his middle, yet his face was gaunt. His cheeks and chin were loose and flabby. There was a telltale tracery of red capillaries in his nose and across his cheekbones. He'd been drinking heavily.

He had never been a fashion plate, dressing with only decency in mind, but now he looked downright seedy. His dishevelment had gone beyond an endearing personality trait. It was evidence of character degeneration. The last time she'd seen him, his hair had been salt-and-pepper. Now it was almost solid white.

She had done this to him.

"Oh, Irish, Irish, forgive me." With a sob, she collapsed against him, wrapping her arms around his solid bulk and holding on tight.

"Your face is different."

"Yes."

"And your voice is hoarse."

"I know."

"I recognized you through your eyes."

"I'm glad. I didn't change on the inside."

"You look good. How are you?" He set her away from him and awkwardly rubbed her arms with his large, rough hands.

"I'm fine. Mended."

"Where have you been? By the Blessed Virgin, I can't believe this."

"Neither can I. God, I'm glad to see you."

Clinging to each other again, they wept. At least a thousand times in her life, she had run to Irish for comfort. In her father's absence, Irish had kissed scraped elbows, repaired broken toys, reviewed report cards, attended dance recitals, chastised, congratulated, commiserated.

This time, Avery felt like the elder. Their roles had been reversed. He was the one who clung tightly and needed nurturing.

Somehow, they stumbled their way to his sofa, though neither remembered later how they got there. When the crying binge subsided, he wiped his wet face with his hands, briskly and impatiently. He was embarrassed now.

"I thought you might be angry," she said after indelicately blowing her nose into a Kleenex.

"I am—damn angry. If I weren't so glad to see you, I'd paddle your butt."

"You only paddled me once—that time I called my mother an ugly name. Afterward, you cried harder and longer than I did." She touched his cheek. "You're a softy, Irish McCabe."

He looked chagrined and irascible. "What happened? Have you had amnesia?"

"No."

"Then, what?" he asked, studying her face. "I'm not used to you looking like that. You look like—"

"Carole Rutledge."

"That's right. Tate Rutledge's wife—late wife." A light bulb went on behind his eyes. "She was on that flight, too."

"Did you identify my body, Irish?"

"Yes. By your locket."

Avery shook her head. "It was her body you identified. She had my locket."

Tears formed in his eyes again. "You were burned, but it was your hair, your—"

"We looked enough alike to be mistaken for sisters just minutes before the attempted takeoff."

"How—"

"Listen and I'll you." Avery folded her hands around his, a silent request that he stop interrupting. "When I regained consciousness in the hospital, several days after the crash, I was bandaged from head to foot. I couldn't move. I could barely see out of one eye. I couldn't speak.

"Everyone was calling me Mrs. Rutledge. At first I thought maybe I did have amnesia because I couldn't remember being Mrs. Rutledge or Mrs. Anybody. I was confused, in pain, disoriented. Then, when I remembered who I was, I realized what had happened. We'd switched seats, you see."

She talked him through the agonizing hours she had spent trying to convey to everyone else what only she knew. "The Rutledges retained Dr. Sawyer to redo my face—Carole's face—using photographs of her. There was no way I could alert them that they were making a mistake."

He pulled his hands from beneath hers and dragged them down his loose jowls. "I need a drink. Want one?"

He returned to the couch moments later with a tumbler three-quarters full of straight whiskey. Avery said nothing, though she eyed the glass meaningfully. Defiantly, he took a hefty draught.

"Okay, I follow you so far. A gross error was made while you were unable to communicate. Once you *were* able to communicate, why didn't you? In other words, why are you still playing Carole Rutledge?"

Avery stood up and began roaming the untidy room, making ineffectual attempts to straighten it while she arranged her thoughts. Convincing Irish that her charade was viable and justified was going to be tricky. His contention had always been that reporters reported the news, they did not make it. Their role was to observe, not participate. That point had been a continual argument between him and Cliff Daniels.

"Somebody plans to kill Tate Rutledge before he becomes a senator."

Irish hadn't expected anything like that. His hand was arrested midway between the coffee table and his mouth as he was raising the glass of whiskey. The liquor sloshed over the rim of the tumbler onto his hand. Absently, he wiped it dry on his trousers leg.

"What?"

"Somebody plans—"

"Who?"

"I don't know."

"Why?"

"I don't know."

"How?"

"I don't know, Irish," she said, raising her voice defensively. "And I don't know where or when, either, so save your breath and don't ask. Just hear me out."

He shook his finger at her. "I may give you that spanking yet for sassing me. Don't test my patience. You've already put me through hell. Pure hell."

"It hasn't exactly been a picnic for me, either," she snapped.

"Which is the only reason I've restrained myself this long," he shouted. "But stop bullshitting me."

"I'm not!"

"Then, what's this crap about somebody wanting to kill Rutledge? How the bloody hell do you know?"

His mounting temper was reassuring. This Irish she could deal with much more easily than the woebegone shell he'd been minutes earlier. She's had years of practice sparring with him. "Somebody told me he was going to kill Tate before he took office."

"Who?"

"I don't know."

"Shit," he cursed viciously. "Don't start that again."

"If you'll give me a chance, I'll explain."

He took another drink, ground his fist into his other palm, and finally relaxed against the back of the sofa, relaying that he was ready to sit still and listen.

"Believing me to be Carole, somebody came to me while I was still in the ICU. I don't know who it was. I couldn't see because my eye was bandaged and he was standing beyond my shoulder." She recounted the incident, repeating the threat verbatim.

"I was terrified. Once I was able to communicate who I really was, I was afraid to. I couldn't tip my hand without placing my life, and Tate's, in jeopardy."

Irish was silent until she had finished. She returned to the sofa and sat down beside him. When he did speak, his voice was skeptical.

"What you're telling me, then, is that you took Mrs. Rutledge's place so you could prevent Tate Rutledge from being assassinated."

"Right."

"But you don't know who plans to kill him."

"Not yet, but Carole did. She was part of it, although I don't know her relationship with this other person."

"Hmm." Irish tugged thoughtfully on the flaccid skin beneath his chin. "This visitor you had—"

"Has to be a member of the family. No one else would have been admitted into the ICU."

"Someone could have sneaked in."

"Possibly, but I don't think so. If Carole had hired an assassin, he would simply have vanished when she became incapacitated. He wouldn't have come to warn her to keep quiet. Would he?"

"He's your assassin. You tell me."

She shot to her feet again. "You don't believe me?"

"I believe you believe it."

"But you think it was my imagination."

"You were drugged and disoriented, Avery," he said, reasonably. "You said so yourself. You were half blind in one eye and—forgive the bad joke—couldn't see out of the other. You think the person was a man, but it *could* have been a woman. You think it was a member of the Rutledge family, but it *could* have been somebody else."

"What are you getting at, Irish?"

"You probably had a nightmare."

"I was beginning to think so myself until several days ago." She took the sheet of paper she'd found in her pillowcase from her purse and handed it to him. He read the typed message.

When his troubled eyes connected with hers, she said, "I found that in my pillowcase. He's real, all right. He still thinks I'm Carole, his coconspirator. And he still intends to do what they originally planned."

The note had drastically altered Irish's opinion. He cleared his throat uncomfortably. "This is the first contact he's had with you since that night in the hospital?"

"Yes."

He reread the message, then remarked, "It doesn't say he's going to kill Tate Rutledge."

Avery gave him a retiring look. "This has been a well-thought-out assassination attempt. The plans were long-range. He'd hardly risk spelling it out. Naturally, he made the note obscure, just in case it was intercepted. The seemingly innocent words would mean something entirely different to Carole."

"Who has access to a typewriter?"

"Everybody. There's one at a desk in the family den. That was the one I used. I checked."

"What does he—or she—mean by 'whatever you're doing'?"

Avery looked away guiltily. "I'm not sure."

"Avery?"

Her head snapped around. She had never been able to fudge the truth with Irish. He saw through it every time. "I've been trying to get along better with Tate than his wife did."

"Any particular reason why?"

"It was obvious to me from the beginning that there was trouble between them."

"How'd you figure that?"

"By the way he treats her. Me. He's polite, but that's all."

"Hmm. Do you know why?"

"Carole either had, or was planning to have, an abortion. I only found out about that last week. I'd already discovered that she was a selfish, self-centered woman. She cheated on Tate and was a disaster of a parent to her daughter. Without raising too much suspicion, I've been trying to bridge the gap that had come between him and his wife."

Again Irish asked, "Why?"

"So I'd know more about what is going on. I had to get to the source of their problem before I could begin to find a motive for a killer. Obviously, my attempts to improve their marriage have been noticed. The killer figures that it's Carole's new tactic to put Tate off guard."

She chafed her arms as though suddenly chilled. "He's real, Irish. I know it. There's the proof," she said, nodding down at the note.

Not yet committing himself one way or the other, Irish tossed the sheet of paper down on the coffee table. "Let's assume there is a killer. Who's gonna ice him?"

"I have no idea," she replied with a defeated sigh. "They're one big, happy family."

"According to you, somebody out there at the Rocking R ain't so happy."

She provided him with a verbal run-down of names and each person's relationship to Tate. "Each has his ax to grind, but none of those axes has anything to do with Tate. Both his parents dote on him. Nelson's the undisputed head of the family. He rules, being stern and affectionate by turns.

"Zee isn't so easy to pigeonhole. She's a good wife and loving mother. She remains aloof from me. I think she resents Carole for not making Tate happier."

"What about the others?"

"Carole might have had an affair with Eddy."

"Eddy Paschal, Rutledge's campaign manager?"

"And best friend since college. I don't know for sure. I'm only going by Fancy's word on that."

"What a cliché. How does this Paschal character treat you?"

"He's civil, nothing more. Of course, I haven't put out the signals Carole did. If they were having an affair, maybe he just assumes it ended with the accident. In any event, he's dedicated to Tate winning the election."

"The girl?"

Avery shook her head. "Fancy is a spoiled brat with no more morals than an alley cat in heat. But she's too flighty to be a killer. Not that she's above it; she just wouldn't expend the energy."

"The brother? Jack, is it?"

"He's extremely unhappy with his marriage," she mused, frowning thoughtfully, "but Tate doesn't figure into that. Although . . ."

"Although?"

"Jack's rather pathetic, actually. You think of him as being competent, good-looking, charming, until you see him next to his younger brother. Tate's the sun. Jack is the moon. He reflects Tate's light but has none of his own. He works as hard as Eddy on the campaign, but if anything goes wrong, he usually gets blamed for it. I feel sorry for him."

"Does he feel sorry for himself? Enough to commit fratricide?"

"I'm not sure. He keeps his distance. I've caught him watching me and sense a smoldering hostility there. On the surface, however, he seems indifferent."

"What about his wife?"

"Dorothy Rae might be jealous enough to kill, but she would go after Carole before she would Tate."

"What makes you say that?"

"I was browsing through family photo albums, trying to glean information. Dorothy came into the living room to get a bottle from the liquor cabinet. She was already drunk. I rarely see her, except at dinner, and then she hardly says anything. That's why I was so surprised when, out of the blue, she began accusing me of trying to steal Jack. She said I wanted to pick up with him where I'd left off before the crash."

"Carole was sleeping with her brother-in-law, too?" Irish asked incredulously.

"It seems that way. At least she was trying to." The notion had distressed Avery very much. She had hoped it was only an alcohol-inspired delusion that Dorothy Rae had drummed up while sequestered in her room with her bottles of vodka. "It's preposterous," she said, thinking aloud. "Carole had Tate. What could she possibly have wanted with Jack?"

"There's no accounting for taste."

"I guess you're right." Avery was so lost in her own musings, she missed his wry inflection. "Anyway, I denied having any designs on Dorothy Rae's husband. She called me a bitch, a whore, a home wrecker—things like that."

Irish ran a hand over his burred head. "Carole must have really been something."

"We don't know for certain that she wanted either Jack or Eddy."

"But she must have put out some mighty strong signals if that many people picked up on them."

"Poor Tate."

"What does 'poor Tate' think of his *wife*?"

Avery lapsed into deep introspection. "He thinks she aborted his baby. He knows she had other lovers. He knows she was a negligent parent and put emotional scars on his daughter. Hopefully, that can be reversed."

"You've taken on that responsibility, too, haven't you?"

His critical tone of voice brought her head erect. "What do you mean?"

Leaving her to stew for a moment, Irish disappeared into the kitchen and returned with a fresh drink. Feet spread and firmly planted, he stood before her. "Are you leveling with me about that midnight caller you had in the hospital?"

"How can you even doubt it?"

"I'll tell you how I can doubt it. You came to me, what was it, almost two years ago, with your tail tucked between your legs, needing a job—any job. You'd just been fired from the network for committing one of the worst faux pas in journalism history."

"I didn't come here tonight to be reminded of that."

"Well, maybe you should be reminded! Because I think that's what's behind this whole damned scheme of yours. You plunged in that time over your head, too. Before you got your facts straight, you reported that a junior congressman from Virginia had killed his wife before blowing his own brains out."

She pressed her fists against her temples as that horrible sequence of events unfolded like a scroll in her memory.

"First reporter on the scene, Avery Daniels," Irish announced with a flourish, showing her no mercy. "Always hot on the trail of a good story. You smelled fresh blood."

"That's right, I did! Literally." She crossed her arms over her middle. "I saw the bodies, heard those children screaming in terror over what they had discovered when they had come home from school. I saw them weeping over what their father had done.''

"Had *allegedly* done, dammit. You never learn, Avery. He *allegedly* killed his wife before blasting his own brains onto the wallpaper.'' Irish took a quick drink of whiskey. ''But you went live with a report, omitting that technical little legal word, leaving your network vulnerable to a slander suit.

"You lost it on camera, Avery. Objectivity took a flying leap. Tears streamed down your face and then—*then*—as if all that wasn't enough, you asked your audience at large how any man, but especially an elected public official, could do such a beastly thing.''

She raised her head and faced him defiantly. ''I know what I did, Irish. I don't need you to remind me of my mistake. I've tried to live it down for two years. I was wrong, but I learned from it.''

"Bullshit,'' he thundered. ''You're doing the same damn thing all over again. You're diving in where you have no authority to go. You're making news, not reporting it. Isn't this the big break you've been waiting for? Isn't this the story that's going to put you back on top?''

"All right, yes!'' she flung up at him. ''That was part of the reason I went into it.''

"That's been your reason for doing everything you've ever done.''

"What are you saying?''

"You're still trying to get your daddy's attention. You're trying to fill his shoes, live up to his name, which you feel like you've failed to do.'' He moved toward her. ''Let me tell you something—something you don't want to hear.'' He shook his head and said each word distinctly. ''He's not worth it.''

"Stop there, Irish.''

"He was your father, Avery, but he was my best friend. I knew him longer and a whole lot better than you did. I loved him, but I viewed him with far more objectivity than you or your mother ever could.''

He braced one hand on the arm of the sofa and leaned over her. ''Cliff Daniels was a brilliant photographer. In my book, he was the best. I'm not denying his talent with a camera. But he didn't have a talent for making the people who loved him happy.''

"I was happy. Whenever he was home—''

"Which was a fraction of your childhood—a small fraction. And you were disconsolate every time he waved good-bye. I watched Rosemary endure his long absences. Even when he was home she was miserable, because she knew it would be for only a short time. She spent that time dreading his departure.

"Cliff thrived on the danger. It was his elixir, his life force. To your mother, it was a disease that ate away her youth and vitality. It took his life quickly, mercifully. Her death was agonizing and slow. It took years. Long before the afternoon she swallowed that bottle of pills, she had begun dying.

"So, why does he deserve your blind adoration and dogged determination to live up to his name, Avery? The most valuable prize he ever won wasn't the fucking Pulitzer. It was your mother, only he was too stupid to realize that.''

"You're just jealous of him.''

Steadily, Irish held her gaze. ''I was jealous of the way Rosemary loved him, yes.''

The starch went out of her then. She groped for his hand, pressed it to her cheek. Tears trickled over the back of it. ''I don't want us to fight, Irish.''

"I'm sorry then, because you've got a fight on your hands. I can't let you continue this."

"I've got to. I'm committed."

"Until when?"

"Until I know who threatened to kill Tate and can expose him."

"And then what?"

"I don't know," she groaned miserably.

"And what if this would-be assassin never goes through with it? Suppose he's blowing smoke? Will you stay Mrs. Rutledge indefinitely? Or will you simply approach Rutledge one day and say, 'Oh, by the way'?"

Admitting to him what she had admitted to herself only a few days earlier, she said, "I haven't figured that out yet. I didn't leave myself a graceful escape hatch."

"Rutledge has got to know, Avery."

"No!" She surged to her feet. "Not yet. I can't give him up yet. You've got to swear you won't tell him."

Irish fell back a step, dumbfounded by her violent reaction. "Jesus," he whispered as the truth dawned on him. "So that's what this is really about. You want another woman's husband. Is that why you want to remain Mrs. Rutledge—because Tate Rutledge is good in bed?"

 # TWENTY-THREE

Avery turned her back to keep from slapping him. "That was ugly, Irish." She moved to the window and was alarmed to notice that it had already grown dark. At the ranch, they'd be finished with dinner. She had told them she was going to shop through the dinner hour. Still, she needed to leave soon.

"It was ugly, yes," Irish conceded. "It was meant to be. Every time I feel like going soft on you, I think about the countless nights following the crash when I drank myself into a stupor. You know, I even considered cashing it all in."

Avery came around slowly, her face no longer taut with anger. "Please don't tell me that."

"I figured, fuck this life. I'll take my chances in the next one. I had lost Cliff and Rosemary. I had lost you. I asked God, 'Hey, who needs this abuse?' If I hadn't feared for my immortal soul, such as it is . . .'' He smiled ruefully.

She placed her arms around him and rested her cheek on his shoulder. "I love you. I suffered for you, too, believe it or not. I knew how my death would affect you."

He gathered her into a hug, not for the first time wishing she was truly his daughter. "I love you, too. That's why I can't let you go on with this, Avery."

She leaned away from him. "I have no choice now."

"If there is somebody who wants Rutledge dead—"

"There is."

"Then you're in danger, too."

"I know. I want to be a different Carole for Tate and Mandy, but if I'm too different, her coconspirator will figure she's betrayed him. Or," she added soberly, "that Carole isn't really Carole. I live in fear of giving myself away."

"You might have failed already and don't know it."

She shivered. "I realize that, too."

"Van noticed."

She reacted with a start, then expelled her breath slowly. "I wondered. I nearly had a heart attack when I opened the door to him."

Irish related his conversation with Van. "I was busy and didn't pay much attention to him at the time. I thought he was just being his usual, obnoxious self. Now, I think he was trying to tell me something. What should I say if he brings it up again?"

"Nothing. The fewer who know, the better—for their sakes, as well as mine. Van knew Avery Daniels. The Rutledges didn't. They don't have anyone to compare the new Carole to. They're attributing the changes in her to the crash and its traumatic aftermath."

"It's still shallow," he said worriedly. "If there is no assassination plot—and I pray to heaven that there isn't—the best you can hope to get out of this is a broken heart."

"If I give it up now and managed to come out alive, I would have done it for nothing. I haven't got the whole story yet. And what if Tate *were* assassinated, Irish? What if I could have prevented it and didn't? Do you think I could live with that the rest of my life?"

He lightly scrubbed her jaw with his knuckles. "You love him, don't you?"

Closing her eyes, she nodded.

"He hated his wife. Therefore, he hates you."

"Right again," she said with a mirthless laugh.

"What's it like between you?"

"I haven't slept with him."

"I didn't ask."

"But that's what you wanted to know."

"Would you?"

"Yes," she replied without equivocation. "From the time I regained consciousness until the day I left the clinic, he was wonderful—absolutely wonderful. The way he treats Carole in public is above reproach."

"What about how he treats her in private?"

"Chilly, like a betrayed husband. I'm working on that."

"What will happen then? If he gives in and makes love to you, don't you think he'll know the difference?"

"Will he?" She tilted her head to one side and tried to smile. "Don't men say that all cats are gray in the dark?"

He gave her a reproving glare. "Okay, let's say he doesn't notice. How will you feel about him making love to you while thinking you're somebody else?"

That hadn't occurred to her. Thinking about it now caused her to frown. "I'll want him to know it's me. I know it's wrong to trick him, but . . ."

Her voice trailed off as she wrestled with the question she hadn't yet found an answer for. Leaving it unresolved again, she said, "And then there's Mandy. I love her, too, Irish. She desperately needs a caring mother."

"I agree. What will happen to her when your job is done and you desert her?"

"I won't just desert—"

"And how do you think Rutledge is going to feel when you do an exposé on his family?"

"It won't be an exposé."

"I'd hate to be around when you try and explain that to him. He'll think you've used him." He paused for emphasis. "He'll be right, Avery."

"Not if I saved his life in the process. Don't you think he could find it within himself to forgive me?"

He swore beneath his breath. "You missed your calling. You should have been a lawyer. You'd argue with the devil himself."

"I can't let my career end in disgrace, Irish. I've got to make restitution for the mistake I made in Washington and earn back my credibility as a journalist. Maybe I am only trying to be daddy's little girl, but I've got to do it." Her eyes appealed to him for understanding. "I didn't pursue this golden opportunity. It was forced on me. I've got to make the best of it."

"You're going about it the wrong way," he said gently, tilting her chin up with his index finger. "You're too emotionally involved, Avery. You've got too much heart to remain detached. By your own admission, you care for these people. You love them."

"All the more reason for me to stay. Someone wants to kill Tate and make Mandy an orphan. If it's within my power, I've got to prevent that from happening."

His silence was as good as waving a white flag of surrender. She consulted his wall clock. "I must go. But first, do you have something belonging to me?"

In under a minute she was slipping the gold chain of her locket over her head. Monetarily it wasn't worth much, but it was her most valued possession.

Her father had brought it back to her from Egypt in 1967, when he had been hired by *Newsweek* to document the conflict between that country and Israel.

Avery depressed the spring and the two disks parted. She gazed at the photographs inside. One was of her father. In the photograph, he was dressed in battle fatigues, a 35-mm camera draped around his neck. It was the last picture taken of him. He had been killed a few weeks later. The other picture was of her mother. Rosemary, lovely and dainty, was smiling into the camera, but sadly.

Hot, salty tears filled Avery's eyes. She closed the locket and squeezed it in her palm. Not everything had been taken away from her. She still had this, and she still had Irish.

"I hoped you had it," she told him gruffly.

"It was in the dead woman's hands."

Avery nodded, finding it difficult to speak. "Mandy had noticed it around my neck. I had given it to her to look at. Just as we were about to take off, Carole became annoyed because Mandy was twirling the chain. She took it away from her. That's the last thing I remember before the crash."

He showed her Carole's jewelry. "Shook my gizzard when I opened that envelope you sent. You *did* send it, didn't you?"

She told him how that had come about. "I didn't know what else to do with it."

"Why didn't you just throw it away?"

"I guess I secretly wanted to make contact with you."

"You want her jewelry?"

She shook her head no, glancing down at the plain gold band on her left ring finger. "It's sudden reappearance would require an explanation. I have to keep things as simple as possible."

He cursed with impatience and apprehension. "Avery, call it off—now. Tonight."

"I can't."

"Hell and damnation," he swore. "You've got your father's ambition and your mother's compassion. It's a dangerous combination—lethal under these circumstances. Unfortunately, you inherited a stubborn will from both of them."

Avery knew he had capitulated completely when he asked regretfully, "What do you want me to do?"

                              *   *   *

Tate was standing in the hallway when she returned. Avery thought he'd prob-ably been waiting and watching for her, but he tried to pass it off as a coincidence.

"Why are you so late?" he asked, barely looking in her direction.

"Didn't Zee give you my message? I told her I had some last-minute things to get for the trip."

"I thought you'd be back sooner than this."

"I had a lot of shopping to do." She was loaded down with shopping bags—purchases she had made before her meeting with Irish. "Could you help me get this stuff to the bedroom, please?"

He relieved her of some of the bags and followed her down the hall. "Where's Mandy?" she asked.

"She's already asleep."

"Oh, I was hoping I'd get back in time to read a bedtime story to her."

"Then you should have come home sooner."

"Did she get a story?"

"Mom read her one. I tucked her in and stayed until she'd gone to sleep."

"I'll check on her in a while." She noticed as she passed the hall windows that Nelson, Jack, and Eddy were conversing over one of the patio tables in the courtyard. Zee was reclined in a lounger reading a magazine. Fancy was cavorting in the pool. "You're missing the conference."

"Eddy's going over the itinerary again. I've already heard it a thousand times."

"Just set those bags on the bed." She slid off her linen jacket, tossed it down beside the shopping bags, and stepped out of her pumps. Tate hovered close, looking ready to pounce.

"Where did you go shopping?"

"The usual places."

He had asked a dumb question, since the glossy sacks had familiar logos on them. For one horrifying moment, she wondered if he had followed her to Irish's house. He couldn't have. She had taken a circuitous route, constantly checking her rearview mirror to make sure she wasn't being followed.

Safety measures like that, which would have seemed absurdly melodramatic months ago, had become second nature. She didn't like living dishonestly, being constantly on guard. Tonight, especially, after the emotionally draining visit with Irish, her nerves were shot. Tate had picked the wrong night to interrogate her and put her on the defensive.

"Why are you giving me the third degree about going shopping?"

"I'm not."

"The hell you're not. You're sniffing like a bloodhound." She came a step closer to him. "What did you expect to smell on me? Tobacco smoke? Liquor? Semen? Something that would confirm your nasty suspicions that I spent the afternoon with a lover?"

"It's happened," he said tightly.

"Not anymore!"

"What kind of sap do you take me for? Do you expect me to believe that an operation on your face has turned you into a faithful wife?"

"Believe what you bloody well want to," she shouted back. "Just leave me alone while you're believing it."

She moved to her closet and almost derailed the sliding door as she angrily shoved it open. Her hands were trembling so badly that her fingers couldn't manage the buttons on the back of her blouse. She softly cursed her unsuccessful efforts to unbutton them.

"Let me."

Tate spoke from close behind her, an underlying apology in his tone. He tipped her head forward, leaving her neck exposed. His hands captured hers and lowered them to her sides, then unbuttoned the blouse.

"It would have been a familiar scene," he remarked as he undid the last button.

The blouse slid off her shoulders and down her arms. She caught it against her chest and turned to face him. "I don't respond well to inquisitions, Tate."

"No better than I respond to adultery."

She bowed her head slightly. "I deserve that, I suppose." For a moment, she stared at his throat and the strong pulse beating there. Then she lifted her eyes to his again. "But since the airplane crash, have I given you any reason to doubt my devotion to you?"

The corner of his lips jerked with a tiny spasm. "No."

"But you still don't trust me."

"Trust is earned."

"Haven't I earned yours back yet?"

He didn't answer. Instead, he raised his hand and, with his index finger, traced the gold chain around her neck. "What's this?"

His touch almost melted her. Taking a real chance by revealing more skin than she ever had, she let the blouse slip from her hands to the floor. Her locket lay nestled in the cleft between her breasts, enhanced by the engineering of her sheer bra. She heard the sharp breath he took.

"I found it in a secondhand jewelry store," she lied. "Pretty, isn't it?" Tate was staring at the delicate gold piece with the hunger of a starved man for the last morsel of food on earth. "Open it."

After a moment's hesitation, he scooped the locket into his palm and depressed the clasp. The two tiny frames were empty. She'd removed the photographs of her mother and father and left them in Irish's safekeeping.

"I want to put pictures of you and Mandy in it."

He searched her eyes. Then he looked long at her mouth while rubbing the locket between his thumb and finger. When he snapped it closed, the sound seemed inordinately loud.

He laid the golden disk back into place against her breasts. His hand lingered. His fingertips skimmed the soft curves, barely maintaining contact with her skin, but where they touched, she burned.

Still touching her, Tate turned his head away. He was fighting a war within himself, attested to by the flexing of his jaw, the turbulent indecision in his eyes, his shallow breathing.

"Tate." Her plaintive inflection brought his gaze back to meet hers. On a whisper, she said, "Tate, I never had an abortion." She raised her fingertips to his lips before they could form an argument. "I never had an abortion because there never was a baby."

The irony of it was that it was the unvarnished truth, but she would have to confess to a lie in order for him to believe it.

This germ of an idea had been cultivating in her mind for days. She had no idea if Carole had conceived and aborted a baby or not. But Tate would never know, either. A lie would be easier for him to forgive than an abortion, and since that seemed to be the thickest barrier to their reconciliation, she wanted to tear it down. Why should she pay the penalty for Carole's sins?

Once committed to it, the rest of the lie came easily. "I only told you I was pregnant for the very reason you cited the other morning. I wanted to flaunt it. I wanted to provoke you." She laid her hands against his cheeks. "But I can't let you go on believing that I destroyed your child. I can see that it hurts you too much.''

After a long, deep, probing stare, he broke contact and stepped back. ''The flight to Houston leaves at seven o'clock on Tuesday. Will you be able to handle that?''

She had hoped her news would release a tide of forgiveness and suppressed love. Trying not to let her disappointment show, she asked, ''Which? The early hour or the flight itself?''

''Both.''

''I'll be all right.''

''I hope so,'' he said, moving toward the door. ''Eddy wants everything to go like clockwork.''

On Monday evening, Irish summoned KTEX's political reporter into his office. ''You all set for this week?''

''Yeah. Rutledge's people sent over a schedule today. If we cover all this, you'll have to give Dekker equal time.''

''Let me worry about that. Your job is to document what's going on in Rutledge's campaign. I want daily reports. By the way, I'm sending Lovejoy with you instead of the photographer originally assigned.''

''Jesus, Irish,'' the reporter whined. ''What have I done to deserve him, huh? He's a pain in the ass. He's unreliable. Half the time he smells bad.''

He continued with a litany of objections. He preferred to be paired with just about anybody over Van Lovejoy. Irish listened silently. At the conclusion of the reporter's petition, he repeated, ''I'm sending Lovejoy with you.'' The reporter slunk out. Once Irish said something twice, there was no use arguing.

Irish had arrived at that decision several days earlier. Before he had even begun, the reporter hadn't had a chance in hell of changing Irish's mind.

Avery might not think she was in any imminent danger, but she was impetuous and headstrong and often made snap judgments for which she later paid dearly. He couldn't believe the mess she'd made for herself now. God almighty, he thought, she had become another woman! It was too late for him to talk her out of assuming Carole Rutledge's identity, but he was going to do all he could to see that she didn't pay for this impersonation with her life.

They had agreed to contact each other through his post office box if telephoning proved risky. He had given her his extra key to the box. Fat lot of good that would do if she needed immediate help. That safety net was no more substantial than a spiderweb, but she had refused his offer to loan her a handgun.

The whole cloak-and-dagger routine made him nervous as hell. Just thinking about it made him reach for his bottle of antacid. These days he was drinking as much of that stuff as he was whiskey. He was too old for this, but he couldn't just stand by, do nothing, and let Avery get herself killed.

Since he couldn't be her guardian angel, he would do the next best thing—he'd send Van along. Having Van around would no doubt make her nervous, but if she got into trouble while on the campaign trail, she'd have somebody to run to. Van Lovejoy wasn't much, but for the time being, he was the best Irish could do.

TWENTY-FOUR

The first glitch in Eddy's carefully orchestrated campaign trip occurred on the third day. They were in Houston. Early that morning Tate had made an impassioned breakfast speech to a rowdy audience of longshoremen. He was well received.

Upon their return to the downtown hotel, Eddy went to his room to answer telephone calls that had come in during their absence. Everyone else gathered in Tate's suite. Jack buried himself in the morning newspapers, scouring them for stories relating to Tate, his opponent, or the election in general. Avery sat on the floor with Mandy, who was scribbling in a Mickey Mouse coloring book.

Tate stretched out on the bed, propping the pillows behind his head. He turned on the television set to watch a game show. The questions were asinine, the contestants frenzied, the host obnoxious, but often something that inane relaxed his mind and opened up new avenues of thought. The best ideas came to him when he wasn't concentrating.

Nelson and Zee were working a crossword puzzle together.

Eddy interrupted the restful scene. He barged into the room, as excited as Tate had ever seen him. "Switch that thing off and listen."

Tate used the remote control to silence the TV set. "Well," he said with an expectant laugh, "you've got everybody's attention, Mr. Paschal."

"One of the largest Rotary Clubs in the state is meeting at noon today. It's their most important meeting of the year. New officers are being sworn in, and wives are invited. Their scheduled speaker called in sick this morning. They want you."

Tate sat up and swung his long legs over the side of the bed. "How many people?"

"Two-fifty, three hundred." Eddy was riffling through the papers in his briefcase. "These are top businessmen and professionals—pillars of the community. Oldest Rotary Club in Houston. Its members have lots of money, even in these depressed times. Here," he said, thrusting several sheets of paper at Tate, "this was a hell of a speech you gave in Amarillo last month. Glance over it. And for God's sake, get out of that chambray and denim and put on a conservative suit."

"This crowd sounds more like Dekker people."

"They are. That's why it's important that you go. Dekker's made you out to be a kid with his head in the clouds, at best, or a wacko liberal, at worst. Show them you've got both feet on the ground and that you don't have horns and a pointed tail." He glanced over his shoulder. "You're invited, too, Carole. Look your charming best. The women—"

"I can't be there."

Everyone's attention abruptly shifted from Eddy to her, where she still sat on the floor with Mandy, holding a selection of crayons in her hand and a picture of Donald Duck in her lap. "Mandy's appointment with Dr. Webster is at one o'clock today."

"Crap." Tate plowed his hand through his hair. "That's right. I'd forgotten."

Eddy divided his disbelieving gaze between them. "You can't even consider throwing away this opportunity. We're up one point in the polls this week, Tate, but we're still trailing by a dismal margin. This speech could mean a lot of campaign dollars—dollars we need to buy TV commercial time."

Jack tossed his folded newspaper aside. "Make another appointment with this doctor."

"What about it, Carole?" Tate asked.

"You know how hard this one was to come by. I probably wouldn't be able to get another one for weeks. Even if I could, I don't believe it would be in Mandy's best interest to postpone.''

Tate watched his brother, father, and campaign manager exchange telling glances. They wanted him to make a speech to this influential crowd of Rotarians, and they were right. These conservatives, staunch Dekker supporters, needed to be convinced that he was a viable candidate and not a hotheaded upstart. When he looked down at his wife, however, he could feel the strength behind her calm gaze. He would be damned either way he went. ''Christ.''

''I could go to the psychologist's office with Carole,'' Zee offered. ''Tate, you make your speech. We can fill you in later on what the doctor has to say about Mandy.''

''I appreciate the offer, Mom, but she's my daughter.''

''And this could mean the election,'' Eddy argued, raising his voice.

Jack stood and hiked up the waistband of his pants, as though he was about to engage in a fistfight. ''I agree with Eddy one hundred percent.''

''One speech isn't going to cost the election. Dad?''

''I think your mother had the most workable solution. You know I don't put much stock in shrinks, so I wouldn't mind a bit going to hear what this one has to say about my granddaughter.''

''Carole?''

She had let the dispute revolve around her without contributing anything to it, which was uncharacteristic. As long as Tate had known her, she had never failed to express her opinion.

''They're both terribly important, Tate,'' she said. ''It has to be your decision.''

Eddy swore beneath his breath and shot her a glance of supreme annoyance. He would rather her rant and rave and fight to get her way. Tate felt the same. It had been much easier to say no to Carole when she was being obstreperous and inflexible. Lately, she used her dark, eloquent eyes to express herself more than she used a strident voice.

Whatever his choice, it would be met with disapproval. The deciding factor was Mandy herself. He looked down into her solemn little face. Even though she couldn't have understood what the controversy was about, she seemed to be apologizing to him for causing such a fuss.

''Call them back, Eddy, and graciously decline.'' Carole's posture relaxed, as though she'd been holding herself in breathless anticipation of his answer. ''Tell them Mrs. Rutledge and I have a previous engagement.''

''But—''

Tate held up his hand to ward off a barrage of protests. He gave his friend a hard, decisive stare. ''My first obligation is to my family. I was guaranteed your understanding, remember?''

Eddy gave him a hard, exasperated stare, then stormed out. Tate couldn't blame him for being pissed. He didn't have a child. He was responsible to no one but himself. How could he possibly understand divided loyalties?

''I hope you know what you're doing, Tate.'' Nelson stood and reached for Zee's hand. ''Let's go try to calm down our frustrated campaign manager.'' They left together.

Jack was just as agitated as Eddy. He glared at Carole. ''Satisfied?''

''Enough, Jack,'' Tate said testily.

His brother aimed an accusing finger at her. ''She's manipulating you with this good-mother routine.''

''What goes on between Carole and me is none of your damned business.''

''Ordinarily, no. But since you're running for public office, your private life is everybody's business. Whatever affects the campaign is my business. I've devoted years to getting you elected.''

''And I appreciate everything you've done. But today I'm taking an hour off for my daughter's sake. I don't think that's asking too much, and even if it is, don't give me an argument about it.''

After casting another hostile glance at Carole, Jack left the suite, slamming the door behind him.

She came to her feet. ''Is that what you think, Tate? That this is just a good-mother routine?''

The hell of it was that he didn't know what to think. Since his first sexual conquest at age fifteen, Tate had exercised control over all his relationships with women. Women liked him. He liked them in return. He also respected them. Unlike most men to whom romantic encounters came easily, his friends among the female sex numbered as many as his lovers, although many in the first category secretly lamented that they'd never joined the ranks of the second.

His most serious involvement had been with a San Antonio divorcée. She sold commercial real estate, very successfully. Tate had lauded her success, but didn't love her enough to compete with it for her time and attention. She had also made it clear from the beginning that she didn't want children. After a two-year court-ship, they had parted as friends.

Jack did most of the hiring and firing at their law firm, but when Carole Navarro had applied, he had solicited Tate's opinion. No living man could look at Carole impassively. Her large, dark eyes captivated his attention, her figure his imagina-tion, her smile his heart. He had given her his stamp of approval and Jack had put her on the payroll as a legal assistant.

Soon, Tate had violated his own business ethics and invited her out to dinner to celebrate a case the jury had found in favor of their client. She had been charming and flirtatious, but the evening had ended at the door of her apartment with a friendly good-night handshake.

For weeks, she had kept their dates friendly. One night, when Tate had with-stood the buddy system as long as he could, he had taken her in his arms and kissed her. She had returned his kiss with gratifying passion. They made a natural pro-gression to bed, and the sex had been deeply satisfying for both.

Within three months the law firm had lost an employee but Tate had gained a wife.

Her pregnancy came as a shock. He had quickly and agreeably adapted to the idea of having a child sooner than they had planned; Carole had not. She com-plained of feeling shackled by an unwelcome responsibility. Her engaging smile and infectious laughter became memories.

Her sexual performance had turned so obligatory that Tate didn't miss it when it was suspended altogether. The had had blistering arguments. Nothing he did pleased or interested her. Eventually, he gave up trying to and devoted his time and energy to the election, which was still years away.

As soon as Mandy was born, Carole dedicated herself to getting her figure back. She exercised with fiendish diligence. He wondered why. Then the reason behind the zeal became apparent. He knew almost to the day when she took her first lover. She made no secret of it, nor of any of the infidelities that followed. His defense was indifference, which, by that time, was genuine. In retrospect, he wished he had gone ahead and divorced her then. A clean break might have been better for everybody.

For months they occupied the same house, but lived separate lives. Then, one night, she had visited him in his room, looking her sexiest. He never knew what had prompted her to come to him that night—probably boredom, maybe spite, maybe the challenge of seducing him. Whatever her reason, sexual abstinence and imprudent drinking with his brother during a poker game had caused him to take advantage of her offer.

During the blackest hours of their estrangement, he had considered resuming his affair with the realtor or cultivating another relationship just for the physical release it would afford him. Ultimately, he had denied that luxury to himself. A sexual dalliance was a pitfall to any married man. To a political candidate, it was an inescapable abyss. Falling into it and getting caught was career suicide.

Whether he got caught or not, vows meant something to him, though they obviously didn't mean anything to his wife. Like a dolt, he had remained faithful to Carole and to the words he had recited to her during their wedding ceremony.

Weeks after that night, she had belligerently announced that she was pregnant again. Although Tate had seriously doubted that the child was his, he had had no choice but to take her word for it.

"I didn't want to be stuck with another kid," she had yelled.

That's when he knew he didn't love her anymore, hadn't for a long time, and never could again. He had reached that momentous conclusion one week to the day before she boarded Flight 398 to Dallas.

Now he shook his head to bring himself out of his unpleasant reverie. He was going to ignore her question about the good-mother routine, just as he had ignored her claim that there had never been a child. He was afraid of the old bait-and-switch con. He wasn't going to commit himself one way or the other until he knew that Carole's recent transformations were permanent.

"Why don't you order up lunch so we won't have to go out before our meeting with Dr. Webster," he suggested, changing the subject.

She seemed just as willing to let the matter drop. "What would you like?"

"Anything. A cold roast beef sandwich would be fine."

As she sat down on the bed to use the phone on the nightstand, she mechanically crossed her legs. Tate's stomach muscles clenched at the sound of her stockings scratching together.

If he still distrusted her, why did he want to have sex with her so badly?

She deserved an A for effort. He would grant her that. Since coming home, and even before, she had done her best to reconcile with him. She rarely lost her temper anymore. She made a concentrated effort to get along with his family, and had taken an unprecedented and inordinate amount of interest in their comings and goings, their habits, their activities. She was the antithesis of the impatient, ill-tempered parent she'd been before.

"That's right, a peanut butter sandwich," she was saying into the receiver. "With grape jelly. I know it's not on the room service menu, but that's what she likes to eat for lunch." Mandy's unwavering love affair with peanut butter and jelly sandwiches was a joke between them. Over her shoulder, Carole flashed him a smile.

God, he wanted to taste that smile.

Recently, he had. Her mouth hadn't tasted of deceit and lies and unfaithfulness. The kisses she returned were sweet and delicious and . . . different. Analyzing them—and he had done that a lot lately—he realized that kissing her had been like kissing a woman for the first time.

What should have been familiar had been unique. Their few kisses had jolted him and left indelible impressions. He had exercised monastic self-discipline to stop with a few, when what he had wanted to do was explore her mouth at leisure until he found an explanation for this phenomenon.

Or maybe it wasn't so phenomenal. She looked different with her hair short. Maybe the plastic surgery had altered her face just enough to make her seem like an entirely different woman.

It was a good argument, but he wasn't convinced.

"They'll be right up," she told him. "Mandy, pick up the crayons and put them back in the box, please. It's time for lunch."

She stooped to help her. As she bent over, the narrow skirt of her suit was pulled tight across her derriere. Desire ripped through him. Blood rushed to his loins. That was understandable, he reasoned quickly. He hadn't been with a woman in so damn long.

But he didn't really believe that, either.

He didn't want just any woman. If that were the case, he could solve his problem with a single phone call.

No, he wanted this woman, this Carole, this wife he was only now becoming acquainted with. Sometimes, when he gazed into her eyes, it was as though he'd never known her before and the antagonism between them had happened to someone else. Impossible as it was to believe, he liked this Carole. Even more impossible to believe, he had fallen a little in love with her.

But he would deny it with his dying breath.

"I'm glad you came with us," Avery said, giving Tate a tentative smile. A receptionist had seated them in Dr. Webster's office to await private consultation.

"It was the only decision I could make."

The psychologist had been with Mandy for almost an hour. Waiting for his prognosis was taking its toll on them. The idle conversation was an attempt to relieve their nervous tension.

"Will Eddy stay mad at me for the rest of the trip?"

"I spoke with him before we left the hotel. He wished us luck with Mandy. I guess Mom and Dad calmed him down. Anyway, he never really gets mad."

"That's odd, isn't it?"

Tate consulted his wristwatch. "How long does his session with her last, for crissake?" He looked at the door behind him as though willing it to open. "What did you say?"

"About Eddy never getting mad."

"Oh, right." He shrugged. "It's just his temperament. He rarely loses control."

"Iceman," she murmured.

"Hmm?"

"Nothing."

She fiddled with the strap of her handbag, weighing the advisability of pursuing the subject. Irish had advised her to learn as much as she could about these people. Her career had been built on her ability to pose pertinent questions, but to phrase them subtly. She had been adroit at squeezing information out of people who were sometimes reluctant to impart their secrets. She decided to test her talent and see if it was still intact.

"What about women?"

Tate tossed aside the magazine he had just picked up. "What women?"

"Eddy's women."

"I don't know. He doesn't discuss them with me."

"He doesn't discuss his sex life with his best friend? I thought all men swapped success stories."

"Boys might. Men don't need to. I'm not a voyeur and Eddy's not an exhibitionist."

"Is he heterosexual?"

Tate hit her with an icy blast of his eyes. "Why? Did he turn you down?"

"Damn you!"

The door swung open. The two of them guiltily sprang apart. The receptionist said, "The doctor is finishing up with Mandy. He'll be in shortly."

"Thank you."

After she withdrew, Avery leaned forward from her chair again. "I'm only asking about Eddy because your niece is throwing herself at him, and I'm afraid she'll get hurt."

"My niece? Fancy?" He laughed with incredulity. "She's after Eddy?"

"She told me so the other night, when she came home with a battered face." His smile disappeared. "That's right, Tate. She picked up a cowboy in a bar. They got high. When he couldn't maintain an erection, he blamed it on Fancy and beat her up."

He expelled a long breath. "Jesus."

"Didn't you notice her black eye and swollen lip?" He shook his head. "Well, don't feel too badly. Neither did her own parents," she said bitterly. "Fancy's like a piece of furniture. She's there, but no one really sees her ... unless she's behaving outrageously. Anyway, she has her sights fixed on Eddy now. How do you think he'll reciprocate?"

"Fancy's just a kid."

Avery gave him an arch look. "You might be her uncle, but you're not blind."

He rolled his shoulders uncomfortably. "Eddy had his share of coeds while we were at UT. He visited the whorehouses in Nam. I know he's straight."

"Is he currently seeing anyone?"

"He goes out with some of the women who work at headquarters, but it's usually a platonic, group thing. I haven't heard any scuttlebutt that he's sleeping with any one of them. Several would probably be willing if he asked.

"But Fancy?" Tate shook his head doubtfully. "I don't think Eddy would touch her. He wouldn't get involved with a woman almost twenty years his junior, particularly Fancy. He's too bright."

"I hope you're right, Tate." After a thoughtful pause, she glanced up at him and added, "And not because I'm interested in him myself."

He didn't have time to comment before the doctor opened the door and entered the office.

TWENTY-FIVE

"Don't feel too, bad, Mrs. Rutledge. Your guilt over past mistakes won't help Mandy now."

"How am I supposed to feel, Dr. Webster? You've all but said that I'm responsible for Mandy's retarded social development."

"You made some mistakes. All parents do. But you and Mr. Rutledge have already taken the first step toward reversing that trend. You're spending more time with Mandy, which is excellent. You're praising even her smallest achievements and minimizing her failures. She needs that kind of positive reinforcement from you."

Tate was frowning. "That doesn't sound like much."

"On the contrary, it's a lot. You'd be amazed how important parental approval is to a child."

"What else should we do?"

"Ask for her opinion often. 'Mandy, do you want vanilla or chocolate?' Force her to make choices and then commend her decisions. She should be made to vocalize her thoughts. My impression is that up till now she's been discouraged to."

He regarded them from beneath rust-colored eyebrows that would have better befitted a cattle rustler with a six-shooter strapped to his hip than a child psychologist with a benign demeanor.

"Your little girl has a very low opinion of herself." Avery pressed her fist to her lips and rolled them inward. "Some children manifest low self-esteem with bad behavior, drawing attention to themselves in that way. Mandy has retreated into herself. She considers herself transparent—of little or no significance."

Tate's head dropped between his shoulders. Bleakly, he glanced at Avery. Tears were rolling down her cheeks. "I'm sorry," she whispered. She was apologizing for Carole, who didn't deserve his forgiveness.

"It's not all your fault. I was there, too. I let lots of things slide when I should have intervened."

"Unfortunately," Dr. Webster said, directing their attention back to him, " the airplane crash only heightened Mandy's anxiety. How did she behave on the flight here the other day?"

"She raised quite a ruckus when we tried to buckle her into her seat," Tate said.

"I was having a difficult time buckling my own seat belt," Avery confessed honestly. "If Tate hadn't talked me through it, I doubt I could have stood the takeoff."

"I understand, Mrs. Rutledge," he said sympathetically. "How was Mandy once you took off?"

They glanced at each other, then Avery answered. "Come to think of it, she was fine."

"That's what I figured. See, she remembers you fastening her into her seat, Mrs. Rutledge, but doesn't remember anything beyond the crash. She doesn't remember you rescuing her."

Avery laid a hand against her chest. "You're saying she blames me for putting her through the crash?"

"To an extent, I'm afraid so."

Shuddering, she covered her mouth with her hand. "My God."

"It will be a real breakthrough when she allows her mind to live through that explosion again. Then she'll remember you rescuing her."

"That would be hell for her."

"But necessary for a complete cure, Mr. Rutledge. She's fighting her memory of it. My guess is that her recurring nightmares lead her right up to the moment of impact."

"She said the fire was eating her," Avery said softly, remembering Mandy's last nightmare. "Is there anything we can do to prod her memory?"

"Hypnosis is a possibility," the doctor said. "What I'd rather do, however, is let her memory evolve naturally. Next time she has one of these nightmares, don't wake her up."

"Christ."

"I know that sounds cruel, Mr. Rutledge, but she's got to experience the crash again to get to the other side of it, to reach safety in the arms of her mother. The terror must be exorcised. She won't overcome her subconscious fear and dread of your wife until then.''

''I understand,'' Tate said, ''but it's going to be tough.''

''I know.'' Dr. Webster stood, signaling that their time was up. ''I don't envy you having to stand by and let her relive that horrifying experience. I'd like to see her back in two months, if that's convenient.''

''We'll make it convenient.''

''And before that, if you think it's necessary. Feel free to call anytime.''

Tate shook hands with Dr. Webster, then assisted Avery from her chair. She wasn't the mother Mandy had the subconscious fear and dread of, but she might just as well be. Everyone would lay Carole's blame on her. Even with the support of Tate's hand beneath her elbow, she could barely find the wherewithal to stand.

''Good luck with your campaign,'' the psychologist told Tate.''

''Thank you.''

The doctor clasped Avery's hands, sandwiching them between his. ''Don't make yourself ill with guilt and remorse. I'm convinced that you love your daughter very much.''

''I do. Did she tell you she hated me?''

The question was routine. He heard it a dozen times a day, particularly from mothers harboring guilt. In this instance, he could provide a positive answer. He smiled a good ole boy's smile. ''She speaks very highly of her mommy and only gets apprehensive when referring to events that took place before the crash, which ought to tell you something.''

''What?''

''That you've already improved as a parent.'' He patted her shoulder. ''With your continued tender loving care, Mandy will get through this and go on to be an exceptionally bright, well-adjusted child.''

''I hope so, Dr. Webster,'' she said fervently. ''Thank you.''

He escorted them to the door and pulled it open. ''You know, Mrs. Rutledge, you gave me quite a start when I first met you. A young women did a television interview with me about a year ago. She bears a remarkable resemblance to you. In fact, she's from your area. By any chance, do you know her? Her name is Avery Daniels.''

Avery Daniels, Avery Daniels, Avery Daniels.

The crowd was chanting her real name as she and Tate made their way through the crowd toward the dais.

Avery Daniels, Avery Daniels, Avery Daniels.

There were people everywhere. She stumbled and became separated from Tate. He was swallowed by the crowd. ''Tate!'' she screamed. He couldn't hear her over the demonic recitation of her name.

Avery, Avery, Avery.

What was that? A shot! Tate was covered with blood. Tate turned to her and, as he fell, he sneered, ''Avery Daniels, Avery Daniels, Avery Daniels.''

''Carole?''

Avery Daniels.

''Carole? Wake up.''

Avery sat bolt upright. Her mouth was gaping open and dry. She was wheezing. ''Tate?'' She fell against his bare chest and threw her arms around him. ''Oh God, it was awful.''

"Were you having a bad dream?"

She nodded, burrowing her face in the fuzzy warmth of his chest. "Hold me. Please. Just for a minute."

He was sitting on the edge of her bed. At her request, he inched closer and placed his arms around her. Avery snuggled closer still and clung to him. Her heart was racing, thudding against his chest. She couldn't eradicate the image of a blood-drenched Tate turning to her with contempt and accusation burning in his eyes.

"What brought this on?"

"I don't know," she lied.

"I think I do. You haven't been yourself since Dr. Webster mentioned Avery Daniels." She whimpered. Tate threaded his fingers up through her hair and closed them around her scalp. "I can't believe he didn't know she died in that crash. He was so embarrassed by mentioning it, I felt sorry for him. He had no way of knowing how much the comparison would upset you."

Or why, she thought. "Did I behave like a fool?" All she remembered after the doctor had spoken her name was the clamorous ringing in her ears and the wave of dizziness that had knocked her against Tate.

"Not like a fool, but you almost fainted."

"I don't even remember leaving his office."

He set her way from him. Her hands slid onto his biceps. "It was a bizarre coincidence that you were on the same airplane with the Daniels woman. Strangers often mistook you for her, remember? It's surprising that no one mentioned her to you before now."

So he had known who Avery Daniels was. That made her feel better somehow. She wondered if he had liked watching her on TV. "I'm sorry I caused a scene. I just get . . ." She wished he was still holding her. It was easier to talk when she didn't have to look him in the eye.

"What?"

She laid her head on his shoulder. "I get tired of people staring at my face all the time. It's an object of curiosity. I feel like the bearded lady in a sideshow."

"Human nature. No one means to be cruel."

"I know, but it makes me extremely self-conscious. Sometimes I feel like I'm still wrapped in bandages. I'm on the inside looking out, but no one can see past my face into me." A tear trickled from the corner of her eye and splashed onto his shoulder.

"You're still upset over the dream," he said, easing her up again. "Would you like something to drink? There's some Bailey's in the bar."

"That sounds wonderful."

He divided the small bottle of Irish cream between two drinking glasses and returned to the bed with them. If he was self-conscious about having only his underwear on, he gave no outward sign of it.

It pleased her that he sat back down on her bed, not the one he had been sleeping in before her nightmare woke him up. Only a narrow space separated the beds, but it might just as well have been the Gulf of Mexico. It had taken an emergency to get him to cross it.

"To your victory, Tate." She clinked her glass with his. The liquor slid easily down her throat and spread warmly through her belly. "Hmm. This was a good idea. Thanks."

She welcomed this quiet interlude. They shared all the problems inherent to any married couple, but none of the intimacy. Because of the campaign, they were always in the public eye and under constant scrutiny. That put an additional strain on an already difficult relationship. They shared no counterbalancing pleasure in each other.

They were married, yet they weren't. They occupied the same space, but existed in separate spheres. Until tonight, Mandy had served as a buffer between them in the confines of the hotel room. She'd slept with Avery.

But tonight Mandy wasn't here. They were alone. It was the middle of the night. They were sipping Irish cream together and discussing their personal problems. For any other couple, the scene would result in lovemaking.

"I miss Mandy already," she remarked as she traced the rim of her glass with her fingertip. "I'm not sure we did the right thing by letting her go home with Zee and Nelson."

"That's what we had planned all along—that they'd take her home after her appointment with Webster."

"After talking to him, I feel like I should be with her constantly."

"He said a few days of separation wouldn't hurt, and Mom knows what to do."

"How did it happen?" Avery mused aloud. "How did she become so introverted, so emotionally bruised?" She asked the questions rhetorically, without expecting a response. Tate, however, took them literally and provided her with answers.

"You heard what he said. He told you how it happened. You didn't spend enough time with her. What time you did spend with her was more destructive than not."

Her temper surged to the surface. In this instance, Carole was getting a bum deal, and Avery felt compelled to take up for her. "And where were you all that time? If I was doing such a rotten job of mothering, why didn't you step in? Mandy has two parents, you know."

"I realize that. I admitted it today. But every time I made the slightest suggestion, you got defensive. Seeing us fight sure as hell wasn't doing Mandy any good. So I couldn't step in, as you put it, without making a bad situation even worse."

"Maybe your approach was wrong." Giving Carole the benefit of the doubt, she played devil's advocate.

"Maybe. But I've never known you to take criticism well."

"And you do?"

He set his glass on the nightstand and reached for the lamp switch. Avery's hand shot out and grabbed his. "I'm sorry. Don't . . . don't go back to bed yet. It's been a long, tiring day for many reasons. We're both feeling the pressure. I didn't mean to lash out at you."

"You probably should have gone home with Mom and Dad, too."

"No," she said quickly, "my place is with you."

"Today was just a sample of what it's going to be like between now and November, Carole. It's only going to get tougher."

"I can handle it." Smiling, she impulsively reached up and ran her finger across the cleft in his chin. "I wish I had a nickel for every time today you said, 'Hi, I'm Tate Rutledge, running for U.S. senator.' Wonder how many hands you shook?"

"This many." He held up his right hand. It was bent into a cramped claw.

She laughed softly. "I believe we bore up very well during that visit to the Galleria, considering we'd just ended our visit with Dr. Webster and told Mandy good-bye."

As soon as they had returned to the hotel from the psychologist's office, they had given Mandy over to her grandparents. Zee went beyond being a white-knuckle flier. She refused to fly altogether, so they had come to Houston by car. They had wanted to start the drive home so they would arrive before dark.

No sooner had she and Tate waved them off than Eddy hustled them into a car and sped toward the sprawling, multilayered shopping mall.

Volunteers, under Eddy's supervision, had heralded their arrival. Tate made a short speech from a raised platform, introduced his wife to the crowd that had gathered, then moved among them, shaking hands and soliciting votes.

It had gone so well that Eddy was mollified after having to decline the Rotary Club's invitation. Even that had turned out well. The civic club had extended Tate an invitation to speak at one of their meetings later in the month.

"Eddy went nuts over all the television coverage you got today," Avery said, reflecting on it.

"They gave us twenty seconds during the six o'clock broadcast. Doesn't sound like much, but I'm told that's good."

"It is. So I'm told," she hastily added.

She'd been stunned to see Van Lovejoy and a political reporter from KTEX at the longshoremen's breakfast. All day, they'd stayed hot on Tate's trail. "Why did they come all the way from San Antonio?" she had asked Eddy.

"Don't knock the free publicity. Smile into the camera every chance you get."

Instead, she tried to avoid Van's camera. But he seemed bent on getting her image on tape. The cat-and-mouse game she played with him all day, coupled with the shock Dr. Webster had dealt her, had chafed her nerves raw. She had been so nervous that, later, when she couldn't find a pair of earrings, she had overreacted.

"I know they were in here the day before I left," she cried to Tate.

"Look again."

She did better than that. She upended the satin pouch and raked through the contents. "They're not here."

"What do they look like?"

They were due to leave for a fund-raising barbecue dinner being hosted by a wealthy rancher outside the city. Tate had been dressed and waiting for half an hour. She was running late.

"Big silver loops." Tate gave the room a cursory once-over. "You won't find them lying on the surface," she had told him with exasperation. "I haven't worn them yet. I brought them specifically for this outfit."

"Can't you substitute something else?"

"I guess I'll have to." She made a selection from the pile of jewelry she'd spilled onto the dresser. By then she was so flustered, she had had difficulty fitting the post into the back. Three attempts proved to be misses. "Shit!"

"Carole, for heaven's sake, calm down," Tate said, raising his voice. Up till then he'd been infuriatingly calm. "You forgot a pair of earrings. It's not the end of the world."

"I didn't forget them." Drawing a deep breath, she faced him. "This isn't the first time something has mysteriously disappeared."

"You should have told me. I'll call hotel security right away."

She caught his arm before he could reach for the telephone. "Not just here. At home, too. Somebody's been sneaking into my room and going through my things."

His reaction was what she had expected. "That's ridiculous. Are you crazy?"

"No. And I'm not imagining it, either. I'm missing several things—small, insignificant things. Like this pair of earrings that I know damn good and well I packed. I checked and double-checked my accessories before I put them in the suitcases.''

Sensitive to any criticism of his family, he folded his arms across his chest. ''Who are you accusing of stealing?''

''I don't mind the missing objects so much as the violation of my privacy.''

Just then a knock had sounded on their door—the perfect culmination for a frazzling day. ''Case in point,'' she had said irritably. ''Why can't we ever finish a private conversation before we're interrupted?''

''Keep your voice down. Eddy'll hear you.''

''To hell with Eddy,'' she had said, meaning it.

Tate pulled the door open and Eddy came striding in. ''Ready, guys?''

By way of explanation for their being late, Tate said, ''Carole lost her earrings.''

She shot him a look that clearly stated she had not lost them.

''Well, wear some others or go without, but we've got to get downstairs.'' Eddy held the door open. ''Jack's waiting with the car. It's an hour's drive.''

They rushed for the elevator. Thankfully, another hotel guest saw them coming and politely held it for them. Jack was pacing the length of the limo parked in the porte cochere.

For the duration of the drive they discussed polls and campaign strategy. She could have been invisible, for all the attention she was given. Once, when she offered an unsolicited opinion, it was met with three impassive stares, then summarily ignored.

Surprisingly, the party had been fun. No press was allowed. Since she didn't have to concentrate on dodging Van's camera, she relaxed and enjoyed herself. There was a plethora of good Texana food, friendly people who likened Tate to a young John Kennedy, and live music. She even got to dance with Tate. Eddy had pressured him into it.

''Come on. It'll look good to the crowd.''

For the time Tate held her in his arms and twirled her around the dance floor, she pretended it had been his idea. Heads thrown back, they had smiled at each other as their feet kept time to the lively music. She believed he was actually enjoying himself. As the music reached a crescendo, he lifted her against him and whirled her around to the exuberant applause of everyone watching. Then he had bent down and kissed her cheek.

When he pulled back, there was an odd expression on his face. He appeared surprised by his own spontaneity.

On the return trip into the city, however, she sat in the corner of the limousine's backseat, staring through the dark patch of tinted window while he, Jack, and Eddy analyzed how well the day had gone and assessed what effect it might have on the outcome of the election.

She had gone to bed feeling exhausted and glum. She'd had difficulty falling asleep. The nightmare—and she could count on one hand the others she had had in her lifetime—was the product of a physically and emotionally taxing day.

She treasured this uninterrupted moment with Tate. They were continually surrounded by other people. Even in their own suite, they were rarely alone.

''I think the Bailey's is going to do the trick.'' She handed him her empty glass and lay back against the pillows.

''Feeling sleepy?''

''Hmm.'' She flung her arms up so that her hands were lying on either side of her head, palms up, fingers curled inward, a position both provocative and defenseless. Tate's eyes turned dark as they moved from her face down the front of her body.

"Thank you for dancing with me," she said drowsily. "I enjoyed you holding me."

"You used to say I had no rhythm."

"I was wrong."

He continued to watch her for a moment, then switched out the lamp. He was about to leave her bed when she laid a restraining hand on his bare thigh. "Tate?"

He froze. His motionless silhoutte was limned by the bluish light leaking through the drapes from the parking lot. Invitingly, she repeated his name on a breath of a whisper. Slowly, he lowered himself to the mattress again and leaned over her. With a soft exclamation, she bicycled her legs to kick off the covers so there would be nothing between them.

"Tate, I—"

"Don't," he commanded gruffly. "Don't say anything to change my mind." His head moved so close that she felt his breath against her lips. "I want you, so don't say a word."

Fiercely possessive, his lips rubbed hers apart. His tongue probed and explored, dipping into her mouth on deep and daring forays. Avery clutched handfuls of his hair and pressed her mouth up into his kiss.

He relaxed his arms, which had been stiffly bridging her head. Gradually, his body stretched out along hers. His hard thigh crowded her hip; she turned her lower body into it. He nudged her moist cleft with his knee.

"Is it me you're wet for?"

Avery gasped, unspeakably aroused by his boldness. "You told me not to say anything."

"Who are you wet for?"

She ran her hand down his thigh, placed it beneath his hip, and invitingly drew him closer.

Groaning in need, he ended the kiss with several rough glances of his lips across hers. He kissed his way down her throat and chest and nuzzled her breasts as he filled his hands with them. His open mouth sought the raised center of one and tugged on it through the fabric of her gown. It beaded against his flicking tongue.

Reflexively, her body bowed off the bed. His hands slid between the pillow and her head, his palms cradling it, his thumbs meeting beneath her chin. He tilted her face up and fastened his mouth to hers again, giving her a scorching, searching kiss as he moved to lie between her spreading thighs.

Avery's body quickened to the splendor of feeling the full extension of his sex stroking the dell of her femininity. There was even a certain sexiness to the friction of his cotton briefs sliding against her silk underpants.

Heat shimmied through her and was conveyed to him through her skin. His kiss delved deeper, and the rocking motions of his body grew more desperate. Too impatient to be leisurely and inquisitive, her hands clutched his sleek, supple back. She fitted his calf muscles into the arches of her feet and receptively angled her hips up.

Hostile, hard, and hot, Tate slid his hand into the damp silk prohibiting his entrance.

The telephone rang.

He withdrew his hand, but she still lay trapped beneath him. While they lay breathing heavily against each other, the phone continued to ring.

Eventually, Tate rolled to the edge of the bed and jerked the receiver to his ear. "Hello?" After a brief pause, he cursed. "Yeah, Jack," he growled. "I'm awake. What is it?"

Avery emitted a small, anguished cry and moved to the far side of the bed, putting her back to him.

━━━━━━━━━━━━━━━━ ✎ TWENTY-SIX

"I'm coming."

Eddy left his comfortable hotel room chair and rounded the matching hassock. Stacked on top of it were computer readouts, newspaper clippings, demographic charts. Thinking the knock signaled the arrival of his room service order, he pulled the door open without first checking the peephole.

Fancy stood on the threshold. "I'd pay to see that."

Not bothering to conceal his annoyance, he barred her entrance by placing his forearm on the doorjamb. "See what?"

"You coming."

"Cute."

"Thanks," she replied cheekily. Then her blue eyes darkened. "Who were you expecting?"

"None of your business. What are you doing so far away from home, little girl?"

The bell on the elevator down the hall chimed, and the room service waiter emerged, carrying a tray on his shoulder. He approached them on soundless footsteps. "Mr. Paschal?"

"Here." When Eddy stepped aside to let him in, Fancy slipped inside, too. She went into the bathroom and locked the door. Eddy scrawled his signature on the bottom of the tab and showed the waiter to the door.

"Have a good night." The youth gave him an elbow-in-the-ribs grin and a sly wink.

Eddy closed the door a little too suddenly and a little too loudly to be polite. "Fancy?" He rapped on the bathroom door.

"I'll be out in a sec."

He heard the commode flush. She opened the door while still tugging the tight, short skirt of her tube dress over her hips. The dress was made of stretchy, clingy stuff that conformed to her body like a second skin. It had a wide cuff across the top that could be worn off the shoulders. She was wearing it way off.

The dress was red. So was her lipstick, her high-heeled pumps, and the dozens of plastic bangle bracelets encircling her arms. With her mane of blond hair even more unruly than usual, she looked like a whore.

"What did you order? I'm starved."

"You're not invited." Eddy intercepted her on her way toward the room service tray the waiter had left on the table near the easy chair. He gripped her upper arm. "What are you doing here?"

"Well, first I was peeking. Now I'm going to scope out what you've got to eat."

His fingers pinched tighter and he strained her name through his teeth. "What are you doing in Houston?"

"It got boring at home," she said, wresting her arm free, "with nobody but Mona and Mother around. Mother's in a stupor half the time. The other half she's crying over Daddy not loving her anymore. Frankly, I doubt he ever did. You know he thought she was knocked up with me when they got married.'' She lifted the silver metal lid off one of the plates and picked up a cherry tomato—a garnish for his club sandwich.

''What's . . . hmm, a chocolate sundae,'' she cooed with pleasure as she investigated beneath another lid. ''How do you eat like this late at night and keep your belly so nice and flat?''

Her practiced eyes moved down his smooth, muscled torso, seen through his unbuttoned shirt. Suggestively, Fancy licked her lips.

''Anyway, Mother believes Daddy has the hots for Aunt Carole, which I think is downright scandalous, don't you?'' She shivered—not from repugnance, but with delight. ''It's so, so Old Testament for a man to covet his brother's wife.''

''The sin of the week, by Fancy Rutledge.''

She giggled. ''Mother's positively morose and Mona looks at me with the same regard she would have for a cockroach in her sugar canister. Grandma, Grandpa, and the little spook were due back, which would only make things worse, so I decided to split and come here, where all the action is.''

Wryly, he said, ''As you can see, there's not much going on tonight.''

Undaunted, she curled up in the easy chair he'd been occupying and popped the tomato into her mouth. It was the same vibrant color as her lips. Her teeth sank into it. The juice squirted inside her mouth.

''The truth of the matter is, Eddy darlin', I ran out of cash. The automatic teller said it couldn't give me any money 'cause my account's overdrawn. So,'' she said, raising her arms over her head and stretching languorously, ''I came to my best friend for a little loan.''

''How little?''

''A hundred bucks?''

''I'll give you twenty just to get rid of you.'' He withdrew a bill from his pants pocket and tossed it into her lap.

''Twenty!''

''That'll buy you enough gas to get home.''

''With nothing left over.''

''If you want more, you could get it from your old man. He's in room twelve-fifteen.''

''Do you think he'd be pleased to see me? Especially if I told him I'd just come from your room?''

Not deigning to answer, Eddy consulted his watch. ''If I were you, I'd start home before it gets any later. Be careful driving back.'' He headed for the door to let her out.

''I'm hungry. Since you've been so stingy with your loan, I won't be able to afford supper. I believe that entitles me to some of this sandwich.'' She took a wedge of the triple-decker sandwich from the plate and bit into it.

''Help yourself.'' He pulled a straight chair from beneth the table, sat down, and began eating a wedge of the sandwich. He perused one of the computer readouts while he chewed.

Fancy slapped at it, knocking it out of his hand. ''Don't you dare ignore me, you bastard.''

The glint in his eyes looked dangerous. ''I didn't invite you here, you little whore. I don't want you here. If you don't like it here, you're welcome to leave any time—the sooner the better—and good riddance.''

''Oh, Eddy, don't talk like that.''

Her knees landed on the carpet as she scooted out of the chair. Suddenly contrite, she walked forward on them until she reached him. She stretched her arms up and slipped her hands inside his shirt, laying them on his bare chest. "Don't be mean to me. I love you."

"Cut it out, Fancy."

His request went unheeded. She wedged herself between his knees and kissed his stomach. "I love you so much." Her mouth and tongue moved avidly over his sleek, hairless belly. "I know you love me, too."

He grunted with involuntary pleasure as her long nails lightly scratched his nipples. She unbuckled his belt and unfastened his trousers.

"Jesus," he moaned when she lifted his hard flesh out of his underwear. His fingers dove into her wealth of blond hair. He roughly twisted bunches of it around his knuckles. From above, he watched her red, red lips slide down over his stiff organ. Her mouth was avaricious, without temperance, modesty, or conscience—an amoral mouth that had never been denied or disciplined.

He gasped her name twice. She raised her head and appealed to him, "Love me, Eddy, please."

He struggled to his feet, drawing her up with him, against him. Their mouths met in a carnal kiss. While her hands worked frantically to get his shirt off, he reached beneath the tube for her panties. Flimsy things, they came apart in his hands.

She cried out with surprise and pain when he crammed two fingers up inside her, but she rode them with crude pleasure. She had already shoved his trousers and underwear past his knees. He pushed them to his ankles and walked out of them as he lifted her to straddle his lap.

Together they fell onto the bed. He shoved up her dress and buried his face in the delta of her body while she wormed her way out of the stretchy tube. Before she had even gotten the dress over her head completely, he began squeezing her breasts, sucking and biting and twisting her nipples.

Fancy writhed beneath him, exulting in his rowdy foreplay. She raked her nails down his back and dug them into his buttocks hard enough to draw blood. He cursed her, called her ugly gutter names. When she drew back her knees, the stiletto heel of her shoe cut a jagged, six-inch gash into the bedspread, but neither noticed or would have cared.

Eddy splayed her thighs wide and thrust into her with enough impetus to drive her into the headboard. His body was already slick with sweat when she wrapped her limbs around him and matched his frenzied bucking. Their bodies slammed together, again and again.

Eddy's face contorted with a grimace of ecstasy. Arching his back, he put all his strength behind his final lunge. Fancy climaxed simultaneously.

"God, that was great!" she sighed as they rolled apart moments later.

She recovered first, sat up, and frowned at the sticky moisture on her inner thighs. She left the bed in search of the small purse she had brought in with her. She took from it a package of condoms and tossed it at him. "Use one of these next time."

"Who says there'll be a next time?"

Fancy, who was unabashedly admiring her naked body in the dresser mirror, gave his reflection an arch smile. "I'm gonna be black and blue tomorrow." She proudly touched the teeth marks on her breasts like they were small trophies. "I can already feel the bruises."

"Don't let on like you're bothered by it. You get off on being punished."

"I didn't hear you complaining, Mr. Paschal."

Still in her heels and bracelets, she strutted to the table and inspected the remnants of the tray. There was nothing left of the sundae except a puddle of white foam muddied by chocolate syrup, with a cherry floating on top.

"Oh, piss," she muttered, "the ice cream's melted."

From the bed, Eddy began to laugh.

Avery woke up before Tate. The room was deeply shadowed. It was still very early, but she knew she wouldn't go back to sleep. She tiptoed into the bathroom and showered. He was still asleep when she came out.

She took the ice bucket and the room key with her and slipped out the door in her robe. Tate enjoyed jogging every morning, even when he was out of town. When he returned, he consumed quarts of ice water. It wasn't always easy to come by in a hotel. She had started having it waiting there for him when he returned from his jog, hot and dehydrated.

She filled the bucket from the ice machine down the hall and was on her way back to their room when another door opened. Fancy stepped out and quietly closed the door behind her. She turned toward the elevators, but drew up short when she saw Avery.

Avery was shocked by the girl's appearance. Her hair was hopelessly tangled. What was left of her makeup was smudged and streaked. Her lips were bruised and swollen. There were scratches on her neck and across her chest, none of which she had made an attempt to hide. In fact, after recovering from her initial shock of seeing Avery, she defiantly tossed back her hair and threw out her chest to better display her wounds. "Good morning, Aunt Carole." Her sweet smile was in vile contrast to her debauched appearance.

Avery flattened herself against the corridor wall, at a loss for words. Fancy swept past her. She smelled unwashed and used. Avery shuddered with disgust.

The elevator arrived almost immediately after Fancy summoned it. Before stepping into it, she shot Avery a gloating smile over her bare, bruised shoulder.

For several seconds Avery stared at the elevator's closed doors, then looked toward the room Fancy had come out of, although she already knew who it belonged to.

Tate was wrong about his best friend. Eddy wasn't as scrupulous as Tate believed. Nor was he as bright.

TWENTY-SEVEN

From Houston the campaign went to Waco, and from Waco to El Paso, where Tate was the undisputed champion of the Hispanic voters. The Rutledges were received like visiting royalty. At the airport, Avery was handed a huge bouquet of fresh flowers. "*Señora Rutledge, como está?*" one of their greeters asked.

"*Muy bien, gracias. Y usted? Como se llama?*"

Her smile over the cordial welcome faltered when the man turned away and she happened to lock gazes with Tate.

"When did you learn to speak Spanish?"

For several heartbeats, Avery couldn't think of a credible lie in any language. She had minored in Spanish in college and was still comfortable with it. Tate spoke it fluently. It had never occurred to her to wonder if Carole had spoken it or not.

"I . . . I wanted to surprise you."

"I'm surprised."

"The Hispanic vote is so important," she continued, limping through her explanation. "I thought it would help if I could at least swap pleasantries, so I've been studying it on the sly."

For once, Avery was glad they were surrounded by people. Otherwise, Tate might have pressed her for details on where and when she had acquired her knowledge of Spanish. Thankfully, no one else had overheard their conversation. Tate was the only one she could trust completely.

Being with Jack, Eddy, and a few of the campaign volunteers as they traveled from city to city had provided her with no more clues as to who Carole's coconspirator was.

Carefully placed questions had revealed little. Innocently, she had asked Jack how he had managed to get into the ICU the night she regained consciousness. He had looked at her blankly. "What the hell are you talking about?"

"Never mind. Sometimes the sequence of events still confuses me."

He was either innocent or an adroit liar.

She had tried the same ploy with Eddy. He had answered by saying, "I'm not family. What would I be doing in the ICU?"

Making threats on Tate's life, she had wanted to say.

She couldn't say that, so she had mumbled something about her confusion and let it go at that, turning up nothing in the way of opportunity for either of them.

She hadn't been luckier in discerning a motive. Even when Tate disagreed with his confidants and advisers, as he often did, they all seemed devoted to him and his success at the polls.

In lieu of a campaign contribution, a private businessman had loaned the entourage his private jet. As they flew from El Paso to Odessa, where Tate was scheduled to speak to independent oil men, the key personnel aired some of their differences.

"At least talk to them, Tate." Eddy was being his most persuasive. "It won't hurt to listen to their ideas."

"I won't like them."

The argument over whether or not to hire professional campaign strategists was becoming a frequent one. Weeks earlier, Eddy had suggested retaining a public relations firm that specialized in getting candidates elected to public office. Tate had been vehemently opposed to the idea and remained so.

"How do you know you won't like their ideas until you've heard what they are?" Jack asked.

"If the voters can't elect me for what I am—"

"The voters, the voters," Eddy repeated scoffingly. "The voters don't know shit from Shinola. What's more, they don't want to. They're lazy and apathetic. They want somebody to tell them who to vote for. They want it drummed into their feeble little minds so they won't have to make a decision on their own."

"Great confidence you're showing in the American public, Eddy."

"I'm not the idealist, Tate. You are."

"Thank God I am. Rather that than a cynic. I believe that people do care," he shouted. "They do listen to the issues. They respond to straight talk. I want to get the issues across to the voters without having to filter the language and phraseology through some bullshitting P.R. jargon."

"Okay, okay." Eddy patted the air between them. "Since that subject is a sore spot, let's table it for now and talk about the Hispanics."

"What about them?"

"Next time you're addressing an audience of them, don't lean so hard on their integrating into our society."

"*Our* society?"

"I'm thinking like an Anglo voter now."

"It's important that they integrate into American society," Tate argued, not for the first time. "That's the only way we can keep society from being distinguished as yours, ours, or theirs. Haven't you been listening to my speeches?"

"Stress that they maintain their own customs."

"I did. I did say that. Didn't I say that?" he asked everyone within hearing distance.

"He said that." It was Avery who spoke up. Eddy ignored her.

"I just think it's important that you don't broadcast the message that they should give up their culture in favor of Anglo America's."

"If they live here, Eddy—if they become citizens of this country—they've got to assume some of the customs, primarily the English language."

Eddy was undeterred. "See, the Anglos don't like hearing that their society is going to be invaded by the Hispanics, any better than the Hispanics like having Anglo customs crammed down their throat, including a new language. Get elected first and then make a point of that integration bit, okay? And try to avoid addressing the drug trafficking problem that exists between Texas and Mexico."

"I agree," Jack said. "When you're a senator you can do something about it. Why wave the drug problem like a red flag now? It gives everybody room to criticize that you're either too harsh or too soft."

Tate laughed with disbelief and spread his hands wide. "I'm running for the U.S. Senate, and I'm not supposed to have an opinion on how to handle the illegal flow of drugs into my own state?"

"Of course you're supposed to have an opinion," Jack said, as though he were humoring a child.

"Just don't bring up your plans to remedy the problem unless specifically asked to. Now, as for this Odessa crowd," Eddy said, consulting his notes.

Eddy was never without notes. Watching him organize them, Avery studied his hands. Had those hands inflicted the scratches and bruises on Fancy, or had she come to him for refuge after another cowboy had worked her over?

"For God's sake, try to be on time to every engagement."

"I explained why we were late to that breakfast speech this morning. Carole had been trying to reach Mom and Dad, and finally caught them at home. They wanted to know everything that was going on, then we each had to talk to Mandy."

Eddy and Jack looked at her. As always, she felt their unspoken criticism, although she had done her best not to cause them any inconvenience on the trip. Out of spite, she said to Jack, "Dorothy Rae and Fancy sent you their love."

"Oh, well, thanks."

She slid a glance at Eddy when she mentioned Fancy's name. His eyes focused on her sharply, but he returned his attention to Tate. "Before we land, get rid of that tie."

"What's the matter with it?"

"It looks like shit, that's what's the matter with it."

For once, Avery sided with Eddy. Tate's necktie wasn't the most attractive one she'd ever seen, but she resented Eddy being so tactless about pointing it out.

"Here, switch with me," Jack suggested, tugging at the knot of his tie.

"No, yours is worse," Eddy said with characteristic candor. "Switch with me."

"Fuck you both and fuck the tie," Tate said. He flopped back in the airplane's plush seat. "Leave me alone." Resting his head on the cushion, he closed his eyes, effectively shutting out everybody.

Avery applauded him for telling them off, even though he had shut her out, too. Since the night in Houston when they had come so close to making love, Tate had taken even greater strides to keep his distance from her. That wasn't always easy because they had to share a bathroom, if not a bed. They went to ridiculous pains to avoid being seen unclothed. They never touched. When they spoke, they usually snapped at each other like two animals who had been sharing the same cage for too long.

Tate's even breathing could soon be heard over the drone of the airplane's engines. He could fall asleep almost instantly, sleep for several minutes, and wake up refreshed—a skill he had developed while in Vietnam, he had told her. She liked watching him sleep and often did so during the night when she found her mind too troubled to give over to unconsciousness.

"Do something."

Eddy had leaned across the narrow aisle of the airplane and roused her from her woolgathering. He and Jack were glaring at her like interrogators. "About what?"

"About Tate."

"What do you want me to do? Start picking out his neckties?"

"Convince him to let me retain that P.R. firm."

"Don't you feel that you're doing an adequate job, Eddy?" she asked coolly.

Belligerently, he thrust his face close to hers. "You think I'm ruthless? Those guys wouldn't take any of your crap."

"What crap?" she shot back.

"Like your screening Tate's calls."

"If you're referring to last night, he was already asleep when you phoned. He needed the rest. He was exhausted."

"When I want to talk to him, I want to talk to him right then," he said, jabbing the space between them. "Got that, Carole? Now, about these professionals—"

"He doesn't want them. He thinks they build a phony, plastic image and so do I."

"Nobody asked you," Jack said.

"When I have an opinion about my husband's campaign, I'll bloody well express it, and you can go to the devil if you don't like it!"

"Do you want to be a senator's wife or not?"

A silent moment elapsed while they collectively cooled their tempers. Eddy went on in a conciliatory tone, "Do whatever it takes to get Tate out of this rotten, short-tempered mood, Carole. It's self-destructive."

"The crowds don't know he's in a foul mood."

"But the volunteers do."

"Jack's right," Eddy said. "Several have noticed and commented on it. It's demoralizing. They want their hero on top of the world and radiating a lust for life, not moping around. Get him right with the world, Carole." Having concluded his pep talk, Eddy resumed his seat and went back to scanning his notes.

Jack frowned at her. "You're the one who's put him in this blue funk. You're the only one who can get him out. Don't play like you don't know how, because we all know better."

The heated exchange left Avery feeling frustrated and unable to do anything about a bad situation they clearly blamed on her.

It was a relief to land and leave the compact jet. She plastered on a smile for the crowd that had gathered to meet them. Her smile dissipated, however, when she spotted Van Lovejoy among the press photographers. He turned up everywhere Tate Rutledge went these days. His presence never failed to unnerve Avery.

As soon as it was feasible, she stepped into the background, where it would be harder for the lens of a camera to find her. From that vantage point, she looked out over the crowd, constantly on the alert for anyone looking suspicious. This crowd was largely comprised of media, Rutledge supporters, and curious onlookers.

A tall man standing at the back of the crowd arrested her attention, only because he looked familiar. He was dressed in a tailored western suit and cowboy hat, and she first took him for one of the oil men Tate was there to address.

She couldn't pinpoint where or when she had seen him before but she didn't think he'd been dressed as he was now. She would have remembered the cowboy hat. But she had seen him recently, she was sure of that. The barbecue in Houston, perhaps? Before she could cite the time and place, he faded into the throng and was lost from sight.

Avery was hustled toward the waiting limousine. At her side, the mayor's wife was gushing like a fountain. She tried to pay attention to what the other woman was saying, but her mind had been diverted by the gray-haired man who had so adroitly disappeared an instant after they'd made eye contact.

As soon as the immediate area was cleared of the senatorial candidate, his entourage, and the media jackals, the well-dressed cowboy emerged from the telephone cubicle. Tate Rutledge was an easy target to follow through the airport. They were both tall, but while Tate wanted to be seen, the cowboy prided himself on his ability to merge into a crowd and remain virtually invisible.

For such a large man, he moved with grace and ease. His carriage alone commanded respect from anyone who happened to fall into his path. At the car rental office, the clerk was exceptionally polite. His bearing seemed to demand good service. He laid down a credit card. It had a false name on it, but it cleared the electronic check system it was run through.

He thanked the clerk as she dropped the tagged key into his hand. "Do you need a map of the area, sir?"

"No, thank you. I know where I'm going."

He carried his clothes in one bag, packed efficiently and economically. The contents were untraceable and disposable; so was the rented sedan, if that became necessary.

The airport was located midway between Midland and Odessa. He headed toward the westernmost city, following the limousine carrying Rutledge at a safe, discreet distance.

He mustn't get too close. He was almost certain Carole Rutledge had picked him out of the crowd while her husband was shaking hands with his local supporters. It was unlikely that she had recognized him from that distance, but in his business, nothing could be taken for granted.

TWENTY-EIGHT

A king-size bed.

"I don't envy the women of Texas. Like the women of every state in this nation, they're faced with serious problems—problems that require immediate solutions. Daily solutions. Problems such as quality child care."

Even as Tate waxed eloquent at a luncheon meeting of professional women, his mind was on that one large bed in the room at the Adolphus Hotel.

After landing at Love Field, they had rushed to check in, freshen up, and make the luncheon on time. The hectic schedule hadn't dimmed his one prevalent thought: tonight he would be sharing a bed with Carole.

"Some corporations, many of which I'm pleased to say are located here in Dallas, have started day-care programs for their employees. But these companies with vision and innovative ideas are still in the minority. I want to see something done about that."

Over the applause, Tate was hearing in his mind the accommodating bellman ask, "Will there be anything else, Mr. Rutledge?"

That's when he should have said, "Yes, I'd prefer a room with separate beds."

The applause died down. Tate covered his extended pause by taking a sip of water. From the corner of his eye, he could see Carole looking up at him curiously from her place at the head table. She looked more tempting than the rich desert he had declined following lunch. He would decline her, too.

"Equal pay for equal work is a tired subject," he said into the microphone. "The American public is weary of hearing about it. But I'm going to keep harping on it until those who are opposed to it are worn down. Obliterated. Banished."

The applause was thunderous. Tate smiled disarmingly and tried to avoid looking up the skirt of the woman in the front row who was offering him a spectacular view.

While they had scrambled to get ready in the limited time allowed, he'd caught an accidental glimpse of his wife through a crack in the partially opened bathroom door.

She was wearing a pastel brassiere. Pastel hosiery. Pastel garter belt. She had a saucy ass. Soft thighs.

She had leaned into the mirror and dusted her nose with a powder puff. He'd gotten stiff and had stayed that way through the wilted salad, mystery meat, and cold green beans.

Clearing his throat now, he said, "The crimes against women are of major concern to me. The number of rapes is increasing each year, but the number of offenders who are prosecuted and brought to trial is lamentably low.

"Domestic violence has been around as long as there have been families. Thankfully, this outrage has finally come to the conscience of our society. That's good. But is enough being done to reverse this rising trend?

"Mr. Dekker suggests that counseling is the answer. Toward reaching a final solution, yes, I agree. But I submit that police action is a necessary first step. Legal separation from the source and guaranteed safety for the victims—most frequently women and children—is mandatory. Then and only then should counseling and reconciliation be addressed."

When the applause subsided, he moved into the final fervent paragraphs of his speech. As soon as this meeting concluded, they were scheduled to go to a General Motors assembly plant in neighboring Arlington, to mingle with the workers as they changed shifts.

After that they would return to the hotel, watch the evening news, peruse the newspapers, and dress for the formal dinner being held in his honor at Southfork. And late tonight, they would return to the king-size bed.

"I'll be expecting your support in November. Thank you very much."

He received an enthusiastic standing ovation. He signaled for Carole to join him at the podium. She took her place beside him. He slid his arm around her waist, as expected. What wasn't expected was the thrill he got from having her that close, feeling small and feminine against his side. She tilted her head back and smiled up at him with what appeared to be admiration and love.

She could put on a hell of an act.

It was almost half an hour before Eddy was able to separate them from the adoring crowd that was reluctant to let them go. The September heat struck them like a blast furnace as they exited the meeting hall.

"Jack is holding a call for me back there," Eddy explained as he herded them toward a car parked at the curb. "Some glitch about tonight. Nothing serious. We'll follow you out to the assembly plant. If you don't leave right now you won't make it in time. Know where it is?"

"Off I-30, right?" Tate shrugged off his suit jacket and tossed it into the backseat of the rented car.

"Right." Eddy detailed the directions. "You can't miss it. It'll be on your right." He glanced at Carole. "I'll call you a cab back to the hotel."

"I'm going with Tate." She slid beneath his arm into the passenger seat.

"I think—"

"It's okay, Eddy," Tate said. "She can come with me."

"She'll stick out like a sore thumb. That's no ladies' club out there."

"Tate wants me there and I want to go," she argued.

"All right," he conceded, but Tate could tell he was none too pleased. "We'll catch up with you shortly." He closed Carole's passenger door and they sped off.

"He never passes up an opportunity to make me feel like a useless appendage, does he?" she said. "I'm surprised he approved of you marrying me."

"He didn't have a chance. We couldn't track him down, remember?"

"Of course I remember," she said crossly. "I only meant . . . oh, never mind. I don't want to talk about Eddy."

"I know he's not one of your favorite people. Sometimes his nagging can be a real pain in the ass. But his instincts are rarely wrong."

"I trust his instincts," she said. "I'm not so sure I trust him."

"What's he ever done to make you mistrust him?"

She averted her head and gazed out the windshield. "Nothing, I guess. Lord, it's hot."

Leaning as far forward as the seat belt would allow, she pulled off her suit jacket. Beneath it was a matching silk blouse. Beneath that, her breasts filled up the lacy yellow brassiere he'd seen while peeping through the bathroom door.

"You were brilliant, Tate," she remarked. "Not condescending or patronizing. They wouldn't have condoned that. As it was, they were eating out of your hand." She glanced at him sideways. "Especially the one in the bright blue dress on the front row. What color were her panties?"

"She wasn't wearing any."

The blunt retort knocked the props out from under her. She hadn't been expecting it. Her teasing smile evaporated. Again, she turned her head forward and stared through the windshield.

He could tell she was wounded. Well, that was fair, wasn't it? He'd been nursing this ache in his groin for days. Why should he be the only one to suffer? An imp was sitting on his shoulder goading him to make her as miserable as he was.

"I avoided the abortion issue. Did you notice?"

"No."

"I didn't know what to say. Maybe I should have called you to the lectern. You could have given us a firsthand account of what it's like."

When she faced him, there were tears in her eyes. "I told you I'd never had an abortion."

"But I'll never know for certain which time you were lying, will I?"

"Why are you being this way, Tate?"

Because there is a *king-size bed* in our room, he thought. Before I share it with you, I've got to remind myself of all the reasons I despise you.

He didn't say that, of course.

He took the cloverleaf at the highway interchange at an indiscriminate speed. Once again on a straightaway, he speeded up even more. If it hadn't been for some quick thinking and daredevil driving, he would have overshot the exit.

There was a delegation waiting for them at the gate to the automotive plant. Tate parked a distance away so he'd have time to collect himself before having to be civil. He felt like a brawl. He wanted to slug it out. He didn't feel like smiling and promising to solve labor's problems when he couldn't even solve his own marital dilemma. He didn't want any part of his wife except *that* part, and he wanted it with every masculine fiber of his body.

"Put your jacket back on," he ordered her, even though he was removing his tie and rolling up his shirtsleeves.

"I intend to," she replied coolly.

"Good. Your nipples are poking against your blouse. Or is that what you had in mind?"

"Go to hell," she said sweetly as she shoved open her car door.

He had to give her credit. She recovered admirably from his stinging insults and conversed intelligently with the union bosses who were there to greet them. Eddy and Jack arrived about the time the shift changed and the doors of the plant began to disgorge workers. Those coming to work converged on them from the parking lot. Tate shook hands with everyone he could reach.

Each time he glanced at Carole, she was campaigning just as diligently as he. She listened intently to whomever was speaking with her. As Eddy had said, dressed in her yellow silk, she did stick out in this crowd. Her dark hair reflected the sunlight like a mirror. Her flawless face didn't distance people, but attracted women workers as well as men.

Tate looked for something to criticize, but could find nothing. She reached for dirty hands and gave them a friendly shake. Her smile was unflagging, even though the crowd was rambunctious and the heat unbearable.

And she was the first one to reach his side when something struck him and he went down.

 # TWENTY-NINE

Avery happened to be watching Tate when his head suddenly snapped backward. Reflexively, he raised his hand to his forehead, reeled, then fell.

"No!"

There were only a few yards separating them, but the crowd was dense. It seemed to take forever for her to push her way through the people. She ruined her stockings and skinned her knees when she landed on the hot pavement beside Tate.''

"Tate! Tate!" Blood was oozing from a wound on the side of his head. "Get a doctor, somebody. Eddy! Jack! Somebody do something. He's hurt!"

"I'm all right." He struggled to sit up. Swaying dizzily, he groped for support, found Avery's arm, and held on tight.

Since Tate could speak and make an effort to sit up, she was sure that the bullet had only grazed him and not penetrated his skull. She cushioned his head on her breasts. His blood ran warm and wet down the front of her clothing, but she didn't even notice.

"Jesus, what happened?" Eddy finally managed to elbow his way through the crowd to them. "Tate?"

"I'm okay," he mumbled. Gradually, Avery released her hold on his head. "Give me a handkerchief."

"They're calling an ambulance."

"No need to. Something hit me." He glanced around him, searching through a forest of feet and legs. "That," he said, pointing to the broken beer bottle lying nearby on the pavement.

"Who the hell threw it?"

"Did you see him?" Avery was prepared to do battle with the attacker.

"No, I didn't see anything. Give me a handkerchief," he repeated. Eddy took one from his pocket. Avery snatched it from him and pressed it to the bleeding gash near Tate's hairline. "Thanks. Now help me up."

"I'm not sure you should try and stand," she cautioned.

"I'm okay." He smiled unsteadily. "Just help me get up off my ass, okay?"

"I could throttle you for joking at a time like this."

"Sorry. Somebody beat you to it."

As she and Eddy helped him to his feet, Jack ran up, huffing for breath. "A couple of the workers don't like your politics. The police have arrested them."

There was a commotion at the far corner of the parking lot. Anti-Rutledge picket signs bobbed up and down like pogo sticks. "Rutledge is a pinko fag," read one. "Vote for a bleeding liberal? You're bleeding crazy!" read another. And "Rutledge is a rutting commie."

"Let's go," Eddy ordered.

"No." Tate's lips were stiff and white from a combination of anger and pain. "I came here to shake hands and ask for votes, and that's what I'm going to do. A couple of bottle throwers aren't going to stop me."

"Tate, Eddy's right." Avery clutched his arm tightly. "This is a police matter now."

She had died a thousand deaths on her headlong rush to reach him. She had thought, "This is it. This is what I wanted to prevent, and I have failed to." The incident brought home to her just how vulnerable he was. What kind of protection could she offer him? If someone wanted to kill him badly enough, he could. There wouldn't be a damn thing she or anyone else could do to prevent it.

"Hello, I'm Tate Rutledge, running for the U.S. Senate." Stubbornly, Tate turned to the man standing nearest him. The UAW member looked down at Tate's extended hand, then glanced around uncertainly at his co-workers. Finally, he shook Tate's hand. "I would appreciate your vote in November," he told the man before moving to the next. "Hi, I'm Tate Rutledge."

Despite his advisers, Tate moved through the crowd, shaking hands with his right hand, holding the blood-stained handkerchief to his temple with the left. Avery had never loved him so much.

Nor had she ever been more afraid for him.

"How do I look?"

Tate asked for her opinion only after dubiously consulting his reflection in the mirror. He'd remained on the parking lot of the assembly plant until those going off duty had left for home and those reporting to work had gone inside.

Only then had he allowed Eddy and her to push him into the backseat of the car and rush him to the nearest emergency room. Jack, who followed in the second car, joined them there, where a resident physician took three stitches and covered them with a small, square white bandage.

Avery had placed a call to Nelson and Zee from the emergency room, knowing that if they heard about the incident on the news they would be worried. They insisted on speaking with Tate. He joked about the injury, although Avery saw him gratefully accept the painkiller the nurse gave him.

A horde of reporters was waiting for them in the lobby of the Adolphus when they returned. They surged forward en masse. "Be sure they get pictures of the blood on your dress," Eddy had told her out the side of his mouth.

For that insensitive remark, she could easily have scratched his eyes out. "You bastard."

"I'm just doing my job, Carole," he said blandly. "Making the most of every situation—even the bad ones."

She had been too incensed to offer a comeback. Besides, they were battling their way through microphones and cameras toward the elevators. At the door to their room, she confronted Jack and Eddy, who were about to follow them inside.

"Tate is going to lie down and let that pain pill take effect," she told them, barring any arguments to the contrary. "I'm going to tell the switchboard not to put any calls through."

"He's got to make some kind of statement."

"You write it," she said to Jack. "You would rewrite whatever he said anyway. Just remember what he told us on the drive back. He doesn't intend to press charges against the man who threw the bottle, although he abhors violence and considers it a base form of self-expression. Nor does he blame the UAW as a group for the actions of a few members. I'm sure you can elaborate on that."

"I'll pick you up here at seven-thirty," Eddy said as he turned to go. Over his shoulder, he added peremptorily, "Sharp."

Tate had dozed for a while, then watched the news before getting up to shower and dress. Now he turned away from the bureau mirror and faced her, lifting his hands away from his sides. "Well?"

Tilting her head, she gave him a thoughtful appraisal. "Very rakish." His hair dipped attractively over the wound. "The bandage adds a cavalier dash to your very proper tuxedo."

"Well, that's good," he muttered, tentatively touching the bandage, "because it hurts like bloody hell."

Avery moved nearer and gazed up at him with concern. "We don't have to go."

"Eddy would shit a brick."

"Let him. Everyone else would understand. If Michael Jackson can cancel a concert because of a stomach virus, disappointing thousands of adoring fans, you can cancel a dinner and disappoint a couple hundred."

"But have Michael Jackson's fans paid two hundred dollars a plate?" he quipped. "He can afford to cancel. I can't."

"A least take another pill."

He shook his head. "If I go, I've got to be in full command of my faculties."

"Lord, you're stubborn. Just like you were about staying there this afternoon."

"It made great video on the evening news."

She frowned at him. "You sound like Eddy now. You're running for public office, not best target of the year for every kook with a grudge against the system. You shouldn't place your life in jeopardy just because it makes for good film at six and ten."

"Listen, it's only because I'm running for public office that I didn't go after that son of a bitch who threw the bottle and beat the crap out of him myself."

"Ah, that's what I like. A candidate who really speaks his mind."

They laughed together, but after a moment their laughter died. Tate's warm gaze held hers. "That's still my favorite dress. You look terrific."

"Thank you." She was wearing the black cocktail dress he had admired before.

"I, uh, behaved like a jerk this afternoon."

"You said some hurtful things."

"I know," he admitted, blowing out a gust of air. "I meant to. Partially because—"

A knock sounded. "Seven-thirty," Eddy called through the door.

Tate looked annoyed. Avery, at the height of frustration, yanked up her evening bag and marched toward the door. Her senses were sizzling. Her nerves were shot. She felt like screaming.

She almost did when one of the first people she spotted among the crowd at Southfork was the man she'd noticed once before, at the Midland/Odessa Airport.

The ranch house made famous by the television series "Dallas" was ablaze with lights. Since this was a special night, the house was open and partygoers were allowed to walk through it. The actual dinner was being held in the adjacent barnlike building that was frequently leased for large parties.

The turnout was better than expected. As soon as they arrived they were informed that it was a capacity crowd. Many had offered to pay more than two hundred dollars for the opportunity to attend and hear Tate speak.

"No doubt as a result of that fantastic news story today," Eddy said. "All the networks and local channels led with it on their six o'clock telecasts." He flashed Avery a complacent smile.

She slid her arm through the crook of Tate's elbow, an indication that he was more important to her than any news story, or even the election itself. Eddy's grin merely widened.

Avery was liking him less every day. His inappropriate dalliance with Fancy was reason enough for her to distrust his Boy Scout cleanliness.

Tate, however, trusted him implicitly. That's why she hadn't mentioned seeing Fancy coming out of Eddy's room, even when Tate had provided her an opportunity to. She could sense a softening in Tate's attitude toward her and didn't want it jeopardized by bad-mouthing his trusted best friend.

She tried to put aside Eddy's remark and all other worries as she walked into the cavernous building with Tate. He would need her to bolster him tonight. The injury was probably causing him more discomfort than he let on. An enthusiastic local supporter approached them. He bussed Avery on the cheek and pumped Tate's hand. It was as she tossed back her head to laugh at a comment he made that she caught sight of the tall, gray-haired man on the fringes of the crowd.

She did a double take, but almost instantly lost sight of him. Surely she was mistaken. The man at the airport had been wearing a western suit and Stetson. This man was dressed in formal clothing. They were probably just coincidental look-alikes.

While trying to appear attentive to the people approaching them to be introduced, she continued to scan the crowd, but didn't catch sight of the man again
before dinner. From the head table it was difficult to see into the darkest corners
of the enormous hall. Even though it was a formal dinner, people were milling
about. Frequently, she had television lights blindingly trained on her.

"Not hungry?" Tate leaned toward her and nodded down at her virtually
untouched plate.

"Too much excitement."

Actually, she was sick with worry and considered warning Tate of the danger he
was in. She regarded the bandage on his forehead as an obscenity. Next time it
might not be an empty beer bottle. It might be a bullet. And it might be deadly.

"Tate," she asked hesitantly, "have you seen a tall, gray-haired man?"

He laughed shortly. "About fifty of them."

"One in particular. I thought he looked familiar."

"Maybe he belongs in one of those memory pockets that hasn't opened up for
you yet."

"Yes, maybe."

"Say, are you all right?"

Forcing a smile, she raised her lips to his ear and whispered, "The candidate's
wife has to go to the ladies' room. Would that be kosher?"

"More kosher than the consequences if she doesn't."

He stood to assist her out of her chair. She excused herself. At the end of the
dais, a waiter took her hand and helped her down the shaky portable steps. As
unobtrusively as possible, she searched the crowd for the man with gray hair while
making her way toward an exit.

As she cleared the doorway, she felt both frustrated and relieved. She was
almost positive he had been the same man she'd spotted in West Texas. On the
other hand, there were tens of thousands of tall Texans with gray hair. Feeling a
little foolish over her paranoia, she smiled to herself ruefully.

Her smile congealed when someone moved in close behind her and whispered
menacingly, "Hello, Avery."

 # THIRTY

At midnight, the McDonald's restaurant at the corner of Commerce and Griffin
in downtown Dallas looked like a goldfish bowl. It was brightly lit. Through
the plate glass windows, everyone inside was as clearly visible as actors standing
on center stage.

The cashier was taking an order from a somber loner. A wino was sleeping it off
in one of the booths. Two giddy teenage couples were squirting catsup on each
other.

Breathless from having walked three blocks from the hotel, Avery approached
the restaurant cautiously. Her formal attire distinguished her from everyone else
who was out and about. It was foolhardy for a woman to be walking the downtown
streets alone at this hour anyway.

From across the street, she peered into the capsulized brilliance of the dining
room. She saw him, sitting alone in a booth. Fortunately, the booth was adjacent
to the windows. As soon as the traffic light changed, she hurried across the broad
avenue, her high heels clacking on the pavement.

"Mmm-mmm, mamma, lookin' good!" A black youth licentiously wagged his tongue at her. With punches and guffaws, his two chums congratulated him. On the corner, two women, one with orange hair, the other with burgundy, competed for the attentions of a man in tight leather pants. He was leaning against the traffic light post, looking bored, until Avery walked by. He gave her a carnivorous once-over. The orange-haired woman spun around, propped her hands on her hips, and shouted at Avery. "Hey, bitch, keep your ass outta his face or I'll kill you."

Avery ignored them all as she walked past, moving along the sidewalk toward the booth. When she drew even with it, she knocked on the window. Van Lovejoy looked up from his chocolate milk shake, spotted her, and grinned. He indicated the other bench of the booth. Avery angrily and vehemently shook her head no and sternly pointed down at the grimy sidewalk beneath her black satin shoes.

He took his sweet time. She impatiently followed his unhurried progress through the restaurant, out the door, and around the corner, so that by the time he reached her, she was simmering with rage.

"What the hell are you up to, Van?" she demanded.

Feigning innocence, he curled both lanky hands in toward his chest. "*Moi*?"

"Did we have to meet here? At this time of night?"

"Would you rather I had come to your room—the room you're sharing with another woman's husband?" In the ensuing silence, he casually lit a joint. After two tokes, he offered it to Avery. She slapped his hand aside.

"You can't imagine the danger you placed me in by speaking to me tonight."

He leaned against the plate glass window. "I'm all ears."

"Van." Miserably, she caught her head with her hand and massaged her temples. "It's too difficult to explain—especially here." The women at the corner were loudly swapping obscenities while the man in leather cleaned his fingernails with a pocketknife. "I slipped out of the hotel. If Tate discovers that I'm gone—"

"Does he know you're not his wife?"

"No! And he mustn't."

"How come?"

"It'll take a while to explain."

"I'm under no deadline."

"But I am," she cried, clutching his skinny arm. "Van, you can't tell anybody. Lives would be put in danger."

"Yeah, Rutledge just might be pissed off enough to kill you."

"I'm talking about Tate's life. This isn't a game, trust me. There's a lot at stake. You'll agree when I've had a chance to explain. But I can't now. I've got to get back."

"This is quite a gig, Avery. When did you decide to do it?"

"In the hospital. I was mistaken for Carole Rutledge. They had done the reconstructive operation on my face before I could tell them otherwise."

"When you could, why didn't you?"

Frantically, she groped for an expeditious way to tell him. "Ask Irish," she blurted out.

"Irish!" he croaked, choking on marijuana smoke. "That cagy son of a bitch. He knows?"

"Not until recently. I had to tell somebody."

"So that's why he sent me on this trip. I wondered why we were covering Rutledge like he was fuckin' royalty or something. It was you Irish wanted me to keep an eye on."

"I guess. I didn't know he was going to assign you this detail. I was stunned when I saw you in Houston. It was bad enough when I answered the door that day at the ranch and you were standing on the porch. Is that when you first recognized me?"

"The day you left the clinic, I noticed how Mrs. Rutledge's mannerisms in front of a camera were similar to yours. It was spooky the way she wet her lips and made that movement with her head just like you used to. After that day of taping at the ranch, I was almost conviced. Tonight I was so sure of it, I decided to let you know that I was in on your little secret."

"Oh, Lord."

"What?"

Over Van's shoulder Avery had spotted a patrolman approaching them on foot.

"Okay, what is it?" Tate asked his brother irritably.

Jack closed the door to his hotel room and shrugged out of his formal jacket. "Drink?"

"No thanks. What's up?"

The moment they entered the lobby of the Adolphus, Jack had cupped Tate's elbow and whispered that he needed to see him alone.

"What, now?"

"Now."

Tate didn't feel like holding a closed-door session with his brother tonight. The only one he wanted to speak with privately was his wife, who had been behaving strangely since their arrival at Southfork. Before that, she had been fine.

Over dinner, she had mentioned a gray-haired man—obviously someone from her past who had inconveniently showed up at the banquet. Whoever he was, he must have confronted her when she had gone to the ladies' room, because she had returned to the head table looking pale and shaken.

She'd been as jumpy as a cat for the remainder of the evening. Several times he had caught her nervously gnawing on her lower lip. When she did smile, it was phony as hell. He hadn't had an opportunity to get to the bottom of it. He wanted to now—right now.

But for the sake of harmony within the camp, he decided to humor Jack first. While they were waiting for an elevator, he had turned to her and said, "Jack wants to see me for five minutes." He shot his brother a meaningful glance that said, "No more than five minutes."

"Oh, now?" she had asked. "In that case, I'm going back to the concierge and ask for some brochures and, uh, hotel stationery to take to Mandy. I won't be long. I'll see you in the room."

The elevator had arrived. She'd dashed off. He'd gone up with Jack and Eddy. Eddy had said good night and gone to his own room, leaving the two brothers alone.

Tate waited expectantly as Jack withdrew a white envelope from the breast pocket of his tux and passed it to him. It had his name handwritten on it. He slid his index finger beneath the flap and ripped it open. After reading the message twice, he looked up at his brother from beneath his brows.

"Who gave you this?"

Jack was pouring himself a nightcap from a bottle of brandy. "Remember the lady—woman—in blue at the luncheon this afternoon? Front row."

Tate hitched his chin toward the liquor bottle. "I changed my mind." Jack handed him a drink. Tate held the note at arm's length and reread it as he polished off the brandy in one long swallow.

"Why'd she ask you to deliver it?" he asked his brother.

"I guess she didn't think it would be proper for her to deliver it herself."

"Proper?" Tate scoffed, glancing again at the brazen wording of the note.

Not even attempting to conceal his amusement, Jack asked, "May I hazard a guess what it's about?"

"Bingo."

"May I offer a suggestion?"

"No."

"It wouldn't hurt to accept her invitation. In fact, it might help."

"Has it escaped your attention that I'm married?"

"No. It also hasn't escaped my attention that your marriage isn't worth shit right now, but you wouldn't welcome my comments about either your wife or your marriage."

"That's right, I wouldn't."

"Don't get defensive, Tate. I've got your interests at heart. You know that. Take advantage of this invitation. I don't know what's going on between Carole and you." He lowered one eyelid shrewdly. "But I know what *isn't*. You're not sleeping together and haven't since long before the crash. There's not a man alive, not even you, who can function at his optimum best if his dick's unhappy."

"Speaking from experience?"

Jack lowered his head and concentrated on the swirling contents of his glass. Tate raked his fingers through his hair, wincing when it pulled against the sutured gash on his temple. "Sorry. That was uncalled for. Forgive me, Jack. It's just that I resent everybody meddling in my business."

"Comes with the territory, little brother."

"But I'm sick of it."

"It's only started. It won't end when you get into office."

Tate propped his hips against the dresser. "No, I guess not." Silently, he studied the nap of the carpet. After a moment, a small laugh started in his chest and gradually worked its way out.

"What?" Jack failed to see the humor in their conversation.

"Not too long ago, Eddy offered to find me a woman to work my frustrations out on. Where were the two of you when I was young and single and could have used a couple of good pimps?"

Jack smiled wryly. "I guess I deserve that. It's just that you've been so uptight lately, I thought a harmless roll in the hay with a lusty, willing broad would do you good."

"It probably would, but no thanks." Tate moved toward the door. "Thanks for the drink, too." With his hand on the doorknob, he asked as an afterthought, "Talked with your family recently?"

"Speaking of 'drink,' hey?"

"It just came out that way," Tate replied, looking chagrined.

"Don't worry about it. Yes, I talked to Dorothy Rae today. She said everything was fine. She can tell that Fancy's up to mischief, but doesn't yet know what it is."

"God only knows."

"Maybe God knows. Sure as hell nobody else does."

"Good night, Jack."

"Uh, Tate?" He turned back. "Since you're not interested . . ." Tate followed his brother's gaze down to the note he still held in his hand. Jack shrugged. "She might be willing to settle for second best."

Tate balled up the paper and tossed it to his brother, who caught it with one hand. "Good luck."

Tate had already removed his jacket, tie, and cummerbund by the time he opened the door to his room. "Carole? I know that took longer than five minutes, but . . . Carole?"

She wasn't there.

When she saw the policeman, Avery averted her head. The sequin trim on her dress seemed to glitter as brilliantly as the golden arches outside the restaurant. "For heaven's sake, put out that cigarette," she said to Van. "He'll think . . ."

"Forget it," her friend interrupted, smiling crookedly. "If you were a whore, I couldn't afford you." He pinched out the burning tip of the joint and dropped it back into his shirt pocket.

While the policeman was busy breaking up the shouting match at the corner, Avery indicated with her head that they should slip around the corner and head back toward the Adolphus. With his slouching gait, Van fell into step beside her.

"Van, I need your promise that you won't reveal my identity to anyone. One night next week, when we're back home, I'll arrange a meeting between Irish, you, and me. He'll want to hear about my trip anyway. I'll fill in the blanks then."

"What do you think Dekker would pay for this information?"

Avery came to an abrupt halt. She roughly grabbed Van's arm. "You can't! Van, please. My God, you can't."

"Until you make me a better offer, I might." He threw off her hand and turned away, calling back, "See ya, Avery."

They were even with the hotel now, but across the street. She trotted after him and caught his arm again, swinging him around. "You don't know how high the stakes are, Van. I'm begging you, as my friend."

"I don't have any friends."

"Please don't do anything until I've had a chance to explain the circumstances."

He pulled his arm free again. "I'll think about it. But your explanation better be damn good, or I'm cashing in."

She watched his sauntering retreat down the sidewalk. He seemed not to have a care in the world. Her world, by contrast, had caved in. Van was holding all the aces and he knew it.

Feeling like she'd just been bludgeoned, she crossed the street toward the hotel. Just before she reached the opposite curb, she raised her head.

Tate was standing in the porte cochere, glaring at her.

THIRTY-ONE

His expression was murderous. After a few faltering steps, Avery moved toward him with the undaunted carriage of a criminal who knows the jig is up but is still unwilling to confess.

"There she is, Mr. Rutledge," the doorman said cheerfully. "I told you she would probably be back any second."

For the doorman's benefit, Tate kept his voice light. "I was getting worried, Carole." His fingers wrapped around her upper arm with the strength of a python.

He "escorted" her through the lobby. In the elevator, they faced forward, saying nothing, while anger arced between them. He unlocked the door to their room and let her precede him inside.

The security lock had a final, metallic sound when he flipped it forward. Neither reached for a light. Neither thought to. For illumination, they relied solely on the weak night-light burning in the bathroom behind a *faux* nautilus shell.

"Where the hell did you go?" Tate demanded without preamble.

"To the McDonald's on the corner. Remember, I didn't eat much dinner at the banquet. I was hungry. As long as you were with Jack, I thought—"

"Who was the guy?"

She started to play dumb, but thought better of it. He had obviously seen her with Van, but hadn't recognized him. While she was deliberating on whether to shoot straight or lie, he advanced on her. "Was he a dealer?"

Her jaw went slack with astonishment. "A drug dealer?"

"I know that on occasion you and Fancy have smoked pot. I hope to God that's all you've done, but a senatorial candidate's wife doesn't buy grass off the street from an unknown pusher, Carole. For God's sake, he could have been an undercover—"

"That was Van Lovejoy!" she shouted angrily. Obviously the name didn't ring any bells. He gave her a blank stare. "The cameraman from KTEX. He shot the video for your TV commercial. Remember?"

She knocked him aside and swept past him, moved to the dresser and began removing her jewelry, dropping the pieces onto the surface with little regard for their value or delicacy.

"What were you doing with him?"

"Walking," she said flippantly, addressing his reflection behind her own in the mirror. In the dim light he appeared dark and intimidating. She refused to be cowed. "I ran into him at McDonald's. He and the station's reporter are. staying at the Holiday Inn, I believe he said." Lying was becoming easier. She was getting lots of practice. "Anyway, he chided me for walking alone and insisted on seeing me back to the hotel."

"Smart fellow. A hell of a lot smarter than you. What the hell were you thinking of to go out alone at this time of night?"

"I was hungry," she said, raising her voice.

"Ever think of room service?"

"I needed air."

"So open a window."

"What does it matter to you if I went out? You were with Jack. Jack and Eddy. Laurel and Hardy. Tweedledee and Tweedledum." She wagged her head from side to side in time to her words. "If it's not one who has something urgent to discuss with you, it's the other. One of them is always knocking on your door."

"Don't get off the subject. We're talking about you, not Jack or Eddy."

"What about me?"

"What made you so nervous tonight?"

"I wasn't nervous."

She tried to sidestep him again, but he wouldn't have it. He blocked her path and caught her by the shoulders. "Something's wrong. I know there is. What have you done this time? You'd better tell me before I find out from somebody else."

"What makes you think I've done something?"

"Because you won't look me in the eye."

"I'm avoiding you, yes. But only because I'm mad, not because I've committed what you would consider a transgression."

"That's been your routine in the past, Carole."

"Don't call me—" Avery caught herself just in time.

"Don't call you what?"

"Nothing." She hated having him address her as Carole. "Don't call me a liar," she amended. Defiantly, she flung her head back. "And just so you'll know from me before you hear it from somebody else, Van Lovejoy was smoking a joint. He even offered it to me. I refused. Now, do I pass muster, Mr. Senator?"

Tate was furiously rocking back and forth on the balls of his feet. "Don't wander off by yourself like that again."

"Don't put me on a short leash."

"I don't care what you do, dammit," he growled, gripping her shoulders harder. "It's just not safe for you to be alone."

"Alone?" she repeated in a harsh, mirthless tone. "Alone? We're never alone."

"We're alone right now."

It occurred to them simultaneously that they were standing chest to chest. One was breathing with as much agitation as the other. Their blood was running hot and their tempers were high. Avery felt her nerves sizzle like fallen hot wires that snaked across a rain-slick street.

His arms went around her, met at the center of her back, and jerked her against him. Avery went limp with desire. Then, moving as one, their mouths came together in a ravenous kiss. She folded her arms around his neck and provocatively arched her body into his. His hands slid over her derriere and roughly drew her up high and hard against the front of his body.

Their breathing was loud. So was the rustle of their evening clothes. Their mouths twisted against each other; their tongues were too greedy to exercise finesse.

Tate walked her backward into the wall, which then served the original purpose of his hands by keeping her middle cemented to him. His fingers curved tightly around her head and held it in place while he gave her a hungry kiss.

The kiss was carnal. It had a dark soul. It touched off elemental sparks that were as exciting to Avery as the first tongues of flame were to primal man. It conveyed that much heat, that much promise.

She attacked the studs on his pleated shirt. One by one they landed soundlessly in the carpeting. She peeled the shirt wide and bared his chest. Her open mouth found the very center of it. He swore with pleasure and reached behind her for the fastenings on her dress.

They eluded his fumbling fingers. Fabric was ripped. Beads scattered. Sequins rained down. Neither was mindful of the damage. He worked the dress down her shoulders and planted a fervent kiss on the upper curve of her breast, then reached for the clasp of her strapless brassiere.

Avery panicked when it fell open. *He would know!* But his eyes were closed. His lips were his sensors, not his eyes. He kissed her breasts, stroking the tips with his tongue, drawing them into his mouth.

He needed her. She wanted him to need her. She couldn't give enough.

She tugged his cuffs over his hands without even unhooking his cuff links. He flapped his arms until he was entirely free of his shirt, then slipped his hands beneath the hem of her underwear, and worked it down. Then his palm was on her, his fingers inside her, and she was gasping hoarse, whimpering, wanting sounds.

"You're my wife," he said thickly. "You deserve a little better than to be banged against the wall."

He released her and stepped away. In seconds he was out of his shoes and socks, leaving his trousers in a heap on the carpet.

Avery shimmied out of her dress, kicked off her shoes, and quickly moved to the bed. The housekeeper had already turned it down. She brushed the chocolate mints off the pillow and slid between the sheets. The lacy black garter belt came off with a snap. Her stockings had barely cleared her toes when Tate reached for her.

She went willingly as he pulled her against his warm, hairy nakedness. Their mouths met for another deep, wet kiss. His sex was hard and smooth. It probed the softness of her belly, nestled in the vee of dark curls.

He cupped her breast, lifted it, ran his thumb lightly back and forth over her nipple, and applied his tongue to it. With no resistance from her, he separated her thighs. The cleft between them was soft and sensitive and creamy. She gasped several short, choppy breaths as his fingers played over her.

Then he rolled her to her back and guided his rigid erection into the moist, oval opening. Her body received him coyly because he was very large and hard and she was very small and soft. Man and woman. As it should be. His power was reduced to weakness; her vulnerability was made strong.

She marveled at the absoluteness of his possession. It was invasive but sweet, unencumbered yet yearning. Her back and throat arched in total surrender. He went farther, touched deeper, reached higher than she believed possible.

Above her, he was straining to withhold his climax, to sustain the pleasure, but that was asking too much of his body, which had been imprisoned by self-imposed abstinence for so long.

He sank into her only a few times before he climaxed.

The room was so silent she could hear the ticking of his wristwatch where his hand lay beside her head on the pillow. She didn't dare look at him. Touching him wasn't even a remote possibility. She lay there and listened as his breathing returned to normal. Except for the rising and falling of his chest, he lay motionless.

It was over.

Eventually she rolled to her side, facing away from him. She tucked the pillow beneath her cheek and drew her knees against her chest. She was hurting, but she couldn't specify how or where or why.

Several minutes elapsed. When she first felt the stroking movement of his hand on her waist, she thought it was because she had wished it so badly that her imagination had made her feel it.

His hand settled in the curve of her waist and applied enough pressure to bring her over to her back again. She gazed up into his face, her eyes large and inquisitive and brimming with misgiving.

"I've always been fair," he whispered.

He drew his knuckles across her cheek, then over her lips. They'd been scraped by his beard stubble. At his tender touch, Avery swallowed emotionally. Her lips parted, but she couldn't speak aloud what she felt in her heart.

Tate lowered his head and kissed her softly. He paused, then kissed her again with the same delicacy. His cheeks were very hot against hers. Acting on instinct and overwhelming need, she reached up and touched the bandage at his hairline. Affectionately, her fingers sifted through his tousled hair. She traced the cleft in his chin with her fingernail.

God, she loved this man.

His lips settled against hers with purpose. His tongue slipped between her lips. Gently, erotically, he worked it in and out, making love to her mouth. She made a small, wanton sound. He responded by drawing her closer to him, close enough for his softened penis to nestle in the humid warmth between her thighs.

He kept kissing her mouth, her neck, her shoulders, while he fondled her breasts. His stroking fingers made the nipples stiff for his mouth. Hotly, wetly, he sucked them with tempered greed, until she was moving beneath him restlessly. He kissed her stomach, her undulating abdomen, the sensitive space between her pelvic bones.

Avery, lost to the touch of his mouth on her skin, threaded her fingers through his hair and held on tight.

Between her thighs, she was absurdly slippery, but his fingers dipped into her without intimidation. He discovered that tiny, distended nubbin of flesh between the pouting lips. He pressed it, feathered it, gently rolled it between his fingers.

She spoke his name on a serrated sigh. Her body quickened. Small shudders began to ripple through her. Reflexively she drew her knees up.

"I'm hard again."

His voice was tinged with wonder. Unintentionally he had spoken aloud the realization that had him mystified. He hadn't expected to need her again so soon, nor to ever need her as violently as he did now.

His entrance was surer than before, yet he took more time. When he was fully buried inside her, he turned his face into her neck and gently pulled her skin between his teeth. Avery's body responded instantly. Her inner muscles flexed, tightly squeezing him. With a low sound, he mindlessly began rocking his hips forward and backward.

She clung to him. Each rhythmic stroke propelled her closer to the light glimmering at the end of a dark tunnel. Her eyelids fluttered. She raced, harder and faster.

The light exploded around her brilliantly and she was consumed.

Tate released a long, low moan. His whole body tensed. He came and came and came, scalding and fierce, until he was completely empty.

He said nothing when he disengaged his body from hers. He turned away, giving her his back and drawing the sheet over his sweat-beaded shoulders.

Avery faced the opposite wall, trying to keep her crying silent. Physically it had been the finest sex imaginable, far surpassing anything she had ever experienced from the few lovers she'd had. There had been pitifully few. Relationships required time, and she'd sacrificed most of hers to the pursuit of her career. The obvious difference with this time was the love she had for her partner.

But for Tate it had started and ended as a biological release. Anger had been his turn-on, not love or even affection. He'd given her a climax, but that had been an obligation considerably fulfilled and nothing more.

The foreplay had been technically excellent but impersonal. They hadn't luxuriated in their repletion, though she'd longed to explore his naked body, familiarize her eyes and hands and mouth with every nuance of it. No endearments had been whispered. No vows of love had been pledged. He hadn't once spoken her name.

He didn't even know it.

THIRTY-TWO

"Tate, I need a minute of your time."

Avery barreled through the previously closed door, interrupting the conference being held in the large den at the ranch house.

Jack, who had been speaking when she made her peremptory entrance, was left standing in the midst of them with his hand frozen in a gesture and his mouth hanging open.

"What is it?" Tate asked, looking particularly ill-tempered.

Eddy was frowning with annoyance; Jack was cursing beneath his breath. Nelson's displeasure was just as clear, but he made an attempt at civility. "Is it an emergency? Mandy?"

"No, Nelson. Mandy's at nursery school."

"Is it something Zee can help you with?"

"I'm afraid not. I need to speak privately to Tate."

"We're in the middle of something here, Carole," he said testily. "Is it important?"

"If it weren't important, I wouldn't have interrupted you."

"I'd rather you wait until we get finished or handle the crisis yourself."

She felt her cheeks grow warm with indignation. Since their return home several days earlier, he had gone out of his way to avoid her. It had come as a vast disappointment but only a mild surprise that he hadn't moved back into the yellow bedroom she occupied. Instead, he'd resumed sleeping alone in the adjoining study.

Their lovemaking hadn't drawn them closer. Rather, it had widened the gap between them. The morning following it, they'd barely made eye contact. Words had been few. The mood had been subdued, as though something nefarious had transpired and neither party involved wanted to own up to it. She had taken her cue from Tate and pretended that nothing had happened in that wide bed, but the effort to remain impassive had made her cantankerous.

He had acknowledged it only once, as they waited for the bellman to come for their luggage. "We didn't use anything last night," he had said in a low, strained voice as he gazed out over the Dallas skyline.

"I don't have AIDS," she had snapped waspishly, wanting to prick his seemingly impenetrable aloofness. She succeeded.

He came around quickly. "I know. They would have discovered it while you were in the hospital."

"Is that why you felt it was okay to touch me? Because I was disease-free?"

"What I want to know," he ground out, "is if you could get pregnant."

Glumly, she shook her head. "Wrong time of the month. You're safe on all accounts."

That had been the extent of the conversation about their lovemaking, although that term elevated the act into something it hadn't actually been, at least for Tate. She felt like a one-night stand—an unpaid prostitute. Any warm, female body would have suited him. For the time being, he was sated. He wouldn't need her for a while.

She resented being so disposable. Used once—well, twice, actually—then thrown away. Perhaps Carole's unfaithfulness had been justified. Avery was beginning to wonder if Tate got off just as easily on the heady thought of becoming a senator as he did on sex. He certainly spent more time in pursuit of that than he did cultivating a loving relationship with his wife, she thought peevishly.

"All right," she said now, "I'll handle it."

She pulled the den door closed with a hard slam. Less than a minute later she was slamming another door in the house—this one to Fancy's bedroom. The girl was sitting on her bed, painting her toenails fire-engine red. A cigarette was burning in the nightstand ashtray. Condensation was collecting on the cold drink can beside the ashtray. Stereo headphones were bridging her head. Her jaws were working a piece of Juicy Fruit to the rhythm of the music.

She couldn't possibly have heard the slamming door over the acid rock being blasted into her ears, but she must have felt the vibration of the impact because she glanced up and saw Avery glaring down at her, holding a gum wrapper in her hand.

Fancy replaced the brush in the bottle of nail polish and draped the headphones around her neck. "What the hell are you doing in my room?"

"I came to retrieve my belongings."

Giving Fancy no more warning than that, Avery marched to the closet and slid open a louvered panel.

"Just a freaking minute!" Fancy exclaimed. She tossed the headphones down onto the bed and came charging off it.

"This is mine," Avery said, yanking a blouse off a hanger. "And this skirt. And this." She removed a belt from a hook. Finding nothing more in the closet, she crossed to Fancy's dressing table, which was littered with candy wrappers, chewing gum foil, perfume bottles, and enough cosmetics to stock a drugstore.

Avery raised the lid of a lacquered jewelry box and began riffling through earrings, bracelets, necklaces, and rings. She found the silver earrings she had reported missing in Houston, a bracelet, and the watch.

It was an inexpensive wristwatch—costume jewelry, really—but Tate had bought it for her. It hadn't been a bona fide gift. They had been browsing through a department store during a break in the campaign trip. She had seen the watch, remarked on its attractive green alligator band, and Tate had passed the star struck salesgirl his credit card.

Avery treasured it because he had brought it for *her*, not for Carole. She had noticed its disappearance from her jewelry box that morning. That had prompted her to storm the meeting in search of Tate. Since he had declined to advise her on how to deal with Fancy's kleptomania, she had taken matters into her own hands.

"You're a lousy thief, Fancy."

"I don't know how your stuff got into my room," she said loftily.

"You're an even lousier liar."

"Mona probably—"

"*Fancy—!*" Avery shouted. "You've been sneaking into my room and taking things for weeks. I know it. Don't insult my intelligence by denying it. You leave unmistakable clues behind."

Fancy looked down at the incriminating gum wrapper now lying on the bed. "Are you going to tattle to Uncle Tate?"

"Is that what you want me to do?"

"Hell, no." She flopped back down on the bed and began vigorously shaking the bottle of nail polish. "Do whatever the hell you want to. Just do it someplace else besides my room."

Avery was on her way out when she reconsidered. Turning back, she approached the bed and sat down. Taking the silver earrings, she pressed them into Fancy's hand and folded her fingers around them.

"Why don't you keep these? I would have loaned them to you if you had just asked."

Fancy flung the earrings as far as she could throw them. "I don't want your goddamn charity." Her beautiful blue eyes turned ugly with dislike. "Who the hell are you to offer me your sorry leftovers? I don't want the earrings or anything else you've got."

Avery withstood the verbal attack. "I believe you. It's not the earrings or any of this stuff that you wanted," she said, nodding down at the possessions she had gathered. "What you wanted was to get caught."

Fancy scoffed. "You've been out in the sun too long, Aunt Carole. Don't you know the sun's bad for your plastic face? It might cause it to melt."

"You can't insult me," Avery returned blandly. "You don't have the power. Because I'm on to you."

Fancy regarded her sulkily. "What do you mean?"

"You wanted my attention. You got it by stealing. Just like you get your parents' attention by doing things you know they'll disapprove of."

"Like fucking Eddy?"

"Like fucking Eddy."

Fancy was taken aback by Avery's calm echo of her cheeky question. She quickly recovered, however. "I'll bet you nearly shit when you saw me coming out of his hotel room. Didn't know I was anywhere near Houston, did you?"

"He's too old for you, Fancy."

"We don't think so."

"Did he invite you to join him in Houston?"

"Maybe, maybe not." She sprayed fixative on her scarlet toenails, then waggled them as she admired her handiwork. Hopping off the bed, she moved to a drawer and took out a bikini. She peeled her nightgown over her head. Her body was marred by bruises and scratches. Her shapely buttocks were striped with them. Avery glanced away, a sick feeling rising in her stomach.

"I've never had a lover like Eddy before," Fancy said dreamily as she stepped into the bikini trunks.

"Oh? What kind of lover is he?"

"Don't you know?" Avery said nothing. She didn't know if Carole had slept with her husband's best friend or not. "He's the best." Fancy hooked the bikini bra, then leaned into the mirror, selected a lipstick off the dressing table, and spread it across her mouth. "Jealous?"

"No."

They made eye contact in the mirror. Fancy looked skeptical. "Uncle Tate's still sleeping in that other room."

"That's none of your business."

"Doesn't matter to me," she said with a malicious grin, "as long as you don't try and take up the slack with Eddy."

"You sound very proprietary."

"He's not sleeping with anybody else." She bent at the waist and, flipping her hair forward, began pulling a brush through the thick, dark-blond strands.

"Are you sure of that?"

"I'm sure. I don't leave him the energy to screw around on me."

"Tell me about him."

Fancy swept her hair to one side and slyly looked up at Avery from her upside down position. "I get it. Not jealous, just curious."

"Maybe. What do you and Eddy find to talk about?"

"Do you chat with the guys you're balling?" She laughed out loud. "Say, you wouldn't happen to have any grass, would you?"

"No."

"Guess not," she said, sighing with disgust as she came erect and threw her hair back. "Uncle Tate went berserk when he caught us smoking that time. Wonder what he would have thought if he'd caught us sharing that cowboy?"

Avery blanched and looked away. "I . . . don't do things like that anymore, Fancy."

"No shit? For real?" She seemed genuinely curious.

"For real."

"You know, when you first came home from the hospital, I thought you were faking it. You were Miss Goody Two Shoes all of a sudden. But now, I believe you really changed after that airplane crash. What happened? Are you afraid you're gonna die and go to hell, or what?''

Avery changed the subject. ''Surely, Eddy's told you something about himself. Where did he grow up? What about his family?''

Fancy propped her hands on her hips and regarded Avery strangely. ''You know where he grew up, same as I do. Some podunk town in the Panhandle. He didn't have any family, remember? Except for a grandma who died while he and Uncle Tate were still at UT.''

''What did he do before he came to work for Tate?''

Fancy had already grown impatient with the questions. ''Look, we screw, okay? We don't talk. I mean, he's a real private person.''

''For instance?''

''He doesn't like me going through his stuff. One night I was searching in his drawers for a shirt to put on and he got really pissed, said for me not to meddle in his stuff again, so I don't. I don't pry, period. We all need our privacy, you know.''

''He's never mentioned what he did between Vietnam and when he came back to Texas?''

''All I've ever asked was if he'd been married. He told me he hadn't. He said he'd spent a lot of time finding himself. I said, 'Were you lost?' I meant it like a joke, but Eddy got his funny look on his face and said something like, 'Yeah, for a while there, I was.' ''

''What do you think he meant by that?''

''Oh, I suspect he freaked after the war,'' Fancy said with breezy unconcern. ''Why?''

''Probably because of Uncle Tate saving his life after their plane crashed. I guess Eddy relives bailing out, being wounded, and having Uncle Tate carry him around in the jungle until a chopper could pick them up. If you've ever seen him naked, you must've noticed the scar on his back. Pretty gruesome, huh?

''He must've been scared shitless they were gonna get captured by the Cong. Eddy begged Uncle Tate to leave him to die, you know, but Uncle Tate wouldn't.''

''Surely he didn't think Tate would,'' Avery exclaimed.

''Well, you know the fighter pilots' motto—'Better dead than look bad.' Eddy must've taken it to heart more than most. Uncle Tate was the hero. Eddy was just another casualty. That must still play on his mind.''

''How do you know all this, Fancy?''

''Are you kidding? Haven't you heard Grandpa tell it often enough?''

''Oh, sure, of course. You just seem to know so many of the fine details.''

''No more than you. Look, I'm going out to the pool. Do you mind?''

Inhospitably, she walked to the door and pulled it open. Avery joined her there. ''Fancy, the next time you want to use something of mine, just ask.'' She rolled her eyes, but Avery ignored her insolence. Touching the girl's shoulder briefly, she added, ''And be careful.''

''Of what?''

''Of Eddy.''

''She said for me to be careful of you.''

The motel room was cheap, dusty, and dank. But as Fancy bit into a fried chicken drumstick, she didn't seem to notice or mind. She'd become accustomed to the shabby surroundings in the last several weeks.

She would rather have had her trysts with Eddy in a more elegant hotel, but the Sidewinder Inn was located on the interstate between campaign headquarters and the ranch, so it was a convenient place for them to meet before going home. The motel catered to illicit lovers. Rooms were rented by the hour. The staff was discreet—out of indifference, not empathy.

Because they had worked through the dinner hour this evening, Fancy and Eddy were sharing their time together with a bucket of Colonel Sander's best. Naked, they were sitting amid the rumpled sheets, eating fried chicken and discussing Carole Rutledge.

"Careful of me?" Eddy asked. "Why?"

"She said I shouldn't be getting involved with a man so much older," Fancy said, tearing off a bite of meat. "But I don't think that's the real reason."

Eddy broke apart a chicken wing. "What's the real reason?"

"The real reason is because she's eaten up with jealousy. See, she wants to play the good wife for Uncle Tate, just in case he wins and goes to Washington. But in case he doesn't, she wants to have someone waiting in the wings. Even though she pretends not to, I know Aunt Carole craves your body." Playfully, she tapped his chest with the drumstick.

Eddy didn't respond. He was staring absently into space, frowning. "I still wish she didn't know about you and me."

"Let's not have another fight about that, okay? I couldn't help it. I walked out of your room and there she was, clutching that stupid ice bucket to her chest and looking like she'd just swallowed her tongue."

"Has she told Tate?"

"I doubt it." A piece of golden-brown crust fell onto her bare belly. She moistened her fingertip, picked up the crumb, then licked it off. "I'll tell you something else," she said in a mysterious whisper, "I don't think she's quite right in the head yet."

"What do you mean?"

"She asks the dumbest questions."

"Like what?"

"Yesterday I mentioned something she should have a vivid memory of, even if she did suffer a concussion."

"What?"

"Well," Fancy drawled, dragging the nearly clean drumstick across her lips, "another ranch was buying some horses from Grandpa. When the cowboy came to look at them, nobody was around. I took him into the stable myself. He was real cute."

"I get the picture," Eddy said drolly. "What does Carole have to do with it?"

"She discovered us screwing like rabbits in one of the stalls. I thought I was sunk, see, because this was a couple of years ago and I was barely seventeen. But Carole and the cowboy connected immediately. You know, snap, crackle, pop. The next thing I know, she's as naked as we are and rolling around in the hay with us."

She fanned her face theatrically. "God, it was fantastic! What an afternoon. But yesterday, when I mentioned it, she looked ready to puke or something. You want some more chicken?"

"No thanks." Fancy tossed her cleaned bone into the box and took out the last chicken leg. Eddy encircled her ankle with his hard fingers. "You didn't give away any of my secrets, did you?"

She laughed and nudged him in the butt with her bare foot. "I don't know any of your secrets."

"So what did you and Carole talk about regarding me?"

"I just told her you were the best I'd ever had." She leaned forward and gave him a greasy kiss on the lips. "You are, you know. You've got a cock of solid iron. And there's something about you that's so exciting—dangerous, almost."

He was amused. "Finish your chicken. It's time you headed home."

Disobediently, Fancy looped her arms around his neck and kissed him languorously. She left her lips in place as she whispered, "I've never done it doggie fashion before."

"I know."

She drew her head back sharply. "Didn't I do it good?"

"You did it fine. But I could tell you were surprised at first."

"I love surprises."

Eddy cupped the back of her head and gave her a searing kiss. Together they fell back onto the sour-smelling pillows. "The next time your Aunt Carole starts asking questions about me," he panted as he pulled on a rubber, "tell her to mind her own frigging business." He plowed into her.

"Yes, Eddy, yes," she chanted, beating on his back with the drumstick she still had clutched in one hand.

 # THIRTY-THREE

"**W**hat the hell," Van Lovejoy said resignedly. He took a final drag on a cigarette he had smoked down to his stained fingertips. "I wouldn't be any better at blackmailing than I am at anything else. I would have fucked up."

"You threatened her with blackmail?" Irish stared at the video photographer with contempt. "You failed to mention that when you told me about your meeting with Avery."

"It's all right, Irish." Avery laid a calming hand on the older man's arm. With a trace of a grin, she added, "Van was miffed at us for not including him in our secret."

"Don't joke about it. This secret is giving me chronic indigestion." Irish left his sofa in pursuit of another shot of whiskey, which he poured into his glass from a bottle on the kitchen table.

"Bring me one of those," Van called to him. Then to Avery, he said, "Irish is right. You're up shit creek and you don't even know it."

"I know it."

"Got any paddles?"

She shook her head. "No."

"Jesus, Avery, are you nuts? Why'd you do such a damn fool thing?"

"Do you want to tell him, or should I?" she asked Irish as he resumed his seat next to her on the couch.

"This is your party."

While Irish and Van sipped their whiskey, Avery related her incredible tale again. Van listened intently, disbelievingly, glancing frequently at Irish, who verified everything she said with a somber nod of his grizzled head.

"Rutledge has no idea?" Van asked when she had brought him up to date.

"None. At least as far as I can tell."

"Who's the traitor in the camp?"

"I don't know yet."

"Have you heard from him anymore?"

"Yes. Yesterday. I received another typed communiqué."

"What'd it say?"

"Virtually the same as before," she answered evasively, unable to connect with Irish's shrewd blue eyes.

The succinct note, found in her lingerie drawer, had read, *You've slept with him. Good work. He's disarmed.*

It had made her queasy to think of that unknown someone crowing over what had happened at the Adolphus. Had Tate discussed their lovemaking with his traitorous confidant? Or was he so close to Tate that he sensed his mood swing and made a lucky guess into the reason for it? She supposed she should be glad that he thought it was a ploy and hadn't figured it for an act of love.

"Whoever he is," she told her friends now, "he still means to do it." Her arms broke out in chill bumps. "But I don't think he's going to do the actual killing." The word was almost impossible for her to speak aloud. "I think someone's been hired to do it. Did you bring the tapes I asked for?"

Van nodded toward an end table where he had stacked several videotapes when he arrived, just a few minutes ahead of Avery. "Irish passed along the note you sent me through his post office box."

"Thanks, Van." Leaving her place on the sofa, she retrieved the tapes, then went to Irish's TV set and VCR and turned them on. She inserted one of the videos and returned to the sofa with a remote control transmitter. "This is everything you shot during our trip?

"Yep. From your arrival at Houston to your return home. If we're going to watch unedited home movies. I've got to have another drink."

"Next time, bring your own bottle," Irish muttered as Van sauntered into the kitchen.

"Screw you, McCabe."

Taking no offense, Irish leaned forward and propped his elbows on his knees. On the television screen Tate was seen emerging from a jetway. Avery and Mandy were at his side. The rest of the entourage was in the background.

"You've got the kid, but where are his parents?" Van asked, returning with a fresh drink.

"They drove down. Zee refuses to fly."

"Funny for an air force wife, isn't it?"

"Not so much. Nelson flew bombing missions in Korea while she was left at home with baby Jack. Then he did some test piloting. I'm sure she was afraid of being widowed. And Nelson's buddy—Tate's named after him—was lost at sea when his plane crashed."

"How'd you learn all that?"

"I went to Tate's office when I knew he wouldn't be there, with the excuse of wanting to have all the pictures reframed. I manipulated his secretary into conversation about the people in—Wait! Stop!"

Realizing that she was controlling the TV with the transmitter, she stopped the tape, backed it up, and replayed it. Very quietly, fearfully, she said, "He was at the airport when we arrived in Houston, too."

"Who?" Irish and Van asked in unison.

Again Avery rewound the tape. "This is still Hobby Airport, right, Van?"

"Right."

"There! See the tall man with gray hair?"

"Yellow polo shirt?"

"Yes."

"Where? I don't see him," Irish grumbled.

"What about him?" Van asked.

Avery rewound the tape. "Does this thing have a stop action?"

"Hell, yes." Irish snatched the transmitter from her hands. "Say when. I haven't seen a goddamn thing to—"

"When!"

"He depressed the button, freezing the action on the screen. Avery knelt in front of the TV set and pointed the man out to Irish. He was standing in the background, at the periphery of the crowd.

"He was in our hotel," she declared as the realization struck her. "We were rushing off to a rally and he held an elevator for us."

That's why she had noticed him in Midland. She had just seen him in Houston, although it hadn't registered at the time that the sweaty man who'd come from a workout in the hotel gym was the same as the man in the western suit.

"So?"

"So he was in Midland, too. He was at the airport when we landed. And I saw him later, in Dallas, at the fund-raising dinner at Southfork."

Van and Irish exchanged worried glances. "Coincidence?"

"Do you really think so?" Avery demanded angrily.

"All right, an avid Rutledge supporter."

"I had just about convinced myself of that," she said, "but I've been dropping by campaign headquarters nearly every day since we got back, and I haven't seen him among the volunteers. Besides, he never approached us while we were away. He was always at the edge of the crowd."

"You're jumping to conclusions, Avery."

"Don't." It was probably the harshest tone of voice she'd ever used with Irish. It startled them both, but she modified it only slightly when she added, "I know what you're thinking and you're wrong."

"What am I thinking?"

"That I'm plunging in, jumping to conclusions before I've lined up all the facts, reacting emotionally instead of pragmatically."

"You said it." Van sat back on his curved spine and propped his tumbler of whiskey on his concave abdomen. "You're good at that."

Avery drew herself up. "Let's look at all the tapes and see just how wrong I am."

When the final tape went to snow on the screen, a sustained silence followed, ameliorated only by the whistling sound made by the video recorder as it rewound the tape.

Avery came to her feet and turned to face them. She didn't waste time by rubbing it in how right she'd been. The tapes spoke for themselves. The man had shown up in nearly every one.

"Does he look familiar to either of you?"

Van said, "No."

"He was in every single city we were," Avery mused out loud. "Always lurking in the background."

"Not 'lurking.' Standing," Irish corrected.

"Standing and staring intently at Tate."

"So were you, most of the time," Van quipped. "You're not going to ice him."

She shot him a baleful look. "Don't you think it's a little odd that a man would follow a senatorial candidate around the state if he weren't actually part of the election committee?"

They glanced at each other and shrugged warily. "It's odd," Irish conceded, "but we don't have any pictures of him with his finger on a trigger."

"Did you see him at the GM plant?" Van wanted to know.

"No."

"That was one of the largest, most hostile crowds Tate addressed," Irish said. "Wouldn't that have been a likely spot for the guy to make his move?"

"Maybe the bottle thrower beat him to it."

"But you said you didn't see Gray Hair there," Van pointed out.

Avery gnawed her lip in consternation. That eventful day was a blur in her memory, punctuated by vivid recollections, like Tate sitting in the emergency room, his shirt stained with blood. The wound had healed in a matter of days; the small scar was faint and hidden by his hair. She shuddered to think how much worse it could have been if Gray Hair—

"Wait! I just remembered," she exclaimed. "I read that day's agenda before we left the hotel," she recalled excitedly. "The trip to the GM plant wasn't printed on the schedule because it was squeezed in later. Nobody except Eddy, Jack, and the union bosses at the plant knew we were going to be there. So even if Gray Hair had intercepted a schedule, he couldn't have known that Tate was going to be in Arlington."

"You two sound like you're talking about a goddamn Indian," Irish said cantankerously. "Look, Avery, this thing is getting too dangerous. Tell Rutledge who you are, what you suspect, and get the hell out."

"I can't." She drew in a catchy breath and repeated with soft emphasis, "I can't."

They argued with her for another half hour, but got nowhere. She enumerated the reasons why she couldn't give up now and rebuked their arguments that she was just doing it for the notoriety it would bring her when it was over.

"Don't you understand? Tate needs me. So does Mandy. I'm not deserting them until I know they're safe, and that's final."

As she prepared to leave, rushing because time had gotten away from her, she hugged them both. "It'll be a comfort to know you're around," she told Van. Irish had assured her that he would assign Van to the Rutledge campaign permanently until after the election. "Be the eyes in the back of my head. Scan the crowds. Let me know immediately if you see Gray Hair."

"Not with the Indian names again," Irish groaned. He pulled her into a bear hug. "You've given me the worst bellyache of my life," he said gruffly. "But I still don't want to lose you again."

She hugged him back and kissed his cheek. "You won't."

Van said, "Cover your ass, Avery."

"I will, I promise."

She left quickly and sped home. But she wasn't speedy enough.

THIRTY-FOUR

"This is becoming an all-too-familiar scene." Tate angrily confronted Avery the moment she cleared Mandy's bedroom door. "I'm pacing the floor, not knowing where the hell you are."

Breathless, she rushed across the room and gingerly lowered herself to the edge of the bed. Mandy was sleeping, but there were tear tracks on her cheeks. "I'm sorry. Zee told me she had another nightmare." Tate's mother had been waiting for her in the hall when she came in.

Tate appeared even more agitated than Zee had been. His face was drawn and haggard, his hair uncombed. "It happened about an hour ago, shortly after she'd fallen asleep."

"Did she remember anything?" she asked, looking up at him hopefully.

"No," he replied in a clipped voice. "Her own screams woke her up."

Avery smoothed back Mandy's hair and murmured, "I should have been here."

"You damn sure should have. She cried for you. Where were you?"

"I had errands to run." His imperative tone of voice grated on her, but she was presently more interested in the child than in arguing with Tate. "I'll stay with her now."

"You can't. The men from Wakely and Foster are here."

"Who?"

"The consultants we hired to oversee the campaign. Our meeting was interrupted by Mandy's nightmare, and their time is expensive. We've kept them waiting long enough."

He propelled her from Mandy's bedroom and toward one of the doors that opened onto the central courtyard. Avery dug in her heels. "What are you most upset over, Tate—your daughter's nightmare, or keeping the bigwigs waiting?"

"Don't test my temper now, Carole," he said, straining the words through clenched teeth. "I was here to comfort her, not you."

She conceded him the argument by guiltily glancing away. "I thought you were against using professional consultants for your campaign."

"I changed my mind."

"Eddy and Jack changed it for you."

"They had their input, but I made the final decision. Anyway, they're here, waiting to talk strategy with us."

"Tate, wait a minute," she said, laying a restraining hand on his chest when he made to move past her. "If you don't feel right about this, just say no to them. Up till now, your campaign has been based on *you*—who you are and what you stand for. What if these so-called experts try to change you? Won't you feel diluted? Homogenized? Even the best advisers can be wrong. Please don't be pressured into doing something you don't want to do."

He removed her hand from the front of his shirt. "If I could be pressured into doing something, Carole, I would have divorced you a long time ago. That's what I was advised to do."

The following morning she stepped out of her tub and loosely wrapped a bath sheet around herself. As she stood in front of the mirror, towel-drying her hair, she thought she saw movement in the bedroom through the partially opened door. Her first thought was that it might be Fancy. She flung open the door, but rapidly recoiled.

"Jack!"

"I'm sorry, Carole. I thought you heard my knock."

He was standing well beyond the door to her room. If he had knocked, she certainly wouldn't have given him permission to come in. He was lying. He hadn't knocked. More angry than embarrassed, she drew the bath sheet tighter around her.

"What do you want, Jack?"

"Uh, the guys left this for you."

Without taking his eyes off her, he tossed a plastic binder on her bed. His intense gaze made her very uncomfortable. It was prurient, but it was also incisive. The bath sheet left her legs and shoulders bare. Could he detect the difference in her body from Carole's? Did he know what Carole's body had looked like?

"What guys?" she asked, trying not to let her discomfort show.

"From Wakely and Foster. They didn't have a chance to give it to you last night before you stormed out of the meeting."

"I didn't storm out of the meeting. I came inside to check on Mandy."

"And stayed until after they'd left." She offered no apology or denial. "You didn't like them, did you?"

"Since you asked, no. I'm surprised you do."

"Why?"

"Because they're usurping your position."

"They work for us, not the other way around."

"That's not what it sounded like to me," she said. "They were autocratic and mandatory. I don't respond to that kind of high-handedness, and I'll be amazed if Tate tolerates it for any significant length of time."

Jack laughed. "Feeling as you do about them and their high-handed advice, you're going to have a tough time stomaching this." He gestured down at the folder.

Curious, Avery approached the bed and picked up the folder. She opened it and scanned the first several sheets of paper. "A list of dos and don'ts for the candidate's wife."

"That's right, Mrs. Rutledge."

She slapped shut the folder's cover and dropped it back onto the bed.

Again Jack laughed. "I'm glad I'm just the errand boy. Eddy's going to be pissed if you don't read and digest everything in there."

"Eddy can go to hell. And so can you. And so can anybody who wants to make Tate a baby-kissing, hand-shaking, plastic automaton who can turn a glib phrase but says absolutely nothing worth listening to."

"You've become quite a crusader for him, haven't you? All of a sudden you're his staunchest ally."

"Damn right."

"Who the hell do you think you're kidding, Carole?"

"I'm his wife. And the next time you want to see me, Jack, knock louder."

He took a belligerent step toward her, his face congested with anger. "Playact all you want in front of everybody else, but when we're alone—"

"Mommy, I drew you a picture." Mandy came bounding in, waving a sheet of construction paper.

Jack glowered at Avery, then wheeled around and strode from the room. She congratulated herself on holding up remarkably well, but now her weak knees buckled and she sank onto the edge of the bed, gathering Mandy against her and holding on tight. She pressed her lips against the top of the child's head. It would be difficult to tell who was drawing comfort from whom.

"Mommy?"

"What did you draw? Let me see." Avery released her and studied the colorful slashes Mandy had made across the page. "It's wonderful!" she exclaimed, smiling tremulously.

In the weeks since her visit with Dr. Webster, Mandy had made tremendous progress. She was gradually emerging from the shell she had sequestered herself in. Her mind was fertile. Her sturdy little body seemed imbued with energy. Though her self-confidence was still fragile, it didn't seem quite so breakable as before.

"It's Daddy. And here's Shep," she chirped, pointing to a dark blue blob on the paper.

"I see."

"Can I have some chewing gum? Mona said to ask you."

"One piece. Don't swallow it. Bring it to me when you don't want it anymore."

Mandy kissed her moistly. "I love you, Mommy."

"I love you, too." Avery gave her another tight hug, sustaining it until Mandy squirmed free and rushed off in quest of her chewing gum.

Avery followed her to the door and closed it. She considered turning the lock. There were those in the house whom she wanted to shut out.

But there were those she had to leave her door open for, just in case. Mandy, for one. And Tate.

Van opened a can of tuna and carried it with him back to his video console. His stomach had finally communicated to his brain that one had to have sustenance to stay alive. Otherwise, he would have been so engrossed in what he was doing, he would never have remembered to eat. He conveyed chunks of the oily fish from can to mouth via a reasonably clean spoon.

Clamping the bowl of the spoon in his mouth, he used both hands at once to eject one tape from one machine and insert a new tape into another. In this capacity, he functioned like a well-coordinated octopus.

He replaced the first tape in its labeled box and turned his attention to the one now playing. The color bars appeared on the screen, then the countdown.

Van swallowed the food he'd been holding in his mouth, took a puff of his smoldering cigarette, a gulp of whiskey, then scooped up another bite of tuna as he leaned back in his desk chair and propped his feet on the edge of the console.

He was watching a documentary he had shot several years earlier for a station in Des Moines. The subject was kiddie porn. This wasn't the watered-down, edited version that had gone out over the air. This was his personal copy—the one containing all the footage he'd shot over a twelve-week period while following around a features producer, a reporter, a grip, and a sound man. It was only one tape of the hundreds in his extensive personal library.

So far, none that he'd watched had justified the niggling notion that he'd seen someone in Rutledge's entourage before, and it wasn't the gray-haired man that had Avery so concerned. Van wasn't even certain what he was looking for, but he had to start somewhere. He wouldn't stop until he found it—whatever "it" was. Until he went back on the campaign trail with Rutledge, he didn't have anything better to do except get wasted.

He could always do that later.

"Where's Eddy?" Nelson asked from his place at the head of the dining table.

"He had to stay late," Tate replied. "He said not to wait dinner on him."

"It seems that we're never all together at dinner anymore," Nelson remarked with a frown. "Dorothy Rae, where's Fancy?"

"She's . . . she's . . ." Dorothy Rae was at a loss as to the whereabouts of her daughter.

"She was still at headquarters when I left," Tate said, coming to his sister-in-law's rescue.

Jack smiled at his parents. "She's been putting in a lot of long hours there, right, Mom?"

Zee gave him a tepid smile. "She's been more dedicated than I expected."

"The work's been good for her."

"It's a start," Nelson grumbled.

Avery, sitting across from Jack, held her peace. She doubted Fancy was working during all the hours she spent at campaign headquarters. She seemed the only one to attach any significance to Fancy and Eddy often coming in late together.

Mandy asked for help buttering her roll. When Avery finished and raised her head, she caught Jack watching her. He smiled, as though they shared a naughty secret. Avery quickly looked away and concentrated on her plate while the conversation eddied around her.

Fancy arrived several minutes later and flopped into her chair, her disposition as sour as her expression.

"Haven't you got a civil word for anybody, young lady?" Nelson asked sternly.

"Jesus, cauliflower," she mumbled, shoving the serving bowl to the other side of the table.

"I will not abide that kind of language," Nelson thundered.

"I forgot," she shouted with asperity.

His face turned an angry red. "Nor will I put up with any of your sass." He shot meaningful glances at Jack, who ducked his head, and Dorothy Rae, who reached for her wineglass. "Show some manners. Sit up properly and eat your dinner."

"There's never anything decent to eat around here," Fancy complained.

"You should be ashamed of yourself, Francine."

"I know, I know, Grandpa. All those starving kids in Africa. Save the sermon, okay? I'm going to my room."

"You'll stay where you are," he barked. "You're part of the family, and in this family, everyone has dinner together."

"There's no need to shout, Nelson," Zee said, touching his sleeve.

Fancy's face swelled up. She glared at her grandfather mutinously, at her parents contemptuously, but she remained seated.

As though nothing had happened, Nelson picked up the conversation where it had left off when she had come in. "The Wakely and Foster team is setting up another trip for Tate." He imparted this piece of information for the benefit of the women, who hadn't heard it firsthand.

Avery looked at Tate. "I just found out this afternoon," he said defensively, "and didn't have time to tell you before dinner. You'll get a schedule."

"Where are we going?"

"Just about every corner of the state."

Zee blotted her mouth. "How long will you be away?"

"A little over a week."

"Don't worry about Mandy, Carole," Nelson said. "Grandpa'll take care of her. Won't he, Mandy?"

She grinned at him and bobbed her head up and down. The child never minded being left with them. Ordinarily, Avery would have had no qualms about leaving her. However, Mandy had had another nightmare the night before—the second that week. If she were on the brink of a breakthrough, Avery hated to be away from her. Perhaps Mandy could go with them. It was something she needed to discuss with Tate before final plans were made.

Eddy suddenly appeared in the arched opening of the dining room. Mona, who was clearing away the main course dishes, told him she had kept his dinner warm. "I'll bring it right out."

"Never mind." His eyes darted around the table, lighting briefly on everyone seated. "I'll have to eat later."

Fancy's mood brightened considerably. A light came on behind her sullen eyes. Her sulky pout lifted into a smile. She sat up straight in her chair and looked at him with admiration and lust.

"I hate to ruin everyone's dinner," he began.

Nelson waved his hand dismissively. "You seem upset."

That was a gross understatement, Avery thought. Eddy was bristling with rage.

"What's the matter? Did we slip in the polls?"

"Is something wrong?"

"I'm afraid so," Eddy said, choosing Zee's question to respond to. "Ralph and Dirk are with me, but I told them to wait in the living room until I'd had a chance to speak with the family privately."

Ralph and Dirk were the two men from Wakely and Foster who were assigned to Tate's campaign. Their names frequently cropped up in conversation. Avery always dreaded hearing them referred to, because she usually had a negative reaction to whatever was subsequently said.

"Well?" Nelson prompted impatiently. "Best to get bad news over with."

"It concerns Carole." Every eye in the room moved to where she sat between Tate and Mandy. "Her abortionist is about to tell all."

THIRTY-FIVE

A quality necessary to bomber pilots is the ability not to crack under pressure. Nelson didn't. Avery reflected on his aplomb later when she reviewed those heart-stopping moments following Eddy's appalling announcement.

His lack of response was remarkable to her, because she had felt like she might very well shatter. She'd been rendered speechless, motionless, unable to think. Her brain shut down operation. It seemed the planet had been yanked from beneath her, and she floated without the security of gravity in an airless, black void.

Nelson, with admirable resilience, scooted back his dining chair and stood up. "I believe we should move this discussion to the living room."

Eddy nodded his head once, glanced at Tate with a mix of pity and exasperation, then left the room.

Zee, drastically pale but almost as composed as her husband, stood also. "Mona, we'll skip dessert tonight. Please entertain Mandy. We might be occupied for some time."

Dorothy Rae reached for her wineglass. Jack took it away from her and returned it to the table. He caught her beneath the arm, lifted her from her chair, and pushed her toward the hall. Fancy went after them. She was fairly bubbling now.

When they reached the archway, Jack said to his daughter, "You stay out of this."

"No way. This is the most exciting thing that's ever happened," she said with a giggle.

"It's none of your concern, Fancy."

"I'm part of this family, too. Grandpa just said so. Besides that, I'm a campaign worker. I have every right to sit in on the discussion. Even more right than her," she said, gesturing toward her mother.

Jack dug a fifty-dollar bill out of his pants pocket and pressed it into Fancy's hand. "Find something else to do."

"Son of a bitch," she mouthed before stamping off.

Tate's face was white with wrath. His movements were carefully controlled as he folded his napkin and laid it next to his plate. "Carole?"

Avery's head snapped up. Denials were poised and ready to be spoken, but the sheer fury burning in his eyes silenced them. Under his firmly guiding hand, she left the dining room and walked across the hall toward the large living room.

It was still twilight. The living room afforded a spectacular view of the western sky, streaked with the vivid shades of sunset. The vista was breathtaking, one

Avery often sat and enjoyed. This evening, however, the endless horizon made her feel exposed and alone.

There wasn't a single friendly face to greet her when she entered the room. The men representing the public relations firm were particularly hostile.

Dirk was tall, thin, saturnine, and had a perpetual, blue-black five o'clock shadow. He looked the stereotype of a hit man from a gangster movie. It appeared that his face would crack if he even tried to smile.

Ralph was Dirk's antithesis. He was round, stout, and jolly. He was always cracking jokes, more to everyone's annoyance than amusement. When nervous, he jangled change. The coins in his pocket were getting a workout now. They rang as noisily as sleigh bells.

Neither of these men, to her knowledge, had ever professed to having a last name. She sensed that omission was to promote a friendly working relationship between them and their clients. As far as she was concerned, the gimmick didn't work.

Nelson took charge. "Eddy, please clarify what you just told us in the dining room."

Eddy went straight to the heart of the matter and turned to Avery. "Did you have an abortion?"

Her lips parted, but she couldn't utter a sound. Tate answered for her. "Yes, she did."

Zee jumped as if her slender body had just been struck with an arrow. Nelson's brows pulled together into a steep frown. Jack and Dorothy Rae only stared at Avery in stunned disbelief.

"You knew about it?" Eddy demanded of Tate.

"Yes."

"And you didn't tell anybody?"

"It wasn't anybody's business, was it?" Tate snapped furiously.

"When did this happen?" Nelson wanted to know. "Recently?"

"No, before the plane crash. Just before."

"Great," Eddy muttered. "This is just fuckin' great."

"Mind your language in front of my wife, Mr. Paschal!" Nelson roared.

"I'm sorry, Nelson," the younger man shouted back, "but do you have any idea what this will do to the Rutledge campaign if it gets out?"

"Of course I do. But we have to guard against responding in a knee-jerk fashion. What good will flying tempers do us now?" After tempers had cooled, Nelson asked, "How did you find out about this . . . this abomination?"

"The doctor's nurse called headquarters this afternoon and asked to speak to Tate," Eddy told them. "He had already left, so I took the call. She said Carole had come to them six weeks pregnant and asked for a D and C to terminate pregnancy."

Avery sank down onto the padded arm of the sofa and folded her arms across her middle. "Do we have to talk about this with them in here?" She nodded toward the public relations duo.

"Beat it." Tate nodded them toward the door.

"Wait a minute," Eddy objected. "They have to know everything that's going on."

"Not about our personal lives."

"Everything, Tate," Dirk said. "Right down to the deodorant you use. No surprises, remember? Especially not unpleasant ones. We told you that from the beginning."

Tate looked ready to explode. "What did this nurse threaten to do?"

"Tell the media."

"Or?"

"Or we could pay her to keep quiet."

"Blackmail," Ralph said, playing a tune with the change in his pocket. "Not very original."

"But effective," Eddy said curtly. "She got my attention, all right. You might have ruined everything, you know," he shot at Avery.

Trapped in her own lie, Avery had no choice now but to bear their scorn. She didn't care what any of the others thought of her, but she wanted to die when she thought of how betrayed Tate must feel.

Eddy strode to the liquor cabinet and poured himself a straight scotch. "I'm open to suggestions."

"What about the doctor?" Dirk asked him.

"The nurse doesn't work for him anymore."

"Oh?" Ralph stopped jingling coins. "How come?"

"I don't know."

"Find out."

Avery, who had given the sharp command, came to her feet. She saw only one way to redeem herself in Tate's eyes and that was to help get him out of this mess. "Find out why she no longer works for the doctor, Eddy. Maybe he fired her for incompetency."

"He? It's a woman doctor. Jesus, don't you even remember?"

"Do you want my help with this or not?" she fired back, bluffing her way through a dreadful error. "If the nurse has been fired, she wouldn't be a very believable extortionist, would she?"

"Carole's got something there," Ralph said, glancing around the circle of grave faces.

"You got us into this jam," Eddy said, advancing on Avery. "What do you plan to do, brazen it out?"

"Yes," she said defiantly.

She could almost hear the wheels of rumination turning throughout the room. They were giving it serious consideration.

Zee broke the silence. "What if she has your medical records?"

"Records can be falsified, especially copied ones. It would still be my word against hers."

"We can't lie about it," Tate said.

"Why the hell not?" Dirk demanded.

Ralph laughed. "Lying's part of it, Tate. If you want to win, you've got to lie more convincingly than Rory Dekker, that's all."

"If I become a senator, I've still got to look myself in the mirror every morning," Tate said, scowling.

"I won't have to lie. Neither will you. No one will ever know about the abortion." Avery stepped in front of Tate and laid her hands on his arms. "If we call her bluff, she'll back down. I can almost guarantee that no local television station would listen to her, especially if she has been dismissed from the doctor's staff."

If the nurse took her story to Irish McCabe—and KTEX would probably be her first choice, because it had the highest ratings—he would nip the story in the bud. If she took it someplace else . . .

Avery suddenly turned to Eddy and asked, "Did she say she had someone to corroborate her story?"

"No."

"Then no credible journalist would break it."

"How the hell would you know?" Jack asked from across the room.

"I saw *All the President's Men.*"

"The tabloids would print it without corroboration."

"They might," she said, "but they have no credibility whatsoever. If we nobly ignored a scandalous story like that, readers would consider it a sordid lie."

"What if it got leaked to Dekker's staff? He'd blast it from Texarkana to Brownsville."

"What if he did?" Avery asked. "It's an ugly story. Who would believe I'd do such a thing?"

"Why did you?"

Avery turned to Zee, who had asked the simple question. She looked stricken, suffering for her son's sake. Avery wished she could provide her with a satisfactory answer to her question, but she couldn't.

"I'm sorry, Zee, but that's between Tate and me," she said finally. "At the time, it seemed like the thing to do."

Zee shuddered with repugnance.

Eddy didn't care about the sentimental aspects of their dilemma. He was pacing the rug. "God, Dekker would love to have this plum. He's got the zealous pro-lifers in his back pocket already. They're fanatics. I hazard to think what he could do with this. He'd paint Carole as a murderess."

"It would look like he was slinging mud," Avery said, "unless he can prove it beyond a shadow of a doubt, which he can't. Voter sympathy would swing our way."

Dirk and Ralph looked at each other and shrugged in unison. Dirk said, "She's brought up some valid points, Eddy. When you hear from the nurse again, call her bluff. She's probably grasping at straws and will scare easily."

Eddy gnawed his inner cheek. "I don't know. It's chancy."

"But it's the best we can do." Nelson got up from his seat and extended a hand down to Zee. "Y'all sort out the rest of this ugliness. I never want to hear it mentioned again." Neither he nor Zee deigned to look at Avery as they went out.

Dorothy Rae headed for the liquor cabinet. Jack was glaring so malevolently at his brother's wife that he didn't notice or try to stop her.

Apparently, no one in the family had known about Carole's pregnancy and abortion until tonight. This development had come as a shock to everyone, even to Avery, who hadn't known for certain herself and had lost by gambling on no one ever finding out.

"You got any more skeletons rattling around in your closet?"

Tate spun around and confronted his brother with more anger than Avery had ever seen him exhibit for anyone in his family. His hands were balled into fists at his sides. "Shut up, Jack."

"Don't tell him to shut up," Dorothy Rae cried, slamming the vodka decanter back onto the cabinet. "It's not his fault your wife's a slut."

"Dorothy Rae!"

"Well, isn't she, Jack? She got rid of a baby on purpose, while mine . . . mine . . ." Tears welled up in her eyes. She turned her back to the room.

Jack blew out his breath, lowered his head, and mumbled, "Sorry, Tate."

He went to his weeping wife, placed his arm around her waist, and led her from the room. For all the aversion she felt toward Jack, Avery was touched by this kind gesture. So was Dorothy Rae. She gazed up at him with gratitude and love.

Dirk and Ralph, impervious to the family drama, had been talking between themselves. "You'll sit this trip out," Dirk told Avery peremptorily.

"I second that," Eddy said.

"That's up to Tate," she said.

His face was cold and impassive. "You stay."

Tears were imminent, and she'd be damned before she cried in front of Dirk, his sidekick, and the indomitable iceman, Eddy Paschal. "Excuse me."

Proudly, but quickly, she walked out. Tate followed her from the room. He caught up with her in the hallway and brought her around to face him. "There's just no limit to your deceit, is there, Carole?"

"I know it looks bad, Tate, but—"

"*Bad?*" Bitter and incredulous, he shook his head. "If you'd already done it, why didn't you just own up to it? Why tell me there'd never been a child?"

"Because I could see how much it was hurting you."

"Bullshit. You saw how much it was hurting you!"

"No," she said miserably.

"Call her bluff. No corroborating witness. Falsified records," he said, quoting her previous suggestions. "If you got caught, you had your escape route all thought out, didn't you? How many other tricks have you got up your sleeve?"

"I made those suggestions so you'd be protected. You, Tate."

"Sure you did." His lips curled with cynicism. "If you'd wanted to do something for me you wouldn't have had an abortion. Better yet, you wouldn't have gotten pregnant in the first place. Or did you think a baby would be your ticket to Washington?"

He released her suddenly, flinging off his hands as though he couldn't bear to touch her. "Stay out of my way. I can't stand the sight of you."

He returned to the living room, where his advisers were waiting for him. Avery slumped against the wall and covered her mouth with her hands to hold back the sobs.

In another attempt to atone for Carole's sins, she had only driven Tate farther away.

The following morning, Avery woke up feeling groggy. Her head was muzzy, and her eyes were swollen and stinging from crying herself to sleep. Pulling on a light robe, she stumbled toward the bathroom.

As soon as she cleared the door, she flattened herself against the wall and, with horror, read the message that had been written on the mirror with her own lipstick.

Stupid slut. You almost ruined everything.

Fear held her paralyzed for several moments, then galvanized her. She ran to the closet and dressed hastily. Pausing only long enough to wipe the message off the mirror, she fled the room as though chased by demons.

It took only a few minutes in the stable for her to saddle a horse. She streaked across the open pasture at a full gallop, putting distance between her and the lovely house that harbored such treachery. Even though the sun's first rays warmed her skin, goose bumps broke out on Avery's arms when she thought of someone sneaking into her bedroom while she slept.

Perhaps Irish and Van were right. She was certifiably insane to continue with this charade. She might pay with her life for another woman's manipulations. Was any story worth that? It was foolish not to leave before she was discovered.

She could disappear, go someplace else, assume a new identity. She was smart and resourceful. She was interested in many things. Journalism wasn't the only worthwhile field of endeavor.

But those were options generated by panic and fear. Avery knew she would never act upon them. She couldn't withstand another professional failure, especially one of this magnitude. And what if Tate's life were lost as a consequence? He and Mandy were now worth more to her than any acclaim. She must stay. With the election only several weeks away, the end was in sight.

As attested to by the message on her mirror, Carole's recent unpredictability had made Tate's enemy angry and nervous. Nervous people made mistakes. She would have to be watchful for giveaways, and at the same time guard against giving herself away.

The stable was still deserted when she returned her mount to his stall. She unsaddled him, gave him a bucket of feed, and rubbed him down.

"I've been looking for you."

Alarmed, she dropped the currycomb and spun around. "Tate!" She splayed a hand across her thudding heart. "I didn't hear you come in. You startled me."

He was standing at the opening of the stall. Shep sat obediently at his feet, tongue lolling.

"Mandy's demanding your French toast for breakfast. I told her I'd come find you."

"I went riding," she said, stating the obvious.

"What happened to the fancy britches?"

"Pardon?"

"Those . . ." He gestured along the outside of his thighs.

"Jodhpurs?" Her jeans and boots weren't fancy, by any means. The shirttail of her simple cotton shirt was hanging loosely over her hips. "I feel silly in them now."

"Oh." He turned to go.

"Tate?" When he came back around, she nervously moistened her lips. "I know everyone is furious with me, but your opinion is the only one that matters. Do you hate me?"

Shep lay down on the cool cement floor of the stable and propped his head on his front paws, looking up at her with woeful eyes.

"I'd better get back to Mandy," Tate said. "Coming?"

"Yes, I'll be right there."

Yet neither made a move to leave the stable. They just stood there, staring at each other. Except for the occasional stamping of a shod hoof against the floor or the snuffling of a horse, the stable was silent. Dust motes danced in the stripes of sunlight coming through the windows. The air was still and thick with the pleasing smells of hay and horseflesh and leather. And lust.

Avery's clothes suddenly seemed constricting. Her hair felt too heavy for her head, her skin too small to contain her teeming body. She ached to go to Tate and place her arms around his waist. She wanted to rest her cheek on his chest and feel the beating of his heart as it had pulsed when he was inside her. She wanted him to reach for her with need and passion again, even if short-term gratification was all he wanted from her.

The desire swirling within her was coupled with despair. The combination was unbearable. She looked away from him and idly reached out to stroke the gelding's velvet muzzle. He turned away from his oats to affectionately bump her shoulder.

"I don't get it."

Her eyes swung back to Tate. "What?"

"He used to breathe fire if you came anywhere near him. You wanted us to sell him to the glue factory. Now you nuzzle each other. What happened?"

She met Tate's gray eyes directly and said softly, "He learned to trust me."

He got the message. There was no mistaking that. He held her stare for a long time, then nudged the large dog with the toe of his boot. "Come on, Shep." Over his retreating shoulder he reminded her, "Mandy's waiting."

THIRTY-SIX

"Be a sweet girl for Daddy." Tate knelt in front of his daughter and gave her a tight hug. "I'll be back before you know it and bring you a present."

Ordinarily, Mandy's grin would have caused Avery to smile, but she found that impossible to do this morning, the day of Tate's departure. He stood up. "Call me if she has any breakthroughs."

"Of course."

"Or any regressions."

"Yes."

"The entire staff's been put on notice that if a call comes in concerning Mandy, I'm to be summoned immediately, no matter what."

"If anything happens, I promise to call right away."

Jack tooted the car horn. He was waiting impatiently behind the steering wheel. Eddy was already sitting in the passenger seat, speaking into the cellular phone that had recently been installed.

"About that other," Tate said, keeping his tone confidential. "Eddy did as you suggested and asked the nurse for irrefutable proof that you'd had an abortion. He grilled her good, gave her a taste of what she would be up against if she went to the press or to Dekker's people with her story.

"He also did some investigating. As you guessed, she was fired from her job and wanted to embarrass the doctor even more than us. Eddy used that as leverage, too, and threatened all kinds of litigation. For the time being, she's cowed."

"Oh, I'm so glad, Tate. I would have hated to have that darken your campaign."

He gave a short laugh. "It couldn't look much darker than it already does."

"Don't get discouraged," she said, laying her hand on his sleeve. "The polls aren't gospel. Besides, they can be reversed at any time."

"They'd better be damn quick about it," he said grimly. "November's going to be here before we know it."

Between now and then, his life was in danger and she couldn't even warn him of it. During this trip she wouldn't be there watching for a tall, gray-haired man. Maybe she should mention that—just give him that much head start against his enemies.

"Tate—" she began. Jack honked the horn again.

"Got to go." He bent from the waist and kissed Mandy's cheek again. "Goodbye, Carole." She didn't get a kiss, or a hug, or even a backward glance before he got into the car and was driven away.

"Mommy? Mommy?"

Mandy must have addressed her several times. By the time Avery stopped staring at the curve in the road where the car had disappeared from view and looked down at her, her little face was perplexed.

"I'm sorry. What is it, darling?"

"How come you're crying?"

Avery brushed the tears off her cheeks and forced a wide smile. "I'm just sad because Daddy's leaving. But I've got you to keep me company. Will you do that while he's gone?''

Mandy nodded vigorously. Together they went inside. If Tate was temporarily beyond her help, she could at least do the best she could for his daughter.

The days crawled by. She spent most of her time with Mandy, but even the activities she invented for them weren't enough to absorb the endless hours. She hadn't been exaggerating when she had told Tate all those weeks earlier that she needed something constructive to do. She wasn't accustomed to inactivity. On the other hand, she seemed to lack the energy to motivate herself into doing anything more than staring into space and worrying about him.

She watched the evening news every night, anxiously looking for the gray-haired man in the crowd shots. Irish would wonder why she hadn't accompanied Tate on this trip, so she had called him from a public phone booth in Kerrville and explained about the abortion crisis.

''His advisers, starting with Eddy, recommended that I stay behind. I'm a pariah now.''

''Even to Rutledge?''

''To an extent, yes. He's as polite as ever, but there's a definite chill there.''

''I've heard of political experts like Wakely and Foster. They give a command and Rutledge barks, is that it?''

''They give a command, Tate snarls at them, then barks.''

''Hmm, well, I'll notify Van and tell him to keep his eye out for that guy you seem to think is significant.''

''I *know* he's significant. Tell Van to call me the instant he spots him.''

''If he does.''

Apparently he hadn't, because Van hadn't called. But all the news stories broadcast by KTEX featured at least one crowd shot. Van was sending her a message. Gray Hair wasn't in the crowds surging around Tate.

That did little to relieve Avery's anxiety, however. She wanted to be beside Tate to see for herself that he was in no imminent danger. At night she experienced graphic visions of him dying a bloody death. During the day, when she wasn't involved with Mandy, she wandered restlessly through the rooms of the house.

''Still in the dumps?''

Avery raised her head. Nelson had come into the living room without her hearing him. ''Does it show?'' she asked with a wan smile.

''Plain as day.'' He lowered himself into one of the easy chairs.

''Admittedly, I haven't been very good company lately.''

''Missing Tate?''

The family's subtle snubbing had made the time pass even more slowly. It had been a little over a week since Tate had left. It seemed eons.

''Yes, Nelson, I miss him terribly. I suppose you find that hard to believe. Zee does. She'll barely look at me.''

He stared straight into her eyes, hard enough and incisively enough to make her squirm. He said, ''That abortion business was hideous.''

''I had no intention of anyone ever finding out.''

''Except Tate.''

''Well, he had to know, didn't he?''

''Did he? Was the baby his?''

She hesitated for only a second. ''Yes.''

''And you wonder why we aren't feeling too kindly toward you?'' he asked. ''You destroyed our grandbaby. I find that impossible to forgive, Carole. You know how Zee feels about Tate. Did you expect her to embrace you for what you did?''

"No."

"Being the kind of mother she's been to the boys, she can't imagine doing what you did. Frankly, neither can I.''

Avery glanced down at the photo album that was spread open over her lap. The pictures she had been looking at when he had come in were from early years. Zee was very young and very beautiful. Nelson looked dashing and handsome in his air force blues. Jack and Tate were pictured as youngsters in various stages. They typified the all-American family.

"It couldn't have been easy for Zee when you went to Korea."

"No, it wasn't, he said, settling more comfortably into his chair. "I had to leave her alone with Jack, who was just a baby."

"Tate was born after the war, right?''

"Just after."

"He was still a baby when you moved to New Mexico,'' she said, consulting the album again, hoping he would elaborate on the few bare facts she knew through painstaking investigation.

"That's where the Air Force sent me, so that's where I went,'' Nelson said. "Desolate place. Zee hated the desert and the dust. She also hated the work I was doing. In those days, test pilots were disposable commodities.''

"Like your friend Bryan Tate.''

His features softened, as though he was mentally reliving good times. Then, sadly, he shook his head. "It was like losing one of the family. I gave up test piloting after that. My heart just wasn't in it anymore, and if your heart's not in it, you can get killed quicker. Maybe that's what happened with Bryan. Anyway, I didn't want to die. There was still too much I wanted to do.

"The air force sent me to Lackland. This was home, anyway. Good place to raise the boys. My daddy was getting old. I retired from the air force after he died and took over the ranching business.''

"But you miss the flying, don't you?''

"Yeah—hell, yeah,'' he said with a self-deprecating laugh. "Old as I am, I still remember what it was like up there. No feeling in the world to rival it. Nothing like swapping beers and stories with the other fliers, either. A woman can't understand what it's like to have buddies like that.''

"Like Bryan?''

He nodded. "He was a good pilot. The best.'' His smile faded. "But he got careless and paid the price with his life.'' His vision cleared as he focused on Avery again. "Everybody pays for his mistakes, Carole. You might get away with them for a while, but not forever. Eventually, they'll catch up with you.''

She looked away uncomfortably. "Is that what you think is happening with me and the abortion?''

"Don't you?''

"I suppose so."

He leaned forward and propped his forearms on his thighs. "You've already had to pay by bearing the shame of it. I'm just hoping that Tate doesn't have to pay for your mistake by losing this election.''

"So do I.''

He studied her for a moment. "You know, Carole, I've jumped to your defense many times since you became part of this family. I've given you the benefit of the doubt on more occasions than one.''

"Your point?''

"Everyone's noticed the changes in you since you came back after your accident."

Avery's heartbeat quickened. Had they been discussing these changes among themselves? "I have changed. For the better, I think."

"I agree, but Zee doesn't think the changes are real. She believes you're putting on an act—that your interest in Mandy is phony and your sudden regard for Tate is merely a tactic to stay in his good graces so he'll take you with him to Washington."

"Not a very flattering commendation from a mother-in-law," she mused aloud. "What do you think?"

"I think you're a beautiful, smart young woman—too smart to lock horns with me." He pointed a blunt finger at her. "You better be everything you've pretended to be." For several moments, his expression remained foreboding. Then he broke into a wide grin. "But if you're sincerely trying to make up for past mistakes, I commend you for it. To get elected, Tate needs his family, especially his wife, behind him one hundred percent."

"I am behind his getting elected one hundred percent."

"That's no more than should be expected." He rose from his chair. At the door he turned back. "Behave like a senator's wife and you'll get no trouble from me."

Apparently he spoke to Zee, because at dinner that evening, Avery noticed a slight thawing in Zee's attitude toward her. Her interest seemed genuine when she asked, "Did you enjoy your ride this afternoon, Carole?"

"Very much. Now that it's cooler, I can stay out longer."

"And you're riding Ghostly. That's odd, isn't it? You've always despised that animal, and vice versa."

"I think I was afraid of him before. We've learned to trust each other."

Mona stepped into the dining room at that moment to call Nelson to the phone. "Who is it?"

"It's Tate, Colonel Rutledge."

Avery squelched a pang of regret that Tate hadn't asked to speak to her, but just knowing that he was on the telephone in the next room made her insides flutter. Nelson was gone for several minutes. When he returned, he looked extremely pleased.

"Ladies," he said, addressing not only his wife and Avery, but Dorothy Rae, Fancy, and Mandy, too. "Get your bags packed tonight. We're leaving for Fort Worth tomorrow."

Their reactions were varied.

Zee said, "All of us?"

Dorothy Rae said, "Not me. Me?"

Fancy leaped from her chair, giving a wild whoop of irrepressible joy. "God, it's about time something good and fun happened around here."

Mandy looked at Avery for a clarification of why everybody had suddenly become so excited.

Avery asked, "Tomorrow? Why?"

Nelson addressed her question first. "The polls. Tate's slipping, losing ground every day."

"That's not much cause to celebrate," Zee said.

"Tate's advisers think the family should be more visible," Nelson explained, "so he doesn't look like such a maverick. I, for one, am glad we're all going to be together again."

"They've changed their minds about me staying in the background?" Avery asked.

"Obviously."

"I'll pack for Mandy and me." All negative thoughts were dispelled by the knowledge that she would soon be with Tate. "What time are we leaving?"

"Soon as everybody's ready." Nelson glanced down at Dorothy Rae, who was obviously panic-stricken. Her face was the color of cold oatmeal and she was wringing her hands. "Mona, please help Dorothy Rae get her things together."

"Do I have to go?" she asked in a quavering voice.

"That's what I was told." Nelson divided a stern stare between her and Fancy, who, unlike her mother, was ebullient. "I don't think I need to remind anyone to be on her best behavior. We're moving into the final days of the campaign. All the Rutledges are going to be under public scrutiny, constantly living under a magnifying glass. Conduct yourselves accordingly."

THIRTY-SEVEN

It was raining in Fort Worth when they arrived.

Nelson drove straight to the downtown hotel, but because the trip from the hill country had taken longer than expected due to the inclement weather and frequent stops, Jack, Eddy, and Tate had already left for the political rally being held that evening.

The travel-weary group checked into their rooms as quickly as possible. Mandy was tired and cranky. She threw a temper tantrum and nothing pacified her—not even the room service meal that was promptly delivered.

"Mandy, eat your dinner," Zee said.

"No," she said petulantly, poking out her lower lip. "You said I could see Daddy. I want to see Daddy."

"He'll be here later," Avery explained for the umpteenth time.

"Come on now, this is your favorite," Zee said cajolingly. "Pizza."

"I don't like it."

Nelson impatiently glanced at his military wristwatch. "It's almost seven. We've got to leave now or get there late."

"I'll stay with her," Dorothy Rae volunteered, her expression hopeful.

"Big help you'd be," Fancy said scornfully. "I say let the little wretch starve."

"Fancy, please," Zee remonstrated. "One difficult child at a time is enough." She pleaded fatigue herself and offered to skip the rally and stay with Mandy.

"Thank you, Zee," Avery said. "That would be a help. I don't think she's fit to meet the public tonight. Nelson, you take Dorothy Rae and Fancy now. I'll come along later."

Nelson began to protest. "Dirk and Ralph said to—"

"I don't care what they said," Avery said, butting in. "Tate wouldn't want me to leave Mandy with Zee while she's behaving this badly. Once she's in bed, I'll take a cab. Tell them I'll get there as soon as I can."

The three of them filed out of Mandy's bedroom, part of a three-room suite assigned to Tate's family. "Now, Mandy," Avery said reasonably, "eat your supper so I can brag to Daddy how good you've been."

"I want my surprise."

"Eat your dinner, dear," Zee pleaded.

"No!"

"Then would you like a nice, warm bath?"

"No! I want my surprise. Daddy said I'd get a surprise."

"Mandy, stop this," Avery said sternly, "and eat your dinner."

Mandy gave the room service tray a push. It went crashing to the floor. Avery shot to her feet. "That settles it." She yanked Mandy out of her chair, spun her around and swatted her bottom hard several times. "I won't put up with that from you, young lady."

At first Mandy was too stunned to react. She looked up at Avery with wide, round eyes. Then her lower lip began to quiver. Enormous tears rolled down her cheeks. She opened her mouth and let out a wail that would awake the dead.

Zee reached for her, but Avery edged her aside and gathered Mandy against her. The child's arms wrapped around her neck. She burrowed her wet face into Avery's shoulder.

Avery rubbed her back soothingly. "Aren't you ashamed of yourself for having to get a spanking? Daddy thinks you're a good girl."

"I *am* a good girl."

"Not tonight. You're being very naughty and you know it."

The crying jag lasted for several minutes. When it finally abated, Mandy raised her blotchy face. "Can I have my ice cream now?"

"No, you can't." Avery pushed back strands of Mandy's hair that tears had plastered to her cheeks. "I don't believe you deserve a treat, do you?" Her lower lip continued to tremble, but she shook her head no. "If you behave now, when Daddy gets here tonight, I'll let him wake you up to give you your surprise. Okay?"

"I want some ice cream."

"I'm sorry," Avery said shaking her head no. "Bad behavior doesn't get rewarded. Understand Mommy?"

Mandy nodded regretfully. Avery eased her off her lap. "Now, let's go take a bath and put your pajamas on so you and Grandma can go to bed. The faster you go to sleep, the sooner Daddy will get here."

Twenty minutes later, Avery tucked her in. Mandy was so tired, she was almost asleep by the time her head hit the pillow. Avery was also exhausted. The incident had sapped her stamina. She was in no frame of mind to quarrel with Zee, whose compact body was quaking with disapproval.

"Tate will hear about the spanking," she said.

"Good. I believe he should."

She was on her way into the connecting room when the telephone rang. It was Tate. "Are you coming, or what?" he demanded without preamble.

"Yes, I'm coming. I had a problem with Mandy, but she's in bed now. I'll get a cab and be there—"

"I'm downstairs in the lobby. Be quick."

She did the best she could in five minutes' time, which was all she dared allow herself. The results weren't spectacular, but good enough to make Tate do a double take as she stepped off the elevator.

The two-piece suit was smart and sassy. The sapphire blue silk enhanced her own vibrant coloring. The curl in her hair had been sacrificed to the humidity, so she'd opted for a sophisticated, dramatic effect and capped it off with a pair of bold, gold earrings.

"What the hell's going on?" Tate asked as he ushered her toward the revolving door. "Dad said Mandy was upset."

"Upset, my foot. Mandy was being an absolute terror."

"Why?"

"She's three years old, that's why. She'd been cooped up in a car all day. I understood why she was behaving the way she was, but understanding only stretches so far. I hate to spoil Zee's surprise, but I spanked her."

They had reached the car parked beneath the porte cochere. He paused with his hand on the passenger door handle. "What happened?"

"It got her attention. It also worked."

He studied her resolute expression for a moment, then bobbed his head and brusquely ordered, "Get in."

He quickly tipped the doorman who'd been keeping an eye on the car, got behind the wheel, and drove cautiously out into the street. The windshield wipers clacked vigorously, but fought a losing battle against the heavy rainfall.

Tate headed north on Main Street, rounded the distinctive Tarrant County Courthouse, then drove across the Trinity River Bridge toward north Fort Worth, where cowboys and cutthroats had made history in its celebrated stockyards.

"Why did you come to get me?" she asked as the car streaked through the stormy night. "I could have taken a cab."

"I wasn't doing anything except hanging around backstage anyway. I thought the time would be better spent doing taxi duty."

"What did Dirk and Ralph say about you leaving?"

"Nothing. They didn't know."

"What!"

"By the time they figure out I'm not there, it'll be too late for them to do anything about it. Anyway, I was goddamn tired of them editing my speech."

He was driving imprudently fast, but she didn't call that to his attention. He seemed in no mood to listen to criticism. His disposition seemed black all around. "Why were we summoned to join you?" she asked, hoping to find the root of his querulousness.

"Have you been following the polls?"

"Yes."

"Then you know that a change of strategy is called for. According to my advisers, desperation measures must be taken. We embarked on this trip to pump up enthusiasm, gain support. Instead, I've lost three points since we started."

"Nelson said something about your maverick image."

He swore beneath his breath. "That's how they think I'm coming across."

"They?"

"Who else? Dirk and Ralph. They thought the bulwark of a family standing behind me would convince voters that I'm not a hothead. A family man projects a more stable image. Shit, I don't know. They go on and on till I don't even hear them anymore."

He wheeled into the parking lot of Billy Bob's Texas. Touted as the world's largest honky-tonk, complete with an indoor rodeo arena, it had been leased by Tate's election committee for the night. Several country and western performers had donated their time and talent to the fundraising rally.

Tate nosed the car up to the front door. A cowboy wearing a yellow slicker and dripping felt Stetson stepped from the alcove and approached the car. Tate lowered the foggy window.

"Can't park here, mister."

"I'm—"

"You gotta move your car. You're in a fire lane."

"But I'm—"

"There's a parking lot across the street, but because of the crowd, it might already be full.'' He shifted his wad of tobacco from one jaw to another. ''Any-how, you can't leave it here.''

''I'm Tate Rutledge.''

''Buck Burdine. Pleased to meet ya. But you still can't park here.''

Buck obviously had no interest in politics. Tate glanced at Avery. Diplomati-cally, she was studying her hands where they lay folded in her lap and biting her lip to keep from laughing.

Tate tried again. ''I'm running for senator.''

''Look, mister, are you gonna move your car, or am I gonna have to kick ass?''

''I guess I'm gonna move my car.''

A few minutes later, he parked in an alley several blocks away, between a boot repair shop and a tortilla factory. As soon as he cut the engine, he looked across the interior of the car at Avery. She glanced at him sideways. Simultaneously, they burst out laughing. It lasted for several minutes.

''Aw, Jesus,'' he said, squeezing the bridge of his nose, ''I'm tired. It feels good to laugh. Guess I have Buck Burdine to thank.''

Rain was coming down in torrents and sheeting against the windows of the car. The streets were virtually deserted on this rainy weeknight. The businesses that sandwiched them were closed, but their neon signs projected wavering stripes of pink and blue into the car.

''Has it been horrible, Tate?''

''Yeah. Horrible.'' Mindlessly, he traced the stitching around the padded leather steering wheel. ''I'm losing ground every day, not gaining it. My campaign's on the wane here in the final weeks, when it should be picking up momentum by the hour. It looks like Dekker is going to pull it off again.'' He thumped the steering wheel with his fist.

Avery shut out everything except him. She gave him her undivided attention, knowing that he needed a sounding board that didn't talk back. He hadn't had to tell her that he was tired. Lines of weariness and worry were etched at the sides of his mouth and around his eyes.

''I've never once doubted that it was my destiny to serve this state in the U.S. Senate.'' He turned his head and looked at her. She nodded in agreement but said nothing, uncertain how she should respond. He wouldn't tolerate banalities and platitudes.

''I even skipped running for state representative and went after what I ultimately wanted. But now, I'm beginning to wonder if I've been listening to people who only told me what I wanted to hear. Have I got delusions of grandeur?''

''Undoubtedly.'' She smiled when he registered surprise over her candor. ''But name one politician who doesn't. It takes someone with enormous self-confidence to assume the responsibility for thousands of people's lives, Tate.''

''We're all egomaniacs, then?''

''You have a healthy self-esteem. That's nothing to be ashamed of or apologize for. The ability to lead is a gift, like being musically inclined or having a genius for numbers.''

''But no one accuses a mathematical wizard of exploitation.''

''Your integrity wouldn't allow you to exploit anyone, Tate. The ideals you espouse aren't just campaign slogans. You believe in them. You're not another Rory Dekker. He's all wind. He's got no substance. In time, the voters are going to realize that.''

''You still think I'm going to win?''

''Absolutely.''

"Yeah?"

"Yeah."

It became very close and still within the car while the rain continued to beat against the roof and lash at the windows. He reached across the car and laid his hand flat on her chest, his thumb and little finger stretching from collarbone to collarbone.

Avery's eyes closed. She made a slight swaying motion toward him as though being tugged by an invisible string. When she opened her eyes again, he was much nearer. He had moved to the center of the bench seat and his eyes were busily scanning her face.

His hand slid up her throat and curled around the back of her neck. When his lips touched hers, spontaneous combustion consumed them. They kissed madly while their hands battled to gain ground. His smoothed down her chest, over the tailored suit jacket, then up again to knead her breasts through the quality cloth.

Avery caressed his hair, his cheeks, the back of his neck, and his shoulders, then drew him against her as she fell back into the corner of the seat.

He unbuttoned the two buttons on her left shoulder and wrestled with the row of hooks running down that side of her torso. When he shoved open the jacket, the gold locket now containing his and Mandy's pictures slipped into the valley between her breasts. The neon lights made a nighttime rainbow of her skin. Streams of rainwater cast fluid shadows across her breasts which were swelling out of her bra.

He bent his head and kissed the full curve, then the dark center. Through the lace, his tongue flicked roughly, hungrily, lustfully.

"Tate," she moaned, as sensations swirled from her breast throughout the rest of her body. "Tate, I want you."

Clumsily, he freed himself from his trousers and carried her hands down. Her fingers encircled the rigid length of his penis. As she caressed its velvety tip with the ball of her thumb, he buried his face between her breasts and gasped snatches of erotic phrases and promises.

His hands slipped beneath her narrow skirt. She helped him get her underpants off. Their lips met in a frantic, passion-driven kiss while they sought a workable position within the impossible confines of the front seat.

"Damn!" he cursed, his voice sounding dry and raw.

Suddenly he sat up and pulled her over his lap. Holding her bottom between his hands beneath her skirt, he positioned her above his erection. She impaled herself. They gave glad cries which, within seconds, diminished to pleasurable groans.

Their lips sought and found each other while their tongues were rampant and quick. He squeezed the taut flesh of her derriere and stroked her thighs above her hosiery and between the lacy suspenders of her garter belt. She used her knees for elevation that teasingly threatened to release his cock before sinking down onto it until it was fully imbedded again. She rode him, milked him.

"Damn, you can fuck."

Having rasped that, he nuzzled his head against her breast until he had worked it free of her brassiere cup. He laved the raised nipple with his tongue, then took it into his mouth. He slid one of his hands between her damp thighs and entwined his fingers in the soft hair, then slipped them into the cleft and stroked the small protuberance.

Avery's breathing became choppy and loud. She bent her head over his shoulder. Tensing around the hardness within her and grinding against the magic stroking finger without, she had a very long, very wet climax that coincided with Tate's.

They didn't move for a full five minutes. Each was too weak. Finally, Avery eased herself off his lap and retrieved her underpants from the floorboard. Wordlessly, Tate passed her a handkerchief.

Self-consciously, she accepted it and said, "Thank you."

"Are you okay? Did I hurt you?"

"No, why?"

"You . . . you feel so small."

Her eyes were the first to fall away after a long, telling stare.

Once she had tidied herself and straightened her helplessly wrinkled clothing, she flipped down the sun visor and looked with dismay at her reflection in the vanity mirror.

Her hairdo had been ravaged. Clumps of moussed hair surrounded her head like a spiked halo. An earring was missing. Carefully outlined lipstick had been smeared over the entire lower third of her face. "I'm a wreck."

Tate made his body as straight as the accommodations would allow and tucked in his shirttail. His necktie was askew and his coat was hanging off one shoulder. He fumbled with his pants zipper and cursed it twice before closing it successfully.

"Do the best you can," he said, passing her the earring he'd just sat down on.

"I'll try." With the cosmetics in her purse, she repaired the damages to her makeup and did what she could with her coiffure. "I guess we can blame my hair on the weather."

"What'll we blame the whisker burns on?" Tate touched the corner of her mouth. "Do they sting?"

She gave a small, unrepentant shrug and smiled shyly. He smiled back, then got out and came around for her.

By the time they reached the backstage area where Eddy was pacing and Ralph was jingling change in both pockets, they truly did look the worse for wear—windblown and rain-spattered, but inordinately happy.

"Where the hell have you been?" Eddy was almost too livid to form the words.

Tate answered with admirable composure. "I went to pick up Carole."

"That's what Zee told us when we called the hotel," Ralph said. He was no longer rattling change. "What possessed you to pull such a damn fool stunt? She said you'd left half an hour ago. What took so long?"

"No place to park," Tate said tersely, disliking this cross-examination. "Where are Jack and the others?"

"Out front trying to keep the hounds at bay. Hear that?" Eddy pointed toward the auditorium, where the crowd could be heard stamping in beat to a patriotic march and chanting, "We want Tate! We want Tate!"

"They'll be all the more glad to see me," Tate said calmly.

"Here's your speech." Eddy tried to thrust several sheets of paper at him, but he refused to take them.

He tapped the side of his head instead and said, "Here's my speech."

"Don't pull that disappearing act again," Ralph warned him bossily. "It's stupid not to let at least one of us know where you are at all times."

Dirk hadn't said a word. His dark face was even darker with fury. It wasn't aimed at Tate, but at Avery. He hadn't taken his beady eyes off her since their breathless arrival. She had withstood his baleful glare with aplomb. When he finally spoke, his voice vibrated with rage. "From now on, Mrs. Rutledge, when you want to be screwed, do it on your time, not ours."

Tate, making a savage, snarling sound, launched himself against the other man. He would have knocked him off his feet if he hadn't flattened him against the nearest wall. His forearm formed a bar as hard as steel against Dirk's throat and his knee plowed high into his crotch. Dirk grunted with surprise and pain.

"Tate, have you gone completely crazy?" Eddy shouted.

He tried to remove Tate's arm from Dirk's throat, but it wouldn't be budged. Tate's nose wasn't even an inch from Dirk's. His face was smooth and blank with the singlemindedness of a man bent on murder. Dirk's face, by contrast, was growing progressively bluer.

"Tate, please," Avery said desperately, laying a hand on his shoulder. "Never mind him. What he says doesn't matter to me."

"For God's sake, Tate." Frantically, Eddy tried to wedge himself between the two men. "Let him go. Now's not the time. Jesus, think!"

"If you ever," Tate said in a slow, throbbing voice, "*ever* insult my wife like that again, you'll die choking on it. You got that, you son of a bitch?" He dug into Dirk's testicles with his knee. The man, whose small eyes were bugging with fear, bobbed his head as much as Tate's arm beneath his chin would permit.

Gradually, Tate's arm relaxed. Dirk bent from the waist, clutching his balls, coughing and sputtering. Ralph rushed to assist his cohort. Tate smoothed back his hair, turned to Eddy, and said coolly, "Let's go." He reached for Avery.

She took his extended hand and followed him on stage.

THIRTY-EIGHT

Mandy insisted on substituting her nightgown for the T-shirt Tate gave her, even though it was long after midnight and closer to breakfast than bedtime.

"Now you're an honorary Dallas Cowboys cheerleader," he said as he slipped it over her head.

She admired the gaudy silver lettering on the front of her new shirt, then smiled up at him beguilingly. "Thank you, Daddy." Yawning hugely, she retrieved Pooh Bear and dropped back onto her pillow.

"She's learning to be a woman, all right."

"Exactly what does that comment imply?" Avery asked him as they went into their bedroom on the other side of the parlor.

"She took the goods, but didn't come across with a hug or a kiss."

Avery propped her hands on her hips. "Should I warn the female voters that behind your public feminist stand on issues, you're nothing but a rotten chauvinist at heart?"

"Please don't. I need all the votes I can get."

"I thought it went very well tonight."

"Once I got there, you mean."

"And before, too." Her confidential inflection brought his head up. "Thank you for defending my honor, Tate."

"You don't have to thank me for that."

They exchanged a long gaze before Avery turned away and began removing her clothes. She slipped into the bathroom, took a quick shower, put on a negligee, then relinquished the bathroom to Tate.

Lying in bed, Avery listened to the water running as he brushed his teeth. From sharing other hotel suites, she knew that he never replaced the towel on the bar, but always left it wadded in a damp heap beside the sink.

When he emerged from the bathroom, she turned her head, intending to tease him about that bad habit. The words were never voiced.

He was naked. His hand was on the light switch, but he was looking at her. She rose to a sitting position, an unspoken question in her eyes.

"In the past," he said in a hoarse whisper, "I could block you out of my mind. I can't anymore. I don't know why. I don't know what you're doing now that you didn't do before, or what you're not doing that you once did, but I'm unable to ignore you and pretend that you don't exist. I'll never forgive you for that abortion, or for lying to me about it, but things like what happened tonight in the car make it easier to forget.

"Ever since that night in Dallas, I'm like an addict who's discovered a new drug. I want you a lot, and I want you constantly. Fighting it is making me crazy and nearly impossible to live with. The last few weeks haven't been fun for me or for anybody around me.

"So, as long as you're my wife, I'm going to exercise my conjugal rights." He paused momentarily. "Is there anything you have to say about that?"

"Yes."

"Well?"

"Turn out the light."

The tension ebbed from his splendid body. A grin tugged at one corner of his lips. He switched out the light, then slid into bed and pulled her into his arms.

Her nightgown seemed to vaporize beneath his caressing hands. Before Avery had time to prepare herself for it, she was lying naked beneath him, and he was stroking her skin with his fingertips. Occasionally his lips left hers to sample a taste of throat, breast, shoulder, belly.

Desire rivered through her, a constant ebbing and flowing of sensation until even her extremities were pulsing. Her body was sensitized to each nuance of his—from the strands of hair that fell over his brow and dusted her skin each time he dipped his head for a kiss, to the power in his lean thighs that entwined with hers before gradually separating them.

When he levered himself above her, poised for entrance, she prolonged the anticipation by bracketing his rib cage between her hands and rubbing her face in his chest hair. Her lips brushed kisses across his nipples. The sound of Tate's hoarse moan was her reward.

Hungrily, their mouths found each other again. His kisses were hot and sweet and deep . . . and that's what he said of her body when he claimed it.

Mandy, riding on Tate's shoulders, squealed as he dipped and staggered as though he were about to fall with her. She gripped double handfuls of his hair, which made him yelp.

"Shh, you two!" Avery admonished. "You'll get us kicked out of this hotel."

They were making their way down the long corridor from the elevator to their suite after having eaten breakfast in the restaurant downstairs. They'd left Nelson and Zee drinking coffee, but Mandy had been getting restless. The formal dining room was no place for an energetic child.

Tate passed Avery the key to their suite. They went inside. The parlor was full of busy people. "What the hell's going on here?" Tate asked as he swung Mandy down.

Eddy glanced up from his perusal of the morning paper and removed the Danish pastry that he'd been holding between his teeth. "We needed to meet and you have the only room with a parlor."

"Make yourselves at home," Tate said sarcastically.

They already had. Trays of juice, coffee, and Danish had been sent up. Fancy was polishing off a bagel as she sat crossed-legged on the bed, flipping through a fashion magazine. Dorothy Rae was sipping what looked like a Bloody Mary and staring vacantly out the window. Jack was on the phone, a finger plugging one ear. Ralph was watching the "Today Show." Dirk was riffling through Tate's closet with the appraising eye of a career shopper at a clearance sale.

"You got a good review last night," Eddy commented around the sweet roll.

"Good."

"I'll take Mandy into the other room." Avery placed her hands on the child's shoulders and steered her toward the connecting door.

"No, you stay," Dirk said, turning away from the closet. "No hard feelings about last night, okay? We've all been under a lot of pressure. Now the air's been cleared."

The man was insufferable. Avery wanted to slap the phony, ingratiating smile off his dour face. She looked at Tate. Ignoring the campaign expert, he told her, "I guess you'd better stick around."

Jack hung up the phone. "All set. Tate's got a live interview on channel five at five o'clock. We need to have him there no later than four-thirty."

"Great," Ralph said, rubbing his hands together. "Any word from the Dallas stations?"

"I've got calls in."

Someone knocked on the door. It was Nelson and Zee. A man, a stranger to Avery, was with them. Fancy bounded off the bed and embraced her grandparents in turn. Since her arrival in Fort Worth, her mood had been effervescent.

"Good morning, Fancy." Zee cast a disapproving glance at Fancy's denim miniskirt and red cowboy boots, but said nothing.

"Who's he?" Tate asked, nodding at the man lingering on the threshold.

"The barber we sent for." Dirk stepped forward and pulled the dazed man into the room. "Sit down, Tate, and let him get started. He can clip while we talk. Something conservative," he told the barber, who whisked a blue-and-white-striped drape around Tate's neck and took a comb to his hair.

"Here," Ralph said, shoving a sheaf of papers beneath Tate's nose. "Glance over these."

"What are they?"

"Your speeches for today."

"I've already written my speeches." No one listened to or acknowledged him.

The phone rang. Jack answered. "Channel four," he excitedly informed them, covering the mouthpiece.

"Zee, Nelson, find seats, please, and let's get down to business. The morning's getting away." In his element, Dirk took the floor. "As Eddy has said, we had a terrific turnout at Billy Bob's last night and raised a lot of campaign dollars. God knows we need them. Once momentum subsides, supporters stop contributing."

"Even though we're currently behind by a substantial margin, we don't want it to look like we're giving up," Ralph said as he bounced the coins in his pocket.

"The people at channel four said they'd be at General Dynamics to get a sound bite of Tate's speech, but that's all they'll promise," Jack reported as he hung up the phone.

Dirk nodded. "Not great, but better than nothing."

"See, Tate," Ralph said, continuing as though the second conversation weren't going on, "even if you lose, you don't want it to look like you gave up."

"I'm not going to lose." He glanced at Avery and winked.

"Well, no, of course not," Ralph stammered, laughing uncomfortably. "I only meant—"

"You're not taking enough off," Dirk sourly told the barber. "I said *conservative.*"

Tate batted the barber's fussing hands away. "What's this?" He pointed to a paragraph in one of the speeches that had been written for him. Again he was ignored.

"Hey, listen to this." Eddy read a passage from the newspaper. "Dekker comes right out and calls you a rabblerouser, Tate."

"I think he's running scared," Nelson said, drawing Dirk's attention to him.

"Nelson, I want you to be a prominent figure on the podium when Tate speaks at General Dynamics this afternoon. Those military contracts keep them in business. Since you're an ex-flier, you'll be a bonus."

"Am I to go? And Mandy?" Zee asked.

"I'll be glad to stay with Mandy," Dorothy Rae offered.

"Everybody goes." Dirk frowned at the empty glass in Dorothy Rae's hand. "And everybody looks his best. Squeaky-clean America. That means you too, missy," he said to Fancy. "No miniskirt."

"Go screw yourself."

"Francine Rutledge!" Nelson thundered. "You'll be sent home promptly if you use that kind of language again."

"Sorry," she mumbled. "But who's this asshole to tell me how to dress?"

Dirk, unfazed, turned to Avery. "You usually do fine as far as wardrobe goes. Don't wear anything too flashy today. These are working people, wage earners. Tate, I picked the gray suit for you today."

"Don't forget to remind him about his shirt," Ralph said.

"Oh, yes, wear a blue shirt, not white. White doesn't photograph as well on TV."

"All my blue shirts are dirty."

"I told you to send them out to be laundered every day."

"Well, I forgot, okay?" Suddenly he swiveled around and snatched the scissors from the barber's hands. "I don't want my hair cut any more. I like it like this."

In a tone of voice he might have used on Mandy, Dirk said, "It's too long, Tate."

He was out of his chair in an instant. "Who says? The voters? Those workers out at GD? Channel five's viewing audience? Or just you?"

Avery wanted to applaud. Unlike everyone else, she hadn't been caught up in the pandemonium going on around her. She'd been watching Tate. The more he read of the papers Ralph had given him to study, the deeper his scowl had become. She had sensed that his temper was about to erupt and she'd been right.

He whipped the drape from around his neck, sending hair clippings flying. He fished into his pocket and came up with a fifty-dollar bill, foisted it on the barber, and walked him to the door. "Thanks a lot." Tate shut the door on him.

When Tate turned back into the room, his expression was as ominous as the low clouds that still scuttled across the sky. "Next time, Dirk, I'll let *you* know when I need a haircut, if I deem it any of your business, which, frankly, I don't. And I would also appreciate it if you'd stay out of my closet and consult me before moving in on my family's private quarters."

"There was no place else to meet," Eddy said.

"The hell there wasn't, Eddy," he shouted, rounding on his friend, who had dared to intervene. "This hotel has several hundred rooms. But since you're already here," he said, picking up the sheets of paper he'd tossed down on the dresser. "I'd like to know what the hell this is supposed to signify?"

Ralph leaned over and read a few lines. "That's your position on the new education bill."

"Like hell it is. This is bullshit. That's what this is." He slapped the sheet of paper with the back of his hand. "Whitewashed, watered down, wishy-washy bullshit."

Zee left her chair. "I'll take Mandy into the other room to watch TV." She led the child away by the hand.

"I have to go potty, Grandma."

"Okay, darling. Fancy, you might want to come with us."

"Hell, no. I wouldn't budge for ten million bucks," she said from her position in the middle of the bed. She opened a fresh stick of Juicy Fruit and added it to the one already in her mouth.

When the door had been closed behind Zee and Mandy, Ralph ventured forth with a conciliatory explanation. "We simply felt, Tate, that your position on some of the campaign issues should be softened."

"Without consulting me?" Tate demanded, bearing down on the much shorter man. "It's *my* position," he said, thumping his chest. "My position."

"You're trailing in the polls," the man pointed out reasonably.

"I was doing that before you were retained to advise me. I've sunk lower since then."

"Because you haven't been taking our advice."

"Uh-uh," Tate said, stubbornly shaking his head. "I think it's because I've been taking too much of it."

Eddy stood up. "What are you implying, Tate?"

"Not a damn thing. I'm outright stating that I don't need anybody to pick out my shirts and suits or hire my barbers. I'm saying that I don't want anybody to put words in my mouth. I'm saying that I don't want anybody softening my position until it's so soft that even I don't recognize it. The people who have pledged their votes to me on the basis of those positions would think I'd gone crazy. Or worse, that I had betrayed them."

"You're blowing this out of proportion."

Tate confronted his brother. "It's not your hair they're trying to cut, Jack," he said heatedly.

"But it might just as well be," he fired back. "I'm in this as much as you are."

"Then you should know how important it is to me that I'm my own man."

"You are," Eddy said.

"The hell I am! What's wrong with the way I dress?" He gestured down to the clothes he'd worn to breakfast. "Do you really think it matters to those workers out at GD what color shirt I have on? Hell, no! They want to know if I'm for a strong defense program or for cutting the defense budget because my Senate vote may determine whether or not they'll have jobs for the next several years."

He paused to draw a breath and plowed his hand through his hair, which, Avery was glad to see, the barber hadn't gotten too much of. "Look, guys, this is me." He held his arms out perpendicular to his body. "This is the ticket. This is how I originally went to the Texas voters. Change me and they won't recognize me."

"We don't want to change you, Tate," Dirk said expansively. "Only make you better."

He clapped Tate on the shoulder. Tate shrugged off his hand. "Gentlemen, I'd like to speak to my family in private, please."

"If there's something to discuss—"

Tate held up his hand to ward off their objections. "Please." They moved toward the door reluctantly. Dirk shot Eddy a telling glance before they went out.

"Carole, would you pour me a cup of that coffee, please?"

"Certainly." As she rose to do so, Tate dropped into an easy chair. She brought the requested cup of coffee and sat down on the upholstered arm of his chair. Tate took the coffee with one hand and casually draped his other over her knee.

Eddy said, "Well, that was quite a speech."

"I tried it your way, Eddy. Against my better judgment, I let you hire them." His gaze was direct and so was his statement. "I don't like them."

"I'll talk to them, tell them to back off a little."

"Wait," Tate said, as Eddy headed for the door. "That's not good enough. They don't listen."

"Okay, I'll tell them that by the end of this tour we want to see drastic improvements in the polls or else."

"Still not good enough."

"Then what do you suggest?"

Tate looked at everyone in the room before saying, "Give them their walking papers."

"Fire them?" Jack exclaimed. "We can't do that."

"Why not? We hired them, didn't we?"

"You just don't shrug off a company like Wakely and Foster. You'll never be able to use them again."

"I don't consider that any great loss."

"You can't do it," Jack said stubbornly.

Eddy pleaded, "Tate, I beg you to think about this carefully."

"I have. I don't like them. I don't like what they're trying to do."

"Which is?" Jack's tone was snide, his stance belligerent.

"Which is to mold me into what they think I should be, not what I am. Okay, maybe I need some grooming. I could use some coaching, some finesse. But I don't like things to be mandated. I sure as hell don't like words put in my mouth when I don't even agree with them."

"You're only being stubborn," Jack said. "Just like when you were a kid. If I told you you couldn't do something, that's exactly what you became damned and determined to do just to show me up."

Tate expelled a long breath. "Jack, I've listened to your advice, and it's always been sound. I don't want to second-guess you on this decision—"

"But that's what you're doing, isn't it?"

"It was my decision, too," Tate said, raising his voice. "Now I'm changing my mind."

"Just like that?" Eddy said, snapping his fingers. "With the election only a few weeks away, you want to switch horses in the middle of the stream?"

"No, dammit, that's what they were trying to do!" He shot out of his chair and pointed toward the door through which the two under discussion had passed.

"They wanted to bend and shape me until I wouldn't be recognizable to the voters who have backed me from the beginning. I'd be selling out. I'd be no better than Dekker. Slicker than owl shit. Two-faced. Double-dealing." He was met with a wall of silent opposition from Eddy and his brother.

He turned to Nelson. "Dad? Help me out here."

"Why ask for my help now? You've already let your temper get the best of you. Don't ever get mad, Tate. Get even."

"How?"

"Win."

"By keeping my mouth shut and taking their advice?"

"Unless you feel that you're being compromised."

"Well, that's exactly where I am. I'd rather lose the election being myself than win and know I've had to compromise on everything I stand for. I'm sorry if none of you agrees."

"I'm on Eddy's side," Fancy said, "if anybody's interested in my opinion."

"Nobody is," Jack said to her.

"Carole?"

She had refrained from entering the verbal melee. Until Tate asked for her opinion, she intended to withhold it. Now that he had, she raised her head and looked up at him with newly formed intimacy and the wordless communication of lovers.

"Whatever you decide is all right with me, Tate. I'm with you all the way."

"Oh, yeah? Since when?" Jack rounded on Tate. "You talk about compromises. Sleeping with her again is the biggest compromise you ever made, little brother."

"That's enough, Jack!" Nelson bellowed.

"Dad, you know as well as I do that—"

"*Enough!* When you can control your own wife, you can start criticizing Tate."

Jack glared at his father, then at his brother, then hunched his shoulders and stormed out. Dorothy Rae rose from her chair unsteadily and followed him.

"I guess you'll walk next," Tate said to Eddy in the tense aftermath of their departure.

Eddy smiled lopsidedly. "You know better than that. Unlike Jack, I don't take these things personally. I think you're wrong, but . . . ." He gave an eloquent shrug. "We'll know on election day." He clapped his friend on the back. "Guess I'd better go break the bad news to our *former* consultants." He left; Fancy was hot on his heels.

Zee brought Mandy in. The atmosphere still crackled with animosity. Uneasily, she remarked, "I heard a lot of shouting."

"We got some things sorted out," Nelson said.

"I hope my decision is okay by you, Dad."

"As you said, it was your decision. I hope you're prepared to live with it."

"For my peace of mind, that's the way it has to be."

"Then stop apologizing for something that's already done."

"I told Mandy we would walk down to Sundance Square for a while," Zee said, interrupting the uncomfortable conversation. "I don't think it's going to rain anymore."

"I'll come along," Nelson said, scooping the child into his arms, his good humor seemingly restored. "I could use the exercise. And we won't mind if it does rain, will we, Mandy?"

"Thanks for backing me up," Tate said to Avery when they were finally alone. "You haven't always."

"As Jack rudely reminded me."

"He was upset."

"More than that, Tate. Jack despises me."

He seemed disinclined to address that. Perhaps he knew, as Avery did, that Jack didn't like Carole, but he desired her. Maybe Tate ignored that calamitous fact in the desperate hope that it would go away.

"Why'd you do it?" he asked. "Why'd you take my side? Did you feel like it was your wifely duty?"

"No," she said, taking umbrage. "I sided with you because I believe you're right. I didn't like them or their meddling or their advice any better than you did."

It had occurred to her that the men from Wakely and Foster might somehow be connected to the plot to assassinate Tate. That was another reason she was so glad to see the last of them.

After the recent heated discussion, the suite suddenly seemed very quiet. Paradoxically, without all the other people, the parlor seemed smaller, not larger. Their silent solitude pressed in on them.

Avery clasped her hands at her waist. "Well, I—"

"Good of Mom and Dad to take Mandy for a walk."

"Yes, it was."

"She'll enjoy the outing."

"And it'll give you a chance to study your speeches without interruption."

"Hmm."

"Although I don't think you really need to study them."

"No, I feel comfortable about today's schedule."

"That's good."

He contemplated the toes of his boots for a moment. When he looked up, he asked, "Do you think it'll rain?"

"I, uh . . ." She gave the window a cursory glance. "I don't think so, no. It—"

He reached for her, pulled her against him, kissed her neck.

"Tate?"

"Hmm?" He walked her backward toward the sofa.

"I thought, after last night, you wouldn't want . . ."

"You thought wrong."

THIRTY-NINE

"**B**oo!"

Fancy sprang out from behind the door as soon as Eddy entered his hotel room. He didn't even flinch. "How'd you get in here?"

"I bribed a maid."

"With what?"

"Uncle Tate's jockstrap."

"You're sick."

"Don't ya love it?"

"What's that?" He pointed to a table in front of the large window. It was draped with a white cloth and had two place settings laid out on it.

"Lunch. Crab salad in cute little avocado halves."

"You should have asked me first, Fancy."

"Aren't you hungry?"

"It wouldn't matter if I were. I've only got a minute." He sat down on the edge of the bed and picked up the telephone. After consulting the piece of scrap paper in his shirt pocket, he punched out the number. "Mr. George Malone, please."

Fancy stood on her knees behind him and ground her pelvis against his spine. "Mr. Malone? This is Eddy Paschal, with the Rutledge campaign. You called?" Eddy ducked his head when she leaned over his shoulder and bit his earlobe.

"Mr. Rutledge's schedule is tight, I'm afraid. What did you have in mind? How many people? Uh-huh."

She kissed his neck, lightly sucking the skin up against her teeth. He covered the mouthpiece with his hand. "Cut it out, Fancy. I'm busy."

Pouting, she flounced off the bed. Moving to the bureau mirror, she paused to plump her hair. Bending at the waist, she flung the thick mane upside down. When she straightened up, she was encouraged to notice that Eddy had been looking at her ass. Facing him with her feet widely spaced, she gathered up her short skirt, flirtatiously raising it an inch at a time.

"How soon do you have to know?"

As Eddy continued to speak smoothly into the telephone, she ran her splayed hands up the fronts of her thighs. Her thumbs met at the red satin triangle covering her pubis. She stroked it once, twice, then peeled the panties off and dangled them in front of his nose.

"I'll speak with Mr. Rutledge and get back to you as soon as possible. In any event, we appreciate your interest. Thank you for the invitation."

He hung up. To Fancy's dismay he brushed past her and went to the bathroom, where he combed his hair and washed his hands.

"What the hell's wrong with you?" she demanded when she joined him.

"Nothing. I'm in a hurry, that's all."

"You're mad because Uncle Tate had you fire those assholes, aren't you?"

"Not mad. I just disagree, that's all."

"Well, don't take it out on me."

"I'm not." He straightened his tie and checked his cuff links.

"Quite a scene this morning, wasn't it? I've never seen Uncle Tate so hot. He's kinda cute when he's in that mood. I love it when a man is on the verge of losing his temper." She slipped her arms beneath Eddy's, reached around him, and pressed her hands against his fly. "That potential violence is so sexy."

"I haven't got time for you now, Fancy." He removed her hands and stepped back into the bedroom.

She flopped down on the bed and watched as he sorted through the papers in his briefcase. He looked so handsome when his brow was furrowed with concentration.

Inspired, Fancy scooted up the bed until her back was against the headboard. She peeled her white cotton sweater over her head and tossed it on the floor beside her discarded panties. Then, left only in her miniskirt and red cowboy boots, she softly called his name. He turned. Slowly, she dragged her tongue over her lower lip and whispered, "Ever had a cowgirl?"

"As a matter of fact, I have," he said blandly. "Last night. In the ass. Or don't you remember?"

Fancy's widespread knees snapped together like the jaws of a sprung trap. She rolled to the edge of the bed, picked up her sweater, and worked it over her head, furiously thrusting her arms into the sleeves.

When she confronted him, her eyes were shimmering with tears. "That wasn't very nice."

"You seemed to think so last night."

"That's not what I meant," she yelled.

Eddy calmly closed his briefcase and picked up the jacket of his suit. "*Nice* is a strange word coming from you." He headed for the door.

She caught his sleeve as he moved past her. "Why are you being so hateful to me?"

"I'm in a hurry, Fancy."

"Then you're not mad?"

He sidestepped her. "I'm not mad."

"Will I see you later?"

"At the rally this afternoon." He patted his pocket to make sure he had his room key, then reached for the doorknob.

She flattened herself against the door. "You know what I mean. Will I see you later?" Smiling seductively, she squeezed him through his trousers.

"Yes, I know what you mean." He brushed aside her caressing hand and opened the door, despite her efforts to keep him from it. "In the meantime, try and stay out of trouble."

As the door closed behind him, Fancy swore liberally. She'd planned an intimate little lunch, then a quick, raunchy tumble. Or, depending on his schedule, a long leisurely afternoon of lovemaking.

So much for that, she thought resentfully. Nobody did or said anything anymore unless it related to the election. She was damn sick and tired of hearing about *the election.* She would be so glad when it was over and done with so Eddy could concentrate solely on her.

She propped herself against the headboard again and turned on the TV. A soap opera couple were smooching beneath satin sheets. Angry and jealous, she mashed the button on the remote control to switch channels. Geraldo Rivera was refereeing a shouting match between a fundamentalist preacher and a cross-dresser. On another station a group of housewives was sniffing open jars of peanut butter. She went back to the soap opera.

She loved Eddy passionately, but admitted that part of his appeal was his remoteness. She'd known guys who screwed their brains out, literally. The building could fall down around them and they wouldn't know it until after they climaxed.

Not Eddy. His physical performance was excellent, but his mind remained detached from his body. Even the most intimate acts never required emotional involvement from him. His participation was almost that of an observer.

That steely control excited her. It was different, intriguing.

But sometimes she wished Eddy would gaze at her with dopey adoration like the hunky male soap star was gazing into the face of the gorgeous ingenue. His eyes spoke volumes of unqualified love while his lips nibbled her fingertips.

Capturing Eddy Paschal's heart would be a real coup. She would delight in knowing that he couldn't take his eyes off her, that they would hungrily follow her as she moved about a room.

She would love for Eddy to be totally absorbed with her like that.

She would love for him to be absorbed with her the way Uncle Tate was with Aunt Carole.

Dorothy Rae launched her attack while they were sitting in the limousine waiting for the men to rejoin them. One second she was staring docilely out the window at the red, white, and blue bunting flapping in the wind, the next she was hissing at Avery like a she-cat.

"You loved it, didn't you?"

Mandy's head was resting in Avery's lap. The child had become tired and restless at the outdoor rally, so she had returned to the car with her before the program was over. Mandy was asleep now. Dorothy Rae, who had accompanied them back to the car, had been so quiet that Avery had almost forgotten she was there.

"I'm sorry, what?" she asked vaguely.

"I said you loved it."

Her meaning escaped Avery completely. She shook her head in confusion. "Loved what?"

"Loved making Jack look like a fool this morning."

Was she drunk? Avery took a closer look at her. On the contrary, she seemed in desperate need of a drink. Her eyes were clear but had the blazing wildness of someone gone mad. She was wringing a damp Kleenex between her hands.

"How did I make Jack look like a fool?" Avery asked.

"By taking Tate's side."

"Tate is my husband."

"And Jack's mine!"

Mandy was roused, but after opening her eyes once, she fell back asleep instantly. Dorothy Rae lowered her voice. "That hasn't stopped you from trying to steal him away from me."

"I haven't tried to steal him."

"Not lately, maybe," she said, taking a swipe at her leaky eyes with the Kleenex, "but before the crash you did."

Avery said nothing.

"The thing that makes it so despicable," Dorothy Rae continued, "is that you really didn't want him. As soon as he became interested, you spurned him. You didn't care that your rejection crushed his ego. You only wanted to get at Tate by flirting with his brother."

Avery couldn't deny the ugly allegations because they were probably true. Carole wouldn't have had any scruples against having an affair with her husband's brother, or, just short of that, making out like she was open to one. Most of her pleasure would be derived from the disharmony and devastation it would cause within the family. Perhaps that was all part of Carole's scheme to destroy Tate.

"I have no designs on Jack, Dorothy Rae."

"Because he's not the one in the limelight." Her hand clenched Avery's arm like a claw. "He never is. Never was. You knew that. Why didn't you just leave him alone? How dare you play with people's lives like that?"

Avery wrenched her arm from the other woman's grip. "Did you fight me for him?"

Dorothy Rae wasn't prepared for a counterattack. She stared at Avery with stupefaction. "Huh?"

"Did you ever fight me for Jack's attention, or did you just drink yourself into a stupor every day and let it happen?"

Dorothy Rae's face began to work convulsively. Her red-rimmed eyes got redder, wetter. "That's not a very kind thing to say."

"People have been kind to you for too long. Everybody in the family turns a blind eye to your disease."

"I don't have a—"

"You've got a disease, Dorothy Rae. Alcoholism is a disease."

"I'm not an alcoholic!" she cried tearfully, echoing the denials that her own mother had used for years. "I have a few drinks—"

"No, you drink to get drunk and you stay drunk. You wallow in self-pity and then wonder why your husband lusts after other women. Look at yourself. You're a mess. Is it any wonder that Jack has lost interest in you?"

Dorothy Rae groped for the door handle. "I don't have to sit here and listen to this."

"Yes, you do." Turning the tables on her, Avery grabbed her arm and refused to let go. "It's time somebody got tough with you, woke you up to a few facts. Your husband wasn't *stolen* from you. You drove him away."

"That's not true! He swore I wasn't the reason he left."

"Left?"

Dorothy Rae looked at her blankly. "Don't you remember, Carole? It wasn't long after you and Tate got married."

"I . . . of course I remember," Avery stammered. "He stayed gone about . . ."

"Six months," Dorothy Rae said miserably. "The longest six months of my life. I didn't know where he was, what he was doing, if he was ever coming back."

"But he did."

"He said he needed time alone to sort out a few things. He had so many pressures."

"Like what?"

She made a small, helpless gesture. "Oh, Nelson's expectations for the law firm, Tate's campaign, my drinking, Fancy."

"Fancy needs a mother, Dorothy Rae."

She laughed mirthlessly. "But not me. She hates me."

"How do you know? How do you know how she feels about anything? Do you ever talk to her?"

"I try," she whined. "She's impossible."

"She's afraid that no one loves her." Avery drew a quick breath. "And I'm afraid she might be right."

"I love her," Dorothy Rae protested adamantly. "I've given her everything she ever wanted."

"You threw her play-pretties to keep her occupied so that rearing her wouldn't interfere with your drinking. You grieve over the two children you miscarried at the expense of the one you have."

Dorothy Rae had mentioned the babies she had lost the night Carole's abortion had come to light. Later, Avery had gleaned the details from Fancy. So much of Dorothy Rae's unhappiness was now understandable. Avery leaned across the plush car seat, appealing to Dorothy Rae to listen. "Fancy is courting disaster. She needs you. She needs her father. She needs someone to take a firm hand. If Jack weren't so worried about your drinking, maybe he would devote more time and attention to being a parent. I don't know.

"But I do know that unless you do something, and quickly, she'll keep on behaving the way she does—doing outrageous things just so she'll get noticed. One of these days, she'll go too far and harm herself."

Dorothy Rae pushed back a strand of lank hair and assumed a defensive posture. "Fancy's always been a handful—more than Jack and I could handle. She's got a willful personality. She's just being a teenager, that's all."

"Oh, really? A teenager? Did you know that she came home the other night after having taken a beating from a guy she picked up in a bar? Yes," Avery emphasized when she saw Dorothy Rae pale with disbelief.

"I'm being an armchair psychologist, but I believe Fancy thinks she deserves no better than that. She thinks she's unworthy of being loved because no one has ever loved her, though she's tried every means she knows to get your attention."

"That's not true," Dorothy Rae said, shaking her head in obstinate denial.

"I'm afraid it is. And there's more." Avery decided to throw caution to the wind. She was, after all, pleading for a young woman's life. "She's sleeping with Eddy Paschal."

"I don't believe you," Dorothy Rae wheezed. "He's old enough to be her father."

"I saw her coming out of his hotel room in Houston weeks ago."

"That doesn't mean—"

"It was dawn, Dorothy Rae. You could tell by looking at her what she'd been doing all night. I have every reason to believe the affair is still going on."

"He wouldn't."

It was a sad commentary that Dorothy Rae didn't question her daughter's morality, only that of the family friend. "He is."

Dorothy Rae took several moments to assimilate this information, then her eyes narrowed on Avery. "You're a fine one to cast stones at my daughter."

"You miss my point," Avery said. "I'm not judging Fancy's morals. I'm worried about her. Do you think a man like Eddy is interested in her except for one reason? In light of his friendship with Tate, do you think he'll continue this relationship for any length of time or let it develop into something more meaningful? No.

"What really concerns me is that Fancy considers herself in love with him. If he dumps her, the rejection would only reinforce her low opinion of herself."

Dorothy Rae laughed scornfully. "If anything, my daughter has a high opinion of herself."

"Is that why she picks up strangers and lets them work her over? Is that why she hops from man to man and lets them use her any way they like? Is that why she has set her cap for a man she can't possibly have?" Avery shook her head no. "Fancy doesn't like herself at all. She's punishing herself for being unlovable."

Dorothy Rae picked at the shredding tissue. Softly, she said, "I never had much control over her."

"Because you don't have control over yourself."

"You're cruel, Carole."

Avery wanted to take the woman in her arms and hold her. She wanted to say, "No, I'm not cruel. I'm not. I'm telling you this for your own good."

Instead, she responded as Carole might. "I'm just tired of being blamed for the lousy state of your marriage. Be a wife to Jack, not a sniveler."

"What would be the use?" she sighed dejectedly. "Jack hates me."

"Why do you say that?"

"You know why. Because he thinks I tricked him into marrying me. I really did think I was pregnant. I *was* late."

"If Jack hated you," Avery argued, "would he have stayed married to you all these years? Would he have come back after a six-month separation?"

"If Nelson told him to," she said sadly.

Ah. Jack always did what his father told him to. He was bound to his wife by duty, not love. He was the workhorse; Tate was the Thoroughbred. The imbalance could breed a lot of contempt. Maybe Jack had figured out a way to get back at his brother and the parents who favored him.

Avery looked at Dorothy Rae from a different perspective and admitted that she might drink, too, if she were caught in a loveless marriage that was held together only by patriarchic decree. The situation was especially demoralizing to Dorothy Rae, who obviously loved Jack very much.

"Here," Avery said, taking a fresh tissue from her purse and passing it to Dorothy Rae, "blot your eyes. Put on fresh lipstick."

Just as she was finishing, Fancy pulled open the car door and got in. She sat on one of the fold-down stools facing them. "God, this campaigning shit really sucks. Look what that frigging wind did to my hair."

Dorothy Rae glanced at Avery with uncertainty. Avery kept her expression impassive. Dorothy Rae took courage and turned to her daughter. "You shouldn't use that kind of language, Fancy."

"How come?"

"Because it's unbecoming to a lady, that's how come."

"A lady? Right, Mom," she said with an audacious wink. "You just go on deluding yourself. Have a drink while you're at it.'' She unwrapped a stick of Juicy Fruit and folded it into her mouth. "How much longer is this going to take? Where's the radio in this thing?''

"I'd rather you left it off, Fancy,'' Avery said. "It will wake up Mandy.''

She swore softly and tapped the toes of her red boots together.

"You'll need to wear something more appropriate to the rally tonight,'' Dorothy Rae said, glancing down at her daughter's shapely bare thighs.

Fancy stretched her arms out on the seat behind her. "Oh, yeah? Well I don't own anything *appropriate*. Thank God.''

"When we get back to the hotel, I'll go through the things you brought and see—''

"Like hell, you will!'' Fancy exclaimed. "I'll wear whatever I damn well please. Besides, I already told you I don't have anything—''

"How about going shopping this afternoon to buy something?'' The two of them looked at Avery, clearly astonished by her sudden proposal. "I'm sure you could find a dress that is suitable but still funky. I can't go, of course, but the two of you could take a cab out to one of the malls while Tate's doing that TV interview. In fact,'' she added, sensing their hesitation, "I have a list of things you could pick up for me as long as you're going.''

"Who said I was going?'' Fancy asked crossly.

"Would you like to, Fancy?''

Fancy looked quickly at her mother, who had spoken quietly, almost shyly. She was clearly astonished. Her eyes were mistrustful, but curious as well. Avery detected a speck of vulnerability behind the worldly façade.

"Why don't we?'' Dorothy Rae urged in a wavering voice. "It's been ages since we've done something like that together. I might even buy a new dress, too, if you'll help me pick it out.''

Fancy's lips parted, as though she was about to nix the idea. After a moment's hesitation, however, she resumed her I-don't-give-a-damn smirk. "Sure, if you want to, I'll go along. Why not?''

She glanced out the window and spotted Eddy as he led the group back toward the waiting limousines. "There sure as hell isn't anything better to do.''

FORTY

"Hello, Mr. Lovejoy.''

Van was bent over, diddling with his camera. He raised his head and shook his long hair out of his face. "Oh, hi, Av . . . uh, Mrs. Rutledge.''

"It's good to see you again.''

"Same here.'' He inserted a blank tape into his camera and hoisted it onto his shoulder. "I missed you the first week of this trip, but the family has been reunited, I see.''

"Yes, Mr. Rutledge wanted us with him.''

"Yeah?'' Van leered with insinuation. "Ain't that sweet?''

She gave him a reproving look. Although she'd seen Van at various times during the day and they'd nodded at each other, she hadn't had an opportunity to speak with him until now. The afternoon had passed in a blur, especially after her enlightening conversation with Dorothy Rae.

"How's it going?" Van asked her.

"The campaign? It's exhausting work. I've shaken a thousand hands today, and that's a fraction of what Tate has done." It was little wonder to her that he had been so tired when she arrived in Fort Worth the evening before. Yet in front of every crowd he had to appear fresh and enthusiastic.

This was the last appearance of the day. Even though the banquet was officially over, the dais was thronged with people who had cheered his speech and now wanted to meet him personally. She commiserated with the demands being placed on him after such a long day, but she was glad for the opportunity to slip away and seek out Van.

"Heard he fired those buzzards from Wakely and Foster."

"News travels fast."

"Paschal already released a statement to that effect. If you ask me, Rutledge didn't oust them a minute too soon. They made it almost impossible to get close to him. It was like screwing with a steel belted radial on your dick instead of a regular rubber."

Avery hoped no one nearby had overheard the simile. It was one he would use with a co-worker, but hardly one suitable for the ears of a congressional candidate's wife. She hurriedly switched subjects. "The commercials you taped at the ranch are running on TV now."

"You've seen them?"

"Excellent photography, Mr. Lovejoy."

His crooked teeth showed when he smiled. "Thanks, Mrs. Rutledge."

"Have you seen anyone here that you recognize?" she asked, casually scanning the milling crowd.

"Not tonight." His emphasis on the second word brought her eyes snapping back to his. "There were some familiar faces in the crowd this afternoon."

"Oh?" She had monitored the crowds carefully, but to her vast relief, hadn't spotted Gray Hair. Obviously Van had. "Where? Here in the hotel?"

"At General Dynamics and again at Carswell Air Force Base."

"I see," she said shakily. "Is that the first time this trip?"

"Uh-huh," he said, nodding his head yes. "Well, you must excuse me, Mrs. Rutledge. Duty calls. The reporter's signaling me, so I gotta split."

"Oh, I'm sorry I detained you, Mr. Lovejoy."

"No problem. Glad to oblige." He took several steps away from her, then turned back. "Mrs. Rutledge, did you ever stop to think that someone's here to see you and not, uh, your husband?"

"Me?"

"Just a thought. But worth considering." Van's eyes telegraphed a warning. Moments later he was sucked into the ebb and flow of people.

Avery stood very still and rolled the chilling theory over and over in her mind. She was impervious to the motion of the crowd, to the noise and commotion, and oblivious to someone watching her from across the room and wondering what she and the disheveled television cameraman had found to talk about for so long.

"Jack?"

"Hmm?"

"Did you notice my new hairdo?"

Dorothy Rae was admiring her reflection for the first time in so long she couldn't even remember. In her youth, when she'd been the most popular girl at Lampasas High School, primping had been her number-one pastime. But for years there had been little to admire when she looked into a mirror.

Jack, reclining on the hotel room bed reading the newspaper, answered mechanically. "It looks nice."

"Today Fancy and I walked past this trendy beauty parlor in the mall. You
know, the kind of place where all the stylists are dressed in black and have several
earrings in each ear." Jack grunted. "On impulse, I said, 'Fancy, I'm gonna have
a make-over.' So we went in and one of the girls did my hair and makeup and
nails."

"Hmm."

She gazed into the mirror, turning her head to one side, then the other. "Fancy
said that I should lighten my hair just a bit, right here around my face. She said it
would give me a lift and take years off. What do you think?"

"I think I'd be wary of any advice coming from Fancy."

Dorothy Rae's reblossoming self-confidence wilted a little, but she resisted the
temptation to go to the bar and pour herself a reviving drink. "I . . . I've stopped
drinking, Jack," she blurted out.

He lowered the newspaper and looked at her fully for the first time that evening.
The new hairdo was shorter and fluffier and flattering. The subtly applied cosmetics had moistened the dry gullies in her face eroded by rivers of vodka, and given
color to the wasteland it had been.

"Since when?"

Her newfound confidence withered a little more at his skepticism, but she
staunchly kept her head erect. "This morning."

Jack folded the newspapers and tossed them to the floor. Reaching for the switch
of the reading lamp mounted to the headboard, he said, "Good night, Dorothy
Rae."

She moved to the bed and clicked the lamp back on. He looked up at her with
surprise. "I mean it this time, Jack."

"You've meant it every time you said you were going to quit."

"This time is different. I'm going to check myself into one of those hospitals
you've wanted me to go to. After the election, that is. I know that now wouldn't
be a convenient time to be committing a member of Tate's family into a hospital
for drunks."

"You're not a drunk."

She smiled sadly. "Yes, I am, Jack. Yes, I am. You should have made me admit
it a long time ago." She put out her hand and tentatively touched his shoulder.
"I'm not blaming you. I'm the one responsible for what I've become."

Then her fine chin, which had somehow withstood the ravages of abusive
drinking and unhappiness, came up another notch. Held at that proud angle, her
face bore traces of the beauty queen she had been and the vivacious coed he'd
fallen in love with. "I'm not going to be a useless drunk anymore."

"We'll see."

He didn't sound very optimistic, but at least she had his attention, which was
something. He didn't listen to her half the time because she rarely had anything
worthy of his interest.

She urged him to scoot over so she could sit at the edge of the bed beside him
and primly folded her hands in her lap. "We've got to keep closer tabs on Fancy."

"Good luck," he snorted.

"I realize we can't put her on a leash. She's too old."

"And too far gone."

"Maybe. I hope not. I want her to know that I care what happens to her." Her
lips parted in a small smile. "We actually got along together this afternoon. She
helped me pick out a new dress. Did you notice the one she was wearing tonight?

It was still flashy, but conservative by her normal standards. Even Zee commented on it. Fancy needs a firm hand. That's the only way she'll know we love her.'' She paused, glancing at him hesitantly. ''And I want to help you.''

''Help me what?''

''Recover from your disappointments.''

''Disappointments?''

''Mostly Carole. You don't have to admit or deny anything,'' she said quickly. ''I'm stone sober now, but I know that your desire for her wasn't a drunken delusion I had. Whether or not it's been consummated doesn't matter to me.

''I couldn't blame you for being unfaithful. There were times when I loved my next drink as much as I loved you—maybe more. I know you're in love with Carole—infatuated, anyway. She's used you and hurt you. I want to help you get over her.

''And I want to help you get over other disappointments, like the one you had this morning when Tate went against your decision to keep those consultants.''

Gaining courage, she touched his face this time. Her hand only shook a little. ''Whether anyone else gives you credit for the fine man you are, I do. You've always been my hero, Jack.''

He scoffed at that. ''Some hero.''

''To me you are.''

''What's all this about, Dorothy Rae?''

''I want us to love each other again.''

He looked at her for a long moment, more meaningfully than he had looked at her in years. ''I doubt that can happen.''

His futile tonality frightened her. However, she gave him a watery smile. ''We'll work on it together. Good night, Jack.''

She extinguished the lamp and lay down beside him. He didn't respond when she placed her arms around him, but he didn't turn away as he usually did.

Insomnia had become the norm since Carole had returned from the hospital. Indeed, these nights of wakefulness were cherished, for the night had become the best time in which to think. No one else was around; there was no motion and noise to clutter the brain. Silence bred insight.

What it obviously failed to instill was logic. Because no matter how many times the data was analyzed, the ''logical'' hypothesis was preposterous.

Carole wasn't Carole.

The hows, whys, and wherefores of it mattered, but not to any extent like the indubitable fact that Carole Navarro Rutledge had been replaced by someone else. Amnesia was the only other explanation for the complete reversal from her former personality. That would explain why she had fallen in love with her husband again, but still wouldn't account for the altered personality traits. Her current persona would only make sense if she were another woman entirely.

Carole wasn't Carole.

Then who was she?

The question was tormenting because so much was at risk. The plan that had taken years to orchestrate was about to come to fruition . . . unless it was thwarted by an impostor. All the elements were in motion. It was too late to turn back, even if that was desired, which it wasn't. Sweet revenge sometimes required bitter sacrifices. Vengeance was not to be denied.

Until the moment it was realized, however, this Carole, this impostor, must be watched. She seemed innocent enough, but one could never be too careful. But who she was and why she would want to assume another woman's identity, if indeed that's what had happened, was puzzling.

As soon as they returned home, answers to these questions must be sought. Perhaps one more carrot should be dangled in front of her just to see how she would respond, whom she would run to. Yes, one more message was called for. She mustn't be put on the alert that she'd been found out. The partner in this would certainly agree. Carole's every move from here on must be scrutinized. They had to know who she was.

A starting point would be to learn who had actually died in the crash of Flight 398 . . . and who had lived.

"Morning."

"Hey, Jack. Sit down." Tate motioned his brother into the chair across the breakfast table and signaled a waiter to pour him some coffee.

"You're not expecting anyone else?"

"No. Carole and Mandy slept late this morning. I got up, went out for my run, and was dressed by the time they woke up. Carole said for me not to wait on them, but to come on down. I hate eating alone, so I'm glad you're here."

"Are you?" To the waiter, he said, "The number three breakfast. Make sure the bacon's crisp and substitute hash browns for the grits, please."

"Certainly, Mr. Rutledge."

"Pays to have a famous brother," Jack commented as the waiter withdrew with his order. "Guarantees better service."

Tate was leaning back in his chair, his hands forming loose fists on either side of his plate. "Mind telling me what you meant by that crack?"

"What crack?" Jack dumped two packets of sugar into his coffee.

"Asking me if I'm really glad you're having breakfast with me."

"I just thought that after yesterday—"

"Yesterday went great."

"I'm referring to the meeting with Dirk and Ralph."

"So you're still pissed because I fired them?"

"It's your campaign," Jack said with an insolent shrug.

"It's our campaign."

"The hell it is."

Tate was about to offer a rebuttal when the waiter appeared with Jack's breakfast. He waited until they were alone again, then leaned across the table and said in a soft, peacemaking tone, "I wasn't belittling your decision, Jack."

"That's what it looked like to me. To everybody else, too."

Tate stared into the cooling remains of his waffles and sausage, but didn't pick up his fork again. "I'm sorry if you took it to heart, but their tactics just weren't working for me. I listened to you, to Eddy, to Dad, but—"

"But you went with Carole's opinion."

Tate was taken aback by Jack's viciousness. "What's she got to do with this?"

"You tell me."

"She's my wife."

"That's your problem."

Tate didn't want to get into a discussion of his marriage with his brother. He addressed the real issue. "Jack, my name is the one on the ballot. I'm ultimately accountable for how my campaign is run. I'll have to answer for my performance in Congress if I'm elected. Tate Rutledge," he stressed, "not anybody else."

"I understand that."

"Then work with me, not against me." Warmed to his topic, Tate pushed his plate aside and propped his forearms on the edge of the table. "I couldn't have done this alone. Hell, don't you think I know how dedicated you are to this?"

"More than anything in the world, I want to see you elected."

"I know that, Jack. You're my brother. I love you. I appreciate your doggedness, your self-sacrifice, and all the details you see to so I won't be bothered with them. I realize, probably more than you know, that I'm sitting on the white horse while you're down there shoveling up the shit."

"I never aspired to ride the white horse, Tate. I just want to be given credit for shoveling the shit pretty damn well."

"More than pretty damn well," Tate said. "I'm sorry we disagreed on that matter yesterday, but sometimes I have to go with my gut instinct, despite what you or anybody else is advising me.

"Would you have me any other way? Would I be a worthy candidate for public office if I could be swayed to go along with something because it would be the popular, expedient, and convenient thing to do, even though I felt strongly against it?"

"I suppose not."

Tate smiled ruefully. "In the final analysis, I'm the one baring my ass to the world, Jack."

"Just don't expect me to bend over and kiss it when I think you're wrong."

The two brothers laughed together. Jack was the first to grow serious again. He summoned the waiter to take away their plates and replenish their coffee cups. "Tate, as long as we're clearing the air . . ."

"Hmm?"

"I get the impression that things are better between you and Carole."

Tate glanced at his brother sharply, then away. "Some."

"Well, that's . . . that's good, I guess. As long as it makes you happy." He fiddled with an empty sugar packet.

"Why am I waiting for the other shoe to drop?"

Jack cleared his throat and shifted uneasily in his chair. "I don't know, there's something . . ." He ran his hand over his thinning hair. "You're going to think I'm crazy."

"Try me."

"There's something out of sync with her."

"What do you mean?"

"I don't know. Hell, you sleep with her. If you haven't noticed it, then I must be imagining it." He paused, waiting expectantly for either a confirmation or denial, neither of which he got. "Did you see her talking to that TV guy last night?"

"What TV guy?"

"The one who did the camera work for the commercial we made at the ranch."

"His name's Van Lovejoy. He's covering my campaign for KTEX."

"Yeah, I know." Jack spread his hands wide and laughed dryly. "It just seemed strange that Carole made a point to speak to him during all that hoopla last night, that's all. She made a beeline for him as soon as she left the dais. He's not exactly her type." Tate quickly averted his head. "What I mean is . . ." Jack stammered, "He's not . . . hell, you know what I mean."

"I know what you mean." Tate's voice was quiet.

"Well, I'd better get back upstairs and light a fire under Dorothy Rae and Fancy. Eddy wants everybody congregated in the lobby, packed and ready to pull out by ten-thirty." He affectionately slapped his brother's shoulder as he walked past him. "I enjoyed breakfast."

"So did I, Jack."

Tate continued to stare sightlessly out the window. Carole had been talking to Van Lovejoy again last night? Why?

He hadn't told his brother that she had had a private conversation with the video photographer once before. For all her glib explanation, their conversation on the sidewalk outside the Adolphus had appeared furtive.

She'd lied her way around it that time. He'd known she was lying, but then he'd kissed her, she'd kissed him back, and he'd forgotten what had started the argument. Things had been going so well between them. Why did this dark cloud have to show up on the horizon?

Their sex had never been as good or as satisfying. It was hot, but it had always been hot. It was dirty, but it had always been dirty. Only now it was like having dirty sex with a lady, which made it even better. She no longer rushed the foreplay. She no longer chanted gutter jargon. She didn't scream like before when she pretended to come, but took catchy little breaths that he thought were infinitely sexier. And he would swear that her orgasms were genuine. There was a newness to their lovemaking, an essence of intrigue, almost like it was illicit. He was embarrassed to even think the cliché, but each time was like the first time. He always discovered something about her that he hadn't realized before.

She'd never been modest, never given a thought to parading around unclothed. Lately, however, she artfully used lingerie rather than nudity to entice him. Yesterday morning, when they'd made love on the parlor sofa, she had insisted that he pull the drapes first. He supposed her self-consciousness stemmed from the nearly undetectable scars on her arms and hands.

The maidenly shyness excited him. She seduced by withholding. He hadn't yet seen in the light what he caressed in darkness with his hands and lips. Damned if the mystery didn't make him want her even more.

He had thought about her constantly yesterday. Prurient thoughts of her had intruded upon high-level discussions and impassioned speeches. Whenever their eyes connected, they seemed to be thinking the same thought, and that was how quickly they wanted the time to pass so they could go to bed again.

He had developed the curious habit of subconsciously knowing where she was at all times, gauging her distance from him and inventing reasons to touch her whenever she was close enough. But was she playing games with him? Was her modesty a sexual gimmick? Why did she have an unexplainable interest in this photographer?

On the one hand, Tate wanted immediate answers. But if answers meant having to give up the peace, harmony, and sex, he was prepared to wait indefinitely for an explanation.

 # FORTY-ONE

Zinnia Rutledge stood gazing at the wall of framed photographs behind the credenza. She loved this office because of those photographs. She could have gazed at them for hours and never tired of it, though of course she never did. The memories they evoked were bittersweet.

At the sound of the door opening behind her, she turned. "Hello, Zee, did I startle you?"

Zee quickly blinked away the tears in her eyes and resealed her emotions in the vault of her heart. "Hello, Carole. You did take me by surprise. I was expecting Tate." They had planned to meet here at his office and go to lunch together—a special date, just the two of them.

"That's why he sent me over. I'm afraid I'm the bearer of bad news."

"He can't make it," Zee said with evident disappointment.

"I'm afraid not."

"There's nothing wrong, I hope?"

"Not exactly. There's been a labor dispute going on within the Houston Police Department."

"I'm aware of that. It's been in all the papers."

"Well, this morning things came to a head. An hour ago, Eddy decided that Tate should go down there, assess the situation, and make a statement. The latest poll shows that Tate is closing the gap. He's only five points behind Dekker now. This volatile situation in Houston presented a perfect forum for Tate to get across some of his ideas, not only on labor versus management, but law enforcement, as well. They're flying down in a private jet and should be back in a few hours, but lunch is out of the question."

"Tate likes to fly as much as his father," she remarked with a wistful smile. "He'll enjoy the trip."

"Will you accept a poor substitute for his company?"

The tentative invitation yanked Zee from her pensiveness. "You mean have lunch with you?"

"Would that be so terrible?"

Zee looked her daughter-in-law up and down, finding little about her appearance to criticize. Carole had refined her image considerably since her recovery. She still dressed with flair, but her emphasis was now more on style than sexiness.

Carole's flamboyance had always repelled Zee. She was glad it had been subdued. The woman inside the impeccable clothing, however, was still just as distasteful as the first time she'd met her.

"I'll pass."

"Why?"

"You never knew when to let something drop, Carole." Zee tucked her handbag beneath her arm.

"Why don't you want to have lunch with me?"

She had taken up a position in front of the door, barring Zee from making a gracious exit. "My heart was set on having lunch with Tate," she said. "I understand why he had to cancel, but I'm disappointed and see no reason to pretend that I'm not. We have so little time together these days, just he and I."

"And that's what's really bugging you, isn't it?"

Zee's small body tensed instantly. If Carole insisted on a confrontation, Zee decided to give her one. "What are you implying?"

"You can't stand that Tate is spending more time with me. You're jealous of our relationship, which is stronger every day."

Zee gave a soft, scoffing laugh. "You would love to believe that, wouldn't you, Carole? You'd prefer to think that I'm merely jealous when you know that I was opposed to your marriage to my son from the beginning."

"Oh?"

"Don't act like you didn't know. Tate does. I'm sure the two of you have discussed it."

"We have. And even if we hadn't, I'd know you dislike me intensely. You don't hide your feelings very well, Zee."

Zee smiled, but it was a sad expression. "You'd be amazed at how well I conceal what I'm thinking and feeling. I'm an expert at it." Carole's gaze sharpened quizzically, putting Zee on alert. She composed her face and said icily, "You've made an effort to patch up your deteriorating relationship with Tate. Nelson is delighted. I'm not."

"Why not? I know you want Tate to be happy."

"Exactly. And he'll never be happy as long as you've got your claws in him. See, Carole, I know that all your loving ways are machinations. They're phony, just as you are."

Zee derived petty satisfaction from watching Carole's face become pale beneath her carefully applied makeup. Her voice was faint. "Phony? What do you mean?"

"Shortly after you married Tate, when I first began to notice a rift between you, I hired a private investigator. Cheesy, yes. It was the most humiliating experience I've ever put myself through, but I did it to protect my son.

"The investigator was a repulsive individual, but he did an excellent job. As you've no doubt guessed by now, he provided me with an extensive portfolio on you before you became a legal assistant at Rutledge and Rutledge."

Zee could feel her blood pressure rising. Her compact body had become an incinerator, fueling itself on her hatred for this woman who had, with the cold calculation of a KGB infiltrator, dazzled all the Rutledge men and duped Tate into loving her.

"I don't believe I need to detail the disgusting contents of that portfolio, do I? God only knows what it omits. Only let me assure you that it encompasses your checkered stint as a topless dancer. Among your other careers," she said as an aside, giving a delicate shudder.

"Your various stage names were colorful but unimaginative, I thought. The investigator stopped digging before he discovered the name you were given at birth, which isn't important anyway."

Carole looked as though she might throw up at any moment. Her difficult swallow could be heard in the silent office, vacant except for the two of them. Tate's secretary had gone to lunch.

"Does anyone else know about this . . . this portfolio? Does Tate?"

"No one," Zee replied, "though I've been tempted on many occasions to show it to him—most recently when I realized that he's falling in love with you again."

Carole drew a soft, whistling breath. "Is he?"

"Much to my dismay, I believe he is. In any case, he's enchanted. Probably against his better judgment. He's falling for this new Carole, who's emerged as a result of the plane crash. Maybe the next name you assume should be Phoenix, since you've risen out of the ashes."

Zee tilted her head to one side and considered her adversary for a moment. "You're an extremely clever young woman. Your transformation from skid row topless dancer into a lady charming enough to be a senator's wife was quite remarkable. It must have taken an enormous amount of planning, studying, and hard work to bring about. You even chose a surname enshrined on the walls of the Alamo—a Spanish name. Very advantageous for the wife of a political candidate in Texas.

"But this most recent change is even more incredible than the first because you seem to believe in it yourself. I could even think that you're sincere until I compare what you were like the morning of the crash to what you're like now, with Tate, with Mandy." Zee gave her head a negative shake. "No one can change that drastically, no matter how clever she is."

"How do you know I haven't changed out of love for Tate? I'm trying to be what he needs and wants."

Shooting her a look, Zee moved her aside and reached for the door. "I know as well as I know my own name that you are *not* what you want us to believe you are."

"When do you plan to expose me?"

"Never." Carole flinched with surprise. "As long as Tate is happy and content with you, I won't disillusion him. The folder will remain our secret. But start hurting him again, Carole, and I assure you I'll destroy you."

"You can't do that without destroying Tate, too."

"I don't intend to make it a public disclosure. Showing the portfolio to Tate would be sufficient. He wouldn't let a whore, even a reformed one, rear his daughter. It's intolerable to me, too, but I have no choice at this point. Rarely are we given real choices."

A look of sheer desperation came over Carole's face. She closed her hand around Zee's arm. "You can't ever tell Tate. Please, Zee, please don't. It would kill him."

"That's the only reason I've resisted so far." Zee wrested her arm free of the younger woman's touch. "But believe me, Carole, if it came to seeing him suffer through a scandal temporarily, or living in misery for the rest of his life, I would spare him the latter at any cost."

On her way out, she added, "I'm sure you'll search for this dossier I have on you. Don't bother destroying it. There's a duplicate in a private safe deposit box, which can be opened only by me, or, in the event of my death, Tate."

Avery unlocked the front door with her key and stepped inside the house. "Mona? Mandy?"

She located them in the kitchen. The cheek she pressed against Mandy's was cold. She'd driven all the way from San Antonio with the car windows down. Her face had been flaming after her unsettling encounter with Zee. The cool air had also warded off the nausea she experienced every time she thought of Carole Navarro's incriminating history.

"Is the soup good, darling?"

"Uh-huh," Mandy replied, slurping up a spoonful of chicken and noodles.

"I didn't expect anyone home for lunch, Mrs. Rutledge, but I can fix you something."

"No thanks, Mona. I'm not hungry." She shrugged out of her coat and sat down in one of the chairs at the table. "I could stand a cup of tea if it's not too much trouble, please."

She nervously wrung her hands until the housekeeper set the steaming cup of fragrant tea in front of her, then folded her bloodless fingers around the mug.

"Are you feeling all right, Mrs. Rutledge? Your cheeks are flushed."

"I'm fine. Just chilled."

"I hope you're not coming down with the flu. There's a lot of it going around."

"I'm fine," she repeated, smiling weakly. "Finish your fruit cocktail, Mandy, then I'll read you a story before your nap."

She tried to respond to Mandy's constant chatter, a sign of her continuing progress, but her mind kept wandering back to Zee and the damning information she had collected on Carole.

"All done?" She praised the two empty bowls Mandy held up for her inspection. Finishing her tea, she led Mandy to her bedroom. After helping her untie her shoes, she lifted her into bed and covered her with a quilt. She settled down beside her with a large picture book.

Her father had read to her from such a book when she was a girl. It was filled with beautiful illustrations of damsels with long, wavy golden hair being rescued from distress by handsome, brave heroes who overcame impossible odds. Her memories of lying beneath covers or sitting on her father's lap while his voice lulled her to sleep were some of her earliest and most precious memories of childhood.

Those had been coveted moments, when Daddy was home and paying attention to her. In the fairy tales he read, the princess always had a doting father. Good was always victorious over the forces of evil.

Perhaps that's why they called them fairy tales. They were a departure from reality, where fathers disappeared for months on end and all too often evil was the victor.

When Mandy fell asleep, Avery slipped from the room and quietly closed the door behind her. Mona retired to her quarters every afternoon for a couple hours of watching soap operas and resting before preparing dinner.

No one else was at home, but Avery stealthily tiptoed along the tile flooring straight from Mandy's room toward the wing of the house Zee shared with Nelson. She didn't weigh the rightness or wrongness of what she was about to do. It was a ghastly invasion of privacy and would have been unthinkable under other circumstances. The circumstances being what they were, however, made it necessary.

She located their bedroom with no problem. A very pleasant room, it was shuttered against the bright autumn sunlight. The floral fragrance she associated with Zee was redolent.

Would Zee keep such explosive documents in the dainty Queen Anne desk? Why not? It looked as innocent as a novice nun. Who would think to violate it? Nelson conducted ranching business at a massive desk in the den down the hall. He would have no reason to go through his wife's seemingly innocuous desk.

Avery took a nail file from the dressing table and applied it to the tiny gold lock on the lap drawer of the desk. She didn't even try to cover her crime. Zee expected her to check. She had said as much.

It wasn't a very sturdy lock. Within seconds, Avery pulled the desk drawer open. Inside there were several thin boxes of stationery engraved with Zee's initials, a book of stamps, an address book, two slender, black Bibles, one with Jack's name embossed in gold block letters, the other with Tate's name.

The manila folder was in the back of the drawer. Avery removed it and pried open the metal bracket.

Five minutes later, she left the room, pale and trembling. Her whole body shook as though she had palsy. Her stomach was queasy. The harmless tea had turned rancid in her stomach. She hastened to her own room and locked the door behind her. Resting against it, she drew in draughts of cleansing air.

Tate. Oh, Tate. If he ever saw the revolting contents of that folder. . . .

She needed a bath. Quickly. Immediately.

She kicked off her shoes, peeled off her sweater, and slid open her closet door. She screamed.

Reeling away from the grotesque sight, she covered her mouth with both hands, though retching noises issued from her throat. Opening the closet door had caused the campaign poster to swing from the end of its red satin cord like a body on a gallows.

In bright red paint, a bullet hole had been painted in the center of Tate's forehead. The paint trickled down his face, hideously incongruent with his smile. Written in bold red lettering across the poster were the words, "Election Day!"

Avery bolted into the bathroom and vomited.

FORTY-TWO

"It was ghastly. So ugly."

Avery sat with her head bowed over a glass of brandy that Irish had insisted would help calm her down. The first unwanted swallow had burned a crater in her empty stomach, but she kept the glass because she needed something to hold on to.

"This whole frigging thing is ugly," her irascible host declared. "I've thought so all along. Didn't I warn you? Didn't I?"

"So you warned her. Stop harping on it."

"Who asked you?" Irish angrily rounded on Van, who was sipping at a joint that Irish had been too upset to notice wasn't an ordinary cigarette.

"Avery did. She called and told me to haul ass over here, so I hauled ass."

"I meant who asked you for your opinion?"

"Will the two of you please stop?" Avery cried raggedly. "And Van, will you please put that thing out? The smell's making me sick."

She tapped her fingertips against her lips, as though contemplating whether or not she was going to throw up again. "The poster terrified me. He really means to do it. I've known so all along, but this . . ."

She set the glass of brandy on the coffee table and stood up, chafing her arms. She had on a sweater, but nothing helped her get warm.

"Who is it, Avery?"

She shook her head hard. "I don't know. Any of them, *I don't know.*"

"Who had access to your room?"

"Earlier this morning and before I came home at noon, anybody. Mona says they should install a revolving door. Everybody's in and out constantly. As the election approaches, they come and go at all hours."

"How do you know someone didn't follow you here?"

"I kept one eye on the rearview mirror and doubled back several times. Besides, no one was home when I left."

"No clues from the folder you found in the old lady's desk?"

Avery answered Van's irreverent question with a dismal shake of her head.

"She's a strange one," he observed.

"What makes you say that?"

"I've got lots of her on tape. She's always smiling, waving at the crowds, but damned if I believe she's all that happy."

"I know what you mean. She's a very private person and says little. At least until today."

"Tell us about Carole Navarro," Irish said. "She's more to the point than Zee Rutledge."

"Carole, or whatever her original name was, was a tramp. She danced in the seediest nightclubs—"

"Tittie bars," Van supplied.

". . . Under a number of spicy and suggestive names. She was arrested once for public lewdness and once for prostitution, but both charges were dropped."

"You're sure of all this?"

"The private investigator might have been slime, but he was thorough. With the information he supplied Zee, it was easy for me to track down some of the places Carole had worked."

"When was this?" Irish wanted to know.

"Before I came here. I even talked to some people who knew her—other dancers, former employers, and such."

"Did any mistake you for her?" Van asked

"All of them. I passed myself off as a long-lost cousin to explain the similarity."

"What did they have to say about her?"

"She had severed all ties. Nobody knew what had happened to her. One drag queen that I spoke to, in exchange for a twenty-dollar bill, said she told him she was going to give up the night life, go to business school and improve herself. That's all he remembered. He never saw her after she quit working at the club where they shared a stage.

"This is pure conjecture, but I think Carole underwent a complete transformation, finessed her way into the Rutledge law firm, then once on the inside, saw a way to take her self-improvement campaign one step further by marrying Tate. Remember the piece I did several years ago on prostitutes, Irish?" she asked suddenly.

"While you were working at that station in Detroit? Sure, I remember it. You sent me a tape. What's it got to do with this?"

"The personality profile of those women fits Carole. Most of them claim to hate men. She was probably no different."

"You don't know that."

"No? Look how she treated Jack. She flirted with him to the extent of damaging his marriage, but I get the impression she never came across. If that isn't malicious, I don't know what is. For the sake of argument, let's say she didn't view men too kindly and set out to ruin one whose future looked the very brightest, while at the same time elevating herself."

"Wasn't she scared that someone would recognize her, that her shady past would eventually catch up with her?"

Avery had thought of that herself. "Don't you see, that would have iced the cake. Tate would really be humiliated if it was revealed what his wife had been before he married her."

"He must be a real dunce," Van muttered, "to have fallen for it."

"You don't understand how calculating she was," Avery said, leaping to Tate's defense. "She became everything he could possibly want. She laid a trap, using herself as the perfect bait. She was pretty, animated, and sexy. But more than that, someone who knew Tate well coached her on the right buttons to push to elevate lust to love."

"The one who wants to kill him."

"Right," Avery said, nodding grimly at Van, who had voiced her hypothesis. "He must have sensed, as Zee did, that Carole was an opportunist."

"When he approached her, why didn't she run to Tate?"

"I'm not sure," she admitted. "My theory isn't without holes. Maybe being the bereaved widow of a public official held more allure than being a senator's wife."

"Same status, but no inconvenient husband," Irish speculated.

"Hmm. Also, she wasn't sure Tate would make it to the Senate. Or maybe her coconspirator made it financially profitable for her. In any case, once they were married, it was her responsibility to make life miserable for Tate—a job she did with relish.''

"But *why* was someone out to make him miserable?'' Irish asked. "It always comes back to that.''

"I don't know.'' Avery's voice was taut with quiet desperation. "I wish to God I did.''

"What do you make of the latest message?'' Irish asked.

She raked a hand through her hair. "Obviously, they're going to make their move on election day. A gun of some kind will be the weapon of choice.''

"That gets my vote. No pun intended,'' Van added drolly.

Irish shot him an irritated glance, then said to Avery, "I don't know. This time the symbolism seems a little too obvious.''

"What do you mean?''

"I'm not sure,'' he admitted, gnawing on his lip. Absently, he picked up Avery's glass of brandy and took a hearty swig. "What happened to the subtlety of the earlier notes? Either he's testing your mettle or he's the cockiest son of a bitch I've ever run across.''

"Maybe he's cocky because it can't be stopped now,'' Van said moodily. "It'll go down no matter what. Everything is already in place.''

"Like Gray Hair?'' Avery asked. Van shrugged.

"What about the footage you shot earlier today in Houston? Any more of him?'' Irish asked Van.

"Nope. He hasn't turned up since Fort Worth. Not since Avery's been staying home.'' His eyes were mellowed by marijuana, but the look he gave her was meaningful enough for Irish to intercept.

"Okay, what don't I know, you two?''

Avery moistened her lips. "Van thinks it's possible that Gray Hair is watching me, not Tate.''

Irish's head swiveled on his thick neck around to the photographer. "What makes you think that?''

"It's just an idea. A little off the wall, but—''

"In every one of the tapes he's looking at Tate,'' she pointed out reasonably.

"Hard to tell. You're always standing right beside him.''

"Avery.'' Irish took her hand, pulled her back down onto the sofa, and squatted in front of her. He covered her hands with his own. "Listen to me now. You've got to notify the authorities.''

"I—''

"I said to listen. Now shut up and hear me out.'' He reorganized his thoughts. "You're in over your head, baby. I know why you wanted to do this. It was a terrific idea—a once-in-a-lifetime chance to make a name for yourself and save lives in the meantime.

"But it's gotten out of hand. Your life is in danger. And as long as you let this continue, so is Rutledge's. So's the kid's.'' Since she appeared to be receptive to his argument, he eased up onto the couch beside her, but continued to press her hands beneath his. "Let's call the FBI.''

"The feds?'' Van squeaked.

"I have a buddy in the local bureau,'' Irish pressed on, ignoring Van. "He usually works undercover, looking for dope coming up from Mexico. This isn't his area of expertise, but he could tell us who to call, advise us on what to do.''

Before he even finished, Avery was shaking her head no. "Irish, we can't. Don't you see, if the FBI knows, everybody'll have to know. Don't you think it would arouse suspicion if Tate were suddenly surrounded by armed bodyguards or Secret Service operatives in opaque sunglasses? Everything would have to come out in the open,''

''That's it, isn't it?'' he shouted angrily. ''You don't want Rutledge to know! And you don't want him to know because you'd have to give up your cozy place next to him in bed.''

''No, that's not it!'' she shouted back. ''The authorities could protect him from people outside the family circle, but they couldn't protect him from anybody within. And as we know, the person who wants him dead is someone close to him—someone who professes to love him. We can't alert Tate to the danger without alerting the enemy that we're on to him.''

She took a deep breath, but it was still insufficient. ''Besides, if you told government agents this tale, they'd think you were either lying or crazy. On the outside chance they believed you, think what they'd do to me.''

''What would they do to you?'' Van wanted to know.

''I'm not sure, but while they were figuring it out, Tate would be exposed and vulnerable.''

''So, what do you plan to do?'' Irish asked.

She covered her face with her hands and began to cry. ''I don't know.''

Van stood up and pulled on a tattered leather biker's jacket. ''I've got some moonlighting to do.''

''Moonlighting?''

Van responded to Irish's question with an indifferent shrug. ''I've been looking through some tapes in my library.''

''What for?''

''I'm working on a hunch.''

Avery reached for his hand. ''Thanks for everything, Van. If you see or hear—''

''I'll let you know.''

''Do you still have that post office box key I gave you?'' Irish asked.

''Yeah, but why would I need it? I see you every day at work when I'm in town.''

''But you might need to send me something when you're out of town with Rutledge—something it wouldn't do to mail to the station.''

''Gotcha. 'Bye.''

As soon as the door closed behind Van, Irish said, out of the side of his mouth. ''That dopehead. I wish we had a more reliable ally.''

''Don't put him down. I get annoyed with him, too, but he's been invaluable. He's been a friend, and God knows I need all of them I can muster.''

She checked her wristwatch—the one Tate had bought for her. Since retrieving it from Fancy, she hadn't taken it off. ''I've got to go. It's getting late. Tate asks questions when I'm late, and I'm running out of plausible excuses. There's only so much shopping a woman can do, you know.'' Her feeble attempt at humor flew no better than a flatiron.

Irish pulled her into a hug. He clumsily smoothed his large hand over her hair while her head rested against his shoulder. ''You love him.'' He didn't even pose it as a question. She nodded her head. ''Jesus,'' he sighed into her hair, ''why does it always have to be so goddamn complicated?''

She squeezed her eyes shut; hot tears leaked onto his shirt. ''I love him so much, Irish, it hurts.''

''I know what that's like.''

Avery was too absorbed in her own misery to acknowledge his unrequited love for her mother. "What am I going to do? I can't tell him, but I can't protect him, either." She clung to Irish for strength. He hugged her tighter and awkwardly kissed her temple.

"Rosemary, all ninety-eight pounds of her, would fly into me if she knew I was letting you stay in a life-threatening situation."

Avery smiled against his damp shirt. "She probably would. She relied on you to watch over us."

"I'm letting her down this time." He clutched her tighter. "I'm afraid for you, Avery."

"After today, seeing that bloodcurdling poster, I'm a little afraid for myself. I'm still considered a conspirator. God help me if he ever discovers otherwise."

"You won't reconsider and let me call the authorities?"

"Not yet. Not until I can point an accusing finger and say, 'That's the one.' "

He put space between them and tilted her chin up. "By then it might be too late."

He hadn't needed to caution her of that. She already knew. It might already be too late to salvage her career as a broadcast journalist and establish a future with Tate and Mandy, but she had to *try*. She hugged Irish once more at his door before telling him good night, kissing his ruddy cheek, and stepping out into the darkness.

It was so dark that neither of them noticed the car parked midway down the block.

FORTY-THREE

The spontaneous trip to Houston to address disgruntled policemen had gone extraordinarily well for Tate and boosted him three points in the polls. Daily, he closed the gap between Senator Dekker and himself.

Dekker, feeling the pressure, began to get nasty in his speeches, painting Tate as a dangerous liberal who threatened "the traditional ideals that we as Americans and Texans hold dear."

It would have been a perfect time for him to use Carole Rutledge's abortion as ammunition. That would have blown Tate's campaign out of the water and probably cinched the race for Dekker. But whatever tactics Eddy had used on the extortionist had apparently been effective. When it became obvious that Dekker knew nothing of the incident, everyone in the Rutledge inner circle breathed a collective sigh of relief.

Dekker, however, had the endorsement of an incumbent president, who made a swing through the state in pursuit of his own reelection. Rutledge supporters feared that the president's appearance might nullify the gut-busting progress they had made.

Actually, the president was fighting for his life in Texas. The rallies where he shared the podium with Dekker had a subliminal edge of eleventh-hour desperation that was conveyed to the uncommitted voters. Tate benefitted rather than suffered from the president's vigorous campaigning. The groundswell gained even greater momentum when the opposing presidential candidate came to Texas and campaigned alongside him.

After an exhausting but exhilarating trip to seven cities in two days, everyone at Rutledge headquarters was reeling with preelection giddiness. Even though

Dekker still maintained a slight margin over Tate in the official polls, the momentum seemed to have swung the other way. Word on the street was that Tate Rutledge was looking better all the time. Optimism was at its highest peak since Tate had won the primary. Everyone was buoyant.

Except Fancy.

She sauntered through the various rooms of campaign headquarters, slouching in chairs as they became available, scorning the party atmosphere, stalking Eddy's movements with sulky, resentful eyes.

They hadn't been alone together for more than a week. Every time he glanced her way, he looked straight through her. Whenever she swallowed her pride and approached him, he did nothing more than assign her some menial task. She was even put on a telephone and told to call registered voters to urge them to go to the polls and vote on election day. The only reason she consented to do the demoralizing work was because it kept Eddy in her sights. The alternative was staying at the house and not seeing Eddy at all.

He was constantly in motion, barking orders like a drill sergeant and losing his temper when they weren't carried out quickly enough to suit him. He seemed to subsist on coffee, canned sodas, and vending machine food. He was the first to arrive at headquarters in the morning and the last to leave at night, if he left at all.

On the Sunday before the election, the Rutledges moved into the Palacio Del Rio, a twenty-two-story hotel on the Riverwalk in downtown San Antonio. From there they would monitor election returns two days later.

Tate's immediate family took the Imperial Suite on the twenty-first floor. The others were assigned rooms nearby. VCRs were installed on all the television sets so newscasts and commentaries could be recorded for subsequent review and analysis. Additional telephone lines were provided. Security guards were posted at the elevators, more to safeguard the candidate's privacy than the candidate himself.

On the mezzanine level, twenty stories below, workers were draping the wall of the Corte Real Ballroom with red, white, and blue bunting. The back wall was covered with larger-than-life-size pictures of Tate. The dais was being decorated with bunting and flags, and bordered with pots of white chrysanthemums nestling in red and blue cellophane. A huge net, containing thousands of balloons, was suspended from the ceiling, to be released on cue.

Over the racket and confusion generated by obsequious hotel employees, meticulous television servicemen, and scurrying telephone installers, Eddy was attempting to make himself heard in the parlor of Tate's suite that Sunday afternoon.

"From Longview you fly to Texarkana. You spend an hour and a half there, max, then to Wichita Falls, Abilene, and home. You should arrive—"

"Daddy?"

"Tate, for crissake!" Eddy lowered the clipboard he'd been consulting and exhaled his annoyance like noxious fumes.

"Shh, Mandy." Tate held a finger to his lips. She had been sitting on his lap during the briefing session, but her attention span had been exhausted long ago.

"Are you listening, or what?"

"I'm listening, Eddy. Longview, Wichita Falls, Abilene, home."

"You forgot Texarkana."

"My apologies. I'm sure you and the pilot won't. Are there any more bananas in the fruit basket?"

"Jesus," Eddy cried. "You're two days away from an election for a Senate seat and you're thinking about bananas. You're too damn casual!"

Tate calmly accepted a banana from his wife and peeled it for Mandy. "You're too tense. Relax, Eddy. You're making everybody crazy."

"Amen," Fancy intoned glumly from where she was curled in an easy chair watching a movie on TV.

"You win the election, then I'll relax." Eddy consulted the clipboard again. "I don't even remember where I was. Oh, yeah, you arrive here in San Antonio tomorrow evening around seven-thirty. I'll make arrangements for the family to have dinner at a local restaurant. You'll retire."

"Do I get to tee-tee and brush my teeth first? I mean, between dinner and retiring?"

Everyone laughed. Eddy didn't think Tate's wisecrack was funny. "Tuesday morning, we'll travel en masse to your precinct box in Kerrville, vote, then return here to sweat it out."

Tate wrestled the banana peel away from Mandy, who was sliding her index finger down its squishy lining and collecting the gunk beneath her fingernail. "I'm going to win."

"Don't get overconfident. The polls still show you two points behind Dekker."

"Think where we started, though," Tate reminded him, his gray eyes twinkling. "I'm going to win."

On that optimistic note, the meeting concluded. Nelson and Zee went to their room to lie down and rest. Tate had to work on a speech he was delivering at a Spanish-speaking church later in the evening. Dorothy Rae had talked Jack into going with her for a stroll along the Riverwalk.

Fancy waited until everyone dispersed, then followed Eddy to his room, which was a few doors down from the command post, as she called Tate's suite. After her soft knock, he called out, "Who is it?"

"Me."

He opened the door but didn't even hold it for her. He turned his back and headed for the closet, where he took out a fresh shirt. She closed the door and flipped the dead bolt.

"Why don't you just leave your shirt off?" She leaned into him suggestively and teased one of his nipples with the tip of her tongue.

"I don't think it would be too suave to show up at campaign headquarters without a shirt on." He crammed his arms through the starched sleeves and began buttoning up.

"You're going there now?"

"That's right."

"But it's Sunday."

He cocked his eyebrow. "Don't tell me you've started observing the Lord's day."

"I was in church this morning, same as you."

"And for the same reason," he said. "Because I told everybody they had to go. Didn't you see the television cameras recording Tate's piety for their viewing voters?"

"I was praying."

"Oh, sure."

"Praying that your dick would rot and drop off," she said with fierce passion. He merely laughed. When he began stuffing his shirttail into his trousers, Fancy tried to stop him. "Eddy," she whined contritely, "I didn't come here to fight with you. I'm sorry for what I just said. I want to be with you."

"Then come to the headquarters with me. I'm sure there's plenty of work to do."

"It wasn't work I had in mind."

"Sorry, that's what's on the agenda from now till election day."

Her pride could only take so much abuse. "You've been brushing me off for weeks now," she said, her fists finding props on her hips. "What gives with you?"

"You have to ask?" He ran a brush through his pale hair. "I'm trying to get your Uncle Tate elected to the U.S. Congress."

"Screw the U.S. Congress!"

"I'm sure you would," he said wryly. "If you had a chance, you'd give every member of the legislature blue balls. Now, Fancy, you'll have to excuse me."

He reached for the door. She blocked his path, pleading again, "Don't go, Eddy. Not just yet, anyway. Stay a while. We could order up some beers, have a few laughs." Wiggling against him, nudging his pelvis with hers, she purred, "Let's make love."

"Love?" he scoffed.

She grabbed his hand and drew it beneath her skirt toward her crotch. "I'm already wet."

He pulled his hand away, bodily lifted her out of his path, and set her down behind him. "You're always wet, Fancy. Peddle it somewhere else. Right now, I've got better things to do."

Fancy gaped at the closed door, then hurled the first available thing her hand landed on, which happened to be a glass ashtray. She threw it with all her might, but it only bounced against the door without breaking and landed dully on the carpeted floor. That enraged her even more.

She'd never been so summarily rejected. Nobody, but nobody, turned down Fancy Rutledge when she was hot. She stormed out of Eddy's room, stayed in hers only long enough to change into a tight sweater and even tighter jeans, then went to the hotel garage and retrieved her Mustang.

She was damned if she was going to stop living for the sake of this confounded Senate race.

"It's me. Anything happening?"

"Hello, Irish." Van rubbed his bloodshot eyes while cradling the telephone receiver against his ear. "I just got in a while ago. Rutledge spoke at a greaser church tonight."

"I know. How'd it go?"

"They loved him better'n hot tamales."

"Was Avery there?"

"Everybody was except the girl, Fancy, all looking as pure as Ivory soap."

"Did Avery get to talk to you?"

"No. There was a throng of jabbering Mex'cans around them."

"What about Gray Hair? Any sign of him?"

Van weighed the advisability of telling Irish the truth and decided in favor of it. "He was there."

Irish muttered a string of curses. "Didn't he stick out like a sore thumb in a Hispanic crowd?"

"He was outside, jockeying for position like the rest of us."

"He posed as media?"

"That's right."

"Did you get close to him?"

"Tall dude. Mean face."

"Mean?"

"Stern. No nonsense."

"A hit man's face."

"We're only guessing."

"Yeah, but I don't like it, Van. Maybe we ought to call the FBI and not tell Avery."

"She'd never forgive you."

"But she'd be alive."

The two men were quiet for a moment, lost in their private thoughts, considering possible options, and coming up with zip. "Tomorrow, you stick around here. No need to go with Rutledge."

"I figured that," Van said of his assignment when Irish finally broke the silence. "I'll be at the airport tomorrow night when he gets back. The press release said he'd be arriving at seven-thirty."

"Good. Try and make contact with Avery then. She said it's hard to phone from the hotel."

"Right."

"Election morning, come to the TV station first. Then I'm posting you at the Palacio Del Rio. I want you to stick to Avery like glue all day. If you see anything suspicious, *anything,* to hell with her arguments, you call the cops."

"I'm not stupid, Irish."

"And just because you have a free day tomorrow," Irish said in a threatening tone, "don't go out and get blitzed on something."

"I won't. I got a lot to do around here."

"Yeah, what?"

"I'm still looking at tapes."

"You mentioned that before. What are you looking for?"

"I'll let you know as soon as I find it."

They said their good-byes. Van got up long enough to relieve himself in the bathroom, then returned to the console, where he had spent nearly every free hour for the last several days. The number of tapes left to view was dwindling, but not fast enough. He had hours of them still to look at.

The wild goose he was chasing didn't even have an identity. As he had told Irish, he wouldn't know what it was till he saw it. This was probably a colossal waste of time.

He'd been dumb enough to start this harebrained project; he might just as well be dumb enough to finish it. He took a drag on his joint, chased it with a swallow of booze, and inserted another tape into his machine.

Irish made a face into the bottom of the glass of antacid he had forced himself to drink. He shivered at the wretched aftertaste. He should be used to it by now since he guzzled the stuff by the gallon. Avery didn't know. Nobody did. He didn't want anyone to know about his chronic heartburn because he didn't want to be replaced by a younger man before he could retire on a full salary.

He'd been in the business long enough to know that management-level guys were bastards. Heartlessness was a requirement for the job. They wore expensive shoes, three-piece suits, and invisible armor against humanism. They didn't give a damn about an old news horse's valuable contacts at city hall or his years of experience beating the bushes for a story or anything else except the bottom line.

They expected dramatic video at six and ten so they could sell commercial time to sponsors, but they'd never stood by and watched a house burn with people screaming inside, or sat through a stakeout while some nut wielding a .357 Magnum held people hostage in a 7-Eleven, or witnessed the unspeakable atrocities that one human being could inflict on another.

They operated in the sterile side of the business. Irish's side was the down-and-dirty one. That was fine. He wouldn't have it any other way. He just wanted to be respected for what he did.

As long as the news ratings kept KTEX number one in the market, he'd be fine. But if the ratings slipped, those bastards in the worsted wool would start sifting out the undesirables. An old man with a sour stomach and a disposition to match might be considered deadwood and be the first thing lopped off.

So he covered his belches and hid his bottles of antacid.

He switched out the light in his bathroom and shuffled into the bedroom. He sat on the edge of his double bed and set his alarm clock. That was routine. So was reaching into the nightstand drawer and taking out his rosary.

The threat of physical torture couldn't make him admit to anyone that this was a nightly ritual. He never went to confession or mass. Churches were buildings where funerals, weddings, or baptisms were solemnized.

But Irish prayed ritualistically. Tonight he prayed fervently for Tate Rutledge and his young daughter. He prayed for Avery's protection, begging God to spare her life, whatever calamity befell anyone else.

Last, as he did every night, he prayed for Rosemary Daniels's precious soul and beseeched God's forgiveness for loving her, another man's wife.

 # FORTY-FOUR

Tate opened the door to the suite and looked curiously at the three people standing just beyond the threshold. "What's going on?"

"Mr. Rutledge, I'm sorry to bother you," one of the uniformed policemen said. "Do you know this young woman?"

"Tate?" Avery asked, joining him at the door. "Who—? *Fancy?*"

The girl's expression was surly. One policeman had a firm grip on her upper arm, but it was difficult to tell if he were restraining or supporting her. She was leaning against him, obviously intoxicated.

"What's the matter?" Eddy approached the door and took in the scene. "Jesus," he muttered in disgust.

"Will you please tell them who I am, so they'll leave me the hell alone?" Fancy demanded belligerently.

"This is my niece," Tate stiffly informed the policemen. "Her name's Francine Rutledge."

"That's what her driver's license said, but we had to take her word for it that she was a relation of yours."

"Was it necessary to bring her here under armed escort?"

"It was either here or jail, Mr. Rutledge."

"On what charge?" Avery asked.

"Speeding, driving while intoxicated. She was doing ninety-five on the loop."

"Ninety-eight," Fancy corrected cheekily.

"Thank you, officers, for seeing her safely here. I speak for her mother and father, too."

Fancy threw off the policeman's hand. "Yeah, thanks a lot."

"How much is it going to cost us to keep this quiet?" Eddy asked the policemen.

One scowled at him disdainfully. The other ignored him completely and spoke only to Tate. "We figured you didn't need the bad publicity right now."

"I appreciate that."

"Well, after that speech you gave in Houston, taking the side of law enforcement officers and all, my partner and me figured it was the least we could do."

"Thank you very much."

"Good luck in the election, Mr. Rutledge." They doffed their caps deferentially before walking down the carpeted hallway toward the elevators and the gawking security guards.

Avery closed the door behind them. Everyone had already gone to bed except the four of them. Mandy was sleeping in the adjoining room. An ominous silence pervaded the suite—the calm before the storm.

"Fancy, where have you been?" Avery asked her softly.

She flung her hands far above her head and executed a clumsy pirouette. "Dancing. I had a wonderful time," she trilled, batting her eyelashes at Eddy. "Of course, nobody here would think so because you're all so old. So straight. So—"

"You stupid little cunt." Eddy backhanded her across the mouth. The force of the blow knocked her to the floor.

"Fancy!" Avery dropped to her knees beside the stunned girl. Blood trickled from the swelling cut on her lip.

"Eddy, what the *hell's* the matter with you?" Tate demanded, catching his arm.

Eddy flung Tate off and loomed above Fancy. "Are you trying to ruin everything? Do you know what could have happened if those two cops hadn't seen fit to bring you here? This childish stunt could have cost us the election," he shouted.

Tate grabbed his collar and hauled him back. "What do you think you're doing?"

"She's got it coming."

"Not from you!" Tate roared. He gave Eddy's shoulders a hard shove that sent him staggering backward. Eddy regained his balance, snarled, and lunged for Tate.

"Stop it, both of you!" Avery shot to her feet and moved between them. "You'll bring this hotel down on our heads, and what kind of headlines will that create?"

The men stood facing each other like two bulls pawing the ground, but at least they were no longer shouting. Avery bent over Fancy again and helped her to her feet. The girl was still so dazed she didn't put up any resistance, but she whimpered with pain and remorse.

Tate touched her cheek briefly, then aimed a warning finger at his friend. "Never, *never,* touch a member of my family like that again."

"I'm sorry, Tate." Eddy smoothed his hands over his ruffled hair. His voice was low, composed, cool. The iceman was restored.

"That's one area of my life where your opinion doesn't count," Tate said angrily, his lips barely moving to form the words.

"I said I was sorry. What else can I do?"

"You can stop sleeping with her."

All were taken by surprise. Eddy and Fancy had no idea that Tate knew. Avery had told him she suspected it, but that was before she knew it for a certainty. The women remained stunned and silent. Eddy walked to the door.

Before he went out, he said, "I think we all need time to cool off."

Avery looked at Tate with undiluted love and respect for coming so quickly to Fancy's defense, then placed her arm across the girl's shoulders. "Come on, I'll walk you to your room."

Once there, she waited while Fancy showered. Emerging from the bathroom, with her hair held away from her scrubbed face by barrettes, and wearing a long T-shirt as a nightgown, she looked young and innocent.

"I improvised on an ice pack for your lip." Avery handed her a plastic bag full of ice and led her toward the turned-down bed.

"Thanks. You're getting good at that."

Fancy propped herself against the headboard and held the ice pack to her lower lip. It had stopped bleeding, but was dark and swollen. She closed her eyes. Tears trickled through her lashes and rolled down her shiny cheeks. Avery lowered herself to the side of the bed and took her hand.

"That son of a bitch. I hate him."

"I don't think so," Avery countered softly. "I believe you thought you loved him."

Fancy looked at her, "*Thought* I loved him?"

"I think you were in love with the idea of being in love with him. How much do you really know about Eddy? You told me yourself you knew very little. I think you wanted to be in love with him because you knew deep down that the affair was inappropriate and had no chance of survival."

"What are you, an amateur shrink?"

Fancy could put a strain on anyone's patience, but Avery evenly replied, "I'm trying to be your friend."

"You're just trying to talk me out of him because you want him for yourself."

"Do you really believe that?"

The girl stared at her for a long moment, and the longer she stared, the more tears filled her eyes. Eventually, she lowered her head. "No. Anybody can see that you love Uncle Tate." She sniffed her drippy nose. "And he's ga-ga over you, too."

She pulled her lower lip through her teeth. "Oh, God," she wailed, "why can't somebody love me like that? What's wrong with me? Why does everybody treat me like shit, like I was invisible or something?"

The floodgate had been opened and all her self-doubt came pouring out. "Eddy was just using me to get his rocks off, wasn't he? I'd hoped that maybe he would love me for something more than just what I was willing to do in bed. I should have known better," she added in a bitter undertone.

Avery pulled Fancy into her arms. Fancy resisted for a second or two, then relented and let herself be comforted while she cried against Avery's shoulder. When her crying subsided, Avery eased her away.

"You know who should be in on this?"

Fancy wiped her wet face with the back of her hand. "Who?"

"Your mother."

"You're kidding, right?"

"No. You need her, Fancy. More than that," Avery said, pressing Fancy's knee for emphasis, "she needs you. She's been trying very hard to make up for past mistakes. Why not give her a chance?"

Fancy thought it over a moment, then nodded sullenly. "Sure, why not, if it'll make the old girl feel significant."

Avery dialed the room. Jack answered sleepily. "Is Dorothy Rae already in bed? Could she come to Fancy's room?"

"What's wrong?"

Avery looked at Fancy's lip and lied, "Nothing. Just a hen party."

In under a minute Dorothy Rae knocked. She was in her nightgown. "What is it, Carole?"

"Come in."

The minute she saw Fancy's face, she stopped dead in her tracks and raised a hand to her chest. "Oh, my baby! What happened to you?"

Fancy's lower lip quivered. A fresh batch of tears filled her eyes. She stretched out her arms and, in a weak, tremulous voice said, "Mommy?"

"I left them crying in each other's arms," Avery told Tate a few minutes later. "This might have been the best thing that could have happened."

"I don't think I've ever seen Eddy so irrational." While she'd been gone, he'd stripped down to his trousers. Barechested, he was was pacing the room, still spoiling for a fight.

"He's determined to get you elected. When something happens that could jeopardize that, his temper is explosive."

"But to strike a woman?" Tate asked incredulously, shaking his head.

"How long have you known that he was sleeping with Fancy?"

"A few weeks."

"He told you?"

"No, I picked up signals."

"Did you say anything to him about it?"

"What could I say? He's a grown-up. So is she. God knows he didn't coerce her or sweet talk his way past her virginity."

"I guess not," Avery sighed. "But for all her sexual experience, Fancy's extremely vulnerable, Tate. He's hurt her."

"Don't get me wrong. I'm not defending—"

"Listen!"

Avery held up her hand and signaled for quiet. Then, moving simultaneously, they rushed toward Mandy's bedroom and burst through the door.

She was flailing her limbs, thrashing them against the bed covers. Her small face was contorted and bathed with sweat. She was weeping copiously, her lips blubbering.

"Mommy! Mommy!" She screamed the name repeatedly.

Instinctively, Avery reached for her. Tate placed a restraining hand on her shoulder. "You can't. This might be it."

"Oh, no, Tate, please."

He shook his head stubbornly. "We have to."

So Avery sat on one side of Mandy and Tate sat on the other. Each lived through the hell the child's subconscious mind was being put through.

"No, no." She gasped for breath, holding her mouth wide. "Mommy? I can't see Mommy. I can't get out."

Avery looked across at Tate. His fingers were steepled over his nose and mouth, his eyes fixed on his tormented daughter.

Suddenly Mandy sat bolt upright, as though a spring action device had catapulted her head off the pillow. Her chest was rising and falling rapidly. Her eyes were open and unblinking, but she was still in the throes of the nightmare.

"Mommy!" she screamed. "Get me loose. I'm scared. *Get me loose!*"

Then her eyelids began to flutter and, though her respiration was still choppy, it no longer sounded as though she'd been running for miles and each breath might be her last.

"Mommy's got me," she whispered. "Mommy's got me now." She flopped back down, and when she did, she woke up.

Once her eyes had focused, she divided her bewildered gaze between Tate and Avery. It was into Avery's arms that she hurled her solid little body. "Mommy, you got me out. You got me away from the smoke."

Avery enfolded Mandy in her arms and hugged her tight. She squeezed her eyes shut and thanked God for healing this child who had become so dear to her. When she opened her eyes, they melded with Tate's. He extended his hand and stroked her cheek with his knuckle, then laid his hand on his daughter's head.

Mandy sat back on her heels and announced, "I'm hungry. Can I have some ice cream?"

Laughing with relief, Tate scooped her into his arms and swung her high over his head. She squealed. "You certainly can. What flavor?"

He ordered ice cream from room service, along with a change of linens from housekeeping to replace the damp, tangled sheets on Mandy's bed. While they waited for the deliveries, Avery changed Mandy into another nightgown and brushed her hair. Tate sat watching them.

"I had a bad dream," Mandy told them pragmatically as she used another hairbrush on Pooh Bear. "But I'm not scared anymore 'cause Mommy's there to get me away."

She'd gotten sleepy again by the time she'd finished her ice cream. They tucked her in and sat at the foot of her bed until she fell asleep, knowing that if Dr. Webster was right, her sleep would be uninterrupted from now on. As they left the room, their arms looped around each other's waists, Avery began to cry.

"It's over," Tate murmured and kissed her temple. "She's going to be okay."

"Thank God."

"Then what are you crying for?"

"I'm exhausted," she confessed with a soft laugh. "I'm going to take a long, hot bath. This day seems like it's lasted twenty years."

He had lived through Fancy's crisis and Mandy's nightmare with her. But Tate didn't know that Avery had experienced an anxiety attack at the Spanish church when she had spotted her nemesis outside the nave, surrounded by clambering media.

Once they had safely reached the limo, she had snuggled close to Tate, linking her arm through his and hugging his firm biceps to her breast. What he'd mistaken for an outpouring of affection had actually been a reaction to stark fear.

When Avery came out of the bathroom a half hour later, her skin was dewy and fragrant from soaking in bath oil. With the light behind her, she provided him with a tantalizing silhouette of her body through her nightgown.

"Still exhausted?" he asked.

The room was dim. The bed had been turned down. Avery's subconscious registered this, because she only had eyes for Tate. His hair was attractively mussed. The single light burning in the bathroom gilded his body hair. It fuzzily smattered his chest, whorled around his navel, then tapered to a stainy stripe that disappeared into the unfastened waistband of his trousers.

"Not that exhausted," she replied huskily. "Not if you have something other than sleep in mind."

"What I have in mind," he said, moving toward her, "is making love to my wife."

When he reached her, he curled one hand around the back of her neck and, without any hesitation, slid the other one inside her nightgown to cover her breast. Holding her eyes with his, he finessed the nipple.

"I don't mean just couple with the woman I happened to be married to," he whispered while his thumb continued giving her nipple glancing blows. "I mean make *love* to my *wife*."

He drew her face up close to his, paused, probed her eyes, then took her lips beneath his. There was a difference in his kiss. The difference was subtle, yet tremendous. Avery sensed it immediately. Technically it was the same, as his tongue gently but possessively mated with her mouth. But somehow it was much more personal, more intimate, more giving.

Minutes later they were in bed. Tate was naked, lying above her, his lips following down her nightgown as he lowered it inch by delicious inch.

When it was completely off, he laid his head on her belly, his shoulders between her thighs, and fervently kissed the yielding softness. "I never thought I could love you again. But after what you've done for Mandy, and for me," he added thickly, "I'll be damned if I don't love you more than ever."

He slid his hands beneath her hips and tilted them up. His parted lips whisked the smooth skin of her abdomen. He kissed the delta of dark curls, nuzzled it with his nose, feathered it with his breath.

Catching his hair with her hands, she arched up, offering her open thighs to his caressing mouth. He drew the silky, slippery, softness between his lips, imbibing her taste and scent, using his flicking, stroking, questing tongue to bring her to one crashing climax after another.

Then she inverted her body and returned the favor. Her lips covered the smooth head of his penis. She sucked it tenderly and used the tip of her tongue to cleave the groove and pick up the pearly drops of fluid already collected there.

Tate prayed to nameless gods when she took him into her mouth completely, and when he filled it with the very essence of himself, he gave hoarse, rasping cries that left them feeling perfectly marvelous and replete.

Later that night, while they lay dozing, he drew her back against his chest. He kissed her warm, soft nape. He nibbled her shoulder. He said nothing, but waited, as though asking her permission to continue.

She merely purred like a drowsy cat and responded when he eased her thigh up toward her chest, leaving her open for his smooth entry. Their bodies gently undulated against each other with no discernible motion. It was a facile, fluid fuck.

Reaching around her, he caressed her breasts, reshaping them with his hand, then fanned his fingertips across the pebbly nipples.

She pressed her buttocks into the curve of his body, and rubbed her smooth flesh against the dense hair spreading outward from the root of his sex. He groaned his approval and drew her up higher, closer.

He manipulated her from the front with breathtaking sensitivity, and sometimes replaced his rigid penis with inquisitive fingers that moved deep inside her, until immense pleasure washed over her like a warm and balmy spring rain, without thunder, without wind, without lightning—cleansing and pure and benevolent.

The rhythmic contractions of her orgasm brought on his. His body tensed. His breathing was suspended for several splendid seconds while the hot tide of his semen bathed her womb.

When it was over and their bodies were relaxed, but still emanating heat, she turned her head toward him. Their seeking mouths came together in a long, slow, wet kiss.

Then they slept.

 # FORTY-FIVE

Since they were scheduled to leave very early that morning, Avery got a head start by waking up before Tate. She disentangled their limbs. Getting her hair unsnarled from his fingers wasn't easy, but she finally managed.

She glanced over her shoulder at him as she left the bed. He was beautiful when he slept, one leg sticking out of the covers, his bearded jaw dark against the pillowcase. Sighing with the sheer pleasure of looking at him, and with the stirring memories of last night's lovemaking fresh in her mind, she crept into the bathroom.

The water taps screeched when she turned them on. Avery winced at the noise. Tate needed as much sleep as he could get. Today's agenda was arduous. He would spend hours in an airplane. In between, he would be delivering speeches, pressing hands, and soliciting votes.

This day before Election Day was possibly the most important one of his campaign. Today the fence-straddlers, vital to the outcome of any election, would make up their minds.

Avery stepped beneath the pounding spray. After shampooing her hair, she lathered her body. It still bore traces of Tate's fervent lovemaking. His mouth had left a faint bruise on her soft inner thigh. The hot water stung her whisker-rasped breasts. She was smiling over that when the shower curtain was suddenly whipped back.

"Tate!"

"Good morning."

"What—"

"I thought I'd shower with you," he drawled, smiling lecherously. "Save time. Save the hotel some hot water."

Avery stood quaking, as guilty in her nakedness as Eve must have been in Eden when God spotlighted her iniquity. The jets of hot water seemed to turn icy and sharp; they pricked her skin like frigid needles. Color drained from her face. Her lips turned blue. Her eyes seemed to recede into her skull, making the sockets appear huge and cavernous. She shivered.

Puzzled, Tate cocked his sleep-tousled head to one side. "You look like you've seen a ghost. Did I scare you?"

She swallowed. Her mouth opened and closed, but she couldn't form a sound.

"Carole? What's the matter?"

He looked for something amiss. His eyes scaled down her pale, trembling body, then back up. Avery's heart sank heavily in her chest as she watched his baffled gaze move down her once again. It was arrested at her breasts, belly, pubis, thighs—places only seen by a lover's eyes, a husband's eyes.

He saw the appendectomy scar, ancient and faint and almost undetectable unless bared to clinical fluorescent lighting. Avery had wondered, but now she knew. Carole had never had her appendix out.

"Carole?" His voice echoed the mystification in his eyes.

Though the protective gesture was a dead giveaway, Avery covered her lower body with one hand and extended the other toward him in appeal. "Tate, I . . ."

As sharp and deadly as swords, his eyes slashed upwards to clash with hers. "You're not Carole." He stated it softly, while his brain still sifted through conflicting facts. Then, when the impact of it hit him full force, he repeated with emphasis, "You're not Carole!"

His arm shot through the shower's spray to grab hold of her wrist and yank her from the tub. Her shins banged into the porcelain; her wet feet slipped on the tiles. She emitted a tortured cry, more of the spirit than the body.

"Tate, stop. I'll—"

He slammed her wet, naked body against the wall and pinned it there with his own. His hand closed tightly around her neck, just beneath her chin.

"Who the fuck are you? Where is my wife? *Who are you?*"

"Don't shout," she whimpered. "Mandy will hear."

"Talk, goddamn you." He lowered his voice, but his eyes were still murderous and his hand exerted more pressure against her adam's apple. "Who are you?"

Her teeth were chattering so badly she could barely speak.

"Avery Daniels."

"Who?"

"Avery Daniels."

"Avery Daniels? The TV . . . ?"

She bobbed her head once.

"Where's Carole? What—"

"Carole died in the plane crash, Tate," she said. "I survived. We got mixed up because we had switched seats on the plane. I was carrying Mandy when I escaped. They assumed—"

He trapped her dripping head between his hands. "Carole's *dead?*"

"Yes," she gulped. "Yes. I'm sorry."

"Since the crash? She died in the crash? You mean you've been living . . . all this time . . . ?"

Again, she gave a swift, confirming nod.

Her heart broke apart like an eggshell as she watched him try to comprehend the incomprehensible. Gradually, he released his stranglehold on her cranium and backed away from her.

She snatched her robe off the hook on the back of the bathroom door and pulled it on, hurriedly knotting the tie belt. She reached into the tub and cut off the faucets, which she instantly regretted doing. The resulting silence was deafening, yet it shimmered with the brassy reverberation of disbelief and suspicion.

Into that silence he threw her one simple question. "Why?"

The day of reckoning had arrived. She'd known it would come eventually. She just hadn't counted on it being today. She wasn't prepared.

"It's complicated."

"I don't give a damn how complicated it is," he said in a voice that vibrated with wrath. "Start talking to me now before I call the police."

"I don't know how or when the initial mix-up was made," she said frantically. "I woke up in the hospital bandaged from head to foot, unable to move or to speak. Everybody was calling me Carole. At first I didn't understand. I was in such pain. I was afraid, confused, disoriented. It took several days for me to piece together what must have happened."

"And when you realized it, you didn't say anything? Why?"

"I couldn't! Remember, I couldn't communicate." She caught his arm in appeal. He slung it off. "Tate, I tried to get the message to you before my face was restored to look like Carole's, but it was impossible. Every time I began to cry, you thought it was from fear over the upcoming surgery. It was that. But it was also because I was being robbed of my own identity and having another imposed on me. I was powerless to get that message across."

"Jesus, this is science fiction." He plowed his fingers through his hair. Realizing he was still naked, he grabbed a towel from the rack and wrapped it around his middle. "That was months ago."

"I had to remain Carole for a while."

"Why?"

She threw back her head and gazed up at the ceiling. The first explanation had been a breeze, compared to what was coming. "It's going to sound—"

"I don't give a shit how it sounds," he said menacingly. "I want to know why you've been impersonating my wife."

"Because someone wants to kill you!"

Her urgent reply took him by surprise. He was still poised to do battle, but his head snapped back like he'd taken an uppercut on the chin. "*What?*"

"When I was in the hospital," she began, clasping her hands together at waist level, "someone came to my room."

"Who?"

"I don't know who. Hear me out before asking me a lot of questions." She drew in a deep breath, but the words continued to tumble rapidly over her lips. "I was bandaged. I couldn't see well. Someone, addressing me as Carole, warned me not to make any deathbed confessions. He said that the plans were still in place and that you'd never live to take office."

He remained unmoved for a moment, then a smile tugged at the corner of his lips. Eventually, he barked a hateful laugh. "You expect me to believe that?"

"It's the truth!"

"The only truth is that you're going to jail. Now." He turned and headed for the telephone.

"Tate, no!" She caught his arm and brought him around. "I don't blame you for what you're thinking about me."

"Your worst guess couldn't even come close."

The invective smarted, but for the time being, she had to ignore it. "I'm not lying about this. I swear it. Someone plans to assassinate you before you take office."

"I'm not even elected."

"As good as, so it seems."

"You can't identify this mystery person?"

"Not yet. I'm trying."

He studied her earnest face for a moment, then sneered, "I can't believe I'm standing here listening to this shit. You've been living a lie all these months. Now you expect me to believe that a total stranger sneaked into your hospital room and put a bug in your ear that he was going to assassinate me?" He shook his head as though marveling over her audacity and his culpability.

"Not a stranger, Tate. Someone close. Someone in the family."

His jaw relaxed. He stared at her with patent incredulity. "Are you—"

"Think! Only family members are allowed into the ICU."

"You're saying a member of my family is plotting my assassination?"

"It sounds absurd, I know, but it's the truth. I didn't make it up. I didn't imagine it, either. There have been notes."

"Notes?"

"Notes left for Carole in places only she would have access to, letting her know that the plan was still in place." She rushed to the luggage rack in the closet and opened a zippered compartment of one of her suitcases. She carried the notes, including the desecrated campaign poster, back to him.

"They were typed on the typewriter at the ranch," she told him.

He studied each one at length. "You could have made these yourself just in case I caught on and you needed a scapegoat."

"I didn't," she cried. "This was Carole's partner's way of—"

"Wait a minute, wait a minute." He tossed the notes aside and held up both hands. "This is getting better all the time. Carole and this would-be assassin were in it together, right?"

"Absolutely. From the time she met you. Maybe before."

"Why would Carole want me dead? She had no political leanings whatsoever."

"This isn't political, Tate. It's personal. Carole set her sights on becoming your wife. She became exactly what you wanted, and once they teamed up she was coached on how to behave so you'd have to fall in love with her. Who introduced you?''

''Jack,'' he said with a small shrug. ''When she came to apply for a job at the firm.''

''It might not have been an accident that she sought employment in your law office.''

''She had impeccable credentials.''

''I'm sure she did. She would have seen to it.''

''She could type,'' he added drolly, ''which shoots your theory all to hell.''

''I know I'm right.''

''I guess you can prove it,'' he said, implying the opposite. He even folded his arms complacently across his chest.

''I don't have to. Zee can.''

He reacted with visible shock. His arms dropped to his sides. ''My mother?''

''She has a whole portfolio on Carole Navarro. I've seen it. Believing me to be Carole, she threatened me with exposure if I made you unhappy.''

''Why would she do that?''

''She seemed to think you were falling in love with your wife again.'' Avery looked at him meaningfully. ''After last night, I have good reason to think that, too.''

''Forget last night. As you well know, it was all a hoax.'' Angrily, he turned away.

Avery quietly gave first aid to the puncture wound in her heart. It would have to be thoroughly nursed later. For now, she had to deal with more critical matters.

''Even if you didn't originally see Carole for what she was, Zee did. She hired a private investigator to delve into her past.''

''And what did he find?''

''I'd rather not discuss—''

''What did he find?'' he asked tightly, spinning around to confront her again. ''For God's sake, don't get squeamish now.''

''She was a topless dancer. She'd been arrested for prostitution, among other things.'' At his stricken expression, she reached for his hand. He jerked it beyond her reach. ''You don't have to believe me about this,'' she said, raising her voice in anger over his stupid, stubborn, masculine pride.

''Ask your mother to show you the data. She was saving it to use against Carole if she ever felt it was warranted. And you can't be all that surprised, Tate, because you have scorned me, as Carole, for having affairs, aborting your child, and using drugs. For months I've borne the brunt of your antipathy for this woman.''

He considered her for a moment, gnawing his inner cheek. ''Okay, let's say for the sake of argument that you're right about this cock-and-bull assassination plot. Do you expect me to believe that you placed yourself in harm's way out of the goodness of your heart? Why didn't you alert me to it months ago, the first chance you got?''

''Would you have believed me then, any more than you believe me now?'' He had no answer, so she answered for him. ''No, you wouldn't have, Tate. I was helpless. I didn't have the strength to protect myself, much less you. Besides, I couldn't afford the risk. When the person, whoever it was—*is*—found out that he'd whispered his plans to Avery Daniels, television news reporter, how long do you think I would have lived?''

His eyes narrowed. Slowly, his head began to nod up and down. ''I think I see now why Avery Daniels, television news reporter, pulled this charade. You did it for the story, didn't you?''

She wet her lips, a signal of guilt and nervousness as good as a signed confession. ''Not entirely. I'll admit that my career factored into it initially.'' She reached for his arm again and held on this time. ''But not now, Tate. Not since I've come to love . . . Mandy. Once I got in, I couldn't get out. I couldn't just walk away and leave things unresolved.''

''So how long were you going to pretend to be my wife? Were we going to fuck with the lights out for the rest of our days? Was I never going to see you naked? How long were you going to live a lie? Forever?''

''No.'' Her hand slid off his arm and she slumped with despair. ''I don't know. I was going to tell you, only—''

''When?''

''When I knew Mandy was okay and that you were safe.''

''So we're back to the assassination plot.''

''Stop saying that so blithely,'' she exclaimed. ''The threat is real.'' She glanced at the poster. ''And imperative.''

''Then tell me who you suspect. You've been living with the same people I have been ever since you came out of the hospital.'' He shook his head again and laughed bitterly at his own stupidity. ''Jesus, this explains so much. The memory lapses. Shep. The riding horse.'' He looked over her body. ''It explains so many things,'' he said gruffly. After clearing his throat, he said, ''Why didn't I see it?''

''You weren't looking. You and Carole hadn't been intimate for a long time.''

He seemed disinclined to address that. He picked up his previous train of thought. ''Who do you suspect of wanting to kill me? My parents? My brother? My best friend? Dorothy Rae? No, wait—Fancy! That's it.'' He snapped his fingers. ''She got pissed off at me a couple years ago when I wouldn't loan her my car, so she wants me dead.''

''Don't joke about it.'' Avery shook with frustration.

''This whole thing's a joke,'' he said, lowering his face close to hers. ''A dirty rotten joke played on all of us by a conniving bitch with big ambitions. Granted, I've been a blind, deaf idiot, but now I'm seeing it all crystal clear.

''Didn't you commit a journalistic faux pas a year or so back—something about making allegations before all the facts were checked out? Yeah, I think you were the one. You devised this scheme to rectify that mistake and reinstate yourself among your colleagues. You're a reporter who needed a hot story, so, when the opportunity presented itself, you cooked this one up.''

She shook her head and whispered mournfully, but without much conviction, ''No.''

''I'll give you credit, Avery Daniels. You go after your story no matter what it takes, don't you? This time you were even willing to whore for it. Probably not for the first time. Do you go down on all your interviewees? Is that their reward for giving you their secrets?''

She wrapped the robe around her tighter, but it did little to protect her from his chilling rebuke. ''I wasn't whoring, Tate. Everything that happened between us was honest.''

''Like hell.''

''It was!''

''I've been fucking an impostor.''

''And loving it!''

''Obviously, because you're as good at that as you are at playacting!''

Her anger had been spent with that one verbal volley. Now tears filled her imploring eyes. "You're wrong. Please believe me, Tate. You must be careful." She pointed down at the poster. "He's going to do it on Election Day. Tomorrow."

He was shaking his head adamantly. "You'll never convince me that somebody in my family is going to put a bullet through my head."

"Wait!" she cried, suddenly remembering something she had forgotten to mention. "There's a tall, gray-haired man who's been following you from city to city." She quickly enumerated the times and places she had seen Gray Hair in the crowds. "Van's got the tapes to prove it."

"Ah, the cameraman from KTEX," he said, smiling ruefully. "So that explains him. Who else is in on your little game?"

"Irish McCabe."

"Who's he?"

She explained their relationship and how Irish had mistakenly identified Carole's body. "He has her jewelry, if you want it back."

"What about the locket?" he asked, nodding at her chest.

"A gift from my father."

"Very clever," he remarked with grudging respect. "You think on your feet and cover tracks well."

"Listen to me, Tate. If I get the tapes from Van, will you look at them to see if you recognize this man?" She told him how they had deduced that a professional assassin had been hired.

"You form quite a trio, all figuring to make big bucks at the expense of the Rutledge family."

"It's not like that."

"No?"

"No!"

The sudden knock on the door brought them both around. "Who is it?" Tate called out.

It was Eddy. "We'll meet downstairs in twenty minutes for a last-minute briefing over breakfast before leaving for the airport." Tate glanced at Avery and held her anxious gaze for several moments. "Is everything okay?" Eddy asked.

She placed her clenched hands beneath her chin and silently beseeched Tate not to say anything. "Please, Tate," she whispered. "You have no reason to, but you've got to trust me."

"Everything's fine," he reluctantly called through the door. "See you in the dining room. Twenty minutes."

Avery collapsed with relief on the nearest sofa. "You mustn't say anything, Tate. Swear to me you won't breathe a word of this to anyone. Anyone."

"Why should I trust you above my own family and confidants?"

She answered carefully. "If what I've told you is true, then your silence could save you from assassination. If it's all a wild scheme, then your silence could save you from public ridicule. Either way, you've nothing to gain right now by revealing me as an impostor. So, I'm begging you not to tell anyone."

He gave her a long, cold stare. "You're as devious as Carole was."

"I hate that you see it that way."

"I should have read the signs. I should have known the changes in you, in *her,* were too good to be true. Like the way you took to Mandy when you came home."

"She's come so far, Tate. Don't I get credit for loving her?"

"You'll get credit for breaking her heart when you leave."

"It will break my heart, too."

He ignored her. "Now I know why you suddenly took an interest in the election, why your opinions were more eloquently expressed, and why . . ." He looked at her mouth. "Why so many things were different." For several moments, he seemed to be struggling against the pull of a powerful magnet that would draw him to her. Then, with a vicious curse, he turned away.

Avery charged after him, catching him before he could lock her out of the bathroom. "What are you going to do?"

"For the time being, not a damn thing. I've come this far. You and your nefarious scheme aren't going to deter me from winning the election for myself, and for my family, and for all the people who've placed their trust in me."

"What about me?"

"I don't know," he answered honestly. "If I expose you, I would expose myself and my family as fools." He grabbed a handful of hair at the back of her head and pulled it back. "And if you expose us, I'll kill you."

She believed him. "I'm not lying, Tate. Everything I've told you is the truth."

He released her abruptly. "I'll probably divorce you, as I'd planned to divorce Carole. Your punishment will be having to remain the former Mrs. Tate Rutledge for the rest of your life."

"You must be careful. Someone is going to try to kill you."

"Avery Daniels has been dead and buried for months. She'll remain dead and buried."

"Watch for a tall, gray-haired man in the crowds. Stay away from him."

"There'll be no career in TV, no smashing story to make you an overnight sensation." His eyes raked over her contemptuously. "You did it all for nothing, Ms. Daniels."

"I did it because I love you."

He shut the door in her face.

FORTY-SIX

Van's search came to an end on the eve of Election Day. For several seconds, he stared at the color monitor screen, not believing that he'd finally found what he had been looking for all this time.

He had taken a catnap at daybreak, realizing when he saw light leaking around the tattered shades in his apartment windows that he had been up all night, viewing one videotape after another. After he had slept for about an hour, he'd drunk a pot of strong, caffeine-rich coffee and returned to his console. The desk area was littered with junk food wrappers, empty soda cans, empty cigarette packs, and rank, overflowing ashtrays.

Van hadn't noticed the untidiness. He didn't care. Nor did it matter to him that he hadn't eaten a square meal or showered in over forty-eight hours. His compulsion to watch videotapes had become his obsession. His passion had grown into a mission.

He accomplished it at nine-thirty P.M. as he sat looking at a tape he had shot three years earlier while working at an NBC affiliate station in Washington state. He didn't even remember the station's call letters, but he remembered the assignment. He had used four tapes in all, each containing twenty minutes of unedited video. The reporter had compressed those eighty minutes into a five-minute special feature for the evening news during a ratings sweep week. It was the kind of piece people shuddered over and woefully shook their heads at, but consumed like popcorn.

Van watched all eighty minutes several times to make certain there was no mistake. When he was positive he was right, he flipped the necessary switches, inserted a blank tape, and began to make a duplicate of the most important, and most incriminating, one of the four.

Since it had to be duplicated at real time, that left him with twenty minutes to kill. He searched through the crumpled packets littering the console and finally produced a lone, bent cigarette, lit it, then picked up the phone and called the Palacio Del Rio.

"Yeah, I need to talk to Mrs. Rutledge. Mrs. Tate Rutledge."

"I'm sorry, sir," the switchboard operator said pleasantly, "I can't put that call through, but if you leave your name and number—"

"No, you don't understand. This is a personal message for Av . . . uh, Carole Rutledge."

"I'll give your message to their staff, who is screening—"

"Look, bitch, this is important, got that? An emergency."

"Regarding what, sir?"

"I can't tell you. I've got to speak to Mrs. Rutledge personally."

"I'm sorry, sir," the unflappable operator repeated. "I can't put that call through. If you leave your—"

"Shit!"

He slammed down the receiver and dialed Irish's number. He let it ring thirty times before giving up. "Where the hell is he?"

While the tape was still duplicating, Van paced, trying to figure out the best way to inform Irish and Avery of what he'd found. It was essential that he get this tape into Avery's hands, but how? If he couldn't even get the hotel operator to ring her suite, he couldn't possibly get close enough tonight to place the tape into her hands. She *had* to see it before tomorrow.

By the time the duplication was completed, Van still hadn't thought of a solution to his dilemma. The only possible course of action was to try to locate Irish. He would advise him what to do.

But after keeping the phone lines hot for half an hour between his apartment, KTEX's newsroom, and Irish's house, he still hadn't spoken to his boss. He decided to take the damn tape to Irish's house. He could wait for him there. It would mean driving clear across town, but what the hell? This was important.

It wasn't until he reached the parking lot of his apartment complex that he remembered his van was in the shop. His companion reporter had had to drive him home after they'd covered Rutledge's return to the San Antonio airport earlier that evening.

"Shit. Now what?"

The post office box. If contact couldn't be made any other way, that was the conveyance he'd been told to use. He went back inside. Among a heap of scrap papers, he found the one he'd scribbled the post office box number on. He sealed the videotape into an addressed, padded envelope, slipped on a jacket, and struck out on foot, taking his package with him.

It was only two blocks to the nearest convenience store, where there was also a mailbox, but even that represented more exercise than Van liked.

He purchased cigarettes, a six-pack of beer, and enough stamps to cover the postage—if not, Irish could make up the difference—and dropped the package into the mailbox. The schedule posted on the outside said that there was a pickup at midnight. The tape could feasibly be in Irish's hands by tomorrow morning.

In the meantime, though, Van planned to keep calling Irish every five minutes until he contacted him. Mailing the duplicate tape was only insurance.

Where could the old coot be at this hour, if not at home or the TV station? He had to show up sooner or later. Then the two of them would decide how to warn Avery of just how real the threat on Rutledge's life was.

Sipping one of the beers en route, Van sauntered back to his apartment, went in, shrugged off his jacket, and resumed his seat at the video console. He reloaded one of the tapes that had solved the mystery for him and began replaying it.

Midway through, he reached for the phone and dialed Irish's number. It rang five times before he heard the click severing the connection. He glanced quickly at his phone and saw that a gloved hand had depressed the button. His eyes followed an arm up to a pleasantly smiling face.

"Very interesting, Mr. Lovejoy," his visitor said softly, nodding at the flickering monitor. "I couldn't quite remember where I'd seen you before."

Then a pistol was raised and fired at point blank range into Van's forehead.

Irish rushed through his front door and caught his telephone on the sixth ring, just as the caller hung up. "Dammit!" He had stayed late in the newsroom in preparation for the hellish day the news team would have tomorrow.

He had checked and rechecked schedules, reviewed assignments, and consulted with the anchors to make certain everybody knew where to go and what to do when. It was this kind of news day that Irish loved. But it was also the kind that gave him heartburn as hot as smoldering brimstone in his gut. He shouldn't have stopped to wolf down that plate of enchiladas on his way home.

He drank a glass of antacid and returned to his telephone. He called Van, but hung up after the phone rang a couple dozen times. If Van was out carousing, getting hopped up on a controlled substance, he'd kill him. He needed him up bright and early in the morning.

He would dispatch Van with a reporter to record the Rutledges voting in Kerrville, then install him at the Palacio Del Rio for the rest of the day and long evening while they waited for the returns to come in.

Irish wasn't convinced that anybody would be so stupid as to attempt an assassination on Election Day, but Avery seemed to believe that's when it would happen. If seeing Van in the crowd alleviated her anxiety, then Irish wanted him there, visible and within easy reach should she need him.

Contacting her by telephone was impossible. He had already tried to call her earlier today, but he had been told that Mrs. Rutledge wasn't feeling well. At least that's the story that had come out of the Rutledge camp when she failed to accompany Tate on his final campaign swing through North Texas.

In a later effort to speak with her, he had been told that the family was out to dinner. Still uneasy, he'd stopped by the post office on the way home and checked his box. There'd been nothing in it, which allayed his concerns somewhat. He supposed that no news was good news. If Avery needed him, she knew where to find him.

He prepared for bed. After his prayers, he tried calling Van once more. There was still no answer

Avery spent Election Eve in tormenting worry. Tate told her peremptorily that she would not be going with him on his last campaign trip, and he stuck to it, heedless of her pleas.

When he returned safely, her relief was so profound that she was weak with it. As they convened for dinner, Jack sidled up to her and asked, "Do you still have the cramps?"

"What?"

"Tate said you weren't up to making the trip today because you got your period."

"Oh, yes," she said, backing his lie. "I didn't feel well this morning, but I'm fine now, thanks."

"Just make sure you're well in the morning." Jack wasn't the least bit interested in her health, only in how her presence or absence might effect the outcome of the election. "You've got to be at your peak tomorrow."

"I'll try."

Jack was then claimed by Dorothy Rae, who hadn't touched a drink in weeks. The changes in her were obvious. She no longer looked frightened and frail, but took pains with her appearance. More self-assertive, she rarely let Jack out of her sight, and never when Avery was around. Apparently she still considered Carole a threat, but one she was prepared to combat for her husband's affections.

Thanks to Tate's ingrained charm, Avery didn't think anyone noticed the schism in their relationship. The family traveled en masse to a restaurant for dinner, where they were seated and served in a private dining room.

For the duration of the meal, Tate treated her with utmost politeness. She plagued him with questions about his day and how he was received in each city. He answered courteously, but without elaboration. The steely coldness from his eyes chilled her to the marrow.

He played with Mandy. He related anecdotes of the trip to his attentive mother and father. He gently teased Fancy and engaged her in conversation. He listened to Jack's last few words of counsel. He argued with Eddy over his Election Day attire.

"I'm not dressing up to go vote—no more than the average guy—and I'll change into a suit and tie only if I have to make an acceptance speech."

"Then I'd better arrange to have the hotel valet press your suit overnight," Avery said with conviction.

"Hear, hear!" Nelson heartily thumped his fist on the table.

Tate looked at her sharply, as though wanting to strip away her duplicity. If he suspected treachery of anyone in this convivial inner circle, it was she. If he harbored any doubts as to where his family's loyalty and devotion lay, he masked it well. For a man whose life could be radically altered the following day, he appeared ludicrously calm.

However, Avery guessed that his composure was a façade. He exuded confidence because he wanted everyone else to remain at ease. That would be typical of Tate.

She longed for a private moment with him upon their return to the hotel, and was glad when his conference with Jack and Eddy concluded quickly.

"I'm going out for a stroll along the Riverwalk," Jack told them as he pulled on his jacket. "Dorothy Rae and Fancy are watching a movie on the TV in our room. It's the kind of sentimental crap I can't stomach, so until it's over I'm going to make myself scarce."

"I'll ride the elevator down with you," Eddy said. "I want to check the lobby newsstand for papers we might have missed."

They left. Mandy was already asleep in her room. Now, Avery thought, she would have time to plead her case before Tate. Maybe his judgment wouldn't be so harsh this time. To her dismay, however, he picked up his room key and moved toward the door.

"I'm going to visit with Mom and Dad for a while."

"Tate, did you notice Van at the airport? I tried calling him at home, but he wasn't back yet. I wanted him to bring the tapes over so—"

"You look tired. Don't wait up."

He left the suite and stayed gone a long time. Finally, because it had been such a long, dreary day, which she'd spent largely confined to the suite, she went to bed.

Tate never joined her. She woke up during the night. Missing his warmth, panicked because she didn't hear him breathing beside her, she quickly crossed the bedroom and flung open the door.

He was sleeping on the sofa in the parlor.

It broke her heart.

For months he had been lost to her because of Carole's deceit. Now he was lost to her because of her own.

FORTY-SEVEN

The bellyache Irish had when he went to bed the night before was mild in comparison to the raging one he had by seven o'clock Election Day morning.

It had dawned clear and cool. Heavy voter turnout was predicted statewide because of the perfect autumn weather.

The climate in the KTEX news department wasn't so clement. Its chief was on the warpath. "Sorry, worthless son of a bitch," Irish mouthed as he slammed down the telephone receiver. When Van failed to show up in the newsroom at six-thirty as scheduled, Irish had started telephoning his apartment. There was still no answer. "Where could he be?"

"Maybe he's on his way," another photographer volunteered, trying to be helpful.

"Maybe," Irish grumbled as he lit a cigarette, which he'd only planned to hold between his lips. "In the meantime, I'm sending you. If you hurry, you can catch the Rutledges as they leave the hotel. If not, drive like hell to catch up with them in Kerrville. And report in every few minutes," he yelled after the cameraman who scrambled out with the reporter. Both were grateful to escape with their scalps intact.

Irish snatched up the telephone and punched out a number he had memorized by now. "Good morning," a pleasant voice answered, "Palacio Del Rio."

"I need to speak to Mrs. Rutledge."

"I'm sorry, sir. I can't put your call—"

"Yeah, I know, I know, but this is important."

"If you'll leave your name and num—"

He hung up on her saccharine spiel and immediately called Van's number. It rang incessantly while Irish paced as far as the telephone cord would reach. "When I get my hands on him, I'm gonna hammer his balls to mush."

He collared a gofer who had the misfortune to collide with him. "Hey, you, drive over there and haul his skinny ass out of bed."

"Who, sir?"

"Van Lovejoy. Who the fuck do you think?" Irish bellowed impatiently. Why had everybody chosen today to turn up either missing or stupid? He scrawled Van's address on a sheet of paper, shoved it at the terror-stricken kid, and ordered ominously, "Don't come back without him."

Avery emerged from the hotel, holding Mandy by one sweating hand. The other was tucked into the crook of Tate's elbow. She smiled for the myriad cameras, wishing her facial muscles would stop cramping and quivering.

Tate gave the cameras his most engaging smile and a thumbs-up sign as they moved toward the waiting limousine parked in the brick paved porte cochere. Microphones were aimed toward them. Bleakly, Avery thought they resembled gun barrels. Tate's voice carried confidently across the city racket and general confusion. "Great Election Day weather. Good for the voters and for the candidates in each race."

He was bombarded with questions regarding more serious topics than the weather, but Eddy ushered them into the backseat of the limo. Avery was distressed to learn that he was riding with them to Kerrville. She wouldn't have Tate to herself, as she had hoped. They hadn't been alone all morning. He was already up and dressed by the time she woke up. He breakfasted in the dining room on the river level of the hotel while she got Mandy and herself dressed.

As the limo pulled away from the curb, she glanced through the rear window, trying to locate Van. She spotted a two-man crew from KTEX, but Van wasn't the photographer behind the Betacam. *Why not?* she wondered. *Where is he?*

He wasn't among the media waiting for them at their polling place in Kerrville, either. Her anxiety mounted, so much so that at one point, Tate leaned down at her and whispered, "Smile, for God's sake. You look like I've already lost."

"I'm afraid, Tate."

"Afraid I'll lose before the day is out?"

"No. Afraid you'll die." She held his gaze for several seconds before Jack intruded on them with a question for Tate.

The ride back to San Antonio seemed interminable. Freeway and downtown traffic was heavier than normal. As they alighted from the limo at the entrance of the hotel, Avery's eyes scanned the milling crowd again. She sighted a familiar face, but it wasn't the one she wanted to see. The gray-haired man was standing in front of the convention center across the street. Van, on the other hand, was nowhere in sight.

Irish had promised.

Something was wrong.

The moment they reached their suite, she excused herself and went into the bedroom to use the telephone. The direct line into the newsroom was answered after ten rings. "Irish McCabe, please," she said with breathless urgency.

"Irish? Okay, I'll go find him."

Having worked election days, she knew what nightmares, and yet what challenges, they presented to the media. Everybody operated on a frantic frequency.

"Come on, come on, Irish," she whispered while waiting. She kept remembering how still and intent Gray Hair had stood, as though maintaining a post.

"Hello?"

"Irish!" she exclaimed, going limp with relief.

"No. Is that who you're holding for? Just a sec."

"This is Av—" When she was abruptly put on hold again, she nearly sobbed with anxiety.

The phone was picked up a second time. "Hello?" a man asked hesitantly. "Hello?"

"Yes, who is—Eddy, is that you?"

"Yeah."

"This is, A—uh, Carole."

"Where the hell are you?"

"I'm in the bedroom. I'm using this line." Evidently, he had picked up the extension in the parlor.

"Well, make it snappy, okay? We've got to keep these lines open."

He hung up. She was still on hold. Her call to the newsroom had been ignored by people with better things to do than track down the boss on the busiest news day of the year. Distraught, she replaced the telephone and went to join the family and a few key volunteers who had assembled in the other room.

Though she smiled and conversed as it was expected of her, she tried to imagine where Van could be. She comforted herself by picturing him downstairs in the ballroom, setting up his tripod and camera to cover what would hopefully be Tate's victory celebration later in the evening.

For the time being there was nothing more she could do. There must be a logical explanation for the switch in plans. Because she hadn't been apprised, she had let her imagination run away with her. Irish and Van knew where she was if they needed to contact her. Resolving to keep her panic at bay, she moved toward the sofa where Tate was sprawled.

True to his word, he'd gone to the polls dressed casually, wearing a leather sports jacket over his jeans. He appeared perfectly relaxed as he told Zee, who was taking orders, what he wanted for lunch.

Avery sat down on the arm of the sofa. He absently draped his arm over her thigh and caressed her knee with negligent possession. When Zee moved away, he glanced up at her and smiled. "Hi."

"Hi."

And then he remembered. She watched as memory crept back into his eyes, eating up the warm glow in his gray irises until they were cold and implacable once again. He gradually lifted his arm away from her.

"There's something I've been meaning to ask you," he said.

"Yes?"

"Did you ever take care of birth control?"

"No. And neither did you."

"Terrific."

She couldn't let his contempt intimidate her into keeping her distance. For the remainder of the day, she didn't intend to get any farther away from him than she was at the moment.

"Irish, line two's for you."

"Can't you see I'm already on the frigging phone?" he yelled across the pandemonium in the newsroom. "Put 'em on hold. Now," he said, speaking into the receiver again, "did you try knocking?"

"Till my knuckles were bloody, Mr. McCabe. He's not home."

Irish ran his hand down his florid face. The gofer was calling in with news that made absolutely no sense. "Did you look through the windows?"

"I tried. The shades are down, but I listened through the door. I couldn't hear a single sound. I don't think anybody's in there. Besides, his van's not here. I already checked the parking lot. His space is empty."

That was going to be Irish's next suggestion. "Christ," he muttered. He had hoped that Van would be at home, sleeping off a night of overindulgence, but obviously he wasn't. If his van wasn't there, he wasn't at home, period.

Irish reasoned they might have gotten their signals crossed and that Van had gone straight to the Palacio Del Rio, but after checking with the crew there, they reported they hadn't seen him either.

"Okay, thanks. Come on back in." He pressed the blinking light on the telephone panel. "McCabe," he said gruffly. He got a dial tone in his ear. "Hey, wasn't somebody holding for me on two?"

"That's right."

"Well, they're not there now."

"Guess they hung up."

"Was it a guy?" he wanted to know.

"A woman."

"Did she say who?"

"No. Sounded kinda ragged out, though."

Irish's blood pressure shot up. "Why the hell didn't you tell me?"

"I did!"

"Jesus!"

Arguing with incompetents wasn't going to help anything. He stamped back into his office, slammed the door behind him, and lit a cigarette. He couldn't be certain it had been Avery on the phone, but he had a gut instinct that it had been. Maybe that's what was making his gut hurt so bad—his rotten instincts.

He took a swig of antacid straight from the bottle and yanked up the telephone again. He dialed the hotel and got the same cool voice as before. When he demanded to be connected to the Rutledge suite, the operator began her same unruffled litany.

"Look, bitch, I don't give a fuck about your fucking instructions or who the fucking calls are supposed to be routed through. I want you to ring her suite now. *Now,* got that? And if you don't do it, I'm gonna come over there and personally take your fucking head off."

She hung up on him.

Irish paced his office, puffing smoke and chugging like a steam locomotive. Avery must be beside herself. She would think they'd deserted her.

Van, that irresponsible bastard, hadn't shown up at the hotel where he was supposed to be, where she would be watching for him, relying on him. His calls weren't being put through to her, so she had no way of knowing that he'd frantically been trying to contact her.

He stormed back into the newsroom as he pulled on his tweed blazer. "I'm going out."

"Out?"

"What, are you deaf? *Out.* If anybody calls or comes looking for me, tell 'em to stay put or leave a message. I'll be back when I can."

"Where are you . . . ?" The subordinate was left talking to wisps of cigarette smoke.

"You're sure he's not there?" Avery was struck with disbelief. "I phoned earlier and—"

"All I know is somebody said he went out, and I can't find him, so I guess he's out."

"Out where?"

"Nobody seems to know."

"Irish wouldn't go out the day of an election."

"Look, lady, it's a madhouse around here, especially since Irish decided to split, so do you want to leave a message, or what?"

"No," she said distantly. "No message."

Feeling that she'd been cut adrift, she hung up and wandered back into the main room. Her eyes automatically sought out Tate first. He was talking with Nelson. Zee was ostensibly listening to their conversation, but her eyes were fixed on Tate with that faraway absorption that often characterized her.

Jack and Eddy were downstairs seeing to the arrangements in the ballroom while carefully monitoring returns as they were reported. It was still several hours before the polls closed, but early indications were that Tate was staying abreast of Dekker. Even if he didn't pull out in front, he'd given the pompous incumbent a good scare.

Dorothy Rae had pleaded a headache earlier and gone to her room to lie down for a while. Fancy was sitting on the floor with Mandy. They were coloring together.

On a sudden inspiration, Avery called her name. "Could you come here a minute, please?"

"What for?"

"I . . . I need you to run an errand for me."

"Grandma told me to entertain the kid."

"I'll do that. Anyway, it's getting close to her nap time. Please. It's important."

Grudgingly, Fancy came to her feet and followed Avery back into the bedroom. Since the incident a few nights earlier, she had been much more pleasant to be around. Every now and then, traces of her recalcitrance asserted itself, but on the whole, she was more congenial.

As soon as she closed the door behind them, Avery pressed a small key into Fancy's hand. "I need you to do something for me."

"With this key?"

"It's a post office box key. I need you to go there and see if there's something inside. If there is, bring it back with you and hand deliver it to me—no one else."

"What the hell's going on?"

"I can't explain right now."

"I'm not gonna go chasing—"

"Please, Fancy. It's terribly important."

"Then, how come you're asking me? I usually get the shit detail."

"I thought we were friends," Avery said, turning up the heat. "Tate and I helped you out of a jam the other night. You owe us a favor."

Fancy chewed on that for a moment, then flipped the key in her palm several times. "Where's it at?" Avery provided her with the address of the post office branch. "Jeez, that's a million miles from here."

"And you said half an hour ago that you were tired of being cooped up in this friggin' hotel suite. And I believe that's a quote. Now, will you do this for me?"

Avery's demeanor must have conveyed some measure of the urgency and importance of the errand because Fancy shrugged. "Okay."

"Thank you." Avery gave her a hard hug. At the bedroom door, she paused. "Don't make a big deal of leaving. Just go as unobtrusively as possible. If someone asks where you are, I'll cover for you."

"Why so hush-hush? What's the big secret? You're not screwing a postman, are you?"

"Trust me. It's very important to Tate—to all of us. And please hurry back."

Fancy retrieved her shoulder bag from the credenza in the parlor and headed for the double door of the suite. "I'll be back," she tossed over her shoulder. No one gave her a second glance.

FORTY-EIGHT

Fancy lifted her hip onto the stool and laid the small rectangular package she'd taken from the post office box on the polished wood surface of the bar. The bartender, a mustached, muscular young man, moved toward her.

The smile she blessed him with had been designed in heaven for angels to wear. "A gin and tonic, please."

His friendly blue eyes looked at her skeptically. "How old are you?"

"Old enough."

"Make that two gins and tonic." A man slid onto the stool beside Fancy's. "I'm buying the lady's."

The bartender shrugged. "Fine with me."

Fancy assessed her rescuer. He was a young executive type—insurance or computers, she would guess. Possibly late twenties. Probably married. Looking for kicks away from the responsibilities he had assumed so he could afford his designer clothes and the timepiece strapped to his wrist.

This was the kind of trendy place that attracted singles or marrieds on the make. It was filled with worthless antiques and glossy, gargantuan greenery. The bar created a vortex during happy hour that sucked in yuppies from their BMWs and Porsches by the scores.

While she was analyzing him, he was analyzing her. The gleam in his eyes as they moved down her body indicated that he thought he'd scored big.

"Thanks for the drink," she said.

"You're welcome. You *are* old enough to drink, aren't you?"

"Sure. I'm old enough to drink. Just not old enough to buy." They laughed and toasted each other with the drinks that had just arrived.

"I'm John."

"Fancy."

"Fancy?"

"Francine, if you prefer."

"Fancy."

The mating ritual had begun. Fancy recognized it. She knew the rules. Hell, she'd invented most of them. In two hours—possibly less, if they got hot sooner—they'd be in bed somewhere.

Following her heartbreak over Eddy, she'd sworn off men. They were all bastards. They wanted only one thing from her, and it was the same thing they could buy from the cheapest whore.

Her mother had told her that one day she would meet a guy who truly cared for her and would treat her with kindness and respect. Fancy didn't really believe it, though. Was she supposed to sit around, bored out of her skull, letting her twat atrophy while she waited for Prince Charming to show up and bring it back to life?

Hell, no. She'd been good for three days now. She needed some laughs. This Jim, or Joe, or John, or whatever the hell his name was, was as good as any to give her some.

Like a freaking Girl Scout, she had run Carole's errand, but she wasn't ready to return to the hotel suite and sit glued to the TV set as the rest would be, watching election returns. She would get there eventually. But first, she was going to have some fun.

Finding a parking place anywhere close to the hotel was impossible. Irish finally found one in a lot several blocks away. He was heavily perspiring by the time he entered the lobby. If he had to bribe his way into the Rutledges' private suite he would do it. He had to see Avery. Together they might figure out what had become of Van.

Maybe all his worries were for nothing. Maybe they were together right now. God, he hoped so.

He waded through the members of an Asian tour group who were lined up to check in. Patience had never been one of Irish's virtues. He felt his blood pressure rising as he elbowed his way through the tourists, all chattering and fanning themselves with pamphlets about the Alamo.

From amid the chaos, someone touched his elbow. "Hi."

"Oh, hi," Irish said, recognizing the face.

"You're Irish McCabe, aren't you? Avery's friend?"

"That's right."

"She's been looking for you. Follow me."

They navigated the congested lobby. Irish was led through a set of doors toward a service elevator. They got inside; the gray doors slid closed.

"Thanks," Irish said, wiping his sweaty forehead on his sleeve. "Did Avery . . ." In the middle of his question, it occurred to him that her correct name had been used. He glanced across the large cubicle. "You know?"

A smile. "Yes. I know."

Irish saw the pistol, but he wasn't given time to register the thought that it was actually being aimed straight at him. Less than a heartbeat later, he grabbed his chest and hit the floor of the elevator like a fallen tree.

The elevator stopped on the lowest level of the hotel. The lone passenger raised the pistol and aimed it toward the opening doors, but didn't have to use it. No one was waiting.

Irish's body was dragged down a short hallway, through a set of swinging double doors, and deposited in a narrow alcove that housed vending machines for hotel employee use. The space was lit from overhead by four fluorescent tubes, which were easily smashed with the silencer attached to the barrel of the pistol.

Covered with shards of opaque glass and stygian darkness, Irish McCabe's body was left there on the floor. The assassin knew that by the time it was discovered, his death would be obscured by another.

Prime time had been given over solely to election returns. Each of the three television sets in the parlor was tuned to a different network. It had turned out to be a close presidential race—still too close to call. Several times, the network anchors cited the senatorial race in Texas between the newcomer, Tate Rutledge, and the incumbent, Rory Dekker, as one of the closest and most heated races in the nation.

When it was reported that Rutledge was showing a slight edge, a cheer went up in the parlor. Avery jumped at the sudden noise. She was frantic, walking a razor's edge, on the brink of nervous collapse.

All the excitement had made Mandy hyperactive. She'd become such a nuisance that someone from the hotel's list of baby-sitters had been hired to keep her entertained in another room so the family would be free to concentrate on the returns.

With her mind temporarily off Mandy, Avery could devote herself to worrying about Tate and wondering where Irish and Van were. Their disappearances didn't make sense. She had called the newsroom three times. Neither had been there, nor had their whereabouts been known.

"Has anyone notified the police?" she had asked during her most recent call. "Something could have happened to them."

"Listen, if you want to report them missing, fine, do it. But stop calling here bugging us. Now, I've got better things to do."

The phone had been slammed down in her ear. She wanted to drive to the station as quickly as she could get there, but she didn't want to leave Tate. As the hours of the evening stretched out, there were two certainties at play in her mind. One was that Tate was about to win the Senate seat. The other was that something dreadful had happened to her friends.

What if Gray Hair *had* been stalking her, not Tate, as Van had suggested. What if he'd noticed her interest in him? What if he'd intercepted Van this morning as he reported to work? What if he'd lured Irish away from the TV station?

It made her nauseated with fear to know that a killer was in the hotel, under the same roof as Tate and Mandy.

And where was Fancy? She had been gone for hours. Had something happened to her, too? If not, why hadn't she at least phoned to explain her delay? Even with Election Day traffic, the round trip to the post office shouldn't have taken much longer than an hour.

"Tate, one of the networks just called the thing in your favor!" Eddy announced as he came barreling through the door. "Ready to go downstairs?"

Avery whirled toward Tate, holding her breath in anticipation of his answer. "No," he said. "Not until it's beyond a shadow of a doubt. Not until Dekker calls and concedes."

"At least go change your clothes."

"What's wrong with these clothes?"

"You're going to fight me on that to the bitter end, aren't you?"

"Till the bitter end," Tate replied, laughing.

"If you win, I won't even care."

Nelson walked over to Tate and shook his hand. "You did it. You accomplished everything I expected of you."

"Thanks, Dad," Tate said a bit shakily. "But let's not count our chickens yet." Zee hugged him against her petite frame.

"Bravo, little brother," Jack said, lightly slapping Tate on the cheek. "Think we ought to try for the White House next?"

"I couldn't have done anything without you, Jack."

Dorothy Rae pulled Tate down and kissed him. "It's good of you to say that, Tate."

"I give credit where credit's due." He stared at Avery over their heads. His expression silently declared just how wrong she had been. He was surrounded by people who loved him. She was the only deceiver.

The door opened again. She spun around, hoping to see Fancy. It was one of the volunteers. "Everything's all set in the ballroom. The crowd's chanting for Tate and the band's playing. God, it's great!"

"I say it's time to break out the champagne," Nelson said.

When the first cork was popped, Avery nearly jumped out of her skin.

*　　　*　　　*

John's arm grazed Fancy's breast. She moved away. His thigh rubbed hers. She recrossed her legs. His predictable passes were getting tiresome. She wasn't in the mood. The drinks no longer tasted good. This wasn't as much fun as it used to be.

I thought we were friends.

Carole's voice seemed to speak to her above Rod Stewart's overamplified, hoarse sexiness and the din the happy hour imbibers were creating.

Carole had treated her decently in the last few months—in fact, since she'd come home from the hospital. Some of the things she'd said about self-respect were beginning to make sense. How could she have any self-respect if she let guys pick her up in joints like this—this was classy compared to some of the dives she'd been in—and do anything they wanted with her, then dispose of her as easily as they threw away a used rubber?

Carole didn't seem to think she was a dimwit. She'd entrusted her to run an important errand. And what had she done in return? She'd let her down.

"Say, I gotta go," she said suddenly. John had leaned over to lick her ear. She nearly knocked him off his stool when she reached for her purse and the padded envelope still lying on the bar. "Thanks for the drinks."

"Hey, where're you going? I thought, well, you know."

"Yeah, I know," Fancy said. "Sorry."

He came off his stool, propped his hands on his hips, and angrily demanded, "Well, what the hell am I supposed to do now?"

"Jerk off, I guess."

She drove toward the hotel with indiscriminate speed, keeping an eye out for radar traps and cruising police cars. She wasn't drunk, but alcohol would show up on a breath analyzer. Downtown traffic made the irregular maze of streets even more of a nightmare, but she finally reached the hotel garage.

The lobby was packed. Campaign posters bearing Tate Rutledge's picture bobbed above the press of people. It seemed that everyone in Bexar County who had voted for Tate Rutledge had come to celebrate his victory.

"Excuse me, excuse me," Fancy wormed her way through the crowd. "Ouch, dammit, that's my foot!" she shouted when someone backed over her. "Let me through."

"Hey, blondie, you gotta wait on the elevators same as everybody else." The complainer was a woman wearing a veritable armor of Rutledge campaign buttons on her chest.

"The hell I do," Fancy called back. "Excuse me."

After what seemed like half an hour of battling through the crowd as alive and working as a bucket of fishing bait, she stood up on tiptoe and was dismayed to find that she still wasn't anywhere close to the bank of elevators.

"Enough of this shit," she muttered. She caught the arm of the man nearest her. "If you can get me into an elevator, I'll give you a blow job you'll never forget."

A sudden hush fell over the room when the parlor telephone rang. All eyes swung toward the instrument. The mood was collectively expectant.

"Okay," Eddy said quietly. "that's him."

Tate picked up the phone. "Hello? Yes, sir, this is Tate Rutledge. It's good of you to call, Senator Dekker."

Eddy raised both fists above his head and shook them like a winning boxer after a knockout. Zee clasped her hands beneath her chin. Nelson nodded like a judge who had just been handed a fair decision from the jury. Jack and Dorothy Rae smiled at each other.

"Yes, sir. Thank you, sir. I feel the same way. Thank you. I appreciate your call.'' Tate replaced the receiver. For several seconds he sat with his hands loosely clasped between his knees, then he raised his head and, with a boyish grin, said, ''Guess that means I'm the new senator from Texas.''

The suite was instantly plunged into chaos. Some of the aides jumped into chairs and began whooping like attacking Indians. Eddy hauled Tate to his feet and pushed him toward the bedroom. ''*Now* you can go change. Somebody go catch an elevator and hold it. I'll call downstairs and tell them to give us five minutes.'' He yanked up the telephone.

Avery stood wringing her hands. She wanted to cheer and shout with joy over Tate's triumph. She wanted to throw her arms around him and give him a kiss befitting the victor. She wanted to share this jubilant moment with him. Instead, she shook like Jell-O, congealed with fear.

When she joined him in the bedroom, he was already stripped to his underwear and was stepping into a pair of dress slacks. ''Tate, don't go.''

His head snapped up. ''What?''

''Don't go down there.''

''I can't—''

She grabbed his arm. ''The man I told you about—the gray-haired man—he's here. I saw him this morning. Tate, for God's sake don't go.''

''I have to.''

''Please.'' Tears formed in her eyes. ''Please, believe what I'm telling you.'' He was buttoning his pale blue shirt. His hands paused. ''Why should I?''

''Because I love you. That's why I wanted to assume the role of your wife. I fell in love with you while I was still in the hospital. Before I could move or speak, I loved you.

''Everything I've told you is the truth. A threat has been made on your life. And yes, a chance for a terrific story presented itself to me and I took it, but . . .'' Here she clutched his shoulders between her hands and appealed to him. ''But I did what I did because I wanted to protect you. I love you and have from the beginning.''

''Tate, they're—'' Eddy came barging in. ''What the hell is going on in here? I thought you'd be dressed by now. They're tearing the place apart downstairs, waiting for you to put in an appearance. Everybody's gone nuts. Come on. Let's go.''

Tate looked from his friend to Avery. ''Even if I believed you,'' he said with quiet helplessness, ''I don't have a choice.''

''Tate, please,'' she begged, her voice tearing like paper.

''I don't have a choice.''

He removed her hands and quickly finished dressing. Eddy coached him on whom to thank publicly. ''Carole, you look like hell. Before you come downstairs, do something with your face,'' he ordered as he pushed Tate through the door.

Disobediently, Avery dashed after them. There were even more people in the suite now. Campaign workers had thronged the corridor and were forcing their way through the double doors to catch a glimpse of their hero. The noise was deafening. Somehow, over it, Avery heard Carole's name and turned in that direction.

Fancy squeezed through the squirming bodies. Inertia propelled her straight into Avery's arms. ''Fancy! Where have you been?''

''Don't lecture me. I've been through bloody hell trying to get here. There's a guy out in the hall who's really pissed off because I welshed on a deal and another one named John who's—''

''Was there anything in the box?''

"Here." The younger woman thrust the package at Avery. "I hope to God it's worth all the hell I've been through to get it here."

"Carole! You, too, Fancy, let's go!" Eddy shouted at them, waving them toward the door above the heads of the celebrants.

Avery ripped into the envelope and saw that it contained a videotape. "Stall them if you can."

"Huh?" Stupefied, Fancy watched her slip into the bedroom and shut the door behind her. "Jesus, is it me, or has everybody else gone fuckin' nuts?" A total stranger danced by and thrust a magnum of champagne into her hand. She took a long gulp.

Inside the bedroom, Avery inserted the tape into the VCR. She backed up toward the bed until the backs of her knees made contact, then sat down on the edge of it. Using the remote control, she fast-forwarded past the color bars to the clapboard. She recognized the station's call letters. Washington state, wasn't it? The reporter's name was unfamiliar to her, but the photographer was listed as Van Lovejoy.

Excitement churned inside her. Van had sent the tape to Irish's box, so it must contain something vitally important. After watching for several minutes, however, she couldn't imagine what that something might be. Was Van playing a joke?

The subject of the piece was a white supremacist and paramilitary group that had a permanent encampment located in an undisclosed spot, deep within the forested wilderness. On weekends, members would meet to plan their annihilation of everybody who wasn't exactly like them. It was their goal to eventually take over America, making it the racially pure, undiluted nation it should be.

Van, who to Avery's knowledge, had no political predilection, must have been alarmed by the ferocity of the hatred the organization espoused, for he had documented on tape the war games they played. He featured them swapping arms and ammunition, training newcomers in guerrilla tactics, and indoctrinating their children into believing that they were superior to everyone. They preached it all in the name of Christianity.

It was captivating video and the news hound inside her regretted having to fast-forward through it. She ran it at normal speed occasionally to make sure she wasn't missing the pertinence of the tape, but she couldn't find a single clue why Van had considered it crucial enough to mail.

His camera panned across a group of men dressed in military fatigues. They were armed to the teeth. Avery backed the tape up, then slowed it down so she could study each face. The commander was screaming swill into the receptive ears of his soldiers.

Van zoomed in for a close-up of one. Avery gasped with recognition. Her head began to swim.

He looked different. His scalp shone through the buzz haircut. Camouflage makeup had been smeared on his face, but it was instantly recognizable because she'd been living with him for months.

"That all men are created equal is a bunch of crap," the instructor ranted into the hand-held microphone. "A rumor started by inferiors in the hope that somebody would believe it."

The man Avery recognized applauded. He whistled. Hatred smoldered in his eyes.

"We don't want to live alongside niggers and kikes and queers, right?"

"Right!"

"We don't want them corrupting our children with their commie propaganda, right?"

"Right!"

"So what are we going to do to anybody who tells us we have to?"

The group, as one body, rose. Van's camera stayed focused on the participant who seemed the most steeped in bigotry and hatred. "Kill the bastards!" he shouted through his mask of camouflage makeup. "Kill the bastards!"

The door suddenly swung open. Avery hastily switched off the tape and vaulted from the bed. "Jack!" She covered her lips with bloodless fingers. Her knees almost refused to support her.

"They sent me back for you. We're supposed to be downstairs now, but I'm glad we have a minute alone."

Avery propped herself up, using the TV set behind her for support. Beyond Jack's shoulder she noted that the parlor was deserted now. Everyone had left for the ballroom downstairs.

He advanced on her. "I want to know why you did it."

"Did what?"

"Came on to me like you did."

Avery's chest rose and fell on a single, life-or-death breath. "Jack—"

"No, I want to know. Dorothy Rae says you never cared about me, that you only flirted with me to drive a wedge between Tate and me. Why, damn you? I nearly ruined my relationship with my brother. I nearly let my marriage fall apart because of you."

"Jack, I'm sorry," she said earnestly. "Truly I am, but—"

"You just wanted to make me look like a buffoon, didn't you? Did it elevate your ego to humiliate Dorothy Rae?"

"Jack, listen, please."

"No, you listen. She's twice the woman you are. Have you noticed how she's quit drinking all by herself? That takes character—something you'll never have. She still loves me, in spite of—"

"Jack, when did Eddy first come to work for Tate?"

He swore beneath his breath and shifted from one foot to the other impatiently. "I'm spilling my guts here and—"

"It's important!" she shouted. "How did Eddy talk himself into the job of campaign manager? When did he first appear on the scene? Did anyone think to check his qualifications?"

"What the hell are you talking about? You know as well as I do that he didn't talk himself into anything. He was recruited for the job."

"Recruited?" she repeated thinly. "By whom, Jack? Whose idea was it? Who hired Eddy Paschal?"

Jack gave her a blank stare, then a quick shrug. "Dad."

FORTY-NINE

The Corte Real was a lovely facility but a poor selection to host Tate Rutledge's victory celebration because it had only one entrance. Between a pair of massive Spanish doors and the ballroom itself was a short, narrow passageway. It formed an inevitable bottleneck.

The newly elected senator was propelled through that channel by a surge of family, friends, and supporters, all raucous, all jubilant over his win. Television lights created an aura around his head that shone like a celestial crown. His smile blended confidence with humility, that mix that elevated good men to greatness.

Tate's tall, gray-haired observer weaved his way toward the decorated platform at the opposite end of the room from the entrance. He elbowed aside media and Rutledge enthusiasts, somehow managing to do so without drawing attention to himself. Over the years, he'd mastered that kind of maneuver.

Recently, he had wondered if his skills weren't getting rusty. He was almost certain Mrs Rutledge had picked him out of the crowd on more than one occasion.

Having thought of her, he suddenly realized that she wasn't among the group following Tate toward the dais. Incisive eyes swung toward the entrance. Ah, there she was, bringing up the rear, looking distraught, obviously because she'd become separated from the rest of the family.

He turned his attention back to the charismatic young man, whose appearance in the ballroom had whipped the crowd into a frenzy. As he climbed the steps of the dais, balloons were released from a net overhead. They contributed to the confusion and poor visibility.

On the stage, Rutledge paused to shake hands with some of his most influential supporters—among them, several sports heroes and a Texas-bred movie actress. He waved to his disciples and they cheered him.

Gray Hair dodged the corner of a bouncing placard that nearly caught him on the forehead and kept his eyes trained on the hero of the hour. In the midst of this orgy of celebration, his face alone was grave with resolution.

Purposefully, he continued to move steadily forward, toward the platform. The pandemonium would have intimidated most, but it didn't faze him. He considered it a nuisance, nothing more. His progress was undeterred. Nothing could stop him from reaching Tate Rutledge.

Avery arrived breathless at the door of the ballroom. The walls of her heart felt as thin as a balloon about to burst. The muscles of her legs were burning. She'd run down twenty flights of stairs.

She hadn't even attempted to take an elevator to the hotel's mezzanine level but, together with Jack, who'd only been told that his brother's life was in imminent danger, had dashed for the stairs. Somewhere in the stairwell, Jack was still trying to catch up with her.

Pausing only a fraction of a moment to draw breath and get her bearings, she madly plunged through the crowd toward the dais. Wall-to-wall bodies formed a barricade, but Avery managed to plow through it.

She saw his head rise above the throng as he took the steps leading to the platform. ''Tate!''

He heard her shout and swirled his head around, but he missed seeing her when someone on the temporary stage grabbed his arm and began pumping his hand enthusiastically.

Avery frantically sought Eddy and found him positioning Nelson, Zee, Dorothy Rae, and Fancy in a semicircle behind the podium. He then motioned Tate toward the speaker's stand, where a dozen microphones were mounted and ready to amplify his first words as a newly elected senator.

Tate moved toward the podium.

''Tate!'' It was impossible for her to be heard over the blaring band. At the sight of their hero, the crowd had gone mad. ''Oh, God, no. Let me through. Let me through.''

A blast of adrenaline strengthened Avery's flagging energy and rubbery legs. With no regard to courtesy, she kicked and clawed her way forward, batting aside drifting balloons.

Jack finally caught up with her. "Carole," he panted, "what do you mean Tate's life is in danger?"

"Help me get to him. Jack, for God's sake, help me." He did what he could to create a furrow through the crowd. When she saw a space opening up in front of her, she jumped into the air and frantically waved her arms. "Tate! Tate!"

Gray Hair!

He was standing near the edge of the dais, partially hidden behind a Texas state flag.

"No!" she screamed. "Tate!"

Jack gave her a boost from behind. She stumbled up the steps, almost fell, caught herself. "Tate!"

Hearing her cry, he turned, wearing his glorious smile, and extended his hand. She rushed across the platform, but not toward Tate.

Her eyes were fixed on his enemy. And his were on her. And the sudden realization that she knew about him caused his eyes to crystallize.

As though in slow motion, Avery saw Eddy reach into his jacket. Her lips formed the word, but she didn't know that she actually screamed "No!" as he withdrew the pistol and took aim at the back of Tate's head.

Avery lunged for Tate and knocked him aside. A millisecond later, Eddy's bullet slammed into her, throwing her into Tate's unsuspecting arms.

She heard the screams, heard Tate's bellowing denial that this was happening, saw Jack's and Dorothy Rae's and Fancy's blank expressions of horror and incredulity.

Her eyes connected with Nelson Rutledge's the same instant Eddy's second bullet struck him in the forehead. It made a neat hole, but its rear exit was messy. Zee was showered with blood. She screamed.

Nelson's face registered surprise, then anger, then outrage. That was his death mask. He was dead before he hit the floor.

Eddy leaped from the dais into the crowd of hysterical spectators. The Lone Star flag fluttered. A man stepped from behind it and fired his previously concealed weapon. Eddy Paschal's head exploded upon impact.

It was Zee's voice that Avery heard from afar.

"Bryan! My God. *Bryan!*"

 # FIFTY

"I thought it would be best if we all met together like this, so I could clarify everything to everyone at once."

FBI Special Agent Bryan Tate addressed the somber group assembled in Avery Daniels's hospital room. Her bed had been elevated so that she was partially sitting up. Her eyes were red and puffy from crying. A bandage covered her left shoulder; her arm was in a sling.

The others—Jack and his family, Zee and Tate—were sitting in the available chairs or leaning against the walls and windowsills. All kept a wary distance from Avery's bed. Since Tate had disclosed her true identity to them, she had become an object of curiosity. After the tragic events of the night before, Mandy had been taken to the ranch and left in Mona's care.

"All of you experienced what happened," Bryan Tate said, "but you don't know the reasons for it. They're not easy to talk about."

"Tell them everything, Bryan," Zee said softly. "Don't leave out anything on my account. I want them, *need* them, to understand."

Tall and distinguished, he was standing beside her chair, a hand on her shoulder. "Zee and I fell in love years ago," he stated bluntly. "It was something neither of us predicted or wanted, particularly. We didn't set out to make it happen. It was wrong, but it was powerful. We eventually surrendered to it." His fingers flexed on her shoulder. "The consequences were far-reaching. They culminated in tragedy last night."

He told them how he had returned home from Korea a few months ahead of his buddy Nelson. "At his request, I checked on Zee periodically," he said. "By the time Nelson got home, the relationship between Zee and me had grown way beyond friendship or simple mutual attraction. We knew we loved each other and would have to hurt Nelson."

"I also knew I was pregnant," Zee said, reaching up to cover Bryan's hand with her own. "Pregnant with you, Tate. I told Nelson the unvarnished truth. He remained calm, but laid down an ultimatum. If I went with my lover and his bastard child, I would never see Jack again."

Tears welled in her eyes as she smiled at her older son. "Jack, you were still a toddler. I loved you, something Nelson knew very well and used to his advantage. When I vowed never to see Bryan again, he said he forgave me and promised to rear Tate as his son."

"Which he did," Tate said.

His eyes locked with Bryan's. The man was his father, though he'd never met him before last night. And the man he had known and loved as his father had been gunned down right before his eyes.

"I didn't know about Nelson's ultimatum," Bryan said, continuing the story. "I just got a note from Zee saying that our affair—and I couldn't believe she'd given it such a shoddy name—was over and that she wished it had never happened."

Despair had prompted him to volunteer for a dangerous overseas mission. When his plane malfunctioned and began spiraling down toward the ocean, he actually welcomed death, since he'd just as soon die as have to live without Zee. Fate intervened, however, and he was rescued.

While recovering from the injuries he had sustained, the FBI approached him. He had already been trained in intelligence work. They proposed that Bryan Tate remain "dead" and start working for them undercover. That's what he'd been doing for the last thirty years.

"When I could, I came to see you, Tate," he said to his son. "From a careful distance, never getting close enough to risk running into Nelson or Zee, I watched you play football a few times. I even tracked you around the base in Nam for a week. I was at your graduation from UT and law school. I never stopped loving you or your mother."

"And Nelson never forgot or forgave me," Zee said, bowing her head and sniffing into a Kleenex.

Bryan touched her hair consolingly, then picked up the story again. His latest assignment had been to infiltrate a white supremacist group operating out of the northwestern states. At the outset, he had come across an extremely bitter Vietnam vet whom he recognized as Eddy Paschal, Tate's former college roommate.

"We already had a thick dossier on him because he had been implicated in several subversive and neo-Nazi activities, including a few ritualistic executions, although we never had enough evidence to indict him.''

"Jeez, and to think I slept with him," Fancy said with a shudder.

"You couldn't have known," Dorothy Rae said kindly. "He had us all fooled."

"I would rather have kept him alive," Bryan said. "He was ruthless, but extremely intelligent. He could have been very useful to the Bureau."

Bryan looked toward Tate. "You can imagine how astonished I was when Nelson contacted him, especially since Paschal's philosophies were antithetical to yours. Nelson cleaned him up, gave him that spick-and-span image, paid for a crash course in public relations and communications, and brought him to Texas to be your campaign manager. That's when I realized that Nelson's intentions weren't what they seemed."

Tate backed into the wall and leaned his head against the pastel plaster. "So he planned to have me killed all along. It was one big setup. He groomed me for public office, instilled in me an ambition for it, hired Eddy, everything."

"I'm afraid so," Bryan said grimly.

Zee left her chair and went to Tate. "Darling, forgive me."

"Forgive you?"

"It was my sin he was punishing, not yours," she explained. "You were merely the sacrificial lamb. He wanted me to suffer and knew that the worst punishment possible for a mother would be to see her child die, especially during a moment of personal triumph."

"I can't believe it," Jack said, also coming to his feet.

"I can," Tate admitted quietly. "Now that I think back on everything, I can believe it. You know how he preached about justice, fairness, paying for one's mistakes, retribution for transgressions? He believed you had made atonement with your life," he said, nodding toward Bryan, "but mother hadn't yet paid for betraying him."

"Nelson was very subtle, very clever," Zee said. "Until last night I didn't realize just how clever or how vindictive. Tate, he manipulated you into marrying Carole, a woman he was sure would remind me of my own unfaithfulness. I had to close my eyes to her flagrant infidelity. I couldn't very well criticize her for committing the same sin I had."

"It wasn't the same, Zee."

"I know that, Bryan," she stressed, "but Nelson didn't. Adultery was adultery in his estimation, and punishable by death."

Jack was upset. His face was pale, ravaged from a night of mourning. "It still doesn't make sense to me. Why, if he hated Bryan so much, did he name the baby Tate?"

"Another cruel joke on me," Zee said. "It would be another constant reminder of my sin."

Jack pondered that for a moment. "Why did he favor Tate over me? I was his real son, but he always made me feel inferior to my younger brother."

"He counted on human nature taking its course," Zee explained. "He made it obvious that he favored Tate so that you would resent him. The friction between you would be another burden for me to bear."

Jack stubbornly shook his head. "I still can't believe he was so conniving. Not Dad." Dorothy Rae reached for his hand and pressed it between hers.

Zee turned toward Avery, who had remained silent throughout. "He was dedicated to getting vengeance on me. He arranged for Tate to marry Carole Navarro. Even after I learned of her shady past, it never occurred to me that Nelson was responsible for her conversion from topless dancer to wife. Now I believe that he engineered that, just as he recruited Eddy. In any case, they formed an alliance at some point.

"Carole was instructed to eat away at Tate's emotions. Nelson knew that the unhappier Tate was, the unhappier I would be. She did everything she was told to do and then some. The only decision she made independently was to have an abortion. I don't think Nelson knew about that. It made him furious, but only because he was afraid it would cost Tate the election."

Zee moved toward the bed and took Avery's hand. "Can you forgive me for the cruel accusations I made against you?"

"You didn't know," she said gruffly. "And Carole deserved your antipathy."

"I'm sorry about your friend Mr. Lovejoy, Ms. Daniels." Bryan's expression was gentle—far different from when he'd taken aim on Eddy and fired. "We had a guy watching Paschal, but he slipped past him that night."

"Van is really the one responsible for saving Tate's life," Avery said emotionally. "He must have viewed hours of video before finding the tape that explained why Eddy Paschal looked familiar to him. Eddy must have eluded your tail on several occasions, Mr. Tate, because he no doubt followed me to Irish's house. That's how he knew they were connected. It also helped him trace who Carole really was."

"Have you heard anything about Mr. McCabe's condition?"

She smiled through her tears. "After I insisted, they let me see him this morning. He's still in an ICU and his condition is serious, but they think he's going to pull through."

"Ironically, McCabe's massive heart attack saved his life. It kept Paschal from shooting him. Paschal's mistake was not making certain McCabe was dead when he dragged him off that elevator.

"May I ask, Ms. Daniels," Bryan continued, "what first clued you that Mr. Paschal was going to make an attempt on Tate's life?"

"She was told," Tate said.

Surprised reaction went through the group like an electric current. Jack was the first to speak. "By whom? When?"

"When I was in the hospital," she replied, "while I was still bandaged and being taken for Carole." She explained her involvement from that time up to the moment the night before when she had rushed up on the stage. When she finished, she glanced at Bryan and apologetically said, "I thought you were a hired killer."

"So you did notice me?"

"I have a reporter's trained eye."

"No," he said, "I was personally involved and not as careful as usual. I took tremendous chances of being recognized in order to stay close to Tate."

"I still can't distinguish the voice, but I believe it was Nelson, not Eddy, who spoke to me that night in the hospital," Avery remarked, "though I'll admit it never occurred to me that he would be the one."

On her behalf, Bryan said, "Ms. Daniels couldn't say anything to anyone at the risk of putting her own life in danger."

"And Tate's," she added, shyly casting her eyes downward when he glanced at her sharply.

Jack said, "You probably thought I was out to kill my brother. Cain and Abel."

"It did cross my mind on more than one occasion, Jack. I'm sorry." Because he and Dorothy Rae were still holding hands, she refrained from mentioning his infatuation with Carole.

"I think it's freaking wonderful how you pulled it off," Fancy declared. "Pretending to be Carole, I mean."

"It couldn't have been easy," Dorothy Rae said, slipping her arm through her husband's. "I'm sure you're glad that everything's out in the open." She gave Avery a look that conveyed a silent thank-you. It made sense to her now why her sister-in-law had been so compassionate and helpful recently. "Is that all, Mr. Tate? Are we free to go and let Avery rest?"

"Call me Bryan, and yes, that's all for now."

They filed out. Zee moved to Avery's side. "How can I ever repay you for saving my son's life?"

"I don't want any repayment. Not everything was faked." The two women exchanged a meaningful gaze. Zee patted her hand and left under Bryan's protective arm.

The silence they left behind was ponderous. Tate finally left his position against the wall and moved to the foot of her bed. "They'll probably get married," he remarked.

"How will you feel about that, Tate?"

He studied the toes of his boots for a moment before raising his head. "Who could blame them? They've been in love with each other for longer than I've been alive."

"It's easy now to understand why Zee always seemed so sad."

"Dad kept her an emotional prisoner." He gave a dry laugh. "Guess I can't refer to him as *Dad* anymore, can I?"

"Why not? That's what Nelson was to you. Whatever his motives were, he was a good father."

"I guess so." He gave her a lengthy stare. "I should have believed you yesterday when you tried to warn me."

"It was too unbelievable for you to accept."

"But you were right."

She shook her head. "I never suspected Nelson. Eddy, yes. Even Jack. But never Nelson."

"I want to mourn his death, but when I hear how cruel he's been to my mother, and that he hired my best friend to kill me . . . Jesus." He exhaled loudly, raking his hand through his hair. Tears came to his eyes.

"Don't be so hard on yourself, Tate. You've got a lot to deal with all at once." She wanted to hold him and comfort him, but he hadn't asked her to and, until he did, she had no right to.

"When you do your story, I have one favor to ask."

"There won't be a story."

"There'll be a story," he argued firmly. He rounded the foot of the bed and sat down on the edge of it. "You're already being hailed as a heroine."

"You shouldn't have revealed my identity during the press conference this morning." She had watched it on the set in her hospital room while it was being broadcast live from the lobby of the Palacio Del Rio. "You could have divorced me as Carole, as you planned to."

"I can't begin my political career with a lie, Avery."

"That's the first time you've ever called me by my name," she whispered, left breathless from hearing it on his lips.

Their gazes held for a moment, then he continued. "So far, no one but the people who were in this room, and I guess a few FBI agents, know that Nelson Rutledge engineered the plot. They've surmised that it was all Eddy's doing and have attributed it to his disillusionment in America after the war. I'm asking you to keep it that way, for my family's sake. Mostly for my mother's sake."

"If anyone asks, I will. But I won't do a story."

"Yes, you will."

Tears started in her eyes again. Fretfully, she groped for his hands. "I can't stand having you think I did this to exploit you, or that I did it for fame and glory."

"I think you did it for the reason you told me yesterday, and which I stubbornly refused to believe—because you love me."

Her heart went a little crazy. She threaded her fingers through his hair. "I do, Tate. More than my life."

He gazed at the bandage on her shoulder and, shuddering slightly, squeezed his eyes closed. When he opened them again, they were misty. "I know."

 # EPILOGUE

"**W**atching it again?"

Senator Tate Rutledge entered the living room of the comfortable Georgetown town home he shared with his wife and daughter. On this particular afternoon, he caught Avery alone in the living room, watching a tape of her documentary.

The story she had produced, at Tate's insistence, aired on PBS stations across the country six months into his term. The facts were presented fairly, concisely, and without any embellishment in spite of her personal involvement.

Tate had convinced her that the public had a right to know about the bizarre chain of events that had started with the crash of Flight 398 and culminated on election night.

He further stated that no one could report the events with more insight and sensitivity than she. His final argument was that he didn't want his first term as senator to be clouded by lies and half-truths. He would rather have the public know than speculate.

The documentary hadn't won Avery a Pulitzer prize, though it was acclaimed by viewers, critics, and colleagues. She was currently considering the offers she had received to produce documentaries on a variety of subjects.

"Still basking in the glory, huh?" Tate laid his briefcase on an end table and shrugged off his jacket.

"Don't tease." She reached behind her for his hand and kissed the back of it as she pulled him around to join her on the sofa. "Irish called today. He made me think of it."

Irish had survived the heart attack he had suffered in the elevator at the Palacio Del Rio. He claimed that he had actually died and come back to life. How else could Paschal have failed to feel a pulse? He swore that he remembered floating out of himself, looking down and seeing Paschal drag his body into the alcove.

But then, everybody who knew Irish well teased him about his Celtic superstition and closet Catholicism. All that was important to Avery was that she hadn't lost him.

At the conclusion of the piece, before the tape went to black, a message appeared in the middle of the screen. It read, "Dedicated to the memory of Van Lovejoy."

"We're too far away for me to put flowers on his grave," she said huskily. "Watching his work is how I pay tribute." She clicked off the machine and set the transmitter aside.

Nelson's machinations had impacted their lives and they would never be completely free from the memories. Jack was still grappling with his disillusionment about his father. He had chosen to stay and manage the law firm in San Antonio rather than join Tate's staff in Washington. Though they were apart geographically, the half brothers had never been closer. It was hoped that time would eventually heal the heartache they had in common.

Tate struggled daily to assimilate Nelson's grand scheme, but also mourned the loss of the man he'd always known as Dad. He adamantly kept the two personas separate in his mind.

His emotions regarding Bryan Tate were conflicting. He liked him, respected him, and appreciated him for the happiness he'd given Zee since their marriage. Yet he wasn't quite prepared to call him father, a kinship he could never claim publicly, even if he acknowledged it privately.

During those moments of emotional warfare, his wife's love and support helped tremendously.

Thinking on it all now, Tate drew her into his arms, receiving as much comfort as he gave. He hugged her close for a long time, turning his face into her neck.

"Have I ever told you what a courageous, fascinating woman I think you are for doing what you did, even though it placed your own life in jeopardy? God, when I think back on that night, to when I felt your blood running over my hands." He pressed a kiss onto her neck. "I had fallen in love with my wife again, and I couldn't understand why. Before I really ever discovered you, I almost lost you."

"I wasn't sure it would matter," she said. He raised his head and looked at her quizzically. "I was afraid that when you found out who I really was, you wouldn't want me anymore."

He pulled her into his arms again. "I wanted you. I still want you." The way he said it left no doubt in her mind. The way he kissed her made it a covenant as binding as the marriage vows they had taken months earlier.

"I'm still finding out who you really are, even though I know you intimately," he whispered into her mouth, "more intimately than I've known any other woman, and that's the God's truth. I know what you feel like inside, and how every part of your body tastes."

He kissed her again with love and unappeasable passion.

"Tate," she sighed when they drew apart, "when you look into my face, who do you see?"

"The woman I owe my life to. The woman who saved Mandy from emotional deprivation. The woman who is carrying my child." Warmly, he caressed her swollen abdomen. "The woman I love more than breath."

"No, I mean—"

"I know what you mean." He eased her back against the sofa cushions and followed her down, cradling her face between his hands and touching her mouth with his. "I see Avery."

BEST KEPT SECRETS

ONE

It wasn't so much the cockroach that made her scream as the chipped fingernail. The cockroach was small. The chip was a dilly. On her manicured nail it looked as deep and jagged as the Grand Canyon.

Alex swatted at the cockroach with the laminated card that displayed the motel's limited room service menu. The reverse side advertised the Friday night Mexican buffet and The Four Riders, a country and western band currently performing in the Silver Spur Lounge nightly from seven till midnight.

Her swipe at the cockroach missed by a mile and it scuttled for cover behind the wood veneer dresser. "I'll get you later."

She found a nail file in the bottom of the cosmetic case she had been about to unpack when the metal clasp had wrecked her fingernail and the cockroach had come out to inspect the new tenant of room 125. The room was located on the ground floor of the Westerner Motel, three doors down from the ice and vending machines.

Once the nail had been repaired, Alex gave herself one last, critical look in the dresser mirror. It was important that she make a stunning first impression. They would be astonished when she told them who she was, but she wanted to create an even stronger impact.

She wanted to leave them stupefied, speechless, and defenseless.

They would undoubtedly make comparisons. She couldn't prevent that; she just didn't want to come out on the short end of their mental measuring sticks. If she could help it, they would find no flaws in Celina Gaither's daughter.

She had carefully chosen what to wear. Everything—clothes, jewelry, accessories—was in excellent taste. The overall effect was tailored but not severe, smart but not trendy; she exuded an aura of professionalism that didn't compromise her femininity.

Her goal was to impress them first, then surprise them with what had brought her to Purcell.

Until a few weeks ago, the town of thirty thousand had been a lonely dot on the Texas map. As many jackrabbits and horned toads lived there as people. Recently, town business interests had generated news, but on a comparatively small scale. By the time Alex's job was done, she was certain Purcell would capture newspaper headlines from El Paso to Texarkana.

Concluding that nothing about her appearance could be improved upon short of an act of God or very expensive plastic surgery, she shouldered her handbag, picked up her eel attaché case, and, making certain she had her room key, closed the door to room 125 behind her.

During the drive downtown, Alex had to creep through two school zones. Rush hour in Purcell began when school dismissed. Parents transported their children from school to dentists' offices, piano lessons, and shopping centers. Some might even have been going home, but the sluggish traffic and clogged intersections indicated that no one was staying indoors that day. She didn't actually mind the stop-and-go traffic. The delays gave her an opportunity to gauge the personality of the town.

Black and gold streamers fluttered from the marquee outside Purcell High School. The caricature of a black panther snarled at the passing cars on the highway and temporary letters spelled out POUNCE PERMIAN. On the field inside the stadium, the football team was working out and running plays. The marching band, its instruments flashing in the sun, was rehearsing Friday night's halftime show on a practice field.

The activity looked so innocent. For a moment, Alex regretted her mission and what its outcome would most likely mean for the community. She dismissed her guilty feelings quickly, however, when she reminded herself why she was here. A harvest of rejection, as well as her grandmother's harsh accusations, were stored in her mind if she ever, even for a second, forgot what had brought her to this point in her life. She could ill afford the slightest sentimental regrets.

Downtown Purcell was almost deserted. Many of the commercial buildings and offices facing the square were closed and barred. Foreclosure signs were too plentiful to count.

Graffiti was scrawled across plate-glass windows that had once been filled with enticing merchandise. There was still a hand-lettered sign on the door of a deserted laundry. Someone had scratched out the *r,* so that the sign now read, 3 SHI TS/ $1.00. It crudely summed up the economic climate in Purcell County.

She parked in front of the country courthouse and fed coins into the meter at the curb. The courthouse had been built of red granite quarried in the hill country and hauled by rail to Purcell ninety years earlier. Italian stonecutters had carved pretentious gargoyles and griffins in every available spot as if the amount of decoration justified the expense of their commission. The results were ostentatious, but gaudiness was one of the edifice's attractions. Atop its dome the national and Texas state flags flapped in the brisk north wind.

Having worked in and about the state capitol of Austin for the last year, Alex wasn't intimidated by official buildings. She took the courthouse steps with a determined stride and pulled open the heavy doors. Inside, the plaster walls showed peeling paint and signs of general disrepair. The aggregate tile floor had faint cracks in it that crisscrossed like the lines in the palm of an ancient hand.

The ceiling was high. The drafty corridors smelled of industrial-strength cleaning solution, musty record books, and an overdose of perfume that emanated from the district attorney's secretary. She looked up expectantly as Alex entered the outer office.

"Hi, there. You lost, honey? I love your hair. Wish I could wear mine pulled back in a bun like that. You have to have real tiny ears. Wouldn't you know it, I've got jug handles sticking out from the sides of my head. Do you put henna on it to give it those reddish highlights?"

"Is this District Attorney Chastain's office?"

"Sure is, honey. Whatcha need him for? He's kinda busy today."

"I'm from the Travis County D.A.'s office. Mr. Harper called on my behalf, I believe."

The wad of chewing gum inside the secretary's cheek got a rest from the pounding it had been taking. "You? We were expecting a man."

"As you can see . . ." Alex held her arms out at her sides.

The secretary looked vexed. "You'd think Mr. Harper would have mentioned that his assistant was a lady, not a man, but shoot," she said, flipping her hand down from a limp wrist, "you know how men are. Well, honey, you're right on time for your appointment. My name's Imogene. Want some coffee? That's a gorgeous outfit, so high-fashion. They're wearing skirts shorter these days, aren't they?"

At the risk of sounding rude, Alex said, "Are the parties here yet?"

Just then, masculine laughter erupted from the other side of the closed door. "That answer your question, honey?" Imogene asked Alex. "Somebody prob'ly just told a dirty joke to let off steam. They're just bustin' a gut to know what this hush-hush meeting is all about. What's the big secret? Mr. Harper didn't tell Pat why you were coming to Purcell, even though they were friends in law school. Is it something to do with ME getting that gambling license?"

"ME?"

"Minton Enterprises." She said it as though she was surprised Alex was not familiar with the name.

"Perhaps I shouldn't keep them any longer," Alex suggested tactfully, side-stepping Imogene's question.

"Shoot, just listen to me running off at the mouth. Did you say you wanted some coffee, honey?"

"No, thank you." Alex followed Imogene toward the door. Her heart started beating double-time.

"Excuse me." Imogene interrupted the conversation by poking her head into the room. "District Attorney Harper's assistant is here. Y'all sure are in for a treat." She turned back toward Alex. One set of eyelashes, gummy with navy blue mascara, dropped over her eye in a broad, just-between-us-girls wink. "Go on in, honey."

Alex, bracing herself for the most crucial meeting in her life, entered the office.

It was obvious from the relaxed atmosphere that the men in the room had been expecting another man. The moment she crossed the threshold and Imogene pulled the transomed door closed, the man seated behind the desk sprang to his feet. He ground out a burning cigar in the thick, glass ashtray and reached for his suit coat, which had been draped over the back of his chair.

"Pat Chastain," he said, extending his hand. " 'Treat' is an understatement. But then, my good buddy Greg Harper always did have an eye for the ladies. Doesn't surprise me a bit that he's got a good-lookin' woman on his staff."

His sexist remark set her teeth on edge, but she let it slide. She inclined her head in acknowledgment of Chastain's compliment. The hand she clasped in a firm handshake was so loaded down with gold-nugget jewelry it could have anchored a fair-sized yacht. "Thank you for arranging this meeting, Mr. Chastain."

"No problem, no problem. Glad to be of service to both you and Greg. And call me Pat." Taking her elbow, he turned her toward the other two men, who had come to their feet out of deference to her. "This here is Mr. Angus Minton and his son, Junior."

"Gentlemen." Confronting them, meeting them eye to eye for the first time, had a strange and powerful impact on her. Curiosity and antipathy warred inside her. She wanted to analyze them, denounce them. Instead, she behaved in the expected civilized manner and extended her hand.

It was clasped by one studded with calluses. The handshake bordered on being too hard, but it was as open and friendly as the face smiling at her.

"A pleasure, ma'am. Welcome to Purcell County."

Angus Minton's face was tanned and weathered, ravaged by blistering summer sun, frigid blue northers, and years of outdoor work. Intelligent blue eyes twinkled at her from sockets radiating lines of friendliness. He had a boisterous voice. Alex

270 SANDRA BROWN

guessed that his laugh would be as expansive as his broad chest and the beer belly that was his only sign of indulgence. Otherwise, he seemed physically fit and strong. Even a younger, larger man would be loath to pick a fight with him because of his commanding presence. For all his strength, he looked as guileless as an altar boy.

His son's handshake was softer, but no less hearty or friendly. He enfolded Alex's hand warmly, and in a confidence-inspiring voice, said, "I'm Junior Minton. How do you do?"

"How do you do?"

He didn't look his forty-three years, especially when he smiled. His straight white teeth flashed and a devilish dimple cratered one cheek, suggesting that he behaved no better than any given occasion called for him to. His blue eyes, a shade deeper than his father's but just as mischievous, held hers long enough to intimate that they were the only two in the room who mattered. She withdrew her hand before Junior Minton seemed ready to relinquish it.

"And over yonder is Reede, Reede Lambert."

Alex turned in the direction Pat Chastain had indicated and located the fourth man, whom she hadn't noticed until now. Flaunting etiquette, he was still slouched in a chair in the corner of the room. Scuffed cowboy boots were crossed at the ankles, their toes pointing ceilingward and insolently wagging back and forth. His hands were loosely folded over a western belt buckle. He unlinked them long enough to raise two fingers to the brim of a cowboy hat. "Ma'am."

"Mr. Lambert," she said coolly.

"Here, sit yourself down," Chastain offered, pointing her toward a chair. "Did Imogene offer you some coffee?"

"Yes, but I told her that I didn't care for any. I'd like to get to the purpose of the meeting, if we could."

"Sure enough. Junior, pull that other chair over here. Angus." Chastain nodded for the older man to sit back down. When everyone was reseated, the district attorney returned to his chair behind the desk. "Now, Miss— Well, I'll be damned. During all the introductions, we failed to get your name."

Alex held center stage. Four pairs of eyes were trained on her, curiously waiting to hear her name. She paused for dramatic effect, knowing that divulging it would cause a profound reaction. She wanted to witness and catalog their individual reactions. She wished she could see Reede Lambert better. He was sitting partially behind her, and the cowboy hat hid all but the lowest portion of his face.

She took a breath. "I'm Alexandra Gaither, Celina's daughter."

A stunned silence followed the announcement.

Pat Chastain, befuddled, finally asked, "Who's Celina Gaither?"

"Well, I'll be a sonofabitch." Angus flopped backward in his chair like a collapsing inflatable toy.

"Celina's daughter. My God, I can't believe it," Junior whispered. "I can't believe it."

"Somebody want to fill me in, please?" Pat said, still confused. Nobody paid him any attention.

The Mintons openly stared at Alex, searching her face for resemblances to her mother, whom they had known so well. From the corner of her eye, she noticed that the toes of Lambert's boots were no longer wagging. He drew his knees in and sat up straight.

"What on earth have you been doing with yourself all these years?" Angus asked.

"How many years has it been?" Junior wanted to know.

"Twenty-five," Alex answered precisely. "I was only two months old when Grandma Graham moved away from here."

"How is your grandma?"

"She's currently in a Waco nursing home, dying of cancer, Mr. Minton." Alex saw no merit in sparing their sensibilities. "She's in a coma."

"I'm sorry to hear that."

"Thank you."

"Where have y'all been living all this time?"

Alex named a town in central Texas. "We lived there all my life—at least, as far back as I can remember. I graduated high school there, went to the University of Texas, and then, straight into law school. I passed the bar a year ago."

"Law school. Imagine that. Well, you turned out fine, Alexandra, just fine. Didn't she, Junior?"

Junior Minton turned on his charming smile full blast. "I'd say so. You don't look a thing like you did last time I saw you," he told her teasingly. "Best as I recall, your diaper was wet and you didn't have a single hair on your head."

Considering the reason for this prearranged meeting, his flirting made Alex uneasy. She was glad when Pat Chastain intervened again. "I hate to butt into such a touching reunion, but I'm still in the dark."

Angus enlightened him. "Celina was a classmate of Junior's and Reede's. They were best friends, actually. Rarely did you see one of them without the other two when they were in high school. Crazy kids."

Then, his blue eyes turned cloudy and he shook his head sorrowfully. "Celina died. Tragic thing." He took a quiet moment to collect himself. "Anyway, this is the first time we've heard a word about Alexandra since her grandma, Celina's mother, moved away with her." Smiling, he slapped his thighs. "Damned if it's not great to have you back in Purcell."

"Thank you, but—" Alex opened her briefcase and took out a manila envelope. "I'm not back to stay, Mr. Minton. Actually, I'm acting in an official capacity." She passed the envelope across the desk to the district attorney, who looked at it with puzzlement.

"Official capacity? When Greg called me and asked if I'd help out his top prosecutor, he said something about reopening a case."

"It's all in there," Alex said, nodding down at the envelope. "I suggest that you peruse the contents and thoroughly acquaint yourself with the details. Greg Harper requests the full cooperation and assistance of your office and local law enforcement agencies, Mr. Chastain. He assured me that you would comply with this request for the duration of my investigation." She closed her attaché with a decisive snap, stood, and headed for the door.

"Investigation?" District Attorney Chastain came to his feet. The Mintons did likewise.

"Are you working with the Racing Commission?" Angus asked. "We were told we'd be carefully scrutinized before they granted us a gambling license, but I thought we had already passed muster."

"I thought it was all over except for the formalities," Junior said.

"As far as I know, it is," Alex told them. "My investigation has nothing to do with the Racing Commission, or the granting of your horse-racing license."

After a moment, when she didn't elaborate, Chastain asked, "Well, then, what *does* it have to do with, Miss Gaither?"

Drawing herself up to her full height, she said, "I am reopening a twenty-five-year-old murder case. Greg Harper asked for your help, Mr. Chastain, since the crime was committed in Purcell County."

She looked into Angus's eyes, then into Junior's. Finally, she stared down hard at the crown of Reede Lambert's hat. "Before I'm finished, I'm going to know which one of you killed my mother."

 # TWO

Alex peeled off her suit jacket and tossed it onto the motel bed. Her underarms were damp and her knees were ready to buckle. She was nauseated. The scene in the D.A.'s office had shaken her more than she wanted to admit.

She had left Pat Chastain's office with her head held high and her shoulders back. She hadn't walked too fast, but she hadn't dawdled. She had smiled good-bye to Imogene, who had obviously been eavesdropping through the door because she stared at Alex bug-eyed, her mouth agape.

Alex's exit line had been well rehearsed, well timed and perfectly executed. The meeting had gone just as she had planned it, but she was vastly relieved that it was over.

Now, she peeled off one cloying piece of clothing after another. She would love to think that the worst was behind her, but she feared it was yet to come. The three men she had met today wouldn't roll over and play dead. She would have to confront them again, and when she did, they wouldn't be so overjoyed to see her.

Angus Minton seemed as full of goodwill as Santa Claus, but Alex knew that nobody in Angus's position could be as harmless as he tried to pretend. He was the richest, most powerful man in the county. One didn't achieve that status solely through benign leadership. He would fight to keep what he'd spent a lifetime cultivating.

Junior was a charmer who knew his way around women. The years had been kind to him. He'd changed little from the photographs Alex had seen of him as an adolescent. She also knew that he used his good looks to his advantage. It would be easy for her to like him. It would also be easy to suspect him of murder.

Reede Lambert was the toughest for her to pigeonhole because her impressions of him were the least specific. Unlike the others, she hadn't been able to look him in the eye. Reede the man looked much harder and stronger than Reede the boy from her grandma's picture box. Her first impression was that he was sullen, unfriendly, and dangerous.

She was certain that one of these men had killed her mother.

Celina Gaither had not been murdered by the accused, Buddy Hicks. Her grandmother, Merle Graham, had drummed that into little Alex's head like a catechism all her life.

"It'll be up to you, Alexandra, to set the record right," Merle had told her almost daily. "That's the least you can do for your mother." At that point she usually glanced wistfully at one of the many framed photographs of her late daughter scattered throughout the house. Looking at the photographs would invariably make her cry, and nothing her granddaughter did could cheer her.

Until a few weeks ago, however, Alex hadn't known who Merle suspected of killing Celina. Finding out had been the darkest hour of Alex's life.

Responding to an urgent call from the nursing home doctor, she had sped up the interstate to Waco. The facility was quiet, immaculate, and staffed by caring professionals. Merle's life-time pension from the telephone company made it affordable. For all its amenities, it still had the grey smell of old age; despair and decay permeated its corridors.

When she had arrived that cold, dismal, rainy afternoon, Alex had been told that her grandmother was in critical condition. She entered the hushed private room and moved toward the hospital bed. Merle's body had visibly deteriorated since Alex had visited only the week before. But her eyes were as alive as Fourth of July sparklers. Their glitter, however, was hostile.

"Don't come in here," Merle rasped on a shallow breath. "I don't want to see you. It's because of you!"

"What, Grandma?" Alex asked in dismay. "What are you talking about?"

"I don't want you here."

Embarrassed by the blatant rejection, Alex had glanced around at the attending physician and nurses. They shrugged their incomprehension. "Why don't you want to see me? I've come all the way from Austin."

"It's your fault she died, you know. If it hadn't been for you . . ." Merle moaned with pain and clutched her sheet with sticklike, bloodless fingers.

"Mother? You're saying I'm responsible for Mother's death?"

Merle's eyes popped open. "Yes," she hissed viciously.

"But I was just a baby, an infant," Alex argued, desperately wetting her lips. "How could I—"

"Ask them."

"Who, Grandma? Ask who?"

"The one who murdered her. Angus, Junior, Reede. But it was you . . . you . . . you. . . ."

Alex had to be led from the room by the doctor several minutes after Merle lapsed into a deep coma. The ugly accusation had petrified her; it reverberated in her brain and assaulted her soul.

If Merle held Alex responsible for Celina's death, so much of Alex's upbringing could be explained. She had always wondered why Grandma Graham was never very affectionate with her. No matter how remarkable Alex's achievements, they were never quite good enough to win her grandmother's praise. She knew she was never considered as gifted, or clever, or charismatic as the smiling girl in the photographs that Merle looked at with such sad longing.

Alex didn't resent her mother. Indeed, she idolized and adored her with the blind passion of a child who had grown up without parents. She constantly worked toward being as good at everything as Celina had been, not only so she would be a worthy daughter, but in the desperate hope of earning her grandmother's love and approval. So it came as a stunning blow to hear from her dying grandmother's lips that she was responsible for Celina's murder.

The doctor had tentatively suggested that she might want to have Mrs. Graham taken off the life support systems. "There's nothing we can do for her now, Ms. Gaither."

"Oh, yes, there is," Alex had said with a ferocity that shocked him. "You can keep her alive. I'll be in constant touch."

Immediately upon her return to Austin, she began to research the murder case of Celina Graham Gaither. She spent many sleepless nights studying transcripts and court documents before approaching her boss, the district attorney of Travis County.

Greg Harper had shifted the smoking cigarette from one corner of his lips to the other. In the courtroom, Greg was the bane of guilty defendants, lying witnesses, and orderly judges. He talked too loud, smoked too much, drank in abundance, and wore five-hundred-dollar pinstriped suits with lizard boots that cost twice that much.

To say that he was flashy and egomaniacal would be gross understatements. He was shrewd, ambitious, ruthless, relentless, and profane, and would therefore probably carve out quite a niche for himself in state politics, which was his driving ambition. He believed in the reward system and appreciated raw talent. That's why Alex was on his staff.

"You want to reopen a twenty-five-year-old murder case?" he asked her when she stated the purpose of the conference she'd requested. "Got a reason?"

"Because the victim was my mother."

For the first time since she'd known him, Greg had asked a question he didn't already know the answer to—or at least have a fairly good guess. "Jesus, Alex, I'm sorry. I didn't know that."

She gave a slight, dismissive shrug. "Well, it's not something one advertises, is it?"

"When was this? How old were you?"

"An infant. I don't remember her. She was only eighteen when she was killed."

He ran his long, bony hand down his even longer, bonier face. "The case remains on the books as officially unsolved?"

"Not exactly. There was a suspect arrested and charged, but the case was dismissed without ever going to trial."

"Fill me in, and make it short. I'm having lunch with the state attorney general today," he said. "You've got ten minutes. Shoot."

When she finished, Greg frowned and lit a cigarette from the smoldering tip of one he'd smoked down to the filter. "Goddamn, Alex, you didn't say that the Mintons were involved. Your granny really believes that one of them iced your mother?"

"Or their friend, Reede Lambert."

"By any chance, did she provide them with a motive?"

"Not specifically," Alex said evasively, loath to tell him that Merle had cited her, Alex, as the motive. "Apparently, Celina was close friends with them."

"Then why would one of them kill her?"

"That's what I want to find out."

"On the state's time?"

"It's a viable case, Greg," she said tightly.

"All you've got is a hunch."

"It's stronger than a hunch."

He gave a noncommittal grunt. "Are you sure this isn't just a personal grudge?"

"Of course not." Alex took umbrage. "I'm pursuing this from a strictly legal viewpoint. If Buddy Hicks had gone on trial and been convicted by a jury, I wouldn't put so much stock in what Grandma told me. But it's there in the public records."

"How come she didn't raise hell about the murder when it happened?"

"I asked her that myself. She didn't have much money and she felt intimidated by the legal machinations. Besides, the murder had left her drained of energy. What little she had went into rearing me."

It was now clear to Alex why, since her earliest recollections, her grandmother had pushed her toward the legal profession. Because it was expected of her, Alex had excelled in school and had ultimately graduated from the University of Texas Law School in the top ten percent of her class. The law was the profession Merle had chosen for her, but thankfully it was a field that intrigued and delighted Alex.

Her curious mind enjoyed delving into its intricacies. She was well prepared to do what she must.

"Grandmother was just a widow lady, left with a baby to raise," she said, building her case. "There was precious little she could do about the judge's ruling at Hicks's competency hearing. With what money she had, she packed up, left town, and never went back."

Greg consulted his wristwatch. Then, anchoring his cigarette between his lips, he stood up and pulled on his suit jacket. "I can't reopen a murder case without a shred of evidence or probable cause. You know that. I didn't snatch you out of law school 'cause you were stupid. Gotta confess, though, that your shapely ass had something to do with it."

"Thanks."

Her disgust was obvious and it wasn't because of his sexism, which was so brassy she knew it was insincere. "Look, Alex, this isn't a teensy-weensy favor you're asking of me," he said. "Because of who these guys are, we're talking earth-shattering shit here. Before I stick my neck out, I've got to have more to go on than your hunch and Granny's ramblings."

She followed him to the door of his office. "Come on, Greg, spare me the legal lingo. You're only thinking of yourself."

"You're goddamn right I am. Constantly."

His admission left her no room to maneuver. "At least grant me permission to investigate this murder when I'm not actively involved in other cases."

"You know what a backlog we've got. We can't get all the cases to court as it is now."

"I'll work overtime. I won't shirk my other responsibilities. You know I won't."

"Alex—"

"Please, Greg." She could see that he wanted her to withdraw the request, but she wouldn't capitulate to anything less than a definite no. Her preliminary research had piqued her interest as a prosecutor and litigator, and her desperate desire to prove her grandmother wrong and absolve herself of any guilt further motivated her undertakings. "If I don't produce something soon, I'll drop it and you'll never hear of it again."

He studied her intent face. "Why don't you just work out your frustrations with hot, illicit screwing like everybody else? At least half the guys in town would accommodate you, married or single." She gave him a withering look. "Okay, okay. You can do some digging, but only in your spare time. Come up with something concrete. If I'm going to win votes, I can't look or act like a goddamn fool, and neither can anybody else in this office. Now I'm late for lunch. 'Bye. "

Her caseload was heavy, and the time she had had to spend on her mother's murder had been limited. She read everything she could get her hands on— newspaper accounts, transcripts of Buddy Hicks's hearing—until she had the facts memorized.

They were basic and simple. Mr. Bud Hicks, who was mentally retarded, had been arrested near the murder scene with the victim's blood on his clothing. At the time of his arrest, he had had in his possession the surgical instrument with which he had allegedly killed the victim. He was jailed, questioned, and charged. Within days there was a hearing. Judge Joseph Wallace had declared Hicks incompetent to stand trial and had confined him to a state mental hospital.

It seemed like an open-and-shut case. Just when she had begun to believe that Greg was right, that she was on a wild goose chase, she had discovered a curious glitch in the transcript of Hicks's hearing. After following up on it, she had approached Greg again, armed with a signed affidavit.

"Well, I've got it." Triumphantly, she slapped the folder on top of the others cluttering his desk.

Greg scowled darkly. "Don't be so friggin' cheerful, and for crissake, stop slamming things around. I've got a bitchin' hangover." He mumbled his words through a dense screen of smoke. He stopped puffing on the cigarette only long enough to sip at a steaming cup of black coffee. "How was your weekend?"

"Wonderful. Far more productive than yours. Read that."

Tentatively, he opened the file and scanned the contents with bleary eyes. "Hmm." His initial reading was enough to grab his attention. Leaning back in his chair and propping his feet on the corner of his desk, he reread it more carefully. "This is from the doctor at the mental hospital where this Hicks fellow is incarcerated?"

"Was. He died a few months ago."

"Interesting."

"Interesting?" Alex cried, disappointed with the bland assessment. She left her chair, circled it, and stood behind it, gripping the upholstered back in agitation. "Greg, Buddy Hicks spent twenty-five years in that hospital for nothing."

"You don't know that yet. Don't jump to conclusions."

"His last attending psychiatrist said that Buddy Hicks was a model patient. He never demonstrated any violent tendencies. He had no apparent sex drive, and in the doctor's expert opinion, he was incapable of committing a crime like the one that cost my mother her life. Admit that it looks fishy."

He read several other briefs, then muttered, "It looks fishy, but it's sure as hell not a smoking gun."

"Short of a miracle, I won't be able to produce any concrete evidence. The case is twenty-five years old. All I can hope for is enough probable cause to bring it before a grand jury. A confession from the real killer—because I'm convinced, beyond a shadow of a doubt, that Bud Hicks did not murder my mother—is a pipe dream. There's also the slim possibility of smoking out an eyewitness."

"Slim to none, Alex."

"Why?"

"You've done enough homework, so you should know. The murder took place in a barn on Angus Minton's ranch. Say his name anywhere in that county and the ground trembles. He's a big enchilada. If there was an eyewitness, he wouldn't testify against Minton because he'd be biting the hand that feeds him. Minton runs about a dozen enterprises in an area of the state where they're gasping their last breath, economically speaking.

"Which brings us to another delicate area, in a case riddled with delicate areas." Greg slurped his coffee and lit another cigarette. "The governor's racing commission just gave Minton Enterprises the green light on building that horse-racing track in Purcell County."

"I'm well aware of that. What bearing does it have?"

"You tell me."

"None!" she shouted.

"Okay, I believe you. But if you start slinging accusations and casting aspersions on one of Texas's favorite sons, how do you think that's going to sit with the governor? He's damn proud of his racing commission. He wants this pari-mutuel thing to get off the ground without a hitch. No controversy. No bad press. No shady deals. He wants everything above reproach and squeaky clean.

"So, if some smart-ass prosecutor starts shooting off her mouth, trying to connect somebody his hand-picked commission has given their coveted blessing to with a murder, the governor is going to be royally pissed off. And if said prosecutor works in this office, who do you think he's going to be the most pissed off at? *Moi.''*

Alex didn't argue with him. Instead, she calmly said, ''All right. I'll resign from this office and do it on my own.''

''Jesus, you're theatrical. You didn't let me finish.'' He pressed his intercom button and bellowed to his secretary to bring him more coffee. While she was carrying it in, he lit another cigarette.

''On the other hand,'' he said around a gust of smoke, ''I can't stand that bastard who's living in the governor's mansion. I've made no secret of it, and it works both ways, though the sanctimonious sonofabitch won't admit it. It would tickle me pissless to watch him squirm. Can you imagine him justifying why his commission picked, from the hordes of applicants, somebody associated with a murder?'' He chuckled. ''I get a hard-on just thinking about it.''

Alex found Greg's motivation distasteful, but she was ecstatic that he was granting her permission. ''So, I can reopen the case?''

''The case remains unsolved because Hicks was never brought to trial.'' He lowered his feet, and his chair rocked forward jarringly. ''I have to tell you, though—I'm doing this against my better judgment, and only because I trust your gut instincts. I like you, Alex. You proved yourself when you were interning here as a law student. Great ass aside, you're good to have in our corner.''

He looked down at the material she'd compiled and fiddled with a corner of one folder. ''I still think you've got a personal grudge against these guys, the town, whatever. I'm not saying it's unjustified. It's just not something you can build a case around. Without this shrink's affidavit, I would have turned down your request. So, while you're out there where the buffalo roam and the deer and antelope play, remember that my ass is in a sling, too.'' He raised his eyes and stared at her balefully. ''Don't fuck up.''

''You mean, I can go to West Texas?''

''That's where it happened, isn't it?''

''Yes, but what about my caseload?''

''I'll put interns on the preparations and ask for postponements. Meanwhile, I'll talk to the D.A. in Purcell. We were in law school together. He's perfect for what you're trying to do. He's not too bright, and he married above himself, so he's always striving to please. I'll ask him to give you whatever assistance you need.''

''Don't be too specific. I don't want them forewarned.''

''Okay.''

''Thank you, Greg,'' she said earnestly.

''Not so fast,'' he said, snuffing her enthusiasm. ''If you trap yourself out there, I'll disclaim you. The attorney general has made no secret that I'm his heir apparent. I want the job, and I'd like nothing better than to have a good-looking, smart broad as chief of one of my departments. That goes down good with the voters.'' He pointed a nicotine-stained finger at her. ''But if you fall on your ass now, I never knew you, kiddo. Got that?''

''You're an unscrupulous son of a bitch.''

He grinned like a crocodile. ''Even my mama didn't like me much.''

''I'll send you a postcard.'' She turned to leave.

''Wait a minute. There's something else. You've got thirty days.''

''What?''

''Thirty days to come up with something.''

''But—''

"That's as long as I can spare you without the rest of the natives around here getting restless. That's longer than your hunch and flimsy leads warrant. Take it or leave it."

"I'll take it."

He didn't know that she had a much more pressing deadline, a personal one. Alex wanted to present her grandmother with the name of Celina's killer before she died. She wasn't even concerned that her grandmother was in a coma. Somehow, she would penetrate her consciousness. Her last breath would be peaceful, and Alex was certain she would at last praise her granddaughter.

Alex leaned across Greg's desk. "I know I'm right. I'll bring the real killer to trial; and when I do, I'll get a conviction. See if I don't."

"Yeah, yeah. In the meantime, find out what sex with a real cowboy is like. And take notes. I want details about spurs and guns and stuff."

"Pervert."

"Bitch. And don't slam—ah, *shit*!"

Alex smiled now, recalling that meeting. She didn't take his insulting sexism seriously because she knew she had his professional respect. Wild man that he was, Greg Harper had been her mentor and friend since the summer before her first semester of law school, when she had worked in the prosecutor's office. He was going out on a limb for her now, and she appreciated his vote of confidence.

Once she had gotten Greg's go-ahead, she hadn't wasted time. It had taken her only one day to catch up on paperwork, clear her desk, and lock up her condo. She had left Austin early, and made a brief stop in Waco at the nursing home. Merle's condition was unchanged. Alex had left the number of the Westerner where she could be reached in case of an emergency.

She dialed the D.A.'s home number from her motel room.

"Mr. Chastain, please," she said in response to the woman's voice who answered.

"He's not at home."

"Mrs. Chastain? It's rather important that I speak with your husband."

"Who is this?"

"Alex Gaither."

She heard a soft laugh. "You're the one, huh?"

" 'The one'?"

"The one who accused the Mintons and Sheriff Lambert of murder. Pat was in a tailspin when he got home. I've never seen him so—"

"Excuse me?" Alex interrupted breathlessly. "Did you say *Sheriff* Lambert?"

 # THREE

The sheriff's department was located in the basement of the Purcell County Courthouse. For the second time in as many days, Alex parked her car in a metered slot on the square and entered the building.

It was early. There wasn't much activity in the row of offices on the lower level. In the center of this warren of cubicles was a large squad room, no different from any other in the nation. A pall of cigarette smoke hovered over it like a perpetual cloud. Several uniformed officers were gathered around a hot plate where coffee was simmering. One was talking, but when he saw Alex, he stopped in midsentence. One by one, heads turned, until all were staring at her. She felt glaringly out of place in what was obviously a male domain. Equal employment hadn't penetrated the ranks of the Purcell County Sheriff's Department.

She held her ground and said pleasantly, "Good morning."

"Mornin'," they chorused.

"My name is Alex Gaither. I need to see the sheriff, please." The statement was superfluous. They already knew who she was and why she was there. Word traveled fast in a town the size of Purcell.

"He expectin' you?" one of the deputies asked belligerently, after spitting tobacco juice into an empty Del Monte green bean can.

"I believe he'll see me," she said confidently.

"Did Pat Chastain send you over?"

Alex had tried to reach him again that morning, but Mrs. Chastain had told her that he'd already left for his office. She tried telephoning him there and got no answer. Either she had missed him while he was in transit, or he was avoiding her. "He's aware of why I'm here. Is the sheriff in?" she repeated with some asperity.

"I don't think so."

"I haven't seen him."

"Yeah, he's here," one officer said grudgingly. "He came in a few minutes ago." He nodded his head toward a hallway. "Last door on your left, ma'am."

"Thank you."

Alex gave them a gracious smile she didn't feel in her heart and walked toward the hallway. She was conscious of the eyes focused on her back. She knocked on the indicated door.

"Yeah?"

Reede Lambert sat behind a scarred wooden desk that was probably as old as the cornerstone of the building. His booted feet were crossed and resting on one corner of it. Like yesterday, he was slouching, this time in a swivel chair.

His cowboy hat and a leather, fur-lined jacket were hanging on a coat tree in the corner between a ground-level window and a wall papered with wanted posters held up by yellowing, curling strips of Scotch tape. He cradled a chipped, stained porcelain coffee mug in his hands.

"Well, g'morning, Miss Gaither."

She closed the door with such emphasis that the frosted-glass panel rattled. "Why wasn't I told yesterday?"

"And spoil the surprise?" he said with a sly grin. "How'd you find out?"

"By accident."

"I knew you'd show up sooner or later." He eased himself upright. "But I didn't figure on it being this early in the morning." He came to his feet and indicated the only other available chair in the room. He moved toward a table that contained a coffee maker. "You want some?"

"Mr. Chastain should have told me."

"Pat? No way. When things get touchy, our D.A.'s a real chickenshit."

Alex caught her forehead in her hand. "This is a nightmare."

He hadn't waited for her to decline or accept his offer of coffee. He was filling a cup similar to his. "Cream, sugar?"

"This isn't a social call, Mr. Lambert."

He set the cup of black coffee on the edge of the desk in front of her and returned to his chair. Wood and ancient springs creaked in protest as he sat down. "You're getting us off to a bad start."

"Have you forgotten why I'm here?"

"Not for a minute, but do your duties prohibit you from drinking coffee, or is it a religious abstinence?"

Exasperated, Alex set her purse on the desk, went to the table, and spooned powdered cream into her mug.

The coffee was strong and hot—much like the stare the sheriff was giving her—and far better than the tepid brew she'd drunk in the coffee shop of the Westerner Motel earlier. If he had brewed it, he knew how to do it right. But then, he looked like a very capable man. Reared back in his chair, he did not look at all concerned that he'd been implicated in a murder case.

"How do you like Purcell, Miss Gaither?"

"I haven't been here long enough to form an opinion."

"Aw, come on. I'll bet your mind was made up not to like it before you ever got here."

"Why do you say that?"

"It would stand to reason, wouldn't it? Your mother died here."

His casual reference to her mother's death rankled. "She didn't just die. She was murdered. Brutally."

"I remember," he said grimly.

"That's right. You discovered her body, didn't you?"

He lowered his eyes to the contents of his coffee mug and stared into it for a long time before taking a drink. He tossed it back, draining the mug as though it were a shot of whiskey.

"Did you kill my mother, Mr. Lambert?"

Since she hadn't been able to accurately gauge his reaction the day before, she wanted to see it now.

His head snapped up. "No." Leaning forward, he braced his elbows on the desk and gave her a level stare. "Let's cut through the bullshit, okay? Understand this right now, and it'll save us both a lot of time. If you want to interrogate me, Counselor, you'll have to subpoena me to appear before the grand jury."

"You're refusing to cooperate with my investigation?"

"I didn't say that. This office will be at your disposal per Pat's instructions. I'll personally help you any way I can."

"Out of the goodness of your heart?" she asked sweetly.

"No, because I want it over and done with, finished. You understand? So you can go back to Austin where *you* belong, and leave the past in the past where *it* belongs." He got up to refill his coffee mug. Over his shoulder he asked, "Why'd you come here?"

"Because Bud Hicks did not murder my mother."

"How the hell do you know? Or did you just ask him?"

"I couldn't. He's dead."

She could tell by his reaction that he hadn't known. He moved to the window and stared out, sipping his coffee reflectively. "Well, I'll be damned. Gooney Bud is dead."

"Gooney Bud?"

"That's what everybody called him. I don't think anybody knew his last name until after Celina died and the newspapers printed the story."

"He was retarded, I'm told."

The man at the window nodded. "Yeah, and he had a speech impediment. You could barely understand him."

"Did he live with his parents?"

"His mother. She was half batty herself. She died years ago, not too long after he was sent away."

He continued to stare through the open slats of the blinds with his back to her. His silhouette was trim, broad-shouldered, narrow-hipped. His jeans fit a little too well. Alex berated herself for noticing.

"Gooney Bud pedaled all over town on one of those large tricycles," he was saying. "You could hear him coming blocks away. That thing clattered and clanged like a peddler's wagon. It was covered with junk. He was a scavenger. Little girls were warned to stay away from him. We boys made fun of him, played pranks, things like that." He shook his head sadly. "Shame."

"He died in a state mental institution, incarcerated for a crime he didn't commit."

Her comment brought him around. "You've got nothing to prove that he didn't."

"I'll find the proof."

"None exists."

"Are you so sure? Did you destroy the incriminating evidence the morning you ostensibly found Celina's body?"

A deep crease formed between his heavy eyebrows. "Haven't you got anything better to do? Don't you already have a heavy enough caseload? Why did you start investigating this in the first place?"

She gave him the same catchall reason she had given Greg Harper. "Justice was not served. Buddy Hicks was innocent. He took the blame for somebody else's crime."

"Me, Junior, or Angus?"

"Yes, one of the three of you."

"Who told you that?"

"Grandma Graham."

"Ah, now we're getting somewhere." He hooked one thumb into a belt loop, his tanned fingers curling negligently over his fly. "While she was telling you all this, did she mention how jealous she was?"

"Grandma? Of whom?"

"Of us. Junior and me."

"She told me the two of you and Celina were like the three musketeers."

"And she resented it. Did she tell you how she doted on Celina?"

She hadn't had to. The modest house Alex had grown up in had been a veritable shrine to her late mother. Noting her frown, the sheriff answered his own question. "No, I can see that Mrs. Graham failed to mention all that."

"You think I'm here on a personal vendetta."

"Yeah, I do."

"Well, I'm not," Alex said defensively. "I believe there are enough holes in this case to warrant reinvestigation. So does District Attorney Harper."

"That egomaniac?" he snorted contemptuously. "He'd indict his own mother for selling it on street corners if it would move him any closer to the attorney general's office."

Alex knew his comment was partially true. She tried another tack. "When Mr. Chastain is better acquainted with the facts, he'll agree that there's been a gross miscarriage of justice."

"Pat had never even heard of Celina until yesterday. He's got his hands full chasing down wetbacks and drug dealers."

"Do you blame me for wanting justice? If your mother had been stabbed to death in a horse barn, wouldn't you do everything possible to see that her killer was punished?"

"I don't know. My old lady split before I was old enough to remember her."

Alex felt a pang of empathy for him that she knew she couldn't afford. No wonder the pictures she'd seen of Reede had been of a very intense lad with eyes much older than his years. She'd never thought to ask her grandmother why he looked so serious.

"This is an untenable situation, Mr. Lambert. You are a suspect." She stood up and retrieved her purse. "Thank you for the coffee. I'm sorry to have bothered you so early in the morning. From now on, I'll have to rely on the local police department for assistance."

"Wait a minute."

Alex, already making her way toward the door, stopped and turned. "What?"

"There is no police department."

Dismayed by that piece of information, she watched as he reached for his hat and coat. He stepped around her, pulled open the door for her, then followed her out.

"Hey, Sam, I'm leaving. I'll be across the street." The deputy nodded. "This way," Reede said, taking Alex's elbow and guiding her toward a small, square elevator at the end of the hall.

They got into it together. The door creaked when he pulled it closed. The sound of grinding gears wasn't very reassuring. Alex hoped it would make the trip.

She tried to help it along by concentrating hard on their ascent. All the same, she was fully aware of Reede Lambert standing so close to her that their clothing touched. He was studying her.

He said, "You resemble Celina."

"Yes, I know."

"Your size, your mannerisms. Your hair's darker, though, and it has more red in it. Her eyes were brown, not blue like yours." His gaze moved over her face. "But there's a striking resemblance."

"Thank you. I think my mother was beautiful."

"Everybody thought so."

"Including you?"

"Especially me."

The elevator jerked to an abrupt stop. Alex lost her balance and fell against him. Reede caught her arm and supported her long enough for her to regain her balance, which might have taken a little too long, because when they separated, Alex felt light-headed and breathless.

They were on the first floor. He shrugged into his jacket as he guided her toward a rear exit. "My car's parked out front," she told him as they left the building. "Should I put more money in the meter?"

"Forget it. If you get a ticket, you've got friends in high places."

His smile wasn't as orthodontist perfect as Junior Minton's, but it was just as effective. It elicited a tickle in the pit of her stomach that was strange and wonderful and scary.

His quick grin emphasized the lines on his face. He looked every day of his forty-three years, but the weathered markings fit well on his strong, masculine bone structure. He had dark blond hair that had never known a stylist's touch. He pulled on his black felt cowboy hat and situated the brim close to his eyebrows, which were a shade or two darker than his hair.

His eyes were green. Alex had noticed that the moment she had walked into his office. She had reacted as any woman would to so attractive a man. He had no paunch, no middle-aged softness. Physically, he looked two decades younger than he actually was.

Alex had to keep reminding herself that she was a prosecutor for the sovereign state of Texas, and that she should be looking at Reede Lambert through the eyes of a litigator, not a woman. Besides, he was a generation older than she.

"Were you out of clean uniforms this morning?" she asked as they crossed the street.

He wore plain denim Levi's—old, faded, and tight—like the jeans rodeo cowboys wore. His jacket was brown leather, and fitted at the waist like a bomber jacket. The fur lining, which folded out to form a wide collar, was probably coyote. As soon as they'd stepped into the sunlight, he'd slid on aviator glasses. The lenses were so dark that she could no longer see his eyes.

"I used to dread the sight of a uniform, so when I became sheriff, I made it clear that they'd never get me in one of those things."

"Why did you always dread the sight of one?"

He smiled wryly. "I was usually trying to outrun it, or at least avoid it."

"You were a crook?"

"Hell-raiser."

"You had run-ins with the law?"

"Brushes."

"So what turned you around, a religious experience? A scare? A night or two in jail? Reform school?"

"Nope. I just figured that if I could outchase the law, I could outchase the lawbreakers." He shrugged. "It seemed a natural career choice. Hungry?"

Before she had a chance to answer, he pushed open the door of the B & B Café. A cowbell mounted above it announced their entrance. It was the place where things were happening, it seemed. Every table—red formica with rusted chrome legs—was full. Reede led her to a vacant booth along the wall.

Greetings were called out to him by executives, farmers, roughnecks, cowboys, and secretaries, each distinguished by his attire. Everyone except the secretaries wore boots. Alex recognized Imogene, Pat Chastain's secretary. As soon as they passed her table, she launched into an animated, whispered explanation of who Alex was to the women seated with her. A hush fell over the room as word traveled from one table to the next.

No doubt this microcosm of Purcell gathered every morning at the B & B Café during coffee-break time. A stranger in the midst was news, but the return of Celina Gaither's daughter was a news bulletin. Alex felt like a lightning rod, because she certainly attracted electric currents. Some, she sensed, were unfriendly.

A Crystal Gayle ballad about love lost was wafting from the jukebox. It competed with "Hour Magazine" on the fuzzy black-and-white TV mounted in one corner. Male impotence was being discussed to the raucous amusement of a trio of roughnecks. The nonsmoking movement hadn't reached Purcell, and the air was dense enough to cut. The smell of frying bacon was prevalent.

A waitress in purple polyester pants and a bright gold satin blouse approached them with two cups of coffee and a plate of fresh, yeasty doughnuts. She winked and said, "Mornin', Reede," before ambling off toward the kitchen, where the cook was deftly flipping eggs while a cigarette dangled between his lips.

"Help yourself."

Alex took the sheriff up on his offer. The doughnuts were still warm, and the sugary glaze melted against her tongue. "They had this waiting for you. Is this *your* table? Do you have a standing order?"

"The owner's name is Pete," he told her, indicating the cook. "He used to feed me breakfast every morning on my way to school."

"How generous."

"It wasn't charity," he said curtly. "I swept up for him in the afternoons after school."

She had unwittingly struck a sore spot. Reede Lambert was defensive about his motherless childhood. Now, however, wasn't the time to probe for more information. Not with nearly every eye in the place watching them.

He devoured two doughnuts and washed them down with black coffee, wasting neither food, nor time, nor motion. He ate like he thought it might be a long time before his next meal.

"Busy place," she commented, unself-consciously licking glaze off her fingers.

"Yeah. The old-timers like me leave the new shopping mall and fast food places out by the interstate to the newcomers and teenagers. If you can't find who you're looking for anyplace else, he's usually at the B & B. Angus'll probably be along directly. ME's corporate headquarters is just one block off the square, but he conducts a lot of business right here in this room."

"Tell me about the Mintons."

He reached for the last doughnut, since it was obvious that Alex wasn't going to eat it. "They're rich, but not showy. Well liked around town."

"Or feared."

"By some, maybe," he concealed with a shrug.

"The ranch is only one of their businesses?"

"Yeah, but it's the granddaddy. Angus built it out of nothing but acres of dust and sheer determination."

"What exactly do they do out there?"

"Basically, they're a racehorse training outfit. Thoroughbreds mostly. Some Quarter Horses. They board up to a hundred and fifty horses at a time, and get them ready for the track trainers."

"You seem to know a lot about it."

"I own a couple of racehorses myself. I board them out there permanently." He pointed down to her half-empty coffee cup. "If you're finished, I'd like to show you something."

"What?" she asked, surprised by the sudden shift in topic.

"It's not far."

They left the B & B, but not before Reede said good-bye to everyone he'd said hello to when they came in. He didn't pay for the breakfast, but was saluted by Pete the cook and given an affectionate pat by the waitress.

Reede's official car, a Blazer truck, was parked at the curb in front of the courthouse. The space was reserved for him, marked with a small sign. He unlocked the door, helped Alex up into the cab of the four-wheel-drive vehicle, then joined her. He drove only a few blocks before pulling up in front of a small house. "That's it," he said.

"What?"

"Where your mother lived." Alex whipped her head around to stare at the frame building. "The neighborhood isn't what it was when she lived here. It's gone to pot. There used to be a tree there, where the sidewalk dips slightly."

"Yes. I've seen pictures."

"It died a few years ago and had to be cut down. Anyway," he said, slipping the truck back into gear, "I thought you'd want to see it."

"Thank you." As he pulled the Blazer away from the curb, Alex kept her eyes on the house. The white paint had grayed. Hot summer suns had faded the maroon awnings over the front windows. It wasn't attractive, but she swiveled her head and kept it in sight as long as she could.

That's where she had lived with her mother for two short months. In those rooms, Celina had fed her, bathed her, rocked her, and sang her lullabies. There, she had listened for Alex's crying in the night. Those walls had heard her mother's whispered vows of love to her baby girl.

Alex didn't remember, of course. But she knew that's how it had been.

Tamping down the stirring emotions, she picked up the conversation they had been having when they had left the B & B. "Why is this proposed racetrack so important to the Mintons?"

He glanced at her as though she'd lost her senses. "Money. Why else?"

"It sounds like they've got plenty."

"Nobody ever has enough money," he remarked with a grim smile. "And only somebody who's been as poor as me can say that. Look around." He gestured at the empty stores along the main thoroughfare they were now traveling. "See all the empty businesses and foreclosure notices? When the oil market went bust, so did the economy of this town. Just about everybody worked in an oil-related occupation."

"I understand all that."

"Do you? I doubt it," he said scornfully. "This town needs that racetrack to survive. What we don't need is a wet-behind-the-ears, blue-eyed, redheaded female lawyer in a fur coat to come along and screw things up."

"I came here to investigate a murder," she lashed out, stung by his unexpected insult. "The racetrack, the gambling license, and the local economy have no relevance to it."

"Like hell they don't. If you ruin the Mintons, you ruin Purcell County."

"If the Mintons are proven guilty, they've ruined themselves."

"Look, lady, you're not going to uncover any new clues about your mother's murder. All you're going to do is stir up trouble. You won't get any help from locals. Nobody's gonna speak out against the Mintons, because the future of this county is riding on them building that racetrack."

"And you top the list of the loyal and close-mouthed."

"Damn right!"

"Why?" she pressed. "Do the Mintons have something on you? Could one of them place you in that horse barn well before you 'discovered' my mother's body? What were you doing there at that time of day, anyway?"

"What I did every day. I was shoveling shit out of the stables. I worked for Angus then."

She was taken aback. "Oh, I didn't know that."

"There's a lot you don't know. And you're far better off that way."

He whipped the Blazer into his parking slot at the courthouse and braked, pitching her forward against her seat belt. "You'd do well to leave the past alone, Miss Gaither."

"Thank you, Sheriff. I'll take that under advisement."

She got out of the truck and slammed the door behind her.

Cursing beneath his breath, Reede watched her walk up the sidewalk. He wished he could relax and just enjoy the shape of her calves, the enticing sway of her hips, and all else that had immediately captured his notice when she had entered Pat Chastain's office yesterday afternoon. Her name, however, had robbed him of the luxury of indulging in pure, masculine appreciation.

Celina's daughter, he thought now, shaking his head in consternation. It was little wonder that he found Alex so damned attractive. Her mother had been his soul mate from the day in grade school when some snotty kid had hurtfully taunted her because she no longer had a daddy after her father's sudden death of a heart attack.

Knowing how ridicule about one's parents could hurt, Reede had rushed to Celina's defense. He had fought that battle and many others for her in the ensuing years. With Reede as the bearer of her colors, no one dared speak a cross word to her. A bond had been forged. Their friendship had been extraordinary and exclusive, until Junior had come along and been included.

So he knew he shouldn't be surprised that the assistant D.A. from Austin had churned up such emotions inside him. Perhaps his only cause for alarm should be their intensity. Even though Celina had borne a child, she had died a girl. Alexandra was the embodiment of the woman she might have become.

He'd like to pass off his interest as purely nostalgic, a tender reminder of his childhood sweetheart. But he'd be lying to himself. If he needed any help defining the nature of his interest, all he had to do was acknowledge the warm pressure that had developed inside his jeans as he had watched her lick sugar off her fingertips.

"Christ," he swore. He felt as ambiguous toward this woman as he'd felt toward her mother, just before she had been found dead in that stable.

How could two women, twenty-five years apart, have such a pivotal impact on his life? Loving Celina had almost ruined him. Her daughter posed just as real a threat. If she started digging into the past, God only knew what kind of trouble would be stirred up.

He intended to trade his sheriff's job for one that would generate wealth and status. He sure as hell didn't want his future shadowed by a criminal investigation.

Reede hadn't worked his butt off all these years to let the payoff slip through his fingers. He'd spent his adult life overcompensating for his childhood. Now, when the respect he'd always wanted was within his grasp, he wasn't about to stand by and let Alex's investigation remind folks of his origins. The sassy lady lawyer could wreck him if she wasn't stopped.

The people who said material possessions weren't important already had plenty of everything. He'd never had anything. Until now. He was prepared to go to any length to protect it.

As he left his truck and reentered the courthouse, he cursed the day Alexandra Gaither had been born, just as he had on that day itself. At the same time, he couldn't help but wonder if her smart mouth wouldn't be good for something besides spouting accusations and legal jargon.

He'd bet his next win at the track that it would.

 FOUR

Judge Joseph Wallace was the Prairie Drugstore's best customer for Mylanta. He knew as he pushed away from the lunch table that he'd have to take a swig or two of the stuff before the afternoon was over. His daughter Stacey had prepared the meal for him—as she did every day of the week except Sunday when they went to the country club buffet. Stacey's dumplings, light and puffy as always, had landed like golf balls in his stomach.

"Something wrong?" She noticed that her father was absently rubbing his stomach.

"No, it's nothing."

"Chicken and dumplings is usually one of your favorites."

"Lunch was delicious. I've just got a nervous stomach today."

"Have a peppermint." Stacey passed him a cut-glass candy dish, conveniently kept on a dust-free cherrywood coffee table. He took out a wrapped piece of red-and-white-striped candy and put it in his mouth. "Any particular reason why your stomach is nervous?"

Stacey had become her father's caretaker when her mother had died several years earlier. She was single and rapidly approaching middle age, but she had never exhibited any ambition beyond being a homemaker. Because she had no husband or children of her own, she fussed over the judge.

She had never been a raving beauty, and age hadn't ameliorated that unfortunate fact. Describing her physical attributes with tactful euphemisms was pointless. She was and always had been plain. Even so, her position in Purcell was well established.

Every important ladies' league in town had her name on its roster. She taught a girls' Sunday school class at the First Methodist Church, faithfully visited residents of the Golden Age Home each Saturday morning, and played bridge on Tuesdays and Thursdays. Her activities calendar was always full. She dressed expensively and well, though far too dowdily for her age.

Her etiquette was above reproach, her decorum refined, her temperament serene. She had weathered disappointments in a style that was noble and worthy of admiration. Everybody assumed that she was happy and content.

They were wrong.

Judge Wallace, a sparrow of a man, pulled on his heavy overcoat as he made his way toward the front door. "Angus called me last night."

"Oh? What did he want?" Stacey asked as she pulled the collar of her father's coat up around his ears to guard against the wind.

"Celina Gaither's daughter turned up yesterday."

Stacey's busy hands fell still, and she took a step away from her father. Their eyes met. "Celina Gaither's daughter?" The voice coming from her chalky lips was high and thin.

"Remember the baby? Alexandra, I believe."

"Yes, I remember, Alexandra," Stacey repeated vaguely. "She's here in Purcell?"

"As of yesterday. All grown up now."

"Why didn't you tell me this last night when I came in?"

"You were late coming home from the chili supper. I was already in bed. I knew you'd be tired, too, and there was no need to bother you with it then."

Stacey turned away and busied herself picking the empty cellophane wrappers out of the candy dish. Her father had an annoying habit of leaving the empties. "Why should the sudden appearance of Celina's daughter bother me?"

"No reason in particular," the judge said, glad he didn't have to meet his daughter's eyes. "On the other hand, it'll probably upset the whole damn town."

Stacey came back around. Her fingers were mutilating a piece of clear cellophane. "Why should it?"

The judge covered a sour belch with his fist. "She's a prosecutor in the D.A.'s office in Austin."

"Celina's daughter?" Stacey exclaimed.

"Helluva thing, isn't it? Who would have guessed that she would turn out that well, growing up with only Merle Graham for a parent."

"You still haven't said why she's come back to Purcell. A visit?"

The judge shook his head. "Business, I'm afraid."

"Does it have any bearing on the Mintons' gambling license?"

He looked away, and nervously fidgeted with a button on his coat. "No, she's, uh, she's gotten the D.A.'s okay to reopen her mother's murder case."

Stacey's bony chest seemed to cave in another inch. She groped behind her, searching for a place to land when she collapsed.

The judge, pretending not to notice his daughter's distress, said, "She had Pat Chastain arrange a meeting with the Mintons and Reede Lambert. According to Angus, she made this grandstand announcement that before she was finished, she would determine which one of them had killed her mother."

"*What?* Is she mad?"

"Not according to Angus. He said she appears to be razor sharp, in complete control of her faculties, and dead serious."

Stacey gratefully lowered herself to the arm of the sofa and laid a narrow hand against the base of her neck. "How did Angus react?"

"You know Angus. Nothing gets him down. He seemed amused by the whole thing. Said there was nothing to worry about—that she couldn't present any evidence to a grand jury because there isn't any. Gooney Bud was the culprit." The judge drew himself up. "And no one can question my ruling that the man was incompetent to stand trial."

"I should say not," Stacey said, rising to his defense. "You had no choice but to commit Gooney Bud to that hospital."

"I reviewed his medical records every year, took depositions from the doctors who treated him. That facility isn't a snake pit, you know. It's one of the finest hospitals in the state."

"Daddy, nobody is pointing a finger at you. Good Lord, all anybody has to do is review your record as judge. For more than thirty years, your reputation has remained unblemished."

He ran his hand over his thinning hair. "I just hate for this to come up right now. Maybe I should retire early, not wait till my birthday next summer to step down."

"You'll do no such thing, Your Honor. You'll stay on that bench until you're ready to retire, and not a day before. No little upstart fresh out of law school is going to run you off."

For all her starchy show of support, Stacey's eyes revealed her anxiety. "Did Angus say how the girl . . . what she looks like? Does she resemble Celina?"

"Some." The judge went to the front door and pulled it open. On his way out he regrettably mumbled over his shoulder, "Angus said she was prettier."

Stacey sat woodenly on the arm of the sofa for a long time after the judge left, staring into space. She completely forgot about cleaning the noon meal dishes.

"Hello, Judge Wallace. My name is Alex Gaither. How do you do?"

Introductions were unnecessary. He had known who she was the minute she had stepped into the office outside his chambers. Mrs. Lipscomb, his secretary, had nodded toward a chair against the opposite wall. Turning, he saw a young woman—twenty-five, if his calculations were correct—sitting in the straight chair with all the poise and self-confidence of royalty. It was an air she had inherited from her mother.

He hadn't had much personal interaction with Celina Gaither, but he knew all about her through Stacey. The girls had been classmates through eleven years of public schooling. Even whittling away Stacey's typical adolescent jealousy, he'd still painted an unflattering picture of a girl who knew she was beautiful, well liked, and who held all the boys in the class in the palm of her hand, including the only two who really mattered, Junior Minton and Reede Lambert.

Too many times to count, Stacey's heart had been broken because of Celina. For that reason alone the judge had despised her. And because this young woman was her daughter, he disliked her on sight.

"How do you do, Miss Gaither."

Judge Wallace shook the proffered hand, but no longer than was necessary to serve propriety. He found it difficult to consider this fashionable woman his colleague. He preferred lawyers who wore white shirts and worsted wool, not chic, short-skirted suits and fur. Viable members of the bar should emanate the faint smell of cigar smoke and leatherbound tomes, not a delicate perfume.

"Has District Attorney Chastain briefed you on why I'm here?"

"Yes. This morning. But I heard from Angus last night."

She tilted her head, as though to say that that information was interesting and worth storing away for future consideration. He could have kicked himself for volunteering it.

The truth was, he was rather dazzled. Angus Minton had been right. Alexandra Gaither was better looking than her mother.

When she moved her head, a shaft of sunlight coming through the window blinds set her dark hair afire. The collar of her fur coat brushed her cheek, giving her complexion a glow as fresh and delectable as ripe apricots. Stacey had a similar coat, but it turned her complexion the color of cold ashes.

"Could I have a moment with you in your chambers, Judge Wallace?" she asked politely.

Needlessly, he consulted his wristwatch. "I'm afraid that's out of the question. Actually, I just stopped by to pick up my messages. I've got an appointment out of the office for the rest of the afternoon." Mrs. Lipscomb started with surprise, a dead giveaway that he was lying.

Alex pondered the toes of her shoes for a moment. "I hate to insist, but I must. This is very important, and I'm anxious to get the investigation underway as soon as possible. Before I can move forward, I need to verify some facts with you. It won't take very long." The corners of her mouth turned up into a smile. "I'm certain your cooperation will be appreciated by my office in Austin."

Judge Wallace wasn't stupid; neither was Alex. She couldn't very well pull rank on him, but she could make him look bad with the Travis County D.A., who hobnobbed with the powers that be in the capitol.

"Very well, please come in." He shrugged off his overcoat, asked Mrs. Lipscomb to hold his calls, then followed Alex into his chambers. "Have a seat."

"Thank you."

His stomach was burning in the center of his gut like a crashed meteor. He'd drunk two swallows of antacid on his way back to the courthouse, but he could stand another kick. Alex didn't appear the least bit rattled. She sat down across the desk from him and gracefully shrugged out of her coat.

"Let's get to it, Miss Gaither," he said imperiously. "What do you want to know?"

Alex opened her briefcase and withdrew a sheaf of papers. Inwardly, the judge groaned. "I've read the transcript of Bud Hicks's hearing, and I have some questions about it."

"Such as?"

"What was your rush?"

"I beg your pardon?"

"Bud Hicks was arraigned on a charge of first-degree murder and held without bail in the Purcell County jail. His competency hearing was held three days later."

"So?"

"Isn't that a rather brief period of time in which to weigh a man's future?"

The judge leaned back in his cordovan leather chair, which had been a gift from his daughter, hoping to impress the young attorney with his composure. "Maybe the docket was loaded and I was trying to clear it out. Or maybe it was a slack time and I was able to act quickly. I don't remember. It was twenty-five years ago."

She lowered her eyes to the notepad resting on her lap. "You had only two psychiatrists examine Mr. Hicks."

"His retardation was obvious, Miss Gaither."

"I'm not questioning that."

"He was, to put it unkindly, the town idiot. I don't mean to sound cruel, but that's what he was. He was tolerated. People saw him, but looked through him, if you know what I mean. He was a harmless fixture—"

"Harmless?"

Again the judge could have bitten his tongue. "Until the night he killed your mother."

"No jury convicted him of that, Judge."

Judge Wallace wet his lips, chagrined. "Of course." He tried to avoid her level gaze so he could collect his thoughts. "I felt that two psychiatric analyses would be adequate, in this particular case."

"No doubt I would agree with you, *if* the analyses hadn't been so divergent."

"Or, if your mother hadn't been the victim of the crime," the judge said, getting in a shot.

She bristled. "I'm going to disregard that, Judge Wallace."

"Well, isn't that what this is all about? Or do you, for some reason unknown to me, want to question my integrity and undermine a judgment I made twenty-five years ago?"

"If you've got nothing to hide, then you've got no reason to believe that your excellent record will be marred by my asking a few questions, do you?"

"Proceed," he said stiffly.

"The two court-appointed psychiatrists disagreed on Mr. Hicks's mental condition the night of my mother's murder. This was the glitch that first intrigued me. After calling District Attorney Harper's attention to it, he agreed that the case should be reinvestigated.

"One psychiatrist clearly believed that Hicks was incapable of committing such an act of violence. The other said he was. Why didn't you seek a third, tie-breaking opinion?"

"It wasn't necessary."

"I disagree, Judge." She paused a moment, then looked up at him without lifting her head. "You were golf partners with the doctor you ruled in favor of. The other psychiatrist was from out of town. That was the first and only time he ever appeared in your court as an expert witness."

Judge Wallace's face became red with indignation. "If you doubt my honesty, I suggest you consult with the doctors themselves, Miss Gaither."

"I've tried. Unfortunately, both are deceased." She met his hostile gaze coolly. "I did, however, consult with the last doctor to treat Mr. Hicks. He says you punished the wrong man, and has given me an affidavit to that effect."

"Miss Gaither." He rose partially from his chair and slapped the top of his desk. He was angry, but he also felt naked and vulnerable. The soft knock on his door was a godsend. "Yes?"

Sheriff Lambert strolled in.

"Reede!" Alex wouldn't have been surprised if the judge had rushed across the room and embraced him. He seemed that glad to see him. "Come in."

"Mrs. Lipscomb said you weren't to be disturbed, but when she told me who was with you, I convinced her that I might be of service."

"To whom?" Alex asked tartly.

Reede sauntered to the chair next to hers and dropped into it. Insolent green eyes moved over her. "To anybody who needs servicing."

Alex chose to ignore the double entendre and hoped he would ignore the mounting color in her face. She directed her attention to the judge.

"Miss Gaither was curious to know why I ruled Mr. Hicks incompetent to stand trial. Since she didn't know him, she can't appreciate how easily he fit the criteria of being unable to understand the charges against him and assist in his own defense."

"Thank you, Judge Wallace," she said, seething, "but I know the criteria. What I don't know is why you made the ruling so hastily."

"I saw no need for a postponement," the judge replied, obviously more at ease now that Reede was there. "I told you earlier that most people in town merely tolerated Hicks. Your mother, to her credit, was kind to him. Gooney Bud latched on to her, in a pathetic way. I'm sure he was often a nuisance, the way he followed her around like a devoted little puppy. Right, Reede?"

The sheriff nodded. "Celina wouldn't let anybody pick on him when she was around. He used to give her presents, you know, mesquite beans, rocks, stuff like that. She always thanked him like he'd given her the crown jewels."

"I figure that Gooney Bud mistook her kindness for a deeper emotion," Judge Wallace said. "He followed her into the Mintons' stable that night and, uh, tried to force his attentions on her."

"Rape her?" Alex said bluntly.

"Well, yes," the judge said, flustered. "And when she rebuffed him, he couldn't handle the rejection, and . . ."

"Stabbed her thirty times," Alex supplied.

"You force me to be insensitive, Miss Gaither." Joe Wallace looked at her reproachfully.

Alex crossed her legs. Her stockings made a slippery, silky sound that drew the sheriff's attention to them. She caught him staring at her hemline, but tried not to let it bother her as she continued to question the jittery judge.

"Let me make sure I understand. It's your contention that the murder wasn't premeditated, but a crime of passion?"

"As you said, it's conjecture."

"Okay, but for the sake of argument, let's say that's the way it was. If Bud Hicks was acting out of extreme provocation, outrage, uncontrollable lust, wouldn't he have utilized a pitch-fork, or a rake, or something else that was handy? What was he doing with a scalpel if he didn't enter that stable with the intention of killing her?"

"That's easy," Reede said. Alex looked at him sharply. "A mare had foaled that day. It was a difficult birth. We called the vet in to assist."

"How? Did he have to do an episiotomy?" she asked.

"In the long run, no. We were finally able to pull the foal. But Doc Collins's bag was right there. The scalpel could have fallen out. I'm guessing, of course, but it's logical to assume that Gooney Bud saw it and picked it up."

"That's a very broad assumption, Sheriff Lambert."

"Not so broad. As I've told you, Gooney Bud collected all kinds of stuff like that."

"He's right, Miss Gaither," Judge Wallace hastened to say. "Ask anybody. Something as shiny as a surgical instrument would have attracted his attention the moment he went into the stable."

"Was he in the stable that day?" she asked Reede.

"Yes. There were people coming and going all day, Gooney Bud among them."

Alex wisely decided that it was time to retreat and regroup. She gave the judge a peremptory thank you and left the chambers. The sheriff followed her out. As soon as they'd cleared the anteroom, she turned to confront him.

"From now on, I'll thank you not to coach whoever I'm questioning."

He assumed an innocent look. "Is that what I was doing?"

"You know damn well it was. I've never heard such a flimsy, farfetched explanation of a murder in my life. And I would eat alive any attorney who attempted to defend a client with it."

"Hmm, that's funny."

"Funny?"

"Yeah." She was subjected to another sly, arrogant once-over. "I was thinking you were the one who looked good enough to eat."

Blood rushed to her head. She attributed it to outrage. "Don't you take me seriously, Mr. Lambert?"

His insolence dissolved along with his insinuating smile. "You're damn right I do, Counselor," he whispered fiercely. "Damn right I do."

FIVE

"Calm down, Joe." Angus Minton was angled back in his red leather recliner. He loved this chair. His wife, Sarah Jo, loathed it.

When he spotted Junior standing in the doorway of his den, he waved him inside. Covering the mouthpiece of the cordless phone he whispered to his son, "Joe Wallace is in a tizzy."

"Now, Joe, you're jumping to conclusions and getting upset over nothing," he said into the mouthpiece. "She's just doing what she thinks is her job. After all, her mama was murdered. Now that she's got a law degree and a high-falutin job as a prosecutor, she's on a crusade. You know how these young career women are."

He listened for a moment. No longer cajoling, he repeated, "Goddammit, Joe, calm down, you hear? Just keep your mouth shut, and all this will blow over. Leave Celina's daughter to me, to *us*," he said, winking at Junior.

"In a few weeks she'll go back to Austin with her tail tucked between her pretty, long legs and tell her boss she struck out. We'll get our racing license, the track will be built on schedule, you'll retire with a perfect record, and this time next year we'll be sitting over drinks, laughing about this."

After saying good-bye, he tossed the portable phone onto the end table. "Jesus, he's a pessimist. To hear him tell it, Celina's daughter put his scrawny neck through a noose and pulled it tight. Fetch me a beer, will ya?"

"Pasty's in the hall waiting to see you."

That piece of news did nothing to improve Angus's sour mood. "Shit. I guess now's as good a time as any. Go get him."

"Don't be too hard on him. He's shivering in his boots."

"For what he did, he ought to be," Angus grumbled.

Junior returned a few seconds later. Pasty Hickam shuffled along behind him, head bowed in contrition, battered cowboy hat in hand. He had come by his nickname by imbibing a whole bottle of Elmer's glue on a dare. His real name had been long forgotten. The deed must have occurred at some point in elementary school, because Pasty had forsaken education before reaching the ninth grade.

He'd ridden the rodeo circuit for several years, but never successfully. What purses he won were small, and quickly expended on drink, gambling, and women. His job at the Minton ranch had been his first venture into gainful employment, and it had endured for almost thirty years, a surprise to everybody. Angus tolerated Pasty's occasional binges. This time, however, he'd gone too far.

Angus let him stand and sweat for several interminable moments before he barked, "Well?"

"Ang . . . Angus," the old ranch hand stuttered, "I know what you're gonna say. I . . . fucked up sumthin' royal, but I swear to God I didn't mean to. You know how it's said that all cats look gray in the dark? Well, damned if it ain't true of horses, too. 'Specially if you've got a pint of Four Roses sloshing around in yore gut." He smiled, revealing that what few teeth he had remaining were black with decay.

Angus wasn't amused. "You're wrong, Pasty. That isn't what I was going to say. What I was going to say is that you're fired."

Junior shot up out of the leather love seat. "Dad!" Angus shot him a hard look that quelled any further interference.

Pasty's face turned pale. "You cain't mean that, Angus. I've been here nigh on thirty years."

"You'll get fair severance pay—a damned sight more than you deserve."

"But . . . but—"

"You put a colt into a paddock with ten high-strung fillies. What if he'd mounted one of them? That one from Argentina was in there. Any idea what that horse is worth, Pasty—over half a million. If she'd been injured or come in foal by that randy colt . . ." Angus blew out a gust of air. "Jesus, I can't even bear to think about the mess that would've put us in. If one of the other hands hadn't caught your mistake, I could have been out millions, and the reputation of this ranch would have been shot to hell."

Pasty swallowed with difficulty. "Give me one more chance, Angus. I swear—"

"I've heard this speech before. Clear your stuff out of the bunkhouse and drop by the office at the end of the week. I'll have the bookkeeper draft you a check."

"Angus—"

"Good-bye and good luck, Pasty."

The old cowboy glanced plaintively at Junior, but knew before looking that there would be no help coming from that quarter. Junior kept his eyes lowered. Eventually Pasty left the room, tracking mud with each step.

When they heard the front door close, Junior got up and headed for the refrigerator built into the paneling. "I didn't know you were going to fire him," he said resentfully.

"No reason you should."

He carried a beer to his father and twisted off the cap of another for himself. "Was it necessary? Couldn't you have yelled at him some, taken away some of his responsibilities, docked his pay? For crissake, Dad, what's an old guy like that gonna do?"

"He should have thought of that before he put the colt in that pasture. Now, let's drop it. I didn't enjoy doing it. He's been around here a long time."

"He made a mistake."

"Worse, he got caught!" Angus shouted. "If you're gonna run this business, boy, you gotta grow steel balls. The job isn't always fun, you know. There's more to it than taking clients out to fancy dinners and flirting with their wives and daughters." Angus took a swig of beer. "Now, let's talk about Celina's girl."

Junior, resigned to accepting Pasty's harsh punishment, even if he didn't agree with it, dropped into an easy chair and sipped at his bottle of beer. "She went to see Joe, huh?"

"Yeah, and notice that she didn't waste any time doing it, either. Joe's jittery as hell. He's afraid his spotless tenure as judge is about to be flushed down the toilet."

"What did Alexandra want with him?"

"She asked some questions about why he rushed up Gooney Bud's incompetency hearing. Reede came to Joe's rescue, which was a smart move on his part."

"Reede?"

"Never asleep at the switch, is he?" Angus removed his boots and dropped them over the padded arm of his chair. They hit the floor with a heavy thud. He had gout, and his big toe was giving him trouble. He massaged it thoughtfully, while looking at his son. "What did you think of the girl?"

"I tend to agree with Joe. She's a threat. She thinks one of us killed Celina, and she's bound and determined to find out who."

"She struck me that way, too."

"Of course, she's got nothing on any of us."

"Of course."

Junior looked at his father warily. "She's sharp."

"As a tack."

"And no slouch in the looks department."

Father and son shared a bawdy laugh. "Yeah, she is good-lookin'," Angus said. "But then, so was her mama."

Junior's smile faded. "Yes, she was."

"Still miss her, don't you?" Angus shrewdly studied his son.

"Sometimes."

Angus sighed. "I don't suppose you can lose a close friend like that without it having a lasting effect on you. You wouldn't be human, otherwise. But it's foolish of you to pine for a woman who's been dead all these years."

"I've hardly pined," Junior countered. "Since the day I figured out how this operates," he said, touching the fly of his pants, "it hasn't gone inactive for long."

"That's not what I'm talking about," Angus said, frowning. "Anybody can get laid on a regular basis. I'm talking about your life. Commitment to something. You were upset for a long time after Celina died. It took you a while to pull your shit together. Okay, that was understandable."

He pushed the footstool of his chair and sat up straight, pointing a blunt finger at Junior. "But you stalled, boy, and you haven't worked up a full head of steam since. Look at Reede. He took Celina's death hard, too, but he got over her."

"How do you know he got over her?"

"Do you see him moping around?"

"I'm the one who's had three wives, not Reede."

"And that's something to be proud of?" Angus shouted, his temper snapping. "Reede's made his life count for something. He's got a career—"

"Career?" Junior interrupted with a contemptuous snort. "I'd hardly call being sheriff of this piss-ant county a career. Big fuckin' deal."

"What would you call a career? Screwing the entire female membership of the country club before you die?"

"I do my fair share of work around here," Junior argued. "I spent all morning on the phone with that breeder in Kentucky. He's this close to buying that colt by Artful Dodger out of Little Bit More."

"Yeah, what did he say?"

"That he's seriously thinking about it."

Angus came out of his chair, booming his approval. "That's great news, son. That old man's a tough son of a bitch, I've heard tell. He's a crony of Bunky Hunt's. Feeds his horses caviar and shit like that after they win." Angus slapped Junior on the back and ruffled his hair as though he were three, instead of forty-three.

"However," Angus said, his frown returning, "that just emphasizes how much we stand to lose if the racing commission rescinds that license before the ink on it is even dry. One breath of scandal and we're history. So, how are we gonna handle Alexandra?"

"Handle her?"

Favoring his ailing toe, Angus hobbled toward the refrigerator to get another beer. "We can't wish her away. The way I see it," he said, twisting off the bottle cap, "we'll just have to convince her that we're innocent. Upstanding citizens." He gave an elaborate shrug. "Since that's exactly what we are, it shouldn't be that hard to do."

Junior could tell when the wheels of his father's brain were turning. "How will we go about that?"

"Not we—you. By doing what you do best."

"You mean—?"

"Seduce her."

"Seduce her!" Junior exclaimed. "She didn't strike me as being a prime candidate for seduction. I'm sure she can't stand our guts."

"Then, that's the first thing we gotta change . . . *you* gotta change. Just seduce her into liking you . . . at first. I'd do it myself if I still had the proper equipment." He gave his son a wicked smile. "Think you can handle such an *unpleasant* chore?"

Junior grinned back. "I'd damn sure welcome the opportunity to try."

 # SIX

The cemetery gates were open. Alex drove through them. She had never been to her mother's grave, but she knew the plot number. It had been jotted down and filed among some official papers that she'd found when she had moved her grandmother into the nursing home.

The sky looked cold and unfriendly. The sun was suspended just above the western horizon like a giant orange disk, brilliant but brassy. Tombstones cast long shadows across the dead grass.

Using discreet signposts for reference, Alex located the correct row, parked her car, and got out. As far as she could tell, she was the only person there. Here on the outskirts of town, the north wind seemed stronger, its howl more ominous. She flipped up the collar of her coat as she made her way toward the plot.

Even though she was searching for it, she wasn't prepared to see the grave. It rushed up on her unexpectedly. Her impulse was to turn away, as though she'd happened upon an atrocity, something horrible and offensive.

The rectangular marker was no more than two feet high. She wouldn't have ever noticed it if it weren't for the name. It gave only her mother's date of birth, and date of death—nothing else. Not an epitaph. Not an obligatory, "In loving memory of." Nothing but the barest statistical facts.

The scarcity of information broke Alex's heart. Celina had been so young and pretty and full of promise, yet she'd been diminished to anonymity.

She knelt beside the grave. It was set apart from the others, alone at the crest of a gradual incline. Her father's body had been shipped from Vietnam to his native West Virginia, courtesy of the United States Army. Grandfather Graham, who had died when Celina was just a girl, was buried in his hometown. Celina's grave was starkly solitary.

The headstone was cold to the touch. She traced the carved letters of her mother's first name with her fingertip, then pressed her hand on the brittle grass in front of it, as though feeling for a heartbeat.

She had foolishly imagined that she might be able to communicate with her supernaturally, but the only sensation she felt was that of the stubbly grass pricking her palm.

"Mother," she whispered, testing the word. "Mama. Mommy." The names felt foreign to her tongue and lips. She'd never spoken them to anyone before.

"She swore you recognized her just by the sound of her voice."

Startled, Alex spun around. Pressing a hand to her pounding heart, she gasped in fright. "You scared me. What are you doing here?"

Junior Minton knelt beside her and laid a bouquet of fresh flowers against the headstone. He studied it for a moment, then turned his head and smiled wistfully at Alex.

"Instinct. I called the motel, but you didn't answer when they rang your room."

"How did you know where I was staying?"

"Everybody knows everything about everybody in this town."

"No one knew I was coming to the cemetery."

"Deductive reasoning. I tried to imagine where I might be if I were in your shoes. If you don't want company, I'll leave."

"No. It's all right." Alex looked back at the name carved into the cold, impersonal gray stone. "I've never been here. Grandma Graham refused to bring me."

"Your grandmother isn't a very warm, giving person."

"No, she isn't, is she?"

"Did you miss having a mother when you were little?"

"Very much. Particularly when I started school and realized that I was the only kid in my grade who didn't have one."

"Lots of kids don't live with their mothers."

"But they know they've got one." This was a subject she found difficult to discuss with even her closest friends and associates. She didn't feel inclined to discuss it with Junior Minton at all, no matter how sympathetic his smile.

She touched the bouquet he'd brought and rubbed the petal of a red rose between her cold fingertips. In comparison, the flower felt like warm velvet, but it was the color of blood. "Do you bring flowers to my mother's grave often, Mr. Minton?"

He didn't answer until she was looking at him again. "I was at the hospital the day you were born. I saw you before they had washed you up." His grin was open, warm, disarming. "Don't you think that should put us on a first-name basis?"

It was impossible to erect barriers against his smile. It would have melted iron. "Then, call me Alex," she said, smiling back.

His eyes moved from the crown of her head to the toes of her shoes. "Alex. I like that."

"Do you?"

"What, like your name?"

"No, bring flowers here often."

"Oh, that. Only on holidays. Angus and I usually bring something out on her birthday, Christmas, Easter. Reede, too. We split the cost of having the grave tended."

"Any particular reason why?"

He gave her an odd look, then answered simply, "We all loved Celina."

"I believe one of you killed her," she said softly.

"You believe wrong, Alex. I didn't kill her."

"What about your father? Do you think he did?"

He shook his head. "He treated Celina like a daughter. Thought of her that way, too."

"And Reede Lambert?"

He shrugged as though no elaboration was necessary. "Reede, well . . ."

"What?"

"Reede could never have killed her."

Alex settled deeper into her fur coat. The sun had set, and it was getting colder by the moment. When she spoke, her breath fogged the air in front of her face. "I spent some time in the public library this afternoon, reading back issues of the local newspaper."

"Anything about me?"

"Oh, yes, all about your Purcell Panther football days."

As he laughed, the wind lifted his fair hair. His was a much lighter blond than Reede's, and it was finer, better controlled. "That must have made for some fascinating reading."

"It did. You and Reede were cocaptains of the team."

"Hell, yeah." He crooked his arm as though showing off muscled biceps. "We thought we were invincible, real hot snot."

"Her junior year, my mother was the homecoming queen. There was a picture of Reede kissing her during halftime."

Studying that photograph had made Alex feel very strange. She'd never seen it before. For some reason her grandmother had chosen not to keep it among her many others, perhaps because Reede Lambert's kiss had been audacious, full-fledged, and proprietary.

Undaunted by the cheering crowd in the stadium, his arm had been curved possessively around Celina's waist. The pressure of the kiss had angled her head back. He looked like a conqueror, especially in the muddy football uniform, holding his battle-scarred helmet in his other hand.

After staring at the photograph for several minutes, she began to feel that kiss herself.

Coming back to the present, she said, "You didn't become friends with my mother and Reede until later on, isn't that right?"

Junior pulled up a blade of grass and began to shred it between his fingers. "Ninth grade. Until then, I attended a boarding school in Dallas."

"By choice?"

"By my mother's choice. She didn't want me picking up what she considered to be undesirable habits from the kids of oil-field workers and cowhands, so I was packed off to Dallas every fall.

"My schooling was a bone of contention between Mother and Dad for years. Finally, when I was about to go into high school, he put his foot down and said it was time I learned there were other kinds of people besides the 'pale little bastards'—and that's a quote—at prep school. He enrolled me in Purcell High School that fall."

"How did your mother take it?"

"Not too well. She was definitely against it, but there wasn't much she could do about it. Where she came from—"

"Which is?"

"Kentucky. In his prime, her old man was one of the most successful breeders in the country. He'd bred a Triple Crown winner."

"How did she meet your father?"

"Angus went to Kentucky to buy a mare. He brought it and my mother back with him. She's lived here for over forty years, but she still clings to Presley family traditions, one of which was to send all the offspring to private school.

"Not only did Dad enroll me at Purcell, he also insisted that I go out for the football team. The coach wasn't too keen on the idea, but Dad bribed him by promising to buy new uniforms for the team if he'd take me on, so . . ."

"Angus Minton makes things happen."

"You can bank on that," Junior said with a laugh. "He never takes no for an answer, so I went out for football. I'd never even touched one, and I nearly got the crap kicked out of me that first day of practice. The other boys naturally resented me."

"For being the richest kid in town?"

"It's a tough job, but somebody's got to do it,' he said with an engaging grin. "Anyway, when I got home that night, I told Dad that I hated Purcell High School and football with equal amounts of passion. I told him I preferred pale little bastards any day of the week over bullies like Reede Lambert."

"What happened?"

"Mother cried herself sick. Dad cussed himself into a frenzy. Then he marched me outside and threw footballs at me till my hands bled from catching them."

"That's terrible!"

"Not really. He had my interests at heart. He knew, even if I didn't, that out here, you've got to play, eat, drink, and sleep football. Say," he interjected, "I'm rambling on. Aren't you cold?"

"No."

"Sure?"

"Yes."

"Want to go?"

"No, I want you to keep rambling."

"Is this a formal interrogation?"

"Conversation," she replied, tartly enough to make him grin.

"At least put your hands in your pockets." Taking one of her hands in each of his, he guided them to the deep pockets of her coat, tucked them inside, and patted them into place. Alex resented the intimate gesture. It was presumptuous of him and, considering the circumstances, highly inappropriate. "I gather you made the football team," she said, deciding to ignore his touch.

"Junior varsity, yes, but I didn't play, not in a single game, until the very last one. It was for the district championship."

He lowered his head and smiled reflectively. "We were down by four points. A field goal wouldn't have done us any good. There were only a few seconds left on the clock. We had the ball, but it was fourth down and miles to go because of penalties. Both the A- and B-string wide receivers had been injured in the previous quarters."

"My God."

"I told you, football's a blood-drawing sport out here. Anyway, they were carting the star running back off the field on a stretcher when the coach looked toward the bench and barked my name. I nearly wet my pants."

"What happened?"

"I shrugged off my poncho and ran out to join the team in a time-out huddle. Mine was the only clean jersey on the field. The quarterback—"

"Reede Lambert." Alex knew that from the newspaper accounts.

"Yeah, my nemesis. He groaned audibly when he saw me coming, and even louder when I told him the play the coach had sent in with me. He looked me right between the eyes and said, 'If I throw you the goddamn football, preppie, you fuckin' well better catch it.' "

For a moment Junior was silent, steeped in the memory. "I'll never forget that as long as I live. Reede was laying down the terms."

"The terms?"

"Of our becoming friends. It was then or never that I had to prove myself worthy of his friendship."

"Was that so important?"

"You bet your ass. I'd been in school there long enough to know that if I didn't hack it with Reede, I'd never be worth shit."

"You caught the pass, didn't you?"

"No, I didn't. In all fairness, I can't say that I did. Reede threw it right here," he said, pointing at his chest, "right between the numbers on my jersey. Thirty-five yards. All I had to do was fold my arms over the football and carry it across the goal line."

"But that was enough, wasn't it?"

His smile widened until it germinated into a laugh. "Yep. That marked the beginning of it."

"Your father must have been ecstatic."

Junior threw back his head and howled with laughter. "He jumped the fence, hurdled the bench, and came charging out onto the field. He swooped me up and carried me around for several minutes."

"What about your mother?"

"My mother! She wouldn't be caught dead at a football game. She thinks it's barbaric." He chuckled, tugging on his earlobe. "She's damned near right. But I didn't care what anybody thought about me, except Dad. He was so proud of me that night." His blue eyes shone with the memory.

"He'd never even met Reede, but he hugged him, too, football pads and all. That night was the beginning of their friendship, too. It wasn't too long after that that Reede's daddy died, and he moved out to the ranch to live with us."

For several moments, his recollections were private. Alex allowed him the introspective time without interruption. Eventually he glanced up at her and did a double take.

"Jesus, you looked like Celina just then," he said softly. "Not so much your features, but your expression. You have that same quality of listening." He reached out and touched her hair. "She loved to listen. At least she made the person talking think she did. She could sit so still and just *listen* for hours." He withdrew his hand, but he didn't seem happy about it.

"Is that what first attracted you to her?"

"Hell, no," he said with a leering smile. "The first thing that attracted me to her was a ninth-grade boy's adolescent lust. The first time I saw Celina in the hall at school, she took my breath, she was so pretty."

"Did you chase after her?"

"Hey, I was dumbstruck, not crazy."

"What about this mad crush you had on her?"

"She belonged to Reede then," he said unequivocally. "There was never any question about that." He stood up. "We'd better go. Regardless of what you say, you're freezing. Besides, it's getting spooky out here in the dark."

Alex, still befuddled by his last statement, let him assist her up. She turned to brush the dry grass off the back of her skirt and noticed the bouquet again. The green waxed paper wrapped around the vivid petals fluttered in the brisk wind. It made a dry, rattling sound. "Thank you for bringing the flowers, Junior."

"You're welcome."

"I appreciate your thoughtfulness to her over the years."

"In all honesty, I had an ulterior motive for coming here today."

"Oh?"

"Uh-huh," he said, taking both her hands. "To invite you out to the house for drinks."

 # SEVEN

She had been expected. That much was evident from the moment Junior escorted her across the threshold of the sprawling two-story house on the Minton ranch. Eager to study her suspects in their own environment, she had agreed to follow Junior home from the cemetery.

As she entered the living room, however, she couldn't help wondering if perhaps she was being manipulated, rather than the other way around.

Her determination to proceed with caution was immediately put to the test when Angus strode across the spacious room and shook her hand.

"I'm glad Junior found you and convinced you to come," he told her as he helped her out of her coat. He tossed the fur jacket at Junior. "Hang that up, will ya?" Looking at Alex with approval, he said, "I didn't know how you'd take our invitation. We're pleased to have you."

"I'm pleased to be here."

"Good," he said, rubbing his hands together. "What'll you have to drink?"

"White wine, please," she said. His blue eyes were friendly, but she found them disquieting. He seemed to see beyond the surface and lay bare the emotional insecurities she kept heavily camouflaged with competency.

"White wine, huh? Can't stand the stuff myself. Just as well be drinking soda pop. But that's what my wife drinks. She'll be down directly. You sit there, Alexandra."

"She likes to be called Alex, Dad," Junior said as he joined Angus at the built-in wet bar to mix himself a scotch and water.

"Alex, huh?" Angus carried a glass of wine to her. "Well, I guess that name suits a lady lawyer."

It was a backhanded compliment, at best. She let her thank-you suffice for both the remark and the wine. "Why did you invite me here?"

He seemed momentarily nonplussed by her directness, but answered in kind. "There's too much water under the bridge for us to be enemies. I want to get to know you better."

"That's the reason I came, Mr. Minton."

"Angus. Call me Angus." He took a moment to study her. "How come you wanted to be a lawyer?"

"So I could investigate my mother's murder."

The answer came to her lips spontaneously, which astonished not only the Mintons, but Alex herself. She had never verbalized that as being her goal before. Merle Graham must have spoon-fed her doses of determination, along with her vegetables.

With that public admission also came the private realization that she was her own chief suspect. Grandmother Graham had said she was ultimately responsible for her mother's death. Unless she could prove otherwise, she would carry that guilt with her for the rest of her life. She was in Purcell County to exonerate herself.

"You certainly don't mince words, young lady," Angus said. "I like that. Pussyfooting is a waste of my time."

"Of mine, too," Alex said, remembering her concurrent deadlines.

Angus harrumphed. "No husband? No kids?"

"No."

"Why not?"

"Dad," Junior said, rolling his eyes, embarrassed by his father's lack of tact.

Alex was amused, not offended. "I don't mind, Junior, really. It's a common question."

"Got an answer to it?" Angus took a swig from his long-neck.

"No time or inclination."

Angus grunted noncommittally. "Around here, we've got too much time and not enough inclination." He shot Junior a withering glance.

"Dad's referring to my failed marriages," Junior told their guest.

"Marriages? How many have there been?"

"Three," he confessed with a wince.

"And no grandbabies to show for any of them," Angus grumbled like a foul-natured bear. He aimed a chastising finger at his son. "And it's not like you don't know how to breed."

"As usual, Angus, your manners in front of company are deplorable."

Simultaneously, the three of them turned. A woman was standing in the open doorway. Alex had painted a mental picture of what Angus's wife would be like—strong, assertive, feisty enough to meet him toe to toe. She would typify the coarse, horsy type who rode to hounds and spent more time wielding a quirt than a hairbrush.

Mrs. Minton was the antithesis of Alex's mental picture. Her figure was willowy, her features as dainty as those on a Dresden figurine. Graying blond hair curled softly about a face as pale as the double strand of pearls she was wearing around her neck. Dressed in a full-skirted mauve wool jersey dress that floated around her slender body as she walked, she came into the room and sat down in a chair near Alex's.

"Honey, this is Alex Gaither," Angus said. If he was put off by his wife's reprimand, he didn't show it. "Alex, my wife, Sarah Jo."

Sarah Jo Minton nodded and, in a voice as formal and cool as her acknowl-edgment of the introduction, said, "Miss Gaither, a pleasure, I'm sure."

"Thank you."

Her pallid face lit up and her straight, thin lips curved into a radiant smile when she accepted a glass of white wine from Junior, who had poured it without being asked. "Thank you, sweetheart."

He bent down and kissed his mother's smooth, proffered cheek. "Did your headache go away?"

"Not entirely, but my nap helped it. Thank you for inquiring." She reached up to stroke his cheek. Her hand, Alex noted, was milky white and looked as fragile as a flower ravaged by a storm. Addressing her husband, she said, "Must you bring talk of breeding into the living room, instead of keeping it in the stable, where it belongs?"

"In my own house, I'll talk about anything I goddamn well please," Angus answered, though he didn't seem angry at her.

Junior, apparently accustomed to their bantering, laughed and circled Sarah Jo's chair to sit on the arm of Alex's. "We weren't talking about breeding, per se, Mother. Dad was just lamenting my inability to keep a wife long enough to produce an heir."

"You'll have children with the right woman when the time comes." She spoke to Angus as much as to Junior. Then, turning to Alex, she asked, "Did I overhear you say you'd never been married, Miss Gaither?"

"That's right."

"Strange." Sarah Jo sipped her wine. "Your mother certainly never lacked for male companionship."

"Alex didn't say she lacked for male companionship," Junior corrected. "She's just choosy."

"Yes, I chose a career over marriage and having a family. For the time being, anyway." Her brow beetled as an original idea occurred to her. "Did my mother ever express any interest in having a career?"

"Not that I ever heard her mention," Junior said, "though I guess all the girls in our class went through that stage of wanting to be Warren Beatty's leading lady."

"She had me so early," Alex said with a trace of regret. "Maybe an early marriage and a baby prevented her from pursuing a career."

Junior placed his finger beneath her chin and raised it, until she was looking at him. "Celina made her own choices."

"Thank you for saying that."

He dropped his hand. "I never heard her say she wanted to be anything other than a wife and mother. I remember the day we talked about it specifically. You should, too, Dad. It was summertime, and so hot you told Reede to take the day off after he'd mucked out the stables. The three of us decided to take a picnic out to that old stock pond, remember?"

"No." Angus left his chair in pursuit of another beer.

"I do," Junior said dreamily, "like it was yesterday. We spread a quilt under the mesquite trees. Lupe had packed us some homemade tamales to take with us. After we'd eaten them we stretched out on our backs, Celina between Reede and me, and stared up at the sky through the branches of those mesquites. They hardly cast a shade. The sun and our full bellies made us drowsy.

"We watched buzzards circling something and talked about chasing them down to find out what had died, but we were too lazy. We just lay there, talking, you know, about what we were going to be once we grew up. I said I wanted to be an international playboy. Reede said that if I did, he was gonna buy stock in a company that made condoms and get rich. He didn't care what he turned out to be, so long as he was rich. All Celina wanted to be was a wife.'' He paused a moment and looked down at his hands. ''Reede's wife.''

Alex started.

''Speaking of Reede,'' Angus said, ''I think I hear his voice.''

EIGHT

Lupe, the Mintons' housekeeper, showed Reede in. Alex turned in time to see him come through the doorway. Junior's startling revelation had left her dazed.

From Grandma Graham, she'd heard that Reede and Celina had been high school sweethearts. The photograph of him crowning her homecoming queen bore that out. But Alex hadn't known that her mother had wanted to marry him. She knew her expression must reflect her shock.

He took in the room at a glance. ''Well, isn't this a cozy little scene.''

''Hey, Reede,'' Junior said from his position near Alex, which suddenly seemed all too close and familiar, for a reason she couldn't explain. ''What brings you out? Drink?''

''Come on in.'' Angus signaled him into the room. Sarah Jo ignored him as though he was invisible. That mystified Alex, since he had once lived with them like a member of the family.

He laid his coat and hat in a chair and moved toward the bar to accept the drink that Angus had poured for him. ''I came to check on my mare. How is she?''

''Fine,'' Angus told him.

''Good.''

There followed a strained silence while everyone seemed to contemplate the contents of their glasses. Finally, Angus said, ''Something else on your mind, Reede?''

''He came out here to warn you about what you say to me,'' Alex said. ''The same way he did Judge Wallace earlier this afternoon.''

''When somebody asks me a direct question, I'll do my own answering, Counselor,'' he said testily. He threw back his drink and set down the glass. ''See y'all later. Thanks for the drink.'' He stamped from the room, pausing only long enough to pick up his hat and coat.

Surprisingly, it was Sarah Jo who filled the silence once Reede had slammed out the front door. ''I see his manners haven't improved any.''

''You know Reede, Mother,'' Junior said with a casual shrug. ''Another glass of wine?''

''Please.''

''Have another drink together,'' Angus said. ''I want to speak to Alex in private. Bring your wine if you want,'' he told her.

She had been helped out of her chair and escorted into the hallway before she quite knew how it had come about. As they moved down the hall, she looked around.

The walls were covered with red flocked wallpaper and held framed photographs of racehorses. A massive Spanish chandelier loomed threateningly overhead. The furniture was dark and bulky.

"Like my house?" Angus asked, noticing that she was dawdling to take in her surroundings.

"Very much," she lied.

"Designed and built it myself when Junior was still in diapers."

Without being told, Alex knew that Angus had not only built but decorated the house. Nothing in it reflected Sarah Jo's personality. Doubtless she countenanced it because she'd been given no choice.

The house was atrociously ugly, but it was in such appalling and unapologetic bad taste that it had a crude charm all its own, much like Angus.

"Before this house was here, Sarah Jo and I lived in a lineman's shack. You could see daylight through the walls of that damn thing. Nearly froze us out in the winter, and in the summer, we'd wake up with an inch of dust covering our bed."

Alex's initial reaction to Mrs. Minton had been dislike. She seemed distracted and self-absorbed. Alex could, however, sympathize with a younger Sarah Jo who had been plucked like an exotic flower out of a gracious, refined culture and replanted into one so harsh and radically different that she had withered. She could never adapt here, and it was a mystery to Alex why either Angus or Sarah Jo thought she could.

He preceded her into a paneled den that was even more masculine than the rest of the house. From their mountings on the walls, elk and deer gazed into space with resigned brown eyes. What space they didn't take up was filled with photographs of horses wearing the Minton colors standing in the winners' circles of racetracks all over the country. Some were fairly current; others appeared to be decades old.

There were several gun racks with a firearm in each slot. A flagpole with a state flag had been propped in one corner. A framed cartoon read: "Tho I walk through the valley of the Shadow of Death, I will fear no evil . . . 'cause I'm the meanest son of a bitch in the valley."

The moment they entered the room, he pointed her toward a corner. "Come over here. I want to show you something."

She followed him to a table that was draped with what looked like an ordinary white bed sheet. Angus unfurled it.

"My goodness!"

It was an architectural model of a racetrack. Not a single detail had been overlooked, from the color-coded seating in the stands, to the movable starting gate, to the diagonal stripes painted in the parking lot.

"Purcell Downs," Angus boasted with the chest-expanding pride of a new father. "I realize you're only doing what you feel like you've got to do, Alex. I can respect that." His expression was belligerent. "But you don't realize how much is at stake here."

Alex defensively folded her arms across her midriff. "Why don't you tell me?"

Needing no more encouragement, Angus launched into a full explanation of how he wanted the track to be built, enumerating its various features. There would be no corners cut, no scrimping. The entire complex was to be a first-class facility from the stables to the ladies' restrooms.

"We'll be the only full-scale track between Dallas/Fort Worth and El Paso, and three hundred or so miles from each. It will be a good stopover for travelers. I can envision Purcell becoming another Las Vegas in twenty years, springing up out of the desert like a gusher."

"Isn't that being a little optimistic?" Alex asked skeptically.

"Well, maybe a bit. But that's what folks said when I started this place. That's what they said when I built my practice track and drew up plans for an indoor swimming pool for the horses. I don't let skepticism bother me. You gotta dream big if you want big things to happen. Mark my words,'' he said, jabbing the air between them for emphasis. ''If we get that license to build this track, the town of Purcell will explode.''

''Not everybody would like that, would they? Some might want to keep the community small.''

Stubbornly, Angus shook his head. ''Several years ago, this town was booming.''

''Oil?''

''Yessiree. There were ten banks. *Ten.* More than in any other town this size. Per capita, we were the richest city in the country. Merchants had more business than they could handle. The real estate market was hot. Everybody prospered.'' He paused to take a breath. ''You want something to drink? A beer? A Coke?''

''Nothing, thank you.''

Angus took a beer from the refrigerator, twisted off the cap, and took a long drink. ''Then, the bottom fell out of the oil market,'' he resumed. ''We told ourselves that it was temporary.''

''To what extent did the oil market affect you?''

''I hold a hefty percentage in several wells and one natural gas company. But thank God, I'd never invested more than I could afford to lose. I'd never liquidated my other businesses to support an oil well.''

''Still, that drop in the price of oil must have caused you a substantial financial setback. Weren't you upset?''

He shook his head. ''I've won and lost more fortunes than you are years old, young lady. Hell, I really don't mind being broke. Being rich is more fun, but being broke is more exciting. It's got built-in challenges.

''Sarah Jo,'' he said, sighing thoughtfully, ''doesn't agree with me, of course. She likes the security of having money collecting dust in a vault. I've never touched her money or Junior's inheritance. I promised her I never would.''

Talking about inheritances was foreign to Alex. She couldn't even conceive of it. Merle Graham had supported them on her salary from the telephone company, and then on her pension after her retirement. Alex's grades had been high enough to earn her a scholarship to the University of Texas, but she'd worked after classes to keep herself dressed and fed so her grandmother wouldn't have those expenses to complain about.

She had received financial assistance for law school, too, because her grades were so impressive. Working in public service didn't provide her with luxuries. She'd struggled with her conscience for weeks before rewarding herself with the fur coat for passing the bar. It was one of the few extravagances she had ever allowed herself.

''Do you have enough capital to finance the racetrack?'' she asked, bringing her mind back around.

''Not personally.''

''Minton Enterprises?''

''Not by itself. We've formed a group of investors, individuals and businesses, that would profit from having the track built here.''

He sat down in his red leather recliner and pointed her into a chair. ''During the oil boom, everybody got a taste of wealth. They're greedy for it again.''

''That's hardly a flattering assessment of the population of Purcell—a group of avaricious carnivores waiting to gobble up horseracing money.''

''Not avaricious,'' he said. ''Everybody would get his fair share, starting with the major investors, and working down to the guy who owns the self-service filling station on the nearest corner. It wouldn't mean just individual gain, either. Think of the schools and hospitals and public facilities the town could build with that increased revenue.''

He leaned forward and curled his hand into a fist, as though grasping at something. ''That's why this racetrack is so damned important. It would set Purcell back on its feet and then some.'' His blue eyes sparkled with enthusiasm for his argument. ''Well, what do you think?''

''I'm not a moron, Mr. Minton, uh, Angus,'' she corrected. ''I realize what the track could mean to the county's economy.''

''Then, why don't you drop this ridiculous investigation?''

''I don't think it's ridiculous,'' she retaliated sharply.

Studying her, he absently scratched his cheek. ''How could you think that I killed your mama? She was one of Junior's best friends. She was in and out of this house on a daily basis. Not so much after she got married, but certainly before then. I couldn't have lifted a finger to hurt that girl.''

Alex wanted to believe him. Despite the fact that he was a suspect in a criminal case, she admired him very much. From what she had read and gathered through conversation, he had started with nothing and built an empire.

His brusqueness was almost endearing. He had a persuasive personality. But she couldn't let his colorful persona influence her. Her admiration for Angus wasn't as strong as her need to know how she, an innocent baby, had prompted someone to murder her mother.

''I can't drop the investigation,'' she said. ''Even if I wanted to, Pat Chastain—''

''Listen,'' he said, scooting forward. ''You bat those big baby blues of yours at him, tell him you made a mistake, and by this time tomorrow, I guarantee that he won't even remember what you came here for.''

''I wouldn't do—''

''Okay, then leave Pat to me.''

''Angus,'' she said loudly, ''you're missing my point.'' When she was assured she had his attention, she said, ''As strongly as you believe in your racetrack, I believe that my mother's murder case was mishandled. I intend to see that rectified.''

''Even though the future of a whole town is at stake?''

''Come on,'' she cried in protest. ''You make it sound like I'm taking bread from starving children.''

''Not as bad as that, but still—''

''*My* future is at stake, too. I can't go on with the rest of it until the case is resolved to my satisfaction.''

''Yes, but—''

''Hey, time out.'' Junior opened the door suddenly and poked his head inside. ''I've had a great idea, Alex. Why don't you stay for supper?''

''Damn you, Junior,'' Angus thundered, pounding the arm of his chair with his fist. ''You wouldn't recognize a business discussion if it bit you in the ass. We're talking seriously here. Don't ever interrupt me when I'm in a private conference again. You know better than that.''

Junior swallowed visibly. ''I didn't know your conversation was so private or so serious.''

''Well, you damned well should have, shouldn't you? For crissake, we were—''

''Angus, please, it's all right,'' Alex said quickly. ''Actually, I'm glad Junior interrupted. I just now noticed how late it is. I need to be going.''

She couldn't stand to watch a grown man get a dressing down from his father, especially in front of a female guest. She was embarrassed for both of them.

Most of the time, Angus was a good ole boy. But not always. He had an explosive temper when crossed. Alex had just witnessed how short his fuse was and just how slight a transgression it took to ignite it.

"I'll see you out," Junior offered woodenly.

She shook hands with Angus. "Thank you for showing me the model. Nothing you've said has diverted me, but you've clarified some things. I'll keep them in mind as I pursue the case."

"You can trust us, you know. We're not killers."

Junior walked her to the front door. After he had held her coat for her, she turned to face him. "I'll be in touch, Junior."

"I certainly hope so." He bent over her hand and kissed it, then turned her palm up and kissed it, too.

She took it back quickly. "Do you flirt like this with every woman you meet?"

"Just about." He flashed her an unrepentant grin. "Are you susceptible?"

"Not in the least."

His grin widened, indicating to her that he wasn't convinced and knew that she wasn't either. After saying another quick good night, she left.

Her car was cold. She shivered inside her coat. As she drove down the private road toward the highway, she noticed the outbuildings on either side of it. Most were stables. There was a faint light burning inside one of them. Reede's Blazer was parked at the door. On impulse, Alex pulled up beside it and got out.

Sarah Jo's bedroom in Kentucky had been duplicated at her Texas home, down to the silk cord tiebacks on the drapes. When the house had been built, she had agreed to let Angus have his heavy, dark furniture, his red leather upholstery, and his hunting trophies in other rooms, but she had flatly refused to let his revolting frontier motif defile their bedroom.

Cheerfully, he had agreed. He liked her fussy, feminine, frilly things around him at night. He'd often told her that if he'd wanted to marry a cowgirl, he wouldn't have had to go all the way to Kentucky to find one.

"Mother, may I come in?" Junior opened the bedroom door after a tentative knock.

"Darling, please do." Sarah Jo smiled, evidently quite pleased over her son's visit.

Junior found her propped up on a mountain of satin pillows, wearing a lace night jacket, smelling of expensive face cream, and reading the biography of some foreign statesman of whom he'd never heard. He'd never even heard of the country from which the man hailed. Probably no one except his mother had.

She took off her reading glasses, laid the book aside, and patted the quilted satin comforter. With a brisk shake of his head, Junior declined to sit down. Instead he remained standing at the foot of the bed, hands in pockets, jingling change, resenting this nightly ritual that was a carryover from his childhood.

Long ago, he'd outgrown the need or desire to kiss his mother good night, but Sarah Jo continued to expect it. Her feelings would be hurt if he didn't. He and Angus went out of their way to spare Sarah Jo's feelings, which were always tenuous.

"It always smells good in here," he commented for lack of anything else to say. The dressing down he'd received in front of Alex still smarted. He was impatient to leave the house and go to one of the local nightspots where he wouldn't have to concentrate on his problems.

"Sachets. I keep them in all my drawers and closets. When I was a girl, we had a maid who made them from crushed dried flowers and herbs. They smelled wonderful,'' she said reminiscently. "Now I have to order them. They use artificial scents in them these days, but I still think they're pretty.''

"How's the book?'' Junior was already bored with the subject of sachets.

"Quite interesting.''

He seriously doubted it, but he smiled down at her. "Good. I'm glad you're enjoying it.''

Sarah Jo sensed his melancholy mood. "What's wrong?''

"Nothing.''

"I can tell when something's wrong.''

"Nothing out of the ordinary. I got on Dad's bad side by interrupting his discussion with Alex.''

Sarah Jo made a moue of displeasure. "Your father still hasn't learned how to conduct himself when there's company in the house. If he can be rude enough to cart a guest out of the living room during the cocktail hour, you can be rude enough to interrupt a discussion.''

She bobbed her head as though she had said her piece and that settled the matter. "What were they discussing so privately, anyway?''

"Something about her mother's death,'' he said nonchalantly. "Nothing to worry about.''

"Are you sure? Everybody seemed so tense tonight.''

"If there's any cause for alarm, Dad'll take care of it, the way he always does. It's certainly nothing for you to worry about.''

He had no intention of telling his mother about Alex's investigation. The men in Sarah Jo's life knew she hated being exposed to anything upsetting or unpleasant, and protected her from it.

Angus never discussed business with her, especially when it was bad. She was disappointed when their horses didn't perform well at the track and celebrated when they did, but beyond that, neither the ranch, nor any of the subsidiary companies comprising Minton Enterprises, held much interest for her.

Indeed, nothing held much interest for Sarah Jo, with the possible exception of Junior. She was like a beautiful doll, sealed inside a sterile room, never exposed to light or any other corrupting element—especially life itself.

Junior loved his mother, but recognized that she wasn't well liked. By contrast, everybody liked Angus. A few of his friends' wives, out of loyalty and obligation, were friendly to Sarah Jo. If not for them, she wouldn't have any acquaintances in Purcell at all.

She'd certainly never gone out of her way to cultivate a friendship. She thought most of the locals were vulgar and coarse, and she made no attempt to conceal her low opinion of them. She seemed perfectly content to reside in this room, surrounded by the soft, pretty, uncomplicated things she liked and understood best.

Junior knew she was the object of derision and gossip. It was said that she drank. She didn't, except for two glasses of wine before dinner. Some, who didn't understand her delicate sensibilities, thought she was odd. Others thought she was just plain "off.''

Admittedly, she was distracted a good deal of the time, as though mentally reliving the privileged childhood she treasured. She had never quite recovered from the premature death of a beloved brother, and had still been mourning it when she had met Angus.

Junior wondered if she had married his father to escape unpleasant memories. He could find no other grounds for two such mismatched people to base a marriage.

Junior was eager to get on his way to having a good time, but he lengthened tonight's visit, curious to know his mother's opinion of their guest that evening. "What did you think of her?"

"Who, Celina's daughter?" Sarah Jo asked absently. Her brows drew together into a slight frown. "She's very attractive physically, though I don't find such flamboyant coloring flattering to a woman."

Thoughtfully, she fingered the fine lace on the bodice of her bed jacket. "She's certainly intense, isn't she? Much more serious-minded than her mother. Celina was a silly little thing, God knows. As I recall, she was always laughing." She paused and cocked her head to one side, as though listening to distant laughter. "I don't remember ever seeing that girl when she wasn't laughing."

"There were plenty of times. You just didn't know her that well."

"Poor darling. I know you were crushed when she died. I know what it's like to lose someone you love. It's sheer misery."

Her voice, so soft, changed suddenly, as did her expression. No longer a shrinking violet, her features hardened with resolve. "Junior, you must stop letting Angus embarrass you, especially in front of other people."

He gave a careless shrug. This was familiar territory. "He doesn't mean anything by it. It's just a habit of his."

"Then, it's up to you to break him of it. Darling, don't you see," she said, "that's what he wants you to do. He wants you to stand up to him. Angus only understands one tone of voice—harsh."

"He doesn't know how to be soft-spoken and genteel, like us. You have to talk to him in a way he understands, like Reede does. Angus wouldn't dare speak to Reede in the condescending way he does to you because he respects Reede. And he respects him because Reede doesn't kowtow to him."

"Dad thinks Reede can do no wrong. To this day, it sticks in his craw that Reede left ME. He'd much rather have Reede than me around to manage things. I never do anything to his liking."

"That's simply not true!" Sarah Jo objected, showing more spirit than she had in weeks. "Angus is very proud of you. He just doesn't know how to show it. He's such a hard man. He's had to be tough to accomplish everything he's done. He wants you to be tough, too."

Junior grinned, doubling up his fists. "Okay, Mother, tomorrow morning I'll come out slugging."

She giggled. His resilience and sense of humor had always delighted her. "Not literally, I hope, but that's the spirit Angus wants to see in you."

Laughter was a good note to leave on. Junior seized the opportunity, said his good night, gave her his promise to drive safely, and left. On the stairs, he met Angus, who was carrying his boots and limping. "When are you going to see a doctor about that toe?"

"What good's a goddamn doctor, except to take your money? I ought to shoot off the sonofabitch and be done with it."

Junior smiled. "Okay, but don't get blood on the carpet. Mother would have a fit."

Angus laughed, all traces of anger gone. It was as if the episode in his den had never happened. He placed his arm across Junior's shoulders and gave them a quick squeeze. "I knew I could depend on you to get that girl out here. It worked out just like I hoped it would. We've put her on the defensive and planted seeds of doubt. If she's smart, and I believe she is, she'll call this thing off before too much damage has been done."

"What if she doesn't?"

"If she doesn't, we'll cross that bridge, too," Angus said darkly. Then he smiled and affectionately slapped Junior on the cheek. "Good night, boy."

Junior watched his father hobble across the landing. Feeling much better, he whistled softly beneath his breath on his way downstairs. Angus wouldn't be disappointed in him this time. The job he had been assigned suited him to a tee.

His experience in handling women was legendary. The challenges that Alex presented would just make the chase that much more exciting and fun. She was a damned attractive woman. Even if Angus hadn't told him, he would have wooed her anyway.

Doing it just right, however, would take some time and thought. He would give himself a few days to come up with a sure-fire strategy. In the meantime, there were lesser worlds to conquer. He saluted his handsome image in the hallway mirror on his way out the front door.

 # NINE

Like the house, the stable was built of stone. The interior was like any other that Alex had seen, except that it was spotlessly clean. Two rows of stalls were divided by a wide center aisle. It smelled, not unpleasantly, of hay and leather and horseflesh.

Low wattage night-lights placed between the stalls made it easy for her to see where she was going—toward a brighter light that was burning in a stall about midway down. Quietly she made her way toward it, passing an open tack room and a door that was labeled PHYSICAL THERAPY. Through a wide opening she also saw a round pen with a walker that would exercise several horses at one time.

Before she saw him, she heard Reede, speaking in a low murmur to the occupant of the stall. Drawing even with it, she looked inside. He was hunkered down, sitting on the heels of his boots, rubbing his large hands up and down the animal's back leg.

His head was bent to one side as he concentrated on his task. His fingers pressed a spot which was obviously sensitive. The horse snuffled and tried to withdraw.

"Easy, easy."

"What's the matter with him?"

He didn't turn around or show the slightest surprise at the sound of her voice. Apparently, he had known all along that she was standing there and was just being obtuse. He gently lowered the injured leg and, standing, patted the animal's rump. "It's a her." He shot her a suggestive smile. "Or aren't you old enough to tell the difference?"

"Not from this angle."

"Her name is Fancy Pants."

"Cute."

"It fits her. She thinks she's smarter than me, smarter than anybody. Fact is, she's too smart for her own good. She goes too far, too fast, and as a result, she ends up getting hurt." He scooped up a handful of grain and let the horse eat it from his hand.

"Oh, I get it. That's a veiled reference to me." He admitted it with a shrug. "Should I take it as a threat?"

"You can take it any way you want it."

Again, he was playing word games, implying double meanings. Alex didn't rise to the bait this time. "What kind of horse is she?"

"A pregnant one. This is the mares' barn."

"They're all kept here?"

"Away from the others, yeah." The mare nuzzled his chest and he smiled as he scratched behind her ears. "Mamas and babies cause a ruckus in a stable."

"Why?"

He shrugged his shoulders, indicating there was no clear-cut explanation. "I guess it's like the nursery floor at the hospital. Everybody goes a little nuts over a newborn."

He ran his hand over the mare's smooth belly. "This is her first time, and she's nervous about being a mother. She got a little skittish the other day when they were walking her and injured her metatarsal."

"When will she foal?"

"In the spring. She's got a while yet. Give me your hand."

"What?"

"Your hand." Sensing her reservation, he impatiently drew her into the stall with him until she was standing as close to the mare as he. "Feel."

He covered her hand with his and flattened it against the mare's sleek coat. The hair was coarse and short, and the vitality and strength of muscle beneath it was evident to the touch.

The animal snuffled and took a hesitant step forward, but Reede shushed her. The stall seemed close and overheated. The fecund smell of new life in the making permeated the square enclosure. "She's warm," Alex commented breathlessly.

"She sure is."

Reede moved closer to Alex and maneuvered her hand, together with his, down the contours of the mare's body to her swollen underbelly. Alex gave a soft exclamation of surprise when she felt movement.

"The foal." Reede was so close his breath disturbed strands of her hair and she smelled the scent of his cologne, mingled with that of the stable.

A swift kick against her palm made Alex laugh with spontaneous delight. She also gave a start of surprise and bumped against Reede. "So active."

"She's breeding me a winner."

"She belongs to you?"

"Yes."

"What about the sire?"

"I paid dearly for his services, but he was worth it. Good-looking stallion from Florida. Fancy Pants took to him right away. I think she was sorry when it was over. Maybe if he was around all the time, I wouldn't have to worry about her getting out of line."

The pressure in Alex's chest was such that she could barely breathe. Her inclination was to rest her cheek against the mare's side and continue to listen to Reede's lulling voice. Thankfully, her reason reasserted itself before she did anything so foolish.

She pulled her hand from beneath his and turned. He was standing so close to her that her clothes brushed against his, and she had to tilt her head back until it was resting against the horse in order to look into his face.

"Do all owners have access to the stables?"

Reede stepped back and allowed her to move toward the opening.

"Since I used to work for the Mintons, I guess they feel they can trust me."

"What kind of horse is she?" Alex said, reverting to her original question.

"A Quarter Horse."

"A quarter of what?"

" 'A quarter of what?' " He tossed back his head and laughed. Fancy Pants danced aside. "Jesus, that's good. A quarter of what?" He unfastened the chain that had secured the mare to a metal ring in the wall, and then joined Alex outside the stall, carefully closing the gate behind him. "You don't know much about horses, do you?"

"Obviously not," she replied tightly.

Her embarrassment seemed to amuse him for only a moment. Then, frowning, he asked, "Was coming out here your idea?"

"Junior invited me."

"Ah, that figures."

"Why should it figure?"

"He's always hot on the trail of the newest available broad."

Blood surged through Alex's veins. "I am not available to Junior, or to anybody else. Neither am I a broad."

He subjected her to a slow and ridiculing once-over. "No, I guess you're not. Too much lawyer and not enough woman. Don't you ever relax?"

"Not when I'm working on a case."

"And that's what you were doing over drinks?" he asked scornfully. "Working on your case?"

"That's right."

"They've sure got funny methods of investigation in the Travis County D.A.'s office." He turned his back on her and swaggered toward the opposite end of the building.

"Wait! I'd like to ask you a few questions."

"Subpoena me," he tossed over his shoulder.

"Reede!" Impulsively, she struck out after him and grabbed the sleeve of his leather jacket. He stopped, glanced down where her fingers were curled into the age-softened leather, then came around slowly and stared at her with eyes as green and sharp as jungle spears.

She let go of his sleeve and fell back a step. She wasn't frightened; rather, she was shocked at herself. She hadn't intended to call his name like that, and she certainly hadn't intended to touch him, especially after what had happened in the stall.

Wetting her lips nervously, she said, "I want to talk to you. Please. Off the record. To satisfy my own curiosity."

"I know the technique, Counselor. I've used it myself. You play chummy with the suspect, hoping that he'll drop his guard and tell you something he's trying to hide."

"It's not like that. I just wanted to talk."

"About what?"

"About the Mintons."

"What about them?"

Standing with his feet widespread, pelvis tipped slightly forward, he slid his hands into the back pockets of his jeans, which pulled his jacket open across his chest. The stance was intimidatingly manly. It aroused her as much as it annoyed her. Alex tried to suppress both responses. "Would you say that Angus and Sarah Jo have a happy marriage?"

He blinked and coughed. "What?"

"Don't look at me like that. I'm asking for your opinion, not an analysis."

"What the hell difference does it make?"

"Sarah Jo's not the kind of woman I would have expected Angus to marry."

"Opposites attract."

"That's too pat. Are they . . . close?"

"Close?"

"Close, as in intimate."

"I've never thought about it."

"Of course you have. You lived here."

"Apparently, my mind doesn't operate on the same prurient track as yours." He took a step closer and lowered his voice. "But, we could change that."

Alex refused to let him provoke her, which she knew came closer to his intention than seduction. "Do they sleep together?"

"I guess so. It's none of my business what they do or don't do in bed. Furthermore, I don't care. I only care about what goes on in my bed. Why don't you ask me about that?"

"Because I don't care."

Again, he gave her a slow, knowing grin. "I think you do."

"I hate being patronized, Mr. Lambert, just because I'm a woman prosecutor."

"Then stop being one."

"A woman?"

"A prosecutor."

Mentally, she counted to ten. "Does Angus see other women?"

She could see annoyance building up behind his green eyes. His patience with her was wearing thin. "Do you take Sarah Jo for a passionate woman?"

"No," Alex replied.

"Do you figure that Angus has a healthy sexual appetite?"

"If it matches his other appetites, I'd say yes."

"Then, I guess you've got your answer."

"Has their relationship affected Junior?"

"How the hell should I know? Ask him."

"He'd only make some glib, dismissive comment."

"Which would be a nice way of telling you that you're interfering with business that doesn't concern you. I'm not as nice as he is. Butt out, lady."

"This does concern me."

He withdrew his hands from his hip pockets and folded his arms across his chest. "I can hardly wait to hear this rationalization."

She didn't let his sarcasm daunt her. "His parents' relationship might explain why Junior has had three failed marriages."

"That's something else that's none of your business."

"It is my business."

"How so?"

"Because Junior loved my mother."

The words reverberated down the corridor of the quiet stable. Reede's head went back with a snap, as if he'd sustained a quick, unexpected uppercut on the chin. "Who told you that?"

"He did." She watched him closely, adding softly. "He said you both loved her."

He stared at her for a considerable time, then shrugged. "In one way or another. So?"

"Is that why Junior's marriages didn't work? Because he was still carrying a torch for my mother?"

"I have no idea."

"Take a wild guess."

"Okay." Arrogantly, he angled his head to one side. "I don't think Celina had shit to do with Junior's marriages. It's just that he can't fuck for recreation without feeling guilty about it later, so to ease his conscience, he takes a wife every few years."

His statement was intended to offend her, and it did. She tried not to show how much. "Why do you think he feels guilty about it?"

"Genetics. He's got generations of southern chivalry flowing through his veins. That makes for a guilty conscience where the ladies are concerned."

"What about you?"

A Cheshire-cat grin lifted one corner of his mouth. "I never feel guilty for anything I do."

"Even murder?"

His grin collapsed and his eyes turned dark. "Get the hell out of here."

"Have you ever been married?"

"No."

"Why not?"

"None of your goddamn business. Anything else, Counselor?"

"Yes. Tell me about your father."

Gradually, Reede lowered his arms to his sides. He gave her a hard, cold stare. Alex said, "I know your father died while you were still in school. Junior mentioned it today. When he died, you came to live here."

"You have a morbid curiosity, Miss Gaither."

"I'm not curious. I'm looking for facts pertinent to my investigation."

"Oh, sure. Pertinent stuff like Angus's sex life."

She gave him a reproving look. "Motives are what I'm after, Sheriff Lambert. As a law officer, you can identify with that, can't you? Ever hear of motive and opportunity?" His eyes turned even colder. "I need to establish your frame of mind the night of my mother's death."

"That's bullshit. What has that got to do with my old man?"

"Maybe nothing, but you tell me. If it's irrelevant, why are you so touchy about it?"

"Did Junior tell you how my old man died?" She shook her head. Reede snorted a bitter laugh. "I can't imagine why not. The nasty details made big news around here. People talked about it for years."

He bent at the waist so they were standing eye to eye. "He choked to death on his own vomit, too drunk to save himself. That's right, look shocked. It was pretty goddamned horrifying, especially when the principal of the high school called me out of class to tell me."

"Reede." In an attempt to stop the flow of sarcastic words, Alex raised her hand. He swatted it aside.

"No, if you're so anxious to open all the closet doors and expose the skeletons, here it is. But brace yourself, baby, this one's a dilly.

"My daddy was the town drunk, a laughingstock, a worthless, pathetic, sorry excuse for a human being. I didn't even cry when I heard he'd died. I was glad. He was a miserable, scummy son of a bitch who never did a single goddamn thing for me except make me ashamed that he was my father. And he wasn't any happier about that than I was. Dickweed—that's what he called me, usually right before he clouted me alongside the head. I was a liability to him.

"But, like a fool, I kept pretending, wishing, that we were a family. I was always after him to come watch me play ball. One night he showed up at a game. He created such a scene stumbling up the bleachers, tearing down one of the banners when he fell, that I wanted to die of embarrassment. I told him never to come again. I hated him. *Hated,"* he repeated, rasping the word.

"I couldn't invite friends to my house because it was such a pigsty. We ate out of tin cans. I didn't know there were things like dishes on the table and clean towels in the bathroom until I was invited to other kids' houses. I made myself as presentable as possible when I went to school."

Alex regretted having lanced this festering wound, but she was glad he was talking freely. His childhood explained a lot about the man. But he was describing an outcast, and that didn't mesh with what she knew about him.

"I've been told that you were a ringleader, that the other kids gravitated to you. You made the rules and set the mood."

"I bullied myself into that position," he told her. "In grade school, the other kids made fun of me, everybody except Celina. Then I got taller and stronger and learned to fight. I fought dirty. They stopped laughing. It became much safer for a kid to be my friend than my enemy."

His lip curled with scorn. "This'll knock your socks off, Miss Prosecutor. I was a thief. I stole anything that we could eat or that might come in useful. You see, my old man couldn't keep a job for more than a few days without going on a binge. He'd take what he'd earned, buy himself a bottle or two, and drink himself unconscious. Eventually, he gave up trying to work. I supported us on what I could earn after school doing odd jobs, and on what I could get away with stealing."

There was nothing she could say. He had known there wouldn't be. That's why he'd told her. He wanted her to feel rotten and small-minded. Little did he know that their childhoods hadn't been that dissimilar, although she'd never gone without food. Merle Graham had provided for her physical needs, but she'd neglected her emotional ones. Alex had grown up feeling inferior and unloved. Empathetically she said, "I'm sorry, Reede."

"I don't want your goddamn pity," he sneered. "I don't want anybody's. That life made me hard and mean, and I like it that way. I learned early on to stand up for myself because it was for damn sure nobody else was going to go to bat for me. I don't depend on anybody but myself. I don't take anything for granted, especially people. And I'm damned and determined never to sink to the level of my old man."

"You're making too much out of this, Reede. You're too sensitive."

"Uh-huh. I want people to forget that Everett Lambert ever lived. I don't want anyone to associate me with him. Ever."

He clenched his teeth and hauled her up to just beneath his angry face by the lapels of her coat. "I've lived down the unfortunate fact that I was his son for forty-three years. Now, just when folks are about to forget it, you come along and start asking nosy questions, raising dead issues, reminding everybody that I crawled up out of the gutter to get where I am."

He sent her backwards with a hard push. She caught herself against the gate of a stall. "I'm sure that no one holds your father's failures against you."

"You don't think so? That's the nature of a small town, baby. You'll find out how it is soon enough, because they'll start comparing you to Celina."

"That won't bother me. I'll welcome the comparison."

"Are you so sure?"

"Yes."

"Careful. When you round a blind corner, you'd better know what's waiting for you."

"Care to be less oblique?"

"It could go one of two ways. Either you won't measure up to her, or you'll find out that being like her isn't all that terrific."

"Well, which is it?"

His eyes swept over her. "Like her, looking at you reminds a man that he is one. And like her, you use that to your advantage."

"Meaning?"

"She was no saint."

"I didn't expect her to be."

"Didn't you?" he asked silkily. "I believe you did. I think you've created this fantasy mother in your head and you expect Celina to fulfill it for you."

"That's ridiculous." Her strenuous denial sounded juvenile and obstinate. More calmly, she said, "It's true that Grandma Graham thought the sun rose and set on Celina. I was brought up to believe she was everything a young woman should be. But I'm a woman myself now, and mature enough to realize that my mother was made of flesh and blood, with flaws, just like everybody else."

He studied her face for a moment. "Just remember that I warned you," he said softly. "You should go back to the Westerner, pack up your designer clothes and your legal briefs, and head for Austin. Leave the past alone. Nobody around here wants to remember that blight on Purcell's history—particularly with that license hanging in the balance. They'd much rather leave Celina lying dead in this stable than—"

"This stable?" Alex gasped. "My mother was killed here?"

It was clear to her that he hadn't intended to let that slip. He cursed beneath his breath before answering curtly, "That's right."

"Where? Which stall?"

"It doesn't mat—"

"Show me, damn you! I'm sick to death of your half answers and evasions. Show me where you found her body that morning, Sheriff." She enunciated the last word carefully, reminding him that it was his sworn duty to protect and serve.

Without another word, he turned and strode toward the door through which she had entered the barn. At the second stall in the row, he halted. "Here."

Alex came to a full stop, then moved forward slowly until she was even with Reede. She turned to face the stall. There was no hay in it, just the rubber-covered floor. The gate had been removed because no horse was occupying the stall. It looked innocent, almost sterile.

"There hasn't been a horse boarded in this stall since it happened." Scornfully, he added, "Angus has a sentimental streak."

Alex tried to envision a bloody corpse lying in the stall, but couldn't. She raised inquiring eyes to Reede.

The skin seemed more tautly stretched across his cheekbones, and the vertical lines that framed his mouth appeared more pronounced than they had a few moments ago, when he had been angry. A visit to the scene of the crime wasn't as easy for him as he wanted to pretend.

"Tell me about it. Please."

He hesitated, then said. "She was lying diagonally, her head in that corner, her feet about here." He touched a spot with the toe of his boot. "She was covered with blood. It was in her hat, on her clothes, everywhere." Alex had heard jaded homicide detectives discussing gory murder sites with more emotion. Reede's voice was hollow and monotonal, but his features were stark with pain. "Her eyes were still open."

"What time was that?" she asked huskily.

''When I found her?'' She nodded, finding it difficult to speak. ''Dawn. Around six-thirty.''

''What were you doing here at that time of day?''

''I usually started mucking the stables around seven. That particular morning I was worried about the mare.''

''Oh, yes, the one that had foaled the day before. So, you had come to check on her and the foal?''

''That's right.''

Tears were shimmering in her eyes as she raised them to his. ''Where were you the night before?''

''Out.''

''All night?''

''Since supper time, yes.''

''Alone?''

His lips narrowed with irritation. ''If you want more answers, Counselor, bring the case to trial.''

''I plan to.''

As she brushed past him on her way to the door, he caught her arm and drew her up against him. He felt hard and powerfully male. ''Miss Gaither,'' he growled in irritation and impatience, ''you're smart. Drop this. If you don't, somebody's likely to get hurt.''

''Namely?''

''You.''

''How?''

He didn't actually move; he just inclined his body closer to hers. ''There are any number of ways.''

It was a threat, only subtly veiled. He was physically capable of killing a woman, but what about emotionally?

He seemed to have a low opinion of women in general, but according to Junior, he had loved Celina Graham. At one time, she had wanted to marry Reede. Maybe everyone, including Reede, had taken for granted that they would marry until Celina had married Al Gaither and gotten pregnant with Alex.

Alex didn't want to believe that Reede could have killed Celina under any circumstances, but she certainly didn't want to believe he had killed Celina because of her.

He was chauvinistic, arrogant, and as testy as a rattler. But a killer? He didn't look like one. Or was it just that she'd always had a weakness for dark blond hair and green eyes; for tight, faded jeans and worn leather coats with fur collars; for men who could wear cowboy boots without looking silly; for men who walked and talked and smelled and sounded and felt consummately male?

Reede Lambert was all of that.

Disturbed more by his effect on her senses than by his cautionary words, she pulled her arm free and backed toward the door.

''I have no intention of dropping this investigation until I know who killed my mother and why. I've waited all my life to find out. I won't be dissuaded now.''

TEN

R eede let loose a string of curses the minute Alex left the stable. Pasty Hickam had overheard them from his hiding place in a nearby stall.

He hadn't planned to eavesdrop on their conversation. When he had come into the barn earlier, he'd only been looking for a place where it was dark and warm and solitary, where he'd have some privacy to nurse his damaged pride, cultivate his resentment of his former employer, and suck on his bottle of cheap rye as if it was mother's milk.

Now, however, his ennui had vanished and his mind was concocting a nefarious plan. Sober, Pasty was merely crotchety. Drunk, he was mean.

He'd barely been able to contain himself as he listened to what that gal from Austin had to say to the sheriff, and vice versa. Lordy be, she was Celina Gaither's daughter, here to investigate her mama's killing.

Thanks to her, and a benevolent God he didn't even believe in, he had been given a golden opportunity to get revenge on Angus and that useless son of his.

He'd busted his ass on this place, worked for miserly wages, and gone without completely when Angus was so broke he couldn't pay him, but he'd stuck it out. He had gone through thick and thin with the bastard, and what thanks did he get? Fired and booted out of the bunkhouse that had been home for almost thirty years.

Well, fortune had finally smiled on Pasty Hickam. If he played his cards right, he could finally have some money for his "retirement fund." Ruby Faye, his current lover, was always after him about never having any money to spend on her. "What's the fun of having an affair if I don't get something out of it besides the thrill of cheating on my husband?" she was fond of saying.

Monetary compensation, however, would be icing on the cake. Revenge would be sweet enough. It was past time that somebody kicked Angus where it hurt.

His impatience was at a near-frantic pitch by the time Reede finished examining his mare and left the stable. Pasty waited several moments to make sure he was alone before leaving the empty stall where he'd been curled up in the fresh hay. He moved down the shadowed corridor toward the wall telephone. He cursed a horse that nickered, spooking him. For all his meanness, courage had never been his strong suit.

He called Information first, then quickly punched out the digits of the number before he could forget them. Maybe she hadn't had time to get there, he thought anxiously after he'd asked the clerk to ring her room. But she answered on the fifth ring, a trifle breathlessly, like she might have come in while the phone was ringing."

"Miz Gaither?"

"Yes, who's this?"

"You don't need to know. I know you, and that's enough."

"Who is this?" she demanded, with what Patsy thought was false bravado.

"I know all about your mama's murder."

Pasty cackled to himself, enjoying the sudden silence. He couldn't have got her attention any sooner or any better if he'd walked up and bit her on her tittie.

"I'm listening."

"I cain't talk now."

"Why not?"

" 'Cause I cain't, that's why."

It was risky to go into it with her now over the telephone. Somebody might pick up another extension somewhere on the ranch and overhear him. That could prove to be unhealthy.

318

"I'll call you back."

"But—"

"I'll call you back."

He hung up, enjoying her anxiety. He remembered the way her mama used to sashay around, like she owned the world. Many a summer day, he'd ogled her lustfully while she frolicked in the swimming pool with Junior and Reede. They'd put their hands all over her and call it roughhousing. But she was too good to even cast an eye in Pasty's direction. He hadn't minded that she got herself killed. He sure as hell hadn't interfered and stopped it when he could have.

He remembered that night and everything that had happened like it was yesterday. It was a secret that he'd kept all this time. Now it would be divulged. And it was gonna tickle him to death to tell that prosecutor all about it.

 # ELEVEN

" **A** re you waiting to give me a parking ticket?" Alex asked as she got out of her car and locked it. She was feeling chipper this morning, due to the unexpected telephone call she had received the night before. Maybe the caller was the eyewitness she'd been praying for. But it could have been a crank call, too, she realistically reminded herself.

If he was genuine, it would be a tragedy if he named Reede Lambert as Celina's murderer. He looked extremely attractive leaning against the parking meter. Actually, since the meter was listing to the right, it might have been leaning on Reede.

"I should change my mind since you're being a smart ass, but I'm such a nice guy . . ." He slipped a canvas hood over the meter. In blue letters it was labeled, CITY OF PURCELL—OFFICIAL CAR. "Take this with you when you leave and use it from now on. It'll save you some change."

He turned and started up the sidewalk toward the courthouse. Alex fell into step beside him. "Thanks."

"You're welcome." They climbed the stairs and went inside. "Come down to my office," he said. "I've got something to show you."

Curious, she followed his lead. They hadn't parted on the best of terms the night before. Yet this morning, he was going out of his way to be hospitable. Deciding that was out of character, Alex couldn't help but be suspicious of his motives.

When they reached the lower level, everyone in the squad room stopped what he was doing to stare. The scene became as still as a photograph.

Reede gave the room one slow, meaningful sweep of his eyes. Activity was immediately resumed. He hadn't spoken a single word, but it was apparent that he wielded tremendous authority over his staff. They either feared or respected him. Alex suspected the former.

Reede stepped around her, swung open a door to the left of the staircase, and moved aside so she could go in. She stepped into a small square, windowless, cheerless office. It was as cold as a meat locker. There was a desk so dented and scarred it looked like it had been made from scrap metal. The particleboard top was ink-stained, and holes had been chipped out of it. Sitting on it were an overflowing ashtray and a black, no-frills telephone. Behind it was a swivel chair she had little confidence in.

"It's yours to use if you want it," Reede told her. "I'm sure you're accustomed to fancier office space."

"No. Actually, my cubicle in Austin is not much larger than this. Whom should I thank?"

"The city of Purcell."

"But it was somebody's idea. Yours, Reede?"

"So what if it was?"

"So," she said, drawing out the word in an effort to ignore the chip he carried on his shoulder, "thank you."

"You're welcome."

Trying to temper the animosity between them, she smiled and said teasingly, "Now that we're in the same building, I can keep a closer eye on you."

He pulled the door shut as he backed out. "You've got it backwards, Counselor. I can keep a closer eye on *you.*"

Alex tossed down her ballpoint pen and vigorously rubbed her chilled arms. The electric space heater she had bought at the hardware store was on full blast, but it wasn't helping much. The square little office was frigid and seemed to be the only dank, damp spot in this otherwise arid climate.

Earlier she had bought office supplies: paper, pencils, pens, paper clips. The office was hardly comfortable, but at least it was functional. It was also much more centrally located than her room at the Westerner Motel.

After checking to see that the heater was indeed working at its maximum, she bent over her notes again. It had taken all afternoon to compile and arrange them according to the individuals involved.

Beginning with her profile on Angus, she reread the briefs. Unfortunately, they were no more concrete or factually based than they had been the first dozen times she'd read them.

What she had was conjecture and hearsay. What few facts she had, she had known when she left Austin. So far, this trip had been a waste of taxpayers' money, and almost a week of Greg's deadline had elapsed.

For the time being, she decided to let the question of opportunity wait. She had to establish motives. All she had learned so far was that the three men had adored Celina. Adoration was hardly motivation for murder.

She had nothing—no evidence, not even a viable suspect. She was certain that Buddy Hicks hadn't killed her mother, yet she was no closer to discovering who had.

After spending time alone with Angus, Junior, and Reede, Alex was convinced that getting a confession would be tantamount to a miracle. Contrition and repentance didn't fit their personality profiles. Nor would one testify against the other. The loyalties were solidly forged, though it was obvious their friendship wasn't what it had once been, which in itself was a clue. Had Celina's death splintered their clique, yet kept them bound to one another?

She still hoped that the person who had called a few nights before was an actual eyewitness. She had waited for days for another call, one that hadn't come, which was a strong indication that it had been a prank.

Apparently, the only people near the stable that night had been Gooney Bud, the killer, and Celina. Gooney Bud was dead. The killer wasn't talking. And Celina—

Alex was suddenly inspired. Her mother couldn't talk—at least, not in the literal sense—but she *might* have something valuable to tell.

The idea made Alex sick to her stomach. She propped her forehead on the palms of her hands and closed her eyes. Did she have the fortitude to do it?

She groped for alternatives, but came up empty-handed. She needed evidence, and she could think of only one place to look for it.

Before she could change her mind, she switched off the heater and left the office. Avoiding the unreliable elevator, she jogged up the stairs, hoping that she would catch Judge Joe Wallace before he left for the day.

She anxiously checked her wristwatch. It was almost five o'clock. She didn't want to put this off until tomorrow. Now that her mind was made up, she wanted to act on her decision before she had the time and opportunity to back out.

The corridors on the second floor were deserted. Jurors had been dismissed for the day. Trials were in recess until tomorrow. Her footsteps echoed loudly as she made her way toward the judge's chambers adjacent to the empty courtroom. His secretary was still in the anteroom, and none too pleased to see her.

"I need to speak with the judge immediately." Alex was out of breath after quickly climbing two flights of stairs, and her voice was tinged with desperation.

"He's fixin' to leave for the day," she was told with a lack of apology. "I can make an appoint—"

"This is vitally important, or I wouldn't bother him at this time of day."

Alex wasn't intimidated by Mrs. Lipscomb's censorious stare or the retiring sigh she emitted as she left her desk and moved to the connecting door. She knocked discreetly, then went inside, closing the door behind her. Alex paced impatiently until she returned.

"He's agreed to see you. Briefly."

"Thank you." Alex rushed past her and into the chambers.

"Well, what is it this time, Miss Gaither?" Judge Wallace barked at her the instant she crossed the threshold. He was pulling on his overcoat. "You seem to have a nasty habit of showing up without an appointment. As you can see, I'm leaving. My daughter Stacey doesn't like to hold dinner, and it would be rude of me to expect her to."

"I apologize to both of you, Judge. As I told your secretary, it's urgent that I talk to you this afternoon."

"Well?" he demanded cantankerously.

"Could we sit down?"

"I can talk standing up. What do you want?"

"I want you to issue a court order to have my mother's body exhumed."

The judge sat down then. Or rather, he dropped down into the chair in front of which he was standing. He stared up at Alex with undisguised dismay.

"I beg your pardon?" he wheezed.

"I believe you heard me, Judge Wallace, although if it's necessary to repeat my request, I will."

He waved his hand. "No. Good Lord, no. Hearing it once was bad enough." He cupped each knee with a hand and continued to stare up at her, apparently thinking she was certifiable. "Why would you want to do such a ghastly thing as that?"

"I don't *want* to. I wouldn't ask for a court order if I didn't think exhumation was absolutely necessary."

Having recovered some of his aplomb, he ungraciously indicated a chair. "You might as well sit. Explain your reasons."

"A crime was committed, but I can find no incriminating evidence."

"I told you you wouldn't," he exclaimed. "You didn't listen. You came charging in here, slinging unfounded accusations, bent on getting vengeance."

"That's not true," she denied evenly.

"That's how I read it. What does Pat Chastain have to say about this?"

"The D.A. is unavailable. It seems he's spontaneously taken a few days' vacation and gone hunting."

The judge harrumphed. "Sounds like a damn good idea to me."

It sounded cowardly to Alex, and she'd been ready to chew nails when the aloof Mrs. Chastain had informed her of it. "Will you permit me to look for evidence, Judge?"

"There is no evidence," he stressed.

"My mother's remains might provide some."

"She was autopsied when she was killed. That was twenty-five years ago, for crissake."

"With all due respect to the coroner at that time, he might not have been looking for clues when the cause of death was so readily apparent. I know an excellent forensic specialist in Dallas. We use him frequently. If there is anything to be found, he'll find it."

"I can guarantee you that he won't."

"It's worth a try, isn't it?"

He gnawed at the corner of his lip. "I'll take your request under advisement."

Alex recognized a brush-off when she saw one. "I'd appreciate an answer tonight."

"Sorry, Miss Gaither. The best I can do is think about it overnight and give you an answer in the morning. Between now and then, I hope you'll change your mind and withdraw the request."

"I won't."

He stood up. "I'm tired, hungry, and damned perturbed that you've put me in this awkward position." He aimed an accusatory index finger at her. "I don't like messes."

"Neither do I. I wish this weren't necessary."

"It isn't."

"I believe it is," she countered stubbornly.

"In the long run, you'll be sorry you ever asked me for this. Now, you've taken up enough of my time. Stacey will be worried. Good night."

He marched from the room. A few seconds later, Mrs. Lipscomb appeared in the doorway. Her eyelids were fluttering with indignation. "Imogene told me you'd mean trouble around here."

Alex swept past her and returned to her temporary office, only long enough to retrieve her belongings. The drive out to the Westerner took longer than usual because she got caught up in Purcell's rush hour. To further complicate the snarled traffic, it began to sleet.

Knowing she wouldn't want to go out again, she picked up a box of carryout fried chicken. By the time she spread the meal on the round table near the windows of her room, the food was cold and tasted like cardboard. She promised herself that she would buy some fruit and healthy snack food to supplement her unbalanced diet, and maybe a bouquet of fresh flowers to brighten the dismal room. She debated taking down the lurid painting of the bullfighter that dominated one wall. The swirling red cape and slavering bull were real eyesores.

Loath to review her notes again, she decided to switch on the TV. The HBO movie she watched was a comedy she didn't have to think about. She was feeling better by the time it was over, and decided to take a shower.

She had just dried off and wrapped her wet hair in a towel when someone knocked on her door. Pulling on her long, white terry cloth robe and knotting the tie at her waist, she peered through the peephole.

She opened the door as far as the chain lock would allow. "What are you, the Welcome Wagon?"

"Open the door," Sheriff Lambert said.

"What for?"

"I need to talk to you."

"About what?"

"I'll tell you when I get inside." Alex didn't move. "Are you going to open the door, or what?"

"I can talk to you from here."

"Open the friggin' door," he shouted. "I'm freezing my balls off."

Alex slid the chain out of its mooring, then pulled the door open and stood aside. Reede stamped his feet and brushed off the ice pellets that were clinging to the fur collar of his coat.

He looked her up and down. "Expecting someone?"

Alex crossed her arms over her middle, a gesture meant to convey her annoyance. "If this is a social call—"

"It isn't." He caught his finger between his teeth and pulled off one leather glove, then the other. He slapped the felt cowboy hat against his thigh to shake off the sleet, then ran a hand through his hair.

He tossed the gloves into the crown of his hat, set the hat down on the table and lowered himself into a chair. He eyed the remains of her supper, then took a bite out of an untouched drumstick. Munching, he asked, "You don't like our fried chicken?"

He was slouched in the chair, looking like he had settled in for the night. Alex remained standing. She felt absurdly exposed in the robe, even though it covered her from jaw to ankles. Having a motel towel wrapped around her head didn't help boost her self-confidence.

She tried to appear indifferent to him and her own dishabille. "No, I didn't like the fried chicken, but it was convenient. I didn't want to go out to eat."

"Smart decision on a night like this. The roads are getting treacherous."

"You could have told me that over the phone."

Ignoring that, he leaned far to one side and looked past her at the television screen, where an unclothed coupled were carnally involved. The camera moved in for a close-up of the man's lips against the woman's breast.

"No wonder you're mad that I interrupted."

She smacked the power button with her palm. The screen went blank. "I wasn't watching."

When she turned back around, he was looking up at her, smiling. "Do you always open your door to any man who knocks on it?"

"I didn't open my door until you swore at me."

"Is that all a man has to do, talk dirty?"

"You're the highest-ranking law enforcement officer in this county. If I can't trust you, who can I trust?" She was thinking she would trust a used car salesman in a green polyester suit before she would trust Reede Lambert. "And was it really necessary to strap that on when you came calling?"

He followed the direction of her gaze down to the holster riding just below his belt. He stretched his booted feet far out in front of him and crossed them at the ankles. Templing his fingers, he peered at her over their tips. "I never know when I might have to use it."

"Is it always loaded?"

He hesitated, his eyes lowering to the vicinity of her breasts. "Always."

They were no longer talking about the pistol in his holster. But more than what was actually being said, the tone of the conversation made her distinctly uncomfortable. She shifted her weight from one bare foot to the other and dampened her lips, only then realizing that she had already removed her makeup. Somehow, that made her feel even more vulnerable. That, and his motionless, broody stare.

"Why did you come here tonight? What couldn't wait until morning?"

"An urge."

"An urge?" she repeated huskily.

He languidly got up out of the chair and moved forward until he stood only inches in front of her. He slipped his rough hand into the parting of her robe and encircled her neck with it. "Yeah, an urge," he whispered. "An urge to throttle you."

Uttering a frustrated grunt Alex removed his hand and stepped aside. By choice, he let her go. "Judge Wallace called me tonight and told me about the court order you asked him for."

Her heart, which had been beating furiously, slowed down, but she muttered a curse of aggravation. "Isn't anything private in this town?"

"Not much, no."

"I don't think I could sneeze without everybody within the city limits offering me a Kleenex."

"You're in the spotlight, all right. What do you expect, going around asking to dig up a body?"

"You make it sound so whimsical."

"Well, isn't it?"

"Do you think I'd disturb my mother's grave if I didn't think it was a vital step toward solving her murder?" she asked heatedly. "My God, do you think it was easy for me to even voice the request? And why did the judge feel it necessary to consult you, *you,* of all people?"

"Why not me? Because I'm a suspect?"

"Yes!" she cried. "Discussing this case with you is highly unethical."

"I'm the sheriff, remember?"

"I never forget it. That's still no excuse for Judge Wallace to go behind my back. Why is he so nervous about having the body exhumed? Is he afraid a forensic investigation will reveal something he helped to cover up?"

"Your request presented him with a problem."

"I'll just bet it did! Who is he trying to protect by keeping that coffin sealed?"

"You."

"Me?"

"Celina's body can't be exhumed. She was cremated."

TWELVE

Reede couldn't figure out why he had elected to go to the seediest tavern along the highway for a drink when he had a perfectly good bottle of whiskey at home. Maybe it was because his frame of mind matched the dark, murky atmosphere of the honky-tonk.

He felt like shit.

He signaled for the bartender to pour him another drink. The Last Chance Bar was the kind of place that refilled glasses; customers didn't get a clean one with each round.

"Thanks," Reede said, watching the whiskey splash into his glass.

"You staking us out undercover, or what?" the bartender quipped.

Without moving anything but his eyes, Reede looked up at him. "I'm having a drink. Is that all right with you?"

The silly grin collapsed. "Sure, Sheriff, sure." The bartender backed away to the opposite end of the bar, where he'd been carrying on a conversation with two friendlier patrons.

Reede noticed that one booth across the room was occupied by women. Surrounding the pool table was a trio of guys whom he recognized as wild well controllers. They were usually a rowdy bunch who partied hard between each dangerous gig. For the time being, they were peaceable enough.

Pasty Hickam and Ruby Faye Turner were cuddled in another booth. Reede had heard in the B & B that morning that Angus had canned the old ranch hand. Pasty had made a damn stupid mistake, but Reede thought the punishment was severe. Apparently, Pasty was being consoled by his latest flame. Reede had doffed his hat in their general direction when he had come in. They gave every appearance of wanting to be ignored as much as he wanted to ignore them.

It was a slow night at the Last Chance, which suited the sheriff just fine for professional as well as personal reasons.

He had gulped his first drink, barely tasting it. This one he sipped because he needed it to last longer. Nursing it delayed going home. Being alone didn't hold much appeal for Reede. Neither did passing time in the Last Chance, but it was better than the first option. At least, tonight it was.

The whiskey had started a slow fire in his belly. It had made the twinkling Christmas lights, strung year-'round over the bar, seem brighter and prettier. The dinginess of the place wasn't so obvious when viewed through whiskey fumes.

Since he was beginning to mellow, he decided this would be his last drink of the night, another reason to savor it. Reede never drank to the point of intoxication. Never. He'd had to clean up after his old man had puked up everything but his toenails too many times for him to think that getting shit-faced was fun.

When he was just a kid, he remembered thinking that he might grow up to be a jailbird or a monk, an astronaut or a post-hole digger, a zookeeper or a big game hunter, but one thing he was *not* going to be was a drunk. They already had one of those in the family, and that was one too many.

"Hiya, Reede."

The sound of the breathy, feminine voice interrupted his contemplation of the amber contents of his glass. He raised his head and immediately saw a plump set of tits.

She was wearing a skin tight black T-shirt with BORN BAD spelled out in glittering red letters. Her jeans were so tight she had difficulty climbing onto the bar stool. She managed, but not without jiggling her breasts and pressing Reede's thigh in the process. Her smile was as brilliant as a zirconium ring, and not nearly as genuine. Her name was Gloria, Reede remembered, just in time to be courteous.

"Hi, Gloria."

"Buy me a beer?"

"Sure." He called out the order to the bartender. Glancing pointedly over his shoulder, Reede called her attention to the group of friends she'd left sitting in the booth across the dim tavern.

"Don't mind them," she said, flirtatiously tapping his arm where it rested on the bar. "It's every girl for herself after ten o'clock."

"Ladies' night out?"

"Hmm." She tipped the long-neck to her glossy lips and drank. "We were headed for Abilene to see the new Richard Gere movie, but the weather turned so bad, we said what the hell, and decided to stay in town. Wha'chu been up to tonight? You on duty?"

"For a while. I'm off now." Reluctant to be drawn into conversation, he returned to his drink.

Gloria wasn't going to be dismissed that easily. She scooted as close to him as the barstool would allow and threw her arm across his shoulders. "Poor Reede. It must get awful lonesome riding around by yourself all the time."

"I'm working when I'm riding around."

"I know, but still . . ." Her breath fanned his ear. It smelled like beer. "It's no wonder you frown so much." A sharp fingernail plowed the deep furrow between his eyebrows. He jerked his head back, away from her touch. She snatched her hand back and uttered a soft, wounded sound.

"Look, I'm sorry," he muttered. "My mood's as bad as the weather. It's been a long day. Guess I'm just tired."

Rather than putting her off, that encouraged her. "Maybe I could cheer you up, Reede," she said with a timorous smile. "Anyway, I'd sure like to try." Again she moved close, sandwiching his upper arm between her cushiony breasts. "I've had the wildest crush on you since I was in seventh grade. Don't make out like you didn't know," she said with a scolding pout.

"No, I didn't know that."

"Well, I did. But you were taken then. What was that girl's name? The one that loony killed in the stable?"

"Celina."

"Yeah. You were real gone on her, weren't you? By the time I got to high school, you were at Texas Tech. Then I got married and started having kids." She didn't notice that he wasn't interested in her chatter. " 'Course, the husband's long gone, and the kids are old enough now to take care of themselves. I guess there never was much chance for you to know I had a crush on you, was there?"

"I guess not."

She leaned so far forward, her perch on the stool became precarious. "Maybe it's time you did, Reede."

He glanced down at her breasts, which were making teasing, brushing contact with his arm. As a result, her nipples made hard, distinct impressions against her T-shirt. Somehow, the blatancy wasn't as enticing as Alex's innocent, bare toes peeking out from beneath her white terry-cloth bathrobe. Knowing that there was nothing but Gloria under the black T-shirt didn't excite him as much as wondering what, if anything, was under Alex's white robe.

He wasn't aroused, not even a little. He wondered why.

Gloria was pretty enough. Black hair curled around her face and emphasized dark eyes that were now lambent with invitation and promise. Her lips were parted and wet, but he wasn't sure he could kiss them without sliding off. They were coated with cherry-red lipstick. Involuntarily, he compared them to lips free of makeup, but still pink and moist, kissable and sexy, without making any attempt to be.

"I gotta be going," he said suddenly. He unhooked his boot heels from the rungs of the stool and came to his feet, fishing in the pocket of his jeans for enough bills to cover the price of his drinks and her beer.

"But, I thought—"

"Better get back to your group, or you're liable to miss the party."

The wild well control boys had ventured toward the women, who were making no secret of being on the prowl and out for a good time. The merging of the two groups had been as inevitable as a hard freeze by morning. The delay had been calculated to build the anticipation. Now, however, sexual innuendos were being swapped at a rate to match the stock exchange on a busy day.

"Nice seeing you, Gloria."

Reede pulled his hat down low over his brows and left, but not before catching her wounded expression. Alex's face had held that same devastated, disbelieving expression when he had told her that her mother's body had been cremated.

Seconds after he had uttered the words, she recoiled against the wall, clutching the lapels of her robe to her throat as if she was warding off something evil. "Cremated?"

"That's right." He watched her face turn pale, and her eyes turn glassy.

"I didn't know. Grandma never said. I never thought . . ."

Her voice dwindled into nothingness. He remained silent and unmoving, figuring that she needed time to digest that sobering piece of information.

He had mentally cursed Joe Wallace for dumping such a rotten task on him. The goddamn coward had called him, fit to be tied, whining and carrying on, asking what he should tell her. When Reede suggested that Alex be told the truth, the judge had interpreted it as volunteering and had been all too willing to abdicate the responsibility.

Alex's numbness hadn't lasted long. Her senses returned abruptly, as though she'd been jarred into consciousness by a thought. "Did Judge Wallace know?"

Reede remembered shrugging with feigned indifference. "Look, all I know is that he called me and said that what you wanted to do was impossible, even if he had handed down a court order, which he would have been reluctant to do."

"If he knew mother's body had been cremated, why didn't he tell me himself this afternoon?"

"My guess would be that he didn't want a scene on his hands."

"Yes," she murmured distractedly, "he doesn't like messes. He told me so." She looked at him without expression. "He sent you to do his dirty work. Messes don't bother you."

Reede, declining to comment, pulled on his gloves and replaced his hat. "You've had a jolt. Are you going to be okay?"

"I'm fine."

"You don't look fine."

Her blue eyes were filled with tears and her mouth trembled slightly. She clasped her hands at her waist, as though forcibly holding herself together. That's when he had wanted to put his arms around her and hold her close, wet hair, damp towel, bathrobe, bare toes, and all.

That's when he had moved forward and, before he even realized what he was doing, forcibly pulled her arms out to her sides. She had resisted, as though wanting to cover a bleeding wound.

Before she reconstructed that barrier, he slid his arms around her and pulled her against him. She was dewy and warm and fragrant, fragile in her grief. She seemed to wilt against him. Her arms dangled listlessly at her sides.

"Oh, God, please don't make me go through this," she had whispered, and he had felt her breasts tremble. She rolled her head toward him, until her face was making an impression on his chest and he could feel her tears through his clothes.

He had angled his head to secure hers against him. The towel wrapping her hair unwound and fell to the floor. Her hair was damp and fragrant against his face.

He told himself now that he hadn't kissed it, but he knew his lips had brushed her hair and then her temple, and rested there.

At that point, a severe case of lust had seized him, and it had been so powerful it was a wonder to him now that he hadn't acted on it.

Instead he had left, feeling like crap for having to tell her something like that and then slinking out like a snake. Staying with her had been out of the question. His desire to hold her hadn't been nobly inspired, and he didn't try to kid himself into believing it was. He'd wanted gratification. He had wanted to cover that hurting, courageous smile with hot, hard kisses.

He swore to his dashboard now as he drove the Blazer down the highway, heading in the opposite direction from home. Sleet froze on the windshield before the wipers could whisk it off. He was driving too fast for the weather conditions—the pavement was like an ice rink—but he kept going.

He was too old for this. What the hell was he doing entertaining sexual fantasies? He hadn't consciously done that since he and Junior had jerked off while drooling over centerfolds. Yet, at no time in recent memory had his fantasies been so vivid.

Completely forgetting who Alex was, he had envisioned his hands parting that white bathrobe and finding underneath it smooth, ivory flesh; hard, pink nipples; soft, auburn hair. Her thighs would be soft, and between them she would be creamy.

Cursing, he squeezed his eyes shut for a moment. She wasn't just *any* woman who happened to be eighteen years younger than himself. She was Celina's daughter, and he was old enough to be her daddy, for crissake. He wasn't, but he could have been. He very well could have been. Knowing that made his stomach feel a little queasy, but it did nothing to decrease the thick hard-on now testing the durability of his fly.

He wheeled the truck into the deserted parking lot, cut the engine, and bounded up the steps to the door. He tried it, and when he discovered it was locked, pounded on it with his gloved fists.

Eventually, the door was opened by a woman as broad-breasted as a pigeon. She was wearing a long, white satin peignoir that might have looked bridal had there not been a black cigarette anchored in the corner of her lips. In her arms she was holding an apricot-colored cat. She was stroking his luxurious fur with an idle hand. Woman and cat glared at Reede.

"What the hell are you doing here?" she demanded.

"Why do most men come here, Nora Gail?" Rudely, he brushed past her and went inside. If he'd been anybody else, he would have been shot right between the eyes with the pistol she kept hidden in the garter belt she always wore.

"Obviously, you haven't noticed. Business was so slow tonight, we closed early."

"Since when has that mattered to you and me?"

"Since you started taking advantage. Like now."

"Don't give me any lip tonight." He was already at the top of the stairs, heading toward her private room. "I don't want conversation. I don't want to be entertained. I just want to be screwed, okay?"

Propping her fist on a generous and shapely hip, the madam's voice dripped sarcasm as she called up to him, "Do I have time to put the cat out first?"

Alex was unable to sleep, so she was awake when the telephone rang. It still alarmed her because of the hour. Instead of turning on the nightstand lamp, she groped in the darkness for the receiver and brought it to her ear. "Hello," she croaked, her voice hoarse from crying earlier. "Hello," she repeated.

"Hidy, Miz Gaither."

Her heart raced with excitement, but she said crossly, "You again? I hope you're ready to talk, since you woke me from a sound sleep." She'd learned from Greg that reluctant witnesses were often more prone to talk when you diminished the importance of what they might have to say.

"Don't go gettin' hoity-toity with me, little lady. I know sumpthin' you want to know. Bad."

"Such as?"

"Such as who did in yore mama."

Alex concentrated on regulating her breathing. "I think you're bluffing."

"I ain't."

"Then, tell me. Who was it?"

"You think I'm stupid, lady? You think Lambert ain't bugged yore telephone?"

"You've seen too many movies." All the same, she looked suspiciously at the receiver she held in her hand.

"You know where the Last Chance is?"

"I'll find it."

"Tomorrow evenin'." He specified a time.

"How'll I know you?"

"I'll know you."

Before she could say anything else, he hung up. Alex sat on the edge of the bed for a moment, staring into the darkness. She recalled Reede's warning about getting hurt. Her imaginative mind conjured up all the horrible things that could happen to a woman alone. By the time she lay back down, her palms were sweating and sleep was even more elusive.

 # THIRTEEN

"You'll never guess what she's up to now."

Purcell County's sheriff lifted the steaming coffee mug to his lips, blew into it, and sipped. It scorched his tongue. He didn't care. He needed a fix of caffeine in the worst way.

"Who are we talking about?" he asked the deputy who was standing in the doorway of his private office, wearing a goofy grin that annoyed the hell out of him. He didn't like guessing games, and he was especially in no mood for one this morning.

The deputy jerked his head in the direction of the other side of the building. "Our resident prosecutor with the baby blues, perky tits, and the legs that go on forever." He kissed the air with a noisy, juicy smack of his lips.

Reede slowly lowered his feet from the corner of his desk. His eyes glittered with a frigid light. "Are you referring to Miss Gaither?"

The deputy didn't have an overabundance of gray matter, but he knew when he'd gone too far. "Uh, yeah. I mean, yes, sir."

"Well?" Reede demanded darkly.

"That funeral parlor man, Mr. Davis, well sir, he just called, raisin' Cain on account of her. She's over there now going through his files and all."

"*What?*"

"Yes, sir, that's what he said, Sheriff Lambert. He's good and pissed off because—"

"Call him back and tell him I'm on my way." Reede was already reaching for his coat. If the deputy hadn't sidestepped quickly, he'd have been run down as Reede rushed through the door.

He was impervious to the inclement weather that had kept schools and most businesses closed. They could handle snow, but an inch-thick sheet of ice covering everything was another matter. Unfortunately, the sheriff's office never closed.

Mr. Davis met him at the door, anxiously wringing his hands. "I've been in business for over thirty years and nothing like this—*nothing,* Sheriff Lambert— has ever happened to me before. I've had caskets disappear. I've been robbed. I even had—"

"Where is she?" Reede barked, cutting short the funeral director's litany.

The man pointed. Reede stamped toward the closed door and wrenched it open. Alex, seated behind a desk, looked up expectantly. "Just what the hell do you think you're doing?"

"Good morning, Sheriff."

"Answer my question." Reede slammed the door and strode into the room. "I've got a hysterical undertaker on my hands because of you, lady. How'd you get here, anyway?"

"I drove."

"You can't drive in this."

"I did."

"What is all this?" With an angry swipe of his hand, he indicated the files strewn across the desk.

"Mr. Davis's records for the year my mother was killed. He gave me permission to sort through them."

"You coerced him."

"I did no such thing."

"Intimidated him, then. Did he ask to see your search warrant?"

"No."

"Do you have one?"

"No. But I can get one."

"Not without probable cause."

"I want proof positive that Celina Gaither's body is not interred in that grave at the cemetery."

"Why didn't you do something sensible, like get a shovel and start digging?"

That silenced her. It took her a moment to recover. At last she said, "You're in a surly mood this morning. Rough night?"

"Yeah, I got laid, but it wasn't very good."

Her eyes dropped to the littered table. "Oh. I'm sorry to hear that."

"What, that I got laid?"

She gazed back up at him. "No, that it wasn't very good."

They shared a lengthy stare. His face looked as rugged and craggy as a mountain range, but it was one of the most appealing she'd ever encountered.

Whenever they were together, she was involuntarily aware of him, of his body, of the way she was drawn to him. She knew her attraction was unethical and reckless, from a professional standpoint, and compromising, from a personal one. He'd belonged to her mother first.

Yet, too often she wanted to touch him or to be touched by him. Last night she'd wanted him to hold her longer while she cried. Thankfully, he'd had better sense and had left.

Who had he gone to? Alex wondered. Where and when had the unsatisfactory lovemaking taken place? Had it been before or after he'd come to her motel room? Why hadn't it been any good?

Several moments elapsed before she lowered her head and resumed sorting through the files.

Not one to be ignored, he reached across the table and placed his hand beneath her chin, jerking it toward him. "I told you that Celina was cremated."

She jumped to her feet. "*After* you and Judge Wallace put your heads together and discussed it. That seems a little convenient to me."

"You enjoy imagining things."

"Why didn't Junior mention that Celina had been cremated when he saw me in the cemetery? I'm thinking that maybe she *is* buried there. That's why I'm going through all these files."

"Why would I lie about it?"

"To keep me from having the body exhumed."

"Again, why? What difference would that make to me?"

"Life imprisonment," she said tightly, "if the forensic report implicated you as her murderer."

"Ah . . ." At a loss for a word foul enough, he slammed his fist into his opposite palm and ground it against the tough flesh. "Is this what they teach you in law school—to start grasping at straws when all else fails?"

"Exactly."

He planted his hands firmly on the desk and leaned far across it. "You're not a lawyer, you're a witch hunter."

That stung because Alex did feel like one. This search had a vigilante desperation to it that left a bad taste in her mouth. She sat back down and laid her hands on top of the open files.

Turning her head away, she stared out at the winter landscape. The naked branches of the sycamore trees on the lawn were encased in tubes of ice. Sleet pellets made tiny pinging sounds against the windowpanes. The sky and everything below it were a dead, dismal gray. Lines of distinction were imprecise. The world was monochromatic—without light and shadows.

Some things, however, were black and white. Chief among them was the law.

"That might be true if there hadn't been a crime, Reede," she said, bringing her head back around. "But there was. Somebody went into that stable and stabbed my mother."

"With a scalpel. Right," he said scoffingly. "Can you envision Angus, Junior or me wielding a surgical instrument? Why not kill her with our bare hands? Strangle her?"

"Because you're all too clever. One of you made it to look like a mentally unbalanced man had done it." She splayed her hand upon her chest and asked earnestly, "In my place, wouldn't you want to know who that someone was and why he did it? You loved Celina. If you didn't kill her—"

"I didn't."

"Then, don't you want to know who did? Or are you afraid that her killer will turn out to be somebody else you love?"

"No, I don't want to know," he said emphatically. "And until you obtain a search warrant—"

"Miss Gaither?" Mr. Davis interrupted, entering the room. "Is this what you're looking for? I found it in a file cabinet in my storeroom." He handed her a folder, then scuttled out under Reede's baleful stare.

Alex read the name typed across the top of the file. She glanced at Reede, then eagerly opened the cover. After scanning the first of several forms, she sank into her chair and reported huskily, "It says here that her body was cremated." Her heart feeling like lead, she closed the folder and rhetorically asked, "Why didn't my grandmother ever mention that?"

"She probably didn't think it was significant."

"She saved everything, Celina's clothes, her things. Why wouldn't she have taken the ashes?"

Suddenly, she leaned forward, rested her elbows on the table, and supported her head with both hands. Her stomach churned mutinously. Fresh tears were building behind her lids, making them sting. "God, this is morbid, but I've got to know. I've *got* to."

After taking a few deep breaths, she reopened the file and began to flip through the various forms. Reading one, she sucked in her breath sharply.

"What is it?"

She lifted the sheet out of the folder and handed it to Reede. "This is a receipt for all of mother's funeral expenses, including the cremation."

"So?"

"Look at the signature."

"Angus Minton," he read softly, thoughtfully.

"You didn't know?" He shook his head. "It appears that Angus paid for everything, and wanted to keep it a secret from everybody." Alex drew a shuddering breath and gazed at Reede inquisitively. "I wonder why."

Across town, Stacey Wallace entered the room that served as her father's office away from the courthouse. He was bent over the desk, poring through a legal tome. "Judge," she chided him affectionately, "as long as you're taking the day off, you should really take it off."

"It's not an official day off," he grumbled, giving the wintry view through the window a disgusted glance. "I've needed to catch up on some reading. Today's the perfect day for it, since I can't get to the courthouse."

"You've been working too hard and worrying too much."

"You're not telling me anything that my ulcer hasn't already."

Stacey sensed that he was extremely upset. "What's wrong?"

"It's that Gaither girl."

"Celina's daughter? She's still pestering you?"

"She came to my office yesterday wanting a court order to have the body exhumed."

"My God!" Stacey exclaimed in a disbelieving whisper. She raised a pale hand to the base of her throat. "The woman sounds like a fiend."

"Fiendish or not, I had to deny the request."

"Good for you."

He shook his head. "I had no choice. The body had been cremated."

Stacey pondered that. "Seems like I remember that now. How'd she take that news?"

"I don't know. Reede delivered it."

"Reede?"

"I called him last night. He volunteered. I would guess she didn't take it well."

"Do Angus and Junior know about this?"

"I'm sure they do by now. Reede would have told them."

"Probably," Stacey murmured. For a moment she was quiet. Then she roused herself and asked, "Can I bring you anything?"

"Not so soon after breakfast, thanks."

"Some hot tea?"

"Not now."

"Cocoa? Why don't you let me—"

"Stacey, I said, no thanks." He spoke with more impatience than he intended.

"I'm sorry I bothered you," she said dejectedly. "If you need me, I'll be upstairs."

The judge gave her an absentminded nod and dipped back into the leather-bound legal volume. Stacey quietly closed the study door. Her hand listlessly trailed the banister rail as she went upstairs to her bedroom. She didn't feel well. Her abdomen was swollen and achy. She'd started her period that morning.

The mid-forties seemed like a ludicrous time to be suffering cramps like a teenager, although Stacey supposed she should welcome these monthly fluxes. They were her only reminders that she was a woman. No children came to her asking for lunch money or help with homework. No husband demanded to know what she had cooked for dinner, or if she'd picked up his cleaning, or if he could expect sex that night.

Daily she lamented not having all that glorious chaos in her life. As regularly as some people said prayers, Stacey enumerated to God the amenities of life that he had denied her. She longed for the racket of children running through the house. She yearned to have a husband reach for her in the night, to nuzzle her breasts and satisfy her hungering, restless body.

Like a priest who takes up self-flagellation, she went to her bureau, opened the third drawer, and took out the photograph album with the embossed white leather cover.

She opened it with reverence. One by one, she fondled the precious mementos—a yellowed newspaper clipping with her picture, a small square paper napkin with silver letters spelling out two names in one corner, a crumbling rose.

She leafed through the plastic binders, gazing at the photographs pressed between them. The people posing for the pictures in front of the altar had changed very little over the years.

After nearly an hour of masochistic reverie, Stacey closed the album and replaced it in its sacred drawer. Stepping out of her shoes so as not to spoil the comforter on her bed, she lay down and drew her pillow against her chest, snuggling it against her curved body like a lover.

Hot, salty tears leaked from her eyes. She whispered a name, urgently and repeatedly. She ground the heel of her hand over her lower body to relieve the pain of emptiness inside her womb, which had been a receptacle for his body, but never his love.

 # FOURTEEN

"**H**ey, what the hell, you two?" Junior exclaimed, dividing his puzzled glance between Alex and Reede. Then, buffeted by a gust of wind, he moved out of the doorway and urged them inside. "Come in. I couldn't imagine who'd come calling on a day like this. Reede, you ought to have your head examined for dragging Alex all the way out here."

He was wearing an ancient pair of jeans with the knees worn through, a cotton sweater, and thick white socks. It looked like he hadn't been up very long. In one hand he was holding a steaming mug of coffee; in the other, a trashy paperback novel. His hair was appealingly mussed. Stubble shadowed the lower half of his face.

Having recovered from the surprise of finding them on his doorstep, he smiled down at Alex. She thought he looked terrific and figured that most of the women in the world would agree with her. He looked lazy and rich, sexy and rumpled, comfortable and cushy. He invited snuggling, and his slow smile suggested that's what he'd been doing when they had interrupted.

"I didn't drag her out here," Reede said touchily. "It was the other way around."

"I was willing to come alone," Alex snapped.

"Well, I wasn't willing to let you become a highway statistic in my county," he shouted. Turning to Junior, who was bemusedly taking in their heated exchange, Reede said, "To make a long story short, I drove her out here because she was determined to come and I was afraid she'd kill herself—or worse, somebody else—on these roads. So, here we are."

"Well, I'm damned glad you're here," Junior said. "I had resigned myself to spending a boring day here alone. I've got a great fire going in the living room, and all the makings for hot toddies. Follow me." He set off, but turned and added, "Ooops, Reede, you know how Mother is about having the floors tracked up. Better take your boots off."

"Fuck that. Is Lupe in the kitchen? I'm gonna try and sweet-talk her out of some breakfast." Giving no regard to Sarah Jo's floors, he tramped toward the back of the house as though he still lived there.

Alex watched him disappear through a doorway. "Did he say *sweet talk?*" she asked caustically.

"Oh, he's in a sunny mood today," Junior remarked negligently. "You ought to see him when he's really pissed. Leave Reede to Lupe. She knows how he likes his eggs. He'll feel better once he eats."

Alex let him help her off with her coat. "I hope this isn't too much of an intrusion."

"Hell, no. I wasn't kidding when I said I'm glad you're here." He threw his arm across her shoulders. "Let's—"

"Actually," Alex said, shrugging off his arm, "this isn't a social call."

"Business, huh?"

"Yes, and extremely important. Is Angus here?"

"He's in his den." His smile was still in place, but it had stiffened.

"Is he busy?"

"I don't think so. Come on, I'll take you back."

"I hate to tear you away from your novel."

He glanced dubiously at the torrid cover. "Doesn't matter. It was getting monotonous."

"What's it about?"

"A legendary cock's sojourn through most of the bedrooms in Hollywood, both male and female."

"Oh, really?" Alex inquired, feigning interest. "Can I borrow it when you're finished?"

"Shame on you," he exclaimed. "I'd be corrupting the morals of a minor, wouldn't I?"

"You're not that much older than I am."

"Compared to Reede and me, you're a baby," he told her as he opened the door to the den. "Dad, we've got company."

Angus glanced up from his newspaper. In the span of several seconds his face registered surprise, irritation, then a smile.

"Hello, Angus. I hate to disturb you on a sleep-in morning like today."

"No problem. There's not much going on. We can't exercise racehorses out-doors when the ground's frozen." He left his red leather recliner and crossed the room to welcome her. "You're a bright spot on a gloomy day, that's for damn sure, hey, Junior?"

"I've already told her as much."

"But as I've told Junior," she hastened to say, "this isn't a social visit."

"Oh? Sit down, sit down." Angus waved her toward a tufted leather love seat. "I'll just—"

"No, Junior, I'd like for you to stay," Alex said before he could withdraw. "This concerns all of us."

"Okay, shoot." Junior straddled the overstuffed arm of the love seat as though it were a saddle.

"I spoke to Judge Wallace again yesterday." Alex thought she saw both men tense, but it was so fleeting, she could have imagined it.

"Any particular reason why?" Angus asked.

"I wanted to have my mother's body exhumed."

There was no mistaking their reaction this time. "Jesus, girl, why in hell would you want to do something like that?" Angus shuddered.

"Alex." Junior reached for her hand, laid it on his thigh, and massaged the back of it. "Isn't this getting a little out of hand? That's . . . that's grue-some."

"The case is gruesome," she reminded him as she eased her hand off his thigh. "Anyway, as I'm sure you know, what I asked for is impossible. My mother's body was cremated."

"That's right," Angus said.

"Why?" Her eyes were bright and intensely blue in the dim room. They reflected the fire burning in the fireplace, making them appear accusatory.

Angus resettled in his chair and hunched his shoulders defensively. "It seemed the best way to handle things."

"I fail to see how."

"Your grandmother planned to leave town with you as soon as everything was tidied up. She made no secret of it. So I decided to have Celina's body cremated, thinking that Merle might want to take the, uh, remains with her."

"You decided? By what right, Angus? Under whose authority? Why was it left to you to decide what would happen to Celina's body?"

His brows beetled with displeasure. "You think I had her body cremated to destroy evidence, is that it?"

"I don't know!" she exclaimed, rising from the love seat.

She moved to the window and stared out at the empty paddocks. Lights shone through the doors of various stables, where horses were being groomed, fed, exercised. She had thoroughly researched Minton Enterprises. Angus had millions invested in this facility. Was he reticent because he had so much to lose if she won an indictment, or because he was guilty, or both?

Eventually, she turned to face the men. "You've got to admit, in retrospect, that it seems an odd thing for you to have done."

"I only wanted to relieve Merle Graham of that responsibility. I felt I should because her daughter had been killed on my property. Merle was out of her mind with grief and had you to take care of. If what I did seems suspicious now, that's just too damn bad, young lady. I'd make the same decision if I had to do it again today."

"I'm sure Grandma Graham appreciated what you did. It was an unselfish thing to do."

Shrewdly, Angus looked at her and said, "But you wish you could believe it was entirely unselfish."

She looked him straight in the eye. "Yes, I do."

"I respect your honesty."

For a moment there was no sound in the room other than the friendly, crackling noise of burning firewood. Alex broke the awkward silence. "I wonder why Grandma didn't take the remains."

"I wondered about that myself when I offered them to her. I think it was because she couldn't face the fact that Celina was dead. An urn of ashes was tangible proof of something she couldn't accept."

Knowing how obsessed her grandmother had been with Celina's life, his explanation was feasible. Besides, unless Merle came out of her coma and Alex posed the question to her, she had no alternative but to accept as truth what Angus told her.

He was absently massaging his big toe through his sock. "I couldn't see storing her ashes in a mausoleum. I never could stand vaults and tombs. Goddamn spooky things. The very thought of them gives me the creeps. Went to New Orleans once. All those cement graves sitting on top of the ground . . . ugh."

He shook his head in repugnance. "I'm not afraid of dying, but when I go, I want to become part of the living again. Dust to dust. That's the natural cycle.

"So it seemed fitting to buy a cemetery plot and have Celina's ashes buried in the soil she grew up on. Guess you figure I'm a crazy old man, Alex, but that's how I felt about it then, and that's how I feel about it now. I didn't tell anybody because I was embarrassed. It was so sentimental, you see."

"Why not just scatter the ashes somewhere?"

He pulled on his earlobe as he pondered the question. "I thought about it, but I reckoned you might turn up one day and want to see where your mama was laid."

Alex felt her spirit slump, along with her posture. Lowering her head, she studied the toes of her suede boots, which were still damp from walking through the sleet. "I guess you think I'm a ghoul for wanting to open her grave. Reede did."

Angus made a dismissive gesture. "Reede's trigger-happy when it comes to forming opinions. Sometimes he's wrong."

She drew a shaky breath. "This time he is. Believe me, it wasn't an easy thing to even consider, much less ask for. I just thought that an extensive forensic investigation might shed some light . . ."

Her voice trailed off. She lacked the will and conviction to continue. Yesterday she had thought that an exhumation might provide the physical evidence she needed. As it had turned out, she was no closer to learning the truth, and all she had to show for her efforts was the traumatic upheaval she'd put herself and everyone else through.

Angus's explanation sounded so damned plausible and guileless. Paying all the funeral expenses, making all the arrangements, had been an act of charity to alleviate her grandmother's grim responsibility and financial burden.

Alex earnestly wanted to believe that. As Celina's daughter, it made her feel good inside. As a prosecutor, however, it left her empty-handed and frustrated and more suspicious than ever that something had been swept under the rug.

"You ready to go back to town, or what?"

Reede was standing in the doorway with his shoulder propped against the frame, insolently maneuvering a toothpick from one side of his mouth to the other. He might have eaten breakfast, but his tone of voice let her know that his foul disposition remained intact.

"Yes, I'm ready, if you'd be so kind as to drive me."

"Good. The sooner I get back to work, the better. Somebody's got to ride herd on the crazy sons of bitches out driving in this."

"As long as you're out here, why don't you spend the day by the fireplace?" Junior suggested to Alex. "We could pop popcorn. Celina used to love that. Maybe we could talk Lupe out of a batch of pralines. I could drive you back later when the roads have cleared."

"It sounds wonderful, Junior, thank you, but I've got work to do."

He wheedled charmingly, but she remained adamant. The Mintons walked her and Reede to the door. She didn't see Sarah Jo. If she were even aware that she had guests in the house, she made no effort to present herself.

Angus looped Alex's arm through his as they made their way down the hall. He spoke softly. "I know this is difficult for you, girl."

"Yes, it is."

"Heard anything about your grandma?"

"I phone the nursing home every day, but there's been no change."

"Well, holler if you need anything, you hear?"

Alex gazed at him with genuine puzzlement. "Angus, why are you being so nice to me?"

"Because of your mama, because I like you, and mainly, because we've got nothing to hide."

When he smiled at her, Alex realized that it was easy to see where Junior had come by his charm. He and Reede were engaged in their own conversation. Alex overheard Reede say, "Ran into one of your old girlfriends last night at the Last Chance."

Her ears picked up at the mention of the tavern where she had an appointment later that day.

"Oh, yes?" Junior was saying. "Who was that?"

"Gloria something. Forgot her married name. Curly black hair, dark eyes, big tits."

"Gloria Tolbert. How'd she look?"

"Horny."

Junior gave a dirty and masculine laugh. "That's Gloria. Takes a strong man to keep her satisfied."

"You ought to know," Reede said drolly.

"Well, what happened last night, you lucky bastard? Did you leave a contented smile on Gloria's pretty face?"

"You know I never discuss my love life."

"That's just one of your traits that irritates the hell out of me."

Alex turned around in time to see Junior playfully sock Reede in the gut. His fist bounced back like he'd struck a drum.

"Is that the best you can do, ol' man?" Reede taunted. "Admit it, Minton, you're losing it."

"Like hell I am." Junior took a swipe at Reede's head. The blow was dodged just in time. Reede tried to catch Junior behind the knee with his boot. They fell against the hall table, almost toppling a ceramic vase.

"Okay, boys, cut it out before you break something," Angus said indulgently, speaking to them as though they were still in grade school.

Alex and Reede pulled on their coats and he opened the door. The frigid wind swirled inside. Junior said, "Sure you can't stay here where it's cozy?"

"I'm afraid not," Alex replied.

"Shoot. Well, good-bye then." He pressed her hand between his and kissed her cheek.

Father and son watched as Reede assisted Alex over the icy stone walkway to where his Blazer was parked. He helped her up into the truck, then went around to the driver's side and vaulted in.

"Brrr," Junior said, shutting the door. "Ready for a hot toddy, Dad?"

"Not yet," Angus answered with a scowl. "It's too early in the day to be drinking hard liquor."

"Since when have you taken into consideration the time of day when you wanted a drink?"

"Get in here. I want to talk to you." Limping to favor his toe, he led his son back into the den. "Stoke up that fire, will ya?"

When the flames were licking fresh logs, Junior faced his father. "What is it? Not business, I hope. I'm taking an official day off," he said around a yawn, stretching like a sleek cat.

"Alex Gaither."

Junior pulled down his arms and frowned. "She was all fired up about that burial business when she came in, wasn't she? But you brought her around."

"I only told her the truth."

"You made it sound as convincing as a good lie."

"Will you be serious for once?" Angus barked.

Junior looked baffled. "I thought I was."

"You listen to me," Angus said sternly, aiming a finger at his son. "Only a damn fool would laugh off her determination to get to the bottom of this thing. Even if she is a good-looking woman, she means business. She looks soft, but she isn't. She's tough as boot leather when it comes to this murder case."

"I'm aware of that," Junior said sulkily.

"Ask Joe Wallace if you don't believe it."

"I do. I just find it hard to take her seriously when she looks as good as she does."

"You do, huh? Well, I don't see you doing anything about that, either."

"I asked her out here for drinks, and she came."

"What have you done since then?"

"What do you want me to do? Court her like some snot-nosed kid? Go the flowers and chocolates route?"

"Yes, goddamnit!"

"She'd never fall for that," Junior snorted, "even if I could do it with a straight face."

"You listen to me, boy. You've got life good. You drive a new Jag every year, wear a big, diamond-studded Rolex, go skiing, deep-sea fishing, and to the horse-races whenever you feel like it, and you gamble big.

"But if this little lady has her way, she'll bust us. Yeah," he said, reading his son's frown correctly, "you might have to go out and get a job for once in your life."

Angus reined in his temper and continued in a more conciliatory tone. "She hasn't got a prayer of turning up any evidence. I think she knows that. She's throwing darts into the dark and hoping to hit one of us in the ass. Sooner or later, hopefully, her arm'll get tired."

Junior chewed on his lip and said glumly. "She probably wants a court trial as much as we want a racetrack. That'd be a real coup for her. It'd launch her career."

"Damn," Angus grumbled. "You know how I feel about that. I don't like all this career bullshit. Women don't belong in courtrooms."

"Where would you keep them? In bedrooms?"

"Nothing wrong with that."

Junior laughed shortly. "You won't get an argument from me, but I imagine you would from millions of working women."

"Alex might not be working for long. It wouldn't surprise me if her career was riding on the outcome of this investigation."

"How do you mean?"

"I know all about Greg Harper. He's ambitious, sees himself in the attorney general's seat. He likes his people to win convictions. Now, if I've got him figured right, he's letting Alex do this because he smells blood, our blood. If we got our tails in a crack over this murder business, he'd get his name in the headlines and gloat every step of the way because there's no love lost between him and the governor. The governor's nose would be rubbed in shit and so would the racing commission's.

"On the other hand, if Alex fails to smoke out any skeletons in our closet, Harper'll have to eat crow. Rather than do that, he'll boot Alex out. And we'll be there with open arms to catch her when she falls," he said, jabbing the air for emphasis.

"I see you've got it all worked out," Junior remarked dryly.

Angus made a grunting sound. "Damn right I do. One of us better be concentrating on more than the fine way she fills out a sweater."

"I thought that's what you wanted me to do."

"You gotta do more than gawk and lust from afar. A love affair would be the best thing that could happen to Alex."

"How do you know she's not involved in one?"

"Because unlike you, I don't leave things to chance. I made it my business to find out. I've had her checked out."

"You cagey old bastard," Junior whispered with grudging admiration.

"Humph. You gotta know what cards the other guy's holding, son, or it does you no good to have a winning hand."

While the fire in the grate popped cheerfully, Junior contemplated all that Angus had said. Then, focusing a narrow gaze on his father, he asked, "Where would you have this love affair lead? To marriage?"

Angus slapped Junior's knee and chortled. "Would that be so bad?"

"Would you approve?"

"Why not?"

Junior wasn't sharing the laugh. He moved to the fire, away from his father's touch and conniving smile. Absently, he poked at the burning logs.

"I'm surprised," he said softly. "You didn't think Celina would make a suitable wife for me. I remember the ruckus you raised when I told you I wanted to marry her."

"You were eighteen then, boy!" Angus shouted. "Celina was a widow with a baby."

"Yes. Alex. And look how fine she turned out. She could have been my stepdaughter."

Angus's brows drew together over the bridge of his nose. They were a dependable gauge of his temper. The steeper the vee, the angrier he was. "There were other considerations."

Junior spun around. "Like what?"

"That was twenty-five years ago, another time, another person. Alex isn't her mother. She's got more beauty, and a hell of a lot more brains. If you were half the man you're supposed to be—if, for once, you'd think with your head instead of your pecker—you'd see how valuable it'd be to have her standing by your side."

Junior blushed with anger. "I *can* see all that. I just wanted to make damn certain before I started a courtship that you would approve of it this time. Whether you want to believe it or not, I loved Celina. And if I start romancing Alex, I might just fall in love with her, too. For real. Not for you, not for the corporation, but for myself."

He stamped toward the door. Angus called his name sharply. Out of habit, Junior stopped and turned around. "You resent this lecture, don't you, boy?"

"Yes," he stormed. "I'm a grown man, not a boy. I don't need your coaching. I know how to handle Alex, or any other woman you can name."

"Oh, you do?" Angus asked silkily.

"Yeah, I do."

"Then why did Alex leave you today and go off with Reede?"

Upstairs, Sarah Jo eavesdropped on the raging conversation. When Junior slunk into the living room and she heard the clatter of glassware, she silently closed the door to her sanctum and leaned back against it. Her chest rose and fell with a heavy, despairing sigh.

It was happening again.

There seemed to be no escaping this nightmare. Junior was going to have his heart broken again, this time by Celina's daughter because she would come between Alex and his father and his best friend. History was repeating itself. The house was in an uproar, and all because of that girl.

Sarah Jo knew she wouldn't be able to stand it. No, she was quite sure she wouldn't. The first time, she had failed to protect Junior from heartache. She wouldn't be able to protect him this time, either.

And that broke her heart.

 # FIFTEEN

She'd had every opportunity to be mugged, raped, or murdered, or any combination thereof, in the Last Chance. Not to mention the chances she'd taken on the roads there and back. Luckily, she had left unscathed, except for her riled temper.

Entering her motel room, Alex slung her handbag and coat in the chair, furious with herself for chasing after what was obviously a red herring. Greg Harper would have a field day if he ever found out she'd been so gullible.

That afternoon, she had called him. He wasn't impressed with her findings so far, and made another pitch for her to return to Austin and reconcile herself to the past. She had held him to the time he'd allotted her.

His disfavor with her lack of results was one reason she had put so much stock in her clandestine meeting tonight. Greg would feel different if she could produce an eyewitness to the murder.

She should have known the instant she pulled into the parking lot of the bar that it didn't hold much promise. Three bulbs were missing from the Texas lone star that blinked off and on above the door. She had hesitated to even go inside the place.

Every head in the room had turned. The men were a rough bunch. They were drawn to her like coyotes to fresh meat. The women looked even rougher, and glowered at her with the blatant unfriendliness of potential rivals. She was tempted to turn and run, but remembering what had taken her there, she walked boldly to the bar.

"White wine, please."

That generated a snicker from everybody within hearing distance. Taking her glass with her, she moved to a booth and slid into the bench that would afford her the best view of the room. Sipping self-consciously, she let her gaze move from one face to another, trying to ascertain which belonged to the voice on the telephone.

Then, to her horror, she realized that some of the men took her close scrutiny of them as encouragement. From then on, she confined her stares to the bottom of her wine glass, wishing that her informant would hurry up and join her and end the suspense. On the other hand, she dreaded meeting him. If he were among this crowd, she didn't think he'd be someone she would enjoy getting to know.

Billiard balls clacked and clattered. She got an overdose of George Strait and Waylon Jennings. She inhaled clouds of smoke, even though she wasn't smoking. And still she sat alone.

Finally, a man who had been seated at the bar when she had come in slid off his stool and moved in the general direction of her booth. He took his own sweet time, stopping at the jukebox to make his selections and pausing beside the pool table to heckle one of the players about a bad shot.

His wandering seemed aimless and casual, but his gaze kept drifting toward her. Her midsection tightened. Instinctively, she knew that his final destination would be her booth.

It was. He propped his hip against the back of the padded bench across the table from her and smiled down as he tilted a long-neck beer bottle to his lips. "You waitin' for somebody?"

His voice sounded different, but then, both times he'd called her, he'd been whispering. "You know I am," she replied in a cold undertone. "Why'd you take so long to come over?"

"I was building up my courage," he said, slurping another draft of beer. "Now that I'm here, wanna dance?"

"Dance?"

"Yeah, dance. You know, a one an' a two." He used the spout of his beer bottle to push up the brim of his cowboy hat. His eyes slithered over her.

Her reaction was negative and chilling. "I thought you wanted to talk."

He seemed momentarily nonplussed, then gave her a slow, sly grin. "We can talk all you want to, honey." He set his bottle of beer on the table and extended his hand down to her. "My truck's right outside."

He was just a cowboy on the make! Alex didn't know whether to laugh or scream. Hastily gathering up her things, she headed for the door. "Hey, wait a minute. Where're you goin'?"

She left him and everybody else at the Last Chance wondering. Now, pacing the worn carpet of her motel room, she berated herself for being such a fool. She wouldn't put it past Reede or one of the Mintons to pay an out-of-work cowboy a few bucks to call her and deliberately throw her off track.

She was still stewing several minutes later when her telephone rang. She yanked it up. "Hello."

"Do you think I'm crazy?" the familiar voice wheezed.

"Where were you?" she shouted. "I waited in that sleazy joint for almost an hour."

"Was the sheriff there the whole time?"

"What are you talking about? Reede wasn't there."

"Look, lady, I know what I seen. I got there just as you was goin' inside. Reede Lambert was tailin' you. Oh, he cruised on past, but made a U-turn down the road a piece. I didn't even stop. It wouldn't do at all for Lambert to see us talkin' together."

"Reede was following me?"

"Damn right. I didn't count on no law, especially Lambert, breathin' down my neck when I called you. He's thicker'n thieves with the Mintons. I've a good mind to call off this whole goddamn thing."

"No, no," Alex said quickly. "I didn't know Reede was anywhere around. We'll meet someplace else. Next time, I'll be certain he's not trailing me."

"Well . . ."

"On the other hand, if what you've got to tell me isn't all that important . . ."

"I seen who done it, lady."

"Then where can we meet? And when?"

He named another bar, which sounded even more disreputable than the Last Chance. "Don't go inside this time. There'll be a red pickup parked on the north side of the building. I'll be in it."

"I'll be there, Mr.— Uh, can't you at least tell me your name?"

"Nope."

He hung up. Alex cursed. She bounced off the bed and went to the window, throwing open the drapes with the flourish of the bullfighter in the terrible artwork.

Feeling foolish, she saw that the only car near her room was her own. The familiar black-and-white Blazer was nowhere to be seen. She closed the drapes, went back to the phone, and angrily punched out another number. She was so furious at Reede for scaring off an eyewitness, she was shaking.

"Sheriff's office."

"I want to speak to Sheriff Lambert."

"He's already left for the day," she was informed. "Is it an emergency?"

"Do you know where he is?"

"At home, I reckon."

"What's that number, please?"

"We aren't s'pposed to give it out."

"This is Ms. Gaither. I must speak with Sheriff Lambert tonight. It's very important. If necessary, I could track him through the Mintons, but I hate to disturb them."

Dropping important names worked miracles. She was given the telephone number without further delay. She intended to put an immediate halt to the sheriff's sneaky surveillance.

Her resolve vanished when a feminine contralto voice answered his telephone.

"It's a woman, asking for you." Nora Gail extended the telephone receiver to Reede. Her pencil-perfect eyebrows formed an inquisitive arch. He had been adding logs to the fireplace across the room. He brushed his hands on the seat of his jeans and pretended not to see the inquiry in her expression as he took the receiver from her.

"Yeah? This is Lambert."

"This is Alex."

He turned his back on his guest. "What do you want?"

"I want to know why you were following me tonight."

"How do you know I was?"

"I . . . I saw you."

"No, you didn't. What the hell were you doing in that honky-tonk?"

"Having a drink."

"And you picked the Last Chance?" he asked scoffingly. "Baby, you hardly look like its typical barfly. That place is reserved for shit kickers and roughnecks looking for fun with dissatisfied housewives. So either you went there to get laid, or to keep a secret appointment. Which was it?"

"I was there on official business."

"So, it was to meet somebody. Who? You'd be wise to tell me, Alex, because whoever it was got scared off when he saw me."

"You admit that you were trailing me?" Reede remained stubbornly silent. "That's just one of many topics we'll address first thing in the morning."

"Sorry. Tomorrow's my day off."

"It's important."

"That's your opinion."

"Where will you be?"

"I said no, Counselor."

"You don't have a choice."

"The hell I don't. I'm off duty tomorrow."

"Well, I'm not."

He cursed and blew out an exasperated breath, making certain she heard both. "If the ground's thawed out, I'll be at the Mintons' practice track."

"I'll find you."

Without another word, he dropped the receiver back into the cradle. He'd trapped her and he knew it. He'd heard her breathing falter when he'd asked how she'd known he had followed her. Whoever she had planned on meeting had chickened out. Who? Junior? It was disturbing how much he disliked that idea.

"Who was that?" Nora Gail asked, adjusting the lush white mink coat around her shoulders. Her beaded sweater had a low neckline. She amply filled it . . . and then some. In the cleft of her breasts nestled an opal as big around as a silver dollar. The gold chain suspending it in that magnificent setting was half an inch wide and studded with small, brilliant diamonds.

She took a black cigarette out of an eighteen-carat gold box. Reede picked up her matching lighter and held it to the tip of the cigarette. She curved her hand around his. The rings on her plump, pampered hand glittered. "Thank you, sugar."

"Don't mention it." He tossed the lighter back onto the kitchen table and returned to his chair across from her.

"That was Celina's girl, wasn't it?"

"What if it was?"

"Ah." She pulled her lips into a ruby pucker and blew a stream of smoke toward his ceiling. "Her ears must have been burning." Tilting her hand downward, she pointed with her cigarette at the letter lying on the table. "What do you think about it?"

Reede picked up the letter and reread it, though its message had been crystal clear the first time. It urged Alexandra Gaither to cease and desist in her investigation. The letter strongly suggested that she suspend all efforts to prosecute Angus Minton, Junior Minton, and Reede Lambert on any criminal charges.

The character of each man mentioned was given a glowing review by the undersigned, who were a group of concerned citizens—among them, his guest. They were concerned not only for their esteemed colleagues who found themselves in this unfortunate circumstance, but also for themselves and their business interests, should the racetrack license be revoked in light of Ms. Gaither's unfounded investigation.

In summation, the letter admonished her to retreat immediately and let them get down to the business of profiting well off the increased revenue a racetrack would mean to their community.

After reading the letter a second time, Reede refolded it and stuffed it into the unsealed envelope. It had been addressed to Alex in care of the Westerner Motel.

He didn't comment on the contents. Instead, he asked, "Did you instigate it?"

"I bounced the idea off a few of the others."

"It sounds like one of your brainstorms."

"I'm a careful businesswoman. You know that. The others thought it was a good idea and took it from there. We all approved the final draft. I suggested that we get your input before we mail it to her."

"Why's that?"

"You've spent more time with her than anybody else in town. We thought you might guess what her reaction will be."

He studied her impassive features for a long moment. She was as sly as a fox. She hadn't gotten as rich as she was by being dumb or careless. Reede liked her, always had. He slept with her on a regular basis to their mutual satisfaction. But he didn't trust her.

Feeding someone like her too much information would not only be unethical, it would be just plain stupid. He had enough street smarts to know better, and it would take more than an extended viewing of her spectacular cleavage to loosen his tongue.

"Your guess is as good as mine how she'll react," he said noncommittally. "She probably won't react at all."

"Meaning?"

"Meaning, I doubt she'll pack her bags and head for Austin the minute she reads this."

"Courageous, is she?"

Reede shrugged.

"Stubborn?"

He gave a sardonic smile. "You could say that, yeah. She's damned stubborn."

"I'm curious about this girl."

"Why?"

"Because you frown every time her name comes up." She sent another stream of acrid smoke ceilingward as she regarded him closely. "You're frowning now, sugar."

"Habit."

"Does she look like her mother?"

"Not much," he said shortly. "There's a resemblance, that's all."

Her smile was slow, feline, crafty. "She bothers you, doesn't she?"

"Hell, yes, she bothers me," he shouted. "She's trying to send me to prison. Wouldn't that bother you?"

"Only if I was guilty."

Reede clenched his teeth. "All right, I've read your letter and given you my opinion. Why don't you haul your ass out of my house?"

Unperturbed by his anger, she leisurely ground out her cigarette in his tin ashtray and pulled her fur coat around her as she stood up. She gathered up her cigarettes, lighter, and the envelope addressed to Alex, and replaced them in her handbag. "I know from experience, Mr. Reede Lambert, that you think my ass is quite something."

Reede's temper abated. Laughing with chagrin, he squeezed a handful of fanny through her clothing and snarled, "You're right. It is."

"Friends?"

"Friends."

As they stood facing each other, she smoothed her hand down his belly and cupped his sex. It was full and firm, but unaroused. "It's a cold night, Reede," she said in a sultry voice. "Want me to stay?"

He shook his head. "We agreed a long time ago that in order to remain friends, I'd come to you to get laid."

She drew a pretty frown. "Why'd we agree to that?"

"Because I'm the sheriff and you run a whorehouse."

Her laugh was guttural and sexy. "Goddamn right, I do. The best and most profitable one in the state. Anyway, I see I took good care of you the other night." She'd been massaging him through his jeans, with no results.

"Yeah, thanks."

Smiling, the madam dropped her hand and moved toward the door. She addressed him over her shoulder. "What was the urgency? I don't recall seeing you in such a dither since you heard about a certain soldier boy in El Paso, name of Gaither."

Reede's eyes turned a darker, more menacing green. "No urgency. Just horny."

She smiled her knowing smile and patted his stubbled cheek. "You'll have to lie better than that, Reede, honey, to put one over on me. I've known you too long and too well." Her voice drifted back to him as she stepped into the darkness beyond his door. "Don't be a stranger, sugar, you hear?"

 # SIXTEEN

It was no longer sleeting, but it was still very cold. Patches of thin ice crunched beneath Alex's boots as she carefully made her way from her parked car toward the practice track. The brilliant sunshine, which had not deigned to appear for the last several days, now blinded her. The sky was a vivid blue. Jets, looking no larger than pinpoints, trailed puffy lines that sometimes crisscrossed, matching the miles of white fencing on the Minton ranch that divided the compound into separate pens and paddocks.

The ground between the gravel road and the practice track was uneven. Tire tracks had worn permanent ruts in it over the years. It was muddy in spots where ice had already surrendered to the sun's rays.

Alex had dressed appropriately in old boots and jeans. Even though her hands were gloved in kid leather, she raised her fists to her mouth and blew on them for additional warmth. She took a pair of sunglasses out of her coat pocket and slid them on to combat the sunlight. From behind their tinted lenses, she watched Reede. He was standing at the rail clocking the horses between the timing poles placed every sixteenth of a mile.

She held back a moment to study him unobserved. Instead of the leather bomber jacket, he had on a long, light-colored duster. One boot was propped on the lowest rail of the fence, a stance that drew attention to his narrow buttocks and long thighs.

The boot she could see was scuffed and well worn. His jeans were clean, but the hems were frayed, their denim threads bleached white. It occurred to her that the flies of all his jeans were similarly worn, and she was shocked to realize that she knew that.

His wrists were propped on the top fence rail, his hands dangling over the other side. He was wearing leather gloves, the same ones he'd had on when he'd pulled her against him the other night and held her while she cried. It was odd, and deliciously disturbing, to reflect on how his hands had moved over her back with nothing except a terry-cloth robe separating them from her nakedness. A stopwatch lay in the palm of the hand that had cupped her head and pressed it against his chest.

He had on the cowboy hat she'd first seen him in, pulled down low over his brows. Dark blond hair brushed the collar of his coat. When he turned his head, she noticed that the angles of his profile were sharp and clear. There were no indecisive shapes, no subtle contours. When he breathed, a vapor formed around the lips that had kissed her damp hair after he'd told her about Celina's body.

"Let 'em go," he shouted to the practice riders. His voice was as masculine as all his features. Whether he was shouting orders or making innuendos, it never failed to elicit a response low in her body.

As the horses came around—four, in all—their hooves pounded and raised clumps of turf that a track conditioner had loosened earlier that morning. Flaring nostrils sent up billows of steam.

When the riders slowed them to a walk, they were directed back toward the stables. Reede called out to one. "Ginger, how's he doing?"

"I've been holding him back. He's bouncy."

"Give him his head. He wants to run. Walk him around once, then let him go again."

"Okay."

The diminutive rider, who Alex hadn't initially realized was a young woman, tipped the bill of her cap with her quirt and nudged her splendid mount back onto the track.

"What's his name?"

Reede's head came around. He speared Alex with eyes shaded against the sun only by the brim of his hat and a natural squint that had left him with appealing crow's-feet at the outer corners of his eyes. "She's a girl."

"The horse?"

"Oh. The horse's name is Double Time."

Alex moved up beside him at the rail and rested her forearms on it. "Is he yours?"

"Yes."

"A winner?"

"He keeps me in pocket change."

Alex watched the rider crouched over the saddle. "She seems to know just what to do," she remarked. "That's a lot of horse for such a tiny person to handle."

"Ginger's one of the Mintons' best gallop boys—that's what they're called." He returned his attention to the horse and rider as they came around the track at a full-out gallop. "Atta boy, atta boy," he whispered. "Comin' through like a pro." He whooped when Double Time streaked past them, a blur of well-coordinated muscle, agility, and immense strength.

"Good work," Reede told the rider when she brought the horse around.

"Better?"

"Several seconds better."

Reede had more encouraging words for the horse. He patted him affectionately and spoke in a language the animal seemed to understand. The stallion pranced off friskily, tail fanning, knowing that a rewarding breakfast was awaiting him in the stable for having performed so well for his owner.

"You seem to have a real rapport with him," Alex observed.

"I was there the day his sire covered the mare. I was there when he was foaled. They thought he was a dummy, and wanted to put him down."

"A what?"

"A dummy's a foal that was deprived of oxygen during the birthing." He shook his head as he watched the horse enter the stable. "I didn't think so. I was right. His lineage indicated that he had every chance to be good, and he has been. Never a disappointment. Always runs his heart out, even when he's outclassed."

"You've got good reason to be proud of him."

"I guess."

Alex wasn't fooled by his pretended indifference. "Do they always run the horses full out like that?"

"No, they're breezing them today, seeing how they run against each other. Four days a week, they're galloped once or twice around the track. Comparable to a jog. Two days after breezing them, they're just walked."

He turned and headed toward a saddled horse that was tied to a fence post. "Where are you going?"

"Home." He mounted with the loose-limbed grace of a range cowboy.

"I need to talk to you," Alex cried in consternation.

He bent down and extended his hand. "Get on." From beneath the brim of his hat, green eyes challenged her.

She pushed her sunglasses higher on the bridge of her nose and approached the horse with an outward show of confidence she didn't actually feel.

Clasping Reede's hand was the tough part. He hauled her up with very little effort, though it was left to her to get situated between his buttocks and the sloping back of the saddle.

That was disconcerting enough, but when he kneed the horse forward, Alex was thrown against his broad back. Out of necessity, her arms encircled his waist. She was careful to keep her hands well above his belt. Her mind wasn't as easy to control. It kept straying to his damned, well-worn fly.

"Warm enough?" he asked her over his shoulder.

"Yes," she lied.

She had thought his long white duster with the steep pleat in the back was all for show. She'd never seen one outside a Clint Eastwood western. Now, however, she realized the coat was designed to keep a rider's thighs warm.

"Who were you meeting in the bar last night?"

"That's my business, Reede. Why did you follow me?"

"That's my business."

Impasse. For the time being, she let it go. She had a file of questions she wanted to ask him, but it was difficult to keep her mind on her task when her open cleft kept bumping into his hips with each rocking motion of the horse. She blurted out the first question that came to mind. "How did you and my mother get to be such close friends?"

"We grew up together," he said dismissively. "It started out on the jungle gym on the school playground and evolved as we got older."

"It never became awkward?"

"Nope. We had no secrets from each other. We'd even played doctor a few times."

" 'I'll show you mine if you'll show me yours'?"

He grinned. "You must've played doctor, too."

Alex didn't rise to the bait, knowing that he was trying to sidetrack her. "I guess the two of you eventually grew out of that stage."

"We didn't play doctor anymore, no, but we talked about everything. No subject was taboo between Celina and me."

"Isn't that the kind of relationship a girl usually has with another girl?"

"Usually, but Celina didn't have many girlfriends. Most of the girls were jealous of her."

"Why?" Alex already knew the answer. She knew even before he shrugged, a move that rubbed his shoulder blade against her breast. Alex was hardly able to speak. She had to force herself to ask. "It was because of you, wasn't it? Her friendship with you?"

"Maybe. That, and the fact that she was by far the prettiest girl around. Most of the girls considered her a rival, not a friend. Hold on," he warned her before guiding the horse into a dry gully.

Inertia pushed her forward, closer to him. Instinctively, she hugged his torso tighter. He made a grunting sound. She asked, "What's the matter?"

"Nothing."

"You sounded . . . uncomfortable."

"If you were a guy sitting astride a horse taking a steep incline and were being crammed against the pommel of the saddle so that your manhood pushed into your lap, you'd be uncomfortable, too."

"Oh."

"Jesus," he swore beneath his breath.

Until the ground leveled out, there was an awkward silence between them, broken only by the horse's clumping tread as he carefully picked his way over the rocky ground. To hide her embarrassment and keep the cold wind off her, Alex buried her face in the flannel-lined collar of his coat. Eventually, she said, "So, Mother came to you with all her problems."

"Yes. When she didn't, and I knew something was wrong, I went to her. One day she was absent from school. I got worried and went to her house during lunch break. Your grandmother was at work, so Celina was there alone. She'd been crying. I got scared and refused to leave until she told me what was wrong."

"What was the matter?"

"She got her period for the first time."

"Oh."

"From what I gathered, Mrs. Graham had made her feel ashamed of it. She'd told her all kinds of horror stories about Eve's curse—crap like that." There was disapproval in his voice. "Was she that way with you?"

Alex shook her head no, but didn't remove it from the protection of his collar. His neck was warm, and smelled like him. "Not that severe. Maybe Grandma had become more enlightened by the time I reached puberty." Until Reede reined in the horse and dismounted, Alex hadn't realized that they'd reached a small frame house. "What about Mother?"

"I consoled her and told her that it was normal, nothing to be ashamed of, that she had officially become a woman." He looped the reins around a hitching post.

"Did it work?"

"I guess so. She stopped crying and—"

"And . . . ?" Alex prodded him to continue, knowing that he had omitted the most important part of the story.

"Nothing. Swing your leg over." He reached up to help her down, taking her around the waist with sure, strong hands and lifting her to the ground.

"Something, Reede."

She clutched the sleeves of his coat. His lips were drawn into a thin, stubborn line. They looked chapped and consummately masculine. She remembered looking at the newspaper picture of him kissing Celina when he crowned her homecoming queen. As before, Alex's stomach swelled and receded like a wave far out in the gulf.

"You kissed her, didn't you?"

He made an uneasy movement with his shoulder. "I'd kissed her before."

"But that was the first real kiss, wasn't it?"

He released her and, crossing the shallow front porch, thrust open the door. "You can come in or not," he said over his shoulder, "it's up to you."

He disappeared through the door, leaving it open. Despondent but curious, Alex followed. The front door opened directly into the living room. Through an arched opening on her left, she could see a dining area and kitchen. A hallway on the opposite side presumably led into a bedroom, where she could hear him rummaging about. Absently, she closed the front door, removed her glasses and gloves, and looked around.

The house had the stamp of a bachelor. Furniture had been arranged for comfort and convenience, not with any decorative flair. He'd set his hat on a table and tossed his coat and gloves onto a chair. Other surfaces were clear, but the bookshelves were cluttered, as though straightening up amounted to cramming anything lying around onto a shelf. There were cobwebs in the corners of the ceiling that caught the sunlight as it poured in through the dusty venetian blinds.

He caught her looking up at one of the cobwebs as he reappeared, carrying a pair of aviator sunglasses. "Lupe sends one of her nieces out here every few weeks. It's about that time." It was an explanation, but hardly an excuse or apology. "Want some coffee?"

"Please."

He went into the kitchen. Alex continued to walk around the room as she stamped circulation back into her frozen feet. Her attention was drawn to a tall trophy in one of the built-in bookshelves. "Most Valuable Player" was engraved on it in block letters, along with Reede's name and the date.

"Is this the right color?" He had moved up behind her. When she turned he was holding a mug of coffee out to her. He had remembered to add milk.

"Fine, thanks." Inclining her head toward the trophy, she asked, "Your senior year, right?"

"Hmm."

"That's quite an honor."

"I guess so."

Alex noticed that he resorted to that catchall phrase when he wanted the conversation to end. He remained an enigma in all other respects. "You're not sure it was an honor?"

He dropped into an easy chair and thrust his feet out in front of him. "I felt then, and still feel, that I had a good team backing me up. The other nominated players were just as valuable as me."

"Junior?"

"He was one of them, yeah," he replied, instantly defensive.

"But you won the award and Junior didn't."

His eyes glared at hers. "Is that supposed to be significant?"

"I don't know. Is it?"

He gave a scoffing laugh. "Stop playing lawyer games with me and say what's on your mind."

"Okay." She leaned against the padded arm of the sofa and considered him carefully as she asked, "Did Junior resent your getting named most valuable player?"

"Ask him."

"Maybe I will. I'll also ask Angus if he minded."

"Angus couldn't have been prouder the night of the awards banquet."

"Except if his son had been named most valuable player instead of you."

Reede's expression turned stony. "You're full of shit, you know that?"

"I'm sure Angus was proud of you, glad for you, but you can't expect me to believe that he wouldn't have rather seen Junior get the trophy."

"Believe whatever you goddamn want to. It makes no difference to me." He emptied his coffee mug in three swallows, set it on the low coffee table in front of him, then stood up. "Ready?"

She set her coffee down, too, but she made no move to leave. "Why are you so touchy about this?"

"Not touchy, bored." He leaned down to put his face close to hers. "That trophy is a twenty-five-year-old, tarnished piece of junk that's good for nothing except to collect dust."

"Then, why have you kept it all these years?"

He plowed his fingers through his hair. "Look, it doesn't mean anything now."

"But it did then."

"Precious little. Not enough to get me an athletic scholarship, which I was counting on to go to college."

"What did you do?"

"I went anyway."

"How?"

"A loan."

"A government loan?"

"No, a private one," he answered evasively.

"Who lent you the money—Angus?"

"So? I paid back every friggin' cent of it."

"By working for him?"

"Until I left ME."

"Why'd you leave?"

"Because I'd paid him back and wanted to do something else."

"That was as soon as you got out of college?"

He shook his head. "The air force."

"You were in the air force?"

"Four years of officers' training during college, then active duty after graduation. For six years my ass belonged to Uncle Sam. Two of those years were spent bombing gooks in Vietnam."

Alex hadn't known he'd been involved in the war, but she should have guessed. He'd been at draftable age during the height of it. "Did Junior serve, too?"

"Junior at war? Can you picture that?" he asked with a rough laugh. "No, he didn't go. Angus pulled some strings and got him into the reserves."

"Why not you, too?"

"I didn't want him to. I wanted to go into the air force."

"To learn to fly?"

"I already knew how to fly. I had my pilot's license before I had my driver's license."

She contemplated him for a moment. The information was coming too fast and furious to absorb. "You're just full of surprises this morning, aren't you? I didn't know you could fly."

"No reason you should, Counselor."

"Why aren't there any pictures of you in uniform?" she asked, indicating the bookcase.

"I hated what I was doing over there. No mementoes of wartime, thanks." He backed away from her, picked up his hat, gloves, and coat, then went to the front door and ungraciously pulled it open.

Alex remained where she was. "You and Junior must have missed each other while you were serving your six years in the air force."

"What's that supposed to mean? Do you think we're queer for each other?"

"No," she said with diminishing patience. "I just meant that you're good friends who, up till that point, had spent a lot of time together."

He slammed the door closed and slung down his outerwear. "By then we were used to being apart."

"You spent four years of college together," she pointed out.

"No, we didn't. We were attending Texas Tech at the same time, but since he was married—"

"Married?"

"Another surprise?" he asked tauntingly. "Didn't you know? Junior got married just a few weeks after we graduated from high school."

No, Alex hadn't known that. She hadn't realized that Junior's first marriage had come on the heels of high school graduation, and consequently, so soon after Celina's murder. The timing seemed strange.

"For a long while, then, you and Junior didn't see much of each other."

"That's right," was Reede's clipped response.

"Did my mother's death have anything to do with that?"

"Maybe. We didn't—couldn't talk about it."

"Why?"

"It was too damned hard. Why the hell do you think?"

"Why was it hard to be around Junior and talk about Celina's death?"

"Because we'd always been a trio. One of us was suddenly missing. It didn't feel right to be together."

Alex weighed the advisability of pressing him on this, but decided to take the plunge. "You were a trio, yes, but if it was ever odd man out, the odd man was Junior, not Celina. Right? You and she were an inseparable duo before you became an inseparable trio."

"You keep the hell out of my life," he ground out. "You don't know a damn thing about it, about me."

"There's no need for you to get mad, Reede."

"Oh, no? Why shouldn't I get mad? You want to resurrect the past, everything from my first real kiss to some fucking football trophy that has about as much value as a pile of horse shit, but I'm not supposed to get mad."

"Most people enjoy reminiscing."

"I don't. I want to leave my past in the past."

"Because it's hurtful?"

"Some of it."

"Is it hurtful to remember the first time you kissed my mother for real?"

He strode toward the sofa and bridged her hips with his hands, keeping his arms stiff. His voice changed from a ranting pitch to pure silk. "That kiss sure as hell intrigues you, doesn't it, Counselor?"

He overwhelmed her. She could say nothing.

"Well, if you're so interested in how I kiss, maybe you should experience it firsthand."

He pushed his hands inside her coat and linked them together at the small of her back. Giving a swift yank, he pulled her to her feet. She caught herself against his chest, gasping soundlessly before he bent his head down low and covered her lips with his.

At first she was so stunned she didn't move. When she realized what was happening, she placed both her fists firmly against his chest. She tried to turn her head aside, but he trapped her jaw in one hand and held it still. His lips expertly rubbed hers apart, then he thrust his tongue between them. He kissed her thoroughly, sweeping her mouth with his tongue and making stabbing motions toward the back of her throat. His lips were chapped. She felt their roughness against hers as well as the thrilling contrast of their sleek lining.

She might have uttered a small whimper of surprise and need. Her body might have become pliant enough to conform to his. He might have made a low, hungry, growling sound deep in his throat. Then again, she might have imagined it all.

But she didn't imagine the feathering sensation between her thighs, or the tingling in her breasts, or the heat spreading through her middle like melting butter. She didn't mistake the rare and wonderful taste of his mouth, or the scent of wind and sunlight that clung to his hair and clothing.

He raised his head and looked into her dazed eyes. His own mirrored her bewilderment. But the smile that lifted one corner of his mouth was sardonic. "Just so you don't feel cheated," he murmured.

He pecked a series of soft quick kisses across her damp lips, then ran his tongue over them lightly and teasingly. He probed the corner of her lips with the tip of his tongue, and the suggestive caress caused a ribbon of sensation in her belly to slowly uncurl.

Then he sealed his open mouth upon hers again. His tongue sank into it, as invasive as her response was involuntary. He stroked her mouth with deeply satisfying leisure while his hands moved over her back, then up her sides to her breasts. He rubbed them softly with the heels of his hands, creating a hunger inside her for him to touch their crests.

Instead, he slid his hands down to her bottom, cupped it, and tilted her hips forward against his. He matched the motions of his tongue with his hips, an ebb and flow that whetted her appetite for fulfillment and eroded her resistance.

Before she could submit to the delicious weakness stealing through her, he abruptly released her. His face still close, he whispered, "Curious to know what I usually do next?"

Alex stepped back, mortified over how close she had come to total capitulation. She wiped his kiss off her lips with the back of her hand. He merely smirked. "No, I didn't think so."

He put on his sunglasses and hat, giving the brim a tug that pulled it low over his eyes. "From now on, Counselor, I suggest you save your cross-examination for the courtroom. It's much safer."

The Derrick Lounge was far worse than the Last Chance. Alex approached it from the south, so when she rounded the corner of the building and saw a battered, rusty, red pickup parked there, she breathed a sigh of relief. She'd already made up her mind that if the eyewitness wasn't there, she wasn't going to hang around waiting on him.

When she had left the Westerner Motel, she'd made certain she wasn't followed. She felt ridiculous playing such cat-and-mouse games, but she was willing to go to any lengths to speak to this man who claimed to be an eyewitness to her mother's murder. If this meeting produced nothing but a telephone prankster looking for new thrills, it would be the crowning touch to a perfectly horrible day.

The longest horseback ride in history had been the one she'd made with Reede back to the practice track where she'd left her car. "Have a nice day," he had called mockingly after she slid from the saddle.

"Go to hell," had been her angry response. As he wheeled his horse around, she could hear him chuckling.

"Arrogant bastard," she whispered to herself now as she got out of her car and moved toward the pickup. She could see the driver sitting behind the steering wheel, and although she was glad he had shown up, she wondered how she would feel if he cited Reede as the man who had killed her mother. It was a disquieting possibility.

She went around the hood of the truck, her shoes crunching noisily in the loose gravel. The Derrick Lounge hadn't spent any money on outdoor lighting, so it was dark at the side of the building. No other vehicles were parked nearby.

Alex entertained a moment's trepidation as she reached for the door handle. Forcibly quelling her uneasiness, she slid inside and pulled the door closed behind her.

Her eyewitness was an ugly little man. He had stark, Indianlike cheekbones with pockmarked craters scooped out beneath them. He was unkempt, and smelled like he didn't shower frequently. He was scrawny and wrinkled and grizzled.

He was also dead.

SEVENTEEN

When it registered why he just sat there staring at her with a vacuous, unfocused, and somewhat surprised expression, Alex tried to scream, but nothing came out. Her mouth had turned to cotton. Reaching behind her, she tried to open the pickup door. It stubbornly resisted.

After frantically tugging on the handle, she gave it her shoulder. It swung open so suddenly that she almost fell out. In her scrambling haste to put distance between her and the bloody corpse, the toe of her shoe caught in the gravel. She stumbled and fell, landing hard on the heels of her hands and scraping her knees.

She cried out in pain and fear and tried to stand. Plunging headlong into the darkness, she was suddenly blinded by a pair of headlights and petrified by the blasting of a horn.

Reflexively, she raised her hand to shield her eyes. Against the backdrop of brilliant light, she made out the outline of a man approaching her. Before she could run or utter a peep, he said, "You get around, don't you?"

"Reede!" she cried in a mix of relief and terror.

"What the hell are you doing here?"

He didn't sound at all sympathetic. That enraged her. "I could ask you the same question. That man," she said, pointing a shaky finger toward the pickup, "is dead."

"Yeah, I know."

"You know?"

"His name is, uh, *was* Pasty Hickam. He's a ranch hand who used to work for Angus." He peered through the bug-splattered windshield and shook his head. "Jesus, what a mess."

"Is that all you can say?"

He turned on her. "No, I could say that the only reason I'm not taking you in on suspicion of murder is because whoever phoned in the tip that Pasty was sitting in his pickup with his throat cut didn't mention that there was a broad with him."

"Somebody tipped you?"

"That's right. Any idea who?"

"I guess whoever knew I was coming here to meet him," she shouted. Then, when another thought struck her, she became still and quiet. "How'd you get here so fast, Reede?"

"You think I headed him off and put a knife to his throat?" he asked with an incredulous laugh.

"It's possible."

Holding her stare, he called for one of his deputies. Alex hadn't realized until then that there was someone with him. She became aware of a couple of things at once—the wail of an approaching siren, the appearance of curious customers, who were rushing out the door of the bar to see what the commotion was about.

"Escort her back to her motel," Reede curtly instructed the deputy. "See that she gets inside her room."

"Yes, sir."

"Keep an eye on her till daylight. Make sure she doesn't go anywhere."

Alex and the sheriff exchanged a hostile stare before she allowed the deputy to lead her back to her car.

"Sheriff?" The deputy tapped hesitantly on the door before daring to open it. The word around the office that morning was that Reede was in a bitch of a mood, and only partially because of Pasty Hickam's death the night before. Everybody was walking on eggshells.

"What is it?"

"I've got some papers for you to sign."

"Give them here." Reede eased up from his half-reclining position in the swivel chair and reached for the stack of official documents and letters. He scrawled his signature where it was called for.

"How's Ruby Faye this morning?"

Pasty's lover had been found in her mobile home when the sheriff arrived there to question her, beaten to a pulp. Before passing out, she named her cuckolded husband as the culprit.

"Lyle did almost as good a number on her as he did on Pasty. She's gonna have to stay in the hospital a week or so. The kids have been packed off to her mama's house."

Reede's expression turned even surlier. He had no tolerance for men who physically abused women, no matter what the provocation. He had been on the receiving end of too many beatings from his old man to stomach domestic violence.

He passed the paperwork back to the clerk. "Any feedback on that APB?"

"No, sir. I'll let you know. And you told me to remind you that you're scheduled to testify in Judge Wallace's court this afternoon."

"Shit, I would've forgotten. Okay, thanks." The deputy gratefully withdrew, but Reede had mentally dismissed him from his mind even before the door clicked shut.

He couldn't hold a thought for longer than a few seconds this morning. The image of Alex left little room for any others.

Swearing liberally, he left his chair and moved to the window. Outside, it was another sunny day. He was reminded of yesterday, when he'd pulled her up on that horse with him and the sunlight had turned her hair a deep, mahogany red. That's what he must have been thinking about when he'd started shooting off his mouth about that stupid football trophy.

Why, for crissake, had he kept it all this time? Every time he looked at it his emotions were split right down the middle, the way they'd been the night he had received it. His elation had been dampened because Junior hadn't been named most valuable player. Crazy as the notion was, he had wanted to apologize to Angus and Junior for winning the award. He'd deserved it because he was the better athlete, but winning over Junior had tainted the prize.

Alex had figured all that out by herself. She was smart, all right. But she wasn't as tough as she pretended to be. She'd had the daylights scared out of her last night, and justifiably so. Pasty had never been a pretty sight, but dead, with blood congealing on his down jacket, he was even uglier.

Maybe it had been good for her to see that. Maybe she wouldn't be so eager to uncover secrets that were none of her concern. Maybe Pasty's grisly murder would scare her out of investigating Celina's. Maybe she'd leave Purcell and never come back.

That possibility should have cheered him. It didn't. It made him angrier with her and with himself.

Kissing her yesterday had been a dumb move. He had let her provoke him. He'd lost his temper. He hadn't been in control of himself. The excuse relieved his conscience, just enough for him to live with what had happened. At the same time, however, it scared the hell out of him. Alex had pushed him over the edge of sound reason. Only one other person had ever been able to do that—Celina.

How had the clever little witch tricked him into mentioning that kiss, he wondered. He hadn't thought about it in years, but all of a sudden, it had been vivid in his mind.

It had been a hot September day, he remembered, when he had gone to check on Celina after she had failed to report to school. The old window air-conditioning unit had labored to cool the stifling little house without much success. The air was hot and humid, instead of hot and dry.

Celina wasn't acting like herself. She had let him in, but had acted subdued, as though this first rite of passage into womanhood had robbed her of girlish animation. Her eyes had been puffy from crying. He had been scared that something was terribly wrong.

When she had told him about her period, he'd been so relieved he had wanted to laugh. He hadn't, though. Her bleak expression had quashed any levity. He had put his arms around her, held her tenderly, stroked her hair, and reassured her that it was something wonderful, not shameful. Seeking comfort, she had wrapped her arms around his waist and nuzzled her face against his collarbone.

For a long time, they had just clung to each other, as they had so many times in the past when it seemed that the two of them were at odds with the rest of the world. But he felt a need to solemnize this occasion, to officially mark her departure from childhood.

He had kissed her cheek first. Tears had left it damp and salty. He kissed his way down. She caught her breath suddenly, and held it, until he pressed his lips firmly upon hers. It was a fervent but chaste kiss.

He had kissed other girls using his tongue. The Gail sisters were already adept at French kissing, and had been eager to share their expertise with him. At least once a week he met the three of them in the abandoned VFW hall and took turns kissing them, feeling their breasts, and slipping his hand into the elastic legs of their cotton panties to touch the hair between their thighs. They quarreled over which one got to undo his pants and fondle him first.

Those sweaty, sordid interludes made life with his father bearable. They were also the only secret he kept from Celina. What he did with the Gail sisters would probably embarrass her if she knew. It might also make her mad. Either way, it was better that she didn't know about the condemned VFW hall and what he did there.

But when he felt Celina's mouth beneath his, and heard that little catch in her throat, he had wanted to kiss her the correct way—the good and exciting and forbidden way. Unable to resist the temptation, his body had overruled his mind.

He'd barely touched the seam of her lips with the tip of his tongue before he felt them separate. Heart pounding, blood boiling, he drew her closer and pushed his tongue into her mouth. When she didn't recoil, he moved it around. She clutched his waist. Her small, pointed breasts burned like brands against his chest.

God, he had thought he was going to die of pleasure. It was immense. The experience rocked the foundations of his adolescent soul. His body had vibrated with volcanic energy. He had wanted to go on kissing Celina Graham forever. But when his penis became so engorged it pressed against her middle, he pushed her away and began babbling apologies.

Celina had stared at him for several seconds, wide-eyed and breathless, then threw herself against him, wrapped her arms around his neck, and told him that she was glad he had kissed her like that. She loved him. He loved her. They were going to get married someday, and nothing was going to come between them, ever.

Now Reede, rubbing his eyes tiredly, returned to his desk and flopped down into the creaky chair. He had been furious with Alex for calling forth memories he had strived for years to keep at bay. It had been his intention to punish and insult her with that kiss.

But, dammit, he hadn't counted on her feeling so good against him—all fur coat and soft wool and warm skin. He hadn't expected her mouth to taste so goddamned sweet. That sweetness still lingered on his tongue. How could he have guessed that her breasts would be that full and soft?

He sure as hell hadn't bargained on his body becoming embarrassingly, instantly aroused for Celina's daughter. It was harder than he'd ever gotten for the Gail sisters—harder than he'd ever gotten period. Hell, he was still hard.

That was just one reason why the impetuous embrace had left him feeling mad as hell at her and not much kinder toward himself. Alex Gaither, the woman he had kissed like crazy yesterday, had all but accused him of two murders, first Celina's, then Pasty's. Even if she couldn't make those allegations stick, she could still spoil all his plans for the future.

He was so close to realizing his dreams. He was about to be where he'd worked hard all his life to get. She could mess it up royally. She didn't even have to finger him. If she indicted any one of them, she would snatch his future away from him before he had fully grasped it. For that, he could easily choke her.

But when he thought about putting his hands on her again, it wasn't to choke her.

*   *   *

"They told me you were in."

"Did they also tell you that I'm due in court in a few minutes, and that between now and then I'm too busy to see anyone?"

Alex stepped into Reede's office and closed the door behind her. "They mentioned it."

"Where'd you get the idea that you're exempt?"

"I thought you'd want to question me about the man who got killed."

"You aren't really a suspect. You were just at the wrong place at the wrong time, something you have a bad habit of doing."

"You don't think there's a connection between me and his murder?"

"No, but obviously you do." Propping his feet on the corner of his desk and stacking his hands behind his head, he said, "Let's hear it."

"I think you already know it. Pasty Hickam witnessed Celina's murder."

"How do you know?"

"He told me over the telephone."

"He was a legendary liar. Ask anybody."

"I believed him. He sounded nervous and terribly afraid. We made an appointment to meet at the Last Chance, but when he saw you following me, he got frightened off."

"So, that makes me Celina's killer?"

"Or someone who's covering up for the killer."

"Let me tell you what's wrong with your theory." He lowered his feet to the floor. "Angus fired Pasty the other day. He was on a revenge trip, something you should be able to relate to, Counselor. He made up some cock-and-bull story that you wanted to believe because so far, your investigation hasn't turned up one goddamn scrap of concrete evidence.

"You think the two murders are connected, right? Wrong," he said. "Think about it. Last night's killing doesn't match Celina's murder. The M.O.'s wrong. The guy who cut Pasty a new smile found out Pasty was humping his wife while he was working over at the potash plant near Carlsbad. We've got an APB out on him."

It sounded so plausible that Alex squirmed under his direct gaze. "Isn't it possible that this ranch hand witnessed my mother's murder? He kept quiet until now out of fear of retribution, or simply because no one ever conducted a thorough investigation. Knowing what he did got him killed before he could identify the killer. That's what I choose to believe."

"Suit yourself. But waste your time on it, not mine." Reede made to stand up, but she said, "That's not all." Resigned, he sat back down.

Alex took an envelope out of her purse and handed it to him. "This came in the mail this morning. It was addressed to me at the motel."

Reede scanned the letter quickly and handed it back to her. She stared at him in amazement. "You don't seem very disturbed by it, Sheriff Lambert."

"I've already read it."

"What? When?"

"Day before yesterday, if I'm remembering right."

"And you let them send it?"

"Why not? It's not obscene. I figure even the postmaster general would agree that it meets postal regulations. It's got the correct amount of postage on it. As far as I can tell, that letter isn't illegal, Counselor."

Alex wanted to reach across his desk and slap the gloating smile off his face. The impulse was so strong she had to curl her hand into a fist to keep from doing so.

"Did you read between the lines? The people who signed this, all—" she paused to count the signatures, "—all fourteen of them, have threatened to run me out of town."

"Surely not, Miss Gaither," he said, feigning shock. "You're just being paranoid because you found Pasty. That letter simply underlines what I've been telling you all along. Angus and Junior Minton mean a lot to this town. So does that racetrack."

"You get somebody's attention quicker by kicking him in the bank account than you do by kicking him in the nuts. You've put some sizable investments in jeopardy. Did you expect folks to stand by and watch all their dreams go down the tubes because of your vindictiveness?"

"I'm not being vindictive. I'm conducting a valid and long-overdue investigation into a severe miscarriage of justice."

"Spare me."

"The district attorney of Travis County sanctioned my investigation."

His eyes drifted over her insultingly as he drawled, "In exchange for what?"

"Oh, that's good. Very professional, Sheriff. When you run out of viable ammunition, you resort to throwing sexist rocks at my character."

With angry, jerky motions, she stuffed the letter back into the envelope and replaced it in her purse, snapping the catch firmly.

"I don't have to explain my reasons to you. Just understand this," she enunciated. "I won't quit until I can draw some satisfactory conclusions about my mother's murder."

"Well, I wouldn't worry about being mugged, if I were you," Reede told her with an air of boredom. "As I've explained, Pasty's killing had absolutely nothing to do with you. The people who signed that letter are pillars of the community— bankers, businessmen, professionals. They're hardly types who would accost you in a dark alley.

"Although," he went on, "I'd recommend that you stop cruising in hotbeds of trouble like you have the last two evenings. If you've just got to have it, there are a couple of fellas I could recommend."

She released a slow, contemptuous breath. "Do you dislike all professional women, or is it me in particular?"

"It's you in particular."

His bluntness was an affront. She was tempted to remind him that his kiss yesterday hadn't conveyed dislike, but she didn't. She didn't want to remind him of it. She hoped to forget it herself, pretend that it had never happened, but she couldn't. It had left her feeling drastically and irrevocably altered.

No, she couldn't forget it. The best she could hope for was to learn to cope with the memory of it, and the addictive craving it had instigated.

His statement hurt her deeply. She heard herself asking, "Why don't you like me?"

"Because you're a meddler. I don't like people who meddle in other people's business."

"This *is* my business."

"How could it be? You were peeing in your diapers when Celina was killed," he shouted.

"I'm glad you brought that up. Since I was only two months old at the time, what was she doing out at the ranch that night?"

His stunned reaction to the question was swiftly covered. "I forget. Look, I'm due—"

"I doubt you ever forget anything, Reede Lambert, much as you pretend that you do. What was she doing there? Please tell me."

He stood up. So did Alex. "Junior had invited her for supper, that's all."

"Was it a special occasion?"

"Ask him."

"I'm asking you. What was the occasion? And don't tell me you don't remember."

"Maybe he felt sorry for her."

"Sorry? Why?"

"For being cooped up with a kid, not getting out. Her social life had gone to zilch. She was only eighteen, for crissake." He stepped around her and headed for the door.

Alex wasn't ready to let it go at that. His answer was too pat. She caught his arm and forced him to face her. "Were you there at dinner that night?"

"Yeah, I was there." He jerked his arm free.

"The entire evening?"

"I left before dessert."

"Why?"

"I don't like cherry pie."

She groaned with frustration. "Answer me, Reede. Why did you leave?"

"I had a date."

"With whom? Does she still live here in town?"

"What the hell difference does it make?"

"She's your alibi. I'd like to talk to her."

"Forget it. I'll never drag her into this."

"You might have to, or plead the Fifth."

"Don't you ever give up?" he asked through bared teeth.

"Never. Did you return to the ranch that night?"

"No."

"Not at all?"

"No."

"Not even to sleep?"

"I told you, I had a date." He put his face close enough to hers that she could feel his breath against her lips. "And she was hot."

He gave a terse bob of his head to emphasize his point, then turned to leave. "I'm due in court. Close the door on your way out, will ya?"

 # EIGHTEEN

"**M**iss Gaither?"

"Yes?"

Alex didn't feel like having company. Her latest altercation with Reede had left her drained. After last night, her nerves were shot. Neither Reede's glib explanation of the Hickam man's murder or any amount of her own sound reasoning had convinced her that she wasn't in danger.

So, when someone knocked on her motel room door, she had approached it cautiously and looked through the peephole. A strange, but evidently harmless couple, were on her threshold. She opened the door and looked at them expectantly.

Suddenly, the man stuck out his hand. Startled, Alex jumped back. "Reverend Fergus Plummet." Feeling foolish, Alex shook hands with him. "Did I frighten you? I'm dreadfully sorry. I didn't mean to."

The reverend's mannerisms were so deferential, his tone of voice so sympathetic, he hardly posed a threat. He had a slight build and was shorter than average, but held himself erect with almost military posture. His black suit was shiny in spots and inadequate for the season. He wore no overcoat and nothing to cover his wavy dark hair, which was fuller than current fashion dictated. In a community where almost every male from the age of twelve wore either a cowboy hat or bill cap, it looked odd to see a man without one.

"This is my wife, Wanda."

"Hello, Mrs. Plummet, Reverend."

Mrs. Plummet was a large woman, with a notable bosom that she'd tried to minimize by covering it with a drab olive cardigan sweater. Her hair was pulled back into a knot on the back of her head, which she kept meekly lowered. Her husband had referred to her with no more personal regard than he might give a lamppost.

"How'd you know my name?" Alex asked, curious about the couple.

"Everybody does," he replied with a brief smile. "There's talk going around town about you."

The minister had a Bible tucked under one arm. Alex couldn't imagine what a minister was doing at her door—recruiting new members?

"I guess you're wondering why I'm here," he said, correctly reading her puzzled expression.

"Frankly, yes. Would you like to come in?"

They stepped into the room. Mrs. Plummet seemed ill at ease and unsure where to sit until her husband pointed her to a corner of the bed. He took the only chair. Alex sat down on the edge of the bed, but far enough away from Mrs. Plummet for both of them to be comfortable.

The preacher gazed about him. He seemed to be in no hurry to disclose the reason he was there. Finally, and with a trace of impatience, Alex said, "Is there something I can do for you, Reverend Plummet?"

Closing his eyes, he raised his hand heavenward and evoked a blessing. "May heaven's rich blessings pour down on this beloved daughter of God," he intoned in a deep, vibrating voice.

He began to pray with loud earnestness. Alex had the wildest impulse to giggle. Merle Graham had seen to it that she was raised with traditional Protestant beliefs. They had attended church regularly. Though she had never embraced the fundamentalist dogma her grandmother adhered to, Alex's Christian faith was well cemented.

"Please, Reverend Plummet," she interrupted when his prayer extended into overtime, "I've had a very long day. Could we get to the point of your visit, please?"

He looked rather piqued over her interruption, but said with a mysterious air, "I can assist you with your investigation of Minton Enterprises."

She was stunned. She had never expected him to be connected in any way to her investigation. She reminded herself, however, to proceed with caution. She was, after all, extremely skeptical. What deep, dark secrets could this weird little man know about Celina, Reede Lambert, or the Mintons? Ministers were privy to confidences, but experience had taught her that professional ethics usually prevented them from revealing any confessions. They strictly abided by the rules of privileged information, and only imparted it in life-threatening situations.

It didn't seem likely that either Angus or Junior would bare his soul to a mousy little man like Plummet. Based wholly on outward appearance, he would have a minimal amount of influence with the Almighty. The thought of Reede Lambert confessing a sin was preposterous.

She responded with a professional detachment that Greg Harper would have been proud of: "Oh, really? How can you do that? Did you know my mother?"

"Unfortunately, no. But I can speed along your investigation just the same. We—my congregation of saints and I—believe that you're on our side. And our side is God's side."

"Th–thank you," she stammered, hoping that was the correct response.

Obviously, it was. It earned a soft amen from Mrs. Plummet, who had been silently praying all this time.

"Reverend Plummet," Alex said uncertainly, "I'm not sure you understand. I'm here at the behest of the district attorney's office to—"

"The Lord uses people as his holy instruments."

"—to investigate the murder of my mother, which occurred here in Purcell twenty-five years ago."

"God be *praised* . . . that this *wrong* . . . will soon be set *right!*" He shook his fists heavenward.

Alex was flabbergasted. She gave a nervous laugh. "Yes, well, I hope so, too. But I fail to see how my investigation concerns you and your ministry. Do you have inside knowledge of the crime?"

"Oh, that I did, Miss Gaither," Plummet wailed. "Oh, that I did, so that we could speed along God's work and punish the iniquitous."

"The iniquitous?"

"Sinners!" he shouted fervently. "Those who would corrupt this town and all the innocent children of God living here. They want to build Satan's playground, fill the precious veins of our children with narcotics, their sweet mouths with foul liquor, their fertile little minds with carnality."

From the corner of her eye, Alex glanced at Mrs. Plummet, who sat with her head bowed, her hands folded in her lap, her knees and ankles decorously pressed together, as though they had been glued that way.

"Are you referring to Purcell Downs?' Alex asked tentatively.

Just as she had feared, the very words opened up a well-spring of evangelical fervor. Prophecies came spewing out of the preacher's mouth like a fountain run amok. Alex endured a sermon on the evils of horserace gambling and all the ungodly elements that accompanied it. But when Plummet began to tout her as a missionary sent to Purcell to vanquish the sons of Satan, she felt compelled to bring the fiery sermon to a halt.

"Reverend Plummet, please." After several attempted interruptions, he stopped speaking and looked at her blankly. She licked her lips anxiously, not wanting to offend him, but wanting to make herself explicitly clear.

"I have absolutely nothing to do with whether or not Minton Enterprises is granted a gambling license. The fact is that they've already been approved by the racing commission. All that remains are the formalities."

"But the Mintons are under investigation for murder."

Choosing her words carefully, and omitting any direct reference to the Mintons, she said, "If enough evidence or probable cause is found as a result of my investigation, the case could be brought before the grand jury. It would be up to it to bring forth an indictment. In any instance, the parties involved are to be presumed innocent until proven guilty, in accordance with our Constitution."

She held up a hand to stave off his interruption. "Please, let me finish. Whatever happens regarding the proposed racetrack after I conclude my investigation will be the responsibility of the racing commission. I will have nothing to do with its final decision on this or any other application for a gambling license.

"Actually, it's coincidental that the Mintons are personally involved with both issues simultaneously. I reopened my mother's murder case because, as a public prosecutor, I was dissatisfied with its resolution, and thought that it warranted further investigation. I do not hold a personal grudge against this town, or anyone in it."

Plummet was squirming with the need to speak, so she let him. "You don't want to see gambling come to Purcell, do you? Aren't you against this device of the devil that snatches food from children's mouths, destroys marriages, and plunges the weak onto paths bound for hell and damnation?"

"My views on pari-mutuel betting—or anything else, for that matter—are none of your business, Reverend Plummet." Alex came to her feet. She was tired, and he was a wacko. She'd given him more time than he deserved. "I must ask you and Mrs. Plummet to leave now."

He wasn't an educated and eloquent churchman, who had researched the issue and drawn enlightened conclusions. There were well-founded arguments for both sides. But whether pari-mutuel gambling came to Purcell County or not, Alex had nothing to do with it.

"We're not giving up," Plummet said, following her to the door. "We're willing to make any sacrifice to see that God's will is carried out."

"God's will? If it's God's will that the Mintons be denied that gambling license, then nothing you do will help or hinder, right?"

He couldn't be trapped with logic. "God uses us to do his work. He's using you, though you might not know it yet." His eyes smoldered with fanatical fire. It gave Alex goose bumps. "You are the answer to our prayers. Oh, yes, Miss Gaither, the answer to our prayers. Call on us. You've been anointed by God, and we're your humble and willing servants."

"I, uh, I'll keep that in mind. Good-bye."

Reverend Plummet's theology was warped. He gave her the creeps. She couldn't get her door closed behind him fast enough. As soon as he did, her telephone rang.

NINETEEN

"How does dinner and dancing sound?" Junior Minton asked without preamble.

"Like a fairy tale."

"It's not. Just say yes."

"You're inviting me out for dinner and dancing?"

"It's the monthly fete at the Purcell Horse and Gun Club. Please say you'll go with me. Otherwise, it'll be boring as hell."

Alex laughed. "Junior, I doubt you're ever bored. Especially when there are women around. Do most of them fall for your b.s.?"

"Almost without exception. If you go with me tonight, it'll be unanimous."

"*Tonight?*"

"Sure, tonight. Did I fail to mention that? Sorry I couldn't give you more notice."

"You're actually serious?"

"Would I joke about something as important as the monthly get-together at the Horse and Gun Club?"

"Of course you wouldn't. Forgive my flippancy."

"All's forgiven if you'll go."

"I really can't. I'm exhausted. Last night—"

"Yeah, I heard about that. Jeez, that must've been awful, you finding Pasty Hickam that way. I want to help take your mind off it."

"I appreciate your consideration, but I can't go."

"I refuse to take no for an answer."

While talking, she had struggled out of her dress and was now standing in her slip and stockings, cradling the telephone receiver between her shoulder and her ear while trying to pull on her robe. The housekeeper always turned off the heat after she cleaned the room. Every evening Alex had a frigid homecoming to dread.

She glanced toward the alcove where her clothes were hanging. "I really can't go, Junior."

"How come?"

"All my dressy clothes are in Austin. I don't have anything to wear."

"Surely a lady as articulate as you isn't resorting to that cliché."

"It happens to be the truth."

"And the occasion calls for casual. Wear that leather skirt you had on the other day. It's a knockout."

Alex had finally managed to wriggle herself into the robe without dropping the phone. She sat down on the edge of the bed and snuggled deeper into the terry cloth. "I still have to say no."

"Why? I know it's rude to put you on the spot like this, but I'm not going to be gracious and let you bow out without giving me a valid reason."

"I just don't think it would be a good idea for us to socialize."

"Because you're hoping I'll soon be a resident of the Huntsville State Prison?"

"No!"

"Then, what?"

"I don't *want* to send you to prison, but you *are* a key suspect in a murder case."

"Alex, you've had time to form an opinion of me. Do you honestly believe that I could commit such a violent crime?"

She remembered how Reede had laughed at the notion of Junior going to war. He was lazy, unambitious, a philanderer. Violent outbursts didn't fit into his image. "No, I don't," she replied softly. "But you're still a suspect. It wouldn't do for us to be seen fraternizing."

"I like that word," he snarled. "It sounds dirty, incestuous. And for your peace of mind, I do all my fraternizing privately. That is, except for a few times, when I was younger. Reede and I used to—"

"Please," she groaned, "I don't want to know."

"Okay, I'll spare you the lurid details, on one condition."

"What?"

"Say you'll go tonight. I'll pick you up at seven."

"I can't."

"Alex, Alex," he moaned dramatically, "look at it this way. During the course of the evening I'll have a drink or two, possibly more. I might start reminiscing, get maudlin, say something indiscreet. When I do, you'll be there to hear it. No telling what stunning confessions I might blurt out in my inebriation. Consider this evening one long interrogation. It's part of your job to wear down the defenses of your suspects, isn't it?

"You'd be shirking your duty if you didn't take advantage of every opportunity to rout out the truth. How can you selfishly languish in the luxury of the Westerner Motel while a suspect is shooting off his mouth over drinks at the Horse and Gun Club? Shame on you. You owe this to the taxpaying public who're footing the bill for this investigation. Do it for your country, Alex."

Again, she groaned dramatically. "If I consent to go, will you promise not to make any more speeches?"

"Seven o'clock."

She could hear the triumph in his voice.

The moment she entered the clubhouse, she was glad she had come. There was music and laughter. She caught snatches of several conversations, none of which were centered around Celina Gaither's murder. That in itself was a refreshing change. She looked forward to several hours of relaxation, and felt that the break had been earned.

Nevertheless, she rationalized being there. Not for a minute did she believe that Junior would make a public spectacle of himself while under the influence. She wasn't likely to hear any startling confessions.

All the same, something beneficial might come out of the evening. The exclusivity of the Horse and Gun Club suggested that only Purcell's upper crust were members. Reede had told her that the people who had signed the letter she had received were local businessmen and professionals. It was conceivable that she would meet some of them tonight, and get a feel for the extent of their animosity.

More important, she would have an opportunity to mingle with locals, people who knew the Mintons and Reede well and might shed light on their characters.

Junior had picked her up in his red Jaguar. He'd driven it with a lack of regard for the speed limit. His festive mood had been contagious. Whether she was acting in a professional capacity or not, it felt good to be standing beside the handsomest man in the room, with his hand riding lightly, but proprietorially, on the small of her back.

"The bar's this way," he said close to her ear, making himself heard over the music. They wended their way through the crowd.

The club wasn't glitzy. It didn't resemble the slick, neon nightclubs that were bursting out like new stars in the cities, catering to yuppies who flocked to them in BMWs and designer couture.

The Purcell Horse and Gun Club was quintessentially Texan. The bartender could have been sent over by Central Casting. He had a handlebar mustache, black bow tie and vest, and red satin garters on his sleeves. A pair of longhorns, which spanned six feet from polished tip to polished tip, were mounted above the ornately carved nineteenth-century bar.

The walls were adorned with pictures of racehorses, prizewinning bulls with testicles as large as punching bags, and landscapes where either yucca or bluebonnets abounded. In almost every instance the paintings featured an obligatory windmill, looking lonesome and stark against the sun-streaked horizon. Alex was Texan enough to find it comfortable and endearing. She was sophisticated enough to recognize its gaucheness.

"White wine," she told the bartender, who was unabashedly giving her a once-over.

"Lucky son of a bitch," he muttered to Junior as he served them their drinks. The grin beneath the lavish mustache was lecherous.

Junior saluted him with his scotch and water. "Ain't I just?" He propped his elbow on the bar and turned to face Alex, who was seated on the stool. "The music's a little too country and western for my taste, but if you want to dance, I'm game.''

She shook her head. ''Thanks, but no. I'd rather watch.''

A few songs later, Junior leaned close and whispered, ''Most of them learned to dance in a pasture. They still look like they're trying to avoid stepping in a pile of cow shit.''

The wine had taken effect. Her eyes were bright, her cheeks flushed. Feeling a pleasant buzz, she tossed her hair over her shoulder and laughed.

''Come on,'' he said, placing his hand beneath her elbow and helping her off the stool. ''Mother and Dad are at their table.''

Alex moved with him along the perimeter of the dance floor to the cluster of tables set up for dining. Sarah Jo and Angus were seated at one. He was puffing on a cigar. Sarah Jo was idly waving the offensive smoke away from her face.

Alex had been apprehensive about wearing the russet leather skirt and matching, leather-trimmed sweater, but she felt more comfortable in them than she would have wearing Sarah Jo's burgundy satin dress and looking out of place in a room where people were stamping out ''Cotton-Eyed Joe,'' yelling ''bullshit'' in the appropriate places, and drinking beer straight from opaque amber bottles.

''Hello, Alex,'' Angus said around his cigar.

''Hello. Junior was hospitable enough to invite me,'' she said as she sat down in the chair Junior was holding out for her.

''I had to do some arm-twisting,'' he told his parents, taking the chair next to her. ''She plays hard to get.''

''Her mother certainly didn't.''

Sarah Jo's cool, catty remark momentarily stifled the conversation. It served to counteract the potency of Alex's glass of wine. Her giddiness fizzled and went flat as day-old soda. She nodded toward Sarah Jo and said, ''Hello, Mrs. Minton. You look lovely tonight.''

Even though her dress was inappropriate, she did look lovely in it. *Not vibrant,* Alex thought. Sarah Jo could never look vivacious and animated. Her beauty had an ethereal quality, as though her visitation on earth was temporary and tenuous. She gave Alex one of her vague, secretive smiles and murmured a thank-you as she took a sip of wine.

''Heard you were the one who discovered Pasty's body.''

''Dad, this is a party,'' Junior said. ''Alex won't want to talk about something nasty like that.''

''No, it's all right, Junior. I would have brought it up myself, sooner or later.''

''I don't reckon it was coincidence that you met him at that honky-tonk and climbed into his pickup with him,'' Angus said, rolling the cigar from one corner of his lips to the other.

''No.'' She paraphrased for them her telephone conversations with Pasty.

''That cowboy was a liar, a fornicator, and worse than all his other vices put together, he cheated at poker,'' Angus said with some vehemence. ''In the last few years he'd gone plumb goofy and irresponsible. That's why I had to let him go. I figure you've got better sense than to put any stock in what he told you.''

In the middle of his monologue, Angus signaled the waiter to bring another round of drinks. ''Oh, sure, Pasty might've seen who went into that stable with Celina, but the one he saw was Gooney Bud.''

Having said his piece, and giving Alex no opportunity to dispute it, he launched into a glowing review of a jockey from Ruidoso that he wanted to ride for them. Since the Mintons were her hosts, Alex graciously let the topic of Pasty Hickam die for the moment.

When they'd finished their drinks, Angus and Junior offered to go through the barbecue buffet for the ladies. Alex would just as soon have gone through the line herself. She found it difficult to make small talk with Sarah Jo, but after the men withdrew, she valiantly made an attempt.

"Have you been members of the club for a long time?"

"Angus was one of the charter members," Sarah Jo supplied distractedly. She kept her eyes on the couples doing the two-step in an eternal circle around the dance floor.

"He seems to have a finger in just about every pie in town," Alex remarked.

"Hmm, he likes to know everything that's going on."

"And be a part of it."

"Yes. He makes things happen and spreads himself thin." She gave a delicate sigh. "Angus has this need to be well liked, you see. He's always politicking, as though it matters what other people think."

Alex folded her hands beneath her chin and propped her elbows on the table. "You don't believe it matters?"

"No." Her entrancement with the dancers ended. For the first time that evening, she looked directly at Alex. "Don't read too much into the way Junior treats you."

"Oh?"

"He flirts with every woman he meets."

Alex slowly lowered her hands to her lap. Anger roiled inside, but she managed to keep her voice low and level. "I resent your implication, Mrs. Minton."

Sarah Jo lifted one shoulder indifferently. "Both of my men are charming and they know it. Most women don't realize that their flirting is meaningless."

"I'm sure that's true of Angus, but I don't know about Junior. Three ex-wives might disagree with you about his flirting."

"They were all wrong for him."

"What about my mother? Would she have been wrong for him?"

Sarah Jo fixed her empty stare on Alex again. "Absolutely wrong. You're a lot like her, you know."

"Am I?"

"You enjoy causing dissonance. Your mother was never content to leave bothersome things alone. The only difference is that you're even better at making trouble and creating ill will than she was. You're direct to the point of being tactless, a trait I've always attributed to bad breeding." She lifted her eyes to someone who had moved up behind Alex.

"Good evening, Sarah Jo."

"Judge Wallace." A sweet smile broke across Sarah Jo's face. One would never guess she had had her stinger out seconds earlier. "Hello, Stacey."

Alex, her face hot with indignation over Sarah Jo's unwarranted criticism, turned around. Judge Joe Wallace was staring down at her with disapproval, as though her being there was a breach of the club's standards.

"Miss Gaither."

"Hello, Judge Wallace." The woman standing beside him looked at Alex with a censure that matched his, though for what reason, Alex couldn't guess. Obviously, Junior was the only friendly face she was going to find in this crowd.

The judge gave the woman's arm a nudge and they moved toward another table. "Is that his wife?" Alex asked, following their progress.

"Good heavens, no," Sarah Jo said. "His daughter. Poor Stacey. Eternally dowdy."

Stacey Wallace was still staring at Alex with such malice that she was captivated by it. She didn't break her stare until Junior's knee bumped hers when he resumed his seat and set two plates of food on the table.

"I hope you like ribs and beans." His gaze followed the direction of hers. "Hey, Stacey." He winked at her and raised his hand in a friendly wave.

The woman's puckered mouth relaxed into a faltering smile. Blushing, she raised her hand to her neckline like a flustered girl and called back shyly, "Hi, Junior."

"Well?"

Though she was still curious about the judge and his chameleon daughter, Junior's one-word inquiry brought Alex's head around. "Sorry?"

"Do you like ribs and beans?"

"Watch me," she laughed, spreading the napkin over her lap.

She did unladylike damage to her plate of food, but her healthy appetite earned her a compliment from Angus. "Sarah Jo eats like a bird. Don't you like the ribs, honey?" he asked, looking into her plate, which had barely been disturbed.

"They're a little dry."

"Want me to order you something else?"

"No, thank you."

After they'd eaten, Angus took a fresh cigar from his pocket and lit it. Fanning out the match, he said, "Why don't you two dance?"

"Are you game?" Junior asked.

"Sure." Alex pushed back her chair and stood up. "But this kind of dancing isn't my forte, so nothing too fancy, please."

Junior drew her into his arms and, disobeying her request, executed a series of intricate turns and dips. "Very nice," he said, smiling down at her when they lapsed into a more sedate two-step. Using the arm he had placed around her waist, he pulled her tighter against him. "Very, *very* nice."

Alex let him hold her close because it felt good to have two strong arms around her. Her partner was handsome and charming and knew how to make a woman feel beautiful. She was a victim of his charms, but knowing it was her safety net.

She could never actually fall for a glib charmer like Junior, but small doses of attention from one was fun temporarily, especially since every time she was around Reede, her confidence and ego took a beating.

"Is Reede a club member?" she asked casually.

"Are you kiddin'?"

"He hasn't been invited to join?"

"Oh, sure, as soon as he won sheriff the first time. It's just that he feels more at home in another crowd. He doesn't give a fuck—excuse me—for society stuff." He stroked her back. "You seem more relaxed than when I picked you up. Having fun?"

"Yes, but you got me here under false pretenses," she accused. "You're a long way from becoming drunk and talkative."

His smile was unrepentant. "Ask me anything."

"Okay. Who's the man over there, the one with the white hair?" Junior identified him by name. Her instincts proved correct. His name had been among those at the bottom of her letter. "Introduce us when the band takes its next break."

"He's married."

She shot him a look. "My interest in him isn't romantic."

"Ah, good, good."

He did as she asked. The banker she had picked out of the crowd seemed disconcerted when Junior introduced her. As she shook hands with him, she said, "I received your letter, Mr. Longstreet."

Her straightforwardness surprised him, but he recovered admirably. "I see that you're taking it to heart." He slid a knowing glance toward Junior.

"Don't let my being here tonight with Junior fool you. I can appreciate what he, his father, and Mr. Lambert mean to Purcell and its economy, but that does not mean I'll suspend my investigation. It'll take more than a letter to scare me off."

Clearly irritated, Junior spoke to her out of the side of his mouth as he escorted her back onto the dance floor a few minutes later. "You could have warned me."

"About what?"

"That you are armed and dangerous. Longstreet's a big wheel who shouldn't be put on the defensive. What's all this about a letter, anyway?"

She explained, reciting as many of the names as she could recall. "I hoped to meet some of them here tonight."

He pulled a deep frown, regarding her with asperity. Eventually, however, he shrugged and fashioned a beguiling smile. "And here I thought I'd swept you off your feet." Sighing in resignation, he added, "Well, I'd just as well help you out. Want to meet the rest of your adversaries?"

Trying to make it appear as casual as possible, Junior moved her through the crowd, introducing her to those there who had signed their names to that subtly threatening letter.

A half hour later they moved away from a couple who owned a chain of convenience stores throughout West Texas. They had invested heavily in Purcell Downs and were the most demonstratively hostile. By that time, though, word had gotten around who Junior's date was, so they'd been laying for her.

"There, that's everybody," he told her.

"Thank God," Alex whispered. "Are the knives still sticking out of my back?"

"You're not going to let that old biddy's rapier tongue get to you, are you? Look, she's a dried up old shrew who hates any woman who doesn't have a mustache as thick as hers."

Alex smiled in spite of herself. "She all but said, 'Be on the next stage leaving town . . . or else.' "

He squeezed her arm. "Come on, let's dance again. It will take your mind off your troubles."

"I need to repair the damages," she said, slipping out of his grasp. "Excuse me."

"Okay. The little girls' room is thataway." He pointed down a narrow hallway.

There was no one in the powder room when she went in, but when she came out of the cubicle, the judge's daughter was standing in front of the dressing table, staring at her reflection in the mirror. She turned and faced Alex.

Alex smiled. "Hi."

"Hello."

Alex moved to the sink and washed her hands. "We haven't been formally introduced. I'm Alex Gaither." She plucked two coarse paper towels from the dispenser.

"Yes, I know."

Alex dropped the used towels into the wastepaper basket. "You're Judge Wallace's daughter." She attempted to break the ice in an atmosphere that was glacial and getting colder by the second. The woman had dropped all vestiges of the shy, insecure maiden she had assumed when Junior had spoken to her. Her face was stony and uncompromisingly antagonistic. "Stacey, wasn't it?"

"Yes. Stacey. But the last name isn't Wallace. It's Minton."

"Minton?"

"That's right. I am Junior's wife. His *first* wife."

 TWENTY

"I can see that's news to you," Stacey said, laughing humorlessly at Alex's dumbfounded expression.

"Yes," she replied in a hollow tone. "No one's mentioned that."

Stacey's composure, always intact, deserted her. Flattening a hand on her meager bosom, she cried out, "Do you have any idea the damage you're doing?"

"To whom?"

"To me," she shouted, pounding her chest. Immediately she dropped her hand and rolled her lips inward, as though mortified by her outburst. She closed her eyes momentarily. When she opened them, they were filled with animosity, but she appeared to have regained control of herself. "For twenty-five years I've had to live down the generally held belief that Junior Minton married me on the rebound from your mother."

Alex didn't state the obvious, but guiltily lowered her eyes.

"I see that you hold to that belief, too."

"I'm sorry, Miss . . . Stacey. May I call you Stacey?"

"Of course," she replied stiffly.

"I'm sorry that my investigation has distressed you."

"How could it not? You're dredging up the past. By doing so, you're airing my dirty linen for all the town to see. Again."

"I had no idea who Junior's first wife was, or that she even lived in Purcell."

"Would it have mattered?"

"Probably not," Alex answered with rueful honesty. "I can't see that your marriage to Junior has any bearing on the case. It's a peripheral association that I can't help."

"What about my father?" Stacey asked, switching subjects.

"What about him?"

"This petty investigation of yours is going to cause him embarrassment. It already has."

"How so?"

"The fact that you're questioning his original ruling."

"I'm sorry. I can't help that, either."

"Can't—or won't?" Stacey held her arms straight at her sides and shuddered with revulsion. "I abhor people who trample on the reputations of others for their own personal gain."

"Is that what you think I'm doing?" Alex asked, taking umbrage. "Do you think I devised this investigation to advance my career?"

"Didn't you?"

"No," she answered, firmly shaking her head. "My mother was murdered in that stable. I don't believe that the man accused of it was capable of committing the crime. I want to know what really happened. I *will* know what happened. And I'll make the one responsible pay for making me an orphan."

"I was prepared to give you the benefit of the doubt, but I see it's only revenge you want, after all."

"I want justice."

"No matter what it costs other people?"

"I've already apologized for any unhappiness it causes you."

Stacey made a scoffing sound. "You want to publicly crucify my father. Don't deny it," she snapped when Alex started to object. "No matter how much you deny it, you're leaving him open to ridicule. At the very least, you're accusing him of making a serious error in judgment."

To deny that would be a lie. "Yes, I believe he made a bad judgment in the case of Buddy Hicks."

"Daddy's got forty impeccable years on the bench that vouch for his wisdom and integrity."

"If my investigation is petty, as you call it, it won't affect his record, will it, Mrs. Minton? A lofty judge couldn't possibly be brought down by a lowly public prosecutor with nothing except spite and vengeance for ammunition. Evidence would be necessary to support my allegations."

"You don't have any."

"I believe I will before I'm finished. If your father's reputation suffers as a result . . ." She drew a deep breath and raised a weary hand to her forehead. Her expression was earnest, her words heartfelt. "Stacey, I don't want to ruin your father's career or besmirch his tenure on the bench. I don't want to hurt anybody's feelings or cause any innocent bystander grief or embarrassment. I only want to see justice done."

"Justice," Stacey sneered, her eyes narrowing with malice. "You've got no right to even speak the word. You're just like your mother—pretty, but shallow. Single-minded and selfish. Uncaring of other people's feelings. Unable to see beyond your own superficial desires."

"I take it you didn't like my mother very much," Alex remarked, her voice laden with sarcasm.

Stacey took her seriously. "I hated her."

"Why? Because Junior was in love with her?"

Alex reasoned that if Stacey were going to hit below the belt, she might as well, too. It worked. Stacey fell back a step and groped for the dressing table to support herself. Reflexively, Alex extended a helping hand, but the judge's daughter recoiled from her touch.

"Stacey, I know that Junior married you only a few weeks after my mother was killed. You must realize how odd that strikes me."

"It might have seemed sudden, but we'd been dating for years."

That surprised Alex. "You had?"

"Yes. And for most of that time, we'd been lovers."

Stacey threw that piece of news at Alex like a dart, sharply and triumphantly. All it served, however, was to make Alex pity her more. She had the full picture now of a plain girl, hopelessly in love with the affable and handsome football hero, willing to sacrifice anything, including her pride, to have even scraps of his attention. She would do anything to keep him near her. "I see."

"I doubt it. Just like Junior, you're blind to the truth."

"What is the truth, Stacey?"

"That Celina was wrong for him. Like everybody else, she constantly compared him to Reede. Junior always came out in second place. I didn't care how he measured up to anybody. I loved him for what he was. Junior didn't want to believe it, but in spite of your father and you, Celina would have always loved Reede."

"If she loved him so much, why did she marry my father?" That question had been plaguing Alex for days.

"Celina and Reede had a falling out the spring of our junior year. As soon as school was out for the summer, she went to visit cousins in El Paso."

"That's where she met my father." Alex knew this much of the story from her grandmother. "He was going through boot camp at Fort Bliss. Soon after they were married, he got shipped to Vietnam."

Stacey sneered, "And after he died, she wanted to take back up with Reede, but he wouldn't have her. That's when she kindled Junior's hopes. She knew he'd always wanted her, but he never would have pursued it, on account of Reede. It was disgraceful how she played up to Junior, involving him with her pregnancy. She might have toyed with the idea of marrying him, but it never would have happened as long as Reede Lambert drew breath.

"Your mother kept Junior dangling by a thread of hope. She made his life miserable. She would have gone on making him miserable if she had lived." The former Mrs. Minton drew a choppy breath that caused her shapeless chest to stagger as it rose and fell. "I was glad when Celina died."

A spark of suspicion leaped into Alex's eyes. "Where were you that night?"

"At home unpacking. I'd just returned from a week's vacation in Galveston."

Would she lie over something so easily checked? "You married Junior right away."

"That's right. He needed me. I knew that I was only a panacea for his grief, just like I'd always known when he made love to me that it was Celina he really wanted. But I didn't care if he used me. I wanted to be used. I cooked his meals, took care of his clothes, nurtured him in bed and out."

Her expression changed as she lapsed into a private reverie. "I overlooked the first time he was unfaithful to me. I was crushed, naturally, but I could understand how easily it had happened. Whenever we went out, women flocked to him. What man could resist such a strong temptation? The affair didn't last long before he lost interest." She clasped her hands and studied them as she spoke softly. "Then there was another. And another. I would have tolerated all his lovers if only he'd stayed married to me.

"But he asked me for a divorce. At first I refused. He kept on and on, telling me that he hated hurting me with his affairs. When I was left no option, I granted the divorce. It broke my heart, but I gave him what he wanted, knowing, *knowing*," she repeated with emphasis, "that no other woman would ever be as right for him as I was. I thought I'd die with the pain of loving him too well."

She shook herself out of the reflective mood and beaded on Alex. "And I still have to stand by and watch him move from woman to woman, all the time searching for what I can and want to give him. I had to watch him dance and flirt with you tonight. You! My God," she sobbed, tilting her face toward the ceiling and pressing her fist to her forehead, eyes squeezed shut. "You want to ruin him, and he still can't see beyond your pretty face and body."

She lowered her hand and glared at Alex. "You are poison, Miss Gaither. I feel the same way about you tonight as I did twenty-five years ago." Closing the distance between them and putting her narrow, angular face close to Alex's she hissed, "I wish you'd never been born."

Alex's attempts to compose herself after Stacey's departure had been in vain. Her face was pale and she was trembling as she walked out of the powder room.

"I was about to come in and get you." Junior was waiting for Alex in the hallway. At first he didn't notice her troubled expression. When he did, he was instantly concerned. "Alex? What's the matter?"

"I'd like to leave now."

"Are you sick? What's—"

"Please. We'll talk on the way."

Without further argument, Junior took her arm and steered her toward the cloakroom, where he asked the attendant for their coats. "Wait here." Alex watched him reenter the club, skirt the dance floor, and move to the table where they had eaten dinner. After a brief exchange with Angus and Sarah Jo, he returned in time to claim their coats.

He hustled her outside and into the red Jaguar. He waited until they were a good distance from the club and the car's heater was pumping warm air before he addressed her across the plush interior. "All right, what gives?"

"Why didn't you tell me that you were married to Stacey Wallace?"

He stared at her until it became a driving hazard, then turned his head and fixed his eyes on the road ahead. "You didn't ask."

"How glib."

She laid her head against the cold passenger window, feeling like she'd just sustained a beating with a chain and was due to enter the ring for round two. Just when she thought she had finished sorting through all the pieces of the various liaisons of Purcell, another intricate twist emerged.

"Is it important?" Junior asked.

"I don't know." She turned her shoulders toward him and rested the back of her head on the window. "You tell me. Is it?"

"No. The marriage lasted less than a year. We parted friends."

"*You* parted friends. She's still in love with you."

He winced. "That was one of our problems. Stacey's love is obsessive and possessive. She shackled me. I couldn't breathe. We—"

"Junior, you screwed around," she interrupted impatiently. "Spare me the banal explanations. I really don't care."

"Then why'd you bring it up?"

"Because she confronted me in the powder room and accused me of ruining her father's life with this investigation."

"For crissake, Alex, Joe Wallace is a big crybaby. Stacey mothers him. I don't doubt for a minute that he's whined and carried on about you something awful in front of her. It's a ploy to get her sympathy. They feed each other's neuroses. Don't worry about it."

Alex didn't like Junior Minton very much at that moment. His cavalier attitude toward a woman's—*any* woman's—love reduced him in Alex's eyes. She'd watched him tonight, doing just as Stacey had described, moving from woman to woman. The young and old, attractive and homely, married and unattached, all seemed to be fair game. He was charming with each, like a small Easter bunny working the crowd, doling out treats to greedy children who didn't realize they'd be better off without them.

He seemed to take their fawning as his due. Alex had never found that kind of conceit commendable or appealing. Junior took for granted that he would elicit a response from every woman he spoke to. Flirting was an involuntary action to him, as natural as breathing. It would never occur to him that someone might misinterpret his intentions and suffer emotional pain.

Perhaps if she hadn't had the conversation with Stacey, Alex would have smiled indulgently, as all the other women had, and accepted his suaveness as part of his personality. But instead, she now felt irritable toward him and wanted him to know she couldn't be so blithely dismissed. "It wasn't just the judge Stacey took issue with. She said I was stirring up memories of her marriage to you, airing her dirty linen. I get the impression that being your ex has been a real trial for her."

"That's not really my problem, is it?"

"Maybe it should be."

Her harsh backlash surprised him. "You sound mad at me. Why?"

"I don't know." The flare of her temper had been short and sweet. Now, she felt drained. "I'm sorry. Maybe it's just that I always pull for the underdog."

He reached across the car and covered her knee with his hand. "An admirable quality that hasn't escaped my notice." Alex picked up his hand and dropped it back onto the leather seat between them. "Uh-oh, I'm not off the hook yet."

She resisted his smile. "Why did you marry Stacey?"

"Is this really what you want to talk about?" He wheeled the car up to the breezeway of the Westerner Motel and shifted the gear into Park.

"Yes."

Frowning, he cut the engine and laid his arm along the seat, turning toward her. "It seemed like the thing to do at the time."

"You didn't love her."

"No shit."

"But you made love to her." He raised an inquisitive eyebrow. "Stacey told me that you'd been lovers for a long time before you got married."

"Not lovers, Alex. I took her out every now and then."

"How often?"

"You want it plain?"

"Shoot."

"I called on Stacey whenever I got horny and the Gail sisters were busy, or had their periods, or—"

"The who?"

"The Gail sisters. Another story." He waved off the questions he could see rising in her mind.

"I've got all night." She settled more comfortably against her door.

"Doesn't anything escape you?"

"Very little. What about these sisters?"

"There were three of them—triplets, in fact. All named Gail."

"That stands to reason."

"No, it wasn't their last name. Their names were Wanda Gail, Nora Gail, and Peggy Gail."

"Is this a joke?"

He drew an *x* across his chest. "Cross my heart. Reede had already initiated them, so to speak, before I arrived on the scene. He introduced me to them." He snickered, as though recalling a particularly sordid incident of his youth. "In short, the Gail sisters put out. They liked putting out. Every guy in Purcell High School must of had them at least once."

"Okay, I get the picture. But when they were unavailable, you called on Stacey Wallace, because she put out, too."

He looked at her levelly. "I've never coerced a woman. She was willing, Alex."

"Only for you."

He shrugged an admission.

"And you took advantage of that."

"Name me one guy who wouldn't."

"You've got a point," she said dryly. "I would venture to say that you're the only man Stacey's ever been with."

He had the grace to look a little ashamed. "Yeah, I'd say so, too."

"I felt sorry for her tonight, Junior. She was hateful to me, but I couldn't help but feel sorry for her."

"I never understood why she latched onto me, but she shadowed me from the day I enrolled into Purcell High School. She was a brainy kid, you know. Always the teachers' favorite because she was so conscientious and never got into trouble." He chuckled. "They'd *never* believe what she was willing to do in the back seat of my Chevy."

Alex gazed distractedly into space, not really listening. "Stacey despised Celina."

"She was jealous of her."

"Mainly because when you made love to Stacey, she knew it was my mother you were wishing for."

"Jesus," he swore softly, his smile collapsing.

"That's what she said. Is that true?"

"Celina was always with Reede. That's just the way it was. It was a fact of life."

"But you did want her, even though she belonged to your best friend?"

After a lengthy pause, he admitted, "I'd be lying if I said otherwise."

Very softly, Alex said, "Stacey told me something else. It was an offhanded comment, not a revelation. She said it as though it was common knowledge—something I should already know."

"What?"

"That you wanted to marry my mother." She refocused on him and asked huskily, "Did you?"

He averted his head for a second, then said, "Yes."

"Before or after she got married and had me?"

"Both." When he saw her apparent confusion, he said, "I don't think a man could look at Celina and not want her for his own. She was beautiful and funny and had this way of making you think you were special to her. She had . . ." He groped for the adequate word. "Something," he said, closing his fist around the elusive noun, "something that made you want to possess her."

"Did you ever possess her?"

"Physically?"

"Did you ever sleep with my mother?"

His expression was baldly honest and terribly sad. "No, Alex. Never."

"Did you ever try? Would she have?"

"I don't think so. I never tried. At least, not very hard."

"Why not, if you wanted her so much?"

"Because Reede would have killed us."

Stunned, she gazed at him. "Do you really think so?"

He shrugged as his disarming smile moved into place. "Figure of speech."

Alex wasn't so sure. It had sounded literal when he said it.

He scooted along the seat of his Jaguar until they were sitting very close. He slid his fingers up through her hair, laid his thumb along her neck and stroked it lightly.

"That's sure a dreary subject. Let's change it," he whispered, brushing an airy kiss across her mouth. "How about leaving the past for a while and thinking about the present?" His eyes wandered over her face while his fingertips touched each feature. "I want to sleep with you, Alex."

For a moment, she was too stunned to speak. "You're not serious?"

"Wanna bet?"

He kissed her in earnest then. At least, he tried to. Tilting his head, he rested his lips upon hers, pressed, tested, pressed harder. When she didn't respond, he pulled back and gave her a puzzled look.

"No?"

"No."

"Why not?"

"You know without my telling you. It would be crazy. Wrong."

"I've done crazier things." He lowered his hand to the front of her sweater and fingered a patch of soft suede. "Wronger things, too."

"Well, I haven't."

"We'd be good together, Alex."

"We'll never know."

He ran his thumb along her lower lip, tracking its slow progress with his eyes. "Never say never." He bent his head and kissed her again—affectionately, not passionately—then returned to the driver's side of the car and got out.

At the door, he gave her a chaste good-night kiss, but his expression was indulgent and amused. Alex knew he thought she was just being coy and that wearing her down was only a matter of time.

She was so befuddled by his come-on that it was several minutes before she noticed that the red message light on her telephone was blinking. She called the motel's front desk, retrieved her message, and called the specified number. Even before the doctor got on the line, she knew what he would say. Nevertheless, his words shocked her.

"Miss Gaither, I'm terribly sorry. Mrs. Graham passed away earlier this evening without ever regaining consciousness."

 # TWENTY-ONE

Alex knocked and waited until Reede called out, "Come in," before entering his office. "Good morning. Thank you for seeing me on such short notice."

She sat down in the chair in front of his desk. Without asking, he poured her a cup of coffee to her liking and placed it in front of her. She thanked him with a nod.

"I'm sorry about your grandmother, Alex," he said as he resumed his seat in the creaky swivel chair.

"Thank you."

Alex had been away for a week, handling the details of her grandmother's funeral. Only Alex, a handful of former coworkers, and a few of the nursing home patients had attended the chapel service. After the burial, Alex had begun the unwelcome chore of clearing out her grandmother's room at the nursing home. The staff had been kind, but there was a waiting list, so they had needed the room emptied immediately.

It had been an emotionally stressful week. As she had sat staring at the modest casket, while organ music played softly in the background, she had felt an overwhelming sense of defeat. She had failed to fulfill the promise she had made to herself and to her grandmother: She hadn't produced Celina's murderer in time.

More defeating than that, she had failed to win her grandmother's absolution and love. That had been her last chance; she wouldn't have another.

She had given serious consideration to throwing in the towel, telling Greg that he'd been right, and that she should have taken his advice from the beginning. He would enjoy seeing her humility, and he would immediately assign her another case.

That would have been the easier course. She would never have to enter the city limits of Purcell again, or cope with the hostility that flew at her like missiles from everyone she met, or look into the face of this man, who generated myriad ambiguous feelings inside her.

From a legal viewpoint, she still had a case too weak to stand up in court. But from a personal perspective, she couldn't quit. She had become intrigued by the men who had loved her mother. She *had* to know which one of them had killed her, and whether or not she was responsible for her mother's murder. She would either have to deny her guilt, or learn to live with it, but she couldn't let it go forever unresolved.

So, she had returned to Purcell. She was staring into the pair of green eyes that had haunted her thoughts for a week, and they were as compelling and disturbing as she remembered.

"I wasn't sure you'd be back," he told her bluntly.

"You should have been. I told you I wouldn't give up."

"Yeah, I remember," he said grimly. "How was the dance the other night?"

His question came out of the blue and evoked a knee-jerk response. "How did you know I went?"

"Word gets around."

"Junior told you."

"No."

"I can hardly stand the suspense," Alex said. "How did you find out I went to the Horse and Gun Club?"

"One of my deputies clocked Junior doing eighty-one that night out on the highway. Around eleven o'clock, he said. He saw you in the car with him." He was no longer looking at her, but studying the toes of his boots. "You sure were in a hell of a hurry to get back to your motel."

"I was ready to leave the club, that's all. I wasn't feeling well."

"The barbecue didn't sit well with you? Or was it the people? Some of them make me sick to my stomach, too."

"It wasn't the food or the people. It was, well, one person: Stacey Wallace . . . Minton." Alex closely watched for his reaction. His face remained impassive. "Why didn't anyone tell me that Stacey had been married to Junior?"

"You didn't ask."

Miraculously, she was able to hold her temper in check. "Didn't it occur to anybody that their hasty marriage might be significant?"

"It wasn't."

"I reserve the right to decide the significance of it myself."

"Be my guest. Do you think it's significant?"

"Yes, I do. The timing of Junior's first marriage always struck me as strange. It's even stranger that the bride turned out to be the judge's daughter."

"That's not strange at all."

"Coincidental, certainly."

"Not even that. Stacey Wallace had been in love, or lust, with Junior since the day she first laid eyes on him. Everybody knew it, including Junior. She certainly made no secret of her devotion. When Celina died, Stacey saw her chance and seized it."

"Stacey didn't strike me as an opportunist."

"Grow up, Alex. We're all opportunists when we want something bad enough.

She loved the guy," he pointed out impatiently. "He was sick over Celina's death. I guess Stacey figured her love could make his hurt go away, that it would be enough."

"It wasn't."

"Obviously. She couldn't make Junior love her back. She sure as hell couldn't weld his zippers shut." Vexed, he gnawed on the corner of his lip. "Who spilled the beans about this, Junior?"

"Stacey herself. She confronted me in the powder room and accused me of upsetting her life by reopening this case."

"Gutsy lady," he said, nodding approval. "I always liked her."

"Oh, really? Did you sleep with her, too? Or did the Gail sisters keep you satisfied?"

"The Gail sisters, huh?" He barked a short laugh. "I know Stacey didn't talk to you about Purcell's notorious triplets."

"Junior filled in the gaps."

"Must have been quite an evening."

"Most revealing."

"Oh, yeah?" he drawled. "What'd you reveal?"

She ignored this well-placed insinuation. "Reede, what was the rush? Junior wasn't in love with Stacey. For the sake of argument, let's say he talked himself into marrying her. Why did they marry when they did?"

"Maybe she wanted to be a June bride."

"Don't make fun of me!" She shot out of her chair and moved to the window.

He whistled low and long. "Boy, are you ever in a rotten mood."

"I just buried my only living relative, remember?" she flared.

He cursed beneath his breath and raked his fingers through his hair. "For a minute there, I did forget. Look, Alex, I'm sorry. I remember how bad I felt when I buried my old man."

She turned to face him, but he was staring at nothing. "Angus and Junior were the only ones out of the whole goddamn town who came to the funeral. We didn't even hold it in a church or the funeral home, just at the grave site. Angus went back to work. Junior returned to school so he wouldn't miss a biology test. I went home.

"Not long after lunch, Celina came to my house. She had skipped school just to come and be with me. She knew I'd feel low, even though I hated the son of a bitch while he was alive. We lay down together on my bed and stayed there until it got dark. She knew if she didn't go home, her mother would get worried. She cried for me because I couldn't."

When he stopped speaking, there was a ponderous silence in the room. Alex was still standing by the window, motionless and transfixed by his story. Her chest hurt with heartache for the lonely young man he'd been.

"Was that the first time you made love to Celina?"

He looked straight at her, got out of his chair, and approached her. "Since you broached the subject of love lives, how's yours?"

The tension snapped, as did her temper. "Why don't you stop beating around the bush and come right out and ask?"

"Okay," he sneered. "Has Junior made it into your pants yet?"

"You bastard."

"Has he?"

"No!"

"I'll bet he's tried. He always tries." His laugh was deep and stirring. "Bingo." He raised his hand and stroked her cheek with the backs of his fingers. "You're blushing, Counselor."

She swatted his hand aside. "Go to hell."

She was furious with herself for blushing like a schoolgirl in front of him. It was none of his business who she slept with. What bothered her most, however, was that he didn't seem to care. If she had to describe that glint in his eyes she would call it amusement, possibly contempt, but certainly not jealousy.

To retaliate, she asked suddenly, "What did you and Celina quarrel about?"

"Celina and I? When?"

"The spring of your junior year. Why did she go to El Paso for the summer and start dating my father?"

"Maybe she needed a change of scenery," he said flippantly.

"Did you know how much your best friend loved her?"

His goading grin vanished. "Did Junior tell you that?"

"I knew before he told me. Did you know, at the time, that he loved her?"

He rolled his shoulders forward in a semblance of a shrug. "Nearly every guy in school—"

"I'm not talking about infatuation with a popular girl, Reede." She grabbed his shirtsleeve to show just how important this was to her. "Did you know how Junior felt about her?"

"What if I did?"

"He said you would have killed him if he'd tried anything with her. He said you would have killed them both if they had betrayed you."

"A figure of speech."

"That's what Junior said, too, but I don't think so," she said evenly. "There were a lot of passions stirring. Your relationships with each other were overlapping and complex."

"Whose relationships?"

"You and my mother loved each other, but you both loved Junior, too. Wasn't it a love triangle in the strictest sense of the word?"

"What the hell are you talking about? Do you think Junior and I are a couple of queers?"

Unexpectedly, he grabbed her hand and flattened it against his fly. "Feel that, baby? It's been hard more than it's been soft, but it's never been hard for a fag."

Stunned and shaken, she pried her hand away, subconsciously rubbing the palm of it against her thigh, as though it had been branded. "You have a redneck mentality, Sheriff Lambert," she said, supremely agitated. "I think you and Junior love each other the way Indian blood brothers do. But you're competitive, too."

"I don't compete with Junior."

"Maybe not consciously, but other people have pitted you against each other. And guess which one of you always came out on top? *You.* That bothered you. It still does."

"Is this more of your psychological bullshit?"

"It's not just my opinion. Stacey mentioned it the other night, and not at my prompting. She said people always compared the two of you, and that Junior always came in second."

"I can't help what people think."

"Your competitiveness came to a head over Celina, didn't it?"

"Why ask me? You've got all the answers."

"You had the edge there, too. Junior wanted to be Celina's lover, but you actually were."

A long silence followed. Reede regarded her with the concentration of a hunter who finally has his quarry in the cross hairs. The sunlight streaming through the blinds glinted in his eyes, on his hair, on his eyebrows, which were slanted dangerously.

Very quietly, he said, "Good try, Alex, but I'm not admitting anything."

He tried to move away then, but she caught his arms. "Well, weren't you her lover? What difference does it make if you say so now?"

"Because I never kiss and tell." His eyes slid down to her pulsing throat, then back up. "And you should be damned glad I don't."

Want surged through her, as warm and golden as the morning sunlight. She craved to feel his hard lips on hers again, the rough, powerful mastery of his tongue inside her mouth. She became dewy with desire and tearful with remorse for what she desperately wanted and couldn't have.

Eyes locked, neither realized that they were being observed from across the street. The sun was as good as a spotlight on them.

Willing herself out of the dubious present and into the disturbing past, she said, "Junior told me that you and Celina were more than just childhood sweethearts." It was a bluff, but she gambled on it working. "He told me everything about your relationship with her, so it really doesn't matter whether you admit it or not. When did you and she first . . . you know?"

"Fuck?"

The vulgarity, spoken in a low, thrumming rasp, sent shafts of heat through her. Never had that word sounded erotic to her before. She swallowed and made an almost imperceptible nod of acknowledgment.

Suddenly, he hooked his hand around the back of her neck and pulled her against him, placing her face directly beneath his. His eyes bore into hers.

"Junior didn't tell you shit, Counselor," he whispered. "Don't try your fancy, courtroom-lawyer bluffs on me. I've got eighteen years on you, and I was born smart. The tricks I've got up my sleeve, you've never even heard about. I'm damn sure not ignorant enough to fall for yours."

His fist clenched tighter around the handful of her hair he was holding. His breath felt hotter and came faster against her face. "Don't ever try to come between Junior and me again, you hear? Fight us both or fuck us both, but don't temper with something outside your understanding."

His eyes narrowed with sinister intensity. "Your mama had a bad habit of playing both ends against the middle, Alex. Somebody got a bellyful of it and killed her before she learned her lesson. You'd do well to learn it before something like that happens to you."

The morning was a washout in terms of discovering new clues. Nothing diverted her mind from the disturbing conversation she had had with Reede. If a deputy hadn't knocked on the office door and interrupted them, she didn't know whether she would have clawed at Reede's eyes or yielded to her stronger urge to press her body close to his and kiss him.

At noon she stopped trying to concentrate and crossed the street to have lunch at the B & B Café. Like most people who worked downtown, that had become her habit. No longer were conversations suspended when she went in. Every now and then she even merited a greeting from Pete if he wasn't too busy in the kitchen.

She dawdled over her meal as long as possible, scooting the yellow ceramic armadillo ashtray back and forth across her table and leafing through Pete's printed brochure on the proper way to prepare rattlesnake.

She was killing time, loath to return to the dingy little office in the basement of the courthouse and stare into space, recounting unsettling thoughts and reviewing hypotheses that seemed more farfetched by the hour. But one thought kept haunting her. Was there any connection between Celina's death and Junior's hasty marriage to Stacey Wallace?

Her mind was steeped in speculation when she left the café. Ducking her head against the cold wind, she walked toward the corner. The traffic light, one of the few downtown, changed just as she reached the corner. She was about to step off the cracked and buckled concrete curb when her arm was caught from behind.

"Reverend Plummet," she stated in surprise. Subsequent events had quickly dismissed him and his timid wife from her mind.

"Miss Gaither," he said in a censorious tone, "I saw you with the sheriff this morning." He could have tacked on any number of deadly sins to account for the accusation smoldering in his deep-set eyes. "You've disappointed me."

"I fail to see—"

"Furthermore," he interrupted with the rolling intonation of a sidewalk evangelist, "you've disappointed the Almighty." His eyes rounded largely, then closed to mere slits. "I warn you, the Lord will not tolerate being mocked."

She nervously moistened her lips and glanced around, hoping to see some avenue of escape, though she didn't know what form it might take. "I haven't meant to offend you or God," she said, feeling foolish for even making such a statement.

"You haven't locked the iniquitous behind bars yet."

"I haven't found any reason to. My investigation isn't complete. And just to set the record straight, Reverend Plummet, I didn't come here to lock anybody behind bars."

"You're being too soft on the ungodly."

"If by that you mean that I've approached this investigation impartially, then yes, I have."

"I saw you this morning fraternizing with that son of the devil."

His maniacal eyes were arresting, if repellent. She caught herself staring into them. "You mean Reede?"

He made a hissing sound, as though the very name conjured up an evil spirit that must be warded off. "Don't be taken in by his wily devices."

"I assure you, I'm not."

He came a step closer. "The devil knows where women are weak. He uses their soft, vulnerable bodies as channels for his evil powers. They're tainted, and must be cleansed by a regular outpouring of blood."

He isn't only nutty, he's sick, Alex thought in horror.

He slapped his hand upon his Bible, causing Alex to jump. Raising his index finger into the air, he shouted, "Resist all temptation, daughter! I command every lascivious impulse to desert your heart and mind and body. Now," he bellowed.

He slumped, as though the exorcism had totally drained him of energy. Alex stood transfixed by disbelief. Coming to her senses, she glanced around uneasily, hoping that no one had witnessed this madness and her unwitting involvement in it.

"As far as I know, I have no lascivious impulses. Now, I must go. I'm late." She stepped off the curb despite the fact that the traffic light was flashing instructions not to walk.

"God is counting on you. He's impatient. If you betray his trust—"

"Yes, well, I'll try harder. Good-bye."

He lunged off the curb and grabbed her by the shoulders. "God bless you, daughter. God bless you and your holy mission." Clasping her hand, he pressed a cheaply printed pamphlet into it.

"Thank you."

Alex worked her hand free and jogged across the street, quickly putting two lanes of traffic between her and the preacher. She trotted up the steps and barreled through the courthouse doors.

Glancing over her shoulder to see if Plummet had followed her, she ran right into Reede.

He caught her against his chest. "What the hell's the matter with you? Where have you been?"

She wanted to lean against him, feel his protective strength, until her heart stopped racing, but didn't allow herself the luxury. "Nowhere. I mean, I went out. To lunch. At the, uh, the B & B. I walked."

He studied her, taking in her windblown hair and ruddy cheeks. "What's that?" He nodded down at the pamphlet she was clutching in her white-knuckled hand.

"Nothing." She tried to stuff it into the pocket of her coat.

Reede snatched it out of her hand. He scanned the cover, flipped it open, and read the message heralding doomsday. "You into this?"

"Of course not. A sidewalk preacher handed it to me. You really should devote some attention to clearing the panhandlers off your city's street, Sheriff," she said haughtily. "They're a nuisance."

She stepped around him and continued downstairs.

TWENTY-TWO

Nora Gail sat up and retrieved the filmy garment she'd worn into the room. "Thanks," Reede said to her.

She gave him a reproving glance over her milky-white shoulder. Drolly she replied, "How romantic." After shoving her arms through the ruffled sleeves of the peignoir, she left the bed and moved toward the door. "I've got to go check on things, but I'll be back, and we can talk." Patting her beehive hairdo, she left the room.

Reede watched her go. Her body was compact now, but in a few years it would go to fat. The large breasts would sag. Her oversized nipples would look grotesque without any muscle tone supporting them. Her smooth, slightly convex belly would become spongy. Her thighs and ass would dimple.

Even though they were friends, he hated her at the moment. He hated himself more. He hated the physical necessity that propelled him through this travesty of intimacy with a woman.

They rutted, probably more mindlessly and heartlessly than some species of animals. The release should have been cleansing and cathartic. It should have felt great. It didn't. It rarely did anymore, certainly not recently.

"Shit," he muttered. He would probably go on sleeping with her through their old age. It was convenient and uncomplicated. Each knew what the other was able to give and demanded nothing more. As far as Reede was concerned, passion was based on need, not desire, and sure as hell not on love.

He got off. So did she. She had often told him he was one of the few men who could make her come. He wasn't particularly flattered because that might be, and probably was, a lie.

Disgusted, he threw his legs over the side of the bed. There was a pack of cigarettes on the bedside table, courtesy of the house. The carefully rolled joints you had to pay for. He lit one of the cigarettes, something he rarely did anymore, and drew the tobacco deep into his lungs. He missed the postcoital cigarettes more than any others, maybe because the tobacco punished and polluted the body that continually betrayed him with a healthy sex drive.

He poured himself a drink from the bottle on the nightstand—that would be added to his bill, even if he did fuck the madam herself—and tossed it down in one swallow. Rebelling, his esophagus contracted. His eyes teared. The whiskey spread a slow, languid heat through his belly and groin. He began to feel marginally better.

He lay back down and stared at the ceiling, wishing he could sleep, but welcoming this coveted time of relaxation when he wasn't called on to speak, move, or think.

His eyes closed, an image of a face, bathed in sunlight and wreathed by loose, dark-auburn hair, was projected on the backs of his eyelids. His cock, which should have been limp with exhaustion, swelled and stretched with more pleasure than it had felt earlier tonight.

Reede didn't whisk the image away, as he usually did. This time he let it stay, evolve. The fantasy was welcomed and indulged. He watched her blue eyes blink with surprise at her own eroticism, watched her tongue nervously flick over her lower lip.

He felt her against him, her heart beating in time with his, her hair tangled in his fingers.

He tasted her mouth again, felt her tongue shyly flirting with his.

He didn't realize that he made a low moan or that his penis twitched reflexively. A drop of moisture pearled the tip. Yearning pressed down on him suffocatingly.

"Reede!"

The door to the room was flung open and the madam rushed back in, no longer looking cool and elegant.

"Reede," she repeated breathlessly.

"What the hell?" He swung his feet to the floor again and stood up in one economical motion. He didn't think to be embarrassed by his evident arousal. Something was desperately wrong.

As long as he'd known her, he'd never seen her rattled, but now, her eyes were wide with alarm. He was stepping into his briefs before she even started speaking.

"They just called."

"Who?"

"Your office. There's an emergency."

"Where?" Already standing in jeans and an unbuttoned shirt, he crammed his feet into his boots.

"The ranch."

He froze and swiveled his head toward her. "The *Minton* ranch?" She nodded. "What kind of emergency?"

"The deputy didn't say. Swear to God he didn't," she added hurriedly when she could see that Reede was about to question that.

"Personal or professional emergency?"

"I don't know, Reede. I got the impression that it's a combination of both. He just said you're wanted out there pronto. Is there anything I can do?"

"Call back and tell them I'm on my way." Grabbing his coat and hat, he pushed her aside and ran into the hallway. "Thanks."

"Let me know what happened," she called down to him, leaning over the banister, watching his hasty descent.

"When I can." Seconds later he slammed the door behind him, leaped over the porch rail, and hit the ground running.

Alex was in a deep slumber, which was why she didn't associate the knocking on her door with reality. Subconsciously, she thought the racket was an extension of her dream. A voice finally roused her.

"Get up and open the door."

Groggily, she sat up and reached for the switch to the bedside lamp, which always seemed to elude her. When the lamp came on, she blinked against the sudden light.

"Alex, dammit! *Get up!*"

The door was vibrating with each fall of his fist. "Reede?" she croaked.

"If you're not up in ten seconds . . ."

She checked the digital clock on the nightstand. It was almost two in the morning. The sheriff was either drunk or crazy. Either way, she wasn't about to open her door to him in his present frame of mind. "What do you want?"

Alex couldn't account for the change in the sound of the thumping until the wood began to splinter, then shatter. Reede kicked the door open and let himself in.

"Just what the hell do you think you're doing?" she shouted, gathering the covers against her as she sat bolt upright.

"Coming to get you."

He grabbed her, covers and all, plucked her off the bed and stood her on her feet, then ripped the covers away from her grasping hands. She stood shivering in front of him, wearing only panties and a T-shirt, her usual sleeping ensemble. It would be difficult to say which of them was the more furious or riveted.

Alex recovered her voice first. "I hope you have a damn good reason for kicking in my door, Sheriff."

"I do." He crossed to the dresser, yanked open a drawer, and began riffling through articles of clothing.

"I'd like to hear it."

"You will." Another drawer fell victim to his searching hands. She moved beside him and pushed the drawer shut with her hip, almost slamming it on his fingers.

"What are you looking for?"

"Clothes. Unless you'd rather go out like that."

He gestured down toward the panties with their high, French-cut legs. The spot where the sheer lace panel tapered between her thighs seemed to capture his attention for several tense seconds before he dragged his eyes toward the alcove where her clothes were hanging. "Where are your jeans?" he asked, his voice thick.

"I'm not going anywhere. Do you know what time it is?"

He jerked the jeans off the hanger. It rocked on the rod, then fell unheeded to the floor. "Yes." None too gently, he tossed the jeans at her. "Put those on. These, too." He threw her casual boots at her feet, then faced her, hands on hips, looking mean. "Well? Want me to do it for you?"

She couldn't imagine what she had done to provoke him. It was obvious, however, that he was livid over something. If he wanted to play out this caveman game, let him. She would go along, but she wouldn't do it graciously.

Turning her back on him, she stepped into her jeans and wiggled them over her hips. She took a pair of socks from one of the ravaged bureau drawers, shook them

out, then pulled them on. The boots came next. Finally, she turned and glared up
at him.

"There, I'm dressed. Now, are you going to tell me what this is all about?"

"On the way."

He yanked a sweater from a hanger and moved toward her as he gathered the
material up to the turtleneck. He pulled it over her head, then shoved her arms into
the sleeves and tugged the hem to her hips. The narrow neck had trapped her hair.
He lifted it out.

Instead of withdrawing his hands, he closed his fingers tightly around her scalp,
then roughly tilted her head up and back. He was shaking with rage.

"I ought to break your neck."

He didn't. He kissed her—hard.

His lips crushed hers, bruised them against her teeth. He thrust his tongue inside
her mouth with no semblance of tenderness. It was an angry kiss, spawned by
angry passion.

It ended abruptly. Her coat was lying across a chair. He tossed it at her. "Here."

Alex was too shaken to think of arguing. She put it on. He pushed her over the
threshold. "What about the door?" she asked inanely.

"I'll send someone to fix it."

"At this time of night?"

"Forget the goddamn door," he roared. Cupping her bottom in his palm, he
boosted her up into the cab of the Blazer, which he'd kept running. The light bar
across the roof of it was flashing a tricolor code of emergency.

"How long before I get an explanation?" she asked as the Blazer careened onto
the highway. Her seat belt did little good. She was thrown against him, and had to
clutch his thigh to keep from being pitched into the floorboard. "For heaven's
sake, Reede, tell me what's happened."

"The Minton ranch has been set afire."

TWENTY-THREE

"Set afire?" she repeated in a thready voice.

"Drop the innocent act, will ya?"

"I don't know what you're talking about."

He banged his fist on the steering wheel. "How could you sleep through it?"

She stared at him, aghast. "Are you suggesting that I had something to do with
it?"

Reede turned his attention back to the road. His face was taut and rigid in the
greenish light emanating from the dashboard. The police radio discharged its
scratchy static. The transmissions were loud and intrusive. There was no other
traffic on the highway, so the siren wasn't necessary, but the lights overhead
continued to whirl and flash, making Alex feel like she was caught in a weird
kaleidoscope.

"I think you had a lot to do with it, you and your close friend and associate."
Her bewilderment only seemed to infuriate him more. "Reverend Fergus Plummet," he shouted. "The preacher's a good friend of yours, isn't he?"

"Plummet?"

" 'Plummet?' " he mimicked nastily. "When did the two of you cook up this idea, the evening he paid a visit to your motel room, or the other day, on the sidewalk in front of the B & B Café.''

She took a series of quick, shallow breaths. "How'd you know?"

"I know, okay? Who called who first?"

"He and his wife showed up at my room. I'd never heard of him before that. The man's a maniac.''

"That didn't stop you from enlisting him to your cause.''

"I did no such thing.''

Swearing beneath his breath, he pulled the transmitter of his radio toward his mouth and notified one of his deputies at the scene that he was only minutes away.

"Ten-four, Reede. When you get here, go to barn number two.''

"How come?"

"Don't know. Somebody said to tell you that.''

"Ten-four. I'm at the gate now.''

They turned off the highway and took the private road. Alex's stomach turned over when she saw a column of smoke rising from one of the horse barns. Flames were no longer visible, but the roof and those of the adjacent buildings were still being doused with fire hoses. Firemen, wearing slickers and rubber boots, were frantically trying to contain the fire.

"They got to it before it did too much damage," Reede informed her harshly.

Emergency vehicles were parked near the smoking stable and in front of the house. Nearly every downstairs window had been broken out. All exterior walls had dire warnings of Armageddon spray-painted on them.

"There were three carloads of them. Apparently they circled the premises several times, throwing rocks through the windows, but only after they'd done their real dirty work. You can see how well K-Mart did tonight in the spray paint department.'' His lip curled snidely. "They dumped shit into the drink troughs. Fine class of friends you've got there, Counselor.''

"Was anybody hurt?" It was a horrendous scene. She was unable to draw sufficient air into her lungs.

"One of the gallop boys.'' Alex turned toward him for elaboration. "He heard the racket, rushed outside the bunkhouse, stumbled, fell and broke his arm.''

Barn number two was the one with the smoldering roof. Reede braked the Blazer in front and left her sitting in the truck when he went inside. Alex, feeling like each limb weighed a thousand pounds, shoved open the door and followed him through the wide doors, shouldering her way through the scurrying firemen.

"What's the matter?" she heard Reede demand as he jogged down the center aisle of the stable.

A horse was screaming, obviously in pain. It was the most hideous sound Alex had ever heard. Reede picked up speed.

The Mintons were gathered in a somber, pajama-clad huddle outside one of the stalls. Sarah Jo was weeping copiously. Angus was fervently, but ineffectually, patting her back. Junior was holding her hand and using his other to cover a yawn. Reede pushed them aside, but drew up short at the entrance to the stall.

"Jesus Christ.'' He cursed a stream of blue words, then let out a tortured roar that caused Alex to shrink back into the shadows.

A pot-bellied, bespectacled man stepped into Alex's line of vision. By all appearances, he'd come straight from his bed. His corduroy jacket had been pulled on over a pair of pajamas. Laying a hand on Reede's arm, he shook his balding head gravely. "There's nothing I can do for him, Reede. We'll have to put him down.''

Reede stared at the man blankly, wordlessly. His chest rose and fell as though he were about to heave up his supper.

Sarah Jo's sobs increased. She covered her face with her hands. "Mother, please let me take you back to the house." Junior placed his arm around her waist and turned her away. Angus's arm dropped to his side. Mother and son moved slowly down the center aisle.

They were almost even with Alex before they noticed her. The instant Sarah Jo saw her, she released a high, keening sound and pointed an accusing finger. "*You.* You did this to us.*"*

Alex recoiled. "I—"

"It's your fault, you meddlesome, spiteful little bitch!"

"Mother," Junior said, not in chastisement, but commiseration. Spent by her outburst, Sarah Jo collapsed against him. He gave Alex a penetrating look, but it seemed more puzzled than accusatory. Without speaking again, he moved on with Sarah Jo, whose head was now bent in misery against her son's chest.

"What happened, Ely?" Reede asked, seemingly unaware of the other drama.

"A falling beam must've landed square on him. He went down hard and broke his shoulder," the man called Ely said quietly. Apparently, he was a veterinarian.

"Give him some painkiller, for crissake."

"I already have. It's strong, but it can't anesthetize this." He gazed down at the suffering animal. "His femur's busted, too. I can only guess at his internal injuries. Even if I could patch him up, he'd likely be sickly from now on, and no use to you as a stud."

They stood silent a moment, listening to the pitiful sounds coming from the animal. At last Angus said, "Thank you, Ely. We know you've done all you could."

"I'm sorry, Angus, Reede," the vet said, meaning it. "Y'all go on outta here. I need to make a quick trip to the office and get the drug, then I'll come back and give him the injection."

"No." The word came hoarsely from Reede's lips. "I'll do it."

"You oughtn't to do that, Reede. The injection is—"

"I can't let him wait that long."

"It won't take me ten minutes."

"I said, I'll do it," Reede shouted impatiently.

Angus intervened, clapping the well-meaning vet hard on the shoulder to stem any further arguments. "Go on home, Ely. Sorry to have dragged you out for this."

"I'm damned sorry. I've been treating Double Time since he was foaled."

Alex's hand flew up to cover her mouth. Double Time was Reede's adored racehorse. The vet left by another door. He didn't see Alex.

Firemen shouted back and forth to each other outside. Other horses snorted fearfully, and restlessly tramped the floors of their stalls. Those sounds seemed distant and detached from the tense silence in that one single stall.

"Reede, you gonna be all right, boy?"

"Yes. Go see to Sarah Jo. I'll take care of this."

The older man looked ready to argue, but finally turned away. He gave Alex a hard, pointed look as he passed her, but said nothing before stamping out.

She wanted to cry as she watched Reede kneel in the hay. He rubbed the injured horse's muzzle. "You were good—the best," he whispered softly. "You gave it all you had, and then some." The animal nickered in what sounded like a plea.

Reede slowly came to his feet and reached for the pistol in his holster. He took it out, checked the chamber, and pointed it down at the racehorse.

"No!" Alex rushed out of the shadows and grabbed his arm. "Reede, no, don't. Let someone else."

She had seen hardened criminals, after being sentenced to death, turn on their prosecutors, the judge, the jury, and vituperatively swear vengeance, even if from beyond the grave.

But she had never seen such deadly intent on a face as when Reede looked down at her. His eyes were glazed with tears and hatred. With uncanny speed, he encircled her waist and drew her backward against his chest. She struggled. He cursed and increased the pressure of his arm across her midriff.

He took her right hand in his left and forcibly wrapped her reluctant fingers around the pistol, so that she was actually holding it when he aimed the barrel between the horse's eyes and pulled the trigger.

"No!"

She screamed the instant the pistol went off in her hand. The deadly sound seemed to ricochet off the stone walls of the stable and reverberate forever. Horses whinnied and tramped in fear. Someone outside shouted, and several of the firemen scrambled through the door to see what the shot meant.

Reede shoved Alex away from him. His voice crackling with rage, he said, "You should have done it clean like that in the first place, and spared him the agony."

"The fire's completely put out, Mr. Minton," the fire chief reported. "We checked all the wiring, insulation, everything in the roof. All the damage was superficial." He clicked his lips against his gums. "Damn shame about Reede Lambert's Thoroughbred, though."

"Thank you for all you've done. I've always said our fire department is the finest in West Texas."

Some of Angus's heartiness had been restored, though his features were heavy with fatigue. He was putting up a good front, as though he was determined not to let this be a setback. Alex could only admire his stamina and optimism.

He was sitting at the kitchen table with Junior, looking like he might have been wrapping up an all-night poker game, instead of holding a wake for a destroyed racehorse and his vandalized property.

"Guess we'll be taking off, then." The fireman picked up his hard hat and moved toward the back door. "Someone will be out tomorrow to look for clues. It's a definite arson."

"We'll cooperate any way we can. I'm just glad you responded so quickly and kept the fire from spreading."

"So long." As the fireman went through the back door, he met Reede coming in. Reede ignored Alex, who was standing self-consciously against the wall, and poured himself a cup of coffee from the pot Lupe had brewed.

"The troughs are pure again. The horses won't be poisoned by their own excrement," he said emotionlessly. "We got all the windows boarded up so you won't freeze tonight. There's still a lot of cleanup to do."

"Well," Angus sighed, coming to his feet, "we can't start on that till daylight, so I'm going up to bed. Thanks, Reede. You went above and beyond your duties as sheriff."

Reede bobbed his head in quick acknowledgment. "How's Sarah Jo?"

"Junior made her take a tranquilizer."

"She's sleeping now." Junior stood up also. "Would you like me to drive you back to town now, Alex? You've got no business being out here at this time of night."

"I wanted her to see her handiwork," Reede said.

"I had nothing to do with it!" she cried.

"Maybe not directly," Angus said sternly, "but this damn fool investigation of yours put things in motion. We've been fighting that loud-mouthed hellfire-and-damnation preacher for years. He was just looking for an excuse to pull a malicious stunt like this. You handed him a golden opportunity."

"I'm sorry if you see it that way, Angus."

The air was thick with tension. No one moved. Even the housekeeper stopped washing empty coffee cups. Finally, Junior stepped forward and took her arm. "Come on. It's getting late."

"I'll take her back," Reede said curtly.

"I don't mind."

"I'm going anyway."

"You'll just harp on what happened here."

"What the hell do you care what I say to her?"

"All right then, you take her home," Junior said testily. "You're the one who brought her, aren't you?" With that, he turned and left the room.

" 'Night, Reede, Alex." An unsmiling Angus followed his son out.

Reede tossed the dregs of his coffee into the sink. "Come on," he ordered her.

Retrieving her coat, she went outside with him and dejectedly climbed into his truck. She wanted to say something to break the dreadful silence, but couldn't bring herself to utter a single word. Reede seemed disinclined to converse. His eyes remained resolutely on the center stripe of the highway.

Finally, the growing knot of anxiety in her chest got to be too much and she blurted out, "I had nothing to do with what happened tonight."

He merely turned his head and looked at her, his expression one of patent disbelief.

"I think Junior believes me," she cried defensively.

"What the hell does he know? You've dazzled him. He took one look into those baby blues of yours and sank like a rock. He's up to his ass in sentimental bullshit about you being Celina's daughter. He remembers how he used to dote on you and wants to do it again—only in an entirely different way. The toy he wants to give you to play with now doesn't rattle."

"You're disgusting."

"It must have given you a thrill to see us coming close to blows over you."

She ground her teeth. "Think what you want to about my designs on Junior and his on me, but I won't have you thinking I was responsible for the damage done to his ranch tonight."

"You were responsible. You incited Plummet."

"Not intentionally. Plummet got it into his head that I was an answer to his prayers—that God sent me to purge Purcell of sinners, the Mintons, anyone connected to or a proponent of pari-mutuel gambling."

"He's crazier than I thought."

She rubbed her upper arms as though recollections of Plummet gave her chills. "You don't know the half of it. He says God is angry because I haven't locked all of you away. He accused me of fraternizing with the devil, meaning you." She refrained from telling him the sexual parallels Plummet had drawn.

Reede parked in front of her motel room. The door was still in shambles and standing ajar. "I thought you said you'd take care of that."

"Prop a chair under the doorknob till morning. You'll be all right."

He didn't turn off the Blazer's engine, but let it idle. The police radio crackled with its monotonous static, but there were no transmissions now. The noise was grating on her nerves.

"I'm sorry about Double Time, Reede. I know how attached to him you were."

His leather jacket made a squeaking sound against the upholstery when he shrugged indifferently. "He was insured."

Alex uttered a small cry of anguish and anger. He wouldn't let her apologize. He wouldn't let her feel sad or sorry because he wouldn't allow himself those emotions. She had witnessed the heartache he had suffered seconds before he put a bullet through the horse's brain. She had heard it when he talked about his father's pathetic funeral.

And that's what Reede couldn't forgive. More than once he had let down his guard and revealed to her that he was a feeling human being after all.

She balled her fists, pressed her wrists together, and thrust them across the console toward him. He looked at her with a dark, questioning frown. "What does that signify?"

"Handcuff me," she said. "Haul me in. Arrest me. Charge me with the crime. You said I was responsible."

"You are," he ground out, his previous rage returning. "Angus was right. If you hadn't come here and started snooping around, none of this would have happened."

"I refuse to take the blame for what happened tonight, Reede. It was the act of an unbalanced man and his misled followers. If my investigation hadn't been their catalyst, something else would have been. I've apologized for the horse. What more do you want from me?"

He gave her a sharp look. She withdrew her hands, snatching them back as though they'd been placed too close to the maws of some terrible beast, and she had realized it in the nick of time.

Inside her mouth was the taste of his kiss—whiskey- and tobacco-flavored. As though it were happening again, she felt the swirling search of his tongue, the possessive pressure of his fingers on her scalp, the solid presence of his thighs against hers.

"You'd better go inside, Counselor." His voice was quiet and husky.

He dropped the truck's transmission into reverse. Alex took his advice and got out.

TWENTY-FOUR

Alex groped for the ringing telephone. She answered it on the fifth ring and said groggily, "Hello?"

"Miss Gaither? I didn't wake you, did I? If so, I'm terribly sorry."

Alex shoved hair out of her eyes, licked her dry lips, blinked puffy eyes into focus, and struggled into a sitting position. "No, I was just, uh, doing some, uh, stuff." The nightstand clock said ten o'clock. She'd had no idea she was sleeping that late, but then, it had been almost dawn before she'd gone to bed. "I'm sorry, I'm not sure—"

"Sarah Jo Minton."

She couldn't hold back her exclamation of surprise. She could name at least a hundred people who might call her before Sarah Jo Minton would. "Are you . . . is everything all right?"

"I'm feeling well, but terribly ashamed for the horrible things I said to you last night."

The confession, spoken so contritely, shocked Alex. "You were understandably upset."

"Would you care to have tea with me this afternoon?"

Maybe she was still asleep, after all, and this was a dream. Nowadays, people said, "Let's do lunch," or "How about a beer?" or "Let's get together for a drink." No one ever said, "Would you care to have tea?"

"That . . . that sounds nice."

"Good. Three o'clock."

"Where?"

"Why, here at the ranch, of course. I'll look forward to seeing you then, Miss Gaither. Good-bye."

Alex stared at the receiver for several seconds before slowly hanging it up. What in the world had prompted Sarah Jo Minton to invite her to tea?

Dr. Ely Collins's office was probably the most cluttered room Alex had ever been in. It was clean but disorganized, and as unpretentious as the veterinarian.

"Thank you for agreeing to see me, Dr. Collins."

"No trouble. I was free this afternoon. Come on in. Sit down." He removed a stack of trade journals from the seat of the straight, wooden chair, making it available for Alex. He sat behind a desk cluttered with mountains of paperwork. "I wasn't all that surprised to hear from you," he remarked candidly.

"Why?"

"Pat Chastain called and said you'd probably get around to asking me some questions."

"I thought he was out of town."

"This was a couple of weeks ago, right after you got here."

"I see."

Alex had decided to utilize the hours before her appointment with Sarah Jo by questioning the veterinarian. When she'd phoned, he had readily agreed to see her.

"Are you familiar with the murder of Celina Gaither?" she began, intentionally playing down her personal involvement.

"Sure am. She was a sweet girl. Everybody was sick about it."

"Thank you. It was your father who attended the foaling at the Minton ranch earlier that day, wasn't it?"

"That's right. I took over his practice after he died."

"I'd like some background information. Do you work exclusively for the Mintons?"

"No, I'm not a resident vet. I have a practice. However, I must be honest and tell you that the Mintons give me so much business I could almost work for them exclusively. I'm out there nearly every day."

"It was the same with your father?"

"Yes, but if you're suggesting that I wouldn't rat on the Mintons at the risk of cutting off my meal ticket, you're wrong."

"I didn't mean to imply that."

"This is horse and cattle country. I have to turn down more business than I can accept. I'm an honest man. So was my daddy."

Alex apologized to him a second time, although it had crossed her mind that he might be reluctant to divulge information that would tend to incriminate his well-paying clients.

"Did your father talk to you about Celina's murder?"

"He cried like a baby when he heard that she'd been killed with one of his instruments."

"Dr. Collins positively identified the murder weapon as his scalpel?"

"There was never any question. Mama had given him that set of sterling silver instruments for their twenty-fifth wedding anniversary. They had his initials engraved on the handles. That scalpel was his, all right. What he couldn't get over is that he'd been careless enough to lose it."

Alex scooted to the edge of her chair. "It would be unlike him to be careless with that scalpel if it was an engraved gift from his wife, wouldn't it?"

He scratched his cheek. "Daddy treasured those things—kept them in a velvet-lined box. I never could figure out how that scalpel fell out of his bag, except that the mare had everyone's attention that day. In all the commotion, I guess it just got jostled out."

"You were there?"

"I figured you already knew that. I'd gone along to observe and assist if Daddy needed me. 'Course, Reede was there, too. He had helped in other births."

"Reede was there?"

"All day."

"Did your father ever leave him alone with his black bag?"

Ely Collins gnawed the inside of his cheek. She could tell he didn't want to answer. "Daddy could have and wouldn't have given it a second thought," he said finally, "but don't get the notion I'm accusing Reede."

"No, of course not. Who else was in the stable that day?"

"Well, now, let's see." He tugged on his lower lip while he thought back. "Just about everybody, at one time or another—Angus, Junior, Reede, all the stable hands and gallop boys."

"Pasty Hickam."

"Sure. Everybody at the ranch was pulling for that mare. Even Stacey Wallace stopped by. As I recall, she'd just gotten back from a trip to the coast."

Everything inside Alex went still. She worked hard at keeping her expression impassive. "Did she stay long?"

"Who, Stacey? No. Said she had to go home and unpack."

"What about Gooney Bud? Was he around?"

"He meandered everywhere. I don't remember seeing him, but that doesn't mean he wasn't there."

"If you didn't see him, weren't you surprised when he turned up with the scalpel covered with Celina's blood?"

"Not really. Daddy hadn't noticed it was missing until they found it on Gooney Bud. We believed what they said—that it had fallen out of Daddy's bag, that Gooney Bud had seen it, picked it up, and killed your mother with it."

"But it's conceivable that someone, in the midst of all the confusion and concern for the mare and her foal, sneaked it out of your father's bag."

"Conceivable, sure."

He admitted it with reluctance because it implicated the men he worked for. Alex remembered how concerned he'd been the night before, over Reede's racehorse. Ely Collins was a friend to all three suspects. Alex had forced him to divide his loyalties because his own integrity and the men who made hand-tooled Lucchese boots affordable. The task was unpalatable, but necessary.

She stood up to leave and extended the doctor her hand. He shook it, and she said good-bye. "Oh, one more thing, Dr. Collins. Would you mind if I looked at the scalpel?"

He was taken aback. "I wouldn't mind at all, if I had it."

"You don't?"

"No."

"Your mother?"

"She never got it back."

"Even after Gooney Bud was incarcerated?"

"She and Daddy didn't press too hard to get it back because of what had happened with it."

"You mean, it's still floating around somewhere?"

"I don't know what happened to it."

The Minton ranch was a beehive of activity. Cleanup crews were sorting through debris and hauling it away. Fire inspectors were picking through the charred lumber and insulation, searching for clues into the origin of the fire.

Around the house, a sandblasting crew was erasing the apocalyptic messages spray-painted on the stone walls. The window openings were being measured for replacement glass.

Reede was in the thick of it, serving in several capacities at once. He was unshaven and unclean; he looked like he'd personally sifted through soot and ash searching for clues. His shirttail was out and unbuttoned; the sleeves had been rolled up. He was hatless, but was wearing leather work gloves.

He spotted Alex, as she alighted from her car, but before he could speak, he was summoned by a fire inspector. "You might want to take a look at this, Sheriff."

Reede made an about-face and walked toward barn number two. Alex followed him. "A rock? What the hell does a rock have to do with the fire?" Reede was asked when she approached.

The fireman scratched his head through his Houston Astros baseball cap. "Looks to me like the fire was an accident. What I mean is, whoever done all this was using something like a slingshot to knock out the windows and such."

"Like David going up against Goliath," Alex murmured. Reede's lips narrowed as he nodded in agreement.

The fireman said, "My guess is that this-here rock went flying, landed in one of the vents on the roof of the stable, and shorted out some of the wiring. That's what caused your fire."

"You don't think it was deliberately set?"

The investigator frowned. "Naw, I can't rightly say it looks that way. If I was gonna start a fire, I'd've pitched a Molotov cocktail or shot a flaming arrow." His frown reversed itself into a silly grin. "I wouldn't've throwed no rock."

Reede bounced the heavy rock in his palm. "Thanks." After the fireman ambled away, Reede said to Alex, "So much for holding Plummet on an arson charge."

Because the day was unseasonably warm, Reede smelled salty and sweaty, but it wasn't an offensive odor. In fact, she liked it. His dense chest hair fanned out over the upper part of his torso and funneled to a narrow line that disappeared into his belt. Up close she could see that perspiration had made it damp and curly. It whorled over the muscles and around his nipples, which the cooling breeze had drawn erect.

Noticing that made her warm inside. She raised her eyes to his face. A bead of sweat trickled from beneath his loose, windblown hair and ran into his eyebrow.

She curbed the temptation to catch it on her fingertip. His day-old beard went well with the grime and sweat on his face.

It was an effort for her to keep her mind on business. "Have you arrested Plummet?"

"We tried," he said. "He's vanished."

"His family?"

"They're all at home, looking guilty as hell, but playing dumb about the preacher's whereabouts. I'm not worried about it. He won't go far. We'll run down the roster of his congregation. Somebody's hiding him. He'll surface sooner or later."

"When he does, I'd like to be there when you question him."

He tossed the rock to the ground. "What are you doing here?"

"I came to have tea with Sarah Jo." In response to his incredulous expression, she said, "Her idea, not mine."

"Well, have fun," he said sardonically. He turned his back on her and sauntered toward the barn.

Angus was standing on the porch of the house, feet widespread, overseeing the activity. As she approached, she tried not to let her apprehension show. She wasn't certain how she would be received.

"You're right on time," he said.

So, he knew she was expected. "Hello, Angus."

"Punctuality is a virtue. So's having guts. You've got 'em, little lady." He nodded his approval. "It took guts for you to show your face around here today." He appraised her through squinted eyes. "In that respect, you're a lot like your mama. She was no shrinking violet."

"No?"

He chuckled. "I saw her hold her own with those two hellions—Reede and Junior—many a time."

His chuckles faded into silent smiles of fond remembrance as he contemplated the horizon. "If she'd lived, she'd've become quite a woman." His eyes came back to Alex. "She'd've been like you, I guess. If I'd ever had a daughter, I'd have wanted her to be like you."

Discomfited by the unexpected statement, she said, "I apologize for being even remotely connected to this, Angus." She made a sweeping gesture that encompassed all the damage. "I hope Reede finds whoever did it. I hope they're prosecuted and convicted."

"Yeah, so do I. Most of it I can overlook." He glanced down at the broken window glass on the porch. "But that was a terrible waste of good horseflesh. I hate like hell that Reede lost him. He took pride in saving up enough to buy him."

"He seemed extremely upset," Alex said, turning to watch as Reede went to his truck and spoke into the radio transmitter.

"More like enraged. He's as jealous as a mama bear when it comes to anything that belongs to him. It's understandable, I guess, considering how he grew up. Didn't have a pot to piss in, not even anybody to look out for him. Lived on hand-me-downs and handouts. Once you've been a scavenger in order to survive, I reckon it's a tough habit to break. He's mean and testy 'cause at times his life depended on it."

Junior breezed through the front door then, beaming his famous smile. He was in an inappropriately jovial mood. Unlike Reede and Angus, his clothes were spotless. If he'd ever broken a sweat, one couldn't tell it by looking at him now.

After greeting Alex warmly, he said, "Y'all wouldn't believe the telephone conversation I just had. One of the owners called to check on her mare that's in foal. Bad news travels fast in racehorse circles," he informed Alex.

"Anyway, she had this high, falsetto voice and was saying, 'My poor baby must have been scared out of her wits.' I reassured her that the mare was in another barn, but she kept me on the phone for half an hour, making me swear that her baby and her baby's baby were okay."

He had imitated the woman's warbling, soprano voice. Angus and Alex were laughing. Suddenly, from the corner of her eye, Alex caught Reede watching them. He was standing perfectly still, and, though it was too far away to tell, she was certain he didn't like what he saw. His resentment seemed to ride the airwaves until they struck her with near-palpable force.

"I'd better go inside or I'll be late for tea," she told the men.

Junior laid a hand on her shoulder. "Mother wants to make amends for her outburst last night. She was tickled pink when you accepted her invitation. She's looking forward to seeing you."

 # TWENTY-FIVE

Lupe took her coat and led her upstairs. The maid paused outside a door and gave it a soft tap.

"Come in."

Lupe swung the door open, but didn't go in. Taking that as her cue, Alex stepped across the threshold into a room that could have been a movie set. Her remark was spontaneous and genuine. "What a beautiful room!"

"Thank you. I like it." Sarah Jo looked beyond Alex's shoulder. "Close the door, please, Lupe. You know I can't stand that draft, and the racket those workers are making is deplorable. Bring up the tea tray right away."

"Yes, ma'am." The housekeeper withdrew, leaving them alone.

Alex stood near the door, feeling self-conscious in her low-heeled suede boots and long wool skirt. There was nothing wrong with her totally black ensemble, but it seemed glaringly modern and out of place in this ultrafeminine Victorian room, which smelled like a perfumery.

Her hostess looked as right in the setting as a whirling ballerina in a musical jewelry box. The ruffles along the neckline of her white blouse were duplicated around her slender wrists. She was wearing a soft beige skirt that fanned out around her where she sat on a robin's-egg-blue damask divan near the window. The afternoon sunlight created a halo around her hair.

"Come in and sit down." She motioned toward a dainty chair near her.

Usually poised, Alex felt gauche as she crossed the carpeted floor. "Thank you for inviting me. This was a very good idea."

"It was mandatory that I apologize as soon as possible for what I said to you last night."

"Never mind. It's forgotten." Junior and Angus seemed to have forgiven her for the unwitting role she had played in the act of vandalism. In return, she could be forgiving toward Sarah Jo.

Curious, she took in her surroundings. "This truly is a lovely room. Did you decorate it yourself?"

Sarah Jo offered a laugh as frail as the hand she raised to her throat to fiddle with the ruffles. "My, yes. I wouldn't let one of those dreadful decorators inside my house. Actually, I copied my room back home item by item, as closely as I could. Angus says it's too fussy."

Alex searched discreetly for something masculine a shred of evidence that a man had been inside the room. There was none. As though reading her mind, Sarah Jo said, "He keeps his things in another room, through there." Alex followed the direction of her gaze to a closed door.

"Come in, Lupe," Sarah Jo said at the housekeeper's soft knock. "Here's our tea."

While Lupe was arranging the silver service on the tea table, Alex asked conversationally, "You mentioned home, Mrs. Minton. Kentucky, right?"

"Yes, horse country. Hunt country. I loved it so."

Her wistful gaze drifted toward the window. The panorama didn't offer much to please the eyes, just miles of dun-colored earth, until it blurred into the horizon. They watched a tumbleweed roll across the stone patio and land in the swimming pool. The landscaping around it was as dead and brown as a cotton field after harvest.

"It's so barren here. I miss the green. Of course, we have acres of irrigated pasture for the horses, but somehow, it's not the same." Her head came back around slowly and she thanked the maid with a nod. Lupe withdrew. "How do you take your tea?"

"Lemon and sugar, please. One lump."

Sarah Jo practiced the ritual that Alex thought had died two generations ago. She did it meticulously. Her pale, translucent hands moved fluidly. Alex realized then why the custom had died in contemporary America. No one would have the time.

"Sandwich? Cucumber and cream cheese."

"Then, by all means," Alex replied with a smile.

Sarah Jo also added two tea cakes to the small plate before passing it to Alex, who had spread a lacy napkin over her lap. "Thank you."

She sipped her tea and pronounced it perfect. The sandwich was only a sliver of crust-trimmed bread, but the filling was cool and creamy. She hoped her stomach wouldn't make a rude noise when it greedily devoured the inadequate portion. She had slept through breakfast; it had seemed superfluous to eat lunch so soon before teatime.

Starting on one of the tea cakes, she asked, "Have you returned to Kentucky often for visits?"

Her hostess prepared her own tea and stirred it idly. "Only twice, for my parents' funerals."

"I didn't mean to bring up a sad topic."

"I have no family left, except for Angus and Junior. Anybody with character learns to live with losses." She replaced her cup and saucer on the table so carefully that the china didn't even clink. Keeping her head lowered, she looked up at Alex from beneath her brows. "Only you haven't, have you?"

Alex returned the uneaten half of the sugar cookie to her plate, knowing intuitively that they had reached the reason behind this invitation to tea. "Haven't what?"

"You haven't learned that it's best to let the dead remain dead."

The lines of battle had been drawn. Alex returned all the tea implements to the silver tray, even the spiderwebby napkin from her lap. "Are you referring to my mother?"

"Precisely. This investigation of yours has upset my entire household, Miss Gaither."

"I apologize for the inconvenience. The circumstances make it unavoidable."

"Thugs vandalized my property, threatening the health and life of every horse we own or board, thereby our livelihood."

"That was an unfortunate incident. I can't tell you how truly sorry I am for it," Alex said, appealing to the woman to understand. "*I* had nothing to do with it. You must believe that."

Sarah Jo drew a deep breath. The ruffles around her neck quivered with suppressed indignation and dislike. Her hostility was so palpable that Alex wondered again what possible reason she had had for inviting her there. The need to apologize had been a ruse. Apparently, Sarah Jo wanted to vent a long-harbored grudge.

"How much do you know about your mother and her relationships with Junior and Reede Lambert?"

"Only what my grandmother told me, coupled with what I've gathered since talking to people here in Purcell."

"They were like a unit," she said, lapsing into a faint, reflective voice, and Alex realized that she had slipped into her own private world. "A little club unto themselves. You rarely saw one without seeing the other two."

"I've noticed that in candid shots in their high school yearbooks. There are lots of pictures of the three of them." Alex had pored over the photographs on those glossy pages, looking for clues, anything, that might benefit her investigation.

"I didn't want Junior to get so deeply involved with them," Sarah Jo was saying. "Reede was a hoodlum, the son of the town drunk, of all things. And your mother . . . well, there were many reasons why I didn't want him to become attached to her."

"Name one."

"Mainly because of how it was between her and Reede. I knew Junior would always be her second choice. It galled me that she could even exercise a choice. She wasn't worthy of the right to choose," she said bitterly.

"But Junior adored her, no matter what I said. Just as I feared, he fell in love with her." Suddenly, her eyes focused sharply on her guest. "And I have a sick feeling that he'll fall in love with you, too."

"You're wrong."

"Oh, I'm sure you'll see to it that he does. Reede, too, probably. That would round out the triangle again, wouldn't it? Don't you want to pit them against each other, like she did?"

"No!"

Sarah Jo's eyes narrowed with malice. "Your mother was a tramp."

Up to this point, Alex had carefully controlled her tongue. But since her hostess was maligning her late mother, she dismissed her manners. "I take exception to that slanderous remark, Mrs. Minton."

Sarah Jo gave a negligent wave of her hand. "No matter. It's the truth. I knew she was common and coarse the first time I met her. Oh, she was pretty, in a lush, flamboyant way. Much like you."

Her eyes moved over Alex critically. Alex was tempted to get up and walk out. The only thing that kept her sitting in that spindly chair was the hope that Sarah Jo would inadvertently impart some scrap of valuable information.

"Your mother laughed too loud, played too hard, loved too well. Emotions were to her what a bottle of liquor is to a drunkard. She overindulged, and had no control over exhibiting her feelings."

"She sounds very honest," Alex said with pride. "The world might be better off if people openly expressed what they were feeling." Her words fell on deaf ears.

"Whatever a man needed or wanted her to be at the moment," Sarah Jo continued, "she was. Celina was an unconscionable flirt. Every man she met fell in love with her. She made certain of it. She would do anything to guarantee it.''

Enough was enough. ''I won't let you disparage a woman who's not around to defend herself. It's ugly and cruel of you, Mrs. Minton.'' The room, which had been as fresh as a greenhouse when she had come in, now seemed suffocating. She had to get out. ''I'm leaving.''

''Not yet.'' Sarah Jo stood up when Alex did. ''Celina loved Reede as much as she was capable of loving anyone except herself.''

''What concern was that of yours?''

''Because she wanted Junior, too, and she let him know it. Your grandmother, that stupid woman, was giddy over the idea of a match between our children. As if I'd let Junior marry Celina,'' she sneered. ''Merle Graham even called me once and suggested that we, as future in-laws, get together and become better acquainted. God, I would have sooner died! She was a telephone operator,'' she said, laughing scornfully.

''There was never any chance of Celina Graham becoming my daughter-in-law. I made that quite clear to your grandmother and to Junior. He moped and whined over that girl until I wanted to scream.'' She raised her small fists, as though she still might do so. ''Why couldn't he see her for what she was—a selfish, manipulative little bitch? And now *you.* ''

She stepped around the small tea table to confront Alex. Alex was taller, but Sarah Jo had years of cultivated anger to make her strong. Her delicate body was trembling with wrath.

''Lately, all he can talk about is you, just like it used to be with Celina.''

''I have not led Junior on, Mrs. Minton. There could never be a romantic entanglement between us. We could be friends, maybe, once this investigation is resolved.''

''Don't you see,'' Sarah Jo cried, ''that's exactly how it was with her? She abused his friendship because he was clinging to the vain hope that it would develop into something deeper. All he is to you is a suspect in a murder case. You'll use him, just like your mother did.''

''That simply isn't true.''

Sarah Jo swayed, as though about to swoon. ''Why did you have to come here?''

''I want to know why my mother was murdered.''

''You're the reason!'' she said, pointing a finger straight at Alex's heart. ''Celina's illegitimate baby.''

Alex fell back a step, sucking in a sharp, painful breath. ''What did you say?'' she gasped.

Sarah Jo composed herself. The suffusion of color in her face receded and it returned to its normal porcelain hue. ''You were illegitimate.''

''That's a lie,'' Alex denied breathlessly. ''My mother was married to Al Gaither. I've seen the marriage license. Grandma Graham saved it.''

''They were married, but not until after she came back from El Paso and discovered she was pregnant.''

''You're a liar!'' Alex gripped the back of the chair. ''Why are you lying to me?''

''It's not a lie. The reason I'm telling you should be clear. I'm trying to protect my family from your vengeful destruction. Being the richest woman in this horrid, ugly little town is the only thing that makes it tolerable. I like being married to the most influential man in the county. I won't let you destroy everything Angus has created for me. I won't let you cause dissent in my family. Celina did. This time, I won't allow it.''

"Ladies, ladies," Junior came into the room, laughing indulgently. "What is all the shouting about? See a spider?"

His manner changed drastically when he sensed the seething animosity between them. It was sulfuric, as real as the ozone in the air after lightning has struck nearby. "Mother? Alex? What's wrong?"

Alex stared at Sarah Jo, whose face was as serene and complacent as a cameo. Alex spun toward the door, sending the small chair toppling over. She rushed from the room and clambered down the stairs.

Junior gave his mother a searching look. She turned her back on him and returned to the divan, picked up her teacup, and took a sip.

Junior raced down the stairs after Alex and caught up with her at the front door, where she was unsuccessfully trying to work her arms into the sleeves of her coat.

He grabbed her upper arms. "What the hell is going on?"

Alex averted her head so he wouldn't see her tears. She tried to disengage his hands. "Nothing."

"You hardly look like you've been to a tea party."

"Tea? Ha!" Alex said, tossing back her head. "She didn't invite me out here to drink tea." She sniffed and batted her eyes in an effort to keep the tears from falling. "I guess I should thank her for telling me."

"Telling you what?"

"That I was a biological accident." Junior's face went blank with shock. "It's true, then, isn't it?" Junior's hands fell away from her arms and he tried to turn away. Reversing their positions, Alex gripped his arm and forced him back around. "Isn't it?" Her tears finally overflowed her eyelids. "Say something, Junior!"

He looked uncomfortable with admitting the truth. It was Alex who verbally pieced together the scenario.

"Celina came back from El Paso. She'd had her fling with a soldier and was ready to reconcile with Reede. They probably would have, too, if it hadn't been for me, right?" She covered her face with her hands. "Oh, God, no wonder he hates me so much."

Junior pulled her hands away from her face and looked at her with sincere blue eyes. "Reede doesn't hate you, Alex. None of us did then, or do now."

She laughed shortly, bitterly. "I'll bet Albert Gaither hated the very thought of me. He was forced to get married." Her eyes went round, and she spoke in a rapid, short-winded, staccato voice. "This explains so much. So *much*. Why Grandma Graham was strict about my dating—who I went with, what time I got home, where I'd been.

"I resented her for being so inflexible because I'd never given her any reason to mistrust me. I guess her overprotectiveness was justified, wasn't it?" Her voice rose to a near-hysterical pitch. "Her daughter got knocked up, and twenty-five years ago, that was still a definite sin."

"Alex, stop this."

"That explains why Grandma never really loved me. I ruined Celina's life, and she never forgave me for it. Celina couldn't have Reede, couldn't have you, couldn't have a future. And all because of me. Oh God!"

The curse, or prayer, was cried in a wailing voice. Alex turned away from him and yanked the door open. She ran across the porch and down the steps toward her car.

"Alex!" He started after her.

"What the hell's going on?" Angus demanded as Alex rushed past him toward her car.

"Leave her alone, you two." Sarah Jo was standing at the top of the stairs, where she had watched and overheard everything.

Junior spun around. "Mother, how could you? How could you hurt Alex that way?"

"I didn't tell her to hurt her."

"What'd you tell her?" Angus asked. He filled up the open doorway, baffled and impatient because no one was answering his questions.

"Of course it hurt her," Junior said. "You knew it would. Why tell her at all?"

"Because she needed to know. The only one who can hurt Alex is Alex herself. She's chasing an illusion. The mother she's looking for didn't exist in Celina Gaither. Merle filled her head with a lot of nonsense about how wonderful Celina was. She forgot to tell the girl how devious her mother was. It was time Alex found out."

"Shit!" Angus cursed. "Will somebody please tell me what the hell is going on?"

 # TWENTY-SIX

Angus quietly closed the bedroom door behind him as he came in. Sarah Jo, propped against the pillows on their bed, laid her book aside and peered at him over the rims of the glasses that were perched on the tip of her nose. "Coming to bed so early?"

She looked about as harmful as a butterfly, but Angus knew that her frail appearance camouflaged an iron will. If she ever gave ground it was out of indifference, not defeat. "I want to talk to you."

"About what?"

"About what happened this afternoon."

She pressed her fingers to her temples. "It gave me quite a headache. That's why I didn't come down to dinner."

"Taken anything?"

"Yes. It's better now."

They had repeated this same exchange regarding her headaches nearly every day of their marriage.

"Don't sit on the bedspread," she scolded as he lowered himself to the edge of the bed. He waited until she had folded back the quilted satin spread, then sat down close to her hip. "My, you look so downcast tonight, Angus," she said with concern. "What's the matter? Not more maniacs on our property, I hope."

"No."

"Thank God the only horse that was injured belonged to Reede."

Angus let that pass without comment. Sarah Jo resented Reede, and Angus knew why. Her feelings toward him would never change, so berating her for the uncharitable remark would serve no purpose.

What he had come to discuss was a delicate subject. He took a moment to choose his words carefully. "Sarah Jo, about this afternoon—"

"I was quite upset by it," she said, drawing her lips into a pretty frown.

"*You* were upset?" Angus forcibly tamped down his impatience. He needed to hear her side of the story before jumping to conclusions. "What about Alex's feelings?"

"She was upset, too, naturally. Wouldn't you be if you'd found out you were a bastard?"

"No," he said with a gruff, humorless laugh. "Wouldn't surprise me if I was. I never checked to see if my parents had a marriage license, and it wouldn't have mattered to me if they didn't." His brows drew together. "But I'm an ornery old cuss, and Alex is a sensitive young woman."

"I felt that she was strong enough to take it."

"Obviously, she wasn't. She ran past me without even seeing me. She was practically in hysterics when she left."

Sarah Jo's smile crumpled. "Are you blaming me for telling her? Do you think it was wrong?"

When she looked up at him with that apprehensive, little-lost-girl look, his heart melted. It always had. Angus took her hand. He could have crushed it like a flower between his rough palms, but he had learned over the years not to exert too much pressure when he caressed her.

"I'm not blaming you for telling her, honey. I'm just questioning the wisdom of it. I wish you had discussed it with Junior and me before you did. It was something she could have gone throughout her life not knowing."

"I disagree," Sarah Jo argued petulantly.

"What difference does it make now if her mama and daddy weren't married until after she was in the oven? Hell, that's so commonplace now it's not even considered a sin anymore."

"It makes a difference in the way she views Celina. Up until now, she's had her on a pedestal."

"So what?"

"Celina hardly deserves a pedestal," Sarah Jo snapped. "I thought it was time everybody stopped pussyfooting around with Alex and set her straight about her mother."

"Why?"

"*Why?* Because she's trying to ruin us, that's why. I decided to stop catering to her and to fight back. I used the only ammunition I had." As usual, during scenes like this, Sarah Jo became overwrought. "I was only trying to protect you and Junior."

Actually, Angus thought, it had taken a tremendous amount of courage for Sarah Jo to confront a self-assured woman like Alex. He still thought Sarah Jo could have refrained from telling Alex about her folks, but her motive had been unselfish. She'd been protecting her family. Her valiant effort deserved better than his criticism. He leaned down and kissed her forehead.

"I appreciate your fighting spirit, but none of us needs your protection, honey." He laughed at the thought. "How could a little thing like you protect one of us big, strapping boys? I've got plenty of money and plenty of know-how to handle any little problem that crops up. A redhead that only stands five feet six inches tall is hardly worth a second's worry."

"If you could resurrect that odious Pasty Hickam, I'm sure he would disagree," she said. "Look what happened to him. Unlike you and Junior, and obviously, every other man, I'm immune to the girl's charms." Her voice developed an edge of desperation. "Angus, can't you see it? Junior is falling in love with her."

"I fail to see why that's so god-awful," he said with a beaming smile.

"It would be a disaster," Sarah Jo cried softly. "Her mother broke his heart. Don't you care about that?"

Frowning, Angus reminded her, "That was a long time ago. And Alex isn't like her mother."

"I'm not so sure." Sarah Jo stared into space.

"Alex isn't fickle and flighty like Celina was," he said. "She's a tad too bossy, but maybe Junior needs that. He walked all over his other wives, and they laid down and let him do it. Maybe he needs a wife who'll tell him what's what."

"Where is he, by the way? Is he still angry with me?" she asked anxiously.

"He was upset, but he'll get over it, like he always does. He said he was going out to get drunk."

They laughed together. Sarah Jo was the first to turn serious again. "I hope he'll drive safely."

"He, uh, will probably be spending the night out."

"Oh?"

"Wouldn't surprise me," Angus said. "Alex needs some time to sort herself out. Junior might be carrying a torch, but he's not dead from the waist down. He'll find a woman who'll give him the comfort he needs tonight."

His gaze lowered to his wife's décolletage, which was smooth and luminescent with the body powder she had used after her bath. "He's got a man's appetites, just like his daddy."

"Oh, Angus," she sighed wearily, as his hand waded through layers of lace in search of her breast.

"I could use some comforting myself."

"You men! Is that all you ever think about? You make me—"

"You make me horny."

"Don't use that kind of language. It's crude. And I don't want to do this tonight. My headache's coming back."

His kiss cut off any further objections. She submitted, as he knew she would. She always put up token resistance, but she never refused him. From the cradle, she had been coached to accept her marital duties, just as she had to properly serve tea.

That she responded to him out of a sense of obligation rather than passion didn't stop him from wanting her; it might even have enhanced his desire. Angus enjoyed a challenge.

He undressed quickly and lowered himself on top of her. He fumbled with the buttons on her gown and finally managed, with no assistance from her, to get it open. Her breasts were as pert and shapely as they had been on their wedding night, when he had first beheld and touched them.

He kissed them now with polite restraint. Her nipples were small. His stroking tongue was rarely successful in coaxing them erect. He doubted she knew they were supposed to get erect, unless some of those novels she read were more sexually explicit than he suspected.

She winced slightly when he entered her. He pretended not to see her grimace. He tried not to sweat or make a sound or do anything that she would consider nasty and unpleasant.

He saved all his raunchiness for the widow lady he supported in the neighboring county. She didn't mind his crude language. In fact, she hooted with laughter over some of his more colorful expressions.

She was as lusty a lover as he. She had large, dark, milky-tasting nipples that she would let him diddle with for hours if he wanted to. She even went down on him and let him go down on her. Each time he mounted her, her round thighs gripped his ass like a vise. She was a noisy comer, and the only woman he'd ever met who could laugh in downright joy while she was screwing.

They'd been together for over twenty years. She never asked for more of a commitment; she didn't expect one. They had a damn good time together, and he didn't know what he would do without her in his life, but he didn't love her.

He loved Sarah Jo. Or, at least, he loved what she was: dainty and pure and refined and beautiful. He loved her as an art collector would love a sculpture of priceless alabaster that was to be touched only on special occasions, and then with the utmost care.

Because she demanded it, he always wore a condom, and when he was done, he removed it carefully so her silk sheets wouldn't get soiled. While he was doing so tonight, he watched Sarah Jo fold down the hem of her nightgown, rebutton the buttons, and straighten the covers.

Angus got back in bed, kissed her cheek, and put his arms around her. He loved holding her tiny body against his, loved touching her smooth, fragrant skin. He wanted to cherish her. To his disappointment, she removed his arm and said, "Go on to sleep now, Angus. I want to finish this chapter."

She reopened her novel, which was no doubt as dry and lifeless as her love-making. Angus was ashamed of the disloyal thought as he rolled to his other side, away from the light of her reading lamp.

It never occurred to him to be ashamed of making the thirty-mile trip to his mistress's house, which he planned to do tomorrow night.

Stacey dropped the ceramic mug. It crashed and broke on the tile kitchen floor. "Good Lord," she breathed, clutching together the lapels of her velour robe.

"Stacey, it's me."

The first knock on the back door had startled her so badly the mug had slipped from her hand. The voice speaking her name did nothing to restore her heart to its proper beat. For several moments she stood staring at the door, then rushed across the kitchen and pushed back the stiff, starched curtain.

"Junior?!"

She didn't have sufficient air to say his name aloud. Her lips formed it sound-lessly. Fumbling with the lock, she hastily unlatched the door and pulled it open, as though afraid he would vanish before she could do it.

"Hi." His smile was uncomplicated and open, as if he knocked on her back door every night about this time. "Did I hear something break?"

She reached up to touch his face and reassure herself he was really there, then shyly dropped her hand. "What are you doing here?"

"I came to see you."

She glanced past him, searching her backyard for a plausible reason for her ex-husband to be standing on the steps.

He laughed. "I've come alone. I just didn't want to ring the bell, in case the judge had already gone to bed."

"He has. He . . . uh, come in." Remembering her manners, she moved aside. Junior stepped in. They stood facing each other in the harsh kitchen light, which wasn't very flattering to Stacey, who had already cleaned her face and prepared for bed.

She had fantasized about him coming to her one night, but now that it had happened, she was immobilized and rendered mute by disbelief. Myriad professions of love and devotion rushed through her mind, but she knew he wouldn't welcome hearing them. She resorted to safe subjects.

"Dad went to bed early. His stomach was upset. I made him some warm milk. I decided to make cocoa out of what I had left over." Unable to take her eyes off him, she gestured nervously toward the stove, where the milk was about to scorch in the pan.

Junior went to the range and turned off the burner. "Cocoa, huh? Your cocoa? There's none better. Got enough for two cups?"

"Of . . . of course. You mean you're staying?"

"For a while. If you'll have me."

"Yes," she said with a rush of air. "Yes."

Usually adept in the kitchen. Stacey clumsily prepared two cups of cocoa. She couldn't imagine why he'd chosen tonight to come see her. She didn't care. It was enough that he was here.

When she handed him his cocoa, he smiled disarmingly and asked. "Do you have any spirits in the house?"

He followed her into the living room, where several bottles of liquor were stored in a cabinet, to be taken out only on the most special occasions.

"This isn't you first drink of the night, is it?" she asked as she tilted the spout of the brandy bottle against his mug of chocolate.

"No, it isn't." Lowering his voice, he whispered, "I smoked a joint, too."

Her lips pursed with stern disapproval. "You know how I feel about dope, Junior."

"Marijuana isn't *dope.*"

"It is so."

"Ah, Stacey," he whined, bending down to kiss her ear. "An ex-wife has no right to scold."

The touch of his lips made her insides flutter. Her censure melted as quickly as ice cream in August. "I didn't mean to scold. I just wondered why, after all this time, you came to me tonight."

"I wanted to." She knew that to Junior's mind, that was reason enough. He sprawled on the sofa and pulled her down beside him. "No, leave the lamp off," he told her when she reached for the switch. "Let's just sit here and drink our cocoa together."

"I heard about the trouble out at the ranch," she said after a quiet moment.

"It's all cleaned up now. Can't tell it ever happened. It could have been a lot worse."

She touched him hesitantly. "You could have been hurt."

He set his empty cup on the coffee table and sighed. "You're still concerned for my safety?"

"Always."

"No one's ever been as sweet to me as you, Stacey. I've missed you." He reached for her hand and pressed it between his.

"You look worn out and troubled."

"I am."

"Over the vandalism?"

"No." He slumped deeper into the cushions of the couch and rested his hand on the back of it. "This mess we're in about Celina's murder. It's depressing as hell." He tilted his head until it was lying on her shoulder. "Hmm, you smell good. It's a smell I've missed. So clean." He nuzzled her neck.

"What bothers you so much about this investigation?"

"Nothing specific. It's Alex. She and Mother had a row today. Mother let it slip that Celina got knocked up and had to get married to her soldier. It wasn't a pretty scene."

His arm slid around her waist. Automatically, Stacey lifted her hand to cradle his cheek and pressed his head against her breasts.

"I lied to her," she confessed in a small voice. "A lie of omission."

Junior mumbled with disinterest.

"I reckon that's it, yes, ma'am."

Alex dropped the drape back into place, slid the chain lock free, and opened the door. "Did he say what he wanted?"

"Sure did. Said for me to tell you that you was to be in Austin tomorrow morning for a ten o'clock meeting."

Alex stared at the clerk, stupefied. "You must have gotten the message wrong. Ten o'clock tomorrow morning?"

"That's what he said, and I didn't git it wrong, 'cause I wrote it down right here." He showed her the slip of paper with the message scrawled in pencil. "The man's been callin' you all afternoon and was p.o.'d 'cause he couldn't git you. Finally, he said he was goin' out for the evenin' and for me to come to your room and hand-deliver the message, which I done. So, good night."

"Wait!"

"Look, I'm s'posed to be tending the switchboard."

"Did he say what kind of meeting this was, why it was so urgent?"

"Naw, only that you're s'posed to be there."

He stood there expectantly. With mumbled thanks, she pressed a dollar bill into his hand, and he loped off in the direction of the lobby.

Thoughtfully, Alex closed her door and reread the message. It made no sense. It wasn't like Greg to be so cryptic. It wasn't like him to call meetings that were virtually impossible to make, either.

When the bafflement began to wear off, the enormity of her dilemma set in. She had to be in Austin by ten o'clock in the morning. It was already dark. If she left now, she would have to drive most of the night, and would arrive in Austin in the wee hours.

If she waited until morning, she would have to leave dreadfully early and then be on a deadline to get there in time. Either choice was wretched, and she wasn't mentally or emotionally fit to make a decision.

Then, an idea occurred to her. Before she could talk herself out of it, she placed a telephone call.

"Sheriff's department."

"Sheriff Lambert, please."

"He's not here. Can anybody else help?"

"No, thank you. I need to speak with him personally."

"Excuse me, ma'am, but is this Miz Gaither?"

"Yes, it is."

"Where are you?"

"In my motel room. Why?"

"That's where Reede's headed. He should be there by now." Then he paused and asked, "Say, are you all right?"

"Of course I'm all right. I think I hear the sheriff pulling up now. Thank you." Alex hung up and moved to the window in time to see Reede get out of his truck and rush toward her door.

She flung it open. He drew up abruptly, almost losing his balance. "Please don't kick it in again."

"Don't be cute with me," he said, glowering darkly. "What the hell is going on?"

"Nothing."

"Like hell." He gestured toward the bedside telephone. Its innocence seemed to provoke him further. He pointed toward it accusingly. "I've been calling for hours, and all I got is a busy signal."

"I took it off the hook. What was so important?"

"I heard what happened this afternoon between you and Sarah Jo."

Her shoulders dropped dejectedly and she released a long breath. She had almost forgotten about that in her perplexity over Greg's summons.

She had never checked the date on her parents' marriage license. It wouldn't necessarily be conclusive, anyway. As an attorney, she knew that dates, even on so-called legal documents, could be falsified. The way everyone had reacted to Sarah Jo's revelation, she knew it was true. She had been conceived illegitimately.

"You should have been there, Sheriff. I made a spectacle of myself. You would have been thoroughly entertained."

Her flippancy didn't improve his mood. "Why'd you take your phone off the hook?"

"To get some rest. What did you think, that I took an overdose of sleeping pills or gave my wrist a close shave?"

He gave the sarcastic question credence. "Maybe."

"Then, you don't know me very well," she told him angrily. "I don't give in that easily. And I'm not ashamed that my parents had to get married."

"I didn't say you were or that you should be."

"That was their mistake. It has nothing to do with me as a person, okay?"

"Okay."

"So stop thinking ... Oh, hell, I don't care what you're thinking," she said, rubbing her temples. She was more annoyed with herself than with him. Lashing out was only an indication of how upset she really was. "I need your help, Reede."

"What kind of help?"

"Can you fly me to Austin?"

The request took him by surprise. He pulled himself upright from where he had complacently slouched against the framework of the recently repaired doorway.

"Fly you to Austin? Why?"

"Business with Greg Harper. I need to be there at ten o'clock in the morning for a meeting."

TWENTY-SEVEN

They were in the air less than an hour later, on a southeasterly course toward the state capital. Alex had used a quarter of that hour to get herself looking human again. She had washed her face in cold water, applied fresh makeup, brushed her hair, and changed into a pair of wool slacks and a sweater. Whatever she wore to the meeting in the morning could come out of her closet at home.

On the way to Purcell's municipal airfield, Reede stopped at a hamburger joint and picked up the order he'd phoned ahead for. There was a single-engine Cessna waiting for them on the tarmac when they arrived at the landing strip. The sheriff knew how to pull strings.

Purcell was no more than a patch of glittering light on the black carpet beneath them before she thought to ask," Does this plane belong to you?"

"Minton Enterprises. Angus gave me permission to use it. Pass me one of those cheeseburgers."

She devoured almost half of hers—Sarah Jo's cucumber sandwich hadn't gone far—before she came up for air. "When did you learn to fly?"

Reede munched a french fry. "I was about eight."

"Eight!"

"I had salvaged an old beat-up bike from a junkyard and repaired it well enough to get around on. I pedaled out to the airfield every chance I got."

"It must be three miles from town," she exclaimed.

"I didn't care. I'd have gone twice that far. The planes intrigued me. The old guy who ran the place was as testy as a rattlesnake, a real loner, but he kept a strawberry soda pop waiting for me in his ancient icebox. I guess I pestered the snot out of him, but he didn't seem to mind all my questions. One day, he looked over at me and said, 'I gotta check out this plane. Wanna go along for the ride?' I nearly peed my pants."

Reede probably didn't realize that he was smiling over the happy memory. Alex remained silent so he wouldn't be reminded that she was there. She enjoyed his smile. It attractively emphasized the fine lines at the outer corners of his eyes and those around his mouth.

"God, it was great," he said, as though he could feel the surge of pleasure again. "I hadn't discovered sex yet, so flying was the best thing that had happened to me. From up there, everything looked so peaceful, so clean."

An escape from the awful realities of his childhood, Alex thought compassionately. She wanted to touch him, but didn't dare. She was about to venture down a rocky, hazardous path. One wrong word or turn of phrase would spell doom, so she felt her way carefully.

Quietly, she asked, "Reede, why didn't you tell me that my mother was pregnant when she came back from El Paso?"

"Because it doesn't make any difference."

"Not now, but it did twenty-five years ago. She didn't want to marry my father. She had to."

"Now that you know, what does it change? Not a goddamn thing."

"Perhaps," she replied uncertainly. After another brief silence, she said, "I was the quarrel, wasn't I?"

He looked at her sharply. "What?"

Letting her head fall back on the headrest, she sighed. "I wondered why the two of you didn't kiss and make up when she got back that summer. Knowing how much and how long you had cared for each other, I wondered what could possibly keep you apart after a silly lovers' spat. Now, I know. It wasn't silly. It was more than a spat. It was me. I kept you apart. I was the quarrel."

"It wasn't you."

"It was."

Grandma Graham had said it was her fault that Celina had been killed. Everything Alex uncovered was bearing that out. Had Celina, by having another man's child, driven her passionate, jealous, possessive lover to kill her?

"Reede, did you murder my mother because of me?"

"Damn," he swore viciously. "I could strangle Sarah Jo for telling you about that. My quarrel with Celina wasn't over you—not originally, anyway."

"Then, what?"

"Sex!" Swiveling his head around, he glared at her. "Okay?"

"Sex?"

"Yeah, sex."

"You were pressuring her to and she wouldn't?"

His jaw tensed. "It was the other way around, Counselor."

"What?" Alex exclaimed. "You expect me to believe—"

"I don't give a rat's ass what you believe. It's the truth. Celina wanted to get a head start on our future, and I wouldn't."

"Next, you're going to tell me that you had an unselfish, noble reason," Alex said, tongue-in-cheek. "Right?"

"My own parents," he said without inflection. "My old man got my mother pregnant when she was barely fifteen. They had to get married. Look how great that turned out. I wouldn't take a chance on the same thing happening to Celina and me."

Alex's heart was thudding with gladness, disbelief and emotions that were too complex to examine. "You mean that you never—"

"No. We never."

She believed him. There was no mendacity in his expression, only bitterness, and perhaps a trace of regret. "Hadn't you heard of birth control?"

"I used rubbers with other girls, but—"

"So there were others?"

"I'm not a monk, for crissake. The Gail sisters," he said with a shrug, "lots of others. There were always willing girls available."

"Especially to you." He shot her a hard look. "Why weren't you concerned that you'd impregnate one of them?"

"They all slept around. I would be one of many."

"But Celina would have slept only with you."

"That's right."

"Until she went to El Paso and met Al Gaither," Alex mused out loud. "He was just a means to make you jealous, wasn't he?" On a humorless laugh, she added, "She overshot her mark and manufactured me."

They lapsed into silence. Alex didn't even notice. She was lost in her turbulent thoughts about her mother, Reede, and their unconsummated love affair.

"It's really beautiful up here at night, isn't it?" she said dreamily, unaware that almost half an hour had passed since they had last spoke.

"I thought you'd fallen asleep."

"No." She watched a bank of clouds drift between them and the moon. "Did you ever take my mother flying?"

"A few times."

"At night?"

He hesitated. "Once."

"Did she like it?"

"She was scared, as I recall."

"They gave her hell, didn't they?"

"Who?"

"Everybody. When word got out that Celina Gaither was pregnant, I'll bet the gossip spread like wildfire."

"You know how it is in a small town."

"I kept her from graduating high school."

"Look, Alex, you didn't keep her from doing anything," he argued angrily. "All right, she made a mistake. She got too hot with a soldier boy, or he took advantage of her. However the hell it happened, it happened."

With the edge of his hand, he chopped the air between them in a gesture of finality. "You didn't have anything to do with the act or the consequences of it. You said so yourself, just a few hours ago. Remember?"

"I'm not condemning my mother or stigmatizing myself, Reede. I feel sorry for her. She couldn't attend school, even though she was legally married."

Alex wrapped her arms around her sides, giving herself a huge hug. "I think she was a very special lady. She could have given me up for adoption, but she didn't. Even after my father was killed, she kept me with her. She loved me and was willing to make tremendous sacrifices for me.

"She had the courage to carry me in a town where everybody was talking about her. Don't bother denying it. I know they did. She was popular; she fell from grace. Anyone harboring malice toward her was delighted. That's human nature."

"If they were, they didn't dare show it."

"Because you were still her knight, weren't you?"

"Junior and me."

"You closed ranks around her."

"I guess you could put it like that."

"Your friendship probably meant more to her then than at any other time." He gave a noncommittal lift of his shoulders.

She studied his profile for a moment. The rocky path had led her to the cliff, and she was about to take the plunge. "Reede, if Celina hadn't died, would you have gotten married?"

"No."

He answered without a second's hesitation. Alex was surprised. She didn't quite believe him. "Why not?"

"Lots of reasons, but essentially, because of Junior."

She hadn't expected that. "What about him?"

"While Celina was pregnant, they became very close. He just about had her talked into marrying him when she . . . died."

"Do you think she would have, eventually?"

"I don't know." He slid Alex a sardonic glance. "Junior's quite a ladies' man. He can be very persuasive."

"Look, Reede, I told Sarah Jo, now I'm telling you, that—"

"Shh! They're passing us off to Austin radar." He spoke into the headset. When the formalities had been dispensed with, he coaxed someone in the airport tower to arrange a rental car for him. By the time he had gone through that procedure, they were approaching the lighted runway. "Buckled up?"

"Yes."

He executed a flawless landing. Alex thought later that she must have been in a daze, because she barely remembered getting from the plane to the rented car. Without having to concentrate, she gave Reede directions to her condo.

It was located in a fashionable, yuppie neighborhood where Evian was the drink of preference, every kitchen had a wok, and membership in a health club was as mandatory as a driver's license.

A line of thunderstorms hadn't hampered their flight, but had moved in over the city by the time they reached her street. Raindrops began to splatter the windshield. Thunder rumbled.

"The one with all the newspapers scattered in the yard," Alex told him.

"You're a public prosecutor. Don't you know better than to advertise to thieves that you're out of town? Or is it your way of drumming up business?"

"I forgot to stop delivery."

He pulled up to the curb, but he didn't turn off the motor. Several days ago, Alex would have been jubilant at the thought of returning home, just for a temporary respite from the Westerner Motel, but as she looked at the front door now, she felt no enthusiasm for going inside. The tears that clouded her vision weren't tears of joy.

"I've been gone for almost three weeks."

"Then I'd better walk up with you." He turned off the ignition and got out, impervious to the rain. He walked with her up the sidewalk, picking up the outdated newspapers as he went. He tossed them into a corner of her covered porch as she unlocked the door. "Don't forget to throw those papers away tomorrow," he said.

"No, I won't." She reached inside and cut off her alarm system, which had begun to hum the moment she opened the door. "I guess that means it's safe inside."

"Do you want to meet at the airport tomorrow, or what?"

"Uh . . ." She couldn't think beyond him driving away, leaving her alone in her condo. "I hadn't thought about it."

"I'll drop by the D.A.'s office around noon and ask for you. How's that?"

"Fine. I should be finished by then."

"Okay, see ya." He turned to leave.

"Reede." Instinctively she reached for him, but when he turned, she pulled her hand back. "Would you like some coffee before you go?"

"No, thanks."

"Where are you going now?"

"I won't know till I get there."

"What did you have in mind?"

"Messing around."

"Oh, well . . ."

"You'd better get inside."

"I haven't paid you yet."

"For what?"

"The plane, your time."

"No charge."

"I insist."

He cursed. "The one thing I'm not going to argue with you about is money. Got that? Now, good night."

He turned and took two long strides before she called his name again. When he came back around, his eyes bore into hers. "I don't want to be alone tonight," she admitted in a rush. Even with all the crying she'd done that afternoon, her supply of tears hadn't been exhausted. They began to roll down her cheeks as steadily as the rainfall. "Please don't go, Reede. Stay with me."

He moved back beneath the overhang, but his hair and shoulders were already damp. Placing his hands on his hips, he demanded, "Why?"

"I just told you why."

"You've got to have a better reason than that, or you wouldn't have asked."

"All right," she shouted up at him. "I feel like crap. Is that reason enough?"

"No."

"I'm hurting for what my mother must have suffered for my sake," she said, making a swipe at her leaking eyes.

"I'm no doctor."

"I need to be held."

"Sorry. I've got other plans."

"Don't you care that I'm appealing to you for help?"

"Not really."

She hated him for making her beg. Nevertheless, she threw down the last vestiges of her pride and said, "My Grandma Graham died resenting me for ruining Celina's life. She wanted her to marry Junior, and blamed my untimely birth when that didn't happen. Now, dammit,'' she said, ''I need to know that you don't despise me, too.

''Can you imagine how terrible I feel, knowing that I'm the reason my mother married another man when she loved you? If it hadn't been for me, you could have married her, had children, loved each other for the rest of your lives. Reede, please stay with me tonight.''

He closed the distance between them, backed her into the wall, and gave her a hard shake. ''You want me to hold you and tell you that everything is okay, and that the sun will come out tomorrow and things will look better?''

''Yes!''

''Well, for your information, Counselor, I don't do bedtime stories. When I spend the night with a woman, it's not because I want to comfort her if she's hurting, or cheer her up if she's sad.'' He took a step closer. His eyes narrowed until they were mere slits. ''And it's for damn sure not because I want to play *daddy*.''

TWENTY-EIGHT

Gregory Harper, district attorney of Travis County, Texas, was clearly furious. He was on his third cigarette in five minutes. His anger was directed toward his assistant, who was seated on the other side of his desk, looking like she'd been socked hard in both eyes.

''Who've you been sleeping with, Dracula? You look like you've been sucked dry,'' Greg remarked with characteristic abrasiveness.

''Could we stick to one crushing blow at a time, please? Don't confuse the issue.''

''Crushing blow? Oh, you mean the part where I told you that your investigation is over and done with and you're to return to Austin pronto, posthaste, lickety-split, do not pass go, do not collect two hundred dollars, haul ass?''

''Yes, that crushing blow.'' Alex flattened her hands on the edge of the desk. ''Greg, you can't ask me to drop it now.''

''I'm not asking—I'm telling.'' He left his swivel chair and moved to the window. ''What the *fuck* have you been doing out there, Alex? The governor called me yesterday, and he was pissed. I mean p-i-s-s-e-d.''

''He's always pissed at you.''

''That's beside the point.''

''Hardly. Greg, everything you do is politically motivated. Don't pretend it isn't. I don't blame you for it, but don't play Mr. Clean with me just because your hand got slapped.''

''The governor thinks his racing commission can do no wrong. To admit that the commission made a mistake in selecting Minton Enterprises for a license is tantamount to the governor admitting that he made an error in judgment, too.''

''Minton Enterprises is above reproach, as far as the horse-racing business goes.''

''Oh, I see. The only hitch is that you suspect one of the Mintons is a murderer, or if not them, a peace officer. Gee, for a minute there, I thought we had a problem.''

''You don't have to get sarcastic.''

He rubbed the back of his neck. "To hear the governor yesterday, Angus Minton is a cross between the tooth fairy and Buffalo Bill Cody."

Alex smiled at the analogy, which was uncannily accurate. "That's a fair assessment, but that doesn't mean he's incapable of killing someone."

"What happened to his barn the other night?"

"How'd you know about that?"

"Just tell me what happened."

Reluctantly, she told him about Fergus Plummet and the vandalism done to the Minton ranch. When she was finished, Greg ran a hand down his face. "You've upset a real big applecart, full of shiny, bright apples." He selected another cigarette and spoke around it. It bobbed up and down with each word, making lighting it difficult. "I didn't like this case to start with."

"You loved it." Alex's nerves were already frayed, so it annoyed her even more than he was shifting all the blame to her. "You thought it might embarrass the governor, and you relished that thought."

He braced his arms on his desk and leaned over it. "You said you were going out there to reopen your mother's murder case. I didn't know you were going to get a loony preacher whipped into a frenzy, a man's barn nearly burned down, a valuable racehorse shot in the head, and offend a respected judge, who has a reputation as spotless as God's."

"Wallace?"

"Wallace. Apparently, he called our esteemed governor and complained about your unprofessional conduct, your handling of the case, and your unfounded accusations." He sucked smoke into his lungs and blew it out in a gust. "Shall I go on?"

"Please," she said wearily, knowing he would anyway.

"Okay. Chastain's scared shitless of Wallace."

"Chastain's scared shitless of his own shadow. He won't even return my calls."

"He's disclaimed you, washed his hands cleaner of you than Ivory soap could have done. He says you've been seen partying with your suspects."

" 'Partying'? I've seen them on a few social occasions."

"Dangerous business, Alex. We've got three gentlemen suspects and one lady prosecutor whose association with each goes way back. It's all as murky as filé gumbo."

She tried not to squirm under his incisive stare. "New tack." Standing, she circled her chair. "This is an unsolved murder case. The investigation is viable, no matter who conducts it."

"Okay," he said complacently, folding his hands behind his head and leaning his chair back, "I'll play. What have you got? No body to dig up. No murder weapon. No—"

"It was lifted out of the vet's bag."

"What?"

"The murder weapon." She told him what Dr. Ely Collins had told her. "The scalpel was never returned to the elder Dr. Collins. I've been meaning to check the evidence room on the outside chance that it's still there, but I doubt that it is."

"So do I. The bottom line is that you've still got no weapon. Has an eyewitness come forward?"

She sighed. "During this telephone call, did the governor mention a ranch hand named Pasty Hickam?"

"So, it's true."

"It's true. And please don't insult me by trying to trap me like that again. I was going to tell you."

"When? When were you going to slip it into the conversation that a representative of this office got involved with a cowboy who turned up dead?"

"Care to hear my side of it?" She told him about Pasty. He was frowning more than ever when she finished. "If you're right, not only is it stupid and politically imprudent to continue this investigation, it's dangerous. I don't suppose anyone's confessed."

She made a face at him. "No. But one of them killed Celina, and probably Hickam."

Cursing, he mashed out his cigarette. "Let's stick to one murder at a time. If you had to arrest one of them tomorrow for killing your mother, who would it be?"

"I'm not sure."

"Why would the old man have iced her?"

"Angus is cantankerous and shrewd. He wields a lot of power, and definitely enjoys being the boss."

"You're smiling."

"He's extremely likable, I'll admit." She kept Angus's comment about having a daughter like her to herself. "He's inordinately rough on Junior. But, a slasher?" she asked rhetorically, shaking her head. "I don't think so. It's not his style. Besides, Angus didn't have a motive."

"What about Junior?"

"There's a possibility there. He's glib and very charming. I'm sure that everything he tells me is the truth, he just doesn't tell me everything. I know he loved Celina. He wanted to marry her after my father was killed. Maybe she said no one too many times."

"Conjecture and more conjecture. So, that leaves Lambert. What about him?"

Alex lowered her head and stared at her bloodless fingers. "He's the most likely suspect, I believe."

Greg's chair sprang forward. "What makes you say that?"

"Motive and opportunity. He might have felt his best friend was displacing him and killed her to prevent it."

"Pretty viable motive. What about opportunity?"

"He was at the ranch that night, but he left."

"Are you sure? Has he got an alibi?"

"He says he was with a woman."

"Do you believe him?"

She gave a short, bitter laugh. "Oh, yes. I can believe that. Neither he nor Junior has a problem with women."

"Except your mother."

"Yes," she conceded quietly.

"What has Lambert's alibi got to say?"

"Nothing. He won't tell me her name. If she exists, she's probably still around. Otherwise, what difference would it make? I'll work on tracking her down when I get back."

"Who says you're going back?"

Up till now, Alex had been pacing. Returning to her chair, she appealed to him. "I've got to go back, Greg. I can't leave it up in the air like this. I don't care if the murderer is the governor himself, I've got to see it through to the finish."

He nodded toward the telephone on his desk. "He's going to call me this afternoon and ask me if you're off the case. He expects me to say yes."

"Even if that would mean leaving a murder unsolved?"

"Judge Wallace convinced him that you've got a bee up your ass and that this is a personal vendetta."

"Well, he's wrong."

"I don't think so."

Her heart stopped beating. "You think that, too?"

"Yep, I do." He spoke softly, more like a friend than a boss. "Call it quits, Alex, while we're all still speaking to each other, and before I get my tail in a real crack with the governor."

"You gave me thirty days."

"Which I can rescind."

"I've got just a little more than a week left."

"You can do a lot of damage in that amount of time."

"I could also get to the truth."

He looked skeptical. "That's a long shot. I've got cases here that need your expert touch."

"I'll pay my own expenses," she said. "Consider this my vacation."

"In that case, I couldn't sanction anything you did out there. You'd no longer have the protection of this office."

"Okay, fine."

He shook his head stubbornly. "I wouldn't let you do that, any more than I'd let my teenage daughter go on a date without a rubber in her purse."

"Greg, please."

"Jesus, you're a stubborn broad." He withdrew a cigarette from the pack, but didn't light it. "You know the one thing that intrigues me about this case? The judge. If he turned out to be as crooked as a dog's hind leg, it'd really get our governor's goat."

"You're mixing metaphors."

"What have you got on him?"

"Nothing more solid than dislike. He's a persnickety little man, nervous and shifty-eyed." She thought a moment. "There is something that struck me as odd, though."

"Well?" he asked, sitting forward.

"Stacey, his daughter, married Junior Minton weeks after Celina's death."

"Unless they're brother and sister, that wasn't illegal."

She shot him a sharp look. "Stacey's not . . . well, not Junior's type, you know? She still loves him." She recounted the incident in the powder room at the Horse and Gun Club. "Junior's very attractive. Stacey isn't the kind of woman he would marry."

"Maybe she's got a golden pussy."

"I'll admit, I never thought of that," Alex said dryly. "He didn't have to marry her to sleep with her. So why did he, unless there was a very good reason? In addition to that, Stacey lied to me. She said she was home unpacking after a trip to Galveston, but failed to mention she'd been in the stable that day."

Greg gnawed on his lower lip, then poked the cigarette in his mouth and flicked the lighter at it. "It's still too weak, Alex." He exhaled. "I've got to go with my gut instincts and call you off."

They stared at each other a moment, then she calmly opened her handbag and withdrew two plain white envelopes. She pushed them toward him. "What's this?"

"My letter of resignation, and a letter of intent to file a civil suit against the Mintons and Reede Lambert."

He almost swallowed his cigarette. "What? You can't."

"I can. I will. There's enough evidence to bring a civil suit against them for the murder of my mother. I'll sue them for so much money in damages that opening a racetrack will be out of the question. Reede Lambert's career will be shot to hell, too. They won't go to jail, but they'll be ruined.''

"If you win.''

"It won't matter if I do or not. In a civil suit, they can't plead the Fifth to avoid incrimination. No matter what they say, everyone will presume they're lying. The racing commission would have no choice but to reverse its decision and revoke the gambling license.''

"So, what this all boils down to is money?'' he cried. "is that what you've been after all along?''

Her pale cheeks sprouted dots of color. "It's beneath even you to say something like that to me. I demand your apology.''

Greg muttered a string of oaths. "Okay, I'm sorry. But, you mean this, don't you?''

"Yes, I do.''

He deliberated for a full minute longer before grumbling, "I ought to have my head examined.'' Pointing a stern finger at her, he said, "Stay the hell out of trouble. Make sure you've loaded both barrels before you go after somebody, particularly Wallace. If you screw up and I get my ass chewed on, I'll claim you were a naughty girl and that I had nothing to do with your actions. And, your original deadline sticks. Got that?''

"Got it,'' she said, coming to her feet. "You'll be hearing from me as soon as I know something.''

"Alex?'' She was already at the door. When she looked back at him, he asked, "What's going on with you?''

"What do you mean?''

"Any reason in particular why you look like the ghost of Christmas, dead and buried?''

"I'm just tired.''

He didn't believe her, but he let it go. After she'd left, he reached for the two envelopes she'd shoved across his desk. He ripped open the first, then, more hastily, the second.

Greg Harper practically hurled his desk and lunged for the door of his office. "Alex, you bitch!'' he roared down the empty corridor.

"She just left,'' his startled secretary informed him. "With a man.''

"Who?''

"A cowboy in a fur-trimmed leather jacket.''

Greg returned to his desk, wadded the two empty envelopes into balls, and shot them at the wastebasket.

It was close to sundown when Reede wheeled his Blazer into the parking lot of the Westerner Motel.

"Just drop me at the lobby, please,'' Alex told him. "I need to check for messages.''

Reede did as she asked without comment. They'd had very little to say to each other since their awkward reunion outside the D.A.'s office. The flight home had been uneventful. Alex had dozed most of the way.

Reede had passed the time watching Alex doze.

No less than a thousand times during the night, he'd almost gone back to her condo. Looking at the crescent-shaped circles beneath her eyes while she slept, he didn't know how he could have walked away from her. She had needed someone with her last night. He'd been the only one available.

But no one had ever presented him a prize for being a good Boy Scout. If he had stayed, he couldn't have kept his hands, or his mouth, or his cock, away from her. That's why he had left. Their needs hadn't been compatible.

Now, she was hesitating, half in, half out of the truck. "Well, thank you."

"You're welcome."

"Are you sure you won't let me pay you?"

He didn't honor that with an answer. Instead, he asked a question of his own. "What was the big powwow about?"

"A case I was working on before I left. The other prosecutor needed some facts cleared up."

"And they couldn't be cleared up over the phone?"

"It was complicated."

He knew she was lying, but saw no reason to pursue it. "So long."

She stepped to the ground and, pulling the strap of her heavy bag onto her shoulder, went into the motel lobby, where the clerk greeted her and handed her a stack of messages. Reede backed up and turned the truck around. He was about to pull out when he noticed that Alex had slowed down to read one of the messages. Her face had grown even paler than it already was. He shoved the transmission into Park and got out.

"What's that?"

She squinted up at him, then hastily refolded the letter and stuffed it back into the envelope. "My mail."

"Let me see it."

"You want to see *my* mail?"

He snapped his fingers rapidly three times and opened his palm. Her exasperation was plain when she slapped the envelope into his hand. It didn't take him long to read the letter. It was short and to the point. Tawny brows merged over the bridge of his nose as he frowned. " 'An abomination unto God'?"

"That's what he's calling me."

"Plummet, no doubt. Mind if I keep this?"

"No," Alex said shakily. "I've memorized it."

"Be sure to keep your door locked."

"You're not taking his threat seriously, are you?"

He wanted to shake her, hard. She was either stupid or naive, and either one could get her hurt. "Damn right, I am," he said. "And so should you. If he makes any attempt to contact you, call me. Understand?"

She looked ready to argue, but eventually nodded her head. Her exhaustion was evident. She seemed on the verge of collapsing in the parking lot. Reede knew he could take partial credit for that, but instead of making him feel smug, it made him feel terrible.

Closing his mind to it, he returned to his truck. He didn't drive away from the motel, however, until Alex was locked safely inside her room.

 # TWENTY-NINE

Reede turned his head when the corrugated tin door of the hangar crashed open. The sinking sun was behind her, so Alex's face was in shadow, but he didn't need to see her expression to know that she was furious. She looked as tense as a pulled hamstring. The vivid light shining through her hair made it appear to crackle like flame.

He calmly finished washing his hands at the industrial metal sink, rinsed them, and reached for a paper towel from the wall dispenser.

"To what do I owe this unexpected pleasure?" he asked pleasantly.

"You're a liar, probably a cheat, possibly a murderer."

"That's been your opinion of me from the beginning. Tell me something I don't already know."

He dropped down onto a stool and hooked the heels of his boots on the lowest rung. Mindlessly, his hands slid up and down the tops of his thighs. He'd never wanted to touch a woman so badly in his life.

She advanced on him militantly, a package of quivering energy. She looked soft, but so goddamn alive and vibrant that he could almost feel her skin against his palms. He wanted to clutch her hair while crushing her smart mouth with nonstop kisses.

She was wearing the fur coat that never failed to elicit an erotic curl deep in his groin. Her tight jeans gloved thighs that he could think of better uses for than supporting a woman obviously on the brink of exploding with rage.

When they were but inches apart, she shook a paper in his face. He recognized the letter she'd received from the concerned citizens soon after her arrival in Purcell. The shit was about to hit the fan, all right. He'd been waiting for it. This showdown had been due to happen the minute she figured it out.

"I knew something didn't jive with this," she said through clenched teeth, "but today as I was poring over the material I have, looking for clues, I finally realized what was out of sync."

Pretending that he didn't smell her tantalizing fragrance, which made him crazy, he folded his arms over his middle. "Well?"

"There is one more business cited in the letter than there are signatures at the bottom. Moe Blakely Airfield," she said, stabbing her finger repeatedly at the typed paragraph. "But Moe Blakely didn't sign it."

"That would have been tough to do, since he died about seven years ago."

"Moe Blakely was the old man you told me about, wasn't he? The one who taught you to fly and treated you to strawberry soda pops."

"You're batting a thousand, so far."

"You own this airfield, Mr. Lambert."

"Right down to the tumbleweeds and tarantulas. Moe willed it to me. Surprised?"

"Flabbergasted."

"Most folks around here were. Pissed off some of them, too—the ones who would have liked to get their hands on the property. That was when they were poking holes in the ground, drilling for oil under every rock."

"We discussed this letter at length," she grated. "You said you'd already seen it, but you failed to mention that your business was listed."

"The people who drafted the letter didn't consult me first. If they had, I would have told them to leave me out of it."

"Why? Your sentiments match theirs perfectly."

"That's right, they do, but I don't make veiled threats. I told you to your face to get your ass back to Austin. Besides, I'm not a joiner, never have been. Group projects aren't my thing."

"That still doesn't explain why you didn't tell me that the airfield was yours, when you've had so many opportunities to do so."

"I didn't because I knew you'd blow it all out of proportion."

She drew herself up. "I am not blowing it out of proportion. You own this airfield free and clear, and you've got big plans for expansion and improvement."

He came off the stool slowly and loomed above her, no longer amused. His eyes were icy. "How do you know about that?"

"I did my homework this afternoon. Representing myself as your secretary, I called three commuter airlines and asked about the status of *our* application for service. If they had never heard of you, I would have known my hunch was wrong."

She gave a dry laugh. "They'd heard of you, all right. They were very anxious to extend their congratulations to you for ME being guaranteed the racing license. All three are excited about your charter service ideas and are currently preparing proposals. They'll be in touch as soon as their market research is completed. By the way, you owe me ten dollars in long-distance charges."

He grabbed her arm. "You had no right to meddle into my business affairs. This hasn't got a goddamn thing to do with your murder case."

"I have every right to conduct this investigation as I see fit."

"Just because I own an airfield that will prosper if that racetrack is built, doesn't mean that I took a scalpel to Celina."

"It might mean that you're protecting whoever did," she shouted.

"Who? Angus? Junior? That's crap and you know it."

She wrestled her arm out of his grip. "You've hampered this investigation every step of the way. You've got a badge, so that's supposed to make you an officer of the law. Ha! Now *that's* crap!

"You don't want me to discover the killer, whoever he is, because any indictment would mean bye-bye racetrack and the end of your money-making schemes. No wonder your loyalty to the Mintons is so steadfast," she said scornfully. "It has nothing to do with friendship or compensation for past favors. You're selfishly protecting your financial interests."

Her breasts quivered beneath her sweater when she pulled in an uneven breath and added, "I might just as well tell you, I think you're it."

"What, the murderer?" His voice was sibilant and sinister. He backed her against the fuselage of the airplane he'd been tinkering with before she had arrived.

"Yes. I think you killed her. I think I know why."

"I'm all ears."

"You loved Celina to distraction, but she betrayed your love. I was a constant reminder of her betrayal, even before I was born. You couldn't forgive and forget, but Junior could. He welcomed the chance to take your place. He began to court her, and his efforts were effective.

"When you noticed that she was falling in love with him, you just couldn't stand losing her to your best friend and chief competitor, so you killed her. If you couldn't have her, then, by God, nobody, especially Junior, was going to."

He let one eyelid sink into a slow, congratulatory wink. "Very good, Counselor. But you got a big, fat problem with that pile of tripe." He took a step closer and lowered his face nearer hers. "You can't prove it, not a frigging bit of it. It's all conjecture. You've got nothing on me, nothing on anybody. So, why don't you just make life easier on all of us and give it up?"

"Because I can't."

He heard the desperation behind her words and knew that he was more than halfway to breaking her. "Why can't you?" he taunted.

"Because I want to punish whoever killed her."

"Uh-uh," he said, shaking his head. "You're not doing this for Celina. You're doing it for yourself."

"I am not!"

"Your granny built Celina up to be larger than life in your eyes, and you can't forgive yourself for coming along at the wrong time in her life and messing it up.''

''Now who's talking psychological bullshit?'' she asked angrily. ''I know enough about you to know that you're selfish, Reede Lambert. The idea of another man touching what you considered your personal property would be intolerable to you.''

Her expression was triumphant and challenging. ''What did you find the hardest to forgive, Reede? That Celina went to bed with another man? Or couldn't you forgive yourself for not taking her when you had the chance?''

''Why are you so hung up on who I did or didn't *take?*'' He nudged her body with his, then inclined forward until they were touching middle to middle. ''I warned you once to keep your curiosity at bay,'' he whispered. ''Isn't that what you've been doing with Junior, satisfying your curiosity about why your mama found him so appealing?'' He took perverse pleasure in watching the color drain from her face.

''No,'' she denied hoarsely.

''I think it is.''

''You're sick.''

''Not me, baby.'' His breath trailed across her lips. ''You're the one who's curious.''

He bent his head and kissed her. She stubbornly resisted the pressure of his mouth, but he finally succeeded in maneuvering her lips apart. His tongue raked her teeth and the inner linings of her lips.

She opened to him. He felt the breath leave her body on a ragged sigh. It was moist and warm and sweet inside his mouth. His erection stretched, pushing painfully against his fly, against hers. He reached inside her coat and covered her breast with his hand. Beneath his revolving thumb her nipple hardened, and when he swept it lightly, a low moan rose out of her throat.

He raised his head and looked down into her face. Her head was resting against the body of the airplane, her throat arched and exposed. She was breathing hard. Her chest rose and fell swiftly. He could feel her heart, like a small, wild, frightened creature that had become trapped in his palm. Her lips were slightly parted, wet and glistening. Her eyes were closed. Slowly, they came open. They looked at each other with wariness and confusion.

Oh Jesus, was Reede's last coherent thought. His mouth lowered to hers again, hungrier, but much more temperate. He pressed his tongue into her mouth, giving, not taking. He fondled her breast with more finesse.

Eventually losing patience with her clothing, he dropped his hand to her waist. Her sweater was pushed up, the cup of her bra was pushed down, and her warm, soft flesh filled his hand. Reflexively, she arched her back, plumping her breast against his callused fingers and palm. He kneaded it and continued to agitate its tight, feverish center with the pad of his thumb.

Kissing her as though this was his first kiss ever, or the last one he would ever be granted, he worked her legs apart with his knee and angled his hips toward her cleft. From the edge of his mind it registered that she made a helpless little sound and lifted her arms to encircle his neck, but he could focus on nothing except her mouth, his invasion of it, and how damn much he wanted to be buried snugly inside her.

His free hand slid over her butt, down the back of her thigh, and caught her behind the knee. He lifted it, propped it on his hip, and made a grinding motion against her. He fit his rigid body into the notch of her thighs and stroked her there until the tempo escalated to a breathless pace. She spoke his name on a sudden, catchy little breath that fanned his passions hotter.

Several seconds later, he heard his name again, coming to him dimly and from afar. Vaguely, he wondered how she had managed to speak when her tongue was so actively engaged with his.

He heard his name called again and realized that it wasn't Alex's voice.

"Reede? Where are you, boy?"

His head snapped up. Alex blinked her eyes back into focus. He hastily withdrew his hand from inside her sweater. She yanked her coat closed.

"In here." His voice sounded like he'd recently gargled nails.

Angus stepped through the door Alex had left open.

Reede noticed that the sun had set.

 THIRTY

To her credit, Alex recovered remarkably well, Angus thought. Except for the dazed expression in her eyes and her slightly swollen lips, she seemed perfectly composed.

"Hello, Angus," she said.

"Hi, Alex. Get things straightened out in Austin?"

"Yes. Thank you for lending me your airplane."

"Don't mention it."

"I, uh, was just on my way out." To Reede she said, "I'll get back to you about this later." She left in a hurry. Reede picked up a wrench and stuck his head into the exposed engine of the small aircraft.

"What's she up to now?" Angus asked as he lowered himself onto the stool Reede had occupied earlier.

"She discovered that I own this place. I never kept it a secret, but I never advertised it, either. She figures I'd have a lot to lose if she takes this case to a grand jury, whether I'm the killer or not."

"She's right," the older man observed. Reede merely shrugged, tossed the wrench on a worktable and closed the motor casing. "Ely told me she came to his office asking questions about his daddy's scalpel and the day of the murder."

"The scalpel, huh?"

"Yeah. Know anything about that?"

"Hell, no, do you?"

"Hell, no."

Reede went to a cabinet where he kept a supply of liquor and beer. He poured himself a hefty shot of Jack Daniels and tossed it down. He tilted the bottle toward Angus. "Want one?"

"Sure, thanks." As he sipped the whiskey, he watched Reede slam back another one.

Catching Angus's curious stare, he said, "It's been that kind of day."

"Alex?"

Reede ran his hands through his hair like a man plagued by demons. "Yeah. Damn, she's tenacious."

"There's no telling what kind of crap Merle Graham filled her head with."

"No wonder she's vengeful." He blew out a breath of extreme agitation. "If ME doesn't get that racetrack, all my future plans will be affected."

"It's that important to you, huh?"

"What did you think, that I want to be a fucking sheriff for the rest of my life?"

"You worry too much, boy!" Angus said heartily. "We'll get it, and your future looks nothing but sunny. That's what I came out here to talk about."

Reede regarded him curiously. "My future?"

Angus finished his whiskey in one hefty swallow and crushed the paper cup in his fist. He pushed his cowboy hat back further on his head and looked up at Reede, smiling devilishly.

"I want you to come back and be an active part of Minton Enterprises again."

For a moment, Reede was rendered speechless by shock. He fell back a step, laughed, and said, "Are you shittin' me?"

"Nope." Angus raised a callused hand. "Before you say anything, hear me out."

He had already outlined in his mind what he was going to say. After receiving disturbing calls from two worried members of the racing commission who had read about Alex's investigation in the Austin newspaper, he'd decided he'd better get more aggressive about putting a stop to it. This thing wasn't going to blow over, like he'd originally hoped.

The long-distance conversation had ended on an optimistic note. He'd pooh-poohed Alex's allegations, told them a few dirty jokes, and had them laughing by the time they hung up. He wasn't gravely concerned yet, but he definitely saw the need for ME to present a solid front. Having Reede as an integral part of the corporation again would be a positive step in that direction.

Now, his rehearsal words flowed smoothly. "You know almost as much as I do about racehorses, and more than Junior ever took the time or effort to learn. You'd come back into the company as an executive. I'd divide responsibilities equally between you and Junior, though you'd have different functions.

"I know how much this airfield means to you. You've got a sentimental attachment to it, but you also see its moneymaking potential. So do I. I'd incorporate it into ME. The corporation could afford to finance the rebuilding and expansion you want to do. We'd also have a lot more clout with the airlines."

His smile broadened. "Shit, I'd even throw in a few shares of ME stock as incentive. You can't pass up a deal like that, boy."

He was disappointed in Reede's reaction, which he had hoped would be astonishment tinged with pleasure. Instead, it appeared to be astonishment tinged with suspicion.

"What brought this on?"

A picture of equanimity, Angus said, "You belong with us—always have. I'm in a position to get things moving for you. You'd be foolish not to take advantage of my offer."

"I'm not a boy who still needs your charity, Angus."

"I never considered you a charity case."

"I know that," Reede said evenly, "but no matter how we dress it up with fancy words, that's what I was." He peered deeply into the older man's eyes. "Don't think I'm not grateful for everything you've done for me."

"I never asked you for gratitude. You always did an honest day's work for anything I sent your way."

"I wouldn't have had any advantages at all if it hadn't been for you." He paused before going on. "But I paid you back, several times over, I think. When I left your company, I did it because I needed independence. I still do, Angus."

Angus was perturbed, and made no secret of it. "You wanna be begged, is that it? Okay." He took a deep breath. "I'm getting close to retirement age. Some would consider me past it. The business needs your leadership qualities to survive.'' He spread his hands wide. ''There. Does that satisfy your confounded ego?''

''I don't need to be stroked, Angus, and you damn well know it. I'm thinking about somebody else's ego.''

''Junior's?''

''Junior's. Have you told him about this?''

''No. I didn't see any reason to, until . . .''

''Until there was nothing he could do about it.''

Angus's silence was as good as an admission.

Reede began to pace. ''Junior is your heir, Angus, not me. He's the one you should be grooming to take over. He needs to be ready when the time comes.''

Angus paced, too, while he collected his thoughts. ''You're afraid Junior won't get ready as long as you're around to do everything for him and cover his tracks when he messes up.''

''Angus, I don't mean—''

''It's all right,'' he said, raising his hand to ward off Reede's objections. ''I'm his daddy. You're his best friend. We should be able to discuss him freely without wading through bullshit. Junior isn't as strong as you.''

Reede looked away. Hearing the truth warmed him inside. He knew how difficult it was for Angus to say it.

''I always wanted Junior to be more like you—aggressive, assertive, ambitious—but. . . .'' Angus gave an eloquent shrug. ''He needs you, Reede. Hell, so do I. I didn't bust my balls all these years to see everything I've built up fall down around me. I've got my pride, but I'm a practical businessman. I face facts, bad as they sometimes are. One of those facts is that you're competent, and Junior isn't.''

''That's my point, Angus. He *can* be. Force his hand. Delegate him more responsibility.''

''And when he fucks up, you know what'll happen? I'll lose my temper, start yelling at him. He'll sulk and run to his mama, who'll mollycoddle him.''

''Maybe at first, but not for long. Junior'll start yelling back one of these days. He'll figure out that the only way to deal with you is to give you tit for tat. I did.''

''Is that what you're doing now, getting back at me for some slight I'm not even aware of?''

''Hell, no,'' Reede answered crossly. ''Since when have I ever been afraid to tell you off, or anybody else, if something wasn't to my liking?''

''All right, I'll tell you since when,'' Angus snapped. ''Since Celina was killed. That changed everything, didn't it?'' He moved closer to Reede. ''I don't think any of us has had an honest conversation with the other since that morning. The thing I always feared most was that she'd come between you and Junior.'' He laughed with rancor. ''She did anyway. Even dead, she put a blight on the friendship.''

''Celina has nothing to do with my decision to say no. I want to feel that what's mine is mine. Completely. Not a part of your conglomerate.''

''So, it's strictly economics?''

''That's right.''

The wheels of Angus's brain were whirring with fresh arguments. ''What if I decided to build an airfield of my own?''

''Then we'd be competitors,'' Reede replied, unruffled. ''But there's not enough business to support two, and both of us would lose.''

''But I can afford to. You can't.''

''You wouldn't get any satisfaction from bankrupting me, Angus.''

Angus relented and snorted a laugh. "You're right. Hell, boy, you're like family."

"*Like* family, but not. Junior is your son, not me."

"You're turning down this opportunity on account of him, aren't you?" It was a shrewd guess and, he saw by Reede's reaction, a correct one.

Reede gave his wristwatch a needless glance. "Look, I've got to run."

"Reede," Angus said, grabbing his arm. "You reckon Junior'll ever realize just how good a friend you are to him?"

Reede tried to sound jocular. "Let's not tell him. He's conceited enough as it is."

Angus smelled defeat, and it was obnoxious to him. "I can't let you do it, boy."

"You've got no choice."

"I won't let you say no. I'll keep after you," he promised, his crafty blue eyes gleaming.

"You're not shook up because you'll miss me. You're shook up because you aren't getting your way."

"Not this time, Reede. I need you. Junior needs you. So does ME."

"Why now? After all these years, why does ME's future rely on me coming back?" Reede's features sharpened with realization. "You're scared."

"Scared?" Angus repeated with affected surprise. "Of what? Of whom?"

"Of Alex. You're sacred that she might pluck the candy apple right out of your hand. You're trying to pack all the power you can behind you."

"Wouldn't we all be stronger against her if we stood together?"

"We are standing together."

"Are we?" Angus fired.

"You've got my loyalty, Angus, just like I've got yours."

Angus stopped closer to Reede. "I damn sure hope so. But I recall the look on your face when I walked through that door a while ago," he whispered. "You looked like you'd been walloped in the nuts, boy. And she looked all rosy and wet around the mouth."

Reede said nothing. Angus hadn't expected him to. He would have considered a babbling denial or an apology a weakness. Reede's strength was one reason he'd always admired him.

Angus relaxed his tension. "I like the girl, myself. She's saucy, and cute as a button. But she's too smart for her own good." He pointed a stern finger at Reede. "See that you don't get your cock up so high you can't look around it at what she's trying to do. She wants to bring us to our knees, make us atone for Celina's murder.

"Can you afford to lose everything you've worked for? I can't. Furthermore, I won't." Ending the discussion on that grim promise, he stamped out of the hangar.

"Where's my boy?" he stormily demanded of the bartender, almost an hour after leaving Reede. During that time, he'd been making the rounds of Junior's haunts.

"In the back," the bartender answered, indicating the closed door at the back of the tavern.

It was a shabby watering hole, but it had the largest poker pot in town. At any time of day or night, a game was in progress in the back room. Angus shoved open the door, nearly knocking over a cocktail waitress carrying a tray of empty long-necks on her shoulder. He plowed through the cloud of tobacco smoke toward the overhead beam that spot-lighted the round poker table.

"I need to talk to Junior," he bellowed.

Junior, a cigar anchored in one corner of his mouth, smiled up at his father. "Can't it wait till we finish this hand? I've got five hundred riding on it, and I'm feeling lucky."

"Your ass is riding on what I've got to tell you, and your luck just ran out."

The other players, most of whom worked for Angus in one capacity or another, quickly swept up their stakes and scuttled out. As soon as the last one cleared the door, Angus banged it shut.

"What the hell's going on?" Junior asked.

"I'll tell you what's going on. Your friend Reede is about to get the best of you again, while you're here in the back room of this dump pissing your life away."

Junior meekly extinguished his cigar. "I don't know what you're talking about."

" 'Cause you've got your head up your ass, instead of on your business, where it belongs."

By an act of will, Angus calmed himself. If he hollered, Junior would only pout. Yelling never got him anywhere. But it was tough to keep his disappointment and anger from showing.

"Alex was at the airfield this afternoon with Reede."

"So?"

"So, if I'd gotten there ten seconds later, I'd've caught them screwing against the side of an airplane!" he roared, forgetting his resolution to restrain his temper.

Junior bolted from his chair. "The hell you say!"

"I know when animals are in heat, boy. I make part of my living breeding them, remember? I can smell when they want each other," he declared, touching the end of his nose. "He was doing what you should have been, instead of gambling away money you didn't even earn."

Junior flinched. Defensively, he said, "Last I heard, Alex was out of town."

"Well, she's back."

"All right, I'll call her tonight."

"Do better than that. Make a date, see her."

"Okay."

"I mean it!"

"I said, okay!" Junior shouted.

"And something else, just so you'll hear it from me first. I've asked Reede to rejoin ME."

"Huh?"

"You heard me."

"What . . . what'd he say?"

"He said no, but I'm not taking that as final." Angus walked toward his son until they were nose to nose. "I'll tell you something else. I haven't decided who'll be working for whom if he takes the job."

Junior's eyes reflected his pain and anger.

Angus poked him hard in the chest. "You'd better get busy and do what I told you to do, or one of two things could happen. Either Reede'll be sitting at your desk, assigning you jobs like cleaning out the stables, or all of us will be making license plates in the Huntsville prison. Either way, you won't have afternoons to while away playing poker."

Angus stepped back and gave the edge of the table a vicious kick with the pointed toe of his lizard boot. It toppled over, sending cards, poker chips, ashtrays, and bottles of beer crashing to the floor.

Then he marched out, leaving Junior to clean up the mess.

THIRTY-ONE

The waitress set down two chicken salads served in fresh, hollowed-out pineapples and garnished with sprigs of mint. She asked Junior Minton if he and his guest needed refills on iced tea.

"We're fine for now, thanks," he said, flashing her his hundred-watt smile.

The country club's dining room offered a view of the golf course. It was one of the few rooms in Purcell County that didn't reek of Texana. The soothing pastel decor would have fit in anywhere. Junior and Alex were among a small number of luncheon diners.

She applied her fork to an almond sliver. "This is almost too pretty to eat. It beats the B & B Café's blue-plate special all to heck," she told him as she munched on the nut. "I'm sure if I ever saw the inside of the kitchen, I'd never eat there. It's probably crawling with roaches."

"Naw, they chicken-fry them and serve them as appetizers," Junior smiled. "Do you eat there often?"

"Often enough. I've had gravy, which comes on everything, and chili up to here."

"Then, since you refused to go out with me last night, I'm glad I insisted on lunch today. I've frequently had to rescue ladies who work downtown from the high-calorie clutches of the B & B. The menu is hazardous to their waistlines."

"Not that this is much more slenderizing," she said, tasting the rich, creamy salad dressing.

"You don't need to worry about that. You're as slender as your mother."

Alex rested her fork on the edge of her plate. "Even after having me?"

Junior's blond head was bent over his plate. He raised it, noticed her earnest curiosity, and blotted his mouth on the stiff linen napkin before answering. "From the back you'd be taken for twins, except that your hair is darker and has more red in it."

"That's what Reede said."

"Really? When?"

His smile faltered. The question had been posed a little too casually to be taken that way. A telltale crease formed between his brows.

"Soon after we met."

"Ah." The furrow between his brows smoothed out.

Alex didn't want to think about Reede. When she was with him, the practical, methodical, professional detachment she prided herself on disappeared. Pragmatism gave way to emotionalism.

One minute she was accusing him of first-degree murder, the next, kissing him madly and wishing for more. He was dangerous, not only from her viewpoint as a prosecutor, but as a woman. Both facets of her, one as vulnerable as the other, suffered under his assault.

"Junior," she said, after they'd finished eating, "why couldn't Reede forgive Celina for having me? Was his pride that badly damaged?"

He was staring out the window at the golf greens. When he felt her eyes on him, he looked at her sadly. "I'm disappointed."

"About what?"

"I thought—hoped—that you accepted my invitation to lunch because you wanted to see me." He let out a discouraged breath. "But you just want to talk about Reede."

"Not Reede, Celina. My mother."

He reached across the table and squeezed her hand. "It's okay. I'm used to it. Celina used to call me and talk about Reede all the time."

"What did she say when she called and talked about him?"

Junior propped his shoulder against the window and began to play with his necktie, idly pulling it through his fingers. "I usually heard how wonderful he was. You know, Reede this, Reede that. After your father got killed in the war, and she was available again, she was afraid that she'd never get Reede back."

"She didn't."

"No."

"Surely, she didn't expect him to be glad about Al Gaither and me."

"No, she knew better than that. Neither of us had wanted her to go away for the summer, but there wasn't much we could do about it once she'd made her mind up," Junior replied. "She went. She was there. We were here, three-hundred-plus miles away. One night, Reede decided to borrow a plane and fly us there to bring her back.

"That son of a bitch had convinced me that he could get us there and back safely before anybody realized the plane was missing. The only person who would notice would be Moe Blakely, and in his book, Reede could do no wrong."

"My God, you didn't do it?"

"No, not then. One of the stable hands—Pasty Hickam, in fact—overheard us plotting it and told Dad. He gave us hell and threatened us within an inch of our lives not to ever try something that crazy. He knew all about Celina trying to make Reede jealous and advised us to let her have her fun. He assured us that she would eventually tire of it and come home, and everything would be just like it had been before."

"But Angus was wrong. When mother came back to Purcell, she was pregnant with me. Nothing was ever the same."

She toyed with her iced tea spoon for a long, silent while. "How much do you know about my father, Junior?"

"Not much. How about you?"

She raised her shoulders in a small shrug. "Only that his name was Albert Gaither, that he was from a coal-mining town in West Virginia, that he was sent to Vietnam within weeks of his marriage to my mother, and that he stepped on a land mine and died months before I was born."

"I didn't even know where he came from," Junior told her regretfully.

"When I got old enough, I thought about going to West Virginia and looking up his family, but I decided against it. They never made any attempt to contact me, so I felt it best to leave it alone. His remains were shipped to them and interred there. I'm not even certain if my mother attended his funeral."

"She didn't. She wanted to, but Mrs. Graham refused to give her the money to make the trip. Dad offered to pay her way, but Mrs. Graham wouldn't hear of that, either."

"She let Angus pay for Mother's funeral."

"I guess she thought that was different, somehow."

"Al Gaither wasn't any more to blame for the hasty marriage than Mother."

"Maybe he was," Junior argued. "A soldier going off to war, that kind of thing. Celina was a pretty girl out to prove her allure."

"Because Reede wouldn't sleep with her."

"He told you about that, huh?"

Alex nodded.

"Yeah, well, some of the girls he did sleep with flaunted it in Celina's face. She was out to prove she was woman enough to snare a man. Gaither no doubt took advantage of that.

"To your grandma, his name was a dirty word. Because of him, your mother missed her senior year of high school. That didn't go down too well with your grandma, either. No, she had a real ax to grind with Mr. Gaither."

"I wish she had at least saved a picture of him. She had thousands of pictures of Celina, but not a single one of my father."

"To Mrs. Graham, he probably represented evil, you know, the thing that changed Celina's life forever. And for the worse."

"Yes," she said, thinking that Junior's words could apply to how her grandmother felt about her, too. "I don't even have a face to associate with the name. Nothing."

"Jesus, Alex, that must be rough."

"Sometimes, I think I just sprang up out of the ground." In an effort to lighten the mood, she said, "Maybe I was the first Cabbage Patch kid."

"No," Junior said, reaching for her hand again, "you had a mother, and she was beautiful."

"Was she?"

"Ask anybody."

"Was she beautiful inside as well as out?"

His brows drew together slightly. "As much as anyone is. She was human. She had faults as well as virtues."

"Did she love me, Junior?"

"Love you? Hell, yes. She thought you were the most terrific baby ever conceived."

Basking in the glow of his words, Alex left the country club with him. As he held open the passenger door of his Jag, he stepped close to her and laid his hand along her cheek. "Do you have to go back to that stuffy old courthouse this afternoon?"

"I'm afraid so. I have work to do."

"It's a gorgeous day."

She pointed at the sky. "You liar. It looks like it's about to rain—or snow."

He bent his head and kissed her quickly. Leaving his lips in place, he whispered, "Then an even more pleasurable way of passing time indoors comes immediately to mind."

He kissed her more firmly, and expertly parted her lips. But when his tongue touched hers, she recoiled. "No, Junior." She was angered by the impropriety of his kiss and shocked by its failure to stir her sensually.

His kiss didn't cause her veins to expand and her blood to pump through them with a new, feverish beat. It didn't cause her womb to contract with a craving so severe she didn't think it could ever be appeased. It didn't make her think that, God, if he didn't become a part of her, she was going to die.

About all Junior's kiss did was alert her to the fact that he had misinterpreted her friendship. Unless she stopped it now, some dangerous groundwork, disturbingly reminiscent of the past, would be laid.

She eased her head back. "I need to work, Junior. And I'm sure you've got work to do, too." He mumbled profanely, but conceded with good humor.

It was as he stepped back so she could get into the car that they saw the Blazer. It had crept up on them, and was now only a few yards beyond the hood ornament of the Jag.

The driver, whom they could see through the windshield, had his hands folded over the steering wheel and was watching them from behind opaque aviator glasses. He was sitting dangerously still and unsmiling.

Reede pushed open the door and stepped to the ground. "I've been looking for you, Alex. Somebody told me you'd left the courthouse with Junior, so I played a hunch and came here."

"What for?" Junior asked touchily, laying his arm across Alex's shoulders.

"We've located Fergus Plummet. One of the deputies is bringing him in now."

"And that gives you the right to interfere with our date?"

"I don't give a shit about your date," Reede said, his lips barely moving. "She said she wanted to be there when I questioned Plummet."

"Will both of you please stop talking about me as though I'm not here?" The tension that had arisen between the two of them because of her was untenable. It resembled the triangle between them and her mother too well. She shrugged off Junior's arm. "He's right, Junior. I want to hear what Plummet has to say for himself."

"Now?" he whined.

"I'm sorry."

"I'll come with you," he said brightly.

"This is official. Duty calls, and I'm on the state payroll. Thank you for lunch."

"You're welcome." He gave her a soft peck on the cheek and said, loud enough for Reede to hear, "I'll call you later."

" 'Bye." She rushed toward the Blazer and climbed in, though her high heels and slender skirt posed some problems. Reede pretended to be impervious to her difficulties. He sat behind the steering wheel glowering at Junior while Junior glowered right back. The second her bottom landed in the seat, Reede floored the accelerator.

When they reached the highway, he swung onto the macadam with enough impetus to plaster Alex against the passenger door. She gritted her teeth and hung on until he straightened out his turn and they were speeding along the center stripe.

"Have a nice lunch?"

"Very," she answered crisply.

"Good."

"Are you upset because you saw Junior kissing me?"

"Hell, no. Why should I be?"

"Exactly."

Secretly, she was glad he had arrived when he had. The interruption had relieved her of having to turn Junior down flat. Feeling a trifle guilty over that, and trying to set things back on a professional track with Reede, she asked, "Where did they find Plummet?"

"Right where I suspected. He was hiding inside one of his deacons' houses. He came up for air, and one of my deputies nabbed him."

"Did he come peaceably?"

"He's no idiot. He's only being questioned. We really can't make a formal arrest yet. They should beat us to the courthouse by just a few minutes."

As moods went, Junior was in the black hole of Calcutta. There was no peace to be found anywhere, though his Jag streaked through the streets of town at an indiscriminate speed in pursuit of it.

Angus was on his back. His mother was on his back because Angus was. Last night she had sternly commissioned him to get off his ass—not in those terms, exactly—and do something that would make his father proud.

Sarah Jo found the idea of having Reede Lambert back at ME untenable and, using a harsher tone than she had ever used with him before, told her son that it simply must never happen.

"Angus wants *you,* not Reede."

"Then, why did he offer him a job?"

"To wake you up, darling. He's only using Reede as a subtle threat."

Junior promised her he'd do his best. But when he had called Alex and asked her to have dinner with him, she'd turned him down, saying she had a headache. She did agree to meet him for lunch today. And then, when everything had been going great, Reede had showed up and snatched her out of his grasp again.

"Business, my ass," he muttered as he pulled into the wide, circular driveway of the judge's home and brought the car to a jarring halt. He jumped the flower bed and landed a hard blow on the front door with his fist.

Stacey didn't get to the door quite fast enough to suit him. He was practically frothing at the mouth by the time she answered.

"Junior!" she exclaimed gladly when she saw him. "This is a sur—"

"Shut up. Just shut up." He slammed the door behind him, rattling every piece of china and glassware in the house. Taking Stacey by both arms, he backed her into the wall of the foyer and covered her stunned, gaping mouth with his.

He kissed her roughly while his hands attacked the buttons on her blouse. They scattered like BBs across the marble floor when he got too impatient to work them out of their holes and ripped them open.

"Junior," she gasped, "what—"

"I gotta have you, Stacey," he mumbled, plunging his face between her breasts. "Please, don't give me a hard time about it. Everybody gives me a hard time about everything. Just shut up and let me fuck you."

He flipped up her skirt and slip, worked down her panty hose, and then opened his trousers. He rammed into her dryly, and she cried out.

He was causing her pain. While he knew it and hated himself for hurting her when she didn't deserve it, he was glad, in a dark part of his soul, that somebody else besides himself was suffering. Why should he be the only person in the whole freaking world to be miserable?

Everybody picked on him. It was time he got to pick on somebody. Stacey was available . . . and he knew he could get away with it.

Her dismay, her debasement made him feel powerful. His release came from subjugating her, not from the sex itself. When it was over, he collapsed against the wall sandwiching her between himself and the floral wallpaper.

He regained his breath and his reason gradually. He eased away from her and stroked her cheek. "Stacey?" Slowly, she opened her eyes. He gave her a disarming smile and a soft kiss. Realizing that she was dressed up, he asked, "Did I keep you from going somewhere?"

"A meeting at church."

The dimple in his cheek grew deeper as his smile widened. Playfully, he tweaked an exposed breast. "You don't look much like going to a church meeting now."

As he knew she would, she responded to his caresses, which got bolder. "Junior," she whimpered breathlessly when he pushed her blouse off her shoulders, yanked down her brassiere, and fastened his mouth to her raised nipple. She chanted his name, interspersing it with avowals of love. He moved his head down her body, pushing aside clothing as he went.

"Junior?" she asked timorously when he dropped to his knees.

He smiled up at her beguiling as he slipped his thumbs between the lips of her sex and spread them apart.

"Junior! Don't. No. I can't. You . . . can't."

"Yes, I can, honey. What's more, you're just dying for me to." He licked her lightly, enjoying the taste of himself on her, the musky smell of aroused female, her uneasiness. "Still want to go to church?" he whispered, nuzzling her with his mouth. "Huh, Stacey?"

When her orgasmic sobs echoed off the walls of the empty house, he pulled her down to straddle him as he lay on his back on the cold marble floor. He emptied himself into her again. Afterward, when she was curled against him like a rag doll, he felt better than he had in weeks.

When he moved to sit up, Stacey clung to him. "Don't go."

"Hey, Stacey," he said teasingly, "look what a mess I've made of you. You'll have to spruce up, or the judge will know the mischief you've been into while he was at work today."

He stood, readjusted his clothing, smoothed back his hair, "Besides, I've got work to do myself. If I stay a minute longer, I'll cart you off to bed and waste the entire afternoon there. Not that it would be a waste, mind you."

"Are you coming back?" she asked plaintively as she trailed him to the door, covering her nakedness as best she could.

"Of course."

"When?"

He frowned, but concealed it from her by turning to open the front door. "I'm not sure. But after the other night and today, you don't think I could stay away, do you?"

"Oh, Junior, I love you so much."

He cupped her face and kissed her lips. "I love you, too."

Stacey closed the door behind him. Mechanically, she headed upstairs, where she bathed her aching body in warm water and scented bubble bath. Tomorrow, she'd likely be black and blue. She would cherish each bruise.

Junior loved her! He had said so. Maybe after all this time, he was finally growing up. Maybe he had come to his senses, and realized what was good for him. Maybe, at long last, he had expunged Celina from his heart.

But then Stacey remembered Alex, and the calf eyes Junior had had for her at the Horse and Gun Club. She recalled how closely he'd held her while they twirled around the dance floor, laughing together. Stacey's insides turned rancid with jealousy.

Just like her mother, Alex was what stood between her and total happiness with the man she loved.

THIRTY-TWO

As soon as Reede and Alex arrived at the courthouse, they went into the interrogation room, followed by a court reporter. Fergus Plummet was seated at a square, wooden table. His head was bowed in prayer over an open Bible, his hands clasped tightly together.

Mrs. Plummet was there, too. Her head was also bowed, but when they came in, she jumped and looked up at them like a startled deer. As before, her face was void of makeup and her hair was drawn back into a severe knot on the back of her head. The clothes she wore were drab and shapeless.

"Hello, Mrs. Plummet," Reede said politely.

"Hello, Sheriff." If Alex hadn't seen her lips moving, she wouldn't have been certain the woman had spoken. She appeared to be scared out of her wits. Her fingers were knotted together in her lap. She was squeezing them so tightly, they had turned bluish-white.

"Are you okay?" Reede asked her in that same kind tone. She bobbed her head and glanced fearfully toward her husband, who was still fervently praying. "You're entitled to have a lawyer present when I and Miss Gaither question you."

Before Mrs. Plummet could offer a reply, Fergus concluded his prayer on a resounding, "Ah-men," and raised his head. He fixed a fanatical stare on Reede. "We've got the best lawyer on our side. I will get my counsel from the Lord God, now and through eternity."

"Fine," Reede said drolly, "but I'm putting it on the record that you waived the right to have an attorney present during questioning."

Plummet's eyes snapped to Alex. "What is the harlot doing here? I'll not have her in the presence of my sainted wife."

"Neither you nor your sainted wife have anything to say about it. Sit down, Alex."

At Reede's directive, she lowered herself into the nearest chair. She was grateful for the chance to sit down. Fergus Plummet was a prejudicial, ill-informed fanatic. He should have cut a comic figure, but he gave her the creeps.

Reede straddled a chair backwards and stared at the preacher across the table. He opened a file one of his deputies had prepared.

"What were you doing last Wednesday night?"

Plummet closed his eyes and tilted his head to one side, as though he were listening to a secret voice. "I can answer that," he told them when he opened his eyes seconds later. "I was conducting Wednesday-night services at my church. We prayed for the deliverance of this town, for the souls of those who would be corrupted, and for those individuals who, heedless of the Lord's will, would corrupt the innocent."

Reede affected nonchalance. "Please keep your answers simple. I don't want this to take all afternoon. What time is prayer meeting?"

Plummet went through the listening act again. "Not relevant."

"Sure it is," Reede drawled. "I might want to attend sometime."

That elicited a giggle from Mrs. Plummet. None of them was more surprised than she by her spontaneous outburst. Mortified, she looked at her husband, who glared at her in reproof.

"What time was prayer meeting over?" Reede repeated in a voice that said he'd tired of the game and wasn't going to be a good sport any longer.

Plummet continued to give his wife a condemning stare. She lowered her head in shame. Reede reached across the table and yanked Plummet's chin around.

"Stop looking at her like she's a turd floating in a punch bowl. Answer me. And don't give me any more bullshit, either."

Plummet closed his eyes, shuddered slightly, greatly put-upon. "God, close my ears to the foul language of your adversary, and deliver me from the presence of these wicked ones."

"He'd better send a whole flock of angels down to save you fast, brother. Unless you start answering my question, I'm gonna slam your ass in jail."

That broke through Plummet's sanctimonious veneer. His eyes popped open. "On what charge?"

"The feds would like to start with arson."

Alex looked quickly at Reede. He was bluffing. Racehorses were considered interstate commerce, and therefore, would come under the Treasury Department's jurisdiction. But government agents didn't usually get involved in an arson case unless damage amounted to more than fifty thousand dollars. Plummet didn't fall for the bluff, either.

"That's ridiculous. Arson? The only fire I've started is in the hearts of my believers."

"If that's so, then account for your time last Wednesday night until today, when Deputy Cappell spotted you slinking out the back door of that house. Where'd you go after prayer meeting let out?"

Plummet laid a finger against his cheek, feigning hard concentration. "I believe that was the night I visited one of our sick brothers."

"He can vouch for you?"

"Unfortunately, no."

"Let me guess—he died."

Plummet frowned at the sheriff's sarcasm. "No, but while I was in attendance, the poor soul was delirious with fever. He won't remember a thing." He made a tsking sound. "He was very ill. His family, of course, could attest to my presence at his bedside. We prayed for him through the night."

Reede's incisive eyes sliced toward Wanda Plummet. She guiltily averted her head. Reede then swiveled around and looked at Alex. His expression said that he was getting about as far as he had expected to. When he turned back around, he asked abruptly, "Do you know where the Minton ranch is?"

"Of course."

"Did you go there last Wednesday night?"

"No."

"Did you send someone out there last Wednesday night?"

"No."

"Members of your congregation? The believers whose hearts you had stoked a fire in during prayer meeting?"

"Certainly not."

"Didn't you go out there and vandalize the place, paint on the walls, shovel shit into the drinking troughs, break windows?"

"My counselor says I don't have to answer any more questions." He folded his arms across his chest.

"Because you might incriminate yourself?"

"No!"

"You're lying, Plummet."

"God is on my side." He worked his eyes like the focusing lens of a camera, making them wide, pulling them narrow. " 'If God is on our side,' " he quoted theatrically, " 'then who can be against us?' "

"He won't be on your side for long," Reede whispered threateningly. Leaving his chair, he circled the table and bent over Plummet. "God doesn't favor liars."

"Our Father, who art in heaven—"

"Come clean, Plummet."

"—hallowed be thy name. Thy—"

"Who'd you send out there to trash the Minton ranch?"

"—kingdom come, thy—"

"You *did* send members of your congregation, though, didn't you? You're too much of a gutless coward to go yourself."

The praying ceased abruptly. The preacher's breathing became choppy and light. Reede had struck a chord. Knowing that, he pressed on. "Did you lead your ratty little army out there, or did you just furnish the spray paint?"

Reede had told Alex earlier that he'd made the rounds of variety and hardware stores, checking out places where spray paint was sold. So far, none of the merchants recalled a significant demand for it on a single day.

Plummet was probably too clever to have bought it all in one store; perhaps he'd gone out of town. Reede couldn't hold him indefinitely because he had no evidence, but Plummet might be fooled into thinking he'd left behind an incriminating clue.

For the second time, however, he called Reede's bluff. Having composed himself, he stared straight ahead and said, "I can't imagine what you're talking about, Sheriff Lambert."

"Let's try this again," Reede said with a heavy sigh, "Look, Plummet, we—Miss Gaither and I—know you're guilty as hell. You all but told her to get tough with the sinners, or else. Wasn't the vandalism out at the Minton ranch the *or else*?"

Plummet said nothing.

Reede took another tack. "Isn't confession supposed to be good for the soul? Give your soul a break, Plummet. Confess. Your wife can go home to your kids, and I'll be able to take off early today."

The preacher remained silent.

Reede began at the top and methodically worked down his list of questions again, hoping to trap Plummet in a lie. Several times, Reede asked Alex if she wanted to question him, but she declined. She had no more to link him to the crime than Reede had.

He got nowhere. The preacher's story never changed. Reede didn't even trip him up. At the conclusion of another exhaustive round of questions, Plummet grinned up at him guilelessly and said, "It's getting close to supper time. May we be excused now?"

Reede, frustrated, ran his hand through his hair. "I know you did it, you pious son of a bitch. Even if you weren't actually there, you planned it. You killed my horse."

Plummet reacted visibly. "Killed your horse? That's untrue. You killed it yourself. I read about it in the newspaper."

Reede made a snarling sound and lunged across the room at him. "You're responsible." He leaned down close to Plummet again, forcing him backward in his chair. "Reading about that probably gave you a real thrill, didn't it, you little prick? You're gonna pay for that animal, if I have to wring a confession from your scrawny neck."

So it went for at least another hour.

Alex's bottom grew tired and sore from sitting in the uncomfortable chair. Once, she stood up and paced the length of the room, just to restore circulation. Plummet's fanatical eyes tracked her, making her feel so ill at ease that she returned to her seat.

"Mrs. Plummet?"

The preacher's wife flinched when the sheriff suddenly spoke her name. Her shoulders had been sagging forward with fatigue; her head had been kept slightly bowed. Both came erect and she looked up at Reede with awe and respect.

"Yes, sir?"

"Do you go along with everything he's told me?"

She shot Plummet a quick, sidelong glance, swallowed hard, and wet her lips nervously. Then, she lowered her eyes and bobbed her head up and down. "Yes."

Plummet's face remained impassive, though his lips were twitching with a smug smile longing to be full-blown. Next, Reede looked down at Alex. She gave him an almost imperceptible shrug.

He stared at the floor for ponderous seconds before barking out a deputy's name. The officer materialized in the doorway as though he'd been expecting his chief's restrained but furious summons.

"Let him go."

Plummet closed his Bible with a resounding clap and stood up. He marched toward the door like a crusader dressed in full battle armor. He ignored his wife, who meekly trailed in his righteous wake.

The deprecations Reede muttered were vile and scathing. "Have somebody keep an eye on the house," he told the deputy. "Let me know if anything he does looks suspicious or even slightly fishy. Damn, I hate to let that bastard walk out of here."

"Don't blame yourself," Alex said sympathetically. "You conducted a thorough investigation, Reede. You knew going in you didn't have any real evidence."

He whirled on her, his eyes stormy. "Well, that sure as hell hasn't ever stopped you, has it?" He stamped out, leaving her speechless with indignation.

Alex returned to her cubicle, fumbled for the key in the bottom of her handbag, and bent to unlock the door. She felt a prickling sensation at the back of her neck that warned her a heartbeat before the sinister whisper reached her ears.

"You've been corrupted by the ungodly. You're consorting with Satan, showing no more shame than a whore who sells herself." She spun around. Plummet's eyes had regained their zealous glint. Spittle had collected to form white foam in the corners of his mouth. His breathing was labored. "You betrayed my trust."

"I didn't ask for your trust," Alex countered, her voice husky with alarm.

"Your heart and mind have been polluted by the ungodly. Your body has been tarnished by the stroke of the devil himself. You—"

He was caught from behind and slammed against the wall. "Plummet, I warned you." Reede's face was fierce. "Get out of my sight or you're going to be spending some time in jail."

"On what charge?" the preacher squealed. "You've got nothing to hold me on."

"Accosting Miss Gaither."

"I'm God's messenger."

"If God has anything to say to Miss Gaither, He'll tell her Himself. Understand? *Understand?*" He shook Plummet again, then released him. He rounded on Mrs. Plummet, who had flattened herself against the wall in horrified silence. "Wanda, I'm warning you, take him home. Now!" the sheriff bellowed.

Demonstrating more courage than Alex would have expected from her, she grabbed her husband's arm and virtually dragged him toward the staircase. Together, they stumbled up the steps and disappeared around the corner at the landing.

Alex didn't realize how shaken she was until Reede's eyes moved to the hand she had pressed against her pounding heart.

"Did he touch you, hurt you?"

"No." Then, shaking her head, she repeated, "No."

"Don't bullshit me this time. Did he make any threats? Say anything I could use to nail his skinny ass?"

"No, just garbage about me selling out to the unrighteous. He considers me the traitor in the camp."

"Get your things. You're going home."

"You don't have to ask me twice."

He took her coat off the rack near the door. He didn't hold it for her; in fact, he almost threw it at her, but Alex was touched by his evident concern for her safety.

He pulled on his leather, fur-trimmed jacket and cowboy hat as they went upstairs and out the front door.

The Plummets must have taken his advice and left. They were nowhere around. Darkness had fallen. Most of the square was deserted. Even the B & B Café had closed for the night. It catered to the breakfast and lunch crowd.

Her car was cold when she slid beneath the steering wheel. "Start your motor to warm it up, but don't leave till I come around in my truck. I'll follow you to the motel."

"That's not necessary, Reede. As you said, he's probably a coward. People who make threats rarely carry them out."

"Yeah. Rarely," he said, stressing the word.

"I can take care of myself. You don't have to worry about me."

"I'm not. It's me I'm worried about. You asked for trouble when you came here, and you're getting it. But no female assistant D.A. is gonna get raped, maimed, or killed in my county. Got that?"

He slammed her car door. Alex watched him disappear down the dark sidewalk, wishing she'd never heard of him or his infernal county. She commissioned him to the fiery hell Plummet frequently expounded upon.

When she saw the headlights of the Blazer approaching, she backed her car into the street and aimed it in the direction of the motel that had been home for far too long. She resented being escorted home.

She let herself into her room and locked the door behind her, without even waving her thanks to Reede. Dinner was a tasteless meal ordered off the room-service menu. She thumbed through the yearbooks again, but was so familiar with them by now that the pictures hardly registered. She was tired, but too keyed up to go to sleep.

Junior's kiss haunted her thoughts, not because it had sparked her sensual imagination, but because it hadn't. Reede's kisses haunted her because he had so effortlessly accomplished what Junior had wanted to.

Angus hadn't needed a script to know the kind of scene he'd walked into when he had entered the hangar and found her with Reede. His expression had been a mix of surprise, disapproval, and something she couldn't quite put a name to. Resignation?

She tossed and turned out of fatigue, frustration, and yes, fear. No matter how many times she denied it, Plummet disturbed her. He was a wacko, but his words held a ring of truth.

She had come to care what each of her suspects thought of her. Winning their approval had become almost as important as winning her grandmother's. It was a bizarre fact, one she had difficult admitting to herself.

She didn't trust Reede, but she desired him and wanted him to reciprocate that desire. For all his laziness, she liked Junior and felt a twinge of pity for him. Angus fulfilled her childhood fantasies of a stern but loving parent. The closer she came to uncovering the truth about their connection to her mother's death, the less she wanted to know it.

Then, there was the cloud of the Pasty Hickam murder lurking on the horizon. Reede's suspect, Lyle Turner, was still at large. Until she was convinced that he had killed the Mintons's former ranch hand, she would go on believing that Pasty had been eliminated as an eyewitness to Celina's murder. His killer considered her a threat, too.

So, in the middle of the night, when she heard a car slowly drive past her door, when she saw its headlights arc across her bed, her heart leaped in fright.

Throwing off the covers, she crept to the window and peeped through the crack between it and the heavy drape. Her whole body went limp with relief and she uttered a small, glad sound.

The sheriff's Blazer executed a wide turn in the parking lot and passed her room once more before driving away.

Reede thought about turning around and going to where he knew he could find potent liquor, a welcoming smile, and a warm woman, but he kept the hood of his truck pointed toward home.

He was sick with an unknown disease. He couldn't shake it, no matter how hard he tried. He itched from the inside out, and his gut was in a state of constant turmoil.

His house, which he had always liked for the solitude it provided, seemed merely lonely when he opened the squeaky screen door. When was he ever going to remember to oil those hinges? The light he switched on did little to enhance the living room. It only illuminated the fact that there was nobody to welcome him home.

Not even a dog came forward to lick his hand, wagging its tail because it was glad to see him. He didn't have a goldfish, a parakeet, a cat—nothing that could die on him and leave another vacuum in his life.

Horses were different. They were business investments. But every once in a while, one would become special, like Double Time. That had hurt. He tried not to think about it.

Refugee camps in famine-ravaged countries were better stocked with provisions than his kitchen. He seldom ate at home. When he did, like now, he made do with a beer and a few saltines spread with peanut butter.

On his way down the hall, he adjusted the furnace thermostat so he wouldn't be frozen stiff by morning. His bed was unmade; he didn't remember what had gotten him out of it so suddenly the last time he'd been in it.

He shed his clothes, dropping them in the hamper in the bathroom, which Lupe's niece would empty the next time she came. He probably owned more underwear and socks than any man he knew. It wasn't an extravagance; it just kept him from having to do laundry frequently. His wardrobe consisted of jeans and shirts, mostly. Having several of each done up at the dry cleaner's every week kept him decently clothed.

While he brushed his teeth at the bathroom sink, he surveyed his image in the mirror. He needed a haircut. He usually did. There were a few more gray hairs in his sideburns than the last time he'd looked. When had those cropped up?

He suddenly realized how lined his face had become. Anchoring the toothbrush in the corner of his mouth, he leaned across the sink and peered at his reflection at close range. His face was full of cracks and crevices.

In plain English, he looked old.

Too old? For what? More to the point, too old for whom?

The name that sprang to mind greatly disturbed him.

He spat and rinsed out his mouth, but avoided looking at himself again before he turned out the cruelly revealing overhead light. There was no need to set an alarm. He was always up by sunrise. He never overslept.

The sheets were frigid. He pulled the covers to his chin and waited for heat to find his naked body. It was at moments like this, when the night was the darkest and coldest and most solitary, that he wished Celina hadn't ruined him for other relationships. At any other time, he was glad he wasn't a sucker for emotions.

At times like this, he secretly wished that he'd married. Even sleeping next to the warm body of a woman you didn't particularly love, or who'd gone to fat months after the wedding, or who had let you down, or who harped about the shortage of money and the long hours you worked, would be better than sleeping alone.

Then again, maybe not. Who the hell knew? He would never know because of Celina. He hadn't loved her when she died, not in the way he'd loved her most of his life up until then.

He had begun to wonder if their love could outlast their youth, if it was real and substantial, or merely the best substitute they had for other deficiencies in their lives. He would always have loved her as a friend, but he had doubted that their mutual dependence was a healthy foundation for a life together.

Perhaps Celina had sensed his reservations, and that had been one of the reasons she'd felt the need to leave for a while. They had never discussed it. He would never know, but he suspected it.

Months before she left for El Paso that summer, he had been questioning the durability of their childhood romance. If his feelings for her changed with maturity, how the hell was he going to handle the breakup? He had still been in a muddle about it when she had died, and it had left him wary of forming any future relationships.

He would never let himself get that entwined with another human being. It was deadly, having that kind of focus on another person, especially a woman.

Years ago, he'd sworn to take what women could expediently give him, chiefly sex, but never to cultivate tenderness toward one again. He would certainly never come close to loving one.

But the short-term affairs had become too complicated. Invariably, the woman developed an emotional attachment that he couldn't reciprocate. That's when he'd started relying on Nora Gail for physical gratification. Now, that had soured. Sex with her was routine and meaningless, and lately, he was having a hard time keeping his boredom from showing.

Dealing with a woman on any level demanded a much higher price than he was willing to pay.

Still, even as he lay there mentally reciting his creed of eternal detachment, he found himself thinking about *her*.

At this advanced stage of his life, he'd started daydreaming like a sap. She occupied more of his thoughts than he would have ever thought possible. At the edges of these thoughts was an emotion very akin to tenderness, nudging its way into his consciousness.

Nipping at the heels of it, however, was always pain: the pain of knowing who she was and how irrevocably her conception had altered his life, of knowing how decrepit he must appear to a woman her age, of seeing her kiss Junior.

"Dammit."

He groaned into the darkness and covered his eyes with his forearm as his mind tricked him into witnessing it again. It had produced such an attack of jealousy, it had frightened him. His fury had been volcanic. It was a wonder he hadn't erupted from the roof of the Blazer.

How the hell had it happened? Why had he let her get to him when absolutely nothing could come of it, except to widen the gulf between him and Junior that had been created by her mother?

A relationship—the word alone made him shudder—between him and Alex was out of the question, so why did it bother him to know that to a smart, savvy career woman like Alex, he must look like a hick, and an *old* one, at that?

He and Celina had had everything in common, but she'd been unattainable, so how the hell did he imagine there was common ground on which he and Alex could meet?

One other small point, he thought wryly. *Celina's murder.* Alex would never understand about that.

None of that sound reasoning, however, kept him from wanting her. An influx of heat surged through his body now, and with it, desire. He wanted to smell her. He wanted to feel her hair against his cheek, his chest, his belly. Imagining her lips and tongue against his skin cost him precious breath, but the lack of sufficient air was worth the image. He wanted to taste her again and tug on her nipple with his mouth.

He whispered her name in the darkness and focused on that instant when he had slipped his hand into the cup of her bra and caressed forbidden flesh. He was consumed by the fire of his imagination. It burned brightly and fiercely.

Eventually, it dimmed. When it did, he was left feeling empty and alone in the cold, dark, lonely house.

THIRTY-THREE

"**G**ood morning, Wanda Gail.''

Fergus Plummet's wife fell back a step. "What'd you call me?''

"Wanda Gail," Alex repeated with a gentle smile. "That's your name, isn't it? You're one of the Burton triplets, informally known as the Gail sisters.''

Mrs. Plummet had answered her door with a dishrag in her hands. Shocked by Alex's knowledge of her past, she took a quick little breath. Her eyes darted about the yard, as though looking for artillery backing Alex up.

"May I come in?''

Alex didn't wait for permission, but used the other woman's astonishment to step inside and close the front door. She had discovered Mrs. Plummet's identity quite by accident while idly perusing the pages of the yearbooks over her morning coffee. After glancing past it a hundred times, the classroom picture had suddenly leaped off the page. She'd thought her eyes were deceiving her until she verified the name in the margin. Wanda Gail Burton.

Hardly able to contain her excitement, she'd consulted the telephone directory for the address and driven straight to the parsonage. She had parked well down the block and hadn't approached the house until Fergus had driven away in his car.

The two women stood face to face in the dim hallway. Alex was curious. Wanda Gail Plummet was clearly afraid.

"I shouldn't be talking to you," she whispered nervously.

"Why? Because your husband warned you against it?" Alex asked softly. "I don't mean to cause you any trouble. Let's sit down.''

Assuming the role of hostess, Alex led Wanda Gail into the drabbest, most unattractive room she had ever been in. There wasn't a single spot of color or gaiety. There were no plants, no pictures—other than one of a bleeding, crucified Christ—no books or magazines. There was nothing to relieve the cheerless atmosphere that pervaded the house. Alex had seen three thin, dejected-looking children leave with their father. She and Wanda Gail were alone.

They sat side by side on a tacky, threadbare sofa that reflected the overall penury of the house. Wanda Gail was wringing the damp towel between her hands. Her face was working with anxiety. She was obviously scared to death, either of Alex, or of her husband's reprisal should he find out she had been in their home.

Alex tried to reassure her by calmly stating, "I just want to talk to you. I accidentally discovered that your name was Wanda Gail Burton."

"Not anymore. Not since I found Jesus."

"Tell me about that. When was it?"

"The summer after I graduated. A bunch of us—"

"Your sisters?"

She nodded. "And some friends. We all piled into somebody's car and drove to Midland. We were looking for fun," she said, casting her eyes downward. "We saw this big tent set up in a cow pasture on the outskirts of town. There was a revival going on. We thought we'd go, see what it was about. We went on a lark, you know, to poke fun at the people and to laugh at the gospel."

She made a grimace of remorse. "It all seemed real funny, 'cause we'd been drinking and smoking pot somebody had brought back from Eagle Pass." She folded her hands together and offered up a brief prayer of repentance.

"What happened? Did you have a religious experience that night?"

She confirmed Alex's guess by briskly nodding her head. "There was this young preacher there. After the singing and praying, he took the microphone." Her eyes assumed a dreamy aspect as she was transported back. "I don't even remember what he preached on. His voice alone put me in a trance. I remember feeling his energy pouring through me. I couldn't take my eyes off him."

Her vision cleared. "The others had had enough and wanted to leave. I told them to go on and pick me up later. I wanted to stay. When he was finished preaching, I went down to the altar with dozens of others. He laid his hands on my head and prayed for my deliverance from sin." Misty-eyed, she announced, "I gave my heart to Jesus and to Fergus Plummet that same night."

"How soon after that were you married?"

"Two days."

Alex didn't know a delicate way to approach her next question. Out of deference to the woman's Christian conversion, she addressed her by her married name. "Mrs. Plummet, you and your sisters . . ." She paused, wet her lips. "I've heard . . ."

"I know what you've heard. We were harlots."

Alex didn't approve of her harsh, condemning estimation of herself and tried to soften it. "I know that you dated a lot of men."

Wanda began to twist the towel again. "I confessed all my transgressions to Fergus. He forgave me, just like God did. HE embraced me in love, in spite of my wickedness."

Alex had a more jaundiced opinion of the preacher's largess. He had probably wanted a wife who felt privileged that he had so unselfishly forgiven her, one who would consider his grace equal to God's.

God forgot sins; Alex doubted that Fergus Plummet did. He probably kept scrupulous accounts of transgressions and used Wanda Gail's past as a tool to keep her under his thumb. He surely made her life miserable with constant reminders of how lucky she was to have his forgiveness.

It was apparent, however, that whatever had happened to Wanda Gail in that revival tent had been profound and irreversible. Her decision that night to create a different life for herself had withstood twenty-five years. For that, she had earned Alex's admiration.

"Two of the boys you dated in high school were Reede Lambert and Junior Minton."

"Yes," Wanda said with a reflective smile, "they were the two best-looking, most popular boys in school. All the girls wanted to date them."

"Including Stacey Wallace?"

"The only boy she could ever see was Junior Minton. It was kinda pitiful, you know, because Stacey was so crazy about him and he was stuck on Celina."

"And Celina belonged to Reede."

"Well, sure. Reede was, and still is, basically good. He didn't treat me and my sister like trash, even though that's what we were. He was always nice about . . . well, you know, whenever he took us out. He always said thank you afterward."

Alex smiled sickly.

"Liked to have drove him plumb nuts when Celina got married. Then, when she died . . ." She sighed sympathetically. "He acts kinda mean sometimes now, but down deep, he's still good." She averted her head. "I know he doesn't like Fergus, but he still treated me nice yesterday."

This woman and Reede were former lovers. Alex looked at her closely. It was impossible to envision Wanda Gail in the throes of ecstasy with any man, but especially with Reede.

Her face retained enough of its former prettiness for Alex to have recognized her picture in the yearbook, but her skin was loose, her throat flabby. The full, teased hairdo she'd been sporting in the class photo had been replaced by the severe and unflattering bun. The eyes that had been dramatically enhanced with cosmetics for the picture wore no makeup at all now. Her waist had thickened to match the dimensions of her bust and hips, which, when she was a teenager, must have been voluptuous.

Wanda Gail looked at least ten years older than her classmates, Reede and Junior—even Stacey. Alex wondered if it had been her previously wild life, or her married life with Plummet that had accelerated her aging process. She would bet on the latter. He couldn't be much fun to live with. For all his piousness, he brought no joy or love to those around him. To Alex, that's what one's faith should be about. Her admiration for this woman was tinged with pity.

It became even more so when Wanda Gail looked up at her and shyly remarked, "You were nice to me, too. I didn't expect you to be nice, 'cause you're so fancy and have such pretty things." She gave Alex's fur coat and eel handbag a wistful glance.

"Thank you," she replied. Then, because Wanda Gail seemed stricken with self-consciousness, Alex resumed the questioning. "How did your sisters react to your marriage?"

"Oh, I'm sure they didn't like it."

"You don't know?"

"Fergus thought it would be best if I didn't mix with them anymore."

"He separated you from your family?"

"It was for the best," Wanda said, immediately rising to his defense. "I left my old life. They were part of it. I had to turn my back on them to prove to Jesus that I was forsaking sin."

Alex chalked up another reason to despise the preacher. He had brainwashed his wife against her family and used her immortal soul as leverage. "Where are your sisters now?"

"Peggy Gail died a few years ago. I read about it in the newspaper. She had cancer," she said, her face sorrowful.

"What about the other one? Nora Gail?"

Wanda's lips narrowed with stern disapproval. "She's still living her sinful ways."

"Here in town?"

"Oh my, yes." Again, she clasped her hands beneath her chin and said a quick prayer. "I pray to God that she'll see the light before it's too late."

"She never married"

"No, she likes men too much, all men. She never wanted one in particular. Maybe Reede Lambert, but he didn't want anything permanent."

"She liked him?"

"Very much. They enjoyed each other physically, but it never amounted to love. Maybe they were too much alike. Stubborn. They both have a mean streak, too."

Alex tried to make the next question sound casual. "Do you know if he still sees her?"

"I expect he does," she said, folding her arms across her middle and sniffing righteously. "He liked us all, but Nora Gail was always his first choice. I don't know if they still sleep together, but they've gotta stay friends 'cause they know too much about each other. Ever since the night Celina was killed, there's been—"

"What about it?" Alex interrupted.

"What about what?"

"The night Celina was killed."

"Reede was with Nora Gail."

Alex's heart fluttered. "He was with your sister that night? You sure?"

Wanda gave her a puzzled look. "I thought everybody knew that."

Everybody but me, Alex thought bitterly.

She asked Wanda where Nora Gail lived. Reluctantly, Wanda gave her directions to the house. "I've never been there, but I know where it is. I don't think you can miss it."

Alex thanked her for the information and rose to leave. At the door, Wanda became nervous again. "I don't think Fergus would like it that I talked to you."

"He won't hear about it from me." Wanda Gail looked reassured until Alex added, "I'd advise him against any more vandalism, and I would appreciate not getting another condemning letter in the mail."

"Letter?"

She appeared not to have any knowledge of the letter that had been waiting for Alex when she had returned from Austin, but Alex felt sure that she must. "I won't place you in a position of having to lie for your husband, Mrs. Plummet, but I should warn you that Reede has the letter and considers it a police matter. I feel certain he'd make an arrest if I received another one."

She hoped the subtle threat would work. By the time she reached her car, however, her mind had already moved forward to her interview with Reede's alibi.

The two-story frame structure reminded Alex of the Prohibition-era roadhouses she'd seen in gangster movies. It had no signs out front and was invisible from the highway, but there were several commercial rigs in the parking lot, along with a few pickup trucks, and even a recent-model Cadillac.

The stone sidewalk was bordered with valiant, dusty pansies. A series of steps led up to a deep veranda. There was an old-fashioned pull bell next to the front door. Muted honky-tonk music wafted through the walls, but the windows appeared to have been blacked out; she couldn't see through them.

The door was answered by a bear of a man with a full, salt-and-pepper beard covering the lower two-thirds of a face as florid as a sirloin steak. He was wearing a white tuxedo shirt and black satin bow tie, over a full white apron. He was also wearing a fearsome, intimidating frown.

"I—" Alex began.

"Are you lost?"

"I'm looking for Nora Gail Burton."

"Whaddaya want with her?"

"I want to talk to her."

"What about?"

"It's personal."

He squinted suspiciously. "You selling something?"

"No."

"You got an appointment?"

"No."

"She's busy."

He started to close the door, but a man approached it on his way out. He squeezed between them, doffing his bill cap to Alex and muttering thanks to the doorman. Alex took advantage of the interruption and stepped over the threshold into a formally decorated vestibule. "I'd like to see Ms. Burton, please. I promise not to take too much of her time."

"If you're looking for work, miss, you'll need to fill out an application and provide pictures. She doesn't see a girl until she's looked over her pictures."

"I'm not looking for work."

He considered her for another long moment before coming to a favorable conclusion. "Name?"

"Alexandra Gaither."

"Wait right here, you hear?"

"Yes, sir."

"Don't move."

"I promise."

He retreated toward the back of the house, moving along the staircase with a grace and lightness of tread unusual for a man his size. His order for her to stay put had been so emphatic that it had nailed her shoes to the floor. She didn't think anything could prise her away.

Within seconds, however, the music beckoned her toward its source. Low conversation and soft laughter lured her toward the violet brocade drapes that separated the hallway from the room beyond. The edges overlapped so she couldn't see anything. Raising her hand tentatively, she pushed them apart and peeked through the slit.

"Ms. Gaither."

She jumped and spun around, dropping her hand guiltily. The bearded giant was looming over her, but his soft, pink lips were twitching with amusement.

"This way," the mammoth said. He led her behind the stairwell and stopped in front of a closed door. After giving it three sharp raps, he pushed it open and stepped aside for Alex to enter. He closed the door behind her.

Alex had expected the madam to be reclining on satin sheets. Instead, she was seated behind a large, functional desk banked by metal file cabinets. From the number of ledgers and folders and stacks of correspondence scattered across the desk, it looked as though she conducted as much business here as in the boudoir.

Nor was her clothing what Alex would have expected. Instead of a scanty article of lingerie, she was wearing a tailored wool business suit. She was, however, elaborately jeweled, and all the pieces were genuine and exquisite.

Her hair had been bleached snow-white and looked like a sculpted mound of cotton candy. Somehow, though, the outdated style suited her. Like her sister Wanda, her figure gravitated toward plump, but she carried that well, too. Her complexion was her best feature. It was flawless, smooth, and milky white. Alex doubted it had ever been exposed to the damaging West Texas sun.

The blue eyes with which she assessed Alex were as calculating as those of the cat that was occupying the corner of the desk nearest her right hand.

"You have better taste than your mother," she said without preamble, giving Alex a slow once-over. "Celina had pretty features, but no sense of style. You do. Sit down, Miss Gaither."

"Thank you." Alex sat down in the chair across the desk. After a moment, she laughed and shook her head with chagrin. "Forgive me for staring."

"I don't mind. No doubt I'm your first madam."

"Actually, no. I prosecuted a woman in Austin whose modeling agency proved to be a prostitution ring."

"She was careless."

"I did my homework. We had an airtight case against her."

"Should I take that as a warning?"

"Your operation doesn't fall into my jurisdiction."

"Neither does your mother's murder case." She lit a slender black cigarette as a man would, with an economy of motion, and offered one to Alex, who declined. "A drink? Forgive me for saying that you look like you could use one." She gestured toward a lacquered liquor cabinet that was inlaid with mother-of-pearl.

"No, thank you. Nothing."

"Peter said you declined to fill out an application, so I guess you're not here looking for a job."

"No."

"Pity. You'd do very well. Nice body, good legs, unusual hair. Is that its natural color?"

"Yes."

The madam grinned wickedly. "I know several regulars who would enjoy you a lot."

"Thank you," Alex said stiffly, the compliment making her feel like she needed a bath.

"I guess you're here on business. Yours," she said with a lazy smile, "not mine."

"I'd like to ask you some questions."

"First, I'd like to ask one of my own."

"All right."

"Did Reede send you here?"

"No."

"Good. That would have disappointed me."

"I found you through your sister."

One eyebrow arched a fraction of an inch higher. "Wanda Gail? I thought she believed that speaking my name aloud would turn her into a pillar of salt, or some such nonsense. How is she? Never mind," she said when she sensed Alex's hesitation.

"I've seen Wanda Gail from a distance. She looks terrible. That little pecker who professes to be a man of God has nearly ruined her health, as well as her looks. Her kids go around like ragamuffins. If she wants to live like that, fine, but why impose poverty on them?"

She was genuinely indignant. "There's no righteousness in being poor. I'd like to help her financially, but I'm sure she would rather starve than take a cent from me, even if her husband would allow it. Did she just come right out and tell you that her sister was a whore?''

''No. She only gave me directions here. I guess she assumed that I already knew your . . . occupation.''

''You didn't?''

''No.''

''My business has been lucrative, but I'm branching out. I used to screw men for fun, Ms. Gaither. I'm still screwing them, but now I do it mostly for money. And you know what? Money's even more fun.'' Her laugh was throaty and complacent.

She had none of Wanda Gail's timidity. Alex got the impression that Nora Gail wasn't afraid of Satan himself, that she would walk up to him and spit in his eye without an ounce of trepidation. After that, she would probably seduce him.

''In fact,'' she continued, ''you were lucky to catch me in. I just returned from a meeting with my banker. No matter how busy he is, he makes room in his schedule to see me.''

She gestured down at the portfolio lying open on top of the desk directly in front of her. Even reading it upside down, Alex recognized the logo on the letterhead.

''NGB, Incorporated,'' she mouthed silently. When her eyes met the madam's again, Nora Gail's were gloating. ''*You* are NGB, Incorporated? Nora Gail Burton,'' she said faintly.

''That's right.''

''You signed the letter the businesspeople sent to me.''

''I helped draft it.'' Her long, beautifully manicured nails sank into the cat's lush fur as she scratched it behind the ears. ''I don't like what you're trying to do here. Miss Gaither. I don't like it at all. You're about to throw a goddamned wrench into all my carefully orchestrated plans for expansion.''

''As I recall, NGB, Incorporated proposes to build a resort hotel near Purcell Downs.''

''That's right. A resort complete with golf course, putting greens, tennis courts, racquetball, swimming. You name it, it'll have it.''

''And does a whore come with every room?''

Nora Gail gave another of her bawdy laughs, taking no offense. ''No. But who knows better how to show folks a good time than an old whore? I've got the best resort architects in the country working on the layout. It'll be spectacular, gaudy as hell, which I've decided the tourist trade likes. Everybody who comes to Texas from out of state, particularly from back east, expects us to be loud, raucous, and tasteless. I don't want my customers to be disappointed.''

''Have you got the money to build a place like that?'' Alex asked, her peevishness giving way to curiosity.

''I've got enough put aside to borrow against. Honey, more cowboys, truckers, roughnecks, white-collar types, statesmen, and would-be statesmen have trooped up those stairs than I could count,'' she said, pointing toward the staircase. ''Actually, I could tell you exactly how many, how long each stayed, what he did, what he drank, what he smoked, whatever you wanted to know. My records are that meticulous.

''I'm a whore, but I'm a goddamned smart one. You don't go into this business just knowing how to make a john come. You go into it knowing how to make him come quickly so you can move on to the next one. You've also got to know how to get him to drop more dollars than he intends to while he's visiting.''

She sat back and stroked the cat. ''Yes, I've got the money. More important, I've got the brains to pyramid it into a fortune. With that resort, I can go legitimate. I'll never have to give a blow job to another stiff cock unless it's one of my own choosing, or listen to another hard-luck story from a man about how his wife doesn't understand him.

"I'm living for the day I can move out of this place and into town, hold my head up, and say, 'Kiss my ass,' to anybody who doesn't like me moving into his neighborhood." She pointed her cigarette toward Alex. "I don't need a cheer-leader like you to come in here and fuck it up for me."

It was quite a speech. In spite of herself, Alex was fascinated, though not cowed. "All I'm trying to do is solve a murder case."

"Not for the sake of law and order you're not. The state doesn't give a damn about Celina Gaither's killing, or it would have been looked into years ago."

"You've just admitted that the case warrants being reopened."

Nora Gail gave an elegant shrug. "Maybe from a legal standpoint, but not from a personal one. Listen, sugar, take my advice. I'm talking to you now like I would to one of my girls when things aren't working out for her." She leaned forward. "Go home. Leave things here the way they were. Everybody'll be happier, especially you."

"Do you know who murdered my mother, Ms. Burton?"

"No."

"Do you believe that Gooney Bud killed her?"

"That harmless idiot? No."

"So, you suspect someone else. Who?"

"I'd never tell you."

"Even under oath on the witness stand?"

She shook her head of glorious white hair. "I wouldn't incriminate my friends."

"Like Reede Lambert?"

"Like Reede Lambert," Nora Gail repeated firmly. "We go way back."

"So I've heard."

Nora Gail's husky chuckle brought Alex's head up. "Does it bother you to know that Reede and I used to screw our brains out?"

"Why should it?"

Without taking her eyes off Alex, Nora Gail sent a plume of smoke ceilingward and ground out her cigarette in a crystal ashtray. "You tell me, sugar."

Alex drew herself up, attempting to reestablish herself as a tough prosecutor. "Was he with you the night my mother was killed?"

"Yes," she answered without a second's hesitation.

"Where?"

"I believe we were in my car."

"Screwing your brains out?"

"What's it to you?"

"My interest is strictly professional," Alex snapped. "I'm trying to establish Reede Lambert's alibi. I need to know where you were, what you were doing, and for how long."

"I fail to see the relevance."

"Let me decide the relevance. Besides, what difference does it make if you tell me now? I'm sure you gave the answers to the officers who questioned you before."

"No one ever questioned me."

"What?" Alex exclaimed.

"No one ever questioned me. I guess Reede told them that he was with me and they believed him."

"Was he with you all night?"

"I'd swear to that in court."

Alex gave her a long steady look. "But was he?"

"I'd swear under oath that he was," she said, her eyes openly challenging.

That was a dead-end street. Alex decided to stop butting her head against the bricks. It was giving her a headache. "How well did you know my mother?"

"Well enough not to cry over her death." Her candor matched Stacey Wallace's. Alex should have been inured to it by now, but she wasn't. "Look, sugar, I hate to put it to you so bluntly, but I didn't like your mother. She knew that Reede and Junior both loved her. The temptation was just too strong."

"What temptation?"

"To play them against each other, see how far she could go. After your daddy got killed, she started playing up to them again. Reede was slow to forgive her for getting pregnant, but not Junior. I guess he saw his chance and took it. Anyway, he started courting her in earnest.

"His folks didn't like it. Stacey Wallace was about to come apart at the seams over it. But it looked like Junior was going to get Celina, after all. He made it known to anybody who wanted to listen that as soon as he graduated, he was going to marry her. Tickled your grandma to death. She'd always been jealous of Reede and fancied Junior Minton as a son-in-law."

She paused to light another cigarette. Alex waited impatiently, a knot of tension drawing tighter in her chest. After Nora Gail's cigarette was lit she asked, "How did Reede feel about the pending marriage between Celina and Junior?"

"He was still pissed at Celina, but he cared—a hell of a lot. That's why he came to me that night. Celina had gone out to the ranch for supper. Reede expected Junior to pop the question. By morning, he expected them to be engaged."

"But by morning, Celina was dead."

"That's right, sugar," Nora Gail replied coolly. "And in my opinion, that was the best solution to their problem."

As though punctuating her startling statement, a shot rang out.

 # THIRTY-FOUR

"**G**ood Lord, what was that?" Alex sprang to her feet.

"A gunshot, I believe." Nora Gail remained admirably calm, but she had already reached the door by the time the man who had greeted Alex flung it open. "Is anyone hurt, Peter?"

"Yes, ma'am. A customer's been shot."

"Phone Reede."

"Yes, ma'am."

Peter lurched toward the telephone on the desk. Nora Gail left the office, Alex followed her. The madam flung open the drapes with a theatrical flourish and took in the scene at a glance. With apprehension and curiosity, Alex peered over Nora Gail's shoulder.

Two men whom Alex assumed were bouncers had subdued a man and were restraining him against the ornate bar. Several scantily clad young women were cowering against the purple velvet furniture. Another man was lying on the floor. Blood was pooling beneath him, making a mess on the pastel Oriental rug.

"What happened?" When Nora Gail got no answer, she repeated her question with noticeably more emphasis.

"They got in a scuffle," one of the prostitutes answered finally. "Next thing we knew, the gun went off." She pointed down. A revolver was lying on the floor near the prone man's feet.

"What were they fighting over?" After a lengthy silence, one of the girls fearfully raised her hand.

"Go to my office and stay there." Nora Gail's tone was as brittle as cracking ice. It suggested that the girl should have known how to prevent an incident like this. "The rest of you get upstairs, and stay there until further notice."

No one argued. Nora Gail ran a tight ship. The young women flitted past Alex like a flock of butterflies. They were met on their way upstairs by several men stampeding down, pulling on their clothes as they ran. Without exception, they looked neither right nor left as they exited through the front door.

It was a farcical scene, but giggling over it was out of the question. Alex was mortified. She had been on the fringes of violence before, but reading about criminal action in a police report was different from experiencing it firsthand. There was something very startling and real about the sight and scent of fresh, human blood.

Nora Gail gestured Peter, who had rejoined them, toward the bleeding man. He knelt beside him and pressed his fingers against the man's carotid artery. "He's alive."

Alex saw some of the starch go out of Nora Gail's posture. She'd handled the situation with aplomb, but she wasn't made of stone. She had been more worried about the situation than she had let on.

Hearing the wail of a siren, Nora Gail turned toward the door and was on the threshold to greet Reede when he came barging in. "What happened, Nora Gail?"

"There was a dispute over one of the girls," she informed him. "A man's been shot, but he's alive."

"Where is he? The paramedics are—" Reede stopped short when he spotted Alex. At first he just gaped at her with patent disbelief; then, his face turned dark with rage. "What the hell are you doing here?"

"Conducting my investigation."

"Investigation, my ass," he growled. "Get the hell out of here."

The wounded man moaned, drawing Reede's attention. "I suggest you tend to your own business, Sheriff Lambert," Alex said tartly.

He cursed as he knelt down beside the man. When he noticed the amount of blood, however, his concentration switched immediately from Alex to the victim. "How're you doing, cowboy?" The man moaned. "What's your name?"

His eyes fluttered open. He comprehended the question, but didn't seem able to answer. Reede gently moved aside his clothing until he found the source of the blood. The bullet had pierced his side at about waist level. "You'll live," he told him. "Just hang in there a few more minutes. An ambulance is on its way."

He came to his feet and walked toward the man still in the bouncers' custody. He was standing with his head bowed. "What about you? Got a name?" Reede asked, jerking the man's chin up. "Well, howdy, Lewis," he drawled. "Thought we'd seen the last of your miserable hide. Didn't take my warning seriously, did you? Can't tell you what a pleasure it's gonna be to have you residing in my jail again."

"Go fuck yourself, Lambert," the man sneered insolently.

Reede hauled back his fist, then reached for the man's spine through about a foot and a half of abdominal tissue. Lewis doubled at the waist, but only until Reede's fist connected with his chin, bringing it up with a powerful blow. He was then lifted by the lapels of his jacket and shoved against the wall.

"You've got a big mouth, Lewis," Reede said calmly, barely winded by the exertion. "We'll see how smart you talk after a month or two in a place where the bad boys will make you eat their dicks for breakfast every morning."

The man whimpered helplessly. When Reede released him, he slid down the wall to form a pathetic heap on the floor. Two deputies stepped into the room, gawking at their plush surroundings.

"He resisted arrest," Reede calmly said, pointing at Lewis, then curtly ordered him handcuffed, Mirandized, and booked for attempted murder. He consulted with the paramedics who had come in behind the deputies and were dealing with the injured man.

"He's lost a lot of blood," one of them reported to Reede as he slid a needle into the victim's arm. "It's serious, but not critical."

Satisfied that everything was being handled properly, Reede's attention reverted to Alex. Taking her upper arm in a firm grip, he hauled her toward the door.

"Let me go."

"Unless Nora Gail hired you on, you've got no business here. Nora Gail, shut down for the night."

"This is Friday, Reede."

"Tough. Don't let anybody leave, either. Somebody'll be along soon to start the questioning."

He roughly shepherded Alex down the steps and into his Blazer, nearly cramming her into the seat before he slammed the door shut. He climbed in behind the wheel.

"My car is over there," she told him stubbornly. "I can drive myself back to town."

"I'll have one of the deputies pick it up later." He ground the key in the ignition. "What in God's name possessed you to come here?"

"I didn't know what it was until I arrived."

"Well, when you figured it out, why didn't you leave?"

"I wanted to talk to Nora Gail. She's a very old and dear friend of yours, I understand," she said with phony sweetness.

At the intersection with the highway, they met one of his patrol cars turning in. He signaled the deputy to stop and rolled down his window. "Give me your keys," he told Alex. She passed them to him because he wasn't going to give her a choice, and because, in spite of her brave front, she was trembling.

Reede tossed her keys to the deputy and instructed him to have his partner drive Ms. Gaither's car to the Westerner Motel when they were finished with the preliminary investigation of the shooting. With that taken care of, he zoomed onto the highway.

"Don't you feel the least bit guilty?" Alex asked him.

"For what?"

"For turning a blind eye to a whorehouse operating in your county?"

"No."

She looked at him, completely flabbergasted. "Why not? Because the madam is an old flame of yours?"

"Not entirely. Nora Gail's place keeps potential troublemakers concentrated in one spot. Her bouncers keep them in line."

"Today they didn't."

"Today was an exception. That scumbag is bad news no matter where he is."

"I should report you for police brutality."

"He had that coming, and then some. He got off on a technicality the last time he passed through our judicial system. This time he'll spend a nice, long time in prison.

"And, by the way, they caught Lyle Turner in New Mexico. He confessed to slitting Pasty's throat for screwing around with Ruby Faye. It had nothing whatsoever to do with you, so you can stop looking over your shoulder for bogeymen."

"Thanks for telling me." The news relieved her, but this latest development was still on her mind. "Don't try to get me off the subject. I'm not going to sweep this under the carpet. Pat Chastain would love to know that there's a bordello operating right under his nose."

Reede laughed. He took off his hat, ran his hand through his hair, and shook his head in dismay over her naïveté. "Have you ever met Mrs. Chastain?"

"What does that—"

"Have you?"

"No. I've talked to her on the telephone."

"She's a country club hag, tanned skin stretched over solid bone. She wears more gold jewelry than a pimp, even when she plays tennis. She thinks her shit don't stink. Got the picture? She likes being the D.A.'s wife, but doesn't like the D.A., particularly in bed."

"I'm not interested in—"

"Her idea of foreplay is, 'Hurry up, but don't mess up my hairdo,' and she would probably rather die than let him come in her mouth."

"You're disgusting."

"Pat's got a favorite out at Nora Gail's who'll swallow it and pretend to like it, so he's not going to lift a finger to shut the place down. If you were smart, which I'm beginning to seriously doubt, you won't embarrass him by letting on you even know that Nora Gail's place is out there. And don't even think about tattling to Judge Wallace. He never partakes, but all his friends do. He sure as hell isn't going to stop their party."

"My God, is everybody in this county corrupt?"

"Oh, for crissake, Alex, grow up. Everybody in the whole goddamn world is corrupt. You might be the only person who ever went through law school and came out believing that the law is still based on morality. Everybody's guilty of something. Everybody's got a secret. If you're lucky, the next guy's secret is juicier than yours. You use his secret to keep him quiet about yours."

"I'm glad you brought that up. It was Nora Gail you were with the night Celina was killed."

"Congratulations. You finally got one guess right."

"It wasn't a guess. Wanda Plummet told me."

He grinned. "When did you figure her out?"

"I didn't," she admitted with some reluctance. "I recognized her picture in the yearbook. You could have told me, Reede."

"I could have, but you'd have started pestering sooner."

"I didn't pester her. She was most cooperative."

"She was scared. You can't tell by looking at her now what a hell-raiser she used to be."

"I'd rather talk about her sister, Nora Gail. The night my mother was killed, were you with her all night?"

"Wouldn't you love to know?"

"What were you doing?"

"Three guesses, and the first two don't count."

"Making love?"

"Screwing."

"Where?"

"Her house."

"Nora Gail said you were in her car."

He whipped his Blazer around a farmer in a pickup truck. "Maybe we were. Car, house, what's the difference? I don't remember."

"You had been to the ranch earlier."

"Yeah, so?"

"You ate dinner there."

"We've been over this already."

"This was a special night—Celina was there for dinner."

"Don't you remember talking about this?"

"I remember. You told me that you'd left before dessert because apple pie wasn't one of your favorites."

"Wrong. Cherry pie. It's still not one of my favorites."

"That's not why you left, Reede."

"No?" He risked taking his eyes off the road to glance at her.

"No. You left because you were afraid Junior was going to propose to Celina that night. You were even more afraid that she was going to accept."

He brought the truck to a jarring stop outside her motel room. He got out and came around to her door, almost jerking it off its hinges when he opened it. Grabbing her arm again, he pulled her to the ground and pushed her toward the door. She resisted and turned to confront him.

"I'm right so far, aren't I?"

"Yeah, I went out with Nora Gail to blow off some steam."

"Did it work?"

"No, so I sneaked back to the ranch and found Celina in the mares' barn. How the hell I knew she was going to be there is something you've yet to figure out, Counselor," he sneered.

"I took the scalpel out of my pocket. Why I'd taken it from the vet's bag when I could have strangled her with my bare hands is something else you'll have to muddle through. While you're at it, think about where I'd hidden it when I took off all my clothes to screw Nora Gail, who would in all probability have noticed a scalpel.

"Anyway, I used the scalpel to stab Celina repeatedly. Then, I just left her body there on the outside chance that Gooney Bud would come wandering by, see her, try to help her, and, in the process, get her blood all over himself."

"I think that's exactly how it was done."

"You're full of shit, and a grand jury will think so too."

He angrily gave her another shove toward her door. In a quavering voice, she said, "There's blood on your hands."

He looked down at them. "I've had blood on them before."

"The night you murdered Celina?"

His eyes moved back to Alex's. His voice was raspy with menace when he lowered his face close to hers and said, "No, the night she tried to abort you."

THIRTY-FIVE

A lex stared at him blankly for several seconds. Then, she attacked him. She went for his face with her nails, his shins with the toes of her shoes. He grunted in pain and surprise as she landed one solid kick against his kneecap.

"You liar! You're lying! *Lying*!" She took a swing at his head. He managed to dodge it.

"Stop it." He grabbed hold of her wrists to protect his face. She tried to wrest her hands free, while still kicking out with her feet and knees. "Alex, I'm not lying to you."

"You are! You bastard. I know you are. My mother wouldn't do that. She loved me. She *did*!"

She fought like a wildcat. Fury and adrenalin pumped through her system, endowing her with additional strength. She was still no match for him. Holding her wrists together in his left hand, he shook her key out of her handbag and used it to open the door. They stumbled inside together. Reede kicked the door shut.

She bucked against him, shouting deprecations, trying to work her hands out of his grip, slinging her head from side to side like someone demented.

"Alex, stop this," he ordered fiercely.

"I hate you."

"I know, but I'm not lying."

"You are!" She twisted and turned and tried to stamp on his feet.

He forced her down on the bed, and secured her there with his own body. Keeping an iron grip on her wrists, he placed his other hand over her mouth. She tried to bite it, so he applied more pressure, making any motion of her jaw impossible unless she wanted to break the bones.

Her eyes were murderous as she glared at him over the back of his hand. Her breasts rose and fell dramatically with each breath. He hung his head above hers, his hair falling over his brow, gulping in draughts of air until he regained his breath.

Finally, lifting his head, he stared deeply into her eyes. "I didn't want you to know," he said in a low, throbbing voice, "but you just kept pushing me. I lost my temper. It's out, I can't take it back, and damn me if it's not the truth."

She tried to shake her head no, the denial in her eyes vehement. She arched her back in an effort to throw him off, but she remained pinioned beneath him.

"Listen to me, Alex," he said, angrily straining the words through his teeth. "Nobody even knew Celina was pregnant until that night. She'd been back from El Paso for several weeks, but I hadn't gone to see her yet, hadn't even called. My pride was still hurting. In a juvenile way, I was letting her sweat it out."

He closed his eyes and shook his head ruefully. "We were playing games with each other, childish, foolish, silly, boy-girl games. Finally, I decided to forgive her." He smiled with bitter self-derision.

"I went to see her on a Wednesday night because I knew your grandmother would be at prayer meeting at the Baptist church. After the service she always stayed for choir practice, so I knew that Celina and I would have a couple of hours alone to sort things out.

"When I got to her house, I knocked several times, but she didn't come to the door. I knew she was there. The lights were on in the back of the house where her bedroom was. I thought maybe she was in the shower or was playing the radio so loud she couldn't hear my knocking, so I went around to the back."

Alex lay still beneath him. Her eyes were no longer narrowed with animosity, but shiny with unshed tears.

"I looked through her bedroom window. The lights were on, but Celina wasn't in there. I tapped on the window. She didn't respond, but I noticed her shadow moving on the bathroom wall. I could see it through the door. It was opened partway. I called her name. I knew she could hear me, but she wouldn't come out. Then—"

He squeezed his eyes shut and bared his teeth in a grimace of pain before going on. "I was getting mad, see, because I thought she was just playing coy. She opened the bathroom door wider, and I saw her standing there.

"For a few seconds I just looked at her face because it had been so long since I'd seen her. She was staring back at me. She looked puzzled, like she was asking, 'What now?' And that's when I noticed the blood. She was wearing a nightgown, and the lower front of it was streaked with red."

Alex's eyes closed. Large, cloudy tears slid from beneath her quivering eyelids and ran onto Reede's fingers.

"It scared the hell out of me," he said gruffly. "I got into the house. I don't even remember how. I think I raised the window and slipped through. Anyway, a few seconds later, I was in her bedroom, holding her. We both ended up on the floor and she just sort of crumpled in my arms.

"She didn't want to tell me what was wrong. I was screaming at her, shaking her. Finally, she turned her face toward my chest and whispered, 'Baby.' Then I realized what all the blood meant and where it had come from. I scooped her up, ran outside, and put her in my car."

He paused for a moment to reflect. When he picked up the story, the emotion that had racked his voice was gone. He spoke matter-of-factly.

"There was this doctor in town who did abortions on the sly. Everybody knew it, but nobody talked about it because abortions were still illegal in Texas then. I took her to him. I called Junior and told him to bring some money. He met us there. He and I sat in the waiting room while the doctor fixed her up."

He gazed down at Alex for a long time before removing his hand. It had left a stark white imprint on the lower half of her face, which in itself was ghostly pale. Her body was now pliant beneath his, and as still as death. With the pads of his thumbs, he wiped the tears off her cheeks.

"Damn you to hell if you're lying to me," she whispered.

"I'm not. You can ask Junior."

"Junior would back you up if you said the sky was green. I'll ask the doctor."

"He's dead."

"Figures," she remarked, laughing dryly. "What did she use to try to kill me?"

"Alex, don't."

"Tell me."

"No."

"What was it?"

"It doesn't matter."

"Tell me, damn you!"

"Your grandma's knitting needle!"

It had started out a soft exchange but ended on a shout. The sudden, resulting silence was deafening.

"Oh, God," Alex whimpered, clamping her teeth over her lower lip and turning her face into the pillow. "Oh, God."

"Shh, don't cry. Celina didn't hurt you, just herself."

"She wanted to hurt me, though. She didn't want me to be born." Her sobs shook her whole body. He absorbed them with his. "Why didn't the doctor just take me while he was fixing her up?"

Reede didn't answer.

Alex turned her head and stared up at him. She caught handfuls of his shirt in her fists. "Why, Reede?"

"He suggested it."

"Then, why didn't he?"

"Because I swore that if he did, I'd kill him."

An emotion zephyred between them. It was so strong it knocked the breath out of her and made her chest ache. She uttered an involuntary, wordless sound. Her fingers momentarily relaxed in the cloth of his shirt, only to grip it tighter and draw him nearer. Her back arched off the bed again, not in an attempt to throw him off, but to get closer.

He sank his fingers into her hair, tilted his dark-blond head, and pressed his open mouth against hers. Her lips were parted and damp and receptive. He sent his tongue deep into her mouth.

Frantically, she worked her arms out of her coat sleeves and locked them around the back of his neck. He raised his head suddenly and looked down at her. There were dark shadows from weeping beneath her eyes, but the blue irises were crystal clear as they steadily gazed back at him. She knew exactly what she was doing. That's all he needed to know.

He ran his thumb over her lips, which were moist and swollen from his hard kiss. All he could think about was kissing her again, harder, and he did.

Her throat was arched and vulnerable to his lips when they left hers. He drew her skin lightly against his teeth, then soothed it with whisks of his tongue. He nuzzled her ear and the base of her neck, and when her clothing got in his way, he pulled her to a sitting position and peeled her sweater over her head.

As they lay back down, their breathing was hard and uneven, the only sound in the room. He unclasped her bra and pushed the cups aside.

His fingers skimmed over her flesh, which was warm and flushed with arousal. He cupped one breast, pushed it up, and took the center between his lips. He sucked it with enough pressure to elicit a tingle in her womb, but with enough finesse to tantalize. When the nipple drew taut, he flicked it roughly with the tip of his tongue.

Alex cried his name in panic and joy. He buried his face between her breasts and held her close while he rolled her above him and fought his way out of his jacket at the same time. She began tearing free the buttons of his shirt. He unzipped and unbuttoned her skirt, then shoved it down over her hips, taking her half-slip along with it. Alex ran her fingers through the thick pelt of hair on his chest, dropped random kisses on his supple muscles, and rubbed her cheek against his distended nipple.

They reversed positions again. She managed to get off her shoes and stockings before he stretched out on top of her. He placed his hand low on her belly and slid it down into her underpants.

His hand covered her mound completely and possessively. With his thumb, he parted the lips of her sex and exposed the tight, responsive kernel of flesh. His fingertips dipped into her creaminess and anointed that tiny nub with the dew of her own desire.

When she moaned her pleasure, he bent his head and kissed her stomach. Removing her panties, he nuzzled the fiery dark curls between her thighs and touched her with his open mouth.

Clumsily, he undid his fly and, taking her hand, pressed it against his erection. He hissed a curse when her fist closed tightly around him. Nudging her thighs apart, he settled himself between them.

The smooth tip of his penis slipped between the folds of her body. He covered her breasts with his hands and lightly ground the raised centers with his palms. He gave a steady, smooth thrust of his hips that should have planted him firmly inside her.

It didn't.

He readjusted his hips slightly and tried again, encountering the same resistance. Levering himself up, he stared at her with disbelief. "You mean . . . ?"

Her breath was choppy, and her eyes fluttered in an effort to stay focused on him. She was making small yearning noises in her throat. Her hands moved restlessly, searchingly, over his chest and neck and cheeks. Her fingertips glanced his lips.

The utter sexiness of all that and the satiny heat that was gloving him so tightly were his undoing. He applied more pressure and sank into her completely. Her ragged sigh of surprise and discovery was the most erotic sound he'd ever heard. It inflamed him.

"Christ," he groaned. "Oh, Christ."

Mating instincts took over and he moved his hips against hers with the ancient compulsion to possess and fill. Sandwiching her head between his hands, he kissed her mouth with rampant carnality. His climax was an avalanche of sensation. It was soul-shuddering. It seemed to go on forever . . . and it still wasn't long enough.

Several minutes elapsed before he roused himself enough to disengage. He didn't want to, but when he gazed down at her, any thoughts of prolonging their coupling fled.

She was lying with her head turned away, one cheek on the pillow. She looked fragile and haunted. Looking down at the faint pulse in her throat, seeing the bruise his kiss had branded there, Reede felt like a rapist. Filled with regret and self-loathing, he worked his fingers free of the snare of her hair.

They both reacted violently to the knock on the door. Alex quickly reached for the rumpled bedspread and pulled it over herself. Reede's feet landed hard on the floor. He hiked his jeans up over his hips.

"Reede, you in there?"

"Yeah," he called through the door.

"I, uh, I got Ms. Gaither's keys here. Remember, you told me to—"

The deputy broke off when Reede opened the door. "I remember." He extended his hand through the crack and the deputy dropped the keys into them. "Thanks," he said tersely, and closed the door.

He tossed the keys on the round table in front of the window. The clatter they made when they landed on the wood veneer was as loud as a cymbal's crash. Reede bent down to retrieve his shirt and jacket, which he'd slung over the side of the bed at some point that escaped his memory now. As he pulled them on, he spoke to Alex over his shoulder.

"I know you're hating yourself right now, but it might make you feel better to know that I wish it hadn't happened either."

She turned her head and gave him a long, searching look. She looked for compassion, tenderness, love. His features remained impassive, his eyes those of a stranger. There was no softness or feeling in his remote gaze. He seemed untouched and untouchable.

Alex swallowed hard, burying her hurt. In retaliation for his aloofness, she said, "Well, we're even now, Sheriff. You saved my life before I was born." She paused, then added huskily, "And I just gave you what you always wanted, but never got, from my mother."

Reede curled his hands into fists, as though he wanted to strike her. Then, with jerky, disjointed motions, he finished dressing. At the open door, he turned back. "Whatever your reason for doing it, thanks. For a virgin, you were a fairly good fuck."

THIRTY-SIX

Junior slid into the orange vinyl booth of the Westerner Motel's coffee shop. His engaging smile collapsed the instant he saw Alex's face. "Darling, are you sick?"

She smiled wanly. "No. Coffee?" she asked, signaling the waitress.

"Please," he told her distractedly. When the waitress tried to hand him a large, plastic menu, he waved it off. "Just coffee."

After she had poured him a cup, he leaned across the table and lowered his voice to a whisper. "I was real tickled to hear from you this morning, but something is obviously very wrong. You're as pale as a sheet."

"You ought to see me without the sunglasses." She bobbed them up and down in an attempt at humor that fell flat.

"What's the matter?"

She leaned back against the bright vinyl and turned her head to gaze through the tinted window. It was bright outside; her sunglasses wouldn't appear out of place. That about exhausted the merits of this day. "Reede told me about Celina's attempted abortion."

At first, Junior said nothing. Then, he cursed expansively beneath his breath. He sipped his coffee, started to say something he thought better of, and finally, shook his head in apparent disgust. "What the hell's wrong with him? Why'd he tell you about that?"

"So, it's true?"

He lowered his head and stared into his coffee. "She was only seventeen, Alex, and pregnant by a guy she didn't even love, a guy on his way to Saigon. She was scared. She—"

"I know the pertinent facts, Junior," she interrupted impatiently. "Why do you always defend her?"

"Habit, I guess."

Alex, ashamed of her outburst, took a moment to compose herself. "I know *why* she did it. It's just incomprehensible to me that she *could.*"

"To us, too," he admitted reluctantly.

"Us?"

"To Reede and me. He gave her only two days to recover before he and I flew her back to El Paso to take care of it." He sipped his coffee. "We met out at the airstrip, right after sunset."

Alex had asked Reede if he'd ever taken Celina flying at night. "Once," he had told her. Celina had been scared, he'd said. "He stole a plane."

"Borrowed is what he called it. I think Moe knew what Reede was up to, but he looked the other way. We landed in El Paso, rented a car, and drove to the army base. Reede bribed the guards into telling Al Gaither that he had relatives waiting to see him. He was off duty, I guess. Anyway, he came to the gate and we, uh, talked him into getting in the car with us."

"What happened?"

He looked at her, shamefaced. "We took him to a deserted spot and beat the shit out of him. I was afraid Reede was going to kill him. He probably would have, if Celina hadn't been there. She was practically hysterical."

"You coerced him into marrying her?"

"That same night. We drove across the border into Mexico." He shook his head wryly at the memory of it. "Gaither was barely conscious enough to recite his vows. Reede and I supported him between us through the ceremony, then dumped him back at the gate of Fort Bliss."

"One thing puzzles me. Why did Reede insist on Celina getting married?"

"He kept saying he wouldn't let her baby be born a bastard."

Alex looked at him intently from behind her shaded glasses. "Then, why didn't he marry her himself?"

"He asked her."

"So, what was the problem?"

"Me. I asked her, too." Seeing her confusion, he blew out his breath. "This all happened the morning following the, uh—"

"I understand. Go on."

"Celina was still real shaken up and said she couldn't think clearly. She begged us to stop badgering her. But Reede said she had to get married in a hurry, or everybody would find out what had happened."

"Everybody found out anyway," she said.

"He wanted to protect her from the gossip as long as possible."

"I must be dense, but I still can't figure it. Celina has two men who love her begging her to get married. Why didn't she?"

"She refused to choose between us." A furrow of concentration formed between his brows. "You know, Alex, that's the first smart, adult decision Celina ever made. We were seniors in high school. God knows Reede didn't have any money. I did, but my folks would have gone ape shit if I'd've gotten married before I even graduated, especially with Celina carrying another man's baby.

"She had another reason, though, more important than finances or parental approval. She knew that if she chose one of us over the other, it would alter the friendship forever. There would be an odd man out. When it came right down to it, she wouldn't break up the triangle. Funny, isn't it? That happened anyway."

"What do you mean?"

"It was never quite the same between the three of us after we got back from El Paso. We were on guard all the time, where before, we were always nakedly honest with each other."

His voice turned sad. "Reede didn't see as much of her as I did while she was pregnant, and that wasn't very often. We were busy with school and she stayed close to home. Oh, we went through the motions of still being best buddies, but when we were together, we tried too hard to pretend that everything was normal.

"That night she tried to abort you stood between us like a solid wall. None of us could ever go up, over, around, or through it. It was there. Conversations became an effort. Laughter was forced."

"But, you didn't desert her."

"No. The day you were born, Reede and I rushed to the hospital. Besides your grandmother, we were the first people you were introduced to."

"I'm glad of that," she said thickly.

"So am I."

"If I'd been Celina, I would have snagged one of you when I had the chance." His grin slowly faded. "Reede stopped asking."

"Why?"

Junior signaled for the waitress to refill his coffee cup. Then, cradling it between his hands, he stared into its dark depths. "He never forgave her."

"For Al Gaither?"

"For you."

Stricken, Alex raised her hand to cover her mouth. The guilt she had borne all her life pressed in on her like a vise.

Junior, sensing her anxiety, rushed to say, "It wasn't because she'd conceived you. He couldn't forgive that abortion business."

"I don't understand."

"See, Alex, Reede's a survivor. Hell, if anybody was ever destined to turn out rotten, it was Reede. He didn't have a snowball's chance in hell of making anything out of himself. Social workers, if Purcell had had any, would have pointed at him and said, 'There goes a wasted life in the making. He'll go bad. Watch and see.' But no, not Reede. He thrives on adversity. He's a scrapper. He's strong. He gets knocked down and comes up fighting.

"Now me," he said with a scoffing laugh, "I can overlook other people's weaknesses because I've got so many of my own. I could understand the panic and fear Celina must have felt. She took desperate measures because she was afraid to stick it out.

"Reede can't understand taking the path of least resistance. He couldn't tolerate that weakness in her. He expects so goddamn much out of himself, he imposes the same standards on everybody else. Those standards are virtually impossible to live up to. That's why he's constantly disappointed in people. He sets himself up to be."

"He's a cynic."

"I can see where you'd think that, but don't let that tough pose fool you. When people let him down, as they invariably do because they're human, it hurts him. When he's hurt, he turns mean."

"Was he mean to my mother?"

"No, never. Their relationship being what it was, she had the power to hurt and disappoint him more than anybody could. But he couldn't turn mean toward Celina because he loved her so much." He looked at Alex levelly. "He just couldn't forgive her."

"That's why he stepped aside and gave you the advantage."

"Which I unabashedly took," he said with a short laugh. "I'm not as hard to please as Reede. I don't demand perfection in myself or anybody else. Yes, Alex, in spite of her mistakes, I loved your mother and wanted her to be my wife on any terms."

"Why didn't she marry you, Junior?" Alex asked, genuinely perplexed. "She loved you. I know she did."

"I know she did, too. And I'm damned good-looking." He winked and Alex smiled. "Few would believe this because of the way I live now, but I would have been faithful to Celina and made you an excellent daddy, Alex. I wanted to try, anyway." He clasped his hands together on the table. "But Celina said no, no matter how many times I asked her."

"And you went on asking her, right up until the night she died."

His eyes snapped up to hers. "Yes. I invited her out to the ranch that night to propose."

"Did you?"

"Yes."

"And?"

"Same as always. She turned me down."

"Do you know why?"

"Yes." He shifted uncomfortably in the booth. "She still loved Reede. Always and forever, it was Reede she wanted."

Alex looked away because she knew it was a painful admission for him to make. "Junior, where were you that night?"

"At the ranch."

"I mean after that, after you took Celina home."

"I didn't take her home. I presumed Dad would."

"Angus?"

"I was upset because she had refused me again. See, I'd told my parents to get used to the idea of having a daughter-in-law and a grandchild in the house soon." He spread his hands in a helpless gesture. "I got mad and stormed out—just flew the coop and left Celina there."

"Where did you go?"

"I hit all the places that would sell liquor to minors. I got drunk."

"Alone?"

"Alone."

"No alibi?"

"Junior doesn't need an alibi. He didn't kill your mother."

They had been so immersed in the conversation that neither had noticed Stacey Wallace's approach. When they looked up, she was standing at the edge of the table. Her stare was even more hostile than it had been at their first meeting.

"Good morning, Stacey," Junior said uncomfortably. He seemed less than pleased by her sudden appearance. "Sit down and have a cup of coffee with us." He moved over to make room for her on his side of the booth.

"No, thank you." Glaring down at Alex, she said, "Stop bothering Junior with your endless questions."

"Hey, Stacey, I'm not bothered," he said, trying to smooth over the situation.

"Why don't you just give it up?"

"I can't."

"Well, you should. It would be best for everybody."

"Especially the murderer," Alex said quietly.

Stacey's thin, straight body quivered like a bowstring just plucked. "Get out of our lives. You're a self-serving, vindictive bitch, who—"

"Not here, Stacey." Junior, intervening quickly, scooted out of the booth and took her arm. "I'll walk you to your car. What are you doing out this morning? Oh, your bridge group is having breakfast," he said, noting the table of women watching curiously. "How nice." He gave them a jaunty little wave.

Alex, as aware as Junior of all the prying eyes, slipped a five-dollar bill beneath her saucer and left the coffee shop only a few moments behind Junior and Stacey.

She gave Stacey's car a wide berth, but watched from the corner of her eye as Junior pulled Stacey into an embrace and rubbed her back consolingly. He gave her a soft kiss on the lips. She clung to him, appealing to him about something that had caused her consternation. His answer seemed to soothe her. She went limp against his chest.

Junior worked himself out of her clutches, but in such a charming way that Stacey was smiling when he tucked her into the driver's seat of her car and waved her off.

Alex was already inside her room when he tapped on the door and said, "It's me."

She opened the door. "What was that all about?"

"She thought I'd spent the night with you, since we were having breakfast together in the coffee shop."

"Lord," Alex whispered. "People in this town certainly have fertile minds. You'd better leave before anybody else gets that impression."

"What do you care? I don't."

"Well, I do."

Uneasily, Alex glanced toward the unmade bed. On any other morning the housekeeper was knocking while she was still in the shower. This morning, of all mornings, she was running late. Alex was afraid that the bed would give away her secret. The room was redolent of Reede. His essence lingered on each surface like a fine coating of dust. She was afraid Junior would sense that.

Gently, he removed her sunglasses and traced the lavender half-moons beneath her eyes. "Bad night?"

That's an understatement, she thought. "You might as well hear it from me. I'm sure it will get around. Late yesterday afternoon I went to Nora Gail's place."

His lips parted with surprise. "Son of a bitch."

"I needed to talk to her. It seems she's Reede's alibi for the night Celina was killed. Anyway, while I was there, a man got shot. There was blood, an arrest."

Junior laughed with incredulity. "You're kiddin' me."

"I wish I were," she said grimly. "Here I am, representing the D.A.'s office, and I get involved in a shootout between two cowboys in a whorehouse."

Suddenly it all collapsed on her. Instead of crying, she began to laugh. Once she started, she couldn't stop. She laughed until her sides ached and tears were rolling down her cheeks. "Oh, God, can you believe it? If Greg Harper ever hears about this, he—"

"Pat Chastain won't tell him. He has a girl out at—"

"I know," she said, "Reede told me. He responded to the call and hustled me out. He didn't seem to think there would be any repercussions." She shrugged in an offhanded manner that she hoped didn't look as phony as it felt.

"It's good to hear you laughing for a change," Junior commented, smiling down at her. "I'd like to stick around and cheer you up even more." He placed his hands on her derriere and began to move them up and down. Alex pushed him away.

"If you wanted to cheer someone up, you should have gone with Stacey. She looked like she could use it."

He glanced away guiltily. "It doesn't take much to make her happy."

"Because she still loves you."

"I don't deserve her."

"That doesn't matter to her. She'll forgive you anything. She already has."

"Of murder, you mean?"

"No. Of loving someone else—Celina."

"Not this time, Alex," he whispered and dipped his head to kiss her. She dodged his well-aimed lips. "No, Junior."

"Why not?"

"You know why."

"Am I still only a pal?"

"A friend."

"Why just a friend?"

"I keep getting the present mixed up with the past. Hearing you talk about wishing you could have been my father stifled my romantic inclinations."

"When I look at you now, I can't relate you to that tiny baby in the crib. You're an enchanting woman. I want to hold you, love you, and not like a daddy."

"No." She shook her head adamantly. "It just doesn't sit right, Junior. It's out of whack."

This was the speech she should have made to Reede. Why hadn't she? Because she was a phony, that's why. And because the same rules didn't always apply to similar situations, even when one wanted them to. And because she didn't have any control over whom she fell in love with. She and Celina had that in common.

"We can never be lovers."

He smiled and said without rancor, "I'm stubborn. Once this is over, I'll make certain that you see me in a whole new light. We'll pretend that we're meeting for the first time and you'll fall hard for me."

If it soothes his ego, let him think so, Alex thought.

She knew it would never be, just as it could never have been with him and Celina.

And in both cases, Reede Lambert was the reason.

⇒ THIRTY-SEVEN

Angus's secretary escorted Alex into his office at ME headquarters. It was an unpretentious complex, situated in a professional building between a dentist's office and a two-partner law firm. He stepped around his desk to greet her.

"Thank you for stopping by, Alex."

"I'm glad you called. I needed to talk to you anyway."

"Would you like a drink?"

"No, thanks."

"Seen Junior lately?"

"Yes. We had coffee together this morning."

Angus was pleased. His lecture had obviously worked. As usual, Junior had just needed a pep talk to get into gear.

"Before we get to my business," Angus said, "what's on your mind?"

"Specifically, the night my mother died, Angus."

His hearty smile faded. "Sit down." He guided her to a small, upholstered couch. "What do you want to know?"

"When I spoke with Junior this morning, he confirmed what I'd already been told—that he proposed to Celina that night. I know that you and Mrs. Minton opposed the idea."

"That's right, Alex, we did. I hate to tell you that. I don't mean to speak badly of your mother because I adored her as Junior's friend."

"But you didn't want her for his wife."

"No." He leaned forward and wagged his finger at her. "Don't think it was snobbishness on my part. It wasn't. Sarah Jo's opinion might have been swayed by class and economic distinctions, but not mine. I would have objected to Junior marrying anybody at that time in his life."

"Then why did you consent to his marriage to Stacey Wallace only a few weeks later?"

No dummy this girl, Angus thought. He assumed an innocent pose. "The situation had changed by then. He'd been emotionally devastated by Celina's death. Stacey worshiped the ground he walked on. I thought she would be good for him. For a while, she was. I don't regret blessing that marriage."

"A prestigious judge's daughter was also a far more suitable match for the son of Angus Minton."

His blue eyes darkened. "You're disappointing me, Alex. What you're suggesting is downright tacky. Do you think I'd force my son into a loveless marriage?"

"I don't know. Would you?"

"No!"

"Even if the stakes were awfully high?"

"Listen," he said, lowering his voice for emphasis, "anything I've ever done for my boy has been for his own good."

"Does that include killing Celina?"

Angus jerked upright. "You've got your nerve, young lady."

"I'm sorry. I can't afford to be subtle. Angus, Junior says he left the ranch that night, angry and hurt, because Celina turned down his proposal."

"That's right."

"It was left to you to drive her home."

"Yes. Instead, I offered her one of the cars and gave her the keys. She told me good-bye and left the house. I assumed she drove herself home."

"Did anyone overhear this conversation?"

"Not that I know of."

"Not even your wife?"

"She went up to bed right after supper."

"Don't you see, Angus? You've got no alibi. There's no witness to what happened after Junior left."

It pleased him enormously that she seemed worried about it. Her features were anxious and drawn. Lately, he'd found it hard to think of this girl as his enemy. Evidently, she was nursing that same ambiguity.

"I slept with Sarah Jo that night," he said. "She'll vouch for that. So will Reede. We were in bed the next morning when he came running in to tell us that he'd found Celina's body in the stable."

"Wasn't my grandmother worried about her? When Celina didn't come home, didn't she telephone the ranch?"

"In fact, she did. Celina had already left the house. She had bragged that you were already sleeping through the night, so I guess Mrs. Graham went back to bed, assuming that she was on her way. She didn't realize until the following morning that Celina hadn't made it home."

"What time did Grandma Graham call?"

"I don't remember. It wasn't very late because I was still up. I usually go to bed early. I was especially tired after the day we'd spent in the stable with that mare."

Alex was frowning in concentration. He grinned. "Sound plausible?"

Grudgingly, she returned his smile. "Yes, but it's riddled with holes."

"It's damn sure not enough to ask a grand jury for a murder indictment. It's nothing like a blood-soaked Gooney Bud holding a scalpel."

Alex said nothing.

Angus reached out and covered her hand. "I hope I didn't hurt your feelings, talking frankly about your mother like that."

"No, you didn't," she replied with a weak smile. "In the last few days I've learned that she was far from an angel."

"I would never have approved of her for Junior. My disapproval didn't have anything to do with whether she was a saint or sinner."

He watched her wet her lips anxiously before asking, "What was your main objection, Angus? Was it because she had me?"

So that's it, he thought. *Alex blames herself for her mother's fate.* Guilt had driven her to get to the bottom of this case. She craved absolution for the sin Merle Graham had laid on her. What a spiteful thing for the old bitch to do to a kid. Still, it served his purpose well.

"My disapproval had nothing to do with you, Alex. It was Reede and Junior." Humbly, he folded his hands and studied them as he spoke. "Junior needs somebody to goad him every now and then. A strong daddy, a strong friend, a strong woman." He looked up at her from beneath lowered brows. "You'd be a perfect mate for him."

"Mate?"

He laughed and spread his arms wide at his sides. "Hell, I might as well come right out with it. I'd like to see a match between you and Junior."

"What!?"

Angus wasn't sure whether she was actually stunned, or a damn good actress. Either way, he was glad he'd chosen to prod this thing along himself. Left alone, Junior wasn't getting the job done.

"We could use a smart lady lawyer in this family. Think what a contribution you'd make to the business, not to mention the empty bedrooms at the ranch. In no time you'd fill 'em up with grandbabies." He lowered his eyes to her pelvic region. "You've got the build for it, and you'd bring new blood to the stock."

"You can't be serious, Angus."

"I've never been more serious in my life." He patted her on the back. "For now, though, let's just leave it at this: I'd be pleased as punch if something romantic was to spark between you and Junior."

She moved away from his touch. "Angus, I don't want to offend you or Junior, but what you're suggesting is . . ." She searched for the right word, then laughed and said, "preposterous."

"Why?"

"You're asking me to play the role my mother was cast for. You rejected her."

"You're suited to the role. She wasn't."

"I'm not in love with Junior, and I don't want the part." She stood up and moved to the door. "I'm sorry if there's been any misunderstanding or if I've misled anybody into thinking . . ." He gave her his darkest, most fearsome frown, the one that usually struck terror into the hearts of those who opposed him. She withstood it well. "Good-bye, Angus. I'll be in touch."

After she left, Angus poured a drink to calm himself down. His fingers closed around the glass so tightly, it was a wonder it didn't shatter under the pressure.

Angus Minton rarely had his ideas questioned, and even less frequently, snickered at. They were sure as hell never called preposterous.

Alex left feeling greatly disturbed. In spite of her best intentions, she had offended him. She regretted that. But what disturbed her most was that she'd seen into the man behind the good ole boy demeanor.

Angus Minton liked to have things go his way. When they didn't move along fast enough, he boosted them. He didn't take kindly to being crossed.

More than ever, Alex pitied Junior, whose pace was so different from his father's. No doubt that had always been a source of friction between them. She could also understand why a man as self-sufficient as Reede had left Minton Enterprises. He wouldn't have functioned well under Angus's heavy thumb.

She returned to her car and began to drive aimlessly, leaving the city limits and taking to the back roads. The scenery wasn't much to brag about. Tumbleweeds were snagged on barbed-wire fences that seemed to stretch forever. Oil wells, black outlines against the colorless earth, pumped desultorily.

The drive helped; it gave her privacy in which to think.

Like her mother, she had become entangled with three men, all of whom she liked. She didn't want to believe one of them was a killer.

Lord, what a muddle. She was gradually peeling away layers of deception. If she kept at it long enough, surely she would eventually get to the truth.

But her time was running out. She had only a few days left before Greg would demand to see some results. If she couldn't produce something concrete, he would demand that she desist.

As she approached the city limits on her return, she became aware that the vehicle behind her was following too close.

"Jerk," she muttered, glancing into her rearview mirror. For another mile the pickup rode her rear end like a shadow. The sun was at an angle to prevent her from seeing the driver. "Come on around if you're in such a hurry."

She tapped her brake pedal, enough for the taillights to blink on. He didn't take the hint. On this rural highway, the gravel shoulder was so narrow it hardly qualified as such. She edged toward it anyway, hoping that the driver of the truck would pass her.

"Thank you very much," she said when the truck straddled the center yellow stripe and sped up to pass her.

It pulled up even with her. She was aware of it from the corner of her eye. She didn't realize that the driver had a more nefarious purpose than vehicular horseplay in mind until he stayed even with her, a hazard at the speed they were driving.

"You fool!" She whipped her head around to glance out the window. The pickup truck accelerated suddenly and deliberately swerved, catching her front left bumper with his right rear one. She lost control of the car.

She clutched the steering wheel and stamped on the brakes, but to no avail. Her car skidded off the loose shoulder and plowed into the deep, dry ditch. Alex was held in by her seatbelt, but flung forward hard enough to bang her head on the steering wheel. The windshield shattered upon impact, showering the back of her head and hands with glass. It seemed to rain down forever.

She didn't think she had lost consciousness, but the next thing she knew, there were voices speaking to her. They were soft and melodious, but she couldn't understand what they were saying.

Groggily, she raised her head. The motion gave her a searing headache. She fought down rising nausea and struggled to focus her eyes.

The men surrounding the car and looking at her with concern were speaking Spanish. One opened her door and said something that was gently inquiring.

"Yes, I'm all right," she answered automatically. She couldn't imagine why they were looking at her so strangely until she felt the wet trickle against her cheek. She raised her hand and investigated. Her trembling fingers came away red.

"I'd rather you spent the night here at the hospital. I can arrange for a room," the doctor said.

"No, I'll be fine in the motel. After a couple of these, I should sleep till morning." She shook the brown plastic bottle of pills.

"You don't have a concussion, but take it easy for a couple of days. No sports, or anything like that."

She winced at the very mention of physical exertion. "I promise."

"In a week, we'll take out the stitches. Good thing that gash was on the top of your head and not on your face."

"Yes," Alex replied uncertainly. He'd had to shave a small patch on her scalp, but with artful combing, her hair would cover it.

"Are you up to having a visitor? There's somebody waiting to see you. Since this is a weeknight, things are kind of slow, so use the room for as long as you like."

"Thank you, Doctor."

He left the treatment room. Alex tried to sit up, but discovered that she was still too dizzy. The sight of Pat Chastain walking through the door didn't help her equilibrium. "Well, Mr. Chastain, long time, no see," she said with sarcasm.

He moved toward the examination table and sheepishly asked, "How are you?"

"I've been better, but I'll be fine."

"Is there anything I can do?"

"No. There was no need for you to come here. How'd you know about it, anyway?"

He pulled forward the only chair in the room and sat down. "Those Mexicans flagged down a passing car. The driver went to the nearest phone and called for an ambulance. The deputy who went out to investigate the accident speaks Spanish, so he heard from them what happened."

"They saw the truck force me off the road?"

"Yeah. Could you identify it?"

"It was white." She met the D.A.'s eyes. "And it had the Minton Enterprises logo stenciled on the side."

He looked troubled and nervous. "That's what the Mexicans said, too. The deputy couldn't locate Reede, so he called me." He nodded toward the bandage on her head. "Is that gonna be okay?"

"In two or three days. I can take the bandage off tomorrow. It required several stitches. And I've got these as reminders." She held up her hands, which were covered with tiny scratches where glass fragments had been tweezed out.

"Alex, did you recognize the driver?"

"No." The district attorney gave her a hard look, testing her truthfulness. "No," she repeated. "Believe me, if I had, I'd be after him myself. I didn't even catch a glimpse. All I could make out was a silhouette against the sun. I think he was wearing some kind of hat."

"Do you think it was a random incident?"

She came up on both elbows. "Do you?"

He patted the air, urging her to lie back down. "No, I guess it wasn't."

"Then don't tax my strength with stupid questions."

He ran a hand through his hair and swore. "When I told my old buddy Greg Harper that you'd have carte blanche, I didn't know that you were going to wreak havoc in my county."

Her patience with him snapped. "It's my head that mountains are being slammed against, Mr. Chastain. Why are you whining?"

"Well, dammit, Alex. Judge Wallace, who didn't like me much in the first place, is hotter than a pistol. I can't win a single point in his courtroom these days. You've all but called three of the county's leading citizens murderers. Pasty Hickam, a fixture in this town, turns up dead while you're with him. You were at Nora Gail Burton's whorehouse when a shooting took place. Goddamn it, why'd you have to open up that hornet's nest?"

She pressed her hand to her throbbing forehead. "It wasn't by choice. I was following a lead." She lowered her head and gave him a pointed look. "And don't worry, your secret interest in Nora Gail's is safe with me."

He squirmed guiltily in his chair. "I tell you, Alex, you've got a bull by the horns here, and it almost got you killed tonight."

"Which should prove that I'm getting closer to the truth. Someone's trying to bump me off to protect himself."

"I guess," he said morosely. "What have you got that you didn't have before you got here?"

"Firmly established motives, for one thing."

"Anything else?"

"A shortage of concrete alibis. Reede Lambert says he was with Nora Gail. She admitted that she would perjure herself if necessary to corroborate that, which leads me to believe that he wasn't with her all night. Junior hasn't produced any kind of alibi."

"What about Angus?"

"He claims he was at the ranch, but so was Celina. If Angus was there all night, he would have had ample opportunity."

"So would Gooney Bud, if he'd followed her out there," Pat said, "and that's what a good defense attorney will tell the jury. No one gets life on probable cause. You've still got nothing that places one of them in that stable with a scalpel in his hand."

"I was on my way to your office this afternoon to talk to you about that when I was run off the road."

"Talk to me about what?"

"The vet's scalpel. What happened to it?"

An expression of surprise came over his face. "You're the second person this week to ask me that."

Alex struggled to prop herself up on one elbow. "Who else asked you about it?"

"I did," Reede Lambert said from the doorway.

THIRTY-EIGHT

A lex's insides lifted weightlessly. She had dreaded the moment she would see him again. It was inevitable, of course, but she had hoped to appear unscathed by what had happened between them.

Lying on a hospital examination table, her hair clotted with blood, her hands painted with pumpkin-colored antiseptic, too weak and muzzy to sit up, didn't exactly convey the impression of invincibility she had desired.

"Hello, Sheriff Lambert. You'll be pleased to know that I took your advice and stopped looking over my shoulder for bogeymen."

Ignoring her, he said, "Hi, Pat. I just got off the radio with the deputy."

"Then you heard what happened?"

"My first thought was that Plummet was involved, but the deputy said her car was struck by an ME truck."

"That's right."

"ME encompasses a lot of companies. Just about anybody in the county could get access to one of those trucks."

"Including you," Alex suggested snidely.

Reede finally acknowledged her existence with a hard stare. The D.A. looked at them uneasily. "Uh, where were you, Reede? Nobody could find you."

"I was out on horseback. Anybody at the ranch could tell you that."

"I had to ask," Pat said apologetically.

"I understand, but you ought to know that running somebody off the road isn't quite my style. Besides me, who do you think could have done it?" he asked Alex pointedly.

It was difficult for her to even conceive of the idea, much less speak it aloud. "Junior," she said quietly.

"Junior?" Reede laughed. "Why in hell?"

"I met with him this morning. He doesn't have an alibi for the night Celina was killed. He admits he was terribly angry." She glanced down. "I also have reason to believe he might be angry with me."

"Why?"

She glared up at him with as much defiance as she could muster. "He came to my room this morning." That's all she was going to supply him. He could draw his own conclusions.

His eyes narrowed fractionally, but he didn't ask what Junior had been doing in her room. Either he didn't want to know, or he didn't care. "Anybody else?" he asked. "Or have you narrowed it down to the two of us?"

"Possibly Angus. I saw him this afternoon, and we didn't part on the best of terms."

"The three of us again, huh? Do you believe we're to blame for everything that happens around here?"

"I don't *believe* anything. I base my suspicions on facts." She was assailed by a wave of dizziness and nausea and had to close her eyes for a moment before going on. "I have another suspect in mind."

"Who?"

"Stacey Wallace."

Pat Chastain reacted like he'd been goosed. "Are you shittin' me?" He glanced toward the door to make certain it was closed. "God, please tell me I'm dreaming. You aren't going to publicly accuse her of anything, are you? Because if you're even thinking about it, I have to tell you right now, Alex, that you'll be on your own. I'm not sticking my neck out again."

"You haven't stuck your neck out for anything, yet!" Alex shouted, causing a blast of pain through her skull.

"Where would Stacey get access to an ME truck?" Reede asked.

"I don't have any solid facts," Alex said wearily. "It's just a hunch."

"Which is all you ever seem to have," Reede said. Alex gave him a menacing look, which she hoped packed more punch than she felt it did.

Pat intervened. "About Stacey, what do you base your allegations on?"

"She lied to me about where she was on the night of the murder." She related what Stacey had told her in the ladies' room at the Horse and Gun Club. "I know she still loves Junior. I don't think I'd get an argument from anyone on that."

The two men exchanged a glance that signified agreement. "She's like a mother hen to her father, and she doesn't want his reputation ruined. And," she added with a sigh, "she hates me for the same reason she hated Celina—Junior. She thinks I'm stealing his affection from her, just as my mother did."

Pat jingled the change in his pockets as he rocked back and forth on the balls of his feet. "Sounds logical when you put it that way, but I just can't imagine Stacey using physical force."

"And here lately, your guesses have been way off base, Counselor."

Alex struggled to a sitting position. "Let's go back to the scalpel." She was so dizzy she had to grip the edge of the table to remain upright. "When did Reede ask you about it, Pat?"

"If you have something to ask, ask me." Reede moved to stand directly in front of her. "I mentioned the scalpel to him a few days ago."

"Why?"

"Just like you, I wanted to know what happened to it."

"If you had located it before me, would you have destroyed it, or turned it over as evidence?"

A muscle in his cheek twitched. "The point is moot. It's no longer in the evidence room."

"You checked?"

"Damn right. I couldn't find a trace of it. It probably hasn't been there for years. Most likely, it was thrown out because the case was."

"Out of consideration to the Collins family, wouldn't someone have offered to give it back?"

"I have no answer for that."

"Was it ever dusted for fingerprints?"

"I took the liberty of asking Judge Wallace that."

"I'm sure you did, Sheriff. What did he say?"

"He said no."

"Why not?"

"The handle was bloody. Gooney Bud's prints were all over it. It was hardly necessary to dust it."

They regarded each other with so much animosity that Pat Chastain broke out in a sweat. "Well, we'd better give these people back their treatment room. Your car is trashed, Alex, so I'll drive you to the motel. Are you up to walking to the car, or should I call for a wheelchair?"

"I'll take her to the motel," Reede said, before Alex could respond to Pat's offer.

"Are you sure?" Pat felt obliged to inquire, though he was obviously relieved that Reede was taking her off his hands. "Since the sheriff has offered," she told Pat, "I'll let him drive me."

The D.A. scuttled out before either could change his mind. Alex watched his rapid departure with derision. "It's no wonder crime is so prevalent in this county. The D.A. is as chicken-livered as they come."

"And the sheriff is corrupt."

"You took the words right out of my mouth." She slid off the edge of the examination table and braced herself against it long enough to get her balance. She tried to take a step, but swayed unsteadily. "The doctor gave me a painkiller. I'm so woozy, maybe you'd better ask them for a wheelchair."

"Maybe you'd better check in for the night."

"I don't want to."

"Suit yourself."

He scooped her into his arms before she could protest and carried her out of the examination room. "My purse." She gestured weakly toward the check-in desk. Reede retrieved it. Then, with the emergency room staff enthralled by the sight, Reede carried her out and deposited her in the front seat of his Blazer.

She rested her head on the back of the seat and closed her eyes. "Where were you this afternoon?" she asked, once they were underway.

"I told you already."

"You were riding even after sundown?"

"I ran some errands."

"You couldn't be reached on your radio. Where were you, Reede?"

"Lots of places."

"Specifically."

"I was at Nora Gail's."

Alex was surprised at how much that hurt her. "Oh."

"I had to question the witness about that shooting."

"Then, you were working?"

"Among other things."

"You still sleep with her, don't you?"

"Sometimes."

She prayed that he would die a slow, painful death.

"Maybe Nora Gail dispatched one of her heavies to do me in," she said, "as a favor to you."

"Maybe. It wouldn't surprise me. If she doesn't like something, she doesn't hesitate to take care of it."

"She didn't like Celina," Alex said softly.

"No, she didn't. But I was with Nora Gail the night Celina died, remember?"

"That's what I'm told."

So, was Nora Gail another suspect for Celina's murder? The thought made her head ache. She closed her eyes. When they arrived at the motel, she reached for the door handle. Reede ordered her to wait and came around to assist her out. With his left arm around her waist, lending support, they made a shuffling trip to the door.

Reede unlocked it and helped her to the bed. She lay down gratefully. "It's freezing in here," he said, rubbing his hands together as he looked for the thermostat.

"It always is when I first come in."

"I didn't notice it last night."

They glanced quickly at each other, then away. Again unable to cope, Alex closed her eyes. When she opened them, Reede was rummaging in the top drawer of the bureau opposite the bed.

"What are you looking for this time?"

"Something for you to sleep in."

"Any T-shirt. It doesn't matter which one."

He returned to the bed, gingerly sat down on the edge, and removed her boots. "Leave my socks," she told him. "My feet are cold."

"Can you sit up?"

She could by leaning heavily against his shoulder while he fumbled with the buttons on the front of her dress. The tiny round things were no bigger than pills, and were covered in the same fabric as her dress. There was a row of them that ran from neck to knee. He was viciously cursing them by the time he got to her waist.

He eased her back down on the pillow, pulled her arms from the tight long sleeves, and worked the dress over her hips and down her legs. Her slip didn't give him pause, but her bra did. Once he seemed to make up his mind about it, he unclasped it with businesslike efficiency and helped her slide the straps off her shoulders.

"I thought you only had a gash on the head and some scratches on your hands?" Evidently, he'd consulted the doctor.

"That's right."

"Then, what's all th—"

He stopped suddenly, realizing that the abrasions on her upper torso were whisker burns. The corner of his mouth twitched with a spasm of regret. She felt compelled to lay her hand against his cheek and reassure him that it was all right, that she hadn't minded having his hot, eager mouth at her breasts, his deft tongue stroking her nipples into stiff rosiness.

Of course she didn't. His dark frown stifled anything she might have said. "You're gonna have to sit up again," he told her curtly.

With a hand behind each shoulder, he pulled her into a sitting position again and propped her against the headboard. He gathered the T-shirt up and tried to pull it over her head. Alex winced the instant he set it against her hair.

"This isn't working," he muttered. Then, with a single, violent motion, he ripped the neck of the shirt wide enough to slip over her head without causing any pain.

When she lay back down, she touched the long tear in the fabric. "Thanks. This was one of my favorites."

"Sorry." He pulled the covers up to her chin and stood up. "Are you going to be all right?"

"Yes."

He looked doubtful. "Are you sure?"

She nodded weakly. "Do you need anything before I go? Water?"

"Okay. Put a glass of water on the nightstand, please."

When he returned to the side of the bed, carrying the glass of water, she had already fallen asleep. Reede stood above her. Her hair, fanned out over the pillow, had bloodstains in it. There was an unnatural wanness to her complexion. It made him sick at his stomach to think how close she'd come to serious injury or death.

He set the glass of water on the nightstand and gingerly lowered himself to the edge of the bed. Alex stirred, murmured unintelligibly, and extended her hand, as though reaching for something. Responding to that silent, subconscious appeal, Reede carefully covered her cut hands with his strong, callused ones.

He wouldn't have been surprised if her eyes had popped open and she had started rebuking him for taking her virginity. How the hell could he have known? *And if I had known,* he thought to himself, *I would have done it anyway.*

She didn't wake up. She only snuffled softly and trustingly curved her fingers over his knuckles. Good sense and impulse warred within him, but the fight didn't last long, and the outcome had been decided before his conscience raised its head.

He eased himself onto the bed, until he was stretched out full beside her, facing her, feeling her gentle, drug-induced breaths against his face.

He marveled over the delicate bone structure of her face, the shape of her mouth, the way her eyelashes lay upon her cheeks.

"Alex." He whispered her name, not to awaken her, but merely for the pleasure of speaking it out loud.

She sighed deeply, drawing his attention down to the torn T-shirt. Through the tear he could see the smooth slope of her breasts. Her cleavage was dusky in the faint lamplight, shadowy and velvety, and he wanted to press his open mouth there.

He didn't. Nor did he kiss her vulnerable mouth, even though his mind was wildly occupied with how softly and deeply and wetly she kissed.

He thought of fondling the tempting mounds of her breasts. He could see the dark impressions of their centers behind the soft cloth of the T-shirt, and knew that with the merest touch of his tongue or fingertips, they would become taut. And that damned T-shirt was far sexier than any fancy negligee and garter belt that Nora Gail had ever worn.

It was hell to lie this close to her and not touch, but it was heaven to have this much access, to stare his fill. When the pleasure and pain of it got to be too much, he reluctantly withdrew his hand from hers and left the bed.

After making certain that she had enough blankets, that the medication had her completely sedated, he slipped quietly out of the room.

THIRTY-NINE

"Come in." Junior was sitting up in bed watching TV and smoking a joint when Reede entered his room. "Hi. What brings you around?" He offered Reede the marijuana.

"No, thanks." Reede dropped into the easy chair and propped his boots on the matching ottoman.

The room had undergone very few changes since the first time Reede had been invited into it, although Junior had updated the furniture when he elected to move home after his last divorce. It was a spacious room, designed with comfort in mind.

"Lord, I'm tired," Reede said, running his fingers through his hair.

Junior pinched out the smoldering cigarette and put it away. "You look it."

"Thanks." He grinned ruefully. "How come I always look like forty miles of bad road and you're always perfectly groomed?"

"Genes. Look at mother. I've never seen her mussed."

"I guess so. God knows my father didn't cotton to good grooming."

"Don't expect any pity from me. You know your rugged good looks are irresistible to the ladies. We're different types, that's all."

"Together, we'd be great."

"We were."

"Huh?"

"Remember the night we shared one of the Gail sisters' behind the National Guard armory. Which one was it?"

Reede chuckled. "Damned if I remember. I'm too tired to think, much less remember."

"You've been putting in a lot of overtime, haven't you?"

"It's taken that," he paused strategically, "just to keep an eye on Alex and keep her from getting hurt."

Reede saw the interest spark in Junior's eyes. "She's a handful, all right."

"I'm not joking. She almost got killed this afternoon."

"What?" Junior swung his feet over the side of the bed to the floor. "What happened? Is she hurt?" Reede told Junior about the incident on the highway. "I'd better call her," he said as soon as Reede finished.

"Don't. When I left her, she was asleep. They gave her a painkiller at the hospital and it was already working."

He could feel the weight of Junior's inquisitive stare, but didn't acknowledge it. He wasn't going to explain why he'd felt it necessary to tuck Alex in. It had taken all his willpower to walk out of that room and deny himself the luxury of lying beside her all night.

"Some Mexicans witnessed the whole thing. They said it was an ME truck, and it deliberately ran her off the road."

Junior looked confused. "My first guess would be that preacher."

"Where would he get one of your company trucks?"

"A devoted member of his flock could be an employee."

"I've got a man checking out that possibility, although I doubt anything'll turn up."

The two friends were silent for a moment. Finally, Reede said casually, "I understand you had breakfast with Alex this morning."

"She called and asked me to meet her."

"Why?"

"She said you told her about Celina's attempted abortion."

Reede averted his head. "Yeah."

"I don't like to second-guess you, friend, but—"

"Then, don't." Reede rolled out of the chair and came to his feet.

"Okay, okay. I just fail to see why it was necessary."

Reede didn't intend to talk about last night at all. "What else did you discuss over breakfast?"

"The night Celina died. Alex wanted to know if I'd proposed." Junior recounted that morning's conversation with Alex.

"Did she believe you when you said you went out and got drunk alone?"

"I guess so. She seemed to. Everybody else believes me."

The look they exchanged lasted a few seconds too long to be comfortable for either. "Yeah, right." Reede gazed out the window. "Alex said Stacey showed up and was none too friendly."

Junior fidgeted. "I've, uh, I've been seeing Stacey lately."

Reede swiveled around, surprised. "Seeing or screwing? Or are they automatically synonymous to you?"

"Guilty to both charges."

Reede cursed. "Why are you fanning that fire?"

"Convenience."

"Nora Gail's is convenient."

"But not free—at least, to no one but you."

Reede's lip curled. "You sorry son of a bitch."

"Look, it's not hurting anybody. Stacey needs the attention. She wants it."

"Because she loves you, you jerk."

"Aww." Junior dismissed that notion with a wave of his hand. "One thing I do know. She's all bent out of shape about Alex. Stacey's afraid she'll ruin all of us, but especially, her old man."

"She might do it. She's determined to find a culprit and send him to prison." Junior slouched against the headboard again. "Does that really worry you?"

"Yes," Reede said. "I've got a lot to lose if ME doesn't get that racing license. So do you."

"What are you getting at, that *I* ran Alex off the road? Is this an interrogation, Sheriff?" he asked in a tone that didn't flatter the office Reede held.

"Well?"

Junior's handsome face flushed with anger. "Good God, are you crazy?" He left the bed and came to stand eye to eye with Reede. "I wouldn't harm a hair on her head."

"Were you in her room this morning?"

"Yes. So?"

"What for?" Reede shouted.

"What do you think?" Junior shouted back.

Reede's head gave a little snap backward. It was a reflexive action, one he couldn't prevent from happening or hide once it had.

Several moments of silence elapsed before Junior said, "She said no."

"I didn't ask."

"But you wanted to," Junior said intuitively. "Does Alex and her reason for being here have anything to do with you turning down Dad's offer to come back to ME?'' He returned to the bed and sat down on the edge of it, giving Reede a wounded and inquisitive look. ''Weren't you even going to mention it, Reede?''

''No.''

''Why?''

''There was no point. When I left the company, it was for good. I don't want to become a part of it again.''

''Of *us,* you mean.''

Reede shrugged. Junior thoughtfully gazed at his friend. ''Because of Celina?''

''Celina?'' Reede whispered with a soft, sad laugh. ''Celina's dead and buried.''

''Is she?''

The friends stared at each other frankly, with all pretense stripped away. After a moment, Reede answered, ''Yes.''

''It hasn't been the same between us since she died, has it?''

''It couldn't be.''

''I guess not,'' Junior said morosely. ''I regret that.''

''So do I.''

''What about Alex?''

''What about her?''

''Is she the reason you won't come back in with us?''

''Hell, no. You know the reason, Junior—or at least, you should. You've heard me talk about it often enough.''

''That crap about independence? That's no reason. You work your way around Angus a lot better than I do.''

Junior sucked in a quick breath, suddenly realizing that he'd hit pay dirt. ''That's it, isn't it? You're steering clear of ME for my sake.''

''You're wrong.'' Reede's denial came a little too fast.

''The hell I am,'' Junior growled. ''You see yourself as a threat to me, the heir apparent. Well, thanks a lot, but don't do me any favors!''

As suddenly as Junior's anger had erupted, it evaporated. ''Who the fuck am I kidding?'' He gave a scoffing laugh. ''Sure as hell not myself.'' He raised his head and looked at Reede imploringly. ''I'd love to have you back. We need you, especially after that racetrack is built.''

''Now who's talking crap?''

''You know I'm right. Dad makes things happen, but he operates like a robber baron. Business doesn't work like that nowadays. I've got charm, but charm is as wasted on a breeding ranch as snow skis in Jamaica. Unless you're a gigolo—a career I've often thought of pursuing—you can't bank charm.''

''It comes in handy.''

''Dad's smart enough to see that you could hold us together, Reede. You could be the buffer between us.'' He looked down at his hands. ''He'd rather have you than me around.''

''Junior—''

''No, let's be honest about this for once, Reede. We're getting too old to lie to ourselves or to each other. Dad would swear on a stack of Bibles that he's proud that I'm his son, but I know better. Oh, I know he loves me, but I'm one screwup after another. He'd rather me be like you.''

''That's not true.''

''I'm afraid it is.''

''Uh-uh,'' Reede said, sternly shaking his head. ''Angus knows that in a pinch, when all the cards are down, you come through. There have been times—''

''What times?''

''Many times,'' Reede stressed, ''when you did what you knew you had to do.

Sometimes it has to get to that last-gasp stage before you accept your responsibility,'' Reede said, ''but when you know it's up to you or else, you do it.'' He laid his hand on Junior's shoulder. ''It's just that sometimes somebody has to put a boot to your butt to get you going.''

It was time to end the discussion, before it got sloppily maudlin. Reede socked Junior's shoulder, then headed for the door. ''Don't go selling that dope to schoolkids or I'll have to haul you in, okay?'' He had opened the door and was on his way out before Junior halted him.

''I was mad as hell the other day when you showed up at the country club to pick up Alex.''

''I know. It couldn't be helped. It was business.''

''Was it? What about the airfield? Was that business, too? That wasn't Dad's impression.''

Reede remained stonily silent, neither admitting or denying anything.

''Jesus,'' Junior breathed, drawing his hand down his face. ''Is it happening again? Are we falling in love with the same woman?''

Reede walked out, quietly closing the door behind him.

 # FORTY

Stacey Wallace slid her father's half-eaten tuna salad out of the way and replaced it with a bowl of fruit cocktail. ''I don't think we'll have her to worry about much longer,'' she said with assurance. The topic of conversation was Alexandra Gaither. ''Did you hear about her accident?''

''From what I understand, it wasn't an accident.''

''All the more reason for her to want to leave town.''

''Angus doesn't think she's going to leave,'' the judge said as he toyed with the cherry floating in the viscous syrup. ''He says she's convinced somebody wanted to scare her into leaving before she exposed the killer.''

''Do you take everything Angus says as carved in granite?'' Stacey asked with exasperation. ''How does he know what she's going to do?''

''He's going by what she told Junior.''

Stacey laid her fork aside. ''Junior?''

''Hmm.'' Judge Wallace sipped his iced tea. ''He sat with her yesterday.''

''I thought she left the hospital and was back at her motel.''

''Wherever she is, Junior's been her only contact with the outside world.'' The judge was so caught up in his own worries, he didn't notice Stacey's suddenly preoccupied gaze.

He pushed away from the table. ''I'd better go or I'll be late. We've got a jury selection this morning and a pretrial hearing for that character who shot a man out at Nora Gail Burton's the other night. I'm expecting a plea bargain, but Lambert's got Pat Chastain pushing for attempted murder.''

Stacey was only half listening. Her mind had lodged on a mental picture of the beautiful Alex Gaither languishing on her motel room bed while Junior waited on her hand and foot.

''By the way,'' the judge said as he pulled on his overcoat, ''did you get that message I left you yesterday?''

''To call Fergus Plummet?''

"Yes. Isn't he that evangelical preacher who raised Cain because they had bingo at the Halloween carnival last year? What'd he want with you?"

"He's canvassing support to keep pari-mutuel gambling out of Purcell County."

The judge snickered. "Does he know he'd just as well try and hold back our next dust storm?"

"That's what I told him when I returned his call," Stacey said. "He knows I belong to several women's organizations and wanted me to plead his case with them. I declined, of course."

Joe Wallace picked up his briefcase and opened the front door. "Reede is convinced that Plummet was responsible for that vandalism out at the Minton ranch, but he's got no evidence to hold him." The judge didn't think twice about discussing cases with Stacey. She had earned his confidence years ago. "I don't think Plummet has the sense to pull off something like that, not without somebody directing him. Reede has been harping on it, but right now, Plummet is the least of my worries."

Concerned, Stacey caught her father's arm. "What worries, Dad? Alex Gaither? Don't worry about her. What harm could she possibly do you?"

He faked a smile. "Absolutely none. You just know how I like things neat and tidy. I've got to run. Good-bye."

Wanda Gail Burton Plummet happened to be sweeping off her front porch when the postman arrived. He handed her the stack of mail and she thanked him. She sorted through it as she made her way back into the house. As usual, all the mail was addressed to her husband. It was mostly bills and church-related correspondence.

One envelope, however, was different from the others. It was made of high-quality beige paper. There was an embossed return address on it, but it had been exed out on a typewriter, making it illegible. Their address had been typed on, too.

Curiosity won out over her husband's strict instructions that he was to open their mail. Wanda tore open the envelope. It contained only a blank piece of paper, folded around five one-hundred-dollar bills.

Wanda stared at the money as though it was a message from an alien planet. Five hundred dollars was more than the offering plate contained after a well-attended revival service. Fergus only took out a pittance to support his family. Almost everything collected went to the church and its "causes."

No doubt this money had been sent by a donor who wanted to remain anonymous. For the last several days, Fergus had been calling up folks on the telephone, asking for volunteers to picket at the gates of the Minton ranch. He solicited money. He wanted to place full-page antigambling ads in the newspaper. Well-publicized crusades were expensive.

Most people hung up on him. Some had called him ugly names before slamming down their receivers. A few had listened and given halfhearted pledges to send a supportive offering.

But, *five hundred dollars.*

He's also spent time on the phone in secretive, whispered conversations. Wanda didn't know what these covert calls were about, but she suspected they had something to do with that business at the Minton ranch. One of the hardest things she'd ever had to do was lie to her old friend, Reede. He had known she was lying, but he'd been gentlemanly enough not to accuse her of it.

Afterward, when she had expressed concern to Fergus about her sin of lying, he had told her that it had been justified. God didn't expect his servants to go to jail, where they would be ineffectual.

She timidly pointed out that Paul had spent a lot of time in prison, and had done some of the most inspired writing in the New Testament while behind bars. Fergus hadn't appreciated the comparison and told her that she should keep her mouth shut about matters that were too complicated for her to comprehend.

"Wanda?"

She jumped at the sound of his voice and reflexively clutched the money to her sagging breasts. "What, Fergus?"

"Was that the postman at the door?"

"Uh, yes." She glanced down at the envelope. The money was surely related to those furtive telephone calls. Fergus wouldn't want to talk about them. "I was just bringing you the mail."

She went into the kitchen. He was seated at the Formica dining table that served as his desk between meals. She laid the stack of mail on the table. When she returned to the sink to finish washing dishes, the fancy envelope and its contents were in her apron pocket.

She would give it to Fergus later, Wanda promised herself, as a surprise. In the meantime, she would fantasize about all it could buy for her three kids.

Alex had had thirty-six hours to think about it. While nursing her debilitating headache, she'd lain in bed, reviewing everything she knew and filling in what she didn't know with educated guesses.

She couldn't continue to run around in circles indefinitely. She was probably as close to the truth as she was ever going to get, short of taking desperate measures. The deadline Greg had set was imminent. It was time to force someone's hand, to get aggressive, even if she had to bluff.

Days ago, she had reached the heartbreaking conclusion that she had been the catalyst for Celina's murder, but she didn't plan to bear the burden of that guilt alone for the rest of her life. Whoever had done the actual deed must suffer for it also.

That morning when she woke up, she still had a headache, but it was one she could live with. She spent the morning reviewing her notes and doing some research, and was waiting in Judge Wallace's anteroom when he returned from lunch. He didn't look pleased to see her.

"I told Ms. Gaither that you had a full schedule today," Mrs. Lipscomb said defensively when he turned a baleful glance on her. "She insisted on waiting for you."

"She's right, Judge Wallace, I did," Alex said. "Can you spare me a few minutes?"

He consulted his wristwatch. "A very few."

She followed him into his office. He took off his overcoat and hung it on a brass coat tree. Not until he was situated behind his desk, trying to look intimidating, did he say, "What is it this time?"

"What did Angus Minton use to entice you?"

His face became instantly mottled. "I don't know what you're talking about."

"Yes, you do. You confined an innocent man to a state mental hospital, Judge Wallace. You knew he was innocent, or at least strongly suspected that he was. You did that at Angus Minton's request, didn't you? And in exchange, you demanded that Junior marry your daughter Stacey."

"This is incredible!" He banged his fists on his desktop.

"It's extremely credible. On the morning after Celina Graham Gaither was found murdered in a stable on the Minton ranch, you received a phone call or a visit from Angus. Bud Hicks had been arrested nearby, covered in blood and in possession of a scalpel presumed to be the murder weapon. That was never ascertained because the scalpel wasn't thoroughly analyzed. The autopsy report specified that she died of repeated stab wounds, but a forensic expert didn't have access to the body before it was cremated, so she could have been stabbed by anything.''

"Gooney Bud stabbed her with Dr. Collins's scalpel,'' he stated stubbornly. "He found it in the stable and killed her with it.''

"Where is it now?''

"Now? It's been twenty-five years. You don't expect it to be lying around in the evidence room, do you?''

"No, but I would expect to have a record of its dispensation. No one ever called the late Dr. Collins or his son, asking if they might want it back, even though it was known to have been a gift from his wife. Doesn't that strike you as unusual?''

"God knows what happened to it, or to the records concerning it.''

"I think that you disposed of it, Judge. You, not the sheriff's office, were the last one recorded to have possession of it. I checked this morning before coming here.''

"Why would I dispose of it?''

"Because if someone came along later—an investigator like me—it would be easy and believable to pass off its disappearance as a clerical error. Better to be accused of sloppy bookkeeping than miscarriage of justice.''

"You are obnoxious, Miss Gaither,'' he said stiffly. "Like most avengers, you're reacting emotionally, and have no basis whatsoever for your horrid allegations.''

"Nevertheless, this is what I intend to present to the grand jury. Actually, I'm doing you a favor by telling you what I have. You'll be able to consult with your attorney ahead of time about the answers you will give. Or will you take the Fifth?''

"I won't need to do either.''

"Do you want to call your lawyer now? I'll gladly wait.''

"I don't need a lawyer.''

"Then I'll proceed. Angus asked you for a favor. You asked for one in return.''

"Junior Minton married my daughter because he loved her.''

"I find that impossible to believe, Judge Wallace, since he's told me himself that he asked my mother to marry him the night she was killed.''

"I can't explain his fickleness.''

"I can. Junior was the trade-off for your ruling on Gooney Bud.''

"The district attorney's office—''

"He was on vacation in Canada at the time. I confirmed that with his widow this morning. His assistant had enough evidence to arraign Bud Hicks for murder.''

"A trial jury would have convicted him, too.''

"I disagree, but we'll never know. You prevented that.'' She drew a deep breath. "Who was Angus protecting—himself, Junior, or Reede?''

"No one.''

"He must have told you when he called that morning.''

"He didn't call.''

"He had to have called as soon as Hicks was arrested. What did Angus tell you?''

"He didn't tell me anything. I never heard from him.''

She came out of her chair and leaned over his desk. "He must have said, 'Look, Joe, I've gotten myself in a jam here.' Or, 'Junior's taken this boys-will-be-boys thing a little too far this time,' or 'Can you help Reede out? He's like a son to me.' Isn't that what happened?''

''No, never.''

''You might have argued that you couldn't do it. You probably asked for time to think about it. Being the nice guy that he is, Angus granted you a few hours to mull it over. That's when you came back saying that you would do this little favor for him in exchange for a marriage between Stacey and Junior.''

''I won't have you—''

''Maybe you even discussed your dilemma with her and Mrs. Wallace.''

''This is defamation of—''

''Or maybe Stacey was the one to suggest the terms of the deal.''

''Stacey never knew anything about it!''

He shot out of his chair and stood nose to nose with Alex, shouting the words in her face. When he realized what he'd admitted, he blinked, wet his lips, then eased away from her and turned his back. Nervously, he ran his fingers over the row of brass studs on the back of his leather chair. It had been a gift from his daughter, his only child.

''You knew how much Stacey loved Junior Minton.''

''Yes,'' he said softly. ''I knew that she loved him more than he deserved.''

''And that her affection wasn't returned.''

''Yes.''

''And that Junior slept with her whenever he felt like it. You thought you had better protect her reputation and the possibility of an unwanted pregnancy by getting her married as soon as possible.''

The judge's shoulders slumped forward and he answered in a low, heartbroken voice. ''Yes.''

Alex closed her eyes and let go a long, silent breath. Tension ebbed from her like a wave receding from the shore. ''Judge Wallace, who killed my mother? Who was Angus protecting when he asked you to hustle Buddy Hicks through the legal system?''

He faced her. ''I don't know. As God is my witness, I don't. I swear it on my years as a judge.''

She believed him and said so. As unobtrusively as possible, she collected her things. When she reached the door of his office, he spoke her name in a thin voice.

''Yes?''

''If this ever comes to trial, will it be essential to your case for all this to come out in court?''

''I'm afraid so. I'm sorry.''

''Stacey . . .'' He paused to clear his throat. ''I wasn't lying when I said she didn't know about my agreement with Angus.''

Alex repeated, ''I'm sorry.''

He nodded gravely. She stepped into the anteroom and closed the door behind her. The secretary shot her a resentful look, which wasn't entirely undeserved. She had badgered him into telling the truth. It had been necessary, but she hadn't enjoyed doing it.

She was waiting for the elevator when she heard the gunshot. ''Oh, God, no.'' She whispered the words, but wasn't even aware of saying them as she dropped her briefcase and raced back toward the end of the corridor. Mrs. Lipscomb was at the door to his office. Alex shoved her aside and ran in ahead of her.

What she saw brought her to an abrupt halt. Her scream froze in her throat, but the secretary's echoed through the chamber and into the hallways.

FORTY-ONE

A stream of secretaries, bailiffs, and other courthouse employees had gathered at the door of Judge Wallace's chambers within sixty seconds of the gunshot.

Reede, the first person to make it upstairs from the basement, shouldered his way through them, barking orders to the deputies who had followed him. "Clear everybody out!"

He instructed one to call an ambulance and another to cordon off the hallway. He placed a comforting arm around Mrs. Lipscomb, who was weeping hysterically, and commissioned Imogene, Pat Chastain's secretary, to take her away. He then bore down on Alex.

"Go to my office, lock yourself in, and stay there, understand?" She stared back at him blankly. "Understand?" he repeated loudly, giving her a shake. Still incapable of speech, she nodded.

To another deputy, he said, "See that she gets to my office. Don't let anybody in."

The officer led her away. Before she left the judge's chambers, she saw Reede look toward the grisly sight at the desk. He ran his hand through his hair and muttered, "Shit."

In his office on the lower level, Alex passed the time by pacing, weeping, gnashing her teeth, staring into space. She agonized in her own private hell over Judge Joseph Wallace's suicide.

Her head was pounding so fiercely, the stitches in her scalp felt like they would pop. She had failed to bring along her medication. A frantic search through the sheriff's desk didn't even produce an aspirin tablet. Was the man totally immune to pain?

She was light-headed and nauseated and her hands refused to get warm, though they perspired profusely. The ancient plaster ceiling conducted every sound from above, but she couldn't identify them. There was an endless parade of footsteps. The office provided her refuge from the confusion, but she was desperate to know what was happening in the rooms and hallways overhead.

She was chin deep in despair. The facts pointed toward an inexorable truth that she didn't want to acknowledge. Judge Wallace's confession to a cover-up further implicated her chief suspects.

Caught in a bind, Angus would have looked out for himself without feeling any remorse. By the same token, he would have bribed the judge in order to protect Junior, and probably done no less for Reede. But of the three, which had actually gone into the stable that night and murdered Celina?

When Reede flung open the door, Alex whirled around, startled. She'd been staring out the window. She didn't know how long she had waited in the room, but she realized suddenly that it was getting dark outside when he flipped on the light switch. She was still ignorant of what was transpiring upstairs and at the front of the courthouse.

Reede gave her a hard look, but said nothing. He poured himself a cup of coffee and sipped from it several times. "Why is it lately that every time something happens in this town, you're involved?"

Tears instantly formed in her eyes. One moment they weren't there, the next they were heavily pushing against her eyelids. She aimed a shaking index finger at his chest. "Don't, Reede. I didn't know that—"

"That when you backed Judge Wallace into a corner he'd blow his brains out. Well, that's what happened, baby. They're dripping over the edge of his desk."

"Shut up."

"We found clumps of hair and tissue on the opposite wall."

She covered her mouth, swallowing a scream behind her hands. Turning her back on him, she shuddered uncontrollably. When he touched her, she flinched, but his hands were firm on her shoulders as he turned her around and pulled her against his chest.

"Hush now, it's done." His chest expanded against her cheek as he drew in a deep breath. "Forget it."

She shoved herself away. "Forget it? A man is dead. It's my fault."

"Did you pull the trigger?"

"No."

"Then it's not your fault."

There was a knock at the door. "Who is it?" Reede asked crossly. When the deputy identified himself, Reede told him to come in. He signaled Alex into a chair while the deputy rolled a sheet of paper into the typewriter. She looked at Reede in bewilderment.

"We have to take your statement," he said.

"Now?"

"Best to get it over with. Ready?" he asked the deputy and got a nod. "Okay, Alex, what happened?"

She dabbed her face with a tissue before she began. As briefly as possible, she told what had transpired in the judge's chambers, being careful not to mention any names or issues that had been discussed.

"I left his office and got as far as the elevator." She stared down at the soggy Kleenex that she'd been mutilating between her hands. "Then, I heard the shot."

"You ran back in?"

"Yes. He was slumped over. His head was lying on his desk. I saw blood and . . . and knew what he'd done."

"Did you see the pistol?" She shook her head. Reede said to the deputy, "Make a note that she answered no and that she couldn't have seen it because it had fallen from the victim's right hand to the floor. That's all for now." The deputy discreetly withdrew. Reede waited several moments. His foot swung to and fro from the corner of the desk where he was seated. "What did you and the judge talk about?"

"Celina's murder. I accused him of tampering with evidence and accepting a bribe."

"Serious allegations. How did he respond?"

"He admitted it."

He took something out of his shirt pocket and tossed it onto his desk. The sterling-silver scalpel landed with a dull, metallic sound. It had oxidized, but was otherwise clean.

Alex recoiled from the sight of it. "Where'd you get that?"

"From the judge's left hand."

They exchanged a long stare. Finally, Reede said, "It was his instrument of self-abuse, kept in his desk drawer, a constant reminder that he was corruptible. Knowing how proud he was of his years on the bench, it's no wonder he cashed in. He'd rather blow off the side of his head than watch his career be ruined."

"Is that all you can say?"

"What do you expect me to say?"

"I expect you to ask me who bribed him? With what? Why?" Her tearful eyes dried instantly. "You already know, don't you?"

He eased himself off the desk and stood up. "I wasn't born yesterday, Alex."

"So, you know that Angus got Judge Wallace to lock Gooney Bud away, presumably as Celina's murderer, in exchange for Junior marrying Stacey."

"Where does that leave you?" Planting his hands on his hips, he loomed above her. "It's speculation. You can't prove it. Neither of them would have been stupid enough to record a conversation to that effect, if one did take place. Nobody wrote anything down. There's enough reasonable doubt there for downtown Dallas to fit into. A man's dead, his reputation as a fine judge has been shot to hell, and you've still got nothing to base a murder rap on."

He tapped his chest, his fingertips making angry stabs at his shirt. "I had to drive to the judge's house and notify Stacey that her old man had emptied his head onto his desk because of your loosely based charges that would probably have been no-billed by the grand jury."

He stopped and regained control of his temper. "Before I get really pissed off at you, I suggest we get out of here and go someplace where it's safe."

"Safe? For whom?"

"For you, dammit. Haven't the repercussions of this sunk in yet? Pat Chastain's near cardiac arrest. Greg Harper has already called three times today, wanting to know if you could possibly have had anything to do with this prominent and respected judge's suicide. Stacey is incoherent with grief, but in her lucid moments, she's cursing you to perdition.

"We've got Plummet and his army of crazies out there on the courthouse steps, carrying pickets that say this is just the beginning of the end. All this chaos is because of you and your half-baked murder case, Counselor."

Alex felt as though her chest was going to cave in, but she fought back. "Was I supposed to let Wallace go free just because he was a really nice guy?"

"There are more subtle ways to handle delicate situations like that, Alex."

"But, no one handled it at all!" she cried. "Is that your philosophy of the law, Sheriff Lambert? Some rules don't apply to some people? When a friend of yours crosses over, do you conveniently look the other way? Apparently so. Case in point—Nora Gail Burton and her whorehouse. Does that same exclusion from justice apply to you, as well?"

He didn't answer. Instead, he went to the door and opened it, saying curtly, "Let's go."

She stepped into the hallway with him; he steered her toward the rear elevator. "Pat loaned me his wife's car," she told him. "It's parked out front."

"I know. There's a swarm of reporters camped right beside it, all of them eager to know the gory details of the judge's suicide. I'm sneaking you out the back door."

They left the building unseen. It was completely dark outside, and Alex wondered what time it was.

They were halfway between the building and the parking lot when a form disengaged itself from the shadows and blocked their path.

"Stacey." Reede exclaimed softly. Subconsciously, his hand closed around the butt of his pistol, although he didn't remove it from the holster.

"I thought I'd catch you trying to hide."

Stacey's eyes were fixed on Alex. The hatred in them made Alex want to cower against Reede for protection, but she maintained her proud stance. "Before you say anything, Stacey, I want you to know that I'm terribly sorry about your father."

"Are you?"

"Very sorry."

Stacey shivered, whether with cold or revulsion, Alex couldn't tell. "You came here to ruin him. Instead of being sorry, you should feel very proud of yourself."

"I had nothing to do with your father's past mistakes."

"You're the reason for the whole mess! Why couldn't you just leave him alone?" Stacey cried, her voice cracking. "What happened twenty-five years ago wasn't important to anybody but you. He was old. He planned to retire in a few months anyway. What harm was he doing you?"

Alex remembered the judge's last words to her. Stacey hadn't known about the shady deal he had struck on her behalf. Alex could spare her that pain, at least until she'd had time to absorb the shock of her father's death. "I can't discuss the case with you. I'm sorry."

"Case? *Case?* This was never about a case. This was about your trashy mother, who used and manipulated people—*men*—until someone got tired of it and killed her." Her eyes narrowed threateningly and she took a malevolent step closer. "You're just like her, stirring up trouble, a user of people and a whore!"

She launched herself at Alex, but Reede stepped between them, catching Stacey against his chest and holding her there until her rage was spent and she was clinging to him weakly, sobbing.

He stroked her back and murmured words of comfort. Behind her back, he passed Alex the keys to his Blazer. She took them and let herself in, locking the door behind her. Watching through the windshield, she saw him lead Stacey around the corner of the building and out of sight. Several minutes later, he came jogging back. She unlocked the door for him and he climbed in.

"Will she be all right?" Alex asked.

"Yeah. I turned her over to some friends. They'll see that she gets home. Someone will stay with her tonight." His lips narrowed into a bitter line. "Of course, the man she wants isn't there for her."

"Her father?"

He shook his head. "Junior."

Because it was all so pitifully sad, Alex began to cry again.

FORTY-TWO

She didn't raise her head until the Blazer jounced over a chuckhole. She tried to get her bearings by looking through the windshield, but it was a dark night, and the road had no markings. "Where are we going?"

"My place." No sooner had he said it than his headlights picked up the house. "Why?"

He cut the truck's engine. "Because I'm afraid to let you out of my sight. People turn up dead or wounded when I do."

He left her sitting in the truck while he went to unlock the front door. She thought about driving off, but he'd taken the keys. In some ways, Alex was relieved she'd been robbed of taking the initiative. She wanted to defy him, but didn't have the physical or mental energy. Tiredly, she pushed open the Blazer's door and got out.

The house looked different at night. Like a woman's face, it fared better under soft lighting that helped camouflage its flaws. Reede had gone in ahead of her and turned on a lamp. He was crouched in front of the fireplace, putting a long match to the kindling beneath the stacked logs.

When the dry wood started crackling, he stood up and asked her, "Are you hungry?"

"Hungry?" She repeated the word like someone unfamiliar with the language.

"When did you eat last? Lunch?"

"Junior brought a hamburger to my room last night."

He made a grumpy, grunting sound and headed for the kitchen. "I don't promise anything as fancy as a hamburger."

Thanks to Lupe's niece, the pantry had been recently stocked with more than peanut butter and crackers. After taking a quick inventory, he recited their choices. "Canned soup, canned spaghetti, frozen tamales, bacon and eggs."

"Bacon and eggs."

They worked in companionable silence. Reede did most of the actual cooking. He had little regard for tidiness and none for culinary finesse. Alex enjoyed watching him. When he slid a plate in front of her and dropped into the chair across the small table, she smiled at him pensively. He noticed her expression and did a double take as he lifted the first forkful to his mouth.

"What's the matter?"

She shook her head and shyly lowered her eyes. "Nothing."

He didn't seem ready to accept her answer. Before he could pursue it, however, the telephone rang. He reached for the wall extension.

"Lambert. Oh, hi, Junior." He looked toward Alex. "Yeah, it was a real mess." He listened. "She, uh, she had a meeting with him right before it happened. . . . I'm afraid she saw everything."

He paraphrased Alex's official statement. "That's all I know. . . . Well, Christ, tell them to calm down. They can read about it in tomorrow's paper, like everybody else. . . . Okay, look, I'm sorry," he said, "it's been a bitch of a day and I'm tired.

"Give Sarah Jo one of her pills and tell Angus he's got nothing to worry about." He caught Alex's frown, but kept his expression bland. "Alex? She's fine. . . . Well, if she doesn't answer her phone, she's probably in the shower. If you want to play Good Samaritan, there's somebody who needs you more than Alex tonight. . . . Stacey, you idiot. Why don't you go over there and sit with her for a while. . . . Okay, see you tomorrow."

After he broke the connection, he left the phone off the hook and went back to his food. Alex asked, "Why didn't you tell him I was here?"

"Did you want me to?"

"Not particularly. I just wondered why you didn't."

"He didn't need to know."

"Will he go see Stacey?"

"I hope so, but you never can tell about Junior. Actually," he said, swallowing a bite, "you seem to be all he's thinking about."

"Me, personally, or what I heard from Judge Wallace?"

"A combination of both, I guess."

"Angus is upset?"

"Naturally. Joe Wallace was an old friend."

"Friend and coconspirator." Reede didn't rise to the bait; he didn't even divert his attention from his supper. "I must talk to Angus, Reede. I want you to drive me over there as soon as we finish eating." He calmly reached for his coffee cup, sipped, returned it to the saucer. "Reede, did you hear me?"

"Yes."

"Then, you'll drive me over?"

"No."

"I've got to talk to him."

"Not tonight."

"Yes, tonight. Wallace implicated him in a cover-up. I've got to question him about it."

"He's not going anywhere. Tomorrow's soon enough."

"Your loyalty is commendable, but it can't protect Angus forever."

He set his silverware on his empty plate and carried it to the sink. "Tonight, I'm more concerned about you than Angus."

"Me?"

He glanced at her plate and, satisfied that she was finished, cleared it away. "Seen yourself in a mirror lately? You look like hell. Several times I've braced myself to catch you, afraid you were about to keel over."

"I'm fine. If you'll just take me back to the motel, I'll—"

"Uh-uh," he said, shaking his head. "You're staying here tonight, where you can get some sleep without being pestered by reporters."

"Do you really think I would be?"

"A judge's death is hot news. A judge's suicide is even hotter. You were the last person to talk to him. You're conducting an investigation that has the racing commission worried. Yeah, I think the press will be tramping down the bushes around the Westerner to get to you."

"I'd be okay if I locked myself in my room."

"I'm not taking any chances. As I've told you before, I don't want one of Harper's pets to get herself killed in my county. You've generated enough negative publicity for us these last few weeks; we sure as hell can't stand any more. Does your head hurt?"

She had rested her head in her hand and was subconsciously massaging her temples. "Yes, a little."

"Take some medicine."

"I don't have it with me."

"I'll see if I can round up something for your pain."

He circled the back of the chair and scooted it away from the table. As she stood up, she said, "You keep a stash of drugs, too? That's against the law, you know."

"Is that all you ever think about—the law? Whether something is right or wrong? Is the line between them so clearly defined for you?"

"Isn't it for you?"

"If it had been, I'd have gone hungry lots of times. I stole food to feed myself and my old man. Was that wrong?"

"I don't know, Reede," she said wearily.

Her head hurt from trying to keep up with their argument. She trailed him down the hallway, not really realizing where he was headed until he switched on the light in his bedroom.

Her face must have registered alarm because he grinned sardonically and said, "Don't worry. I'm not trying to seduce you. I'll sleep on the sofa in the living room."

"I really shouldn't stay here, Reede."

"We could both be grown up about this ... if you were a grown-up to start with."

Not in the least amused, she lashed out at him. "There are a million reasons why I shouldn't spend the night here. Number one on the list is that I should be questioning Angus right now."

"Give him one more night of grace. What could it hurt?"

"Pat Chastain will probably expect to hear from me."

"I told him you were near collapse and that you would contact him in the morning."

"You planned ahead, I see."

"I wasn't taking any chances. When allowed to roam free, you're dangerous."

She leaned against the wall and closed her eyes for a moment. Too proud to capitulate, but too exhausted not to, she compromised. "Just answer one question."

"Shoot."

"May I use your shower?"

Fifteen minutes later, she turned off the taps and reached for a towel hanging on the bar. He had loaned her a pair of pajamas to put on. They looked brand new.

When she had commented on it, he said, "Junior brought them to me in the hospital when I had my appendix taken out several years ago. I only wore them so I could get out of that ass-baring gown. Can't stand the things."

Smiling at the distasteful face he'd made when he'd said that, she slid her arms into the blue silk top and buttoned up the front. Just then he tapped on the bathroom door. "I found some pain pills."

Well covered to midthigh, she opened the door. He handed her the prescription bottle. "This is strong stuff," she remarked, reading the label. "You must have been in severe pain. The appendectomy?"

He shook his head. "Root canal. Feeling better?"

"The shower helped. My head's not hurting so bad anymore."

"You washed your hair."

"Against doctor's orders. I wasn't supposed to for a week, but I couldn't stand it any longer."

"Better let me take a look at your stitches."

She tipped her head forward and gently parted her hair. His fingers were light and deft. The most pressure she felt was his breath against her scalp.

"Everything looks all right."

"I washed around it."

Reede stepped away, but continued to look at her. She looked back. They stayed that way for a very long, silent time. Eventually, in a low, rough voice, Reede said, "Better take your pill."

She turned toward the sink and filled his toothbrush glass with tap water. She shook a tablet from the plastic bottle, tossed it back, and took a long drink. As she was bringing her head forward, she caught his eyes in the mirror. She replaced the snap-on lid of the pill bottle and turned, drying her mouth on the back of her hand.

Inexplicably, and totally unexpectedly, tears formed in her eyes. "I know you don't regard me too highly, Reede, but you must know how terrible I feel about what Judge Wallace did." Her lower lip began to tremble; her voice became husky with emotion. "It was awful, horrible."

She stepped toward him, put her arms around his waist, and laid her cheek against his chest. "Be kind for once and just hold me. Please."

He groaned her name and curled his arm around her waist. His other hand cradled the back of her head to hold her face against his chest. He massaged her scalp soothingly and pressed soft kisses on her brow. At the first touch of his lips, she tilted her head up. She kept her eyes closed, but she could feel the heat of his gaze on her face.

His lips brushed hers, and when hers separated, he murmured another low groan and kissed her deeply. His hands sifted through her wet hair, then caressed her neck.

"Touch me again, Reede," she pleaded.

He unbuttoned the pajama top, then slid his hands inside it, encircling her body and drawing it up high against him. His shirt lightly rubbed against her nipples. She felt the cold bite of his belt buckle on her bare belly and the bulge of his fly nudging her mound as it nestled in the soft hair between her thighs.

Each sensation was more electrifying than the last. She wanted to savor each one individually, but the combination of them was too immense and overwhelming for her to concentrate. Every blood vessel in her body expanded with passion. She was inundated with him.

Suddenly, he moved away from her. She looked up at him, bewildered, wide-eyed, and already feeling the loss. "Reede?"

"I have to know."

"What?"

"Have you been to bed with Junior?"

"I don't have to answer that."

"Yes, you do," he said resolutely. "If you want this to go one step further, you do. Have you been to bed with Junior?"

Desire won out over pride. She shook her head and gave him a soft, whispery answer. "No."

After several ponderous seconds, he said, "Okay, then, this time we're going to do it right."

Taking her hand, he led her into the living room, which surprised her because the bed had been turned down while she was in the shower. In the living room, the only light was from the fire burning in the fireplace. He had already made up the couch for himself, but he whipped the bedding off now and spread it out on the floor in front of the hearth. She knelt on the pallet while he calmly began to undress.

His boots, socks, shirt, and belt were cast aside with dispatch. Alex, acting on impulse, moved aside his hands when they went to undo his fly. Slowly, her fingers pushed the stubborn metal buttons through the holes. When all were undone, she opened the wedge wider, leaned forward and kissed him.

Groaning, Reede gently cupped her head between his hands. Her mouth opened warmly and wetly over his belly, just below his navel. "That's my favorite thing," he rasped.

Sliding her hands into the back of his jeans, she eased them over his buttocks, while her lips continued to whisk airy, breathy kisses over his lower body. Finally, her tongue glanced the tip of his penis.

"Stop, Alex. Stop," he moaned. "That's killing me, baby."

Quickly, he stepped out of the jeans and kicked them aside. Naked, he was tall and rangy and rugged, the appendectomy scar only one of many.

His body hair caught the glow of the fire. It showed up as a golden fuzz over his tanned skin, except around his sex, where it was dark and dense. Lean muscles rippled with each movement.

"Get out of that goddamned pajama top before I tear it off."

Sitting back on her heels, Alex eased the pajama jacket off her shoulders and let it go. The sensuous fabric pooled around her. Reede dropped to his knees in front of her. His eyes drank in every inch of her.

Alex thought he seemed hesitant to touch her, but finally, he lifted his hands to her hair and rubbed the damp auburn strands between his fingertips. He watched his hand's slow progress down her neck and chest to her breast. His thumb made light, deft passes across the nipple until it hardened.

Catching her breath, she sighed, "I thought you weren't trying to seduce me."

"I lied."

They lay down together. He pulled the covers up over them, took her in his arms, drew her close, and kissed her with more tenderness than passion.

"You're very small," he whispered against her lips. "Did I hurt you the other night?"

"No." He angled his head back and looked at her suspiciously. She ducked her head timidly. "Only a little."

His hand curved around her throat; he stroked it with his thumb. "How was I supposed to know you were a virgin?"

"You weren't."

"How come you were, Alex?"

She tilted her head to one side and gazed up at him. "Are the reasons why so important, Reede?"

"Only because you let me."

"*Letting* you never entered my mind. It just happened."

"Any regrets?"

She laid her hand along his cheek and drew his head down. They kissed long and avariciously. His hand had found its way to her breast again by the time he ended the kiss. Pushing back the covers, he watched his fingers caress her nipple.

"Reede," she said, her voice tentative, "I'm embarrassed."

"I want to look. Just tell me if you get cold."

"I'm not cold."

She was making small, yearning sounds even before he lowered his head and closed his lips around her nipple. He sucked on it with masterful skill. His hand moved down to appreciate the curve of her waist, then smoothed over the shape of her hip and thigh. He touched her navel playfully, and lightly scrubbed the area beneath it with his knuckles. He touched the delta of springy hair, and his eyes turned dark.

"I want you to come this time," he murmured.

"I want to."

He slid his hands between her thighs. She raised her hips slightly to accommodate him. She was already wet. He slipped his fingers inside her.

"Reede," she gasped with pleasure.

"Shh. Just enjoy."

His thumb idly fanned back and forth across that vulnerable gem of flesh while he planted kiss after fervent kiss on her fertile mouth.

"I think it's about to happen," she panted between kisses.

"Not yet. Talk to me. I never get to talk in bed."

"Talk?" She couldn't even think. "About what?"

"Anything. I just want to hear your voice."

"I . . . I don't . . ."

"Talk, Alex."

"I like watching you cook," she blurted.

"What?" He chuckled against her lips.

"It was very manly, the way you banged and rattled the pans. You're messy. You didn't crack the eggs, you smashed them. Your ineptitude was endearing."

"You're crazy."

"You're making me crazy."

"Am I?"

He inched his head down and stroked her belly with his tongue. His thumb continued to finesse her slowly, provocatively, maddeningly, while his fingers slid in and out. Sensations began to bubble warmly within her lower body. The pressure centered on the idle movement of his thumb, so that when he replaced it with the tip of his tongue, she cried out.

She clutched handfuls of his hair and tilted her hips upward toward the heat of his avid mouth, toward the swirling magic of his tongue.

Not until the aftershocks had subsided did she open her eyes. His face was bent low over hers. Damp strands of hair clung to her cheeks and neck. He lifted them away and laid them on the pillow.

"What does a woman say at a time like this, Reede?"

"Nothing," he replied gruffly. "Your face said it all. I've never watched a woman's face before."

Alex was deeply touched by his admission, but tried to make light of it. "Good. Then you won't know if I did it right or not."

He glanced down at her flushed breasts, at the moisture that had caused her pubic hair to glisten. "You did it right."

Lovingly, she combed her fingers through his hair. "It could have happened before it did, you know—like, that evening at the airfield. And the time in Austin when you took me home. I begged you to stay with me that night. Why didn't you?"

"Because you wanted me there for the wrong reasons. I wanted a woman, not a little lost girl looking for her daddy." He studied her doubtful expression. "You don't seem convinced."

Unable to meet his incisive eyes, she looked at a point beyond his shoulder. "Are you positive that's the reason? Or were you looking for somebody else?"

"You don't mean somebody, you mean Celina." Alex turned her head aside. Reede gripped her jaw and forced her to look at him. "Listen to me, Alex. You made me mad as hell by saying what you did the other night, that crap about taking from you what I'd always wanted from Celina. I want you to understand something. We're the only two people here now. There's nobody between us. No ghosts, either. You got that?"

"I think—"

"No." He shook his head so emphatically that strands of dark blond hair fell over his green eyes. "Don't just think—*know*. You're the only woman in my head right now. You're the only woman that's been in my head since I met you. You're the only woman I'm dying to fuck every minute I'm awake and that I dream about fucking when I'm asleep.

"I'm too old for you. It's stupid and probably wrong for me to want you. It's complicated as hell. But, right or wrong, no matter whose daughter you are, I want you." He imbedded himself firmly inside her. "Understand?" He pushed higher, harder, hotter, and groaned, "Understand?"

He made himself understood.

Junior woke up before sunrise, a rarity for him. He'd had a bad night. Following Reede's suggestion, he'd spent several hours with Stacey. Her physician had given her a sedative, but it hadn't worked well enough. Each time Junior thought she was asleep and left his chair at her bedside, she would wake up, clutch his hand, and beg him not to leave her. He hadn't gotten home until well after midnight. Then he'd slept fitfully, worrying about Alex.

The instant his eyes opened, he reached for the telephone on his nightstand and dialed the Westerner Motel. He instructed the clerk, who was tired and cranky during those waning minutes of his long shift, to connect him with her room. The phone rang ten times.

Breaking the connection, he called the sheriff's office. He was told that Reede hadn't come in yet. He asked to be patched into his mobile unit, but the switchboard operator told him it wasn't in use. He called Reede's house and got a busy signal.

Frustrated, he got out of bed and began to pull on clothes. He couldn't stand not knowing where Alex was. He would find out for himself, starting with Reede.

He crept past his parents' bedroom, although he heard stirrings behind the door. He was sure Angus would want to talk to him about the deal with Judge Wallace concerning his marriage to Stacey. Junior didn't feel up to discussing that yet.

He left the house and climbed into his Jag. It was a clear but cold morning. The drive to Reede's house took him no more than a few minutes. He was glad to see that the Blazer was still parked out front and that smoke was curling out of the chimney. Reede was an early riser. Hopefully, he had a pot of coffee already perking.

Junior jogged across the porch and knocked on the front door. He stood there, hopping from one foot to another and blowing on his hands in an effort to get warm. After a long wait, Reede pulled open the door. He was wearing only a pair of jeans and a rumpled, sleepy, disagreeable expression.

"What the hell time is it?"

"Don't tell me I got you out of bed," Junior said incredulously, opening the screen door and stepping into the living room. "It's late for you, isn't it?"

"What are you doing here? What's going on?"

"That's what I was hoping you could tell me. Alex hasn't answered her phone all night. Do you have any idea where she is?"

From the corner of his eye, he noticed the pallet in front of the hearth, then a movement. Turning slightly, he saw her standing in the hallway leading to Reede's bedroom. Her hair was tousled, her lips full and red, her legs bare. She was wearing the top to the pajama set he'd given Reede when he'd had his appendectomy. She looked wanton and well-screwed.

Junior fell back a step as the breath left his body. Slumping against the wall, he looked toward the ceiling and uttered a short laugh.

Reede laid a hand on his arm. "Junior, I—"

Junior angrily shook off his friend's hand. "It wasn't enough you had her mother, was it? You had to have her, too."

"It's not like that," Reede said in a steely voice.

"No? Then, you tell me, what's it like? You gave me the green light the other night. You said you didn't want her."

"I said nothing of the kind."

"Well, you damn sure didn't say hands off. You moved faster than a sidewinder when you found out I was interested, didn't you? What was your rush? Were you afraid that if she slept with me first, she'd never want to give up quality for low life?"

"Junior, stop it!" Alex cried.

Junior didn't even hear her. He was focused on Reede. "Why is it, Reede, that whatever I want, you take? Football trophies, my own father's respect. You didn't even want Celina anymore, but you made damn sure I didn't get her, didn't you?"

"Shut up," Reede snarled, taking a threatening step forward.

Junior aimed his finger at the center of Reede's chest. "Stay away from me, you hear? Just stay the hell away from me."

He slammed out the front door. The racket echoed through the small house. After the Jag's roar had faded, Reede headed toward the kitchen. "Want some coffee?"

Alex was stunned by what Junior had said, and even more shocked by Reede's cavalier reaction. She ran into the kitchen. Coffee grounds showered from the metal scoop when she grabbed his arm and spun him around.

"Before I fall completely in love with you, Reede, there's something I've got to ask one final time." She took a sharp breath. "Did you kill my mother?"

Several heartbeats later he replied, "Yes."

FORTY-THREE

Fergus Plummet stood at the side of the bed, looking down at his sleeping wife, his body quivering with indignation. "Wanda, wake up." His imperious tone of voice could have awakened the dead.

Wanda opened her eyes and sat up, groggy and disoriented. "Fergus, what time—" Everything sprang into clarity when she saw what he was holding in his hand—five incriminating one-hundred-dollar bills.

"Get up," he ordered before marching from the room.

Trembling in fear, Wanda got out of bed. She dressed as quickly as she could and ruthlessly raked her hair back, not wanting him to find more fault with her.

He was waiting for her in the kitchen, sitting straight and tall at the table. Like a penitent, she timorously approached him.

"Fergus, I . . . I was saving it as a surprise."

"Silence," he bellowed. "Until I tell you to speak, you will remain silent and soul-searching." His accusing eyes pierced straight through her. She bowed her head in shame.

"Where did you get it?"

"It came in the mail yesterday."

"In the mail?"

Her head wobbled up and down in a frantic nod of affirmation. "Yes. In that envelope." It was lying on the table beside his cup of coffee.

"Why did you hide it from your husband, to whom you are supposed to be submissive, according to holy scripture?"

"I," she began, then stopped to wet her lips, "I was saving it to give you as a surprise."

His eyes smoldered with suspicion. "Who sent it?"

Wanda raised her eyes and looked at him stupidly. "I don't know."

He closed his eyes and swayed as though entranced. "Satan, I command you to release her from your evil power. You have control of her lying tongue. Give it back, in the name—"

"No!" Wanda shouted. "I'm not lying. I thought it probably came from one of those folks you've been talking to on the phone about what you did out at the Minton ranch."

He was out of his chair like a shot. Rounding the table, he bore down on her. "How dare you mention that? Didn't I tell you never, *never* to utter a word about that?"

"I forgot," she said, cowering. "I thought maybe the money came from somebody who appreciated what you did."

"I know who it came from," he hissed.

"Who?"

"Come with me." He grabbed her hand and dragged her toward the door that connected the kitchen to the garage.

"Where are we going, Fergus?"

"Wait and see. I want the sinners to meet face-to-face."

"The kids are—"

"God will watch over them until we get back."

With Wanda sitting shivering in the front seat beside him, Plummet drove through the sleeping streets of town. At the highway, he headed west. He seemed unaware of the cold, warmed by his coat of righteousness. When he took the turnoff, Wanda stared at him in total disbelief, but he shot her a look of such condemnation that she wisely refrained from uttering a peep.

He pulled up in front of the large house and ordered his wife to get out of the car. His footsteps landed hard on the hollow steps and his knock rang out loudly in the stillness of early morning. No one answered his first knock, so he pounded harder on the door. When still no one came, he emphatically banged on the window nearest him.

Nora Gail herself pulled open the door and aimed the barrel of a small handgun directly at his forehead. "Mister, you'd better have damned good reason for beating down my door and getting me out of bed at this ungodly hour."

Fergus raised his hands above his bowed head and called upon God and a host of angels to cleanse the sinner of her wrongdoing.

Nora Gail pushed him aside and moved toward her sister. They faced each other. Nora Gail, her platinum hair radiant, looked marvelous for someone who had just gotten out of bed. The constant use of expensive night creams guaranteed her a glowing complexion. She was resplendent in a rose satin robe trimmed with seed pearls. By contrast, Wanda looked like an overweight brown wren.

"It's cold out here," Nora Gail remarked, as though they'd seen each other only yesterday. "Let's go inside." She led her gawking sister across the threshold of the whorehouse. Nudging Fergus in his skinny ribs as she went past, she said, "Preacher, if you don't shut up that noisy praying, I'm going to shoot your balls off, you hear?"

"Ah-men!" he cried, suddenly ending his prayer.

"Thank you," Nora Gail said with amusement. "I'm sure I can use the prayers. Come on in. I've been wanting to talk to you."

Several minutes later, they were collected around the table in her kitchen, which looked very ordinary and not the least bit sinful. Coffee had been brewed and poured into fine china cups. Fergus commanded Wanda to avoid it, as though it was a poisonous concoction.

"You can't defeat us," Fergus said heatedly. "God is on our side, and He's sorely provoked at you, a whore who leads weaker brothers astray."

"Save it," Nora Gail said with a casual wave of her hand. "I fear God, all right, but what's between Him and me is personal, and no business of yours. The only thing that scares me about you, preacher, is your stupidity."

He took umbrage. His face puffed up like an adder. "Did you send my wife some of your ill-gotten money?"

"Yes. From the looks of her and your kids, I thought she could put it to good use."

"We don't need your money."

Nora Gail sat forward and, with a lazy smile, spoke softly to Fergus. "You haven't thrown it back in my face, either, have you?"

His mouth puckered like a drawstring purse. "I never reject a gift that God so generously bestows."

"No, I'm sure you don't." Nora Gail complacently dropped two cubes of sugar into her coffee. "That's why I want to make a deal with you, *Reverend* Plummet."

"I don't deal with the ungodly. I came here as a messenger of God, to warn you of His wrath, to hear your confession of—"

"How would you like a new church?"

The flow of evangelism ceased abruptly. "Huh?"

Idly, Nora Gail stirred her coffee. "How would you like a new church? A big, grand church that would put all the others in town to shame, even the new First Baptist." She paused to sip her coffee. "I can see I've left you speechless, which in itself is a blessing."

Again, she smiled like a cat that had just licked clean a saucer of cream. "As soon as Purcell Downs is completed, I'm going to be very rich and very respectable. It would be to your benefit, preacher, to accept my generous donations, which would be sizable and given on a regular basis. Then, when *Texas Monthly* or '60 Minutes' comes out here to interview me as one of the state's richest businesswomen, they can also report what a generous and benevolent person I am.

"And in return for this fancy church I'll build you," she said, leaning forward again, "I would expect you to keep your loud mouth shut about racetrack gambling. There are plenty other sins to keep you occupied. If you run out of sermon material, I'll be more than glad to provide you a list of sins, because I've committed them all, sugar."

He was gaping like a fish washed ashore. The madam definitely had his attention.

"And, you wouldn't be pulling any more stunts like you did at the Minton ranch a week or so back. Yes," she said, holding up her heavily jeweled hand to stem his denials, "I know you did it. You caused a valuable horse to get put down, and that really chaps my ass."

Her eyes narrowed on him. "If you do anything that stupid again, I'll pull the pulpit right out from under you, preacher man. I make plans, see, and I knock down anybody who stands in the way of them. If you have a problem you want solved, come to me. Leave the revenge-getting to somebody who knows how to get it and not get caught." She leaned back in her chair. "Well?"

"You've . . . you've given me a lot to think about."

"Not good enough. I want your answer today. Right now. Do you want to become a religious big shot with a shiny new church, or do you want to go to jail? Because, you see, if you don't say yes to my offer, I'll call my good buddy Reede Lambert and tell him I've got an eyewitness to that vigilante raid out at the ranch. What's it gonna be, sugar—a pulpit or prison?"

Fergus swallowed visibly. He struggled with himself, with his conscience, but not for long. His head gave one swift nod of agreement.

"Good. Oh, one other thing," Nora Gail continued in the same lilting voice. "Stop treating my sister like a doormat. You were overheard dressing her down in public at the sheriff's office the other night. If I ever get wind of it happening again, I'll personally cut off your pitiful pecker and feed it to the next dog I see. Okay?"

He swallowed hard.

"I'm sending Wanda Gail to a spa up in Dallas, where she'll stay and be pampered for two weeks, which is little enough vacation from you. How do you expect to attract folks to your new church if your own wife looks like a downtrodden toad? This summer your kids'll go to camp. They're gonna have new bicycles and baseball gloves, because I'm overturning your rule about no games of any kind and signing them up for Little League next spring." She winked. "Their Aunt Nora Gail is gonna be the best goddamn thing that ever happened to those kids. Are you getting all this, preacher?"

Again, Plummet gave a brusque nod.

"Good." She sat back in her chair, calmly swinging a shapely leg back and forth through the slit of her robe. "Now that we've cleared the air, let's talk terms. You'll receive the first donation the day the licensing is finalized, and one on the first of each month after that. The checks will be drawn on the NGB, Incorporated account. I'm going to need the tax deduction," she said with a throaty laugh.

Then, dismissing Fergus, she looked at her sister. "Wanda Gail, don't wait till I send you to Dallas. Use the money I sent you the other day to buy you and your kids new clothes. And for crissake, do something with your hair. It looks like shit."

Wanda's eyes misted. "Thank you, thank you."

Nora Gail reached out to touch her sister's hand, but thought better of it and lit one of her black cigarettes instead. Through a dense cloud of acrid smoke, she replied, "You're welcome, sugar."

FORTY-FOUR

"Junior?"

He turned away from the bar, where he'd been mixing his second drink in ten minutes. "Good morning, Mother. Would you like a Bloody Mary?"

Sarah Jo crossed the room and yanked the bottle of vodka from his hand. "What's the matter with you?" she asked, speaking in a much harsher tone than she usually used with him. "Why are you drinking this early?"

"It's not that early, considering what time I got up."

"You went out. I heard you leave. Where'd you go?"

"I'd like to know that myself," Angus said, coming into the room. "I need to talk to you."

"Let me guess," Junior said with feigned cheerfulness, "it's about Judge Wallace."

"That's right."

"And my marriage to Stacey."

"Yes," Angus said reluctantly.

"I'll bet you're going to tell me why it was so all-fired important that I marry her when I did."

"It was for your own good."

"That much you told me twenty-five years ago. It was a trade-off, wasn't it? You got him to close Celina's murder case in exchange for my marriage to Stacey. Am I getting warm? Apparently, so was Alex. When she confronted the judge with her hypothesis, he killed himself."

Looking faint, Sarah Jo covered her mouth. Angus responded with anger. His hands flexed into fists at his sides. "It was the best thing to do at the time. I couldn't allow an in-depth investigation. To protect my family and my business, I had no choice but to ask the judge that favor."

"Did Stacey know about it?"

"Not from me. I doubt that Joe ever told her."

"Thank God for that." Junior dropped into a chair. His head hung dejectedly. "Dad, you know as well as I do that Gooney Bud was innocent."

"I know no such thing."

"Come on. He was harmless. You knew he didn't kill Celina, but you let him be punished for it. Why didn't you just let things take their natural course? In the long run, we'd all have been better off."

"You know that's not so, Junior."

"Do I?" He raised his head and looked at his parents with hot, intense eyes. "You know who Reede has in his bed this morning, looking all soft and sexy and satiated? Alex." He flopped back against the easy chair's cushions and rested his head. With a bitter, humorless laugh, he said, "Celina's *daughter*. Jesus, can you beat that?"

"Alex spent the night with Reede?" Angus thundered.

Sarah Jo made a sniffing sound of disgust. "That doesn't surprise me."

"Why didn't you keep it from happening, Junior?" Angus demanded.

Junior, sensing his father's rising temper, shouted, "I tried!"

"Evidently, not hard enough. It's your bed she's supposed to be in now, not Reede's."

"She's a grown woman. She didn't need my permission to go to bed with him. With anybody." Junior pushed himself out of the chair and headed for the bar.

Sarah Jo blocked his path. "I don't like the girl. She's as trashy as her mother, but if you wanted her for yourself, why did you let Reede Lambert have her?"

"It's more critical than that, Sarah Jo," Angus said tightly. "Our future rested on Alex's opinion of us. I was hoping she would become part of the family. As usual, Junior fell down on the job."

"Don't criticize him, Angus."

"Why the hell not? He's my son. I'll criticize him if I damn well feel like it." Then, curbing his impatience with her, he exhaled a heavy sigh. "Too late now to be bawling over spilled milk. We've got a bigger problem than Junior's love life. I'm afraid we're extremely vulnerable to prosecution." He left the room and slammed out the front door.

At the bar, Junior poured himself a straight vodka. Sarah Jo grabbed his arm as he raised the glass to his lips. "When are you going to learn that you're as good as Reede? *Better.* You've disappointed your father again. When are you going to do something to make him proud of you? Junior, my darling, it's time you grew up and seized the initiative for a change."

Alex stared at Reede with wordless disbelief. He calmly swept the spilled coffee grounds off the counter with the back of his hand and continued to fill the filtered basket of the coffee maker. Once it was dripping boiling coffee into the glass carafe, he turned to face her.

"You look like you've swallowed a marble. Isn't that what you expected to hear?"

"Is it true?" she asked hoarsely. "Did you kill her?"

He looked away, staring at nothing for several moments, then back into her eyes, penetrating them. "*No*, Alex. I did not kill Celina. If I had wanted to, I would have done it before that night, and with my bare hands. I would have felt that it was justifiable homicide. I wouldn't have gone to the trouble of stealing a scalpel. I sure as hell wouldn't have let that unfortunate retarded man take the rap for me."

She stepped into the circle of his arms and hugged him tight. "I believe you, Reede."

"Well, that's something, I guess." Holding her close, he moved his hands over her back. She nuzzled his chest.

He made a low sound of arousal, but set her away from him. "The coffee's ready."

"Don't push me away, please. I'm not ready to stop hugging."

"Neither am I," he said, stroking her cheek, "but hugging isn't all I want to do, and I have a strong feeling that our conversation isn't going to be conducive to romance." He poured two mugs of coffee and carried them to the table.

"Why do you say that?" She sat down across from him.

"Because you want to know if I know who went into the barn that night."

"Do you?"

"No, I don't," he said with an emphatic shake of his head. "I swear to God I don't."

"But you know it was either Junior or Angus."

He shrugged noncommittally.

"You've never wanted to know which, have you?"

"What difference does it make?"

She was aghast. "It makes a difference to me. It should to you."

"Why? Knowing won't change a damn thing. It won't bring Celina back. It won't alter your unhappy childhood or mine. Will it make your grandmother love you? No."

Reading her horrified expression, he said, "Yes, Alex, I know that's why you've appointed yourself Celina's avenger. Merle Graham always had to have a scapegoat. Whenever Celina did something she considered wrong, I usually caught the blame for it. 'That Lambert kid,' she used to call me, always with a sour expression on her face.

"So it doesn't surprise me that she laid a lifelong guilt trip on you. She wouldn't take the blame for Celina's mistakes upon herself. And she wouldn't admit that Celina, like every other human being ever to grace this earth, did what she damned well pleased when she damned well felt like it, with or without motivation. That left you, the only real innocent in this whole goddamned affair, to place the blame on."

He drew in a deep breath. "So, with all that in mind, what good can it possibly do anybody to know who killed her?"

"I've got to know, Reede," she said, close to tears. "The murderer was also a thief. He robbed me. My mother would have loved me if she had lived. I know she would have."

"For crissake, she didn't even want you, Alex," he shouted. "No more than my mother wanted me. I didn't go on any quests after her."

"Because you're afraid to," she yelled back.

"Afraid?"

"Afraid of being hurt by what you find out."

"Not afraid," he said. "Indifferent."

"Well, I'm not, thank God. I'm not as cold and unfeeling as you."

"You thought I was hot enough last night," he sneered. "Or did you stay a technical virgin this long by going down on all your dates?"

She flinched as if he'd struck her. Hurt beyond belief, she stared at him across the table. His expression was closed and hostile, but her vulnerability defeated him. He muttered a string of swear words and dug into his eye sockets with his thumb and middle finger.

"I'm sorry. That was uncalled for. It's just that you're so goddamn aggravating when it comes to this." He lowered his hand. His green eyes appealed to her. "Give it up, Alex. Relent."

"I can't."

"Won't."

She reached for his hand. "Reede, we're never going to agree on this, and I don't want to argue with you." Her face turned soft. "Not after last night."

"Some people would think that what went on in there," he said, indicating the living room, "would erase the past."

"Is that why you made it happen, hoping that I'd forgive and forget?"

He yanked his hand away. "You're dead set on pissing me off, aren't you?"

"No, I'm not trying to provoke you. Just please understand why I can't give up when I'm this close."

"I *don't* understand."

"Then just accept it. Help me."

"How? By pointing a finger at either my mentor or my best friend?"

"Junior didn't sound like a best friend a while ago."

"That was injured pride and jealousy talking."

"He was jealous the night Celina was killed, too. She had injured his pride. She turned down his marriage proposal because she was still in love with you. Could that have driven him to murder her?"

"Think about it, Alex," he said with annoyance. "If Junior did blow his top at her, would he have had that scalpel handy to start slashing? And do you honestly think, no matter how enraged he was, that Junior could kill anybody?"

"Then, it was Angus," she said softly.

"I don't know." Angrily, Reede slung himself out of his chair and began to pace. This was a familiar, haunting hypothesis. "Angus was against Junior marrying Celina."

"Angus is more volatile than Junior," she said, almost to herself. "I've seen him angry. I imagine that when he's crossed, he could be capable of killing, and he certainly took desperate measures to have the case closed before the evidence could come around to him."

"Where are you going?" Reede jerked to attention when she left her chair and headed toward the bedroom.

"I've got to talk to him."

"Alex!" He went after her. He rattled the knob of the bathroom door, but she'd locked it behind herself. "I don't want you to go over there."

"I've got to." She opened the door, already dressed, and stuck out her hand. "Can I borrow your Blazer?"

He stared at her hard. "You'll wreck his life. Have you thought of that?"

"Yes. And every time I feel a pang of regret, I remind myself of the lonely, loveless childhood I spent while he was prospering." She closed her eyes and pulled herself together. "I don't want to destroy Angus. I'm only doing my job, doing what's right. I actually like him. If circumstances were different, I could grow very fond of him. But the circumstances are what they are, and I can't change them. When a person does something wrong, he's got to be punished."

"All right." He grabbed her arm and drew her up close. "What's the punishment for a prosecutor sleeping with a suspect?"

"You're no longer a suspect."

"You didn't know that last night."

Furious, she wrested her arm free and ran through the house, grabbing his keys off the end table where she'd seen him drop them the night before.

Reede let her go and placed a call to his downtown office. Without preamble, he barked, "Get me a car out here on the double."

"They're all out, Sheriff. All except the Jeep."

"That'll do. Just get it here."

FORTY-FIVE

Stacey Wallace Minton shocked her friends by walking into the living room fully dressed, dry-eyed, and seemingly composed. They had been speaking in hushed tones in deference to her suffering. They had believed that she was getting some much-needed rest in preparation for the ordeal facing her.

Tupperware and Pyrex dishes, filled with salads and casseroles and desserts, had been delivered to the house by a steady stream of concerned acquaintances. Without exception, all had asked, "How's she taking it?"

By all appearances, Stacey was taking her father's death very well. As always, she was impeccably dressed and groomed. Except for the grayish circles beneath her eyes, she could have been on her way to a club meeting.

"Stacey, did we wake you? We put a note on the door, asking people to knock instead of ringing the bell."

"I've been awake for a while," she told her friends. "What time did Junior leave?"

"Sometime during the night. Would you like something to eat? Lordy, there's enough food in there to feed an army."

"No, thank you, nothing right now."

"Mr. Davis called. He needs to discuss the funeral arrangements with you, but said that could be at your convenience."

"I'll contact him later this morning."

As her friends watched in stupefaction, she went to the hall closet and took out her coat. They exchanged concerned and bewildered glances.

"Stacey, dear, where are you going?"

"Out."

"We'll be glad to run errands for you. That's what we're here for."

"I appreciate the offer, but this is something I've got to do myself."

"What are we supposed to tell people when they drop by to see you?" one asked, anxiously following her to the front door.

Stacey turned and calmly replied, "Tell them whatever you like."

Angus didn't seem surprised to see Alex when she walked into his den unannounced. He was seated on the leather sofa, massaging the toe that continued to give him pain. "I didn't hear you come in," he said. "I just got in from the stables myself. We've got a two-year-old gelding with shin bucks, which can't be a damn bit more painful than gout."

"Lupe told me you were back here."

"Do you want some breakfast? Coffee?"

"No, thank you, Angus." Hospitable to the bitter end, Alex thought. "Is this a convenient time for us to talk?"

He laughed. "As convenient a time as any, I reckon, considering what we're going to talk about." She sat down beside him on the sofa. He studied her with shrewd blue eyes. "Did Joe spill his guts before he killed himself?"

"He didn't invite me to his office to take a confession, if that's what you mean," she answered, "but I know about your deal with him. How did you talk Junior into going along with it, Angus?"

"At that point in time," he said, making no effort to deny her allegations, "the boy didn't care what happened to him. Celina's death hit him so hard, he was married to Joe's girl almost before he realized it. Know what? I'm not sure he could have made it those first few months if Stacey hadn't taken such good care of him. I never regretted making that deal with Joe."

"Who were you protecting?"

Changing the subject abruptly, he said, "You look a little worse for wear this morning. Did Reede ride you that hard last night?"

Embarrassed, Alex ducked her head. "Junior told you?"

"Yes." He pulled on his boot, wincing as he worked the sore toe into it. "Can't say that I'm surprised—disappointed, but not surprised."

She lifted her head. "Why?"

"Like mother, like daughter. Reede always had an edge over every other man with Celina. Who knows why? That's just the way it was. Chemistry, I think they call it nowadays." He set his foot on the floor and leaned back against the tufted sofa. "What's between you two?"

"It's more than chemistry."

"So, you love him?"

"Yes."

He drew a worried expression. "I'll caution you like a daddy would, Alex. Reede's not an easy man to love. He has a tough time showing affection, and an even tougher time of accepting it. As old as he is, he's still bitter about his mama up and leaving him when he was a baby."

"Is that why he found it impossible to forgive Celina for getting involved with Al Gaither and having me?"

"I think so. He tried not to let on like it hurt him. Walked around here with a chip on his shoulder as big as Texas. He hid his feelings behind that I-don't-give-a-damn veneer, but he was crushed just the same. I could tell. He didn't hold it against you, you understand, but he could never quite forgive your mother for cheating on him."

"What about Junior?"

"Junior couldn't forgive her for loving Reede more than she loved him."

"But neither one of them killed her." She met him eye to eye. "It was you, wasn't it?"

He stood up and moved to the window. He gazed out on all that he had built from nothing and was liable to lose. The ponderous silence in the room lasted for several minutes. Finally, he said, "No, I didn't." Then, turning slowly, he added, "But I wanted to."

"Why?"

"Your mother played games, Alex. She liked to. When I first met her, she was still a little tomboyish. Things might have gone fine if she'd stayed like that. But she grew older and realized that she had a power over both of those boys—sexual power. She began to use that in her games."

Alex's heart began to ache. She scarcely breathed. It was like watching a horror movie and waiting for the monster to finally rear his head. She wanted to see the whole picture, but yet, she didn't. It would probably be ugly.

"I could see it happening," Angus was saying, "but there wasn't much I could do about it. She played them against each other."

His words echoed what Nora Gail had told her. *The temptation was just too strong.*

"The older they got, the worse it got," Angus continued. "The solid friendship between the boys was like a shiny apple. Celina ate away at the core of it like a worm. I didn't like her very much." He returned to the sofa and sat down. "But I desired her."

When Alex was sure her ears hadn't deceived her, she couldn't hold back her gasp. *"What?"*

Angus smiled crookedly. "Remember, this was twenty-five years and thirty pounds ago. I didn't have this,'' he said, rubbing his protruding belly, ''and I had more hair. If I do say so, I was still considered a lady-killer.''

''It's not that I doubt your appeal, Angus, it's just that I had no idea—''

''Neither did anyone else. It was my little secret. Even she didn't know . . . until the night she died.''

Alex groaned his name. The monster of truth wasn't only ugly, it was hideous.

''Junior stormed out on his way to drown his sorrows in booze. Celina came into this room. She sat right there, where you're sitting now, and cried. She told me she didn't know what to do. She loved Reede in a way she'd never love another man. She loved Junior, but not enough to marry him. She didn't know how she was going to raise you alone. Every time she looked at you, she was reminded of the mistake that had changed her future forever.

''On and on she went, expecting me to sympathize, when all I could see was what a selfish little bitch she was. She'd brought all her hardships on herself. She didn't give a damn how she hurt other people or played with their lives. She only cared about how things affected her.''

He shook his head with self-derision. ''That didn't stop me from wanting her. I wanted her more than ever. I think I justified it to myself because I figured she deserved no better than lust from a horny old man like me.'' He took a deep breath. ''Anyway, I made my pitch.''

''You told her you . . . desired her?''

''I didn't come right out with it, no. I offered to set her up in a house out of town, someplace close. I told her I'd pay for everything. She wouldn't have to lift a finger, just be accommodating when I could come see her. I expected her to bring you along, of course, and Mrs. Graham, too, though I doubt your grandma would ever have agreed to it. In short,'' he concluded, ''I asked her to be my mistress.''

''What did she say?''

''Not a goddamn thing. She just looked at me for several seconds, and then she burst out laughing.'' His eyes chilled Alex to the bone when he added raspily, ''And you know how I hate having my ideas laughed at.''

''You filthy old son of a bitch.''

Simultaneously, they turned toward the intrusive voice. Junior, his face contorted with outrage, was standing in the open doorway. He pointed a shaking, accusatory finger at his father. ''You didn't want me to marry her because you wanted her for yourself! You killed her because she turned down your despicable proposal! You goddamn bastard, you killed her for that!''

The road seemed bumpier than usual. Or maybe she was just hitting all the ruts because her eyes were blurred with tears. Alex fought to keep the Blazer on the road to Reede's house.

When Junior had launched himself at Angus and begun to beat him with his fists, she had run from the room. She couldn't stand to watch. Her investigation had turned son against father, friend against friend, and she simply couldn't stand any more. She had fled.

They'd all been right. They'd tried to warn her, but she had refused to listen. Compelled by guilt, headstrong and fearless, armed to the teeth with an unshakable sense of right and wrong, cheered on by the recklessness of immaturity, she had excavated in forbidden territory and disturbed its sanctity. She had aroused the ire of bad spirits long laid to rest. Against sound counsel, she had kept digging. Now those spirits were protesting, making themselves manifest.

She had been brainwashed to believe that Celina was a fragile heroine, tragically struck down in the full bloom of womanhood, a heartbroken young widow with a newborn infant in her arms, looking out on the cruel world with dismay. Instead, she had been manipulative, selfish, and even cruel to the people who had loved her.

Merle had made her believe that she had been responsible for her mother's death. With every gesture, word, and deed, whether overt or implied, she had made Alex feel inadequate and at fault.

Well, Merle was wrong. Celina was responsible for her slaying. By an act of will, Alex unburdened herself of all guilt and remorse. She was free! It no longer really mattered to her whose hand had wielded that scalpel. It hadn't been because of her.

Her first thought was that she must share this sense of freedom with Reede. She parked the Blazer in front of his house, got out, and ran across the porch. At the door, she hesitated and knocked softly. After several seconds, she pulled it open and stepped inside. "Reede?" The house was gloomy and empty.

Moving toward the bedroom, she called his name again, but it was obvious that he wasn't there. As she turned, she noticed her handbag, lying forgotten on the nightstand. She checked the adjoining bathroom for items she might have left behind, gathered them up, and dropped them into her handbag.

As she snapped it closed, she thought she heard the familiar squeak of the screened front door. She paused and listened. "Reede?" The sound didn't come again.

Lost in sweet reverie of the night before, she touched Reede's things on the nightstand—a pair of sunglasses, a comb that was rarely used, an extra brass belt buckle with the state seal of Texas on it. Her heart swelling with love, she turned to go, but was brought up short.

The woman standing in the doorway of the bedroom had a knife in her hand.

FORTY-SIX

"**W**hat the hell is going on here?"

Reede grabbed Junior's collar and hauled him off Angus, who was sprawled on the floor. Blood was dribbling down his chin from a cut on his lip. Oddly enough, the old man was laughing.

"Where'd you learn to fight like that, boy, and why haven't you done it more often?" He sat up and extended his hand to Reede. "Help me up." Reede, after giving Junior a warning glance, let go of his collar and assisted Angus to his feet.

"One of you want to tell me what the devil that was all about?" Reede demanded.

When the Jeep had arrived, he had driven straight to the ranch house, where an anxious Lupe had greeted him at the door with the news that Mr. Minton and Junior were fighting.

Reede had run into the den and found the two men locked in combat, rolling on the floor. Junior had been throwing earnest, but largely ineffectual, punches at his father's head.

"He wanted Celina for himself," Junior declared, his chest heaving with exertion and fury. "I overheard him telling Alex. He wanted to set Celina up as his mistress. When she said no, he killed her."

Angus was calmly dabbing at the blood on his chin with a handkerchief. "Do you really believe that, son? Do you think I would sacrifice everything—your mother, you, this place—for that little chippy?"

"I heard you tell Alex that you wanted her."

"I did, from the belt down, but I didn't love her. I didn't like the way she came between you and Reede. I sure as hell wouldn't gamble away everything else in my life by killing her. I might have felt like it when she laughed at my offer, but I didn't." His eyes roved over both the younger men. "My pride was spared when one of you did it for me."

The three men exchanged uneasy glances. The past twenty-five years had dwindled down to this crucial moment. Until now, none of them had had the courage to pose the question. The truth would have been too painful to bear, so they had let the identity of the murderer remain a mystery.

Their silence had been tacitly agreed upon. It had protected them from knowing who had ended Celina's life. None had wanted to know.

"I did not kill that girl," Angus said. "As I told Alex, I gave her the keys to one of the cars and told her to drive herself home. The last time I saw her, she was leaving by the front door."

"I was upset because she turned me down," Junior said. "I made the rounds of the beer joints and got shit-faced. I don't remember where I was or who I was with. But I think I would remember slashing Celina to ribbons."

"When dessert was passed around I left," Reede told them. "I spent the night humping Nora Gail. I got to the stable about six that morning. That's when I found her."

Angus shook his head in bafflement. "Then everything we've told Alex is true."

"Alex?" Reede exclaimed. "Didn't you say she was just here?"

"Dad was talking to her when I came in."

"Where is she now?"

"She was sitting right there," Angus said, pointing at the empty spot on the sofa. "I didn't see anything after Junior came sailing toward me and knocked me down. Felt like a goddamn bull falling on me," he said, jovially socking his son beneath the chin. Junior grinned with boyish pleasure.

"Would you two cut it out and tell me where Alex went?"

"Calm down, Reede. She's gotta be around here somewhere."

"I didn't see her when I came in," he argued stubbornly as he rushed into the hall.

"It couldn't have been but a couple of minutes in between," Junior said. "Why are you so anxious about—"

"Don't you get it?" Reede asked over his shoulder. "If none of us killed Celina, whoever did is still out there, and he's just as pissed off at Alex as we've been."

"Jesus, I didn't think—"

"You're right, Reede."

"Come on."

The three men rushed through the front door. As they were clambering down the steps, Stacey Wallace wheeled into the drive and stepped out of her car.

"Junior, Angus, Reede, I'm glad I caught you. It's about Alex."

Reede drove the Jeep like a bat out of hell. At the crossroads of the highway and the Mintons' private road, he caught up with the deputies who had delivered him the Jeep and flagged down the patrol car.

"Have you seen my Blazer?" he shouted to them. "Alex Gaither was driving it."

"Yeah, Reede, we did. She was headed back toward your place."

"Much obliged." To his passengers he shouted, "Hang on," and executed a hairpin turn.

"What's going on?" Stacey asked. The Jeep's top was off, so she was clinging to the roll bar for dear life. In her staid world, nothing this death-defying had ever happened.

Trying to detain the Mintons and Reede had been impossible. They had almost mowed her down in their haste to scramble into the Jeep. She'd been summarily told that if she must speak with them right then, she had to go along. She had climbed into the backseat with Junior, while Angus sat in the front seat, next to Reede.

"Alex could be in danger," Junior shouted into Stacey's ear to make himself heard. The cold north wind sucked the words out of his mouth.

"Danger?"

"It's a long story."

"I went to her motel," Stacey shouted. "The desk clerk told me she might be at the ranch."

"What's so important?" Reede asked over his shoulder.

"I didn't get everything off my chest last night. She didn't hold the pistol or pull the trigger, but she caused Daddy's suicide."

Junior placed his arm around her, drew her close, and kissed her temple. "Stacey, let it drop. Alex isn't the reason Joe killed himself."

"It's not just that," Stacey said, distraught. "Her investigation has raised questions about . . . well, we got married so soon after Celina got killed. People thought . . . you know how suspicious and narrow-minded they can be. They're talking about it again." She gazed up at him imploringly. "Junior, why did you marry me?"

He placed a finger beneath her chin. "Because you're a beautiful, dynamic woman, the best damn thing that ever happened to me, Stacey," he said, meaning it. He couldn't love her, but he appreciated her kindness and goodness, and her unflagging love for him.

"Then, you do love me a little?"

He smiled down at her and, for her sake, said, "Hell, girl, I love you a lot."

Her eyes glistened with tears. The radiance with which her face shone made her almost pretty. "Thank you, Junior."

Angus suddenly leaned forward and pointed toward the horizon. "My God, that looks like—"

"Smoke," Reede grimly supplied, and floored the accelerator.

FORTY-SEVEN

"Sarah Jo!" Alex cried. "What on earth are you doing?"

Sarah Jo smiled placidly. "I followed you here from my house."

"Why?"

Alex's eyes were on the knife. It was an ordinary kitchen knife, but it didn't look at all ordinary in Sarah Jo's hand. Always before, her hand had looked feminine and frail. Now it looked skeletal and ominous around the handle of the knife.

"I came to rid my life of another nuisance." Her eyes opened wide, then narrowed. "Just like I did back in Kentucky. My brother got the colt I wanted. It wasn't fair. I had to get rid of him and that colt, or I could never be happy again.''

"What . . . what did you do?''

"I lured him into the stable by telling him the colt had colic. Then, I locked the door and started the fire.''

Alex swayed in terror. "How horrible.''

"Yes, it was, actually. You could smell burning horseflesh for miles. The stench hung on for days.''

Alex raised a trembling hand to her lips. The woman was obviously psychotic, and therefore, all the more terrifying.

"I didn't have to start a fire the night I murdered Celina.''

"Why not?''

"That idiot man, Gooney Bud, had followed her to the ranch. I met him on my way out of the stable. He scared the living daylights out of me, standing there in the shadows so quiet. He went in and saw her. He fell down on top of her and started carrying on something awful. I saw him pick up Dr. Collins's knife.'' She smiled gleefully. "That's when I knew I wouldn't have to start a fire and destroy all those lovely horses.''

"You killed my mother,'' Alex stated tearfully. "You killed my mother.''

"She was a trashy girl.'' Sarah Jo's expression changed drastically, becoming spiteful. "I prayed every night that she would marry Reede Lambert. That way, I'd get both of them out of my life. Angus didn't need but one son, the one I gave him,'' she cried, thumping her chest with her free fist. "Why did he have to keep that mongrel around?''

"What did that have to do with Celina?''

"That stupid girl let herself get pregnant. Reede wouldn't have her after that.'' She clenched her teeth, distorting her delicate features. "And I had to watch when Junior stepped in to take Reede's place. He actually wanted to marry her. Imagine a Presley marrying a lowlife with an illegitimate baby. I wasn't going to let my son ruin his life.''

"So, you looked for an opportunity to kill her.''

"She dropped it into my lap. Junior left the house that night, disconsolate. Then, Angus made a complete fool of himself over her.''

"You overheard their conversation?''

"I eavesdropped.''

"And you were jealous?''

"Jealous?'' she said with a musical little laugh. "Good heavens, no. Angus has had other women for almost as long as we've been married. I might not even have minded him having Celina, so long as he set her up out of town and away from Junior. But that silly bitch laughed at him—laughed in my husband's face after he had poured out his heart to her!''

Her eyes were blinking rapidly now, and her meager breasts were rising and falling with each strenuous breath. Her voice had grown shrill. Alex knew that if she was going to talk herself out of this, she had to tread softly. She was still trying to choose her next words when she caught the first whiff of smoke.

Her eyes moved beyond Sarah Jo to the hall. It was filling with smoke. Flames were licking up the walls of the living room beyond.

"Sarah Jo,'' Alex said in a quavering voice, "I want to talk to you about this, but—''

"Stay where you are!'' Sarah Jo commanded sharply, brandishing the knife when Alex took a hesitant step. "You came here and started causing trouble, just like her. You favor Reede over my Junior. You're breaking his heart. Angus is upset and worried over Joe Wallace's death, which is all your fault. You see, Angus thought one of the boys killed her.''

She smiled impishly. ''I knew he would. I knew that the boys wouldn't ask any questions, either. I depended on their loyalty to each other. It was the perfect crime. Angus, thinking he was protecting the boys, made his deal with the judge. I hated that Junior had to get married so young, but I was glad it was to Stacey rather than Celina.''

The smoke was growing thicker. It was swirling around Sarah Jo, though she seemed unaware of it. ''You started asking too many questions,'' she told Alex, drawing a sad face. ''I tried to scare you off with that letter. I made it look like it had come from that crazy Reverend Plummet, but I sent it.'' She seemed quite pleased with herself. Alex used her complacency to creep forward, moving slowly, one step at a time.

''You still didn't take the hint, so I ran you off the road with one of the company pickups. Judge Wallace would probably still be alive, and the deal Angus made with him would still be a secret, if only you had died when your car crashed.'' She seemed genuinely perturbed. ''But, after today, I won't have to—''

Alex lunged forward and struck Sarah Jo's wrist. She was stronger than she appeared. She managed to maintain her grip on the knife. Alex grabbed her wrist and hung on, trying to dodge the stabbing motions aimed toward her body.

''I won't let you destroy my family,'' Sarah Jo grunted as she plunged the knife toward Alex's midsection.

The two women struggled over control of the knife. They fell to their knees. Alex tried to dodge the downward arcs of the blade, but the smoke was getting too thick for her to see it well. Her eyes filled with tears. She began to choke. Sarah Jo knocked her into the wall. Upon impact, she felt the stitches in her scalp pop open.

Somehow, she managed to get to her feet, and began dragging Sarah Jo down the hallway, where smoke was billowing around them. All the rules of fire escape fled Alex's mind. She tried to hold her breath, but her lungs demanded oxygen for the difficult task of pulling Sarah Jo along with her.

They had almost reached the living room before Sarah Jo realized that Alex had gained the upper hand. She renewed her efforts and came back stronger than ever. The knife slashed Alex's ankle and she screamed. Its serrated edge caught her again in the calf, and she staggered back toward the living room.

Suddenly, she lost her grip on Sarah Jo. While seconds ago, she'd been fighting for her freedom, she now panicked at the thought of losing her attacker in the suffocating black smoke. It was so thick that she couldn't even distinguish an outline of the other woman.

''Sarah Jo! Where are you?'' Alex gagged on a mouthful of smoke. Stretching her arms far out in front of her, she groped for the woman, but touched nothing except the searing air.

Then, survival instincts took over. She turned, ducked, and plunged through the hallway. In the living room, she dodged burning furniture and ran blindly in the direction of the door. The door was intact, but smoldering. She grabbed the knob; it branded the palm of her hand.

Screaming in fear and pain, she barreled through the door and out onto the porch.

''Alex!''

She stumbled in the direction of Reede's voice and saw through smoke-damaged eyes the wavering image of a Jeep coming to a screeching halt only yards in front of her.

"Reede," she croaked, reaching for him. She fell. He leaped from behind the steering wheel and bent over her. "Sarah Jo," she wheezed. With an effort, she raised her hand and pointed toward the house.

"My God, Mother!" Junior went over the side of the Jeep and hit the ground at a run.

"Junior, come back!" Stacey screamed. "No, God, no!"

"Son, don't!" Angus reached for Junior's arm as he sped past. "It's too late!"

Reede was already on the porch when Junior knocked him aside. Reede fell backward down the steps and onto the ground. He made an unsuccessful grab for Junior's ankle. "Junior, you can't!" he roared.

Junior turned and looked down at him. "This time, Reede, I'll get the glory."

He flashed Reede his most beautiful smile, then ran into the burning house.

EPILOGUE

"I thought you might be here."

Reede gave no impression of having heard Alex approach until she spoke to him. He glanced at her over his shoulder, then back at the two fresh graves. For a moment, there was an awkward silence, then he said, "I promised Angus I would come out every day to check on things. He's not feeling quite up to it yet."

Alex moved nearer. "I stopped by to see him this afternoon. He made a feeble attempt to be the hale fellow well met," she remarked sadly. "He's entitled to grieve. I told him so. I hope he took it to heart."

"I'm sure he appreciated your visit."

"I'm not so sure." Reede came around to face her. She nervously swept back her hair, which the strong wind was blowing across her face. "If I'd never come here, never reopened the case—"

"Don't do that to yourself again, Alex," he said fiercely. "None of it was your fault. Nobody guessed the extent of Sarah Jo's insanity, not even Angus, and he was married to her. Junior. . . . Well. . . ." He stopped speaking, his throat working convulsively.

"You'll miss him."

"Miss him?" he repeated with phony nonchalance. "The dumb bastard. Running into a burning house about to collapse. Only a goddamn fool would do something that stupid."

"You know why he did it, Reede. He felt he had to." The tears shimmering in his eyes made Alex's throat ache with the need to cry. She stepped forward and laid a hand on his arm. "You loved him, Reede. Is that so hard to admit?"

He stared down at the flower-banked grave. "People always talked about how jealous he was of me. Nobody ever guessed how jealous I was of him."

"You were jealous of Junior?"

He nodded. "Of the advantages he had." He gave a dry, derisive laugh. "I stayed mad at him most of the time for squandering those advantages."

"We love people in spite of what they are, not because of what they are. At least, that's the way it should be."

She dropped her hand from his arm and, trying to keep her voice light and conversational, said, "Angus told me that he plans to go ahead with the race-track."

"Yeah. He's a stubborn old cuss."

"Your airfield will prosper."

"It better. I'll be out of a job by the end of the year," he told her. In response to her puzzled expression, he said, "I resigned. I can't sheriff and make anything out of that airport at the same time. It was time I either tackled it or let it go. I decided to tackle it."

"Good. I'm glad for you. Angus says you're considering incorporating with him."

"We'll see. I'm going to buy another racehorse with Double Time's insurance money. I'm thinking about training it myself. Angus wants to help."

She wasn't fooled by his casual treatment of the subject, but she didn't pressure him about it. If she were a gambler, she'd put her money on a future alliance. This time it would be for Angus's benefit more than Reede's.

"What about you?" he asked. "When will you be going back to work?"

She dug her hands into her coat pockets and drew her shoulders up. "I'm not sure. In light of my injuries—"

"How are they, by the way?"

"Everything's healing fine."

"No pain?"

"Not any longer. Basically, I'm as good as new, but Greg told me not to rush back to work. He knows the strain I've been under." She plowed into the soft earth with the toe of her boot. "I'm not sure I want to go back at all." Sensing his start of surprise, she smiled up at him. "You'll find this amusing, Sheriff. I've recently realized how much empathy I have for the accused. I might try defense law for a change."

"Public defender?"

"Possibly."

"Where?"

She looked deeply into his eyes. "I haven't decided."

Reede began to rearrange the freshly turned earth beneath his boots, too. "I, uh, I read your statement in the newspaper. It was decent of you to close the case for lack of evidence," he said in a low voice.

"It really wouldn't serve much purpose to quarrel with the original ruling, would it?"

"No, it wouldn't, especially not now."

"Probably from the beginning, Reede." He raised his head and gave her an appraising look. "You were right, all of you. This investigation was self-serving. I used it and the people involved to prove my grandmother wrong." She drew a shaky breath. "It's too late for Celina to rectify her mistakes, but I can certainly do something about mine."

She inclined her head toward the nearby grave, the older, overgrown one, which now had a single red rose lying at the base of the headstone. "Did you put that there?"

Reede looked across the two fresh graves toward Celina's. "I thought Junior would like sharing a flower with her. You know how he felt about the ladies." It was healthy that he could smile when he said it.

"You know, I didn't realize that this was the Minton family plot until the funeral the other day. Mother would like that, being here with him."

"And he's where he always wanted to be. Near Celina, with nobody between them."

Emotion welled up in Alex's throat and eyes. "Poor Stacey. She never had a chance with Junior, did she?"

"No woman did. For all his philandering, Junior was a one-woman man."

By tacit agreement, they turned and started down the hill toward their cars.

"Was it your idea for Stacey to move into the ranch house for a while?" Alex asked, as she picked her way across the grass.

He seemed reluctant to admit it. An affirmative rolling motion of his shoulders was all he gave her for an answer.

"That was a thoughtful suggestion, Reede. She and Angus will be good for each other." The late judge's daughter would never feel kindly toward her, but Alex understood and could forgive her animosity.

"Stacey needs somebody to fuss over," Reede said, "and Angus needs that kind of attention right now."

Having reached her car, Alex turned to him and asked huskily, "What about you? Who'll fuss over you?"

"I've never needed it."

"Oh, yes, you have," she said, "you just never let anybody." She took a step closer to him. "Are you going to let me leave town, walk out of your life, without making any effort to stop me?"

"Yes."

She regarded him with love and frustration. "Okay, I'll tell you what, Reede. I'll just go on loving you for as long as I live, and you just go on resisting it." It was spoken as a dare. "See how long you can hold out."

He angled back his head and gauged the determination in her posture, her voice, her eyes. "You're too big for your britches, you know that?"

Her responding smile was tremulous. "You love me, Reede Lambert. I know you love me."

The wind lifted the tawny hair on his head as he nodded slowly. "Yeah, I do. You're a pain in the ass, but I love you." He cursed beneath his breath. "That still doesn't change anything."

"Like what?"

"Like our ages. I'll get old and die long before you, you know."

"Does that matter today—this very minute?"

"It sure as hell should."

"It doesn't."

Infuriated by her calm logic, he crammed his fist into his opposite palm. "God, you're persistent."

"Yes, I am. When I want something badly enough, when I feel that it's right, I never give up."

For several long moments he stared at her, at war with himself. He was being offered love, but he was afraid to accept it. Then, swearing liberally, he grabbed a handful of dark auburn hair and pulled her toward him.

He reached inside her coat, where she was warm and soft and giving. "You make a damn strong argument, Counselor," he growled.

Backing her into the side of the car, he touched her heart, her belly, then placed a hand on her hip and bowed her body against his. He kissed her with passion and love and something he'd always had very little of—hope.

Breathlessly tearing his lips from hers, he buried his face in the warmth of her neck. "In my whole life, I've never had anything that belonged to me first, that wasn't a hand-me-down or a handout—nothing, until you. Alex, Alex. . . ."

"Say it, Reede."

"Be my woman."

SLOW HEAT
IN HEAVEN

~~≫ ONE

A t first she wasn't sure he was real.

    She had been dozing. Her head rested on her bent arm, which had gone to sleep and had started to tingle. She woke up and opened her eyes, then stretched languorously and turned her head. That's when she saw him. She immediately forgot her discomfort.

She thought he was a trick of her unfocused eyes or a product of late afternoon drowsiness and midsummer ennui. She blinked several times. The image remained.

The outline of his body was as detailed as a silhouette cut out of black construction paper with tiny manicure scissors. It was cast against a showoff sun that was making one hell of an exit. The horizon was as gaudily striped as a sultan's turban. It boasted every vibrant hue ranging from vermilion to gold.

Like the pines, he was motionless. The trees stood as majestic and tall as sentinels. Their spiky branches were still. There wasn't a breath of breeze. Above from where Schyler lay, Spanish moss drooped from the sprawling limbs of the live oak, looking more desolate than usual, mourning the unrelenting humid heat.

The unmoving form was undeniably male. So was the stance. Ah, yes, his stance was definitely, arrogantly masculine. One knee was bent, throwing his hip slightly off center.

It was intimidating to wake up from a nap and discover someone standing not twenty yards away watching you with the silence and patience of a predator. It was doubly disconcerting to find that that someone was a self-assured and cocky male who clearly saw you as the trespasser.

Most disturbing was the garden hoe that lay across his shoulders. It appeared innocuous. His wrists were hooked over the handle, his hands dangling carelessly. On the streets of London, a man carrying a garden hoe across his shoulders would attract attention. In rural Louisiana during the summertime, it was a common sight.

But there wasn't so much as an onion patch on this section of Belle Terre. The fields where sharecroppers cultivated vegetables were miles away. So Schyler had reason to be alarmed. The sun was going down, she was alone and, relatively speaking, a long way from the house.

She should challenge him, demand to know who he was and what he was doing on her property. But she said nothing, perhaps because he looked more a part of Belle Terre than she did. He blended into the landscape, was one with it. By comparison, she seemed out of place and conspicuous.

She didn't know how long they had been staring at each other. At least she thought they were staring at each other. She couldn't distinguish his face, much less tell what he was looking at so intently. But instinct told her he was watching her and that he had been for quite some time. That unnerving thought goaded her to act. She sat up.

He started toward her.

His footsteps hardly rustled the ankle-deep grass. Moving silently and sinuously, he slid the hoe off his shoulders and gripped the long handle with both hands.

All the self-defense instructions Schyler had ever heard burrowed cowardly into the farthest corners of her mind. She couldn't move, couldn't speak. She tried to suck in a deep breath so she could scream, but the air was as dense as quicksand.

Instinctively she shrank against the massive tree trunk and shut her eyes tightly. Her last impression was that of the sharpened blade of the hoe. It glinted in the remnant rays of sunlight as it made its swift, downward arc, making a thunking sound when it landed. She waited for the agonizing pain to assault her before she keeled over dead. But it never came.

"Get your nap out, *pichouette*?"

Schyler blinked her eyes open, amazed that she was still alive. "What?"

"Get your nap out, Miss Schyler?"

She shaded her eyes against the brilliant sunset, but she still couldn't distinguish his face. He knew her name. His first language had been a Cajun dialect. Other than that, she didn't have a clue as to who he was.

Snakes slithered out of the bayous. She'd been taught from infancy to consider all of them poisonous. That reasoning seemed to apply to this situation.

The thunking sound had been made by the sharp blade when it bit into the grass. The man was leaning on the hoe now, both hands innocently folded over the blunt end of the handle. His chin was propped on them. But his benign stance made him no less dangerous.

"How do you know me?" she asked.

A pair of saturnine lips cracked open briefly. The fleeting facial expression wasn't a bona fide smile. It was too sardonic to pass for genuine.

"Why, it's common knowledge around Laurent Parish that Miss Schyler Crandall has come home from Londontown."

"Only temporarily and only because of my father's heart attack."

He shrugged, supremely indifferent to her comings and goings. Turning his head, he glanced at the rapidly sinking sun. His eyes reflected it like the motionless waters of a bayou when sunlight strikes it at the right angle. At that time of day the surface of the water looks as solid and impenetrable as brass. So did his eyes.

"I don't repeat gossip, Miss Schyler. I only listen to it. And I only pay attention when I hear something that could affect me."

"What are you doing here?"

His head came back around. "Watching you sleep."

"Before that," she said sharply.

"Gathering roots." He slapped the small leather pouch attached to his belt.

"Roots?" His answer made absolutely no sense, and his cavalier attitude irritated her. "What kind of roots?"

"Doesn't matter. You've never heard of them."

"You're trespassing on private property. You've got no business on Belle Terre."

Insects hummed noisily in the silence that followed. His eyes never wavered from her face. When he answered, his voice was as soft and elusive as the wished for breeze. "Oh, but I do, *pichouette*. Belle Terre is my home."

Schyler stared up at him. "Who are you?"

"You don't remember?"

Comprehension dawned. "Boudreaux?" she whispered. Then she swallowed hard, not really relieved to know who she was talking to. "Cash Boudreaux?"

"*Bien*! You recognize me now."

"No. No, I didn't. The sun's in my eyes. And it's been years since I've seen you."

"And then you had good reason not to remember." He grunted with amused satisfaction when she had the grace to look away, embarrassed. "If you didn't recognize me, how did you know who I was?"

"You're the only person living on Belle Terre who isn't . . ."

"A Crandall."

She ducked her head slightly, nervous at being alone with Cash Boudreaux. For as long as she could remember, her father had forbidden her sister Tricia and her to even speak to him.

His mother was the mysterious Cajun woman, Monique Boudreaux, who lived in a shanty on Laurent Bayou that wound in and about the forested acreage of Belle Terre. As a boy, Cash had had access to the outlying areas but had never been allowed to come this close to the house. Not wanting to take issue with that just yet, Schyler asked politely, "Your mother, how is she?"

"She died."

His blunt reply startled her. Boudreaux's face was inscrutable in the descending twilight. But had it been high noon, Schyler doubted his features would have given away what he was thinking. He'd never had a reputation for being loquacious. The same aura of mystery that cloaked his mother had cloaked him.

"I didn't know."

"It was several years ago."

Schyler swatted a mosquito that landed on the side of her neck. "I'm sorry."

"You'd better get yourself home. The mosquitoes will eat you alive."

He extended his hand down to her. She regarded it as something dangerous and was as loath to touch it as she would be to reach out and pet a water moccasin. But it would be unspeakably rude not to let him assist her to her feet. Once before she had trusted him. She hadn't come to any harm then.

She laid her hand in his. His palm felt as tough as leather and she felt raised calluses at the bases of his fingers that closed warmly around her hand. As soon as she was on her feet she withdrew her hand from his.

Busily dusting off the back of her skirt to cover the awkward moment, she said, "Last I heard of you, you were just out of Fort Polk and on your way to Vietnam." He said nothing. She looked up at him. "Did you go?"

"*Oui*."

"That was a long time ago."

"Not long enough."

"Uh, well, I'm glad you made it back. The parish lost several boys over there."

He shrugged. "Guess I was a better fighter." His lip curled into a facsimile of a smile. "But then I always had to be."

She wasn't about to address that. In fact, she was trying to think of something to say that would graciously terminate this uncomfortable conversation. Before she did, Cash Boudreaux raised his hand to her neck and brushed away a mosquito that was looking for a sumptuous spot to have dinner.

The backs of Cash's fingers were rough, but their touch was delicate as they whisked across her exposed throat and down her chest. He looked for her reaction with frank interest. His gaze was sexual. He knew exactly what he was doing. He had brazenly committed the unpardonable. Cash Boudreaux had touched Schyler Crandall . . . and was daring her to complain about it.

He said, "They know the best places to bite."

Schyler pretended to be unmoved by his insinuating stare. She said, "You're as ornery as ever, aren't you?"

"I wouldn't want to disappoint you by changing."

"I couldn't care less."

"You never did."

Feeling severely put down, Schyler stiffened her posture. "I need to get back to the house. It's suppertime. Good seeing you, Mr. Boudreaux."

"How is he?"

"Who? My daddy?" He nodded curtly. Schyler's shoulders relaxed a degree. "I haven't seen him today. I'm going to the hospital after supper. I spoke with one of his nurses by telephone this morning who said he'd had a comfortable night." Emotion dropped her voice to a husky pitch. "These days even that is something to be grateful for." Then in her most refined, Sunday-company voice she said, "I'll tell him you inquired, Mr. Boudreaux."

Boudreaux's laugh was sudden and harsh. It startled a bird into flight from the top of the live oak. "I don't think that'd be a very good idea. Not unless you want the old man to croak."

If her swift calculations were correct, Cash Boudreaux was approaching forty, so he should have known better than to say something so flippant about a seriously ill man. His manners hadn't improved with maturity. He was as coarse, as rude, as undisciplined as he'd been in his youth. His mother had exercised no control over him whatsoever. She had let him run wild. He was constantly into mischief that had ceased to be cute by the time he reached junior high school, where he fast became the scourge of the public school system. Heaven, Louisiana had never spawned such a hellraiser as Cash Boudreaux.

"I'll say good evening, then, Mr. Boudreaux."

He executed a clipped little bow. "Good evening, Miss Schyler."

She gave him a cool nod, more characteristic of her sister than of her, and turned in the direction of the house. She was aware of him watching her. As soon as she was a safe distance away and beneath the deep shadows of the trees, she glanced back.

He had propped himself against the trunk of the live oak, which half a dozen men standing hand to hand couldn't span. She saw a match spark and flare in the darkness. Boudreaux's lean face was briefly illuminated when he lifted the match to the tip of his cigarette. He fanned out the match. The scent of sulfur rode the currents of Gulf humidity until it reached Schyler's hiding place.

Boudreaux drew deeply on the cigarette. The end of it glowed hot and red, like a single eye blinking out of the depths of hell.

 TWO

Schyler slipped through the trees, stumbling over dense undergrowth in her hurry to reach the security of the house. On the creaky footbridge, her head was engulfed by a buzzing cloud of mosquitoes. The bridge spanned the shallow creek that separated the woods from the manicured lawn surrounding the house with a neat apron.

Reaching the emerald carpet of thick St. Augustine grass, Schyler paused to regain her breath. The night air was as heavily perfumed as a Bourbon Street hooker. Honeysuckle lined the banks of the creek. Gardenias were blooming somewhere nearby, as well as wild roses, waxleaf ligustrum, and magnolia trees.

Schyler cataloged the individual smells. They were resurrected out of her childhood, each attached to its special memory. The scents were achingly familiar, though she was long past childhood and hadn't set foot on Belle Terre in six years.

No English garden smelled like this, like home, like Belle Terre. Nothing did. If she were blindfolded and dropped into Belle Terre, she would recognize it immediately by sound and scent.

The nightly choir of bullfrogs and crickets was warming up. The bass section reverberated from the swampy creek bottom, the soprano section from overhead branches. Out on the spur, a mile or so away, a freight train's whistle hooted. No sound was as sad.

Schyler, closing her eyes and leaning against the rough bark of a loblolly pine, let the sensations seep into her. She crossed her arms over her chest and hugged herself, almost afraid that when she opened her eyes she would awaken from a dream to find that she wasn't at Belle Terre in the full bloom of summer, but in London, shrouded in a cold, winter mist.

But when she opened her eyes she saw the house. As pure and white as a sugar cube, it stood serenely in the heart of the clearing, dominating it like the center gem in a tiara.

Yellow lamplight, made diffuse by the screens, poured from the windows and spilled out onto the deep veranda. Along the edge of the porch were six columns, three on each side of the front door. They supported a second-story balcony. It wasn't a real balcony, only a facade. Tricia frequently and peevishly pointed that out. But Schyler loved it anyway. In her opinion the phony balcony was necessary to the symmetry of the design.

The veranda wrapped around all four sides of the house. It was enclosed with screens in back, made into what had once been called a sleeping porch. Schyler remembered hearing her mother, Macy, talking about the good times she'd had there as a child when all her Laurent cousins would sleep on pallets during family get-togethers.

Personally Schyler had always preferred the open veranda. Wicker chairs, painted white to match the house, were strategically placed so that whoever sat in one might enjoy a particular view of the lawn. There were no eyesores. Each view was worthy of a picture postcard.

The porch swing that Cotton had suspended for Tricia and Schyler to play on was in one corner of the veranda. Twin Boston ferns, each as plush as a dozen feather dusters tied together, grew out of matching urns on either side of the front door. Veda had been so proud of those ferns and had fussed over them endlessly, scolding anyone who brushed past them too quickly and too close. She took it as a personal injury if a cherished frond was torn off by a careless passerby.

Macy was no longer at Belle Terre. Nor was Veda. And Cotton's life hung in the balance at St. John's Hospital. The only thing that remained unchanged and seemingly eternal was the house itself. Belle Terre.

Schyler whispered the name like a prayer as she pushed herself away from the tree. Indulging a whim, she paused long enough to slip off her sandals before continuing barefoot across the cool, damp grass that the automatic sprinkler had watered that afternoon.

When she stepped off the grass onto the crushed shell drive, she winced at the pain. But it was a pleasant discomfort and evoked other childhood memories. Running down the shell drive barefooted for the first time each season had been an annual rite of spring. Having worn shoes and socks all winter, her feet would be tender. Once it was warm enough and Veda had granted permission, the shoes and socks came off. It always took several days for the soles of her feet to toughen so that she could make it all the way to the public road without having to stop.

The sound and feel of the shell drive was familiar. So was the squeak as she pulled open the screened front door. It slapped closed behind her as she knew it would. Belle Terre never changed. It was home.

And then it wasn't. Not anymore. Not since Ken and Tricia had made it their home.

They were already in the dining room, seated at the long table. Her sister set down her tumbler of bourbon and water. "We've been waiting, Schyler," Tricia said with exasperation.

"I'm sorry. I went for a walk and lost all track of time."

"No problem, Schyler," Ken Howell said. "We haven't been waiting long." Her brother-in-law smiled at her from the sideboard where he was topping off his glass from a crystal decanter of bourbon. "Can I pour you something?"

"Gin and tonic, please. Heavy on the ice. It's hot out."

"It's stifling." Crossly, Tricia fanned her face with her stiff linen napkin. "I told Ken to reset the thermostat on the air conditioner. Daddy's such a fussbudget about the electric bill. He keeps us sweltering all summer. As long as he's not here, we might as well be comfortable. But it takes forever for this old house to cool down. Cheers." She tipped her glass in Schyler's direction when Ken handed her the drink.

"Is it all right?"

Schyler sipped from her drink but didn't quite meet Ken's eyes as she replied, "Perfect. Thanks."

"Ken, before you sit back down, please tell Mrs. Graves that Schyler finally put in an appearance and we're ready to be served."

Tricia waved him toward the door that connected the formal dining room with the kitchen. He shot her a resentful look but did as he was told. When Schyler dropped her sandals beside her chair, Tricia said, "Honestly, Schyler, you haven't been home but a few days and already you're resuming the bad habits that nearly drove Mama crazy up until the day she died. You're not going to sit at the dinner table barefooted, are you?"

Tricia was already aggravated with her for holding up dinner. To maintain peace, Schyler bent down and put her sandals back on. "I can't understand why you don't like to go barefooted."

"I can't understand why you do." Though Michelangelo could have painted Tricia's smile on an angel, she was being nasty. "Obviously there's some aristocratic blood in my heritage that is grossly lacking in yours."

"Obviously," Schyler said with rancor. She sipped from her drink, appreciating the gin's icy bite and the lime's tart sting.

"Doesn't that ever bother you?" Tricia asked.

"What?"

"Not knowing your background. Sometimes you behave with no better manners than white trash. That must mean that your folks were sorry as the day is long."

"Tricia, for God's sake," Ken interrupted with annoyance. Returning from his errand in the kitchen, he slid into the chair across the table from his wife. "Let it drop. What the hell difference does it make?"

"I think it makes a lot of difference."

"The important thing is what you do with your life, not who gave it to you. Agreed, Schyler?"

"I never think about my birth parents," Schyler replied. "Oh, I did now and then when I was growing up, whenever I had my feelings hurt or was scolded or—''

"Scolded?" Tricia repeated with disbelief. "I don't recall a single time. Exactly when was that, Schyler?"

Schyler ignored her and continued. "I'd get to feeling sorry for myself and think that if my real parents hadn't given me up for adoption, I would have had a much better life." She smiled wistfully. "I wouldn't have, of course."

"How do you know?" Tricia's sculptured fingernail lazily twirled an ice cube inside the tumbler, then she sucked her fingertip dry. "I'm convinced that my mother was a wealthy society girl. Her mean old parents made her give me up out of jealousy and spite. My father was probably someone who loved and adored her passionately but couldn't marry her because his shrewish wife wouldn't divorce him."

"You've been watching too many soap operas," Ken said with a droll smile, which he cast in Schyler's direction. She smiled back.

Tricia's eyes narrowed. "Don't make fun of me, Ken."

"If you're convinced that your birth parents were so wonderful, why haven't you tracked them down?" he asked. "As I recall, Cotton even encouraged you to."

Tricia smoothed the napkin in her lap. "Because I wouldn't want to upset their lives or cause them any embarrassment."

"Or because you might find out they aren't so wonderful. You couldn't stand to eat that much crow." Ken took a final drink from his highball glass and returned it to the table with the smugness of a gambler laying down the winning ace.

"Well if they weren't rich," Tricia snapped, "at least I know they weren't trashy, which I'm sure Schyler's real parents were." Then she smiled sweetly and reached across the table for Schyler's hand. "I hope I didn't hurt your feelings, Schyler."

"No. You didn't. Where I came from never mattered to me. Not like it did to you. I'm just glad that I became a Crandall through adoption."

"You always have been so disgustingly grateful that you became the apple of Cotton Crandall's eye, haven't you?"

Mrs. Graves's appearance gave Schyler an excuse not to acknowledge Tricia's snide remark. The housekeeper's name was appropriate, since Schyler was sure a more dour individual had never been born. Schyler had yet to see the stick-figure woman crack a smile. She was as different from Veda as possible.

As the taciturn housekeeper went around the table ladling vichyssoise out of a tureen, Schyler felt a stab of longing for Veda. Her smiling face, as dark as chicory coffee, was a part of Schyler's memory as far back as it went. Veda's ample bosom was as comfortable as a goose down pillow, as protective as a fortress, and as reassuring as a chapel. She always smelled of starch and lemon extract and vanilla and lavender sachet.

Schyler had looked forward to being enveloped in one of Veda's bear hugs the moment she crossed Belle Terre's threshold. It had come as a crushing disappointment to learn that she'd been replaced by Mrs. Graves, whose meager bosom looked as hard and cold and uninviting as a granite tombstone.

The vichyssoise was as thin and spiritless as the woman who had prepared it, served it, and then slunk back into the kitchen through the swinging door. After one taste of the chilled soup, Schyler reached for the salt shaker.

Tricia immediately leaped to the cook's defense. "I told Mrs. Graves to stop cooking with salt when Daddy's blood pressure started getting too high. We're used to it by now."

Schyler shook more salt into her bowl. "Well I'm not." She tested the soup again, but found it unpalatable. She laid her spoon in the underserver and moved the plate aside. "I remember Veda's vichyssoise too well. It was so thick and rich, you could stand your spoon in it."

With controlled motions, Tricia blotted her lips with her napkin, then carefully folded it into her lap again. "I might have known you'd throw that up to me."

"I didn't mean—"

"She was old, Schyler. You hadn't seen her in years, so you're in no position to question my judgment. Veda had become slovenly and inefficient, hadn't she, Ken?" She asked for his opinion rhetorically and didn't give him time to express it. "I had no choice but to let her go. We couldn't go on paying her salary when she wasn't doing her work. I felt terrible about it," Tricia said, pressing a hand against her shapely breasts. "I loved her, too, you know."

"I know you did," Schyler said. "I didn't mean to sound critical. It's just that I miss her. She was such a part of Belle Terre." Because she'd been living abroad at the time, Schyler couldn't countermand Tricia's decision. But a slovenly and inefficient Veda Frances was something Schyler couldn't fathom.

Tricia paid lip service to loving the housekeeper, but Schyler couldn't help but wonder if she had been acting out of spite when she let Veda go. There had been numerous occasions when her sister had been anything but loving toward Veda. Once she had rebuked Veda so insultingly that Cotton lost his temper with her. There had been a terrific row. Tricia had been banished to her room for a full day and had been grounded from a party she had looked forward to for weeks. Although Tricia was capable of carrying grudges indefinitely, Schyler was sure there had been a more serious reason for Veda's dismissal.

No amount of salt or pepper made the chicken casserole that followed the cold potato soup taste good to Schyler. She even tried seasoning it with Tabasco sauce straight from the bottle, which was a staple on any table belonging to Cotton Crandall. The red pepper sauce didn't help either.

However, she gave Mrs. Graves's culinary skills the benefit of the doubt. She hadn't had much appetite since she had received the overseas call from Ken, informing her that Cotton had suffered a heart attack.

"How is he?" she had asked fearfully.

"Bad, Schyler. On the way to the hospital, his heart stopped beating completely. The paramedics gave him CPR. I won't bullshit you. It's touch and go."

Schyler had been urged to come home with all possible haste. Not that she needed any encouragement. She had pieced together frustrating flight schedules that eventually got her to New Orleans. From there, she had taken a small commuter plane to Lafayette. She had rented a car and driven the remaining distance to Heaven.

When she arrived, her unconscious father was in an ICU at St. John's, where he remained. His condition was stable, but still critical.

The worst of it for Schyler was that she wasn't sure he even knew she had come home to see him. He wafted in and out of consciousness. During one of her brief visits to his room, he had opened his eyes and looked at her. But his face had remained impassive. His eyes had closed without registering recognition. His blank stare, which seemed to look straight through her, broke her heart. She was afraid Cotton would die before she had a chance to talk to him.

"Schyler?"

Startled, she looked up at Ken, who had addressed her. "Oh, I'm sorry. Yes, I'm finished, Mrs. Graves," she said to the woman who was staring down censoriously at her virtually untouched plate. She took it away and replaced it with a blackberry cobbler that looked promising. Hopefully the sugar cannister hadn't been discarded along with the salt box.

"Are you still going to the hospital after supper, Schyler?"

"Yes. Want to come with me?"

"Not tonight," Tricia said. "I'm tired."

"Yeah, playing bridge all day is hard work."

Ken's dig was summarily ignored. "Daddy's Sunday school teacher brought by a get well card from the class and asked us to deliver it. He said it was a shame that Cotton had to recover in a Catholic hospital."

Schyler smiled at the deacon's religious snobbery, though it was typical of the area. Macy had been Catholic and had raised her adopted daughters in the church. Cotton, however, had never converted. "Heaven doesn't have a Baptist hospital. We have no choice."

"Everybody in town is worried about Cotton." Ken's waistline had expanded marginally since Schyler had last seen him but that didn't deter him from pouring heavy cream over his cobbler. "I can't walk down the sidewalk without a dozen people stopping to ask about him."

"Of course everybody's worried," Tricia said. "He's about the most important man in town."

"I had someone ask me about him this afternoon," Schyler added.

"Who was that?" Tricia asked.

Tricia and Ken stopped eating their cobbler and looked at Schyler expectantly. "Cash Boudreaux."

 # THREE

"**C**ash Boudreaux. Well, well." Tricia turned her spoon upside down inside her mouth and, with her tongue, leisurely licked it clean. "Were his pants zipped?"

"Tricia!"

"Come now, Ken, don't you think nice ladies like me know about him?" She flirtatiously batted her eyelashes at her husband. "Everybody in town knows about Cash's escapades with women. When he broke off with that Wallace woman, she told the whole Saturday morning crowd at the beauty shop about their sordid little affair." Tricia lowered her voice secretively. "And I do mean every detail. We were all embarrassed for her because the poor dear was more than just a little drunk. But still we hinged on every scintillating word. If he's half as good as she claimed, well . . ." Tricia ended with a sly wink.

"I take it that Mr. Boudreaux is the town stud," Schyler said.

"He nails everything that wears a skirt."

"That's where you're wrong, honey," Tricia said, correcting her husband. "From what I hear, he's very particular. And why not? He can afford to pick and choose. He has women all over the parish practically throwing themselves at him."

"Heaven, Louisiana's equivalent to Don Juan." Dismissing the topic, Ken returned to his cobbler.

Tricia wasn't yet ready to shelve it. "Don't sound so sour. You're just jealous."

"*Jealous*?" Jealous of a no 'count, bastard, ne'er-do-well, who doesn't have two nickels in his jeans?"

"Honey, when talk comes around to what he has in his jeans, the ladies are not referring to money. And apparently what he's got in his jeans makes him more valuable than pure gold." Tricia gave her husband a feline smile. "But you've got no need to worry. The earthy type has never appealed to me. You must admit, though, that Cash is a fascinating character." She turned to Schyler. "Where'd you run into him?"

"Here."

"Here?" Ken's spoon halted midway between his bowl of cobbler and his mouth. "At Belle Terre?"

"He said he was gathering roots."

"For his potions."

Schyler stared at Tricia, who had supplied what she seemed to think was a logical explanation. "Potions?"

"He took up where Monique left off." Schyler continued to stare confusedly at her sister. "Don't tell me you didn't know that Monique Boudreaux was a witch."

"I'd always heard the rumors, of course. But they were ridiculous."

"They were not! Why do you think Daddy let trash like that live on Belle Terre all those years? He was afraid she'd put a curse on us all if he ran her off."

"You're guilty of melodrama as usual, Tricia," Ken said. "Actually, Schyler, Monique was what is known as a *traiteur,* a treater. It's a Cajun custom. She cured people, or so they claimed. Right up till the day she died she was doling out tonics and tinctures."

"Traditionally, treaters are left-handed and usually women, but folks around here seem to believe that Cash inherited his mama's powers."

"She didn't have any *powers,* Tricia," Ken said impatiently.

"Listen," she said, slapping the edge of the table with her palm for emphasis, "I happen to know for a fact that Monique Boudreaux was a witch."

"Malicious gossip."

Tricia glared at her husband. "I know it firsthand. One day in town, she looked at me with those big, dark, evil eyes of hers and that afternoon I got my period. It was two weeks early and I've never had cramps that bad before or since."

"If Monique possessed any special powers, she used them to make people feel better, not worse," Ken said. "Her potions and incantations had been passed down since the eighteenth century from the Acadians. They're harmless and so was she."

"Hardly. Those healing traditions were combined with African voodoo when the Acadians came to Louisiana. Black magic."

Ken frowned at Tricia. "Monique Boudreaux wasn't into voodoo. And she wasn't evil. Just different. And very beautiful. Which is why most of the women in this town, including you, want to believe she was a witch."

"Who actually knew her, you or me? You'd only been living here a little while before she died."

"I've heard tell."

"Well, you've heard wrong. Besides, she was getting old and all her former beauty had faded."

"That's a woman's point of view. I tell you she was still a good-looking woman."

"What about Cash?" Schyler cut into what she could see was becoming a full-fledged marital disagreement. It hadn't taken long for her to realize that the Howells' marriage fell short of being sublime. She tried her Christian best not to take pleasure in that.

"What does Cash do for a living?" Schyler could tell the question surprised them. They stared at her for a moment before Ken answered.

"He works for us, for Crandall Logging."

Schyler assimilated that. Or tried to. Cash Boudreaux was on her family's payroll. He had hardly behaved deferentially that afternoon. His manner hadn't befitted an employee in the presence of an employer. "Doing what?"

"He's a logger. Plain and simple." Having demolished the cobbler, Ken wiped his mouth and tossed down his napkin.

"Not quite that plain or that simple, Schyler," Tricia amended. "He's a sawhand, a loader, he drives the skidder. He selects the trees for cutting. He does just about all of it."

"Shame, isn't it," Ken said, "that a man his age, and as smart as he seems to be, has no more ambition than that?"

"Does he still live in that shanty on the bayou?"

"Sure does. He leaves us alone. We leave him alone. Cotton has to deal with him down at the landing, but other than that we all give each other wide berth. Can't imagine him coming close to the house today. He and Cotton had words when Monique died. Cotton wanted to move Cash out. Somehow Cash talked Cotton into letting him stay. Cotton's trust is commendable."

"It's also selfish," Tricia said. "He needs Cash."

"He might need him, but he doesn't like it. I think he's a fool for trusting the man. I wouldn't trust Cash Boudreaux as far as I could throw him." Suddenly Ken leaned across the table and looked at Schyler with concern. "He didn't do or say anything offensive, did he?"

"No, no. We just exchanged a few words." And a touch. And a gaze. Both had conveyed as much contempt as sensuality. Schyler didn't know which disturbed her the most, his interest or his suggested animosity. "I was curious about him, that's all. It's been years since I'd heard anything about him. I didn't expect him to still be around."

"Well, if he ever gets out of line with you, you let me know."

"And what will you do? Beat him up?" Tricia's laughter ricocheted off the crystal teardrops of the chandelier overhead. "Some say Cash stayed in the jungles of Vietnam a tad too long. He kept reenlisting in the marine corps because he loved the fighting and killing so much. Came back meaner than he went, and he was already meaner than sin. I doubt you could pose a threat to him, honey."

Schyler could feel the undercurrents of enmity between husband and wife rising again. "I'm sure that's the last I'll see of Mr. Boudreaux." She scooted back her chair. "Excuse me, please. I'm going to freshen up before I go to the hospital."

The bedroom she was sleeping in now was the same one she had as a child. Through three large rectangular windows she had a view of the back of the property, the greenhouse, what had at one time been a smokehouse and now served as a toolshed, the barn that housed several horses, and the detached garage. Beyond the outbuildings which were all painted white to match the main house, was the woods, and beyond the trees, the bayou.

She closed the bedroom door behind her and stood with her back against it. She paused to appreciate the room she'd missed so much. The hardwood floor was dotted with area rugs that were worn and faded and would bring a premium price should they ever be sold, which they wouldn't be. Schyler would never part with anything that belonged in or to Belle Terre.

All the furniture in the room was made of oak, aged to a golden patina that kept the pieces from looking heavy and masculine. The walls were painted saffron, all the woodwork white. The bedspread, chair cushions, and drapes were white as well. She had insisted on that the last time the room had been redecorated. She hadn't wanted any of the furnishings to detract from the simple beauty of the room itself.

The only modern touch was the bookshelf. It was still cluttered with childhood and teenage memorabilia. She had resolved to clean out and throw away the yearbooks and dried corsages and yellowing party invitations many times. But nostalgia would always override her pragmatism. Nevertheless, she decided that before she returned to London she would give this room a thorough housecleaning and get rid of that junk.

The small adjoining bathroom hadn't been changed. It still had a white porcelain pedestal sink and claw-foot bathtub. She rinsed her face and hands in the sink and, using the framed mirror over it, retouched her makeup and brushed her hair. When she lifted the loose, dark blond curls off her neck, she noticed the pink bump on the side of her throat. A mosquito bite.

They know the best places to bite, she remembered Cash saying.

She tossed down the hairbrush impatiently and, picking up her purse and rental car keys off the bureau in the bedroom, went downstairs. Tricia was speaking animatedly into the telephone receiver in the formal parlor. It was joined to the informal parlor by sliding wooden doors that disappeared into the connecting walls. The doors were always kept open, making one large room out of the two, but each half was still referred to by its traditional name.

The adoptive sisters waved good-bye to each other. Schyler walked through the wide hallway and out onto the veranda. She was on the second step down when Ken spoke to her. He left the rocker he'd been sitting in and came to join her on the step. Encircling her upper arm, he led her toward her car, which was parked in the drive. It made a semicircle in front of the house, then ran along one side of it to the back and the garage.

"Let me drive you to the hospital," he offered.

"No thanks. You and Tricia went this morning. It's my turn."

"I don't mind."

"I know, but there's no need."

He turned her to face him. "I didn't offer because I thought you needed a ride. I offered because we haven't had a second alone since you got here."

Schyler didn't like the direction the conversation was taking, nor Ken's confidential tone. She politely but firmly disengaged her arm. "That's right, Ken. We haven't, And I think that's best, don't you?"

"Best for whom?"

"For all of us."

"Not for me."

"Ken, please." Schyler tried to sidestep him, but he headed her off. Facing her again and standing close, he ran his fingers down her cheek.

"Schyler, Schyler. I've missed you like hell. Jesus, can you imagine what it was like for me to see you again?"

"No, what was it like?" Her voice was harsh as were her accusing eyes.

He frowned with chagrin and withdrew his hand. "I can imagine how you felt when we found out that Tricia was pregnant."

Schyler's laugh was bitter. "No, you can't. Not unless you've been betrayed like that. Not unless the planet has been jerked out from under you. You can't know what I felt like at all." She wet her lips and shook her head as if to ward off an attack of insurmountable depression. "I've got to go."

Again she tried to walk around him and again he impeded her. "Schyler, wait. We've got to talk about this."

"No."

"You hightailed it to London without ever giving me a chance to explain."

"What was there to explain? We were about to announce our engagement to be married when Tricia upstaged us by announcing that she was pregnant with your baby. Your baby, Ken," she repeated, stressfully enunciating each word.

He gnawed his lower lip, his only concession to a guilty conscience. "We'd had a fight, remember?"

"A quarrel. A stupid, lovers' quarrel. I don't even remember what it was about. But it must have been over a real bone of contention with you because you wasted no time in sleeping with my sister."

"I didn't know she would get pregnant."

Schyler was speechless. She didn't remember obtuseness being one of Ken's character traits. Six years was a long time. She had changed. Apparently so had Ken. Still, it was incredible that he missed the point.

"It was inconsequential that she conceived, Ken. It hurt me just as much to know that she *could* be pregnant with your baby."

He took a step closer and caught her shoulders. "Schyler, you're blaming the wrong party here. Tricia came on to me something fierce. Hell, I'm only a man. I was depressed. I was missing you. At first I thought she just wanted to comfort me, you know, sympathize, but then—"

"I don't want to hear this."

"But I want you to," he said, shaking her slightly. "I've got to make you understand. She, well, you know, started flirting with me, flattering me. One thing led to another. She kissed me. Next thing I know, we're making out. It just happened once." Schyler looked at him with patent disbelief. "Okay, maybe a few times, but it never meant anything. I screwed her, yeah, but I loved you." He tightened his grip on her shoulders. "I still do."

Angrily, Schyler threw off his grasping hands. "Don't you dare say that to me. It insults us both. You are my sister's husband."

"But we're not happy."

"Tough. I am."

"With that Mark character you work for?"

"Yes. Yes, with that Mark character. Mark Houghton has been wonderful to me. I love him. He loves me."

"Not like we loved each other."

She laughed shortly. "Nothing like the way we loved each other. Mark and I share a kind of love you would never understand. But whatever my relationship with Mark, it has no bearing on ours. You're married to Tricia. Whether or not your marriage is happy or dismal is no concern of mine."

"I don't believe you."

He quickly drew her to him and kissed her. Hard. She recoiled and made a small choking sound when his tongue speared into her mouth. But he didn't stop kissing her.

For a moment she allowed it, curious as to what her reaction would be. She discovered, quite surprisingly, that Ken's kiss evoked nothing but revulsion. She dug her fists into his chest and pushed him away. Saying nothing, she quickly got into the rented Cougar and started the motor. She floorboarded the accelerator and put the car into motion with a spray of crushed shells.

FOUR

From the cover of a palmetto, Cash watched Schyler drive away, leaving Ken staring wistfully after her. He waited until Howell had dejectedly climbed the steps and entered the house before he slipped into the deeper shadows of the woods and headed toward the bayou.

"So that's how the wind blows," he said to himself.

In Heaven everybody knew everybody's business. The scandal six years ago involving the Crandall sisters had started tongues wagging. The town had buzzed with gossip for months after Schyler's defection to London and speculation on when she would return had varied. Some said weeks. Others said she might sulk for a month or two. No one betted on it being years before she came home, and only then because her daddy's life was in jeopardy.

But Schyler Crandall was back at Belle Terre and, apparently, back in her old lover's arms. If that kiss was any indication, it didn't matter to her that Howell was married to her sister. Maybe she rationalized that she had had him first and that turnabout was fair play.

What mystified Cash was why either woman would want Ken Howell. He must pack more of a punch than it seemed he could. Howell had been known to frequent the upstairs bedrooms of the area honky-tonks, but no more than any other man. He never chased after women who were married, single, or somewhere in between. And he always paid for his extramarital dalliances. Women weren't one of his vices.

Whatever made Ken Howell attractive to the Crandall sisters escaped Cash. In his opinion, Howell was a sanctimonious son of a bitch. He'd been raised to look down his nose at anybody who wasn't in the social register. Howell had conveniently forgotten that when his folks died in a plane crash, they had left behind more liens than legacy. He still considered all but the upper crust of society inferior to him.

Maybe he also considered himself above morality and felt justified in having a wife in the house and a lover on the veranda.

Deep in thought, Cash continued walking through the forest. He moved through the trees with a stealth that had been developed in childhood and refined with taxpayers' money. The marine corps had honed his natural talent and developed it into a fine art. He didn't have to think twice about finding his way, which was good since he was lost in thought about Schyler Crandall.

It didn't make sense to him that that much woman would want a pompous wimp like Howell. Not that Schyler was a lot of woman physically. He was certain he could almost close his hands around her waist and he would welcome a chance to prove it. Her hips were full enough to make a sensual curve from her slender waist. While her breasts weren't large enough to win a wet T-shirt contest, he was sure she'd find it uncomfortable to sleep on her stomach without making adjustments. He'd been well aware of their shape beneath her blouse.

Thinking of that made Cash smile. Was there a set of tits on any living woman that he didn't take notice of? With that expertise to qualify him, he could say that Schyler Crandall's figure wasn't voluptuous, but remarkable just the same.

She put that figure to full advantage, too. It wasn't so much her body that made her wholly woman, but what she did with it. The graceful way she moved. The feminine gestures she unconsciously made with those slender, ringless hands. The long legs and narrow feet. The expressive movements of her light brown eyes. And all that sweet, honey blond hair.

She was woman through and through. Cash wondered if she knew that. It was doubtful she did. But he sure as hell did.

Irritated with himself for dwelling on her, he stepped into the pirogue that he'd left on the bank of the bayou. He picked up the long pole and used it to push off. As silent as his guerrilla progress through the nighttime jungle, the canoe cut as cleanly as a blade through the still, murky waters of Laurent Bayou.

Since he was several years older than Schyler—he wasn't sure just how many because Monique hadn't been a stickler for dates and was never sure exactly what his birthday was—Cash had watched her grow up from a pretty little girl with flaxen braids into the woman she now was.

As a child, being driven around by proud papa Cotton in his newest Cadillac convertible, she had always worn hair ribbons that matched her lace-trimmed dresses. Always so prim. While Cotton looked on proudly, she had entertained his friends with her precociousness.

But she hadn't been like that all the time. Every now and then the little doll had stepped out of her bandbox. From his hiding places in the woods, Cash had often seen her riding Cotton's horses barebacked and barefooted, hair flying, face flushed and sweaty.

He wondered if she still rode horseback. And if she did, did she ride hell-bent for leather like she used to when nobody but him was looking?

That image of her made his sex stretch and grow hard against his zipper. He wiped the sweat that beaded his forehead on his sleeve and cursed the vicious heat. Ordinarily he wouldn't have even noticed it.

But Schyler Crandall had come home. Nothing was ordinary.

Schyler noticed how stifling the heat was as she left the car and made the short walk to the air-conditioned lobby of the two-story hospital. By the time she stepped through the automatic doors, her clothes were sticking to her. Maybe she should have showered and changed before coming to the hospital.

As she waited for the elevator, she surreptitiously checked herself in the mirrored wall and decided that she looked far from outstanding, but okay. There was a grass stain on the hem of her full cotton skirt and her sleeveless blouse was wrinkled, but in this part of the country everybody wore cotton in the summertime. Everybody looked wilted by late afternoon. It was a given that the heat and humidity would inflict their damages, so they were generally ignored.

The very thought of wearing stockings was suffocating. She'd left on her sandals. Her only pieces of jewelry were a plain watch with a leather strap and the gold hoops in her ears. They were eighteen carat but unostentatious. Her shoulder bag was expensive and of the highest quality, but since the designer's signature wasn't obvious, no one would be impressed, even if he recognized the Italian's name.

In the mirror Schyler saw a woman who looked perilously close to her thirtieth birthday. It wasn't the maturity in her face that bothered her, but that she didn't have more to show for those thirty years. No career to speak of. No husband. No children. Not even an address she could call her own.

Her accomplishments added up to nil. She hadn't been able to move forward because of the memories that kept her shackled to the past. By coming home, she had wanted to lay to rest the most disturbing of those memories. She had hoped that the ambiguities surrounding her feelings for Ken Howell would be resolved.

Instead, his kiss had only confused her further. She no longer loved him, not with the intensity she had before. That she knew. What she didn't know was why.

She couldn't pinpoint the reason why her heart didn't trip over itself each time he looked at her, why she hadn't dissolved at the touch of his lips on hers.

For six years Ken Howell had been preserved in her mind as she had first seen him, a dashing student leader on the Tulane campus, a stunning basketball star. He was from a good family, in solid with New Orleans society. He was a business administration major; his future had held nothing but bright promise. And he had chosen Schyler Crandall, the reigning bell of Laurent Parish, to pin his fraternity pin on.

They went together for two years. As soon as both had graduated, marriage seemed a natural progression. Then they had had a silly falling out, a misunderstanding over something so trivial as to be insignificant. They didn't date each other for several months.

Schyler never considered the break irrevocable and she had viewed the temporary separation as healthy for the relationship. It gave them time to date others and make certain that they wanted each other for life.

When Ken finally relented and called her, he wanted desperately to see her. Their reconciliation was tender and passionate by turns. He was impatient to get married; she felt the same. They set a tentative date for their wedding and asked both families to gather at Belle Terre for a party.

But Tricia stole the show.

She wore blue that day, a shade exactly the color of her eyes. Schyler had told her earlier how pretty she looked. Schyler had loved the entire world that day. Everybody and everything was beautiful.

In the midst of all the gaiety, Tricia had sidled up to Ken and taken his hand. "Everybody, everybody, can I please have your attention?" When the laughter and conversation died down, she smiled up at Ken and said, "Honey, I suppose I should have told you first and in private, but it seems so appropriate to tell you now, when the people we love most dearly are here with us." Then she had drawn a deep breath and, with a jubilant smile, announced, "I'm going to have your baby."

According to his facial expression, Ken was as stunned as anyone there. He looked flabbergasted, embarrassed, ill. But he didn't deny his responsibility, not even when Schyler turned to him with disbelief and silently begged him to.

Any solution other than marriage was out of the question. Within days and with very little fanfare, Tricia and Ken were married in a civil ceremony. Eight weeks later Tricia miscarried.

But by that time, Schyler had left for Europe. When news of the miscarriage reached her, she felt nothing. Her heart had been as empty as Tricia's womb. Their betrayal had left her numb.

In many ways, she still was. So when the bad memories darkly obscured the good ones, Ken's kiss evoked nothing but revulsion.

Stepping off the elevator on the second floor of the hospital, Schyler thought that if Cotton didn't pull out of this, that if he died as a result of the massive heart attack, at least he would die in the knowledge that his life had amounted to something. So far, the same could not be said of her.

Before she returned to England, she must come to terms with her feelings for Tricia and Ken and their treachery. If she didn't, she might remain stagnant forever. Until her mind and heart had finally closed the door on the past, she would be like a stalled engine, going nowhere, accomplishing nothing.

"Good evening," she said to the nurse she met in the hallway. "How is my father?"

"Hello, Miss Crandall. There's no change. The doctor asked earlier if you had come in. He wants to see you."

"He can find me outside my father's room."

"I'll tell him."

The nurse moved away to find the doctor. Schyler continued down the corridor toward the last ICU. Through a narrow window she saw Cotton lying in a bed, connected to machines that bleeped and blinked his discouraging vital signs.

Schyler's own heart ached to see the man she adored in this condition. Cotton, if he was aware of it, would hate being helpless. He had never been dependent on anyone. Now, the most elemental body functions were being done for him by sophisticated machinery. It didn't seem possible that such a robust man could be laying there motionless, colorless, useless.

Laying her palm against the cool glass, Schyler whispered, "Daddy, what's wrong? Tell me."

Their estrangement had roots in that horrible day when the gods had decided that Schyler Crandall had had enough good luck and had hurled a life's worth of misfortune at her in the space of one afternoon.

After the bewildered guests had departed, after Ken and Tricia had left to handle the necessary legal aspects of getting married, Schyler had gone to Cotton, expecting him to envelope her in his loving and sympathetic embrace.

Instead he'd metamorphosed into a stranger. He refused to look directly at her. He brusquely set her aside when she collapsed against his wide chest. He treated her coolly. Until that day Schyler had been the apple of his eye. But on that miserable afternoon, when Schyler suggested that she go abroad for a while, Cotton had approved the idea. He hadn't been angry. He hadn't ranted and raved. She wished he had. That would have been familiar. She could have dealt with his short temper.

But he had treated her with indifference. That had pierced Schyler to the core. Cotton was indifferent only to people he had absolutely no use for. Schyler could not understand why her father no longer showed the tender affection she so desperately needed.

So she had left Belle Terre and moved to London. The rift between Cotton and her had grown wider with each year. Other than a letter every several months, and a few civil but chilly telephone conversations on holidays, they had had no formal contact.

He didn't seem to mind. It was as though he'd dismissed her from his life for good. She didn't want him to die harboring the secret grudge. Her greatest fear was that she would never know what had turned him against her, what had changed her from pet to pariah.

"I'm not going to have two patients on my hands, am I?"

The doctor's voice roused her. She raised her bowed head and wiped tears off her cheeks. "Hello, Dr. Collins." She smiled waveringly. "I'm fine. Just very tired." He looked skeptical but didn't pursue it, for which Schyler was grateful. "Any change?"

Jeffrey Collins was a young man who had decided to set up practice in a small community hospital rather than battle the competition in a large city. As he studiously consulted the chart on Cotton Crandall, he reminded Schyler of a boy about to give an oral book report in front of the class, wanting to do well.

"Nothing significant."

"Is that good or bad?"

"Depends on which way you look at it. If it's a change for the worse, we'd rather do without."

"Of course."

"What the patient needs is bypass surgery. Triple, maybe quadruple. The pictures of his chest indicate that." He snapped closed the metal cover of the chart. "But he isn't strong enough yet. We've got to wait, build up his strength, and hope that he doesn't have another attack before we can go in."

" 'We'?"

"The resident cardiologist, the general surgeon, and I."

She looked away, trying to think of a graceful way to put what she had to say. "Dr. Collins, at the risk of sounding ungrateful for everything you've already done, and doubtful of your ability—"

"You wonder if I know what the hell I'm doing?"

She smiled helplessly. "Yes. Do you know what the hell you're doing?"

"I don't blame you for wondering. We're a small hospital. But the financial backers who built this facility, your father included, spared no expense. The equipment has the latest technology available. The staff is well paid. We're not doctors and surgeons who couldn't find jobs anywhere else. It's just that we wanted a small-town environment for our families."

"I'm sorry, I didn't mean to imply that you weren't competent or qualified."

He held up his hand, indicating that no offense had been taken. "When the time comes for surgery, if you want to have Mr. Crandall moved to another hospital, I'll be glad to make the arrangements for you and do whatever it takes to move him safely. I wouldn't advise that he be moved now, however."

"Thank you, doctor. I appreciate your candor. I hope you appreciate mine."

"I do."

"And I don't think it'll be necessary to have him transferred."

"That's gratifying to know."

They smiled at each other. "Can I go in and see him now?"

"Two minutes. By the way, I recommend that you catch up on your meals and start getting more rest. You look none too healthy yourself. Good night."

He set off down the hall with a confident stride that belied his wet-behind-the-ears appearance. Schyler took comfort in that as she nodded a greeting to the nurse monitoring the life-support equipment and stepped into the ICU. Despite the bright fluorescent lighting, the room was sepulchral.

She tiptoed to the bed. Cotton's eyes were closed. A tube had been inserted into his mouth, held in place by tape across his lips. Smaller tubes had been placed in his nostrils. Wires and conduits and catheters attached to the various machines disappeared beneath the sheet covering him. She could only guess at their unpleasant functions.

The only thing that was familiar was his shock of white hair. Tears blurred her eyes as Schyler reached out and ran her fingers through it. "I love you, Daddy." He didn't stir. "Forgive me for whatever I did." She used up the full two minutes before she kissed his forehead and quietly left the room.

Only after the door closed behind her did Cotton Crandall open his eyes.

FIVE

Tricia and Ken were in the throes of an argument. From the steps of the veranda, Schyler could see them through the parlor windows. An authentic Aubusson rug was their arena. They were squared off across its muted, pastel pattern. Their voices were muffled, so she couldn't distinguish individual words. She didn't have to. They were gesturing angrily.

Stepping out of the wedge of light coming through the window, she went back down the steps. She didn't want to intrude or have them see her, especially if she were the source of the squabble.

Surely Tricia hadn't seen Ken kissing her before she left for the hospital. Tricia wouldn't have stayed undercover, waiting until Schyler left to confront her husband. She would have charged out of the house immediately and challenged them both.

The visit to the hospital had left Schyler emotionally drained. She didn't want to join the fracas going on in the formal parlor, so she left her purse and keys lying on the hood of her car and struck out across the lawn.

Maybe the exercise would exhaust her enough to make her sleep. She had been tired every night since her arrival but had lain awake, thinking about Cotton, thinking about Tricia and Ken, thinking about them sleeping together in the room down the hall from hers. She hated herself for still caring about that. But she did.

And because she did, it was curious that Ken's kiss hadn't affected her more than it had. For the last six years she had fancied herself still in love with him. The first kiss, after so long and heartbreaking a separation, should have electrified her, regardless that she was kissing her sister's husband. Yet all she felt was a vague sadness, a sense of loss, which she couldn't explain.

That was just one of the things troubling Schyler as she made her way across the wide lawn and entered the surrounding forest. The evening air was sultry, only marginally cooler than it had been at sunset. Her footsteps disturbed patches of mist that hovered above the ground. Ethereally, it swirled around her ankles and climbed her calves. It could have been a spooky sensation, but Schyler regarded these patches of fog as friendly.

She followed the narrow path that paralleled the road for a few hundred yards before angling off to the left. From there, it meandered through the woods on a gradual decline until it reached the fertile banks of the bayou.

Here, on the higher terrain, there were a few hardwoods, trailing the harmless Spanish moss from their branches. But mostly there were pines, reproducing themselves prolifically until they gave way to the cypress and willow and cotton-wood that claimed the muddy shore of the bayou as their domain.

Almost as soon as she could say her ABCs, Schyler could name every tree in the woods. She had never forgotten them. She remembered Cotton's forestry lessons well. She knew the forest by sight, touch, and smell. Her ears could still attach a label to each familiar sound.

Except one.

And it came upon her so swiftly that she didn't even have time to wonder about it until the vicious, snarling dog was blocking her path.

The animal had seemingly emerged from hell and sprung out of the marshy ground to stand only a few feet in front of her. His body was sturdy, with a deep and heavily muscled chest. His face was triangular and had a blunt snout. His sharply pointed tail curved in an upward arc that was aggressive and hostile. He was short-haired, an unattractive, mottled blend of black and brown and tan. Wide-set eyes glittered up at her. His snarling mouth drooled. He stood with his feet planted far apart, like a sailor on the deck of a tall ship. He was ugly, extremely ugly, the most menacing creature Schyler had ever seen. His sinister growl was terrifying in itself.

Instinctively she sucked in and held her breath. Her heart was pounding so hard it hurt. When she raised her hand to it, the animal lurched forward and gave three sharp, rapping barks.

She froze, not wanting to alarm the dog by moving a muscle. "Down, boy, down." The words were ridiculously trite. This wasn't an amiable pet. There wasn't a single friendly aspect to his character. The animal was a killer. His growl modified to a low vibration in his throat, but Schyler wasn't foolish enough to think that he was backing down.

Crying out for help would be futile. She was too far from the house. Besides, the sudden noise might provoke the short-tempered animal to attack her. But this Mexican standoff couldn't last forever. She decided to chance a half step backward. The dog didn't seem to notice, so she took another. Then another.

When she had put several yards between them, she decided to turn and make her way swiftly along the path toward the house. She wouldn't break into a run because he was certain to chase her. But she wouldn't waste any time either.

Dreading the risky result, she turned. The instant she did, the dog barked another sharp threat. The sound was so abrupt, so startling and loud, that she stumbled and fell. The dog lunged at her. Schyler rolled to her back, covered her face with her forearm, and knocked the powerful animal aside with the other.

Actually coming into physical contact with him was like living a hideous nightmare. His moist breath was hot on her arm. She felt the scrape of sharp teeth on her skin. Either his saliva or her own blood felt sticky and wet as it trickled over her wrist. The bone in her arm almost cracked upon impact with the dog's broad skull. The blow numbed the nerves for several seconds.

She had no doubt that the animal would rip out her throat if she couldn't stop it. Acting on sheer survival instinct, she groped behind her and picked up the first thing she laid her hand on, a fallen pine branch about as big around as her wrist. When the dog launched his next attack, she whacked him in the face as hard as she could. The blow landed solidly but didn't deter him. Indeed, it only infuriated him more.

Swinging the pine branch wildly and, as a consequence, ineffectually, Schyler struggled to her feet and started to run. As she slashed her way through the trees, the dog was literally on her heels. She felt his teeth snapping at her thrashing ankles. Several times she barely escaped his clenching jaws.

Suddenly, from out of nowhere, two brilliant lights cut through the forest as smoothly as a scythe through tall grass. They stopped on her like a searchlight that had found its target, blinding her. Mist and dust danced eerily in the twin beams. Reflexively, Schyler crossed her arms over her eyes.

A piercing whistle rent the still, humid air. She sensed the dog's immediate attention. He ceased his snarling and barking and came to an abrupt standstill. Another shrill whistle galvanized him. He sped past her. His sweaty body brushed against her bare leg, nearly knocking her down. He plunged through the undergrowth in the direction of the bright lights.

Schyler realized then that in her headlong plunge, she had almost reached the road. The lights belonged to a vehicle that had pulled to the shoulder. The steering wheel had been cut sharply to direct the headlights into the woods. She blinked into focus the shape of a pickup truck, made spectral by the cloud of dust that swirled around it.

The noises coming from the truck were surreal. The engine was wheezing and knocking. And from the back of the truck came the raucous sound of barking dogs. They were in a frenzied state, rattling their metal cages as they clambered to get out. Schyler couldn't tell how many there were, but it sounded like every hound in hell.

She reversed her direction and fled in terror, certain that soon the whole blood-thirsty pack would be unleashed on her. She risked looking over her shoulder. The truck was backing up, the gears grinding. Then it turned onto the road and lumbered away. The forest was plunged into darkness again.

But the barking continued, so Schyler kept running from it, blindly clawing her way through the dense trees that had become alien. The moss that brushed against her cheek now was terrifying. Roots and vines were snares that wrapped around her ankles and tried to trap her in this nightmare. In vain, she fought off the mist that rose to embrace her in its ghostly arms.

She actually screamed when she was brought up hard against a solid, impregnable body. She fought it, struggling to scratch and claw her way free. She was lifted up; her feet left the ground. She used them to kick.

"Stop it! What in hell's name is the matter with you?"

Despite her terror, Schyler realized that this phantom in her nightmare had a very human voice. He felt human, too. She flung her head back and looked up at him. It was the devil, all right.

Cash Boudreaux was gazing down at her curiously. Several seconds lapsed, then he swung her up in his arms. Schyler was too relieved to argue. The dog's attack was still too recent for her not to welcome a larger, stronger presence than herself.

Her breath came in short, swift pants that fanned his throat. She clutched the front of his shirt. She shuddered with revulsion at the recollection of the dog's slobbering, snarling mouth. But when the remnant horror began to recede, embarrassment set in.

She drew in a long, unsteady breath. "You can put me down now, Mr. Boudreaux. I'm fine." He didn't set her down. He didn't even stop but kept walking in the direction of the bayou. "Did you hear me?"

"*Oui.*"

"Then please put me down. This is nice of you, but—"

"I'm not being nice. It's just more convenient to carry you than drag you along behind me."

"That's my point. I can manage alone."

"You couldn't stand up. You're shaking too bad."

That was true. From the marrow out, she was quaking like a dead leaf in a gale. Willing, at least for the moment, to concede the point to him, she let him carry her. "You're going the wrong way. The house is back there."

"I know where the house is." There was a trace of sarcasm in his voice. "I thought you might be running scared from something or someone there."

"What would I be afraid of there?"

"You tell me."

"For your information, I was attacked by a . . . a dog." Her voice cracked. It was mortifying to feel tears in her eyes but she couldn't help it.

Boudreaux stopped in his tracks. "A dog? A dog attacked you?" She nodded. "I heard the barking," he said. "Were you bitten?"

"I think so. I'm not sure. I ran."

"Jesus."

He started down the path again, walking more quickly now. The chorus of bullfrogs grew louder. Schyler recognized the willows, whose long, trailing branches bent toward the still, murky waters like a penitent paying homage. This branch of the bayou was distributary, drawing water out of the wider, freer flowing Laurent Bayou. It was a narrow creek. The waters flowed sluggishly if at all, making it appear almost stagnant.

There was a pirogue lying half in, half out of the water. Agilely, Cash put one foot in it and leaned down to deposit Schyler in the narrow, canoe-type boat. Taking a book of matches from the breast pocket of his shirt, he struck one and lit a kerosene lantern. The yellow light made his eyes appear as sinister as the wildcats that prowled the swamps. He blew out the match and turned up the lantern.

"What were you doing here?" she asked with a detached curiosity.

"Hauling in the day's catch." He nodded toward a net trap that was partially submerged in the shallow water. Several dozen red swamp crayfish were squirming inside.

"You seem to have a propensity for trespassing where you don't belong."

He didn't defend himself. "Here, have a drink."

A pint bottle of bourbon was lying in the bottom of the pirogue. He twirled off the cap and passed the bottle to her. She regarded it blankly. "Go on," he said impatiently. "It's not moonshine and it's not bootleg. I bought it this afternoon from a respectable liquor store."

"I'd rather not."

He leaned forward, his face looking satanic in the lantern light. "When you plowed into me you looked like you'd seen a ghost. I don't have any crystal glasses or silver ice buckets like up at Belle Terre. I'm sure it's not as fancy a cocktail as you're used to, but it'll give you a good, swift kick in the gut, which is what you need to stop your shakes. Now take a drink, goddammit."

Not liking anything he had said, liking less the imperious way he'd said it, Schyler yanked the pint of liquor from him and tipped it to her mouth. Cotton had taught her to drink, just like he'd taught her to do everything else. But he'd taught her to drink like a lady, in a manner Macy had approved of. The hefty swig of bourbon she drew out of Cash Boudreaux's pint scalded her throat and every inch of her esophagus along its way to her stomach where it exploded with the impetus of a dying sun.

She gave a hoarse, unladylike cough, wiped her mouth with the back of her hand, and passed the bottle to him. He took it from her and, staring at her with amusement, drank from it himself. "More?"

"No, thank you."

He took another drink before recapping the bottle and tossing it into the bottom of the pirogue. He climbed in and crouched down in front of Schyler. "Did he get you anywhere beside the arm?"

Schyler gasped when he reached out and encircled her wrist, drawing her arm closer to the lantern. His touch elicited a tingle, but what alarmed her was that her arm was oozing blood from several ugly scratches. "I didn't realize. My God."

His fingers were warm, strong, and gentle as he probed the wounds, examining them carefully. "What did it look like?"

"The dog?" Schyler shivered. "Horrible. Ugly. Like a boxer. Sort of like a bulldog."

"Must've been one of Jigger's pit bulls." Cash's gaze rose to meet hers. "You were lucky to get off with no more than this. What'd you do to it?"

"Nothing!" she cried. "I was walking, through my own woods, and suddenly it sprang out of nowhere."

"You didn't provoke it?"

The dubious inflection in his voice made her angry. She jerked her arm free and surged to her feet. "I'm going to the hospital. Thank you—"

Cash shot up and loomed above her. His splayed hand landed solidly in the center of her chest and gave a slight push. "Sit down."

 # SIX

H er bottom landed hard on the rough seat that spanned the floor of the canoe. Incredulous, she stared up at him. "I'll take care of you," he said.

Schyler wasn't accustomed to being manhandled. Nor was she accustomed to someone dictating to her. In light of the fact that she was on eye level with the fly of his tight jeans, she said as calmly as possible, "Thank you for what you've done, Mr. Boudreaux, but I think I need to let a professional look at this."

"Some consider me a professional." He knelt down in front of her again. "Besides, I refuse to take you to the hospital and you'd never get there under your own power." His eyes lifted to hers again. His were mocking. "Of course you could always get your brother-in-law to take you." He returned his attention to the bleeding wounds. "But you'd have to get to Belle Terre first, and I don't think you'd make it."

"I'll need a rabies shot." Even as she spoke the sudden realization aloud, she felt ill at the prospect of getting the series of painful shots.

Reaching around her for a leather pouch at the rear of the pirogue, Cash shook his head negatively. The light picked up strands of gold in his long, brown, wavy hair.

"None of Jigger's dogs would have rabies. They're too valuable."

She watched with mingled fear and curiosity as he withdrew several opaque brown bottles from the pouch. None were labeled. "Are you referring to Jigger Flynn?"

"*Oui.*"

"Is he still around?"

Cash snorted a laugh. "Every whore in the parish would be out of business if he ever left."

Jigger Flynn's name conjured up childhood fears. Flynn was a reputed pimp and bootlegger, the occupation from which he'd derived his nickname. "My mother used to tell my sister and me that Jigger Flynn kidnapped little girls who didn't behave," Schyler said.

"She wasn't far off."

"At our house, he was one and the same with the Boogey Man. We would stare at his house with awe and fear whenever we drove past."

"It's still there."

"Somebody should have locked that reprobate behind bars years ago."

Cash smiled around a soft chuckle. "Not a chance. The sheriff's office provides some of Jigger's most frequent customers."

Knowing that he was probably right, Schyler nodded vaguely. She'd also been distracted by Cash's low laugh. It had touched an erogenous spot deep inside her. She pulled her arm from his grasp. "What is that?"

He had soaked a wad of cotton with the clear liquid from one of the brown bottles. He lifted it to her nose. The smell was pungently recognizable. "Plain ol' everyday rubbing alcohol. And it's going to burn like hell. Feel free to scream."

Before she could properly brace herself for it, he applied the alcohol to the scratches on her forearm. She felt the wave of pain approaching before it crashed over her full force. She was determined not to scream, but she couldn't hold back the choking sound that escaped before she rolled her lips inward and forcibly held it back.

Her stoicism seemed to amuse him. He was grinning as he laid aside the blood-soaked cotton. "This will help stop the stinging." Quickly he uncorked another of the bottles he'd taken from the bag and, and using his fingers, dabbed the contents onto her wounds. Now cleaned of blood, they didn't look so serious. After liberally smearing them with the unguent, he bound her arm from wrist to elbow with gauze. "Keep it clean and dry for several days."

"What was that you put on it?" Amazingly the wounds had stopped stinging.

"One of my mother's homemade salves." At her startled expression, he grinned sardonically. "It's got bat's eyes and ground spleen of warthog in it." His eyes glittered in the lantern light. "Black magic," he whispered.

"I never believed that your mother practiced black magic."

His grin settled into a hard line of bitterness. "Then you were among few. Did the dog bite you anyplace else?"

Schyler nervously wet her lips. "He snapped at my ankles, but—"

She didn't get a chance to finish before he flipped back her skirt and lay the hem well above her knees. Cupping the back of her calf in one hand, he lifted her foot to his thigh and turned it this way and that beneath the light.

"The scratches aren't as deep. I'll clean them, but they won't need a bandage." Checking the other ankle and finding that it only had one faint mark, he doused another ball of cotton with alcohol.

Schyler watched his capable left hand swab the scratches and bites on her ankles. She tried to think of what Ken had called these Cajuns who healed. She tried to think of anything except the intimacy of having her foot propped high on Cash Boudreau's thigh and his face practically in her lap.

"You said I was lucky to get off this light," she said. "Has that dog attacked people before?"

"There was a kid, a few months back."

"A child? That dog attacked a child?"

"I don't know if it was that particular dog. Jigger's got pit bulls with just enough mongrel in them to make them meaner than junkyard dogs."

"What happened to make the dog attack the child?"

"They say the kid provoked it."

"Who said that?"

He shrugged uncaringly. "Everybody. Look, I don't have the details because it was none of my business."

"Some of that gossip that doesn't apply to you," she said snidely.

"That's right."

"What happened to the child?"

"He got okay, I guess. I didn't hear anything more about it after they took him to the hospital."

"He had to be hospitalized? And no one did anything?"

"About what?"

"About the dogs. Didn't Jigger have to pay a fine, anything like that?"

"It wasn't Jigger's fault. The kid was in the wrong place at the wrong time."

"It's Jigger's fault if the dog was running free."

"I guess you've got a point. Those dogs are mean sons of bitches. He trains them to be. They have to be mean to fight in the pit."

"The pit?"

He looked at her with derision and gave a dry, coughing laugh. "Haven't you ever heard of pit bull terrier fights?"

"Of course I've heard of them. They're illegal."

"So is spitting on the sidewalk in front of the courthouse, but that doesn't stop folks from doing it."

He had finished treating the wounds on her ankles and was restoring his supplies, including Monique's homemade, anesthetizing salve. Schyler shoved her skirt down over her knees. That didn't escape his attention.

Ignoring his lecherous smile, she said, "You mean that pit bull fights are held around here?"

"Have been for years."

"Jigger Flynn breeds dogs to kill and be killed?"

"*Oui.*"

"Well, somebody's got to put a stop to that."

Cash shook his head, obviously amused by the suggestion. "That wouldn't sit too well with Jigger. His pit bulls are one of his most lucrative sidelines. They aren't defeated in the pit too often."

"As soon as I get to Belle Terre, I'm calling the sheriff."

"I'd let it drop if I were you."

"But that animal could have killed me!"

Moving suddenly, Cash closed his fingers around her throat and drew her face closer to his. "You haven't been back very long, Miss Schyler. I'll save you the trouble of finding this out for yourself." He paused and stared deeply into her eyes. "Nothing in Laurent Parish has changed since you left. Maybe you've forgotten the first unwritten rule. If you don't like something, you look the other way. Saves you a lot of grief. Got that?"

Because she was concentrating so hard on his fingers touching her skin, it took her a moment to comprehend his warning. "I hear you, but I won't change my mind about this. I hate to think what would have happened if Flynn hadn't come along when he did and called the dog back to the truck."

"You'd've been chewed to pieces, and that would have been a damn shame, wouldn't it? 'Cause you look pretty damn good just like you are."

His thumb made a slow stroke along the base of her neck. When the pad of it swept over the rounded welt, he went back to investigate more closely. He rubbed it several times. "That mosquito got you, didn't it?"

Schyler felt herself quickly losing control of the situation. The intensity in his eyes was thrilling, but it made her uncomfortable. She liked the structure of his stern face and the sexy inflection of his voice very much. She had covertly admired the breadth of his chest and the tapering shape of his torso. His thighs were lean and hard. The bulge between them testified that his reputation as a stud was well-founded.

But she was Schyler Crandall and knew better than to fall for Cash Boudreaux's disreputable charm.

"Kindly let me go."

He kept stroking her throat. "Not before I put something on that bite."

"That won't be necessary."

However, she didn't move when he removed his hand from around her neck and went foraging through the bag again, coming up with a small vial. He uncorked it. The scent of the oily substance was familiar and evoked memories of summer camp.

"You're a phony witch doctor, Mr. Boudreaux. That's Campho-Phenique."

He grinned unapologetically. "Close."

Schyler never knew why she didn't deflect the hand that moved toward her neck again, why she sat still and let the pad of his index finger, slippery with the camphor-laden substance massage that small, red bump on her neck. She didn't know why, having done that, she let his fingers explore her neck and chest for other welts, and, finding one beneath the neckline of her blouse, let him unbutton the first button. He slipped his hand inside and liberally coated the raised spot with the lotion.

His hand remained in the opening as he asked, "More?"

It was a loaded question. "No."

"Sure?"

"Very sure."

Slitted eyes revealed glints of amusement as he withdrew his hand and replaced the vial in his bag. Standing, he stepped out of the pirogue and offered a hand down to her. This time she declined to take it and came to her feet without assistance. But the moment she stood up, she swayed. Only his quick reaction prevented her from falling. Once again, he lifted her in his arms.

"Put me down. I'm fine."

"You're drunk."

She was. A near impossibility on one swallow of booze. "You lied to me. That drink you gave me wasn't liquor store whiskey." He made a noncommittal sound that could have meant anything.

The three-quarter moon had risen above the tree line. As a result, the forest was brighter than it had been earlier. Cash made rapid progress through it, seeming to know even better than Schyler did where each curve in the path was and anticipating each low limb.

The frightening ordeal with the dog, not to mention the potent liquor, had left her listless and dizzy. She gave up trying to hold her head erect. Her cheek dropped to his chest. Her body went limp. Her shape molded pliantly against his. She couldn't keep her eyelids open and they closed. When he came to a stop, she kept them closed for several seconds longer before opening them. They were standing in the shadow of the gazebo.

His face was bending low over hers. "Can you make it the rest of the way on your own?"

Schyler raised her head. Belle Terre looked like an iridescent pearl nestled in green velvet. It seemed very far away. The prospect of covering that distance under her own steam wasn't very appealing, but she said, "I'll be fine," and slid to her feet when he relaxed his arms and released her.

"I'd be glad to carry you the rest of the way, but your daddy would rather have somebody piss in the well than to have Cash Boudreaux's shadow fall on Belle Terre."

"You've been very kind. Thank you for—"

The breath left her body when he planted the heels of his hands in the center of her midriff and backed her against the latticed wall. His fingers closed hard around her narrow rib cage. His breath was hot as it fell on her startled face.

"I'm never kind to a woman. Beware, *pichouette*. My bite is much more dangerous to you than Jigger Flynn's dog."

*　　　*　　　*

"You call that making love?"

Cash rolled away from the woman lying beneath him. Her body was shiny and slick with his sweat and bore the reddish markings of rowdy sex. Reaching for the pack of cigarettes on the nightstand, he lit one and drew deeply on it.

"I never have called it making love." He left the bed, peeling off the condom and dropping it into the wastebasket. He was only semi-soft. His body was still taut, still hungry.

Rhoda Gilbreath sat up and pulled the sheet over her breasts. The ludicrously demure gesture was wasted on him. He was standing at the window with his back to her, naked, calmly smoking his cigarette and staring sightlessly at the gaudy, animated, pink neon sign in the parking lot of the Pelican Motel.

"Don't pout." Her purr was conciliatory. "I like it hard and fast sometimes. I wasn't complaining."

His head, with its shaggy, gold-streaked hair, came around. Scornfully he gazed at her over his shoulder. "You've got no reason to complain, Rhoda. You got off three times before I lost count."

In the span of a second her expression went from seductive to furious. "First you sulk, then you get nasty. One would think you'd be grateful."

"What do you want, a tip?"

She glowered at him. "It wasn't easy for me to drop everything and come running tonight. I only accommodated you because when you called it sounded like an emergency."

"It was," he muttered, remembering the state he'd been in when he left Schyler at Belle Terre. Leaving the window and placing the cigarette between his broody lips, he reached for his jeans and stepped into them.

The woman reclining against the headboard sat up at attention. "What are you doing?"

"What does it look like?"

"You're leaving?"

"That's right."

"*Now?*"

"Right again."

"But you can't. We just got here."

"Don't sound so put out, Rhoda. You rushed over because you were hot to get laid. You always are."

"Aren't you?"

"Yes. But I admit it. You make it sound like meeting me here was an act of charity. We both know better."

She took another tack, reverting to seduction. Raising one knee, wagging it back and forth slowly and enticingly, she said, "I told Dale that I was going to sit with a sick friend and probably wouldn't be home until morning." She let the sheet fall. "We've got all night."

Indifferent to her allure, Cash pulled on a pair of muddy cowboy boots and shoved his arms into a shirt, which he left unbuttoned. "You've got all night. I'm leaving."

"Damn you."

"The room's paid for. There's cable TV. You've got an ice machine right outside. What more could you want? Enjoy." He tossed the room key onto the bed beside her.

"You bastard."

"That's exactly right. Ask anybody." He gave her a cynical smile and a mocking salute before slamming the motel door behind him.

SEVEN

They laughed at her.

Breakfast was being served on the screened portion of the veranda at the back of the house. When Schyler made her outlandish statement, Tricia dropped the spoon she was using to dig out a Texas Ruby Red grapefruit. Ken clumsily replaced his coffee cup in the saucer. For a moment they stared at her with amazement, then simultaneously began laughing.

Only minutes earlier Schyler had put in an appearance, already dressed for the day. By eight-thirty the humidity had topped ninety percent. It had made her hair wave and curl and cling to the back of her neck. Just in the few days since her arrival, the southern sun had streaked the strands nearest her face to a pale and appealing blond. The bandage on her arm had drawn attention immediately.

"What in the world happened to your arm, Schyler?" Tricia had asked.

Pouring herself a cup of coffee from the silver pot on the trolley and declining Mrs. Graves's stilted offer of a hot breakfast, she said, "I was attacked in the woods last night by a pit bull terrier."

Tricia's eyes widened. "You're kidding!"

"I wish I were."

"They're vicious dogs."

"I don't know about the whole breed, but this one was. It scared the living daylights out of me. It could have killed me."

"The dog was in our woods?" Ken asked. "On Belle Terre?"

"Yes. Only a few hundred yards from the house." Schyler recounted the incident for them, omitting any reference to Cash Boudreaux.

"You should have those bites looked at," Ken said worriedly.

"They've been looked at. I had them treated last night." She was deliberately unspecific and hoped that neither of them would ask her for details. To avoid that, she said, "I intend to press charges against that Flynn character."

That's when they reacted first with astonishment, then laughter. "Schyler, you can't sic the law on Jigger Flynn." Ken smiled at her patronizingly.

"Why not?" she demanded. "There must be a local or state law he's violating by keeping those dogs."

"There's not. Folks have been fighting pit bulls around here for a hundred years or more. Jigger doesn't let them roam free."

"One was free last night."

"It probably just got out of its pen by mistake."

"A costly mistake. And that's not the first time. I heard that a child was attacked not long ago."

"The kid was riding his bike past Jigger's place."

"And that justifies him getting mauled?" she cried angrily. "I intend to see that something is done to guard against that happening again."

"Calling the sheriff won't do you any good. Oh, he might make a token visit out to Jigger's place, but they'll likely end up sharing a drink and a dirty joke."

Schyler divided her disgust between her sister and Ken. "You expect me to just let this drop, pretend that it never happened, let bygones be bygones?"

"That would probably be best, yeah." Ken got up, gave Tricia a perfunctory kiss on the cheek and Schyler a pat on the shoulder. "I'm due to tee off at ten. Bye-bye, girls."

Schyler watched him leave with a blend of dismay and resentment. His dismissive attitude toward the dog attack made her furious and all the more determined not to let it pass without taking action against the animal's owner.

She had rolled over and played dead only once in her life, when Tricia announced her pregnancy. Never again. She had learned there was no percentage in being a martyr. As often as not it earned one contempt, not respect.

"I can't believe Ken wants me to let this drop. He's always been ready to crusade for the underdog, no pun intended."

"When he was in college, Schyler. He grew up."

"So you're suggesting that I grow up, too."

"Yes," Tricia declared. "This isn't a campus. We're not trying to end a war or start one or find relief for migrant workers or equal education for black children." Tricia returned the uneaten half of her biscuit to her plate and licked the dripping butter and honey off her fingers. "You haven't been back a week yet. Don't go stirring up trouble, please."

"I didn't start this. I wouldn't have even known that the damn dogs existed if one hadn't attacked me on my own property."

Tricia let out a long sigh. "You just can't leave things alone, can you? You always were poking your nose into business that didn't concern you. Cotton encouraged your activist goings on, but they drove Mama and me to distraction. They were an embarrassment. So ... so unrefined." She leaned forward for emphasis. "This is my home, Schyler. Don't you dare do anything that's going to embarrass me. I want to be able to hold my head up when I go into town."

Schyler scraped back her chair and tossed her unused napkin into her empty plate. "If I can't get the authorities to do something about that menacing bootlegger and his vicious animals, I'll do something about it myself. And I don't give a damn how much embarrassment it causes you with the Junior League, Tricia."

"He has showed signs of improvement in the last twelve hours," Dr. Collins told her when she arrived at the hospital. "I'm being guardedly optimistic. If his condition continues to improve, even this gradually, we should be able to operate within a week."

"That's wonderful."

"I said guardedly optimistic. He's still a very sick cardiac patient."

"I understand." The doctor smiled at Schyler sympathetically. When someone's loved one had been as close to death as Cotton Crandall had been, relatives grasped at shreds of hope. "Can I see him?"

"Same rules. Two minutes max every hour. But you might want to hang around for a while. He's been semiconscious all morning."

Schyler went to the pay telephone and notified Tricia of the good news, putting aside the argument they'd had earlier that morning. Then she was allowed into her father's ICU for two minutes. She was disappointed that he didn't wake up or otherwise acknowledge that he knew she was at his bedside, but she was encouraged by the doctor's report. Even the nurse's reassuring smile seemed more genuine.

Tricia and Ken arrived early in the afternoon. The three of them whiled away the hours in the hospital waiting room, taking turns going into the ICU once every hour. Boredom set in. Eventually Ken said, "Schyler, why don't you come on home with us?"

"You two go ahead. I'll be home in time for dinner. I'd like to see him one more time before I leave."

"All right." Ken led his wife to the elevator. They waved at Schyler before the doors slid closed. Sick of looking at the same four walls, Schyler strolled along the gleaming corridors, thinking that she should call Mark.

He had been generous to let her leave without having any idea how long she would be gone. He hadn't even asked. He had helped her pack, had driven her to Heathrow, had kissed her good-bye, and told her to call if she needed anything. He had been as concerned for her as he was for Cotton, whom he'd never met but had certainly heard a lot about.

Schyler decided to wait until Cotton's prognosis was more definite before she called him. There was no sense in phoning until she had something substantial to report, except that she missed him terribly. She would take comfort just in hearing the familiar sound of his nasal Boston accent.

"Miss Crandall?"

She spun around. "Yes?" The nurse was smiling. "Daddy?"

"He's awake. Hurry."

Schyler followed the nurse's rapid footsteps down the corridor and into the ICU. Cotton didn't look much better than he had last night, though Schyler thought his complexion didn't look quite so waxy and that the blue tinge of his lips had faded somewhat. Being careful of the IVs, she lifted his hand and pressed it between both of hers.

"Daddy, hi. It's Schyler. I've been here for several days. How are you feeling? We've all been so worried. But the doctor says you're going to be fine."

The lines in his face were etched deeper. The skin beneath his stubborn, square chin was looser. His hairline had receded. But it was his eyes that arrested her. They had undergone the most remarkable change since she'd last seen him. The change made her own heart sink heavily in her chest. His eyes were the same vivid color of blue, but there was no light in them, no spark of mischief, no life.

His heart condition wasn't responsible for that lifelessness. Schyler knew that she had extinguished that light in his eyes. What she didn't know was what she had done to put it out.

"You've come back." His voice was as whispery and fragile as ancient paper. There wasn't a degree of warmth behind it.

"Yes, Daddy, I'm back. I'm at Belle Terre. For as long as you need me."

He stared up at her for a long moment. Then his veiny eyelids closed over those condemning blue eyes and he turned his head away.

The nurse stepped forward. "He's gone back to sleep, Miss Crandall. We'd better not disturb him anymore."

Schyler reluctantly released her father's hand and moved away from the bed. She watched the nurse make adjustments on the IVs. Feeling empty and alone, she left the room and the hospital.

No daughter had ever loved her father more than Schyler loved Cotton. And vice versa. Only he had stopped loving her. Six years ago. Why? She had been the injured party. Why had he turned against her? *Why?*

The accumulated heat inside her car was unbearable. Even set on high, the air conditioner wasn't sufficient to cool it off, so she rolled down the windows. The wind tore at her hair punishingly. She took the winding road that was as familiar as her own face in a mirror. Her heart began to beat with glad expectation as she crossed the Laurent Bayou bridge. The road came to a dead end in front of Crandall Logging.

It was Saturday afternoon. The landing was deserted. No one was working in the yard or on the loading platforms that lined the railroad tracks. The rigs were parked beneath the enormous shed, their trailers folded up and riding piggyback on the cabs. The air wasn't punctuated by the racket of loggers hauling the timber from the surrounding forests. There was no sound of machinery, no clank of metal wheels on the rails. Except for a few chirping birds, everything was still and silent.

She left her car door open and went toward the small, square, frame building that housed the office. The key that was still on her key ring fit the lock. It hadn't been changed in six years. The door swung open and she stepped inside.

It was stifling. She left the door open behind her. The late afternoon sun cast her shadow across the dull, scarred floor and over the top of Cotton's desk. Unfiled paperwork and unopened correspondence littered it. It always had. He would procrastinate doing the clerical chores for months. Schyler would catch up with them during school holidays and summer vacations.

She crossed to the desk, picked up the telephone and dialed the number that was engraved on her memory forever.

"Belle Terre."

"Hello, Mrs. Graves, this is Schyler. I won't be home for a while. Don't hold dinner for me."

The housekeeper appeared not to have any curiosity and nothing to say; the call was completed within fifteen seconds. Replacing the telephone receiver, Schyler gazed about her. The windows overlooking the railroad tracks needed washing. They were without adornment of any kind, even venetian blinds. Cotton had always insisted on an unobstructed view. He wanted to know what was going on at any given time.

Schyler ran her fingertip along the windowsill and picked up an inch of dust. She should arrange for someone to come in and clean. Returning to the desk, she stood behind the chair and laid her hands on the tall, tufted back.

Cotton's chair.

Years of use had made the brown leather glove-soft and pliable beneath her squeezing fingers. She closed her eyes. Hot, salty tears welled up behind her eyelids as she recalled the times she had sat in Cotton's lap in this chair, listening patiently while he explained the different types of wood and to which lumberyard or paper mill the timber would be shipped.

He had been delighted with his attentive pupil. Tricia hated the landing. She called it a dirty, noisy ol' place and had grown sullen if she ever had to go near it. Macy hadn't cared about the business, even though it had originally belonged to her family. Cotton had audaciously changed its name. No sooner had Mr. Laurent been buried than Cotton set himself up as sole owner and operator.

Macy hadn't cared about much at all, not her family's business, not her husband, not even the two daughters she had adopted out of desperation when she learned that she was barren and could not give Cotton the offspring he desired.

Macy had seen to it that her two daughters were better dressed than any other girls in the parish. They had been educated in an elite private school. Parties held in their honor were more lavish than any the old-timers could remember. She had provided their material needs, but she had neglected their emotional ones. If it hadn't been for Cotton, Schyler would never have known parental love.

But he no longer loved her.

She opened her eyes and wiped the tears from them. Suddenly noticing the long shadow stretched across the untidy desk, her head snapped up. She gave a soft gasp that seemed unnaturally loud in the stillness. Then, recognizing the man indolently leaning against the doorjamb, she frowned.

EIGHT

"**I** wish to heaven you'd stop sneaking up on me. It's giving me the creeps."
"What are you crying about?"
"Cotton."
Cash's body tensed. His brows formed a low shelf over his enigmatic eyes. "He died?"
Schyler shook her head. "No. He regained consciousness. I spoke with him."
"I don't understand."
"You're not supposed to," she said shortly. "Stop meddling in my business."
"All right. The next time you get a dog bite, I'll let your arm rot off."
Schyler pressed the heel of her hand against her temple, where a headache was off to a good start. "I'm sorry. I should have thanked you."
"How is it?" He nodded toward her bandaged arm.
"Okay I guess. It hasn't hurt at all."
"Come here." She only stared at him. He arched one brow and repeated softly, "Come here."
She hesitated a moment longer before stepping around the desk and approaching the open door, where he still had a shoulder propped against the frame. She stuck out her injured arm with about as much enthusiasm as she would thrust it into a furnace.
Her aversion to having him touch her made him smile sardonically as he unwound the gauze bandage he had fashioned the night before. Schyler was amazed to see that the skin had almost completely closed over the wounds and that there was no sign of infection. He touched the scratches lightly with his fingertips. They were painless.
"Leave the bandage on tonight." He rewrapped her arm. "Tomorrow morning, take it off and wash your arm carefully. It should be okay after that." She looked up at him inquiringly. "It's the spleen of warthog that does the trick."
She jerked her arm away. "You're left-handed."
His grin widened. "You believe the legend, do you? That all *traiteurs* are left-handed." Without a smidgen of apology or hesitation, he moved aside the square nautical collar of her dress and brushed his fingers across the top of her breast, where he had located the welt the night before. "How are the mosquito bites?"
Schyler swatted his hand away. "Fine. Was Monique left-handed?"
"*Oui.* She was also a woman. That's where I break with tradition." His voice dropped seductively. "Because I am a man. And if you have any doubts as to that, Miss Schyler, I'd be more than glad to prove it to you."
She looked up at him and said wryly, "That won't be necessary."
"I didn't think so."
His conceit was insufferable, Schyler thought as she watched his lips form a lazy, arrogant smile. What was she expected to do, unravel because big, bad Cash Boudreaux, the man most feared by fathers of nubile daughters, had turned his charm on for her? She was a little old to grow giddy and faint in the face of such blatant masculine strutting.
Still, no one needed to sell her on Cash's masculinity. It was evident in the rugged bone structure of his face, the width of his shoulders, the salty scent that he emanated in the afternoon heat. A bead of sweat rolled from beneath the hair curving over his forehead. It slid down his temple and disappeared into his thick eyebrow.
His walk, all his movements, were masculine. Schyler watched his hands as they

went for the pack of cigarettes in his breast pocket and shook one out. He offered it to her, but she wordlessly declined. His lips closed around the filtered tip. He replaced the pack in his pocket and pulled out a matchbox. He struck the match on the doorjamb, then cupped his hands around the flame while he lit the cigarette.

She remembered his hands on her midriff, pressing into the tender center of her stomach, the hard, dominant fingers lying against her ribs. He had imprisoned her against the wall of the gazebo without exercising any force. The only bruises her body bore this morning were a result of her struggles with the pit bull. It made her uneasy to know that Cash Boudreaux could be so overpowering without hurting her.

As he drew on his cigarette, staring at her through the smoke that rose from it, she lowered her eyes. There was a knotted bandanna around his strong, tanned throat. His chest tapered into a narrow waist and lean hips. The soft, washed denim of his Levi's cupped his sex as intimately as a lover's hand.

Schyler knew that his eyes were boring a hole into the crown of her head, just as certainly as she knew that there was something sexual going on. But then, if rumor was correct, everything that Cash Boudreaux had done since he was about thirteen years old had been sexually motivated.

She wasn't flattered. She wasn't afraid. If he'd wanted to assault her, he'd had plenty of opportunities in the past twenty-four hours to do so. Mostly, she was offended. Obviously he had lumped her into the ranks of women who were flattered by his indiscriminate attention.

If she were being entirely honest, however, she had to admit that the prospect of experiencing something sexual with Cash Boudreaux had a certain allure. He was disreputable and dangerous, aggravating and arrogant. He was rude and disrespectful and treated women abominably. Perhaps that was his attraction, what made him desirable.

Geographically they'd grown up in the same place, but the realms of their upbringings were worlds apart. They had nothing in common except these sexual undercurrents, which were invisible but as real as the shimmering heat waves that radiated out of the ground. She was a woman. Cash Boudreaux was indisputably a man.

She raised her head and gave him a direct look, as if by doing that she could nullify the subliminal sparks. "Did you follow me here?"

"No. I just happened by. Thought I'd check on things."

"Check on things? I'm sure Ken is capable of handling things while Daddy is ill."

"Ken isn't capable of finding his ass with both hands."

"Mr. Boudreaux—"

"To keep everybody from discovering that, he shut the place down."

Her protests died on her tongue. "*What?* What do you mean he shut the place down?"

"I mean he told all the employees on the payroll that they were laid off until further notice. He told the independent loggers to find other markets for their timber. He said that Crandall Logging was temporarily out of operation. Then he locked the door and left. Don't you think that amounts to shutting the place down?"

Schyler fell back a step. She gazed about the office with dismay, realizing now why it had an abandoned look. It bore the empty sadness of a house that hadn't been occupied in a while. "Why would Ken do that?"

"I just told you why."

"I'm serious."

"So am I." Cash flicked his cigarette out the door behind him. It made a red arc before dying in the dust of the deserted yard. "The day after they took Cotton to the hospital, your brother-in-law paid everybody off and hightailed it outta here."

"Does Cotton know about it?"

"I doubt it."

"So do I." She gnawed the inside of her cheek, trying to figure out what could have motivated Ken to shut down. Cotton had had to ride out economic crunches before, but he had never laid off employees. "That must have put scores of men out of work."

"Goddamn right it did."

Schyler pulled her fingers through her hair. "I'm sure Ken had his reasons. They just aren't apparent."

"Well, let me tell you what *is* apparent, Miss Schyler." He stopped slouching in the doorway and advanced into the room. "About half the families in the parish are running out of groceries. Prospects aren't looking too good that they'll have money to buy more any time soon. While your brother-in-law is languishing around the country club swimming pool, swizzling glass after glass of Lynchburg, Tennessee's finest, kids are doing without breakfast, dinner, and supper."

Ken left the house every morning and returned every afternoon. Schyler had assumed he was at work during those hours. It galled her to think that he was living off the profits Cotton had put a lifetime into earning. But perhaps she was being unfair by jumping to conclusions. Ken had begun working for Crandall Logging when he married Tricia. When his parents were killed, he had sold everything in New Orleans, severed all connections there, and moved to Heaven. He had several years of his life invested in this business. There must be a logical explanation for his shutting down operation.

"Come up with any good excuses for him yet?"

"I won't have you disparaging my brother-in-law, Mr. Boudreaux," she lashed out.

He whistled softly. "Listen to her defend him. That's what I call real family loyalty."

Willfully restraining her temper, Schyler said, "I assure you that I'll look into the matter immediately. I know Cotton wouldn't approve of families going hungry, families who depend on him for their livelihoods."

"I know he wouldn't either."

"I assure you something will be done."

"Good."

She gave Cash a long, steady look. He irritated the hell out of her. He was no better than he had to be. He was a lowlife who seemingly had no scruples. She could use just that kind of man.

"I guess you're off the payroll, too."

"I don't think your brother-in-law likes me. I was the first one to get notice."

"Then I'm sure you're running low on money and could use some." He shrugged noncommittally. She drew herself up importantly. "I've got a job for you."

"You do?"

"Yes, I do. I'll pay you well."

"How well?"

"You tell me."

"Well, now that all depends on what the job entails." His voice was thick with lewd suggestion. "What do you want me to do for you?"

"I want you to destroy the dog that attacked me last night."

He didn't blink for several moments, only held her in a stare. His eyes, she noticed now, were hazel, but with more yellow and gray than green. They were like cat eyes, predatory cat eyes.

"Kill it?"

"That's what destroy usually means."

"You want me to kill one of Jigger Flynn's pit bulls?"

She raised her chin and answered firmly. "Yes."

He hooked both thumbs into his tooled leather belt and leaned down until his face was almost on a level with hers. "Have you lost your frigging mind?"

"No."

"Well, then you must think I've lost mine."

"I want that animal killed before it kills someone."

"Last night was a freak accident. Jigger doesn't let those dogs run free."

"So Ken told me. But that—"

"Ah!" He held up his hands to forestall her and looked at her through narrowed eyes. "You bounced this idea off your brother-in-law first?"

"Not exactly."

"You asked him to do it. He crapped in his britches at the very thought, so now you're coming to me. Is that it?"

"No!" She drew an exasperated breath. "I told Tricia and Ken about the dog attacking me. They noticed the bandage."

"Did you tell them where you got it?"

"No."

"I didn't think you would," he drawled.

Ignoring him, she rushed on. "I insisted that something be done about those dogs. Ken thought I should let the matter drop."

"Well, for once I agree with the son of a bitch. Let it drop."

"I can't."

"You'd better. Stay away from Jigger Flynn. He's meaner than hell."

"So are you."

An abrupt silence followed her raised voice. Cash treated her to another long, penetrating stare. She moistened her lips and forced herself to speak. "What I mean is, you have a reputation for . . . too much fighting. You went to war and stayed longer than you had to. You must be good with guns."

"Damn good," he whispered.

"I don't know anybody else to ask. I don't know anybody else who has . . . has . . . killed . . ."

"You don't know anybody else low enough to do your dirty work."

"I didn't say that."

"But that's what you meant."

"Look, Mr. Boudreaux, you've spent the better part of your life cultivating a short-tempered, violent image. By all accounts you're as testy as a cobra. Don't blame me for responding to your reputation. I know you must have broken the law before."

"Too many times to count."

"So why do you have a conscience against destroying a public menace, a killer dog?"

"Not a conscience. Common sense. I have the good sense not to provoke Jigger Flynn's wrath."

"Because you're afraid of him," she shouted up at him.

"Because it's not my quarrel," he shot back.

Schyler could see that yelling was a one-way street leading to a dead end. She took another tack. One could always fall back on greed for motivation. "I'll pay you one hundred dollars." His face remained unmoved and unimpressed. "Two hundred."

"Stuff it, Miss Schyler. I don't want your goddamn money."

"Then what?"

His lecherous grin was as good as an invoice. And the sum total of it couldn't be measured in dollars and cents.

"Read my mind."

Furious, Schyler shoved past him on her way to the door. "Jerk. I should have known better than to ask you."

He closed his fingers around her upper arm and brought her up against him hard. "You're quite a hothead, aren't you?" His eyes rapaciously scanned her face. "Are you just as eager to make love as you are to make war?"

"Not with you."

"Never say never."

"Let me go," she said through her teeth.

"Come with me."

"Come with you? Where?"

"I'll show you why no sane person would kill one of Jigger's dogs."

"I'm not going anywhere with you."

"How come? What are you afraid of?"

NINE

"**W**here are we going?"

Cash was behind the steering wheel of his faded blue pickup truck. Schyler still couldn't guess what had prompted her to accept his invitation. Perhaps because it had been posed in the form of a challenge. Before she took into account the possible consequences, she had locked the office, left her car parked at the landing, and stepped up into the cab of Cash's battered truck.

In answer to her question, he consulted the watch strapped to his right wrist. "It's early yet. Hungry?"

"I thought this had to do with Jigger Flynn."

"It does. Be patient. That's a common trait with you people. You're always in a hurry."

" 'You people'?"

He looked at her across the stained, threadbare upholstery. "Rich folks, Miss Schyler."

She refused to acknowledge or address the disparity between their economic levels, so she took issue with the appositive he continued to use with such phony obsequiousness. "Why don't you drop the Miss and call me just plain Schyler?"

He casually took a hairpin curve in the road before turning his sly grin on her. "Because I know it annoys the shit out of you."

"And is that your main goal in life? To be annoying?"

"How come you don't spell it like it sounds?" he asked, ignoring her question. "Why not Skyler?"

"I didn't have any choice. That's how Mother and Daddy entered my name on my birth certificate."

"When they adopted you?"

She wasn't surprised that he knew. Everybody in the parish knew. She was, however, automatically defensive. "I was only three days old."

"That's still not the same, is it?"

"The same as what?"

"As being their natural born."

Deliberately or not, Cash was rubbing salt into an old wound. "It's the same to me."

He shook his head. "Nope. It's not the same." Before Schyler could argue with him, he whipped the pickup off the road and braked to a hard stop. "There it is."

Schyler hadn't realized where they were going and drew in a sharp, quick breath when she noticed the ramshackle house. It had been in disrepair for as long as she could remember. It was constructed of unpainted cypress. The gray, weathered wood added to the overall dreary appearance of the place.

The window screens were torn; they curled outward toward the snaggle-toothed batten shutters. Forlorn lace curtains hung in the windows. They were tattered and dingy, as pathetic as an aging whore's last fancy dress.

A collection of hubcaps had been nailed on the exterior walls. Once shiny, they were now corroded. A potpourri of junk littered the yard. Tools and utensils lay neglected in the grassless dirt. A disemboweled car was providing a roost for several scraggly hens. An empty Frigidaire on the sagging porch was serving no purpose except to support a dusty wisteria vine, which valiantly struggled for life amid the decay. Behind the house was a dog kennel made of rusty, cyclone fencing. There were no dogs in it presently. In fact, the place appeared to be deserted.

"We picked a good time to come calling. Jigger's not at home."

Schyler rubbed her arms as though chilled. "I used to be afraid to even drive past this place."

"I don't blame you. Jigger's been known to do target practice on motorists from his front porch out of sheer meanness."

"How does he get by with things like that?" Schyler cried angrily. "I didn't know that the saying, 'Justice is blind,' meant that it turned a blind eye? Why hasn't he ever been prosecuted?"

"Simple. People are afraid of him."

"I'm not."

"Well, you damn sure ought to be." Cash slipped the truck into first gear and set off down the rough gravel road in the direction of town. "You didn't answer my question. Are you hungry?"

Schyler was glad to leave Flynn's place behind. Even deserted, it unnerved her. "I hadn't thought about it. I guess I am."

"I'll treat you to supper at a place you've never been to before."

"Oh?"

"Red Broussard's."

"Is the floor still covered with peanut shells?" she asked with a mischievous smile.

He looked at her with astonishment. "Don't tell me."

"Oh, yes. Daddy used to take me to Broussard's often."

Cash's grin faded gradually. "I forgot. Cotton likes Cajun food, doesn't he?"

"Yes, he does. And so do I."

"I never saw you at Broussard's."

"We usually went before sundown."

"Hell, the place doesn't start warming up until after sundown."
She laughed. "That's why he always took me before then."

The accordion music was loud, repetitive, and raucous. It seemed to expand and recess the walls of the clapboard restaurant like the wolf in the tale of the three little pigs, huffing and puffing and trying to blow it down. Cash was humming the French Acadian tune as he came around and opened the passenger door for Schyler.

"Saturday night," he remarked. "They're tuning up for a *fais-dodo*. Drinking, dancing, a party," he said by way of explanation.

She took offense. "I know what it is."

"You're acquainted with Cajun customs?"

"Belle Terre isn't an ivory castle, you know."

"No. I don't know." Having made that oblique statement, he placed his hand in the small of her back and nudged her toward the entrance.

"I hope I'm dressed properly," she remarked uneasily.

"Not quite." When she shot him a swift, worried glance, he added. "They might ask you to take off your shoes."

The square building was set on stilts. Dancing footsteps drummed through the floorboards and echoed in the hollow space underneath. Red Broussard, a barrel-chested, potbellied, bearded man with a Santa Claus countenance and garlic breath, greeted them personally, giving each a boisterous shout of welcome and a rib-crunching hug. He pressed icy bottles of beer into their hands and ushered them toward a table in the corner of the room, affably elbowing aside dancers who blocked their path.

Schyler moved through the crowd self-consciously, but no one stopped to stare as she feared they might. No one seemed to think it noteworthy that she was with Cash Boudreaux. But then, this was his crowd, not hers. If she'd taken him to the country club tonight it would have caused quite a stir. It was much easier to move down a notch in society than it was to move up.

They reached their table and Red held her chair for her. The upper two-thirds of the walls of the building were screened. The hinged, exterior walls had been raised and propped open by two-by-fours. They were only lowered during a severe Gulf storm and the coldest days of winter. Maddened insects, frantic to reach the lights burning inside, kamikazied themselves against the screens.

"Boudin sausage, *mon cher*?" Red asked with a beatific smile that split his furry red beard and revealed nicotine stained teeth.

Schyler smiled up at him. "No thanks." She hadn't been able to eat the sausage since a Cajun rig driver had bartered some timber for a hog and had insisted that Cotton oversee the slaughtering. Schyler had begged to go along. Over Macy's vehement protests Cotton had taken her. She'd regretted it ever since. "Crawfish, please."

Red threw back his rusty head and bellowed a deep laugh. Then, pointing a meaty finger down at her, he teased, "I seen de day you pack away dem crawfish, don't cha know. More dan your papa, *oui*."

"Bring us a platter, Red."

Red gave Cash's shoulder an affectionate and mighty wallop, then lumbered off toward the bubbling vats where the day's catch of crawfish was boiling in water seasoned with spices that made one's eyes water and nose itch. Over the music, Red shouted at his patrons to eat and drink some more.

Cash reached for the bowl of peanuts in the center of the table, cracked the shell between his fingers, and shook the roasted nuts out of the pod. He tossed them into his mouth, then took a swig of beer to wash them down. He swallowed gustily. His eyes, glowing in the light cast by the red glass candle holder, dared Schyler to do the same.

She accepted the silent dare, dropping the peanut shells onto the floor as Cash and every other customer had done. She didn't request a glass for her beer but drank directly from the bottle.

He said, "I thought you'd be horrified at the thought of coming here."

"Because I'm too snooty and would look down my aristocratic nose at the people here?"

"Something like that." He took a drink of beer, watching her. "So is this an act just to prove me wrong?"

"No. I miss the food."

That's all they had time to say to each other before Red sent a waitress over with a platter of crawfish. She scooted aside the candle and the bowl of peanuts and set the platter between them in the center of the table. Before moving away, she gave Cash a seductive sidelong glance.

Schyler watched her walk away. "Is she one of yours?" She selected a crawfish. Without needing a refresher course on how it was done, she broke off the tail, dug her thumbs into the seam of the shell and split it apart. Then used her fingers to pull out the rich, white meat.

Cash followed suit. "She could be if I wanted her." He tossed the remainder of the crustacean body back onto the platter and picked up another.

Schyler blotted her mouth with the paper napkin she took from the metal dispenser. "It's that easy for you? Any woman you want is yours for the taking?"

"Interested?"

"Curious."

"Curious to know what attracts them?"

"No, curious to know what attracts you."

"Curiosity."

With belying composure, Schyler ate another crawfish, took another sip of beer, and blotted her lips before she looked at him.

He took a long drink from his beer bottle first. Then, lowering the bottle back to the table, his eyes captured and held hers. They intimated, "Come and get it."

Up from Schyler's stomach rose a trill of sensation that had nothing to do with the spicy ethnic food and beer. Cash Boudreaux was dangerous in a variety of ways. His allure was undeniable; he was sexually attractive. He was also street smart and cunning, wise in the art of bullshitting. But he was no slouch in serious verbal warfare either.

"You don't like me, do you?"

He answered her intuitive question honestly. "No. I guess I don't. Don't take it personally."

"I'll try to remember that," she said dryly. "Why don't you like me?"

"It's not so much you I dislike. It's what you represent."

"And what is that?"

"An insider."

She hadn't expected so succinct and simple an answer. "That's not so much."

"To an outsider it is."

His prejudice struck her as being unfair. "I had nothing to do with that."

"Didn't you?"

"No. I didn't even know you."

His eyes narrowed accusingly. "You didn't make a point to get to know me either."

"That's not my fault. You weren't ever exactly friendly."

Her flare of temper seemed to amuse him. "You're right, *pichouette*. I guess I wasn't."

She used that to get them off the track the conversation had taken and onto something else. "You've used that word before. What does it mean?"

"*Pichouette*?" He hesitated, watching her face. "It means little girl."

"I'm hardly that."

He twirled the neck of the beer bottle between his fingers as he stared at her across the candlelit table. "I remember you as a little girl. You had long blond hair and long skinny legs."

Schyler responded spontaneously and smiled. "How do you know?"

"I used to watch you playing on the lawn at Belle Terre."

She knew better than to ask why he hadn't joined her to play. He would have been ordered off the place by her parents if she hadn't run inside out of fear first. Neither Cotton, nor Macy, nor Veda would have allowed her to play with Monique Boudreaux's boy. Not only had he been several years older, he was an unsuitable companion for a young girl under any circumstances. His reputation as a trouble-maker was well founded and well known.

"I remember one particular birthday party you had," Cash said. "I think it was the day you turned four. There must have been fifty kids at that party. Cotton was giving them rides on a pony. A clown performed magic tricks."

"How do you remember that?" she explained.

"I remember because I wasn't invited. But I was there. I watched the whole thing from the woods. I wanted like hell to see those magic tricks up close."

His antipathy was understandable, she supposed. He carried a chip on his shoulder, but it was justified. Whether overtly or not, he had been slighted. She hadn't been directly responsible for it, but she intuitively knew how it would affect her now. "You're not going to kill Jigger Flynn's dogs for me, are you?"

"No, I'm not."

She twisted her damp napkin. "I guess it was unfair of me to ask you to do my dirty work, as you put it."

"Yeah, I guess it was."

"I didn't mean to insult you."

He merely shrugged and nodded toward the platter between them.

"Finish eating."

"I'm finished."

Red chastized them for not eating enough and invited them back soon. As they went down the rickety steps of the restaurant, Schyler thanked Cash for bringing her. "I haven't had a good-tasting meal since I got here. The new housekeeper my sister hired took an instant dislike to me. The feeling is mutual. I can't stomach her any more than I can the food she serves."

"Just how weak is your stomach?"

The serious tone of his question brought Schyler's head around. "Why?"

"Because it's about to be tested."

 TEN

"I thought I knew every road in the parish, but I've never been on this one." Schyler braced herself against the dashboard as the pickup jounced over the road. "Where in God's name are you taking me?"

"To a place you've never been." He gave her a sidelong glance. "And this time I'm sure of it."

It was a hot, still night. Away from the town's lights, the stars were visible, a panoply of brilliance. Having lived in a city for the past six years, Schyler had forgotten just how dark it could get in the country once the sun went down. Beyond the beams of the pickup's headlights, there was nothing but inky blackness.

But then the pickup topped a rise, and she spotted the building. She looked at Cash inquisitively but he said nothing. To reach the building, they crossed a narrow wooden bridge that she prayed would hold up until they were safely on the other side. Despite the difficulty in reaching it, the corrugated tin structure was a popular place.

It was built like a barn and may have served that purpose at one time. Apparently it was some kind of meeting place because there were dozens of cars parked on the flat, marshy ground surrounding it.

Cash drew the pickup alongside a sleek new Mercedes, which seemed ridiculously out of place in this remote rural area. Schyler looked at him for an explanation. He gave her a smirking grin.

Ill at ease, she alighted when he came around for her, and they started toward the entrance. It was distinguished only by one bare bulb suspended above the uninviting door. There were no signs posted, nothing to indicate what was going on inside the building.

She wanted to turn around and leave. But she wouldn't give Cash the satisfaction of seeing her back down or showing any fear or reservation about stepping through the tin door he held open for her.

It was suffocatingly hot inside, as dank and humid and airless as a sauna. And dark. So dark that Schyler nearly stumbled into the table that was positioned a few steps inside the door. She would have walked right into it if Cash hadn't placed both his hands on her hips and stopped her.

"Hiya, Cash."

The toad of a man sitting in the folding chair behind the table looked Schyler over with a grin so lecherous it made her skin crawl. "Who's the new broad?"

"Two please."

He added Cash's ten-dollar bill to a metal box that was already stuffed with money. "We can always count on you to find fresh meat. Yessiree, that we can do," he said in a singsong voice.

"How'd you like to eat your balls for breakfast tomorrow morning?" Cash's steely tone of voice wiped the grin right off the man's face.

"I was just jokin' with ya, Cash."

"Well don't."

"Okay, sure, Cash. Here're your tickets." The man carefully reached past Schyler to hand Cash two tickets he'd ripped off a roll.

Suddenly a roar issued up from behind the partial wall in back of the table. It rocked Schyler, who wasn't expecting it. Again Cash placed his hand on the curve of her hip just below her waist. The ticket seller glanced over his shoulder at the wall behind him.

"Y'all are just in time for the next fight. If you hurry, there'll be time for the little lady to place a bet before it starts. Be more fun for her that way, don'tcha know."

"Thanks. We'll keep that in mind." Cash nudged Schyler toward the end of the partition. When she seemed reluctant to move, he pushed a little harder.

She did an angry about-face and hissed, "What is this?"

She had been to the Soho district of London. She had seen the pornographic stage shows there, but it had been her choice to go. She had been in the company of several friends. It had been harmless. She had known what she was getting into when she paid her admission.

This was vastly different. All her life she had lived in southwestern Louisiana, but she had never heard of a place such as this, much less been to one. She was afraid of what she would find beyond the partition and afraid of the man who had brought her here. His hard, sardonic face did nothing to reassure her that his intentions were good.

"It's a dog fight."

Her lips parted in shock. "Pit bulls?"

"*Oui*."

"Why'd you bring me here?"

"To show you what you're up against if you hold to that fool notion to even the score with Jigger."

That was tantamount to calling her a fool. Schyler resented that, especially coming from someone with as tainted a history as Cash Boudreaux. "I told you I wasn't afraid of him and I meant it." Turning her back to Cash, she led him around the end of the partition.

From the outside the building had looked large. Even so, Schyler was astonished by just how immense it was. It was rimmed by crude bleachers, ten or twelve rows deep. It was difficult to count exactly how many because the whole place was dark except for the pit located in the center of the arena. It was lit by brilliant overhead spotlights. The large rectangular pit had a dirt floor and was enclosed by wooden slats that were bloodstained.

On opposing sides of the pit, the owners and trainers were readying their pit bull terriers for battle. Though it had been years since she had seen him, she recognized the trainer facing her as Jigger Flynn.

Cash moved up close behind her. "Want to place a bet on your favorite dog?"

"Go to hell."

He merely laughed and edged her toward the nearest set of bleachers. There was room enough for them at the end of the fourth row. Those around them were distracted from the activity in the pit when Schyler climbed the bleachers and took her seat. Realizing that she was one of notably few women in the place, she assumed a haughty, parochial school posture that Macy would have been proud of and tugged her skirt down over her knees.

"That won't help," Cash said close to her ear. "You stick out like a sore thumb, baby. If you cover your knees, they'll ogle your tits."

Her hair whipped across his cheek when she brought her head around with a snap. "Shut up."

His eyes glowed threateningly in the darkness. "Be careful how you talk to me, *mon cher*," he said silkily. "When they get all riled up," he nodded toward the crowd, "I might be the only thing standing between you and gang rape."

By an act of will, she kept her face composed, not wanting him to see her anxiety. She returned her attention to the pit. A shudder went through her when she recognized the dog snarling across the dirt floor of the pit at his opponent as the one who had attacked her.

Uglier and meaner looking than the two pit bulls, however, was Jigger Flynn. Schyler watched him in fearful fascination as he closed his hands around his dog's jaws and, straddling the animal's back, lifted it up until only its back feet touched the ground.

Flynn's thinning, gray hair had been slicked back with oil that made his pink scalp glisten beneath the spotlights. His eyes were deep-set, small, and dark.

Surrounded by puffy flesh, they looked like raisins set in bread dough. His nose was fleshy, his lips thin and hard. Schyler doubted they could form a smile. His chin melted into the loose, wobbly flesh beneath it. He wasn't tall. Generally, he was a small man, but his neck was thick, and he had a beer gut that hung over his belt. His baggy trousers looked as though they were losing a battle to stay up on his hips that were unsupported by a butt. He had thin, bandy legs and comically small feet.

No one knew his worth, but it was estimated that he was one of the richest men in the parish, all of his money earned through illegal enterprises. Whatever his wealth, he certainly didn't flaunt it. His clothes could have been salvaged from a welfare bin. They were old and soiled. He reeked of malevolence.

"What's he doing with that dog?"

Cash, who had been intently studying Schyler, glanced toward the pit. Jigger was holding his dog to face the other. He shook the animal slightly while continuing to squeeze its broad face between his hands. The other trainer was doing likewise. The dogs' back legs were thrashing, kicking up puffs of dirt whenever their sharp claws touched.

"That's called scratching. The trainers are deliberately provoking them, rousing their inbred instincts to fight, infuriating them so they'll charge each other. The fight is over when one dog kills the other or when one refuses to scratch and charge."

"You mean—"

"They try to rip one another's throat out."

The only thing that kept Schyler sitting on the bleacher was her stubborn determination not to lose face in front of Cash. A man whom she assumed was a referee signaled for quiet and enumerated the rules. Obviously this was a routine practice and of no interest to anyone except her. Everyone was shifting restlessly, ready for the action to begin.

She actually jumped when the two animals were released and charged across the pit toward each other. By nature of the sport she had expected violence, but nothing to equal the ferocity with which they attacked each other. The dogs were amazingly strong and tenacious. Time and again they went for each other, but their stamina never seemed to flag.

When first blood was drawn, Schyler turned her head away and pressed her face into Cash's shoulder. She was revolted, but also horrified, realizing how lucky she was to have come away with only superficial wounds from the dog's attack.

Shaken, she raised her head and watched until Jigger's dog clamped down on the other's shoulder. The opposing dog closed his jaws on Jigger's dog's back. They held on.

"That's the way they rest," Cash told her. "They'll be given a minute, but it won't last long. See?"

Both trainers entered the pit. Each had a wedge-shaped stick about six inches long, which he put in his dog's mouth and pried open the jaws. "That's called a break stick. Rest time's over."

The dogs were separated and the scratching process started again. "Do the dogs ever turn on their trainers?" Schyler asked. She was mesmerized by the evil light in Flynn's eyes as he purposefully antagonized his pit bull.

"I've known it to happen."

"Little wonder. They put them in that pit to die."

Cash continued to watch her, even after the dogs had launched another attack on each other. The noise in the tin building began to mount in proportion to the violence going on in the ring. The Saturday night crowd had filled the hall to capacity. Men and dogs were sweating profusely. The dogs waiting to fight sensed the tension. They smelled the blood and anticipated tasting it. They barked with ferocious and crazed intent from their wire cages.

The crowd's sudden gasp drew Cash's attention back to the pit. This time, more than blood had been drawn. Hide and tissue had been ripped from the shoulder of the dog opposing Jigger's. Once the initial shock passed through the crowd, a cheer went up. Jigger's dogs were usually favored to win. Hard-earned wages were riding on this fight and gamblers holding those vouchers smelled victory.

So did Jigger's dog. It went after its foe with renewed vigor. It sank its teeth into the other dog's neck and tore out a chunk of flesh, severing the jugular. Blood spurted from the wound and splattered the slat walls of the pit.

Schyler covered her mouth and turned her head away again. Cash's left hand came up reflexively, cupped the back of her head, and pressed her face into the crook of his shoulder. His right arm slid around her waist and drew her closer. He glanced over his shoulder and cursed viciously when he saw that the crowd had doubled since their arrival. Between them and the exit was a squirming, shouting sea of men with necks craned to see the finish of the fight.

Schyler couldn't breathe, but that was all right because she didn't want to. The walls of the crowded auditorium pressed in on her. The unventilated air was fogged with the smoke from hundreds of foul cigars. The stifling heat concentrated the unpleasant smells until she tasted them with each breath she drew. Sweat, dog, smoke, blood.

Her fingers curled inward and came up with a handful of Cash's shirt. "Please."

The hoarsely spoken appeal went through him like a rusty nail. It touched a soft spot that he thought had calloused over forever when he was in Nam, where seeing men die was a daily occurrence.

"Hold on. I'll get you out of here."

Caring little now for her pride, Schyler clung to him, listening to his heartbeat in the hopes that it would drown out the yelling of the maniacal, bloodthirsty crowd. It was a futile hope. When the mortally wounded dog fell, the racket reached a crescendo that was deafening.

"Okay, that's it. But take a good look, Schyler, at what you're up against."

Cash hooked a finger beneath her chin and forced it up. In the pit, Jigger was leading his dog around by a leash while receiving accolades from the crowd. The dog's coat was lathered and smeared with blood. Flynn's gloating smile sickened Schyler more than the blood and gore.

When she turned toward Cash, her face was pale. He said to her, "That animal isn't a pet. It's a machine trained to kill. It's a moneymaker. If you harm one of his dogs, Jigger will kill you."

He waited a moment, to make certain she had understood, then he leaped off the end of the bleacher and extended his arms up for her. Placing her hands on his shoulders, she let him lift her down. Holding her close against him and trying to shield her with his own body, he shouldered his way toward the exit. It was bottlenecked with men either coming in or going out, counting their winnings or cursing fate for their defeat, congratulating or commiserating with each other.

From out of that mass of bodies Schyler heard, "Jesus Christ, Schyler, what the fuck are you doing here?"

ELEVEN

She stopped, turned in the direction of the familiar voice, and stood still while the crowd eddied around her, Cash, and Ken Howell. Her brother-in-law was looking at her through eyes that were red and glazed by alcohol. Slack-jawed, he gaped at her incredulously, then at Cash, then back at her. "Answer me! What the hell are you doing here?"

"I could ask you the same question," she replied.

"Help me get her out of here, huh, Howell? We're blocking traffic."

Ken gave Cash a withering glance, then clumsily grabbed Schyler's hand and began shoving people aside as they wiggled their way through the exit. Outside, men were milling around, drinking, laughing and joking, and discussing the fights that had already taken place and those yet to come. Ken propelled Schyler toward the corner of the building and away from the crowd before he drew her around and repeated his original question.

"What are you doing here? Especially with him." He hitched his chin toward Cash contemptuously.

"Stop shouting at me, Ken. You're not my keeper. I'm a grown woman, and I don't have to answer to you or to anybody else."

He wasn't hearing too clearly. Either that or he wasn't paying attention. "Did you ask him to bring you here?"

She faltered. "Well no, not exactly, but—"

He whirled toward Cash. Spittle showered from his mouth as he sneered, "You stay away from her, you hear me, boy? You goddamn Cajun bastard, I'll—"

Ken never had the satisfaction of stating his threat. In one fluid motion, Cash came up with a knife that had been concealed in a scabbard at the small of his back and, at the same time, slammed Ken into the wall with enough impetus to knock the breath out of him and to rattle the tin. The gleaming blade of the knife was placed so strategically that reflexive swallowing would give Ken's Adam's apple a close shave.

Schyler fell back a step, astonished and afraid. Cash's nostrils flared with each breath he drew. Ken's glassy, bloodshot eyes were bugging. Sweat ran down his face as copiously as a baby's tears.

"Before I cut you real bad, you son of a bitch, you'd better get out of here." The voice, tinged with the musical rhythm of his first language, sounded as sinister as the razor-sharp knife looked. Cash eased the blade away from Ken's throat and stepped back. Ken clutched his neck as though to reassure himself that it hadn't been dissected. He cowardly slumped against the tin wall.

"Get out of here," Cash repeated. His eyes sliced to Schyler. The cold glint of them made her blood run cold. "And take her with you."

Cash turned his back on them, not the least bit concerned that either would launch a counterattack. Schyler watched him thread his way through the parked cars until he disappeared.

"Where's your car, Ken?"

He raised an unsteady hand to indicate the general direction. She took his arm and pulled him away from the support of the wall. Together they made their way toward his sports car. When they reached it, she asked for the keys.

"I'll drive," he mumbled.

"You're drunk. I'll drive." His prideful resistance snapped her patience in two. "Give me the damn car keys."

He belligerently dropped them into her extended palm. She slid behind the wheel. Once he had closed the passenger door, she peeled out. She didn't even take the insubstantial bridge slowly but roared across it.

She was angry—angry at Ken for behaving like such a fool, angry at Cash Boudreaux for putting her through this ordeal, and angry at herself for letting him lead her to slaughter like a naive lamb.

"What were you doing with him?"

"For godsake, Ken, we just came away from a place where one animal wantonly killed another for the amusement of cheering men. There was illegal gambling going on, and God only knows what else. And you want to talk about what I was doing with Boudreaux?"

Her voice had risen a note on each word until she realized she was virtually screeching. She took a composing breath. "Boudreaux wanted to make a point. I tried to hire him to kill the dog that attacked me. I guess he wanted to show me how important those dogs are to Jigger Flynn."

"Jesus," Ken swore, running a hand through his hair. "I told you to drop that. Kill one of Jigger's pit bulls? You might just as well challenge him to a duel on Main Street."

"Don't worry. Cash declined my offer."

"Thank God. He's right. Leave it alone, Schyler."

She switched topics. "What were *you* doing there, Ken?"

He squirmed in the expensive leather car seat and turned his head away from her. "It's Saturday night. Don't I deserve a chance to unwind every now and then?"

"Were you gambling?"

"Anything wrong with that?"

"No. But there are more wholesome environments for it. The racetrack in Lafayette, a private poker game."

"Don't get on my back." He hunched lower in the seat, looking like a petulant child. "Tricia bitched at me tonight because I wouldn't take her to a goddamn country club dance. I don't need bitching from you, too."

Schyler let it go. It wasn't any of her business what Ken did in his leisure time. She needed to ask him why he had suspended operation of Crandall Logging, but now wasn't the time or place to bring up that delicate subject. He was sullen, no doubt feeling demoralized and emasculated after being so badly shown up by Cash.

"Did he hurt you?" she asked quietly.

He swung his head around. "Hell no! But you stay away from him. See what kind of man he is? He's poison, as low and vicious as those fighting dogs. You can't trust him. I don't know what he's after, or why he's sniffing around you all of a sudden, but he has his reasons. Whatever they are, they're self-serving." He jabbed an index finger at her for emphasis. "I can guarantee you that."

"I'll see who I want to see, Ken," she said icily. "I told you why Cash took me to that fight."

He tilted his head cockily. "Did he also tell you how much money he had riding on the outcome?"

Schyler brought the car to an abrupt halt in the center of the road and turned to her brother-in-law. "What?"

Ken smiled smugly. "I can see that he failed to mention his sizable wager."

"How do you know?"

"Boudreaux always bets on Jigger's dogs, so he won big tonight. I don't know what he told you, but he had a vested interest in that pit bull fight."

"No wonder he turned down my offer," she muttered.

"Right. You think he's gonna kill a dog that earns him winnings like that?" Seeing Schyler's disillusionment, he touched her shoulder sympathetically. "Listen, Schyler, Boudreaux always covers his ass first. Count on that. He has the survival instincts of a jungle animal. You can't trust the conniving Cajun bastard."

She shrugged off Ken's consoling hand and put the car into motion again. Ken reached across the seat and laid his hand on her thigh, giving it an affectionate squeeze that wasn't entirely brotherly.

"You've only been home a short while. There are reasons for the wide gaps in the social structure around here, Schyler. They're not meant to be crossed." He patted her thigh. "Just be sure you remember where you belong, and you'll be back in the swing of things in no time. Stay away from the white trash. And don't provoke the likes of Jigger Flynn. That's only asking for trouble."

Heaped onto what he'd told her about Cash, his condescending, patronizing, chauvinistic tone enraged her. She didn't waste energy on that, however. She let his humoring attitude work to make her more resolute.

Since she hadn't succeeded in enlisting anyone else for her cause, she would take action into her own hands.

TWELVE

She knew that once the dogs started barking, she wouldn't have much time. Flynn would come charging out to see what had caused the ruckus in his yard. It was going to be tricky. She had to get close enough to be effective with the shotgun, but keep enough distance between her and the house so the dogs wouldn't pick up her scent. Once she had accomplished what she had come to do, she would gladly own up to it, but she didn't want to alert Flynn beforehand.

Undertaking this alone probably wasn't very smart. Schyler realized the risks involved and was willing to face them. On the other hand, every time she thought of the evil that Jigger Flynn embodied, she shivered involuntarily.

Last night she had retrieved her car from the landing. Tonight she had left it parked in front of Belle Terre and walked to Flynn's house through the woods. She had dressed for her mission, in old jeans and a dark T-shirt. She had thought about covering her light hair with a cap, but thought that might be a trifle melodramatic.

Earlier in the day, when both Ken and Tricia were away from the house and Mrs. Graves was outside sweeping the veranda, Schyler had gone into Cotton's den and taken a shotgun from the gun rack. She had given the twelve gauge a cursory inspection, certain that it was cleaned and oiled and in prime condition. Cotton had always kept his hunting guns in working order, ready to load and fire. Schyler hated guns, hated touching their cold, impersonal surfaces of wood and metal. But she had put her aversion aside and concentrated on what she felt compelled to do.

The Howells and she had eaten a large Sunday dinner at midday, so supper consisted of cold fried chicken and fruit salad. Ken and Tricia, who was still peeved because Ken hadn't accompanied her to the dance the night before, had bickered throughout the light meal.

"I got to watch the Saturday night movie on TV all by myself," Tricia complained sarcastically, "while you went out to God knows where."

Schyler's eyes met Ken's across the table. Tacitly they agreed not to mention to Tricia where he had been. "I told you I was with friends," Ken said.

Since they had returned to Belle Terre in separate cars, Tricia didn't know that Ken and her sister had been together. Keeping that a secret smacked of an illicitness that made Schyler uneasy, but she still thought it best for Tricia to remain unenlightened of last night's activities. In this case what she didn't know couldn't hurt her, or anyone else.

The secret that they shared hadn't drawn Ken and her closer. On the contrary, he had been querulous and standoffish all day. That suited her fine. She thought it best that they give each other breathing room after what had happened last night, when neither had been seen in the most favorable light.

As soon as she had eaten supper, Schyler excused herself and went upstairs. In her room, she changed clothes, then sneaked out of the house by way of the back stairs. She wanted to avoid having to explain where she was going toting a shotgun. Besides, if she thought about it much longer, she might chicken out.

Now, standing hidden behind a clump of blackberry bushes several hundred yards and across the road from Flynn's house, her hands were slick with perspiration and her heart was racing. She didn't take lightly what she was about to do. The thought of killing anything made her sick to her stomach. Even the idea of maiming an animal turned her stomach.

Only the memory of how viciously the provoked dog had attacked her, and the possibility that another defenseless child might suffer such an attack, propelled her closer to Flynn's house. His pit bulls weren't ordinary household pets. They were life-threatening animals, bred to attack and kill. If Flynn demanded it afterward, she would compensate him for his loss, within reason. Apart from that she would offer no apology. She would personally see to it that action was taken to prohibit pit bull fights in the area, even if it meant appealing directly to her congressman.

Flynn's pickup was parked in the yard. A mangy cat was curled on the hood of it. There were no lights on outside the house, but enough light was coming through the windows to illuminate the yard and cast long, eerie shadows. As she crept closer, she could hear a TV or radio playing inside. Every now and then a shadow moved past a window. The tacky lace curtains rose and fell reluctantly whenever the desultory breeze touched them. Schyler could smell pork cooking. She counted on that pervasive smell to keep the dogs from picking up her scent.

From the opposite side of the road, she gave the house wide berth, having planned to approach it from the back side. She hadn't selected the shotgun at random. A pistol was out of the question. She would have to get too close. A rifle would have meant firing with precision accuracy, and since it had been years since she'd fired one, her skill was questionable. Using the double-barreled shotgun to blast the kennel where the dogs were penned would guarantee hits. If the shots didn't kill the dogs, they would at least inflict serious damage.

Crouching low, Schyler watched the house for another five minutes. She could see movement inside. The dogs were prowling their pens restlessly, but not a single bark had been uttered. Drawing a deep breath, she stepped from behind the bushes and onto the gravel road. She was fully exposed for the length of time it took her to run across it. Making it to the back of a dilapidated shed, she flung herself flat against the wall of it, drinking in oxygen through her wide, gasping mouth.

One of the dogs growled. Their movements became more restless. One whined a sound that had a question mark at the end of it. Schyler sensed their mounting skittishness. They couldn't smell her, but they seemed to know she was there. They sensed impending danger, danger she tried not to think about as she checked the shotgun one final time. Two shells were loaded, two riding in her waistband waiting to be. Holding her breath, she pulled back both hammers. The soft metallic clicks elicited another growl from the dog pens.

It had to be now.

She stepped from behind the shed and aimed the shotgun at the fenced enclosure. It was about seventy-five feet away from her. Her finger was so wet with perspiration, it slipped off the trigger the first time she tried to pull it; however, she finally squeezed off the shot.

She had forgotten how deafening a sound it made. The gunshot exploded in the stillness and reverberated like a cannon. She had also forgotten to anticipate the kickback and was painfully reminded of it when the stock rammed into her shoulder with bruising force, nearly knocking the breath out of her.

In the periphery of her mind, she was aware of the racket that erupted around her, the frantic yapping coming from the kennel, the livid cursing and shouting from inside the house. She disregarded both and concentrated only on aiming the shotgun a second time.

As soon as she fired, she flipped the release and the barrels dropped forward. Reaching inside, she pinched out the two empty shells and replaced them with the two she had easily accessible in the waistband of her jeans. She locked the barrel into place again. Her practice that afternoon had paid off. She'd completed reloading in under eight seconds. She fired the third shot and had just gotten off the fourth when Jigger Flynn came tearing out the back door of the house.

He was almost farcically outraged. His face was a florid mask, his sparse hair was standing on end. He was barefooted and was wearing a ratty, ribbed knit tank T-shirt over his drooping trousers. Far from funny, however, was the pistol he was brandishing. Dire threats issued from a mouth that sprayed spittle with each blue word.

Schyler froze in terror. She hadn't counted on him having a gun. She had expected him to be upset, angry, even furious, but she had planned to reason with him once the initial shock had worn off and he had calmed down. One couldn't reason with a madman waving a pistol. The man cursing and damning the whole world to hell looked like he would never be reasonable again.

He hadn't spotted her yet. His first concern was for the dogs. Because none had charged out to attack her through the holes the shotgun had made in the fencing, Schyler assumed that she had inflicted serious damage. Some of the animals were still alive. Their pitiable whimpering would ring in her ears for years to come.

"My dogs . . . What motherfuckin' bastard . . . I'll kill you." Flynn spun around and fired aimlessly into the darkness, intent on killing the culprit who had suspended his lucrative sideline. "I'll kill you, goddamn you to hell. You shithead, you'll wish you were dead when I get through with your miserable, goddamned hide. I'll kill you."

Schyler saw movement beyond Flynn's shoulder. "What's happened?" the woman asked from the window.

Schyler, recognizing her, gasped.

"Shut up, you black bitch! Call the sheriff. Some cocksucker's shot my dogs!" The curtain fell back into place. Flynn, sputtering in his rage, fired the pistol again. This time the bullet slammed into the wall of the shed. Schyler heard the brittle wood splinter near her head. Giving thought to nothing except running for cover, she dashed toward the road, putting the shed between her and Flynn.

Seconds later, she could hear his choppy breathing and knew that he had seen movement. He ran across the yard after her, cursing the obstacles in his path.

All thought of diplomatic negotiating vanished. Schyler ran for her life. Her only chance to escape unharmed was to get across the road and take cover in the dense woods. She slid from the shallow ditch and scrambled up the other side. When she reached the road, the pounding heels of her tennis shoes crunched in the gravel. She prayed she wouldn't twist an ankle, which was a ridiculous prayer. Why worry about a sprain when at any second she could be shot? Jigger Flynn was in hot pursuit and firing the pistol as he hurled vile curses at her.

She had reached the center of the road when a pickup truck careened around the bend, almost running over her. It swerved away just in time and came to a partial stop with a theatrical shower of gravel and a cloud of dust. The passenger door was flung open.

"Get in, you idiot!" Cash shouted at her. Schyler tossed the shotgun into the bed of the truck, grabbed hold of the open door, and hauled herself inside. A bullet struck the door. "Keep your head down!"

"Come back, you goddamned murderer," Flynn yelled. He fired the pistol repeatedly but was too angry to be accurate. By the time he had calmed down enough to take careful aim, the truck had been obscured by a curtain of dust.

Inside the cab of the pickup, Schyler was bent double, her head between her knees, arms crossed over her head. She couldn't stop shaking, even when she knew that they were out of range and Flynn's hysterical cursing could no longer be heard.

Cash was piloting the old truck as though it were a Porsche on a smooth racetrack, taking the twisting turns in the washboard road at a daredevil speed and without the aid of headlights, making it impossible for anyone to follow them. The roads crisscrossed the bayous as intricately as a weaving pattern of the cotton yarn in a Cajun blanket. He knew each one and had no difficulty navigating them.

"You okay?" His eyes left the road for a split second, only long enough for him to glance down at his passenger.

"I'm unwell."

"Unwell? What the hell does that mean?"

Schyler raised her head and glared at him. "It means I'm about to puke."

The truck came to another screeching halt. Cash reached across her and shoved open the door. Schyler leaped from the cab and retched into the dusty bushes that lined the edge of the road.

Hands propped on her knees, she remained bent at a forty-five-degree angle while the spasms gripped her until she was entirely empty. Her ears were on fire. Her skin broke out in a clammy sweat. She was trembling all over. She waited for the terror to subside. It didn't, but eventually it waned. Finally, she opened her eyes. A bottle of whiskey came into focus.

She accepted the bottle and lifted it to her chalky lips. She filled her mouth with the fiery liquor, swished it around, then spat it out. Or tried to. Most of it dribbled down her chin.

"Hell." Cash removed the bandanna that was knotted around his neck and passed it to her. She blotted her chin with it, then dabbed her eyes. They were leaking tears, though she wasn't actually crying. "You can't spit worth a damn. But you can damn sure shoot. There were four holes wider than washtubs in the side of that kennel. Hide and guts were splattered—"

"Please, shut up," she begged weakly. Her stomach heaved again.

"Are you going to vomit again?" She shook her head no. "If you are, tell me so I can pull over. I don't want you doing it in my truck."

She looked at the fresh bullet hole in the door of his pickup, then glanced up at him disparagingly. "Take me back."

"To Belle Terre?"

"To Flynn's place."

He stared at her with patent disbelief. "Have you got shit for brains, lady?"

"Take me back, Cash."

"Like hell. I'm getting tired of rescuing you."

"I didn't ask you to!"

"You'd be dead by now if I hadn't," he shouted back.

"I've got to go back. I've got to offer to pay for—"

"Forget it." His voice sliced the humid air as precisely as his hands did when he made the negative chopping motion. "You don't want Jigger to ever find out who did that to his dogs."

"But I can't just—"

He took her by the shoulders. "Look, why do you think I went in there with the headlights off? I didn't want to spotlight you. I hope to God he didn't recognize my truck."

"I heard him say he was going to call the sheriff. If the sheriff is there, I can explain. Surely—"

Cash shook her hard, and she fell abruptly silent. "Schyler, you don't realize the kind of man you're dealing with. He doesn't settle out of court. He goes for the jugular just like his dogs. I advised you to leave it alone, but now it's done. Stay away from him and don't admit doing this to a soul."

"I've got to go back," she repeated tearfully.

"Shit," he cursed viciously. "Haven't you heard anything I just said?"

"I saw Gayla. Through the window."

"Gayla Frances?"

"Yes, Veda's daughter. You know her? She was inside Flynn's house."

"That's right." Cash released her and stepped back. Clinging to the open door for support, Schyler looked at him incomprehensively. "Gayla's been living with Jigger the last few years."

The earth slipped off its axis. The dark trees spun around her. "*Gayla?* With Jigger Flynn? That's impossible."

"Get in."

Without a shred of compassion, he pushed her into the cab of the truck and slammed the door. He came around and slid beneath the wheel. He had left the motor running, so within seconds they were underway again. He still didn't turn on the headlights. They drove along roads so narrow that sometimes the tree branches slapped against the pickup and interlaced to form a tunnel around them. Schyler didn't suggest that he turn the headlights on; he seemed to know exactly what he was doing. It was a relief to let someone else handle the decisions for a while.

Exhausted, she rested her head against the open window and let the breeze cool her face. "Tell me about Gayla. How did she come to live with that reprobate?"

"When we get home. My home."

"I'd rather not."

"Yeah, well I'd rather not have been staking out Flynn's place tonight, waiting for you to pull some damn fool stunt like you did."

"You were—"

"Parked just around the curve in the road."

"You were that sure I'd do it?"

"I had a strong suspicion you'd try something."

"Even after you had warned me not to?"

He gave her a wry look. "Because I had warned you not to."

After a moment she said, "I guess I owe you another thank you."

"*Oui.* I guess you do."

THIRTEEN

He stopped the car. The emergency brake pedal made a grinding noise when he pushed it toward the floorboard. He turned to face her. For a long, tense moment they stared at each other.

"What'll you give me for saving your life again?" he asked softly. "You're running up quite a bill."

Schyler stared him down stonily, though her insides felt as light and airy as meringue. Her mouth was dry and it wasn't because of her recent nausea.

After several seconds, his lips curved into his characteristically cynical smile. "Relax. I won't collect tonight."

"How kind."

"It's not that. We haven't got that much time." He pushed open his door. "We walk from here, Miss Schyler."

He had deliberately avoided the roads leading back to Belle Terre, so they had approached his house from the far side. Taking her hand, he led her down the overgrown path toward the bayou and the small house that sat on its banks, nestled among the trees.

It had been built of cypress and was probably as old as the plantation house. Like Red Broussard's café, the house was set off the ground on enormous cypress stumps. The metal roof extended over a recessed porch lined with posts, which helped support it. The batten shutters had been left open and revealed screened windows. An exterior staircase, located at one end of the porch, led to a second story.

Cash guided her up the wooden steps, across the porch, and through a door into the central room. At one end there was a fireplace and small kitchen. The room served as both living room and eating area. It was neater than Schyler had expected it to be, but it definitely bore the stamp of Cash's heritage.

She had toured reconstructed Cajun houses, which were a staple tourist attraction in that part of Louisiana. The architecture of this house was typical, even to the *galerie,* or screened porch, that ran the length of the central room at the back of the house. Through a narrow connecting door, she could see into a bathroom, obviously a modern addition to the original floor plan.

On the *galerie,* there was an iron double bed, a bureau, and a rickety table with a small, portable TV and a deck of cards on it. A bookcase was stocked with best-selling paperback novels and recent-issue magazines. In addition to his tidiness, his reading matter, too, surprised her. She gathered that the *galerie* was where Cash spent most of his time when he was at home. It overlooked the bayou.

"What's upstairs?" she asked.

"My mother's bedroom."

Some of the furniture was obviously handmade, but by master craftsmen. There were touches of modernity, like the TV, the microwave oven, and the fan with cane blades that was suspended from a beam in the ceiling of the main room. He reached for the string and gave it a yank. The fan began circulating the still air.

"Drink?" He crossed to the cabinet in the kitchen, parted the calico curtain that was gathered on a rod, and took down a bottle of whiskey.

"Please. Add some water."

"Ice?"

She shook her head no. He came back, bringing the bottle with him, and handed her the drink. "Sit down." He indicated a chair that was upholstered in a regular, all-American fabric, a chair that could have been purchased in any furniture store in the nation. It seemed absurdly out of place in this interesting house beside the bayou, but Schyler sank into it, grateful for the familiarity. Nothing so far this evening had seemed normal. Her teeth clicked against the glass as she took a sip of her drink. "Thank you."

He plopped into the matching chair facing hers and took a swallow of his own drink, having placed the bottle on the low table between them. He propped his booted feet there, too, stacking one ankle on top of the other.

"Where did you learn to shoot?"

"Cotton taught me."

He had been about to raise his glass to his mouth for another drink. He paused momentarily, then drank before he said, "He did a good job of it."

"I'm not proud of what I did tonight."

"Your daddy would be."

"Probably," she admitted grudgingly. Studiously, she ran her finger around the rim of her glass. "We had a disagreement over it, my shooting," she told Cash with a wistful smile. "He wanted me to go hunting with him every fall, but I couldn't bring myself to shoot anything except inanimate targets. He was disappointed in me." She took another swift swallow, then set her empty glass on the low table beside Cash's feet and stood up.

"Another drink?"

"No thanks," She made a slow, exploratory circle around her chair, trailing her finger over the nubby fabric. "Tonight was different. I had to do it. But I don't want to be complimented on my marksmanship."

Restlessly she prowled the room, making her way toward the window over the kitchen sink. In the sill an herb garden was growing. Apparently it was carefully tended. Inquiringly she glanced at him over her shoulder. He shrugged and poured himself another straight whiskey. "My mother always had things growing in that window."

"You use the herbs to make your potions?"

She asked the question teasingly, but his answer was serious. "Some of them."

Next to the outdated refrigerator, which hummed noisily, there was a corkboard hanging on the wall. Several old pictures had been thumbtacked there. Schyler leaned forward to get a better look at them. There was one of a woman and a child, a young boy with unruly, wavy hair and mature, serious eyes.

"You and your mother?"

"*Oui.*"

The woman's hair was black and curly around her triangular face that tapered from a wide forehead to her impishly pointed chin. Her long, exotic eyes made her look as though she was privy to a thousand secrets. Her mysterious smile said she was sharing none of them. Her lips were heart-shaped, full and voluptuous, enticing and sexy.

Schyler could remember Monique, but never as being this young. And she'd only seen her from a distance. She was captivated by the photograph. "Your mother was very beautiful."

"Thanks."

"How old were you here?"

"Ten maybe. I don't remember."

"What was the occasion?"

"I don't remember that either."

Schyler looked at the other pictures. Several were snapshots of marines in battle fatigues, dogtags hanging from chains around their necks, grinning, acting silly. One had assumed a batter's stance and was holding his rifle like a baseball bat. Another had his middle finger raised to the camera. She recognized Cash in some of the pictures.

"Vietnam?"

"*Oui.*"

"You all seem to be enjoying yourselves."

He made a scoffing sound. "Yeah, we had a helluva good time over there."

"I didn't mean to be facetious."

"The guy with the mustache got it in the gut the day after the picture was taken. The medics didn't even bother to fix him up, just tried to pile all the parts back into the carcass before the chopper got there to cart it out." From across the room, he pointed at one of the other pictures. "I'm not sure what happened to the guy wearing the funny hat. We were out on patrol. When we heard his screams, the rest of us got the hell out of there."

Stunned by his blasé attitude, she asked, "How can you talk about deceased friends like that?"

"I don't have any friends."

She recoiled as though he had socked her. "Why do you do that?"

"What?"

"Retaliate. Repay concern with cruelty."

"Habit, I guess."

"Take me home."

"You don't like it here?" He spread his arms to encompass the modest room.

"I don't like you."

"Most people in your class don't."

"I'm not in a *class*. I'm me. And the reason people don't like you is because you're such a snide, sarcastic son of a bitch. Where's your phone? If you won't drive me to Belle Terre, I'll call someone to pick me up."

"I don't have a phone."

"You don't have a telephone?"

He smirked at the incredulity underlying her question. "That way I don't have to talk to somebody I don't want to."

"How do you survive without a telephone?"

"When I need one, I go to the office at the landing and use that one."

"That door is always kept locked."

"There are ways around that."

Schyler was aghast. "You pick the lock? You break in and mooch off us?" His unrepentant grin was as good as a signed confession. "Not only are you unlikable, you're a thief."

"So far no one has seemed to mind."

"Does anyone know?"

"Cotton knows."

Schyler was surprised. "Cotton lets you bleed utilities off Belle Terre? In exchange for what?"

"That's between him and me." Abruptly he placed his glass on the table and sat forward, propping his elbows on his knees. "You aren't planning to do anything crazy about Gayla Frances, are you?"

"At the very least I'm going to talk to her."

"Don't. She won't welcome your interference."

"I damn well will interfere. I want to hear from her own lips that she chooses to live with that man. Until then I won't believe it. I can't understand why Veda allows it."

He gave her a strange look. "Veda's dead."

The breath deserted Schyler's body. Her knees unhinged and she dropped into the chair again. She stared at him blankly. "You must be mistaken."

"No!"

"Veda's dead?" He nodded. She lowered her gaze and stared into near space, trying to imagine a world without Veda in it. Solid, dependable, loving Veda, who had nursed her through colic and scraped knees and affairs of the heart that had gone awry. "When?"

"Several years ago. Not long after you left. Didn't your sister tell you?"

A cold numbness, like death, stole over her. She shook her head. "No, she didn't. She told me she had had to let Veda go."

He muttered a foul word. "She let her go, all right. That was the beginning of the end. Veda took sick soon after that. Personally I think it was because that bitch you call a sister booted her off Belle Terre."

He flopped back against the cushions of his chair. "Veda was too old to get another job. Then she got too sick to work. Gayla had to leave college and come home to take care of her. Jobs were scarce. Gayla took what she could find. She got hired to serve drinks in a honky-tonk. That's where she caught Jigger's eye. He liked what he saw and took her under his wing. He coached her in a more profitable occupation."

Schyler stared with disbelief. "You're lying."

"Why would I? Ask anybody. It's the truth. Gayla turned tricks in the cheapest dive in town."

"She would never do that."

"She did, I tell you."

Schyler vehemently denied the possibility. "But she's so pretty, so intelligent and sweet."

"I guess that's why she became such a favorite." Schyler clamped her teeth over her lip and tried to keep the tears out of her eyes. "Among Jigger's girls, Gayla shone like a new penny. That's why he took her for his own. Now he only occasionally loans her out and then at a premium price." Schyler's head dropped into her waiting hand.

Without mercy, Cash went on. "Veda died, mostly of shame and grief. Tricia Howell had spread it around that she was old and incompetent and had almost burned Belle Terre to the ground by negligently leaving an iron on. Then there was Gayla. Veda couldn't stand what her daughter had become."

It wasn't possible. Schyler had known Gayla since she was born to Veda, a late-in-life child. Together they'd cried when Mr. Frances was killed in an explosion at the oil refinery where he worked. That's when Cotton had invited Veda to move into the quarters at Belle Terre. Schyler had watched Gayla blossom into a lovely teenager. She had just seen her off to college when Schyler left for England.

"What about Jimmy Don?" she asked.

Jimmy Don Davison had been Gayla's sweetheart since kindergarten. He'd become the star running back on Heaven's high school football team. He had been known as the Heathen of Heaven on the gridiron. He was such an outstanding athlete that a coach from LSU had drafted him and given him a full, four-year scholarship. He was a handsome, intelligent young man who was popular with black and white students alike. But it had always been understood that he belonged to Gayla Frances and vice versa.

"He's doing time."

"Time? You mean in prison?" Schyler wheezed. "For what?"

"He was still at school while all this was going on. When he heard that Gayla had moved in with Jigger, he got drunk, went berserk, and busted up a bar and just about everybody in it. Nearly killed one guy for boasting that he'd been with Gayla and telling all who would listen what a juicy piece she was. Jimmy Don pleaded guilty to all the charges and is serving his sentence. Three years, I think."

Schyler covered her face with her hands. It was too much to assimilate at one time. Veda. Gayla. Jimmy Don. Their lives had been ruined. And, although indirectly, Tricia was responsible. Schyler felt guilty by association.

She raised her head and looked at the man slouching in the chair opposite her. He seemed to take perverse pleasure in tormenting her. "You relished telling me all that, didn't you?"

He conceded with a nod. "Just so you'll know the caliber of folks you're living with in that big, fancy house. Your sister is a spiteful bitch. Her dick-less husband is a joke. Cotton . . . hell, I don't know what's wrong with him. He stood by and let Tricia do with people's lives what she damn well pleased."

Schyler's chin went up a notch. It was all right for her to acknowledge her family's weaknesses, but it was something else for an outsider to, especially Cash Boudreaux. "What the people at Belle Terre do is no concern of yours. I won't have you bad-mouthing my family." She stood up and looked down at him, her expression imperious and haughty.

It nudged his temper over the edge. One second his spine was conforming to the cushions of the chair, seemingly indifferent. The next, he was looming over Schyler, gripping her shoulders hard. "I'll say what I goddamn want to about anybody or anything."

"Not about my family."

His fingers slid up through her hair and pressed against her scalp, holding her head in place. He lowered his face to within inches of her. "All right. For the time being, I'll tell you what I think of you."

"I don't care what you think of me."

His lips brushed across hers. "I believe you do."

"Stop that."

Smiling, he briefly touched his lips to hers a second time. "I think you're just about the most interesting woman I've come across in a long time, Miss Schyler."

"Let me go." She tried to dodge his roaming, sipping lips, but they wouldn't be eluded. They gently struck her face with petal softness. She tried to push him away, but her efforts were wasted.

"Any woman who'd go up against Jigger Flynn, hell, she's somebody I've just got to know better." He thrust his hips forward and up, using the fly of his jeans to suggestively nudge the cleft of her thighs.

"You're disgusting."

His laugh was low, deep, dirty. "Ask around, Miss Schyler. Most women don't think so. And I think you're just dying to find out for yourself."

She tried to squirm away, but he pressed his fingers against her head, hard enough to cause some mild discomfort and to effectively stop her from trying to pull it free. Then he tilted her face up and kissed her, covering her lips with his.

She made a strangled sound of protest when his tongue slid between her lips and into her mouth. His tongue's lazy, swirling penetration shocked her. She reeled and clutched his shoulders for support.

After a long, thorough kiss, he raised his head. "Just what I thought," he said roughly. "You put on all those ladylike airs, but you're just like a firecracker on the Fourth of July, ready to ignite, ready to explode." His hands slid from her head, down her shoulders and arms to her waist, which he clasped. He jerked her forward and rubbed against her. "Feel that? I've got just the match to light your fuse." She slapped him hard. His eyes narrowed dangerously. "What's the matter, not used to—"

"Filth, Mr. Boudreaux. No, I'm not used to filth."

"Doesn't your brother-in-law talk dirty to you in bed?" Schyler's face went white with indignation. Cash snickered, adding, "How does Howell manage to service both you and your sister?"

"Shut up!"

"Folks in town are wondering, you know. Does he traipse back and forth between bedrooms, or do y'all sleep in one big, happy bed?"

Schyler pushed against his chest so hard that he was forced to release her. She ran out the front door and clambered down the steps. He followed close behind. Encircling her waist, he brought her up short. "No need to run off. I don't want Howell's leftovers. Now get in the truck. I'll drive you home."

"I wouldn't go anywhere with you."

"Afraid you'll be seen with me?"

"Yes. I'm afraid people would think that your lying, cheating ways might rub off on me."

"Lying, cheating ways?"

"You had bet money on Jigger's dog last night."

"I don't deny that."

"Why didn't you tell me you gambled on those fights when I asked you to kill the dog?"

"It was none of your business."

"You manipulated me!" she cried. "Taking me there, urging me for my own good not to do anything against him. But all the time you were protecting your own interest."

"One had nothing to do with the other."

"Liar. You won a lot of money."

"I damn sure did."

She shuddered with fury over his calm admission. "You're every bit as unscrupulous as people say."

She wrested her arm free. She truly loathed this man. She had tried to communicate with him as an equal, but he wouldn't let her. Ken was right in that respect. The differences between the classes were as deeply ingrained as the rings in an oak tree and seemingly as impenetrable. The system was feudalistic, it was unacceptable, but it was undeniable. Cash Boudreaux had dragged her down to his level and she felt soiled.

"Now that you've told me off, get in the truck," he said.

"Like hell I will."

"Where are you going?"

"Home."

Cash went after her. "Don't be stupid. You can't walk all the way to Belle Terre in the middle of the night."

"Wanna bet?"

He pulled her around again. "You're mad because I said the things you know but don't want to hear. People call me trash. Fine. I don't give a goddamn about anybody's opinion of me but my own. I'll go to hell for some of the things I've done, but I never dumped on an aging black woman who depended on me for her livelihood like your sister did. I wouldn't stand by and let it happen either like that gutless wonder, Howell, did. I wouldn't turn a blind eye like Cotton did."

Schyler glowered at him. Even in the darkness, she could see that he was sneering at her. His kiss had been blatantly erotic, but not sexually prompted. He had used it to insult her, to punish her for being what she was and for what he wasn't and never would be.

"Stay away from Belle Terre and everybody in it. Especially me. If you don't, I'll shoot you for trespassing."

With that, she took the shotgun from the bed of his pickup and struck out for home on foot.

 # FOURTEEN

G ayla sat in the ladder-back chair in the corner. Like a child, Jigger expected her to be seen and not heard, especially when he had company—unless he was using her to entertain his company. Tonight their company was the sheriff. She knew from experience that the sheriff liked his sex straight. He was a swine, but a finicky one. Tonight, though, he was on duty, which relieved Gayla of hers.

"Made any enemies recently, Jigger?"

Sheriff Pat Patout looked longingly at the glass of whiskey Jigger was drinking, but he had declined the offer to join him. He had barely squeaked past his opponent in the last election. He was already sweating the outcome of the next one. Lately he was being as prudent and conscientious as an old-maid school marm.

"I don't have an enemy in the world, Sheriff," Jigger said blandly. "You know that."

They both knew quite the opposite. The sheriff cleared his throat loudly and cast a lustful glance at Gayla. Her face remained impassive, as though she were too stupid to grasp the meaning of their conversation. That passivity was the only way she had survived the last few years. She sat there and let the sheriff ogle her high, pointed breasts. They were as symmetrical and well defined as two sno–cone cups growing out of her chest. Their shape was ill-concealed by the thin, tight dress Jigger made her wear. Gazing back at the sheriff with lifeless eyes, her mind actively conjured up epithets that applied to him.

Patout wiped his mouth with the back of his hand and fidgeted uncomfortably in his chair. "Maybe I will have just a touch of that." He nodded toward the bottle. "It's a thirsty night. So goddamn hot." Jigger poured him a hefty drink. He downed it in one swallow. Almost immediately beads of sweat popped out on his forehead. "You might not have any enemies, Jigger," his stinging vocal cords wheezed, "but you sure as hell pissed off somebody. I only had to take a gander at those dog pens to ascertain that."

"Bastards," Jigger muttered.

"You think there was more than one?"

"One did the shooting. One did the driving the pickup."

"Did you recognize the vehicle?"

Jigger shook his shiny, oily head. "Too dark. Too fast."

"Did *you* see anything?"

Gayla jumped when she realized that Patout had addressed her. She tucked her bare feet beneath the chair and curled her toes downward, pressing them into the cracked, scummy linoleum floor. Her hands were balled together into twin coffee-colored fists. Straightening her arms, she pressed her fists between her thighs as though to hide evidence. She relaxed her arms and withdrew her hands, however, when she realized that the pose made her breasts more prominent. The goat with the badge pinned to his shirt pocket was staring bug-eyed at her chest.

In answer to his question, she shook her head no. They could torture her, but she would never supply them the name they wanted. That name was Schyler Crandall. Schyler had been in Jigger's yard shooting up his kennel with a shotgun.

It didn't make a lick of sense, but it was true. She would recognize Schyler anywhere. She just prayed to God that Schyler hadn't seen her. Schyler wouldn't spit on her shadow now. Schyler's return had nothing to do with her, but somehow it was heartening to know that her former friend was home.

"I didn't see nothin', Sheriff," Gayla mumbled, deliberately using bad grammar.

Jigger scowled at her over his shoulder. "Where are your manners, gal?" He pronounced it "mannahs." "Fix the sheriff some supper."

"No, thanks, Jigger. I already ate down at the café."

"Fix him some supper." Jigger's eyes were as piercing as pins that impaled Gayla against the tattered wallpaper with the cabbage rose print.

"He don't want none."

"I said fix him some supper," Jigger roared, banging his fist on the table and jiggling the amber contents of the whiskey bottle.

Gayla came to her feet. They whispered across the dirty floor. From the shelf above the old gas stove, she took down a plate. She lifted a graying, greasy pork chop from the pan, dropped it onto the plate, and ladled a spoonful of collard greens beside it. She broke off a piece of cold cornbread from what had been left over and set the chunk on top of the greens, then carried the unappetizing platter to the table and unceremoniously thunked it down in front of the sheriff.

"Thank ya." Patout gave her an uncertain smile.

Jigger wrapped his arm around her waist and jerked her against him. His shoulder gouged her belly. He patted her rump and let his hand linger, caressing her, squeezing the firm flesh through the threadbare dress.

"She's a good girl. Most of the time. And when she ain't . . ." He soundly swatted her fanny with his palm, making it hard enough to sting. Gayla didn't flinch.

A housefly buzzed around the sheriff's plate, which he voraciously attacked once he'd doused the greens with Tabasco. He mopped up the green pot liquor with a hunk of cornbread until it was soggy, then stuffed it into his corpulent mouth. While Jigger continued to maul her, Gayla concentrated on the fly. She watched it light on the dented metal top of the salt shaker. Her mamma would have died before she let a fly invade the kitchen at Belle Terre.

But then her mama would have died before she let a lot of things happen, like her girl becoming a whore.

Jigger slipped his calloused hand beneath her dress and ran it up the back of her thigh. She reacted reflexively, though she didn't alter her expression to let her revulsion show.

"How many of your pit bulls were killed?"

"Two. Had to shoot another myself, he was wailing so pitiful like. His brains was hanging out. One more won't fight again. Just as well be dead." He laughed nastily. "But the pregnant bitch wasn't even hit. When she whelps, I'll have the finest litter of fighting pit bulls around."

The sheriff continued to gorge. Occasionally he grunted to let Jigger know he was listening. "I'll do what I can, but there aren't many clues."

"You find the bastards what ruint my dogs, and Gayla and me'll give you a little present, won't we, honey?"

Patout stopped chewing long enough to glance up at her. His lips and chin were shiny with pork grease. She stared down at him, wondering if her eyes revealed just how much she despised all men.

The sheriff swallowed hard and pushed the cleaned plate away. He stood up, tried to hitch his britches over his belly, and reached for his straw cowboy hat. "Then I'd better git on it. I'll keep an eye out for a pickup with a bullet hole in it."

"That accounts for just about every pickup in the parish." Jigger accompanied the sheriff at the screened back door, negligently pushing Gayla aside in the process. "You'll have to do better than that, don'tcha know."

"I don't need you telling me how to do my job, Jigger."

Jigger's mean eyes turned even meaner. "Then I'm tellin' you that whoever done it will be a lot better off if you find them before I do."

The men exchanged a stare of understanding. Patout put on his hat, gave Gayla one last, slavering glance, then went through the door. With a creak and a slap of old wood, it shut behind him. "Bury these dead dogs in the mornin'. They're already stinking in this heat," he said over his shoulder.

"Come out here and bury them your ownself, you blubber gut," Jigger said beneath his breath as he waved the sheriff off.

Jigger wanted the dead animals to stink. He wanted them to stink to high heaven. He wanted everybody in the parish to smell them, to know about what had happened, and the ones who'd done it to be forewarned that he was out for vengeance. He'd get them, but good. He'd show no mercy. He'd set them up as examples. Nobody crossed Jigger Flynn and got away with it. Then he'd see to it that that litter of pups became the meanest sons of bitches in the state of Louisiana and beyond. The thought of the prestige he would gain, not to mention the money, was arousing.

He turned toward Gayla, who was at the sink, scraping off the sheriff's plate. "Time for bed."

Ordinarily she would have dropped what she was doing and followed him into the bedroom. The sooner she capitulated, the sooner it was over with. But she remembered Schyler, who, for unknown reasons, had gone up against him. Schyler's courage had rubbed off on her.

"I c . . . can't tonight, Jigger. I got my period."

He was on her in a flash, backhanding her across the mouth. Her teeth cut her lip and drew blood. "You lying bitch. You got your period last week. What do you think, I'm stupid? You think I don't remember?" He gave her a swift kick in the buttocks that sent her flying face first into the wall.

"Stop it, Jigger. I ain't lyin'." He drove his fingers into her cap of short, curly hair. She kept it short, having learned that when it was long, he could use it as a weapon. He got enough of a grip on it now to bring tears to her eyes.

"I said, time for bed. That means now."

Hand over hand she felt her way along the wall, guided by the twisting, pulling fingers in her hair. She fell through the doorway into the living room. He gave her head a mighty push that almost snapped her neck in two. She stumbled into the bedroom.

Docile now, she stood beside the bed and unbuttoned her dress. She peeled it off her shoulders and let it drop to her feet. Naked she crawled onto the bed and lay down on her back, hoping that's all he wanted her to do tonight.

He undressed. The bed springs rocked noisily when he mounted her. Grunting like a hog, he dryly pushed himself into her. In pain, she arched her back and gripped the coarse sheet beneath her; her heels dug into the thin mattress. But she didn't utter a single sound. He liked her to cry out when he hurt her. She refused to give him the satisfaction. After that initial reaction to his brutal penetration, she lay perfectly still.

This, this gross rutting, bore no resemblance to the loving act she and Jimmy Don had started doing together when she was barely fifteen. They had been so young, so much in love. They couldn't keep their eyes and hands off each other. Their blood had run as hot and sweet as pralines bubbling in a double boiler. Kissing and petting weren't enough. They had followed the urgent dictates of their bodies. And, oh, Jesus, it had felt good.

From that first time, they made love regularly. Afterward she had never felt dirty. With Jigger she always felt as nasty as a spittoon. Mating with Jimmy Don had made her feel pure, loved, cherished. It had not made her feel tainted, or so filthy she would never get clean, or so vile that she wanted to die.

She had thought about it frequently. Killing herself had been a preoccupation ever since she had come to live with Jigger. The only thing that prevented her from ending her own life was the hope, the faint hope, that one day she would see Jimmy Don again and win his forgiveness.

She had also thought about killing Jigger. When he fell into one of his drunken stupors, she had fantasized about driving a butcher knife through his bloated gut and putting an end to her misery. Nothing they could do to her afterward would be as bad as what she lived with daily.

But Veda had made her attend church faithfully, twice on Sundays and Wednesday night prayer meeting. The doctrines were steeped into her. Thundering sermons about hell and damnation had kept her on the straight and narrow for most of her life. She wasn't sure what brimstone was, but she was terrified of having to spend eternity in its midst.

God would forgive her for loving Jimmy Don and "doing it" before they got married. God understood that she was married to Jimmy Don in her heart. And she reasoned that God would forgive her for letting men use her body as a receptacle for their lust. Mama's doctor bills and medicine had been so expensive. Black girls, no matter how smart, rarely got jobs in offices and banks and retail stores. During a recession in the economy they didn't get jobs at all. She was too pretty, her looks too sensual, to get a job cleaning houses. No sane housewife wanted her around a husband or son. So she had done what she had to do. God knew her heart and would understand that.

It might stretch the boundaries of even His understanding and forgiveness if she murdered Jigger Flynn in cold blood. So she hadn't. She had tolerated what he was doing to her now, hoping that she would die a natural death and get out of this life without jeopardizing her chances for spending the next one in heaven with Papa and Mama and maybe even with Jimmy Don.

It was taking longer than usual tonight. Jigger's foul breath soughed against her clammy neck. He sweated like a pig. It dripped from his body and trickled over her breasts.

She couldn't stand it any longer.

Gayla lifted her long, elegant legs and folded them across his back, hugging his pumping hips tightly. She made a moaning, passionate sound that was a tragic parody of the sighs she had once moaned against Jimmy Don's strong, hard, smooth chest.

Her feigned passion worked. Jigger Flynn climaxed, throwing back his ugly, flat head and braying like a jackass. He collapsed on top of her before rolling off, precariously rocking the bedsprings. He lay on his back, as white and plump and slimy as a slug.

Gayla turned to her side away from him and gathered her limbs against her body protectively. She held herself still, grateful that it was over and that she had suffered no more tonight than a wallop in the lip and a kick in the rear end.

But she didn't cry until Jigger was snoring beside her. Then she cried silently. While she mouthed her prayers, her tears, remorseful, bitter, and hopeless, slid noiselessly down her satiny cheeks.

 FIFTEEN

"There was a telephone call for you while you were out," Mrs. Graves informed Schyler. "I put the message on Mr. Crandall's desk in the study."

"Thank you."

Schyler's footsteps echoed off the hardwood floors in the wide central hall as she went toward the back of the house to the small, square room that was tucked behind the sweeping staircase.

The paneled room was dominated by a massive desk. Schyler dropped her handbag and car keys on top of the mounting pile of unopened mail and settled herself in the tufted leather chair. It resembled the one in the office at the landing, but not as many treasured memories were associated with it. Cotton hadn't used this chair as often.

Macy didn't want the girls' heads to be cluttered with talk of timber and its various markets. She had objected to frequently finding Schyler enclosed in this den talking shop with Cotton, so he had done his tutoring at the landing instead. That had helped maintain peace in the household.

Schyler's thoughts focused on her father now. There was still no change in his condition. Less than an hour earlier, the cardiologist had told her that was something to be glad about.

"It's like a tie score, like kissing your sister," he had said. "His condition is nothing to cheer about, but we can be glad he's not getting any worse."

"You still have no idea when you'll be able to do the surgery?"

"No. But the more time we give him to build up his strength, the better. In this case, each day we delay is to our advantage."

After a brief visit to Cotton's ICU, she had returned home. She was dispirited. She missed Mark. The heat was oppressive. She was starved for something good to eat. She was tired of Ken's and Tricia's incessant squabbling. She longed for a good night's sleep.

As she punched out the telephone number Mrs. Graves had jotted down for her, she acknowledged two of the prevalent reasons she hadn't been sleeping well. One was Gayla Frances. The other was Cash Boudreaux.

"Delta National Bank."

Schyler realized her call had gone through. "Uh, pardon?"

"Delta National Bank. May I help you?"

She hadn't expected the call to be of a business nature. On the notepad in front of her was written an individual's name. She referred to it now. "Mr. Dale Gilbreath please," she said with a shade of inquiry in her voice.

"His line is busy. Do you care to hold?"

"Yes, please."

While she waited, Schyler slipped off her shoes and ground her numb toes against the carpet to restore circulation. Tomorrow she would revert to wearing sandals. In this heat, pantyhose and high heels were masochistic.

Who the devil was Dale Gilbreath? The name didn't ring any bells. She searched her memory but couldn't come up with a definite recollection, so she gave up trying and turned her thoughts to matters more pressing.

She had to do something about Gayla. But what? The tale Cash had told her was too outlandish not to be true. He was probably right about Gayla not welcoming her interference. Still, something had to be done. Gayla couldn't continue living with that wretched excuse for a man. The insulting way he had spoken to her was indicative of how horrid her life with him must be. Schyler couldn't stand by and do nothing. The problem was in deciding what to do and how to go about it in a manner that could be acceptable to Gayla. For the moment, she shelved that dilemma, too.

Cash Boudreaux. Lord, what should she do about him? On the surface she could answer that question with, "Nothing." Do nothing. He'd been living on Belle Terre all her life and she'd barely known he was there. Why was it starting to bother her now? So he had kissed her. So what? Forget it.

The problem was that she couldn't forget it. It was like an itch coming from an undetermined source. She didn't know where to scratch to relieve herself of the memory. She shouldn't have liked the kiss. But she had. She couldn't leave the memory of it alone until she had figured out why every time she thought about his kiss, she got a sexual thrill.

"I can ring Mr. Gilbreath now."

Schyler jumped. "Oh. Oh, thank you."

"Gilbreath."

"Mr. Gilbreath? This is Schyler Crandall returning your call."

The tonal quality changed drastically. It went from brusque to ingratiating in a heartbeat. "Well, Miss Crandall, a pleasure to talk to you. A real pleasure. Thank you for calling me back."

"Do I know you?"

He laughed at her straightforwardness. "I've got you at a disadvantage. I've heard so much about you I feel like I know you."

"You're with the bank?"

"President."

"Congratulations."

Either her sarcasm was lost on him or he chose to ignore it. "Cotton and I do a lot of business together. He told me you've been living in London."

"That's right."

"How is he?"

She related the latest doctor's report. "All we can do at this point is wait."

He made a commiserating sound. "Things could be worse."

"Yes, much worse." The conversation lagged. Schyler was anxious to get off the phone and take an aspirin for her nagging headache. "Thank you so much for calling, Mr. Gilbreath. I'm sure Cotton will appreciate your asking about him."

"This isn't strictly a courtesy call, Miss Crandall."

She could have told that by another sudden switch in his inflection. He no longer sounded like he was bending over backward to be cordial. "Oh?"

"I need to see you. Banking business."

"With me? Surely you're aware that my brother-in-law handles—"

"The financial affairs of Crandall Logging, certainly. But since this matter could directly affect Belle Terre, I thought I ought to consult you. As a favor."

More than a headache caused her brows to pull together and form a deep crevice. "What matter is that?"

"An outstanding loan. But look, I think we should discuss this in person."

She didn't like him. Instinctively she knew that. His deference was phony. She wanted nothing more than to tell him to go to hell. Well, not quite. What she wanted most was to undress, take a tepid shower, and lie on the cool sheets of her bed until supper, maybe nap off her headache. But all thoughts of relaxing were tabled. "I'm on my way."

"But I haven't got time this—"

"Make time."

An hour later Schyler entered the fake pink marble foyer of the Delta National Bank. The building was new to her and now took up a whole block right downtown where the five-and-dime had once been. It was a shame that a vault now stood in the spot where the soda fountain had been, that credit applications were dispensed instead of lemon Cokes and triple-decker club sandwiches. She was swamped with homesickness for the old bank lobby that had been paneled in dark wood and filled with subdued furnishings. One could almost smell the currency.

In her opinion this stark, modern lobby was hideous. It was as sterile as an operating room, and as clinical. It had no character or personality. Islands of chrome chairs with stiff mauve cushions floated on a carpet of sea green. Cotton had often said that no chair was worth its salt unless the wood creaked a little when you planted your butt in it. Schyler was of the same mind.

She was led to one of these chairs by a smiling receptionist who was a stranger to her. After situating herself, she glanced around and spotted a few familiar faces. They smiled at her from glass cubicle offices and tellers' windows. She drew encouragement from each familiar face. The words "Belle Terre" and "outstanding loan" kept circling in her head like buzzards waiting for helpless prey to succumb.

"Ms. Crandall, please come this way."

She was led across the lobby and into one of the gold fishbowl offices, this one occupied by Mr. Dale Gilbreath, president of Delta National Bank. He smiled unctuously as they shook hands.

"Miss Crandall, you were lucky I was able to work you in. Sit down, please. Coffee?"

"No thank you."

He bobbed his head to the receptionist and she withdrew. He took a seat behind his desk in the reclining chair and linked his hands over his stomach. "It's a pleasure to finally meet you."

She wasn't about to lie and say, "Likewise." She replied with a cool, "Thank you." Her intuition had proven right. She despised him on sight. He was going to bring bad tidings, cause her trouble.

He assessed her for a moment longer than was flattering. It verged on being insulting. "Well, what do you think of our new bank?"

"Impressive." It had made an impression on her, all right. She didn't feel inclined to expound.

"It is, isn't it? We're proud of it. It's about time downtown Heaven got a facelift, don't you think?"

"I'm sentimental."

"Meaning?"

The man didn't know when to quit. "Meaning that I liked downtown the way it was."

His smile deflated and his reclining chair bounced to an upright position. "What a surprising attitude for a modern woman like you."

"I confess to having an old-fashioned streak."

"Yes, well, there's something to be said for antiquity, but I always think there's room for improvement."

Schyler was savvy enough to know when she was being baited. Rather than enter into a difference of opinion with a man she didn't know and whose opinion was of absolutely no interest to her, she declined his subtle invitation to spar by picking a nonexistent piece of lint off her hem.

Gilbreath pulled on a pair of eyeglasses and opened a folder lying on the desk. "I regret having to call you, Miss Crandall." Intimidatingly, he glanced up at her over the rim of the glasses. She met him eyeball to eyeball over the glossy surface of the desk and didn't even blink until he looked down to refer to the contents of the folder again. "But it's my responsibility to protect the interest of the bank, no matter how unpleasant that responsibility might sometimes be."

"Why don't you get to the point? No matter how unpleasant."

"Very well," he said briskly. "I wondered if Cotton's unforeseen illness would have any bearing on the payout of the loan I extended him."

Buying time, Schyler recrossed her legs. She tried to maintain her composure, though any time a shadow fell on Belle Terre, she got a sick, sinking sensation in the pit of her stomach. "I don't have any knowledge of the loan. Exactly what were the specified terms?"

He angled his reclining chair back once again. "We call it a balloon note. In this case, Cotton borrowed three hundred thousand dollars a year ago. We set it up for him to make quarterly interest payments. All were made on time."

"Then I fail to see the problem."

Leaning his forearms on the desk, he gazed at her with the earnestness of a funeral director. "The potential problem, and I stress potential, is that the balance of the note, in addition to the final interest payment, comes due on the fifteenth of next month."

"I'm sure my father is aware of that and has the money set aside. I can authorize a transference of funds, if that's what you want."

His sympathetic smile did nothing to calm her jittery stomach. "I wish it were that easy," he said, making a helpless gesture. "Cotton's personal account won't cover the amount of the loan. Not even the interest."

"I see."

"Nor will the Crandall Logging account."

"The bank couldn't be that much at risk. I'm sure a loan of that size was collateralized."

"It was." She held her breath, but she knew what was coming. "He put up Belle Terre as collateral."

She saw stars, as though she'd been struck in the head. "How much of it?"

"The house and a sizable amount of the acreage."

"That's ridiculous! The house alone is worth far more than three hundred thousand. My father would never have agreed to that."

Again Gilbreath made that helpless little gesture, a lifting of his pale hands and a shrug of his shoulders. "At the time he applied for the loan, he had no choice. He was suffering a severe cash flow problem. Those were the best terms I could give him. He did what he had to do. I did what I had to do."

"Usury?"

He made a wry face. "Please, Miss Crandall. I want to make every effort to keep this friendly."

"We're not friends. I seriously doubt we'll ever be friends." She stood up and looked down at him. "Rest assured, I'll see that the loan is paid off in time."

Coming to his feet, he frowned. "I don't blame you for getting upset. You don't need any more bad news. But you can't blame me for being worried in light of Cotton's illness and the shutdown of the business. That could go on indefinitely."

"There is no cause for alarm on either account," she said, wishing such were the case. "The loan will be paid off in time."

Her smile was as fraudulent as the watercolor painting hanging on the wall behind his desk. Schyler wasn't deceived by either. "It would be a tragedy if we had to foreclose."

"Never." Her smile was no more genuine than his. "And you can engrave that on one of those phony pink pillars in your tacky lobby. Good-bye, Mr. Gilbreath."

SIXTEEN

What Dale Gilbreath had told Schyler was the dismal truth. She spent the remainder of the afternoon in Cotton's study at Belle Terre, checking the balances in all his bank accounts. He had virtually no cash at his disposal, not anywhere close to three hundred thousand dollars.

She was staring down at the alarmingly low total at the end of the adding machine tape, when Ken breezed in. "Drinks before dinner now being served on the veranda."

During the first days following the pit bull fight, Ken had been sullen and crotchety. Recently, he'd had a turnaround and had gone out of his way to be jocular. That jocularity grated on her now like a pumice stone.

"Ken, I need to talk to you." She tossed down the pencil she'd been using and linked her hands together over the desktop. "Why did you cease operation of Crandall Logging when Daddy had his heart attack?"

Ken's wide grin faltered and showed signs of deterioration in the corners, but he managed to hold it intact. "Who told you that?"

"What difference does it make who told me? I would have found out sooner or later. Why, Ken?"

"What brought this on?"

She sighed in resignation. "A phone call from Mr. Gilbreath at Delta National Bank."

"That asshole. He had no right to—"

"He *did* have a right, Ken. We owe his bank a lot of money. And *I* have a right to know what the hell is going on around here, which I'm waiting for you to tell me.''

''Well, I have a right to know what you've been up to lately, too.'' For one heart-stopping moment she thought Ken had found out about her visit to Cash's house on the bayou, possibly even about the kiss. It was almost a relief when he said, ''The big news around town is that somebody shot up Jigger Flynn's kennel and killed three of his dogs. He's foaming at the mouth to find out who did it.'' His eyes narrowed on her. ''You wouldn't know anything about that, would you?''

''When did it happen?'' she asked, stalling.

''Sunday night.''

''I went to bed early, remember?''

He sat on the corner of the desk and carefully gauged her facial expression. ''Yeah, I remember.'' He picked up a brass paperweight and shifted it from hand to hand. ''According to Jigger, a pickup truck came barreling down the road like a bat outta hell and picked up the fellow who shot his dogs. He says he fired at the truck with his pistol and hit it on the passenger side.'' He crossed his arms over his thigh and leaned down low, whispering, ''Now guess whose truck is sporting a fresh bullet hole?''

''Whose?''

''Cash Boudreaux's.''

''Is Mr. Boudreaux responding to any allegations that he was responsible?''

''Yeah, he's responding. He says he got shot at while fleeing a married man's bedroom, or more specifically, fleeing a married man's wife inside the bedroom.''

''Nobody can dispute that.''

Ken flashed her a grin. ''Not the probability of it anyway. But you know what I think?'' Stubbornly and calmly she waited him out. He lowered his voice another decibel. ''I think you killed those dogs and that Boudreaux helped you. What I'm wondering is what kind of currency you exchanged, 'cause that Cajun doesn't do anything for nothing.''

She came out of her chair like a shot and, feeling trapped, circled the end of the desk. ''You're changing the subject.''

He grabbed her wrist. All pretense disappeared. His face had turned ugly. ''I thought I told you to steer clear of him, Schyler.''

She pulled her wrist free. ''And I told you that I don't need a keeper. But apparently you do, or my father's business wouldn't be in the shambles it's in.''

''It's my business, too.''

''Then why did you shut it down?''

''For godsake, what is all the shouting about?'' Tricia entered the room, exuding Shalimar and petulance in equal strengths. ''Kindly keep your voices down.'' She closed the door behind her. ''Mrs. Graves doesn't talk much around here, but she's probably a blabbermouth when it comes to spreading gossip. Now, what's going on?''

''Nothing you need to concern yourself about,'' Ken snapped.

''It is something she should concern herself about,'' Schyler contradicted. ''She lives here. She should know that Belle Terre is in jeopardy.''

Tricia looked from one to the other. ''What in the world are y'all talking about?'' She sipped at her highball while Schyler summarized for them her conversation with Gilbreath.

Ken spat the banker's name. ''I might have known he'd get you all wound up. He's a persnickety old Scrooge. Only sees the bottom line. Probably a fag, too.''

''I don't care if he sleeps with sheep,'' Schyler declared angrily, ''the facts are the same. We have a note coming due and no way that I can see to pay it.''

"I'll take care of it," he grumbled.

"How, Ken, how?" Schyler went around the desk again and sat down. Shuffling through the accounts she had just gone over, she raised her hands in surrender and said, "We're broke."

"Broke!" Tricia said on an incredulous laugh. "That's impossible."

"Daddy used Belle Terre to cover a three-hundred-thousand-dollar loan. I can't imagine him doing it, but he did."

"He was desperate," Ken said. "I thought it was foolish myself at the time, but he wouldn't listen to my advice. Not that he ever does."

Schyler jumped to Cotton's defense. "I'm sure he did what he thought was necessary. He couldn't foresee that he would have a heart attack or that you'd close the doors on the business the minute he did."

"You keep waving that at me like a red flag. Well, you finally succeeded in getting me angry, if that's what you're after."

"It isn't. We can't afford the luxury of getting angry at each other. I want an explanation."

Ken gnawed on the inside of his cheek. He shoved his hands into the pockets of his slacks and hunched his shoulders defensively. "It's simple economics. We were losing more money than we were making. No contracts were coming in, but Cotton was paying the regulars the same wages he always had. He was paying the independents a premium price on timber, too."

"He wouldn't cut back on them."

"And that's probably why Crandall Logging is in the shape it's in," Ken said heatedly. "I thought it was better to quit while we were ahead instead of pouring good money after bad."

Ken's explanation didn't quite gel, but Schyler was in no position to dispute it. Cotton had always been a shrewd businessman. It was unlike him to let things get so far beyond his control. Unless he was getting senile, which also seemed an absurd possibility. In any case, the problem was urgent. Solving it had to take precedence over finding its source.

"How are we going to pay this note? We've got until the fifteenth of next month to come up with the cash."

Tricia dropped into a chair and nonchalantly examined her fingernails. Ken moved to a window and nervously jangled the change in his pants pocket. "You could have brought me one of those," he said to his wife, nodding down at her drink.

"When you start being an attentive husband, I'll be an attentive wife."

If they launched into one of their verbal skirmishes, Schyler thought she would scream. She was spared. Ken turned to face her and said, "You and Tricia have money from your mother's legacy."

"Forget it," Tricia said. "I'm not risking my inheritance to get Crandall Logging out of hock or to save Belle Terre. I'd sell it first."

"Don't even say such a thing!" Schyler wanted to slap her. Tricia had never cared for the property the way Schyler did. Her nonchalance now pointed up just how uncaring she was.

But Tricia was right in one respect. Schyler couldn't use her mother's legacy to pay off this note. If Cotton died, she would need that money to maintain Belle Terre in the future.

"What about that guy in London?"

Schyler looked at Ken. "Mark? What about him?"

"He's rich, isn't he?"

"I can't ask Mark for the money."

"How come? You're sleeping with him, aren't you?"

Ignoring the slur, Schyler shook her head adamantly. "Out of the question. I can't and won't ask Mark for the money."

"Then what do you propose to do?"

She resented his condescending tone. "I propose to reopen Crandall Logging and to earn the money to pay off the loan."

"Excuse me?"

"You heard me, Ken."

"You can't do that."

Tricia snickered. "That would be right down her alley, honey, going to that dirty old landing every day. Mama used to have to drag her away from there."

"I forbid it," Ken shouted angrily.

Only minutes ago, Schyler couldn't see a way out of this unexpected dilemma. Now the solution was brimming crystal clear in her mind. The decision was made; it felt right. She wanted to do this for her father. She needed to do it for her own peace of mind.

"You can't forbid me to do anything, Ken," she said tightly. "Tomorrow I want the business records of the last several years brought to the office at the landing. Everything. Contracts, payroll accounts, tax returns, expense receipts, everything."

"Cotton will hear about this," Ken ground out.

Schyler aimed an accusing finger at him. "You're damn right he will. I want to know why Crandall Logging went from a productive business to a nonrevenue-producing company on the brink of ruin in just six short years."

"I guess you think it's my fault. That the company's decline started the day I came aboard."

"Please, Ken, don't be childish," she said wearily. "I'm not blaming anybody."

"Sounds like it to me," Tricia said in unusual defense of her husband.

"It's the economy's fault," Ken said. "You don't understand the economy around here anymore, Schyler. Things have changed."

"Then maybe we should change with them."

"We're up against the big guys. Weyerhauser, Georgia Pacific, huge conglomerates like that."

"There's still a place in the market for small operations like us. Don't try to tell me otherwise."

Ken plowed his fingers through his hair in frustration. "Do you have any idea how complicated running a business like this is?"

"I'm sure I'll find out."

"You're going to make me look like a damn fool. While Cotton's indisposed, Crandall Logging is my responsibility!" he shouted.

"It was," Schyler replied coolly, coming to her feet. "If you wanted to wear the pants in the family, you should have put them on the day Daddy went to the hospital."

She left the room. Ken, fuming, watched her go, then turned on his wife, who was still indolently curled up in the chair sipping her drink. She gave a disdainful shrug toward the entire situation and drained her glass.

SEVENTEEN

"Schyler?"

"Hmm?"

"What are you doing out here?"

"Thinking."

Hesitantly, Ken sat down beside her in the porch swing. It was after eleven o'clock. Tricia was indoors watching Johnny Carson.

"I guess I owe you an apology," Ken said, staring beyond the veranda at the dark lawn.

Schyler's breasts rose and fell with a deep breath. "I don't want your apology, Ken. I want your help." She turned her head and looked at him. "I need to do this. Don't fight me. Help me."

He reached for her hand and covered it with his. "I will. You know I will. I blew my top, that's all. It's not every day a woman just moves in and takes over, you know."

"Is that what you think I'm doing? I don't intend to usurp your authority."

"That's how it'll look to folks."

"I'll make sure it doesn't."

He traced the delicate bones in the back of her hand with his fingertip. "Why do you feel like you have to do this?"

"I don't really have a choice, do I? That note has to be paid or we'll lose Belle Terre. You were right about Gilbreath. He is an asshole and would show no mercy if it came down to foreclosing."

"I'm sure we could figure out another way to come up with the cash if we put our minds to it."

"Probably. But time is so short, I can't go exploring. I don't want to borrow money to cancel this loan. That would only dig us in deeper and postpone the inevitable. And I don't want to liquidate bits and pieces of Belle Terre. The very thought of parting with one saucer of the china collection, or selling one acre of land makes me shudder. Besides what that would mean to us personally, I have to think about the sharecroppers. I can't sell their homes out from under them."

"You can't burden yourself with everybody's problems."

She smiled at him to relax the mood. "I need something to do. I'm going stir crazy around here between visits to the hospital."

He pressed her hand affectionately. "I know you're accustomed to staying busy, but I'm afraid you're biting off more than you can chew."

"Then if I fall on my face, or make a bigger mess of things, you'll have the supreme satisfaction of saying, 'I told you so.' "

"This is no joking matter, Schyler."

"I know," she said softly, ducking her head.

"I don't think Cotton will find it funny either."

"I'm sure he won't."

Cotton. He was her main motivation. He loved Belle Terre more than he loved anything. He had come to it an outsider and made it his. If Schyler was successful in saving it, maybe his love and affection for her would be restored. He might forgive her for whatever transgression she had unwittingly committed. Their relationship would revert to the loving one it had been before she left for London. As soon as possible, she wanted to present him with the canceled note and watch the love and gratitude well in his eyes. She didn't want that for her sake, but for his.

"You're an exciting woman, Schyler." Her head snapped around at Ken's soft

578

proclamation. It so closely echoed what Cash had said to her only a few nights before. Unlike Cash, however, Ken was smiling gently. "You're a pain in the ass sometimes, but exciting."

"Thank you. I think."

He inched closer, until his thigh was pressing against hers on the bench. The swing rocked slowly. "What I mean is, you're hardheaded. Gutsy. That determination is aggravating as hell. But it's the thing that makes you so damn appealing, too." He reached out and stroked her cheek with a feather-light touch. "Remember all those hours we spent picketing this or that? Lambasting or advocating one cause or another."

"We were a pair of crusaders, weren't we?"

He shook his head in denial. "You were the crusader. I only tagged along so I could be with you."

"That's not true. You were every bit as strong in your convictions as I was. You just don't remember."

"Maybe," he conceded doubtfully.

Honestly, she doubted it, too. But she didn't want to. She wanted to believe that he was uncompromising, that his integrity had been as steadfast as the Rock of Gibraltar. "I've really stuck my neck out this time, Ken. I need your strength and support."

He lightly closed his fingers around her neck. "You make me feel strong." His eyes came to rest on hers. "I made a bad choice. I married the wrong woman, Schyler."

"Don't, Ken."

"Listen to me." Schyler heard the anxiety in his voice, felt it in his touch. He leaned closer. "I regret that indiscretion with Tricia every day of my life. She's not you. She's petty and shallow. Superficial."

"Stop there, Ken."

"No. I want you to hear this. She doesn't even come close to being you. She's nice to look at, she's okay in bed, but she's selfish. She doesn't have your spirit and fire, your zest for living and loving."

Schyler thrilled to the words, but squeezed her eyes shut as though to block them out. "Don't say anything more. Please. I can't stay here if you—"

"Jesus, don't leave. I need you so much."

Closing the short distance between them, he kissed her with passion and desperation. Her initial reaction was to stiffen woodenly, but gradually she relaxed. Her mouth accepted his probing tongue. His hand slid from her neck to her breast. He kneaded it through her clothes. He lifted his lips from hers and, whispering her name endearingly, covered her face with quick, light kisses. She submitted until he tried to reclaim her lips. Then she pushed him away and left the swing.

Encircling the corner column with her arms, she rested her cheek against the cool, fluted wood. "We might regret the way things turned out between us, Ken, but there's no going back. Don't touch me like that ever again."

She heard the chains of the swing squeak as he left it. He moved up behind her and placed his hands on her waist, murmuring her name in her hair. She spun around to face him. "Don't! I mean it."

The light coming through the windows was sufficient for him to see the resolve on her face and in her eyes, which held his without flinching. Disappointment, then anger, caused his lips to shrink into a tight, narrow line. He stormed across the veranda and down the steps. Getting into his car, he gunned it to life and sped off. Schyler watched until the red brake lights disappeared at the bend in the lane.

She didn't realize how exhausted she was until she tried to move away from the column. She had to push herself away from its support. Sluggishly she went inside and climbed the stairs to her bedroom. Once ready for bed, she settled against the pillows and pulled the telephone into her lap. She would beat Mark's alarm clock by an hour or so, but that couldn't be helped. She needed to talk to him now.

"Hi, it's me," she said when the transatlantic call had gone through to the flat she shared with Mark Houghton.

"Schyler? God, what time is it?"

"Here or there?" She laughed, envisioning his blond hair sticking up all around his head and his clumsy, sleepy groping for the bedside clock.

"Just a sec. Let me light a cigarette."

"You promised you were going to quit while I was away."

"I lied." In under a minute he was back. "You don't have bad news I hope."

"About Daddy, no. He's stable."

"That's wonderful."

"But I won't be coming home anytime soon."

"That's not so wonderful."

"He's got to have bypass surgery." She explained Cotton's prognosis. "I can't leave until he's completely out of danger."

"I understand, but I miss you. At home and in the gallery. Some of our customers won't deal with anybody but you. If I don't produce you soon, I'm afraid they'll lock me in the Tower."

She had first met Mark when he hired her to work as his assistant in his antique gallery. He'd not only been her employer, but also her teacher. She had been an astute pupil with a natural eye and excellent taste. Before long, she knew as much or more about their inventory as he. That's why his flattery was particularly gratifying, if not entirely truthful.

"I know several high-ticket customers who trample over me to get to you." Toying with the coiled telephone cord, she collected her thoughts. "I'll be overseeing the family business until Cotton gets better." She threw out that piece of information like a baited fishing line.

He whistled. "Quite an undertaking. What about Ken?"

Mark knew the entire story, everything. "He resented my interference and objected to the idea at first, but I think he'll come around once he gets used to it."

"You can handle him and the work load."

"Can I?"

"I don't doubt it for a minute."

"Don't be so hasty. There's more. A bank loan is coming due and the coffers are empty."

There was a significant pause. Then, "How much do you need?"

"I wasn't asking."

"But I'm offering."

"No, Mark."

"Schyler, you know that anything I have is yours. Don't be proud. How much? I'll have my attorney draft a check in the morning."

"No, Mark."

"Please let me help you."

"No. I need to do this on my own."

I need to earn the right to live at Belle Terre is what she meant. She hadn't realized it until that very second.

Belle Terre was hers by chance. If another child had been born hours ahead of her, a child who filled the criteria just as well as she. Macy and Cotton Crandall would have been given that baby instead of her. When Cotton died, she and Tricia would inherit Belle Terre. Tricia would consider it her due.

But not Schyler. No bloodlines linked her to the house and land. She would have to earn it. Pressed, she couldn't have explained to anyone, not even to herself, why she felt working for it was necessary. It was simply a compulsion she had no choice but to act upon.

"Can you do without me for a while longer, Mark?"

He sighed with forbearance. "What choice do you leave me?"

"None, I'm afraid."

"So there's nothing more to discuss."

"I need a hug," Schyler said in a frightened, little girl's voice. "Mark, what the hell do I know about managing a logging company?"

He laughed. "About as much as you knew about antiques before you came to work for me. You're a fast learner."

"In the case of the antiques, I had an excellent teacher."

His voice grew husky with remembrance of good times shared. "I love you, babe."

"I love you, too."

She extended the conversation as long as it was economically feasible, telling him about Jigger Flynn and the pit bulls, which he found difficult to believe. "You mean this young woman, Gayla, is virtually enslaved? I thought the South was decadent only in Tennessee Williams plays and William Faulkner novels."

"Don't judge us all by Jigger Flynn."

He expressed concern for her safety. That's when she mentioned Cash. "I've known him forever. I mean, I've know about him forever. He's somebody who has always been lurking in the background."

"Are you sure you can trust him? He sounds almost as dangerous as this Flynn character."

She plucked at the embroidery on the hem of the sheet. "I guess he's trustworthy, in his own fashion."

Trustworthy? Perhaps. He was certainly dangerous. Dangerous to be alone with if you were a woman emotionally overwrought and temporarily unsure of yourself, when you deliberately compared his kiss to the former lover's and discovered that the former lover's took a distant second place.

Out of sheer curiosity, she had let her lips respond to Ken's kiss to see what would happen. And nothing did. But every time she even recalled Cash's kiss, her heart started beating fast, her nipples tightened, and her insides quivered.

She thought about telling Mark. He was adult about these things. He wasn't judgmental. He would understand. Nevertheless, she changed her mind. She couldn't put into words exactly how she felt about Cash's kiss.

"Schyler?"

"I'm still here, but I've got to hang up. Here I am on the brink of dispossession and I'm running up an astronomical phone bill."

"Call collect next time."

"I apologize for calling so early. Try to go back to sleep."

"Hell, it's time to get up now."

"Sorry."

"I'm not. Call again whenever you need to talk. Whenever you need anything."

"I will."

"Promise?"

"Promise."

Hanging up, she wished all the relationships in her life were as open and uncomplicated as the one she shared with Mark. She switched out the lamp and lay staring at the constantly shifting patterns of moonlight and shadow on the ceiling.

First thing in the morning, she would put out a notice that Crandall Logging was back in operation. The loggers who wanted to work would be immediately reinstated. She would call the independent loggers and tell them that she was actively buying timber. She could get their names from the files. Then the markets would have to be analyzed and contacted. Sales calls would have to be made.

So much to do.

So much to think about . . . namely that Ken's kiss, for all its passion, hadn't disturbed her nearly as much as Cash Boudreaux's.

 # EIGHTEEN

"**H**ey, boy!"
Every muscle in Jimmy Don Davison's athletic body tensed with the sudden realization that he was the only one left in the shower room. That was a dreadful mistake. He lifted his head out of the sputtering stream of lukewarm water and looked toward the man who had addressed him. "You talkin' to me?"

The hulking, muscular man bore a remarkable resemblance to Mr. Clean. He was indolently propped against the damp tile wall. A towel dangled from his extended right hand. "None other, sweetheart."

Jimmy Don ignored the endearment and cranked the rusty handles of the faucet to cut off the shower. He sluiced water off his skin, aware of being watched as his hands skimmed over the muscles he kept supple and strong by daily workouts in the prison yard. He reached for the towel. Razz snatched it out of reach at the last second. After several attempts to take it from the other man, who childishly withheld it, Jimmy Don managed to catch hold. He immediately wrapped it around his waist and tucked the end inside. Without letting his nervousness show, he quickly scanned the shower room. As he had feared, he and Razz were alone.

"Wha'cha looking for, boy? A guard? Don't bother. I brought him a new porno magazine. He's in the crapper happily jacking off." His ribald laughter echoed in the empty, tile chamber.

" 'Excuse me, Razz. I'm busy."

Jimmy Don brushed past the other inmate, but Razz's meaty fist wrapped around his bicep and stopped him. The former all-star football player was in excellent physical condition. On the running track, he could beat Razz by a mile and not even get winded. Here, however, he was far outsized. The man, whose skin was as pink and smooth as a baby's bottom, outweighed him by nearly a hundred pounds and was as strong as an ox. While Jimmy Don's muscles were kept well honed and sinewy, Razz worked at pumping his up to abnormal proportions. He shaved and oiled his head and body. He was a brute.

Unctuously, he crooned, "What's your hurry, sweetheart?"

"Leave me alone."

For a moment Razz's smile faded and his piggish eyes bore into Jimmy Don's handsome face. Then the nasty smile reappeared. He playfully punched Jimmy Don's arm. "It'd be real stupid of a niggah boy to get Razz mad, now wouldn't it?" he trailed a finger over Jimmy Don's beautifully sculpted chest. " 'Specially since I know what I know."

Jimmy Don shifted away from Razz's touch but said nothing, nor did his face reveal the murderous hate and revulsion he felt. Early enough he had learned the unwritten law of the prison, which was as brutal as the law of the jungle. Only the fittest survived. To survive, one did what was necessary. One found oneself being submitted to unspeakable cruelty by his fellow prisoners, but one stoically withstood the abuse if one wanted to live to get out.

And he did want to get out—just long enough to finish what he had to do. After that, he didn't care what happened to him in this lifetime or in the one hereafter for that matter. Once his scores were settled, the devil could have him.

"Ain't you the least bit curious 'bout this juicy secret I've got concernin' you?" Razz scraped Jimmy Don's nipple with his thumbnail. The muscles surrounding it leaped reflexively, but Jimmy Don's face didn't even flinch. Such molestation was a common occurrence. He had learned to stomach it because to resist was as good as a death sentence according to those in the cell block.

The electric chair was humane compared to what could happen to you at the hands of the inmates, those who governed the prison. Razz was one of them. He was a lifer; the prison was his dukedom. He exercised despotic control over other prisoners and many of the guards. Only the highest administrative officials were ignorant of, or indifferent to, the power Razz and the men like him wielded. Terror was the tactic they used.

"Ask me nice and I'll tell you what I know," Razz taunted.

"What you know ain't worth shit."

Jimmy Don was quick. He could break the hundred in ten seconds. But he hadn't learned to fight in alleys. Razz had. Before Jimmy Don could react, Razz had his hand under the towel and was squeezing Jimmy Don's testicles in a fist as strong as a vise.

"You sure?" He twisted his hand, Jimmy Don came up on his toes. "Ask me nice to tell you," Razz panted close to Jimmy Don's face. Grinning, he applied even more pressure to his fingers. Jimmy Don winced. "Ask me nice or I'll tear 'em off."

"Please. Please tell me." Jimmy Don hated himself for capitulating, but he didn't want to die, and he didn't want to leave there maimed. "Please."

"That's more like it." Razz gradually relaxed his hand, but he didn't remove it. He stepped closer and leaned down to impart his secret. "You're coming up for parole, boy. Soon. Real soon."

Jimmy Don had thought his heart was dead. It wasn't. It sparked involuntarily. His breath rushed in and out. He blinked repeatedly. "You bullshittin' me?"

"Would I do that?" Razz asked, looking wounded.

Hell yes, he would. "How do you know?"

"A little birdie told me." Razz pulled a sad face. "I knew you'd be real glad to hear it, but that piece of news makes me real sad. I kinda like havin' pretty black boys like you around." His hand squeezed Jimmy Don again. This time it was a caress.

Jimmy Don batted Razz's groping hand aside. "Keep your hands off me, you son of a bitchin' fag."

He was lifted bodily and thrown up hard against the shower wall. His cheekbone caught it. The pain was immense. One arm was twisted up behind him. Razz shoved his hand up between his shoulder blades and Jimmy Don cried out in pain in spite of his determination never to show it.

"The only thing that keeps me from cracking your face against this wall like a pecan is that I hate to spoil something so pretty," Razz hissed.

Jimmy Don gouged him in the gut with his elbow. Razz grunted, but his grip on

Jimmy Don didn't lessen one degree. He sandwiched the younger man between his massive body and the wall and pressed his lips against Jimmy Don's ear. His voice was sibilant and sinister.

"You'd better be nice to me, sweetheart. You'll do what Razz says when Razz says it, or I'll see that your chances of parole go down the shit hole. You got that? I ain't got much time to enjoy you, but while you're here, you're mine, understand?"

Jimmy Don nodded. Fighting Razz was a waste of energy and time. Fighting only got you hurt and prolonged the inevitable. In this case fighting could mean losing his chance for parole.

Number twenty-one, the Heathen of Heaven, heard Razz's zipper being opened. He felt brutal hands on his flesh. For what was coming, he braced himself, mentally as well as physically.

He could endure it. He *would* endure it. He would endure anything. He had to get out. He lived for the day he would get revenge on Jigger Flynn and his whore, Gayla Frances.

NINETEEN

"Did you do it?"

"Do what?" Cash asked around the sharp fingernail that was seductively rimming his lips. Rhoda Gilbreath smiled at him. It was as bloodthirsty a smile as he'd ever seen. She needed only fangs to make the picture complete.

"Did you kill Jigger Flynn's pit bull terriers?"

"They're not really terriers, you know. That's a misnomer."

"Quit playing word games. Did you?"

"No."

Cash pushed her aside and moved further into the room. She had barely let him in through the back door of her house before molding herself against him. After only one kiss she had posed her question.

"That's what's going around."

"I can't help what's going around. I didn't shoot his dogs."

"Do you expect me to take your word for it?"

"Jigger did."

Rhoda's carefully made-up eyes registered surprise. "You've talked to Jigger?"

"Not more than an hour ago. Get me a beer."

Once she had gotten the can of beer from the kitchen refrigerator, she followed Cash into the formal living room. He plopped down on her finest sofa and propped his boots on the smoked glass coffee table. He sipped at the cold can of beer.

Rhoda sat down beside him. Avid curiosity eked from her like resin out of a pine tree. "Where?"

"Where what?"

"Where did Jigger confront you?"

"He didn't confront me. I was out on the edge of town and saw his pickup parked outside one of his beer joints. I stopped and went in."

"What did he do when he saw you?"

Cash shrugged nonchalantly. "He threw out some fairly strong accusations. I denied them, told him I would have to be nuts to kill off his dogs when they frequently won me money.'' He slurped at the beer while Rhoda sat hinging on every word. ''He said he hadn't thought of it that way. Then he asked me where I got that bullet hole in the side of my truck.''

''Where *did* you get it?''

''Some goddamn fool up in Allen Parish got it into his head that I'm humping his wife.''

''Are you?''

His grin neither admitted nor denied. He enjoyed tormenting Rhoda. It was rotten of him, granted, but no more rotten than she was for being an unfaithful wife. Cash never seduced a loving wife away from her husband. He took to bed only those he knew were on the make. Rhoda Gilbreath had hit on him one night at the country club. He was hardly a regular with that crowd and had only been there at a divorcée's invitation.

During a break in the penny-ante poker tournament, the divorcée went into the ladies' room. Cash went outside to smoke. Rhoda Gilbreath followed him.

''What do you think of the poker party?'' she had asked.

''Boring.''

''What do you think of these?'' She whipped her sweater over her head and stood before him topless.

While inhaling deeply on his cigarette, he gave her braless breasts a casual once-over. ''The best money can buy.''

She slapped him. He slapped her back. She cooly replaced her sweater. Holding his hazel gaze, she said, ''Tomorrow afternoon, three o'clock, the Evangeline Motel.''

He put his index and middle fingers together at his temple and gave her a quick and mocking salute. She went back inside. He finished his cigarette before rejoining the party.

The windows of room two eighteen of the Evangeline Motel steamed up the following afternoon. When Rhoda left, she felt bruised, battered, beautiful, and never better.

Since that afternoon, they had met in a variety of motels, but he liked coming to her house. He derived pleasure from violating the domicile she shared with Dale Gilbreath. He enjoyed putting his muddy boots on her expensive furniture. He could get by with mistreating her because she had more to lose than he did and both knew it.

She was attractive. When they split, she would find another lover, one who would appreciate her frosted blond hair and frosty blue eyes; one who would adore her implant-enhanced figure; one whose smile wasn't always tinged with contempt.

Rhoda's face was arresting, but there was a hard aspect to it that kept it from being pretty. There was a calculating glitter in her eyes that never went away, even in the throes of passion. Cash had detected it the night they met. That was part of her attraction. This woman couldn't be wounded too deeply. He never took up with a woman who wasn't tough enough to take the crap he dished out.

Rhoda was. He had her pegged correctly the instant she started sending him it-itches-and-I'd-like-you-to-scratch-it looks across the card table. Women like her castrated their husbands, making them feel inadequate to provide all they wanted in the bank and in the bedroom. They were socially rapacious, fanatical about their looks, money mad, and sexually dissatisfied. They were hungry, restless, selfish harpies. Rhoda Gilbreath led the pack. She deserved no respect.

She deserved no better than Cash Boudreaux.

He drained his beer and set the empty can on the coffee table. ''Unless you've started drinking beer, don't forget to throw that away before Dale gets home.''

She ran her finger down the placket of his shirt and dug beneath his belt in search of his navel. "Maybe I'll let him discover that I have a lover.''

One of Cash's eyebrows rose skeptically. "Don't you imagine he already knows?''

"Probably.'' She flashed a teasing smile. "Maybe I'll let him worm it out of me who my lover is. That might be exciting. I'd like to see you square off with Dale the way you did with Jigger Flynn.''

"Such a thing would never happen.''

"Oh? Why not?''

"Because Jigger loved his dogs.''

Her coy smile went as flat as a punctured soufflé. She glared at him coldly. "You son of a bitch. You'd better tread lightly with me. I haven't forgiven you for leaving me stranded the last time we met at that seedy motel.''

He stacked his hands behind his head and rested it on the back of the sofa. "You can't threaten a man who has absolutely nothing to lose, Rhoda. I don't even have a good reputation at stake.''

She angrily pondered his handsome profile for a moment, then laid her head on his chest in conciliation. "That's the hell of it. The more like a bastard you behave, the more attractive you are. I read all about your type in this month's *Cosmo*. They call it 'heel appeal.' '' He barked a short laugh.

She plucked at the buttons of his shirt, undoing them one by one. "But you might have something to lose. If the Crandalls lose Belle Terre, you'll be evicted. I doubt if the next—''

He covered her roving hand with his, flattening it against his belly to keep it still. It was a sudden, reflexive move, lightning quick. "What the hell are you talking about? The Crandalls losing Belle Terre?''

She worked her hand free and started on the buttons again. "Dale said Cotton Crandall borrowed money from him last year. He's been making interest payments on it, but the principal is coming due. Dale was worried about it because Ken Howell shut down the business, so he met with that girl, the oldest one, what's her name?''

"Schyler.''

"Whatever. Anyway she didn't even know about the loan. He said she nearly had a caniption when she found out Cotton had used Belle Terre for collateral. Cool as a cucumber and real hoity-toity, you understand, but Dale said she went as pale as death. Right now, it looks like the bank might have to foreclose.''

That was one of the reasons Cash had kept meeting Rhoda Gilbreath. Every now and then she supplied him with a tidbit of valuable information. Apparently Dale had no qualms about discussing confidential banking matters with his wife, who in turn had no hesitancy in sharing them with her lover.

Cash stared sightlessly at the ceiling. Rhoda's head moved over his chest, dropping light kisses on the thick carpet of hair. "What would the bank want with an old plantation house like Belle Terre?'' he asked.

"Hmm? I don't know.'' She swirled her tongue around his nipple. "Sell it, I guess.''

"Wonder what it would take to buy it?'' he mused aloud.

Rhoda lifted her head and looked at him with amusement. "Why? You interested, Cash?''

He knotted his fingers in her hair, drew her mouth up to his, and kissed every single cunning thought out of her head. His tongue swept each malicious idea from her mind and left her thinking of only one thing. Her brain was too fertile a field to sow a single seed of suspicion in. The most farfetched speculation mustn't be given a chance to take root in Rhoda's conniving mind.

"Why don't you finish what you started?" He fished in the pocket of his jeans and tossed her the foil packet he was never without. No bastard kids for Cash Boudreaux. Never.

Holding his hot stare, Rhoda licked her lips. So adroit was she that she didn't even have to look down to unfasten his belt buckle and undo his zipper. She did it all by feel. Palming his testicles, she lifted him free of his jeans, then lowered her face over his lap.

Cash's head fell back against the sofa again. He stared up through the crystal teardrops of the ostentatious chandelier overhead. He became entranced, not by the rhythmic movements of Rhoda's greedy mouth, but by the name that was chanted in his head like a call to vespers. *Belle Terre. Belle Terre . . .*

"Belle Terre," Cotton Crandall proudly pronounced.

"It's a beautiful name for a beautiful house."

Monique Boudreaux smiled up at him, her eyes glowing. Cotton bent his tow head and kissed her lips softly. "You understand why I wanted it, why I married Macy?"

"I understand, Cotton."

Cash, his bare toes curling in the warm earth, angled his head back and watched his mother's smiling face turn sad, though she made sure Cotton couldn't see her smile fade. Cash had hoped that when they moved from New Orleans to this new town where the tall man with the white hair lived that his mother wouldn't be sad anymore. He had hoped that she wouldn't cry and lie listlessly on her bed in the afternoons until it was time to get up and go to work in the barroom where she served bottles of beer to rough, boisterous merchant marines.

She had always told him that one day the man she called Cotton would send for them. Then they would be happy. And she was—happier, anyway. The day she'd gotten that letter from Cotton, she'd squeezed Cash so hard he could barely breathe.

"Look, *mon cher,* do you know what these are? Tickets. Train tickets. See, didn't *maman* tell you? He wants us to come live with him in a wonderful place called Belle Terre." Bubbling and animated with emotion, she had covered Cash's face with eager, exuberant kisses.

Two days later, which was all it had taken to finalize their affairs and pack their meager belongings, they dressed in their best clothes and boarded the train. The ride hadn't lasted long enough for Cash. He had loved it. When they arrived at their destination, he had stood warily against the belly of the steam-belching engine, suspiciously eyeing the man his mother ran to.

She flung herself into his arms. He lifted her up and swung her around. Cash had never seen a man so tall or so strong. Monique threw back her head, laughing more musically than Cash had ever heard. Her dancing, dark curls had glistened iridescently in the sunlight.

She and the man kissed for so long that Cash thought his mother had forgotten him. The man's large hands moved over her, touching her in ways that she wouldn't let the customers of the barroom touch her. Many kisses later, she disengaged herself and eagerly gestured him forward. Taking reluctant baby steps, he moved toward the towering man. He smiled down at Cash and ruffled his hair.

"I don't think he remembers me."

"He was just a baby when you left, *mon cher,*" Monique said softly. Her eyes brimmed with shiny tears, but her mouth was wide and smiling. Cash's young heart lifted. His *maman* was happy. He had never seen her so happy. Their lives had taken a new direction. Things were going to be just as she had said—wonderful. They would no longer live down a dark, dingy hallway in a roach-infested apartment. They were going to live in a house in the country surrounded by grass and trees and fresh air. They were finally at Belle Terre.

But the house Cotton had driven them to wasn't quite as wonderful as Monique had expected. It was a small gray house sitting on the banks of a bayou that he called Laurent. The sunny atmosphere had turned stormy. Monique and Cotton had had a shouting match. Cash had been sent outside to play. He grudgingly obeyed but went no further away than the porch, still distrustful of this man he'd just met.

"It's a shack!" Monique said in a raised voice.

"It's sturdy. A family of moss harvesters used to live here, but it has stood vacant for years."

"It smells like the swamp."

"I can help you fix it up. See, I've already started. I added a bathroom."

Monique's voice had cracked. "You won't live here with us, will you?"

After a short pause, Cotton sighed. "No, I won't. But this is the best I can do."

Cotton had married a lady named Macy and Monique didn't like it. She yelled at him and called him names Cash had overheard in the barroom, but had been forbidden to repeat. She lapsed into her native "Frenglish" and spoke it with such heated emphasis that even her son, who was accustomed to hearing it, could barely translate.

As darkness fell, he gave up trying and concentrated on catching lightning bugs. His mother and Cotton went upstairs to the bedroom and stayed a long time. He fell asleep curled up on the rough board of the porch. When they finally came downstairs, they had their arms around each other's waists. They were smiling. The tall man bent down and touched Cash's cheek, then kissed Monique good-bye and left in his car.

They watched it disappear into the dark tunnel of trees. Monique draped her arm around Cash's narrow shoulders. "This is our home now, Cash." And if she didn't sound very happy about it, at least she sounded content.

Monique worked wonders on the house. In the months that followed, she turned it from an empty, dreary place into a home full of color and light. Flowers bloomed in window boxes. There were rugs on the floor and curtains on the windows. Just as she kept her secret heartache hidden, she disguised the shortcomings of the shanty.

It seemed they had lived there for a long time before Cotton finally gave in to Monique's pestering and walked them through the forest to see the plantation house.

The day would forever stand out in Cash's memory because, up to that point, he'd never seen a house so large. It was even grander than the estates on St. Charles Avenue that Monique had pointed out to him from the streetcar. He was awed by how clean and white Belle Terre was. In his wildest imagination, he couldn't have fathomed a house like Belle Terre.

Standing in the shadows of the trees, with moss serving as a screen, Monique rested her cheek against Cotton's chest as she stared at the large house. "Tell me about it. What does it look like on the inside?"

"Ah, it's beautiful, Monique. The halls have floors that are polished as smooth and shiny as mirrors. In the dining room, the walls are covered with yellow silk."

"Silk?" she had repeated in a reverent whisper. "I wish I could see that."

"That's impossible." Cotton set her away from him and sternly looked down into her face. "Never, Monique, do you understand? The house is Macy's domain. You and Cash can never go beyond this point right here."

Monique's glossy head bowed. "I understand, Cotton. I was just wishing I could see something so fine."

Cotton's face changed. He clasped her to him fiercely. He hugged her tight, lowering his head to cover hers. Cash gazed back at the house, wondering what it would hurt if he and his *maman* went inside to see the yellow silk walls and why they couldn't because of this Macy woman. It was probably because she was married to Cotton.

"Does she dress up for supper?" Monique wanted to know.

"Yes."

"In fancy clothes?"

"Sometimes." Monique inched closer to Cotton, as though to prevent him from seeing her plain cotton dress. He lovingly stroked her riotously curly hair. After a moment, he placed his finger beneath her chin and tilted it up. "Speaking of supper, didn't you tell me you had cooked jumbalaya for me?"

She gave him a brilliant smile. "*Oui.*"

"Then let's go back. I'm starving." They turned as one and headed back toward the bayou. "Cash, you comin', boy?" Cotton called back when he realized that Cash wasn't following them.

"I'm comin'."

But he remained where he was, transfixed by the beautiful house. Belle Terre. . . .

Rhoda's mouth was avid. She was unaware that Cash's mind wasn't on her, only on the sensations she coaxed from his body. When he swelled to the fullest proportion, when everything went dark around him, when he squeezed his eyes shut and focused only on release, when he bared his teeth in a gripping climax, it wasn't Rhoda's name, but another, that rang in his head.

 # TWENTY

Schyler's head dropped forward. Closing her eyes, she stretched the back of her neck, then rolled her head around her aching shoulders to work out the kinks of fatigue. Trying to refocus on the fine print of the contracts in front of her proved to be impossible. Her tired eyes refused. She left the desk and moved to the coffee maker across the room.

She poured a cup, more for the distraction and the exercise than because she wanted the coffee. She only took a few sips before setting down the mug and restlessly walking to the window.

She had hired a cleaning team to attack the landing office. They had washed the grime off the windows, but the view was no more encouraging through clean glass. She stared at the inactive platform. Even the railroad tracks were collecting dust. Trains avoided the spur because there was no Crandall timber to pick up and haul to market.

It had been three days since she had asked the newspaper to print a notice that Crandall Logging was open for business. She had anticipated having to turn independent loggers away, thinking she would be unable to buy timber from all of them until she had several contracts in hand. Her optimism had been misplaced.

As yet, not a single one had brought a rig loaded with logs to the landing. She had personally notified the former employees by telephone. None had come to reclaim his job. Without an inventory to sell, it would be senseless to contact the markets.

Dejectedly, she rubbed her bloodshot eyes. Last night she had stayed late at the hospital, hoping to catch Cotton awake. She had only had the opportunity to speak to him that one time. Then he had turned away, not caring that she had returned home to see him. Every time she thought about it, she despaired.

She suspected that he was faking the deep sleeps he lapsed into whenever she was at the hospital. Dr. Collins's prognosis was still guarded but basically favorable. Tricia and Ken had each engaged Cotton in brief conversations. But to Schyler, he still had nothing to say.

Her trips to the hospital were washouts. So was each working day. She spent hours in this office at the landing, waiting for something to happen. Nothing ever did. But she refused to give up. She had to succeed at this even if it meant hiring a forester, someone to coordinate everything, someone who talked the loggers' language, someone who could motivate them to work harder than they'd ever worked in their lives.

It meant rehiring Cash Boudreaux.

His name cropped up everywhere. Like the proverbial bad penny, it kept coming around. She'd heard it so many times in the last few days, she had begun hearing it in her sleep. It was the first thing that came to her mind when she woke up.

The first saw hand she had telephoned said, "You want me back at work? Great! Soon as I hear from Cash, I'll—"

"I'm afraid that Mr. Boudreaux isn't coming back."

"Whadaya mean, Cash ain't coming back? He's the main man."

"Not any longer."

"Oh, well, uh, see, I got this temporary job."

And it had gone downhill from there. By the time she had reached the fifth name on her list, word had apparently gotten around through the grapevine, which had it all over Ma Bell as far as transmitting information expeditiously went.

"Now, Cash, he—"

"I always work with Boudreaux. He—"

"Boudreaux ain't working for you no more? Well, ya see, he—"

She had called every logger Crandall Logging had ever had on its payroll but with no success. She got nowhere. Out of frustration, she had consulted Ken. "I'm beginning to think all Cash Boudreaux had to do was look at a tree and the damn thing would fall down. Exactly what did he do for Crandall Logging?"

"Generally caused trouble."

She curbed her impatience. "Specifically."

"Specifically he . . ." Ken made an encompassing gesture. "He more or less did everything."

"Do you mean at the sites, at the landing, in the office? What?"

"Hell, Schyler, I don't know. My office is downtown. I rarely go to the landing. I wasn't in on the day-to-day operation. Mine is a white-collar job."

"I realize that, Ken. Sorry to have bothered you. Thank you for the information and forgive the interruption." She turned to leave, uncomfortable now every time she was alone with Ken.

"Schyler?"

"Yes?"

Ken seemed to debate with himself before saying, "I overheard Cotton say . . ."

"Well?"

"I once overheard him say that Boudreaux has forgotten more about forestry than other foresters ever knew."

"Coming from Cotton, that's a staggering compliment," Schyler mused out loud.

"But he's a born troublemaker. He continually kept the loggers riled up over something. A day hardly went by that he and Cotton weren't at each other's throats. If you ask me, we're better off without him."

At the time, Schyler had thought they were better off without him, too. He was a disruptive force, especially to her. On principle, she would never approach him about working for her family again.

Staring out the window now, watching the rigs rusting in the garage when they should have been loaded to groaning capacity with timber, she admitted that she couldn't afford to avoid him any longer. The X's on her calendar were multiplying toward the deadline. No amount of principle was going to get Belle Terre out of hock. If getting the money meant humbling herself in front of Cash, then she would be humble. All other alternatives had been exhausted.

Before she lost her nerve, she locked the landing office door behind her. The mare was still tied to the tree across the wide yard, grazing on the short grass in the shade. Schyler mounted. She and Mark had ridden together occasionally, but not so regularly that she wouldn't be saddle sore tomorrow. She didn't care. The muscle discomfort would be well worth the thrill of riding over the acreage of Belle Terre as she had since she was old enough to sit in a saddle and duplicate Cotton's patient instructions.

She set out. The best place to start looking for Cash Boudreaux was at his house. If he wasn't there, she would leave a note. It was damned aggravating not to be able to call him on the phone. Sooner or later she would be forced to look into his gloating face.

Rather than take the roads, she cut across the open fields, wending her way through the copses of trees. As the mare daintily picked her way through a particularly dense patch of forest, Schyler heard the wine of a chainsaw. Curious, she led the mare in that direction.

Cash saw her the moment she cleared the trees, but he didn't acknowledge her. He returned his attention to the chain saw he was applying to the branches of a felled tree. Piqued because he had so blatantly ignored her, Schyler drew the mare up but remained in the saddle, watching him.

He wasn't wearing a shirt. The skin of his back and chest was baked a deep brown. His face was beaded with sweat, despite the handkerchief he had tied around his forehead to act as a sweatband. His biceps bunched and strained as he held the saw steady while it ate its way through the pine and sent up a plume of acrid blue-white smoke. Sawdust was sprayed against his shins and over his boots.

When the last major branch had been severed, he cut the power and the saw's whine silenced. He took it in one hand. It weighed down his arm, stretching the skin so thin that Schyler could see each strong vein standing out. He raised his free arm and wiped perspiration off his brow.

"I should have you arrested for stealing timber off my property."

A white grin split his grimy, tanned face. "You should thank me for getting rid of this blowdown for you."

He set the chain saw on the ground beside the trunk of the tree. Over his jeans he was wearing the knee-length suede chaps that served to protect a saw hand's thighs from mishap, at least theoretically. From a wide leather belt around his waist hung a plastic bottle of chain saw propellant. There was a tape measure, used to record the length of felled trees, attached to the back belt loop and riding above his hip pocket. He had on work gloves, which, disconcertingly, only called more attention to his bare torso.

He sauntered to the mare's side and propped an elbow up on the pommel of the saddle. "You want damaging bugs eating away at your forest, Miss Schyler?"

To keep from looking at his chest and its sexy covering of damp, curly hair, she eyed the dismembered pine. "When was it blown down?"

"We had a bad storm about two months back. There's already larvae under the trunk. I checked."

"What are you going to do with it?"

"I'll bring a skidder down here tomorrow and drag it out." He glanced up at her again. "If I can borrow a skidder that is."

"She was determined not to be provoked. "I need to talk to you."

"Not from up there, you don't."

"Pardon?"

"I don't look up to anybody. Get down."

She was about to protest when he peeled the yellow leather work gloves off his hands and dropped them to the ground. He extended his hands up to her. "I can manage," she said, swinging her right leg over the saddle and landing on her right foot. She lifted her left foot out of the stirrup and turned around. He was still standing close, allowing her no extra room.

"Funny-looking britches."

She had on black twill jodhpurs and smooth brown leather riding boots. "I left them behind when I moved to England."

"Yeah, from what I hear you left in a big hurry."

Difficult as it was to ignore that, she did. "I'm glad I did. Left the riding clothes, I mean. They came in handy today." A horsefly buzzed past her nose. She fanned it away. Cash didn't move a muscle. "They're a little hot though."

"You used to ride barebacked and bare-legged."

Schyler began to notice another kind of heat. It spilled through her system, making her veins run as hot as rivers of lava. "Mama made me stop doing that. She said it didn't look ladylike."

His eyes lowered to the delta of her thighs, then unhurriedly climbed back up. "Your mama was right. It looked downright dirty."

"How do you know what it looked like?"

"I used to see you."

"Where?"

"Everywhere. All the time. When you didn't know anybody was watching."

Schyler moved away from the horse, away from the man. Both seemed to emanate a musky, animalistic scent. The atmosphere was redolent with sexuality and she couldn't say why, except that the last time she had stood this close to Cash, he'd been kissing her.

Every time he looked at her, his eyes seemed to remind her of that. He remembered that kiss, and knew that she did, too. Restlessly, she rolled back the wide sleeves of her white shirt and pulled away the collar to allow air inside.

"Want a drink?" He bent at the waist to pick up his discarded gloves and tucked them into his low-riding waistband.

"No, thank you. I came here on business."

He walked to the bed of his pickup. It was parked nearby in the shade. The tailgate was down. There was a large, blue thermos sitting on it. He uncapped it and dipped a plastic glass inside. It came up full to overflowing with ice water. He gulped it down thirstily. Some of it ran down his chin and sweaty throat. It formed glistening drops on his chest hair, drawing strands of it into wet clumps.

Intentionally looking elsewhere, Schyler's eyes fell on the hard hat with the screened visor. It was designed to protect a logger's eyes from flying wood particles. "Your hard hat isn't doing you much good in the back of your truck. Why aren't you wearing it?"

"Didn't feel like it."

"But if you had gotten hurt on my land, you would have sued me."

"I don't hold anybody responsible for me, but me, Miss Schyler."

"I've asked you not to call me that."

"That's right. You have." Grinning like a sinner who had no plans to repent, he drained another glass of water. "Sure you don't want a drink?"

The water looked delicious, and so did his cold, wet lips. "Okay, all right. Thanks."

He dipped the glass into the top of the thermos again and passed it to her. She took it from him but didn't drink right away. Instead she gazed dubiously at the dripping glass in her hand. Cash's brows drew together angrily.

"My tongue has been halfway down your throat," he growled. "It's too late for you to worry about drinking after me."

She had never gotten so angry so fast in her life. With one vicious flick of her wrist she threw the entire icy contents of the glass onto the ground. "You are scum."

"That's a British word. Around here people like me are referred to as white trash."

"And worldwide you're called bastards." A muscle in his cheek twitched. A vein in his temple popped out. Schyler immediately regretted her choice of words. "I didn't mean it that way. Not literally." She felt an impulse to reach out and touch him in conciliation, but she didn't. She was afraid to.

He grabbed the glass away from her and tossed it into the pickup's bed. "You came all the way out here, in this heat, to call me names?"

She shook her head. "I came on business."

"Who do you want me to kill this time?"

She deserved that, she supposed, so she disregarded it. "I want you to come back to work for Crandall Logging."

"Why?"

"Because I need you." His eyes snapped to hers. They were disconcertingly incisive. She plunged on. "I've reopened the business. I can handle the paperwork because I used to do it for Cotton."

She tried to wet her lips, but her tongue, like the inside of her mouth, was arid. "But I don't know how to organize the loggers. I don't know where to tell them to cut, or what to cut, or how much to cut. I won't be a good judge of the quality when they bring timber in and won't know whether I'm over- or underpaying them. From what I understand, you've been in charge of all that."

"That's right."

"Well, then, I need you to pick up where you left off before Cotton had his heart attack."

"In other words, you want me to save your ass."

She drew herself up straight. "Look, I'm sorry for what I said earlier. I didn't mean to call you a bastard. It just slipped out. If you're going to carry that chip on your shoulder, if you're going to hold that against me and be obnoxious—"

"You want me to save Belle Terre from Dale Gilbreath's clutches."

Schyler fell abruptly silent. For long moments they stared at each other. Cash's expression was belligerent, hers bewildered. "How did you know about that?"

"I know."

"Did Cotton tell you that he had borrowed money from Gilbreath?"

He turned his back on her and went to retrieve his chain saw. "Your daddy doesn't confide in me."

"Then where did you hear it?"

Heaven was a small town. Everybody meddled into everybody else's business, but to think that the people of the town were sitting back like Romans at the Coliseum, waiting to see if Belle Terre survived the jaws of the lion, was untenable. She'd been away from it just long enough to resent destructive, small-town gossip.

Angrily, Schyler caught Cash's forearm and spun him around. He glanced down at her hand. Her fingers were biting into his flesh. The hairs on his arms were curled over them. Her nails were making crescent-shaped impressions in his skin. He lifted his eyes back to hers, but she wasn't intimidated by the dangerous glint in them.

"Where did you hear about that loan?"

"In bed."

Schyler snatched her hand back. He smiled a crooked, sardonic smile before continuing on his way back to the pickup. He laid the chain saw in the back. Item by item, he took off his gear and laid it with the saw in the pickup. He pushed the thermos past the hinge and slammed the tailgate shut. He picked up a T-shirt from where he'd left it draped in the truck's open window and pulled it over his head. As he worked it down his torso, he asked, "Want the details? Time, place, with whom?"

"No."

He gave her a lazy smile. She wanted to wipe it off his mouth with the palm of her hand. "Bet you do." She only glared at him. He laughed. "Pity you're not more curious. It's juicy stuff. You might have gotten a kick out of it." He lowered his eyelids to half-mast. "We both might have."

The man was insufferable. He had the manners of a pig and the sexual discretion of a tomcat. If she didn't need him, and need him desperately, she would see to it that he was off Belle Terre by nightfall, and she didn't care what previous arrangements Cotton had made with him.

As it was, she had no choice but to tolerate him and his arrogance, temporarily she hoped. She lifted her heavy, wavy hair off her neck, hoping a breath of air would find it. "Are you coming to work for me or not, Mr. Boudreaux?"

"Depends."

"On what?"

"On who's in charge."

"I believe you were foreman. You will be again."

"Will I have Howell breathing down my neck?"

"Ken's responsibilities will remain what they've always been."

"As the company do-nothing?"

"For your information," she flared, "he spoke very highly of your qualifications as a forester."

"He'd be lying if he said otherwise."

"Don't bother to thank him," she said sarcastically.

"I won't." He gave her another arrogant smile. "But I guess I should be flattered that the two of you took time out from your stolen time together to talk about me."

Schyler clenched her fists to keep from screaming. She forced her voice to remain temperate. "Ken will stay in his downtown office."

"And where will you be?"

"I'll be working out of the office at the landing. I'll handle the contracts and the shipping schedules. You just supply me the loggers and the timber."

"What about the independents?"

"We'll use them as we always have."

"Will the pay scale stay what it was?"

"Yes. And so will the wages of those who work exclusively for us."

"And I'm in charge, right?"

Schyler had the uneasy feeling she was being backed into a corner. He was pressing her for a verbal commitment, but she was unsure why. She hesitated but finally answered. "Right. You're in charge."

"Okay then." While the negotiating was going on, he had been leaning against the tailgate, arms folded over his chest, ankles crossed. Now he pushed himself away and started toward her. It took all her willpower not to back down. She stood her ground until they were standing toe to toe.

"Stop wearing blouses you can see through."

"What?"

"That lacy brassiere you've got on isn't worth a damn. The only thing it's good for is to make a man crazy. If you want full production out of the loggers, we can't have them getting hard and horny. I don't care if they screw their wives and girlfriends through the mattress over the weekend, as long as they report to work bright and early every Monday morning and don't let up till Friday afternoon."

His eyes raked over her hair. "And smooth your hair back. That just-got-laid hairdo will have them sneaking off into the woods by themselves to jerk off."

"You're—"

"No," he interrupted, catching her shoulders, "*you're* going to listen to me." He lowered his face to within inches of hers. "You're up shit's creek without a paddle, Miss Schyler. If you want my help in saving your company from bankruptcy and Belle Terre from foreclosure, you're going to keep your butt to the ground, your mouth shut, and do things my way, understand?" He shook her slightly and raised his voice. "Understand?"

"Yes!"

He released her as suddenly as he had grabbed her. "Good. We start tomorrow."

TWENTY-ONE

"**G**ilbreath."

"Hello. It's Schyler Crandall. Thank you for taking my call so late in the day."

The banker angled back his reclining chair and propped his feet on the corner of his desk. "No thanks are necessary, Ms. Crandall. I hope you have good news for me."

"I think so."

"You're prepared to pay off the loan?"

"The news isn't that good, I'm afraid."

Dale's pause was calculated and lengthy. "That's a shame. For both of us."

"Crandall Logging starts full-scale production in the morning, Mr. Gilbreath," she informed him briskly. "I've rehired the previous foreman."

"Mr. Boudreaux, I believe."

"That's correct. My father has a tremendous amount of confidence in him. So do the loggers. I've compiled a promising list of markets. I'll be contacting them as soon as we have enough board feet to make some impressive sales. That shouldn't take but a few days of cutting. Everyone is eager to get back to work."

"This is all very interesting, Ms. Crandall. You've obviously taken some positive steps to reorganize your family's business. But I fail to see how these measures directly affect the bank."

"If I can present you with enough contracts to cover the amount of the loan, would you be willing to let me pay the interest and rollover the principal for a while longer? Six months max."

This was no faint-hearted southern belle with hominy grits for brains. Schyler Crandall was not to be underestimated. She had seized the bull by the horns. It was time to get tough.

"I'm afraid I can't do that, Ms. Crandall, even if you get the contracts, which is doubtful."

"Let me worry about getting them. A signed contract is as good as cash."

"Not quite," he said, oozing chauvinistic condescension. "You might not be able to deliver the orders."

"I would."

"But I would have no guarantee."

"You'd have Belle Terre as collateral."

"I've already got Belle Terre. What would be my incentive?"

"How about decency?"

"That was uncalled for, Ms. Crandall."

She sighed heavily, but didn't apologize. "Deal with me, Mr. Gilbreath," she said imperatively. "It's unrealistic to hope that I can fill enough contracts to come up with that much cash in such a short time."

"That's hardly my problem." He tried to keep a gloating tone out of his voice. He could almost hear her mind working during the ensuing silence.

"What if I paid you the interest and a portion of the principal?"

"Ms. Crandall," he said expansively, "please stop to consider the awkward position you're placing me in. You're making me out to be the heavy. I regret that. This isn't solely my decision to make. I have to answer to the bank's directors. They, as much as I, have been lenient with Crandall Logging and Cotton.

"He's been a customer in good standing for years, but sentiment can only stretch so far. *If* we went out on a limb and extended the loan, we would be placing ourselves in a vulnerable position with the bank examiners. We have to answer to them for every transaction. They don't know Cotton Crandall. They won't be sentimental. They will view this as a nonproducing loan. With the economy being as sluggish as it is—"

"Thank you, Mr. Gilbreath, you've answered my question. Good-bye."

She hung up before giving him a chance to respond. Smiling smugly, Gilbreath replaced the receiver. He enjoyed seeing the mighty humbled and headed for a fall.

When he moved to Heaven from Pennsylvania three years ago, the pillars of the community had treated him with attitudes ranging from mild derision to outright snobbery. Rhoda and he had soon learned that one wasn't considered to have roots in Heaven unless there was a moth-eaten Confederate uniform packed in an attic trunk. Family trees had to have branches sprawling across several generations before the stigma of being an outsider was removed.

Unless one met these criteria, one wasn't embraced by the socially prominent—which is what Dale and Rhoda wanted to be. They wanted to be in the very bosom of Heaven's social circle.

They had been virtually forced to leave their home in Pennsylvania. The couple they had been swapping partners with for several years became born-again Christians during a citywide crusade. In a tearful testimony in front of a large, spiritually emotional congregation, they had confessed everything, naming their partners in sin. The very next day, Dale had been discreetly asked by the staid officers of the bank where he had been a second vice-president to tender his resignation. They agreed to provide a letter of recommendation if he left promptly.

So he had come to the Delta National Bank of Heaven, Louisiana, overqualified and underimpressed. At the time, however, he hadn't had the financial luxury of turning down any job in his chosen field, particularly that of bank president. He had swayed the board of directors with ingratiating charm and gave as his reason for leaving his former place of employment a desire to move to a more temperate climate.

No sooner had the Mayflower van delivered his furniture, than he regretted his decision. He hated the town, hated the heat, hated the narrow-minded people and their closed cliques.

The only person who had treated him in a friendly fashion was Cotton Crandall. Gilbreath had discovered that Cotton was somewhat of a newcomer and outsider himself. Cotton had firmly established himself in the community by marrying the last surviving Laurent in the parish.

Gilbreath had had no such opportunity, but he saw a way to cement his position in this town. It wasn't a perfect town, but since the Pennsylvania episode wasn't the first time he and Rhoda had been asked by moral do-gooders to leave a community, they were determined to stay in Heaven. And if he could help it, they wouldn't remain there as second-class citizens. This was a small pond, but he was going to make sure he was the biggest fish in it.

If he owned Belle Terre, people would have to regard him and Rhoda with deference. It made him giddy just thinking about a couple of Yankees living in Belle Terre. That would set the town on its ear. And there wouldn't be a damn thing that anybody could do about it but kiss his ass and pretend to love him.

Taking Schyler Crandall's phone call was his last piece of business for the day. With a springy gait he left the bank building and walked the two blocks to the parking lot where he left his car each day. Except for his Lincoln, the lot was empty. He opened the door and slid behind the wheel.

"Jesus, it's about time," the person sitting in the passenger side said. "Turn on the air conditioner. It's hotter than hell in here. I thought you said five o'clock. It's almost fifteen after. What took you so long?"

Chuckling, Dale turned on the motor and adjusted the air-conditioning controls. "Believe it or not, I was talking to Schyler."

"To Schyler? At the bank?"

"She called me."

"What about?"

"She feels the undertow and is trying to keep her head above the surface. I think she's afraid that everything she holds near and dear is about to be taken away from her."

"Well, she's right, isn't she?"

"For your good, as well as mine, you'd better hope so."

"What did she want with you?"

"To bargain." He recapped their telephone conversation.

"You turned her down, I hope."

Dale's smile was evil. "Of course, but with a great deal of commiseration."

"She won't fall for that. She's smart."

"You're worried about that, are you?"

"You're damn right I am. What are you grinning about? This is serious."

"You're telling me?" Dale snapped. "Schyler's got her foreman back." He glanced at his passenger. "She's confident that she'll line up some good contracts in the next few days."

"They'll have to be more than just good."

Dale nodded in agreement. "Contracts or not, what she hasn't got is time. I don't think we have a problem."

"We do if we don't keep close tabs on Schyler."

"Exactly. That's why I need you to tell me every move she makes. Even things that you don't consider important, I want to know about."

"You want me to spy on her."

"Yes. Not only that, sabotage whatever you can get away with. Just don't get caught at it."

"All right."

"We need something to distract her."

"Like what?"

"I don't know. A love affair? Of course, it would be most fortuitous if Cotton died. That would take her mind off the business for a while." Dale carefully gauged the other's violent reaction. His eyebrows rose inquiringly. "Would that upset you so much?" No answer. Dale frowned. "I can see that it would. Are you sure that your loyalties aren't divided?"

"I'm only loyal to myself. Why shouldn't I be?"

"Then if it gets unpleasant or dangerous before it's over, you won't object?"

"No."

"I hear uncertainty in your voice."

"No!"

"That's better," Dale said, his smile restored.

"Schyler shot Jigger Flynn's dogs."

After a moment of stunned silence, Dale asked, "Are you sure? I'd heard a rumor that—"

"The rumors are false. Schyler did it. She used one of Cotton's shotguns."

"How do you know?"

"I know, okay?"

Dale knew when to back off. He did so, and at the same time, pondered this valuable piece of information and considered its useful applications. "Jigger would love to know that."

"Meaning?"

"Don't play innocent. You're thinking the same thing I am. That's why you told me. I've used Jigger Flynn before to handle sticky situations. He's extremely efficient and relatively inexpensive. If he knew Schyler was responsible for killing his pit bulls, he would do just about anything to retaliate. He would consider Schyler fair game." Dale's thin lips parted in a ferret's smile. "Wouldn't he?"

"I've got to go," the passenger said brusquely, shoving open the door.

"No matter how ambiguous your feelings for Cotton might be, you won't let them stand in your way, will you?"

"No. I won't let anything stand in my way."

"That's what I wanted to hear."

Supremely satisfied with the way the interview had gone, Dale watched his informant disappear into the alley.

⟋⟋ **TWENTY-TWO**

Ken had a pleasant buzz going when he left the Gator Lounge. He wasn't staggering, but he was drunk enough to fumble and drop his keys as he approached his car. They landed in the gravel. He bent to pick them up, but before he touched them, a shiny black shoe came out of nowhere and stamped on them. His hand was nearly crushed. It froze.

"Hey, Kenny."

Ken straightened slowly. Glancing swiftly over his shoulder, he confirmed what he already suspected. The first man, the one with the expensive shoe, wasn't alone. These types always traveled in pairs, like nuns; except this duo was unholy.

"Hi." Ken gave a nervous little laugh. He shrugged innocently and raised his hands in surrender. "Now before you get pissed, I'll tell you right off that I don't have the cash toni—"

A rock-hard fist landed a solid blow to Ken's guts. He bent over double, clutching his middle. The thug who'd been standing in the background grabbed a handful of Ken's hair and pulled him upright. He yelped with pain. There was no one to hear him. The parking lot, bathed in the ruby light of the neon sign, was deserted. But even if someone had heard his cry for help, he wouldn't have interfered. These guys were deadly.

The first man, obviously the spokesperson, moved forward to stand nose to nose with Howell. "I'm already pissed off. You're three days late paying me what you owe me, Kenny." His voice was silky, but contemptuous. "It does something to me when you lie." The hand he used to cover his heart glittered with diamond rings. "In here, deep inside, it hurts me when you lie to me."

"I can't help it," Ken gasped. "Money's tight. I've had to pay the old man's hospital bills. Doctors."

"Kenny, Kenny, you're breaking my heart." The sullen face turned ugly. "Know what you are? Besides being a liar, you're a loser. You lost bad on that pit bull fight last week. And that nag you bet on in the daily double at Lafayette belongs in the glue factory." He spat in Ken's face. "You're a goddamn loser. I hate losers. They make me want to puke."

Ken was sweating bullets. "Look, man. Give me more time. I—"

He rammed his knee into Ken's groin. Ken screamed in agony. "I don't want any more of your lame excuses. I can't cover my expenses with excuses. I want cash. When do I get my money?"

"S . . . soon," Ken stuttered. "Something big is about to break."

"Something big? Like what? You gonna win at bingo?" The man holding Ken's hair chuckled.

"No," Ken gasped, still in excruciating pain. "Something really big."

"This sounds like more of your bullshit."

"No, swear to God, but I can't give you the details. I haven't worked them all out yet. The logging company—"

"Is reopening. Yeah, yeah, I know. Old news. Boudreaux is back doing his thing." He flashed an oily smile. "Is he bangin' that sexy sister-in-law of yours?"

"No!" Ken angrily put up a struggle against the man who restrained him. The thug only knotted his fingers tighter in Ken's hair and pulled his head back further. "If that's what you've heard, it's a goddamn lie."

His tormentor laughed nastily. "She kicked you outta her bed and outta your position in the family business. Now ain't that a shame?"

"That's not true. None of it. I'm still in control of the books. I'm still vice-president of the company."

"But she's running the show. With Boudreaux coaching her in soft whispers while he's screwing her. Ain't that the way it is?"

Ken tried to shake his head in denial, but the motion only pulled his hair tight enough to bring tears to his eyes. "No. I'm in charge."

"You?" The thug barked a laugh, which he silenced as abruptly as he flicked open the switchblade and slid it between Ken's thighs, directly beneath his manhood.

Ken squealed and rose up on tiptoes. The man behind him, who had been threatening to tear his hair out, now relaxed his grip at a time when Ken wanted to be held up. "I'll get your money," Ken whimpered in panic. "But you gotta give me more time."

"Time's run out on you, Kenny." He pressed the knife's blade against Ken's zipper.

"No, no, please, for the love of God, no. I'll get you your money."

"All of it?"

"Every blessed cent."

"When?"

"A . . . a month." The man behind him opened his fist and let go of his hair. Ken barely kept himself from falling onto the blade. "Two weeks," he amended breathlessly.

Gradually, with a motion that sickeningly resembled a slow, slicing movement, the loan shark withdrew the knife. "Okay, I'm easy. Two weeks." He grinned broadly, then drew his face into a scowl. "Don't bother calling us. We're gonna be on top of you like flies on a pile of dogshit, Kenny." He flashed Ken a hungry crocodile smile. Even his teeth looked like they'd been filed to points. Then he and his comrade stepped out of the pool of neon light and disappeared into the darkness.

With no more spine than a blob of ectoplasm, Ken dropped to his knees. He vomited in the gravel. When the spasms subsided to dry heaves, he crawled around on hands and knees until he located his keys.

The headlights roused Schyler. Sitting on the porch swing, occasionally giving it a desultory push with her bare toes, she'd almost been lulled to sleep. She hadn't known what fatigue was until she had started working at the landing every day. She rarely left until well after dusk and was always the first one to arrive in the morning.

She smiled at Ken as he trudged up the steps. "Hi. You look as ragged out as I feel."

"I, uh, my stomach's upset."

"Nothing serious, I hope." When he shook his head, she asked, "Is that why you weren't here for supper?"

"No. I just got sidetracked." Crossing the veranda, he reached for the handle of the screen door.

"If you've got a minute, there's something I want to ask you about."

Ken's hand fell to his side and he turned to face her. "There's something I want to ask you about too," he said heavily.

"Shoot."

"Are you sleeping with Cash Boudreaux?"

Schyler's smile collapsed. She was affronted, not only by his assumption that her bed partners were his business, but also by the insult his question implied. "Certainly not."

His tread was slow and deliberate and angry as he moved toward the swing. "Well you might as well be. That's the gossip going around town."

Darkness concealed the sudden flush of heat in her cheeks. With admirable skill she kept him from seeing how much his comment upset her. She made a dismissive gesture. "You know as well as anybody how people around here love to talk."

"There's usually some basis for gossip."

"Not this time."

"You spend all day with him."

"But not all night!" The instant her temper erupted, she squelched it. She was too tired for an argument tonight, especially since she had nothing to defend. "I work with Cash. I'm required to spend time with him. I've worked with a lot of men, but that doesn't mean I sleep with them."

"Mark Houghton is one exception that springs to mind."

Schyler got out of the swing so fast that it rocked crazily behind her. "I'm not about to discuss my private life with you, Ken. As I've said before, it's none of your damned business. Good night."

He caught her arm as she stalked past him. "Schyler, Schyler," he pleaded, "don't go. Stay and talk to me."

"Talk? Okay. Refute allegations that I'm sleeping with Boudreaux or with anybody, no."

"Hell, what do you expect people to think?"

"I expect people to think exactly what they please. But I expect better from you."

"I can't stand having your name connected to his."

"What would you have me do about that? We're working together."

"Fire him."

"I can't," Schyler cried incredulously. "I don't want to. I need him too much."

"You didn't think so at first."

"I know better now. He's an excellent forester. He does even more than he gets paid for."

"Then *you* quit. Let me take over."

Schyler was surprised by how intensely she loathed that idea. As exhausting as her work at the landing was, she wouldn't think of giving it up. Her efforts to obtain large contracts from former markets had so far met with little success. But the thought of quitting now was untenable. Nor did she trust anyone else, not even Ken, to fight as diligently as she was fighting to keep Belle Terre.

It would be churlish to come right out and say that, so she tried to decline his offer diplomatically. "You can't be two places at one time."

"I'll move my work to the landing office."

"You can't handle both jobs, Ken."

"I can," he argued insistently. "Give me a chance."

"It's unnecessary to wear yourself out. Especially when I'm willing to—"

He squeezed her arm hard. "I'm not willing. I'm not willing to let you turn into a ball-breaking, career broad."

"I'm not like that."

"Fast becoming." He pulled her close. "I remember how sweet and feminine you were when—"

"Ken, please."

"Let me finish, Schyler. I still lo—"

"I thought I heard your voice out here. It's about time you dragged yourself home." Ken jumped away from Schyler and guiltily spun around and faced his wife. "Well, well, well," Tricia laughed lightly, pushing through the screen door. "What are you two up to?"

For a sustained moment, no one said anything. Then Schyler replied smoothly, "I was asking Ken about some files that are missing from the batch he brought to the landing for me."

Only a brief few weeks ago, Schyler would have welcomed hearing a profession of love from Ken's lips. It would have been icing on the cake for him to profess it within Tricia's hearing.

Now, that kind of reward seemed as cheap and insignificant as a plastic trophy. Having him say he still loved her was no longer worth the tumult it would cause. She no longer wanted to hear it. His love just wasn't valuable to her anymore.

"I'll look for those missing files to be on my desk sometime tomorrow then, all right?" she asked him.

"Uh, sure, okay."

"Good." She bent down and picked up the sandals she'd left beneath the swing. "I'm exhausted. Six o'clock comes early, so I'm off to bed. 'Night." She went inside and padded upstairs.

Tricia, leaning against one of the columns, gave her husband an accusatory and uncharitable look. "It's been a long day for me, too," he said quickly. "I'm going—"

"You, stay where you are, Mr. Howell." Tricia's tone had a ring of authority to which Ken automatically responded. For the second time in only a few minutes, his hand fell away from the handle of the screen door. "You smell like a tavern."

He plopped down heavily in the swing and massaged his eyesockets with his middle finger and thumb. "Makes sense. That's where I've been."

"Drowning your sorrows in an ocean of bourbon?"

"Yeah," he said scornfully, "the chief sorrow being my bitch of a wife."

"Forget me. I'm the least of your problems."

"What do you mean?"

"You're going to let her waltz in here and take over, aren't you?"

"What? Who?"

"Schyler, you idiot. Can't you see what she's doing? Don't you care?"

"I care, but she doesn't listen to me, Tricia."

"Then you're not talking loud enough." She turned her back on him and crossed her arms as though holding in her temper. After a moment she glanced back at him over her shoulder. "Have you ever mentioned to her what we discussed?"

He laughed scoffingly, shaking his head in disbelief. "About selling Belle Terre?"

"Belle Terre, Crandall Logging, and everything else."

"Schyler would never hear of it."

"How do you know? You haven't asked her."

"Neither have you." He made it a challenge.

"She has never listened to me. If anybody holds sway over her, it's you." Her eyes narrowed. "Or are you losing ground to Cash Boudreaux? My, my, are the tongues in town flapping about *that.* Imagine what strange bedfellows the two of them make. Schyler Crandall, former belle of Laurent Parish, and Monique Boudreaux's bastard boy. Who'd ever believe it?''

"Nobody who's got any sense.''

"You sound so sure.''

"I am. I just asked her. There's no truth to the rumor.''

"You think she'd tell you?''

"Yes,'' he said with more surety than he felt. "I think she would.''

"Doesn't matter,'' Tricia said airily. "If folks think they're sleeping together, it's as good as fact.'' Her smile changed direction and turned downward. "And it would be just like her to lie down with white trash. She never had any discrimination.'' She gnawed the corner of her lip. "She'll drag our reputation right down into the swill with hers. I wouldn't be surprised if that's why she took up with Cash. To come back here and ruin us for doing . . . for what happened when we got married.''

Tricia thumped her fists on the column. "Well, I won't have it. She's provided us even more reason to get away from here. Belle Terre,'' she sneered. "A pretty name for . . . what?'' She waved her hand to encompass the lawn and beyond. "A pile of dirt. Trees. A stinky old bayou that's good for nothing but breeding mosquitoes and crawfish. The house isn't even an original. It's a replica of one the Union army burned down when they were done with it. There's nothing special about it.''

"Except that Schyler loves it.'' Ken gave his wife a calculating look. "Which I believe is the very reason you insisted we live here.''

She counterattacked. "Well, I haven't heard you complaining. You haven't had to pay rent, have you? You haven't had to buy groceries. Not one red cent of your money goes into keeping up the place. You've had it pretty damn good for the six years we've been married.'' She paused before playing her trump card. "Up until now that is.''

"Don't threaten me, Tricia.''

"Take it as fair warning. If you're not careful, Schyler will replace you, sugar pie. She'll barge right in and make you superfluous. You'll be deadwood around here and Cotton won't hesitate to cut you off.''

Because she teased him with his greatest fear, Ken got up and headed for the front door again. As he went past her, Tricia caught his arm and detained him. Changing her tactic, she snuggled against him and laid her cheek on his chest, disregarding the sour smell.

"Don't go huffing off, baby. Don't get mad at me. I'm telling you this for your own good. Our own good. Talk Schyler into getting rid of Belle Terre. What do we need a great big old house like this for? We're sure as hell not going to fill each bedroom with a grandbaby like Cotton expected us to. With our share of the sale money we could buy a modern condo in any city we want. We could travel. We—''

"Tricia,'' he interrupted wearily, "even if Schyler agreed, which she won't, what about Cotton? He will never agree to selling this place.''

"Cotton might die.'' Ken stared down into his wife's face. It was cold and unfeeling enough to make him shiver. Her expression softened only marginally when she said, "We have to prepare ourselves for that eventuality. It could happen any day. Now, will you approach Schyler with the idea of putting Belle Terre up for sale or not?''

"I've got a lot on my mind,'' he mumbled evasively. "But I promise to think about it.''

He disengaged himself and went inside. Tricia watched him go, despising the dejected manner in which he climbed the stairs, head down, shoulders stooped, hand dragging along the banister like a lifeless appendage.

By comparison, Tricia felt like a kettle about to boil. Flattening herself against the wall of the house, she clenched her fists and clamped her teeth over her lower lip to keep from screaming in frustration. She wanted and wanted and wanted and never got any satisfaction. She thought the people around her, especially her husband, were so unambitious and dull.

No one seemed to care that life was passing them by with the speed of a zephyr, while they had no more forward motion than the waters of the bayou. They were willing to settle for so little when there was so much out there waiting to be had. They seemed content to rot in Heaven.

Her impatience to get away and change her life was so strong that her skin itched from the inside.

 # TWENTY-THREE

Heart patients were robbed of all dignity.

Spending weeks in a hospital ICU had made Cotton Crandall expertly familiar with humiliation. His body's weakness, assisted by powerful medications, had kept him drifting in and out of consciousness. But he knew that having his ticker on the blink was as debasing and emasculating as castration.

He pretended to be woozier than he actually was while the nurse exchanged IV bottles because he was only mildly curious about what was being dripped into his veins. His thoughts were more with the nurse. She wasn't one of the bossy nuns who ran the place like military generals. She was young and pretty. From an advantageous angle, Cotton could appreciate the shape of her breasts while she took his blood pressure. He wondered what she would do if he tented the covers with an erection.

He wanted to laugh at the thought but couldn't quite garner the energy, so he satisfied himself with a smile that never quite creased his lips.

There was little hope of an erection, though, since he had a tube running up his cock to drain his bladder for him. "Shit," he thought scornfully. He wasn't even able to piss by himself.

Satisfied with his current condition, the nurse gave his shoulder a kindly pat and left the room. He was left in peace, if not in silence. The computerized machines that monitored all his vital statistics beeped out their information on small, green screens.

How long before he could leave? How soon could he go home to Belle Terre? *God, at least grant me the blessing of dying there,* he prayed.

But he seriously doubted that God, if there even was one, remembered Cotton Crandall's name.

Still, he hoped. His dream death had him sitting on the veranda of Belle Terre, a tall glass of neat bourbon in one hand, his other arm around Monique.

The beeping signals faltered. He heard the glitches before he even felt the palpitation inside his chest. To be safe, he pushed the thought of Monique aside.

Instead, he thought about those living at Belle Terre. As usual his thoughts centered on Schyler. Her name evoked profound love and glaring resentment.

These two emotions warred within him, each so strong as to cancel out the other and leave him numb.

When he had regained enough of his faculties to realize that she had come home, his ailing heart had swelled with gladness. But his heart attack hadn't erased his memory. When he recalled why she had gone away, all the bitter anguish returned. He couldn't forgive her.

He thought it was odd that she kept coming to see him. Even though he never acknowledged that she was there, she faithfully visited him each day. He didn't want to admit it, but her visits were the brightest spots of his endless days for in this place there were no sunrises or sunsets. The hours were measured not by the position of the sun in the sky, which couldn't even be seen, but by the switching shifts of nurses and technicians. One could spend months in the hospital and never know the seasons had changed.

Perhaps a season was too much to ask for, but he hoped he lived to see another sunset at Belle Terre. Jesus, he remembered the first sunset he'd viewed from the veranda like it was yesterday.

He had been working for old man Laurent, the stingiest bastard ever to draw breath. The wages he had been earning as a saw hand were paid out in scrip, which could only be used at the company store. The system stunk, but he had been grateful for the job.

Macy Laurent had pulled up at the landing one day in a sleek red convertible. She epitomized forbidden fruit. With her blond hair and banana-yellow sundress, she looked ripe for the picking. But there might just as well have been a barbed wire fence around her since no one of Cotton's caliber could even get close to her. She didn't notice him any more than she noticed all the other loggers who ogled her while she weaseled her daddy out of a crisp twenty-dollar bill, more than most of them earned in a week.

Cotton credited fate with the flat tire that crippled Macy's red convertible a few days later. He'd been walking to work from the boardinghouse he lived in—it was also company owned—when he spotted her on one of the back roads. She was wearing a swimming suit. Her legs rivaled Betty Grable's, and he'd been a big admirer of Miss Grable for years. He offered to change her tire. Even though he would be docked in pay for being late to work, he considered this good deed an investment.

It paid off. Macy was impressed by his tall, brawny build and intrigued by his pale, almost white, hair. For changing her tire, she offered to pay him a dollar. He declined. So she invited him to her house for fresh peach ice cream that evening instead. He accepted.

"Anytime after supper," she had said, giving him a wave as she sped off.

Supper was at six o'clock at the boardinghouse. He didn't know that rich folks didn't eat until seven-thirty, so he arrived much too early. A massive black woman of indeterminate age—he was later amazed to discover that Veda Frances wasn't nearly as old as he had initially thought; her bearing was more indomitable than some of the sergeants he'd served under in combat in France—sternly told him to wait for Miss Macy on the veranda. He was given a glass of lemonade to quench the thirst he'd worked up on the long, dusty walk from town.

Sipping from that tall, cool glass of lemonade, he had experienced his first sunset at Belle Terre. The colors had dazzled him. He had wanted to share it with Monique, but she was back in New Orleans where he had left her until he could send for her.

Then Macy stepped out onto the veranda and spoke his name in a drawl that was as thick as honey and soft as a feather and he forgot all about Monique Boudreaux.

Monique was as vibrant and vivid as a red rose. Macy was as sweet and subdued as a white orchid.

Her skin was just about that translucent, too. He nearly burst with the protective, possessive instinct that seized him. She was so slightly built, so ethereal, that she barely disturbed the air as she moved to one of the fan-back wicker chairs and gestured him into the one beside it.

The first time he kissed her, which came little more than a week later, he told her she tasted like honeysuckle. Her laughter tinkled like a tiny bell. She called him a foolish poet.

The first time he touched her small, pointed breasts, she whimpered and told him that she felt faint and that if her daddy caught him at that, they'd have to get married.

And Cotton said that was okay with him.

News of their engagement rocked the town, of course. To placate their dainty as china, but stubborn as a mule, daughter, the Laurents allowed her to marry Cotton Crandall. To save face, they created a past for him that included a clan from Virginia. The fictitious family history was rife with calamity. Poor Cotton was the sole descendant of the unlucky bunch.

He didn't care what the Laurents told their snooty friends about him. He was in love, with Macy, with Belle Terre. He didn't care that Macy's mother retired to her room in the evenings to keep from watching him desecrate the hallowed rooms of Belle Terre with his white trash mannerisms and rough language. When she died, he didn't mourn her passing, nor that of his father-in-law only three months later.

Like a well-greased piston, Cotton slipped into the managerial slot of the logging company. The first thing he banished was the scrip system. He sold the company store and had the ratty boardinghouses condemned. When the board of directors unanimously disapproved his innovations, he solved that problem by disbanding the board.

He promised the loggers that he would always put their interests first. They were wary but soon came to learn that Cotton Crandall was a man of his word. His promise was as long lasting as gold. The name on the company letterhead was changed as a sign of Cotton's sincerity and the dissolution of Laurent's autocracy. Considering the immensity of the changes in company policy, the transition was made smoothly.

The same was not true in the mansion. Cotton discovered that his fair lady was accustomed to and fond of being pampered. To a man who had grown up believing in a strong work ethic, whose next meal depended on whether or not he did an honest day's work, her idleness was incomprehensible.

Equally as puzzling to him was Macy's aversion to sex. In that respect, she was as different from Monique as night to day. Of course Monique hadn't been a virgin. He had met her in a seedy nightclub in the French Quarter during the closing days of the war. The place had been crawling with soldiers and sailors, but she had picked him out.

She flirted vivaciously; he offered to buy her a drink. He boasted his feats in battle; she'd acted suitably impressed. They made love that first night. Godalmighty, she'd wrung him out. He had never met a woman with so generous an attitude toward sex. She loved fiercely but faithfully. From that first night Monique's bed was reserved for him.

They had set up housekeeping in a rundown apartment house and hadn't spent a night apart until he had been forced to leave to look for work. By that time they had lived together for three years. The subject of marriage had never been broached. She didn't seem to expect or require it for her happiness.

And in the back of Cotton's mind, he had known that something better was in store for him.

He thought he had found it in Laurent Parish. The irony was that Macy hadn't been exaggerating when she told him his caresses made her faint. She almost fainted on their wedding night when he, after hours of unsuccessful persuasion and coercion, forcibly consummated their marriage.

While she wept, he remorsefully promised that the worst was over. But it never got better. No matter what he did, she never liked it. Intimate foreplay repulsed her. She refused to touch him "there" because it was so ugly and nasty. She either accepted him with scathing contempt or sacrificial stoicism. He distinctly remembered the day Macy cut him off completely.

"Cotton?"

"Hmm?"

It had been raining, so he wasn't at the landing. His head had been bent over the ledgers on his desk in the study behind the stairs at Belle Terre.

"Would you please look at me when I speak to you?"

He raised his head. Macy was standing in the doorway. Her slender form was limned by the light in the hallway. "I'm sorry, darling. I was lost in thought." He laid down his pencil. "What is it?"

"I moved your things today."

"My things?"

Nervously, she clasped her hands at her waist. "Out of the master suite and into the one across the hall."

He never recalled a time in his life when he was angrier. "That'll cause you a helluva lot of trouble, my dear. Especially since you'll have to move every single goddamn thing right back where it friggin' belongs."

"I've asked you not to use profanity—"

When he lunged out of his chair, it went rolling backward and crashed into the paneled wall. "What the hell are you trying to pull?"

Her narrow chest rapidly rose and fell with indignation. "Mama and Daddy never shared a bedroom. Civilized people don't. The kind of ... of ... nightly rutting you're accustomed to is—"

"*Fun.*" He stamped across the room and loomed over her. "Most people think it's fun."

"Well I find it revolting."

That cut him to the quick. He admitted that one of Macy's attractions had been her unattainability. That was probably most of his attraction, too. He'd been different from all the smooth-talking college boys who had courted her. It was the Cinderalla story in reverse. He had thought he had scaled the walls of the castle and won the princess, but he hadn't. To her, he was still a redneck saw hand, uncouth and unprincipled—in a word, revolting.

His ego wouldn't allow her to see how deeply she had wounded it. "What about children?" he asked coldly. "What about the dynasty we want to establish?"

"I want to have babies, certainly."

He lowered his face to within inches of hers. "Well, to have babies, Macy, you gotta fuck."

He took perverse pleasure in watching her face drain of all color. She swayed as though he'd backhanded her. He had to admire the grit it took for her to stand her ground, though he wasn't surprised. One of her ancestors had been a Confederate hero.

"I'll let you know the days each month when I'm fertile." Without a sound, without a rustle of her clothing, she left him.

A few months later, he discovered the abandoned house on the bayou. He sent for Monique. To this day, he recalled that lusty afternoon when she arrived with her boy. It hadn't all been rosy. She'd pulled a knife on him and threatened to cut off his pecker when he broke the news that he was married. But he'd talked his way clear, and the fight had only heightened their passions.

Naked as jaybirds and sleek as otters, they had loved away that afternoon in the sweltering upstairs bedroom. That was the last time he ever made love to her without using a rubber. All his seed had to be conserved for those periodic visitations he made into Macy's unresponsive, rigid, dry body.

Cotton had never gone into Macy's bedroom without being invited. After they adopted the girls, he never went into it at all. He kept his word to Macy even after she died. Monique had lived according to the conditions he laid down the day of her arrival on Belle Terre.

To the day she died, she had never complained about their arrangement. Each time he made the trip from the mansion to the house on the bayou, whatever time of day or night he arrived unexpectedly, she dropped whatever she was doing and gave him what he needed, whether it be a meal, a fight, sympathy, laughter, conversation, sex.

Her curiosity about Macy never waned, but she wasn't jealous of her. Jealousy wouldn't have improved her situation. It would have been a wasted emotion, and Monique poured all her emotion and energy into loving Cotton.

Jesus, he had loved that woman.

She'd been dead for almost four years, but the pain of her death was as keen as it had been when her smiling lips whispered his name for the last time and her fingers relaxed their grip on his hand.

Now, the guilty memory of her last smile squeezed tightly the fragile walls of his damaged heart.

 # TWENTY-FOUR

"Cash?" He stopped and turned. Schyler was poised in the doorway of the office. "Are you on your way home?"

He squinted against the setting sun. "It's quitting time, isn't it?"

"Yes, but if you can spare a minute, I'd like to talk to you."

She thought he was going to ignore her because he turned his back and sauntered toward his pickup truck. He left it parked at the landing nearly every day and drove one of the company trailer rigs to wherever they were cutting.

"Have you been cooped up inside that office all day?" he asked over his shoulder.

"Yes."

He leaned over the side of the truck and opened a cooler. He took an iced-down six-pack of beer out of it. "Come on. I'll treat you to a beer."

"Where?"

He looked at her long and hard. "Does it matter?"

Schyler wouldn't back down from a challenge, no matter how subtly it was issued. "Just a sec." She went back inside and turned off all but one light, then locked the office for the night before joining him beside the pickup. He had already downed one can of beer. He crushed the can in his fist and tossed it into the pickup's bed. It landed with a hollow, metallic clatter. He worked a can out of the plastic webbing for her and took another for himself before replacing the six-pack in the cooler.

"Where are we going?"

"Over the river and through the woods."

"To grandmother's house?" Laughing, Schyler fell into step beside him.

"I never had a grandmother."

Both her smile and her footsteps faltered. "Neither did I." He stopped in his tracks and gazed at her. "At least none I knew about," she said in an undertone. He began walking again. After a moment, she asked, "Why do you do that?"

"What?"

"Throw all your deprivations in my face."

"To make you mad."

"You admit it?"

"Why not? It's true. I don't need a priest to confess my sins to."

"You're a Catholic?"

"My mother was."

"And you?"

"I can do without it. My mother's religion didn't do her any good, did it? I prized a rosary out of a dead soldier's hand in Nam. What good did prayers do him?"

"How can you be so callous?

"Practice."

They walked on, but Schyler wasn't ready to quit. "What about your mother's people?"

"What about them?"

"Where were they from?"

"Terrebonne Parish, but I never met any of them that I remember."

"Why?"

"They kicked her out."

Again Schyler stopped and faced him in the darkening twilight. "They kicked her out?"

"*Oui*. Because of me. When my old man deserted us, her folks didn't want to have anything to do with us either."

Not a trace of sadness was registered on his uncompromisingly masculine features, but she knew that he must hurt. Somewhere deep down inside himself, Cash Boudreaux must feel the pain of rejection.

They continued down the overgrown path that meandered through the woods. "Maybe that's why my real mother gave me up for adoption," she said. "Maybe her family threatened to disown her if she kept her illigitimate baby. Your mother must have loved you very much and wanted to keep you in spite of her family."

"She did. But wanting to keep me sure as hell made life tough on her." He held aside a low dogwood branch for her. "There."

He pointed toward the shallow and narrow tributary at the bottom of a slight decline. Trailing willow branches bent toward the water to tickle the knobby knees of cypress trees that poked out above the surface.

"It's beautiful here," Schyler whispered. "And peaceful. The nearest town could be miles away."

"Have a seat."

She sat down on the boulder he indicated, close to the water's edge. Fragrant, yeasty vapor was belched out of the can of beer when she pulled the tab off. Foam spewed. She sipped it off the back of her hand. She drank from the can, then licked her lips. Cash was leaning against the trunk of a cypress, studying her. She looked up at him and asked, "How do you find these places?"

He gazed around. "I was as wild as an Indian when I was growing up. My favorite place to be was in the woods. I've tramped all over these bayous." He slid down the tree trunk until he was sitting on his haunches. He picked up a stick and dug the tip into the soft mud at the water's edge. Bubbles popped up. When they burst, tiny holes were left. "Crawfish," he said.

Schyler stared at him. This man intrigued her. He was an enigma, a study of contradictions. He was a diligent worker, but money wasn't his motivation. He didn't seem to mind living with scarcely any amenities. He neither scorned nor coveted material possessions but seemed genuinely indifferent to them.

"Did you ever think of doing something else, Cash?"

He slurped his beer. "About what?"

"With your life. I mean, didn't you ever have any ambition to go somewhere else?"

"Like where?"

"I don't know," she said in exasperation. "Somewhere. Didn't you explore other career opportunities?"

He shook his head. "I always wanted to work in the forest."

"I know. You're excellent at your job. So you could have gotten work anywhere there is timber. Didn't you ever think of leaving Heaven?"

He stared at the still surface of the water for a long time before answering. "I thought about it."

"Then why didn't you go?"

He finished his beer. "It just didn't work out."

Dissatisfied with his answer, Schyler pressed. "What didn't work out? A promised job?"

"No."

"Then what?"

"I couldn't leave." Impatiently, he rose to his feet.

"Of course you could leave. What was holding you here?"

He made several restless movements, then propped his hands on his hips and stared at his booted feet. He drew a deep breath and let it out. "My mother. I couldn't leave because of her."

That was a more thorough answer than Schyler had hoped for, but it still didn't shed much light. She ran her fingertip around the top of the aluminum beer can. "And after she died? Why didn't you leave then?"

He didn't answer her. She looked up expectantly. He was staring down at her. "I had promised her that I wouldn't." They stared at each other for so long that Schyler began to feel uncomfortable. Intuitively she knew that his reply implied something important, something that involved her, but she doubted she would ever know what it was. Cash Boudreaux was a mystery that would remain unsolved.

That reminded her of why she had detained him. "Cash, didn't you tell me that two of the rigs had flat tires when you got to the landing yesterday morning?"

"*Oui,* but they've been taken care of. I changed the flats myself. The tires are being repaired at Otis's garage."

"I'm not worried about the tires," she murmured absently. "Doesn't that strike you as unusual and unlikely?"

"What?"

"That two rigs would have flat tires on the same morning."

"Coincidence." Her worried frown indicated that she wasn't so sure. "You don't think so?"

The deep breath she drew lifted her breasts and delineated them against her blouse. She wasn't aware of that, nor that the involuntary motion had drawn his eyes. Since the day she had asked him to resume his position with the company, she had been careful to wear modest clothing, not because she felt bound to obey his high-handed directives, but because she didn't want to warrant his criticism.

"I suppose it's just a crazy coincidence. I probably wouldn't have thought any more about it except . . .''

"Go on. What?"

Feeling rather foolish, she looked directly at him. "This morning when I got here, the office door was standing ajar. You didn't arrive before me, did you?"

He shook his head. His brows were pulled into a *V* across his forehead. "Wind?"

"What wind?" she asked with a soft laugh. "I would give my eye teeth to feel a good stiff breeze. Besides, the door was locked. I make certain of that every night before I leave. Did you come in behind me last night to use the telephone?"

He smiled lopsidedly and shook his head no. "What are you getting at? That the truck tires could have been tampered with?"

"No, I guess not. It sounds ridiculous, doesn't it?" She rubbed the back of her neck. The nagging suspicions she had nursed all day sounded ludicrous when spoken aloud. She wished she had heeded her earlier instinct and kept them to herself.

"Was anything in the office missing?"

"No."

"Disturbed?"

"No."

"No signs of vandalism?"

She denied that, too, with a shake of her head. "It just made me feel creepy."

"I'm sure it's nothing to worry about. But maybe you'd better start going home earlier. Don't stay here so late by yourself."

"Ken said the same thing. He's been driving over to follow me home every night."

"Howell?" Cash's brows drew even closer together. "Was he here the night before last?"

"Yes," she replied, mystified by the question. "Why?"

"Did he go anywhere near the garage?"

She shot him a sour look. "Don't be absurd."

"It's not so absurd. Howell has got two good reasons to be severely pissed off."

"What?"

"You taking over the management of Crandall Logging. And the gossip circulating about us."

"Us?" She knew what was coming. The only reason she had asked was that she was curious to see how much he knew. She braced herself for whatever he might say.

"Us. You and me. Folks say that business isn't all we're doing together. They've put us in the same bed. And they say we're having a damn good time there."

Her preparations fell short. She didn't sustain the blow of his words at all. In fact they caused her breath to catch. She said nothing; she couldn't, no more than she could escape his compelling stare, which, like a chameleon, changed color to match the background. One second it was gray, the next mossy green, the next agate.

"Now if you were Howell, wouldn't you be feeling like shit?"

"Ken's got no reason to hold a grudge. I haven't infringed on his work at the downtown office. As for the other, even though it's silly gossip, it's none of his business. He's married to my sister.''

"Right," Cash drawled, taking a long drink from his beer. "But he can't stand the thought of me sampling what he threw away. Finished?''

Schyler had once again been rendered mute. Finally she asked hoarsely, "What?''

"Finished?" He nodded down at the can of beer she was mindlessly strangling with both hands.

"Oh, not quite.''

"Well, what have we here?''

Schyler was shakily raising the can of beer to her mouth, when Cash bent from the waist and scooped something up from the muddy ground near her feet. She went rigid with terror when she saw the writhing body of the snake dangling by its tail from his hand. Its dark-banded body was a good two feet long. Its head was black. Inside its open mouth Schyler could see the pinkish-white membrane from which it drew its nickname.

Cash casually swung the snake backward, then let his hand fly as though he were fishing with a casting rod. The cottonmouth tumbled end over end in the air before making a splash in the center of the viscous bayou.

Schyler's eyes backtracked from the dark green splash it made to Cash. "That was a water moccasin,'' she wheezed.

"Um-huh. Ready to head back?''

"And you just picked it up.''

Then he noticed her apparent dismay and said wryly, "I was raised on the banks of the bayou, Schyler. I'm not afraid of snakes. Any snake." He reached down and drew her up. He ran his warm, rough palms over her upper arms. "I guess you are, though. You've got goose bumps." As his hand continued to rub the raised flesh, he whispered, "Not too many snakes make it as far as the mansion, do they?''

Keeping one hand around her elbow, he guided her back toward the landing. Her knees were trembling. The altercation with the cottonmouth had been unsettling. So had his cavalier treatment of it. So was his soft touch and his hot stare and every sexy word that came out of his mouth.

When they reached his pickup, she slumped against the side of it. "Before I forget,'' she said, "there's something else I wanted to talk to you about.''

"I'm listening.''

"Today I made an appointment to meet with Joe Endicott, Jr. at his paper mill.''

"Over in East Texas?''

"Yes. We've dealt with them before.''

"I remember. They gave us several good contracts.''

"That's been a few years ago. Do you know why they stopped doing business with us?''

"No.''

"Neither do I. He treated me coolly, but I finally wore down his resistance and he granted me an appointment. It's on the twelfth." She paused to draw a breath. "Cash, will you go with me?''

He looked surprised but replied quickly, "Sure.''

"I would appreciate it. I'll need your expertise. I got the impression that they need quality timber and have just about depleted their regular suppliers. This could mean a big contract for us. If we can fill their requirements, I might be able to pay off the note at the bank with this order alone.''

She was no longer sensitive to discussing family business with him. Since they'd been working together, she had discovered that if anybody had the inside track on Crandall Logging, it was Cash. He knew what dire straits she was in and there was no sense in putting up a falsely optimistic front.

"Glad to oblige," he said. "Aren't you finished with that beer yet?"

She nodded and passed him the can, which was still a third full. He drank the rest of it himself and tossed the empty into the back of the truck with the two of his.

He curled his fingers over the edge of the truck and straightened his arms, bracing himself against it. His taut, well-shaped rear stuck out. One knee was bent. He turned only his head and looked at her. "You never did come to like beer much, did you?" Schyler looked away. "I guess that beer bust at Thibodaux Pond turned you against it forever."

She stared at the first evening star, showing up silver and shiny against the indigo sky. "I wondered if you remembered that."

"I remember."

She bowed her head so far that her chin nearly touched her chest. "When I thought about it later, I got so scared for what could have happened."

"You were about to get into a heap of trouble and you were only . . . what? Fourteen? Fifteen?"

"Fifteen."

He let the tension in his arms go slack. With an economy of movement, he turned and propped one side of his body against the truck so that he was now facing her. Schyler didn't look at him, but she could feel his eyes on her.

"My mother had died only a few months before that." She couldn't understand why she felt she owed him an explanation for her behavior that night so long ago. But she couldn't hold it back. "She . . . my mother . . . never was a very attentive parent. What I mean is," she rushed to say, "she didn't dote on us the way Cotton did. She was always distracted by other things."

Cash said nothing. "But she was the rule-maker, the disciplinarian. She and Cotton disagreed more often over how Tricia and I should be raised than they did over anything else."

Of course one of their disagreements had resulted in Cotton's banishment from Macy's bedroom. But that had been before she came along. Schyler had never known a time when she'd shared a bedroom. She remembered being shocked to learn at age eight that in most families the mama and daddy slept not only in the same room, but also in the same bed."

"Anyway," she continued, "when Mama died, Tricia and I started testing the perimeters of Cotton's control. I knew that he wouldn't approve of the beer bust. He had bought me a new car, even though my license was restricted. I wanted to go to that party at the pond and show my new car off to all those older kids. I guess I wanted them to think that my mother's death hadn't fazed me." She drew a staggering little breath. "So I went."

"And met up with Darrell Hopkins."

Laughing derisively, she glanced up at him. "How do you remember that?"

"I remember a lot of things about that night." His voice turned husky. "You had on a white dress. I remember how the light from the bonfire picked you out from everybody else. It was made of that material with the little holes in it."

"Eyelet."

"I guess. Your hair was longer than it is now and was sorta pulled up here with a clip." He made a gesture.

"I can't believe you remember that well."

"Oh, I remember. Because I'll never forget that horny kid's hands groping your backside while you danced with him."

Schyler stopped laughing. She lowered her gaze. "Things went too far before I realized what was happening. One minute it all seemed very romantic, dancing under the sky on the shore of the pond with an 'older man.' The next minute, he was grabbing at me. I panicked and started fighting him off."

She lifted her eyes to his. "That's when you interfered. You came out of nowhere. I remember wondering later, when I was lucid, where you had come from and what you were doing there. I hadn't seen you in ages."

"I was home on leave from Fort Polk."

Her memory quickened. "You had a GI haircut."

He ran his hand through his long hair, smiling. "*Oui.* I was cruising the drag downtown and heard about a helluva party with plenty of beer going on out at the pond, thought I'd go out there and see what kind of action I could scare up."

"You ended up taking me home to Daddy."

"Not before pounding the crap out of Darrell Hopkins. You know, last time I saw him, which wasn't too long ago, he crossed the street to avoid me. He still has a chipped front tooth." Cash closed the fingers of his left hand into a tight fist. "He should have known not to engage in a fight with a soldier on his way to jungle warfare."

Schyler's mellow expression turned serious. "You barely knew me. What made you do it, Cash?"

The air between them seemed to grow thick and electric, as expectant as right before a thunderstorm. His eyes wandered over her face. "Maybe I was jealous. Maybe I wanted to dance with you so I could be the one feeling you up."

He meant to be insulting. Schyler felt like crying and wasn't sure why. "I don't believe that, Cash. I think you did it to be nice."

"I told you before, I'm never nice. Especially with a woman."

"But I was a girl then. I think you interfered because you didn't want an innocent girl to get hurt."

"Could be." He tried to sound nonchalant, but his voice was deep and low. He couldn't keep his eyes away from hers. "But I don't think so."

"Why?"

"Because I liked having your head in my lap too much. Remember that?"

"No."

"Liar."

"I don't remember!"

"Well you should. On the drive home, you laid your head on my thigh. I can still see your hair spread out over my lap. It looked and felt so silky, so sexy. It went ... everywhere." His eyes turned dark and moved down to her mouth. "I should have taken what I felt I had coming while I had the chance, what I felt I was owed for doing my good deed."

"And what was that?"

Slowly his hand came up out of the darkness. His fingers closed around the back of her neck. His thumb stroked her throat. He drew her forward, until the tips of her breasts grazed his chest. "A taste of you."

"Is that why you kissed me the other day? You felt you had it coming?"

"I kissed you for the same reason I do everything else, because I damn well wanted to."

"Obviously you wanted to the night of the beer bust. Why didn't you then?"

The shield that often screened his eyes dropped into place. "Other things got in the way."

"Like Cotton."

"Yeah, like Cotton."

"Why did he get so angry with you? If it hadn't been for you, I could have lost my virginity to a beer-guzzling, randy kid. I hadn't drunk much. Maybe two beers, but that was enough to make me tipsy and to cloud my judgment."

"So you don't remember everything about that night?"

Schyler was puzzled by the wariness in his expression. "Not really," she answered slowly, probing her memory for evasive facts. "I remember seeing Darrell lying unconscious on the ground, bleeding from his mouth and nose. I wanted to help him, to make sure he was all right, but you practically dragged me to my car. *My* car," she exclaimed. "You drove me home in my car?"

"*Oui.*"

"Then how'd you get back to Thibodaux Pond to pick up your own?"

"I walked from Belle Terre to the highway and hitched a ride."

She had never pieced together all the sketchy details of that night. Now it seemed important that she do so, though she couldn't say why.

Cash had saved her from disgrace, but had characteristically turned the situation to his advantage. It had been in the front seat of the shiny, new Mustang Cotton had given her that she had lain her head in Cash's lap. That made it seem even more forbidden, more erotic, more reason for Cotton to have lost his temper.

She looked at Cash again. "Cotton got angry, didn't he?"

"Not surprising. His pride and joy was brought home drunk."

"Yes, but he was furious with you. Why? It wasn't your fault." Her mind went on a frustrating search for tidbits of memory. "When we got to Belle Terre, you half carried me up the front steps. The veranda lights came on. And ..." She paused, closing her eyes, conjuring up a mental picture. "And Cotton was standing there."

"Looking as fearsome as Saint Peter at the pearly gates," Cash supplied caustically. "Without even waiting for an explanation, he started thundering at me. Veda came out and hustled you inside and upstairs."

"I remember." Laughing softly, Schyler added, "She undressed me and tucked me into bed. She scolded me for exercising poor judgment and condemned white trash boys who showed no respect for decent young girls like the Crandall sisters."

She recalled Veda brushing the "so silky, so sexy" blond hair that had been spread across Monique Boudreaux's bastard son's lap just minutes earlier.

God rest Veda, Schyler thought, smiling pensively. She would have given Cash a thrashing herself that night if she could have. As it was, he had taken a tongue-lashing from Cotton. While she was upstairs being lulled to sleep by Veda, Cash was being unjustly accused.

"You took the blame, didn't you?" she asked him, puzzled. "You bore the brunt of Cotton's wrath." Gazing into near space, she continued as recollections, like pages of a book, unfolded for her. "I remember hearing the two of you all the way upstairs shouting at each other. Cotton didn't understand that you weren't the one who gave me beer."

"Cotton refused to understand it," Cash said bitterly.

"He should have been thanking you, but he just kept yelling about—" The book was suddenly slammed shut. The pages stopped turning. Her search had led to a dead end, and like all dead ends, it was frustrating. "What was Cotton yelling at you about that night?"

"Bringing you home drunk."

"Something else," she insisted.

"I don't remember," he said curtly. He swiftly ducked his head and brushed a kiss across her lips. "What the hell difference does it make anyway? It's ancient history."

It made a difference. She knew it. There was something significant here being left unsaid, something more important than Cash wanted to let on.

"Why won't you help me remember?"

"I'd rather make some memories," he whispered against her neck. "But if you want to re-create the past, we'll go for a ride in your car now. I'll drive. You can lay your head in my lap again." He cupped her head between his hands and gave her a brief, but thorough, kiss. "While it's there, maybe you can think of something else to do with your mouth besides talk about days gone by."

"Don't!" she cried, angry over his easy dismissal of the subject. "I need to talk to you about this, Cash."

"Talking's a waste of time between a man and a woman." He coiled his arm around her waist and drew her closer. "Tell you what, if it's a walk down memory lane you want, let's take the rest of the six-pack to Thibodaux Pond." He dropped a quick kiss on the tip of her nose. "We could drink some beer. Get naked. Skinny-dip." He kissed her mouth, thrusting his tongue between her lips. "We'll roll in the grass. Engage in some heavy foreplay. I'll kiss you all over. My tongue will stroke you senseless." His lips claimed hers again. The kiss was as rough and wanton as his fingertips on the raised center of her breast. "Who knows? I might get luckier than Hopkins."

Schyler pushed him away and wiped his kiss off her mouth. Her breasts rose and fell with indignation, and to her mortification, arousal. "I should have shot you when I had the chance."

He gave her a slow, lazy smile. "And I should have raped you when I had my chance. 'Night, Miss Schyler." He turned his back on her and sauntered off into the darkness.

Schyler was still fuming over their encounter hours later as she lay in bed, trying to sleep. Cash Boudreaux was the most infuriating man. She wanted to kill him for all his crimes against her, chief of which was making her blood run hot every time she came near him.

He had caused problems for her from their first personal encounter all those years ago. Her memory had kindly obscured that night he had brought her home from the pond. But tonight the memories had flashed like brilliant patches of light in the dark recesses of her brain.

Still, that most significant point, that inexplicable *something* that Cash had said to her father, eluded her. It was vitally important, though Cash obviously didn't want her to remember it. That was curious. What could it be, and why was it important even now?

She was still searching for a plausible explanation when the phone on her nightstand rang hours later. After fumbling for it in the darkness, she said, "Hello?"

"Ms. Crandall?"

"Yes."

"This is Dr. Collins."

She gripped the receiver hard.

TWENTY-FIVE

"**D**addy?" she asked fearfully.

"We need you at the hospital as soon as you can get here," Dr. Collins told her. "He's suffered another massive heart attack. We have no choice now but to operate. Even then . . . I just don't know."

"I'm on my way."

She allowed herself five seconds of numbing, immobilizing grief before swinging her feet to the floor. Barefooted, she ran out into the hall. Ken was in his underwear, standing just outside the bedroom he shared with Tricia. "I picked up the extension in our room and heard the end of your conversation," he said. "We're coming, too."

"I'd like that. Downstairs in five minutes."

Even at that hour of the night, the hospital was well lit, though sepulchrally quiet. The trio in the elevator were silent as they rode up to the second floor, where they'd been frequent visitors for several weeks. The women looked pale without their makeup. The fluorescent lighting didn't flatter either. Ken's eyes were puffy and his jaw was shadowed with stubble.

They erupted from the opening doors of the elevator like news hounds on the scent of a big story. Schyler outdistanced the other two and reached the nurses' station first.

"Where's Dr. Collins?"

"He's already scrubbing. He left this consent form for you to sign."

Schyler, barely glancing over the necessary document, scribbled her name on the dotted line. "Has my father been taken into the operating room yet?"

"No, but the orderlies are in his room now."

"Can I see him?"

"He's heavily sedated, Ms. Crandall."

"I don't care. I've got to see him." She didn't add the qualifying words "once more." But that's what she feared it would be.

The stark anxiety on her face appealed to the nurse's compassion. "Okay. Just don't detain them."

"I won't." She turned to her sister and Ken. "Do you want to see him?"

Tricia, vigorously rubbing her hands up and down her chilled arms, shook her head no. Ken looked from his wife to Schyler. "Why don't you go alone? Seeing him in pain like that the first time it happened wasn't pleasant for either of us."

Schyler jogged down the corridor. The door to Cotton's room was open. Two orderlies were transferring him from his hospital bed to a gurney. His body looked as frail as a child's. He was strung with tubes and wires. It was a macabre sight. But that didn't even slow Schyler down. She rushed into his room. The orderlies looked at her curiously.

"I'm his daughter."

"We're taking him to the OR," one of them said.

"I understand, but the nurse gave me permission to speak to him. Is he conscious?"

"I don't think so. They gave him a pre-op shot."

While they were adjusting the IVs and covering Cotton with a stiff white sheet, Schyler moved to the side of the gurney, standing far enough away not to hamper the orderlies, but close enough to take Cotton's hand. The back of it was bruised for having had needles in it for so long. It lay in hers listlessly.

The palm of it, however, was beautifully familiar. She knew each callus personally. A thousand memories were associated with that hand. It had proudly patted her head for getting an A in math. It had soothed her after taking a fall off a frisky colt. It had wiped away her tears while he explained that Macy did love her, she just didn't know how to show it.

She raised his hand to her cheek. "Why'd you stop loving me, Daddy?" Schyler whispered the words so softly that no one could have heard them. But, as though in answer, Cotton's eyes opened and he looked directly at her. She gave a soft, joyful cry and smiled brilliantly through her tears. He wouldn't die without knowing how much she loved him.

"Schyler?" Cotton rasped.

"We've got to go now, miss," the orderly said, trying to edge her aside.

"Yes, I know, but . . . What is it, daddy? What are you trying to say?" *He still loved her!* He was trying to tell her so in case this was his last chance.

"Why did you . . ."

"Miss?"

"Please!" she shouted in frustration. The orderly stepped back. Schyler bent over Cotton again. "What, Daddy? Why did I what?"

"Why . . . did . . . did you destroy my grandchild?"

"Boudreaux!"

Cash had been so lost in thought that he hadn't heard the pickup approaching his house, nor the footsteps on his porch. He'd been drinking coffee since three-thirty, waiting until dawn so he could report for work at the landing. Recently, at idle moments such as this, his thoughts turned to the woman he worked for.

That's why he kept himself so busy.

His name had boomed out of nowhere. Now someone was pounding on his door and repeating his name in a voice as finely tuned as a concrete mixer. Cursing his predawn visitor, he left his hot cup of coffee on the table.

Jigger Flynn was standing on the other side of the door Cash angrily pulled open. His eyelids contracted suspiciously, but he was careful to appear nonchalant.

"*Bon jour,* Jigger. What brings you calling so early in the morning?"

Without any kind of greeting, Jigger snarled, "I need something for my woman."

"Which woman?"

"That black bitch who lives with me, which one you think?"

Cash's eyes turned cold. "Gayla?" Jigger grunted and bobbed his head. "What's the matter with her?"

"She's bleeding."

"Bleeding?" Cash repeated in alarm. "Bleeding where?"

"Everywhere. Wake up, I do, with blood in my bed. She says she slipped a kid."

"Jesus."

Cash ran his hand down his face. This wasn't the first time Jigger had come to him asking for medicine for one of his prostitutes who had either botched a self-induced abortion or taken a beating from a customer who got off on bondage and violence. Jigger avoided doctors because such incidents warranted police reports. Most of the law enforcement officers in the parish were in his back pocket, but Jigger didn't take unnecessary risks.

"If she miscarried a fetus she needs a doctor," Cash told him. "You'd better get her to the hospital fast."

"Your *maman,* she gave me the medicine before, don'tcha know. Fixed them whores right up."

"She knew more about it than I do."

Jigger's eyes gleamed with malevolence. "Be a shame, Gayla should die in a pool of her own blood."

That was his way of telling Cash that he had no intention of taking her to the hospital. He was smart enough not to come right out and say so, but his grin was amoral.

Cash gnashed his teeth. "Wait here."

A few minutes later, he was back with a paper sack. "There are two different bottles in here for her to take. I wrote out the directions." He extended Jigger the sack. Jigger took hold of it, but Cash didn't release it. Jigger looked at him inquisitively. "Leave her alone until she's completely well," Cash said tightly. "Do you understand what I'm saying?"

"No fucking."

"That's right. Otherwise you could kill her."

Jigger leered at him. "You like Gayla? Tell you what, Boudreaux, I'll let you enjoy her for one night. In exchange for the medicine."

Cash's face turned dangerous. He abruptly released the sack. "Give me twenty bucks instead."

Shrugging, Jigger fished a twenty-dollar bill out of his pants pocket and handed it to Cash. "Sure you wouldn't rather have Gayla?" Cash said nothing. Jigger cackled and turned to leave. He had taken only one step, however, when he turned around and asked, "Why do you work for that Schyler Cran-*dall?*"

"The hours are good and she pays well."

Jigger's eyes narrowed to slits. "Did that lady shoot my dogs like Gilbreath said?" Cash said nothing, but he tucked away that piece of information. "She'll pay for it," Jigger hissed threateningly.

"Leave Schyler Crandall to me."

Jigger threw back his head and laughed. He pointed a chipped, yellow index fingernail at Cash. "I forgot. You got an ax to grind with the Cran-*dalls,* too."

"And I'll grind it my own way. You stay away from them."

Jigger winked. "We're on the same side of the fence, Boudreaux, don'tcha know. The same side of the fence."

He ambled down the porch steps to where his truck was parked. He gave another nasal laugh and waved to Cash before driving off.

Cash finished dressing for work, unplugged the coffeepot, and left his house only minutes after Jigger. He was surprised that Schyler wasn't at the landing when he drove up. He let himself into the office, wondering if he should mention Jigger's visit to her. He decided against it. The news about Gayla would only upset her and more than likely provoke her into doing something reckless. Besides, the less Schyler knew the better.

When the loggers began to report for work and she still wasn't there, Cash dialed the phone number at Belle Terre and was told by the dour housekeeper that Ms. Crandall wasn't at home.

"Where is she?" he asked.

"She's at the hospital. Mr. Crandall had another heart attack and isn't expected to live."

Absently Cash replaced the telephone. He dropped into Cotton's chair behind the desk and stared into near space. Eventually one of the loggers stamped in to get his orders for the day. He took one look at Cash's face and withdrew without saying a word. Something was wrong with the boss, and God help the man who disturbed him when he was in such a mood.

TWENTY-SIX

H er father's words echoed in her head.
"Why did you destroy my grandchild?"

As many times as she had mentally repeated them, they still made no sense. It was too critical a problem to puzzle through now because her mind could not sustain a thought for more than a few seconds. Her energy had to be used for one purpose, that of holding herself together until the surgery was over.

She covered her face with her hands and drew in a deep breath. He couldn't die before she had another chance to talk to him. He couldn't. God couldn't be that cruel.

"Coffee, Schyler?"

She lowered her hands. Ken was bending over her. "No thanks." He squeezed her shoulder reassuringly, then returned to the other vinyl sofa and sat down beside Tricia. He took his wife's hand and pressed it between his. Schyler watched, feeling a pang of envy. She needed that kind of oneness with someone right now—anyone; anyone who could share her fear and help get her through this.

Tricia happened to catch Schyler's longing stare. She scooted closer to Ken and clung to his arm possessively. Schyler ignored the smug gesture but looked closely at her sister. Without her makeup, Tricia appeared older, harder. There were no cosmetics to alleviate the bitter lines around her mouth or to warm the cold calculation in her eyes.

And then Schyler knew.

In one explosive split second of clarity, she *knew*. Tricia was the culprit.

"Did you . . ." Schyler's voice was as dry and rattly as dead corn stalks blowing in a hot August wind. She tried to work up enough saliva to swallow. "Tricia, did you, at any time, tell Daddy that I had had an abortion?"

Tricia's cheeks, unenhanced by blushing powder, paled even whiter. Her lips went slack and separated slightly, making her look dim-witted. Her blue eyes blinked once, twice. In wordless trepidation, she stared across the waiting room at the woman who was her sister in name only.

"You did. You did."

The knowledge struck Schyler in the middle of her chest. She gasped with pain and sucked in a sharp breath. Her head fell back against her shoulders. She squeezed her eyes shut. Tears rolled down her chalky cheeks.

"Ms. Crandall?"

She raised her head and opened her eyes. Dr. Collins was standing there, looking down at her with concern. He was still wearing his green scrubs. The surgical mask had been untied and was lying flat on his chest like a bib. "The surgeon sent me out. He's closing now."

"Is my father still alive?"

The young doctor smiled. "Yes he is. He survived a quadruple bypass."

Several knots inside her chest unraveled and she took her first comfortable breath in hours. "Will he be all right?"

The doctor scratched his cheek indecisively. "If he recovers, he'll definitely be better than he was. But it'll be touch and go for several days."

"I understand. Thank you for being honest with me."

"Would you like to talk to the surgeon?"

"At his convenience. It's not really necessary, is it?"

"No." He studied her a moment. "It's been a long night for you. I suggest you go home and get some . . ."

His voice dwindled to nothingness. Schyler was stubbornly shaking her head. "No. When Daddy wakes up I have to be here."

"It might be—"

"I have to be here," she repeated adamantly.

The doctor could see that combating such resolve was a waste of time. "I'll keep you posted. He'll be in recovery for thirty-six hours or so. That's an ugly scene, but you can go in periodically if you want to."

"I want to."

"Okay. Then be outside the door every even hour at ten of."

He nodded at the Howells who had remained curiously silent, gave Schyler one last look, and left the waiting room with his characteristic briskness.

Schyler swallowed with difficulty. She didn't want to break down and weep now, though sobs pushed at the back of her throat until it ached. She willed her pounding heart to slow down. She dried her perspiring palms on the handkerchief that was already twisted and soggy with the sweat of anxiety. Her fingertips were white and cold. They felt bloodless.

Making a valiant effort, she stood up. She only took three steps, halving the distance that separated her from her sister and brother-in-law. She looked Tricia straight in the eye. "Get out of my sight." Speaking in a precise, clipped, clear voice, she enunciated each word.

Then she left the waiting room with her dignity and her rage intact.

Schyler became the resident ghost on the recovery floor of the hospital. She refused to leave it. She prowled it endlessly, restlessly, unceasingly, anticipating each report on Cotton's condition, which remained aggravatingly unchanged.

Dr. Collins had tried to prepare her, but nothing he said could have diluted the horror of the recovery room. It was a high-tech torture chamber. She watched from a distance as Cotton struggled against the breathing tube in his throat, which gave him a choking sensation when he regained consciousness. His arms had to be restrained to keep him from jerking free of the necessary needles and catheters and electrodes. She didn't know how any patient survived the recovery room. She didn't know how she did.

The first day, she thought of little else except her father. She was so afraid that the machines monitoring his heartbeat would fall silent and he would die. Every hour he stayed alive was encouraging, the doctors told her. She clung to that hope. On the second day, she started believing it. To help pass the long hours of the second night, she went to the bank of pay telephones and called Mark. Upon hearing his kind and concerned voice, her restraint crumbled and she burst into tears.

"Is he gone, darling?"

"No, no." She brought him up-to-date with wet, noisy slurpy phrases.

"I hope he recovers. I'm sure he will. The doctors are optimistic, aren't they?"

"Yes. They've said as much anyway."

"But what about you? You sound done in."

"I am," she confessed. She didn't have to pretend with Mark. "I'm exhausted. But I want to be here until I'm sure he's out of danger."

"What good will you be to him if you're on the verge of collapse?"

"I must stay here with him."

He knew better than to argue with her when she assumed that particular tone of voice. Tactfully, he switched subjects. "What about the business? Any progress being made there?"

She filled him in on that, too. "Of course I haven't been to the landing since Daddy's surgery. I assume that Cash has everything under control."

Mark offered her money again. Again, she refused it. Finally he said, "I miss you, Schyler."

"I miss you, too. I need to be held."

"Come home and I'll hold you."

She clamped her teeth over her lower lip and tried to keep from crying again. Very expensive tears, these. It was wasteful to cry long distance, but she was dismally homesick for Mark. "I can't, Mark. Not yet. Probably not for quite a while. I need to be here for Daddy. One way or another."

"He doesn't deserve this much loyalty from you."

"Yes he does." He didn't know about Tricia's treachery and she didn't want to go into it over the telephone. "My place right now is at Belle Terre. I have to stay."

They ended the conversation by him telling her a dirty joke. Mark was good at that, at coaxing a smile out of her when she was feeling her lowest. Before she met him, he had experienced his own disillusionment and pain. His suffering had spawned a droll sense of humor and a pragmatic way of looking at life and the rotten pranks it played on people. It was that unique ability of his that had drawn her to him in the first place and that had saved her on more than one occasion from debilitating despair.

But after she hung up, Schyler felt more depressed than ever. Her head was bowed despondently as she made her way down the sterile, over-air-conditioned corridor toward the waiting room, which had become her headquarters.

She didn't see Cash until she walked right into him. He caught her upper arms to steady her. She gazed at him blankly. He stared down at her with dismay, making her realize just how frightful she must look. She had been avoiding mirrors in the ladies restroom for two days. Defensively she asked, "What are you doing here?"

His hands fell away from her arms and his lip curled sardonically. "This is a public hospital, isn't it? Don't they let Cajun bastards come inside?"

"Oh, that's just great. That's just what I need. Your rank sarcasm." She tried to go around him, but he blocked her path.

"Why didn't you call me when it happened?"

She laughed dryly with disbelief. "Well, I was sort of busy. I had a few other things on my mind."

"Okay, since then. What else have you had to do? Didn't you think I'd want to know?"

"Apparently you found out."

"After calling Belle Terre to check on you."

"So what are you upset about?"

"All that uptight bitch who answered the phone would tell me was that Cotton had suffered another heart attack and that it would probably be fatal."

"Much as I hate to defend Mrs. Graves, that's all she knew at the time."

"Well, word got around to everybody else fast enough. I found out the details of the surgery at the goddamn filling station where I went to have my truck gassed up."

The nursing nun behind the desk raised her head and peered at them reprovingly over her granny glasses. Cash glared back at her. "You need something, lady?"

"Please keep your voice down, sir."

He resented authority; the look he sent the woman proved it. Taking Schyler's arm, he roughly pulled her down the hallway and through a set of swinging doors that led to an atrium courtyard. It was filled with plastic plants and stone benches. He batted aside a tacky palm frond that happened to get in his way and ignored the benches.

"How is he?"

Each of Schyler's nerve endings felt as raw as an open wound. Everything irritated her.

It was especially aggravating to discover that she was glad to see Cash Boudreaux.

If he wasn't such an ass, if his manners weren't so atrocious, if he knew how to behave like a gentleman instead of a street thug, she would enjoy having him here with her. His wide chest seemed like a perfect resting place for her tired head. If he had placed his arms around her, she would have moved into his embrace because she wanted so much to be held. She would welcome any comfort he offered. But he wasn't doling out comfort; he was being his critical, obnoxious self.

"I said, how is he?"

He barked the question so sharply that she jumped. "He's fine."

"Shit."

"Okay, not so fine," she shouted, flinging out a hand in agitation. "They cut open his chest, prized apart his ribs, and did four bypasses on his heart, which was weak to begin with. How do you think he is? The two of you have never had a kind word for each other. So what do you care anyway?"

His face moved to within inches of hers. "Because I want to know if the business I'm busting my balls for is going to go belly up when the owner of it croaks."

Schyler whirled around. Cash plowed through his hair with all ten fingers, holding it back off his face for several seconds before letting it fall back into place. He swore beneath his breath, in English, in French, in the mixed language he'd learned from his mother.

"Look," he said, catching up with her at the door, "the loggers are asking about him. I couldn't get anything out of the hospital when I called. Howell has been as tight-lipped as a friggin' clam. I need something to tell the men."

Schyler, her composure restored, turned to face him again. Her expression was stony. "Tell them that he's doing as well as can be expected. The doctor said that by tomorrow we should see a change for the better." Her face softened a degree when she added, "If there's to be one."

"Thank you."

"You're welcome."

"Have they assigned you a bed yet?"

"Pardon?"

"A hospital bed. You look like crap that's been run through the blender."

"How charmingly phrased, Mr. Boudreaux."

"I was putting it mildly. How long since you've had a hot meal? A few hours' sleep? A bath? Why are you punishing yourself for Cotton's illness?"

"I'm not!"

"Aren't you?"

"No. And I don't need you to tell me how bad I look." She drew herself up. "I'll have Ken deliver the payroll checks on Friday. So while you're busting your balls for the company, rest assured that you'll be well paid for your efforts."

She left him cursing amid the artificial forest.

*   *   *

Dr. Collins sought her out the next afternoon at a little past two o'clock. She was in the waiting room, resting her head against the wall. He sat down beside her and took her hand. She braced herself to hear the worst.

"I don't want to be too optimistic," he began, "but he's showing marked signs of improvement."

Her breath escaped in a gust of profound relief. "Thank God."

The doctor squeezed her hand. "I want to keep him in an ICU for another week at least. But I think he's past the critical stage."

"Can I see him?"

"Yes."

"When?"

"In five minutes. During which I suggest you brush your hair and put on some lipstick. We don't want to scare the poor man to death after all he's been through." She laughed shakily.

Five minutes later she entered the ICU where Cotton had previously resided. She noticed his improved color immediately. His skin had lost its grayish pallor. The attending nurse withdrew respectfully, allowing Schyler a modicum of privacy with her father.

She bent over him and touched his hair. His eyes opened and found her. "You're going to be fine," she whispered. Her fingertip smoothed over one of his shaggy white eyebrows, which disobediently sprang back up. "When you get better, I'll explain everything." She licked her lips to moisten them, even though she had just applied lipstick. "But I want you to know something, and it's the truth." She paused to make certain that he was lucid and that she had his full attention. "I've never been pregnant. I've never had an abortion. I would never have killed your grandbaby." She laid her hand along his cheek. "Daddy, do you hear me?"

His eyes clouded with tears. She had her answer.

"I've never lied to you in my life. You know that. What I'm telling you is the truth. I swear it on Belle Terre, which you know I dearly love. I've never been pregnant. It was all a . . . an unfortunate misunderstanding."

The change that came over his face was as dramatic as the first dawn of light breaking out of darkness. His features fell into restful, peaceful repose. His eyes closed. A tear eked from between the wrinkled lids. Schyler wiped it away with her thumb, then bent down and lovingly kissed his forehead.

Exhausted as she was, she left the hospital feeling better than she had in six years.

TWENTY-SEVEN

The first thing Schyler did when she returned to Belle Terre was take a scalding and soapy shower. She ruthlessly massaged her itchy scalp with shampoo, shaved her legs, and got to feeling human again.

Then she went directly to bed and slept for sixteen hours.

When she woke up the following morning, she was ravenous. She dressed in a casual skirt and top, then went downstairs to the kitchen. The three-egg, ham and cheese omelet was almost ready when Mrs. Graves came in.

"Good mroning," Schyler said pleasantly as she deftly slid the omelet out of the pan and onto the plate. The housekeeper, incensed that her kitchen had been invaded, made no reply but turned on her heels and stalked out. Amused, Schyler sat down at the kitchen table and consumed every speck of food on her plate, washing it down with orange juice she had squeezed fresh and two cups of coffee.

It was raining, she noted as she cleaned up after her breakfast. The sky was dark with low, scuttling clouds. A good day to sleep late. And apparently that's what Tricia and Ken were doing.

She left the house without seeing them and drove to the hospital. At the door of Cotton's ICU, she came to an abrupt standstill. Using a slender nurse as his crutch, he was standing beside his bed. He raised his head and smiled at his daughter.

"Hurts like bloody hell but feels great."

Dropping her purse on the floor, Schyler rushed forward and hugged him for the first time since Tricia had married Ken.

They were spared a highly emotional scene by the nurse saying, "I hope you have better control over him than I do, Ms. Crandall. He's the most cantankerous, profane patient I've ever had."

"That's a goddamn lie."

The women winked at each other behind Cotton's back. Together they eased him back into bed. For all his bravado, the exercise had exhausted him. Almost as soon as his head touched the pillows, he began snoring gently. Schyler watched him sleep for a while, then left his room and went to the lobby gift shop to order flowers for him. They had a lot of sorting out to do. But there would be time for that later. Thank God, there would be time.

She waited around for several hours, but he didn't wake up. Dr. Collins and the cardiac surgeon assured her that the best thing for him now was sleep. She left without speaking to Cotton again, but the fond smile he'd given her when she entered his room had been her reassurance that he remembered what she had told him the day before and that his faith in her had been restored.

She was anxious to attend to business at the landing, but it would keep for another few hours. There was something she must do first. It had been put off long enough. Six years in fact.

It was shortly after noon when she returned to Belle Terre from the hospital. The weather was still inclement. She ran from her car to the veranda through a hard rain. The rooms of the lower story were empty. She heard Mrs. Graves moving about the kitchen but avoided her. She went upstairs. A radio was playing behind Tricia's bedroom door. Schyler opened the door without knocking and stepped inside.

Tricia, wearing a satin kimono over her slip, was sitting at a vanity table applying makeup. She was humming along with Rod Stewart. When Schyler appeared in her mirror, Tricia dropped the eye crayon and spun around on the tufted velvet cushion of the stool.

"I didn't hear you knock."

"I didn't knock."

Tricia's hand moved to the lapels of her robe and pulled them together, a giveaway of her nervousness, though none of it showed up on her face. "How rude. Has associating with white trash made you forget common courtesy?"

Schyler refused to be provoked or put on the defensive. She went to the radio and switched it off with an angry flick of her wrist. The silence was abrupt and absolute. Schyler confronted her sister.

"You don't deserve my courtesy. Be glad you won't get what you deserve." Schyler was angry, angry enough to cross the room and tear out Tricia's glossy hair strand by strand. But overriding her anger was perplexity. "Why Tricia? What possible motive could you have had for telling Cotton that I had aborted a baby?''

"What makes you think I did?''

"No more games,'' Schyler lashed out. "I know. What I don't know is *why*. For godsake, why would you make up such a lie?''

Tricia rose to her feet and gave the belt of her kimono a vicious yank. She went to the window, moved aside the drapes and gazed out at the dreary day. The drape dropped back into place when she let it go. Finally she faced Schyler.

"To get him off my back, that's why. So he would stop condemning me for snatching Ken away from you. Not that I had to do much snatching.'' She raised her chin haughtily. Her hair swung against her shoulders.''Once he had been to bed with me, there was no question of him ever going back to you.''

A statement like that would have destroyed Schyler several years ago, but now her mind concentrated on something else. "Cotton berated you for taking Ken away from me?''

Tricia laughed shortly and without humor. "Berated. Badgered. Bitched. Call it whatever you want. For the way he carried on, you would think I'd driven a stake through your heart. He went on and on about how I had betrayed you, how I had deliberately set out to get Ken only because you wanted him.''

Schyler ran her fingers over the carved rosewood back of a chaise longue. She could remember Macy reclining on its linen cushions, distracted and distant, when her daughters came to kiss her good night. Schyler could still feel her mother's cool lips barely grazing her cheek. Tricia had always pushed Schyler aside, clambering to claim those dispassionate kisses that were so miserly dispensed.

"And wasn't he right?'' she asked her sister softly. "Didn't you want Ken only because I had him?''

"No!'' Tricia answered shrilly. "I fell in love with Ken. You're just like Daddy, always ready to think the worst of me.''

"You give people no choice but to think that, Tricia. You've schemed all your life. But this . . . this . . .'' Her eyes searched the beautiful room, looking for words suitably descriptive of Tricia's betrayal. She came up empty. "How could you do something so mean?''

"I didn't do it to hurt you, Schyler.''

Schyler gaped at her incredulously. "How could it not?''

"Because you're a survivor. You moved to London and started a new life. I thought Daddy would get over it.''

"Over his daughter having an abortion?''

"Oh, for heaven's sake! I just said the first thing that popped into my head when he asked me how I could do such a thing to poor little Schyler.'' Mockingly, she laid a hand against her breast.

"I don't believe you. I think you told him that because you knew it would drive a permanent wedge between us.''

"That's bull.'' Tricia turned to the dressing table and picked up the eye crayon again. Leaning toward the mirror and pulling down her lower lid, she applied color to it. "Don't make such a federal case out of it. An abortion just seemed like a believable reason for you and Ken to have quarreled. I didn't know Daddy was going to mope about it forever.''

"When it became apparent that he was, that he was holding it against me, why didn't you tell him the truth?''

"Because I didn't want him to hate me.''

"But you let him hate *me*.''

Tricia whirled around. "Well it was about time those tables were turned, wasn't it?"

Schyler fell back a step, astonished by Tricia's obvious hatred. Her face was taut with it. "What do you mean?"

"Wasn't it my time to have his approval? To have his attention? To have his love?" Her shapely chest rose and fell beneath the satin. The words had been pent up inside her for years. Now they poured out. "He doted on you. Everything you did was right, perfect. When he happened to see past you and look at me, he didn't like what he saw."

"Tricia, that's not true."

Tricia ignored her. "When he spoke to me, it was always to criticize. But you, you could do no wrong."

She flung off her robe and went to her closet. She jerked a dress off its hanger and stepped into it. Schyler noticed what a beautiful woman Tricia was. Her body was well made. Her figure was slender and compact. Her face would have been beautiful, too, were it not for the bitterness that prevented it from being femininely soft.

Tricia went back to the dressing table and picked up a lipstick. She twirled it out of the gold tube and applied it in smooth rapid strokes to her lower lip. "I don't know why the hell they got me." She rubbed her lips together and dropped the tube of lipstick back onto the dressing table with a clatter.

"They wanted you."

Tricia made a scornful sound. "Your naïveté confounds me, Schyler. Mama was half loony because she couldn't have a baby of her own."

"She wanted to give Daddy children."

Tricia groaned in derision. Wrapping a belt around her waist, she latched and adjusted it. "She didn't give a damn about giving Daddy anything but a hard time. She wanted to have a baby because that would guarantee a Laurent heir to Belle Terre. At least half a Laurent, which was the best she could do. Being unable to have a child made her less than perfect. She couldn't accept that about herself. So she went a little nuts when she couldn't conceive."

"Don't say that. Mama wasn't a very happy woman, but—"

"Dammit, Schyler, she was miserable. *Yes!*" she stressed when she saw that Schyler was about to contradict her. "She was a miserable, self-centered bitch. Her main occupation in life was to make everybody else miserable, too. She didn't love us. She loved herself. Period. Cotton loved you. You worshiped the ground he walked on. So where do you think that left me? Huh? Out in the cold. Every single day of my life. And when Ken Howell came along with his pedigree in one hand and his broken heart in the other, you're damn right I wanted him. Why shouldn't I? It was my turn," she screamed, flattening a hand against her chest. "You bet I went after him. I would have done anything to keep you from having him."

"*Anything?* There was never a baby, was there, Tricia? You never were pregnant. That was a lie, too. There was no miscarriage after the wedding, was there?"

"What difference—"

"Tell me!"

"*No!*"

Their animosity was palpable. Tricia's one-word confirmation of Schyler's long-held suspicion served as a bell ending a round, signaling each to return to her corner. They caught their breath. Schyler was the first to speak.

"Does Ken know you deceived him?"

Tricia shrugged as she lit a cigarette. "I imagine so. He's no Einstein, but he's not that stupid. We've never talked about it." She blew out a cloud of smoke, aimed ceilingward. "I think he prefers to believe that a heavy period was a miscarriage. I say let him, if that makes him feel better about losing you."

She gave Schyler a once-over. "Actually between the two of us, I'm a much better wife to him than you ever would have been. Your self-sufficiency threatens him. He admires it, but he doesn't like it. It makes his shortcomings too apparent."

"Don't you dare tell me what kind of wife I would have made Ken. I loved him. Deeply."

Tricia's mouth turned up at the corners. "Yes," she said softly, "I know."

"He came back to me. You couldn't stand that." Schyler's words struck home. Tricia angrily flicked an ash into a Waterford ashtray on the vanity. "That's why you made up the lie about being pregnant. You wanted to hurt us both. You saw a way to emotionally destroy me and to trap Ken."

As Schyler sifted through her thoughts, she moved to the windows. The rainfall was heavier than before. Puddles were forming in the grass on the lawn. Even in the rain, Belle Terre was beautiful. Nothing diminished its beauty in her eyes.

"But then you had to justify yourself to Daddy. You knew that what he valued above everything was Belle Terre. He talked constantly about establishing a dynasty. Even though they wouldn't bear his name, he wanted generations of children to grow up in this house. You knew he wanted that more than anything. You knew the thing that would hurt him the most was to find out that one of us had aborted his grandchild."

"Oh, Jesus," Tricia swore as she ground out her cigarette. "You're as sentimental as he is. Our children wouldn't be his grandchildren. Because we're not his! All that dynasty and generational talk was ridiculous. It was embarrassing to hear him carry on about it like a babbling fool. He doesn't belong to Belle Terre any more than we do. Everybody in the parish knows that he only married Macy Laurent to get Belle Terre."

"That's not true. He loved Mama."

"And he screwed Monique Boudreaux!"

Schyler spun around and looked at Tricia with patent disbelief.

Tricia burst out laughing. "Gracious sakes alive. You didn't know, did you? I can't believe it," she said, flabbergasted. "You honestly didn't know that she was Cotton's mistress? Amazing." Shaking her head, she made a scornful sound. "What do you think he is, a monk? Saint Cotton? Did you think he went without a place to stick it all those years he and mama didn't sleep together?"

"You're vulgar."

"You're right," Tricia purred. "That's why it was so easy to lure Ken out of your bed and into mine."

"That's not altogether true."

Both women reacted to Ken's voice. They turned simultaneously to find him standing in the open doorway. He had addressed Tricia. But he was looking at Schyler. "Let me refresh your memory, Tricia. You came on to me like a bitch in heat."

"Which you seemed to like."

"You also told me the same lie you told Cotton."

"She told you that I had aborted your child?" Schyler asked.

"Out of pique, she said."

"And you believed her?"

Schyler looked at the man standing before her and wondered how she could have ever loved him. He was weak. He was pathetic. That was glaringly obvious now. He had allowed a spiteful woman to dominate his mind and dictate his future. A real man wouldn't have been led around by the nose like that. Cash Boudreaux wouldn't.

Ken made a helpless gesture. "Hell, Schyler, it was easy to believe her. You were always demonstrating for womens' rights, saying a woman had a right to choose."

"Yes, the right to *choose*. That didn't mean that I—" She broke off. There was no sense in rehashing that now. The damage had been done years ago. But thank God it hadn't been permanent.

"I told Daddy the truth yesterday. We've been reconciled." For the time being she ignored Ken and spoke directly to Tricia. "There was never any reason for you to think that Daddy didn't love you. He does and always did. In addition, you've got Ken. The hatchet is buried as of this second, but I'll never forgive you for adversely manipulating my life."

She turned to leave, but Tricia lunged after her. She stepped between Schyler and the door. "I don't give a good goddamn whether you forgive me or not. I just want my share of this place free and clear. Then I'll be all too happy to get out of your adversely manipulated life forever."

"Your share of this place? What are you talking about?"

"Tricia," Ken said, "this isn't the time."

"We want to sell Belle Terre."

For a moment, the meaning of Tricia's statement didn't register with Schyler. The idea was so inconceivable as to be ludicrous. It was so preposterous that she laughed. "Sell Belle Terre?" She expected them to smile, to let her in on what was surely a private joke.

Rather, it appeared to be a private conspiracy. Tricia hatefully stared her down. She looked toward Ken for an explanation. He looked away guiltily.

"Have you both gone mad?" she asked hoarsely. "Belle Terre will never be sold."

"Why not?"

"Because it's ours. It belongs to Cotton and to us."

"No it doesn't," Tricia sneered. "It belonged to the Laurents. They're all dead."

Schyler drew herself up. "Cotton might not own it through bloodlines, but he has poured his whole life into Belle Terre. He will never sell it."

She tried to go around Tricia, but the other woman, with surprising strength, caught her arm. "Cotton's mind can be changed."

"Never. I wouldn't even try." She shook off Tricia's hand.

"He's an old man, Schyler. He's been critically ill. His business is suffering as a result. He's got himself in debt so deep he'll never get out."

"Your point?"

"We can have him certified incompetent."

Schyler wanted to strike Tricia so badly that she clenched her fists to keep from doing it. "If anything happens to Cotton, then you will truly have an adversary, Tricia. You will have *me* to contend with."

TWENTY-EIGHT

Schyler gripped the steering wheel so tightly her knuckles turned white. She was driving far too fast, but she didn't care. Besides, it seemed only fair that the car keep pace with the windshield wipers. They flapped back and forth furiously, but had little effect in the downpour.

From a sane corner of her mind, she reasoned that she must still be exhausted even after her long sleep. That's why she felt that she had been flayed alive. Her confrontation with Tricia and Ken had left her feeling raw and exposed. Her self-control was tenuous. She feared that it might slip at any moment.

In the meantime, she felt driven to act. If she stalled, she might never get into motion again. If she let herself think about all that had been said in the last hour, she would go stark, staring mad. She had to keep moving to keep her mind from petrifying around one thought: they wanted to sell Belle Terre.

Her objective was clear. She had her sights set on a goal and nothing would keep her from achieving it. She had to preserve Belle Terre, keep it safe, intact, save it for Cotton. She had to work until she dropped. That's what she must do.

Her course of action was so definitely blueprinted in her mind that when she reached the landing side of the Laurent Bayou bridge, she floorboarded the brake pedal. The car skidded several yards before coming to a complete standstill. The windshield wipers continued to clack out their steady beat. The torrential rain drummed to clack out their steady beat. The torrential rain drummed against the roof of the car. Schyler, breathing through her mouth as though she had run the distance from the mansion, stared at the landing.

The inactive scene was so out of keeping with the energy churning inside her, she couldn't believe what she was seeing. It was incomprehensible. There was absolutely nothing being done. The place was deserted.

The office door was dead-bolted, the windows dark. The heavy doors of the hangarlike building that housed the rigs when they weren't in use were chained closed. The loading platforms along the railroad tracks were deserted. The entire area looked as forlorn as a ghost town, desolate, empty, and dead.

Schyler swallowed her dismay and tried desperately to remember what day of the week this was. She had lost track of the days, surely. The time she had spent in the hospital had put her off track. Mentally she tallied days against the calendar. No, this was a work day.

Then why wasn't any work being done? Where the hell was Cash? Goddamn him!

She was so upset that she began to shake uncontrollably. She took her foot off the brake and gave the steering wheel a vicious turn. She stepped on the accelerator; the rear wheels spun, trying to gain traction on the soggy ground. They threw up a shower of mud behind the car.

"Dammit it!" Schyler thumped her fist on the steering wheel and dug her toe into the accelerator. Finally the wheels found a foothold. The car lurched forward. Its rear end fishtailed and swerved dangerously close to a concrete support of the bridge. Schyler jerked the wheel again and straightened the car out as it shot onto the main road. She met no other cars, and that was a blessing because she positioned her car over the yellow stripe.

Visibility was severely limited by the dark day and the driving rain. She saw the turnoff she wanted too late and slammed on the brakes. The car slid past the side road. Cursing lividly, she shoved it into reverse and backed up.

The side road was a sea of mud, but she aimed the hood ornament down its center and plowed through it. Her fury gained as much momentum as her car.

When she brought it to a teeth-jarring stop, she wrenched the door open and cannoned out. Heedless of the rain, she marched toward the house. It was the same color as the gray sky and blended into its setting so well as to be almost invisible.

He was sitting on the covered porch but far enough back to keep dry. Rainwater was rolling off the tin roof and dripping over the eaves, splashing in puddles that bordered the porch. The chair he was sitting in had a cane seat and a ladder back. It was reared back to a precarious angle. He had balanced himself by propping his bare feet on a cypress post that supported the overhang.

He was without a shirt. His jeans were zipped, but unsnapped. A bottle of whiskey and a glass with two fingers' worth in the bottom of it were sitting beside his chair. A cigarette was occupying one corner of his sullen lips. His eyes were squinted against the smoke that curled from its tip. They widened a trifle when Schyler bounded up onto the porch and yelled her first question.

"Just what the hell do you think you're doing?"

In no apparent hurry, Cash took the cigarette from between his lips and looked at it curiously. "Smoking?"

Schyler quivered with outrage. Her arms were stiff at her sides, and she kept opening and closing her fists. She seemed impervious to her chilled, wet skin and her hair, which dripped rain onto her rigid shoulders.

With an angry, grunting sound, she reached out and knocked his feet away from the post. The front legs of his chair landed hard on the porch. As though catapulted from the seat, Cash was instantly on his feet and towering over her. He flicked his cigarette over the porch railing.

"You live dangerously, Miss Schyler." His voice had the sinister lisp of a sword being withdrawn from its scabbard.

"I ought to fire you on the spot."

"For what?"

"For goofing off when you thought I'd be away. Why isn't any work being done? Where are the loggers? The rigs haven't even been out today. I went to the landing. The office is closed. The garage is locked. Nothing is going on. Why the hell not?"

Cash's temper had never had a very long fuse. He didn't take reprimands well and had never walked away from a fight. On any application, he filled in the blank space after RELIGIOUS PREFERENCE with the word Christian, but the concept of turning the other cheek was alien to his nature. The army had trained and sharpened reflexes that were already lightning quick.

He might have appeared to be totally relaxed, a man enjoying a smoke, a whiskey, and a good, hard rain, but in fact, Cash's nerves were as frazzled as Schyler's. For the last few days, he hadn't slept any more than she. His short supply of patience had been used up days ago; he was fresh out. He had consumed more whiskey than was prudent for a man to drink in the middle of the day. He had been spoiling for a fight even before Schyler had charged into his territory slinging unfounded accusations.

Had she been a man, she would already be picking herself up out of the mud and spitting out teeth. But Cash, for all his meanness, had never physically abused a woman. He resorted to contempt. He was oozing it when he said, "The weather, lady. Do you expect me to let loggers work in this?" He made a broad, sweeping gesture with his hand; water running off the leaves splattered it.

"I hired you to work in any kind of weather."

"This isn't a brief April shower."

"I don't care if it's a hurricane, I want the loggers out there cutting timber."

"Are you *crazy?* The forests become death traps when it rains this much this quick. We can't even get rigs in. The mud—''

"Are you going to put them to work or not?''

"I'm not.''

Her breasts heaved with the extent of her anger and frustration. "I should have listened to everybody. They told me you were worthless.''

"Maybe so. But saw hands can't cut, haul, or load in this kind of rain. If you've ever been around loggers you damn well know that. Cotton wouldn't send men out in this and neither am I.''

Suddenly remembering Tricia's words, Schyler drew a staggering breath. "Your mother. And my father. Is it true? Were they . . . ?''

"Yes.'' He pushed the *s* through his teeth. "They were.''

Schyler sucked back a sob. "He was *married.* He had a family,'' she cried with anguish. "She was a slut.''

"And he's a son of a bitch,'' Cash snarled. "I hated him being with her.'' He moved forward threateningly, backing Schyler into the cypress post. "But I had to live with it day in and day out practically all my life. You didn't. You were protected up there at Belle Terre, while I had to watch him use and hurt my mother for years. There wasn't a damn thing I could do about it.''

"Your mother was a grown woman. She made her choice.''

"A rotten one in my estimation. She chose to love a stinking son of a bitch like Cotton Crandall.''

Schyler raised her chin. "You wouldn't have the guts to call him that to his face.''

"I have. Ask him.''

"I want you off Belle Terre by the end of the week.''

"Who's going to get your timber ready for market?''

"I will.''

"Wrong. You can't do doodledee squat without me.'' He took a step closer. "And you know it. You knew it when you came driving over here, didn't you?'' He braced one hand against the post near her head and leaned into her, brushing his body against hers. "Know what? I don't think that's why you came over here at all. I think you came over here for something altogether different.''

"You're drunk.''

"Not yet.''

"I meant what I said. I want you gone—''

She had moved away from the post. He caught her arm and slammed her back up against it, hard enough to halt her condescending speech. His palm supported her chin while his fingers bracketed her jaw.

"The trouble with you, Miss Schyler, is that you just don't know when to quit. You keep pushing and pushing, until you drive a man over the edge.''

His mouth covered hers in a hard kiss. Schyler reacted violently. She struggled against his hand to release her jaw, while her body bucked against his. Her arms flailed at him.

"Admit it.'' He lifted his mouth off hers only far enough to speak, "This is what you came here for.''

"Let me go.''

"Not a chance, lady.''

"I hate you.''

"But you want me.''

"Like hell I do.''

"You want me. That's what got you as mad as a hornet."

He kissed her again. This time he succeeded in getting his tongue inside her mouth. The rain beat loudly against the roof, drowning out her whimpers of outrage and then of surrender.

It wasn't a conscious decision. She didn't voluntarily capitulate. Her emotions superseded her will and responded on their own. For days they'd been seeking an outlet. It had just presented itself, and they eagerly funneled toward it.

Still, her stubborn nature balked at total compliance. She succeeded in tearing her mouth free. Her lips felt swollen and bruised. When she dragged her tongue over them, she tasted whiskey. She tasted him. Cash Boudreaux.

The thought was untenable. She laid her hands on his bare shoulders, intending to push him away. But he lowered his head again. His lips ate at hers. Her fingers curled inward, forming deep furrows in the tense muscles of his upper arms.

When the kiss ended, she rolled her head to one side. "Stop," she moaned.

He did. At least he stopped kissing her lips. But he laid his open mouth against her neck. "You want this as much as I do."

"No."

"Yes." He flicked her earlobe with his tongue. "How long has it been since you got fucked real good?"

A low groan escaped her. It dissolved against his lips. They kissed ravenously, engaging in an orgy of kissing, cruel and carnal. He swept her mouth with his tongue, as though to rid it of pride and resistance.

His hands moved down her chest until each covered a breast. He massaged them roughly. He wasn't easy on the buttons of her damp blouse, nor on the clasp of her bra. He wasn't too much kinder to the soft flesh that filled his hands. "Jesus," he sighed as he kneaded her. He supported her breasts with his palms while he whisked the erect nipples with his thumbs.

"Very nice, Miss Schyler."

"Go to hell."

"Not yet. Not until we've finished what we've started here."

Schyler's head ground against the post. Her eyes were squeezed shut, but she blindly knotted her fingers in his dense chest hair. He grunted, with pain, with pleasure. He bit her lower lip. She went in search of a full-fledged, open-mouth, tongue-thrusting kiss, and got it.

Abruptly they broke apart and gazed into each other's eyes. Their rapid breaths soughed together. It was the only sound they could hear over the incessant rain.

He bent at the knees and lifted her into his arms. The front door crashed open when he landed his bare foot against it. The rooms of the house were dim and shadowed and stuffy. He carried her straight through it to the screened back porch.

The iron bed had been left unmade. The sheets were white and clean, but had a rainy-day rumpledness that was as sexy as the heat their two bodies generated. His knee made a deep dent in the mattress. Springs creaked like settling wood in a beloved old house. The instant her wet hair made contact with the pillows, his body covered hers with mating possessiveness. Their mouths came together hungrily as Cash gathered her beneath him.

Kissing her deeply, he slid his hand beneath her skirt and up her smooth thigh. He palmed her. She was warm, damp. He gently squeezed her mound. Her responding gasp was soft and yearning. Quickly he sat up and plunged his other hand beneath her skirt. Hooking the fingers of both hands in the elastic of her panties, he peeled them down her legs.

Then he straddled her, planting his knees soldily on either side of hers. Schyler's heart was fluttering wildly as she gazed up at him. His thighs looked hard and lean inside the faded jeans. From her perspective his shoulders looked broader, his arms more powerful, like he could break her in two if he wanted to.

His belly was flat and corrugated with muscles. Copper nipples nestled in a forest of light brown hair. He was wearing no expression, but intensity had made the bone structure of his face more pronounced. His eyes seemed to be the only spot of color in the gray room. They burned.

She focused on them as he pulled her blouse open. Immediately he tugged it out of the waistband of her skirt and pushed aside the flimsy lace cups of her brassiere. Her breasts lay softly upon her chest, but the areolas were wrinkled and puckered with arousal. Her nipples were very pink and very hard.

Cash bent over her and stroked one with his tongue. Schyler's back arched off the bed. He touched her again and again with the pointed tip of his tongue, then he drew one of the shiny, wet nipples into his mouth.

The pleasure was so exquisite, the heat so fierce, Schyler clutched at him. Her seeking hands came to rest on his upper thighs. Her thumbs settled in the grooves of his groin. He bridged her body with his stiff arms and dipped his head low over her breasts. His hair fell forward, tickling her skin.

"Unzip me," he directed huskily between the soft, damp caresses he was giving her breasts. After a few moments, when it became apparent that she wasn't going to, he stood on his knees again and reached for his fly. He winced as he worked the zipper down. Schyler stared, fascinated, as the wedge widened. It filled up with body hair that was darker and denser than that on his chest.

When the zipper was undone, he hooked his thumbs into the cloth and pulled the jeans down over his hips. Schyler caught her breath and held it, shocked by his flagrant immodesty and the fullness of his erection. The tip was as round and smooth and voluptuous as a ripe plum.

He reversed the position of their knees until hers were on the outside. He raised the hem of her skirt to her waist. Schyler closed her eyes.

At that instant, she wanted desperately to call it off.

But then he touched her there. His fingers lightly tweaked clumps of dark blond curls, then slid between the soft folds of her body and up inside, stretching into the wetness.

He made a groaning sound before he said, "You'd better hold on. This is going to be a rough ride." He moved her hands to the iron rails of the headboard behind her head and folded her fingers around them. She gripped the cool metal.

His hands spread wide on the insides of her thighs and separated them. She made a small, helpless sound. "Open your eyes. I want you to know who this is."

Her eyes sprang open in direct challenge to his insulting words. But there was no doubt as to who drove into her. She was wet, but she was tight. She winced with momentary pain. He tensed with momentary surprise. Then he gave another swift thrust and embedded himself inside her with absolute possession.

He withdrew, almost leaving her, before sinking into her again. "My name is Cash Boudreaux."

"I know who you are."

"Say it." He ground his pelvis against hers. "Say it." She caught her lower lip between her teeth. Sweat dotted her upper lip. She tried to keep her hips on the bed, but involuntarily she raised them to meet the next plunging stroke of his strong, smooth penis. "You're going to say my name, damn you."

He flattened his hand low on her belly, fingers pointed toward her breasts, and worked it downward until the heel of his hand was at the very lowest point of her body. He rubbed it back and forth slowly. A low, choppy moan rose out of

Schyler's chest. Warm sensations began to spiral up through her middle and
radiate outward until her fingertips and toes began to throb with an infusion of
blood. She gripped the headboard tighter.

"Say my name." His forehead was bathed with sweat, his teeth clenched in
restraint. He lowered his head to her breasts and nuzzled them with his nose. His
stubbled chin rasped the delicate skin. His buttocks rose and fell with each rhythmic stroke. The heel of his hand caressed her until he felt moisture against it. He
swept his thumb downward, over the tuft of hair, and into the source of that
moisture. The pad of his thumb was soft and sensitive against that softer, more
sensitive spot.

Pleasure speared through Schyler. She gave a sharp cry.

"Say my name," he panted.

"Ca . . . Cash."

Her eyes closed. Her neck arched. Her head thrashed on the pillow. Her thighs
hugged his buttocks tight. Cash stared down at her. Yielding to an urge he had
never had before, he lowered himself over her and buried his face in the hollow of
her shoulder. His hands joined hers on the headboard. Their fingers interlaced over
and around the iron rods. His chest crushed her breasts. Their breathing escalated
and turned harsher. He hammered into her. The walls of her body milked him.

When the climax came, neither said anything coherent, but their moans of
gratification were simultaneous and long.

 # TWENTY-NINE

On the one hand, he stayed inside her far too long.
On the other hand, it was much too brief.

Cash eased himself away from her. He glanced down into her face. Her eyes
were closed. Her face was smooth and still. Resisting an impulse to kiss her mouth,
he slowly disengaged their arms and legs and rolled to one side of the bed.
Automatically he reached for the pack of cigarettes and lighter on the bedside
table.

As he lit one, Schyler sat up and threw her legs over the opposite side of the bed,
keeping her back to him and her head averted. She shoved down her skirt and
groped between the twisted sheets for her panties. Finding them, she bent at the
waist and stepped into them. She pulled them on in the same motion she used to
stand up. She replaced the cups of her bra, clasped it, then rebuttoned her blouse.
She didn't tuck it in.

She turned around and looked down at him as though there was something she
wanted to say. She swallowed visibly. Her lips opened but closed without uttering
a single sound. He stuck the cigarette in his mouth and stacked his hands behind
his head in a pose that looked insolent and uncaring, especially since his jeans were
still bunched around his thighs.

He would have bet a month's salary on what she would do next, and he was
right. She turned her back on him and left the house. He listened to her footsteps
fade as she went through the front door and across the porch. Shortly, he heard her
car's motor starting.

He lay motionless for a long time, until the cigarette between his lips became a
fire hazard. He ground it out. He took off his jeans, balled them up, and angrily

threw them as far as he could. They hit the opposite wall and dropped to the floor.

Naked, he rolled to his side and stared sightlessly through the screen. It was raining harder than ever. He could barely see the opposite bank of the bayou through the silver curtain. The limbs of the trees drooped with the weight of the rainwater.

His eyes moved to the pillow beside his. He laid his hand in the imprint her head had made. It was still warm.

"Schyler."

Schyler. Cash remembered the day he first heard that name. He had thought it was a funny name for a baby girl. So had Monique. They had talked about it later, after Cotton left.

It had been a cold November day. The bayou was shrouded in fog. Cash had made white clouds of vapor by blowing into the cold air. He had pretended he was smoking Camels like the older boys at the pool hall did.

Cotton had caught him at it. "Why aren't you in school, Cash?" he had asked the minute he alighted from his long, shiny car.

"*Maman* didn't make me go today. Are those doughnuts?" He pointed to the white bakery sack Cotton was carrying. Cotton rarely came empty-handed. He usually brought something for both of them, like flowers, a trinket, a bottle of perfume for Monique; comic books, a sack of candy, a small toy for Cash.

But he never gave them money. He had tried, but Monique would never take it. They'd had fights over it, but Monique always won.

They didn't fight that day. Monique stepped out onto the porch, drying her hands on a dish towel. "You must have smelled my roux," she teased Cotton. "How can you always tell when I'm making gumbo?"

Cotton smiled back at her. "Good day for gumbo." Then his light eyebrows furrowed. "Why isn't Cash in school?"

Monique shrugged one shapely shoulder. "We slept late."

"He should be in school, Monique. You'll have the truant officer back out here."

She laughed her deep contralto laugh and bent down to hug Cash's disheveled head against her warm breasts. "I need him to deliver medicines today. Everybody's sick with the croup."

"Medicines my ass," Cotton muttered, stamping the mud off his boots as he came upon the porch. "What you're selling folks is mumbo jumbo, voodoo bullshit."

Laughing and sandwiching the eight-year-old boy between them, she caught the lobe of Cotton's ear between her strong, white teeth. "It works on you, *mon cher.*"

Cotton sighed. "It sure as hell does." He kissed her long and deeply, rubbing her back with his large, work-worn hands. "When will the gumbo be ready?"

"Hours. Can you stay that long?"

He looked down at Cash. The lad read the gravity of Cotton's expression. "I need to talk to you about something."

At the table in front of the fireplace, while they demolished the doughnuts and a fresh pot of coffee, Cotton broke the disturbing news.

"We're getting a baby."

Cash, who had been licking powdered sugar off his fingers, quickly looked at his mother. Instinctively he knew that she would be distressed. She was. He watched her delicate hands come together. She interlaced her slender fingers and held them so tightly that her knuckles turned the color of bones.

"A *bébé?*"

"Yes. We're adopting a child. Macy . . . Macy . . . " Cotton sighed and stared into his coffee cup for a long moment before going ahead. "It appears she's barren. It eats on her." His blue eyes spoke eloquently to Monique. "Especially since she knows about you. She wants children. Belle Terre needs children."

Monique glanced down at Cash. "*Oui*, it does," she said quietly. "You should fill it with as many children as possible."

Cotton forced a laugh. "Well, we're only starting with one. It's a baby girl. Macy wanted a boy, but . . ." He shrugged. "This girl was born and she jumped at the chance to get her. Father Martin is handling the adoption for us. I had to agree to raise her a Catholic."

"Better than a Baptist."

Her teasing was as forced as his laugh had been. He cleared his throat noisily. "She's only three days old."

"What does she look like?"

"She was born in Baton Rouge, so we haven't seen her yet. But Macy had already named her Schyler."

"A strange name for a baby girl. But pretty," Monique said with hollow enthusiasm.

"It's a Laurent family name."

Their mouths were saying one thing, but their eyes were communicating quite another. Finally both fell silent. The logs in the fireplace popped and crackled. Cash's eyes warily shifted between his mother and her lover.

After a time, Cotton reached across the table and covered Monique's clasped hands. "This doesn't change anything."

"It must."

"It doesn't. You know it doesn't. You *know*." She continued to stare into his eyes, hurt and unsure. He continued to send her unspoken assurances. "When did you say the gumbo would be ready?"

Her face brightened. Her jet-black eyes sparkled through unshed tears. "Can you stay?"

"I can stay."

"Until it's ready?"

"Until I've had at least two bowls."

She flew from her chair and threw her arms around his neck. They kissed with a passion made stronger because it was illicit. Then she hurried to get the fish, shrimp, vegetables, and spices into the pot, where they would simmer together in the roux until they were tender and the gumbo was rich and thick and properly murky.

Meanwhile Cotton helped Cash load the red wagon he was often seen pulling through the streets of town. In the back of it bottles of unguents and potions, salves and tinctures clinked together musically. His mother was a *traiteur*. He was her delivery boy.

"You're not smoking for real, are you?" Cotton asked him, referring to the clouds of make-believe smoke he'd been blowing earlier.

"No, sir." Monique had coached him on how to address Cotton respectfully.

"Good. It's a nasty habit and very bad for you."

"How come?"

"It damages your lungs."

"You smoke sometimes."

"I'm a grown-up."

Cash gazed up at Cotton, hoping that someday he would be that tall, that strong. "will the new baby live in the big white house?"

"Of course."

Cash thought about that, envying the baby a little. "Will you still come to see us after you get her?"

Cotton stopped what he was doing. He gazed down into Cash's earnest, anxious face. With a half smile, he reached out and touched the boy's cheek. "Yes, I'll still come to see you. Nothing could keep me from coming to see you."

Cash gauged the honesty behind Cotton's answer and decided it was genuine. "What'd you say the baby's name was?"

"Schyler."

Cash laid his hand in the bowl her head had made in the pillow. Her wet hair had left the pillowcase damp. He closed his fist. It came up empty. There was nothing there.

For Monique Boudreaux's bastard boy, there never had been.

 # THIRTY

"You're restless tonight. If you don't stop pacing you'll wear a path in the carpet." Dale Gilbreath missed the dirty look his wife sent him. He had chastised her from behind his newspaper. He tipped the corner of it down and smiled at her in the patronizing manner she loathed. "Is something wrong, dear? Don't you feel well?"

"I feel fine." Rhoda's strained tone of voice wasn't very convincing.

"You've been on edge and out of sorts all evening." With only bland interest he scanned the page of newsprint he'd been reading.

"It's the rain." Rhoda moved to the window and jerked on the tasseled cord. The drapes swished open. "God, the weather in this place is wretched. The humidity is so goddamn high, it's like trying to breathe lentil soup. It threatens to rain. It doesn't. Then when it does, it's a goddamn flood."

"We traded severe winters for a little stickiness."

Dale was on the receiving end of another withering glance. She could do without his half-baked philosophy tonight, especially when she knew he hated the Louisiana climate as much as she.

"Shoveling a few feet of snow wouldn't hurt you," she said snidely. "You're beginning to get a real gut. Which is no wonder since you sit on your ass behind a desk all day. Don't you ever feel the need to exercise?"

Rhoda attended a workout class every weekday morning. The strain and sweat and self-abuse was like a religious rite to her. To point up to him just how superior her physical condition was to his, she sucked in her tummy, tightened her derriere, and thrust out her breasts.

Dale exchanged his newspaper for a pipe and calmly began filling it with his special blend of tobaccos, scooping it from a leather pouch. "When you're right, you're right. I could use some exercise." He put a match to the bowl of his pipe and drew on the stem. Fanning out the match as he watched her through the rising cloud of smoke, he asked, "But do you really want to swap insults with me tonight, Rhoda?"

Dale could get nasty. He didn't take pot shots but hit below the belt every time with well-aimed punches. Rhoda wasn't in a frame of mind to suffer one of his soft-spoken, but malicious attacks. Her ego was bruised. She didn't think it could withstand further injury.

Cash had told her he would call this afternoon and arrange a time and place for them to rendezvous. He hadn't. She couldn't call him; he didn't have a damn telephone. She had often wondered if the sole reason he didn't have one installed was so he could avoid a woman when he wanted to. That was probably it. The Cajun was a class A son of a bitch.

She would have driven to his out-of-the-way house, but she wasn't sure where it was. He'd been aggravatingly unspecific about that when she had asked him for directions. As the dreary afternoon had worn on, she had given serious thought to gambling her reputation and sacrificing her pride for one roll in the sack with him, but damned if she was going to risk getting her BMW stuck to the hubs on one of the backwoods quagmires. They were called roads. Some even had designated state highway numbers, but she considered them pig trails that were to be avoided at all costs.

Now, just thinking about her thwarted plans for the afternoon heated her temper back up to a slow simmer. And apparently Dale wanted to swap insults whether she wanted to or not.

Casually he said, "For instance, I could start with this juvenile fixation you've developed for your latest lover."

Rhoda's posture stiffened marginally, but she was adroit at controlling knee-jerk reactions. Dale wanted her to fly into a tirade of denial. He loved pricking her with innuendo and half-truths. He enjoyed provoking her until she blew.

Slowly she turned to face him, affecting bewilderment with admirable skill. "Latest lover?"

He puffed at his pipe and smiled around the stem clenched between his teeth. "You really should have pursued an acting career, Rhoda. You're very good. But I know you better than you know yourself. I can smell when you're in heat. You exude a musky odor like an animal."

"Well I'm glad you didn't pursue a career as a poet. Your phraseology is revolting."

"You're also very good at changing the subject."

"I find your subject tiresome."

Dale chuckled. "Rhoda, you and your lovers are never tiresome."

"How do you know there is a current lover?" she challenged. Hands on hips, she faced him where he sat in an easy chair.

"There's always one." Drolly, he added, "At least one."

"Jealous?"

"You know better."

"Ah, that's right," Rhoda said with a catty smile. "You were always a much better spectator than participant."

"Because you always put on such an entertaining and engrossing show."

It wasn't a compliment and Rhoda was smart enough not to mistake it for one. "Let's talk about something else. Or better yet, let's don't talk at all. You're in a foul mood tonight."

Dale puffed the pipe with deceptive contentment. "You'd be well advised not to anger me, my dear." Just as Dale had intended, that got her attention.

Figuratively she laid down her weapons. "Oh? Why not?"

"I'm about to pull off a big deal."

"At the bank?"

"Hmm. Something you'll be extremely pleased about."

"Is it legal?"

He frowned at her, but neither one of them took his reproachful expression seriously. "Shame on you. Of course it's legal. In fact it will be the culmination of a year's work."

"What does it mean to me?"

"Nothing short of the realization of a dream. For both of us. Instead of us being on the outside of Heaven's social circle looking in, these rednecks will be kissing our asses. There won't be anything we can't do and get away with."

Rhoda tingled with an excitement that was almost sexual. She sat down on the arm of his chair and wiggled close to him. "Tell me about it."

"Not yet. I'm saving it for a surprise." He emptied the bowl of his pipe into an ashtray and turned out the lamp on the end table.

Rhoda fell into step behind him as he left the chair and headed toward the bedroom. "Damn you, Dale. I hate it when you dangle carrots in front of me like this."

"On the contrary, darling, you love it. You thrive on intrigue."

"I can't if I don't know about it. Let me in on what you're up to."

"I'll give you a hint." He switched the light on in their bedroom. "What's the hottest topic of conversation around town these days?"

She thought for a moment, watching with detachment as Dale took a 35mm camera from a glass shelf in the étagère. He loaded a roll of film and reset the ASA. Suddenly Rhoda's throat vibrated with a low, nefarious laugh. "Not Cotton Crandall!" she exclaimed. "Your scheme doesn't involve Crandall and Belle Terre, does it?"

"Why shouldn't it?" Dale adjusted the lamp shades on the bedside tables to his satisfaction. He looked at his wife pointedly. She began removing her clothes.

"*Belle Terre?* You mean there's a chance—"

Dale reached out and cupped his hand over her mouth. "It's not to be discussed outside this room, understand?" She nodded her head. He removed his hand and began undoing the buttons of her blouse.

"That daughter," Rhoda whispered. "I understand she's a firecracker, that Cotton coached her well."

"Schyler? Not to worry," Dale replied with dismissive smugness. "She's being taken care of."

"What do you mean?"

"That's one of the details you needn't be concerned about. The stakes are high on this one, Rhoda. That's why we must be extremely careful." He slipped her blouse off and tossed it onto a chair. He ran his hands over her breasts. "It would be regrettable if a senseless indiscretion screwed this up, wouldn't it?" He tweaked her nipple, a pinch too strong to be classified as foreplay. She winced. "And screw is the operative word."

"Be specific."

"All right. Find a lover who isn't so personally involved with the Crandalls and preferably one who didn't crawl out of a trash can."

She met him eye to eye without flinching. She wasn't alarmed that he knew about her affair with Cash. In fact she was pleased. Dale knew that Cash's reputation with women was legendary. That Cash had chosen her from so many elevated her desirability.

"You've never cared who my lovers were before," she said in a voice as sultry as the weather.

"They've always come from a suitable strata of society before. You're scraping scum off the bayou this time."

By tacit agreement the name Cash Boudreaux would never be uttered. They had learned from experience that mentioning names was unwise. Names could result in more complicated resolutions once affairs were over. Admit nothing was the credo that each adhered to.

"He could be useful to us."

"He is," Dale said. "Extremely useful. But I'm using him my way. He's of more value to us someplace other than your bed. He can't be screwed by both of us at the same time."

Again she laughed deep in her throat. "We've used that tactic before."

"But not with this kind of man. I don't think he'd like that, do you?"

"No," she said without a second's hesitation. "He definitely would not."

"I don't blame you for selecting him. He's attractive, if you like the vulgar, brutal type. But until all the details are finalized, amuse yourself with someone who's closer to being your social equal."

"And yours." Rhoda knew that that was at the crux of this entire discussion. Dale didn't mind being a cuckold. He did mind who made him one. It was a matter of ego.

"And mine," he admitted. He helped her step out of her skirt and paused to admire the dark hosiery, the lacy garter belt, and the patch of hair in between. He slid his hand between her thighs. "You're wet."

"You knew I would be."

Stroking her, he laughed. "Money hungry, bitch. You can come just talking about money."

"We share the same ambition, darling."

"I remember the time you told me that if my cock were as monstrous as my ambition, you wouldn't have to seek outside diversions."

"And in reply you said that my sexuality was one of your greatest assets."

"It's served its purpose profitably many times."

Later, as she languished against the pillows on the bed, the lips of her sex as rosy and glistening as those of her mouth, Dale moved in for a closeup with the camera. He snickered as he clicked the shutter.

"Let me in on the joke."

"I was just thinking what some of the bank board members would say if they saw you this way."

Rhoda reached out and stroked his cheek in a parody of affection. "Most of them have, my dear, most of them have."

THIRTY-ONE

It was the dead cats that did it.

Schyler had returned to Belle Terre after being with Cash and went straight to her room. She filled her bathtub to the rim and soaked until the hot water turned cold. She asked Mrs. Graves to bring her dinner up to her on a tray. She ignored both the housekeeper's long-suffering sigh and the dinner. She wasn't hungry. She doubted she ever would be again.

How could she have done something so stupid?

Not that she was new at making severe errors in judgment. She had underestimated her sister's jealous hatred and ability to manipulate. She had given Ken up too easily, but had clung to a dead love for too long. She had almost let Tricia destroy her relationship with their father. But of all the serious mistakes she had made in her life, going to bed with Cash Boudreaux championed them all.

To save herself from having to think about it that night, she took a sleeping pill and went to bed early. Before the effects of the mild narcotic overpowered her, though, she suffered through several replays of the afternoon.

In her imagination, she felt again his hands, his lips, his body. Beside hers. Inside hers. She kept remembering him naked and strong and hard and beautiful. He made love as he did everything else, with intensity and passion and a total absence of discipline. His reputation as a stud was well earned. Even the memory of the act was more potent than any other sexual encounter Schyler had ever had. She had never felt so bloody marvelous in her life.

That is, until it was over. Then she'd never felt so wretched. She hadn't cried, but she had wanted to. Thank God she had held back her tears. They would have spelled her final and absolute humiliation and Cash's unqualified victory because what had happened on that bed had been a battle. He had set out to prove that there was a way he could best her, and he had.

He had fought to win. If there had been one kind and tender word spoken, she might not have taken defeat so hard. Nothing had softened the blow to her pride, not even that she had been forced or coerced. No, when he had carried her to his bed, she had wanted to go.

She had left his house and driven home under her own power. She had spoken intelligently with Dr. Collins over the telephone, and had even had a brief and animated conversation with Cotton. Under the circumstances, she had done well. She was confused and angry, but she was made of stern stuff. The matrix of her spirit had held her together. She hadn't crumbled; she hadn't broken apart.

But when she saw the dead cats she began to shake.

Mrs. Graves's scream rattled the crystal in every chandelier in the house. It was a clear morning, promising a better day than the one preceding it. Birds were splashing in the rain puddles on the lawn. A new sun was disintegrating sheer pink clouds. God was in his heaven . . . but all was not right with the world.

The scream woke Schyler up. She bolted out of bed. She was naked, so she grabbed a robe and charged out her door, almost colliding with Ken and Tricia. By the looks of them, they had been roused by the housekeeper's scream, too.

"What the hell is going on?" Ken mumbled.

"I don't know."

Schyler beat them downstairs. Mrs. Graves was standing in the open front door, her face in her hands. She was making retching sounds. Schyler pushed her aside and stepped across the threshold.

Her empty stomach contracted. She tasted bile in her throat. No more than three feet behond the front door lay the two cats. The female was on her back, spread-eagled beneath the male. The symbolism was blatant and crude. The female's throat had been slit. Blood and gore still oozed from the wide wound. Black fur was clotted with it. Her dead eyes were crawling with ants. The male was dead, too, but whatever had killed him wasn't apparent.

"Jesus!" Ken hissed. "Stay back, Tricia. And for chrissake, shut her up." Impatiently he gestured toward Mrs. Graves who was still gagging behind her hands.

The two women gladly withdrew. Ken stepped around Schyler, who seemed rooted to the threshold. He bent down on one knee and investigated the macabre sight. He looked up at Schyler. "Do you know anything about this?"

"Of course not." But she was afraid she did. Two dead cats found on the front porch could be attributed to teenage pranksters, playful vandalism. Two dead cats, brutally murdered and arranged to depict human beings making love, was the product of a sick mind. The question was, whose?

"Guess we ought to call the sheriff."

Schyler shook her head. "No. He wouldn't do anything. Just get rid of them. Clean up the mess."

"Like hell!" Ken exclaimed. "I'm not a yard nigger."

Schyler began to tremble. Her hands balled into fists. She could feel herself losing control. "Clean it up," she angrily enunciated. "Unless you'd rather go to the landing and deal with the loggers."

Ken's face worked with indignation, but in the end, he stamped off the porch and toward the toolshed. He crossed the wet grass in his bare feet, having to dodge mud puddles in his path. Schyler looked down at the floorboards of the veranda. They were clean. There were no muddy footprints on the steps either. Whoever had placed the cats there could have come from inside the house. Either way, the perpetrator was clever—very, very clever.

She went back inside and upstairs to her room. She returned to the bed, but she didn't give in to the second impulse to hide beneath the covers. Instead, she sat on the edge of it and folded her arms over her middle. Rocking back and forth, she indulged in a good crying jag.

Someone knew about Cash and her. Someone knew that they'd been to bed together. But who except the two of them?

Cash? She had fired him. He hadn't liked her in the first place. But could he be so violent as to wantonly kill two cats? Of course he could. That's why she had asked him to do away with Jigger's pit bull terriers. She had witnessed him pulling the knife on Ken. He had a reputation for violence.

Jigger Flynn could be violent, too. But he wouldn't know about Cash and her going to bed together. Would he? How?

Tricia and Ken were no doubt furious with her after the confrontation yesterday. They stood on opposing sides regarding the sale of Belle Terre. But they wouldn't resort to something like this even if they knew about Cash and her.

Suddenly Schyler realized that there were several people in Heaven, and on Belle Terre in particular, who would have been much happier if she had never come home from England.

But it was going to take more than a couple of grisly dead cats to scare her off. She had to pay back the loan before the deadline. Yesterday's production had been sacrificed to the weather so they would have to work twice as hard today to make up for it. Now that Cash was out of the picture, she would have to handle everything alone. That shouldn't slow her down. She had been relying solely on herself for a long time.

Wiping the salty tear tracks from her cheeks, she removed her robe and headed for her closet.

When she arrived at the landing three loggers were there. They were hoisting chains and pulleys into a flat trailer. It was obvious they were wasting no time. Their expressions were grim. They didn't even take time to stop and speak to her. Something was wrong.

"What's going on?" she called out as she left her car.

"Accident," one informed her around a wad of tobacco. " 'Xcuse me, ma'am." Moving her aside, he slung a coil of heavy rope over his head and threw it onto the truck.

"An accident? Where? What kind of accident?"

"Rig overturned."

"Did anyone get hurt?"

"Yes, ma'am. One man's down."

She didn't need more details than that. This was an emergency. Loggers loved to swap horror stories of work-related accidents. She had hung around the landing enough to know that. The tales rarely needed embellishment to make them gory. Logging accidents were usually disastrous, if not fatal.

"Is he badly hurt? Why wasn't I notified?"

"We called the house. You'd already left."

"Did you call an ambulance?"

"Sure did. Told 'em where we're cuttin'. It's back deep in the woods. Be tough to get anything that's not four-wheel drive in there, but they said they could. Hey, Miz Schyler ma'am, whadaya doin'?"

"Since I can't take my car, I'll ride there with you." She was met with three argumentative stares.

"No sense in you goin' at all, ma'am."

"A cuttin' site ain't no place for a woman."

"We're wasting time." She stepped into the cab of the truck and decisively slammed the door behind her.

Shrugging and muttering that it was no skin off his ass what the boss lady did, the driver slid in beside her. The other two climbed onto the trailer.

The truck labored its way along a twisting, narrow highway. Once they made it to the turnoff, it had the muddy, bumpy skid rows to navigate. They drove for what seemed like miles through a forest so dense that daylight barely penetrated. The driver colorfully cursed the truck's reluctance as it chugged over the rough terrain toward the site where they had been cutting towering pines.

"Up yonder," the driver told Schyler with a nod of his head.

Logs were scattered about the clearing like a giant's set of pick-up sticks. The floor of the forest was littered with severed branches and pine needles. The air was damp. The skidder, a piece of machinery that dragged the logs through the woods to be loaded onto the rig, had left the earth freshly plowed. The scent of pine was as pungent as a Christmas candle. Later in the day, the site turned hot and dusty, but at this early hour it was verdant.

Schyler had always enjoyed being in the woods early, but today she didn't pause to enjoy its green freshness. In the middle of the clearing the overturned rig looked like a fallen dinosaur lying on its side. She didn't wait until the truck came to a full stop before putting her shoulder to the cranky door and shoving it open. She jumped to the ground. Her shoes were immediately swallowed by the mud. She worked them free and, lifting her skirt above her knees, tramped toward the silent group of men.

"Excuse me, excuse me." She elbowed her way through the somber huddle of loggers. The sound of her voice acted like Moses' rod. The men parted as cleanly as the waters of the Red Sea to let her through.

She drew up short when the last crewman stepped aside and she saw what was in the center of the ring of men. A massive pine log had pinned down a logger's leg. He was lying on his back, obviously in excruciating pain. Taking a deep breath, she moved to his side and dropped to her knees.

His lips were rimmed with a thin, white line of agony. His face was as waxy and pale as a peeled onion. Each hair follicle on his dark beard stood out in contrast. He was drenched with sweat. His teeth were clamped shut, but bared, and his hand was gripping another as though his life depended on maintaining that grip.

He was holding on to Cash Boudreaux for dear life.

Cash was speaking softly. ". . . the fanciest whorehouse I've ever seen. Right there in downtown Saigon. Did you get to any of those whorehouses while you were over there, Glee? Those Asian girls have got tricks—''

The logger screamed.

''Where's the goddamn whiskey I asked for?'' Cash roared. Through the crowd of men a bottle of Jack Daniels was passed from hand to hand until it reached Schyler. She handed it to Cash. His eyes locked with hers. Something odd happened to her insides. They experienced a flurry.

Cash said nothing to her but took the bottle and uncapped it. He held it to the man's lips and used his other hand to support his head.

''Where's the fucking ambulance?'' Cash asked her out of the side of his mouth.

''The men said they called. It should be here soon.''

''Cash?'' the injured man asked, refusing any more liquor. ''Will they take it off. My leg? Will it have to come off?''

''Shit, this little scratch? It ain't nuthin'.'' Cash passed the whiskey bottle back to Schyler and wiped the man's drooling lips with his bare fingers.

''Don't bullshit me. Will they take it off?''

Cash dropped the false joviality. ''I don't know, Glee.''

The man's lips quivered. ''It hurts like hell, Cash. No foolin'.'' He gasped with pain.

''I know it does. Hang in there.''

''How am I gonna feed my kids, with my leg all fucked up, Cash? Huh?''

''Don't worry about it.'' He smiled and winked. ''Worry about something important, like how you're going to keep the rest of these buzzards from flocking around Marybeth at the next dance. You might have to sit that one out.''

''Marybeth's pregnant again. Seven months gone. She can't work. How am I gonna feed my kids?''

The man began to cry. Schyler stared down at him. His despair was tangible, real, basic. Disappointing love affairs, sad movies, disillusionments. Dead cats. Those were the things one cried over. She had never seen anyone cry because he might not be able to feed his children.

My God, where had she been? This was life. People suffered. People actually went hungry. She had marched and picketed on behalf of the downtrodden and unfortunate, but this was the first time she'd ever experienced human misery firsthand. His tears touched something deep inside her.

''Feeding your family will be the least of your problems,'' Cash said softly. ''I'll see to it that they don't go hungry. I swear that on my mother's grave.'' He raised his head suddenly. ''Well, thank Jesus, Mary, and Joseph. I hear an ambulance. Hear that, Glee? You're on your way to a nice, long vacation.''

''Cash?'' The man gripped the front of Cash's shirt. ''You won't forget your promise?''

''I won't forget,'' he said, squeezing tighter the hand he held.

Glee's anguished face relaxed a second before he passed out.

Cash eased the man's head to the ground, then surged to his feet. ''Get out of the way,'' he shouted, waving the loggers aside. He didn't mince words with the tardy paramedics. ''You took your goddamn time.''

''We were eating breakfast.''

''What were you having? Pussy? Give this man something for his pain, something to keep him knocked out.''

''We know what to do,'' one of them said defensively.

''Then do it,'' Cash said through his teeth. ''Tank, Chip . . . where are you?'' Two men sprang forward with the discipline of young Nazi troopers. ''Did you get the loader into place?''

"Set to go, Cash."

"All right, everybody knows what to do."

Everybody but Schyler. She stood there, looking around her stupidly and help-lessly, while the men scrambled in 360 different directions. Cash spun around, nearly knocking her down. "Move. You're in the way," he said harshly.

She opened her mouth to speak, but knew that now wasn't the time to take issue with his high-handedness. With as much dignity as she could muster, she waded through the mud back toward the truck that had transported her there from the landing. This scene clearly belonged to men. No amount of legislated equality between the sexes would change the fact that she was as glaringly out of place as one of the loggers would be at a quilting bee.

She watched as Cash, sitting in the knuckle boom of the loader, maneuvered the crane himself and carefully lifted the log off Glee's leg with the enormous pinch-ers. Glee's shin was shattered. It was a mass of crushed bone and torn flesh, barely held together by his shredded trousers. He remained blessedly unconscious as the paramedics lifted him out of the mud and onto a stretcher.

The others watched somberly as the stretcher was loaded into the ambulance. The cheerul chatter of birds seemed grossly inappropriate in the respectful silence. It lasted until the ambulance disappeared into the forest on its way back to town.

Then Cash bellowed, "What's going on here? A frigging holiday? Get to work." Then, to soften the order, he added, "Cold beer on me if we make up half of what we missed yesterday." A roar of approval went up. "Haul ass. Get that rig back on its feet. We'll need a new bolster on the rear. And keep the loads light. Everybody look alive."

He watched to see that his orders were being carried out to his satisfaction, then consulted his wristwatch. He seemed impervious to everything except the tremen-dous task at hand.

"I fired you yesterday. Apparently you've forgotten."

His head snapped around. "What are you still doing here?"

"I'm the boss. Did you hear what I said?"

The once-over he subjected her to was purely sexual. "*Oui,* I heard you. And in answer to your question, I haven't forgotten anything that happened yesterday."

She tried to peel away the layers of deception in his eyes and get to the truth, but there were no layers of deception masking them. They were clear, cool, incisive. Either he didn't know anything about two dead cats being obscenely placed on the veranda of Belle Terre, or he felt no guilt over doing it.

Neither was a comforting thought. If Cash hadn't done it, then the culprit was still a mystery. And if Cash wasn't ashamed of doing such a hideous thing, then he was psychotic. But it just didn't seem his style to sneak around like that, leaving symbolic messages. He usually issued his threats in a straightforward manner.

"I fired you," she repeated. "Why did you report to work this morning?"

"Because it's not that easy to get rid of me, Miss Schyler. You hired me to do a job and I'm going to do it. Not for you, and not for Cotton, but for me," he said, tapping his chest. "I've got more years of my life than I like to count invested in this company. It's not going to go bankrupt without a helluva fight from me."

"And it doesn't matter what I say about it?"

He smiled arrogantly. "Say whatever makes you happy. The bottom line is that you need me. We've both known that from the beginning."

She glanced at the well-oiled team of loggers, who were attaching pulleys to the overturned trailer. "I guess I can't fire you after the way you handled this emer-gency. Thank you for what you did for that man."

"His name is Glee."

"I know that," she said in angry reaction to his subtle rebuke. "Glee Williams. I'll see that his family is compensated fully while he's in the hospital."

"He'll probably lose his leg." It was a gauntlet Cash threw down to see how far she would go.

"For as long as it's necessary, he'll draw full wages."

Cash stared down at her. For some inexplicable reason she felt like she was on the witness stand pleading her innocence to an unforgiving judge. "What else can I do?" she shouted up at him.

"We shouldn't have been cutting today." He hitched his head backward in the direction of the overturned rig. "I knew it was dangerous. The ground is too soft. If the logs shift a fraction of an inch while they're being loaded, the rig can go over because it's got no ground support. That's exactly what happened. My bad judgment cost me a good man. It cost Glee his leg.

"But I didn't want you bitching at me about goofing off and letting valuable work days go by. I didn't want you to call me worthless." He pulled on his yellow leather gloves with, quick, angry motions. "Think about that every time you sign a paycheck made out to Glee Williams."

He flipped down the screened visor on his hard hat and turned his back on her.

THIRTY-TWO

Jigger came home in a bad mood. He was also drunk. Sober, he was mean. There was no one meaner in the world compared to Jigger Flynn when he was drunk. At those times Gayla thought he must be the devil incarnate, the Antichrist she'd read about in the Book of Revelations.

Sometimes she felt feisty enough to stand up to him and give him some sass, but never when he was drunk. Then, she did nothing that might provoke him.

Tonight was one of those nights. The screen door slammed closed behind him. He stumbled to the kitchen table and yanked out a chair. It barely cleared the table before he dropped into it.

Silently Gayla filled a plate with food and set it in front of him. With an oath of digust, he shoved the plate aside and demanded whiskey. She poured him a glass.

"That bastard Boudreaux," he grumbled between deep swallows of straight whiskey. "Mighty smart, that Cajun."

Gayla pieced together the almost unintelligible words and phrases until some sense emerged from them. Earlier that evening, Cash Boudreaux had bought beer for all the loggers who worked for Crandall Logging. It was their reward for doing two days' work in one.

"Big shot, he thinks he is." Jigger's bleary eyes found Gayla and squinted her into focus. "I tell you, he's headed for a fall, he is. He brags now, but wait. All his work goes up like that." He clapped his hands together loudly. His face turned darker and his eye glittered as he unsteadily tipped the whiskey bottle toward his glass again. "And that Schyler Cran-*dall*. Bitch."

Gayla ran her moist palms down her thighs, drying them on her cheap cotton dress. "What's Schyler ever done to you?"

"Killed my dogs that bitch did." He swigged more whiskey. "I get her. Good, I get her."

"What are you going to do to Schyler?"

He looked up at her and cackled the evil laugh that sent chills down her spine. "You think 'cause your mammy work at Belle Terre the Cran-*dalls* have anything to do with you? Ha! That highfalutin bitch, she spits on black whores like you."

Gayla's head dropped forward in shame. He was probably right. It had been her daily prayer since she had seen Schyler toting the shotgun that her old friend hadn't recognized her before she ducked out of sight. Schyler was fine and good. She would never understand or forgive what Gayla had become.

"What are you going to do to Schyler?" she repeated, keeping her head bowed. If she knew what Jigger's plans were ahead of time, she might be able to thwart them. She could warn Schyler anonymously, prevent her from being hurt. Gayla had lived with Jigger long enough to know that he kept his vows of vengeance. He wouldn't be afraid to take on Belle Terre and everybody in it, especially with Cotton laid up and that worthless Ken Howell in charge.

"That's my business, don'tcha know," he growled. He stood, swaying so that he had to brace himself against the edge of the table to remain upright. "Your business is to get ready for that fancy gentleman that's coming to pick you up."

Fearfully, Gayla backed against the wall. "I can't go with nobody, Jigger. You know that. I'm not healed up yet."

He made a snarling sound. "That sorry Cajun gave me sorry medicine. I git him for that, too." He aimed a finger at Gayla. "You're goin' tonight. Earn your keep."

"I can't!"

He weaved forward and backhanded her across the breasts. He was gifted at inflicting wounds that wouldn't spoil the perfection of her face. "He's paid one hunerd dollars for you. You're going."

Tears rolled down Gayla's cheeks. "I can't, Jigger. I'm still bleeding. Please don't make me go. Please."

"I do bizness with this man. You're part of our deal."

Her pitiful pleas had no effect on him. At the sound of tires crunching on the gravel road outside, he grabbed her hand and dragged her across the kitchen floor and through the screen door. She tried to wrest her hand free. Her heels dug into the rain-softened earth. She stumbled along behind his staggering tread toward the long car with the opaque tinted windows.

The headlights almost blinded her. It was God, she knew, spotlighting her sin. She averted her head. Jigger pulled open the passenger door and shoved her inside. The air-conditioning had made the upholstery cool. It surrounded her in a clammy caress.

"Is there a problem, Jigger?" asked the man behind the steering wheel. Gayla recognized the voice. She'd been loaned out to him before.

"No problem," Jigger told him. "She likes you."

"Good," the man said softly. "Because I like her, too."

Gayla kept her head down. She didn't see the threatening look Jigger gave her before he closed the door. The man put the car in motion, but they'd barely driven out of sight of the house before he braked and turned toward her. He ran the backs of his fingers down her cheek and felt the wetness of her tears.

"I won't hurt you, Gayla."

She knew he wouldn't. He wasn't one of the violent ones. He just liked to take dirty pictures. He would barely touch her.

He wouldn't affect her emotionally at all. She had collapsed into herself, like a dying star, leaving a black void of such density that no light could escape or enter.

She couldn't be touched. That's the only way she had survived. She didn't allow herself to feel.

"Joe Jr., he's a cagey son of a bitch," Cotton said from the pillows of his hospital bed. "Inherited old man Endicott's shrewdness. Arrogant as hell, too. A real smart-assed buck. He'll haggle you down to bottom dollar if you let him."

Schyler smiled, glad to see that her father had reverted to his normal speech patterns. He was regaining strength each day. The stronger he got, the more profane his language became.

That afternoon he'd been moved from the ICU to a regular room. His prognosis was favorable, if guarded. He was now holding court like a king who had defied death and lived to rule again. Schyler liked to think that one cause for his vast improvement was that she had begun talking shop with him. Dr. Collins had agreed to the idea when she broached the subject. Cotton shouldn't be made to feel like an invalid, he had said.

"Heart patients go through a period of depression that is almost as debilitating as their physical illness. By all means, discuss business with him. Nothing catastrophic, you understand, but let him feel like a useful human being. Don't mollycoddle him."

She had brought Cotton up-to-date on the progress Crandall Logging was making in his absence.

"I'm sorry I saddled you with that balloon note, Schyler," he had said. "Jesus, I didn't realize how soon it was coming due."

"You could hardly schedule a heart attack around a bank loan," she had said with a smile. "Don't worry. We'll make it."

"How?"

"I've got several irons in the fire."

He didn't press her for details, so she was spared having to tell him that none of the irons she boasted having were large enough to cover the debt. Timber was leaving the landing daily on the train, but the accounts she had negotiated were peanuts compared to the sizable contract she desperately needed from Endicott.

Cotton didn't seem to resent her management. On the contrary, he seemed pleased that she had seized control. She'd been careful not to mention Cash's name, unsure how Cotton would feel about him playing such a vital role in their business.

That's just what his role was—vital. As difficult as it was for her to admit, Schyler didn't know how she would have managed without him. He worked circles around every other logger. She saw him several times each day at the landing, but they hadn't engaged in any lengthy conversations since Glee's accident. Things seemed to go more smoothly when they stayed out of each other's way.

Something Ken said drew her back into the present. "Maybe I should go to East Texas with Schyler tomorrow," he offered.

Tricia and he had joined Schyler in Cotton's room, in a sort of celebration over his rapid progress. It was the first time the three of them had been in the same room since their argument. For Cotton's benefit, they pretended to be as staunchly devoted to each other as the three musketeers. "I've dealt with Joe Jr. before."

"Which might be the reason we're in dutch with Endicott's," Cotton said crossly. "Let Schyler handle it herself."

"She doesn't have any experience," Ken argued.

Cotton looked at his daughter with affection and admiration. "Then she'll get some, won't she? Dealing with Joe Jr. will be a baptism of fire."

"Well, if she blows this deal, don't blame me."

"No one would think of it," Cotton said sharply.

Schyler intervened to keep her father from getting upset. "I visited with Glee Williams before coming up here."

"How is he?"

She had told Cotton about the accident, but not until after she'd been told by the doctors that Glee's leg had been spared amputation. During a painstakingly and lengthy operation, his fibula had been knit back together with the help of synthetic materials. He would always walk with a pronounced limp, and it was still undetermined what jobs he would be physically capable of handling, but at least he wouldn't be an amputee.

It was gratifying to learn that Cotton had taken an interest in the logger's welfare. He had known Glee personally. He'd even referred to the man's wife by name.

"He looked much better than he did yesterday," Schyler told him. "He said he wasn't in pain, but they're keeping him heavily sedated. The flowers you ordered have been delivered. He and Marybeth sent their thanks. She doesn't look old enough to vote, much less to have three children and one on the way."

"I don't think she is," Cotton said, laughing. "Glee knocked her up when they were in the eighth grade."

Tricia rolled her eyes heavenward. Schyler smiled. Despite Macy's admonitions, Cotton had never ameliorated the saltiness of his language in front of his daughters.

"The insurance company will probably raise our premiums after what they had to shell out for that operation." Ken made a face. "Schyler brought in an orthopedic specialist from New Orleans."

"And he worked a miracle to save that leg," she said, annoyed that Ken had placed her in a position to defend her decision.

He ignored her and spoke directly to Cotton. "Then she offered to pay Williams full wages. Indefinitely. That's going to cost us a fortune and we won't be getting anything in return."

"I approve of her decision," Cotton said in the ironclad voice that indicated the subject was closed to further discussion.

Sensing the mounting tension, Schyler again acted as a deflector. "Tricia is organizing the Junior League to gather used clothes for the Williams children and to give the family a pounding. I'm sure they could use the extra groceries, especially with another baby due in a few weeks."

Cotton looked at his younger daughter appraisingly. "That's right decent of you, Tricia. They'll appreciate that."

Flustered, Tricia replied, "I'm glad I could help in some small way."

"Well, we'd better go and let you rest." Schyler gathered her handbag and leaned over to kiss Cotton's cheek. "Good night, Daddy. Sleep well."

"Can't help but sleep like a frigging corpse after absorbing that goddamn suppository they shove up my ass every night." His querulousness didn't camouflage his fatigue. They left a few moments later.

As soon as the heavy door closed behind them, Tricia's hand clamped like a talon around her sister's arm. "Why in hell did you tell him that? I'm organizing nothing, do you understand me? Pounding, indeed. Do you think any of my friends would be caught dead toting bags of groceries into that rundown neighborhood?"

Schyler slung off Tricia's hand. "Then don't. I thought it would make Daddy happy to know that you were taking part in company business. And I was right. It did make him happy."

"I don't need you to make me look good in front of Daddy, thank you very much.'' Tricia spoke through thin, tight lips. She looked ready to kill. ''I'm taking part in company business, all right, but in ways you might not like, big sister.''

She headed toward the elevator, where she endangered her sculptured fingernail on the button she punched. Ken touched Schyler's elbow. ''Sure you don't want me to go with you tomorrow? That's a big deal you're negotiating all by yourself.''

Schyler had kept it to herself that Cash was going to Endicott's with her. That had been one of the smartest decisions she had made lately. She wasn't certain he still planned to go. If he didn't, she wouldn't have to explain the reason to anybody. If he did, Ken could find you after the fact. She didn't want to justify her reasons to him now.

''No, thank you, Ken. I'd rather you stay here and oversee things while I'm away.''

Sighing, he ran a hand through his hair. ''You're still mad at me, aren't you?''

''No. This isn't personal.''

He gazed at her longingly. ''Let's bury this hatchet, Schyler. I can't stand all this tippy-toeing around each other.''

''You and Tricia took one stand. I took another.''

''Forget Tricia. I'm talking about us. I don't want to quarrel with you anymore.''

''I have only one quarrel with you, Ken, and that's over Belle Terre. If you and Tricia persist in wanting to sell it, I'll fight you. Otherwise, we remain friends.''

''Just friends?'' he asked, lowering his voice.

''Just friends.'' She gave him a cool stare. ''The elevator's here.'' She walked away from him and joined Tricia, who was impatiently waiting for them in the open elevator.

Fuck you, bitch.

Schyler stared up at the words. They'd been ineptly scrawled in spray paint on the door of the landing office. She glanced around. No one was in sight. It was well past nine o'clock. She hesitated to go inside, but reasoned that the vandal had done his dirty work for the day. It was unlikely he would still be lurking around. She unlocked the door and stepped inside.

The red glowing tip of a cigarette winked at her out of the darkness. With her heart in her throat, she reached for the light switch and turned it on. Cash was sitting behind the desk, his boots propped on the corner of it.

''I guess you got the message.'' He nodded toward the door she was holding open.

''Did you leave it there for me?''

He snorted a laugh and swung his feet to the floor. ''Hardly. I wouldn't waste good paint on what I could easily say to your face.''

She closed the door. ''I don't guess you would sacrifice two perfectly healthy cats either, would you?''

His brows drew together as he eased himself out of the chair. ''What are you talking about? Two cats?''

She told him. ''Ken disposed of the carcasses. He told me later that the male had been gutted. Do you use cat guts in any of your potions?''

Cash's face remained impassive, his reply noncommittal. ''None that I recall. I've strung a few fiddles with them though.''

She tossed her purse and keys onto the desk and stepped around him. ''I could use a drink. How about you?''

''I've had one already. But I'll take another.''

Schyler shook her head ruefully when she spied the glass on the desk. There was a fraction of an inch of amber liquid in the bottom of it. She took a secreted bottle of bourbon out of the lowest desk drawer and poured them each a drink. "Besides stealing my liquor, what were you doing here?"

"Homework." He flipped open the manila file folder lying on the desk.

Schyler sat down in the chair he had recently vacated. The leather still retained his body heat. It felt wonderful against the backs of her thighs and buttocks. She forced herself not to squirm.

"Endicott," she said, reading the letterhead on the top sheet of correspondence.

Cash sat down on the corner of the desk, facing her. "According to those letters, Cotton's initial dealings with the senior Endicott went well. Both parties came away happy."

Schyler dragged her eyes away from the crotch of Cash's jeans, which rested against the corner of the desk. She reached for her glass of whiskey and took a quick drink. "Cotton said Joe Jr. was a cagey son of a bitch, but he seemed to respect him, too."

"How is he? Cotton," he elaborated when she looked up at him quizzically.

"Much better. He's been moved out of the ICU."

Cash nodded. He pointed down at the file with his highball glass. "I've read through all the correspondence. I can't figure out what soured the Endicotts on us."

"Well, I guess we'll find out tomorrow."

"We?"

"Aren't you going with me?"

"You still want me to?"

It cost her some pride to admit it, but she did want him along. For Crandall Logging and Cotton. For Belle Terre. And—who was she kidding?—for herself. "Yes, Cash. I do."

Staring at her over the rim of his glass, he tossed back the rest of his whiskey. "What time in the morning?"

"I'll meet you here at nine."

"Okay." He stood up. "Let's go for now."

"I'm not finished here." She waved her hand over the cluttered desktop. "I need to catch up on some paperwork."

"I don't think you should stay here by yourself. Let's go." He hooked his thumbs into his belt and assumed a stance that said arguing would be futile.

"I am tired," she confessed.

"And tomorrow is going to be a long day. Besides, the bully might still be around."

Or the bully might be standing right in front of her, shoulders pulled back, pelvis thrust forward, looking like a wolf in sheep's clothing. Before capitulating, she drained her glass just as he had. When she stood up, he was smiling as though he knew that last draught was a gesture of defiance.

She went ahead of him out the door. "I'll have someone take care of this first thing in the morning," he told her.

"Thank you, Cash."

"You're welcome."

His phony obsequiousness was irritating, but she let it pass. When they reached her car, he drew her around and pulled her close. "Whoever the son of a bitch is," he said, hitching his thumb over his shoulder toward the door, "he's got a damn good idea."

Schyler's temper went off like a rocket. "You want to talk about it, I suppose?"

"About what? Fucking you?"

"Yes."

His grin formed slowly. "Sure. Why not? Let's talk about it."

"All right." She drew a deep breath to show him how bored she was with the subject. "It was a mistake to go to bed with you. I regret it. It happened. I wish it hadn't, but it did. I take full responsibility for my actions, but I intend to forget the whole thing. I expect you to as well."

"You do?"

"Yes I do."

His whiskey-flavored breath was as balmy as the night air when he laughed into her stormy face. He leaned forward, aligning his body against hers. "Not bloody likely. Do you know what it means to a poor white trash, bastard kid like me to make Miss Schyler Crandall come?"

She shoved him away from her and yanked open the car door. "Don't flatter yourself. It had been a long time for me, that's all."

She peppered his boots with gravel as her car peeled out of the lot. He watched her red taillights disappear in the darkness.

Cash drank straight from the brown paper sack. The liquor sloshed in the bottle, indicating that the pint was almost empty. He belched sourly.

Where was that bitch?

After Schyler left he had gone back into the office, snickering at the crude message written on the door, and made a phone call. That had been an hour ago. He was at the filling station and liquor store on the Lafayette highway. Across the street was the motel. He was waiting for Rhoda.

She had been pathetically happy to hear from him. Oh, she'd acted aloof at first. She'd obviously been pissed off. He explained how busy he'd been. She hadn't been impressed or sympathetic and kept making snotty comments that had made him want to strangle her.

He had said something to the effect of, "Fine. In the dark, one honey pot is as sweet as another. You don't want to play tonight? Fine." That had knocked her on her elegant ass. He named the time and place and she had agreed quicker than a sailor's zipper on shore leave.

But now he wished he had just drowned his anger in the bottle of cheap whiskey and left Rhoda out of it. The newness was wearing off their affair. He was bored with her, especially since she had become possessive and clinging. She had served her purpose. He didn't need her anymore.

Except tonight.

Tonight he needed something or someone to work out his frustration on. Damn Schyler Crandall. She had loved cutting him down like a loblolly sapling, reminding him that she had only used him as a substitute for the boyfriend in London who kept her sexually satisfied and in uptown style.

"Shit." He drained the bottle and tossed it into the overflowing oil drum that served as a trash can outside the men's toilet.

So, Schyler wanted to forget their afternoon together? She didn't want anybody to know about it. Well, that suited him fine. He would never let himself become an object of ridicule like Cotton Crandall had. People kowtowed to Cotton because he was rich and powerful, the biggest timber contractor around. Behind his back, however, they still remembered him as the redneck logger who'd romanced his way into Belle Terre. In these parts "money marries money" was the eleventh commandment. Cotton had had the gall to break the unwritten law and hadn't been forgiven for it yet.

That wouldn't satisfy Cash Boudreaux. He wanted to be able to look himself in the mirror without knowing that his wife's last name had earned the respect he was shown. Schyler's slender, silky thighs opened to the sweetest, tightest piece of woman he'd ever had, but he wouldn't use it as a portal by which to enter Belle Terre.

He'd get what he had rightfully coming to him in his own way and under his own terms.

Amid his brooding he noticed Rhoda's black BMW pulling into the motel parking lot. He watched her alight. She kept the engine running. She went inside to check in and did so, using her gold card. Clasping the room key like a wino with a handout, she returned to her car, her phony tits ajiggle beneath her sleeveless sweater.

Cash felt a yearning to fondle, to kiss, to suck—but not Rhoda's breasts. Cursing his susceptibility, he went to his pickup and got inside. He stared down at the ignition key lying in his palm and gave serious consideration to standing up Rhoda and driving home to nurse his misery in private.

Cutting his eyes across the highway, he watched her enter a room. She'd be hot, eager, grasping, willing to please, *determined* to please.

What the hell was he waiting for?

Resolve thinning his lips, he crammed the key into the ignition and revved the motor. A hazard to other motorists, he sped across the highway and brought the pickup to a bucking stop outside the door Rhoda had gone into.

Wanting Schyler Crandall, he went inside to join the banker's unfaithful wife.

THIRTY-THREE

"What's the matter? Have I got egg on my tie?"
   "Your tie is fine."

"Then why do you keep staring at it?"

"Because it's there."

Cash, failing to see Schyler's humor, scowled. "I might have grown up with bayou mud between my toes, I was poorer than Job's turkey, but I'm not ignorant. On good days I can even read and write. I know when the occasion calls for a necktie."

"Do you want me to drive?"

"No."

"You don't mind driving?"

"I told you I didn't."

"I thought maybe that's why you're being such a pain in the butt today."

"Why should today be any different?"

"Right."

She flopped back in the passenger seat and turned her head to stare out the window at the scenery. It whizzed past her car, a blur of colors. Cash drove too fast. She remembered that from the night he'd picked her up at Jigger Flynn's house. They'd been escaping a derelict's wrath then. She couldn't account for his excessive speed now, except that he had been in a grumpy mood since she'd met him at the landing earlier that morning.

He had mumbled his replies when she asked him about the assignments he'd given the loggers for that day. He accepted her offer to drive with a grunt. Beyond that, he hadn't spoken three words to her.

His expression was surly, his attitude defensive. His shoulders were hunched as though he were ready to take offense at the slightest affront. His eyes were glued to the road. At least Schyler assumed they were on the road. She couldn't see them behind his aviator sunglasses.

"Maybe I should have taken Ken up on his offer," she mused out loud. Cash didn't bite. She elaborated anyway. "He offered to come with me."

"Maybe you should have."

"He would have been better company."

"He's quite a charmer, all right. Can charm the pants off anybody." He gave her a sidelong glance. "The Crandall girls seem to be particularly vulnerable to his charm."

"You just love being vulgar, don't you?"

"Too bad your hero can't fight worth a damn."

"You pulled a knife on him!"

"You're always jumping to his defense, aren't you?"

Schyler ground her teeth, angry at herself for letting him draw her into an argument. It was obvious he was ready to do battle. She watched all ten of his fingers extend and stretch, then curl back around the padded steering wheel, gripping it tightly, as if he wanted to uproot it from the dashboard.

"You're a sore loser, Mr. Boudreaux."

His head came around abruptly. "What's that supposed to mean?"

"I turned you down last night. Apparently most women don't say no to you."

By slow degrees his whole demeanor changed. His posture relaxed until it became a veritable slouch. He laid his arm along the back of the seat. He no longer looked like he might, at any minute, ram his head through the windshield in the throes of a tantrum.

"You're right about that, Miss Schyler. In fact, the second one I asked last night said yes."

This time it was Schyler's head that snapped around. The teasing smirk had been wiped right off her face. She felt like she'd been clubbed in the middle with a two-by-four. She recovered quickly and hoped Cash hadn't seen her stunned expression. "Congratulations."

He flashed her a killer smile. "Thanks. Coffee?" He nodded toward the rest stop complex they were approaching at an unsafe speed.

"Yes, please."

As soon as he braked, Schyler alighted and headed for the ladies' room. She used the toilet even though she really didn't need to. As she washed her hands in the lavatory, she addressed herself in the mirror. "If you didn't want to know, you shouldn't have provoked him."

It was unrealistic of her, having become one of Cash Boudreaux's conquests, to demand his respect. Fidelity, of course, was never even a possibility. His women were as disposable as the coarse paper towel she was drying her hands on. One was as easy to come by as another.

In order to salvage her ego, before she left the restroom she smoothed the wrinkles out of her linen business suit and applied fresh lipstick. She even ran a hairbrush through her hair. When he looked at her today, she wanted him to see his boss, not a has-been lover.

"Can you drink that in the car?" Cash asked, passing Schyler a Styrofoam cup of coffee when she rejoined him in the refreshment area of the convenience store. "Sure."

"Good. I can't take the smell of those hot dogs."

There was a rotisserie on the counter, slow-cooking fat, red frankfurters for the lunch trade. Cash replaced the sunglasses, which he'd pushed to the top of his head when he went inside. Schyler noticed his tired eyes, the green cast to his skin.

"Now I know what's wrong with you," she said as they walked back toward the car. "You've got a hangover."

"A real bitch." He grimaced.

"It must have been some night."

"A real bitch." This time he smiled.

Sliding into her seat while he held the car door open for her, Schyler wondered at what point Cash's other affairs had become such a bone of contention with her.

"I guess we have a deal, Mr. Endicott," Schyler said, "if that's the very best price you can give us."

"That's top dollar. Compare us with other markets. I'm not bullshitting you."

She resented his taking the liberty to use that kind of language in front of her in a strictly business situation. One slightly raised eyebrow indicated her displeasure. If he saw the censure, he ignored it. What could one expect from a man who was thoroughly obnoxious and continually cracked his knuckles?

Joe Endicott, Jr. was a pompous ass, leaning back in his chair, a smug expression on his face. He seemed to think that he held all the aces. Unfortunately he did.

One thing he didn't know, however, was that the deal they had negotiated would put Crandall Logging in the black with some left over. Schyler was elated, but she carefully concealed her excitemknt from Joe Endicott, Jr.

"We've always thought Crandall's timber was top grade."

"I'm delighted to hear that," Schyler replied to the compliment. "Now to the terms of our contract, would you prefer paying us upon receipt of each delivery, or would you rather send us a check at the end of each week for the cumulative amount?"

"Neither one."

"Neither one?"

Joe Jr. popped a knuckle badly. "I didn't stutter."

"I don't understand."

"I'm not paying you at all until I receive every board foot of the order."

"Then you must think we're stupid." Cash was slumped in the second chair across the desk from Endicott. Up until now he hadn't said much, only muttered in direct response to a question or comment Schyler made to him.

"I know you're not stupid, Mr. Boudreaux."

"Then how can you expect us to ship you timber for nothing?"

"You'll get your money, Ms. Crandall. I get my timber. *All* my timber."

"We can't operate that way."

Endicott spread his hands wide and smiled pleasantly. "Then we've got no deal."

Schyler glanced at Cash. He was staring at Endicott over his tented fingers as though he wanted to pulverize him beneath his boot like any other cockroach. His solution to this dilemma was likely to be violent. With as much composure as she could garner, Schyler turned back to Endicott. "May I ask why you're placing this restriction on us?"

"Certainly. You don't always deliver the goods."

"I beg your pardon."

"I didn't—"

"He didn't stutter," Cash supplied in a tight voice.

Endicott smiled at him, but his smile wavered beneath Cash's steady stare. "Crandall Logging took us for several thousand dollars. My old man advanced you money on an order, but we never received the last shipment. That's why we haven't done business with you folks the last coupla years.''

Schyler drew herself up straight. "I assure you, Mr. Endicott, that there must have been an oversight or a bookkeeping mistake. My father's reputation as an ethical and honest businessman has stood for decades. If Crandall was advanced a check—''

"It was. And it came back endorsed and cashed.

"By my father?''

"Yep.''

"I don't understand.'' She was at a loss. Cotton was competitive. He believed in free enterprise and capitalizing on every business opportunity. But he played by the rules. He wasn't dishonest. He didn't have to be. "Why didn't you inquire as to why—''

"Don't you think I did?'' Knuckle pop, knuckle pop. "All our letters and threatening notices went unanswered.''

"Why didn't you file suit?''

"Because my daddy has a sentimental streak.'' Joe Jr. shrugged. "He always said ol' Cotton Crandall was one of the best contractors in southwest Loosiana. He'd been doing business with him for a long time. He said to let it drop, so I let it drop. Against my better judgment.''

"Well I don't intend to let it drop,'' Schyler informed him firmly. "I'm going to dig until I get to the bottom of it and am able to offer you a full explanation. In the meantime, your refusal to pay us on each shipment is unrealistic. How are we supposed to pay our operating expenses?''

Resting his linked hands on top of his head, he said, "That's not my problem, is it?''

"So we won't receive any money until the last shipment is delivered?''

"Right down to the pulp wood.''

"Nobody does business like that.'' Cash almost came out of his chair, like a testy animal whose leash had just snapped.

"I don't . . . usually.'' Endicott made a half turn in his swivel chair to look through the wall of glass behind him. It overlooked the railroad yard where logs were unloaded before being run through the paper mill. "But I've got to cover my own ass. I want the shipments to be delivered on a specified schedule, but I won't give Crandall one red cent until the whole order has been filled.'' He spun his chair around. "*Comprende,* y'all?''

Schyler looked helplessly toward Cash. He looked at her, then back at Endicott. "I need a smoke.'' He came to his feet abruptly. "Schyler?'' He extended a hand down to her. She took it. He helped her out of her chair and they headed for the door.

"Hey, do we have a deal or not? You're taking up my valuable time here. What am I supposed to do while you're out smoking?'' Endicott demanded.

"Relax, Junior,'' Cash said. "Take a nap. Take a leak. We'll be right back.''

He slammed the door behind them. The secretary looked up reprovingly. She was ignored as they went through the reception area. The long hallway opened into various offices. At the end of it there was a large window and a seating area. It was there that Cash escorted Schyler. He shook a cigarette out of the pack in his breast shirt pocket. Schyler watched him light it. He angrily exhaled toward the skylight overhead.

"Well?'' she asked. "What do you think?''

"I think I'd like to put my heel to his nuts and send him and that rolling chair straight through that glass wall.''

"What should I tell him?"

"To eat shit and die."

"Cash! I'm serious."

"So am I." When he saw her retiring expression, he said, "Okay, okay, I'll get serious."

"Do you know anything about us welshing on a deal?"

"I guess you think I'm the company crook."

"I wasn't making an accusation. I just asked you a straight question."

He took a long drag on the cigarette, then unmercifully ground it out in the nearest ashtay. "No, I don't know anything about why that shipment wasn't delivered, or letters going unanswered, etcetera, etcetera. Want to strip search me?"

Signing, she rubbed her temples. After slowly counting to ten, she appealed to him for advice. "Should I accept his terms? And don't tell me what you think I want to hear. What do you think I should do?"

"What are your alternatives?"

"To go back home and start making calls. That's backtracking, of course. It took me days to set up this appointment. I really haven't got time to start over from scratch."

"There are plenty other markets, Schyler."

"I know, but none on this scale. I could fill a small order here, another one there like I've been doing. We'd work ourselves to death and it would still be piecemeal, just barely enough to meet payroll and stay open. This one order could pay off the bank note and give us comfortable operating capital for months."

"Then I guess you have your answer."

"What if we deliver all the timber, but he doesn't pay us the full amount?"

"He wouldn't dare. We'd have it in writing. Besides," Cash added, cracking his own knuckles in imitation of Joe Jr., "he values his life."

"*Can* we fill the order?"

"Let me do some quick figuring." He sat down on the edge of a small sofa and reached for a magazine lying on the spindly coffee table. Using its back cover as his scratch sheet, he did some quick calculations. "We've got six rigs hauling every day. That's not including any independents we pull in. At five thousand board feet per load, that's—"

"Thirty thousand board feet."

"Times three loads per day." He glanced up at her. "We can ship ninety thousand board feet each day, in addition to what we buy from independents."

"He's ordering over two million. We've got under a month before the loan comes due."

"Say thirty days."

"It's less than that, Cash."

"So we'll work some overtime."

"What about the weather?"

"We'll be really screwed if it rains."

"Oh, Lord."

He rechecked his figures. "We can do it, Schyler," he said.

"Are you sure?"

"I'm sure."

"By the deadline?"

"Yes."

"I'm placing a lot of trust in you."

He stared at her for a long moment. "I know."

His expression and his soft, almost sad, tone of voice disconcerted her. For a moment she was distracted by them. Then she asked him, "If I weren't here, if you had to do this alone, if you were responsible for this decision, what would you do?"

He stood up, moved to the windows, and stared out. He slid his hands into his pockets, a gesture that parted his unbuttoned sport coat. His dress slacks fit his seat as well as the jeans he always wore. His shoes looked new, as though he might have bought them especially for this business appointment. That was endearing. Schyler was touched.

He turned around slowly. "I hate kissing anybody's ass, particularly a guy like that." He jutted his chin toward the executive office at the other end of the hall. "I'd be tempted to tell him to shove it. I guess it would come down to how badly I wanted or needed the deal. How important is it to you?"

Suddenly she remembered the expression on Cotton's face when he looked up at her from the gurney and asked, "Why did you destroy my grandchild?" She would never forget that as long as she lived. Cotton's faith in her, his love, had been shattered. She needed to restore it completely.

"It's very important, Cash," she said huskily. "Not just to me. But to Cotton. To Belle Terre. Its future is at stake. I'll do anything, sacrifice anything, even my pride, for Belle Terre. Can you understand that?"

A muscle in his cheek twitched. *Oui,* I can understand that."

"Then shall we go back in and sign Joe Jr.'s contract?"

"I'm right behind you."

Ken Howell collapsed on top of his wife the second after his climax. When he regained his breath, he raised his head and dusted kisses along her hairline. "That was great. Was it good for you?"

She pushed him off her and rolled to the side of the bed. She thrust her arms into a peignoir. "Did you ask Schyler that every time you made love to her?"

His face, already flushed from intercourse, turned a deeper red. "With Schyler, I didn't have to ask."

Tricia cast him a glance over her shoulder. "Touché." Her mules slapped against her bare heels as she walked into the bathroom. Over the sound of running water, she called out to him, "Are you still in love with her?"

Ken padded naked to the bathroom. He stood in the doorway and waited until Tricia finished brushing her teeth. "Do you care?"

She straightened and blotted her mouth on a towel, watching him in the mirror over the sink. "Yes, I think I do."

"Only because you don't want her to have something that you can't."

She shrugged and dropped the sheer robe. "Probably."

"At least you're honest."

Tricia turned on the shower. Reaching in to test the water temperature, she swiveled her head around and looked at him over her smooth shoulder. He was morosely staring at the tile floor. "I haven't always been."

He raised his head. "What, honest? Yes, I know."

For a moment husband and wife stared at each other across the bathroom that was rapidly filling up with steam. Their expressions were tinged with regret, maybe remorse, but neither kidded himself for long. Neither was righteous and never would be.

"When did you know?"

"That there never was a baby?" he asked. Tricia nodded. He pushed back his touseled hair. "I don't know, maybe from the beginning."

"But you still married me."

"I didn't see an easier way out of the mess. It was more expedient and less trouble to go along with your lie."

"You would rather be stuck with me than to beg Schyler's forgiveness for screwing me."

"I never claimed any medals for heroism."

"What about those cats?"

He looked at her quizzically. The question was seemingly out of context. "Disposing of them made me sick to my stomach."

"Don't play dense, Ken. Did you do it?"

"Of course not. Did you?"

"Of course not."

Neither was convinced of the other's innocence. Tricia stepped into the shower but didn't close the door. "You've got to stop her, you know."

"I'm trying," Ken said defensively.

"Try harder. She's in East Texas today negotiating a deal that will get Crandall Logging out of hock. We'll have a harder time convincing Cotton to sell if everything is solvent."

Ken gazed at his reflection in the mirror, running a hand over his stubbled jaw, not liking what he saw. He was beginning to look jowly, old, soft, dissipated. He looked useless.

"Cash Boudreaux bears watching, too," Tricia said from the shower. "I understand that he and Schyler are thick as thieves."

"He works for her, that's all. She depends on him to manage the loggers."

Tricia's laugh echoed loudly in the shower when she shut off the water. "How naive you are, Ken. Or are you burying your head in the sand? You don't want to believe that they're lovers."

"Who says?"

"Everybody." She wrapped herself in a bath sheet and began applying baby oil to her wet limbs. "Any woman Cash's shadow falls on eventually goes to bed with him. If he wants her, that is. Those who have been with him say that he's the best lover they've ever had. They say his cock's a good ten inches."

Ken frowned at her as he stepped into the shower and twisted the taps wide open. "Female bullshit. Is that all you and your cronies talk about? Men and the size of their cocks?"

"No more than men talk about tits and ass."

"That's a male prerogative."

"Not anymore, baby," she chortled.

Ken shook his head in disgust, then thrust it beneath the needle spray. Tricia finished drying and sailed the towel in the general direction of the hamper in the corner.

She left the bathroom, confident in the knowledge that what she wanted, she went after, and usually got. If Ken couldn't or wouldn't keep up with her, he would be left behind. That would be all right, too.

THIRTY-FOUR

"Having chateaubriand and asparagus tips for lunch was decadent."
Cash indulgently propelled Schyler toward her parked car. She was comically tipsy. They'd stopped at the steakhouse to have a celebratory, late lunch. When they discovered that it did't open until four, they had decided to wait, passing the time by milling around the parklike setting on the edges of a national forest. Even though the contract they had obtained from Endicott had a definite drawback, it had boosted their spirits.

The meal had been delicious, the portions generous to a fault. They had demanded and gotten the royal treatment, being the only customers in the place at that early hour. Schyler had ordered champagne to toast their success. Cash figured the two bottles she had bought probably depleted the restaurant's wine cellar of its stock. There wasn't much call for champagne in a restaurant that catered mostly to upper-crust tourists and local regulars.

One bottle had washed down their steak dinners. Schyler was affectionately clutching the other to her breasts now as she sashayed toward the car.

"Let's roll down the windows and drive real fast," she said excitedly.

Her eyes were more animated than Cash had ever seen them. They sparkled with amber lights. Champagne was good for Schyler Crandall's soul. She had shed her snooty air along with her inhibitions. She wasn't the boss lady. She wasn't the reigning princess of Belle Terre. She was one hundred percent pure woman. And one hundred percent of his body knew it. Her effect on him was being felt from the top of his head to the soles of his new shoes, which were almost as tight as she was.

"Okay, but I'll do the driving." Smiling to himself, he opened the car door for her and stood aside as she got in. "Why don't you take off your jacket?"

"Good idea." She set the bottle of champagne beside her on the seat and shrugged out of the linen jacket. Leaning forward, she shimmied her shoulders to get the sleeves off. Her breasts swayed beneath the blouse.

His penis took notice.

He laid her discarded jacket in the back seat along with his. As he went around the car, he whipped off the necktie and unbuttoned the first few buttons of his shirt. By the time he steered the car out onto the highway, Schyler's alligator heels were lying on their sides on the carpeted floorboard and her head was lolling against the seat. One foot was tucked up under her opposite thigh. Her knees were widely spread. It wasn't indecent. Her skirt was bunched between them.

What Cash was thinking was decidedly indecent.

"Such an odious man," she said around a wide yawn that would have mortified Macy Laurent. Schyler didn't even attempt to cover it.

Two of her jaw teeth had fillings, he noticed. He had never been in a dentist's chair until he went into the army. It hadn't mattered because he'd been blessed with good teeth. Neglecting semiannual checkups would have been unheard of in the mansion at Belle Terre.

"Who's odious? Me?" he asked.

Her head remained on the seat, but she turned it to look at him. A placid little smile was curving her lips upward. She had eaten off her lipstick. He liked her lips better without it. She had a real bedroom mouth, suitable for kissing, suitable for lots of things.

"No, not you. Joe Endicott, Jr."

"He's a prick."

She giggled. "Crude but true." For a moment she studied him. "How come when you say bad words they don't sound bad?"

"Don't they?"

"No," she replied, puzzled. "Just like Cotton. He cusses something terrible. Always has. Some of the first words I learned to say were swear words I'd overheard him using. Mama nagged him to clean up his language all the time." She yawned again. "I never thought bad language sounded bad coming from Cotton."

"Is the wind too strong?"

Her breasts rose on a deep, supremely lazy breath. They strained against her linen blouse, which by now had lost its starch. It looked touchable. Cash ached to feel her. He couldn't understand why he didn't, why he didn't just reach across the short distance and cover one of those soft mounds with his hand, pinch up one of her nipples with his fingertips. He had never exercised caution with a woman before. What he saw and wanted, he took. He usually got away with it, too.

"No, the wind feels wonderful," Schyler sighed. Her eyes slid closed. "Wake me up when we get to Heaven." She giggled again and began to sing, "When I get to Heaven, gonna put on my shoes, gonna walk all over God's Heaven." Her smile was winsome. "Veda used to rock me in the chairs on the veranda and sing that spiritual."

Cash thought she'd fallen asleep, but after a moment she said, "Silly name for a town, isn't it? Heaven. I love it and I hate it, know what I mean?"

He took her question seriously, *"Oui."*

"It's like this mole I have on my hip. It's ugly. I don't like it, but ... but it's a part of me. It wouldn't do any good to have it removed because every time I looked at that spot, I'd be reminded of that mole anyway. That's how I feel about Heaven and Belle Terre. I can leave, go to the other side of the world, but they're always there. With me." Her eyes popped open. "Am I drunk?"

He couldn't keep from laughing at her alarmed expression. "If you're sober enough to wonder, then you're not too far gone."

"Oh, good, good." Her eyes closed again. "It was delicious champagne, wasn't it?" She dragged her tongue over her lower lip.

Cash shifted the swollen flesh in his trousers to a more comfortable position. *"Oui, delicieux."*

"Are we home?" Schyler sat up, groggy and disoriented.

"Not quite. I want to show you something."

"There's nothing to see," she said querulously.

Beyond the car in any direction was dense woods. Judging by the long slanting shadows the tree trunks cast on the ground, it was getting close to sunset.

Cash pushed open his door and got out, taking the unopened bottle of champagne with him. "Come on. Don't be a spoilsport. And don't forget your shoes." Schyler put her heels back on and got out but leaned against the side of the car unsteadily, holding her head. "You okay?" Cash asked as he came around the rear of the car.

"A bowling tournament is being played inside my head. My eyeballs are the pins."

He laughed, disturbing the birds in the nearest tree. They set up a chattering protest. "What you need is the hair of the dog." He wagged the bottle of champagne in front of her face and she groaned. Taking her arm, he led her forward, into the temple of trees that surrounded them.

"These aren't hiking shoes, Cash," she complained. Her high heels sank into the soft ground. Milkweed stalks broke against her legs, spilling their white sap on her stockings.

He strengthened his grip on her arm and helped her along. "It's not far."

"To what?"

"To where we're going."

"I don't even know where we are."

"On Belle Terre."

"Belle Terre? I've never been here."

They were working their way up a gentle hill. The ground was garnished with purple verbena. Wild rosebushes were tangled around lesser shrubs, their pink blooms fragrant in the dusty, shimmering heat of late afternoon.

They crested the hill. Cash said, "Careful. It's steeper going down on this side."

At the bottom of the hill, Laurent Bayou made a gradual bend. Between there and the higher ground on which they stood grew hardwoods and pines, then, along the muddy banks of the bayou, cypresses. Late sunlight dappled the floor of the forest with golden light. It was lovely, wild, and primeval—a place for pagan worship.

"Cash!" Schyler exclaimed in fright when a winged animal went sailing from one tree to another not far from them. "Was that a bat?"

"A flying squirrel. They usually don't come out until dark. He's getting a head start."

She watched the squirrel's acrobatics until it disappeared among the leafy branches. Stillness descended. One could almost hear the beetles crunching paths through blowdowns. Iridescent insects skimmed along the brassy surface of the water. Bees buzzed among the flowering plants. A cardinal flitted through the trees like a red dart.

Schyler stood in awe of this spot unsullied by man. It was Nature in balance. Left alone it had beautifully perpetuated itself century after century, eon upon eon. She must still be drunk, she thought ruefully. She was waxing poetic. She commented on her observations to Cash. He didn't seem particularly surprised or amused.

"It does that to me, too. We're seeing a transformation take place." She looked around her but did't see any drastic changes in progress. He laughed. "We'd have to stay here several centuries to see it completed."

She consulted her wristwatch. "I probably should get back before then." He actually laughed at her joke. She liked that. It was the first time he had laughed without it being tinged with sarcasm. "What transformation?"

He propped his foot up on a boulder as his eyes swept the forest surrounding them. "I speculate that the original forest was destroyed by fire. It happened, oh, maybe a hundred years ago. See back there behind us," he said, pointing. "What kind of trees do you see? Mostly."

"Oak. Other hardwoods."

"Right. But after the fire, the first ones to grow back were pines, loblolly mainly. They were probably as thick as a nursery in just a few years after the fire. The saplings brought in birds, who carried seeds from the hardwoods of neighboring forests."

"And they took over."

He looked pleased that she knew. "Do you know why?"

She searched her memory, but shook her head. "I remember Cotton telling me that the deciduous usually outlive pines."

"The pine seeds germinate quickly in sunny soil. But deprived of sunlight, the saplings die out."

"So the taller the hardwoods get, the shadier the forest floor gets and—"

"You end up with what we've got here. The pines eventually giving way to the hardwoods."

"Then why don't all forests eventually become deciduous?"

"Because man tames most of them. This," he said with a sweep of his hand, "happens when a tame forest reverts to wilderness.

"It is untamed." She was impressed with his knowledge. Gazing up at him she said, "You like it best this way, don't you?"

"Yes. But it's damned hard to earn a living by admiring a view." He extended her his hand. "Come on."

He led her down the steep incline. They waded through pine needles that were ankle deep. He guided her to a blowdown near the water's edge. She could now see that the bayou wasn't really stagnant at this point, as she had thought when looking down on it from above. But the current was so lacking in energy, the water appeared motionless.

"I thought you didn't allow blowdowns to remain in the forest."

He tore the foil off the bottle of champagne, carefully putting it in his pocket. He disposed of the wire the same way after twisting it off. "Ordinarily I don't. Not here." He looked around him with reverence and awe, as one does in a cathedral. "Everything here is left alone. Nature works out its own problems. Nobody messes with the natural order of things here."

"But this is part of Belle Terre."

The cork popped out. The champagne spewed over his hand and showered Schyler. They laughed.

In that same jocular vein, she asked, "Aren't you taking a rather proprietary attitude over my land?"

He looked down at her for a long moment. "I'd kill anybody who tried to bother this place."

Schyler believed him. "You shouldn't say that. You might have to."

He shook his head. "Cotton feels the same way I do about it."

"Cotton?" Schyler asked, surprised.

"My mother is buried up there."

Schyler followed the direction of his gaze to the top of the hill they'd descended minutes earlier. "I had no idea."

"The priest wouldn't let her be buried in consecrated ground because she . . ." Cash took a drink of the champagne straight out of the bottle. "He just wouldn't."

"Because she was my father's mistress."

"I guess."

"She must have loved him very much."

He blew out a soft puff of air that sufficed as a bitter laugh. "She did that. She loved him." He took another drink. "More than she loved anything. More than she loved me."

"Oh, I doubt that, Cash," Schyler protested quickly. "No mother would put a man who wasn't even her husband above her child."

"She did." He set his foot on the log, almost but not quite touching her hip, and leaned down, propping himself on his knee. "You asked me why I've stuck around all this time."

"Yes."

"You want to know why I still live around here where everybody knows me as a bastard."

"I've wondered, yes."

His eyes penetrated hers. "Before she died, my mother made me promise never to leave Belle Terre as long as Cotton Crandall was alive. She made me swear that I wouldn't.''

Schyler swallowed emotionally. ''But why . . . why would she ask you to do that?''

He shrugged. ''Who knows? I guess I'm supposed to act as his guardian angel.''

''Guarding him against what?''

''Himself maybe.'' He switched subjects suddenly. ''Want some champagne?''

''I shouldn't.''

''What the hell?''

He nudged her shoulder with the bottle. She took it from him and drank. The wine foamed in her mouth, in her throat. ''It's too warm.''

Schyler passed the bottle back to him, but was arrested by the intensity with which he was watching her. The forest, which had been full of activity only moments ago, fell absolutely still. Nothing moved. She could feel the heat waves emanating up from the ground, through the dead log, through her clothing and entering her body through her thighs. Her ears began to ring with the profound silence. Despite the drink of champagne she'd just swallowed, her mouth was as dry as cotton.

''We'd better go.'' She stood up. Cash lowered his foot to the ground, but he didn't make a move to retrace their path. He continued to stare at her. Nervous, and eager to fill the silence, she started babbling, ''Thank you for helping me out with Endicott and for showing me this place. I would have never known it was here. It's beautiful. It's—''

He still had the bottle of champagne in his fist when he threw his arm around Schyler's neck and trapped her head in the crook of his elbow. He sealed her lips closed with a hot, wet kiss.

Schyler's arms closed around his lean torso. Her fingers dug into the supple muscles of his back. They turned toward each other until one's body was imprinted onto the front of the other.

They shared an eating kiss, where lips and tongues tried to taste as much as they could as quickly as possible. They came up for air and gazed deeply into each other's eyes. Their breathing was harsh and uneven.

''I broke all my rules with you.'' Cash watched his own hand slide down to her breast. He cupped it, lifted it, used his thumb to bring the nipple to a hard peak against her clothing. ''I didn't use a rubber. I never do that,'' he confessed, mystified by his own neglect. ''My motto is fuck 'em and forget 'em.'' Swiftly his eyes came back to hers. ''I can't forget it. I've tried.'' His hand slid over her belly; he pressed the *v* at the top of her thighs. ''Damn you, I want it again,'' he said gruffly.

''Me too.''

''*Oui?*''

''Yes. Where?''

''Here.''

''Here?''

''*Oui.*''

''*T—*''

''*Oui.*''

They started kissing again. His tongue probed the silky recess of her mouth with carnal implication. The muscles of her cheeks contracted, squeezing his tongue. He groaned and rubbed his erection against her belly. She reached down to touch him and made of her hand a gentle, caressing, sliding fist. He uttered a hoarse cry. As one, with mouths clinging, they dropped to their knees on the forest floor.

He pressed her shoulders between his hands and angled her backward. She landed on a bed of fallen leaves and pine needles that rustled more enticingly than satin sheets. Responding to a primitive masculine need to possess and dominate, Cash stretched out on top of her.

Schyler reacted with the same degree of passion, though her response was purely feminine. She opened her thighs. He burrowed, hard and urgent, against the warm, vulnerable softness of woman. The elements that made them different made this wonderful. Each released a long, soughing sound that was usually reserved for climaxing.

Raising her hips, Schyler struggled to work her skirt up her legs and out of his way. Cash was roughly rubbing his face against her breasts, his mouth open, moist and hot. He grappled with his belt buckle, but his desperation to be inside her made him clumsy and ineffective.

Between choppy gasps for breath, he cursed with frustration. Schyler knocked his hands aside and attacked the stubborn buckle herself. But she wasn't very dexterous either. Their hands batted at each other in their rush to undo his belt.

And then, simultaneously, they realized that their agonized sighs weren't all that they heard. Abruptly, Cash rolled off her and sat up.

"Cash? Did you hear—"

"Shh!" He held up one hand for quiet.

They listened. It came again—a low, unrecognizable sound.

Cash stood up. As fleet-footed as a deer and as silent as a shadow, he slipped away from Schyler and through the trees in the direction of the noise. His training as a jungle fighter served him well. He didn't even disturb the leaves of the plants he skimmed past. He drew his knife from the scabbard at the small of his back. He crept along the muddy banks of the bayou and circled the ropy trunk of a cypress.

"Jesus."

Schyler, leaving the love nest their bodies had ground into the undergrowth, scurried after him, sliding in the mud. "What is it?" she asked, stepping around him. *"Gayla!"*

 # THIRTY-FIVE

The young black woman looked up at them fearfully. Her eyes were red. Swelling and bleeding scratches had distorted one whole side of her face. Her clothes were in tatters. The exposed skin was covered with abrasions and cuts. She was missing one shoe.

Cash scanned both banks of the bayou and the hill above them. His eyes were as sharp as a machete. Schyler dropped to her knees in the mud. "Gayla, my God, Gayla." She repeated the name softly and reached out to touch her childhood friend. Gayla flinched.

"Don't be afraid, Gayla. It's me, Schyler." Distraught, Schyler glanced up at Cash. "She doesn't know me."

"Yes I do, Schyler." Gayla ran her tongue over the deep and nasty cut on her lower lip. It had dribbled blood onto her chest. "Don't look at me. Just go away. Please."

Tears welled in her chocolate-colored eyes. She gathered her limbs against her body and curled inward in an effort to make her shame invisible. Schyler lifted

Gayla's head onto her thigh and laid her hand along the smooth uninjured cheek. It was the only feature that made her recognizable. Schyler hoped the disfigurement done to her face would be temporary.

"Oh, I'm going to look at you plenty," Schyler whispered, "because I've missed you so much. We're going to talk. We're going to reminisce about old times and, when you're feeling better, we're going to giggle like girls."

A tear slid into one of the scratches on Gayla's cheek. "I'm not a girl anymore, Schyler. I'm a—"

"You're my friend," Schyler stressed.

Gayla closed her eyes and began to cry in earnest. "I don't deserve to be."

"Thank God none of us gets what she deserves." While she continued to hold Gayla, gently stroking her head, Schyler looked up at Cash. He'd been scouting around the immediate area. "Do you see anybody?"

"No." He knelt down and assessed the madman's handiwork. He touched Gayla's shoulder. "Did Jigger do this to you?" Gayla nodded. "That filthy son of a bitch," Cash mouthed. "He must have beat her up, then dumped her. Looks like she slid down the hill."

There was forest debris ensnared in her tight cap of hair. Twigs and leaves clung to her clothes. Her bare arms and legs were streaked with dirt.

"No, Mr. Boudreaux." Gayla pronounced his name correctly, in a musical, contralto, West Indian voice that was made even huskier because of her tears. "I slid down the hill, but Jigger didn't dump me here. I ran away from him."

"You came all this way on foot?"

"Yes."

"Is he looking for you?"

"No. I don't know. Just leave me alone. Forget you saw me. Let me die lying right here and I'll be happy. I can't go back. He'll kill me. I don't want to live, but I don't want to give him the pleasure of killing me."

"He's not going to kill you. He's not going to do anything to you because I'm going to protect you. And I'm damn sure not going to leave you here to die," Schyler said sternly. "Can you carry her up the hill?" she asked Cash. "If we can get her that far, I'll stay with her while you go call an ambulance."

"No!" Gayla nearly came up off the ground. "No, Jesus, no, please. He'll find me and kill me."

"You'll be safe in the hospital, Gayla."

Gayla, bordering on hysteria, shook her head emphatically, despite the pain it must have caused. "Jigger beat me, then locked me in the toolshed. But I got out. When he discovers I'm gone, he'll go crazy."

"He's already crazy."

"He'll find me no matter where I am. He'll kill me for running away, Schyler. Swear to God he will. He's told me he would and he will." She clutched double handfuls of Schyler's blouse. "If you help me, he'll hurt you, too. Go away, please. Don't touch me. I'm dirty. You don't want to mess with a whore like me."

"That's enough!" Schyler cried. "I'm not afraid of Jigger Flynn. Let him come anywhere near us and I'll shoot him myself." Gayla began to weep again; Schyler softened her tone of voice. "If you won't feel safe in the hospital, we'll take you to Belle Terre. I promise to keep you safe there."

Cash nudged Schyler aside. "Come on, Gayla. Can you put your arms around my neck? Yes you can," he urged gently, when she shook her head no. "Try. That's it. Clasp your hands now. That's good." He slid his arms beneath her back and knees and lifted her up.

"Cash, she's bleedin'," Schyler gasped. The back of Gayla's dress was soaked with bright red blood. "Gayla, what did he do to you?"

"She fainted," Cash told her. Gayla's head was lolling against his shoulder. "It's just as well. This is going to be a rough trip."

He started up the hill. Schyler picked up the bottle of champagne that he'd dropped and scrambled after him. Her high heels were caked with mud. Branches snagged the cloth of her expensive skirt. She paid them no heed. She was wondering how Gayla had survived tumbling down the steep hillside.

After what seemed like a trek up Mount Everest, they reached the car. Schyler hobbled ahead and wrenched open the back door. She jumped inside. "Lay her head in my lap. Get to the hosptial as fast as you can. I don't care what she said, she's got to get to the emergency room."

Cash laid Gayla on the back seat as Schyler had instructed, but he didn't withdraw his head and shoulders from the door. He stayed bent over, looking at her. "Well, what is it? Get going," she ordered curtly.

"They'll take care of her injuries at the hospital, but they'll have to call the sheriff about this." He nodded down at the unconscious woman. "He'll conduct a routine investigation, but he won't do a frigging thing to Jigger. In a few days the hospital will release her. Jigger wil be waiting for her. Next time it'll be worse."

Schyler stared down into Gayla's brutalized face and knew that he was right. "All right, let's take her to Belle Terre. I don't know if I can get a doctor to come out there—"

"I can."

Cash slammed the door and ran around to the driver's side of the car. Within seconds they were under way, speeding down the highway through the closing twilight.

"Another drink, Tricia?"

"No thank you, darlin'. Mrs. Graves should be calling us in to supper any minute now."

Tricia was fanning herself with the insubstantial afternoon edition of *The Heaven Trumpet*. There had been a full accounting of the generous pounding the Junior League had sponsored for the Glee Williams family. Tricia was feeling smug and piqued—smug because she was given credit for the astounding outpouring of generosity, piqued because Schyler had been the one who had actually organized the benevolent gesture and had done most of the legwork involved in collecting the food, staples, and used clothing.

"It's really getting tiresome," she said petulantly, "having to hold supper for Schyler every night. She's always late."

"She didn't know for sure when she'd be getting back from Endicott's." Ken sucked on a bourbon-flavored ice cube he'd shaken from the bottom of his glass. "It's a long drive."

"You'd think she'd at least call."

"Relax. Here she comes now." Ken set his empty glass on a wicker table and stepped off the veranda onto the steps. "Driving like a bat outta hell, too. That's not like her."

"Maybe she finally got the message about being perpetually late." Languidly Tricia laid down the newspaper and left her chair to go inside.

"What the hell?" Ken asked rhetorically.

Cash pulled the car to a jarring halt just a few feet from the steps. He opened his door, rolled out, and wrenched open the rear door. Bending at the waist, he reached inside and lifted Gayla out.

"What the hell is going on here?" Ken blocked Cash's path as he set his foot on the first step leading up to the veranda. "Schyler, I'm waiting for you to tell me—"

"Move out of the way, Ken. Tricia, are any of the guest rooms made up?" Both Howells were staring at Cash and Gayla as though they were aliens who had hatched in the bayou. "Well, answer me," Schyler demanded. "Are any of the guest rooms made up?"

Tricia's eyes found her sister's. "What's the matter with that girl?"

"She's been beaten to within an inch of her life. Which bedroom should I put her in?"

"You don't mean to bring her inside the house, do you?"

Schyler emitted a breath of disbelief and disgust. She looked toward Ken for support. He was glaring at Cash where they stood eye to eye on the steps, Ken one up from Cash and directly in his way.

"What is the matter with you two?" Schyler exclaimed. "Don't you recognize Gayla?"

"I know who she is," Tricia snapped.

"She's seriously hurt."

"Then I suggest a hospital."

"She's coming inside."

Schyler went around Ken and indicated to Cash that he should do the same. She was glad that he was holding Gayla in his arms; otherwise he would have used physical force to move Ken out of his path. From the murderous look in his eyes, he would have enjoyed that immensely.

Schyler crossed the veranda and reached for the handle on the screen door. Tricia stepped in front of her and flattened herself against the door to hold it shut. "Mama would turn over in her grave if she knew you were bringing them inside Belle Terre."

"Gayla's been inside. Many times. We used to play with her, remember? Her mother ironed your clothes, washed your dishes, cooked the food you ate. And Veda was blacker than Gayla."

"This has got nothing to do with race."

"Then what?"

"You force me to be unkind, Schyler. She's Jigger Flynn's whore," Tricia shouted.

Schyler went hot with fury. "And whose fault is that?"

Tricia faltered but recovered quickly. "I suppose you're going to suggest it's mine."

"Well isn't it?"

"You blame me for everything that goes wrong around here!"

"I can't argue with you about anything now, Tricia," Schyler said, having lost patience with Tricia's childish tantrum. "This is a house. It isn't the holy of holies. Neither Gayla nor Cash can or will defile it. Mama will never know who comes inside. Even if she's watching with disapproval from on high, there's not a damn thing she can do about it. Now get out of my way."

Schyler pushed her sister aside and jerked open the door.

"You know what Cotton thinks of *him*," Ken shouted behind her.

She turned and thought about that for a moment. Then she said, "There's nothing Cotton can do about it now either." Schyler looked at Cash and inclined her head toward the spacious foyer beyond the door. For the first time in his life, Cash Boudreaux stepped over the threshold of Belle Terre.

Mrs. Graves was standing in the foyer, looking like the last formidable guard at the gates of heaven. "Are any of the guest rooms made up?" Schyler asked her.

"Not for the likes of her." She crossed her arms over her shriveled breasts as though visibly withdrawing any responsibility for what was about to take place.

"Then she can use my room." Schyler said calmly. "Make up a guest room for me." She headed for the stairs. "By the way, Mrs. Graves, that will be your last official duty at Belle Terre. Kindly rid the quarters of all your personal belongings. I'll have a severance check waiting for you on the hall table within an hour."

Schyler ran ahead of Cash up the sweeping staircase. He took the stairs two at a time. Mrs. Graves was left standing slack-jawed in the hall. Tricia and Ken were stone-faced. Schyler ignored their glares from below as she reached the second-story landing and pointed out her room to Cash. He went ahead of her. By the time she reached the doorway, he was already depositing Gayla on her bed.

"It's going to make a helluva mess." When he withdrew his arms from beneath Gayla's limp body, the front of his shirt was bloodstained.

"It doesn't matter. I just made a bigger mess downstairs," Schyler muttered as she bent over Gayla. "While I undress her, you call the doctor."

"No doctor."

"What?" Schyler sprang erect and stared at him incomprehensively.

"Have her undressed by the time I get back." He headed for the door.

"Wait!" Schyler charged after him. Her fingers slipped on his bloody sleeve, but she managed to stop him. "I thought you said you could get a doctor here. Where are you going?"

"I'm the doctor, but I've got to go get my stuff."

Her face turned pale. "Are you crazy? She needs professional help. She's bleeding and I don't even know—"

"It's vaginal bleeding. She's had a miscarriage." Schyler sucked in a sharp breath and held it. She gaped at him speechlessly. "I recognize it. My mother lost a baby. There was nobody else to take care of her. I had to. She told me what to do. I know how to deal with it."

Schyler spun around and lurched for the phone. She picked up the receiver, but before it ever made it to her ear, Cash yanked it out of her hand and slammed it back down. "You promised Gayla."

"I can't take responsibility for this."

"You promised."

"But I didn't know it was anything this bad. What if she dies?"

They'd been shouting at each other. Cash pressed her shoulders between his hands and lowered his voice drastically. "I can help her. Trust me." He gave her shoulders a hard squeeze. "Trust me."

For ponderous moments, Schyler stared into his eyes. She glanced down at Gayla. When her eyes moved back to his, her posture went as limp as her linen blouse. Lips barely moving, she said, "If anyone downstairs tries to stop you—"

"I'll take care of it. Nothing would give me greater pleasure."

Schyler watched him go, praying that she had made the right decision. Then she turned back to the bed and the grim chore ahead of her.

THIRTY-SIX

Schyler had time to sponge Gayla off before Cash returned. Dirt and dried blood had concealed evidence of previous beatings. With each swipe of the wet cloth, Schyler's pity for her friend increased in proportion to her hatred for Jigger Flynn. By the time Cash came rushing through the door, there were tears of pity standing in Schyler's eyes.

"She's got marks and scars all over her," she told him.

"I doubt Jigger is a tender lover."

"He's an animal that should be locked up."

"Don't hold your breath." He sat down on the edge of the bed and studied Gayla's face. "How is she otherwise?"

"No more bleeding."

"Good. Shown any signs of coming around?"

"She's conscious. She moaned while I was washing her."

Cash laid his hand on Gayla's forehead and called her name softly. "Gayla, wake up and talk to me. I need to ask you some questions." Her eyelids flickered open. She looked at him, then over his shoulder at Schyler. "You're at Belle Terre. Safe."

"Safe." They watched her cut and swollen lips form the disbelieving word. Her eyes closed peacefully.

"Don't go back to sleep yet," Cash said, shaking her awake. "I'm going to treat you, but I have to ask you some questions first."

She struggled to keep her eyes open. "Okay."

He opened his leather pouch and took out a jar of salve. He folded back the sheet and began applying the waxy, yellow substance to the scratches on her chest and arms. "How far along was your pregnancy?"

Tears sprang into her eyes as the old fears swamped her again. Her face twisted in anguish. "I couldn't have his baby. Devil man that he is, I just couldn't."

"There is no baby. Not anymore." Cash clasped her hand reassuringly. "How far along were you before you started bleeding? How late was your period?"

"Six, eight weeks maybe."

"*Bien.*"

"I took the medicine you sent me."

"Medicine?" Schyler exclaimed. She turned on Cash. "You knew about this before today?"

He shushed her. Gayla was still speaking in a faint, faraway voice. "Jigger said you told him it would fix me right up."

Schyler demanded Cash's attention again. "You gave that man medicine for her?"

"*Oui,* now shut up."

"You dealt with him?" Schyler asked, flabbergasted.

Cash whipped his head around. "I did. He came to my house, told me Gayla was bleeding. That she'd had a miscarriage. What was I supposed to do, ignore him?"

"You could have told me."

"So you could do what? Go butting into business that didn't concern you? So you could shoot up his place one more time and get him really pissed off at you?" She fell silent, but she was still fuming. "Besides, that was when Cotton was at his worst. It didn't look like he was going to pull through. You had your hands full and didn't need anything more to worry about."

He went back to his unpleasant task. He laid his finger against a circular scar on the side of Gayla's breast. "Cigarette burn," he said softly. Gayla whimpered with a terrible memory. Cash's face turned compassionate. "What brought on the miscarriage?"

Gayla rolled to her side and buried her face in the snowy pillowcase. Schyler and Cash looked at each other, puzzled. She had said she didn't want Jigger's baby, but now she seemed upset at the mention of her miscarriage. Cash touched her bare shoulder and turned her over. "Gayla, tell me. What happened? Did Jigger get too rough with you?"

She shook her head slowly from side to side. Tears rolled down her ravaged cheek, liquifying dried blood. "I did it myself. I started the bleeding."

"Jesus," Cash breathed.

Schyler raised both hands to her lips and pressed them until they were white.

"I couldn't have his baby," Gayla averred in a hoarse voice. "I'll go to hell, won't I, for killing it? God'll send me to hell for murdering my own baby."

She was on the brink of hysteria. Cash leaned over her pressing her back onto the pillows. "You're not going to hell, Gayla. You're not the sinner. You're the one sinned against. Did the medicine I sent help you?"

"Yes. Thank you, Mr. Boudreaux. I was real sick till Jigger brought me the medicine. I followed the directions and took it all. It stopped the bleeding. I was feeling better, but then . . ."

She looked around the room warily, as though she were in the witness box and the defendant on trial was likely to kill her on the spot if she told the truth.

"Then what, Gayla?" Cash prompted softly, dabbing at a cut on her shoulder with peroxide-soaked cotton.

Gayla looked up at Schyler. Her dark eyes were shimmering with tears of remorse. "He made me go with one of the gentlemen." The words were almost inaudible. "I didn't want to. I told him I couldn't because I wasn't completely healed up yet, but—" She turned her face into the pillow again. "The man paid a hundred dollars for me. Jigger made me go."

Cash glanced at Schyler. She shook her head in wordless incredulity. Gayla's tale was medieval. That kind of subservance couldn't occur in the twentieth century. But it had.

"Did this gentleman," Cash said with a sneer, "make you have sex with him?" Gayla nodded her head. Cash swore viciously. "Why did Jigger beat you today?"

"I refused to go again today. I told Jigger I wasn't feeling good, that I'd started bleeding again. But he didn't want to make the man mad."

"Was it the same man as before?"

"I think so. I saw his car."

"Who? Who is he?"

"I don't know his name. But he . . ."

"What?"

"He . . . he takes pictures of me."

Schyler shivered. Cash mentally filed the information. "Exactly what happened this afternoon?"

"I said I wouldn't go. The man got tired of waiting and went away. After he left, Jigger whipped me with his razor strap. He did this," she gestured at her swollen jaw, "with his fist. It had a chain wrapped around it."

Cash called Jigger a gutter name, which Schyler thought was well deserved.

"He told me to reconsider my decision while I was locked in the shed." Gayla's lips began to quiver. "That's the worst beating he's ever given me. The next time, he'll kill me. I know it. I had to run away while I had the chance." Her face contorted with anxiety. "He'll kill me when he finds me."

"He can't touch you as long as you're here." Schyler laid a reassuring hand on Gayla's arm. "You don't have to ever be afraid of him again."

Gayla didn't look so certain. "You don't hate me, Schyler, for what I've done?"

"Of course not. You were victimized."

"Mama couldn't work. She was sick. I had to feed her, buy her medicine. I couldn't find a job, so I took one serving drinks in the beer joint. Mama would have killed me if she'd known what I was doing. I told her I was working at the Dairy Mart."

She wet her lips and twisted the hem of the sheet Cash had pulled up over her. "Mama got sicker. I asked Jigger for a raise. He said there was only one way I could make more money."

"Shh, Gayla, don't," Schyler said.

"I went with that first man 'cause I was gonna get fifty dollars out of it. I cried and cried afterwards because of Jimmy Don. I knew he would hate me if he ever found out. I thought it would just be that once. That's all, I swear. I didn't set out to become a whore."

"I know. You don't have to tell me anymore."

"But that fifty dollars went fast. And I needed some more." Her shoulders shook. "I went with another man. Then another. Jigger kept bringing them to me."

"Gayla, nobody needs to hear a confession," Cash said. He cradled the sobbing woman in his arms and said to Schyler, "I need to examine her. Can you bring her something to drink? Hot tea? Something?"

Schyler pressed Gayla's arm once more before withdrawing. Outside the door she pulled closed behind her, she let go a long, deep breath and for a moment leaned back against the wall. She was fatigued, physically and emotionally, but she couldn't rest yet. She went downstairs.

Ken was nowhere in sight. Tricia was in the front parlor. She stopped pacing when she saw Schyler and stormily followed her into the kitchen. Schyler put the kettle on the stove and turned on the burner beneath it.

"You weren't serious when you fired Mrs. Graves, were you?"

"Thank you for reminding me, Tricia. I need to write her a check."

"I won't let you fire her."

"I already have. I despise the woman. I have ever since I came home."

"But you can't fire her just like that," Tricia said, snapping her fingers inches in front of Schyler's nose, "just because she expressed out loud what Ken and I were thinking. Something's happened to you, Schyler. You've gone off the deep end. Lately, you've become unreasonable."

"I fired Mrs. Graves because she insulted a friend of mine. And even though the friend was unconscious at the time and didn't hear the insult, I did. As to being unreasonable," she said reflectively, "perhaps you're right." She calmly set the pot of hot tea she'd prepared on a tray. Picking up the tray, she faced her sister. "Mrs. Graves can wait until morning to leave. I really don't have time to write out a check now."

Tricia's face fell. She was right on Schyler's heels as she headed toward the stairs. "You won't get away with this, Miss High-and-Mighty. Where do you get off, coming home after six years and throwing your weight around, undoing everything that I've done?"

Schyler turned and confronted her. "Everything you've done needs undoing, Tricia."

Tricia went as straight and rigid as an arrow. Through clenched teeth she warned, "First thing in the morning, Cotton will hear about this."

Schyler set the tray on the hall table and backed Tricia into the wall. "Cotton will hear about nothing," she said through clenched teeth. "Do you understand me?"

"Watch and see."

"If you go barging into the hospital and upset him, what might happen? He could have another heart attack, right? He could die. Suddenly. And then where would all your plans for selling Belle Terre be? Out the window. Because I'm sure Daddy's will divides it equally between us, and I'll see you in hell before I'll ever let my half of it be sold. Your chances of talking Cotton into it are so slim as to be negligible. But your chances with me are positively zero." She picked up the tray again. "Think about that, baby sister, before you go to Cotton and start tattling."

Inside the bedroom, Cash was gently tucking the covers around Gayla. Schyler looked at him for information.

"I don't think she did much damage, though God knows how she kept from it." He ran his hand through his hair, which was already untidy. "Believe me, you don't want to hear the details. It's a miracle she didn't bleed to death."

"Does she need a transfusion?" Schyler asked, looking down at Gayla and keeping her voice low.

"I was afraid she might, but I don't think so. If I did, I'd drive her to the hospital myself. She wasn't bleeding from her uterus. She'd been . . . well . . . scratched up inside." Schyler winced. "Those scratches had opened up, thanks to the shutter-bug. I found some Kotex in the bathroom. Change the pad often. If the bleeding increases, let me know. If she stays in bed a few days, she'll be all right."

"What about her face?"

"No structural damage. Once the swelling goes down, she'll be as pretty as ever. The scratches and cuts will heal."

"After the trauma she's lived through the last few years, I don't know if she'll ever be completely healed." Schyler extended him the tray. "Here's the tea."

Cash reached into his bag again and took out a small vial. He uncorked it and poured several drops of the contents into the tea. "What is that?" Schyler asked.

"The narcs don't know about this one. It's an ancient recipe handed down through generations of *traiteurs*. It'll keep Gayla asleep for several hours." He cupped Gayla's head in his hand and lifted it off the pillow. "Gayla, drink this." He placed the rim of the china cup between her battered lips. "It'll make you feel like you're on a flying carpet headed for Nirvana."

Gayla sipped the strong, potion-laced tea. She gazed up at Schyler. "How come you're doing this for me?"

"Stupid question, Gayla. I loved your mother. And I love you."

"I don't deserve anybody's love," she said solemnly. "Not even God's."

"He loves you, too."

Gayla shook her head with conviction. "Not after I killed my baby. That's a mortal sin." She lapsed into a moment of self-examination. "It doesn't matter though. Jimmy Don couldn't ever love me again after all the men who've had me. And I loved Jimmy Don more than I loved God." She gazed up at them, her eyes now made lambent by Cash's potion. "Do you think that's why God let Jigger get me? Was God jealous of Jimmy Don?"

Cash set the empty cup on the nightstand. "I'm a long way from being a prophet, Gayla. But I don't think God shits on people the way other people do."

Gayla seemed to take comfort in that unorthodox piece of theology. Her eyelids closed. Seconds later, her entire body went limp. "She's out," Cash said, standing up.

Schyler looked at him, noticing for the first time how tired he seemed. He had changed shirts while he was gone, but otherwise, he looked worse for wear. She cleared her throat and began awkwardly, "Cash, I don't know how to thank you."

"Forget it. I didn't do it for you."

"Yes, but—"

The sudden pounding on the door halted whatever she was about to say. She was too stunned to respond. Cash grunted a dangerous, "Who is it?"

"Deputy Sheriff Walker."

Cash uttered an expletive beneath his breath. Then he called out, "Hold on a sec."

His hand caught Schyler around the back of the neck and yanked her forward. He kissed her mouth soundly, rolling his tongue over her lips until they were red and wet and shiny. He roughly rubbed his stubbled chin against her throat. He tore open two buttons of her blouse, reached inside and pushed down her bra strap.

"Try to look like you've been screwing."

THIRTY-SEVEN

"What the hell do you want, Walker? It better be damned important." Deputy Sheriff Walker flinched when Cash Boudreaux querulously yanked open the door. He cursed his rotten luck. Sheriff Patout would have his ass if he didn't follow through on this call, but, hell, he didn't want a hassel with Boudreaux. From the looks of it, the Cajun was in a tetchy state of mind, too. He was a far cry from a good ol' boy any day of the week. Anybody who went up against the ornery cuss was likely to get a knife between his ribs. Still, it was his duty to check out this complaint.

Cash had one arm braced on the doorjamb. His body was blocking the narrow opening. The deputy peered around him, trying to look stern and official. That wasn't easy for a man who had to shave only every other day.

"Hiya, Cash, Miss Schyler." He tipped his hat at her. She was standing in the background wearing whisker burns around her mouth and a dazed expression in her eyes. Damn Boudreaux's luck. His legendary dick got him invited between even the classiest thighs.

Walker drew his thoughts back to professional matters. "Domestic quarrel in here. Is that right?"

"A domestic . . ." Cash rolled his eyes and cursed. "That dumbass. Is he talking about Gayla? Gayla just had a little accident. She got banged up a little. A few scratches. I'm hurting a whole helluva lot worse than she is."

"Whadaya mean, Cash? What's goin' on?"

"Well," Cash drew out the word and glanced over his shoulder at Schyler, "I don't have to tell you *everything,* do I?"

The deputy cleared his throat importantly and said, "Yeah, you do. Everything."

Cash stared him down, then cursed in apparent exasperation. "All right. You see me and Schyler were having a little picnic out in the woods." He tilted his head.

Walker followed the direction he indicated and spotted the half-full bottle of champagne standing on the nightstand. "I wasn't exactly nibbling on fried chicken. Understand what I'm saying?" Walker swallowed hard and bobbed his head. "In fact," Cash said, "I was really getting with it, when here comes one of Jigger's whores tumbling down the hill."

Walker guffawed. "You and me both've seen whores with their heels in the air."

Cash's face changed. His eyes turned cold. Walker began sweating and cursed his stupidity. He'd gone too far.

But Cash went on easily. "Right. I didn't think anything about it. I was anxious to continue what we'd been doing." He frowned. "I'd forgotten that Schyler knows Gayla from way back. She got upset because Gayla was hurt and asked me to fix her up. So, we called off our . . . uh, *picnic* and brought Gayla here. She's sleeping, but if you want to come on in and look for yourself . . ." He stepped aside and swept his arm wide.

The deputy glanced at the bed, where Jigger's whore was indeed sleeping peacefully. He looked at Schyler and blushed to the tips of his ears. Sure enough, she looked like she could have been the main course at a picnic with Cash Boudreaux. Her clothes and hair were in a mess. She seemed embarrassed and guilty as hell to be caught seen with Boudreaux. Shifting from one foot to another, she raised one hand to her blouse and nervously fidgeted with an unfastened button. A spectacular amount of cleavage was showing. He'd like to get a closer look, but the Cajun probably wouldn't want him ogling his current woman. Cash was touchy about things like that.

"No, that's okay, Cash. I don't need to come in." Walker started to move away, but paused. "Only . . . Well, Mr. Howell said that maybe Jigger Flynn was involved."

"Jigger? Did you see Jigger anywhere around, Schyler?" Boudreaux consulted with her over his shoulder.

"Uh, no." She self-consciously smoothed her hand over her touseled hair. "I didn't see him."

Cash shrugged. "All we saw was Gayla barreling down that hill end over end."

"What was she doing out in the woods all by herself?"

"How the hell should I—No, wait. On the way here, she mumbled something about communing with God."

"God?"

"Look, I don't know what the hell she was muttering about, okay?"

"Uh, yeah, okay."

"So is that it?"

"Well—"

"If so, beat it. We've got better things to do." He leaned forward and whispered, "Give me a break, Walker. I've got a hard-on that's stiff as a pike and I'm beginning to fear this just ain't my day to get laid."

Walker laughed and jabbed Cash in the ribs. "I know what that's like, man."

"Then have a little pity and get the hell out of here."

Louder than was necessary, Walker said, "Well, I'd better let y'all get about your business. Sorry to have bothered y'all." He gave Cash a broad wink. "Miss Schyler, ma'am." He tipped his hat and turned away. He had almost reached the top of the stairs when she surprised him by catching up.

"I'll show you out, Mr. Walker."

She fell into step with him. Walker thought that showed real moxey. Catch a lady with her pants down and she's still a lady. As they went downstairs side by side, he gazed about him. He hadn't done too badly. He had parted company with Boudreaux on a friendly basis and he'd got to take a gander at the inside of Belle Terre.

He would have something exciting to tell the wife after his shift. She would pester him with questions, wanting to know what this and that looked like. Damn! He hadn't noticed the color of Miss Schyler Crandall's bedroom. What the hell, he'd make something up. The wife would never know the difference.

There was a tense moment when they went past the parlor. Ken and Tricia watched from the arched opening. "Well?" Ken demanded, stepping into the foyer.

"Cash and I explained everything to Deputy Walker. He's agreed that Gayla should stay here," Schyler said smoothly. She guided the deputy to the door. "Thank you so much for stopping by."

The door was closed behind Walker before he fully realized what had happened. Schyler turned to face the Howells. They both looked ready to bludgeon her. Before she could give it much thought, something at the top of the stairs attracted her attention. Cash was coming down them, casually trailing his hand along the banister.

Tricia and Ken turned to stare with open animosity. His appearance only fueled their hostility. "I won't have that black whore sleeping under my roof," Tricia ground out.

"You have no choice," Schyler said evenly. "Gayla is here to stay for as long as she wants to. When I've had a chance to explain the situation to Cotton, I'm sure he'll be in full agreement with my decision." Tired as she was, Schyler dared either of them to take issue with her.

Ken accepted the challenge. "What about him? Have you asked him to spend the night, too?"

"Thanks, but I've already made other plans," Cash replied politely, a sardonic smirk on his lips.

Tricia looked at Cash with condescending speculation as she passed him on her way upstairs. "Excuse me," she said with hauteur.

Ken was less subtle when he went past. "You'll be sorry, Boudreaux."

"I doubt it."

Seconds later, the slamming of their bedroom door reverberated through the house. Schyler blew out her breath. "I won't be winning any popularity contests around here any time soon."

"Does it matter?"

"Not if I'd have to do anything differently, no." She stood facing him awkwardly, clasping and unclasping her hands at her waist. She was able to stand up to her sister's and Ken's angst, but she faltered beneath Cash's steady stare, especially in light of the lie he'd told the deputy. She could feel the whisker burns around her lips. She hadn't looked in a mirror lately but knew they must be obvious. At the very least she looked well kissed. That couldn't have won her any points with either Ken or Tricia.

"I don't like being indebted to you," she told Cash candidly.

"What'll you give me?"

"What do you want?"

"You know damn well what I want," he growled. "But for now, one drink would cancel all debts."

"This way."

She turned and led him toward the formal parlor; however, he paused in the doorway of the dining room with the yellow silk walls. Schyler, turning, watched him curiously for several seconds. "Cash? Coming?"

"Oui," he replied absently. Beneath his breath he whispered, "For you, *Maman.*"

Schyler went to the sideboard that served as a liquor cabinet and withdrew a decanter of bourbon. She poured a generous portion into a tumbler. "Ice? Water?"

When he didn't answer, she turned and caught him pivoting slowly, taking in every aspect of the room. "Cash?" she repeated. He came to attention with a start. "How do you want your drink?"

"Neat." He came to her, took the glass from her hand and tossed back the contents. He extended the glass, she poured more of the liquor. He drank it the same way.

"That's two drinks," she remarked.

"Then I guess I'll be indebted to you."

"That would be a switch." Since he had set his glass down, she capped the Waterford decanter.

"You're not having one?"

"Ice water." The two ice cubes she took from the silver bucket rattled noisily in the glass. She splashed water over them and took a drink. "Champagne always makes me thirsty."

"And drunk."

"I should have warned you."

"I didn't mind."

He was the first to look away from their long stare. He took in the luxurious surroundings, which bespoke wealth and refinement that was generations old. "You've never been inside Belle Terre before, have you?"

"No," he answered tersely. "Pretty fancy."

"Most of the furniture and accessories in this room are replacements of the originals. The Union army didn't have much of an appreciation for the house. When they left it, they burned what little could have been salvaged. Only the rug and that clock on the mantel are originals. An enterprising Laurent was able to sneak them out."

"How'd they get so rich to start with?"

"There was always timber, of course. But they invested the money they brought from France in several plantations. Sugarcane. Rice. Most of the family never even saw those. They were miles away. They only grew their household crops around here."

"Who's that?"

She glanced toward the oil portrait hanging above the marble mantel. "Macy's great-grandmother."

Cash gazed at the thin, pale woman in the portrait. "Not bad. Not a knockout, but not bad."

"How sexist!"

He looked down at Schyler, letting his eyes rove over her hair and face and figure. Unlike Walker, he didn't avoid looking at her exposed cleavage. He even touched the smooth skin with his fingertip and watched it glide over the soft curves as he asked, "Will your portrait hang up there some day? Will a couple of descendants stand in this spot and discuss your attributes?"

"I doubt if I'll ever have a portrait painted. And if I did, it wouldn't be right to hang it up there."

"How come?"

"I'm not a Laurent. Not even half of one. I came to live at Belle Terre purely by chance."

He studied her for a long moment, then abruptly withdrew his caressing hand. "I gotta go. Gayla should be fine in a few days. I left some ointment on the table by the bed. Apply it twice a day to those scratches on her arms and legs."

"Do you think Jigger will come looking for her?"

"I wouldn't be surprised. Be careful."

He had made it to the front door before Schyler caught up with him. She was puzzled over his rush to leave. She was also irrationally disappointed. "Will you be at the landing in the morning?"

He shook his head no. "I'll go straight to where we're cutting and start marking trees. We've got that order to fill, remember?"

"Actually, I didn't. So much has happened since our meeting with Joe Jr." She trailed Cash out onto the veranda, inexplicably reluctant to have him go. "Cash?" He turned. "That lie you told the deputy . . ."

"It wasn't exactly a lie, was it?"

"Yes, yes it was. And I didn't approve."

"Tough. I didn't have time to consult you first."

"It'll be all over town tomorrow that we were making out in the woods."

"That's the price you'll pay for taking in Gayla. Sorry?"

"No, of course not. Only . . ."

"Only . . . ?"

"I just wish you had told Walker something else."

"I had to get his mind on us and off her."

"Well your lie certainly worked to do that."

"*Oui*, it did."

She wet her lips. They still tasted like him. The whisker burns stung. "Do lies always come to you that easily?"

He backed into the darkness and was swallowed up by it. "Always."

THIRTY-EIGHT

"I suppose you expect me to wait on her hand and foot."

"On the contrary, Tricia. I expect you to pretend that Gayla isn't here."

"Good. That's what I plan to do."

The two sisters were in the downstairs hall. Schyler was dressed and ready to go to work. She had just spoken to Cotton over the telephone, promising to visit him that afternoon with a full account of her interview with Endicott.

"Gayla only drank tea for breakfast and then went back to sleep," Schyler told Tricia. "I imagine she'll sleep most of the day. I've left fruit juice on the night-stand beside her bed, along with the muffins Mrs.Graves baked yesterday. If Gayla gets hungry before I come home, she can eat those without having to disturb you. I've left her a note to call the office if she needs me."

"Mrs. Graves left this morning."

"Good. That's one less thing I have to worry about."

"Don't expect me to do any housekeeping. This place can rot and fall down for all I care."

"I'll start looking for a housekeeper as soon as I get to the office."

"And what am I supposed to do in the meantime?"

Impatiently Schyler said, "In the meantime, you can fend for yourself or go hungry."

Tricia's eyes narrowed. "You can't order me around like you do everybody else, including my husband. It's going to stop, Schyler, do you hear me?"

"I'm sure everyone in the neighboring parish heard you, Tricia. Kindly stop yelling at me."

"I have every right to yell. You've got Cajun white trash and a nigger whore traipsing through my house."

Schyler came close to slapping her. Perhaps she would have had the telephone not rung just then. Instead of raising a hand to Tricia, she yanked up the receiver. "It's for Ken." Laying the receiver on the table, she picked up her handbag and left before she submitted to an impulse to throttle her adopted sister.

Ken took the call upstairs. "Hello?"

"Yiya, Kenny."

Sweat popped out on his forehead. "I've got it, Tricia." He waited to make sure that she had hung up the extension downstairs before he said anything more. "What the hell do you think you're doing by calling here? I told you never to call me here."

"What you told me ain't worth shit. If it was, Kenny, I'd have my money by now, wouldn't I? It really pisses me off when people don't keep their word to me."

"I asked you for more time." Ken slumped down on the unmade bed and massaged his forehead.

"And like a sap I granted you more time. Have I got my money yet? No."

"I'll get it to you."

"Tomorrow."

"But—"

"Tomorrow."

The telephone went dead. Ken stared vacantly at it for a long time before hanging it up. He didn't have the energy to move, so he sat dejectedly on the edge of the bed. When he finally raised his head, he saw that Tricia was standing in the doorway looking at him curiously.

"Who was that?"

"Nobody." He stood up and went to his closet, randomly selecting a tie. As he did it, he was uncomfortably reminded of a noose.

"It was somebody," she said petulantly. "I didn't like the sound of his voice."

"I don't like the sound of yours," Ken said, shooting her a hateful look. "Not when it's got that edge to it and not this early in the morning."

"We need to talk."

"We talked until the wee hours last night."

"And nothing was resolved. What are you going to do about her?" She aimed a finger in the direction of Schyler's bedroom where Gayla Frances lay recovering.

"There's not much I can do. We called the sheriff. You saw how that turned out. Personally I don't want to get involved with Jigger Flynn. If you're smart you won't either."

Lighting a cigarette, Tricia snorted. "Hardly. All we need around here is another lowlife. They seem to be taking over Belle Terre. If Schyler had her way we'd become a branch of the Salvation Army."

Ken laughed. For once Tricia wans't flattered that her joke had gone over.

"I'm glad you think all this is funny," she snapped. She was on his heels as he went downstairs. "I don't think it's at all amusing that we've got a former servant's daughter residing here like she was the Queen of Sheba. Or that my sister," she sneered the word, "has her trashy lover strutting around here like he owned the place."

"Boudreaux isn't her lover."

Tricia laughed out loud. "Will you grow up? Of course he's her lover. Didn't you see the way she looked at him when he came down those stairs? Are you blind? Or is it that you just close your eyes to what you don't want to see?"

On top of his recent telephone call, Ken didn't need Tricia's harping. "Look, I don't like the way Schyler has come in and taken over everything either, but I don't know how to stop her."

Tricia flung back her hair and faced him challengingly. "Well you'd better find a way, darling."

"Or what?"

"Or I'll take matters into my own hands." She gave him a feline smile. "And you're a lot nicer than I am."

"Knock, knock?"

Schyler, holding the phone in the crook of her shoulder, signaled for Ken to come in. He closed the door of the landing office behind him. If he noticed the fresh coat of paint on it, he made no remark.

"That will be wonderful, Mrs. Dunne," Schyler said into the receiver as she smiled at Ken. "Yes, it does seem like providence, doesn't it? . . . And we'll look so forward to having you at Belle Terre . . . This afternoon then? . . . Very good. Good-bye."

She hung up and whooped loudly. "I can't believe it. Mrs. Dunne was a cook in the public school cafeteria and comes highly recommended. She quit several years ago so she could stay at home with her ailing husband. When he died, she contacted an agency in New Orleans that specializes in domestics. When I called them, they referred her. Isn't that a coincidence? She won't have to relocate, except to move into the quarters. And I won't have to exhaust myself with interviews. She won't mind looking after Daddy either." She paused for breath and smiled broadly. "Well, what do you think?"

"Will all our meals taste like school cafeteria food?"

"It can't be any worse than what Mrs. Graves served." She shuddered. "Where did Tricia find that stick woman?"

"Search me. That's Tricia's department."

She let him get seated comfortably before asking, "Why didn't you interfere when she fired Veda, Ken?"

"It wasn't my place to," he said defensively. "I didn't grow up sitting on Veda's knee the way you did. To me she was just a housekeeper."

"To me she was a member of the family," Schyler said sadly. "I'm surprised Tricia didn't feel that way about her, too." Then, forcing herself out of her unsettling reflections, she asked, "What brings you to the landing? While you're here, you can take this. It's your copy of the Endicott contract."

"You didn't even mention it last night."

"I hardly had a chance, Ken."

"Boudreaux went with you, didn't he?"

"Yes, he did," she confessed with chagrin. "His assistance was invaluable."

"Hmm. You were with him all day then."

"It's a long drive."

He had more questions to ask but lost his nerve. "How'd it go?"

"I know you'll be pleased."

She handed him a copy of the contract and braced herself for criticism when he got to the clause about receiving no payment before the entire shipment was received. Ken barely glanced at it before folding it and stuffing it into his breast pocket of his summer blazer.

"Aren't you even going to read it?"

"I'll go over it later," he said. "I'm sure everything is in order." He wouldn't look her in the eyes and he was fidgeting as nervously as a kid at a piano recital. "Actually, I came here this morning to talk about something personal."

Schyler sighed and rose from her chair. "If it's about Gayla, I've said all I have to say."

"It's not about that."

Schyler sat down on the corner of the desk, her legs at a alant in front of her. "Then what?"

"Money." He finally looked up at her. "I need some money."

"Don't we all?" she asked lightly.

His grin was half formed and fleeting. "No, I mean now. Immediately."

He was serious. This was no laughing matter. Schyler matched her mood to his. "How much, Ken?"

He shifted in his chair and cleared his throat. "Ten grand."

"Ten thousand dollars?" She didn't even attempt to disguise her dismay.

"It rounds off to that." Again, his smile vanished as soon as it was formed. "It's for a good cause."

"Your health?"

He seemed to find that funny and laughed out loud. "In a manner of speaking."

"Ken?" She stood up and placed a hand on his shoulder. "You're not ill, are you? Is something—"

"No, no, nothing like that." He came to his feet. "But it's important, Schyler, or I wouldn't come crawling to you like a goddamn beggar. Trust me, you're better off not knowing what it's for. And I'll repay you. I promise."

"I don't want guarantees or explanations from you. If you need the money, you need the money. If your reasons for needing it are personal, I honor your privacy."

"Then you'll loan it to me?"

"I wish I could, but I can't."

"Can't?"

"I don't have it."

"Don't have it?"

His echo was bothersome, but she tried not to show her irritation. "I'll barely have enough to live on until I get my next check."

Ken ran his hand through his hair in befuddlement. "What next check?"

"I put my legacy from Mama in a trust. My attorney in London doles out allotments on the first of every month. Those allotments come out of the interest. I've never touched the principal and don't intend to unless it's absolutely necessary."

"You mean you can't have use of your own money when you want it?"

"I could, but I'd have to pay costly penalties to take out lump sums and later replace them. Besides, if Crandall Logging doesn't pull out of this slump and pay off the loan, I'll have to use part of my inheritance as collateral on another loan. I can't start depleting the account."

"Doesn't that Mark character you work for pay you anything?"

"Yes, but I insisted on working strictly on commission. As you know I haven't been there for almost a month."

He began to pace. He looked like a man who had run out of options. Schyler took sympathy on him. "I'm sure you could make arrangements for a personal loan at the bank."

"My old man didn't trust me with my own inheritance. I can't touch it until I turn forty. I don't have shit to use for collateral."

"Tricia?"

He softened. "She spent the last of the money her mother left her years ago. Since then she's been sponging off Cotton and the paltry salary he pays me."

"When the business is in the black again, I'll see that you get a well deserved raise."

"That's not going to help me now, Schyler," he shouted. At her stunned expression, he moved toward her and clasped her shoulders. "I'm sorry. I didn't mean to yell at you."

"Ken, you're frightening me. Just how desperate are you for cash?"

Her concern set off warning bells. He couldn't afford to reveal too much. His face relaxed and he forced himself to smile. "Not so desperate that you need to worry about it." He ironed the wrinkle of worry out of her forehead with his index finger. "It'll take care of itself. Something will turn up."

His finger didn't stop with the furrow on her forehead, but slid down her cheek and then along the rim of her lower lip. "So pretty. And so strong." He drew a deep breath of longing. "My God, Schyler, do you know how sexy you are? The air fairly crackles when you walk into a room."

Schyler tried to move away. "Ken, stop it. I've asked you more than once not to touch me."

"You know I still want you. I know you still want me."

She denied that with a hard shake of her head. "Your come-ons are not only wrong, but tiresome. We've said everything that need be said . . . repeatedly. Now for the last time, cut it out!"

Again, he refused to take no for an answer. If anything, he seemed more determined than ever. He moved forward and embraced her tightly. She pushed him away. He only clasped her tighter.

"Schyler, don't snub me. Let me love you." His breathing accelerated. "Damn! Wouldn't it be exciting to make love right here? Right now." He backed her against the edge of the desk.

"Have you lost your mind?" she gasped.

"Yes. I'm crazy about you."

"Don't you see how wrong this is?"

"It's not wrong. It can't be. Not when I love you so much. What we had is still there. You'll see."

Schyler had too much dignity to engage in a sophomoric, physical struggle. Sternly she said, "No, Ken."

"Why not? We're alone here."

"Not quite."

They sprang apart at the sound of the intrusive third voice.

THIRTY-NINE

C ash Boudreaux was lounging against the doorjamb.

"I hate to break up such a tender scene, but I need to see you about something, Miss Schyler."

She tried to appear composed, but doubted that she pulled off the act. "That's all right, Cash. Ken was just leaving."

Ken's jaw dropped. "You're sending me packing so you can talk to *him*?"

She would have to make amends for the slight later, but she couldn't have Cash believing that she was carrying on an affair with her brother-in-law. "Cash and I need to talk business. What you and I were discussing can wait till later."

He glared at her furiously. "Okay, sure," he said curtly. He nudged Cash aside on his way out the door.

Cash waited until Ken's car had cleared the other side of the bridge and the dust had settled before he turned back to Schyler. "Is that how he earns his salary these days, by keeping the boss lady's hormones well tuned?"

"What Ken was doing here is between him and me."

"That much was obvious."

"And none of your business, Mr. Boudreaux."

The atmosphere in the room was explosive. If one had struck a match, the whole place would have gone up in flames. Cash's eyes flayed her with censure. She stared him down. She would be damned before stammering any self-defensive explanations. Let him think what he would.

"I just don't get you, lady," he said.

"Not that I'm all that interested, but what don't you get?"

"You've got a house like Belle Terre, but you run off and live on the other side of the world."

"I had my reasons."

"For leaving, *oui*. But why'd you stay so long?" He slid his hands, palms out, into the rear pockets of his jeans and tilted his head arrogantly. "But I guess that guy you live with over there has something to do with that."

"Mark has a great deal to do with that, yes."

His lip curled cynically. "What's your game, huh? What are you doing, playing Howell and this English dude against each other, and taking on anybody else who gives you a crotch throb in the process?"

"I'm not playing anybody against anybody," Schyler said, seething. "Ken is my sister's husband. As for Mark, he's not English. In the second place, a man like you couldn't begin to understand our relationship. There's much more to it than lust and sweat."

"Lust and sweat should be enough."

"Maybe for you, but not for me. And not for Mark."

He nodded slowly, still treating her to a judgmental stare. "Something else confounds me. You take in a woman with Gayla's past when most respectable ladies wouldn't spit on her if she was on fire, but you have no conscience against screwing your sister's husband."

Schyler wanted to launch herself at him, scratching and clawing, but she knew that's what he wanted her to do. He wanted to drag her down to his level. She wasn't about to let him do that. If she didn't need him to keep Crandall Logging running smoothly, she would fire him on the spot. Sadly, she did need him. If she had to suffer his insults for the sake of Belle Terre, she would.

"You overstep your position, Mr. Boudreaux," she said loftily. "If you've come to me with a business concern, kindly state what it is. If not, then we both have better things to do.''

His eyelids were still half-closed and his expression sardonic, but he removed his hands from his jeans pockets. ''How's Gayla?''

''She slept through the night. Drank some tea this morning. Went to the bathroom. Slept again.''

''Anymore bleeding?''

''No.''

''Good. Let me know if there's any change.''

''I will.''

By now he was standing close. He smelled like the forest at daybreak. She could feel the edge of the desk against her buttocks. She wanted him to back her against it, and that made her angry with herself. ''Is that all?''

''No.''

''Well?'' Her heart was beating rapidly, thinking that he might kiss her yet.

''This was tacked to the office door this morning when I got here. You were late. I've been holding on to it. Thought you ought to see it.''

He reached into the breast pocket of his shirt and came up with a snapshot. He passed it to her. Disappointed, she took the photograph from him and studied it, but after a moment quizzically looked up at him. ''The significance escapes me.''

''It's a pit bull bitch and her litter. Four puppies, if I'm counting teats right.''

The significance of it struck her full force then. ''Jigger,'' she said softly.

''*Oui.* Guess he wanted you to know he's not quitting the gambling trade, even though he's suffered a setback.''

''I called the state representative's office several times, but never got through to him personally. His secretary didn't seem impressed by my problem and suggested that I take it up with local authorities.''

''And?''

''I got nowhere. Jigger's probably laughing up his sleeve at me.''

''I warned you.''

She thumped the snapshot with her finger and dropped it onto her desk. ''He's still holding a grudge.''

''I told you he would.''

''Would you kindly stop rubbing my nose in your superior knowledge of the subject,'' she snapped. ''If you want to say something, tell me what I should do.''

''All right.'' He bent over her, until she had to reach back and support herself on the desk. ''You want my advice? Get the hell out of here and go back to England.''

''What?!''

''Things have been shot to hell ever since you got here.''

''That's not my fault.''

''Isn't it?''

''No.''

''Name one mess you haven't made messier.''

''What would all those loggers be doing for work if it weren't for me?''

Because what she said was true, Cash straightened suddenly. He spun around and rammed his fist into the nearest wall. He shook his head to clear it of angry frustration, then looked back at her. ''Why didn't you just leave well enough alone?''

''Because everything wasn't 'well enough.' ''

''It was a freak accident that Jigger's dog attacked you.''

"I doubt you would have thought so if it had been you. Or your child."

"I don't have a child."

"That's not my fault either."

They fell back strategically to plan their next attack. Cash came out fighting first.

"Cotton would have figured out a way to pay off that loan."

"How? He was out of cash."

"That's bull. He's got friends, friends with money, drinking buddies, who would have covered that note for him in a minute. But no, you had to go butting in. You had to undertake all this," he shouted, waving his hand to encompass the entire landing. "To feed your own goddamn ego."

"It has nothing to do with ego."

"Then why are you doing it?"

"That's my business."

"Why? Why didn't you just leave us the hell alone?"

"It was something I had to do!"

"And fuck up everybody else's life in the process!"

He headed for the door. Schyler stepped between him and it. "Cash, don't fight me. Help me. Just how ruthless could Jigger be?"

"You saw Gayla."

"Ruthless enough to jeopardize the Endicott shipment if he got wind of it?"

"Probably."

Laying her hand on his arm, she looked up at him in appeal. Anger and pride were diminished by worry. "What am I going to do?"

His eyes reflected no emotion. They seemed uncaring and indifferent to her problems, as if they had no direct bearing on him. "You're a smart lady." Cruelly he shook off her restraining hand. "You'll land on your feet."

Rhoda's long fingernail twirled a clump of body hair on Cash's lower belly. Her tongue lapped at his nipple like it was the curly tip on the top of a frozen custard cone. She made snuffling noises that gave the impression she thought it was just as sweet.

"We haven't had a nooner in so long," she sighed, taking a love bite of his tough, heavily veined bicep. "I'm glad you called."

Cash had one arm crooked behind him, his head resting in the palm of his hand. His eyes were focused on the water rings on the ceiling as the smoke from his cigarette snaked upward toward them. He was wondering if Rhoda knew, that for all her talent and trouble, he was still soft. His jeans were unsnapped, but so far she hand't investigated inside them. She would be mad as hell when she discovered he wasn't loaded and ready to fire.

His cock was lusting for somebody else. Rhoda wasn't going to appease it. He had known that before he had called her, but on the outside chance that she would temporarily distract him, he called her anyway.

So far nothing she had done had worked. That left him feeling mad as a hornet and mean as hell. He pushed Rhoda off him and left the bed.

"Where are you going?"

"It's hotter than hell in here."

"It is not. If anything it's too cold. The air conditioner is blowing full blast."

"All right then, it's too cold." He located an ashtray on the dresser and ground out his cigarette, wishing he could put out the fire in his belly as easily.

"You're in another stinky mood."

"It's been a stinky twenty-four hours."

Not really. This time yesterday he'd been watching Schyler get delightfully tipsy on champagne, becoming softer, sexier with each sip. He'd watched her reclining in the car with her knees spread wide, her hair tangled and blowing in the wind, her lips slightly parted while she gently snored through them. All her defenses had been down.

"Cash?"

"What? Goddamn it. Can't you see I'm thinking?"

"I thought you came here to think about me," Rhoda said shortly.

He was ready to hammer home a scathing comment, but he checked himself. What the hell was the matter with him? He had a hot and willing broad in bed waiting for him. She was naked and she was nasty, and he was moping around like a dumb-assed kid with a big red zit on prom night.

"That's right, Rhoda, I did. Give me something to think about."

He dove on top of her and covered her mouth with his. He held her head between his hands. His kiss was rapacious. Cruelly he ground his pelvis against hers.

"Cash, my God," she gasped several moments later when she came up for air. "Calm down, baby. We don't have to rush it, do we?"

"Yes," he muttered against her neck. "We do." He fumbled to draw out a semi-erection that was showing promise. He had to get it inside Rhoda before he remembered she wasn't his first choice.

"Wait, I want to show you somehting." She ignored his cursing impatience and smiled seductively. "Look at these." She reached for her handbag on the nightstand, letting her nipple drag across the starched sheet. When she lay back down, both nipples stood out.

Cash sat up, snarling with disgust for himself, for her, for everything. Apprehensively he stared down at what she had handed him. "Pictures?"

His attitude changed after glancing at the first snapshot. He thumbed through the stack of photographs, carefully studying each one before going on to the next. Without moving his head, he glanced up at Rhoda from beneath his brows. Her smile defined licentiousness. He went back to the photographs and looked at all of them a second time.

"That's a really wide ... smile you've got there, Rhoda." His pause was deliberately timed so that his observation had an insulting double entendre.

Rhoda, however, was too in love with the pictures to notice his intentional slur. "Guess who took them?"

"I don't like guessing games."

"Dale," she said on a high giggle.

"He likes to take pictures of naked women?" Cash's passions hadn't just cooled. They'd gone cold. He thoughtfully tapped the pornographic prints against his thumbnail, remembering Gayla's tearful account of a john who got his highs with a camera. A rage inside him was being stoked, but Rhoda didn't know that.

She lay back against the pillows in one of the indolent poses captured on film. "Which one do you like best?"

"I couldn't begin to choose."

"What's the matter? Jealous?"

"Pea green with it."

She frowned. "You don't seem very excited over the pictures."

"Oh, I am, I am." He bent over her and took both her hands. "Put one hand here," he said, placing it on her breast. "And the other one here, just like in the picture." He laid her hand between her splayed thighs. "And before you know it, you won't even miss me."

He had his jeans buttoned and was pulling on his shirt before Rhoda realized what was happening. "You can't do this to me again, you bastard."

Cash slammed out the motel room door. Rhoda lunged off the bed and flung open the door, uncaring that she was stark naked and in full view of anyone on the highway. In a voice that disturbed truckers napping in the neighboring rooms, she screamed, "Screw you, Boudreaux! I'll get even with you for this."

"Schyler got a contract from Endicott Paper Mill."

Dale Gilbreath hissed a curse beneath his breath. "How large?"

"First I have to know if our deal still stands."

"It does," the banker said. "I get the house. The rest of Belle Terre you can do with as you wish."

"The *bank* will get Belle Terre."

Dale dismissed the clarification. "It'll be as good as mine."

"How so?"

"There'll be a foreclosure auction. Private bids."

"And you'll act as the auctioneer."

"Precisely," he said with an evil grin.

"You'll see to it that your bid is the highest." Dale nodded. "What if the bids are checked?"

"I'll fudge them."

"Even then, you'll have to come up with a tidy sum of cash. Will you have it?"

"The acquisition of Belle Terre is just one of my, uh, hobbies. I've always got more than one deal going."

"You're very clever, aren't you, Mr. Gilbreath?"

"Very."

Dale gauged the individual across from him. His own motivations for participating in this scheme were clear. He wanted Belle Terre because of the power and respect that went with the address. But what about the other's motivations? Were they as clearly defined as his, or were they murky, linked to the past, and related to the emotions? It didn't matter to him really. He was simply curious. Did one have to have concrete reasons for one's actions? Probably not. His co-conspirator held a grudge. He couldn't care less where it had its roots, as long as it resulted in the downfall of the Crandalls and Belle Terre.

"How large is the Endicott contract?" Dale asked.

"It's sufficient to pay off the loan and then some."

"Damn!"

"But there is a catch. Crandall Logging has to deliver the entire order before Endicott lets go of one red cent."

"How do you know all this?"

"I know."

Dale examined the other's face and decided that the information wasn't speculation, but fact. He expulsed a deep breath. "So the key is to make sure that the last shipment doesn't go through."

"Right. A shipment will go out every day or so on the train. But, as you said, stopping the last one is the key."

"How soon will that be?" Dale asked.

"The order is so large, she'll be working right up to the deadline. And that means everybody working overtime and the weather holding out. She'll barely be able to get the timber there before the note comes due."

"You'll help me see that she doesn't succeed?"

"She's dumped on me for the last time. I'll do whatever needs to be done."

Gilbreath smiled, tasting victory that was only a few weeks away. "I'll speak to Jigger again. He was agreeable when I first mentioned our little project to him."

"Something else the two of you should know. Gayla Frances is at Belle Terre, lying in Schyler's own bed."

"Jesus. Flynn would love to know that."

"Wouldn't he though?"

"What happened to the girl?"

"Why?"

"Just curious."

"Are you sure? You look pale. You're not a regular customer, are you?"

"What happened to the girl?" Dale repeated with an implied threat.

"Jigger beat her up. She ran away from him. Schyler took her in. That's two strikes against Schyler as far as he's concerned. He'll be more than willing to help us out."

"And if anything should go wrong and he's caught—"

"He'll be the one to take the rap."

"Not quietly, he won't. He'll implicate us."

"And we'll say he's lying. It'll be our word agaisnt his. Who's going to take Jigger's word for anything?"

Gilbreath smiled at his conspirator. "Keep me posted."

"Don't doubt that for a minute. Schyler Crandall's comeuppance is long overdue."

Jimmy Don Davison stared at the envelope for a long time before opening it. It had been unsealed and the contents read by prison officials before being delivered to him. The flap on the stiff, cream-colored envelope was embossed with the return address: *Belle Terre, Heaven, Louisiana.* Now who in hell at Belle Terre would be writing to him in prison? Who at Belle Terre knew or cared that he was there?

Finally, slumped on his bunk with his back against the wall and his heels at the edge of the thin, lumpy mattress, he took out the single sheet of stationery. Before reading the lines of neat, cursive script, he glanced down at the signature.

"Schyler Crandall?"

"D'you say somethin', Jimmy Don?" his cell mate asked from the bunk above his.

"Nothin' to you, Old Stu."

"Dear Mr. Davison," the salutation read. In between that and the unexpected signature, he was apologetically reacquainted with the sender, as though anybody from Laurent Parish needed to be reminded who Schyler Crandall was. She inquired after his well-being. Then she got down to the purpose of the letter. It had been sent to inform him that Gayla Frances was living at Belle Terre for an indefinite period of time and that, should he want to contact her, all correspondence should be addressed to her there.

He read the puzzling letter several times to make certain he understood its meaning. On the surface it amounted to a change of address notification, but what Miss Schyler was telling him in a roundabout way was that he should get in touch with his old girlfriend. Some girlfriend; Gayla was a whore. Apparently she'd sunk so low that even Jigger Flynn wouldn't have her under his roof any longer.

Jimmy Don coined epithets for Gayla and the rich, white bitch who went meddling into other folks' business. The embossed cream paper became a wadded ball in his fist. He hurled it against the wall opposite him.

"Hey, man, what's in the letter?"

"Shut up," Jimmy Don growled to Old Stu.

Schyler Crandall seemed to think he was interested in Gayla's whereabouts. He was, but only to the extent of knowing where he could find her in a hurry when he got out. He'd have to move fast. She must have no warning. His revenge must be as swift and sure as the sword of God.

His black eyes snapped with anger. His fists clenched and opened subconsciously. He probed at Gayla's betrayal like a tongue poking at a sore tooth. No matter how much it hurt, he kept returning to it and asking how, how she could have ever resorted to that kind of life.

They'd talked about graduating college, getting married, having kids. Hell, they'd even named the first three or four. She'd been a virgin the first time they went all the way. He hadn't been far from one. They'd coached each other on how to make love, frankly expressing what felt nice, when to rush, when to tarry.

The idea of her applying those sexual skills for hire made him sick to his stomach. That she could be loving Jigger Flynn with the same sweetness and consideration that she had once loved him made him livid enough to kill them both and laugh while he was doing it.

He was so steeped in thoughts about their slow and torturous executions that he didn't notice the group of prisoners that collected outside his cell. It was free time and all the cell doors were opened. Prisoners were at liberty to walk about in unrestricted areas. Jimmy Don didn't see the nefarious group until they came strolling into his cell, crowding together to fit into the small space. Razz propped his elbow on the upper bunk and smiled down at him.

"What's happenin', boy?"

"Nobody invited you in, Razz."

Jimmy Don didn't like the odds. Razz and three of his lieutenants against Old Stu and him. If the prison were a microcosm, Old Stu was the village simpleton. He had been given life for killing a cop, almost assuredly a frameup. Old Stu didn't seem to mind the injustice. He had no family. The prison was his home. He was useless; he was harmless. His credo was to hear no evil, see no evil, speak no evil, and by doing so, survive.

Razz smiled down at Jimmy Don. "That don't sound very friendly. We came by to give you a going away party, right?" The other three brutes nodded their heads in agreement.

"I'm not going anywhere."

"You're outta here, boy. Soon. Paroled. Ain't you heard about it yet?"

Jimmy Don had an appointment with the parole board, but he wasn't going to divulge the date to Razz. "I haven't heard anything official."

"No?" Razz asked, feigning surprise. "Well now, it would be a damn shame if you caused a fuss right before meeting with the parole board, wouldn't it?" He touched Jimmy Don's cheek affectionately. Jimmy Don jerked his head aside. When he did, he happened to catch one of the other inmates leafing through his Bible.

"Get your filthy hands off that," he said testily.

"Hey man, don't go messin' with Jimmy Don's Bible," Razz said to the other prisoner. "His mama must have give it to him, right, Jimmy Don?"

Jimmy Don moved to the edge of his cot. "I said to leave the Bible alone."

The other prisoner, ignoring his warning, read the inscription on the inside cover. "Say what? Now ain't that sweet? You into religion, Jimmy Don?" He ripped out the illuminated page and crumpled it in his fist, just as Jimmy Don had done the letter from Belle Terre.

"Goddamn you!" Jimmy Don lunged off the cot, hands aimed at the other prisoner's throat.

Razz caught him by the neck of his T-shirt and held him back. Mockingly he scolded Jimmy Don's tormentor. "Leave the boy's Bible alone. Didn't you know he's into all that? It's always revival time at Jimmy Don's church. They get baptized, speak in tongues, handle serpents, all that weird shit."

Several more gilt-edged pages of the Bible were maliciously ripped out and divided between the prisoners. Laughing at their own cleverness, they tore them to shreds before letting them flutter to the floor.

"You sons of bitches," Jimmy Don snarled.

"Now is that any way to talk to your friends? Hmm?" Razz cooed. "We come to give you a little going away present."

"Make that a *big* going away present." The prisoner stroked the fly of his pants. The joke earned him loud, approving laughter.

Jimmy Don put up a fierce struggle, but it was a token struggle and he knew it. He was as strong as a young bull, but he couldn't overpower the four of them. It would be useless and even more dangerous to call for a guard becasue the guard, out of fear of retribution, would side with Razz. If Jimmy Don called attention to himself or caused any trouble in the cell block, he wouldn't make parole. If he didn't make parole, he wouldn't have the chance to do what God had sanctioned him to do to Jigger and Gayla.

So he gritted his straight, white teeth and endured the gang rape while Old Stu lay in the bunk above him, picking his toenails, and thanking the Lord he was too old and ugly for any of Razz's gang to want him.

 # FORTY

"**D**amn!"
  Schyler's terse expletive was directed toward the bank statement she had been trying to balance for the last hour. Either she had no head for figures or her calculator was broken or several thousand dollars in the Crandall Logging account was indeed missing.

She needed Ken's help with this. He was the accountant. He was being paid to track down misplaced money. She reached for the telephone on her desk but before she touched it, it rang.

"Hello?"

"Schyler? Jeff Collins."

She and the doctor had been on a first-name basis since Cotton's surgery. "There's nothing wrong I hope."

"Why do people always think the worst when a doctor calls?"

She laughed. "Sorry. Are you the bearer of good news?"

"I hope you'll think so. Your father can leave tomorrow."

"That's wonderful," she exclaimed.

"You might want to check with the nurses before you say that," the doctor remarked around a chuckle. "Within a week you might want to send him back. Not that we'd take him back. He's gotten to be a real pain in the ass."

"Feisty old codger, isn't he?"

"The feistiest."

"I can't wait to have him home."

"If you want to come by this afternoon, I'll have all the release forms ready for you to sign. That way you won't bottleneck with the other dismissed patients in the morning.''

"Thanks for the consideration, Jeff. I'll be right over.''

Before she could hang up, he said, "We haven't told him yet. I thought you might want to break the good news yourself.''

"Thanks, I appreciate that. See you shortly.''

Grimacing with distaste, she folded all the canceled checks back into the folder, along with the bank's computerized printout of her account. The damn thing would have to remain unreconciled for the time being.

In fact, everything could be put on hold. Cotton Crandall was coming home.

"Seen Ms. Crandall?'' Cash asked a logger who was weighing in the load on his rig. The scale at the landing was so delicate, the amount of board feet the load contained could be measured precisely.

"She left 'bout five minutes ago,'' he answered around a chaw of tobacco. "What are you doing here?''

"I brought Kermit back,'' Cash replied absently. It was unusual for Schyler to leave this early in the afternoon. "Did Ms. Crandall happen to say where she was going?''

"The hospital.''

Cash, who'd been wiping his perspiring face with his bandanna, froze. The logger had his back turned and was shouting directions to the driver of another rig. Cash caught his shoulder and turned him around. "The hospital?''

"That's what she said, Cash.''

"Did she say why? Did it have something to do with Cotton?''

"The lady don't inform me of her comin's and goin's. All I know is that she was in a big hurry. Shouted out to me that she'd be at the hospital if anybody asked, then herded that car of hers outta here lickety split.''

Cash's face settled into a deep frown. His brows were pulled down low over his eyes. He stared toward the bridge in the direction Schyler had taken.

"Anything wrong, Cash?'' the logger asked worriedly.

"No. Probably nothing.'' He roused himself from his private thoughts and tried to appear casual. "Keep an eye on things here, okay? Get all this timber ready to load on the train before quitting time. If I don't come back, see that the office is locked for the night before you leave. And tell Kermit to sit in there for the rest of the afternoon and man the phone. He got red in the face because of the heat, but he doesn't want to miss out on the overtime.''

"Okay, Cash, but where're you goin'?''

Cash didn't hear him. He was already running toward his pickup.

"I'm going to turn the downstairs study into a bedroom for you. It might not be finished by tomorrow, but when I get through with it, you'll be able to lie in bed and look outside at the back lawn of Belle Terre.''

"I liked my old bedroom.''

Cotton sounded grumpy, but Schyler knew how pleased he was to be going home. She tried to hide her indulgent smile. "Dr. Collins said you shouldn't be climbing the stairs.''

He aimed an adamant index finger at her. "I won't be babied. Not by you. Not by anybody. I've had enough of that in here. I'm not an invalid.''

That's exactly what he was. He knew that's what he was, but Schyler knew better than to let on that he was. "You're damn right you're not. Don't expect to be pampered. I'm going to put you to work as soon as you're rested up.''

"From what I hear you've got more help around the place than you can use."
He shrewdly gauged her reaction from beneath his bushy white eyebrows.

"Tricia told you about Mrs. Dunne?"

"She did. Said she's bossy as all get out."

"Maybe that's why I like her so much. She reminds me of Veda."

" 'Xcept she's white."

"Well, yes, there is that difference," Schyler said, laughing.

"Can she cook as good as Veda?"

"Yes." She waved a sheet of paper in front of him. "She can cook everything on this diet Jeff gave me for you."

"Shit."

"Come now, it's not that bad," she teased. "But there'll be no grits and sausage gravy for you. And I won't have you bribing Mrs. Dunne either. Her first loyalty is to me. She won't be swayed, no matter how persuasive or ornery you get."

Cotton's expression remained disagreeable. "I wasn't just referring to the housekeeper when I mentioned the new help."

Schyler kept her smile intact. Was he referring to Cash? Had Tricia, in spite of Schyler's warning, come tattling?"

"Veda's girl," Cotton grunted. "I hear she's taken up residence at Belle Terre."

The tension in Schyler's chest receded. "Yes, Gayla's there at my invitation. I felt like we Crandalls were responsible for her misfortunes."

"I heard she's trashy as the day is long."

"I'm sure you have," she said, thinking of Tricia's vicious tongue. "But there were extenuating circumstances. Jigger Flynn's been abusing her for years. This time he nearly killed her. Luckily she was able to get away from him. While she's recuperating, I want her to stay with us."

"That's mighty generous of you."

She pretended not to notice his sarcasm. "Thank you."

Schyler's motives were not purely unselfish. She treasured Gayla's friendship. Lately, her list of friends had dwindled drastically. Because of their most recent altercation, every time Tricia looked at Schyler, resentment wafted from her like cheap perfume.

As for Ken, Schyler apparently had bruised his pride when she asked him to leave her alone with Cash. On the heels of turning down his request of a loan, she had added insult to injury. He, too, was avoiding her these days. He spoke only when it was absolutely necessary and then with rigid politeness.

Cash had dispensed with their coffee-drinking sessions in the mornings. She knew he had been in the landing office ahead of her each day when she arrived, but since their latest quarrel, he had made it a point to leave before she got there. If he returned to the landing before she left in the evenings, he spent the time in the yard among the men, making daily inventory of the timber that had been cut, weighing the loads, recording the figures, and supervising the loading of it onto the freight cars.

If it was necessary for him to consult with her on something pertaining to business, he did so as briefly as possible. His face looked like it would crack if he smiled. His hazel eyes seemed to look straight through her. He was as remote and quick to take offense as when they had first met. His hostility was sexually charged. She knew it, felt it, and recognized it because she felt the same way.

She was restless. During the hot days, she used exhausting work to keep that internal turmoil on simmer. But at night she tossed and turned in bed, unable to sleep, her mind occupied with disturbing thoughts and even more disturbing fantasies. She hated acknowledging how much she missed Cash. Even having him around when he was surly and insulting was preferable to not having him around at all. Also, recollections of that rainy afternoon kept her in a constant state of dissatisfaction.

So she had taken solace in the quiet talks she shared with Gayla. She talked frequently about Mark and their life in London. Gayla, tearfully and over a period of days, revealed what her nightmarish life with Jigger Flynn had been like. Schyler urged her to press charges against him, but Gayla wouldn't hear of it.

"He'd kill me, Schyler, before he ever came to trial. Even if he was in jail, he'd find a way. Besides, who would believe me?" she had asked.

Who indeed? Gayla's tales were unbelievable.

"There was a girl who worked in the Pelican Lounge," Gayla had told her one afternoon. "Jigger strangled her for not giving him his fair cut of what she earned. One morning she was found dead in a dumpster out behind the building. Her murder went down as an unsolved crime. I even tipped the sheriff with an anonymous phone call, but nothing was ever done about it."

"How could a law officer just blow off a murder like that?"

"Either he was scared of Jigger, or, most probably, he thought the girl had it coming for holding out on him."

Gayla had also told her, "Another of the girls got pregnant by one of her johns. Only he wasn't just a customer to her. She loved him and wanted to have the baby. Jigger found out about it and knew that if she carried the baby, he'd lose a valuable employee. He beat her with his fists until she aborted.

"He gets crazy if somebody welshes on a bet. One man owed him a lot of money over a pit bull fight. Jigger sent thugs out to get it, but they couldn't collect. The man went out in his fishing boat one day and never was seen again. They ruled it an accidental drowning and dragged the lake for his body. I guarantee you, it's anchored to the bottom and never will be found."

Day by day, with the help of Cash's ointment and Mrs. Dunne's plentiful meals, Gayla recovered physically. The scratches on her face diminished and eventually disappeared. The swelling went down until her beautiful bone structure was evident again. The bleeding stopped, but she was jittery; she jumped at every loud noise. Schyler realized that it would take months, maybe years, for Gayla to get over her recurring fears and to recover emotionally from the hellish existence she'd been subjected to.

Still, she was fiercely proud. "I can't stay here indefinitely, Schyler," she had insisted on more than one occasion.

Schyler had been just as insistent. "I want you here, Gayla. I need a friend."

"But I can't ever repay you."

"I don't want you to."

"I can't take your charity."

Schyler had considered it for a moment. "I can't afford to pay you a salary just now. Would you be willing to work for room and board?"

"Work? You just hired Mrs. Dunne."

"But there's plenty for you to do."

"Like what?" Gayla had asked skeptically. "You've got a crew that takes care of the yard. Somebody else tends to the horses. What is there for me to do?"

"I'd like the books in the small parlor to be cataloged. Those shelves haven't been inventoried in years. No telling what's up there. You can start on that. And don't rush it. Don't wear yourself out now that you're regaining your strength. Work only when you feel like it."

Gayla had seen through Schyler's ploy. She knew the job had been invented and was unnecessary. "All right. I'll inventory the books. Some of the houseplants need attention, too," she had said, holding her chin at a proud tilt. "Mama would have a fit if she could see how they've been neglected. And there's mending that needs to be done. I've noticed tears in some of the bed linens."

Gayla had moved out of Schyler's bedroom and into a small room off the kitchen. She refused to eat with the family in the dining room as Schyler had wanted her to. Instead she stubbornly ate her meals with Mrs. Dunne in the kitchen. They had established a fast friendship because Mrs. Dunne's kindness was extensive.

"Gayla has fit in beautifully," Schyler told her father now. "In fact, I don't know how I managed without her. I think you'll find everything at Belle Terre to your liking."

He frowned doubtfully. "You'll hear about it if I don't."

"I'm sure I will." She eased herself off the edge of his bed. "See you in the morning. Not too early. You'll have breakfast here. Take your time getting showered and shaved. I'll be here around ten, okay?" She bent down and kissed him good-bye.

He caught her hand. "I'm proud of that Endicott deal. You did a good job, Schyler."

She hadn't told him why Endicott had stopped using them as a supplier. Until she could satisfy herself with an explanation, she didn't want to get Cotton worked up over it. "Thanks, Daddy. I'm glad you approve."

For the first time in days, Schyler's step was springy as she crossed the hospital lobby on her way out. She had almost reached the sliding glass doors when they opened for a man coming in.

Upon seeing him, she stopped dead in her tracks. "Mark!"

Cash lit a cigarette with the smoldering butt of his last one. He inhaled the acrid smoke while staring at the facade of St. John's Hospital. At any moment, he expected someone to appear with a black wreath to hang over the sliding glass doors.

For the last half hour, he'd been sitting in a widening puddle of his own sweat in the cab of his pickup, smoking, and trying to work up enough courage to cross the street and inquire at the front desk whether or not Cotton Crandall had died.

He didn't want to know.

But he had a strong suspicion that's why Schyler had left the landing in the middle of the day. She wouldn't have done that unless there was a crisis of some kind. Her periodic reports to him on Cotton's condition had been fairly optimistic.

His heart was stronger, but still weak.

He was improving, but not altogether out of the woods.

The operation had been a success, but there was a limited amount of repair that could be done.

Cash knew that Cotton's life was still in danger. Any little thing could go wrong; obviously something had.

The endless cigarettes had made his throat dry and irritated. Impatiently he tossed the one he'd just lit out the open window of his truck. When he did, he noticed a man walking toward the entrance to the hospital.

He was arresting in that he was so different. He fit into the southwestern Louisiana backdrop about as well as an Eskimo would in Tahiti. He looked out of place in his white slacks and navy blazer. He had on white shoes. White shoes, for chrissake! A jaunty red handkerchief was sticking out of his breast pocket. His hair was blond and so straight it could have just come off an ironing board. It was neatly parted on one side and glistened in the sunlight. He was wearing dark sunglasses, but the eyes they shaded would have to be as blue as the sky.

He jogged up the steps of the entrance with the self-confidence of a man who knew that everyone he passed turned to get a better look. He looked polished and cosmopolitan enough to be at home in cities that the people who gawked at him had never even heard of. He was so handsome he could have stepped off the cover of a flashy magazine.

Cash got a real sick feeling deep in his gut.

His worst suspicion was confirmed when the man came face-to-face with Schyler in the doorway. Cash heard her squeal his name in surprise. A smile of pure delight broke across her face a split second before she launched herself against the man's chest. Well-tailored sleeves enfolded her. They hugged each other tightly, rocking together joyfully. Then the man kissed her full on the mouth.

Even from across the street, Cash could see that her face was radiant as she gazed up at the blond god, babbling questions while quick, excited little laughs bubbled out of her smiling lips.

One thing was for damn certain—the broad wasn't in mourning.

Cash nearly broke off the key in the ignition when he cranked it on. He nearly stripped the transmission of his pickup, making it to third gear before he reached the stop sign at the nearest corner. He wanted to get Schyler's attention. He wanted her to see just how unimpressed he was with her affluent, well-dressed, sophisticated roommate.

When Cash glanced in his rearview mirror, however, he saw that she hadn't even noticed him. She was engrossed with her lover.

 # FORTY-ONE

"My God, it's Tara."

Schyler beamed beneath Mark's praise. "It's lovelier than Tara."

Mark Houghton glanced at her from the passenger side of her car. "And you're lovelier than Scarlett."

"You're an angel for saying so, but that's crap. I'm exhausted and it shows."

He shook his head. "You're gorgeous. I'd forgotten how much."

Schyler had forgotten how nice it was to hear a compliment. Her face glowed around her smile. "If I look pretty it's because I'm so happy to see you."

He clasped her right hand. "Hurry. I can't wait to take the grand tour."

She began honking the horn when she was only halfway down the lane. By the time she braked the car, Mrs. Dunne and Gayla were waiting expectantly on the veranda to see what all the commotion was about.

"Good news," Schyler called out to them as she alighted and ran around the hood of the car. "Mark is here. And Daddy's coming home tomorrow."

Mark placed his arm around her waist, not only in affection, but as a means of holding Schyler earthbound as she ran up the steps. She was as exuberant as a child at her first circus.

"You must be Mrs. Dunne," Mark said, addressing the housekeeper. "I'm the one you spoke with on the phone a while ago. As you said, I found Schyler at the hospital. Thank you."

"Throw another chicken in the pot, Mrs. Dunne. There will be a guest for supper."

"What a coincidence. I'm baking Cornish hens with wild rice stuffing and I just happen to have an extra one," she said, smiling at the attractive blond couple.

"Good. Is the guest room still made up?"

"I changed the linens today."

"Then you go see to the extra hen. We'll get Mark's bag upstairs. He travels light." Mrs. Dunne went back inside. "Mark," Schyler said, "this is my dear friend Gayla Frances. Gayla, Mark Houghton."

"I'm delighted to meet you, Miss Frances." Mark lifted her hand and kissed the back of it.

"Pleased to meet you, too, Mr. Houghton," Gayla said, flustered. "Schyler has told me a lot about you."

"All good I hope." He smiled disarmingly.

Gayla looked nervously toward Schyler for help. She still found it difficult to make small talk, especially with men. She was spared having to when Tricia stepped out onto the veranda.

"What in tarnation is—" She broke off and gaped at Mark, her eyes going wide with stupefaction and then narrowing with feminine approval. "Hi, y'all." Her slow, honeyed accent matched her smile.

"Hello," Mark said blandly. He was accustomed to having people stare at him. He wasn't obnoxiously vain, but he wasn't oblivious to his good looks. He knew that the way he looked had been either an asset or a hindrance, depending on the situation.

Schyler conducted the introductions. Tricia laid a self-conscious hand at her neckline. "You should have told me, Schyler."

"I didn't know. Mark's visit is a complete and delightful surprise."

"I hope it's not an inconvenience," he said to Tricia politely.

"Oh, no, no. It's just that if I'd known we were going to have company, I would have dressed."

"You look very attractive to me, Mrs. Howell."

"Please call me Tricia." She glanced down at her designer dress with chagrin. "I just put this on to attend a meeting in town. I'll go call right now and tell them I'm not coming."

"Not on my account, please."

"Oh, I wouldn't hear of missing supper with you. Schyler's just raved about you so much," Tricia gushed breathlessly. "Excuse me while I change. Honey, would you bring up that dress I asked Mrs. Dunne to press for me?" She directed that to Gayla before disappearing through the screen door.

"Tricia," Schyler called out in vexation.

Gayla laid a hand on Schyler's arm and said, "It's all right. I was going upstairs anyway to check the guest room. You visit with Mr. Houghton."

"But you are not Tricia's handmaiden. The next time she orders you to do something, tell her to go to hell."

"I'll sell tickets to that," Gayla said, laughing good-naturedly as she went inside.

"Lovely woman," Mark observed when Gayla was out of earshot. "Is she the one who—"

"Yes." During one of their lengthy overseas calls, Schyler had told him about Gayla.

"Hard to believe," he said, shaking his head. "You've worked wonders for her."

"I've been her friend. She would have done the same for me."

Mark faced her and ran his hand over her hair. His eyes were full of love and adoration. "Is that a habit of yours?"

"What?"

"Collecting people who desperately need befriending? I recall a certain aimless wanderer in London, an expatriated American who was terribly lonely. You nurtured him, too."

"Your memory is bad. That's what *he* did for *me*." She went up on tiptoes and kissed his lips softly. "I'll never be able to repay you for all you've meant to me, Mark. Thank you for coming. I didn't realize how much I needed you until I saw you."

As always, when he didn't have an audience, his beautiful smile was tinged with sadness and self-derision. "Before this gets too pithy, show me Belle Terre."

"Where should we start?"

"Did you mention horses?"

Ken was the last one to meet Mark.

By that time they were having predinner drinks in the formal parlor. Mark had been given the grand tour of the house, including all the outbuildings. When they returned, Schyler had excused herself to freshen up before dinner. Mark, already impeccable, had nonetheless gone to his room, ostensibly to do the same.

When Schyler came downstairs wearing a cool, frothy voile print dress, Mark was being entertained by Tricia in the parlor. Schyler was amused by her sister's transformation. Tricia's dress was fancier than the occasion warranted, but Schyler wasn't surprised that Tricia had chosen to wear it. It showed off her voluptuous figure and an immodest amount of suntanned cleavage.

When Schyler entered the parlor, Tricia was saying, "I don't actually remember when Mr. Kennedy was president, but I've watched old films of him. You sound just like him. Of course you probably think *I* have an accent."

Mark's eyes lit up when Schyler entered. He went to greet her, taking both her hands and kissing her cheek. "You look wonderful. This stifling climate suits you like a hothouse does an orchid. Drink?"

"Please." Blushing with pleasure over his compliment, she sat down on one of the love seats while Mark, making himself at home at the sideboard, prepared her a tall gin and tonic. His thoughtfulness didn't escape Tricia, whose effervescence had fizzled since Schyler had come in. Schyler said to her, "Mark actually knows the Kennedys. Did he tell you that?"

Tricia's eyes went round with amazement. "No! *Those* Kennedys? Why I think that's simply fascinating." Mark carried Schyler her drink. He started to sit down beside her, but Tricia was patting the cushion next to her. Politely he sat down beside her again. "Tell me how you met them. Did you know Jackie, too?"

"Actually the Kennedys were neighbors of ours. My parents have a home at Hyannis Port."

"Really? Oh, I've always wanted to go there." She laid a hand on his thigh. "Is it truly beautiful?"

"Well—"

Just then Ken walked in. He took in the parlor scene with one sour glance. Schyler said, "Hello, Ken."

"I called the landing. The ignoramus who answered the phone said there was an emergency at the hospital. I called there. Nobody knew anything about it."

"No emergency. Daddy's coming home tomorrow." That piece of news did nothing to lighten Ken's dark frown. "Mark paid me a surprise visit," Schyler said hastily. "Everything happened so fast, I didn't have a chance to call you."

She introduced him to Mark. Mark stood up, causing Tricia's hand to slide off his thigh. He met Ken halfway and the two men shook hands. Ken's face was sulky. Schyler had known that Ken was prepared to hate Mark on sight, and it was obvious that he did. He took one look at Mark's bandbox appearance and excused himself to go upstairs.

When he came back down, he was dressed in a summer suit and pastel tie. He had also showered; his hair was still damp, and he smelled like the men's cologne counter at Maison-Blanche in downtown New Orleans.

"Can I refill anyone's drink?" he asked, crossing to the sideboard.

He glared at his wife who was monopolizing Mark and prattling on about her reign as Laurent Parish's Mardi Gras Queen. "I was eighteen that summer. Lordy, has it been that long?" she said with a sigh. "I can remember how anxious I was to get all my dresses made in time. You can't imagine how many parties there are. My parade float has never been equaled. Everybody says so. I loved it." She pursed her lips sadly. "Schyler missed out on all that. They passed her up for . . . Who was queen that year, Schyler?"

"Dora Jane Wilcox, I believe."

Schyler was furious. For almost an hour she had watched Tricia's hand slide up and down Mark's thigh. She had watched her simper and flirt until she wanted to throw up. Her sister's saccharine performance for Mark was nauseating.

Whether Tricia was doing it to make her jealous, or Ken jealous, or for the sheer fun of it, it was aggravating the hell out of Schyler. Tricia was dominating Mark and he was too polite to excuse himself from her.

"That's right," Tricia exclaimed. "Dora Jane Wilcox. Well I told you, Schyler, that you spent too much time with Daddy at the landing and not enough time at the country club getting to know the people on the selection committee."

"And I told you, Tricia, that I didn't give a damn about that society stuff. Then or now."

"I was involved for Mama's sake. Before she died, all she talked about was our coming-out parties and such. I felt like we owed it to her to participate in the things she loved."

Tricia made a tsking sound and shook her head at Mark as if to say that Schyler was a hopeless case. "She still spends all her time at the landing. I invited her to join my clubs, but she won't hear of it.

"All she does is work, work, work. She's taken it upon herself to run Belle Terre even though it just wears her out. About the best thing you could do for her is whisk her right back to London." Flirtatiously she gazed at him through her eyelashes. "Not that I'm anxious for you to leave, of course."

"Dinner's ready, Ms. Crandall," Mrs. Dunne announced from the archway.

"Thank you." Schyler was so angry she could barely speak. "We're coming."

Tricia shot the housekeeper a dirty look for announcing dinner to Schyler instead of to her. Possessively she latched onto Mark's arm as they stood up. She nestled it against her breasts. "Mark can escort me to the dining room. Ken, you bring in Schyler."

Ken, who had been slamming back straight double bourbons at a reckless rate, carried the decanter with him. He gripped Schyler's elbow with his other hand. Together they crossed the wide entry hall and went into the dining room. Mark was holding out Tricia's chair. She was smiling up at him over her shoulder.

"Sit here beside me, Mark. Ken and Schyler can take the other side. Daddy always sits at the head of the table. It would be just about perfect if he was here, wouldn't it?"

Things were far from perfect. In fact they started off badly with the fruit compotes when Tricia, with no small amount of asperity, told her husband he was drinking too much. After that, she ignored him and directed her animated conversation to Mark, who responded with noble charm.

With each wonderfully prepared course, tension around the table mounted. Schyler got angrier, Ken was mad at the world, it seemed, and Mark was anxious because the light had gone out of Schyler's eyes. Tricia was the only one having a good time.

That came to an abrupt finish during dessert.

She had said something she thought incredibly witty. As she giggled, she leaned toward him, mashing her breasts against his arm. Mark laughed with her, but it was strained laughter. Then he blotted his mouth with the stiff linen napkin and said, "I'll spare you anymore efforts, Tricia."

Her laughter ceased abruptly and she gazed at him blankly. "Efforts? What do you mean?"

"You can stop pressing my thigh beneath the table. Give your fluttering eyelids a rest. And stop giving me glimpses of your breasts. I'm not interested."

Tricia's fork clattered to her plate. She looked at him whey-faced.

He smiled pleasantly. "You see, I'm gay."

FORTY-TWO

"That wasn't very kind."

Schyler was leaning against the corner pillar of the veranda. Her hands were folded behind her lower back. The balmy breeze blew against her, molding the soft dress to her body. Fair strands of hair stirred against her cheeks.

The night was almost as beautiful as the woman. The sky was studded with brilliant stars. The moon limned the branches of the live oaks with silver light. The orchestra of insects had tuned up and was in full swing. Floral scents hung heavily in the sultry air.

"What she was doing to you wasn't very kind either." Mark was lounging in one of the fan-back wicker chairs. He'd been appreciating a snifter of brandy for the last half hour. He now drained it and set it on the small round table at his elbow. "You know that it's not like me to be unkind. I couldn't help myself. I stood it for as long as I could. Tricia deserved to be taken down a peg for what she was doing to you."

"Which was?"

"Trying to steal me."

He was right. It was just painful for Schyler to admit it. She stared off into the distance. "You took her down more than a peg. You knocked the slats out from under her."

Mark raised his hands above his head and stretched, shoving his feet out in front of him at the same time. "That's probably why she flounced upstairs. The look she gave me was so venomous I should be dead by now. Your sister is a viper."

"You shouldn't say things like that about her to me."

"I refuse to apologize."

"As her husband, Ken should have jumped to her defense. Instead he laughed."

"Yes," Mark said wryly, drawing his long, elegant limbs back in. "Your brother-in-law was delighted by my announcement. Now he knows that I don't pose a threat.''

"A threat?'' Schyler's head came around. "To whom?''

"To him. Don't you realize that the man was eaten up with jealousy?''

"Over Tricia.''

Mark's blond head reflected moonlight as he shook it. "Over you. He still loves you, Schyler.''

"I don't think so.'' Pulling her hands from behind her, she made a dismissive gesture. "Maybe he thinks he still loves me, but I think what he feels is something else. I'm an anchor, something he needs to hold on to.''

"Why? Is he slipping?''

Mark had intended that as a joke, but Schyler answered him seriously. "Yes, I think he is. At least he feels that he is. There's something wrong . . . no, that's too strong a word. There's something *not right* with Ken. I'm not sure what.''

"I do.'' She glanced at him inquiringly. "He knows he made a grave error. He married the wrong woman. He has let Tricia and your father make all his decisions for him. His life isn't worth shit. That's hard for a man to take.''

One of the things she had always admired about Mark was that he didn't mince words. Even when it hurt to be blunt, he was. "I think you're probably right,'' she said softly. "He's made several advances.''

"Of a romantic nature?''

"Yes.''

"How pathetic. What was your reaction?''

"I've warded them off, of course.''

"On moral grounds?''

"Not entirely.''

"Then you don't love him any longer?''

"No,'' she said sadly. "I don't. There wasn't so much as a spark when he touched me. I think I had to come back to realize it though.''

"Want to know a secret?'' He didn't wait for her reply. "I think you stopped loving him a long time ago, if you ever loved him at all.''

"Why didn't you tell me?''

"I was tempted, but you wouldn't have believed me. You had to find it out for yourself.''

"I wasted so much time,'' she said with regret.

"I don't believe time is wasted when one is healing. You had a lot of healing to do. Does the brandy come with the room?'' He nodded at the silver tray Mrs. Dunne had brought out bearing two snifters and a decanter.

"Please help yourself.''

"You?''

"No thanks.'' Schyler watched him pour himself another drink. He took a sip, leaned his head back against the wicker and closed his eyes to fully appreciate the bouquet of the potent liquor. "Mark?'' His eyes came open. "I believe what you said about Ken is right. But I hope you weren't obliquely referring to anyone else I know when you said his life isn't worth shit.''

He smiled at her ruefully. "Live with a woman for six years and she thinks she knows you.''

"I do know you.''

He held up the snifter and studied the moon through its amber contents. "Perhaps you do.''

"I recognize the melancholia.''

"Don't be too alarmed. You know I go through these phases periodically.

They're almost as regular as your menstrual cycle. I'll get over this funk in a day or two. In the meantime I'll wallow in self-pity. I'll wonder why I didn't let my parents go on deluding themselves that I was straight and marry the woman they had chosen for me. Everyone would have been much happier.''

"No one would have been happier, Mark. Especially not the woman. You couldn't have fooled her for long. And certainly not you. As honest as you are with everyone, including yourself, you would have been miserable living a lie.''

"But my mother and father would have been happy. They wouldn't have looked at their only son and heir with horror and disgust.''

Schyler's heart ached for him. He'd been banished by his parents, who maintained a high profile among Boston's elite. That their son was gay had been an abomination, something untenable. Like a malignancy, they had cut him out of their lives.

"Have you heard from them recently?''

"No, of course not,'' he said, draining the snifter for the second time. "But that's not why I'm melancholy.''

"Oh?''

"No. I'm depressed over losing my roommate.''

Schyler smiled wanly and ducked her head. "How did you know?''

Mark left his chair and came to stand in front of her. He laid his hands against her cheeks. "My analogy comparing you to a hothouse orchid was outrageously poetic, but accurate, I believe. You've flourished here, Schyler.'' He gazed around him, taking in the density of the night. "This is where you belong.''

She sighed deeply. "I know. For all its drawbacks, I love it.'' Tears formed in her eyes. "The ratty little town, the narrow-minded people, the forests, the bayou, the smell of the earth, the humidity and heat. Belle Terre. I love it.''

He hugged her hard, pressing her head into the crook of his shoulder. "God, don't apologize for it. Stay here, Schyler, and be happy.''

"But I'll miss you.''

"Not for long.''

"Always.''

He tilted her head away from him and wiped the tears off her cheeks with his thumbs. "When we met we were emotional cripples. Whether you had come home or not, I'm not sure it was healthy for us to go on depending on each other for support and safekeeping. We had a mutually beneficial arrangement. You didn't have to fight off unwelcomed attention from men. I hid my homosexuality behind your skirts. Most married couples aren't as good friends as we are.'' His smile was wistful. "But we can't go on living together indefinitely. You need more than that. You need more than I can give you.'' He leaned forward and whispered. "You need Belle Terre.''

"It needs me, too.''

She had kept him abreast of her tribulations because she knew he was genuinely interested. During their tour of the house, he had listened patiently while she brought him up to date.

"Tomorrow Daddy will be home. I'm delighted. But that means I'll be dividing my time between him and my work at the landing. I can't sacrifice one to the other. I want to include him on decisions so he doesn't feel useless, but I can't let him become too emotionally involved or he could suffer another attack. It'll be a real juggling act.''

"You can handle it.''

"Do you really think so?''

"I really think so." He combed his fingers through her hair. "When were you going to tell me that you were here to stay, Schyler?"

"I don't know. I'm not even sure I knew for certain myself until you said that about losing your roommate. I guess my final decision was lying there in my subconscious, waiting for someone to pull it out."

"Hmm." He nodded thoughtfully. "Does your subconscious decision to stay have anything to do with the cigarette?"

"The cigarette?"

He hitched his chin in the direction of the woods beyond the yard. "There's been one glowing out there for as long as we've been on the veranda."

Schyler whipped her head in that direction. "Cash," she whispered.

"Mr. Boudreaux," Mark said dryly. "His name pops up frequently in your conversation. I wonder if you realize how often it's, 'Cash says this,' or 'Cash does that.' "

She couldn't quite meet the amusement in his eyes, so she stared at the carefully knotted necktie at his throat. "Its not what you think. It's very complicated."

"It usually is, love."

"No, Mark, it's more than just boy-girl games. He's . . ."

"Wrong for you."

"That's an understatement."

"His reputation with women is dubious."

"Not dubious at all. It's definite. Quite definite. He nails everything that moves."

"Is that a quote?"

"Roughly."

"I thought so. It didn't sound like you."

"It's not only that Cash is a womanizer. He's—"

"From the wrong side of the tracks. In this case, the wrong side of the bayou."

"I'm not a snob," she said defensively.

"But most people are," he reminded her gently. "And, after all, you're a Crandall from Belle Terre. What would people think?"

"It's not even as simple as that. I've never given too much thought to what other people think. Mama did. Cotton was just the opposite. He never gave a flying—I'll skip that quote." Mark laughed and it was good to hear his laughter. Shrugging, smiling, she said, "I guess I fall somewhere in between them. I don't really care what people think, but I feel a responsibility to Belle Terre to keep us respectable."

"You're getting off the subject. What about Cash Boudreaux?"

"I don't know. He's . . . It's . . ." She closed her eyes and gritted her teeth. "So damned confusing. I don't trust him and yet . . ."

"You lust for him."

She opened her eyes and gazed up at him. She'd never been able to lie to Mark. She couldn't even stretch the truth. His bald honesty with himself demanded honesty from everyone else. "Yes," she confessed softly. "I lust for him."

Mark embraced her. "Good. I'm glad. A case of raw lust is going to be very healthy for you." Chuckling, he added, "This is going to be interesting to watch, even from afar." He kissed her temple, then her lips. "Be happy, Schyler."

He released her and moved across the veranda toward the screen door. "Don't bother showing me upstairs. I know the way. Forgive me for abandoning you tonight, but I'm exhausted. The flight and all." He blew her a kiss, then stepped inside.

Schyler remained where she was, staring at the empty doorway. After several moments, she turned, still keeping contact with the pillar, and looked out across the lawn.

The red glow of a cigarette winked at her.

She was down the steps and walking through the damp, cool grass before she even realized the fluted column was no longer supporting her. It seemed to take forever for her to reach the woods, but then before she could prepare herself for it, she brushed aside a clump of crepe myrtle blooms and came face-to-face with Cash. He tossed down his cigarette and ground it to powder with the toe of his boot.

"What are you doing skulking around out here in the dark?" Schyler angrily demanded. "If you were spying on me, why—"

"Shut up."

FORTY-THREE

He took her jaw between his hard fingers, backed her into the trunk of a pine, and forced her lips to open beneath his kiss. His tongue arrowed toward the back of her throat as his lips rubbed kiss after hot kiss upon hers. Her arms went up around his neck. She drove her fingers through his hair and held his head fast. He released her jaw and moved both hands up and down her body, touching as much of her as he could.

He tore his mouth free and locked his lustful gaze with hers. Their breaths made a thrashing sound in the dark stillness.

"Goddamn you, say you want me."

Schyler moistened her swollen, vandalized lips. "I want you. That's why I'm here."

He enclosed her wrist in the circle of his fingers and dragged her deeper into the forest. She stumbled along behind him, half laughing, half crying. She wasn't frightened. Her heart was churning with exhilaration, not fear. She didn't feel a sense of being dragged away from everything that was familiar and safe, but rather toward something that was new and exciting. And though he had her wrist imprisoned in his grasp, she felt free and unfettered.

He took her to the place on the bayou where he'd treated the dog bites a few weeks earlier. The same lantern was there, the same pirogue.

"Get in."

She stepped into the small boat and unsteadily lowered herself onto the seat. Cash pushed the boat away from the bank and stepped into it in one fluid motion. Taking up the long pole, he moved the pirogue through the shallow, murky waters by pushing along the bottom with the pole.

He stood in the prow, never taking his eyes off of Schyler. His silhouette looked large and dangerous and dark against the moonlit sky. The moon played in and among the trees that lined the bank, so that the surrounding forest was a constantly shifting pattern of light and shadow. The waters of the bayou swished pleasantly against the pirogue. Bullfrogs croaked from their natural barges and night birds called to each other.

"Why did you leave him and come to me?"

"Mark?"

"Did you break it off with him?"

"There was nothing to break off."

"You could get hurt playing me for a fool, Schyler."

She didn't doubt that for an instant. "Mark is gay. Our living arrangement was purely platonic."

He didn't laugh. He didn't accuse her of lying. He didn't express disbelief.

She would have expected any of those reactions. He said nothing, and only continued to help the slow-moving current by applying the pole to the muddy bottom of the bayou.

Sometimes the channel was so narrow that tree branches interlaced above them and formed a canopy. The bayou took twists and turns until Schyler lost all sense of direction. Even the moon seemed to change position in the sky.

She experienced sights and sounds and smells that she had never experienced before. The air felt different, still, but teeming with energy, with life unseen. It was an alien world, Cash's world. He was lord of it, so she wasn't afraid.

At last the pirogue nosed against the bank. He stepped out and dragged it to more solid ground. Dropping the pole, he reached for Schyler's hand and helped her alight. Carrying the lantern in his free hand, he led her up the incline toward his house.

They entered through the screened porch. He set the lantern on his bedside table and turned to face her. For endless moments they said nothing, just stood there, staring at each other, feeling apprehensive about what was about to happen.

Moving simultaneously, they fell on each other hungrily. His fingers sank into her hair and folded around her scalp. He angled her head back and kissed her mouth, then her throat, than her mouth again. In between those explicit kisses, he murmured even more explicit words. Some were spoken in the language of his mother's ancestors. If the words were indistinguishable, his inflection was easily understood. Schyler responded to the sexual dialect, demonstrating her willingness by arching her body against his.

The fabric of her dress was so soft, so sheer, that it seemed as insubstantial as cotton candy against the hard, demanding toughness of his body. Schyler wanted to be wrapped in his virility.

His kisses gentled. He moved his tongue in and out of her mouth with deliberate leisure, savoring each nuance, the sleek texture, the sweet taste.

"Last time, you didn't know what hit you," he said gruffly. "This time, lady, I want you buzzing."

"I'm already buzzing." She gasped as his hands moved down the front of her dress. His palms were hot. They seemed to melt the fabric.

He looked down at her and smiled. "Good. That's good." He bent his head and kissed her mouth again. He reached for her buttons. Ending the kiss, his eyes followed the movements of his hands as he meticulously released each button from its hole. When they were all undone, he parted the bodice. Her demi-bra was pastel and floral and all for show. It seemed to disintegrate beneath his deft fingers.

And then her breasts were lying in his palms and his thumbs were sweeping back and forth over their tips. "Cash." Softly crying his name, she placed her hands at either side of his waist as her body angled back.

He made small sounds of arousal and gratification as her nipples turned as hard and rosy as pink pearls against his brushing fingertips. He bent his head toward them and laved them quickly with his tongue. He drew one into his mouth and sucked firmly.

"I can't get enough," he groaned, flinging his head up. He pressed her face between his hands and glared down at her, his intense desire bordering on fury. "I can't get enough," he repeated before assaulting her mouth again.

Locked together they fell on the bed. He worked her dress down to her hips, then he tossed it over the bed. He took only an instant to visually admire her skimpy lingerie before helping her remove it.

When she was naked, he laid his hand on her belly and rubbed his calloused palm across it. He stroked the wedge of tight, blond curls. They ensnared his fingertips. Then he curved his strong dark hand around her breast.

Holding his stare, Schyler pulled his shirt out of his waistband and slid her hands beneath it. She combed her fingers through the thick curly pelt. His eyes narrowed with increasing passion. His breath made a whistling sound through his compressed lips.

With rapid, jerky motions, he ripped his shirt buttons out of their holes and shrugged his shirt off. The buckle of his belt required a little more dexterity. He cursed it numerous times before it and his jeans became unfastened. He quickly rolled to his back and, raising his hips off the bed, pushed the jeans down his thighs. He kicked free of them, sending his boots to the floor at the same time.

Naked, warm, and hard, he rolled on top of Schyler and pinned her hands on either side of her head. His kiss would have been ravishment had she not participated with equal ardor.

"I'll kill you if you're lying to me about him."

"I'm not. I swear I'm not."

"Then this is for me? You're hot for me?"

"Yes," she cried out.

Inching his way down, he kissed her neck and chest. She laid her hands on his shoulders and gripped them hard while he stimulated her breasts with his lips and tongue until her nipples were stiff. He kissed his way down her middle, nipping her lightly with his teeth. His tongue flicked over her navel until she was gasping for breath.

Then it became impossible to breathe at all because he planted a hot, wet kiss just above her pubic hair, kissing her so strongly that he drew her delicate skin against his front teeth and made a mark. Her reaction was electric and involuntary. Raising her knees, digging her heels into the mattress, she tilted her hips up and forward.

Cash slid his hands beneath her derriere, pressed his fingers into the supple flesh, and drew her against his open mouth. He ate her with gentle avidity, letting her know he derived as much pleasure from it as he gave. Mindless as she was, and drowning in sensation, Schyler realized that Cash wanted her in the most intimate way.

His tongue pressed high into the giving folds of her body, sliding in and out in a delicious tongue-fuck. When he allowed it to slip free, he made sharp, stabbing motions with it against that kernel of flesh that had become exposed.

She clutched his hair. "Stop. Stop. Cash. No." Her belly grew taut. Her throat and breasts grew flushed. She felt as if she were poised on the edge of a cliff, looking down.

"Come," he grated hoarsely. "I want you to. Come against my mouth."

She couldn't have stopped it if she had wanted to.

When the last wave receded and she opened her eyes, his face was bending close above hers. She saw herself reflected in the swirls of gray and green and gold in his eyes. She smiled tentatively.

"What?" He playfully nudged her belly with the smooth, velvety tip of his iron penis.

"I look thoroughly debauched."

He grinned. "You certainly do." Then he sobered as his eyes wandered over her face. It was rosy and dewy with perspiration. Her lips were full and moist and slightly battered from his kiss and her own teeth. "You look beautiful."

He wasn't a man who handed out compliments frequently, if at all. Schyler had the feeling that he'd never told another woman that she was beautiful, at least not after he had succeeded in getting her in bed.

Her eyes turned smoky with the thought. Moving her fingers over his chest she said, "I think you're beautiful, too." She drew his head down and kissed his lips, licking the taste of herself off them.

Cash, hissing in sexual agony, caught her hand. He carried it down between their bodies and filled it with his erection. "Hold me. Squeeze me. Tight." He said the last word between clenched teeth, because her hand was already caressing the smooth, thick shaft. She discovered a drop of moisture on the very tip and spread it in and around the cleft.

Chanting love words, swear words, Cash reached between their bodies and separated the moist lips of her sex with his fingers. He planted himself so solidly inside of her that their body hair meshed.

He whispered, "You're tighter than a fist. Wetter than a mouth."

She massaged him with the walls of her body, contracting and releasing her muscles in an undulating motion that reduced him to a whimpering, quivering male animal, defeated by his own superb sexuality.

"Damn you," he breathed as he began to stroke her harder. "Damn you."

Again and again he delved into her body. Each time he almost withdrew, stretching and opening to give them ultimate sensation when he sank back into her. Schyler arched up to meet each deep thrust. Soon her choppy breathing matched his. When climax was imminent, they clung together and helplessly surrendered to each other, and to the rampant desire that neither wanted.

FORTY-FOUR

Lying face-to-face, Schyler lovingly examined him. "What caused this?" She touched a knick of a scar on his chest.

"Knife fight in Vietnam."

"You got that close to the enemy?"

"Not the enemy. Another GI."

"What were you fighting over?"

"Hell if I know. It didn't matter. We invented reasons for fighting."

"Why?"

"To let off steam."

"Wasn't there enough of a fight going on in the battle zones?"

"*Oui.* But that wasn't a fair fight. Most of the skirmishes in the barracks were."

"Were you a regular soldier?"

"I was *ir*regular. All of us had to be to survive."

"I meant did you specialize in something."

"Munitions and explosives." His jaw tensed. "I guess I did my share to get the body count up."

She tried to smooth the hair on his eyebrow, but it was too unruly. "If you felt that way about the war, why did you volunteer to go? I was told you kept reenlisting.''

He shrugged. ''It seemed like the thing to do at the time. I wasn't doing anything else.''

''What about college?''

''I was enrolled, but I knew more about my major than the professors.''

''What was your major?''

''Forestry.''

''You didn't have to go to Vietnam to get out of college, Cash. You could have stayed here and worked.''

He was shaking his head before she finished. ''Cotton and I had had a falling out.''

''Cotton was partly responsible for you going to war? How? What did you argue over?''

He gazed at her for a long time, then said, ''Over your mother's death.''

''*My* mother's death? What did that have to do with you?''

He rolled to his back and stared at the ceiling. Propping herself on one elbow, Schyler looked down at him inquisitively. He avoided looking at her. ''After Macy died, I expected Cotton to marry my mother. He didn't. Wouldn't.''

She rested her hand on Cash's breastbone, opening and closing her fingers like the pleats of a fan, snaring curly strands of chest hair between them. ''I don't know what to say about that, Cash. I don't know much about it.''

''Well I sure as hell knew what to say. I said it all to Cotton's face. We had a helluva fight. We would have come to blows if my mother hadn't intervened.''

From what she knew of Monique, Schyler imagined how she must have felt when the two men she loved were at each other's throats. ''What did she do?''

''Do? She defended Cotton, of course. She always defended him. She had justifications for everything he ever did. She never saw what a son of a bitch he is.''

Her lover was calling her father a son of a bitch, but Schyler didn't jump to Cotton's defense. It was little wonder that Cash resented Cotton for not marrying his mother. Under similar circumstances, she would have felt the same way.

Cotton had been a good father to her and Tricia. She adored him in spite of his shortcomings. But she was no judge on how he conducted his personal life outside of Belle Terre. Until a few weeks ago, she didn't even know about his relationship with Monique Boudreaux and her volatile son. Each man was strong-willed and Schyler clearly imagined how vehemently they could disagree.

''The night we brought Gayla to Belle Terre, you mentioned that your mother had miscarried a baby.''

''*Oui.*''

''My father's baby?''

His eyes flashed defensively. ''*Oui.* My mother might have been unmarried, but she wasn't a whore. She didn't sleep with anybody but him.''

''I didn't mean to imply—''

''I'm hungry. Are you?'' He rolled off the bed and snatched up his jeans.

Troubled, Schyler took the shirt he tossed her and pushed her arms through the sleeves. ''Yes, I'm hungry. What have you got?''

''Red beans and rice.''

''Sounds delicious.''

''Leftovers, but I'll heat it up.''

Together they padded through the house, switching on lights as they went.

Schyler sat in a chair at the table and watched while Cash moved about the small kitchen heating up a pan of the fragrant, hearty ethnic dish. When he passed her a plateful she saw that the beans and rice were complemented by large disks of spicy sausage.

"Just the way I like it," she said, digging in. "Hmm, wonderful. Who made it?"

"I did." She stopped chewing. He laughed at her incredulous expression. "Did you think the only recipes my mother left me were cures for warts and dyspepsia?"

Schyler ate with an unladylike appetite and finished everything on her plate. As Cash was carrying it to the sink, she studied the graceful lines of his back, the natural swagger of his narrow hips, and his long, lean legs.

He turned around and caught her looking at him with dreamy, misty eyes. "See anything you like?" he asked cockily.

"You're conceited, but, yes, I like everything I see."

"You don't sound too happy about it. What's the matter?"

"What's going to happen tomorrow?"

"Tomorrow?"

Suddenly embarrassed, Schyler glanced down at her hands, which were nervously clasping and unclasping in her lap. The hem of his shirt barely skimmed her thighs. She resisted the urge to modestly tug it down.

"I mean, what's going to happen between us? Daddy's coming home."

"I know." She looked up hastily. "I called the hospital," Cash said by way of explanation. "When you left the landing in such a hurry, I thought something might be wrong."

"On the contrary, he's doing much better. But he's still a heart patient. He can't get upset." She ran her tongue over her lips. "I don't know how he would take to something, you know, an affair, between you and me."

"He'll go apeshit."

Cash's response was not very encouraging. She continued anyway. "You know how busy we're going to be for the next few weeks. We've got to get that Endicott order filled in time. I can't let anything, particularly my personal life, stand in the way of that. There won't be much time for . . . for . . ."

Cash, leaning against the old-fashioned, corrugated cast-iron drain board, crossed his bare ankles and folded his arms over his hairy chest. His silence urged her to continue. "I'm not sure I'm ready for any kind of emotional entanglement. The relationship I had with Mark was special, even though it wasn't sexual. I'll miss him. I know you see other women."

She hoped he would enlighten her as to who and how many. Better yet, she wished he would tell her that he was through with other women now that he'd slept with her. But he remained as silent and still as a wooden Indian. It piqued her that he revealed nothing while she held nothing back.

"Dammit, say something."

"All right." He pushed himself away from the drain board. When his bare toes were only inches from hers, he reached down and grabbed a fistful of his shirt, hauling her up by it. "Get back to bed."

Minutes later, they were lying amid the sheets that smelled muskily of him, of her, of sex. She was lying on her side, facing him. His face was nestled between her breasts. He was softly caressing her nipple with his tongue.

"I've wanted to do this for a long time," he mumbled.

Schyler had conveniently dismissed her concerns for the time being. Cash had the right idea. Ignore tomorrow. Let the devil take it. Live for the moment. She might have to pay the piper a king's ransom later, but right now, with his mouth warm and urgent against her breasts, she didn't care.

"You're not going to say something corny like, 'Since the moment we met,' are you?"

"No. I wanted to do it even before we met."

"Before we met?" She looked at him with a puzzled expression. He eased her to her back and propped himself up on one elbow, leaving his other hand free to fondle.

"The first time I remember noticing that you weren't a little girl anymore, we were in the Magnolia Drug. I must have been eighteen, nineteen. You came in with a group of your friends. You were all acting silly, giggling. I guess you were still in junior high. You ordered a chocolate soda."

"I don't remember."

"No reason you should. It was just an ordinary day to you."

"Did you speak to me?"

He laughed bitterly. "Hell no. You would have run in terror if the scourge of Heaven had spoken to you."

"Is that when you rode the motorcycle?" He nodded and she laughed. "You're right. It would have been compromising to my good reputation to even say hello."

"If Cotton had gotten wind of it, he'd've had me castrated. I was banging everything in skirts that said yes. In fact, I was in the drugstore buying rubbers. I'd just paid for them when you came in. I decided to stick around. I ordered a drink at the fountain."

"Just so you could watch me?"

He nodded. "You had on a pink sweater. Fuzzy. A fuzzy pink sweater. And your breasts, or tits as I thought of them then, were making me crazy. They were small. Pointed. But they made two distinct impressions on the front of your sweater." He played with her, his motions as idle as his speech. "I made that vanilla Dr. Pepper last for more than an hour, watching you while you fed quarters into the jukebox and gossiped with your girlfriends. And the whole time, I was wishing I could reach up under your sweater, where your skin would be warm and smooth, and touch your pretty little breasts."

Schyler was mesmerized by the story. Cash stared into her wide, glassy gaze for a long time before leaning down and moistening her tight nipple with his tongue. Years of wanting went into each damp stroke.

"I knew better than to fantasize about you," he murmured. "I'd already been with more than my share of girls, but they'd all been willing partners. I never took unfair advantage of any of them. You were way too young for a man with my vast experience." He moved his face back and forth in the valley of her breasts. "Do you think I was perverted?"

"Very."

He raised his head and grinned. "But you like it?"

"Yes," she admitted with a self-conscious laugh. "I guess every woman likes to think she's been the object of a fantasy at least once."

"You were that, Miss Schyler. You were that. I was a white trash, bastard scum. You were the reigning princess of Belle Terre. I was grown. You were just a kid. You were so far out of my league, it wasn't even funny. But I had no control over myself. I wanted to touch you."

"Because you couldn't."

"Probably."

"We always want what we can't have."

"All I know is, I got so hard I hurt," he rasped, brushing a rough kiss across her lips. "After you and your friends left the drugstore, I got on my bike and drove to the edge of town. I parked and masturbated." He kissed her hard. "One phone call and I could have had a girl under me in five minutes. But I didn't want one. I wanted to get off, thinking about Schyler Crandall." Again, he kissed her. Harder.

"I've never seen Belle Terre at dawn from this side of the yard," Schyler remarked from the cab of Cash's pickup. "I've viewed sunrises from my upstairs window, but never from the outside looking in."

"I've never seen it any other way."

Her head came around quickly, but his expression didn't suggest hostility. It didn't suggest anything. She tried to lighten the mood. "I feel foolish, sneaking in at dawn."

"I wonder what your company thinks about you being out all night."

"Mark! I forgot about him. I really should be there when he wakes up." She placed her hand on the door handle, but was reluctant to officially end the night. "What are you going to do? Go back to bed?"

"No."

"Surely you're not going to work this early." The sky was still gray at the horizon.

"I've got other things to do."

"At this hour?" His eyes became even more remote. It was a visible transformation. "Excuse me," Schyler said testily, "I didn't mean to pry." She shoved open the door, which still bore Jigger Flynn's bullet hole, and got out.

"Schyler?"

"What?" She spun around, angry with Cash for not being more affectionate and angry with herself for wanting him to be.

"I'll see you later."

His steamy look melted her thighs and her resentment. His expression and tone of voice intimated he would be seeing a lot of her later. With a slow, possessive smile, he shoved the pickup into gear and drove off.

 # FORTY-FIVE

Jigger woke up with a painful erection. Before he remembered that she was no longer there, he rolled over and reached for Gayla. Instead of warm, wonderful woman, he came up with a handful of grubby sheets.

Cursing her for not being available when he wanted her, he stumbled into the bathroom and relieved himself. Glancing in the mirror over the chipped, stained sink, he hooted in laughter at his reflection. "You'd make a vulture puke." He was uglier than sin. His beard stubble showed up white on his loose, flabby jaw.

Too much whiskey last night, he thought. He released a vile-tasting belch. His eyes were rivered with red streams. There was a large hole in his dingy tank T-shirt. It was a miracle that his voluminous boxer shorts kept their grip on his skinny ass.

He was hobbling back to bed, when he abruptly stopped and stood still. He had just realized what had woken him.

"What the hell?" he mumbled. He had never heard anything like that sound. He shoved aside the tacky curtains and peered through the grimy glass. A ray of sunlight pierced his red eyes, stinging him as if he had been speared through the back of his skull. He cursed viciously.

Once his eyes adjusted to the light, he blinked the yard into focus. Nothing unusual was going on. The puppies were yapping at their dam, demanding breakfast. Everything was normal.

Everything but that sound.

Jigger's gut knotted with foreboding. He had razor-sharp instincts about these things. He could smell trouble a mile away. That sound meant bad news. Menace. But where the hell was it coming from?

Compelled to find out, he didn't bother with dressing. Knobby knees aiming in opposite directions, he walked through his shabby house. It had really gone to seed since Gayla's defection. Mice scattered like a sack of spilled marbles across the linoleum floor when he entered the kitchen. Jigger cursed them, but otherwise ignored them. He pulled open the back door and pushed through the screen. The dogs in the backyard pens began barking.

"Shut up, you sons of bitches." Couldn't they tell his head was splitting? He raised a hand to his thudding temple. "Jesus." The blasphemy was still fresh on his lips when he spotted the oil drum.

It was a fifty-five gallon drum, silver and rusty in a few spots, but otherwise in good condition. It was ordinary.

Except for the sound it emitted.

Jigger recognized it now. It was a rattler. A hell of a one if the racket it was making was any indication of its size.

The drum had been left square in the middle of his yard between the back door and the toolshed. But by whom, Jigger wondered as he stood there with his hands propped on his nonexistent hips, staring at the drum in perplexity. Whoever it was had been a cagey bastard because his dogs hadn't made a racket. Either it was somebody who was used to handling dogs or it was somebody, or some*thing* spooky. Whatever it was, it was fuckin' weird. Goose bumps rose on his arms.

"Shit!"

It was just a snake. He wasn't afraid of snakes. When he was younger he'd traveled all the way to West Texas several times to go on rattlesnake roundups. That had been a helluva good time. There had been lots of smooth booze and coarse broads, lots of snake handling and one-upmanship. He'd lost count of the rattlers he'd milked of their venom.

No, it wasn't the snake that bothered him. What was giving Jigger the shivers was the manner in which the snake had been delivered. If somebody wanted to give him a present, why didn't he just come up and hand it to him outright? Why leave it as a surprise for him to discover while he still had a bitchin' hangover and before his morning coffee?

Coffee. That's what he needed, coffee dark as Egypt and strong as hell. He needed a woman here every morning to get his coffee. Yes, sir. He'd look into that today. He'd find a new woman. He had put up with that black bitch far too long. He needed one who didn't sass, one who kept her mouth shut and her thighs open. He was coming into some money soon, a goddamn fair amount, too. Nothing to sneeze at. With that, he could buy the best pussy in the parish.

This mental monologue had given Jigger time to walk all the way around the drum, inspecting it from all angles. Thoughtfully, he scratched his nose. He scratched his crotch. The lid of the drum was anchored down with a large rock. He reckoned he ought to open it and look inside to see just how monstrous this rattler was.

But damned if that sound wasn't getting to him. It was playing with his nerves something fierce. That snake was good and pissed off for being confined to that drum. He tried to remember just how far rattlers could strike.

He recalled one guy who was a fanatic about rattlers. He'd told Jigger that one could strike as far as he was long. Jigger hadn't believed him at the time. He was a born liar, and a Texan to boot. Besides, he'd been drunk as a fiddler's bitch and his tales had been nearly as tall as the blond broad who'd been straddling his lap and licking his ear.

But now, when such information was critical, Jigger wondered if the fellow knew what he was talking about. Yet it could be that it only sounded noisy because it was in the bottom of that hollow drum.

"Hell yeah, that's it, don'tcha know. It just sounds big."

He approached the drum with garnered bravery, but as a precaution, he carried a long stick of firewood with him. His nerves were jangling as energetically as the rattler's tail when he knocked the rock to the ground, using the piece of firewood.

He moved the stick from one hand to the other, while alternately wiping his palms on the saggy seat of his boxers. Then, reaching far out in front of him, he eased the end of the stick under the rim of the drum's lid and carefully levered it up.

A bluejay squawked raucously from the tree directly overhead. Jigger nearly jumped out of his boxer shorts. He dropped the stick of firewood on his bare big toe.

"Goddammit to hell!" he bellowed. His cursing sent the pit bull bitch into a frenzy. Snarling and slavering, she repeatedly threw herself against the kennel's fence. It took several minutes for Jigger to quiet her and the litter and to scare off the territorially possessive bluejay.

Scraping together his courage again, Jigger picked up the stick and wedged it under the rim of the lid. He prized it up no more than an inch, but the volume of the sinister sound increased ten times. Jigger approached the drum on tiptoes, trying to see into it, but he could see only the opposite inside wall.

Taking a deep breath and checking to see that nothing was behind him, he flipped the lid to the ground. At the same time, he leaped backward like an uncoordinated acrobat. His heart was beating so quickly it reverberated in his eardrums, but nothing drowned out that deafening, nerve-racking, bloodcurdling sound.

No snake came striking out. He crept closer to the drum and peered over the edge, leaning forward as far as he dared.

"Jesus H. Christ."

He couldn't see all of it. He could see only a portion of a body that was as thick as a muscle builder's bicep. Quickly he scouted the yard for something to stand on. Spotting a bucket in a pile of junk, he brought it back to the drum at a run and uprighted it. Then he stood on it, still a safe distance away, and got his first full look at his snake.

It was a monster, all right. Coiled several times around the bottom of the drum, he estimated it to be eight feet long. Six minimum. It filled up a good third of the drum. Sticking up out of the center of that deadly concentric coil was a rattling tail that looked like it would never stop. It shook so rapidly, it was impossible to count the individual rattles. But it was a great-granddaddy of a rattlesnake; it was mad as hell, and it was *his*.

Jigger clapped his hands in glee. With childlike delight, he clasped them together beneath his chin. He stared in wonder and awe at his marvelous gift. Eve's serpent couldn't have had any more sinister allure. It was entrancing to watch something so consummately evil, so gloriously wicked.

Everything about it was corruptly beautiful—the geometric pattern of its skin, the obsidian eyes, the forked tongue that flicked in and out of the flat lips, and that incessant rattle that was ominous and deadly.

Quickly, but cautiously, Jigger replaced the lid of the drum and weighted it down with the rock. He wasn't really worried that the snake could get out. If it was capable of striking over the rim of the drum, it would have by now. That snake was mean, diabolically so. Jigger instantly developed an attachment to it.

He loved his snake.

He ran for the house, full of plans on how to capitalize on the gift. It was a gift. He was sure of that now. Whoever had left it meant him no harm. He reasoned that it had been left by somebody who owned him money. That could be just about anybody in southwestern Louisiana. He wasn't going to worry about that now. His head was too full of commercial plans.

First, he'd have a flyer printed up advertising it. By nightfall his yard would be crawling with customers who wanted to see his rattler. What should he charge? A buck a peek. That was a neat, round figure he figured.

He entered his house through the back. The squeaky screen door slammed shut behind him, but he didn't hear anything over the clacking noise that his fabulous rattler made. In Jigger's opinion, it was music.

 # FORTY-SIX

Cotton was a trying invalid even on his good days. Within a week of his homecoming everybody at Belle Terre was tempted to smother him in his sleep.

Tricia's affected bedside manner, never very extensive, was expended after the first day. She met Schyler in the hall. "He's always been a contrary old son of a bitch." She spoke under her breath so he wouldn't hear her through the walls of the study-bedroom. "He's even worse now."

"Tolerate his moods. Don't do or say anything to get him angry."

Schyler feared that her sister and Ken would become impatient about selling Belle Terre and broach the subject with Cotton. Dr. Collins had reiterated when she brought Cotton home that he was still a heart patient and must be treated carefully no matter how irksome he became.

Tricia didn't take Schyler's admonition kindly. "You're worried about that, aren't you? Is that what's keeping you up nights?"

"What are you talking about?"

"Come now, don't play innocent. Clever as you've been," Tricia said with a sly smile, "you haven't hidden your comings and goings in the middle of the night from us." She shook her head and laughed lightly. "Honestly, Schyler, you have the most appalling taste in men. A fairy antique dealer and a tom-catting white trash."

"And your own husband," Schyler shot back. "Insult my taste in men and you're insulting yourself. Don't forget that I picked Ken before you."

"I never forget that." Tricia smiled complacently. "And apparently neither do you."

Schyler let the argument die instantly. Insult swapping with Tricia was a tiresome exercise in futility. She could never top her sister's pettiness. As long as Tricia left Cotton alone, Schyler didn't care what she thought of her or the company she kept.

Ken avoided seeing Cotton after paying one obligatory visit to the sickroom soon after Cotton arrived. In fact, Ken kept to himself most of the time. His mood was volatile. He drank excessively and frequently carried on furtive, whispered telephone conversations.

He was particularly acerbic toward Schyler. She supposed he was still pouting because she hadn't loaned him the money he had requested. The telephone calls were probably from impatient creditors. Because of his financial difficulties she felt sorry for him. He was a grown man, though; it was time he learned to sort out his own problems.

At first Gayla was so shy around Cotton she could barely be persuaded to enter his room, but they had soon fallen into an easy rapport. He seemed to have entirely dismissed her years with Jigger and teased her often, recounting times in her childhood when she'd been a trial to Veda.

Eventually Gayla's guard relaxed. An unspoken bond developed between the two of them, which wasn't completely surprising. Each was recuperating from an assault. When no one else could convince Cotton to eat food he didn't like or to take his medication or to do his regimen of mild exercises, Gayla could.

He and Mrs. Dunne nearly came to blows the first day he was home. She had a tendency to mother him as she had her sick husband. Cotton couldn't stomach that and let her know it in no uncertain terms. Mrs. Dunne's maternal instincts gave way to a military bearing that clashed with Cotton's temper. Once the air had been cleared, however, they developed a mutual, if grudging, respect for each other.

But of everyone in the household, Schyler best handled the recalcitrant patient. She seemed to know how to molify his temper when something set it off and how to boost his morale when he fell victim to depression. By turns she kept him calm and encouraged.

He was allowed to watch newscasts on the portable television that had been placed in his room. One of Gayla's duties was to bring him the local newspaper the moment it was delivered. But Schyler kept her answers vague whenever he asked about Crandall Logging.

"Everything's going very well," she parroted each evening when she came in to visit with him.

"Any problems on getting that order to Endicott?"

"None. How are you feeling?"

"Trains running on schedule?"

"Yes. Mrs. Dunne said you ate all your lunch today."

"Does it look like good timber their cutting?"

"Highest Crandall quality. Did you get a good rest this afternoon?"

"Are we gonna make that loan payment in time?"

"Yes. I'm sure of it. Now settle down."

"Jesus, Schyler. I hate that you're having to undo my mistakes."

"Don't worry about it, Daddy. The hard work is good for me. I'm actually enjoying it."

"It's too much for a woman to handle."

"Chauvinist! Why shouldn't I be able to handle the business?"

"Guess I'm just old-fashioned in my thinking. Behind the times." He glared at her from beneath his brows. "Like when I was your age, queers were avoided. Normal women sure as hell didn't move in with them. Is that why I never got to meet Mark Houghton? You were hiding him from me?"

"That's not the reason at all." She kept her voice even, but inside she was fighting mad. Tricia or Ken had tattled. It was probably Tricia, in retaliation for the putdown she'd received from Mark. "Mark had to leave before you got home, that's all."

She had returned home that morning from Cash's house to find a note pinned to her undisturbed pillow. In it Mark expressed his hope that she'd had an enjoyable evening. He wrote that he had been struck by a sudden case of homesickness in the middle of the night, had packed and called Heaven's one taxi, promising an enormous tip if he were driven to Lafayette where he could make flight connections the following day.

Schyler could read through the lines of the cryptic message. Mark hadn't wanted to say good-bye to her. She belonged at Belle Terre; he didn't.

Their bittersweet parting had occurred the night before, though neither had wanted to admit that's what the conversation on the veranda had been. A sad, lengthy, weepy good-bye would have put them through an unnecessary and emotional ordeal. Distressed as she had been to find his note, Schyler was glad Mark had taken the easy way out. She was sad, but relieved.

"How could you live with a guy like that?"

" 'A guy like that'? You don't know what kind of guy Mark is, Daddy. You never met him."

"He's a queer!"

"A homosexual, yes. He's also intelligent, sensitive, funny, and a very dear friend."

"In my day, if one of those crossed our path, we'd beat the hell out of him."

"I hope that's not something you're proud of."

"Not particularly, no. But I'm not particularly ashamed of it either. That's just what us regular guys did. That was before all this social consciousness bullshit got started."

"High time, too. We've come a long way from rolling queers in alleys."

Cotton didn't find her attempted humor very funny. "You've got a real smart mouth, Miss Crandall."

"I learned it from you."

He studied her for a moment. "You know I was real upset about you and Ken not getting together. But now I'm glad. Damn glad. He's a pussy. Drinks too much, gambles too much. Lets Tricia run roughshod over him. She likes that arrangement just fine. But you would have hated it, and soon enough you'd have come to hate him. You're too strong for Ken Howell." He sighed in aggravation. "But once you were rid of him, what do you go and do? You shackle yourself to a man who's even weaker."

"You're wrong. Mark is a very strong individual, one of the strongest men I've ever met. It took tremendous courage for him to leave the life he led in Boston. I moved in with him because I liked him, we got along extremely well, and both of us were lonely. Believe it or not, I didn't consider your feelings about it at all. I didn't become Mark's roommate to spite you."

Cotton frowned at her skeptically. "Kinda looks like that, doesn't it? When are you going to get you a real man, one who can plant some grandbabies in you?"

"Mark could have, if he wanted to. He didn't want to."

"I reckon that's one reason you were attracted to him. He didn't pose a threat."

"I liked him for what he was, not for what he wasn't."

"Don't play word games with me, young lady," he chided her sharply. "Your problem is that you've always loved the unlovely."

"Have I?"

"Ever since you were a kid. Always taking up for the underdog. Like Gayla. Like Glee Williams."

Glad for the chance to switch subjects, Schyler said, "Speaking of Glee, he's doing very well. I called today. The doctors are going to release him from the hospital soon. He'll have to report every few weeks for physical therapy. I'm hoping we can find a desk job for him to do."

"Who's we?"

"We?"

"You said you hoped 'we' can find Glee a desk job."

"Oh, uh, you and I." Cotton's eyes shrewdly searched for the truth. Schyler squirmed. "Glee doesn't like taking a salary without earning it."

He grumbled, a sign that he wasn't satisfied with her glib answer. "You didn't inherit that generous nature from me. Certainly not from Macy. Her heart was about as soft as a brass andiron. Where'd you get your kindheartedness?"

"From my blood relations, I suspect. Who knows?" The conversation had taken a track that made Schyler distinctly uncomfortable. She consulted her wristwatch. "It's past your bedtime. You're intentionally dragging out this conversation to postpone it. Really, Daddy, you're worse than a little kid about going to bed on time."

She leaned over him and fluffed his pillow. Kissing his forehead, she switched off the bedside lamp. Before she could step away, he caught her hand.

"Be careful that your benevolence doesn't work against you, Schyler," he warned.

"What do you mean?"

"Vast experience has taught me that folks dearly love to bite the hand that feeds them. It gives them a perverse satisfaction that's just plain human nature. You can't change that." He wagged his finger at her. "Make sure nobody mistakes your love and charity for weakness. Folks claim they admire saints. But fact is, they despise them. They gloat in seeing them stumble and fall flat on their asses."

"I'll keep that in mind."

Cotton had a spit-and-whittle club philosophy. Schyler wanted to smile indulgently, say, "Yes, sir," and dismiss his advice as the ramblings of an old man. But it weighed on her mind as she stepped out onto the veranda through the back door. She had a strong intuition that Cotton was beating around the bush about something—specifically Cash Boudreaux. He was reluctant to bring it into the open.

She still hadn't mentioned the extent of Cash's involvement in the business or how much she depended on him. Cotton wouldn't like it. And what Cotton wouldn't like, she wasn't telling him. Careful as she'd been to keep Cash's name out of their conversations, Cotton was too smart not to pick up signals. Piecing information together had always been his forte. He must know that Cash was running the daily operation of Crandall Logging. He no doubt resented that, but realized that Cash's experience and knowledge were necessary to Schyler ssuccess.

What he suspected, but obviously didn't want confirmed, was Schyler's personal involvement with Cash. Because of his long-standing relationship with Monique, Cotton would certainly have misgivings about an alliance between them.

Schyler had more than misgivings. She was downright terrified of her feelings for Cash.

She had a voracious physical appetite for him. She looked forward to his stolen kisses and their hungry lovemaking. She had never felt more alive than when she was with him, nor more confused when she wasn't. He was the most intriguing man she'd ever met, but it was confounding not to know all his secrets. He was passionate and perplexing. She depended on him; yet she didn't completely trust him. His lovemaking was frightening in its intensity, but he was often aloof afterward.

When the heat of their desire had been extinguished and she languished in his postcoital embrace, the moment was invariably spoiled by her niggling doubts. She feared that Cash wanted her only because she represented something he'd always been denied. He'd been with legions of women. Certainly many of them were more fascinating, pretty, and sexy than she. What made her so attractive to him? When he entered her body, was he loving her or was he trespassing on Belle Terre?

That thought was so disturbing, it made her warm. Needing air, she stepped outside and drifted soundlessly along the veranda. As she rounded the corner, she bumped into Gayla. The young woman let out a soft scream and flattened herself against the wall of the house.

"Gayla, my God, what's the matter with you?" Schyler said, catching her breath. "You scared me."

"I'm sorry. You scared me, too."

Schyler looked at her friend closely. Gayla's eyes were round with genuine fear. "What's the matter?"

"Nothing. I was just taking the evening air. Guess it's time I went in."

Gayla eased away from the wall and turned as if to run. Schyler caught her arm. "Not so fast, Gayla. What's wrong?"

"Nothing."

"Don't tell me nothing. You look like you've seen a ghost."

Gayla's mouth began to work emotionally. Tears formed in her large, dark eyes. "I wish it was a ghost."

Schyler moved in closer, concerned for her friend's mental stability. "What happened?"

Gayla reached into the deep pocket of her skirt and took something out. Enough light from the window fell on it so Schyler could see what it was. It was an ugly little handmade doll that bore an uncanny resemblance to Gayla. There was a vicious-looking straight pin stuck in the brightly painted red heart on its chest.

"Voodoo?" Schyler whispered. She glanced up at Gayla incomprehensively. "Is that what it is?" She didn't believe in such nonsense. "Where did you get it?"

"Somebody left it on my pillow."

"In your room? You found it in your room? Are you saying that somebody in the house did this?" The cruelty of it was inconceivable, even for Tricia. There was no love lost between the two women, but . . . black magic?

"No. I don't think it was anybody in the house," Gayla replied.

"When did you find it?"

"Last night."

"Tell me."

"I heard something out here on the veranda."

"What time?"

"I don't know. After you left." The two women shared a guilty glance, then looked away. "It was late."

"Go on."

"I thought I heard a noise out here." Gayla glanced around apprehensively. "I wasn't sure. I thought it could have been my imagination. I've been real spooked lately. I think I see Jigger behind every bush."

"That certainly isn't a figment of your imagination," Schyler said grimly, nodding down at the doll.

"I worked up my courage and came out here to investigate."

"You shouldn't have done that alone."

"I didn't want to make a fool of myself by waking up everybody."

"Don't worry about that the next time. If there is a next time. What happened when you came out here?"

"Nothing. I didn't see or hear anything. When I went back inside, this was lying on my pillow." She crammed the doll back in her skirt pocket and tucked her hands under her opposite arms.

"Do you think Jigger did it?"

"Not him personally. He's not that subtle." She thought for a moment. "But he might've hired somebody to do it, to let me know he hasn't forgotten."

"Who does that kind of thing these days?"

"Lots of the blacks."

"Christians?"

Gayla gravely nodded her head. "The early slaves believed in black magic before they ever heard of Jesus. It's been passed down."

"Does Jigger believe in it?"

"I doubt it. But he knows that other folks do, so he uses it to scare them."

"Then he's used these scare tactics before?" Schyler was remembering the two dead cats found on the veranda.

"I think so, yes."

"Do you know who he gets to do his black magic for him?" Gayla looked everywhere but at Schyler. Schyler clasped her arm and shook it. "Who, Gayla?"

"I don't know. I'm not sure."

"But you have a fair idea. Who?"

"Jigger only mentioned one hex to me in all the time I lived with him."

"And?"

"He was probably lying because it isn't a black."

"Who? Give me a name."

Gayla wet her lips. When she spoke, her voice was as soft and fitful as the Gulf Breeze. "Jigger said Cash Boudreaux did it for him."

Cash heard the old board on his porch squeak under weight. He laid down his magazine and casually slipped the knife from the scabbard at the small of his back. Pressed flat against the inside wall, he inched toward the front of his house. The door was opened. Insects dived toward the screen, making small pinging sounds when they struck. He didn't hear anything else. It didn't matter. He knew with a guerrilla fighter's instincts that somebody was out there.

Moving so fast that his limbs were flesh-colored blurs, he whipped open the screen door and lunged outside. The other man was cowering against the wall. Cash's shoulder gouged his midsection. As he doubled over, Cash pressed the tip of his knife against the man's navel.

"Jesus, Cash," he cried out in fear. "It's me."

Adrenaline stopped its chase through Cash's body. His brain telegraphed his hand not to send the knife plunging in and up. He eased to his full height and slid the weapon back into the scabbard. "Goddammit, I almost gutted you. What the hell are you doing sneaking around out here?"

"I thought that's what you hired me to do. Sneak around."

Cash grinned and slapped the other man on the shoulder. "Right. But not around me. Want a drink, *mon ami?*"

"I could damn sure use one. Thanks."

They went inside. Cash poured two straight bourbons. "How'd it go?"

"Just like you said." The man tossed back his drink and, with a wide smile, added. "They never knew I was there."

FORTY-SEVEN

"What's so amusing?" Rhoda Gilbreath asked her husband from her end of the dining table. She laid her fork on her plate and reached for her wineglass. "They lock people who laugh to themselves into tiny, padded rooms, Dale."

Unperturbed, he blotted his mouth with his napkin and pushed his plate aside. Because Rhoda wanted to stay stick-figure thin, she expected him to eat as sparingly as she did. Not that he wanted huge portions of the health food she served at home. He ate surgary bakery doughnuts every morning for breakfast and a high-caloric lunch so that he wouldn't starve to death in the evenings.

"Sorry, darling. I didn't mean to exclude you from the joke." He washed down his last tasteless bit with a swallow of tepid white wine. It, too, was low cal and had no sting. "Have you heard about the latest entertainment attraction in town?"

"They've reopened the drive-in theater. Old news, Dale."

"No, something else."

"I'm holding my breath," she said drolly.

"Jigger Flynn's got a pet snake."

"Bully for him."

Dale leaned back in his chair. "This isn't any ordinary snake. It's a rattlesnake. Gruesome-looking thing."

"You actually went to see Jigger Flynn's snake?"

"I didn't want to be the only one in town who hadn't seen it," he chuckled. "That's all anybody's talking about."

"Which is a clear indication of the intelligence level in this community."

"Don't be snide. This really is a remarkable snake."

"You're dying to tell me all about it, aren't you? Well, go ahead." When he was done, Rhoda was impressed in spite of herself. "And he doesn't know who left it in his yard?"

"Claims not to. Of course Jigger is a bald-faced liar, so you can never be sure if he's telling the truth or not. Still," Dale said, recalling Jigger's giddiness as he showed off his prized possession, "I think this is more than just another of his moneymaking schemes."

"How so?"

"I'm not sure. This snake seems to have touched Jigger in some way."

"Touched? You mean mentally?"

"Psychologically." Dale leaned forward and said in a hushed voice, "I think it was supposed to."

"Isn't this where the spooky music is supposed to come up full? Doo-doo-doo-doo, doo-doo-doo-doo."

Dale ignored his wife's sarcasm. His expression was reflective, as though he were reasoning through an intricate riddle. "Whoever left that rattler for Jigger to find wanted him to be hyped up about it. Jesus, it wouldn't take long for that monster to fuck with my mind. You can hear the thing from two hundred yards. Never heard such a creepy sound in all my life."

Rhoda's slender, beringed fingers slid up and down the stem of her wineglass as she shrewdly regarded her husband. "You don't know anything about it, do you?"

Dale feigned surprise. "Who, me? No. Certainly not." At her skeptical expression, he laughed. "Honest. I don't know anything about Jigger's snake."

Rhoda took a sip of wine. "If you did, you wouldn't tell me."

"What makes you think that?"

"Because you're a provoking son of a bitch, that's why."

Dale frowned at his wife. She wasn't a cheerful drunk. Indeed, she got more surly by the glass. "I'd like to know what burr has been stuck up your ass for the last week or so. You've been impossible to live with."

"I've got a lot on my mind."

"Not the least of which is who your next extramarital lover is going to be."

He had pushed himself away from the table and left the dining room before Rhoda came to her senses. She stumbled from her chair and chased after him. She caught up with him in the den where he was calmly lighting his pipe. Before he could apply the match to the filled bowl, she caught his arm.

"What do you mean, who my next lover is going to be?"

Dale jerked his arm free, lit his pipe, and fanned out the match, meticulously dropping it in the ashtray, before giving his wife his attention. "It's all over town that your most recent stud is humping the Crandall woman. Tough luck, Rhoda."

"What does it mean?"

"Humping? It means—"

She punched him in the chest. "Stop it! You know what I meant. What does this mean to us? To your plans for the takeover of Belle Terre?"

He glowered at her for striking him, but he puffed his pipe docilely. "Their affair falls right into place with my own plans. He might be nailing her, but he has an ulterior motive. There's bad blood between him and the Crandalls, having to do with his mother and Cotton I believe."

Rhoda's spirits lifted marginally. She had cause to want the sky to fall on both Cash and Schyler. As Dale had said, it was all over town that they were sleeping together. Rhoda herself had heard it at a meeting of the Friends of the Library. Helping to spread the salacious tidings was Schyler's own sister. Tricia Howell had held court to an enthralled audience while she dragged Schyler's name through the muck.

Oh, she had put on a great act, making her avid listeners drag the information out of her, bit by juicy bit. But once she'd confirmed the gossip, she said, "Everybody at Belle Terre is thoroughly disgusted. Cash is so trashy. I mean, think what his mama was."

Rhoda wasn't fooled. Tricia was jealous of her older sister, and probably envious of her affair with Cash. The catty little bitch had then launched into a story about Schyler's life in London with a homosexual, while Rhoda sat and stewed in her own juice. Schyler Crandall was the reason behind Cash's peculiar switch in personality. He had dumped *her* for Schyler Crandall. For that, she'd pay them back in spades.

"You can play one off the other," she suggested to Dale now.

Dale stroked his wife's cheek affectionately. "You're a vicious bitch, my dear. Vicious, but so clever."

SANDRA BROWN

"Is there anything I can do to help further things along?"

"Thank you, but I have everything under control. I'm keeping a very close eye on the situation. I'm being kept well informed."

"By someone you can trust, I hope."

"By someone who stands to gain as much as we do."

Rhoda laid her hands on his lapels and moved close to him, nuzzling his crotch with her middle. "Be sure to let me know if there's any way I can help you, darling."

Dale set his pipe aside and reached for the fly of his trousers. "Actually there is. It also might serve to improve your disposition.

He pushed her to her knees, but she went willingly.

The blast of a car horn woke Schyler up. She threw off the covers and ran out into the hall. Looking out the landing window, she saw Cash's pickup below. He was standing in the wedge made by the open door.

"Get dressed," he shouted up to her. "We've got a problem."

"What?"

"I'll tell you on the way."

She made it downstairs within minutes. Tossing her shoes in first, she jumped into the cab of his pickup. "You certainly raised a ruckus inside this house. I hope this is important."

"A chain on one of the rigs busted. Both bolsters gave way under the pressure. We've got a helluva log spill out on Highway Nine. I called out a crew. They're working to clear the road now."

"Was anybody hurt?"

"No."

"Thank God." If the accident hadn't occurred so early in the morning, when the highway wasn't busily traveled, it very well could have cost lives. Schyler shuddered to think of the consequences. "You had a rig loaded this early in the morning?"

"I've got every man putting in extra hours. A team comes on as soon as it gets light. We've got less than a week to get the rest of that order to Endicott's, remember?"

"And if we don't get the mess on the highway cleared up, a whole crew won't be free to cut today."

"That's right. Every hour counts." Cash was driving the pickup with no regard for traffic law or speed regulations.

"How long do you think it will take?"

"I don't know." He glanced across at her. "I should have told you to dress in jeans. You might end up lumberjacking today."

"Gladly, skirt or not. We've got to get that timber cut while the weather holds out." Gnawing the inside of her jaw in vexation, she muttered, "Why did the blasted chain have to break now."

"It didn't." Schyler looked at him in surprise. "It was sawed through," Cash told her. "Clean as a whistle. The truck had no more than pulled onto the highway than the logs started rolling off."

"Cash, are you sure?"

"I'm sure."

"Who did it?"

"How the hell should I know?"

"Who was driving?"

He named the man and shook his head firmly. "He's been with the company for years. Thinks Cotton Crandall hung the moon."

"But what about Cotton Crandall's daughter? What does he think of her?"

He turned to her with a leering smile. "Sure you want to hear it word for word?"

The way he asked made her certain she didn't want to know. "He's loyal?"

"Loyal as they come."

"What about the others on that crew?"

She gave him time to run through the list of names mentally. "I'd trust any of them with my life. What would be a logger's motivation to deliberately screw things up? He would lose his job permanently if Crandall Logging goes out of business."

"Not if he were bribed with a large amount of money."

"Sudden riches would be a dead giveaway. The traitor would never survive the others' revenge. None of them would be stupid enough to try it. Besides, they're as loyal to each other as they are to your daddy."

"An independent?"

"Again, what's his motivation? You've created an active, local market. He's making more profit because his hauling expenses are reduced."

"But you still think it was sabotage?"

"Don't you?"

"Jigger?" she asked. They stared at each other, knowing the answer.

That was the last quiet moment they had for the next several hours. A state trooper was already on the scene when Cash and Schyler arrived. He was engaged in a heated argument with the logging crew.

Cash shouldered his way through. "What's going on?"

The trooper turned around. "You in charge?"

"I am."

"I'm gonna ticket you, mister. This rig was overloaded."

"Find me one that isn't."

"Well you got caught," the trooper said in a syrupy voice.

"A chain busted."

"Because you were overloaded. And just because everybody else overloads doesn't make it right. I'll make an example out of you." He took a citation pad out of his pocket. "While I'm doing it, tell your driver to get his rig off the road."

As it was, the trailer rig and the logs were blocking both lanes of the two-lane state highway. "Look," Cash said, with diminishing patience, "we can't just scoot that timber aside. It's got to be reloaded onto another trailer."

"Yeah?"

"Yeah. We'll have to scare up a loader that's not in use and get another rig out here. It'll take awhile. They're not built for speed."

"We can't shut down this highway. You'll have to do that at night."

"I'm afraid that's out of the question. I wouldn't risk the lives of my men by having them work after dark."

At the sound of the feminine voice, the trooper spun around. He gave her a once-over that was calculated to intimidate. "Who are you?"

"Schyler Crandall."

The name worked like a splash of water on a growing fire. "Oh, Ms, Crandall, ma'am," he stammered, tipping his hat, "well I was just telling your man here—"

"I heard what you told him. It's unacceptable." The startled trooper opened his mouth to protest, but before he could say a word Schyler went on. "I suggest a compromise. Could you keep open the east-bound lane and close only the west-bound? That might slow traffic down, but it will slow down because of gawking drivers anyway. Having only one lane closed wouldn't stop traffic and it would be a tremendous help to us. I think we can move all our equipment in and work from one side of the road. We could get this cleared much sooner and that would be to everyone's advantage. Am I right?''

"Am I right?" Cash mimicked her moments later, fluttering his eyelashes.

"You weren't getting anywhere with him," she said. "It was a macho, Mexican standoff. What was I supposed to do?"

"Well, a blow job might have done the trick quicker. As it is, what you did worked okay.''

She gave him a fulminating look, but he missed it. He was already stalking away from her, issuing orders. Though it seemed like little was being done at any given time and confusion reigned, one by one the immense pine logs were lifted by crane and swung from the highway to the trailer rig. Cash himself sat in the knuckle boom and operated the loader. He carefully chose each log before loading it and stacked them all to achieve the perfect balance.

The accident did stop traffic, but it was the fault of rubbernecked drivers and not Crandall Logging. By midmorning the state trooper was literally eating out of Schyler's hand since she brought him a doughnut when she catered a snack to the crew assisting Cash.

"Thanks," Cash said curtly as he opened the soda Schyler handed him. Unlike the others, who were taking a ten-minute break, lounging on the shoulder of the highway in the shade of trees, Cash was checking the bolsters and chains on the rig that had arrived to replace the damaged one. He drank the cold drink in one long swallow. "Wish it was a beer," he said, handing Schyler the empty can.

"I'll buy you a case of it if you make up this morning's quota before dark."

Staring her down, he grimly pulled on his beaten leather gloves and put the hard hat back on his head. Turning away from her, he shouted, "All right, up off your asses. This isn't a goddamn picnic. Back to work." The loggers grumbled, but they complied with his orders. Schyler had seen only one other man who commanded both obedience and respect from his crews—Cotton.

As the morning progressed, the heat became unbearable. Waves of it shimmered up off the pavement. The humidity was high; there wasn't a breath of air. The men removed their shirts when they became sodden and plastered to their backs. Handkerchiefs were used as sweatbands beneath hard hats. The state trooper kept his uniform intact, but large rings of perspiration stained his shirt beneath his arms. Frequently he removed his hat to mop his forehead and face. Schyler stayed busy at the bed of Cash's pickup dispensing ice water.

He never took a break, so she carried a cup of water out to him. He put a chunk of ice in his mouth and poured the water over his head. It dribbled off his head and shoulders and through his chest hair. His discarded shirt had been tucked into his waistband. It hung over his hips like a breechcloth.

"You shouldn't be out here," he said after giving her a critical look. "You'll cook. The tip of your nose is already sunburned."

"I'm staying," she replied staunchly. She wouldn't desert her men.

But as she walked back to the pickup, she pulled the tail of her blouse from the damp waistband of her skirt. Sweat trickled between her breasts and behind her knees. Her hair felt hot and heavy on her neck. Luckily she found a rubber band in her purse and used it to hold together a wide single braid. She'd never felt grittier or more uneasy. Even after gathering her hair off her neck, it continued to prickle with sensations that were so unpleasant as to be uncomfortable, almost as though someone had her in the cross hairs. Slowly, warily, she turned her head and looked toward the woods behind her.

Jigger Flynn was standing partially hidden behind the trunk of a pecan tree. He was staring at her, clearly laughing to himself.

Schyler sucked in a quick breath of stark fear, though she retained enough control over her reaction not to let Jigger see it. His malice toward her was palpable, but Schyler held his stare. His eyes were so small and so deeply embedded that she couldn't really distinguish them. It was his overall expression that conveyed his silent message of vengeance. He was mocking her, gloating over the havoc she was sure he had caused. He was daring her to confront him and warning her that if she did, he would retaliate. This was only a mild example of the cruelty of which he was capable.

She briefly considered running to the trooper and pointing out Jigger as the one responsible for the log spill, but she vetoed it as a futile idea. Jigger was an adroit liar; he would only deny the charge and produce an alibi. She needed proof.

As for alerting Cash, he already knew that Jigger was the most likely culprit and had made no effort to go after him. She doubted he would.

Jigger seemed to discern her dilemma because he smiled. The devil's face couldn't look any more sinister than that smile. Schyler actually shuddered, as though the evil he embodied were passing through her body. She felt it as an assault and physically reacted to it.

Panicked, she spun around. She opened her mouth to summon Cash, but she realized he was involved in loading the last log onto the rig. The trooper was speaking into the microphone of his patrol car radio. She was alone. She had to deal with her fear of Jigger Flynn by herself. She had to face him.

Drawing a deep breath, she turned around to confront him, but there was nothing beneath the pecan tree except its branches and their leaves, dropping in the heat. All Schyler saw were shadows and dappled sunlight. Jigger Flynn had disappeared without a sound through the tall, dry grass. It was as if hell had opened up and taken him home.

Schyler was brought around by the cheer that went up from the men as the last log was placed on the rig and the load was secured.

"Get that rig unloaded at the landing and then bring it back to the site," Cash shouted to the driver as he ran toward his pickup. To the other men he said, "Hitch a ride on the loader. I'll meet you at the site after I drop Schyler off. When I get there I want to see trees dropping like whores' panties."

He jumped into the cab of his truck. "Get in," he barked at Schyler, who was still standing and trembling with fear. She got in. Cash slipped the truck into first gear and pulled out onto the highway. As they drove past the trooper, Schyler waved her thanks to him.

"Did you two make a date?" Following so closely on the heels of seeing Jigger, his acerbity was too much for her nerves.

"Do you care?"

"Damn right." His arm shot across the seat and his hand plunged between her thighs. He squeezed her possessively. "This is mine until I get through with it, understand?"

Enraged, Schyler removed his hand, throwing it away from her. "Keep your hands off me. And while you're at it, go to hell."

"What would you do without me if I did?"

She averted her head and didn't look at him again. As soon as the pickup came to a stop on the other side of the Laurent Bayou bridge, she bolted out the passenger door. Cash was hot on her trail and caught up with her at the door of the office. He spun her around and, pressing her shoulders between his hands, drew her against his bare, damp chest. He kissed her hard enough to take away her breath.

His tongue ground its way between her unwilling lips. Schyler's resistance slipped a notch, then snapped. He tasted like salty, sweaty, unrefined, fearless man. Feeling a desperate need for a mighty warrior's protection, she greedily kissed him back.

As suddenly as he had grabbed her, he pushed her away and released her. "I warned you that I was never kind to women. Don't expect me to be any different with you."

He drove off, leaving a cloud of white powdery dust swirling around her.

FORTY-EIGHT

Schyler watched until the lights of the caboose disappeared in the tunnel of trees. Wearily pushing back a wispy strand of hair that had escaped her clumsy braid, she turned around, but instantly stopped short.

Cash was leaning against the exterior wall of the office. She hadn't known he was there, though she should have smelled the smoke from his cigarette. It was dangling precariously from the corner of his lips. His shirt was unbuttoned. He had his thumbs hooked into the waistband of his jeans.

"Well, we did it," Schyler said. "We recovered the production time we lost this morning."

"*Oui.*"

"Several times today I doubted that we would."

He took one last drag on the cigarette before flicking the butt into the gravel bed between the train tracks. "I never doubted it."

"Thank the men for me."

"One of the drivers brought back word to the site that you mentioned a bonus."

"I did."

"They'll hold you to it."

"They'll get it. As soon as I get a check from Endicott and the bank note is paid in full."

"You owe me a case of beer."

"Is tomorrow soon enough?"

"Fine."

She entered the landing office by the back door. She didn't sit down behind the desk, fearing that if she did, she would lay her head on top of it and fall asleep right there. Instead she switched off the lamp, picked up her purse, and made her way toward the front entrance.

"You still mad at me?" Cash followed her out, making certain the door was locked behind them.

"Why should I be mad?"

"Because I don't court you with flowers and presents."

She turned to face him. "Do you think I'm that shallow? That silly? If you gave me flowers I'd know you were mocking me, not courting me. All that aside, I don't want to be courted by you. By anybody."

"Then why are you mad?"

"I'm not."

Schyler headed toward her car, only to realize that her car was at Belle Terre. She reversed her direction. Cash caught her arm. "Where're you going?"

"To call Ken to come pick me up."

"Get in the truck. I'm taking you home."

"I—"

"Get in the truck, dammit."

Schyler knew that it would be lunacy to stand there and fight with him when she felt this tired and this grimy. It was grossly unfair of a man to engage a woman in an argument when a hard day's work had left him looking ruggedly appealing and left her looking like hell. If she'd had access to a lipstick and a hairbrush, then maybe she would have stayed to fight. As it was, the deck was stacked against her. She was too exhausted to think, much less argue with him. She got in his pickup.

"Want to go by Jigger's and see his rattlesnake?"

Jigger was the last topic she wanted to talk about. She still shuddered every time she recalled his leering grin. But what Cash had suggested was so out of context and so preposterous, she couldn't help asking an astonished, "What?"

"His rattlesnake. Jigger's got a new pet rattler. I hear it's a helluva snake. He's even charging admission to look at it. Want to stop by on the way home?"

"I hope you're joking. If you are, it's in very poor taste. I don't want to have anything to do with him, except maybe to bring charges against him for assaulting Gayla . . . and that only tops a very long list of offenses. I can't believe you'd go near him either. He might have been responsible for sabotaging that rig this morning."

"I thought of that."

"And you still pander to him?" She spread her arms wide. "Oh, but I forgot. He's a customer of yours, isn't he?"

"You mean the medicine?"

"Yes, the medicine."

"I was doing Gayla a favor, not Jigger."

"But you took Jigger's money."

"It's green. Same as anybody else's."

"Money is money, is that it?"

"*Oui.* To somebody who's never had it, that's it, Miss Schyler. You wouldn't know what poverty is like."

"You grab at money no matter where it comes from?"

"It matters. I didn't kill those pit bulls for you, remember?"

"So there are a few things you wouldn't do for money."

"Very few, but some."

What about making a hideous little doll and placing it on someone's pillow, Schyler wondered. Cash had at least a smattering knowledge of voodoo. Gayla had heard his name in connection with it, but surely he didn't know anything about that doll. He could't have treated Gayla so kindly the day they found her in the woods, only to later put a curse on her. On the other hand, could anyone count on Cash's loyalty? It seemed to extend only to himself.

Schyler turned her head away and stared through the open window, letting the wind cool her down for the first time that day. Cash was practically inviting her to tell him about the doll. She didn't because she didn't trust him enough. That disturbed her deeply. There were no boundaries to their physical intimacy, but she couldn't trust him with her secrets. She didn't even want to mention Jigger's appearance at the site of the accident that morning.

He pulled the truck to a stop while they were still a distance away from the mansion. "I don't want to give Cotton another heart attack by coming any closer," he said bitterly.

"You drove right up to the front door this morning."

"This morning there was an emergency. Even Cotton could understand and forgive that."

"Better than he could understand and forgive you for delivering his inebriated teenaged daughter?"

He laughed shortly. "I could deny it till kingdom come and he'll always believe that I was the one who got you drunk that night at the lake. He probably thinks I took sexual liberties, too."

"But that's not what you argued about."

His grin evaporated. His eyes homed in on her face as though it were the target and they were a laser weapon. "what did you say?"

Obviously that night was a sore spot with him. She considered dropping the subject then and there, but she was compelled to solve this riddle, to find the clue that had always been missing. "I said that's not what you and Daddy argued about that night."

"How do you know what we argued about?"

"I overheard you yelling at each other."

He stared at her for a long moment. "Oh, really? Then you tell me. What did we argue about?"

"I can't remember." A crease formed between her eyebrows as she strained her memory. "I was so woozy. But I remember you shouting at each other. It must have been an argument over something important. Was it Monique?"

"That's been over ten years ago." He slumped down in the seat behind the steering wheel and cupped his hand over his mouth, staring out into the darkness. "I've forgotten what it was about."

"You're lying," Schyler said softly. His head snapped around. "You remember. Whatever you argued with Daddy about still isn't resolved, is it?" Cash didn't answer her. He looked away again.

"Ah, to hell with it," Schyler muttered. It was between the two of them. Let it fester. She was too tired to try to lance that ancient wound tonight. "Thanks for everything you did today. Bye."

Schyler put her shoulder to the door. It was necessary for without that boost, she doubted she would have had the strength to open it. As soon as her feet hit the ground, she bent down and slipped off her shoes. The grass felt wonderfully cool and clean and soothing beneath her feet.

Keeping within the shadows beneath the trees, she made her way toward the house. The purple twilight made the painted white bricks of Belle Terre look pink and ethereal, like the castle in Camelot. The windows shone with mellow, golden light. The bougainvillea vine that garnished one corner column of the veranda was heavy with vivid blossoms.

A pang of homesickness and love seized Schyler until it was painful to breathe. Physical and mental fatigue had brought her emotions to the surface. She braced herself against a chest-high live oak branch and stared through the balmy dusk at the home she loved, but which always seemed just beyond her grasp.

She had lived there most of her life. The walls had heard her weeping and her laughter. The floorboards had borne her weight when she learned to crawl and when she learned to waltz. She'd watched the birth of a foal and received her first kiss in the stable. Her life was wrapped around the house as surely as the bougainvillea was wrapped around the column.

But the spirit, the heart, of the house eluded her. She could never touch it. It was inexplicable, this feeling of being an interloper in her own home, yet it was undeniably there, a part of her she couldn't let rest. It was like being born without one of the senses. She couldn't miss it because it had never belonged to her, but she knew she was supposed to have it and felt the loss keenly. A sense of loss that made her sad was perpetually in the back of her mind.

She knew Cash was there before he actually touched her. He moved up behind her and folded his hands around her neck. "What's bothering you tonight, Miss Schyler?"

"You're a bastard."

"I always have been."

"I'm not referring to the circumstance of your birth. I'm referring to *you*. How you behave. How you treat other people."

"Namely you?"

"What you did and said to me this morning was crude, unnecessary, and unconscionable."

"I thought we settled this at the landing."

She made an impatient gesture with her shoulders. "I don't want hearts and flowers from you, Cash, but I do expect a little kindness."

"Don't."

Her head dropped forward in defeat. "You don't give an inch, do you? Never. You never give anything."

"No. Never."

She should have walked away from him, but she couldn't coax her feet to move, not when he was a solid pillar to lean against. She needed a shoulder to cry on. He was available, and he, more than anyone except her father, would understand how she felt.

"I'm afraid, Cash."

"Of what?"

"Of losing Belle Terre."

His thumbs centered themselves at the back of her neck and began massaging the tension out of the vertebrae. "You're doing everything you possibly can to make sure you don't."

"But I might. In spite of everything I do." She tilted her head to one side. He massaged the kinks out of her shoulder. "I take one step forward and get knocked back two."

"You're about to cash in on the deal that'll put Crandall Logging in the black and free up Belle Terre. What are you afraid of?"

"Of failing. If we don't get it all there, then the timber we've already shipped doesn't count. This last week is the most crucial. My saboteur knows that as well as I do." She breathed deeply and clenched her fist. "Who is it? And what does he have against me?"

"Probably nothing. His quarrel might be with Cotton."

"That's the same thing."

"Hurt Cotton, hurt you?"

"Yes. I love him. I couldn't love him any more if he were my natural father. Maybe because I understand why he loves this place so much. He came here an outsider, too. He had to prove himself worthy of Belle Terre."

Cash said nothing, but his strong fingers continued to knead away her tension and distress. The massage loosened her tongue as well.

"Macy was never a mother to me. She was just a lovely, but terribly unhappy, woman who inhabited the same house and laid down the rules of conduct. Cotton was my parent. My anchor.'' She sighed deeply. ''But our roles have switched, haven't they? I feel like a mama bear fighting to protect her cub. I'm desperately inadequate to protect him.''

''Cotton doesn't need your protection. He'll have to pay for his mistakes. And there won't be a damn thing you can do about it when the time of reckoning comes.''

''Don't say that,'' she whispered fiercely. ''That frightens me. I can't let him down.'' Cash had moved up close behind her. His lips found a vulnerable spot on the back of her neck beneath her braid. He lifted her hands to the branch of the tree and placed them there. ''Cash, what are you doing?''

''Giving you something to think about besides all your troubles.'' Now that her arms were out of the way and he had an open field, he slid his hands up and down her narrow rib cage, grazing the sides of her breasts.

''I don't want to think about anything else. Anyway, I'm still angry with you.''

''Anger's made for some of the best sex I've ever had.''

''Well I don't think of it as an aphrodisiac.'' She sucked in her breath sharply when he reached around her and cupped her breasts. ''Don't.'' Responding to the feebleness in her voice and not to the protest itself, he pulled her blouse apart, unfastened her bra, and laid his hands over her bared breasts. ''This is . . . no. Not here. Not now. Cash.''

Her objections fell on deaf ears. His open mouth was moving up and down her neck, taking love bites, while his fingers lightly twisted her nipples. He tilted his hips forward. Reflexively she pressed her bottom against his erection.

''You want me,'' he growled. ''You know you do. I know you do.''

He slipped one hand beneath her skirt. He pushed down her panties and palmed the downy delta at the top of her thighs. She sighed his name, in remonstration, in desire. ''No,'' she groaned, ashamed of the melting sensation that made her thighs weak and pliant.

He hissed a yes into the darkness as his fingers sought and found the slipperiness that made her a liar. He raised her skirt and pulled her against him. The cloth of his jeans against her derriere was rough, soft, wonderful.

Then his thumbs, stroking her cleft, down, down until they parted the swollen lips. She pressed her forehead into the hard wood of the branch and gripped it with her hands. ''Cash.'' His name was a low, serrated moan of longing.

He deftly unzipped his jeans. His entry was slow, deliberate. He was ruthlessly stingy with himself until his own passions governed him and he sheathed himself within the moist, satiny fist of her sex. He ground against her. The hair on his belly tickled her smooth skin.

Schyler flung her head back, seeking his lips with hers. Their open mouths clung together; tongues searched out each other. He fanned one tight, raised nipple with his fingers. His other hand covered her mound. His stroking middle finger quickly escalated her to an explosive climax.

His coming was long and fierce and scalding. When it was over, he slumped forward and let her support him. Both might have collapsed to the carpet of grass had not Schyler been braced against the limb of the tree.

Eventually he restored her clothing and his. Schyler let him. She was too physically drained to move. And too emotionally unstrung to speak.

My God, what she had just done was unthinkable. Yet it had happened. She wasn't sorry, only deeply disturbed, because while he'd been holding her she'd been inundated with him. She had forgotten her problems. She had forgotten everything, including Belle Terre.

She spun around when she heard the engine of his pickup being gunned to life, not realizing that he'd slipped away. It was just as well, she thought, as she watched the truck disappear down the lane. She wouldn't have known what to say to him anyway.

Parked on the edge of the ditch, Cash waited until the last of Jigger's gawking customers left before he pulled up in front of the derelict house. Even over the noise of the pickup's motor, he could hear the rattlesnake in the drum.

He cut the motor and got out. Through the screened back door, he could see Jigger hunched over the kitchen table counting the day's take. Cash knocked loudly. The old man whirled around. He was holding a pistol aimed directly at the door.

"Calm down, Jigger. It's me."

"I nearly blew your fool head off, don'tcha know." He dropped his money on the table and shuffled toward the door.

"What do you do with all your money, Jigger? Stuff it in mayonnaise jars and bury it in your yard? Or maybe under your kennel?"

The old man's eyes glittered. "You want to know, Boudreaux," he taunted, slowly waving the pistol back and forth just beneath Cash's nose, "you try to find out."

Cash laughed. "Do I look stupid to you?" Then his smile disappeared altogether. "I assure you, I'm not."

Jigger lowered his head and peered up at Cash from hooded eye sockets. "I should shoot you anyway. You helped my black bitch get away. You took her to Belle Terre."

"You nearly killed her."

"That's none of your business."

"Oh, but it is. You didn't leave her alone after the miscarriage like I told you to. I take that personally, Jigger."

"It wasn't me. It was a customer."

"It's still your fault."

Jigger executed a Gallic shrug. "She's just a woman. I'll get me another one."

"Fine with me," Cash said with deceptive nonchalance. "But if you ever work over another woman the way you did Gayla Frances, I'll come here, cut off your cock, and stuff it down your throat until you choke. Understand, *mon ami?*" Cash leaned against the door frame where the paint was chipped and peeling. His eyes didn't blink, but there was a trace of a smile on his lips.

"You threaten me?"

"*Oui.* And you know I don't threaten lightly."

Jigger's face split into a parody of a grin. "You got the hots for the bitch, hey Boudreaux?" Then he shook his head. "No. You're fuckin' Schyler Cran-*dall.*"

"That's right, I'm fucking Schyler Crandall," Cash said tightly. "But I'm still looking out for Gayla."

The two men eyed each other antagonistically. Finally Jigger threw back his head and cackled. Cash Boudreaux was perhaps the only man in the parish who intimidated him. Jigger was smart enough to know when retreat was prudent. He didn't want to test the other man's reputed temper and skill with the knife that always rode in the small of his back. If one were measuring meanness, they were equal, but Cash was twenty years younger, thirty pounds lighter, and much swifter. Physically, Jigger was no match for him.

Cash relaxed his tense stance and eased himself away from the doorjamb. "Are you going to show me your rattler or did I drive out here for nothing?" He angled his head in the direction of the oil drum.

Jigger shoved the pistol in the waistband of his trousers. He strutted across the yard toward the drum. A light cord had been strung from the house. A bare bulb dangled over the drum. Jigger switched it on. With a proud flourish he knocked the rock off the lid and prised it open with a tire tool.

"Look at that son of a bitch, Boudreaux. Ever see such?"

Unlike most spectators, Cash approached the oil drum with a casual, intrepid stride. He walked right up to it and peered over the rim. The rattler's tail was flicking, filling the still night air with its insidious racket. Even the nocturnal birds and insects in the trees had fallen silent out of respect and fear. The pit bull bitch barked, then whined apprehensively.

Jigger waited excitedly to hear Cash's reaction. He was sorely disappointed when Cash shrugged, unimpressed. "Fact is, I have seen such, lots of times, in the bayous."

"Bloody hell."

"I'm not lying. Once a flood washed up a whole colony of cottonmouths. *Maman* wouldn't let me play outdoors for days. The yard was working alive with those snakes. All sizes. Some as big or bigger than this. Could have swallowed a dog whole.

He leaned over the barrel for a closer look and stayed a long time. Jigger peered over his shoulder. When Cash spun around abruptly, Jigger dropped his short crowbar and leaped backward.

Cash smiled with sheer devilment. "Why, Jigger, I do believe this snake makes you nervous."

"Bull*shit*." Angrily Jigger picked up the lid, tossed it back onto the drum and maneuvered it into place with the crowbar he'd retrieved from the ground. When he was done, he stuck out his hand. "One dollar."

"Sure." Never breaking his stare, Cash fished in his tight jean pocket and came up with a crumpled one-dollar bill. "It was well worth a dollar just to see you jump like that." He strolled toward his parked truck.

"Boudreaux!" Cash turned around and faced the man standing in front of the drum. "You know who sent me this snake?"

Cash only grinned through the darkness before disappearing into it.

 # FORTY-NINE

Schyler slept late. When her alarm went off at the regular time, she rolled over, shut it off, and promptly went back to sleep. Hours later she woke up. She glanced at the clock and discovered that it was closer to lunch than breakfast. She should feel ashamed; but after the hellish day she had had yesterday, she decided that she deserved to take a morning off. She showered and dressed quickly and was soon in the kitchen doing damage to a honeydew melon.

"You can have chicken salad for lunch, if you'll wait an hour for it to chill," Mrs. Dunne told her.

"Thanks, but I need to get to the office." Sometime during the night, in her subconscious, a thought concerning their last shipment to Endicott's had struck her. Luckily she remembered it this morning and was eager to discuss it with Cash.

"Well if you ask me, you're working too hard."

"I didn't ask," she retorted, but kindly, as she winked at the housekeeper on her way out. As she went past the parlor doors, she saw Gayla in there dusting the books on the shelves. "Gayla, I asked you to catalog those books, not dust them. That's what I pay Mrs. Dunne to do."

"I don't mind. I ran out of chores. I feel guilty just sitting around mooching off you."

"You're not mooching." Schyler smiled up at Gayla, who was perched on a ladder. She got only a faint smile from Gayla in return. "Is something wrong? No more voodoo dolls, I hope."

"No." Distractedly Gayla gazed through the wide windows. The expansive lawn, full of sunlight and serenity, hardly looked threatening. "It's just that I . . . I . . ." She sighed and shook her head in self-derision. "Nothing."

"What?"

Gayla made a helpless gesture with her dust cloth. "The yard looks so peaceful and harmless now. But when it gets dark outside, I have the eerie feeling that something or someone is out there watching us."

"Gayla," Schyler chided gently.

"I know it's stupid. I jump at my own shadow."

"That's understandable after all you've been through. The doll was a very real threat. I was reluctant to call the sheriff's office to come out and investigate, but if you want me to I will."

"No," Gayla exclaimed. "Don't do that. Besides, it wouldn't do any good. The sheriff is a friend of Jigger's."

"Then you're certain he was responsible?"

"He probably paid somebody to put it in my room."

"I'm sure he just wanted to scare you. I doubt it'll go any further than that. For all his chicanery, Jigger Flynn wouldn't dare set foot on Belle Terre."

"I hope not." There wasn't much conviction behind Gayla's voice.

Schyler lowered herself to the padded arm of an easy chair. "That's not all, is it?"

"No."

"Tell me."

Gayla climbed down the ladder and dropped her cloth into a basket of cleaning supplies. Her narrow shoulders lifted and fell on a deep sigh. "I don't know if I can pinpoint what's wrong, Schyler."

"Try."

"You're too busy to listen to my whining."

"I've got time. What's on your mind?"

Taking a moment to collect her thoughts, Gayla said, "I've just been wondering what I'm going to do with the rest of my life. I don't have enough college to get a good job. I'm too old to go back to school. Even if I wasn't, I couldn't afford it." She raised troubled eyes. "What is there for me to do? Where should I go? How will I live?"

Schyler rose and embraced her fondly. "Don't rush yourself to make a decision. Things will get sorted out in time. Something will turn up. In the meantime you have a home here."

"I can't go on living off you, Schyler."

"It makes me angry when you say that."

She tilted Gayla's head up. Looking into Gayla's eyes was like looking into twin cups of chicory coffee. They were that large, that dark, that fluid. They should be laughing; instead they were full of despair.

It was disappointing to Schyler that Jimmy Don Davison hadn't responded to that letter she had mailed him in prison. She had hoped that once he knew Gayla had left Jigger in fear of her life, he would contact her. She had gambled on him being curious about his lost love at the very least. Obviously he wasn't.

A forgiving letter from Jimmy Don would be like a tonic to Gayla. It would imbue her with optimism for the future. Schyler had no way of knowing how Jimmy Don felt about his former sweetheart, but surely once he was acquainted with the circumstances, he wouldn't hold Gayla's recent past against her.

"It's too pretty a day to worry about the future," Schyler said softly. "I don't want to think about you leaving Belle Terre. It makes me sad. I don't know what I would have done without your friendship these past few weeks."

Gayla's eyes cleared of misery, but they flashed with anger. "Tricia's been so hateful to you. How do you stand it?"

"I try to ignore the swipes she takes at me."

"I don't see how you can. And her husband just stands there and lets her get by with it." Gayla shook her head. With a wisdom beyond her years that was probably inherited from Veda, she added, "There's something wrong there."

"Wrong where?"

"With them."

"Like what?"

"I'm not sure. They're sneaky. Both of them. They carry on whispered telephone conversations. Are you aware of that? When I walk past, they hang up, or start talking real loud, like I'm too stupid to tell that they're faking it." She looked at Schyler worriedly. "I wouldn't trust them if I were you."

Those furtive telephone conversations were probably being placed to realtors. Gayla didn't know about the Howells' plan to put Belle Terre up for sale. Schyler laughed off her warning. "I doubt they're plotting to smother me in my bed."

"Mr. Howell hasn't got the balls. But she does. She hates you, Schyler. I don't know how two girls can be raised as sisters and turn out so differently."

"We come from different stock."

"Well I think Tricia is a bad seed. Mark my words."

"She's just insecure about her self-worth." Gayla's intuition made Schyler more uneasy than she wanted to acknowledge. Still, and to Gayla's annoyance, she defended Tricia. "Mother ignored both of us, but Daddy made no secret of favoring me. Years of living with that turned Tricia sour."

"I respect you for taking up for her. But don't give her your back."

With that warning echoing in her ears, Schyler left Gayla in the parlor and headed toward the back of the house. She checked Cotton's room, but he wasn't there. She found him outside, sitting in a lawn chair and feeding shelled pecans to squirrels that ate the treats right out of his hand. When Schyler appeared, they scattered across the lawn and into the nearest trees.

"Spoilsport," Cotton said, frowning at her.

"Good morning to you, too." She leaned down and gave him a quick kiss before dropping into the chair beside his. "How are you this morning? I feel glorious." Pointing her toes far in front of her and reaching high over her head with both arms, she stretched luxuriously.

"You should. You've slept away half the day."

"Well after yesterday, I thought I deserved it."

"Reckon you do. Quite a mess, wasn't it?"

"How did you know?" He'd already been asleep when she came in last night. She followed his gaze down to the morning newspaper lying on the small table between their chairs. Even reading upside down, Schyler could see that the front page was dominated by an account of the Crandall Logging rig accident. The accompanying picture featured Cash, standing astride one of the massive logs, overseeing the chore of clearing the highway.

"Cash was right there in the thick of it, I see."

Schyler knew better than to take her father's comment at face value, but she pretended to. "He's a born organizer. The other loggers would walk through a wall of fire for him."

"Hmm." One of the squirrels had decided that Schyler posed no danger and had crept back for more nuts. Cotton leaned out of his chair and tossed it a pecan half.

"Does Mrs. Dunne know you've got those? Pecans that pretty should be going into a pie."

"Don't change the subject," Cotton said crossly.

"I didn't know there was one," Schyler fired right back.

"Why didn't you tell me about this accident?"

"I haven't seen you since the accident."

"Why didn't you ask for my advice when Boudreaux came roaring up here yesterday morning?"

"I'm sorry. Did he disturb you?"

"He's always disturbed me."

She ignored that and answered his original question with forced calm. "I didn't tell you about it or ask your advice because frankly I didn't think about it."

"I'll have you know, young lady, that I'm still the head of this goddamn company," he bellowed.

"But you're temporarily out of commission."

"So you've turned the whole operation over to that Cajun bastard."

"Now wait a minute, Daddy. I depend on Cash, yes, but I still make the decisions. On most of the major ones, I've consulted you. Yesterday was an exception. I had to act spontaneously. I didn't have time to weigh my options. There were no options."

"You could have phoned. You could have kept me posted."

"I could have, I suppose, but since your surgery I've tried to insulate you from the day-to-day hardships of running the business."

"Well don't do me anymore goddamn favors. I don't want to be insulated. I'll be insulated for a long time when they seal me in a friggin' casket. Don't rush it."

It took an enormous amount of self-control for Schyler to remain silent and let that go by without comment. Like a catechism, she mentally recited all the reasons why she should overlook his unfair allegations. He wasn't to be excited or upset. Stress of any kind could be dangerous, if not deadly. He was prone to depression and contrariness when his pride was in jeopardy.

In a carefully regulated voice she said, "Now that you're obviously feeling so much stronger, I'll consult you on business matters. It was only out of consideration for your health that I hadn't before now."

"That's bullshit." He jabbed a finger in her direction. "You didn't consult me because you've got Cash to talk to." A vein in his temple began to throb, but neither of them noticed. "Do the two of you talk shop in bed?"

Schyler flinched guiltily. She stopped breathing for a moment. When her involuntary responses eventually took over again, she raised her chin a notch and bravely challenged her father's censorious stare.

"I'm a grown woman. I won't discuss my personal life with you."

He banged his fist on the arm of his chair. "We're not talking about your personal life. You got passed over for your sister. She duped us all into believing Howell had knocked her up. You lived with a goddamn fairy for six years. After all that, why would I start caring about who you're screwing? I don't.''

''Then what are you shouting at me for?''

He moved his face closer to hers. ''Because this time your bedmate is Cash Boudreaux.''

''And that makes a difference?''

''You're damn right it does. He's too close to my business, my home. Your affair with him affects everything I've worked my ass off for.''

''How?''

''Because that Cajun bastard—''

Schyler shot out of her chair and bore down on him. ''Stop calling him that! He can't help being born illegitimate.''

Cotton flopped back in his chair and looked up at his daughter with disbelief. ''God almighty. You've in love with him.''

Her face went blank. She continued staring at her father a few thudding heartbeats longer, then turned away. She braced her arms on the back of the chair she'd been sitting in, leaning against it for additional support.

Cotton wasn't finished with her yet. He sat up straight and scooted to the edge of his seat. ''You dare to defend that man to me. To *me*.'' He thumped his chest. Inside it, shooting pains were leaving fissions in the walls of his heart. He was too irate to notice. ''Have you made the pitiful blunder of falling in love with that skirt chaser, with Cash Boudreaux?''

She flung herself away from the chair and angrily confronted Cotton again. ''Why not? You were in love with his mother.''

They glared at each other so hard that neither could stand the open animosity for long. They lowered their eyes simultaneously. ''So you know,'' Cotton said after awhile.

''I know.''

''Since when?''

''Recently.''

''He told you?''

''No, Tricia did.''

He sighed. ''What the hell? I'm surprised you didn't know all along. Everybody else in the parish did.'' Cotton cracked another pecan, dug out the meat and passed it to an inquisitive and intrepid squirrel. ''I committed adultery with Monique for years. I made her an adulteress.''

''Yes.''

''And I would do it again.'' Father and daughter looked at each other. ''Even if it meant burning in hell for eternity. I would love Monique Boudreaux again.'' He leaned back in his chair again and rested his head against the wicker. ''Macy wasn't a . . . a warm woman, Schyler. She equated passion with a loss of self-control. She was incapable of feeling it.''

''Monique Boudreaux was?''

A ghost of a smile lifted his pale lips. ''Ah, yes,'' he breathed. ''She was. She did everything passionately, laugh, scold, make love.'' Schyler watched his eyes become transfixed, as though he were looking into a mirror of memory, seeing a happier time. ''She was a very beautiful woman.''

Schyler was amazed by the expression on his face. She'd never seen Cotton's features look that soft. His vulnerability affected her deeply. ''I think Cash is a beautiful man.''

Instantaneously Cotton's expression changed again. It grew hard and ugly. His smiling lips turned downward with contempt. "He's done a real number on you, hasn't he? You actually trust him."

"He's been invaluable to me. I depend on him. He's the most intelligent, instinctive forester around. Everybody says so."

"Dammit, I know that," Cotton snarled. "I depend on his professional judgment, too, but I don't crawl into bed with him. I don't even turn my back on him for fear I'll get a knife in it."

"Cash isn't like that," she said, wishing she believed it herself.

"Isn't he? When he was telling you about Monique and me, did he mention all his threats?"

"Threats?"

"I see he didn't."

"I know the two of you have had several vicious arguments. One being the night he brought me home from Thibodaux Pond. Remember that? It was right after Mama died."

"I remember," he answered guardedly.

"Cash helped me that night. He wasn't the one who plied me with beer. You unfairly blamed him for my condition."

"Cash never does anything out of the goodness of his heart. He might not have been the one that got you drunk, but don't be misled into thinking he was concerned with your welfare."

"What did the two of you argue about that night?"

"I don't remember."

He was lying, too, just as Cash had. "Monique?"

"I don't remember. Probably. When Macy died, Cash demanded that I marry his mother."

Schyler searched his face, looking for the soft expression of love that had been there only moments ago. "Why didn't you, Daddy? If you were so in love with her, why didn't you marry her when Mama died?" Feeling guilty she asked, "Because of Tricia and me?"

"No. Because of a pledge I had made Macy."

"But she was dead."

"That didn't matter. I'd given her my word. I couldn't marry Monique. She understood and was resigned to it. Cash wasn't."

"Can you blame him? You made his mother's life hell. Did you know she had miscarried your child?"

Cotton's eyes clouded with tears. "Damn him for telling you that."

"Is it true?"

"Yes. But I didn't know she was pregnant until afterwards. I swear to God I didn't."

She believed him. He might have lied by omission, but he'd never told her a lie that was an outright contradiction to truth. "Monique lived in a very gray area, an outcast of society. She couldn't even observe her religion because of her life with you."

"It was her choice as much as mine to live as she did."

"But when Mama died, when you had a chance to rectify that, you didn't."

"I couldn't," he repeated on a shout. "I told Cash that. Now I'm telling you. I *couldn't*." Cotton paused to draw a deep breath. "That's when Cash swore on his mother's rosary that he would get vengeance. He accused me of making her a whore. He promised not to stop until he's brought ruination to me and to Belle

Terre.'' He gasped for sufficient oxygen. ''Why do you think a man with his expertise has hung 'round here all these years, living like white trash down there in that shanty on the bayou?''

''I asked him that.''

''And what did he say?''

''He said he had promised his mother on her deathbed that he would never leave Belle Terre as long as you were alive. She asked him to watch over you.''

That gave Cotton pause. For a moment, he stared sightlessly at Schyler, then into near space. Finally, he shook his head stubbornly. ''I don't believe that for a minute. He's been biding his time. Waiting like a panther about to pounce. You came back from England with sex-deprived gonads and *bam!*, he saw his opportunity to finally get his revenge. Because I was laid up, he had access to you that he'd never had before. He took full advantage, didn't he?''

''No.''

''Didn't he?''

''*No!*''

Cotton's eyes narrowed to slits. ''Didn't he seize a golden opportunity to pay me back for screwing his mother? Everybody around here knows how I feel about you, Schyler. The boy's not dense. If he wanted to fuck me real good, the best way he could do it was fuck the daughter I love best.''

Schyler crammed her fist against her lips and shook her head vehemently while tears of doubt filled her eyes.

''He's as cunning as a swamp fox, Schyler,'' Cotton rasped. ''Monique was proud. She never would take any money from me. They barely scraped by. Growing up as he did messed with Cash's mind. He's warped. He hates us. He has all Monique's charm, but none of her compassion or sweetness.''

Cotton wagged his finger at her in warning. ''You cannot trust him. Do, and we're doomed. He'll do anything, say anything, to bring us down. Don't doubt that for a single instant.''

Schyler, unable to tolerate another word, turned and fled.

 # FIFTY

It wasn't true, she told herself.

By the time Schyler reached the landing office, however, the doubts that Cotton had raised obscured her certainty like a thundercloud blotting out the sun.

She braked and shoved open the car door. Cash's pickup was parked beside one of the scales. He was here, not in the forest. She was glad she wouldn't have to chase him down. This confrontation couldn't wait. She wanted to know, and know immediately, that Cotton was wrong. She needed to know that she was right.

She bolted into the office and swung the door closed behind her with a loud crash. Cash was sitting at the desk, entering data into an adding machine. He glanced up. His brow was beetled, his lips a hard, narrow line. ''You're not going to believe this, Schyler. Ken Howell's been screwing you.''

''So have you.''

Her voice was soft, but chilly and taut. It was obviously not what he had expected. His brow gradually smoothed itself out. He regarded her carefully. She was standing rigidly against the door, blinking rapidly with indignation, like a temperance marcher who'd just detected demon rum in the punch. His eyes lei-surely swept down her highly strung posture, then back up. He casually tossed the pencil he'd been using onto the littered desk and stacked his hands behind his head.

"That's right, I have. And so far I haven't heard you complaining about it."

Her breasts shuddered with her uneven breath. "Why do you? Why did you want to in the first place?"

"Why?" he repeated on an incredulous laugh. When he saw that she wasn't being facetious, he answered flippantly. "It feels good."

"That's the only reason, because it feels good?" Her voice was hoarse. "Then any woman would do, right? So why me?"

He lowered his hands and stood up. Coming around the corner of the desk, he propped himself against the edge of it, studying her all the while. "What brought this on all of a sudden? A bad case of cramps?"

"Just answer me, Cash," she said in a shrill, impatient voice. "Just about any woman could give you an erection and make it feel good, so why me?"

He gnawed on the corner of his lip. "You want it straight?"

"I want it straight."

"Okay," he said insolently. "I guess you just make it feel better than anybody has in a long time. I wanted you that day I saw you sleeping under the tree. Every time I saw you after that, I wanted you a little bit more. Until I had you."

"That must have been thrilling for you. My capitulation."

"It was," he said with brutal honesty. "It was thrilling for you, too."

She bit her lip hard to keep from crying. "Why didn't you say anything?"

"When?"

"After the first time."

"Because you looked down at me like you expected an apology. I never apol-ogize to a woman. For anything. But especially not for screwing her."

"You had what you wanted. I had surrendered. I'd even come to you. Why didn't you just leave it at that?"

He looked at her strangely. "Because I wasn't satisfied. I'm still not. I like your tits, your legs, your ass, your mouth, those breathy little sounds you make when you come, and the way you give head. Now should I go on or stop with that?"

Schyler's emotions waged war. The lady that Macy had groomed wanted to slap his face and storm out. The woman in her wanted to fling herself against him, kiss him, love him. Cotton's daughter wanted to scratch and claw at him. She wanted to inflict pain that would hurt him as much as the cold detachment in his voice was hurting her.

"Why . . . why did you take me last night at Belle Terre?"

"I got the urge."

"Why in that particular way?"

"Don't pretend you didn't like it. You were dripping."

"I didn't say I didn't like it," she yelled. "I asked you why you did it then and there."

"Because it felt—"

"Good?"

"*Oui!*" he shouted. "And right. It felt right. I went with the flow, okay? I didn't stop to reason it out. My cock was doing my thinking."

"From what I hear, it usually does."

He made a hissing sound through his teeth. "Look, you wanted it. I wanted it. I was hard. You were creamy. We did it and it was fine with both of us at the time." He stood up and advanced on her. The lock of hair hanging over his brow was trembling with anger. "So what's the big fuckin' deal, huh? Why the cross-examination? Can we drop this and talk about something important, like how your brother-in-law has been cleverly skimming off the books for years?'' His eyes turned dark. ''Or better yet, why don't you climb on my lap and do something about this monstrous hard-on I've grown as a result of our conversation?''

''That's not funny.''

''You're damn right it's not.''

Seething, Schyler said tightly, ''Tell me about Ken.''

''Simple. He's a crook. He's the reason the company's been losing money in spite of steady business. I don't know if Cotton knew and overlooked it because Howell is family, or if he's gone dotty in his old age. It was Howell who robbed Endicott. Apparently he endorsed Cotton's signature on their check, cashed it and pocketed the money, but failed to mention that order and advance payment to anybody.'' He waved his hand toward the ledgers on the desk. ''Those records are shot full of holes that he made.''

''How do you know all this?''

''Glee uncovered the number-juggling Howell had done to make the sums come out right.''

''Glee?''

''You said he needed something to do. I took duplicate records over to him. He's been going over them. He said they weren't—''

''Who gave you the authority to do that?'' Schyler was furious.

''What?''

''You heard me.''

He tossed back his hair with a jerk of his head. ''Let me get this straight.'' His left knee unhitched, throwing him slightly off center and into an arrogant stance. ''You're upset because Glee turned up the goods to send your ex-lover to jail?''

''No,'' she ground out. ''I'm upset because you assumed authority that I didn't give you.''

''Oh, I see,'' he said coldly, ''I overstepped my bounds.''

''That's right.''

''Does this have anything to do with our previous discussion? Am I overstepping my bounds every time I take Miss Schyler Crandall to bed?''

''Isn't that part of the kick for you? Overstepping bounds? Flaunting authority? Trespassing? Isn't that why you make love to me?''

''I don't make love.''

Schyler tried not to flinch. ''I see. You don't make love. You rut.''

He made a dismissive motion with his shoulder. ''I guess that's as good a word as any.'' He saw the pale, bleak expression settle over her face. It brought a soft curse to his lips. ''I call a spade a spade. I don't believe in the word love, so I don't use it. It doesn't mean anything. All I've ever seen people do in the name of love is hurt each other. Your father claimed to love my mother.''

''He did. He told me so this morning.''

''Then why did he stay with a woman he didn't love, didn't even like? Because this grand love he claimed to have for my mother wasn't as strong as his own goddamn ambition and greed. My mother claimed to love me.'' He swiped the air in front of him to cancel out the protestation he saw rising from Schyler's lips.

''But when she died, you know who she was crying for? Cotton. Cotton! Who'd treated her like shit. She cried because she didn't want to leave Cotton.'' He shook his head in bewilderment and disgust. He laughed bitterly. ''There's just no percentage in this love bullshit. The inventor of it got nailed to a cross. So explain its attraction. Sure, you can toss the word around if it makes things look prettier than they are. If it justifies the reason people do things, go ahead. Use the word. But it doesn't mean a damn thing.''

Schyler said gruffly, ''I'm sorry for you.''

''Save it. I don't want anything to do with love. Not if it means letting people mop up the floor with me and then begging them to do it again. Fuck passive resistance. Cash Boudreaux fights back.''

''An eye for an eye.''

''Precisely. And then some.''

''So since Cotton used your mother, you felt justified to use me the same way.'' Her eyes moved up to meet his. There was no life in them, no compassion or human warmth. They reflected only her own disillusioned features. ''Didn't you?''

''Is that what you think?''

She nodded slowly. ''Yes. That's what I think.'' Her heart begged him to deny it. He didn't.

''I take it Cotton opened your eyes to me,'' he said calmly.

''He said you threatened to ruin him. Did you?'' Cash said nothing. ''You swore on your mother's rosary to destroy him and Belle Terre. Does that include frightening me? Tampering with the equipment? Causing delays? Making certain that a contract that would put the company on solid footing again doesn't get filled.''

His eyes glittered. ''You're a smart lady. You figure it out.''

''And it would be a big joke on all of us if you were sleeping with me at the same time, wouldn't it?''

''It brings a smile to my face just thinking about it.''

But his face wasn't smiling. It was remote and cold. Wanting to crumple, Schyler forced herself to stand tall. ''I want you out of here immediately. Don't come back. Don't go around the loggers either.''

''You think you can stop me?''

''I won't have to. You wield tremendous influence over them. You could probably get them to walk off their jobs this afternoon.'' She tipped her head to one side. ''But I wonder if they would go on strike if it meant giving up those promised bonuses. I wonder what they'd do to you if they suspected you of sabotaging the shipments and preventing them from getting those bonuses.''

''I see you've got it all thought out.''

''I want you off Belle Terre within a week. Vacate that house. Burn it to the ground for all I care. Just don't come back. If I ever see you on my property again, I'll shoot you.''

He tried to stare her down, but she didn't succumb. He shrugged, went to the door, and pulled it open. ''You'll never make the deadline without me, you know.''

''I'll die trying.''

He gave her a slow, assessing glance. ''Maybe so.''

Even the click of the latch when he closed the door behind him sounded as ominous as a gunshot.

FIFTY-ONE

Schyler walked into the dining room at Belle Terre. Without a word, she slapped a manila folder on the table in front of Ken. ''What's that?'' he asked.

''Enough incriminating evidence to send you to jail.''

Across the table, Tricia's fork halted midway between her plate and her mouth. Ken played innocent and smiled sickly. "What the hell are you talking about, Schyler?"

"I don't want to talk about anything in here where we might be overheard by Mrs. Dunne or Gayla. I'll meet you in the parlor."

Minutes later she was seated in a wing chair. Her bearing was indomitable, but she felt more like the feathery ball of a dandelion blossom on the verge of disintegration. She was ready to fly apart.

As Ken and Tricia entered the room, she said, "Please slide the doors closed."

"My, we're being so dramatic tonight." Tricia snuggled into a chair across from Schyler and draped her legs over the arm of it. She plucked several white grapes off the stalk she had brought in with her and popped them into her mouth. "I adore all this intrigue, but why is it necessary?"

"I'll let Ken tell you." Schyler, ignoring Tricia's irritating insolence, looked at her former fiancé. Comparisons were unfair, but she couldn't help measuring his failure against Cash's success. Ken had had all the advantages. He'd come from a good family, had a private school education, had money. He had squandered all those advantages. Cash had begun with nothing, not even legitimacy, and had built a successful life for himself. He still didn't have many material possessions, therefore his success couldn't be measured in dollars and cents. But he had earned more respect than ridicule.

She had loved both men. Both were liars and cheats. That was a worse reflection on her than on them. Obviously she had a tendency toward choosing the wrong men to love.

Ken tapped the edge of the folder against his palm. "Look, Schyler, I don't know what you think this file proves, but—"

"It proves that you've been embezzling money from Crandall Logging almost since my father put you on the payroll."

Tricia sat up straight and swung her feet to the floor. *"What?"*

"I don't know what the hell you're talking about," Ken sputtered.

"The figures are there in black and white, Ken," Schyler said evenly. "I've seen Father's forged signature on canceled checks."

Ken nervously wet his lips. "I don't know who put this . . . this outlandish idea into your head, but . . . it was Boudreaux, wasn't it? That son of a bitch," he spat. "He'll stop at nothing to cause disruption. Don't you see what he's doing? He's trying to turn you against me."

Schyler bowed her head and massaged her drumming temples. "Ken, stop it. Please. I've known for weeks, ever since I went to Endicott's, that there were discrepancies in the bookkeeping. I couldn't figure out why Daddy had ignored them until the company was on the brink of bankruptcy."

"I'll tell you."

All heads turned toward the sound of Cotton's voice. He hadn't parted the wide sliding doors that separated the parlors, but stood in the doorway that led into the hall. He was thinner than before his illness, but when he stood at his full height, as now, he could still be intimidating and seemingly invincible.

He came into the room. "I ignored it because I didn't want to admit that there was a thief living under my own roof."

"Now just a—"

"Shut up," Cotton commanded his son-in-law. "You're a goddamn thief. And a liar. You're a gambler, which I could forgive if you were any good at it. But you don't gamble any better than you do anything else. I know all about the heavies you owe money to."

Ken had started to sweat. At his sides his fists opened and closed reflexively. "What's he talking about, Ken?" Tricia asked.

It was Cotton, however, who answered her. "He's in debt up to his ass with a loan shark."

"Is that why you asked me for money?" Schyler wanted to know.

Ken foundered for an answer. Cotton frowned at him disparagingly. "I was kinda hoping they'd get rough and scare some sense into you. But you're too stupid to take their warnings seriously. Then I started hoping they would go ahead and kill you. This family would have been shed of you and we could pass it off as robbery and murder."

"You better stop right there, old man," Ken warned.

Cotton paid no attention to him. "I never could stomach you, Howell. You might have hoodwinked both my daughters, but I had your number the day you let that little bitch," he said, pointing to Tricia, "get by with that lie about carrying your kid. You're a weakling, a sorry excuse for a man, and I can't stand the sight or the smell of you. You stink of failure."

Schyler left her chair. "Daddy, sit down." Cotton's face was florid. He was gasping for breath. She took his arm and led him to the nearest chair, easing him into it.

Her ministrations annoyed him. "You all seem to think that when my heart went on the blink, my brain did, too. You've been pussyfooting around this house, not wanting the old man to get drift of what was going on. But I know, all right. I know everything. And I can't say I like much of it."

"All the trouble started when Schyler came home," Tricia said peevishly. "Things were rocking along fine until then. She just moved in and took over."

"What did she take from you?" Cotton asked.

"My husband," Tricia replied venomously.

"That's a lie!" Schyler cried.

Cotton gave Schyler a baleful look. "Do you still want him?"

"No."

He looked back at Tricia. "She doesn't want him. I'd think she was crazy if she did. What else have you got to bellyache about?"

"She took over the management of this house. She fired the housekeeper."

"Thank Jesus, Mary and Joseph," Cotton said. "That Graves woman was a shriveled-up, dried-up old shrew who couldn't cook worth a damn. I say good riddance."

"What about that black person who's living with us?"

"Veda's girl? What about her?"

"Thanks to Schyler she's got the run of the place. God only knows what kind of diseases she brought with her."

"That's a dreadful thing to say," Schyler exclaimed furiously.

Tricia glared up at her. "You'd turn this house into a refuge for every color of riffraff if we'd let you. Mama would roll over in her grave."

"Your mother never had a kind thought for anybody," Cotton said to Tricia. "And neither have you. At least Schyler doesn't have your prejudices."

Tricia's breasts heaved with indignation. "Of course. Sure. Certainly. Take up for Schyler. No matter what she does, it's okay with you, isn't it?" Her blue eyes flashed. "Well, did you know she's sleeping with Cash Boudreaux? *Cash Boudreaux!* I mean, my God, that's scraping the bottom of the barrel, isn't it? What do you think about your precious Schyler now, Daddy?"

"I didn't come in here to discuss Schyler's love life."

"No," Tricia shouted. "Of course not. Schyler's perfect even if she's bedding down with lowlife."

"That's enough!"

"Daddy, calm down."

"Tricia, just shut up," Ken yelled.

"I won't," Tricia screamed at her husband. "Daddy's right. You are a weakling to just stand there and not even defend yourself. Why don't you defend me?" She jabbed her index finger into her breast. She was bristling with rage. Spittle had collected in the corners of her lips. "I stayed here in this tacky, rundown old house for years while Schyler was living the high life in London. I stayed and took care of you," she said, turning to Cotton, "when Schyler deserted you. And this is the thanks I get. You still throw her up to me as an example to live by."

Cotton's gaze penetrated Tricia to the core of her being. "You stayed here with me so Schyler couldn't come home. That's the only reason. It wasn't out of affection."

She collected herself and drew in several deep breaths. In a small voice she said, "Why that's simply not true, Daddy."

Cotton's white head nodded. "Oh, yes it is. You didn't want Ken. You just knew that Schyler did. And you didn't want to live at Belle Terre. You knew that it killed Schyler's soul to leave it." Staring at her, he shook his head sadly. "You've never had a single unselfish thought, Tricia. If you ever had a drop of charitable blood in your veins, Macy polluted it with her autocratic philosophy. You're a self-indulgent, spiteful, lying bitch, Tricia. Much as it grieves me to say so."

Tricia shuddered under his verbal attack. "Whatever I am, it's your fault. You knew Mama didn't love us. You made up for it with Schyler. But not with me. You ignored me. You couldn't see me through Schyler's golden aura."

"I tried to love you. You won't let anybody love you. You're too busy being defensive about not coming out of Macy's womb. It never mattered to me that I didn't spawn you, but it sure as hell mattered to you."

Tricia came out of her chair slowly. Her eyes glowed with evil fire. "I'm glad I'm not your real daughter," she hissed. "You're coarse and crude, just like Mama always said you were. No wonder she wouldn't let you darken the door of her bedroom. You strut around like God almighty, but you're little better than white trash. That's exactly what you'd be if you hadn't married a Laurent."

She turned to Schyler. "And I'm glad I'm not your blood sister. You weren't content to come back and upset the household that I'd kept together even though I despise this place. You made my husband look like a fool for not seizing control of the business. Now you're accusing him of being a thief."

"He is a thief," Cotton barked.

It was easy for Schyler to disregard Tricia's vindictiveness. She was concerned for Cotton. This stress was what he needed least. "Daddy, we can talk about all this later."

"We'll talk about it now," he shouted, banging the arm of his chair. At the risk of upsetting him more, Schyler held her peace. Cotton focused his attention on Ken again. "You've bled my business for years. I should have put a stop to it when I first figured it out. I guess I hoped you'd grow some balls and stop before someone caught you at it."

"I wouldn't have had to dip into the company till if you'd paid me a decent salary."

"A decent salary?" Cotton repeated in a raised voice. "Goddamn you. What I pay you is more than three times what an average logger gets. And he sweats and strains and ruins his back and risks his life for every friggin' dollar." Cotton leaned forward in his chair. "What did you ever do to earn your handsome salary? I'll tell you. Play golf three afternoons a week and keep your butt folded over a padded pink leather stool in the country club bar."

"I've given six good years to Crandall Logging."

"With nothing to show for it," Cotton yelled back. "Nothing, that is, except a criminal record."

"If you had treated me like a man—"

"You never acted like a man."

"If you had given me more responsibility like you did Boudreaux, I'd've—"

"You'd've fucked up even worse," Cotton finished curtly.

That was like the final blast of steam out of a factory whistle. It was followed by a profound silence. Schyler spoke first. "We're all tired and short-tempered tonight. Maybe airing our differences has been good for us." She glanced down at her father. It hadn't been good for Cotton. He was leaning against the back of his chair, looking utterly exhausted. "Let's not talk anymore tonight. I think once this Endicott order is filled, we'll all feel a lot better."

"Is that all you ever think about?" Tricia asked.

"Right now that's all there is," Schyler replied shortly. "If we don't get the last shipment there in time, we don't get paid. If we don't get paid—"

"Belle Terre will be foreclosed upon. Well that would suit me just fine." Tricia's statement roused Cotton from his brief respite. He raised his head and looked at her as though he hadn't heard correctly. "In fact I hope that's exactly what happens."

"Tricia, shut up."

"Daddy, may just as well know now how Ken and I feel, Schyler."

"Not now."

"Why not? We might not get another chance at a family discussion like this." She looked at Cotton. "Ken and I want to sell Belle Terre. We want our portion of the money and then we want to leave here and never come back."

Schyler knelt down in front of her father's chair. She grasped his hands. "Don't worry about it, Daddy. It'll never happen. I swear that to you."

"Careful, Schyler," Tricia taunted. "With all the things that have been going wrong, I'm not so sure you can get that order filled in time."

Schyler surged to her feet and confronted Tricia. "I can and I will. We've got several more days before the note at the bank comes due."

"Not much time."

"But enough."

"Not if something else causes a delay."

"I'll make sure nothing does. In fact, I'm not going to wait until the last minute. Today I ran a quick inventory of the timber we've got at the landing. I think I can ship enough to fill the order by Wednesday. No need to wait until next week."

That was the plan she had wanted to discuss with Cash. Now, even without his advice, she had decided to act on it. She would get the jump on anyone who had notions of seeing her fail.

"Tomorrow morning, I intend to step up operations. Start an hour earlier, work an hour later. With the bonuses I'm offering as incentive, I think everyone will be more than willing to put in the overtime."

"Leave organizing the loggers to Cash." Cotton was absently rubbing his chest.

Schyler noticed. She mentally flipped a coin on whether or not to tell him she had fired Cash. She decided that it would relieve Cotton to know that she was no longer involved with him. "Cash won't be acting as foreman any longer. I fired him today."

The three were stunned by her announcement, Cotton most of all. "You fired Cash?"

"That's right. I ordered him off Belle Terre. He'll be gone within a week."

"Cash is leaving Belle Terre?" Cotton parroted in a thready voice.

"Isn't that what you wanted?"

"Of course, of course," he said. "It's just that I'm shocked to hear that he agreed."

Her announcement hadn't been met with the reaction she had expected. She wanted to pursue it with Cotton, but Tricia distracted her.

"You're going to bring this about all by yourself?"

"That's right."

Tricia snickered. "If nothing else, it's been highly entertaining to watch the rise and fall of Schyler Crandall. And about that sale of Belle Terre, Daddy, I don't think the choice will be left up to us. Not even to you. Coming, Ken?" She glided out of the room.

Schyler rushed to the doorway and called for Mrs. Dunne. "Help Daddy get to his room and into bed," she said the moment the housekeeper appeared. "He's upset, so give him his medication even if it is an hour early. He needs to go to sleep."

"Don't fuss, Schyler," he said cantankerously as he labored to get out of his chair. "I'm still standing. It'll take more than Tricia, Ken, and their hush-hush plans for Belle Terre to kill me."

"You knew they'd been talking about it?"

He smiled at her, tapping his temple, and winked. "I'm a mean son of a bitch. I learned to take care of myself on the docks of New Orleans. Not much gets past me."

"You own Belle Terre. Nobody is going to take it away from you."

He shook his head, his expression reflective. "No one can own Belle Terre, Schyler. It owns us."

He let himself be led away by Mrs. Dunne. Schyler watched him go. He looked frail as he shuffled down the hall. She wasn't ready for him to be aged and feeble. Her daddy was strong. Nothing could bring him down.

More than ever she regretted the years they'd been separated by the misunderstanding based on Tricia's lie. She echoed the sentiment Tricia had voiced earlier. She was very glad the same blood didn't flow through their veins.

Her shoulders stooped with fatigue, she turned into the room again. She had almost forgotten that Ken was still there. "I thought you went upstairs with your wife."

He was pulling his lower lip through his teeth. "No, uh, we left a matter up in the air."

"What matter?"

"That." He nodded down at the file. Schyler had forgotten about it.

"I'll cover for you, just as Cotton has."

"Don't do me any favors," he said sarcastically.

"Then you'd rather go to jail?" Schyler's nerves were shot. Ken should have known better than to press her when he was ahead.

Apparently her tone of voice brought him to that same conclusion. "No, of course not. But I want you to know, Schyler, that I'm not a thief."

"You stole something that didn't belong to you. That's the generally accepted definition of a thief."

"I only took what I felt I had coming."

"You only took what you needed to keep the loan sharks from breaking your legs."

"And to keep Tricia off my back about money. That woman thinks she's a Vanderbilt and has to live like one. Cotton's a stingy bastard. He never paid me according to my ability."

Schyler looked away, not wanting to point up the obvious, but Ken saw her expression and took issue with it. "I guess you're going to say that my contribution wasn't worth even what I got."

"I'm not going to say anything except good night. I'm exhausted."

He barred her way to the door. "I know what you're thinking."

"What?"

"That I've been putting moves on you just for the money."

"Haven't you?"

"No."

"You're right. That's what I was thinking. Not very flattering to either of us, is it?" She looked him in the eye. "Not that it matters. I would have rejected you anyway."

She tried to go around him. Again he blocked her way. "Are you going to fire me? Is that your next duty as CEO of Crandall Logging?"

"I haven't really thought about it, Ken. I can't think about anything until I get a check from Endicott and endorse it over to Gilbreath."

"But firing me would be just your style, wouldn't it? You like throwing your weight around. You must have what the shrinks call penis envy. You want to be the son your daddy never had, don't you? That's probably what went wrong between you and Boudreaux. There can't be two studs in one bed."

"Good night, Ken." When she tried pushing him aside, he caught her arm roughly.

"Tricia was right. Everything turned to shit when you came back. Why didn't you stay with your gay friend? That relationship was more suited to you. You could be the man. Why'd you have to come back here and screw everything up?"

Schyler wrenched her arm free. "I came back to find everything already screwed up, thanks to you and Tricia. I'm going to put things back the way they should have been all along. And nothing is going to stop me."

FIFTY-TWO

From where she stood out on the veranda, Gayla heard Schyler's exit line. Through the windows, she watched her enter the hall and head toward her father's bedroom. Gayla saw Ken Howell in the parlor, working free the knot of his necktie with one hand and pouring himself a stiff bourbon with the other. He muttered deprecations to Schyler, to Cotton, to his wife.

Gayla considered Ken a dangerous man. He was like a wounded beast. He would lash out at anything or anyone, even someone who tried to help him. Weak men were often the most dangerous. They felt threatened from every direction. They had something to prove.

Gayla hadn't been eavesdropping intentionally. She and Mrs. Dunne had been drinking coffee together in the kitchen when the hue and cry went up in the back parlor. They'd glanced at each other, then took up their conversation, trying to ignore the raised voices and what they might signify. After Mrs. Dunne had been summoned to take Mr. Crandall to bed, Gayla had slipped out the back door.

It had become her nightly ritual to walk the entire veranda several times before going to bed. It was a masochistic exercise. Nothing scary had happened since the appearance of the doll on her pillow. She never saw anything unduly alarming on these nightly excursions.

But she knew that someone, something, some *presence* that bore malice toward the people of Belle Terre was out there in the darkness, lurking, watching, biding his time.

Schyler, she knew, passed off her skittishness to ethnic superstition at best and to her remnant fear of Jigger at worst. Gayla was sure that in the latter respect, Schyler was right. She was terrified that one day he would seek retribution for her desertion.

She had ridden into town with Mrs. Dunne for the first time only the day before. When they arrived at the supermarket, however, she had refused to go inside with her. Instead she had sat in the car, sweltering in the noon heat, with all the windows rolled up, anxiously glancing around.

Her fears were childish. But one glance at her scarred naked body was sufficient to remind her that they were justified. The worst of her scars didn't show. They were on her mind and in her heart. Jigger had marred her soul. She prayed for his death each night. She would burn in hell for that, and for being his whore, and for betraying Jimmy Don's sweet, pure love.

The only comfort she could derive was that Jigger would burn in hell, too. Hopefully there were stratas of hell, where those who sinned because they had no choice were dealt with more kindly than those who sinned out of meanness.

She only hoped that before she was consigned to hell, she would know that Jimmy Don was out of that awful place. Gayla felt guiltily responsible for Jimmy Don's imprisonment.

She had just about come full circle. She rounded the corner of the veranda, but immediately she ducked back, clamping her hand over her mouth to keep from uttering a squeal of fright. A tall shadow had made a dent in the rhododendrons the instant she'd stepped around the corner.

Her instinct was to run as fast as she could for the nearest door, but she forced herself to stay where she was. After several seconds, she peered around the corner again. Every leaf on the shrub had fallen back into place. The blossoms were motionless. There was no shadow, no evidence that anybody had been on the veranda.

Maybe she had imagined it. She crept forward, inching along the wall. At the parlor window, she glanced inside. Ken was pacing the floor, drinking and bad-mouthing his misfortunes beneath his breath.

Gayla slipped past the window unseen. She figured that anyone on the inside couldn't see out onto the veranda because the lights in the parlor were so bright. But anyone on the outside could see inside clearly, as well as hear everything that was said. It would be like watching a picture show.

But there hadn't been anybody there. A bird had probably disturbed those rhododendron bushes. She had imagined the shadow. Her overactive nerves were making her see things that didn't exist.

Gayla had almost convinced herself of that when she turned and caught, on the still evening air, the unmistakable fragrance of tobacco smoke.

At two minutes past nine the following morning, Dale Gilbreath took a telephone call at his desk.

"What do you mean she's going to ship ahead of time!" He sat bolt upright in his reclining chair.

"She's sending the timber out on Wednesday."

"Why?"

"Why do you think?" his caller asked impatiently. "She's a damn clever bitch. She's trying to avoid exactly what we had planned for that last shipment."

Dale quickly assimilated the information. "I don't think this will cause any problems. Flynn's agreed to our price. He's willing to do it. More than willing since that Frances girl is at Belle Terre."

"Are you sure he knows how to use the materials?"

"Yes. You just see to it that he gets them. I'll notify him about the change in the date. What time Wednesday?"

"If the train is on schedule, it arrives Wednesday afternoon at five-fifteen. I rechecked this morning."

"You know," Dale said thoughtfully, "that if anyone on that freight train gets killed, it'll be murder."

"Yes. Too bad Schyler won't be on it."

Wednesday dawned hot and still. The hazy sky was the color of saffron. Area bayous seemed to lack the energy to flow at all. Their viscous surfaces were unbroken except for an occasional insect skimming them. Thunderheads built up on the horizon in the direction of the Gulf, but at five-ten in the afternoon, the sun was still beating down.

The explosion occurred a mere quarter of a mile from the Crandall Logging landing. It blew the glass out of the office windows and showered the desk with flying shards that ripped the leather upholstery of Cotton's chair.

A large column of black smoke rose out of the pile of twisted metal. It could be seen for miles. The boom was loud enough to have heralded the end of the world. The impact of it rattled the beer bottles behind the bar at Red Broussard's café.

One of Red's frequent customers, sitting alone at a table, smiled with supreme satisfaction. He'd done a damn fine job.

 FIFTY-THREE

"Stop looking at me like that, Daddy. I'm fine."

Cotton's cheeks were flushed. He was propped up against the pillows on his bed. Schyler was glad he wasn't up and moving about.

"You don't look fine. What happened to your knees?"

She glanced down, noticing for the first time that her knees were raw and bleeding, as were the heels of her hands. There were particles of gravel embedded in the flesh. She brushed them off, trying not to wince at the stinging pain.

"I was standing out on the platform, watching the train approach. The blast knocked me off my feet. I landed on my hands and knees beside the tracks."

"You could have been killed."

She thought it best not to tell him that she probably would have been if she'd been sitting behind the desk in the office. "Thank God no one was."

"No one on the train?"

She shook her head. "It was pushing two empty locomotives. They sustained the worst damage. The engineers in the third diesel weren't even bruised. Scared, naturally. It was a costly, uh, accident, but thankfully not in lives or injuries.''

"Accident, my ass. What happened, Schyler?" He frowned at her. "And don't sugarcoat it for the heart patient. What the hell really happened?''

"It was deliberately set," she admitted with a deep sigh. "They used—''

"They?"

"Whoever . . . used some kind of plastic explosive. Once the smoke had cleared and we had made sure nobody was hurt, the sheriff conducted a preliminary investigation.''

"Investigation," Cotton scoffed. "Patout doesn't know shit from shinola. He wouldn't recognize a clue if it bit him in the butt.''

"I'm afraid you're right, so I stayed right there with him. That's one reason I'm so grubby." She swept her hand down the front of her dress. "There are a thousand and one unanswered questions. Since the train is interstate, several government agencies will be going over the scene with a fine-tooth comb. It'll take weeks, if not months, to sort through all the debris.''

"And in the meantime, the tracks are unusable.''

"The tracks look like iron hair ribbons all knotted together." Dejectedly, she sat down on the foot of his bed. "What I can't figure out is why the explosives were set to go off before the train reached the landing. If someone wanted to stop that shipment, why didn't the explosion occur after the train was loaded with Crandall timber and not before?''

"Somebody wanted to put us out of commisson, and they did.''

"Like hell," Schyler said, with a burst of enthusiasm. "I swore to you, I swore to myself, that I was going to meet that deadline and I'm going to.''

"Maybe you should let it go, Schyler." Cotton's face looked heavy and old with defeat. The familiar zest was absent from his blue eyes. There was a hopeless lassitude in his posture that had nothing to do with his repose. He didn't look at rest; he looked resigned.

"I can't let it go, Daddy," she said huskily. "To let it go is tantamount to letting Belle Terre go. I can't. I won't.''

"But you can't do this alone.''

He struck at the heart of her most basic fears. She was utterly alone. Cotton could coach from the sidelines but, through no fault of his own, he was a weak and unreliable ally. She wished she had someone to act as a backboard for her ideas, her apprehensions.

She wished she had Cash.

She desperately needed his counsel on what action to take next. But he might be the very one who had blown up the tracks. She tried to forget his telling her that he'd been an explosives expert in Vietnam. He was clever enough to have disabled Crandall Logging without hurting anybody. But was he capable of such wanton destruction? And why would he destroy all he had built?''

She recalled his face the last time she'd seen it, hard and cold, reeking contempt. There hadn't been a spark of human feeling in the eyes that bore into her. Yes, he was capable of doing anything. Mere pride wouldn't prevent her from going to him on her knees and begging his advice, but consulting him now was out of the question. He was a suspect.

She thought of calling Gilbreath and humbly appealing to his emotions, but she seriously doubted he had any. If he wouldn't extend the deadline of the load in light of Cotton's heart illness, what would compel him to do it in light of this catastrophe? Besides, for all his unctuous mannerism, she suspected him of celebrating each mishap that had befallen her and Crandall Logging.

Most unsettling of all was that only a handful of people knew that she had changed the day of the shipment. They were the people closest to her, people she should have been able to trust.

Ken. There was hostility there to be sure. Her discovery of his embezzlement had only stoked his resentment. He had hurled vicious insults at her, but Schyler doubted there was a violent bone in Ken's body. He was all talk and no action. An explosioh just didn't seem in keeping with his personality. Besides, he would lack the ambition and knowledge to pull it off successfully.

Tricia. She was certainly vindictive enough. She would rejoice in the company's failure because it would expedite the sale of Belle Terre. But again, she wouldn't have the expertise to do something of that caliber.

Jigger Flynn. Motive, yes. But no opportunity. He couldn't have known about her secret change in plans.

Cash wasn't among those who knew either, but Cash could have found out. The loggers must have known something was in the wind by the way she'd been pushing them the last few days. They drank together in the local watering holes in the evenings. Cash could have overheard tongues lubricated by too much liquor.

Whoever the culprit, he was still around and very close to her.

"I'm afraid for you," Cotton's raspy voice jostled her out of her brooding.

She forced a confident smile. Through his socks, she massaged his feet. "I'm more afraid for Belle Terre. If we were forced out, we'd have to change our personal stationery. Imagine what a hassle that would be."

He didn't crack a smile at her attempted humor. "Did Cash do this to us?" The disillusionment in his expression made his whole face appear ravaged.

"I don't know, Daddy."

"Does he hate me that much?" Cotton turned his head and stared out the window. "I probably haven't been fair to the boy."

"He's not a boy. He's a man."

"He could be a better one. Monique was so proud, she wouldn't let me buy him clothes, wouldn't let me pay for anything. When he started school, he was laughed at. Made fun of." He squeezed his eyes shut. "That works on a kid, you know. It either makes him a pansy or a mean son of a bitch. Cash started fighting back. That was good. I knew he'd have to be tough to make it in this world. But Jesus, that boy has turned into a pain in the ass."

"Whatever tiffs you've had with him, nothing warrants what happened today," Schyler remarked. "If it's ever proved that he was involved, I'll see to it that he's punished to the full extent of the law."

Cotton's chest rose and fell heavily. "Monique would hate to see him locked in some goddamn jail. Cash belongs in the forest, on the bayous. That dark water flows in his veins instead of blood, she used to say." He gnashed his teeth. "Christ."

Schyler stroked his thick white hair out of compassion for his suffering. "Don't worry about Cash. Tell me what I should do. I need your guidance."

"What can you do?"

She thought a moment. "Well, the timber is still intact at the landing. They were hauling the last—"

Suddenly she broke off. Her mind halted and then backtracked as she recalled the last half hour before the explosion when the landing had been a beehive of activity. "Daddy, when you first took over the company, how did you transport the timber?"

"That was before I built the landing and weaseled the railroad into laying the spur."

"Exactly. How did you haul the timber to the various markets?"

His blue eyes flickered. "Like most of the independents do now. Rigs."

"That's it!" Schyler bent down and planted a smacking kiss on his lips. "We'll drive that shipment to Endicott's. Right up to Joe Jr.'s front door."

"Why wasn't it done right?" the caller hissed into the telephone receiver.

Gilbreath had been sitting hunched over his desk, asking himself the same question. "Jigger must have been drunk. He misunderstood our instructions. Something. I don't know. For some reason he didn't realize that he was supposed to blow the tracks after the shipment was loaded, not before."

"We were fools to depend on him."

"We had to."

"I think I'm a fool to depend on you, too, I can do this by myself and cut you out entirely."

"Don't threaten me," Dale said coldly. "We haven't lost anything yet. It didn't go as we expected, but there's no way in hell she can get that shipment off in time."

"Want to bet? Tomorrow night."

"*What?*"

"Yes. Tomorrow night. By truck."

"Crandall's doesn't have that many rigs."

"Schyler's been mustering them all day. Everybody in the parish who owns or has access to a rig, she's enlisting. Paying top dollar. She'll make it, I tell you, unless she's stopped."

Gilbreath's palms began to sweat. "We'll have to use Jigger again."

"I guess so. I'll let you handle that, but you make damn certain he knows what he's doing this time."

"I'll see to it. Don't worry."

"Funny. I do."

Gilbreath, choosing to disregard the dig, asked, "What time tomorrow?"

"I don't know yet. I'll have to call you when I find out."

"That means Jigger will have to use a timer."

"Probably."

"The stakes are higher this time. There will be men driving those rigs."

"I can live with a guilty conscience if you can."

"Oh, I can," Gilbreath said with a chuckle. "I just wanted to be sure you could."

"Don't doubt it."

"After your call tomorrow, I don't think we should speak to each other again. And for a long time after this is over."

"I agree. Too bad we won't be able to have a celebration drink."

"When Rhoda and I are ensconced in Belle Terre, we'll invite you out for cocktails."

There was a laugh. "You do that."

"I'll get back some time tomorrow," Schyler squeezed Cotton's hand affectionately. "I can tell you're worried. Don't be. Endicott is expecting us. I explained why the convoy would be arriving in the wee hours. He thinks I'm crazy, but I think he's a jerk, so we're even," she said with a laugh.

Cotton didn't laugh. His expression was grave. "I'll feel much better when you're back safe and sound."

"So will I. I've got a lot of hard work ahead of me before then."

"Why do you have to go yourself?"

"I don't have to. I want to. This will be the culmination of everything I've worked for. I want to accept that nice, fat check in person. I promise to ride with the best driver. Whom do you recommend?"

"Cash."

"Cash?" she asked in surprised. "He won't be going."

"I know. But he's who I would recommend you ride with if I had first choice."

Cash would be her first choice as well. He should be there beside her when Joe Jr. handed over that check. Tonight would be the culmination of all Cash's hard work, too. Or had his hard work been a screen just like his lovemaking?

Correction. Cash didn't make love. He'd said so with brutal explicitness: *I don't make love.*

Schyler cleared her throat of a tight constriction and put on a phony, bright smile. "Who would be your second choice?" Cotton named an independent logger. "I'll ride with him then. Now," she said, placing her hands on Cotton's shoulders and easing him back against the pillows of his bed, "you get a good night's sleep. Not long after you wake up in the morning, I'll be home." She kissed him good-bye. "Good night, Daddy. I love you."

At the door she turned to give him a thumbs-up sign, but his eyes were closed.

"What a marvelous idea," Rhoda cooed as she languished in the bubble bath her husband had drawn for her. She reached for her stem of chilled champagne and sipped, then rolled her tongue over her lips, intentionally making the movement seductive. "There's room for two in here, if we get real chummy."

"No. I'd rather watch."

"And take pictures?"

"Yes. Later."

"Are we celebrating?"

Dale knelt beside the tub and parted the mountain of bubbles so that Rhoda's surgically edified breasts were visible. The nipples bobbed upon the surface of the water. He stuck his finger in her glass of champagne and dribbled the cold wine over them until they tightened.

"We are."

"What are we celebrating?"

Dale removed the champagne from her hand and replaced it with a bar of scented soap. "Wash yourself."

Eyes lowered to half-mast, Rhoda took the soap between her wet hands and began rubbing them back and forth until they were dripping foamy lather. She laid them on her breasts and squeezed the stiff, red nipples between her slippery, soapy fingers.

Dale's eyes glazed over. His breathing accelerated. "We're celebrating our success."

"Hmm. Does our success have anything to do with the explosion at the Crandall landing the other day?"

"No, that didn't go quite as planned."

"Oh?"

"Wash down there, too," he instructed raspily as he unfastened his trousers to accommodate his erection.

Rhoda smiled indulgently as she parted her thighs and rested her feet on opposite rims of the tub. She slid the bar of soap between her thighs. Dale groaned.

"What went wrong at the landing?"

In panting bursts of dialogue, he explained the snafu. "It slowed her down, but it didn't stop her. We're stopping her tonight. Nothing's going to go wrong this time. We've got the timing right, everything."

"Good." She blew aside a clump of bubbles so Dale would have an unrestricted view. She would have enjoyed his bedazzled expression more if she hadn't been puzzling through her own thoughts. "That doesn't sound like Cash. To make a drastic error like that."

"Move your hand faster, darling. Yes, that's it," he panted. "Boudreaux? What has he got to do with it?"

"Everything, I thought. Wasn't he the one who set the explosives?"

"Hell no. Jigger Flynn did."

Water sloshed over the rim of the tub as Rhoda suddenly sat up. "But Cash planned it, showed him how, right?"

"No."

"I thought you were using Cash. You said you had plans for him."

"Initially I did. But I changed my mind. He's too closely tied to Belle Terre. I couldn't be sure how loyal he is to Schyler."

"He's sleeping with her."

"He sleeps with everybody," Dale yelled defensively, not liking Rhoda's tone. It suggested he was stupid. He added silkily, "So far Cash Boudreaux hasn't shown much discrimination."

"You bastard." Rhoda stepped out of the tub, splattering Dale with water and reaching for a towel. "So you hired that Flynn character."

"He can be trusted because he wants to see Schyler Crandall ruined."

"But does Cash?" Rhoda demanded of her husband. "Where is he tonight?"

"Out of the picture. She fired him."

"You fool!" Rhoda cried. "He might be pissed off at her, but he's not going to stand by and idly watch as Belle Terre falls into our hands. He wants the place himself. He told me so. Who's keeping an eye on him tonight?"

Dale, realizing what a serious blunder he'd made, left the bathroom at a run. He knocked the bedroom telephone to the floor in his haste to dial.

"What's all this?"

Ken entered his bedroom to find it in a state of utter chaos. Two suitcases were lying opened on the bed. The clothes from Tricia's closet were draped across chairs and every other conceivable surface. Bureau drawers had been disemboweled, their lacy entrails spilling over their sides. Tricia was busily picking and sorting.

"What does it look like I'm doing? I'm packing."

"For where?"

"New Orleans. Dallas. Atlanta." Tricia shrugged and smiled prettily. "I haven't really decided. I think I'll drive to Lafayette, then head out on the interstate and see what strikes my fancy."

"What the hell are you talking about?" As she sailed past him, Ken caught her arm. She jerked it free.

"Freedom. I'm talking about getting out of Heaven and never looking back."

"You can't just leave."

"Watch me." For emphasis, she tossed a pair of shoes into one of the suitcases. They landed with a plop that sounded final.

"You haven't got any money."

"I'll use plastic money until I get some cash."

"And where will that come from?"

"Don't worry about it, honey. I'm not asking you for any." She ran her palm down his clammy cheek.

When she stepped away, however, he caught her against him again. "I'm your husband. Where do I fit into all your plans?"

"You don't. Our marriage is over."

"What do you mean over?"

Tricia sighed with vexation. She didn't want to waste time explaining to him what should be obvious. "Look, Ken, we started out this marriage on a lie. Let's at least end it on a truth. We don't love each other. We never have. I tricked you into marrying me. The only reason I wanted you was because you and Schyler wanted each other. Well she doesn't want you anymore, so neither do I."

"You bitch!"

"Oh, please. Spare me a theatrical scene and don't look so wounded. You've lived the life of Riley these last six years. Personally I don't like it, but Belle Terre is considered to be a fine mansion by most people's standards. You've had the privilege of residing here without paying a dime in rent. You haven't had to pursue a career. You've bled the family coffers of God knows how much money and got off scot-free.

"We each knew what we were getting when we got married. You know I am manipulative and selfish. I know you are weak and unambitious. Our sex life has been adequate. To my recollection I never said no and when you visited the bawdy houses, I looked the other way.

"The arrangement worked well for us while it lasted, but it's time to call it quits." She went up on tiptoe and kissed his lips softly. "You'll do just fine without me. Lay off the bourbon for a month or two and firm up your belly. You're still good looking. You'll find a wealthy woman just dying to take care of you."

"I don't want a woman to take care of me."

"Why of course you do, sugar. That's what you've always wanted, somebody to make all your tough decisions for you."

The telephone on the nightstand rang. Smiling her rehearsed Mardi Gras Queen smile, Tricia dismissively patted Ken's cheek and went to answer it. But her smile collapsed; she barely got out a hello before she fell silent and listened intently.

Jigger woke up with a roaring headache and a hairy tongue. He rolled over and buried his face in the pillow. It smelled sourly of him and hair oil and sweat. The ringing in his head wouldn't stop. When, after several minutes it became apparent that he couldn't go back to sleep, he sat up on the edge of the bed, gripping the mattress for balance.

His head was muzzy. He tried to shake off the grogginess. He tried to yawn away the ringing in his ears. It persisted. He shouldn't have drunk that pint of whiskey so fast. He chastised himself for it as he stumbled through the dark house.

He had returned home from his nefarious errand at dusk. It was full-fledged nighttime now, but he didn't turn on any lights in deference to his headache. He bumped into several pieces of furniture before he made it to the kitchen sink and turned on the faucet. He had to get that foul, furry taste out of his mouth.

He didn't begrudge guzzling a whole pint. He'd been due a drink. He had risked getting caught by placing those explosives when all that activity was going on at the landing. Several times he'd spied that Crandall bitch herself sashaying in and out and about, issuing orders like a goddamn drill sergeant. It wouldn't be long before she'd get hers.

Smiling evilly, he filled a glass with tap water and raised it to his mouth. It was only halfway there when he realized what had awakened him. It wasn't the noise in his head. It was the lack of it.

His rattlesnake had stopped rattling.

The glass shattered when Jigger dropped it. Water splashed over his muddy shoes, but he didn't notice as he lunged through the back door. In his haste, he almost fell down the concrete steps. At the bottom of them he drew up short, chest heaving.

It was still there. The oil drum was glowing silver in the pale moonlight. The lid was on top of it and anchored down by the large rock. He glanced around the yard. Just as on the morning the snake had been mysteriously delivered, everything appeared normal. He glanced toward his kennel. The pit bull bitch looked at him curiously. Her ears had perked up when he came barreling through the door, but she lay quietly letting her litter suck.

She hadn't barked all evening. His nap had been a deep sleep, but not so deep that a yelping dog wouldn't have roused him. He could swear his snake had been in that drum, making that bloodcurdling sound when he got home at dusk.

So why not now? What was it doing in there that prevented it from making its characteristic sound? Was it digesting that field mouse he'd tossed in there? No, that had been days ago. Why had that son of a bitch stopped rattling?

Was it dead? Shit! It seemed like everything he touched here lately turned to shit. He had planned to use the snake to take up the slack while he was training his pit bull pups to fight. He had thought about taking it on a tour, puttng it in a carnival sideshow, or working up an act with it and one of his whores. Now if his snake was dead, all his fancy planning wouldn't be worth a damn.

Or maybe it wasn't in there at all. Maybe some lowdown, sneaky bastard had heard of his plans and had come along and swiped his snake while he'd been in there sleeping off a pint of cheap whiskey! He would find him, he would. . . .

Cursing, he ran toward the drum and pushed the rock off. It landed with a hard thud on the ground, sending up a little cloud of dust. Jigger grabbed the lid, ready to swing it off. He caught himself just in time. As much as he admired his snake, it was still a helluva rattler. He respected its deadliness. He let go of the lid quickly and snatched his hands back. They had begun to sweat. He wiped them on his pants legs.

Why wasn't it rattling?

Was it even in there?

Muttering, he went to the woodpile and picked up a stick of firewood. For the sake of his paying customers, he'd courageously dispensed with that precaution, but he felt better about having it in his hands now. Again he approached the drum. It looked the same, but damed if it didn't seem spookier now that the sound had stopped.

He had to relieve himself badly. His breath was choppy. He stood staring at the lid of the drum for a long time before he poked it once, quickly, with the stick of firewood. There was not even one little rattle.

The snake wasn't in there. Was it? Jesus, he was going fuckin' nuts. He had to know.

Using the stick, he pushed against the rim of the lid. It didn't budge. It was stuck. Swearing, Jigger applied more force. The lid didn't move a fraction. He dug his heels in and put his weight behind it.

Suddenly the lid slid off and clattered to the ground.

Inertia propelled Jigger forward. He fell against the silver drum belly first. His head went over the rim. He yelled in startled fright.

Regaining his balance, he laughed nervously at himself. Goda'mighty, he was edgy tonight! He was relieved to see that his snake was still there, all right, coiled up in the bottom of the drum. But why wasn't it rattling? Was it dead?

He leaned against the drum and peered over the rim.

When he did, an iron hand clamped down hard on the back of his neck.

Jigger squealed like an impaled pig.

"He's still in there, you cock-sucking son of a bitch." The voice was whispery, laced with hate and rife with malevolence. "He's asleep now on gasoline fumes. But when he wakes up, he's gonna be mad as hell and he's gonna take it out on you."

Jigger screamed. Panicked, he kicked his feet out backward and flailed his arms. His struggles did him no good. His head and shoulders were being held over the open drum by a strong arm with a body sufficient to back it up.

"Before he wakes up, you'll have a while to think about all the mean things you've done. This is Judgment Day for you, Jigger Flynn, and your road to hell is going to be long and scary."

The chain landed heavily on Jigger's neck. He grunted with pain. Terror made him weak. His efforts to escape were ill-timed and ineffectual. An ordinary pair of handcuffs had been linked to the end of the chain. Jigger watched in horror as they were clamped to his wrists. His arms were stretched across the drum and down the other side until his head and shoulders were bridging it. He was staring facedown at his splendidly wicked snake. The chain was wound around the drum, securing his feet and legs to it.

Jigger tried to keep his eyes closed, but he couldn't. He gaped at the oily coil of muscle beneath him. Those muscles were beginning to ripple. He screamed and peed in his pants.

"That's right, scream. Scream real loud. Scream so every devil in hell hears you." Jigger was swacked across his buttocks with the stick of firewood. "I ought to cram this up your ass, but I don't want you to die that way. I want you to die looking eyeball to eyeball with a snake just like yourself. Wonder how many times he'll get you before you die?"

"Let me up. God, Jesus, please. Let me up. Sweet Jesus. Hail Mary, Mother of God, blessed art thou . . ."

"That's it, Jigger, pray."

"Oh, Jesus God. What'd I ever do to you? Who are you, you son of a bitch?"

"I'm an angel of the Lord. I'm a demon from hell. It doesn't matter to you who I am." He opened his hand wide over Jigger's head and pushed his face down farther into the drum. He whispered with insidious delight, "You're gonna die. You're gonna die in excruciating pain."

"Oh, Jesus, Jesus," Jigger whispered. "I'll do anything. Please. Please. I'm begging. I'll give you anything. Money. All my money. Every friggin' cent. Oh, Jesus, help me."

The vindicator got tired of Jigger's screams and his pleas for mercy. He unwound the bandanna around his throat and stuffed it into Jigger's mouth. Jigger tried to spit it out, but all he succeeded in doing was gagging himself on scalding whiskey that his stomach tried to reject. Jigger squirmed frantically, bucking against his restraints.

"You won't be alone for long, Jigger. You'll have company real soon. You know how swelled up your head is gonna be by morning? Your face'll look like a meat platter, with those twin holes all over it. Bye-bye Jigger. Next time we see each other, we'll be in hell."

The vindicator stopped at the kennel to hand-feed the pit bull bitch a snack. She'd come to expect that from him. He spoke to the puppies; they licked his hands with affection and trust. Then he slipped into the darkness of the forest, becoming one with all the tall dark shadows.

Jigger wiggled against the barrel as much as the chain would allow. He screamed, but it only echoed inside his terrified brain. His heart knocked painfully against his ribs. The acrid sweat of stark fear ran into his eyes. He blinked it away only to see the slitted black eyes of his beautiful snake.

The rattling tail began to twitch.

Gayla would be glad when this night ended.

Lordy, what a night. First Schyler had left for the landing. Gayla thought she was crazy for going back there after the explosion. It would be a tremendous load off her mind when Schyler got through with her business in East Texas and came home.

Schyler would have been enough to worry about, but then Tricia had pulled her stunt. She had run out of the house like the devil was after her, only to come storming back inside seconds later. "Where the hell is my car?"

Gayla had had the misfortune of being the only one available to answer her. "Mrs. Dunne took it to town."

"What!" Tricia shrieked.

"Her car broke down. This is her night off. Schyler said she could take your car since you weren't going out."

"Well I *am* going out."

"Then I guess you'll have to drive Mr. Howell's car."

"I can't," Tricia said through her teeth. "It's a stick shift. I never learned to—" Exasperated, she raked her hand through her hair. "Why in God's name am I standing here explaining it to *you?*"

She whirled on her heels and stalked out the front door, letting the screen door bang shut behind her. Gayla watched her run across the yard and disappear into the barn. A few minutes later, she rode out barebacked on one of the horses. Wherever she was going, it was in a hell of a hurry.

Then Ken had come downstairs and gone into the parlor. Gayla heard him scraping open drawers and banging them closed, apparently searching for something. She didn't dare cross paths with him. He seemed as upset as Tricia. Gayla watched him leave the house and, looking like a man with a purpose, drive off in his sports car.

She would have been relieved to see them go, if their stormy departures hadn't left her alone in the house, except for Mr. Crandall, who had been sleeping peacefully the last time she checked on him. Schyler had asked her to keep a close eye on him and to call Dr. Collins if he showed any signs of pain or distress.

She didn't mind the duty. In fact, she enjoyed taking care of him. She seemed to have an instinct for knowing when he needed something but was too proud to ask for it. He rarely thanked her out loud for her unasked for attention, but he looked at her kindly.

When darkness fell, Gayla's nervousness increased. She patrolled the house, checking to see that all the doors and windows were locked. She didn't take her nightly stroll around the veranda. She couldn't bring herself to step outside.

She tried to watch television, but the programming didn't hold her interest. She tried to read, but couldn't sit still for any length of time. She was glad when the clock in the hall chimed the hour, indicating that it had been an hour since she'd last checked on Mr. Crandall.

She went to his bedroom and opened the door. Craning her neck around it, she peered through the darkness. His form was clearly delineated beneath the covers. His medication had worked well; he was sleeping soundly. She listened closely until she was certain she heard his breathing, then backed out of the room, pulling the door closed.

The attack was so sudden, she didn't have time to scream before a hand was clamped over her mouth. The arm that curled around her waist was as supple as a tentacle and as strong as a vise.

She was dragged backward down the hallway. When she scraped her heels along the door trying to get traction, she was lifted up and carried. She clawed at the hand over her mouth and kicked her feet, doing some damage to her attacker's shins, but not enough to be released.

She was pulled into the parlor, spun around, and slammed back against the wall.

Reeling and dizzy with fear, gulping for breath, she raised her head. Her eyes went round with disbelief and apprehension. Her mouth formed the name, but no sound came out.

"Jimmy Don!" she finally whispered.

FIFTY-FIVE

He was probably drunk. Some drunks imagined seeing pink elephants. He was imagining he saw a woman on horseback, a blond woman on horseback. She reminded him of Schyler. His gut curled with desire and his loins got thick and tight and he wished to hell he would stop having these physical reactions every time he thought about her.

He took a deep swallow of his drink. It was the third or fourth bourbon he'd had since he'd returned to his house only a short while ago. It was a hot, humid night and he had had a lot of ground to cover. He had slogged through swamps and tramped through dense forests for hours, but he had a niggling suspicion that he had left one stone unturned. It was the important stone, the one that counted. It pestered him like a gnat. He couldn't brush it away.

What had he overlooked?

Pacing restlessly, drinking steadily, he had tried to push his worries aside. Hell, it wasn't even his problem anymore. Why was he letting it bother him? Yet he couldn't relax. The steady intake of booze wasn't helping. It was only making him see things. A blond woman riding barebacked. Jesus!

Once again, he paused at the window. This time, he slowly lowered the glass from his lips. Damned if there wasn't a woman sliding off the back of a horse and running up to his door. He set his glass down and went to answer her knock.

"Hi, Cash," she said breathlessly, splaying her hand over her bosoms.

"Are you lost?" He would have had to be blind not to notice that she was braless beneath her snug T-shirt.

She appeared to be out of breath, as though she'd been jogging instead of riding horseback. Spreading her hands wide, she shrugged, a movement that did great things for the nice set of tits. "In fact I am," she said around a giggle. "Can you tell me how to get back to Belle Terre?"

Cash stepped through the screen door. "I don't know," he drawled. "Can I?"

Tricia simpered as Cash backed her up against the cypress post. "From what I hear about you, Cash Boudreaux, you can lead a woman just about anywhere. Even some places she doesn't want to go."

"Is that a fact?"

Her glance lowered to his impressive chest, seen through his unbuttoned shirt. "Um-huh. That's what I hear." She looked up at him through her eyelashes. " 'Course I don't know that for sure."

"You could ask your sister."

Tricia's smile faltered. "Schyler? Are you referring to her? She's not my real sister, you know."

Cash propped his shoulder against the post and leaned in close. He ran the knuckle of his index finger across her collarbone. "You could still ask her."

Tricia invitingly leaned into his caress and gazed up at him provocatively. "There are some things I'd rather find out for myself."

Cash, giving her a cool, steady stare and a sly grin, eased himself away. "Want a drink?"

"Thank you, I'd love one. I'm fairly parched."

He held open the screen door. "After you."

She went past him, dragging her body against the front of his and giving him a knowing, sidelong glance. "Why, this is just charmin'. Absolutely charmin'. Look at that cute little chair. Handmade?"

"*Oui*. Bourbon okay?"

"And just a splash of water. Ice, too, please." She pivoted slowly, taking in the quaintness of his house, with its pronounced Cajun flavor. "So this is where my daddy spent so many passionate hours with your mama."

"Now the way I see it," Cash said, deliberately thunking two ice cubes into a glass and covering them with liquor and water, "is that if Schyler isn't your sister, then Cotton isn't your daddy." He turned in time to catch Tricia's hostile glare, which hastily righted itself into a smile.

She took the glass from him, deliberately brushing his fingers with hers. "I guess you're right." She immediately took a sip of her drink, as though she desperately needed it. Her eyes darted around furtively. She kept trying to steal glances through the windows. "Fact is, I don't feel like I have any attachments here anymore."

"Oh?"

"I'm leaving Heaven."

"Alone?"

"Yes. Ken and I are finished."

"Too bad."

"I don't think so."

"When are you going?"

"Tomorrow probably."

"Where?"

"I'm not sure."

"You picked a funny time to go horseback riding."

"Well, I . . ." she stammered, "I got tired of packing. Besides, I guess I wanted to say a formal good-bye to Belle Terre."

"Hmm, and you got lost."

She took another drink, looking at him over the rim of her glass while she drained it. Her voice was husky when she said, "You know why I came here, Cash."

"You want to get laid."

His ability to see through her was disconcerting. His candor was unkind and offensive. She pretended it was flattering. Pressing a hand over her heart again, she said, "My goodness, you're so blunt. Shame on you, Cash Boudreaux. You know I'm nervous. You plumb take my breath."

Cash started unbuckling his belt as he moved toward her. "I've known you since Cotton and Macy adopted you. You never gave me the time of day, Miss Tricia. Each time we passed on the street, you made it a point to turn up your nose and look the other way. If you've got such a powerful crotch throb for me, what took you so long?"

Tricia followed the slow, deliberate movements of his hands as he unsnapped his jeans. She moistened her lips. "I've heard other women talk about you."

"And just what do they say?"

"That you're the best. I wanted to find out."

"You could have found out sooner. Why'd you wait?"

"I guess I was working up my courage."

Cash was standing directly in front of her now. His eyes were half-closed as he looked down at her. He reached for the hem of her T-shirt and began working it up. "What I can't figure out is why you came here tonight, since you were so busy getting packed and all." He peeled the shirt over her head and dropped it to the floor.

Tricia draped her arms over his shoulders and arched her lush body against his. "We're wasting time with all these silly questions."

Cash sank the fingers of one hand into her hair and pulled her head back. His breath was hot and flavored with fine bourbon as he lowered his mouth close to hers. "One thing you ought to know about me, Miss Tricia. I never waste my time."

She should have known things were going too smoothly. Something disastrous was bound to happen. Schyler had wondered what form the first sign of trouble would take. A half hour before they were scheduled to leave, she found out. It didn't come from outside the ranks of the trusted, but from within.

The loggers stubbornly refused to drive the timber to East Texas unless Cash was in the lead rig.

"Mr. Boudreaux no longer works for us," she told the disgruntled group. That didn't faze them. There were nearly a dozen of them facing her, unresponsive to her reasoning. "He doesn't want to work for us."

"Boudreaux don't quit on a job 'ntil it's did," one said from the back of the crowd. Others murmured in agreement.

Before she had a bona fide strike on her hands, Schyler reminded them of the bonuses. "You won't get them. None of the loggers, the saw hands, the loaders, the drivers, nobody will get a cent if this deal with Endicott falls through. You all know the terms of the contract."

"Everybody's behind us. We're authorized to speak for everybody. We ain't budgin' if Cash don't go." The ultimatum was punctuated by a stream of tobacco juice. They all chorused their agreement.

Schyler's shoulders slumped with defeat. She couldn't drive the whole convoy to East Texas. She didn't have time to recruit other drivers from outside the parish, and it seemed that all the locals had pledged fealty to Cash. It was the eleventh hour.

She had no choice.

"All right, wait for me. I'll be back. By the time I get here, I want every rig ready to roll. Got that? Check your chains and bolsters every few minutes while I'm gone. Keep an eye out for anybody lurking around who doesn't belong here."

She had carefully timed their departure and arranged with Sheriff Patout to provide them with a police escort to the state line. At ten o'clock two units from his office were to meet them on the other side of the Laurent Bayou bridge. As she ran to her car, she consulted her wristwatch. It was twelve minutes till ten.

She floorboarded the accelerator of her car and sent it skimming over the rough dirt road that led to Cash's house. There were endless negative possibilities of what she would find when she arrived. He could laugh at her. He could slam the door in her face. He could have already left town. He could be sick, drunk, asleep, or all of the above.

Her headlights made a sweeping arc over the front of his house when she pulled up. There were no lights on inside. God, please let him be here.

She left the car's motor running and the door open as she raced for the front porch, calling his name. She banged on the frame of the screen door.

"Cash?" she called out. Seconds later, he materialized behind the screen. "Cash, thank God you're here. Listen to me, please. I know I don't have any right to ask. I don't want to ask. But you've got to help me. You've got to—"

The rushing fountain of words dried up the instant Tricia appeared beyond Cash's shoulder. She pulled her T-shirt over her head. Schyler watched as she smoothed it over her breasts and cleared her hair from the neck of it. Seeing Tricia in this place was so astonishing that Schyler stared at her with bewilderment.

Then her eyes moved back to Cash. She noticed his unbuttoned shirt, his unfastened jeans, his rumpled hair, the insolent expression on his face. And the smug one on Tricia's.

She actually fell back a step. "My God." She couldn't catch her breath. Unconsciously she gripped a handful of her shirt directly over her heart as if to hold it together. It seemed to be collapsing inside her chest. She closed her eyes and prayed to God she wouldn't disgrace herself by fainting. She didn't want to give either of them that satisfaction.

She was reliving that nightmarish moment at her engagement party when Tricia had announced her pregnancy by Ken. She felt herself being sucked into that chasm of despair again. The woman she had called her sister was wearing the same gloating smile now as then. And as before, the other guilty party was saying nothing, neither confessing nor denying. Cash would never feel the need to justify himself. It would never occur to him to make apologies or amends. He would watch her sink into that black pit and do nothing to help lift her out.

Schyler's impulse was to turn and run until she fell down dead. Instead she drew upon resources she didn't know she possessed. Taking a deep breath she said, "Forgive the intrusion. I didn't know you had . . . a guest."

"What's the problem?"

She gripped her hands together, swallowed, and said the hardest words she'd ever had to say. "I need you." Once those three words were out, the rest seemed relatively easy. "The drivers refuse to drive the rigs unless you're with them. I can't change their minds. They won't be swayed by threats or promises. I'm running out of time to negotiate. The sheriff will give us an escort to the state line, but we've got to go now. So tell me yes or no. There's no time to think about it. I've got to know now. Will you help me one last time?"

He didn't say anything. He gave the screen door the heel of his hand and stalked across the porch past her, refastening his clothes along the way. Schyler fell into step behind him.

"What about me?" Tricia trotted after them. "Cash, come back here. You can't just leave me here by myself."

"Get home the same way you got here," he told her as he slid behind the wheel of Schyler's car.

"Cash, why are you going with her?" Tricia wailed. "What do you care what happens to that wretched timber? Schyler fired you. Don't you have any pride? Cash, don't you dare leave me here."

"If you don't want to get left behind then get in the goddamn car." Fuming, Tricia scrambled in. Cash executed a hairpin turn before she had even closed the back door.

Schyler kept her knuckles pressed against her lips for the duration of the trip. She wanted to rail at both of them. She wanted to physically punish them. Except for her secret love for this man, she had no right to. The pain of this second betrayal might very well kill her, but later. Not tonight. Once she had Belle Terre's future secured, she might die of her twice-broken heart. She wouldn't succumb tonight; she wouldn't let herself.

The loggers were sitting around glumly, smoking, talking desultorily among themselves when the car pulled into the clearing. They rose from their sullen postures and looked toward the car expectantly. A cheer went up when Cash stepped out.

"What the hell is going on around here?" he bellowed. "Get off your fat asses and climb behind the wheels of these rigs. You want that timber to take root before we get it to Endicott's?"

His harsh words galvanized them like a sprinkling of fairy dust. Their lassitude vanished and they sprang into action. Laughing and slapping each other on the back, they ran toward the cabs of their rigs.

"Which one do you want me in?" Cash asked Schyler.

"The lead one." She fell into step beside him.

"Where are you going?"

"Where do you think?"

"Endicott's?"

"Yes, and I'm riding with you. Cotton recommended that I should."

He stopped. She did likewise. They turned to face each other and exchanged a puissant stare. Schyler didn't look away until the two sheriff's cars pulled to a stop on the far end of the bridge. "It's time to go." Without waiting for his assistance, she climbed up into the cab of the lead truck.

Cash went around and got behind the steering wheel. He started the motor. He checked the rearview mirrors on both sides, stepped on the clutch, and pushed it into first gear. They moved forward only a few feet.

"Wait!" Schyler cried. Cash braked. "That looks like Ken's car."

"What the hell is he doing?"

They watched through the wide windshield of the rig as Ken sped between the two sheriff's cars and braked in the center of the bridge. The rear end of his car swerved to one side before shuddering to a halt. Cash tooted the horn of the truck. Schyler leaned out the window and waved her arms.

"Ken, what are you doing? We're on our way out. Don't block the bridge."

Ken got out of his car. Schyler shaded her eyes against his headlights. She could barely make out his silhouette against the glare that filtered through the cloud of dust he'd raised.

"What on earth is he doing?" she asked rhetorically.

"Beats the hell outta—Oh, *shit!*"

In the same instant, Schyler saw what Cash had. She gasped. "Oh, my God, no."

Ken raised a revolver to his temple. He took a few steps forward. "You all thought I was stupid." His speech was slurred. He'd been drinking. But his gait was steady and so was the hand holding the pistol to his head. "You thought I didn't have any balls. No brains. I'll show you. I'll show you all. You'll know I've got brains when I splatter them all over this motherlovin' bridge."

"We've got to do something." Schyler opened her door.

Cash grabbed her arm and held her inside. "Not yet."

"But he could pull the trigger any second."

"He will if you go barging across the bridge and freak him out."

"Cash, please," she said, trying to wrest her arm free.

"Give me a sec," he said. "Let me think."

"Get off the bridge, you idiot!"

They turned in the direction of the scream. Up until then, they had forgotten Tricia. They spotted her cowering against the exterior wall of the office building.

"What's the matter with her?" Schyler wondered out loud. "Why isn't she—"

"Get off the bridge!" Cupping her hands, her voice frantic, Tricia shouted to her suicidal husband. "Ken! Do you hear me? Get off the bridge."

Schyler whipped her head around to look at Ken again. "I don't understand her. What—"

"Jesus!" Cash shoved open his door. Dragging Schyler across the cab, he jumped to the ground. "Get out of the truck!" He pulled her to the ground with him. She hit it at a dead run.

A split second later the explosives Jigger had meticulously set blew the Laurent Bayou bridge to smithereens.

 # FIFTY-SIX

Gayla ran her hands over Jimmy Don's chest, his face, down his arms. "I can't believe you're here. That I'm actually touching you. And ... and that you don't despise me." Tears filled her eyes. By now she should have cried herself dry. Since Jimmy Don had appeared out of nowhere, she'd been crying. First in fear, then in shame, now out of love.

"I don't despise you, Gayla. At first I did. All the time I was in prison I hated you. But I got a letter from Cash the very same day I got one from Schyler. He told me to come see him when I got paroled." His hand lovingly grazed her cheek. "He told me how it had been with you, why things had turned out the way they had."

"Then why have you been spying on me?"

He grinned in the darkness and gave the porch swing a push. "Cash hired me to."

"He hired you to spy on Belle Terre?"

"To keep an eye on it. He was scared Jigger was gonna do something to get revenge."

She digested that. "Cash was worried about Schyler?"

"About everybody. Schyler, you, the old man."

"You made me afraid. I knew somebody was out there, watching, waiting till the time was right to do something terrible to us."

"There was." His nostrils flared. "It wasn't just me sneaking around. Jigger was, too. One night I saw him go inside."

"So he did leave the doll on my bed."

"A doll?"

"Voodoo."

"I didn't know what he was doing in there. There wasn't anything I could do to stop him without letting him know I was watching him. I just made sure he came out without hurting you and then I followed him home."

"A few nights ago someone was eavesdropping outside the parlor."

"That was Jigger, too. I saw you come out onto the veranda. I held my breath, wanting to warn you not to step around the corner, but Cash had told me to lay low until Jigger tipped his hand."

"But he hasn't."

Jimmy Don shrugged. "It's too late for him to. That timber goes out tonight. Cash has been as jumpy as a cat these last few days. I don't know how many times he's scouted the area around the landing.

"Looking for what?"

"That's just it. He didn't know. He was just convinced that somebody had it in for Schyler. Whoever blew up the railroad tracks wasn't going to stop there. Cash was sure they would do something to stop that convoy."

"They?"

"Cash didn't think Jigger was working alone."

Out of habit, Gayla shivered at the mention of his name. "You've got to stay away from Jigger, Jimmy Don. If you're seen with me, he'll want to kill you, too."

Her hand was protectively sandwiched between the ones that had carried a football across the goal line more times than anyone in Heaven High School history. "Jigger isn't gonna hurt you, or anybody else, ever again."

He spoke with such surety that Gayla's heart froze. She gazed up at him apprehensively. "Jimmy Don, you didn't . . . ?"

He laid his finger vertically along her lips. "Don't ever ask me."

For a moment they stared at each other, then she made a small sound of gratitude and pressed her face into the hollow of his throat. He held her.

Eventually she eased herself out of his embrace. She went to stand against one of the columns. "I've been to bed with too many men to count, Jimmy Don."

He came to his feet and moved to stand beside her. "It doesn't matter."

"It does to me." She looked down at her hands through eyes blurred with tears. "Before I went to work in that beer joint, I'd never had anybody else but you. Swear to God."

He laid his hands on her shoulders. "I know that. We both suffered 'cause of that evil man, Gayla." He turned her to face him. "Things were done to me in prison that . . ." His voice tapered off. The memories were too painful for him to vocalize.

Intuitively she knew that. "You don't have to tell me anything," she whispered.

"Yeah, I do. I love you, Gayla. And I want to be with you. I want to marry you like we always talked about. But I can't ask you to marry me." She tilted her head to one side, gazing up at him inquiringly. He cleared his throat, but he couldn't blink away the tears in his own eyes. "There were men in prison who forced themselves on me." He turned his head aside and squeezed his eyes shut. "That killed something inside me. I, uh, I don't know if I can . . . if I can be with a woman anymore. I think I might be, uh, impotent.''

Gayla laid her hands on his cheeks and turned his face toward her again. He opened his tearful, troubled eyes. ''I don't care about that, Jimmy Don,'' she said with soft earnesty. ''Believe me, baby, I've been worked over so many times I don't even remember what it's like to want a man in that way. Just be gentle and tender and sweet with me. Love me. That's all I want from you.''

Tears streamed down his smooth, dark cheeks. He clasped her to him and held her tightly. At that moment nothing could have parted them except the explosion that rattled the windows at Belle Terre and lit up the night sky like the Fourth of July.

''Good God!'' Jimmy Don cried. ''Looks like Cash was right.''

''Schyler!''

''You stay here.'' Jimmy Don set her away from him.

She reached out. ''I want to go with you.''

''You've got to stay with the old man.'' He vaulted over the railing of the veranda.

''All the cars are gone.''

''I'll run.'' His powerful, record-breaking legs started churning.

''Be careful, baby. Call when you know something.'' He waved to her to let her know he'd heard. She watched until he disappeared around the bend in the lane. At the squeaking sound of the screen door, she spun around. ''Mr. Crandall, get back to bed!'' She rushed forward and braced him up on one side. He seemed on the verge of collapse. The red glow of the fire was reflected in his eyes.

''That's the landing.''

''I'm sure everything's all right. Jimmy Don's gone to check. He said he would call.''

Cotton didn't ask about Jimmy Don. It didn't seem to register with him that an ex-convict had spent the last few hours in his house. Either that or he didn't care. He was staring at the hellish red light rising above the treetops.

''I've got to get to the landing,'' he wheezed.

''You'll do no such thing. You're going back to bed.''

''I can't.'' He wrestled with her, though he was so weak it was no contest.

''Mr. Crandall, even if I'd let you go, we don't have a car. You've got no way of getting there.''

''Goddammit!'' He slumped against the doorjamb. His breathing was rough. His hand was making squeezing motions over his heart.

Gayla was frightened. ''Come on back to bed now.''

''Leave me alone,'' he rasped, shaking off her assisting hands. ''I'm not a baby. Stop treating me like one.''

Any further badgering would only cause him stress. Gayla relented. ''Okay. We'll sit out here on the veranda. We can hear the phone ringing from here.''

Cotton let himself be led to one of the wicker chairs. Once he was settled, Gayla sat down on the top step and wrapped her skirt around her shins. Together and in silence they watched the night sky turn the color of blood.

The pickup rumbled up to the front walk. Gayla was still sitting on the top step, leaning against the column, alseep. She didn't come awake until the door of the pickup was closed. She raised her head and shielded her gritty eyes against the morning sunlight.

Cash and Schyler were coming up the front walk. Both looked like they'd been in a combat zone. Jimmy Don climbed out of the bed of the pickup and jumped to the ground. She smiled at him shyly. He smiled back.

"Daddy!" Schyler exclaimed. She ran the rest of the way up the steps and onto the veranda. "What on earth are you doing out here? Why aren't you in bed?"

"He refused to go back inside, Schyler," Gayla told her. "Even after Jimmy Don called and told us that you were all right, he flat refused to go back to his room.'"

"You've been out here all night?" Gayla nodded in answer to Schyler's question. The women exchanged a worried glance. Cotton didn't look well. "Well, I won't hear of such shenanigans from you," Schyler said bossily. "You might have intimidated Gayla, but you don't intimidate me. You're going back to bed immediately."

Cotton pushed his daughter aside. "I want to know one thing." Though his voice was as fragile as tissue paper, it stunned them all with its impact. Using the arms of the chair for support, he struggled to stand at his full height. "Did you do this to me?"

He looked directly at Cash. His blue eyes were deeply hooded by scowling brows. Cash returned his stare. One was as steady and antagonistic as the other. "No."

"It was Jigger Flynn, Daddy," Schyler said quickly.

She was trying to outrun a storm about to break. The air was sulfurous. The instant Cotton and Cash came face-to-face, the scene had becomne as still and electric as the atmosphere before a tornado. She had known there was antipathy between them, but she'd never expected it to be so palpable that it could be tasted.

In short, concise sentences, she related to Cotton what had happened during the night. She didn't go into details. They could be doled out to him like medication when he was well enough to hear them. She didn't tell him that Ken had been killed in the explosion seconds before he planned to take his own life. She didn't tell him that Tricia, months earlier, had formed an unholy alliance with Dale Gilbreath. At that very moment Tricia was giving her deposition to the sheriff in the presence of her attorney. He was already planning to plea bargain. Tricia hoped she would get a lesser sentence if she turned state's evidence. If not, she would stand trial with Gilbreath and Jigger Flynn for the murder of her husband among a variety of other charges.

No, all that could wait until later, when Cotton wasn't swaying on his feet.

"The fire looked much worse than it was, Daddy," Schyler concluded anxiously. "Most of the timber was saved. We'll deliver it to Endicott in good time, but we don't have to worry about the deadline at the bank."

Cotton seemed not to have heard a single word. He raised his hand and pointed a finger at Cash. "You're trespassing."

"Daddy, what's the matter with you? Cash has done the work of ten men for you tonight."

His pointing hand began to shake. "You . . . you . . ." Gasping, Cotton clutched his pajama jacket and fell back a step."

"Daddy!" Schyler screamed.

Cotton went down on one knee, then fell backward onto the veranda. Schyler dropped to her knees beside him.

"I'll call the doctor," Gayla said and ran inside. Jimmy Don bolted after her.

"Daddy, Daddy." Schyler moved her hands over her father frantically. His pasty face was beaded with sweat. His lips and earlobes had an unhealthy bluish cast. His breath whistled through his waxy lips.

Schyler raised her head and looked up at Cash in desperate appeal. His taut expression startled her. His face was suffused with color, as though he had an overabundance of blood while Cotton didn't have enough.

Kneeling, he reached down and secured a handful of Cotton's pajama top in his fist and yanked him up. "Goddamn you to eternal hell if you die now. Don't you die, old man. Don't you die!"

"Cash, what are you doing?"

Cash shook Cotton. His white head wobbled feebly. His eyes were fixed on Cash's tortured face. The younger man's sun-tipped hair had fallen over his brows. Tears were making his hazel eyes shimmer.

"Don't you die until you've said it. Look at me. Say it!" He clenched the pajama top tighter and pulled Cotton up closer to him. He lowered his head and ground his forehead against Cotton's. His voice cracked with yearning when he pleaded through clenched teeth. "Say it! Just once in my whole godforsaken life, say it. *Call me son.*"

With an effort, Cotton lifted his hand. He touched Cash's stubbled cheek. The bloodless fingertips caressed it, but the name he rasped wasn't his son's. Drawing a rattling breath, he sighed, "Monique."

And then he died.

His hand fell away from Cash's face and landed with a thud on the boards of the veranda. Gradually the muscles of Cash's arms relaxed and he lowered the sagging form. He kept his head bending over it for a long time, staring into the sightless blue eyes that had always refused to see him.

Then he pushed himself to his feet and staggered down the steps of the veranda. He drove away, but not before Schyler, speechlessly kneeling at Cotton's side, had had a glimpse of his shattered expression.

⟾ FIFTY-SEVEN

Every sunset at Belle Terre was beautiful.

Today's was more gorgeous than most. It had rained earlier in the day, but the sky overhead was clear now. On the western horizon enormous violet thunderheads looked like a cluster of hydrangea blooms. The sun was shining through them to create a sunset that was celestial.

It reaffirmed one's belief in God.

Schyler gazed at the spectacular sunset through her bedroom window. Long shadows were cast along the walls and floor. Dust motes spun in the glow of the warm, fading sun. The house was quiet. It usually was. She and Mrs. Dunne didn't create much noise.

Gayla had moved out. She and Jimmy Don were living as newlyweds in a duplex nearer town. Gayla was planning to enroll in a nursing school in the fall. Jimmy Don was working for Crandall Logging. He had taken over the bookkeeping responsibilities that Ken Howell had once had. His parole officer was pleased. Schyler had high hopes for the couple. They would make it, especially since they had been extricated from the blight of Jigger Flynn.

Schyler had been shocked to hear the horrible and mysterious circumstances surrounding his death. Though it was one of the grisliest murders to ever occur in Laurent Parish, not a single clue had turned up. Most everybody had formed an opinion and had made their list of possible suspects, but none were coming forward. Jigger had cultivated enemies like most folks cultivated summer gardens. Few lamented his ghastly demise. His murder would be entered in the record books as an unsolved crime.

Cotton Crandall's funeral was one of the largest the parish had experienced in decades. The First Baptist Church had been filled to capacity. Extra chairs had been set up in the aisles. When they were filled, the crowd stood on the grounds outside. The service had been abundant in pomp and circumstance. The preacher had never been so eloquent. The whole choir had sung. When they reached the last verse of "Amazing Grace," even those who had called Cotton an opportunist who had married well had tears in their eyes.

But his funeral wasn't what had people all abuzz; it was his private interment. He hadn't been buried beside his wife in the Laurent family cemetery as everybody had expected him to be. He's been laid to rest in an undisclosed and undisturbed spot on Belle Terre. Only Schyler knew where. Only she knew that another grave lay beside his.

She also knew Cotton approved her decision.

The day before his funeral, she had gone to New Orleans to entomb the body of Ken Howell with his family. Pitifully few attended. Tricia remained tearless. She had refused to look at or speak to her sister. She was led away by policemen as soon as the brief service was concluded. Schyler was paying for Tricia's defense attorney. Beyond that, her sister wouldn't accept her help. She had refused to see her when Schyler tried to visit her in jail.

During the darkest days of her bereavement, Schyler had telephoned Mark in London. He'd been sympathetic and consoling, but there was a difference in their friendship now. Each knew it and each was saddened by it, but each accepted that they couldn't return to the way they'd been before.

So Schyler was very much alone in the large house and never more alone than this evening. She'd taken a lingering bath in the old tub. Her clothes were carefully folded into neat piles on the bed. All that was left to do was place those neat piles in her suitcase and go to bed. But she would put that off as long as she could because tonight was the last night she would ever spend under Belle Terre's roof.

When the sun finally gave up its valiant struggle to survive one more second and sank beyond the edge of the earth, she shook off her despair-induced lethargy and turned away from the window.

He was standing in the doorway of her bedroom, one shoulder propped against the frame, silently staring at her. He was dressed as always in jeans and boots and a casual work shirt, which made her feel even more uncomfortable being caught in nothing more than her slip.

"I see your manners haven't improved since the last time I saw you," she remarked. "Couldn't you have at least knocked?"

"I've never needed to knock to get into a lady's bedroom."

He levered himself away from the door and swaggered into the room. He withdrew an envelope from the breast pocket of his shirt and tossed it onto her dressing table. "I got your letter."

"Then there's nothing left for us to say to each other, is there?"

He picked up a crystal perfume bottle and sniffed its contents. "I think so. That kind of news is usually delivered in person."

Schyler felt naked, not just her body, but her spirit. His presence in the feminine room was unsettling. He prowled it, touching things, making her feel violated. "I thought it would be best for us not to see each other. My attorney advised me to notify you by mail."

"Did he vote in favor of your decision to sign over Belle Terre to me?"

"No."

"Because I'm Cotton's bastard."

"That wasn't his objection. He . . . he thought I should let Daddy's will stand as it was written."

"Dividing the property equally between you, me, and Tricia?"

"Yes."

"But you didn't think so?"

"No."

"How come?" He sprawled on a linen-covered chaise and propped one booted foot on the end of it. The other he left on the floor. His bent knee swung from side to side.

"It's difficult to explain, Cash."

"Try."

"My father . . . *our* father . . . treated you abominably."

"You're trying to right his wrongs?"

"In a manner of speaking."

"A kid born on the wrong side of the blanket has no rights, Schyler."

"You were more than that to him."

He laughed bitterly. "A living guilty conscience."

"Perhaps. When he left New Orleans, he didn't mean to desert you and your mother. He loved her. Fiercely. His will proved that he loved you, too."

"He never even had a kind word for me," he said angrily.

"He couldn't afford to." That got his attention. The insolent knee stopped wagging. His eyes held hers, begging to be convinced. "He loved you, Cash. He just couldn't let himself get too close. He knew if he allowed himself to show his love just a little, it would be obvious to everybody." Schyler's brow wrinkled in puzzlement. "I don't understand why that would have been so bad. Why didn't he acknowledge you when he was alive?"

"He had sworn to Macy that he wouldn't. That was their bargain. Cotton could have my mother as his mistress, but he couldn't have his son."

"But after Mama died, why didn't he recognize you then?"

"Macy's deal was for life. Cotton's life. At least that's what he told Mother and me when I wanted him to marry her. Macy had no choice but to leave him Belle Terre. She just made damn certain he wouldn't be too happy in it."

"He placed Belle Terre above his own happiness. Above his own son," Schyler said sadly. "He loved you, Monique, me. But he loved Belle Terre more than anything."

Looking down at him she said quietly, "And so do you, Cash. That's why you've stayed here all this time. In the back of your mind, you knew Belle Terre was rightfully yours. You've been waiting all your life to claim it, haven't you?" He said nothing, just stared at her. "Well, you don't have to wait any longer. I gave up my share of it to you. It says so in that letter.

"Everything's in the clear," she went on after a short pause. "The deed to the house is no longer tied up as collateral. It's written out in your name now. Endicott's check covered the bank note. You've got plenty of operating capital. With an honest bookkeeper taking care of the budget, I'm sure that you'll make Crandall Logging what it was in Cotton's heyday. Probably even better. Daddy taught you well. And what he didn't teach you, you learned on your own. He always said you were an instinctive forester. The best. He was proud of you."

She smiled at him faintly. "You'll probably want to change the name of the business, won't you, now that you've inherited Belle Terre?"

"I'd rather have a woman than a house."

Schyler took a quick little breath. "What?"

He rolled his spine off the chaise and stood up. He moved so close she had to tilt her head back to look up at him. "I didn't sleep with Tricia," he said. "I never wanted to. In any event, that bitch wouldn't have let my shadow fall on her before that night. I knew she had probably been sent as a decoy. I was just going through the motions until she cracked under pressure and I could get information out of her."

He reached around Schyler with both hands and took hold of her hair, pulling her head back. "You love this place, Schyler. Why'd you give it to me?"

"Because I've always felt like it was on loan to me. I sensed, always, *always,* that it didn't really belong to me. I didn't know why. Now I do. You're Cotton's flesh and blood. His son." She shook her head at her own stupidity. "You're so like him. Why didn't I see it?"

She gazed into his face, loving it so much it was painful and she had to look away. "After he died, I finally remembered what had been said the night you brought me home from Thibodaux Pond. It had never made sense before. Daddy told you to stay away from the house. You shouted back, 'I've got more right to be here than they do.' You were referring to Tricia and me, weren't you?"

"*Oui.* I lost my temper."

"But you were right. You belonged here. Not us."

"I've been obsessed with Belle Terre since the first time my mother said the words to me." He brushed a kiss across her lips. "But I'm not going to be like my daddy. I'm not going to place Belle Terre above everything else. It's not what I want most. I knew what I wanted most when I saw you asleep under that tree."

"Cash?"

"Why'd you give me Belle Terre?"

"You know why," she groaned against his lips. "I love you, Cash Boudreaux."

He kissed her. His lips were warm and sweet as they parted above hers. His tongue gently explored the inside of her mouth. He combed his fingers through her hair, then let them drift over her shoulders and down her chest to her breasts. He caressed them, touched their centers with his fingertips, then slid his hands down her ribs to her waist. Holding their kiss, he pulled her forward as he backed up. When the backs of his knees made contact with the mattress, he sat down on the edge of the bed and positioned her between his spread thighs.

He kissed her breasts through her slip, flicking the ivory silk charmeuse with his tongue. "You aren't going anywhere," he growled as he planted a kiss between her breasts. "You're staying here with me. And when we die, our children will bury us here together. On Belle Terre."

Tears stung Schyler's eyes. Joy and love pumped through her. She tunneled her fingers in his hair and held his head against her.

Cash nuzzled the giving softness of her belly. "Schyler?"

"Yes?"

"Several ponderous heartbeats later, he whispered, "I love you."

ABOUT THE AUTHOR

SANDRA BROWN has been a model, actress, TV personality, and, since her first book was published, a bestselling novelist. Under the pseudonyms Rachel Ryan, Erin St. Claire, and Laura Jordan, as well as her own name, Sandra has wooed and won the loyalty of fans and critics alike. This year she has had three books simultaneously on *The New York Times* hardcover and paperback Bestseller lists. A Silver Pen and Gold Certificate recipient from *Affair de Coeur,* Sandra Brown won the Waldenbooks' award for the best-selling single title release of 1988 with her novel *Slow Heat in Heaven.*

Married to video producer Michael Brown and currently living in Arlington, Texas, Sandra has a daughter Rachel and son Ryan, from whom she borrowed her first pen name.